HUMAN BODY!

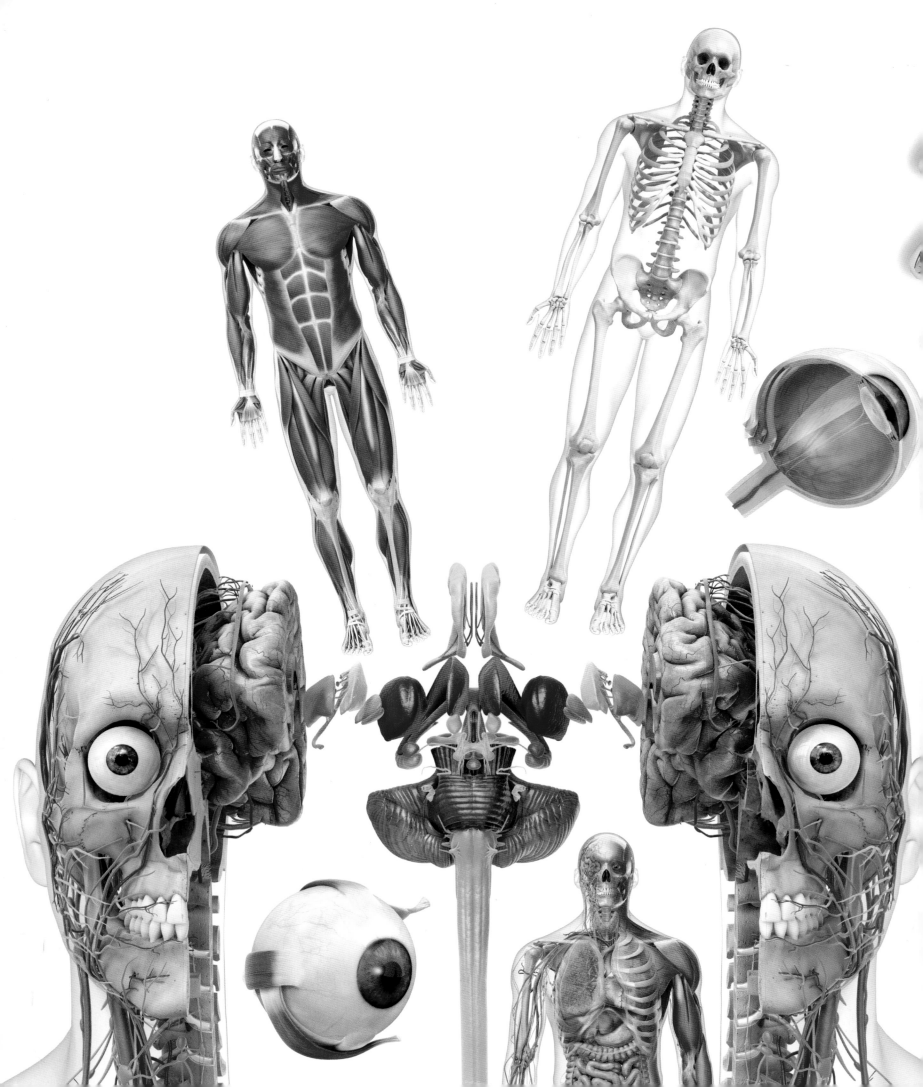

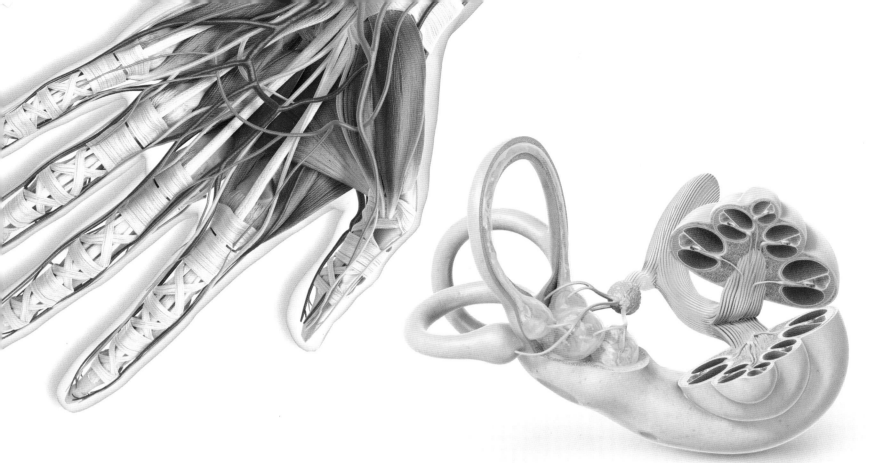

DK SMITHSONIAN ✱
HUMAN BODY!

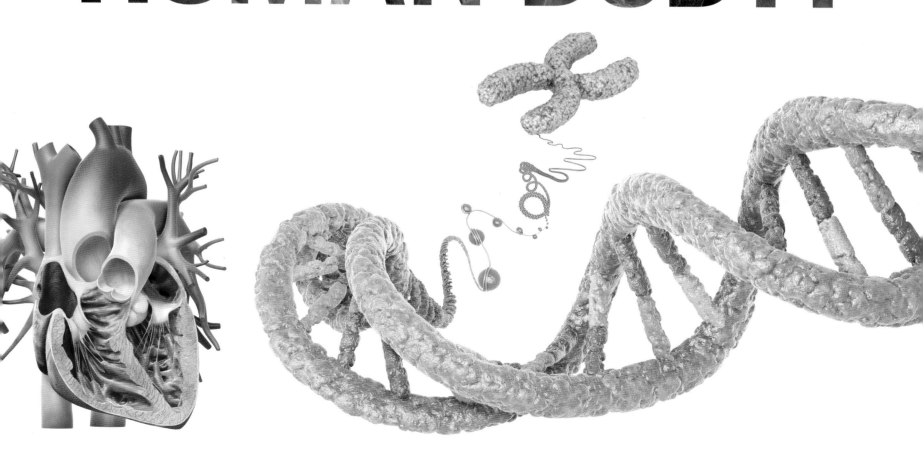

Penguin Random House

Senior Art Editor Smiljka Surla
Senior Editor Rona Skene
US Editors Megan Douglass, Margaret Parrish
Medical Consultant Dr Kristina Routh
Contributors Anna Claybourne, John Farndon,
John Friend, Nicola Temple
3D illustrators Arran Lewis, Rajeev Doshi
Additional Illustrations Michael Parkin,
Maltings Partnership
Editors Tim Harris, Andrea Mills
Designer Simon Murrell
DK Picture Library Romaine Werblow
Picture Researcher Deepak Negi
Managing Editor Lisa Gillespie
Managing Art Editor Owen Peyton Jones
Producer, Pre-Production Catherine Williams
Senior Producer Anna Vallarino
Jacket designers Suhita Dharamjit, Surabhi Wadhwa
Jackets design development manager Sophia MTT
Senior DTP designer Harish Aggarwal
Jackets editorial coordinator Priyanka Sharma
Jackets editor Claire Gell
Publisher Andrew Macintyre
Art Director Karen Self
Associate Publishing Director Liz Wheeler
Design Director Phil Ormerod
Publishing Director Jonathan Metcalf

First American Edition, 2017
Published in the United States by DK Publishing
1450 Broadway, Suite 801, New York, NY 10018

Copyright © 2017 Dorling Kindersley Limited
DK, a Division of Penguin Random House LLC
22 23 24 10 9 8 7 6 5 4 3 2 1
001–334974–Jan 23

A catalog record for this book is available from the Library of Congress.
ISBN: 978-1-4654-6239-8

DK books are available at special discounts when purchased in bulk for
sales promotions, premiums, fund-raising, or educational use.
For details, contact: DK Publishing Special Markets,
1450 Broadway, Suite 801, New York, NY 10018
SpecialSales@dk.com

Printed and bound in China

For the curious
www.dk.com

THE SMITHSONIAN
Established in 1846, the Smithsonian—the world's largest
museum and research complex—includes 19 museums and galleries
and the National Zoological Park. The total number of artifacts, works of art,
and specimens in the Smithsonian's collection is estimated at 154 million.
The Smithsonian is a renowned research center, dedicated to public education,
national service, and scholarship in the arts, sciences, and history.

MIX
Paper from
responsible sources
FSC™ C018179

This book was made with Forest Stewardship
Council™ certified paper – one small step
in DK's commitment to a sustainable future.
For more information go to
www.dk.com/our-green-pledge

CONTENTS

BODY BASICS

BODY SYSTEMS

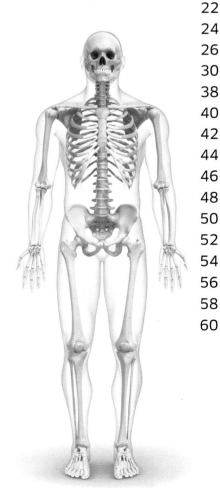

HEAD AND NECK

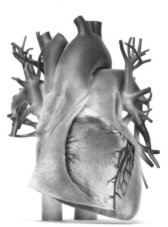

CHEST AND BACK

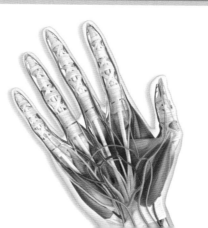

ARMS AND HANDS

ABDOMEN AND PELVIS

LEGS AND FEET

BODY SCIENCE

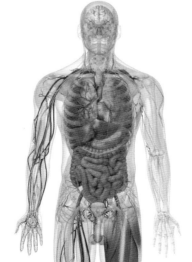

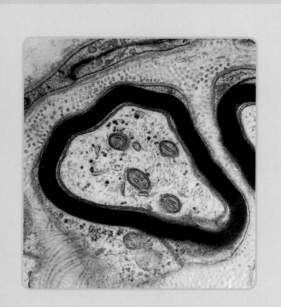
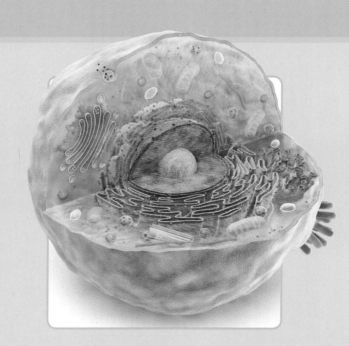

BODY BASICS

The smallest structure found in living things is the cell, and trillions of them make up each human body. These building blocks of life each have a specific job. They are constantly dividing to produce new cells that allow the body to grow and repair itself.

MAKING A HUMAN

Everything in the body is made up of atoms, the tiniest building blocks of matter. Atoms combine to form molecules. Millions of molecules form every cell in the body. There are more than 200 types of cell, with similar cells working in teams called tissues. The body's many organs and systems are made up of different tissues.

Atoms and molecules

The smallest parts in the body are atoms. These tiny building blocks form the elements in the body, such as carbon. Atoms from different elements can also join together in groups called molecules–for example, water is a molecule, made from a combination of hydrogen and oxygen atoms.

Cell

Molecules build up to create body cells. There are about 37 trillion cells in the average human, with different types of cells carrying out a variety of body functions, from transporting oxygen to sensing light and color in the eye.

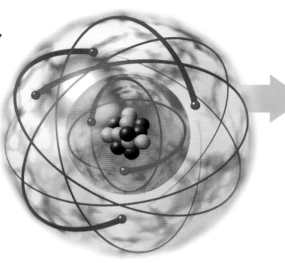

ATOM

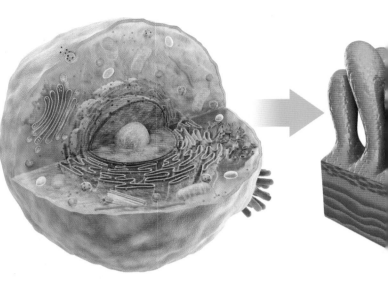

CELL

WHAT MAKES A BODY?

The human body is made from the same components as every other living thing. It is the way that they are put together that makes our bodies uniquely human. The basic materials are simple chemicals such as water, carbon, and oxygen, but they join to create more complex compounds. Trillions of microscopic cells become the building blocks of life, grouping together to form skin, bone, blood, and organs, until the body becomes complete.

TYPES OF TISSUE

Tissues are groups of connected cells. Many tissues are made entirely from one type of cell. The four main types of tissue in the human body are connective, epithelial, muscular, and nervous.

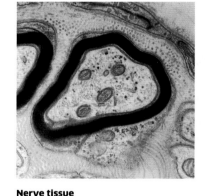

THE HARDEST **TISSUE IN THE** HUMAN BODY **IS TOOTH ENAMEL.**

Nerve tissue
Large groups of nerve cells create nervous tissue. This forms the brain, spinal cord, and masses of nerves that work together in the nervous system, the body's high-speed communications network.

BODY BASICS

More than 93 percent of the human body consists of three chemical elements–oxygen (65%), carbon (18.5%), and hydrogen (10%). Nitrogen (3%), calcium (1.5%), and phosphorus (1%) are also present in significant amounts. At least 54 chemical elements feature in total, but most of these are tiny traces.

A 10-YEAR-OLD'S BODY CONTAINS **66 GRAMS OF POTASSIUM, THE SAME AMOUNT AS IN 156 BANANAS.**

Others 6.5%

Hydrogen 10%
The most common element in the universe, hydrogen has the tiniest atoms, and is mostly bonded with carbon or oxygen in the body.

Other elements = less than 1.0%
Iron 0.006%
Sodium 0.2%
Potassium 0.4%
Phosphorus 1%
Calcium 1.5%
Nitrogen 3%

ENLARGEMENT

Oxygen 65%
About two-thirds of the body is oxygen. Most of the oxygen is bonded with hydrogen to form H_2O–the chemical formula for water.

Carbon 18.5%
Nearly one-fifth of the body is carbon, the same element that coal, diamond, and the lead of pencils are made from.

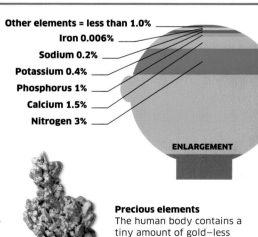

Precious elements
The human body contains a tiny amount of gold–less than the weight of a grain of sand. Most of the body's gold is in the blood.

Tissue

Cells performing the same function are grouped together to form body tissues, such as skin, fat, or heart muscle. Blood is also a tissue, in liquid form.

Organ

Different kinds of tissue combine to make larger structures called organs. Each organ works like a machine, performing its own role. An example of an organ is the stomach, which plays a part in the process of digesting food.

Body system

Organs are at the center of 12 internal body systems. Each system has a specific job to keep the body in working order. The stomach is one of the main organs of the digestive system.

Complete human

When this complex combination of integrated systems, organs, and tissues works together, the human body is complete. Each individual component plays its part in maintaining a fully functioning body.

STOMACH TISSUE

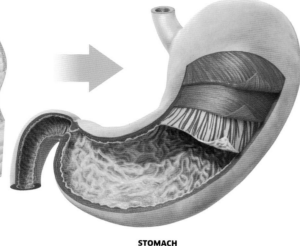

STOMACH

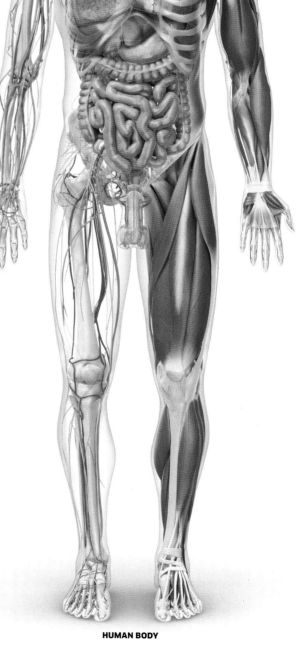

DIGESTIVE SYSTEM

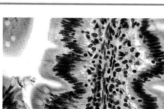
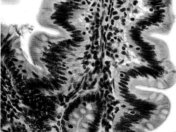

Epithelial tissue

Made up of three main shapes of cell, epithelial tissue lines and covers surfaces inside and outside the body. It forms skin and the linings of body cavities such as the gut and lungs.

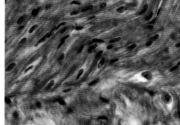
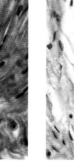

Muscle tissue

Built from long, thin cells, muscle tissue can relax and contract to allow muscles to move bones. It also helps sustain blood pressure and carry food through the digestive system.

Connective tissue

This dense tissue is the body's "glue," filling the space between other tissues and organs, and binding them together. Examples include adipose tissue (fat), bone, and blood.

CARBON COMPOUNDS

The human body is made from chemicals containing the element carbon. Called organic compounds, they often contain hydrogen and oxygen, too. Although these organic compounds are based on only a few elements, they produce more than 10 million different compounds. Four main types of carbon compound exist inside the human body.

Proteins

Proteins are vital body molecules. Organs such as the brain are made of protein, as well as muscles, connective tissues, hormones that send chemical messages, and antibodies that fight infection.

Fats

Fats are made from carbon and hydrogen atoms. They form the outer barrier of cells. The layer of fat beneath the skin stores energy and helps the body to keep out the cold.

Nucleic acids

The molecules DNA and RNA carry all the instructions for making the proteins that our bodies are made of. They also carry code that controls how cells work and reproduce.

Carbohydrates

Carbohydrates are made from carbon, oxygen, and hydrogen and are the body's main source of energy. Carbohydrates circulate in the blood as sugars or are stored in the liver and muscles.

HUMAN BODY

10 body basics ∘ **INSIDE A CELL**

37 trillion (37,000,000,000,000)—the approximate
number of cells in the human body.

Types of cell

Each type of cell has a shape and size related to its own vital task in the body.

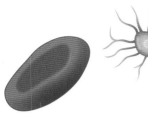

Red blood cells
are doughnut shaped, and this lets them pick up and carry oxygen easily.

Nerve cells
are long, thin, and carry electrical signals over long distances.

Muscle cells
can contract (shorten) and relax to produce movement.

Epidermal cells
in the skin fit tightly together to form a protective layer.

Fat cells
are filled with droplets of liquid fat as an energy store.

Cone cells
in the eye detect light, enabling us to see.

Cell life spans

Different types of body cell have different life spans. Some, such as skin cells, are worn away. Other cells wear out and self-destruct. They are replaced with more of their kind by special cells called stem cells.

Less than 1 day
White blood cells fighting infection

30 days
Skin cells

12–18 months
Liver cells

15 years
Muscle cells

A whole lifetime
Some nerve cells in the brain

Inside a cell

The body is made of trillions of cells, each too small to see without a microscope. These cells aren't all the same. There are about 200 different types, each with its own size, shape, and contents. Each type of cell has a particular task.

Just as the body has organs, such as the heart, the cell has organelles, such as mitochondria. These parts work together to make the cell a living unit. In addition, tiny rods, including microtubules, move organelles and form a kind of "skeleton" that supports and shapes the cell.

Golgi apparatus
The Golgi apparatus processes and packages proteins made on ribosomes, ready for use inside or outside the cell.

Vesicle
This bag takes proteins from the Golgi apparatus and carries them to where they are needed.

Cell membrane
This flexible membrane surrounds the cell and controls what enters and exits. It consists of a double layer of lipid (fat) molecules containing proteins that have different jobs to do.

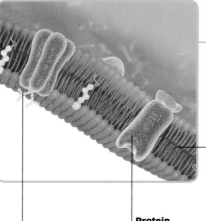

Lipid layer
A double layer of lipid (fat) molecules forms the main part of the membrane.

Protein
This protein channel transports substances into and out of the cell.

Glycoprotein
This "tag" identifies the cell to other cells.

1 million years—the time it would take to count all the **body's cells** at a rate of one per second.

Red blood cells make up about **70% of the total number of cells** in the body.

11

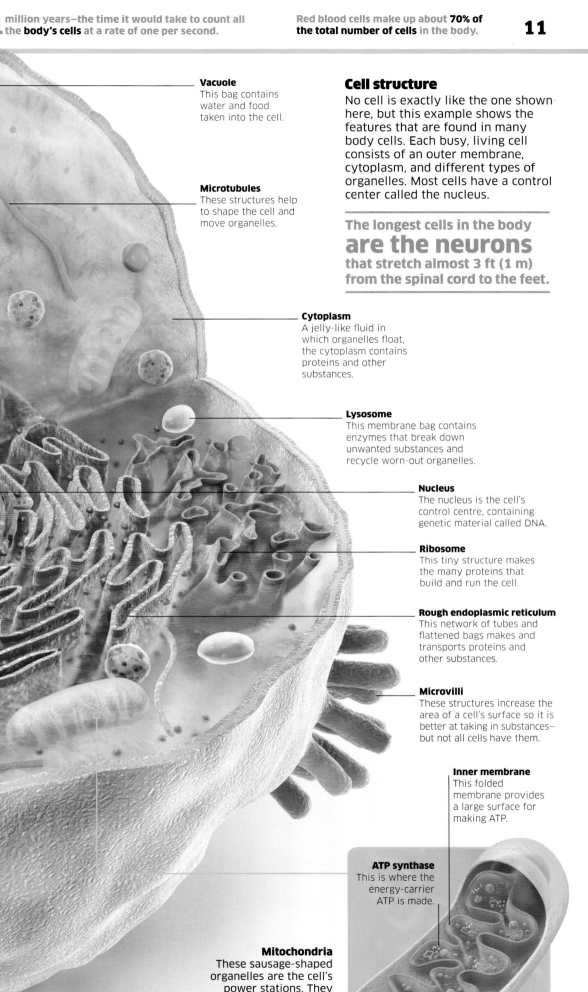

Vacuole
This bag contains water and food taken into the cell.

Microtubules
These structures help to shape the cell and move organelles.

Cell structure
No cell is exactly like the one shown here, but this example shows the features that are found in many body cells. Each busy, living cell consists of an outer membrane, cytoplasm, and different types of organelles. Most cells have a control center called the nucleus.

The longest cells in the body **are the neurons** that stretch almost 3 ft (1 m) from the spinal cord to the feet.

Cytoplasm
A jelly-like fluid in which organelles float, the cytoplasm contains proteins and other substances.

Lysosome
This membrane bag contains enzymes that break down unwanted substances and recycle worn-out organelles.

Nucleus
The nucleus is the cell's control centre, containing genetic material called DNA.

Ribosome
This tiny structure makes the many proteins that build and run the cell.

Rough endoplasmic reticulum
This network of tubes and flattened bags makes and transports proteins and other substances.

Microvilli
These structures increase the area of a cell's surface so it is better at taking in substances—but not all cells have them.

Inner membrane
This folded membrane provides a large surface for making ATP.

ATP synthase
This is where the energy-carrier ATP is made.

Mitochondria
These sausage-shaped organelles are the cell's power stations. They release the energy from glucose and other foods that cells use to drive their many activities.

Centrioles
These two bunches of microtubules play a key part in cell division.

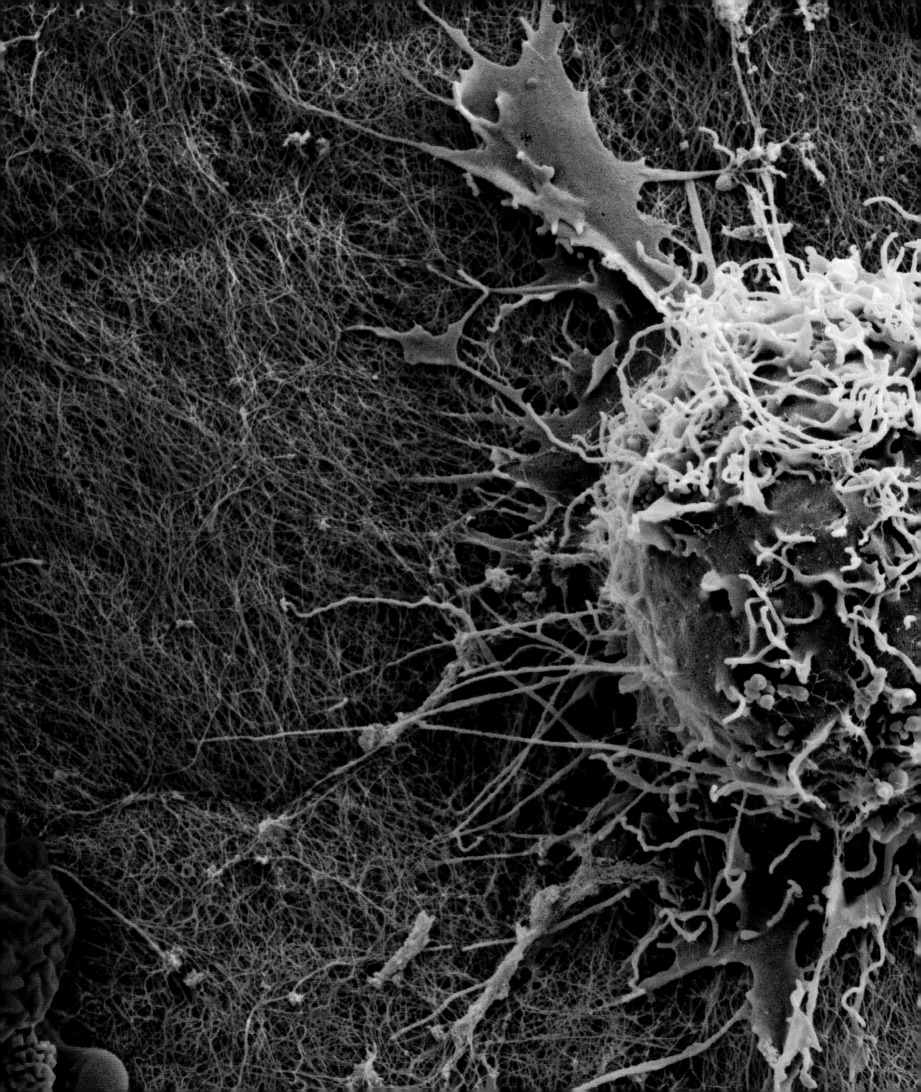

STEM SUPPORT

Inside the human body are special "master cells" called stem cells. They can either renew themselves or grow into one of more than 200 different types of body cell. Stem cells help the body stay healthy by repairing damaged tissue or organs.

This image from a scan shows a stem cell (colored brown) from adult bone marrow on the surface of cartilage tissue (colored pink). Bone marrow is a spongy tissue inside the bones, where all the different blood cells are produced by stem cells. The blood cells leave the bone marrow to enter the bloodstream.

DNA—instructions for life

The nucleus of every human cell carries a set of unique codes for making new cells to build and maintain the body. These instructions are called genes, and they are made of a substance called DNA.

Inside the cell nucleus, there are 46 tiny structures called chromosomes. These are made of tightly coiled strands of DNA, which contain all the information the cell needs to make a new, identical version of itself. Every time a cell divides so the body can grow or repair itself, a DNA strand "unzips" down the middle. Each unzipped half then rebuilds itself into a new DNA strand, identical to the original and carrying all the same codes.

The sequence of DNA bases is different for everyone—except **identical twins**, whose DNA is exactly the same.

Chromosome
Inside a cell nucleus there are 46 chromosomes (23 pairs), made of tightly packed DNA.

The DNA molecule

Magnified, a strand of DNA looks like a twisted ladder, with two long, thin strands connected by rungs. These rungs are called bases and are made up of four different chemicals. The bases interact to form instructions for making proteins—the building materials that make up our organs, muscles, blood, bones, and hair.

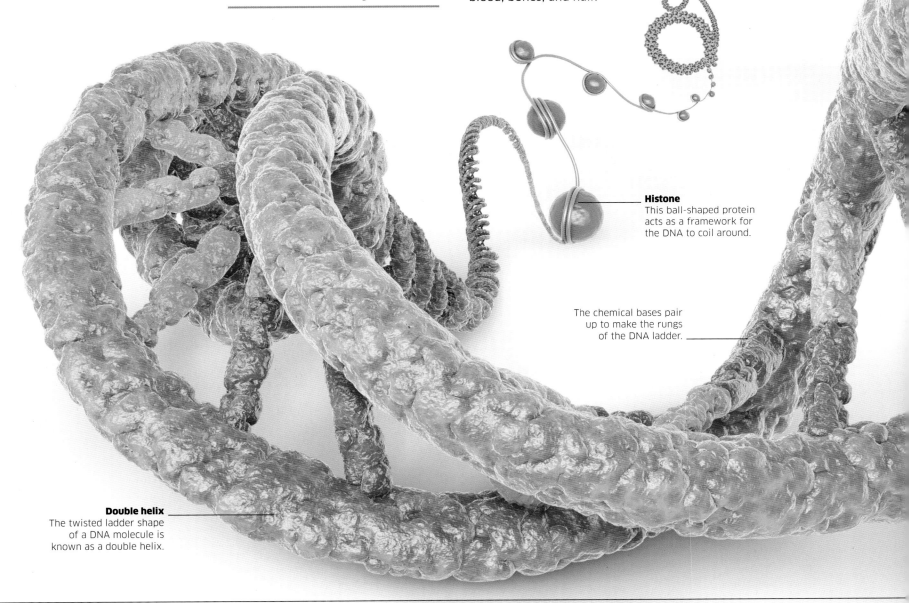

Histone
This ball-shaped protein acts as a framework for the DNA to coil around.

The chemical bases pair up to make the rungs of the DNA ladder.

Double helix
The twisted ladder shape of a DNA molecule is known as a double helix.

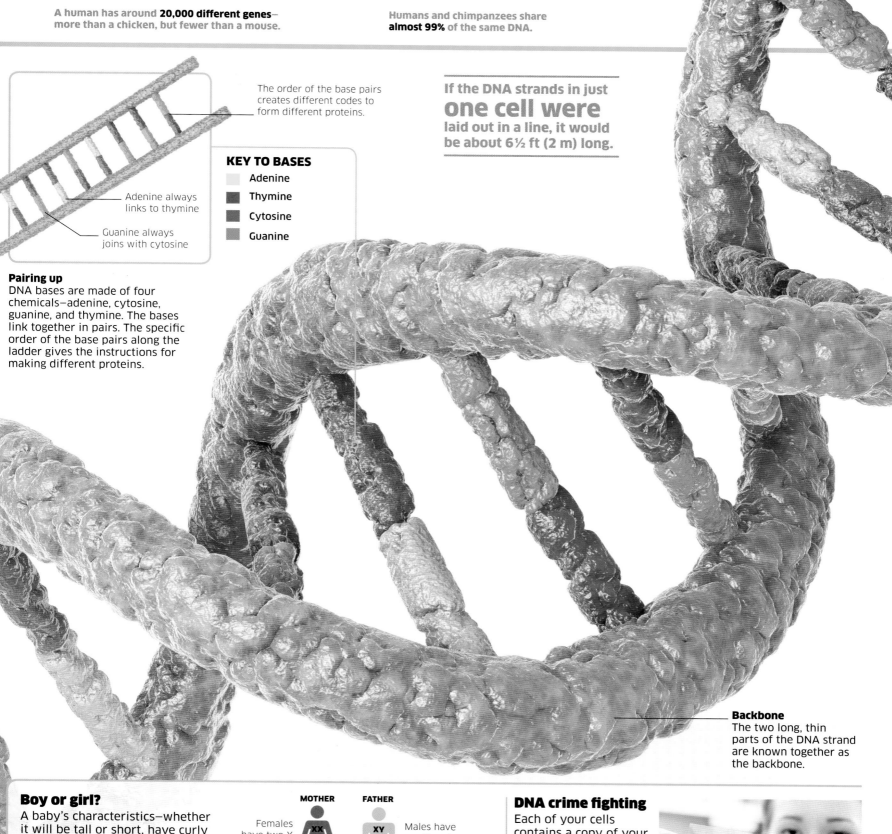

A human has around **20,000 different genes**—more than a chicken, but fewer than a mouse.

Humans and chimpanzees share **almost 99%** of the same DNA.

The order of the base pairs creates different codes to form different proteins.

If the DNA strands in just **one cell were** laid out in a line, it would be about 6½ ft (2 m) long.

KEY TO BASES

- Adenine
- Thymine
- Cytosine
- Guanine

Adenine always links to thymine

Guanine always joins with cytosine

Pairing up

DNA bases are made of four chemicals—adenine, cytosine, guanine, and thymine. The bases link together in pairs. The specific order of the base pairs along the ladder gives the instructions for making different proteins.

Backbone

The two long, thin parts of the DNA strand are known together as the backbone.

Boy or girl?

A baby's characteristics—whether it will be tall or short, have curly or straight hair, or brown or blue eyes—are set by the DNA it inherits from its parents. Two special chromosomes, called X and Y, determine whether a baby will be male or female.

Genetic mix

An embryo is created when a sperm cell fertilizes a female egg. All eggs contain an X chromosome, but a sperm can carry either an X or a Y chromosome. So it is the sperm that determines the baby's sex.

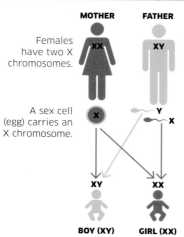

MOTHER

FATHER

Females have two X chromosomes.

Males have one X and one Y chromosome.

A sex cell (egg) carries an X chromosome.

Sex cells (sperm) can carry either an X or a Y chromosome.

XY
BOY (XY)

XX
GIRL (XX)

A baby receives an X chromosome from its mother and an X or Y chromosome from its father.

DNA crime fighting

Each of your cells contains a copy of your genome—all the DNA that you inherited from your parents. Just like a fingerprint, everyone (except an identical twin) has a slightly different, unique genome. This means that a criminal who leaves hair, skin, blood, or saliva at a crime scene can be identified by their DNA.

Matching DNA

A DNA fingerprint from a sample is recorded as a series of rungs, similar to a supermarket bar code. Crime investigators use software to search databases of offenders' DNA to look for a match.

STAGES OF LIFE

Throughout life, the human body is constantly changing as it experiences different stages of development. From a single cell, the body goes through a process of cell division and multiplication as it grows and develops. By adulthood the body is fully grown, and cells no longer divide for growth. Instead, they divide to replace worn out or damaged cells.

HOW CELLS MULTIPLY

We each start out as a single cell. To develop different organs and tissues for the body to grow, our cells must multiply. As adults, cells need to be replaced when damaged or when they complete their life cycle.

Mitosis

The body produces new cells by a process called mitosis. This is when a cell's DNA, which carries all the instructions to build and run a new cell, duplicates itself. The cell then splits to form two identical cells. This is how cells grow—by making exact copies of themselves.

1 CHECKING
The parent cell gets ready for mitosis. It checks its DNA for damage and makes any necessary repairs.

6 OFFSPRING
Two daughter cells are formed. Each one contains a nucleus with an exact copy of the DNA from the parent cell.

5 SPLITTING
A membrane forms around each group of chromosomes. The cell membrane starts to pull apart to form two cells.

THE CHANGING BODY

From babyhood to old age, the body changes as it grows and ages. At the age of around 20–30, humans have reached maximum height and are physically at their strongest. After that, the body very gradually decreases in power with age. However, the brain actually continues to improve over several more years. As it gains more experience, it gets better at analyzing situations and making decisions.

ONLY A FEW **BODY CELLS LAST** A LIFETIME—THEY **INCLUDE NEURONS IN** THE BRAIN AND **HEART MUSCLE CELLS.**

Standing tall
A surge in hormones produces a big growth spurt.

Making a man

Here are the stages of life for a human male, from a baby to an elderly man. Size and height are the most obvious changes, but there are many other changes on the way to adulthood and old age.

Permanent teeth
Baby teeth are replaced by adult teeth by the age of about 11.

Starting small
Learning to stand and walk is a gradual process for growing babies.

1 BABY
Babies have a large head and short arms and legs. By around 18 months, they have gained enough strength and muscle control to stand and start to walk.

2 TODDLER
At about age 2, the arms and legs grow so the head no longer looks as large. The brain develops rapidly, and children learn to talk and use their hands with more precision.

3 CHILD
From the ages of 5–10, children continue to grow and learn complex physical skills, such as riding a bike and swimming.

4 TEENAGER
During puberty, hormones trigger major changes: height increases, the body takes on more adult features, and emotional swings are common.

2 PREPARATION
The chromosomes duplicate themselves, then the originals join together with their copies.

3 LINING UP
Each doubled chromosome attaches to special fibers, which help them to line up in the center of the cell.

4 SEPARATION
The chromosomes break apart at the point where they were attached. Each half is pulled to the opposite end of the cell.

HEALTHY CELL

CELL SHRINKS AND BREAKS APART

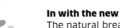

FRAGMENTS EATEN BY CLEANER CELL

OUT WITH THE OLD

When cells reach the end of their natural life span, they undergo a process of shrinking and breaking down into small fragments. These pieces are then eaten up by special cleaner cells called phagocytes.

In with the new
The natural breakdown of cells and the cleanup operation by phagocytes leaves room for new cells to replace them.

USE IT OR LOSE IT

The speed of aging varies widely between people. Although genetics plays its part, evidence suggests that keeping both mind and body active can help to slow down the aging process and may help you live longer.

Staying active
Briton Fauja Singh holds many senior running records, including marathons. In 2013, he ran in the Mumbai Marathon at the age of 102.

5 YOUNG ADULT
The body reaches its adult height, and bones stop growing. People are physically capable of reproducing—having children.

6 ADULT
Humans are physically strongest between 20 and 35 years of age. Muscle development is complete and body systems continue to function well.

7 MIDDLE-AGED ADULT
Between the ages of 50 and 70, the skin becomes less stretchy and wrinkles appear. Muscles weaken. Vision and hearing begin to deteriorate.

8 ELDERLY ADULT
A person gets shorter as they age because their spine shortens. Their muscles also get weaker, and together with stiff joints this can make movement slower.

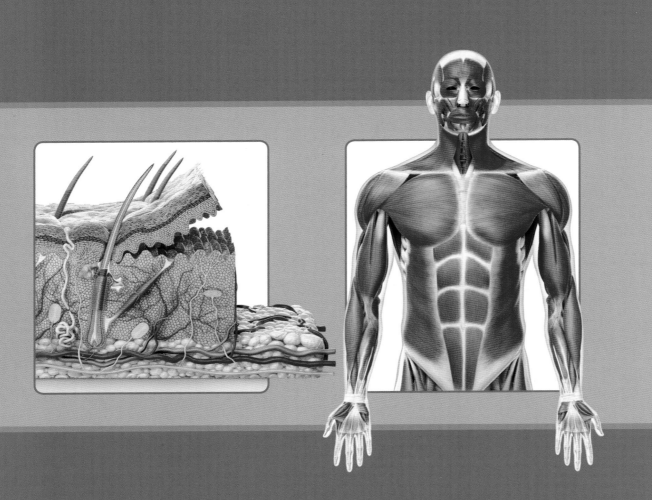
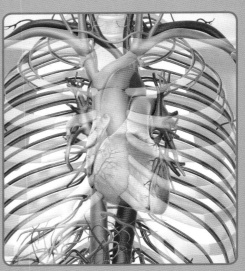

BODY SYSTEMS

The human body works like a machine, running multiple systems at once to keep it operating at optimum levels. Each body system has its own unique function, but also depends on all the other systems to perform at its best.

The kidneys make urine and also release hormones, so they belong to both the **urinary and the endocrine** systems.

All systems go

Humans could not survive without all 12 of the body systems—groups of body parts that carry out different tasks. The systems communicate continually by passing instructions to each other, so the body works as one.

The 12 systems are the skin, hair, and nails; muscular; skeletal (bones); nervous (brain and nerves); cardiovascular (heart and blood); lymphatic (drainage); immune (defense); respiratory (lungs and breathing); digestive (processing food); urinary (kidneys and bladder); reproductive (sex); and endocrine (hormones) systems.

Working together

Body systems are interdependent, which means they rely on each other to function. Some organs belong to more than one system—the pancreas plays a role in digestion but also releases hormones, so it belongs to both the digestive and endocrine systems.

Every single part of the human body is connected to the central **nervous system.**

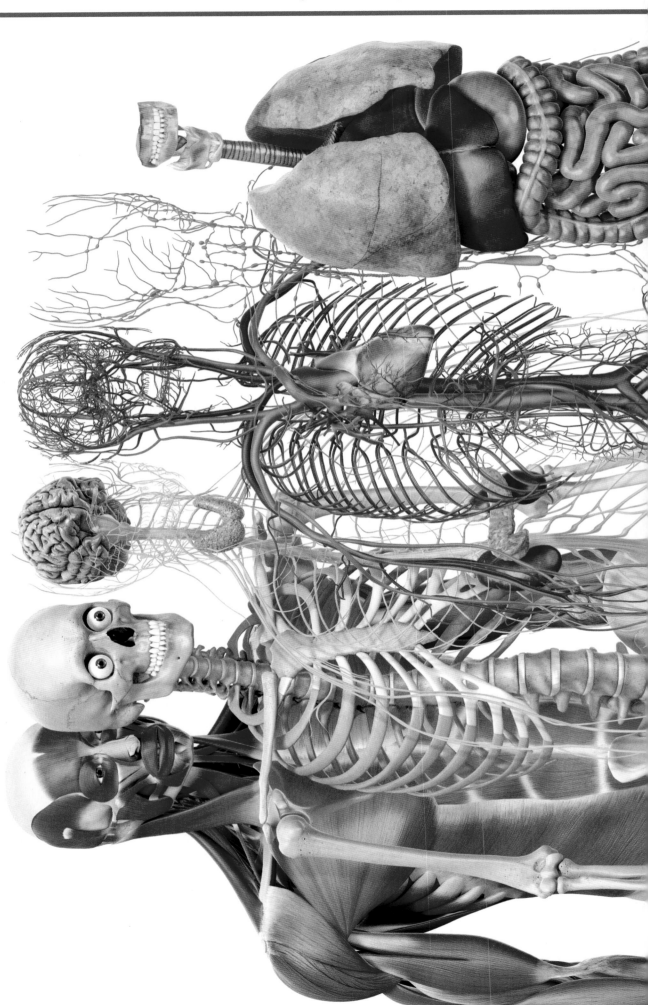

Muscles **push food through your system** so efficiently that food would reach your stomach even if you ate standing on your head.

Your body makes **two million new red blood cells** every second, to replace the same number that die.

21

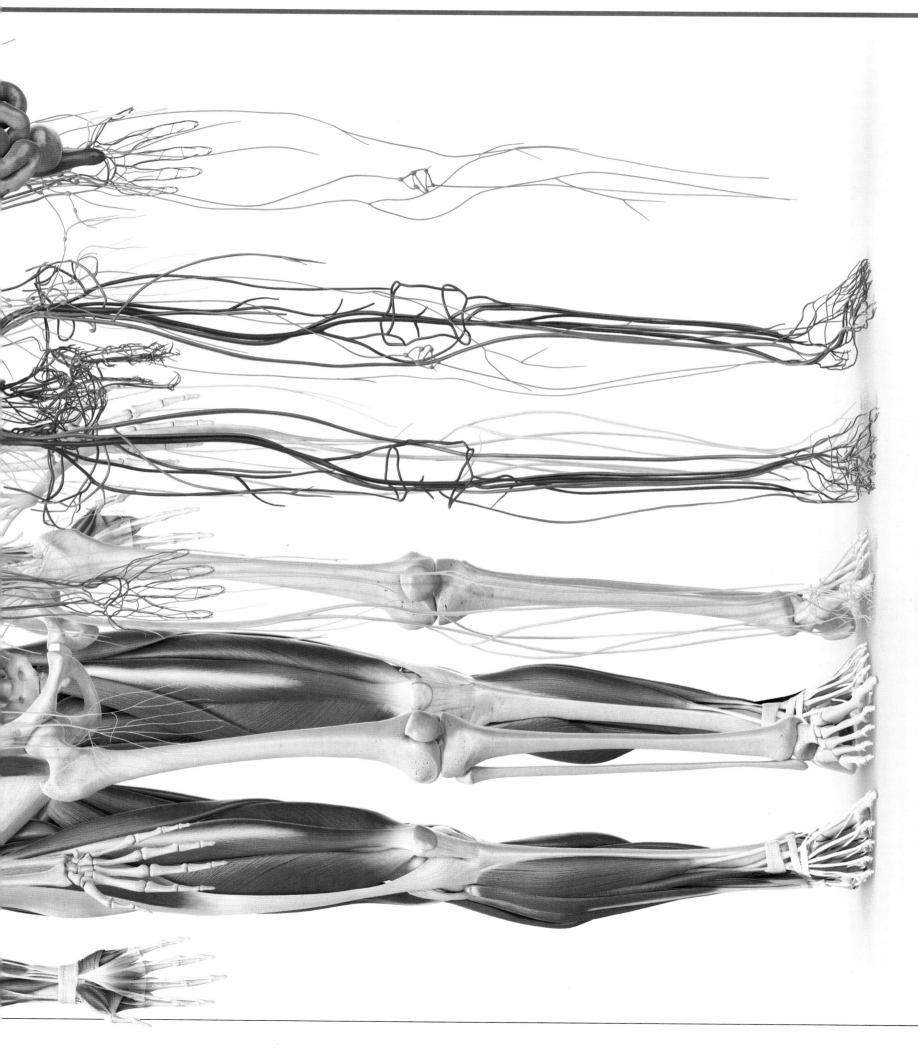

Skin and hair

The skin has two main layers. The epidermis is the thin, protective outer covering, made up mostly of dead, scaly cells. Beneath it lies the thicker dermis, which is rich in blood vessels and nerve endings to sense pressure, temperature, and pain. Strands of bendy hair cover almost all the body's surface. Hair grows from follicles, which are deep pits in the skin.

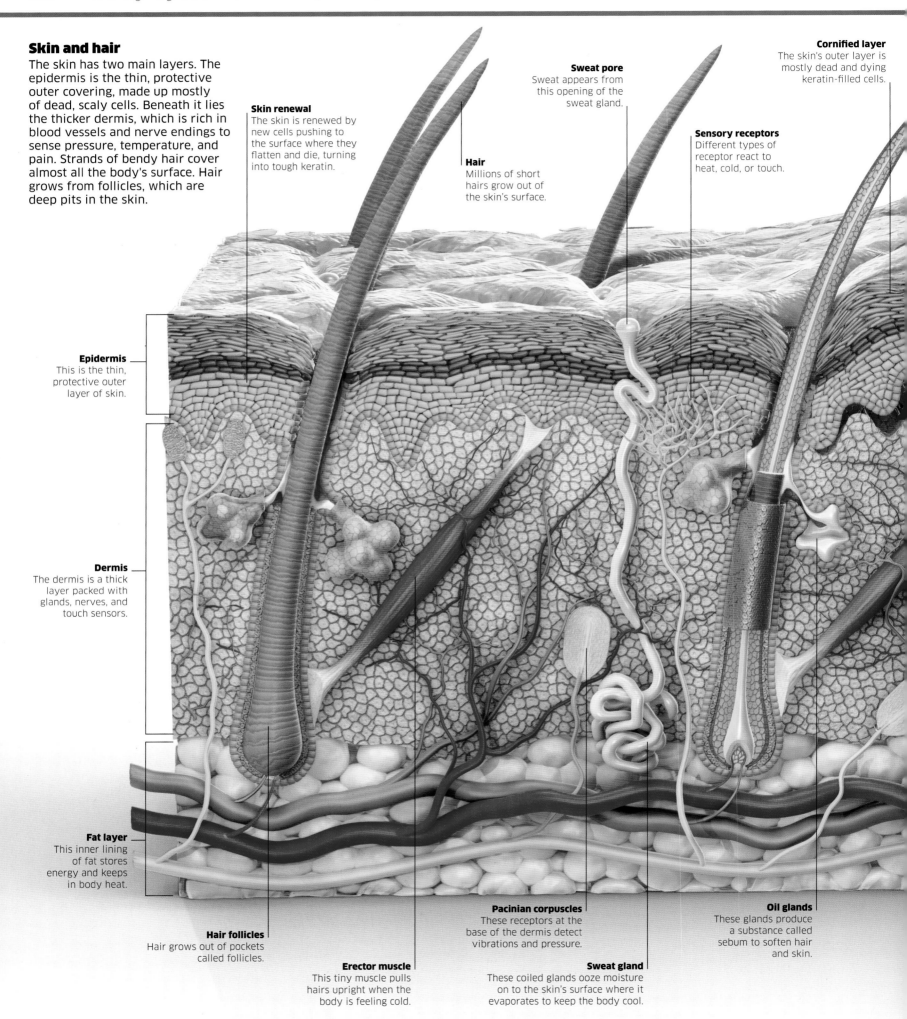

Skin renewal
The skin is renewed by new cells pushing to the surface where they flatten and die, turning into tough keratin.

Sweat pore
Sweat appears from this opening of the sweat gland.

Cornified layer
The skin's outer layer is mostly dead and dying keratin-filled cells.

Hair
Millions of short hairs grow out of the skin's surface.

Sensory receptors
Different types of receptor react to heat, cold, or touch.

Epidermis
This is the thin, protective outer layer of skin.

Dermis
The dermis is a thick layer packed with glands, nerves, and touch sensors.

Fat layer
This inner lining of fat stores energy and keeps in body heat.

Hair follicles
Hair grows out of pockets called follicles.

Erector muscle
This tiny muscle pulls hairs upright when the body is feeling cold.

Pacinian corpuscles
These receptors at the base of the dermis detect vibrations and pressure.

Sweat gland
These coiled glands ooze moisture on to the skin's surface where it evaporates to keep the body cool.

Oil glands
These glands produce a substance called sebum to soften hair and skin.

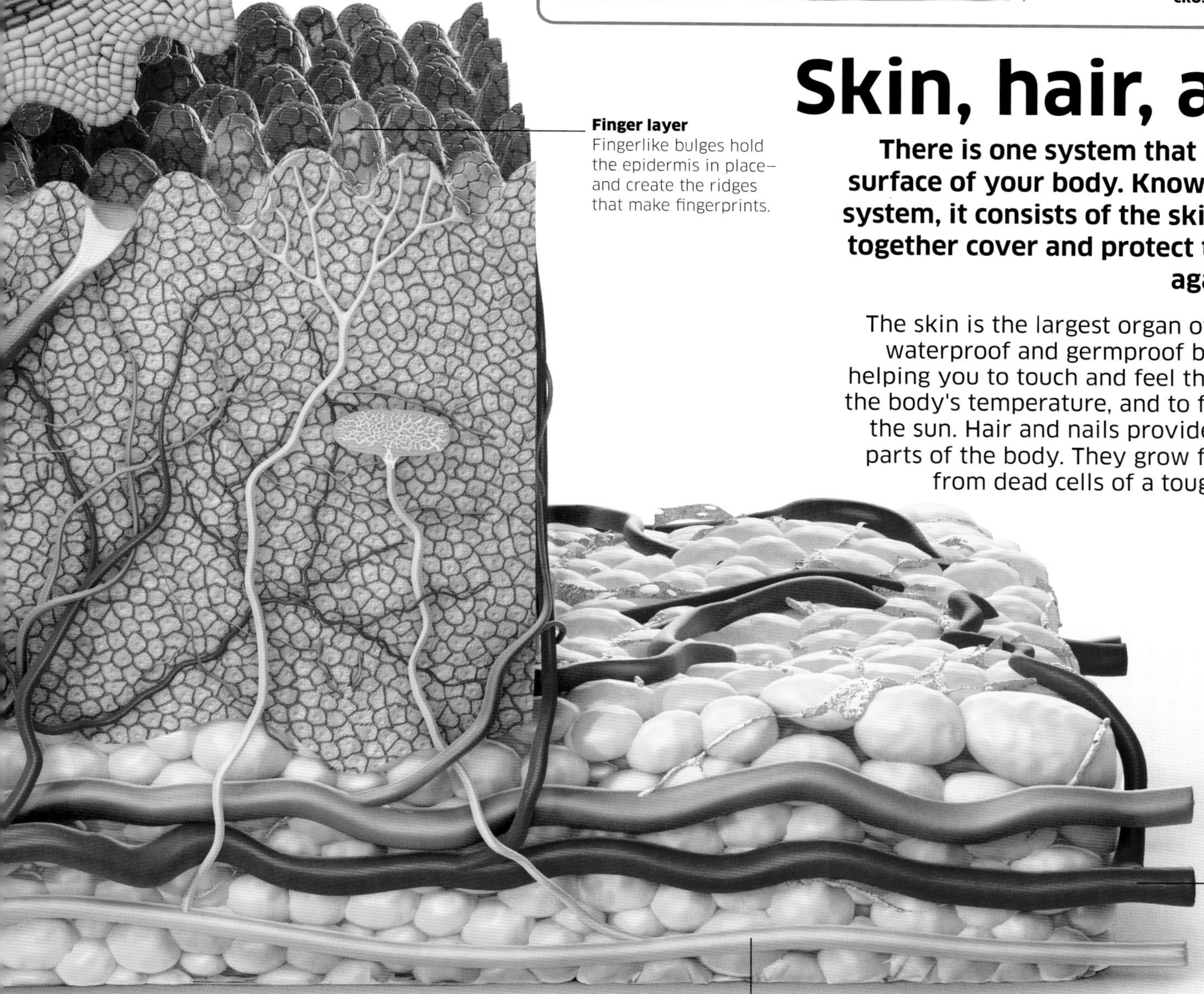

Base layer
New skin cells are formed in the base of the epidermis, ready to move up to the surface.

Protective shield

Skin protects the body, while being flexible enough to let you move around easily. The hair on your head keeps you warm and gives the scalp an extra layer of defense. Fine hairs on the rest of your body make you more sensitive to touch.

Nail structure

Nails are hard plates of dead cells that protect the ends of your fingers and toes. They also help you to grip and pick things up. New cells grow in the root of the nail, and as these cells move forward, they harden and die. It takes about six months for cells to move from the base of a nail to the tip.

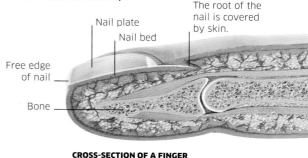

The root of the nail is covered by skin.

Nail plate

Nail bed

Free edge of nail

Bone

CROSS-SECTION OF A FINGER

Skin, hair, and nails

There is one system that extends over the entire surface of your body. Known as the integumentary system, it consists of the skin, hair, and nails, which together cover and protect the other body systems against the outside world.

Finger layer
Fingerlike bulges hold the epidermis in place— and create the ridges that make fingerprints.

The skin is the largest organ of the body, wrapping it in a waterproof and germproof barrier. It is also essential in helping you to touch and feel things around you, to control the body's temperature, and to filter out harmful rays from the sun. Hair and nails provide extra protection for some parts of the body. They grow from the skin and are made from dead cells of a tough substance called keratin.

Artery
This supplies oxygen and nutrients to the skin.

Nerves
These networks carry signals between touch receptors and the brain.

16% of your total body mass is made up of skin.

BODY COVER

The human body is almost entirely covered in a layer of skin and hair for protection and warmth. Together, the skin and hair form the body's largest sensory organ, with an advanced array of sensors that give the brain detailed data about the body's surroundings. The body has different skin and hair types, depending on where they are and their role.

HAIRY OR SMOOTH

The main skin types are hairy or hairless (also called glabrous skin). Most of the body is covered in hairy skin, even though the hair is sometimes too fine for us to see it easily.

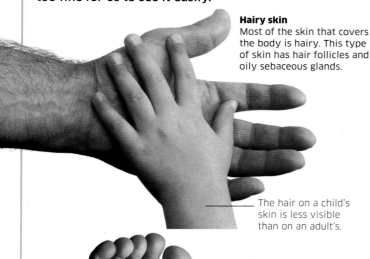

Hairy skin
Most of the skin that covers the body is hairy. This type of skin has hair follicles and oily sebaceous glands.

The hair on a child's skin is less visible than on an adult's.

Glabrous skin
Without any hair follicles, glabrous skin is much smoother than hairy skin. It provides padding for the lips, palms of the hands, and soles of the feet.

Glabrous skin has no hair.

THE BODY'S THINNEST SKIN IS ON THE EYELIDS, AND THE THICKEST IS ON THE SOLES OF THE FEET.

BODY TEMPERATURE

When it's too hot or cold, skin and hair play important roles in keeping the temperature at a safe and comfortable level. A thermostat in the brain's hypothalamus monitors signals from the body's sensors. It then sends signals for the body to act to cool itself down or stay warm.

Sweating
Sweat cools the skin as it evaporates.

SUN SHIELD

One of the skin's many functions is to make vitamin D by harnessing the sun's rays. However, ultraviolet light from the sun can damage the skin, so the body produces a substance called melanin to protect it. Melanin is what makes skin look darker or lighter.

Skin color

Human skin has adapted to suit the conditions on Earth. Near the equator, the Sun's rays are most intense. The body produces lots of melanin for maximum protection, so skin is darker. Far from the equator, less melanin is needed, so skin is lighter.

Dark skin
Lots of melanin is produced by cells called melanocytes.

Pale skin
The skin produces smaller amounts of melanin pigment.

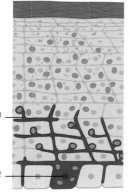

Melanin

Melanocyte

Keeping cool
If the temperature rises above 100.4°F (38°C), sweat glands produce watery sweat to cool the skin. Blood vessels at the skin's surface widen, so heat can escape easily. Hair relaxes, so heat is released into the air.

Hair is flattened

Muscle relaxes

Blood vessels are wide

Sweat gland releases droplets of sweat

Hair stands upright

Skin forms goose bumps

Muscle contracts

Blood vessels narrow

Keeping warm
When the temperature drops, skin goes into heat-retention mode. Blood vessels become narrower to prevent heat loss from the warm body. Muscles contract to make the skin's hairs stand upright to trap warm air. These muscles pull on the skin above, making lumps known as goose bumps.

HAIR
Unlike most warm-blooded land animals, humans have no fur to keep them warm— most of the hair that covers our bodies is very fine. Bare skin is good for keeping the body cool, but in colder climates, humans need to wear clothes to maintain their body temperature.

Hair growth
Each hair grows out of a deep, narrow shaft called a follicle. At the base of the hair, living cells divide and push the hair upward. Hair does not grow constantly. Instead it grows in spurts and has periods of rest in between.

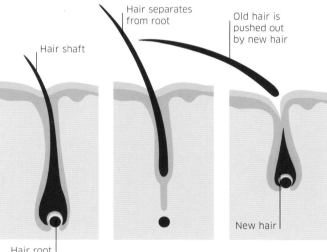

Hair separates from root

Old hair is pushed out by new hair

Hair shaft

Hair root

New hair

1 ACTIVE FOLLICLE The active follicle creates new cells inside the hair root. As these die, they are pushed out to form the shaft, which gets longer and longer.

2 RESTING STAGE The follicle becomes narrower, and the hair stops growing. The hair gets pulled away from the root, losing its blood supply.

3 NEW GROWTH The follicle begins a new cycle. As people age, their hair becomes thinner because fewer follicles reactivate and grow new hairs.

Hair types
There are two main types of hair on the human body—vellus and terminal. Vellus hairs are the fine, soft hairs that are usually found covering the skin of children and women. Terminal hairs are thicker, and are found on the head, in the armpits and pubic area, and on other parts of the body, especially in men.

Hair styles
The type of hair you have depends on the shape and size of the follicle it grows from. Small follicles produce fine hair, while bigger follicles produce thick hair. Hair on the head can be straight, wavy, or curly. About 100 head hairs are lost every day, and these are replaced by new growth.

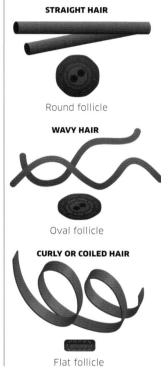

STRAIGHT HAIR

Round follicle

WAVY HAIR

Oval follicle

CURLY OR COILED HAIR

Flat follicle

Freckles
Some people have a gene for freckles. These small dots show where many melanocyte cells have grouped together. They can become more visible when exposed to sunlight.

Freckled face
Freckles are most common on the face, but they appear on arms and shoulders, too.

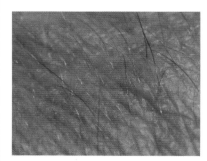

Vellus hair
Fine, short vellus hairs are pale-colored or translucent and grow over most areas of the body.

Terminal hair
Thicker hair on top of the head provides warmth and gives cover from the sun.

Skeletal system

The skeleton shapes and supports the body, allows it to move, and protects internal organs. It is constructed from 206 bones that, far from being dry and dusty, are moist, living organs. Together, those bones create a framework that is strong but light.

Without a skeleton, the body would collapse in a heap. Yet it is not a rigid structure. Flexible joints between bones allow the body to move when those bones are pulled by muscles. The skeleton has other roles. It protects delicate organs such as the brain and heart. Its bones also make blood cells and store calcium, a mineral that is essential for healthy teeth.

Skeleton front view
This is the front view of an adult male skeleton. The female skeleton is usually smaller and lighter than a male's, with a wider pelvis, which makes childbirth easier.

Cranium
This contains and protects the brain, eyes, ears, and nose.

Lower jawbone (mandible)
The only part of the skull that can move is the mandible.

Spinal column
A flexible series of bones holds the head and upper body upright.

Clavicle
This long bone is also called the collarbone.

Scapula
Also called the shoulder blade, this connects the arm to the shoulder.

Humerus
This is the upper arm bone.

Ulna
This is the inner bone of the forearm.

Radius
This is the outer bone of the forearm.

Carpal
There are eight of these small bones at the wrist.

Sternum
Also called the breastbone, it supports the ribs at the front of the body.

Ribs
The 12 pairs of curved rib bones protect the heart and lungs.

Pelvis
These connected bones support the abdominal organs.

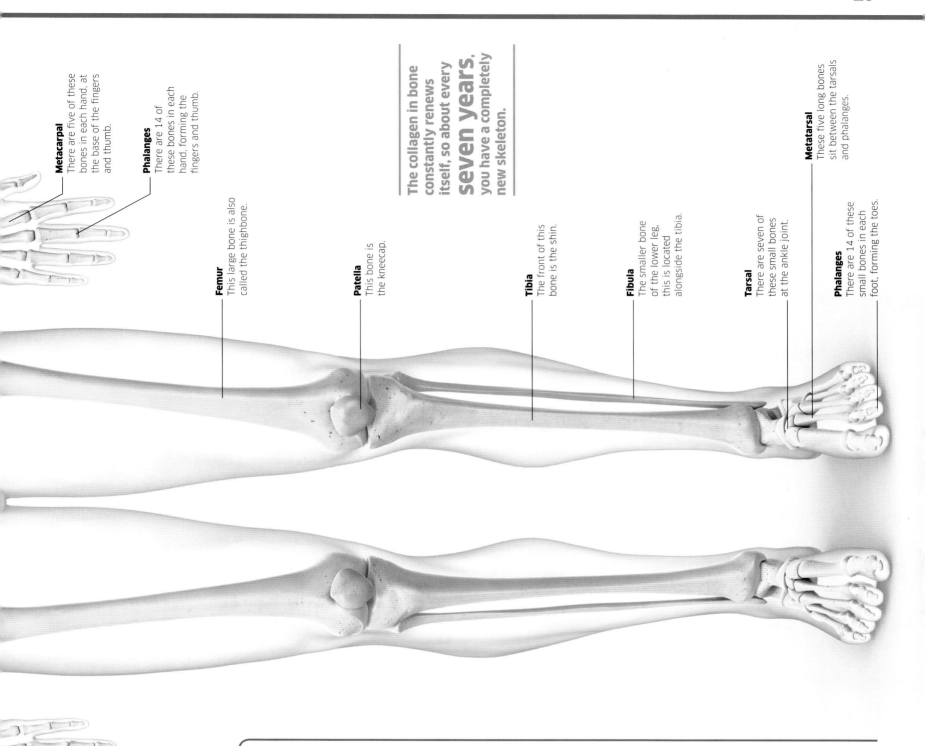

Metacarpal
There are five of these bones in each hand, at the base of the fingers and thumb.

Phalanges
There are 14 of these bones in each hand, forming the fingers and thumb.

Femur
This large bone is also called the thighbone.

Patella
This bone is the kneecap.

Tibia
The front of this bone is the shin.

Fibula
The smaller bone of the lower leg, this is located alongside the tibia.

Tarsal
There are seven of these small bones at the ankle joint.

Phalanges
There are 14 of these small bones in each foot, forming the toes.

Metatarsal
These five long bones sit between the tarsals and phalanges.

The collagen in bone constantly renews itself, so about every **seven years,** you have a completely new skeleton.

Two skeletons in one

The skeleton can be divided into two parts. The axial skeleton (red) forms a central core that supports the upper body and protects important organs. The appendicular skeleton (blue) consists of the arm and leg bones, and the bony girdles that connect them to the axial skeleton.

Axial skeleton
This is made up of the 80 bones of the skull, vertebral column, ribs, and breastbone.

Appendicular skeleton
This consists of the 126 bones of the upper and lower limbs, and the shoulder and hip girdles.

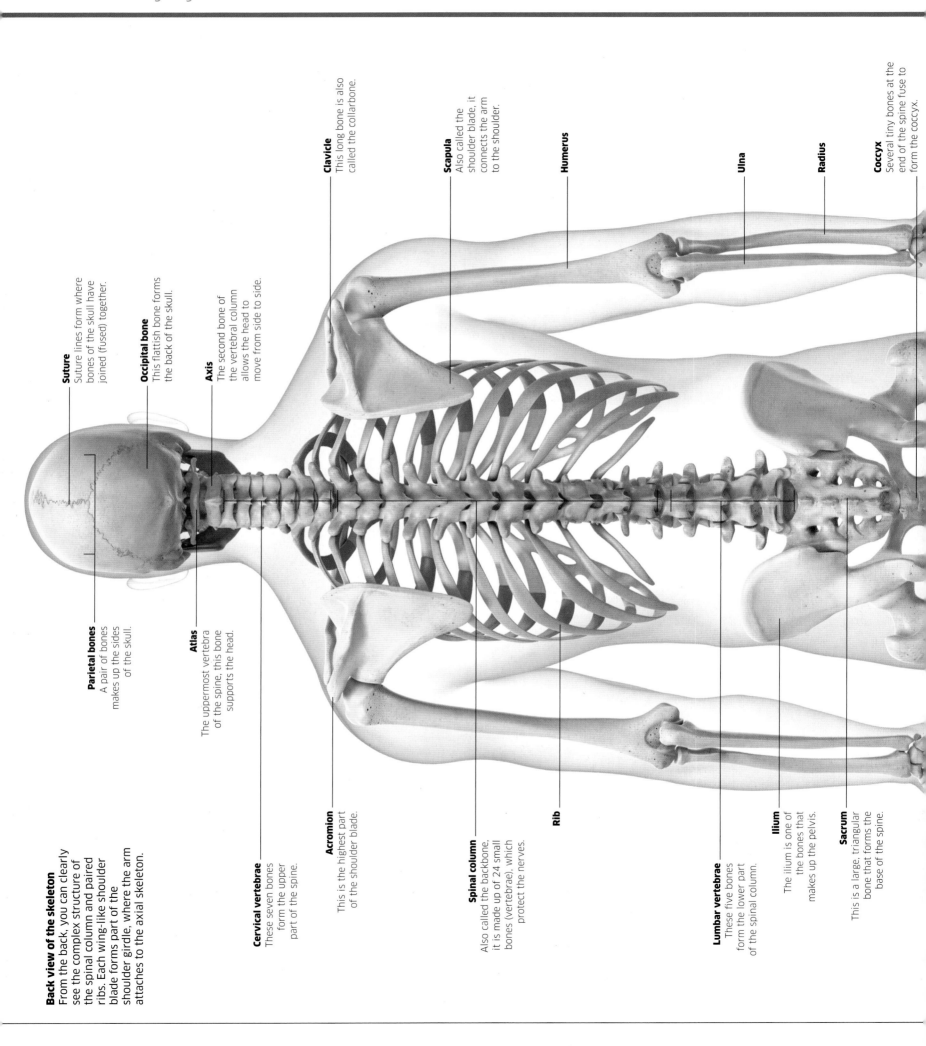

Back view of the skeleton
From the back, you can clearly see the complex structure of the spinal column and paired ribs. Each wing-like shoulder blade forms part of the shoulder girdle, where the arm attaches to the axial skeleton.

Suture
Suture lines form where bones of the skull have joined (fused) together.

Occipital bone
This flattish bone forms the back of the skull.

Axis
The second bone of the vertebral column allows the head to move from side to side.

Clavicle
This long bone is also called the collarbone.

Scapula
Also called the shoulder blade, it connects the arm to the shoulder.

Humerus

Ulna

Radius

Coccyx
Several tiny bones at the end of the spine fuse to form the coccyx.

Parietal bones
A pair of bones makes up the sides of the skull.

Atlas
The uppermost vertebra of the spine, this bone supports the head.

Cervical vertebrae
These seven bones form the upper part of the spine.

Acromion
This is the highest part of the shoulder blade.

Spinal column
Also called the backbone, it is made up of 24 small bones (vertebrae), which protect the nerves.

Rib

Lumbar vertebrae
These five bones form the lower part of the spinal column.

Ilium
The ilium is one of the bones that makes up the pelvis.

Sacrum
This is a large, triangular bone that forms the base of the spine.

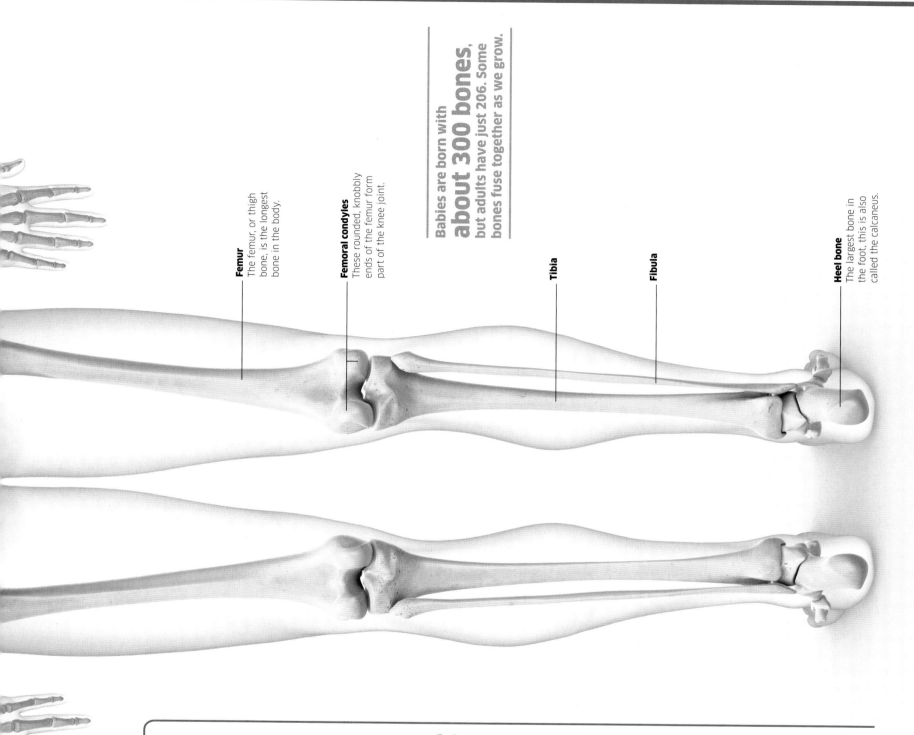

Femur
The femur, or thigh bone, is the longest bone in the body.

Femoral condyles
These rounded, knobbly ends of the femur form part of the knee joint.

Babies are born with **about 300 bones,** but adults have just 206. Some bones fuse together as we grow.

Tibia

Fibula

Heel bone
The largest bone in the foot, this is also called the calcaneus.

Types of bone

Bones have different shapes and sizes, depending on their functions. There are five kinds of bone in the human skeleton.

Long bones
These bones are longer than they are wide and are found in the arms, hands, legs, and feet. They support the body's weight and allow it to move.

FEMUR
(thigh bone)

Short bones
Roughly cube-shaped bones in the wrist and ankle allow some movement and provide stability to the joints.

TARSAL BONES IN THE FOOT

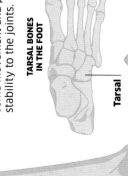

Tarsal

Flat bones
Shield-like flat bones protect organs such as the heart and brain.

SCAPULA
(shoulder blade)

Irregular bones
These bones have complex shapes to perform specific roles. For example, the vertebrae allow the back to bend and rotate, and protect the spinal cord.

VERTEBRA

Sesamoid bones
These small, roundish bones protect tendons and joints from wear and tear. The patella protects the knee joint. It sits inside the tendon that attaches the thigh muscle to the tibia.

PATELLA
(kneecap)

Muscular system

Every single movement your body makes is produced by the muscular system. Muscles are layers of hardworking tissue that shape the body, keep it upright, and move it around.

Muscle tissue is made of long cells called fibers, which use energy to contract, or shorten, pulling different parts of the body into position. Movements are controlled by nerve signals from the brain. Sometimes you move your muscles consciously, such as when you sit down, or turn to look at something. But other muscle movements, such as your heartbeat, or when you blink your eyes, happen without you thinking about them.

Deep muscles, front view

This front view of the skeleton shows the body's deepest layer of skeletal muscles. Skeletal muscles in the back and neck work to keep the body upright, while those in the arms and legs are used for walking, running, and all kinds of other physical activities.

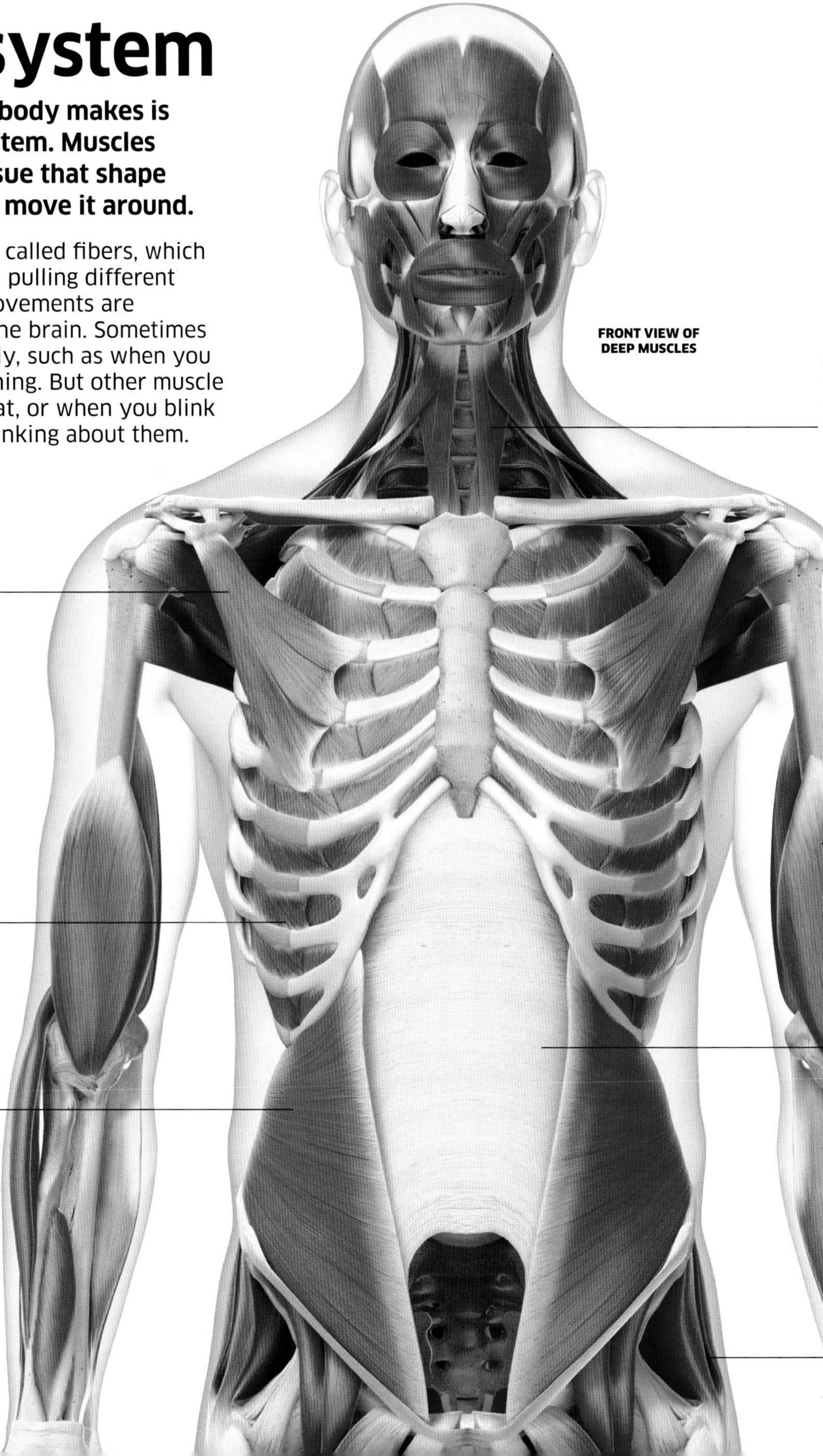

FRONT VIEW OF DEEP MUSCLES

Sternothyroid
This straplike muscle at the front of the neck pulls the larynx down.

An adult's body weight is made up of about **40% muscle.**

Brachialis
The brachialis helps to bend the elbow.

Posterior rectus sheath
This tissue is formed by the tendons of the abdominal muscle.

Flexor digitorum profundus
This muscle helps to bend the fingers.

Gluteus medius
This muscle moves the thigh outward.

Pectoralis minor
This muscle helps to stabilize the shoulder blade when the arm moves.

Intercostal muscles
These muscles between the ribs help with breathing by raising the ribs up and out.

Transversus abdominis
This muscle helps to stabilize the pelvis and lower back when moving.

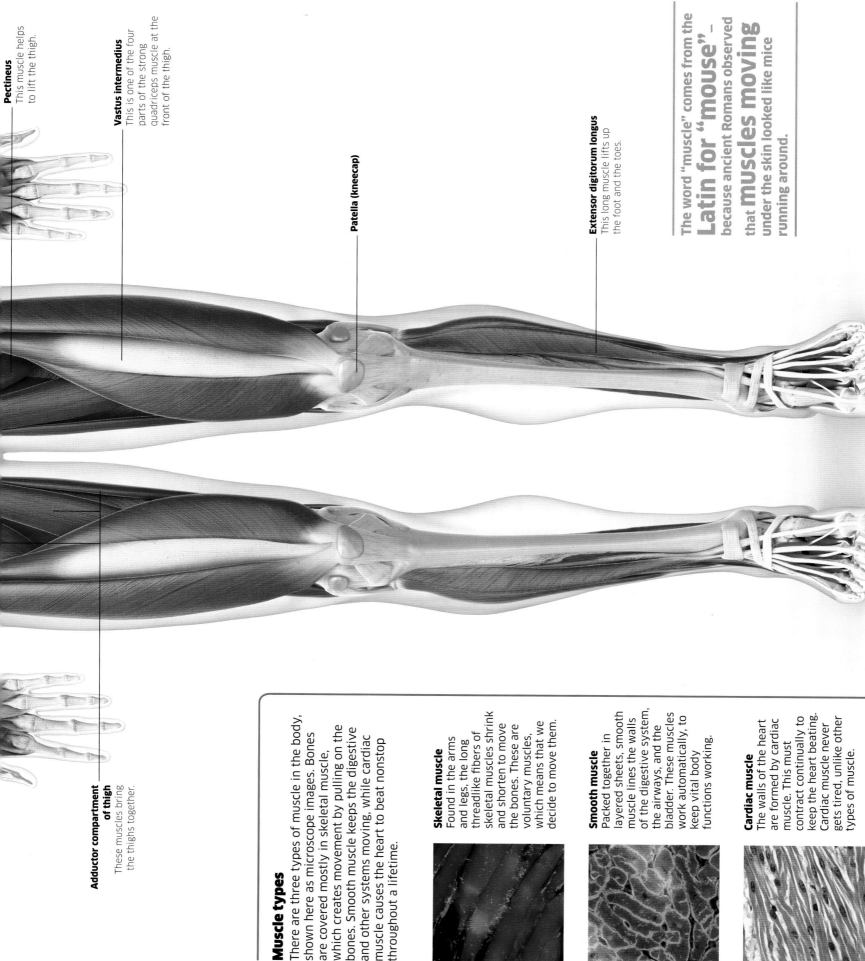

Pectineus
This muscle helps to lift the thigh.

Vastus intermedius
This is one of the four parts of the strong quadriceps muscle at the front of the thigh.

Patella (kneecap)

Extensor digitorum longus
This long muscle lifts up the foot and the toes.

The word "muscle" comes from the **Latin for "mouse"** – because ancient Romans observed that **muscles moving** under the skin looked like mice running around.

Adductor compartment of thigh
These muscles bring the thighs together.

Muscle types

There are three types of muscle in the body, shown here as microscope images. Bones are covered mostly in skeletal muscle, which creates movement by pulling on the bones. Smooth muscle keeps the digestive and other systems moving, while cardiac muscle causes the heart to beat nonstop throughout a lifetime.

Skeletal muscle
Found in the arms and legs, the long threadlike fibers of skeletal muscles shrink and shorten to move the bones. These are voluntary muscles, which means that we decide to move them.

Smooth muscle
Packed together in layered sheets, smooth muscle lines the walls of the digestive system, the airways, and the bladder. These muscles work automatically, to keep vital body functions working.

Cardiac muscle
The walls of the heart are formed by cardiac muscle. This must contract continually to keep the heart beating. Cardiac muscle never gets tired, unlike other types of muscle.

Deep muscles, back view

This rear view of the deep muscles shows skeletal muscles from the head to the feet. They hold the head and back upright, keep the shoulders steady, pull the arms back, straighten the thighs, bend the knees, and point the toes down.

If all the body's muscles pulled in the same direction at once, they could create a force strong enough to **lift a small truck.**

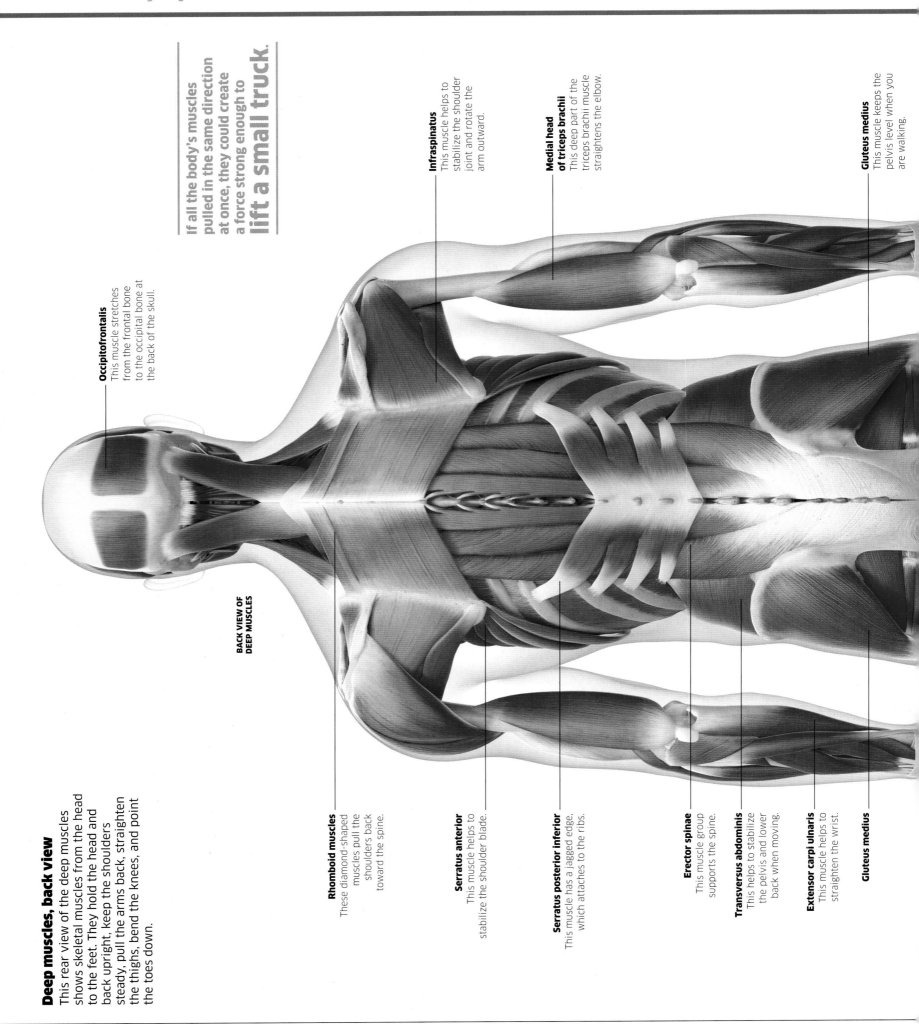

BACK VIEW OF DEEP MUSCLES

Occipitofrontalis
This muscle stretches from the frontal bone to the occipital bone at the back of the skull.

Infraspinatus
This muscle helps to stabilize the shoulder joint and rotate the arm outward.

Medial head of triceps brachii
This deep part of the triceps brachii muscle straightens the elbow.

Gluteus medius
This muscle keeps the pelvis level when you are walking.

Rhomboid muscles
These diamond-shaped muscles pull the shoulders back toward the spine.

Serratus anterior
This muscle helps to stabilize the shoulder blade.

Serratus posterior inferior
This muscle has a jagged edge, which attaches to the ribs.

Erector spinae
This muscle group supports the spine.

Transversus abdominis
This helps to stabilize the pelvis and lower back when moving.

Extensor carpi ulnaris
This muscle helps to straighten the wrist.

Gluteus medius

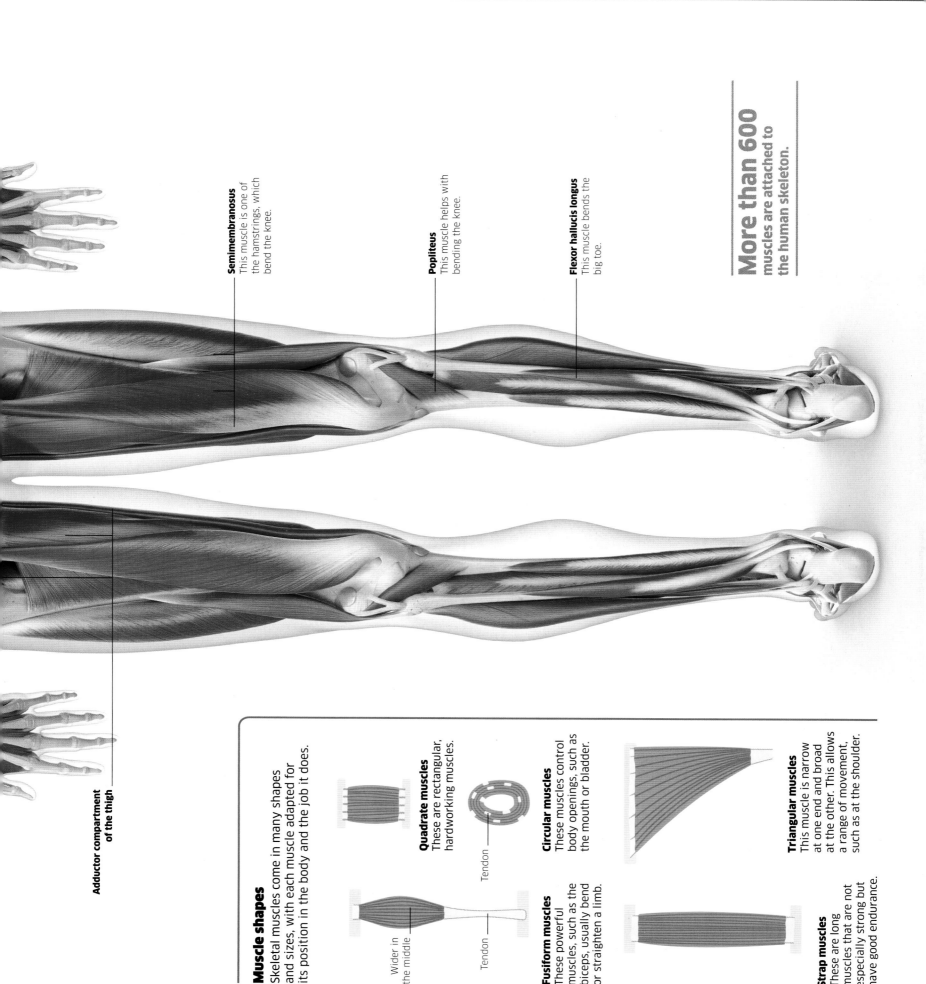

Semimembranosus
This muscle is one of the hamstrings, which bend the knee.

Popliteus
This muscle helps with bending the knee.

Flexor hallucis longus
This muscle bends the big toe.

Adductor compartment of the thigh

More than 600
muscles are attached to the human skeleton.

Muscle shapes
Skeletal muscles come in many shapes and sizes, with each muscle adapted for its position in the body and the job it does.

Quadrate muscles
These are rectangular, hardworking muscles.

Tendon

Circular muscles
These muscles control body openings, such as the mouth or bladder.

Triangular muscles
This muscle is narrow at one end and broad at the other. This allows a range of movement, such as at the shoulder.

Fusiform muscles
These powerful muscles, such as the biceps, usually bend or straighten a limb.

Wider in the middle

Tendon

Strap muscles
These are long muscles that are not especially strong but have good endurance.

Superficial muscles, front view

Superficial muscles are just beneath the skin. Those at the front of the body create different facial expressions, move the head forward and sideways, bend the arms and move them forward, bend the body forward and sideways, bend the legs, straighten the knees, and lift the feet.

Your eye muscles move more than 100,000 times every day.

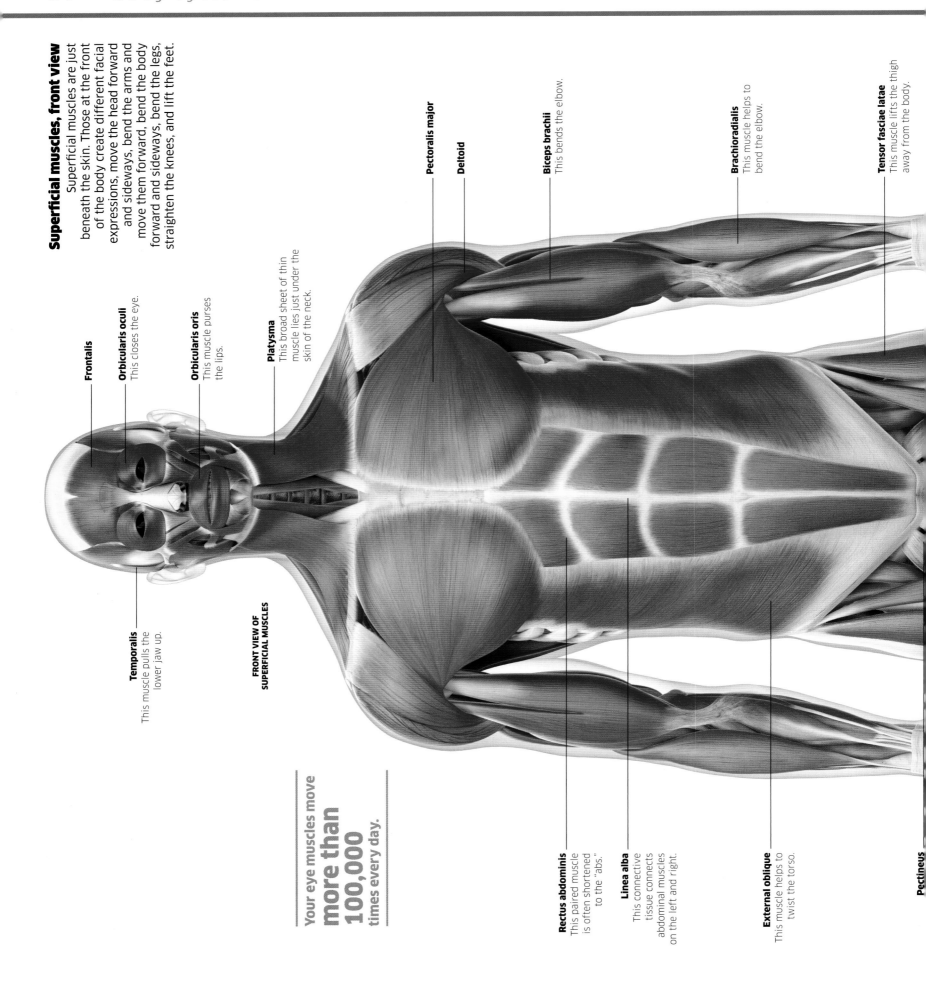

FRONT VIEW OF SUPERFICIAL MUSCLES

Frontalis

Orbicularis oculi
This closes the eye.

Orbicularis oris
This muscle purses the lips.

Platysma
This broad sheet of thin muscle lies just under the skin of the neck.

Temporalis
This muscle pulls the lower jaw up.

Pectoralis major

Deltoid

Biceps brachii
This bends the elbow.

Brachioradialis
This muscle helps to bend the elbow.

Tensor fasciae latae
This muscle lifts the thigh away from the body.

Rectus abdominis
This paired muscle is often shortened to the "abs."

Linea alba
This connective tissue connects abdominal muscles on the left and right.

External oblique
This muscle helps to twist the torso.

Pectineus

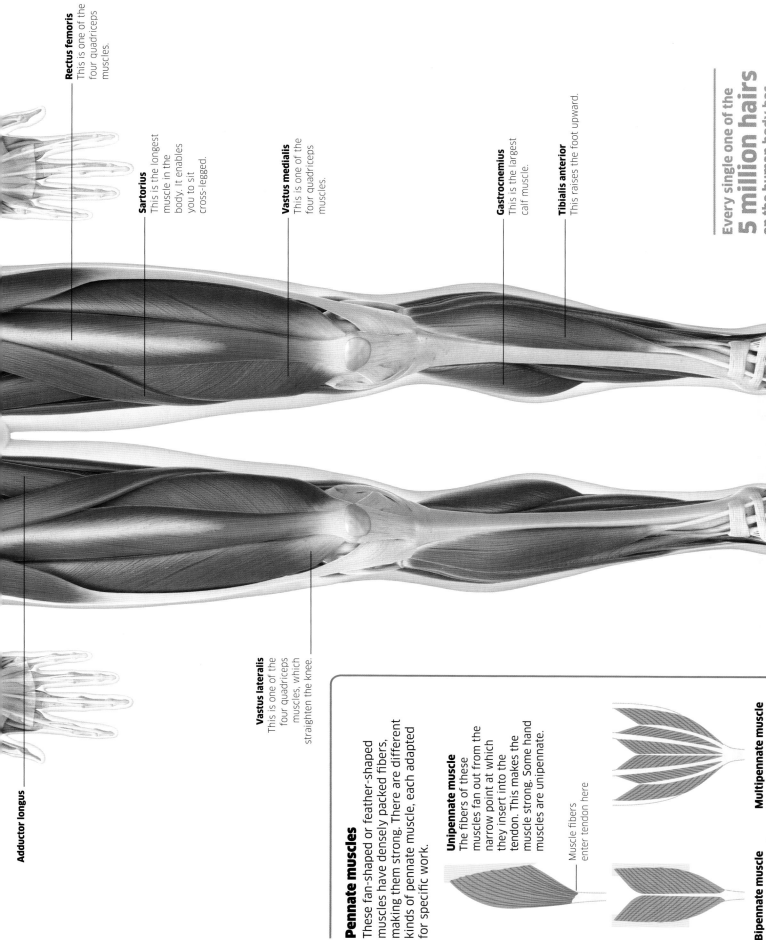

Rectus femoris
This is one of the four quadriceps muscles.

Sartorius
This is the longest muscle in the body. It enables you to sit cross-legged.

Vastus medialis
This is one of the four quadriceps muscles.

Gastrocnemius
This is the largest calf muscle.

Tibialis anterior
This raises the foot upward.

Adductor longus

Vastus lateralis
This is one of the four quadriceps muscles, which straighten the knee.

Every single one of the
5 million hairs
on the human body has its own muscle.

Pennate muscles

These fan-shaped or feather-shaped muscles have densely packed fibers, making them strong. There are different kinds of pennate muscle, each adapted for specific work.

Bipennate muscle
This has fibers running diagonally from each side of a tendon, like a feather. This makes the muscle even stronger, but less mobile. The rectus femoris muscle at the front of the thigh is bipennate.

Unipennate muscle
The fibers of these muscles fan out from the narrow point at which they insert into the tendon. This makes the muscle strong. Some hand muscles are unipennate.

Muscle fibers enter tendon here

Multipennate muscle
This powerful muscle has many rows of fibers running from a central tendon. The deltoid (shoulder) muscle is multipennate.

Superficial muscles, back view

At first glance, muscle names may appear difficult to read, but they have all been given a unique Latin name to describe them. This name can be understood around the world. The chosen name relates to specific characteristics of the muscle, such as its size, shape, location, and what it does.

There are three times as many **skeletal muscles** as there are bones in the human body.

BACK VIEW OF SUPERFICIAL MUSCLES

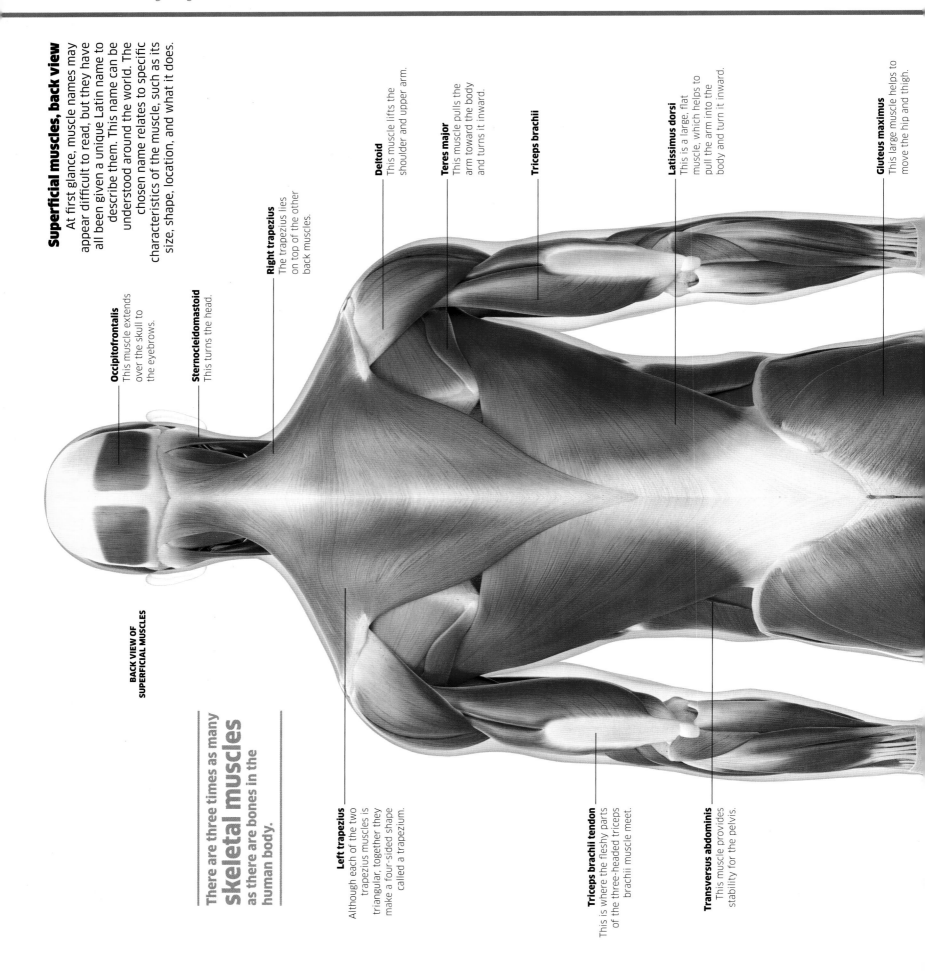

Occipitofrontalis
This muscle extends over the skull to the eyebrows.

Sternocleidomastoid
This turns the head.

Right trapezius
The trapezius lies on top of the other back muscles.

Deltoid
This muscle lifts the shoulder and upper arm.

Teres major
This muscle pulls the arm toward the body and turns it inward.

Triceps brachii

Latissimus dorsi
This is a large, flat muscle, which helps to pull the arm into the body and turn it inward.

Gluteus maximus
This large muscle helps to move the hip and thigh.

Left trapezius
Although each of the two trapezius muscles is triangular, together they make a four-sided shape called a trapezium.

Triceps brachii tendon
This is where the fleshy parts of the three-headed triceps brachii muscle meet.

Transversus abdominis
This muscle provides stability for the pelvis.

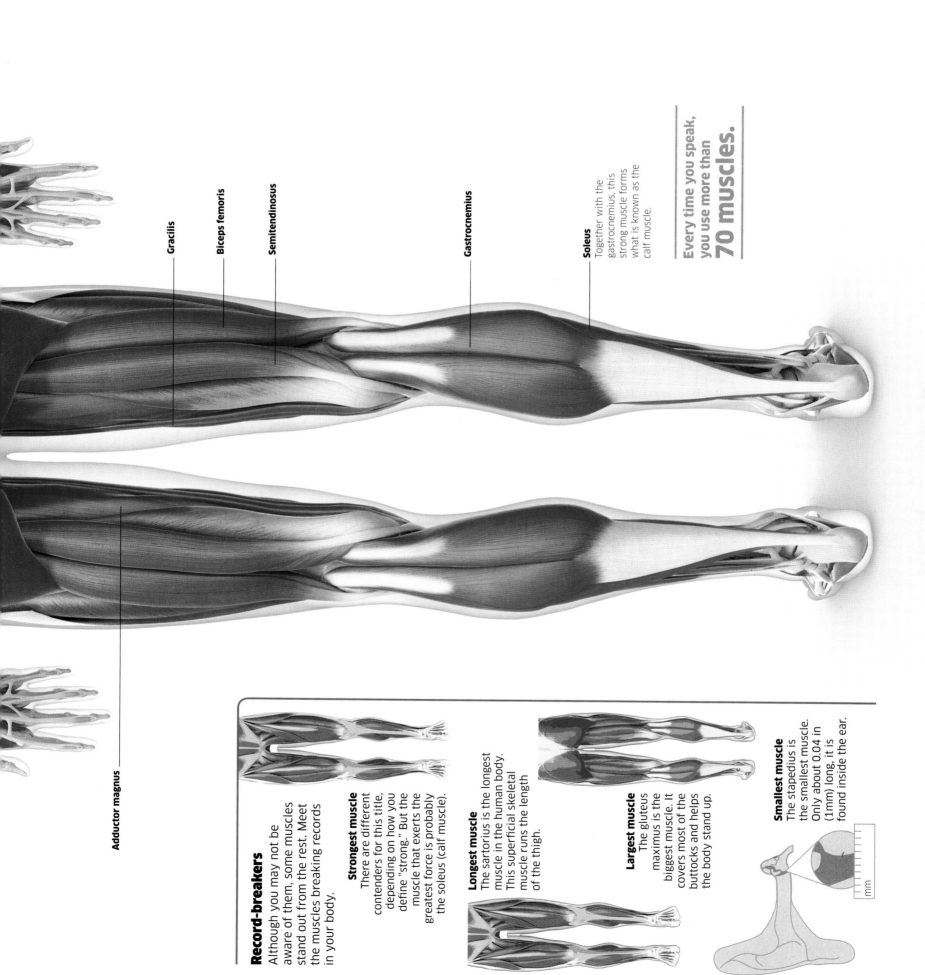

Gracilis

Biceps femoris

Semitendinosus

Gastrocnemius

Soleus
Together with the gastrocnemius, this strong muscle forms what is known as the calf muscle.

Adductor magnus

Every time you speak, you use more than **70 muscles.**

Record-breakers

Although you may not be aware of them, some muscles stand out from the rest. Meet the muscles breaking records in your body.

Strongest muscle
There are different contenders for this title, depending on how you define "strong." But the muscle that exerts the greatest force is probably the soleus (calf muscle).

Longest muscle
The sartorius is the longest muscle in the human body. This superficial skeletal muscle runs the length of the thigh.

Largest muscle
The gluteus maximus is the biggest muscle. It covers most of the buttocks and helps the body stand up.

Smallest muscle
The stapedius is the smallest muscle. Only about 0.04 in (1mm) long, it is found inside the ear.

mm

Nervous system

This is the body's communication and control network. The brain sends and receives messages along the spinal cord and billions of interconnecting nerve cells wired up to every part of the body.

The nervous system works like high-speed internet, sending electrical signals at great speed through nerve cells called neurons. Sensory nerves send signals to the brain from sense receptors all over your body. At the same time, going in the opposite direction, motor nerves send signals from the brain, telling the muscles to move.

Bundle of nerves
The brain and the spinal cord—the mass of nerves running down the backbone—make up the central nervous system (CNS). This coordinates most of the body's activities, from blinking and breathing to seeing and standing. Nerves branch out to the rest of the body via the peripheral nervous system (PNS).

Brain
The control center of the nervous system, this is home to more than 100 billion neurons.

Cranial nerves
Twelve pairs of cranial nerves relay signals between the brain and the head, face, and neck.

Spinal cord
The body's primary communications highway, this carries all nerve signals between the body and brain.

Musculocutaneous nerve
This nerve supplies muscles in the upper arm and gives feeling in the forearm.

Axillary nerve
The axillary nerve supplies muscles and sensation in the shoulder.

Phrenic nerve
Messages to and from the diaphragm are carried by this nerve.

Ulnar nerve
Supplying muscles in the forearm and hand, this nerve gives the "funny bone" tingle if you hit your elbow.

Sciatic nerve
The thickest and longest nerve in the body, this links the spinal cord to muscles in the legs and feet.

Brachial plexus
This collection of nerves supplies the muscles and skin of the arm and hand.

Intercostal nerve
The intercostal nerve supplies the muscles and skin of the thorax (chest).

Median nerve
Most of the muscles in the forearm and hand, and some skin of the hand, is supplied by this nerve.

Radial nerve
This nerve supplies muscles in the back of the arm and the skin of the lower arm.

Lumbar plexus
A "plexus" is a branching network. The lumbar plexus supplies the skin and muscle of the lower back.

Femoral nerve
This supplies sensation and muscles in the thigh and inner leg.

Sacral plexus
The skin and muscle of the pelvis and leg are supplied by this web of nerves.

Saphenous nerve
The saphenous nerve supplies the skin on the inner leg.

Common peroneal (fibular) nerve
A branch of the sciatic nerve, this supplies the front and side of the lower leg.

Superficial peroneal nerve
Supplying the skin and muscles of the leg and foot, this is one of the fibular nerves.

Deep peroneal (fibular) nerve
This nerve supplies the muscles of the leg and foot.

Tibial nerve
This is the biggest branch of the sciatic nerve. It produces a "pins and needles" feeling in the legs if it is squashed.

Plantar nerve
The plantar nerve is responsible for the tickling sensation when the soles of the feet are touched.

The body's nervous system can **transmit signals** at speeds of 220 mph (350 kph).

Neuron fibers

Each neuron has thousands of fibers extending from its cell body. One large fiber, called an axon, carries outgoing electrical signals, while smaller branching fibers, called dendrites, carry incoming electrical signals. The neurons connect with each other at junctions called synapses. Signals cannot jump across these tiny gaps without the help of chemicals called neurotransmitters.

Nerve cell
Each neuron has a nucleus at the center and fibers projecting from it.

Synapse
This is the junction between the axon of one neuron and the dendrite of another.

Axon
An axon is a large fibre that transmits an electrical signal to the next neuron.

Dendrite
These smaller fibres receive signals from nearby neurons.

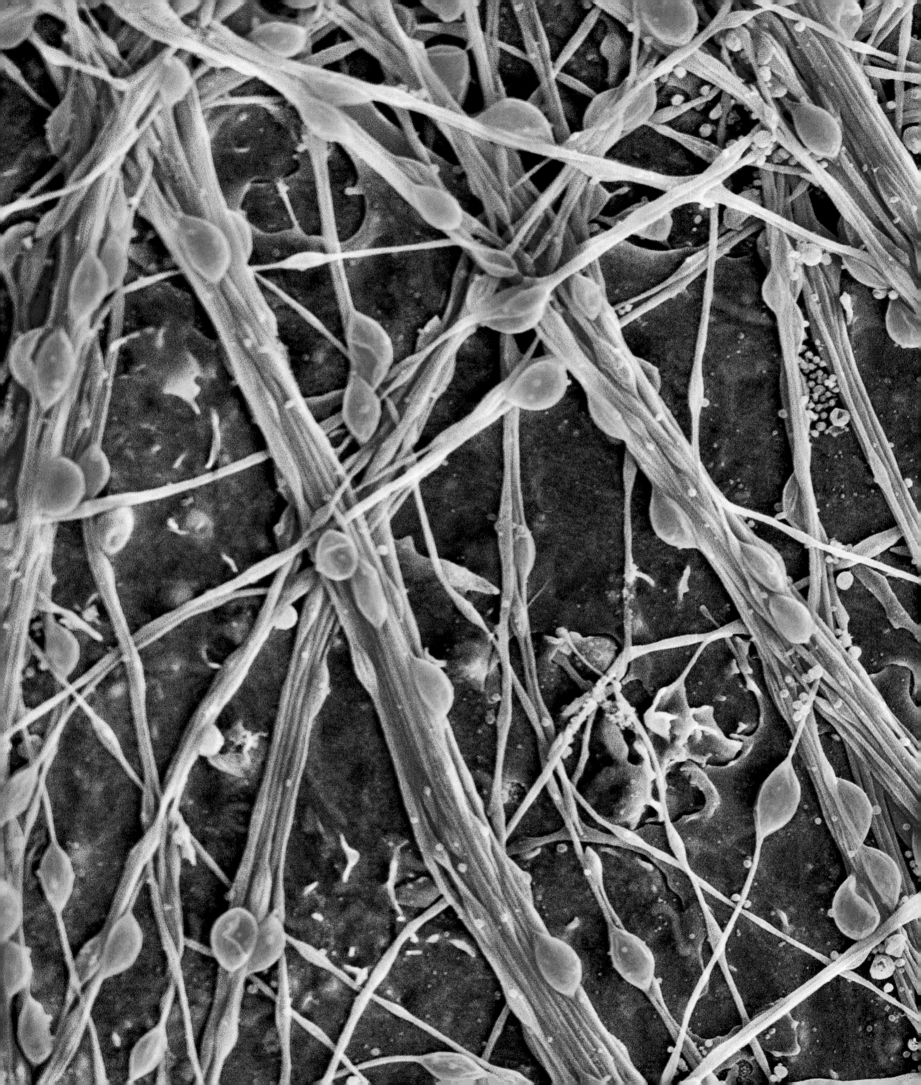

NEURON NETWORK

This image shows the network of nerve cells called neurons. Every nerve is made up of neurons, and there are billions of them. If all the body's neurons were put end to end they would stretch 37 miles (60 km).

Electrical signals pass from one neuron (colored green) to another by moving down their long extensions, which are called axons (colored blue). Signals cross a tiny space to the receiving parts of the next neuron, which are called dendrites (also blue). Messages travel at high speeds, going all the way from the brain to the feet in 0.01 seconds.

Endocrine system

In addition to sending high-speed signals along the nervous system, the body also uses chemicals called hormones to carry messages to specific parts. These hormones are produced and released into the bloodstream by the tissues and glands of the endocrine system.

There are about 50 different kinds of hormone, made by a dozen or so major glands as well as some organs. As it travels around the body, each hormone targets a particular cell or tissue to alter how it works. Hormones control growth, hunger, sleep, reproduction, and many other functions of the body.

Stroking a pet dog or cat releases the hormone oxytocin, which lowers blood pressure and reduces feelings of anxiety.

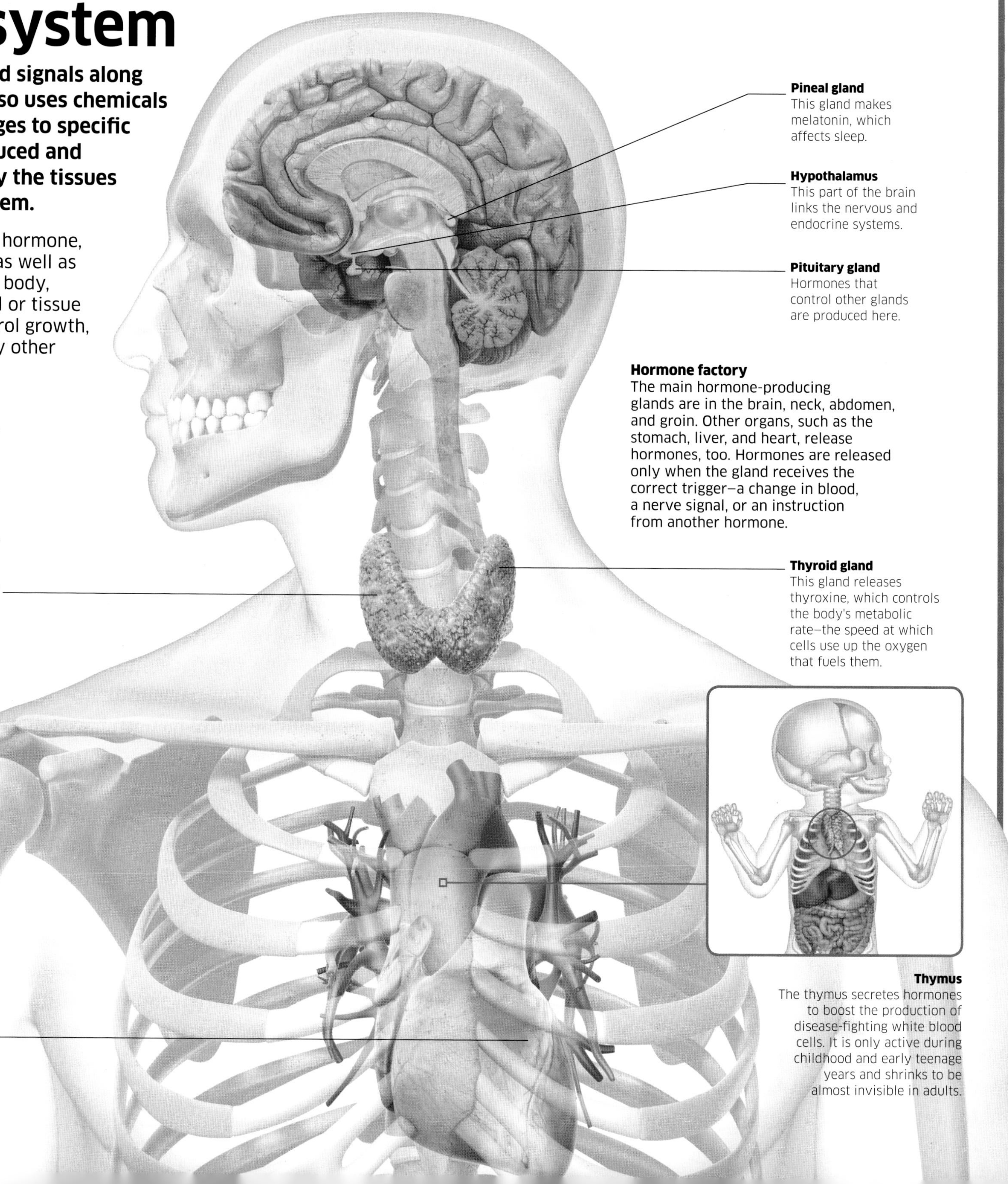

Pineal gland
This gland makes melatonin, which affects sleep.

Hypothalamus
This part of the brain links the nervous and endocrine systems.

Pituitary gland
Hormones that control other glands are produced here.

Hormone factory
The main hormone-producing glands are in the brain, neck, abdomen, and groin. Other organs, such as the stomach, liver, and heart, release hormones, too. Hormones are released only when the gland receives the correct trigger—a change in blood, a nerve signal, or an instruction from another hormone.

Thyroid gland
This gland releases thyroxine, which controls the body's metabolic rate—the speed at which cells use up the oxygen that fuels them.

Thymus
The thymus secretes hormones to boost the production of disease-fighting white blood cells. It is only active during childhood and early teenage years and shrinks to be almost invisible in adults.

Parathyroid glands
These four small glands regulate levels of calcium, which is vital for healthy teeth and bones.

Heart
The heart releases hormones that control blood pressure.

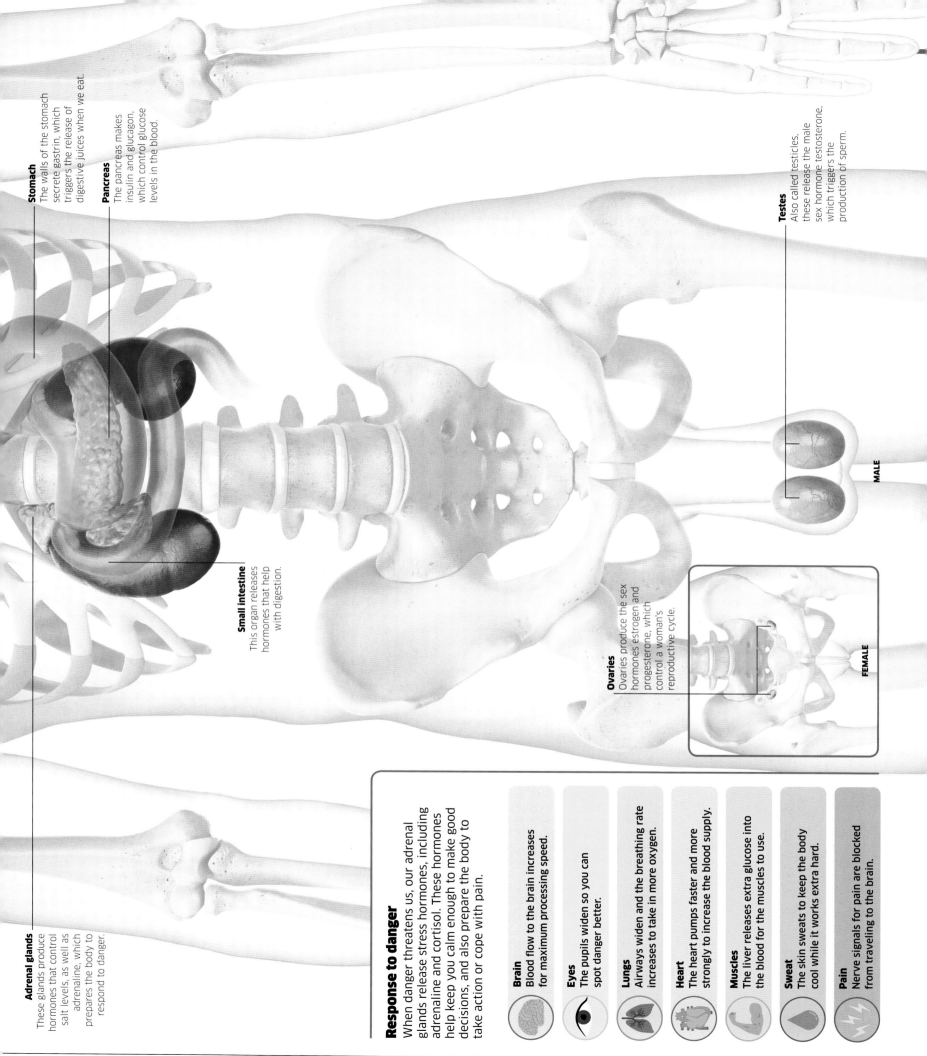

Stomach
The walls of the stomach secrete gastrin, which triggers the release of digestive juices when we eat.

Pancreas
The pancreas makes insulin and glucagon, which control glucose levels in the blood.

Testes
Also called testicles, these release the male sex hormone testosterone, which triggers the production of sperm.

Adrenal glands
These glands produce hormones that control salt levels, as well as adrenaline, which prepares the body to respond to danger.

Small intestine
This organ releases hormones that help with digestion.

Ovaries
Ovaries produce the sex hormones estrogen and progesterone, which control a woman's reproductive cycle.

MALE

FEMALE

Response to danger

When danger threatens us, our adrenal glands release stress hormones, including adrenaline and cortisol. These hormones help keep you calm enough to make good decisions, and also prepare the body to take action or cope with pain.

Brain
Blood flow to the brain increases for maximum processing speed.

Eyes
The pupils widen so you can spot danger better.

Lungs
Airways widen and the breathing rate increases to take in more oxygen.

Heart
The heart pumps faster and more strongly to increase the blood supply.

Muscles
The liver releases extra glucose into the blood for the muscles to use.

Sweat
The skin sweats to keep the body cool while it works extra hard.

Pain
Nerve signals for pain are blocked from traveling to the brain.

HORMONES FOR GROWING UP

The human body goes through many changes from birth to old age. The glands and organs of the endocrine system produce the hormones that trigger different stages of development. The most important period of change is adolescence—the transition from a child to an adult. During this stage of rapid growth, called puberty, the body changes shape and the reproductive system develops. A hormone in the brain triggers puberty, while other hormones regulate functions, such as growth, mood, and sleep.

HORMONES FOR PUBERTY

Hormones are the chemical messengers that travel between the body's organs and tissues. They can only instruct cells that have the right receptors to detect them, so many different hormones are involved in the chain of events of puberty.

The starting point

Puberty begins in the brain. Between the ages of about 9 and 12, an area of the brain called the hypothalamus sends messages to the pituitary gland to release hormones that start the process of puberty by instructing other glands to produce hormones.

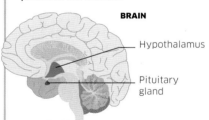

BRAIN

— Hypothalamus

— Pituitary gland

Growth hormone

The body grows very fast during puberty—and growth hormone (hGH) is the driver of growth spurts. It is released by the pituitary gland, and affects all parts of the body, making muscles and organs larger, and bones longer.

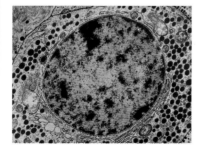

Hormone cell
Growth hormone is made by cells in the pituitary gland. The brown spots in the outer part of the cell are storing newly made growth hormone.

Getting ready to reproduce

This chart shows the chain of some of the hormones that turn children into adults capable of having their own children. Luteinizing hormone (LH) and follicle-stimulating hormone (FSH) play a major role, stimulating different hormones in boys and girls that control the necessary changes.

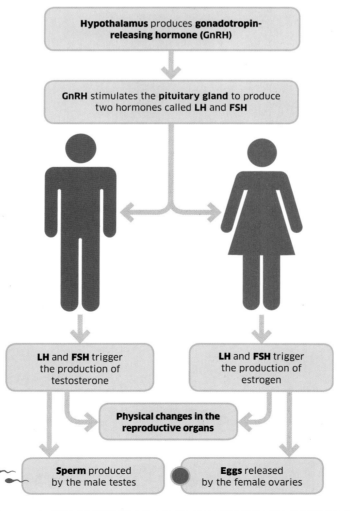

Hypothalamus produces **gonadotropin-releasing hormone (GnRH)**

↓

GnRH stimulates the **pituitary gland** to produce two hormones called **LH** and **FSH**

LH and **FSH** trigger the production of testosterone

LH and **FSH** trigger the production of estrogen

Physical changes in the reproductive organs

Sperm produced by the male testes

Eggs released by the female ovaries

BODY TRANSFORMATION

Puberty marks the start of the process of preparing the body for reproduction later in life. In the reproductive organs, girls begin to produce eggs, while boys start to produce sperm. Puberty starts at different ages and takes different amounts of time to complete, so friends of the same age can often be very different heights and shapes.

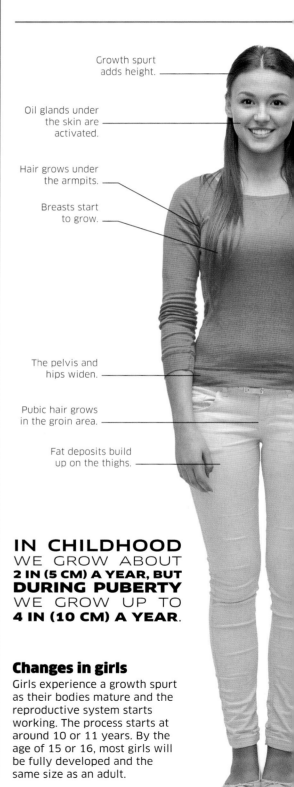

Growth spurt adds height.

Oil glands under the skin are activated.

Hair grows under the armpits.

Breasts start to grow.

The pelvis and hips widen.

Pubic hair grows in the groin area.

Fat deposits build up on the thighs.

IN CHILDHOOD
WE GROW ABOUT **2 IN (5 CM) A YEAR, BUT DURING PUBERTY** WE GROW UP TO **4 IN (10 CM) A YEAR**.

Changes in girls

Girls experience a growth spurt as their bodies mature and the reproductive system starts working. The process starts at around 10 or 11 years. By the age of 15 or 16, most girls will be fully developed and the same size as an adult.

Teenage acne

During puberty, hormones called androgens stimulate the skin's oily sebaceous glands. Before they settle down to normal production, the newly activated glands can produce too much oil. Skin pores become blocked, causing blackheads. If the trapped oil gets infected, the area becomes inflamed and pimples appear.

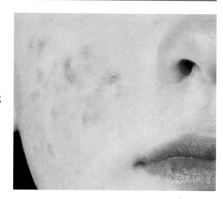

Pimples
Pimples and blackheads on the face, back, and chest are very common in puberty.

Changes in boys

Boys enter puberty between the ages of 9 to 12, and most have completed the stage by the time they are 17 or 18 years old.

Oil glands under the skin are activated.

Facial hair begins to grow.

The enlarged larynx produces a lump on the neck, called an Adam's apple.

Shoulders become broader.

Hair grows under the armpits.

Muscles build in the chest and limbs.

Pubic hair begins to grow.

Male genitals get bigger.

Hair grows on the legs.

Deeper sounds

The hormone testosterone affects boys' voices in adolescence. Vocal cords grow thicker, so they vibrate at a lower frequency and the voice sounds deeper. The larynx tilts and sticks out, forming the Adam's apple.

Breaking voices
As boys go through puberty, their voices can fluctuate between high and low as they learn to control their thicker vocal cords.

◉ MATURING BRAIN

As hormone levels go up and down, teenagers can experience emotional highs and lows. Adolescence is a time of great upheaval in the brain, too. It is clearing out millions of neural connections that are no longer needed, forming more efficient networks of nerve pathways, and learning to control rapidly growing limbs and muscles. These factors affect thinking and behavior, and many teenagers often feel clumsy and moody.

Gray to white

The brain is rewired dramatically during puberty, as these scans show. The red areas show the highest volume of gray matter, while blue and purple areas have lower gray matter volume. As unused brain circuits are pruned away, gray matter is reduced. With less gray matter and more white matter, the brain does not learn new skills so quickly, but it is much better at using the skills it already knows.

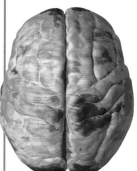

BRAIN OF 13-YEAR-OLD

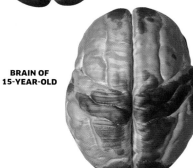

BRAIN OF 15-YEAR-OLD

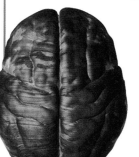

BRAIN OF 18-YEAR-OLD

Raging hormones

In addition to affecting the physical makeup of the brain, hormones alter the behavior of teenagers.

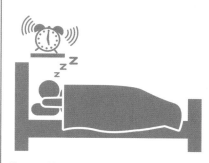

Sleep patterns
Teenagers need more sleep than children or adults. A hormone called melatonin helps people fall asleep. This is released later in the evening for teenagers, which is why they struggle to get up in the morning.

Taking risks
Teens sometimes do risky things without thinking of the consequences. They lack judgment because although the thrill-seeking part of the brain is fully formed, the decision-making area is still maturing.

Moodiness
Alterations in hormone levels, together with changes in parts of the brain that deal with emotions, can cause teenage mood swings and impulsive or aggressive behavior.

Clumsiness
Teens may feel clumsy and uncoordinated at times. This happens because their body shapes are changing, and the brain is struggling to make new neuron connections fast enough to keep up.

Cardiovascular system

The cardiovascular, or circulatory, system is the body's blood transport network. Blood delivers oxygen and nutrients to cells so they can convert them into energy. Then it carries away waste products created by this energy-making process.

Together, the heart, blood, and an intricate network of hollow tubes called blood vessels make up the circulatory system. The heart beats constantly to pump blood through the vessels to every part of the body.

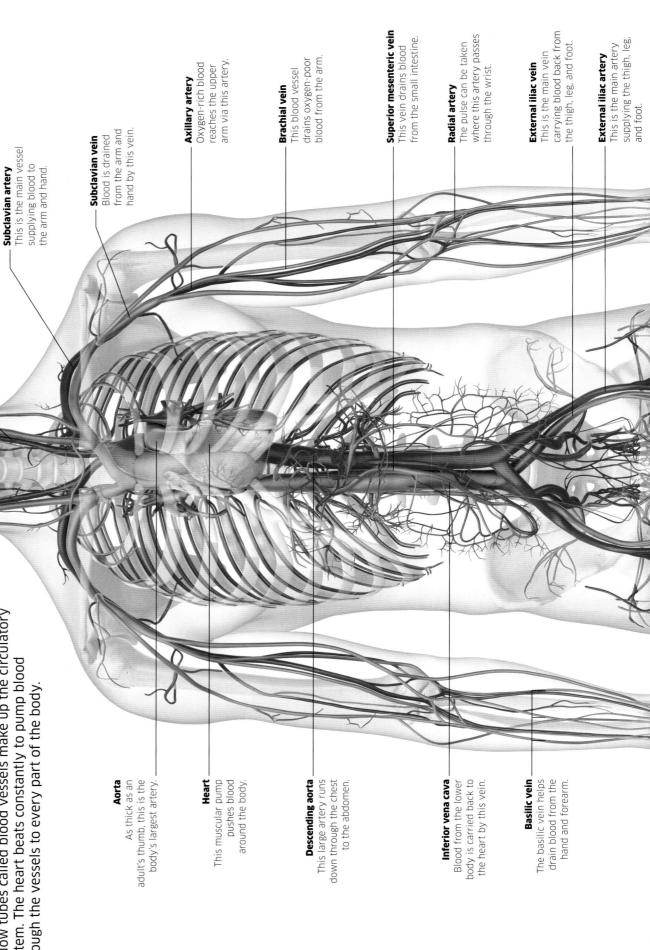

Never-ending circuit
Blood travels round the body via blood vessels. Arteries, shown in red, carry blood from the heart, branching into smaller and smaller vessels to deliver oxygen-filled blood to the body's cells. Veins, shown in blue, deliver blood back to the heart. This process is called circulation because the same blood flows around and around.

External jugular vein
Blood is carried away from the face and scalp by this vein.

Common carotid artery
This large vessel supplies blood to the head and neck.

Subclavian artery
This is the main vessel supplying blood to the arm and hand.

Subclavian vein
Blood is drained from the arm and hand by this vein.

Axillary artery
Oxygen-rich blood reaches the upper arm via this artery.

Brachial vein
This blood vessel drains oxygen-poor blood from the arm.

Superior mesenteric vein
This vein drains blood from the small intestine.

Radial artery
The pulse can be taken where this artery passes through the wrist.

External iliac vein
This is the main vein carrying blood back from the thigh, leg, and foot.

External iliac artery
This is the main artery supplying the thigh, leg, and foot.

Aorta
As thick as an adult's thumb, this is the body's largest artery.

Heart
This muscular pump pushes blood around the body.

Descending aorta
This large artery runs down through the chest to the abdomen.

Inferior vena cava
Blood from the lower body is carried back to the heart by this vein.

Basilic vein
The basilic vein helps drain blood from the hand and forearm.

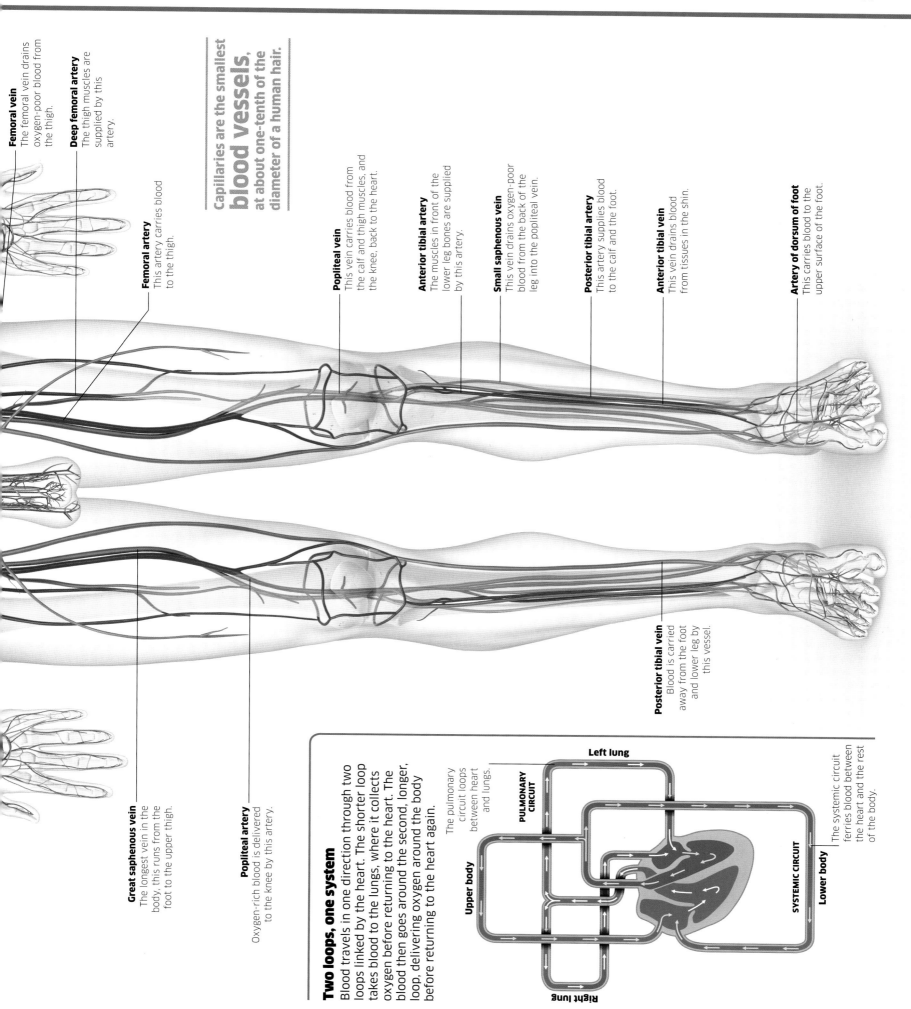

Femoral vein
The femoral vein drains oxygen-poor blood from the thigh.

Deep femoral artery
The thigh muscles are supplied by this artery.

Femoral artery
This artery carries blood to the thigh.

Capillaries are the smallest **blood vessels**, at about one-tenth of the diameter of a human hair.

Popliteal vein
This vein carries blood from the calf and thigh muscles, and the knee, back to the heart.

Anterior tibial artery
The muscles in front of the lower leg bones are supplied by this artery.

Small saphenous vein
This vein drains oxygen-poor blood from the back of the leg into the popliteal vein.

Posterior tibial artery
This artery supplies blood to the calf and the foot.

Anterior tibial vein
This vein drains blood from tissues in the shin.

Artery of dorsum of foot
This carries blood to the upper surface of the foot.

Great saphenous vein
The longest vein in the body, this runs from the foot to the upper thigh.

Popliteal artery
Oxygen-rich blood is delivered to the knee by this artery.

Posterior tibial vein
Blood is carried away from the foot and lower leg by this vessel.

Two loops, one system

Blood travels in one direction through two loops linked by the heart. The shorter loop takes blood to the lungs, where it collects oxygen before returning to the heart. The blood then goes around the second, longer, loop, delivering oxygen around the body before returning to the heart again.

The pulmonary circuit loops between heart and lungs.

Left lung

PULMONARY CIRCUIT

Upper body

Right lung

SYSTEMIC CIRCUIT

Lower body

The systemic circuit ferries blood between the heart and the rest of the body.

Lymphatic system

The lymphatic system collects and drains away excess fluid that has passed from the blood into tissues. It also carries cells that fight infection by helping to stop disease-causing germs, called pathogens, from spreading around the body.

All body tissues are bathed in a watery liquid that comes from the surrounding blood vessels. Most of it drains back into the veins, but the rest becomes a clear fluid called lymph. This is transported along a network of vessels, called lymphatics, back to the bloodstream. The lymph passes through lymph nodes, which contain cells that target and destroy germs in the lymph fluid.

The average human body returns **6½ pints (3 liters)** of lymph fluid back to the bloodstream every day.

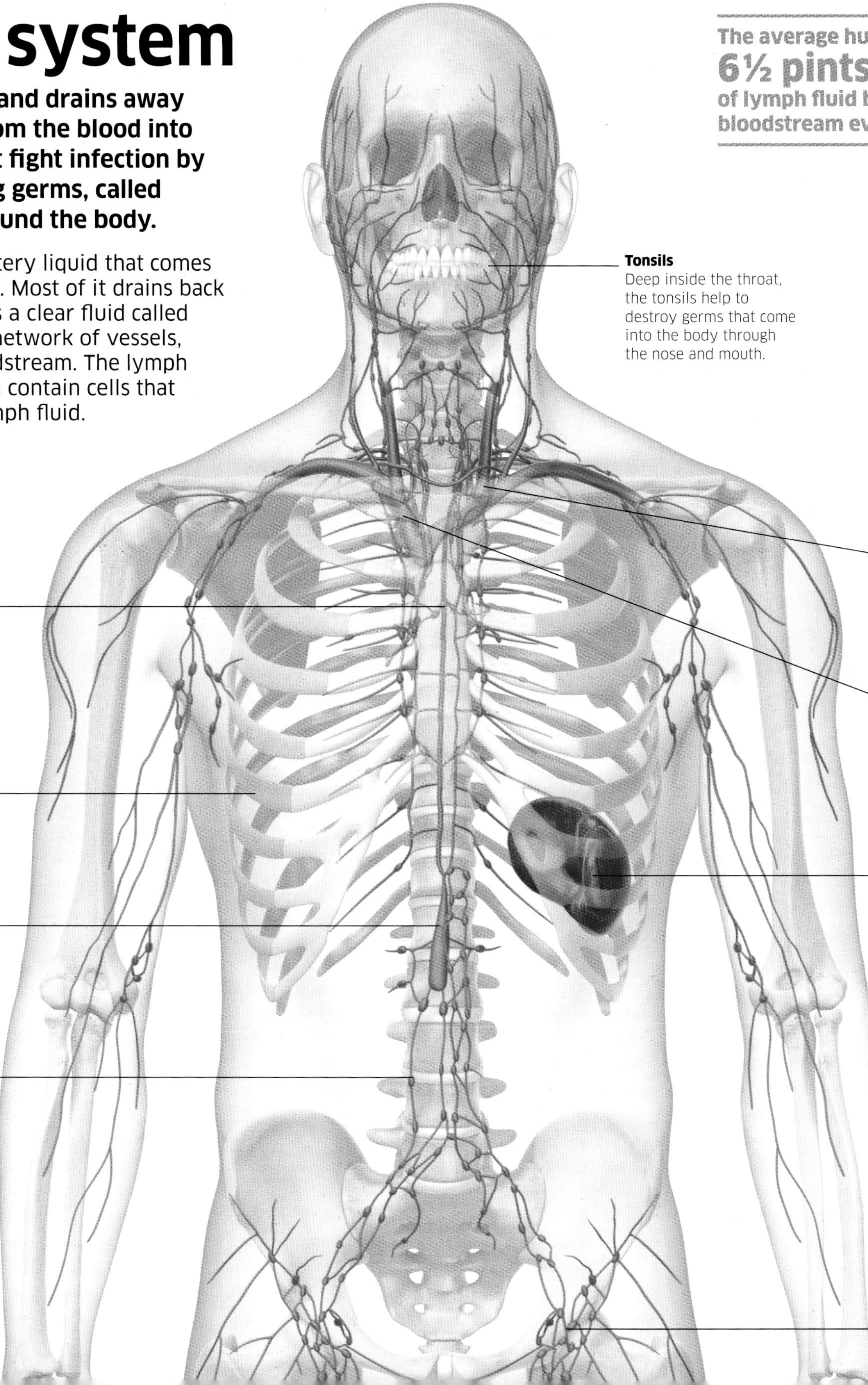

Tonsils
Deep inside the throat, the tonsils help to destroy germs that come into the body through the nose and mouth.

Left subclavian vein
This drains blood from the left arm and collects lymph from the left side of the body and the lower half of the right side.

Right subclavian vein
This drains blood from the right arm and collects lymph from the upper half of the right side of the body.

Spleen
The largest organ in the lymphatic system, the spleen produces cells that help to fight infection.

Inguinal nodes
Lymph from the legs passes through these nodes.

Thoracic duct
Lymph drains into the left subclavian vein through this tube.

Rib cage
Red bone marrow in the ribs produces white blood cells.

Cysterna chyli
This collects lymph from the lower half of the body before it goes up into the thoracic duct.

Lymph node
Lymph is processed and cleaned as it passes through lymph nodes.

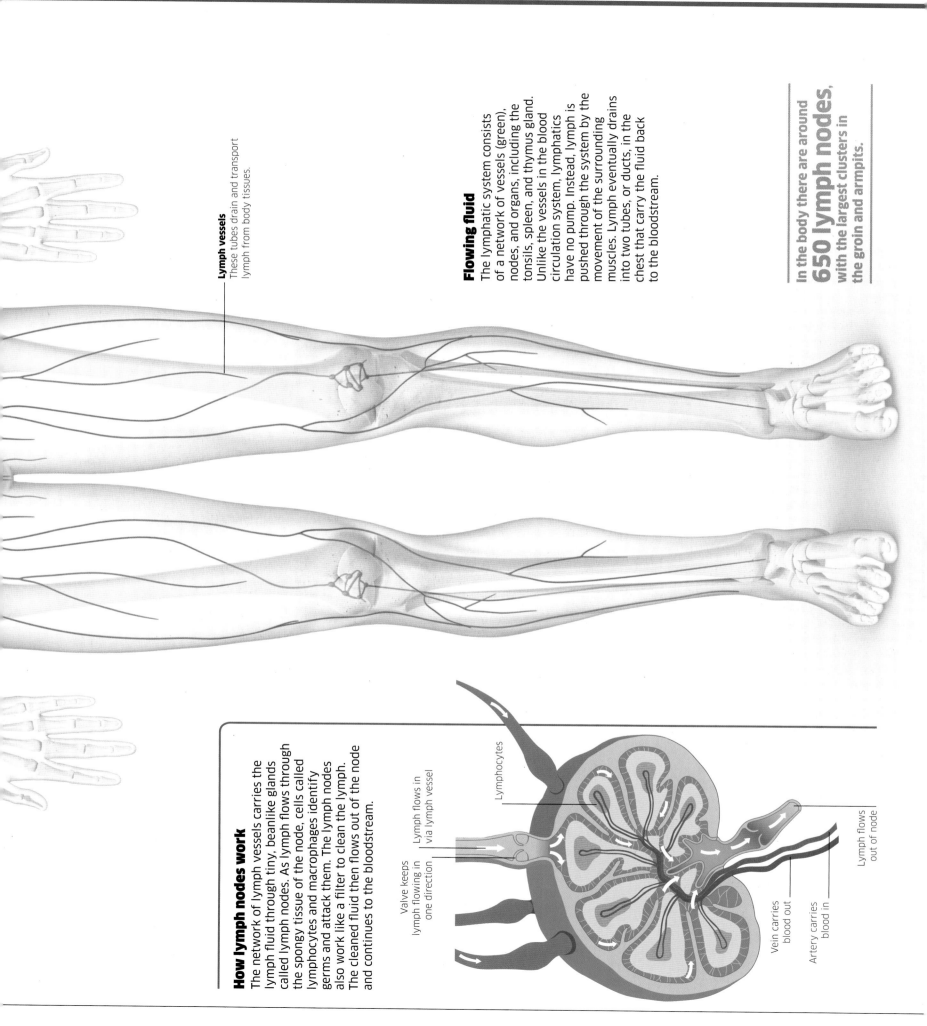

Lymph vessels
These tubes drain and transport lymph from body tissues.

Flowing fluid

The lymphatic system consists of a network of vessels (green), nodes, and organs, including the tonsils, spleen, and thymus gland. Unlike the vessels in the blood circulation system, lymphatics have no pump. Instead, lymph is pushed through the system by the movement of the surrounding muscles. Lymph eventually drains into two tubes, or ducts, in the chest that carry the fluid back to the bloodstream.

In the body there are around **650 lymph nodes,** with the largest clusters in the groin and armpits.

How lymph nodes work

The network of lymph vessels carries the lymph fluid through tiny, beanlike glands called lymph nodes. As lymph flows through the spongy tissue of the node, cells called lymphocytes and macrophages identify germs and attack them. The lymph nodes also work like a filter to clean the lymph. The cleaned fluid then flows out of the node and continues to the bloodstream.

Lymphocytes

Valve keeps lymph flowing in one direction

Lymph flows in via lymph vessel

Vein carries blood out

Artery carries blood in

Lymph flows out of node

BODY INVADERS

Pathogens are bacteria and viruses that cause disease. Most bacteria are simple and harmless, and some are helpful, such as those that live in the gut to help with digestion. However, some bacteria invade and damage body tissues. Viruses are chemical packages much smaller than bacteria that take control of body cells and multiply, causing illness and disease.

Cocci
These round bacteria can live in the body without a problem, or cause serious diseases such as scarlet fever and pneumonia.

Bacteria

Bacteria are simple, single-celled organisms that can multiply rapidly. A few can cause serious diseases by invading the body, and some release poisons called toxins.

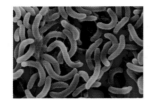

Bacilli
These rod-shaped bacteria often live harmlessly in the gut. Other bacilli cause illness, such as bladder infections and typhoid.

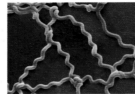

Spirilla
Small, spiral-shaped bacteria, called spirilla, come from uncooked shellfish or stale water. These cause stomach upsets and diarrhea.

ATTACK AND DEFENSE

Every day the human body comes under attack from a range of microscopic invaders that cause disease. All kinds of defensive measures are in place to stop them. Skin and membranes form physical barriers. Fluids such as saliva, tears, and mucus provide chemical warfare. If these lines are passed, the immune system fights back. Armies of special cells target and destroy enemy attackers to make the body healthy again.

Viruses

Viruses reproduce by invading a body cell. The hijacked cell is turned into a factory where more viruses are produced. These are then released to infect more and more cells.

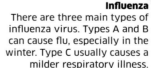

Adenovirus
This virus can infect lungs to produce coughs, eyes to give conjunctivitis, and the digestive system to trigger diarrhea.

A large outbreak of a disease is called an **epidemic.** If it spreads worldwide, it is known as a pandemic.

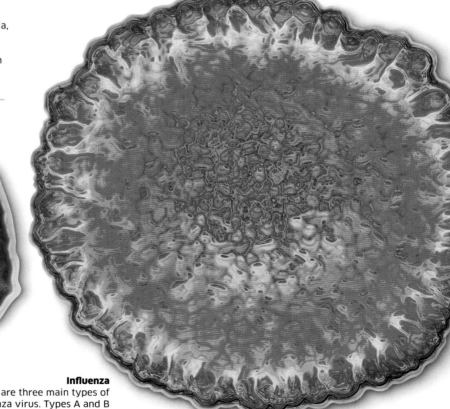

Influenza
There are three main types of influenza virus. Types A and B can cause flu, especially in the winter. Type C usually causes a milder respiratory illness.

Fungi, protists, and parasites

Although most fungi grow in soil or rotting food, some live on or inside humans. Protists are simple organisms, some of which cause human disease. Parasites are other living things that live on or in our bodies.

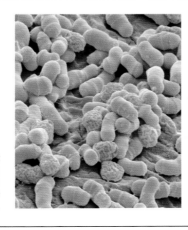

Athlete's foot
This fungus, called *Trichophyton*, grows as a network of threads in damp skin, especially between the toes. It causes an itchy infection.

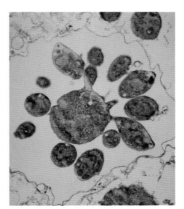

Plasmodia
Single-celled plasmodia live inside mosquitoes. A mosquito bite can bring plasmodia into the human bloodstream where they infect red blood cells.

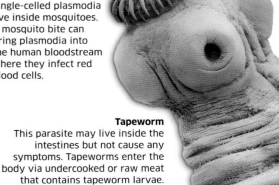

Tapeworm
This parasite may live inside the intestines but not cause any symptoms. Tapeworms enter the body via undercooked or raw meat that contains tapeworm larvae.

BODY BARRIERS

Bacteria, viruses, and other pathogens face huge resistance from the human body. The first line of defense is the skin and the linings of the eyes, mouth, nose, throat, and stomach.

Inner defenses

Pathogens can enter the body through the food we eat or the air we breathe. To stop germs from gaining access, internal passageways are lined with protective fluids, such as saliva, mucus, and tears.

Tears
Salty tears form to wash away eye pathogens.

Mucus
The nose is lined with sticky mucus to trap germs.

Saliva
This slimy substance has chemicals to kill mouth bacteria.

Wax
Ears contain thick wax to deter invaders.

Skin
The body's outer covering is a barrier against infection.

Blood
Different types of white blood cells unite to attack invaders.

Stomach
Powerful acid in the stomach destroys germs in food.

IMMUNE SYSTEM

The body's collective defense measures are known as the immune system. This works by identifying and targeting pathogens. Over time, the body remembers some germs and gives immunity so the same diseases do not return.

Antibodies

The body makes weapons called antibodies. These defensive chemical proteins attach themselves to invaders to identify them as enemies for white blood cells to eat.

Armies of antibodies
When the body recognizes a pathogen, about 10,000 trillion antibodies are released into the bloodstream and attach themselves to the known germs.

Antibody
The antibody sticks to the germ it is targeting.

Germ

White blood cell
This surrounds and eats the marked germ.

ALLERGIES

The immune system can go wrong when harmless substances that we swallow, breathe in, or touch are targeted by our body's defenses. This overreaction is called an allergy.

Allergens

Substances that trigger an allergic reaction are called allergens. Common allergens include nuts, pollen from flowers, and animal fur.

Automatic response
Common allergic reactions are sneezing; coughing; or red, itchy skin. Reactions are sometimes severe enough to cause breathing problems and be life-threatening.

FIGHTING BACK

Even if some pathogens manage to get past the body's first line of defense, they are unlikely to beat the many millions of white blood cells.

White blood cells

The immune system is run by white blood cells, which move through the bloodstream and other bodily fluids looking for bacteria and viruses to kill. Most white blood cells are made inside bone marrow tissue, and more are produced when germs are present.

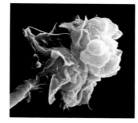
Macrophage
This type of white blood cell kills bacteria and other germs by engulfing them and eating them.

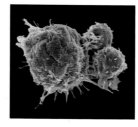
Lymphocyte
This type learns to attack only one type of germ by filling it with poison or releasing antibodies.

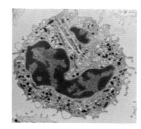
Neutrophil
This is the most common type of white blood cell. Neutrophils help to fight bacteria and fungi.

Appetite for destruction

Macrophages hunt invading bacteria by following the chemical trails they leave behind. If these hungry white blood cells track down an invader, they surround and swallow it. Each macrophage eats about 200 bacteria before it dies.

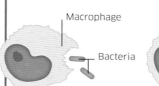
Macrophage
Bacteria

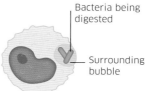
Bacteria being digested
Surrounding bubble

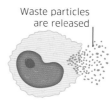
Waste particles are released

1 PLAN OF ATTACK
A macrophage identifies bacteria as enemies and prepares to attack.

2 KILLER CHEMICALS
The bacteria are captured, surrounded, and digested by powerful chemicals.

3 HUNGRY HUNTER
The macrophage expels harmless waste and carries on hunting for invaders.

Fighting inflammation

When the skin is broken by a cut, the body's defense team responds at once. Damaged tissues release chemicals to attract white blood cells, ready to destroy pathogens. Blood vessels allow blood to leak out, so platelets and white blood cells can reach the site of the wound.

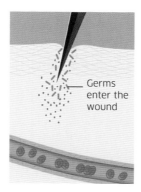
Germs enter the wound

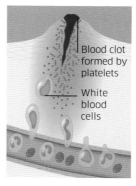
Blood clot formed by platelets
White blood cells

1 INJURY
The skin is pierced. Blood vessels respond by getting wider to increase blood flow to the site. Exposed tissue leaves germs and dirt free to enter.

2 BLOOD CLOT
Platelets thicken the blood to create a clot that seals the wound. White blood cells arrive, looking for pathogens to destroy.

3 GERM EATERS
The white blood cells consume the pathogens. The tissue and skin can now begin to repair itself.

MACROPHAGE

Hungry hunter cells, called macrophages, patrol the human body on the alert for microscopic invaders to engulf and eat.

Part of the immune system, macrophages are white blood cells that target and destroy bacteria to protect the body against infection. In this scan, a macrophage (shown in red) is overwhelming harmful tuberculosis (TB) bacteria (shown in greenish-yellow). TB bacteria usually infect the lungs and can cause serious illness if they are allowed to flourish.

Respiratory system

Every cell in the human body needs a constant supply of oxygen to survive. The lungs and airways of the respiratory system deliver this oxygen and also expel waste carbon dioxide.

We take in air through the mouth and nose into the lungs. Oxygen from the air seeps through the lung membranes into the bloodstream, where it is carried to all the body's cells. These cells burn oxygen to make energy, in a process called cellular respiration. This process causes cells to release another gas–carbon dioxide. This is carried back in the blood to the lungs to be exhaled.

Air intake

The respiratory system is a vast network of millions of airways, spreading like the branches of a tree into the lungs. With each breath, air sucked in through the nose or mouth rushes down the windpipe, or trachea. This carries air to a fork deep inside the chest where the airways divide in two. One of the branches, or bronchi, leads to the left lung, while the other leads to the right. Air comes in when the lungs expand and is pushed out when they shrink back.

A glassful of mucus forms in your airways each day–and **you swallow it!**

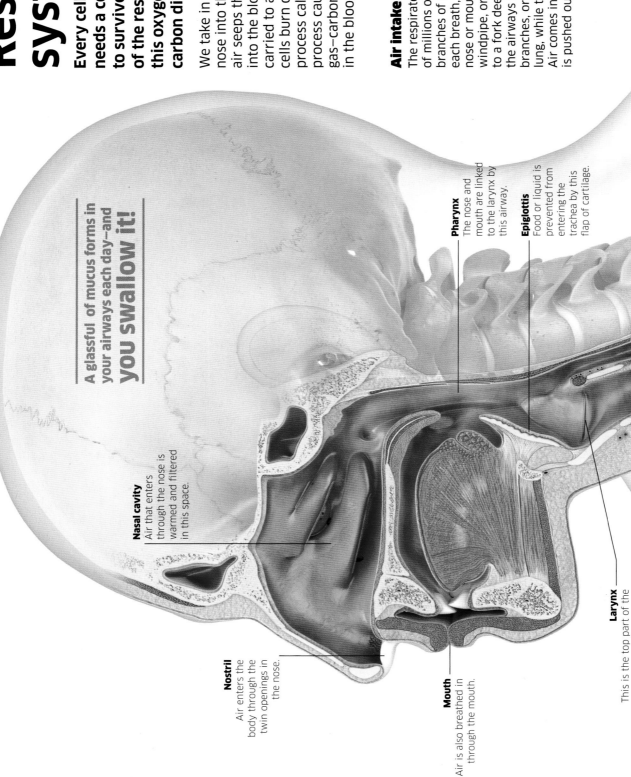

Nasal cavity
Air that enters through the nose is warmed and filtered in this space.

Nostril
Air enters the body through the twin openings in the nose.

Mouth
Air is also breathed in through the mouth.

Larynx
This is the top part of the trachea. It has bands, called vocal cords, which contract and relax to create sounds.

Pharynx
The nose and mouth are linked to the larynx by this airway.

Epiglottis
Food or liquid is prevented from entering the trachea by this flap of cartilage.

Intercostal muscles
During breathing, muscles between the ribs pull the rib cage up and down.

Trachea
The windpipe, a strong tube of muscle and rings of cartilage, carries air from the larynx to the lungs.

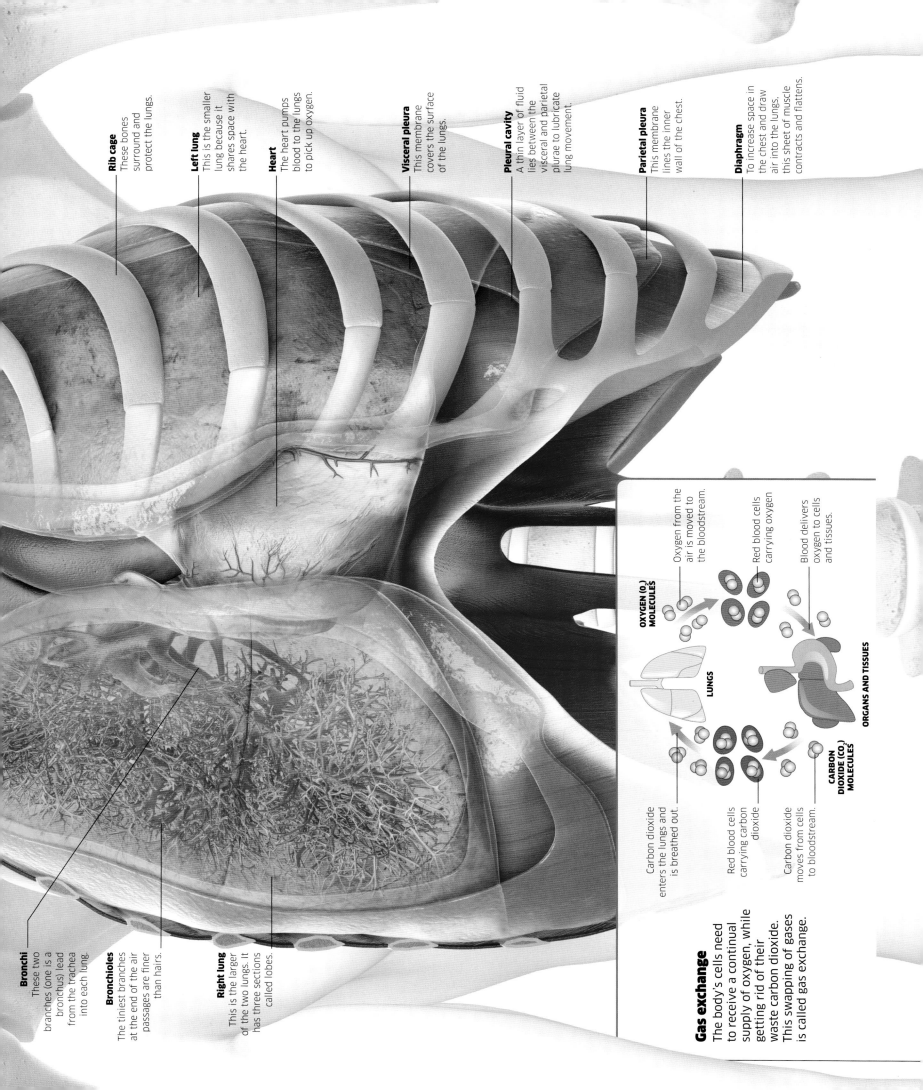

Bronchi

These two branches (one is a bronchus) lead from the trachea into each lung.

Bronchioles

The tiniest branches at the end of the air passages are finer than hairs.

Right lung

This is the larger of the two lungs. It has three sections called lobes.

Gas exchange

The body's cells need to receive a continual supply of oxygen, while getting rid of their waste carbon dioxide. This swapping of gases is called gas exchange.

Carbon dioxide enters the lungs and is breathed out.

Red blood cells carrying carbon dioxide

Carbon dioxide moves from cells to bloodstream.

Oxygen from the air is moved to the bloodstream.

OXYGEN (O₂) MOLECULES

Red blood cells carrying oxygen

LUNGS

Blood delivers oxygen to cells and tissues.

CARBON DIOXIDE (CO₂) MOLECULES

ORGANS AND TISSUES

Rib cage

These bones surround and protect the lungs.

Left lung

This is the smaller lung because it shares space with the heart.

Heart

The heart pumps blood to the lungs to pick up oxygen.

Visceral pleura

This membrane covers the surface of the lungs.

Pleural cavity

A thin layer of fluid lies between the visceral and parietal plurae to lubricate lung movement.

Parietal pleura

This membrane lines the inner wall of the chest.

Diaphragm

To increase space in the chest and draw air into the lungs, this sheet of muscle contracts and flattens.

Digestive system

Food gives the body the nutrients and energy it needs. The job of the digestive system is to break food down into simple substances the body can use. These are then absorbed into the bloodstream, while any indigestible waste is removed.

The main part of the digestive system is a long tube, called the digestive tract. It starts in the mouth, travels down the esophagus to the stomach, then runs through the small and large intestines to the anus. Other organs also play a role in digestion: these are the teeth, tongue, salivary glands, liver, pancreas, and gallbladder.

Stages of digestion

There are four main stages along the digestive tract. The first is the mouth, which cuts and chews food into small chunks. The second is the stomach, where food is churned into a liquid called chyme. Inside the small intestine, the chyme is broken down into nutrients that can be absorbed and carried to the body's cells. Finally, anything not used enters the large intestine, where it dries out to become feces.

From the mouth at one end to the anus at the other, an adult's digestive tract is around 23 ft (7 m) long.

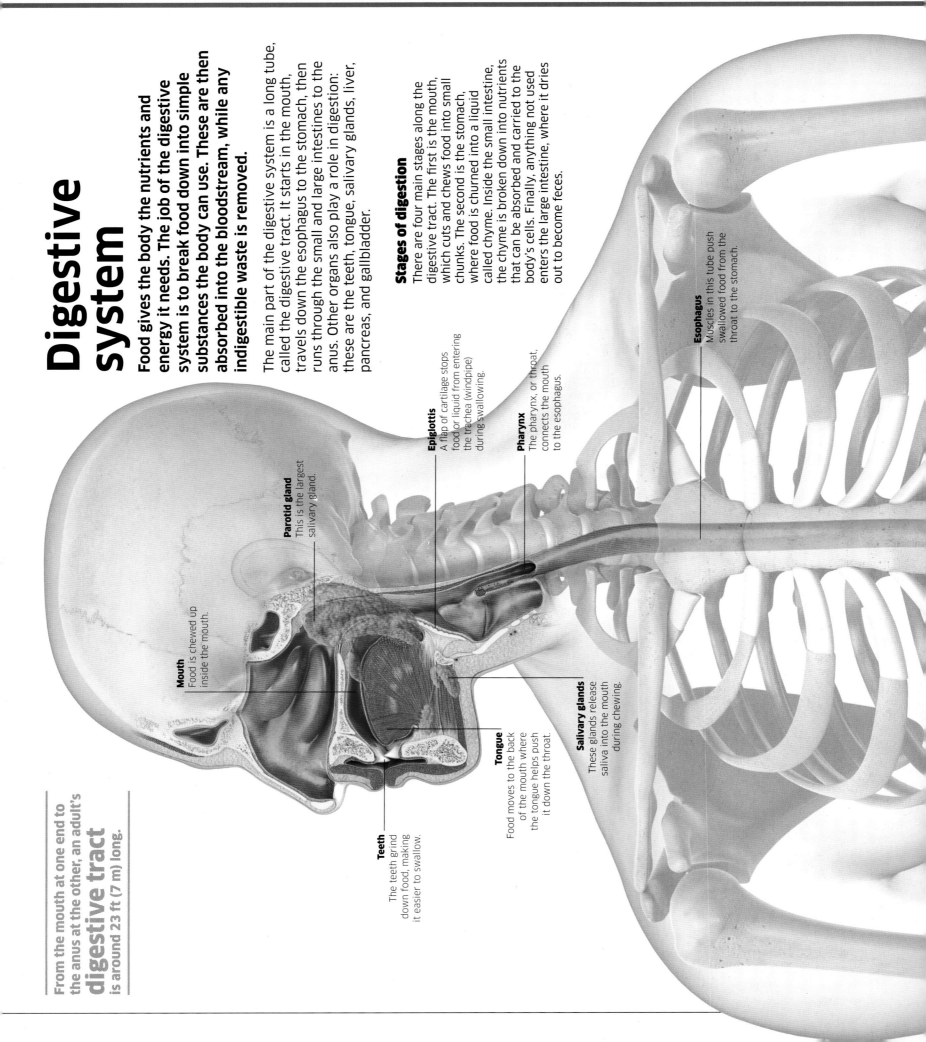

Mouth
Food is chewed up inside the mouth.

Parotid gland
This is the largest salivary gland.

Teeth
The teeth grind down food, making it easier to swallow.

Tongue
Food moves to the back of the mouth where the tongue helps push it down the throat.

Epiglottis
A flap of cartilage stops food or liquid from entering the trachea (windpipe) during swallowing.

Salivary glands
These glands release saliva into the mouth during chewing.

Pharynx
The pharynx, or throat, connects the mouth to the esophagus.

Esophagus
Muscles in this tube push swallowed food from the throat to the stomach.

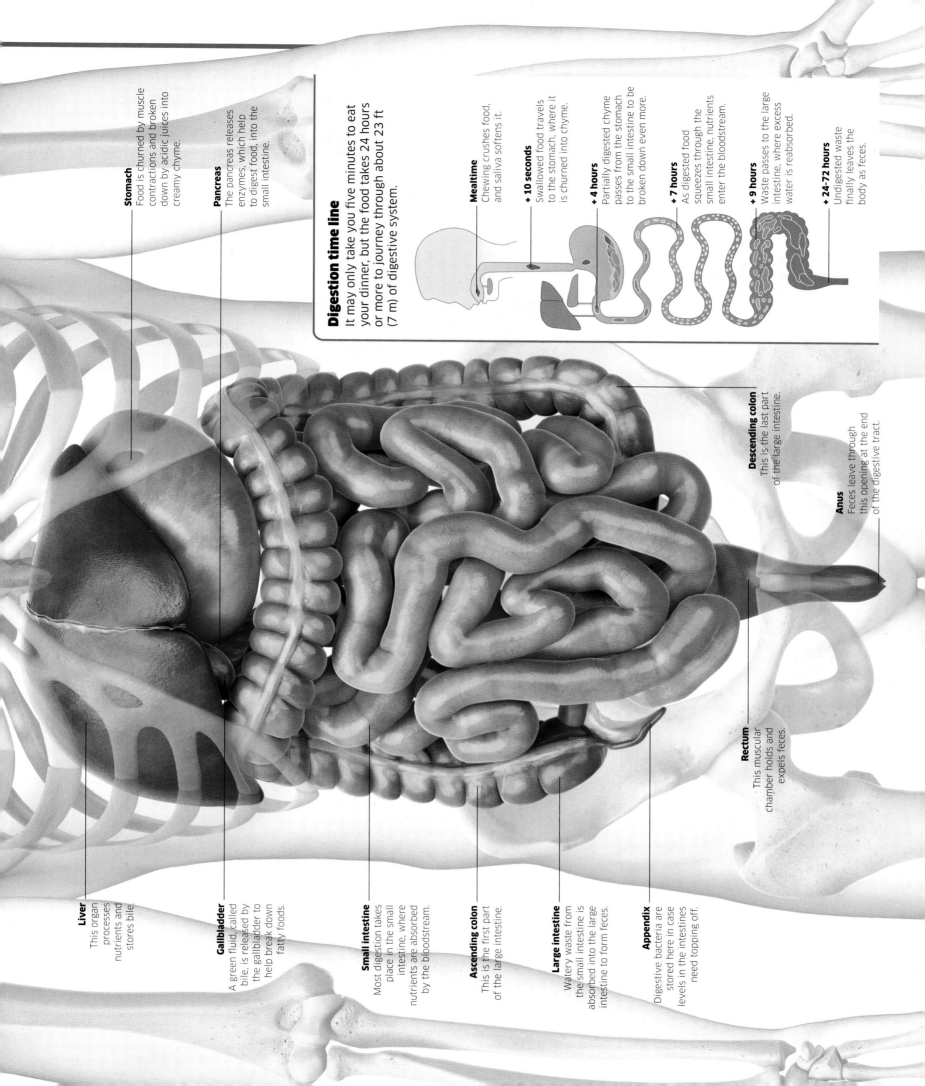

Stomach
Food is churned by muscle contractions and broken down by acidic juices into creamy chyme.

Pancreas
The pancreas releases enzymes, which help to digest food, into the small intestine.

Digestion time line

It may only take you five minutes to eat your dinner, but the food takes 24 hours or more to journey through about 23 ft (7 m) of digestive system.

Mealtime
Chewing crushes food, and saliva softens it.

+ 10 seconds
Swallowed food travels to the stomach, where it is churned into chyme.

+ 4 hours
Partially digested chyme passes from the stomach to the small intestine to be broken down even more.

+ 7 hours
As digested food squeezes through the small intestine, nutrients enter the bloodstream.

+ 9 hours
Waste passes to the large intestine, where excess water is reabsorbed.

+ 24–72 hours
Undigested waste finally leaves the body as feces.

Descending colon
This is the last part of the large intestine.

Anus
Feces leave through this opening at the end of the digestive tract.

Rectum
This muscular chamber holds and expels feces.

Liver
This organ processes nutrients and stores bile.

Gallbladder
A green fluid, called bile, is released by the gallbladder to help break down fatty foods.

Small intestine
Most digestion takes place in the small intestine, where nutrients are absorbed by the bloodstream.

Ascending colon
This is the first part of the large intestine.

Large intestine
Watery waste from the small intestine is absorbed into the large intestine to form feces.

Appendix
Digestive bacteria are stored here in case levels in the intestines need topping off.

Urinary system

In addition to delivering nutrients around the body, the blood also collects waste products from cells and delivers them to two hardworking organs called kidneys. There, waste and excess fluids are filtered out and processed into a liquid called urine, then passed out of the body.

The urinary system also keeps the volume and pressure of the blood stable by holding water back when there is a shortage, and making more urine when there is too much. This system also maintains a healthy balance of minerals and salts in the body.

Waste disposal

The urinary system consists of two kidneys, two ureters, a bladder, and a urethra. The kidneys process the blood's waste into urine, which passes through the ureters to the bladder. When the bladder is full, pressure sensors send signals to the brain. Humans are not born with the ability to control the urge to urinate. Children start to learn bladder control at around the age of two.

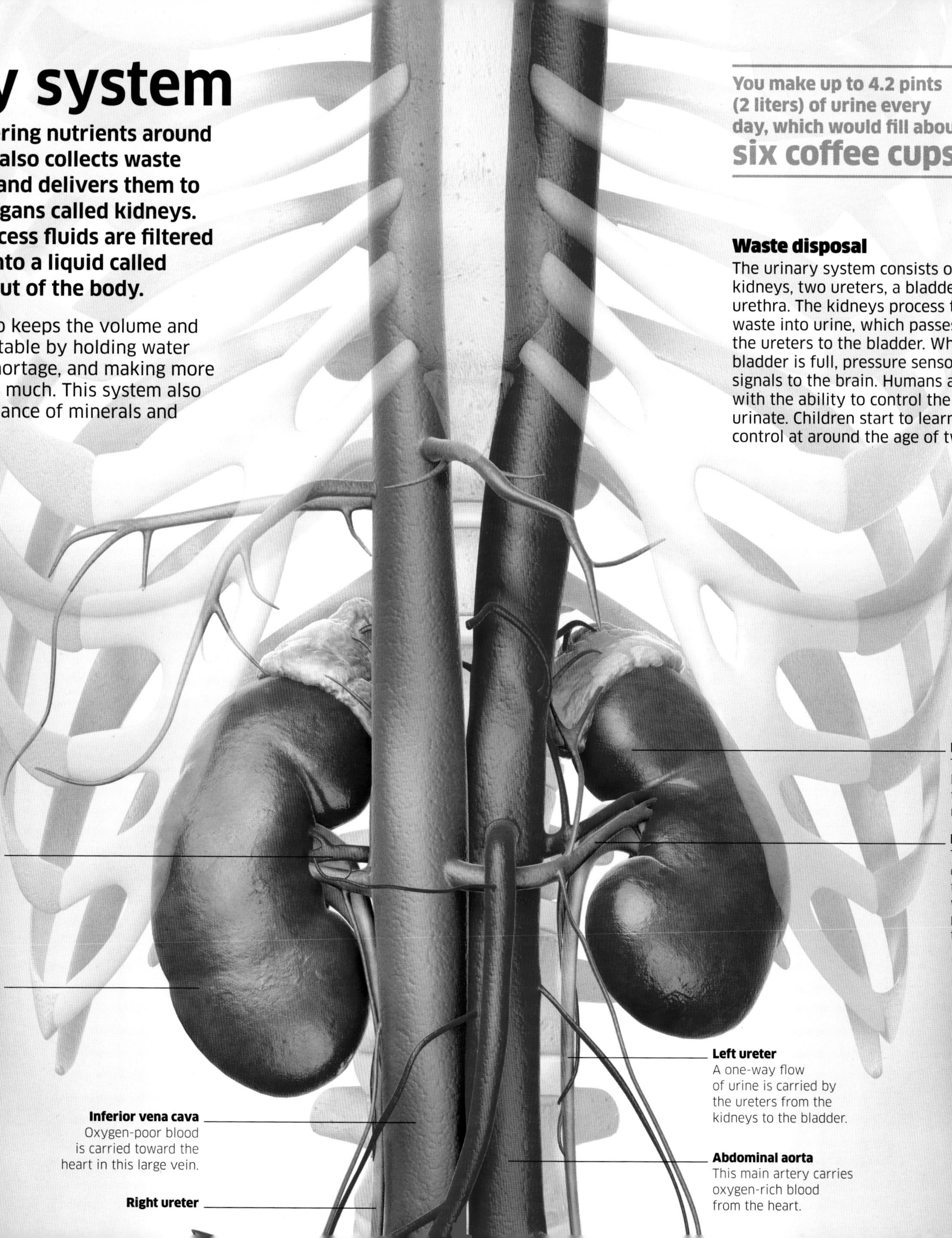

You make up to 4.2 pints (2 liters) of urine every day, which would fill about **six coffee cups.**

Left kidney
This is one of two bean-shaped organs that filters blood to make urine.

Renal vein
The two renal veins carry filtered blood to the heart, from where it can be pumped around the body again.

Left ureter
A one-way flow of urine is carried by the ureters from the kidneys to the bladder.

Abdominal aorta
This main artery carries oxygen-rich blood from the heart.

Renal artery
The renal arteries bring unfiltered blood to the kidneys.

Right kidney
This organ sits slightly lower than the left kidney, beneath the liver.

Inferior vena cava
Oxygen-poor blood is carried toward the heart in this large vein.

Right ureter

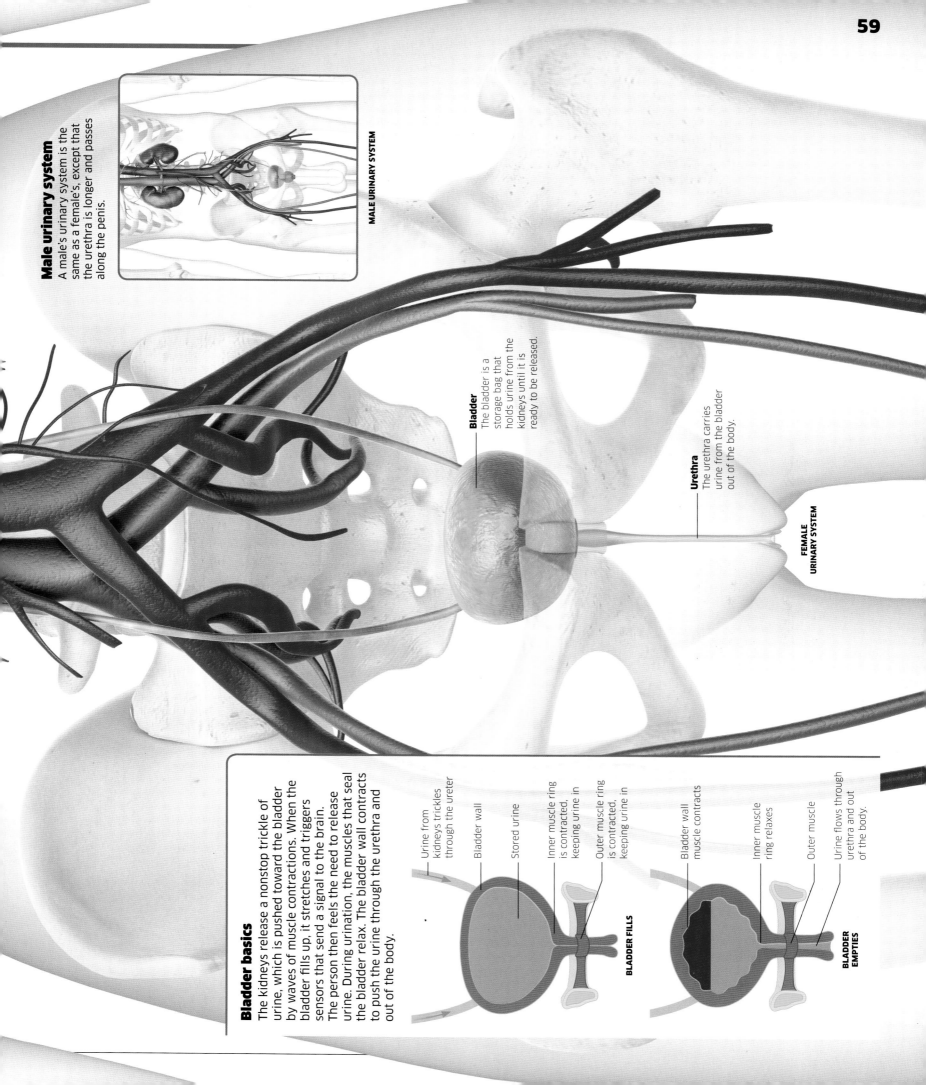

Male urinary system

A male's urinary system is the same as a female's, except that the urethra is longer and passes along the penis.

MALE URINARY SYSTEM

Bladder
The bladder is a storage bag that holds urine from the kidneys until it is ready to be released.

Urethra
The urethra carries urine from the bladder out of the body.

FEMALE URINARY SYSTEM

Bladder basics

The kidneys release a nonstop trickle of urine, which is pushed toward the bladder by waves of muscle contractions. When the bladder fills up, it stretches and triggers sensors that send a signal to the brain. The person then feels the need to release urine. During urination, the muscles that seal the bladder relax. The bladder wall contracts to push the urine through the urethra and out of the body.

Urine from kidneys trickles through the ureter

Bladder wall

Stored urine

Inner muscle ring is contracted, keeping urine in

Outer muscle ring is contracted, keeping urine in

BLADDER FILLS

Bladder wall muscle contracts

Inner muscle ring relaxes

Outer muscle

Urine flows through urethra and out of the body.

BLADDER EMPTIES

Reproductive system

The reproductive system consists of the body parts used to create new life. Humans cannot reproduce on their own—both male and female cells are needed to make a baby. The reproductive organs are different in men and women, as they have different roles in the reproductive process.

Adults have special sex cells called gametes. The creation of a new baby begins when a male sex cell (sperm) unites with a female sex cell (egg). This process is called fertilization. The male reproductive system makes the sperm to fertilize the female egg. The female system produces eggs and sustains the baby during its development in the uterus. After a baby is born, the mother's mammary glands, in the breasts, produce milk to feed the baby.

Reproductive organs

A woman's reproductive organs sit inside her body. They consist of the uterus, two ovaries and two fallopian tubes, the vagina, the breasts, and the milk-producing glands. The male reproductive system is much simpler, and most of it is outside the body. It manufactures and provides sperm to fertilize the female egg.

Secretory lobule
These tissues contain clusters of milk-producing glands called alveoli.

Milk duct
Many of these tiny tubes carry milk from the glands to the nipple.

Nipple
The nipple is the opening of the milk ducts, where the baby sucks out milk.

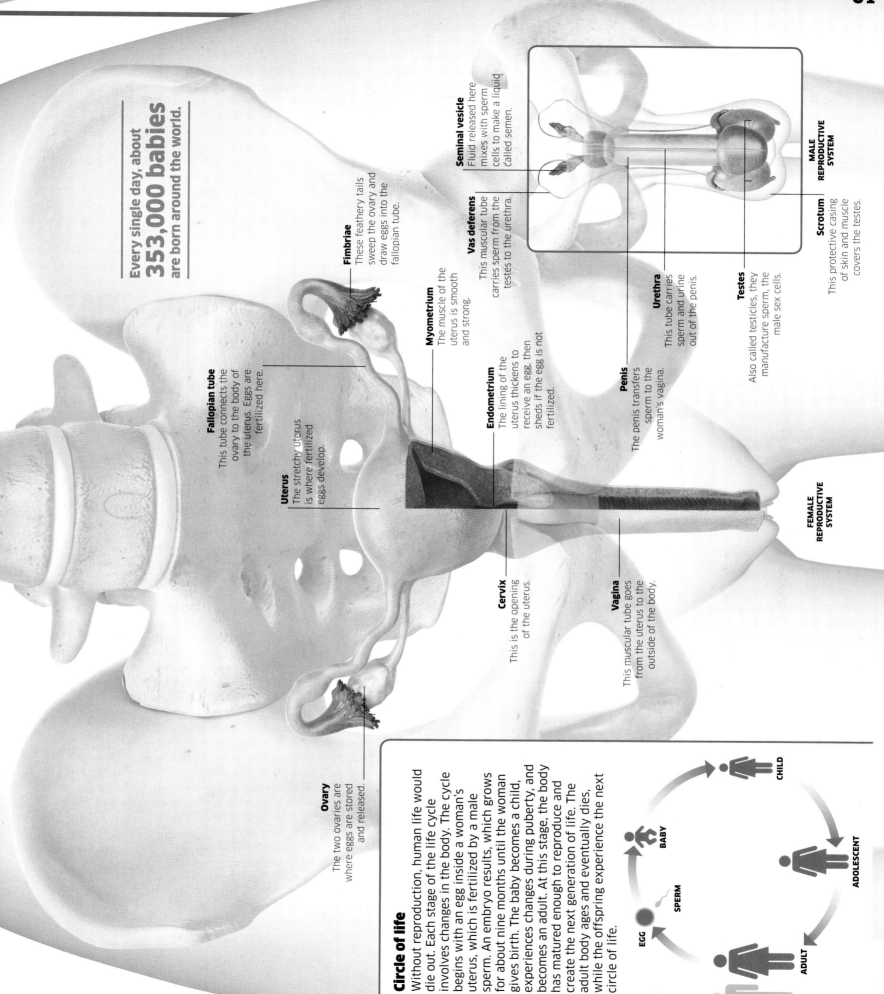

Every single day, about
353,000 babies
are born around the world.

Fimbriae
These feathery tails sweep the ovary and draw eggs into the fallopian tube.

Seminal vesicle
Fluid released here mixes with sperm cells to make a liquid called semen.

Vas deferens
This muscular tube carries sperm from the testes to the urethra.

Myometrium
The muscle of the uterus is smooth and strong.

MALE REPRODUCTIVE SYSTEM

Fallopian tube
This tube connects the ovary to the body of the uterus. Eggs are fertilized here.

Uterus
The stretchy uterus is where fertilized eggs develop.

Endometrium
The lining of the uterus thickens to receive an egg, then sheds if the egg is not fertilized.

Penis
The penis transfers sperm to the woman's vagina.

Urethra
This tube carries sperm and urine out of the penis.

Testes
Also called testicles, they manufacture sperm, the male sex cells.

Scrotum
This protective casing of skin and muscle covers the testes.

Cervix
This is the opening of the uterus.

Vagina
This muscular tube goes from the uterus to the outside of the body.

FEMALE REPRODUCTIVE SYSTEM

Ovary
The two ovaries are where eggs are stored and released.

Circle of life

Without reproduction, human life would die out. Each stage of the life cycle involves changes in the body. The cycle begins with an egg inside a woman's uterus, which is fertilized by a male sperm. An embryo results, which grows for about nine months until the woman gives birth. The baby becomes a child, experiences changes during puberty, and becomes an adult. At this stage, the body has matured enough to reproduce and create the next generation of life. The adult body ages and eventually dies, while the offspring experience the next circle of life.

CHILD

BABY

ADOLESCENT

SPERM

EGG

ADULT

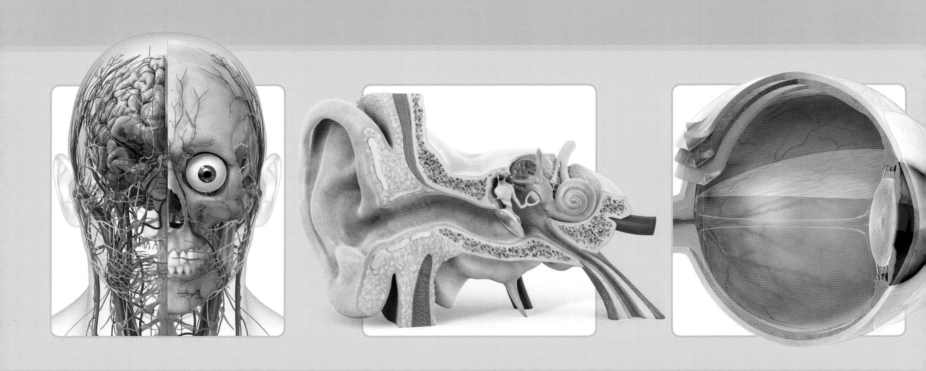

HEAD AND NECK

The control center of the body is the brain. It processes thoughts and interprets information from our surroundings. The skull protects this vital organ and the body's most important sensory organs. The neck supports the head, providing a communications highway between the brain and the body.

64 head and neck ∘ **SKULL**

24 months—the age at which the **gaps in a baby's skull** close up and the **bones fuse** together.

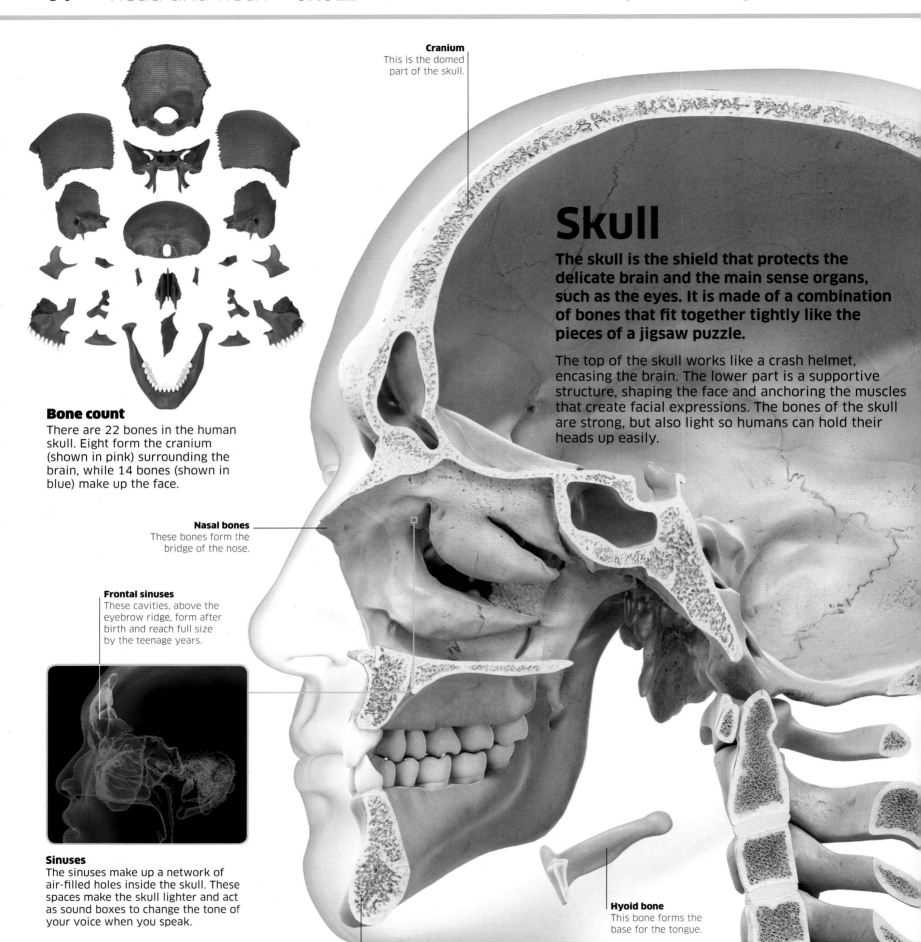

Cranium
This is the domed part of the skull.

Skull

The skull is the shield that protects the delicate brain and the main sense organs, such as the eyes. It is made of a combination of bones that fit together tightly like the pieces of a jigsaw puzzle.

The top of the skull works like a crash helmet, encasing the brain. The lower part is a supportive structure, shaping the face and anchoring the muscles that create facial expressions. The bones of the skull are strong, but also light so humans can hold their heads up easily.

Bone count
There are 22 bones in the human skull. Eight form the cranium (shown in pink) surrounding the brain, while 14 bones (shown in blue) make up the face.

Nasal bones
These bones form the bridge of the nose.

Frontal sinuses
These cavities, above the eyebrow ridge, form after birth and reach full size by the teenage years.

Sinuses
The sinuses make up a network of air-filled holes inside the skull. These spaces make the skull lighter and act as sound boxes to change the tone of your voice when you speak.

Lower jaw
Also called the mandible, this is the largest bone in the skull, and the only one that can move.

Hyoid bone
This bone forms the base for the tongue.

The **hyoid bone** anchors the root of the tongue; the bone is held in place purely by **muscles**.

The **rounded shape** of the skull gives it extra strength, similar to **the arch of a bridge**.

65

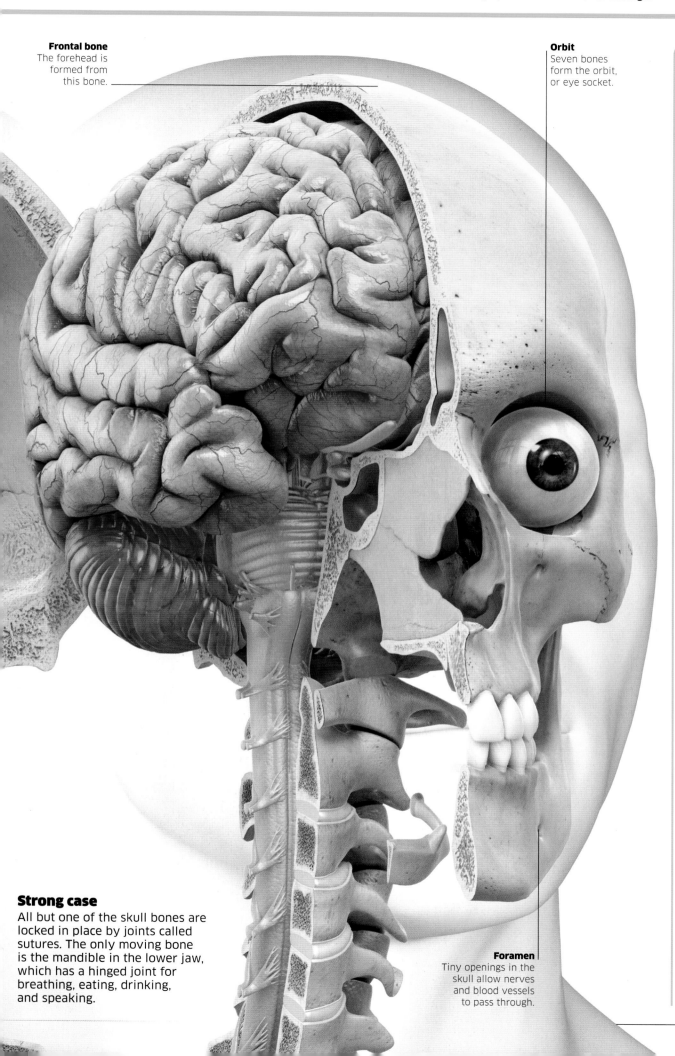

Frontal bone
The forehead is formed from this bone.

Orbit
Seven bones form the orbit, or eye socket.

Strong case

All but one of the skull bones are locked in place by joints called sutures. The only moving bone is the mandible in the lower jaw, which has a hinged joint for breathing, eating, drinking, and speaking.

Foramen
Tiny openings in the skull allow nerves and blood vessels to pass through.

Squishy skulls

Human babies have big heads compared to their bodies, but their heads are flexible enough to squeeze through the birth canal during birth. Newborns have gaps, called fontanels, between the skull bones. These spaces, loosely joined by soft tissue, allow the brain to grow fast—a baby's brain doubles in size in the first years after birth.

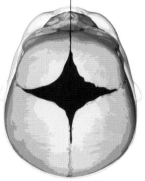

Fontanel
This gap allows the skull to change shape as the baby is being born.

SKULL OF A TWO-MONTH-OLD BABY

Hole in the head

The hole at the base of the skull is called the foramen magnum. The spinal column, which carries messages between the brain and the body, passes through it.

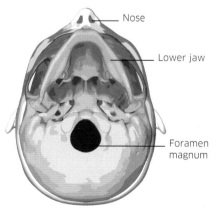

Nose

Lower jaw

Foramen magnum

SKULL FROM BELOW

THERE ARE NO BONES **SHAPING THE** NOSE OR EARS. **INSTEAD, THESE PARTS** ARE MADE OF **TOUGH, FLEXIBLE CARTILAGE.**

66 head and neck ○ **FACIAL MUSCLES**

50—the **number of muscles** you use to make facial expressions.

Facial muscles

The bones of the face are covered in layers of facial muscles. Flexing these muscles allows us to blink, talk, and eat, as well as make a range of facial expressions for communication.

The facial muscles are unique within the body because one end is usually attached to the skin rather than another bone. A small contraction of a facial muscle pulls the skin of the face to form a different expression. The ability to make—and understand—so many different facial expressions helps humans to communicate better.

Taking shape

The shape of a human face is mostly defined by its facial bones and muscles. Forensic sculptors can reconstruct a face from a skull to give a good idea of a person's appearance when they were alive. This can be achieved by modeling with clay or by using computer software programs.

New faces
Modelers use their knowledge of how muscles are arranged over the skull to re-create a face. The model face on the right has been built up, layer by layer, from the skull on the left.

Pulling faces

The facial muscles pull the skin and change the position of the eyes, eyebrows, and lips to make us smile and scowl. These expressions are hard to fake because we make them automatically.

Key

■ MUSCLE CONTRACTS

■ MUSCLE RELAXES

Corrugator supercilii
When this short, narrow muscle is flexed it pulls the eyebrows together and down to form a frown.

Orbicularis oculi
The circular muscle around the eye socket closes the eye.

Zygomaticus
The zygomaticus muscles raise the corners of the mouth to smile.

Buccinator
This muscle keeps food in the mouth by holding the cheek close to the teeth during chewing.

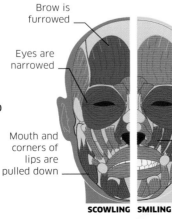

Brow is furrowed

Eyes are narrowed

Mouth and corners of lips are pulled down

Eyes are crinkled

Upper lip is lifted

Mouth and corner of lip are pulled up and sideways

SCOWLING SMILING

Micro-expressions are facial muscles that last less than a second, and may tell us about a person's **true emotions**.

The word **"levator"** in a muscle's name means it pulls upward, while **"depressor"** tells us the muscle pulls downward.

67

Layered muscles

The facial muscles are arranged in thin layers. Superficial muscles lie just under the skin, and beneath them is a layer of deep muscles. In some parts of the face, these two layers are connected by dense fibers.

Only about 20% of humans can **wiggle their ears** voluntarily, using the auricularis muscles.

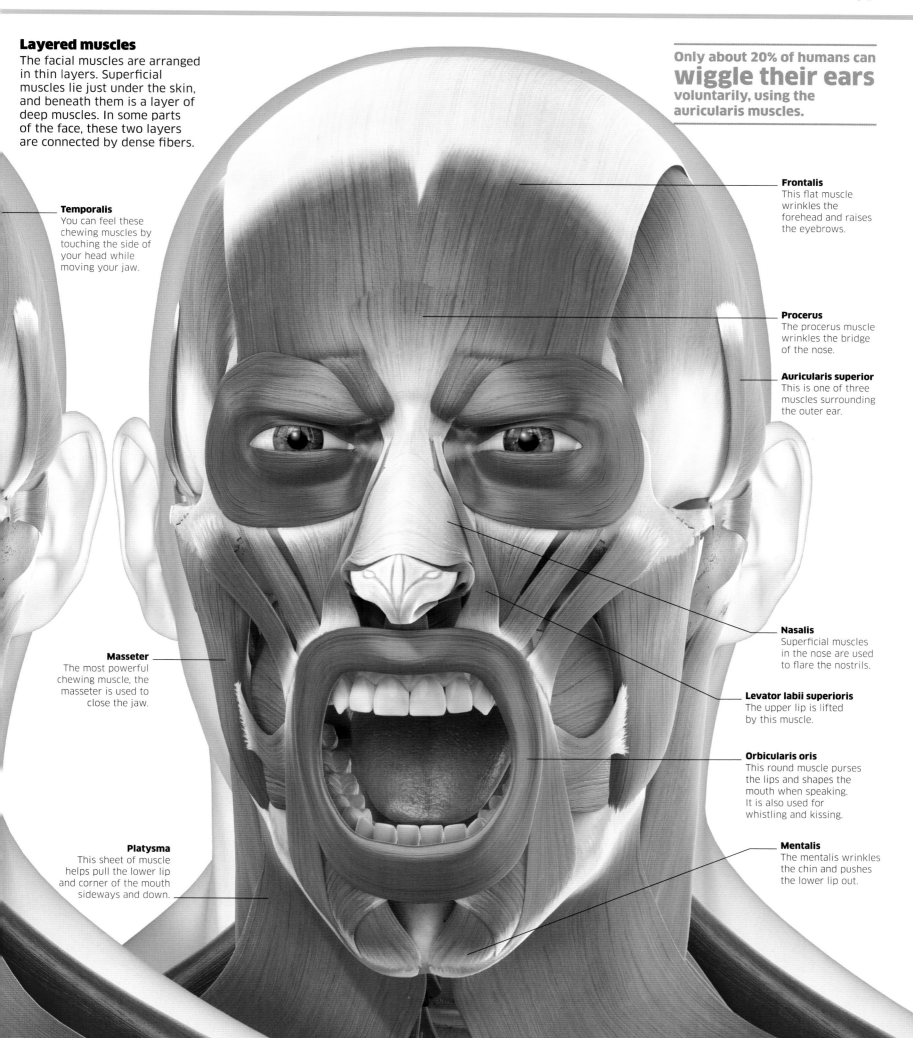

Temporalis
You can feel these chewing muscles by touching the side of your head while moving your jaw.

Frontalis
This flat muscle wrinkles the forehead and raises the eyebrows.

Procerus
The procerus muscle wrinkles the bridge of the nose.

Auricularis superior
This is one of three muscles surrounding the outer ear.

Nasalis
Superficial muscles in the nose are used to flare the nostrils.

Masseter
The most powerful chewing muscle, the masseter is used to close the jaw.

Levator labii superioris
The upper lip is lifted by this muscle.

Orbicularis oris
This round muscle purses the lips and shapes the mouth when speaking. It is also used for whistling and kissing.

Platysma
This sheet of muscle helps pull the lower lip and corner of the mouth sideways and down.

Mentalis
The mentalis wrinkles the chin and pushes the lower lip out.

68 head and neck ○ **INSIDE THE HEAD**

20% of the **body's oxygen supply** is used by the **brain**.

Inside the head

Some of the body's most important—and delicate—organs are in the head and neck area. The brain is the center of operations for the body, and sits within the skull's protective case of bone. The head also houses the eyes, ears, mouth, and nose—our main sense organs.

The area is served by a complex network of blood vessels and nerves. Blood supplies the fuel needed to power the muscles, nerves, and organs in this part of the body. Nerves transmit messages between the brain and the sense organs in the head, enabling us to see, hear, smell, and taste.

Head and neck
This image shows the head and neck with the skin and muscles removed. One side shows the skull bones, while the other exposes the brain. The neck, through which the spinal cord passes, provides a communication channel between the brain and the rest of the body.

Temporal artery
This blood vessel provides a blood supply to the scalp.

Temporal vein
Blood is carried away from the scalp by this vessel.

Eye socket (orbit)
The two hollow eye sockets surround and protect the eyeballs.

Nasal cavity
This hollow area is filled with smell-detecting sensors.

Frontal bone
The front of the skull and the upper part of the eye sockets are formed by this bone.

Brain
The body's center of operations, this controls movement, thinking, emotions, and memory.

Eyeball
The eyes detect light and send signals to the brain, enabling us to see.

Brain stem
The brain stem controls automatic functions such as breathing.

Facial vein
This vein carries blood away from the face.

Buccal (cheek) nerve
This relays sensations from the cheek to the brain.

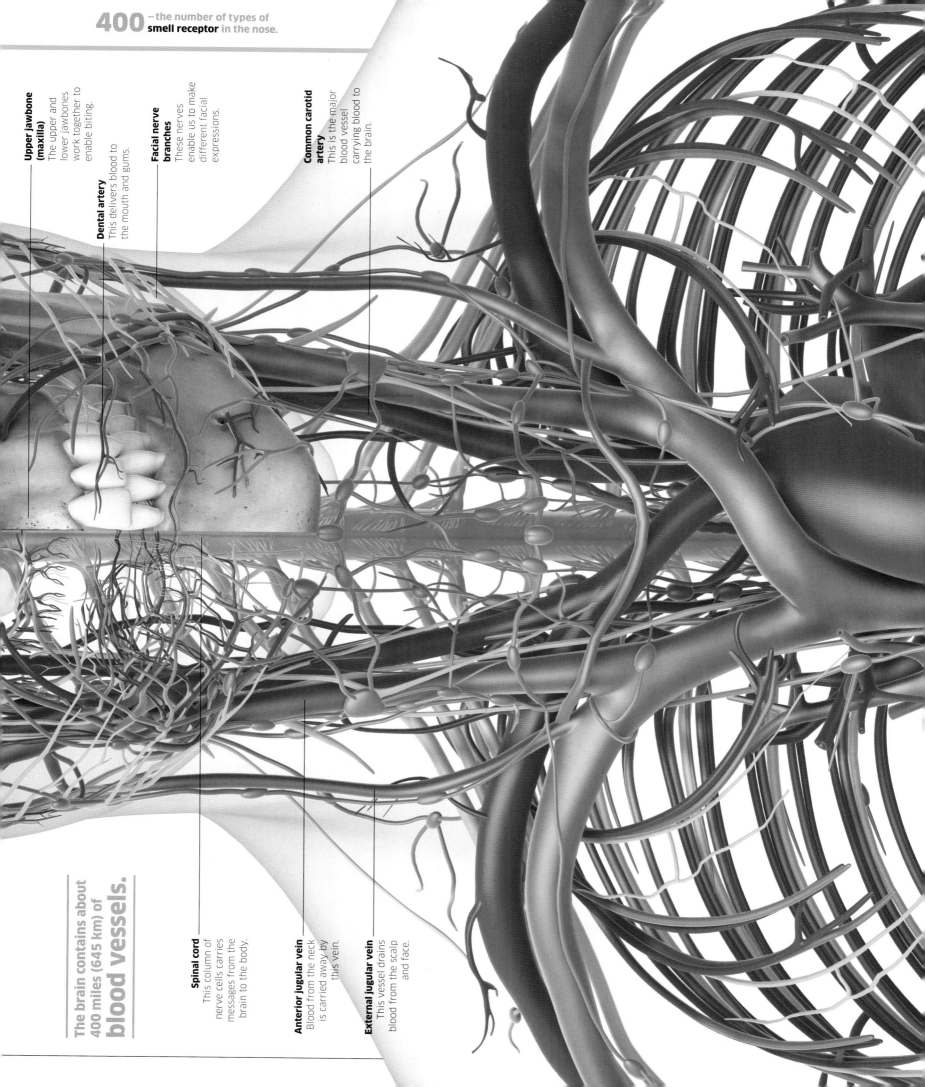

Upper jawbone (maxilla)
The upper and lower jawbones work together to enable biting.

Dental artery
This delivers blood to the mouth and gums.

Facial nerve branches
These nerves enable us to make different facial expressions.

Common carotid artery
This is the major blood vessel carrying blood to the brain.

The brain contains about 400 miles (645 km) of **blood vessels.**

Spinal cord
This column of nerve cells carries messages from the brain to the body.

Anterior jugular vein
Blood from the neck is carried away by this vein.

External jugular vein
This vessel drains blood from the scalp and face.

70 head and neck ○ **BRAIN**

3 lb (1.5 kg)—the **average weight** of an adult's brain.

100 billion—the number of **nerve cells** in the human brain.

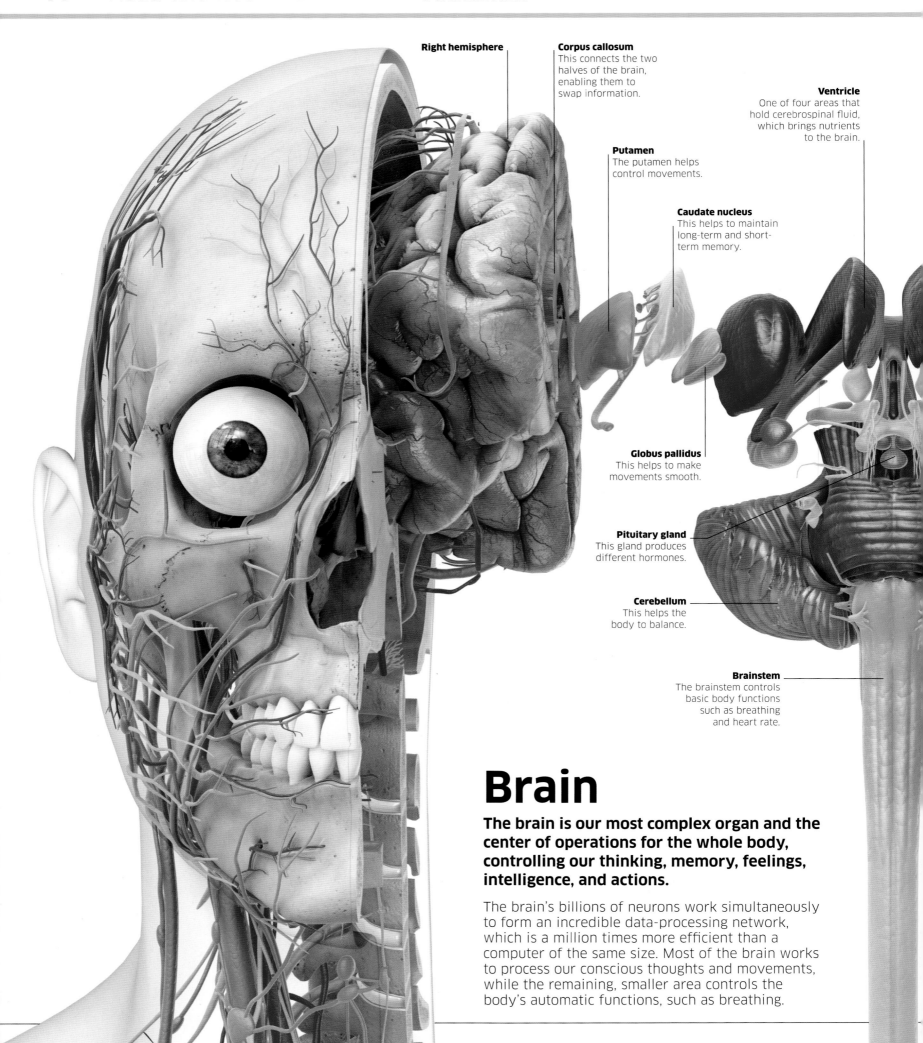

Right hemisphere

Corpus callosum
This connects the two halves of the brain, enabling them to swap information.

Ventricle
One of four areas that hold cerebrospinal fluid, which brings nutrients to the brain.

Putamen
The putamen helps control movements.

Caudate nucleus
This helps to maintain long-term and short-term memory.

Globus pallidus
This helps to make movements smooth.

Pituitary gland
This gland produces different hormones.

Cerebellum
This helps the body to balance.

Brainstem
The brainstem controls basic body functions such as breathing and heart rate.

Brain

The brain is our most complex organ and the center of operations for the whole body, controlling our thinking, memory, feelings, intelligence, and actions.

The brain's billions of neurons work simultaneously to form an incredible data-processing network, which is a million times more efficient than a computer of the same size. Most of the brain works to process our conscious thoughts and movements, while the remaining, smaller area controls the body's automatic functions, such as breathing.

A newborn baby's brain grows by **1% each day** until it is about 3 months old.

By the age of nine, a **child's brain is already 95%** of the size of an adult's.

71

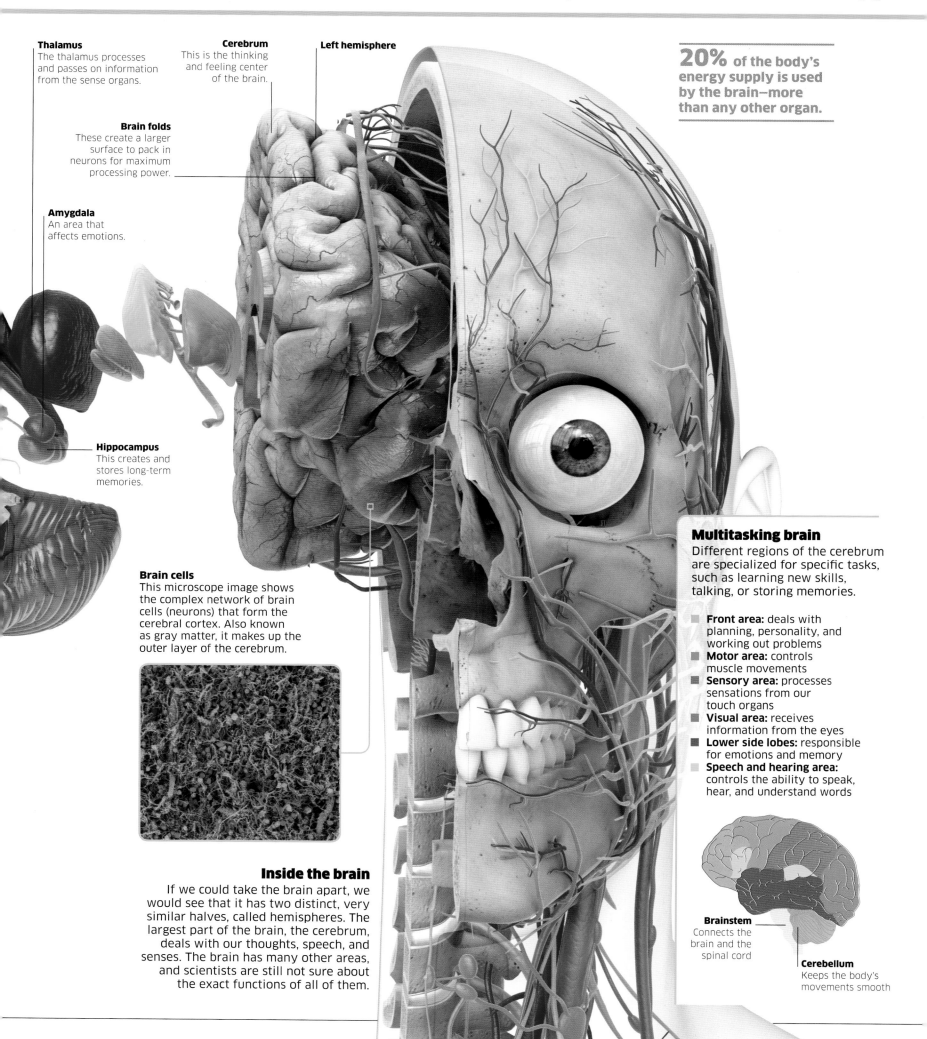

Thalamus
The thalamus processes and passes on information from the sense organs.

Cerebrum
This is the thinking and feeling center of the brain.

Left hemisphere

20% of the body's energy supply is used by the brain—more than any other organ.

Brain folds
These create a larger surface to pack in neurons for maximum processing power.

Amygdala
An area that affects emotions.

Hippocampus
This creates and stores long-term memories.

Brain cells
This microscope image shows the complex network of brain cells (neurons) that form the cerebral cortex. Also known as gray matter, it makes up the outer layer of the cerebrum.

Multitasking brain
Different regions of the cerebrum are specialized for specific tasks, such as learning new skills, talking, or storing memories.

- **Front area:** deals with planning, personality, and working out problems
- **Motor area:** controls muscle movements
- **Sensory area:** processes sensations from our touch organs
- **Visual area:** receives information from the eyes
- **Lower side lobes:** responsible for emotions and memory
- **Speech and hearing area:** controls the ability to speak, hear, and understand words

Inside the brain
If we could take the brain apart, we would see that it has two distinct, very similar halves, called hemispheres. The largest part of the brain, the cerebrum, deals with our thoughts, speech, and senses. The brain has many other areas, and scientists are still not sure about the exact functions of all of them.

Brainstem
Connects the brain and the spinal cord

Cerebellum
Keeps the body's movements smooth

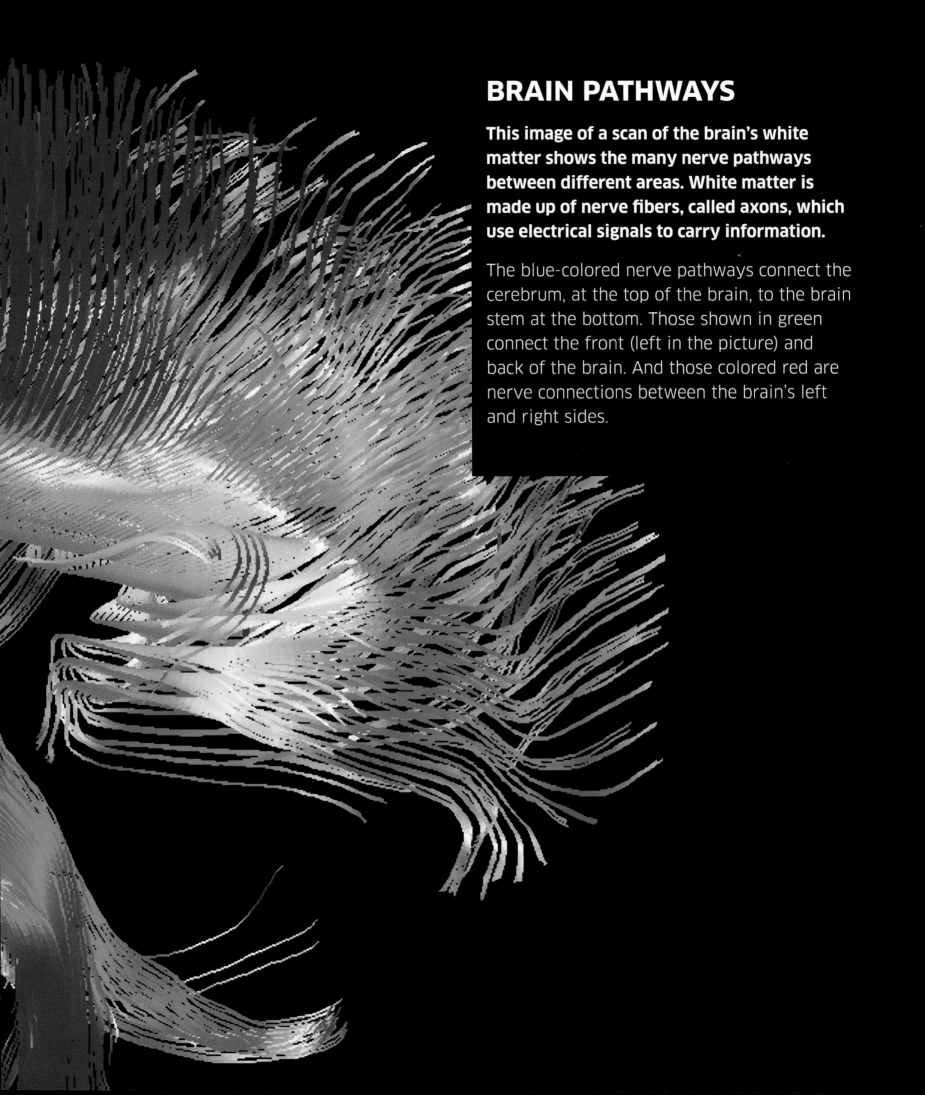

BRAIN PATHWAYS

This image of a scan of the brain's white matter shows the many nerve pathways between different areas. White matter is made up of nerve fibers, called axons, which use electrical signals to carry information.

The blue-colored nerve pathways connect the cerebrum, at the top of the brain, to the brain stem at the bottom. Those shown in green connect the front (left in the picture) and back of the brain. And those colored red are nerve connections between the brain's left and right sides.

CONTROL CENTER

The human brain is a million times more efficient than a computer the same size. This busy control center is responsible for our thoughts, movements, and memories. The brain needs a lot of energy to fuel its amazing processing power. Trillions of electrical impulses pass along the neural networks every second. These networks must be maintained and alternative routes planned, so if there is a problem, the signals can still get through.

MAKING MOVES

Body movement is stimulated by electrical impulses carried along nerve cells, called motor neurons. The impulse to move begins in the brain's cerebral cortex, travels down the spinal cord, along the motor neuron, and to the muscle. As muscles contract, the body moves.

Unconscious movement

Sometimes the body must respond so quickly to sensory information that it does not wait to involve the brain. This is an automatic reflex that protects the body in times of danger, such as touching something hot.

Conscious movement

Sometimes the body does not move until it receives specific sensory information. This prevents a player from swinging at a tennis ball before it reaches the racket. Nerves carry electrical impulses from the brain to the muscles to make sure the body moves at the right time.

Returning serve
As the tennis ball is coming, a signal is sent to the brain to predict where the ball will land and move the body into position.

RIGHT OR LEFT?

The cerebrum is divided into the right and left hemispheres. They communicate with each other through a thick bundle of nerve fibers called the corpus callosum. The right hemisphere controls the left side of the body, while the left hemisphere controls the right side.

Brain divide

The brain's left side tends to control verbal and written skills and logical thought. The right side tends to be where creative and emotional impulses come from. But the sides work together in a complex way that we don't yet fully understand.

LIFE EXPERIENCE

The brain organizes and stores experiences as memories. These put information into context, such as whether you have been somewhere before or met someone previously. They also repeat useful information, such as the way to school. The brain does not keep every memory. If a memory is unimportant or the memory is not revisited, it is soon forgotten.

Memory bank

Memories are not stored in a single part of the brain—in fact, recalling just one memory can involve several different parts of the brain.

Language
Fluency with spoken words is controlled by the left hemisphere.

Writing
The left hemisphere controls your ability to express yourself in written words.

Logical thought
The left side is responsible for thinking logically and finding solutions to problems.

Math and science
The left side handles numbers, problems, and scientific thought.

Spatial skills
The right side of your brain deals with 3-D shapes and structures.

Imagination
Creativity and imaginative thoughts are fueled by your right side.

Music
The right hemisphere is more active when you listen to music or play an instrument.

Art
Your artistic streak shows up on the right whenever you draw or paint.

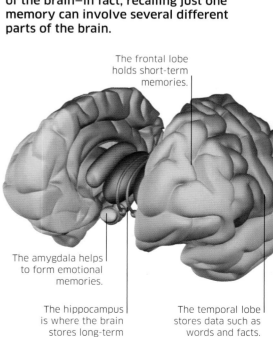

The frontal lobe holds short-term memories.

The amygdala helps to form emotional memories.

The hippocampus is where the brain stores long-term memories.

The temporal lobe stores data such as words and facts.

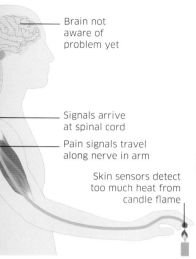

Brain not aware of problem yet

Signals arrive at spinal cord

Pain signals travel along nerve in arm

Skin sensors detect too much heat from candle flame

Pain registers in brain

Brain still not aware of pain or movement

Reflex link in spine

Signals to arm muscle make it contract

Hand withdraws to a safe distance

Signals race to brain

1 BURNING HOT
When you touch something very hot, the pain signal travels through the sensory nerve to the spinal cord.

2 AUTOMATIC RESPONSE
A nerve signal is sent from your spinal cord to your arm muscle, which contracts to pull the hand away.

3 PAIN SIGNAL
The pain signal reaches the brain after the hand has moved away, and you now start to feel pain.

Setting a pattern
An experience will cause a certain set of brain cells to fire together. This creates a distinct neural pattern of activity in the brain. The information is bundled up and encoded as a memory.

Nerve signal

More cells join the network

New connection

Brain cell

THE BRAIN CAN STORE THE SAME AMOUNT OF INFORMATION AS 3 MILLION HOURS OF TELEVISION PROGRAMS.

1 NEURAL PATTERN
A new experience triggers a neuron to send signals to other brain cells, forming a connected neuron network.

2 STRONG CONNECTION
When this experience is remembered, the same network is used. It grows bigger and the connection becomes stronger.

Making memories
Experiencing a memorable moment stays in the memory because a unique pattern of neural activity is created and reinforced.

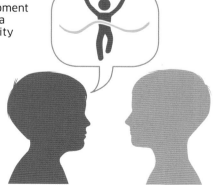

1 FORMATION
If you win a race, everything you experience—the way your body feels, the people around you, the weather on the day—combines to create a unique pattern of neural activity in the brain.

2 CONSOLIDATION
Afterward, when you talk about winning the race with a friend, you revisit the experience and add emotions, which makes the memory even stronger.

3 REVISITING
You replay the memory by looking at a photograph from the day. The more often you revisit this memory, the stronger the neural connections become, ensuring you don't forget it.

ENERGY RUSH
Although the brain makes up less than three percent of our body weight, it uses 20 percent of our total daily energy supply. Energy is required to fire neurons, and the brain has more than 100 billion of them. Two-thirds of the energy used by the brain fuels this neuron activity. The remaining third is used to repair and maintain neurons.

Full power
Scientists have found that the best way to maintain a healthy brain is to keep using it. Activities can be intellectual, such as learning a new language, or physical, such as running a race. Providing the brain with different kinds of challenges helps the growth, maintenance, and regeneration of neurons.

Cube challenge
A Rubik's cube stimulates neuron activity. Challenging the brain lifts the mood, reduces stress, and speeds up thinking.

A good night's sleep
Nobody knows exactly how and why we sleep, but most experts agree that sleep is probably important for the health of the brain. Sleeping and dreaming may give the brain the chance to store memories, process information taken in during the day, and delete data.

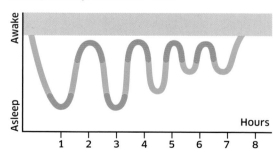

Awake

Asleep

Hours

1 2 3 4 5 6 7 8

Sleep cycle
We pass through the different stages of sleep several times a night, from light to deep sleep and back again.

Light sleep—Body processes slow down; waking up is easy.

REM sleep—The eyes flicker under the eyelids; dreams occur at this stage.

Deep sleep—Body systems slow even more; waking is more difficult.

Mouth and throat

The mouth is the gateway for food and drink to enter the body. It also helps to carry air in and out, and we shape the mouth to produce different sounds when we speak.

The mouth is bounded by the lips, the roof and floor of the mouth, and the cheek muscles. It opens into the throat, a muscular tube that runs down the neck. Only air travels in the top section, which connects to the nose. Both air and food pass through the middle section, but not at the same time. The bottom section divides into two branches—the esophagus, which carries food to the stomach, and the windpipe, which channels air to the lungs.

More than 700

species of bacteria have been found in the mouth, but most healthy people host about 70 different varieties.

Inside the oral cavity

This cross section through a head shows the mouth, the oral cavity (space inside the mouth), and throat. At the back of the throat are the tonsils, which help destroy harmful bacteria that are carried into the mouth with food or in the air. The tongue is not shown, so the other organs can be seen more clearly.

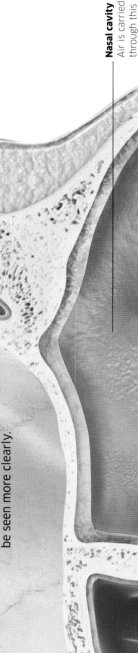

Nasal cavity
Air is carried through this space between the nostrils and throat.

Swallowing food

When we eat, it's important that food does not enter our airways and make us choke. So as we swallow, the body automatically closes off the airways in the throat and nose. A flap of tissue called the epiglottis drops over the entrance to the windpipe. The soft palate lifts up to block access to the nasal cavity, too.

1 Chewing food

While we chew food, we can still breathe because the positions of the epiglottis and soft palate allow air in through the nose. As we prepare to swallow, the tongue pushes the food back into the throat.

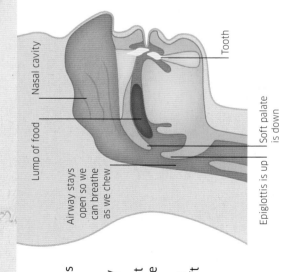

Nasal cavity

Lump of food

Airway stays open so we can breathe as we chew

Tooth

Epiglottis is up | Soft palate is down

2 Swallowing

As the food hits the back of the throat, it triggers a reflex action in the body. The soft palate rises to block the nasal cavity, while the epiglottis folds down to cover the windpipe. The food is directed safely down the esophagus, toward the stomach.

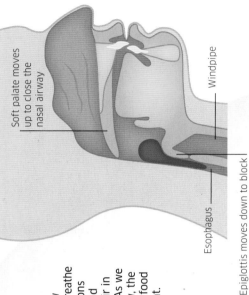

Soft palate moves up to close the nasal airway

Windpipe

Esophagus

Epiglottis moves down to block entrance to the windpipe

7 seconds is how long it takes food to travel **from your mouth** to your stomach.

The salivary glands produce **less saliva at night** than they do during the day.

77

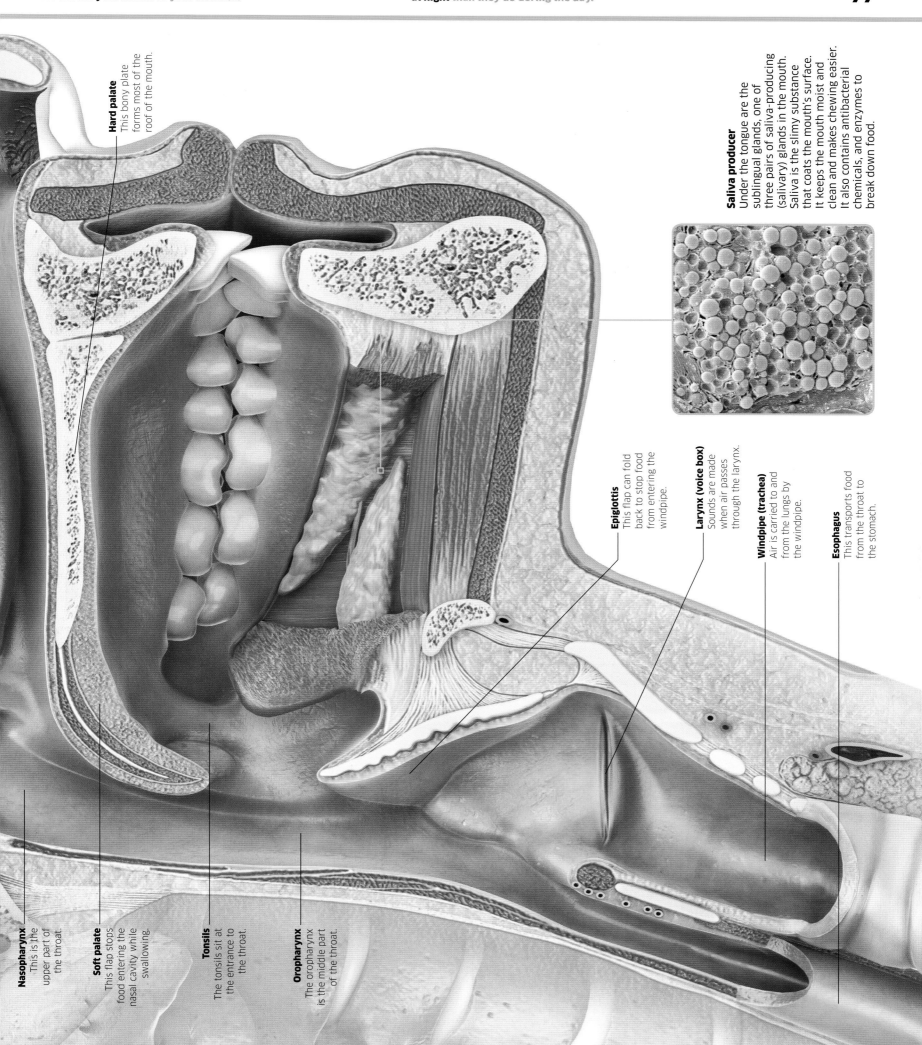

Hard palate
This bony plate forms most of the roof of the mouth.

Saliva producer
Under the tongue are the sublingual glands, one of three pairs of saliva-producing (salivary) glands in the mouth. Saliva is the slimy substance that coats the mouth's surface. It keeps the mouth moist and clean and makes chewing easier. It also contains antibacterial chemicals, and enzymes to break down food.

Epiglottis
This flap can fold back to stop food from entering the windpipe.

Larynx (voice box)
Sounds are made when air passes through the larynx.

Windpipe (trachea)
Air is carried to and from the lungs by the windpipe.

Esophagus
This transports food from the throat to the stomach.

Nasopharynx
This is the upper part of the throat.

Soft palate
This flap stops food entering the nasal cavity while swallowing.

Tonsils
The tonsils sit at the entrance to the throat.

Oropharynx
The oropharynx is the middle part of the throat.

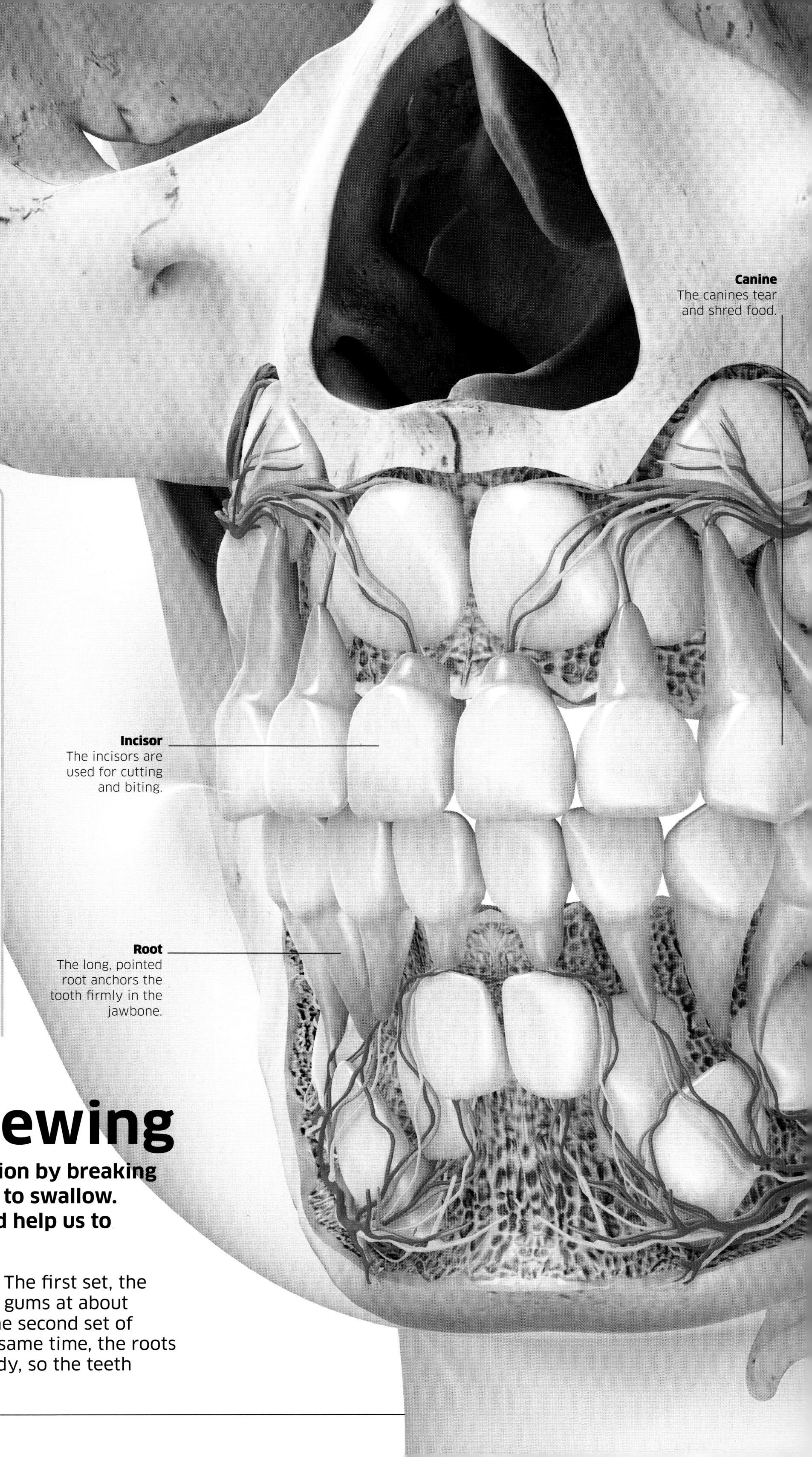

Canine
The canines tear
and shred food.

Tooth arrangement
Different shaped teeth perform specific tasks.
Sharp-edged incisors at the front cut into foods,
while pointed canines are good for tearing. The
cut food is then pushed back to the molars and
premolars for grinding and chewing.

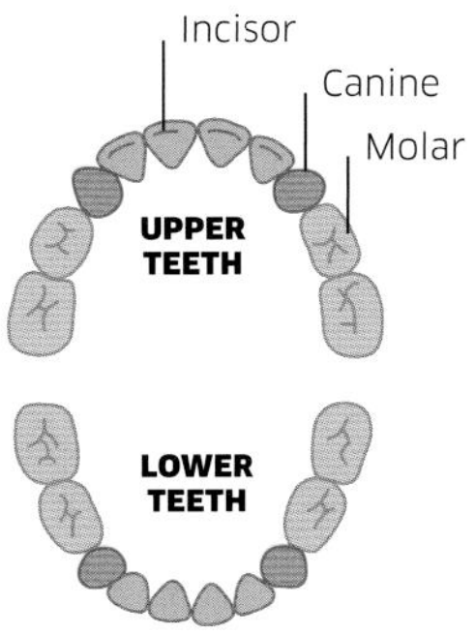

Incisor

Canine

Molar

**UPPER
TEETH**

**UPPER
TEETH**

Molar

**LOWER
TEETH**

Wisdom tooth

Premolar

**LOWER
TEETH**

Incisor
The incisors are
used for cutting
and biting.

Baby teeth
A set of baby teeth
consists of 20
teeth—10 each in the
upper and lower jaw.
There are 4 molars
for chewing food, but
no premolars.

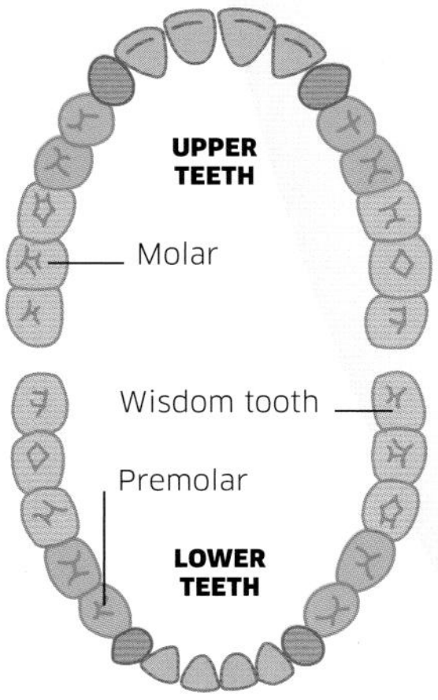

Permanent teeth
By the age of about 11, a child
has a set of 28 permanent teeth.
In the late teens, 4 more molars—
the wisdom teeth—may appear,
making a set of 32.

Root
The long, pointed
root anchors the
tooth firmly in the
jawbone.

Teeth and chewing

**The teeth start the process of digestion by breaking
food down into pieces small enough to swallow.
Teeth also give shape to the face and help us to
pronounce sounds when we speak.**

We grow two sets of teeth in our lifetime. The first set, the
baby teeth, start to emerge from a baby's gums at about
six months of age. Then from six years, the second set of
permanent teeth starts to emerge. At the same time, the roots
of the baby teeth are absorbed by the body, so the teeth
become loose and eventually fall out.

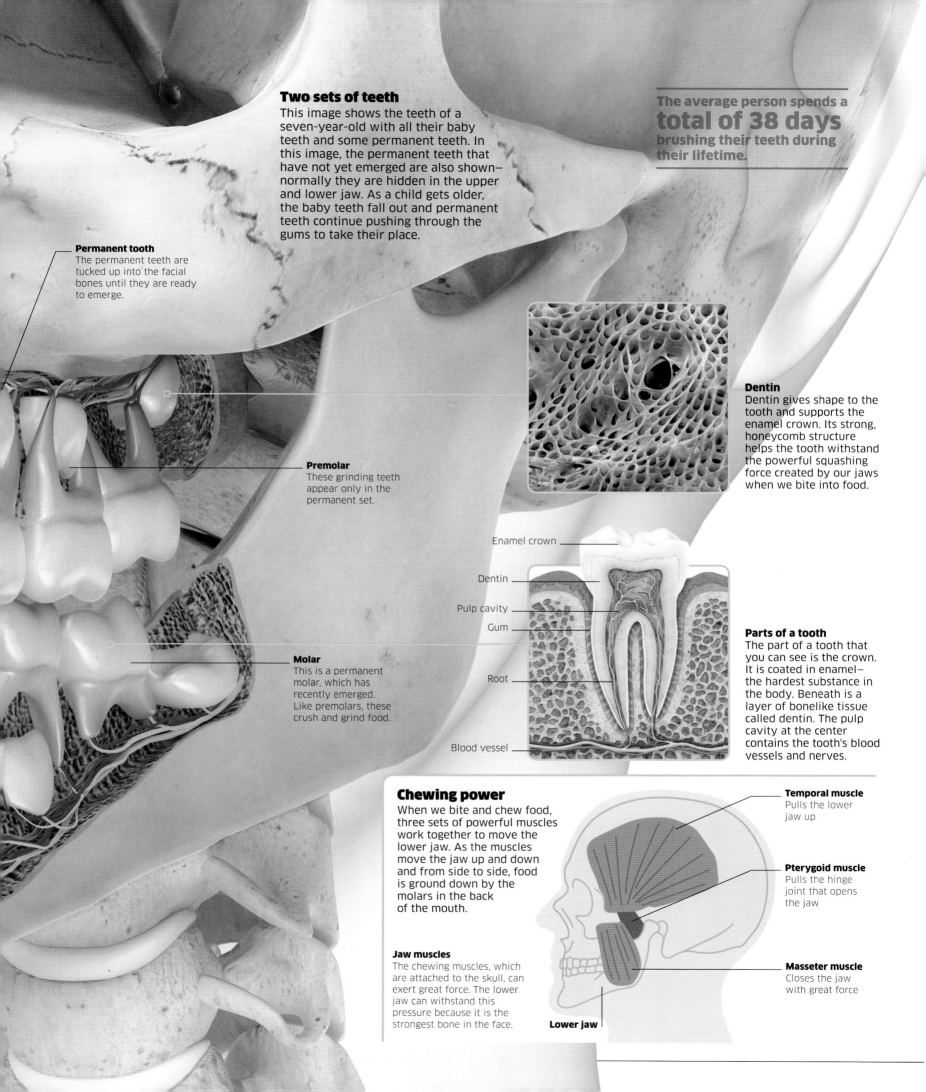

Two sets of teeth

This image shows the teeth of a seven-year-old with all their baby teeth and some permanent teeth. In this image, the permanent teeth that have not yet emerged are also shown—normally they are hidden in the upper and lower jaw. As a child gets older, the baby teeth fall out and permanent teeth continue pushing through the gums to take their place.

The average person spends a total of 38 days brushing their teeth during their lifetime.

Permanent tooth
The permanent teeth are tucked up into the facial bones until they are ready to emerge.

Premolar
These grinding teeth appear only in the permanent set.

Molar
This is a permanent molar, which has recently emerged. Like premolars, these crush and grind food.

Dentin
Dentin gives shape to the tooth and supports the enamel crown. Its strong, honeycomb structure helps the tooth withstand the powerful squashing force created by our jaws when we bite into food.

Enamel crown

Dentin

Pulp cavity

Gum

Root

Blood vessel

Parts of a tooth
The part of a tooth that you can see is the crown. It is coated in enamel—the hardest substance in the body. Beneath is a layer of bonelike tissue called dentin. The pulp cavity at the center contains the tooth's blood vessels and nerves.

Chewing power

When we bite and chew food, three sets of powerful muscles work together to move the lower jaw. As the muscles move the jaw up and down and from side to side, food is ground down by the molars in the back of the mouth.

Jaw muscles
The chewing muscles, which are attached to the skull, can exert great force. The lower jaw can withstand this pressure because it is the strongest bone in the face.

Temporal muscle
Pulls the lower jaw up

Pterygoid muscle
Pulls the hinge joint that opens the jaw

Masseter muscle
Closes the jaw with great force

Lower jaw

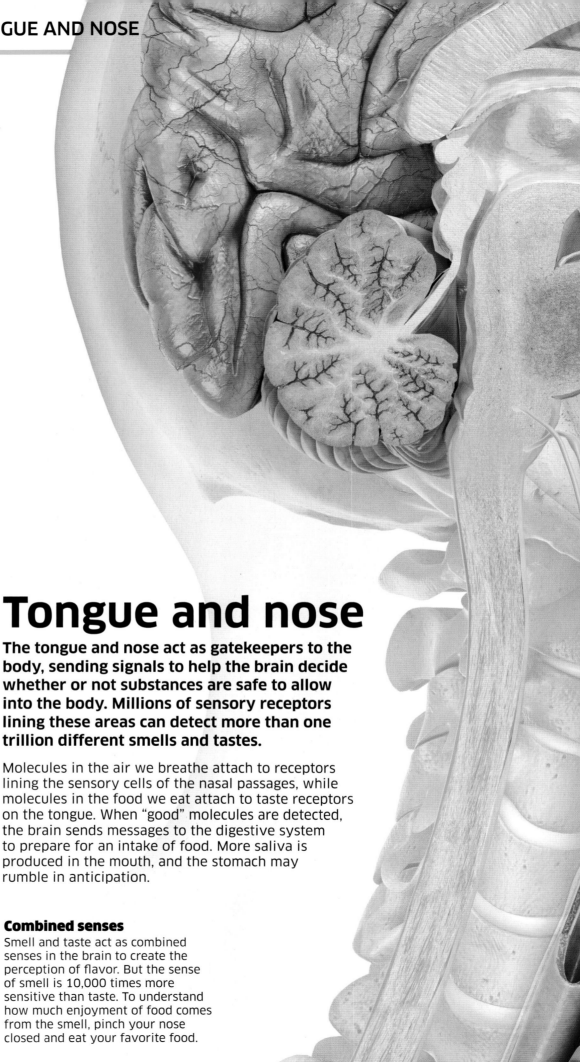

Taste test
The tongue has thousands of taste buds, but these receptors can recognize only five different basic tastes.

Bitter
Tasting something bitter can stop us from eating harmful food. But some people enjoy bitter tastes like coffee.

Salty
This taste comes from sodium, which helps regulate muscle contractions, nerve signals, and keeping the right balance of water.

Sour
Acidic foods, such as lemons and vinegar, taste sour. Humans are the only animals to enjoy sour food.

Sweet
Sweetness is naturally attractive as it indicates the presence of sugar, which provides a swift energy boost.

Umami
This is a mouthwatering savory taste, found in foods such as grilled meat, mushrooms, or soy sauce.

Sensing danger
We use our senses of smell and taste to ensure we don't eat harmful things. Our sense of smell can also detect other potentially dangerous substances, such as smoke or toxic chemicals. The brain processes these smells and warns the body to steer clear.

Warning signal!
When fresh foods such as milk spoil, the sour smell quickly lets us know. Wrinkling the nose in disgust partly blocks off unpleasant, potentially harmful odors.

Tongue and nose

The tongue and nose act as gatekeepers to the body, sending signals to help the brain decide whether or not substances are safe to allow into the body. Millions of sensory receptors lining these areas can detect more than one trillion different smells and tastes.

Molecules in the air we breathe attach to receptors lining the sensory cells of the nasal passages, while molecules in the food we eat attach to taste receptors on the tongue. When "good" molecules are detected, the brain sends messages to the digestive system to prepare for an intake of food. More saliva is produced in the mouth, and the stomach may rumble in anticipation.

Combined senses
Smell and taste act as combined senses in the brain to create the perception of flavor. But the sense of smell is 10,000 times more sensitive than taste. To understand how much enjoyment of food comes from the smell, pinch your nose closed and eat your favorite food.

20,000,000 —the total number of **smell receptors** in a person's nose.

81

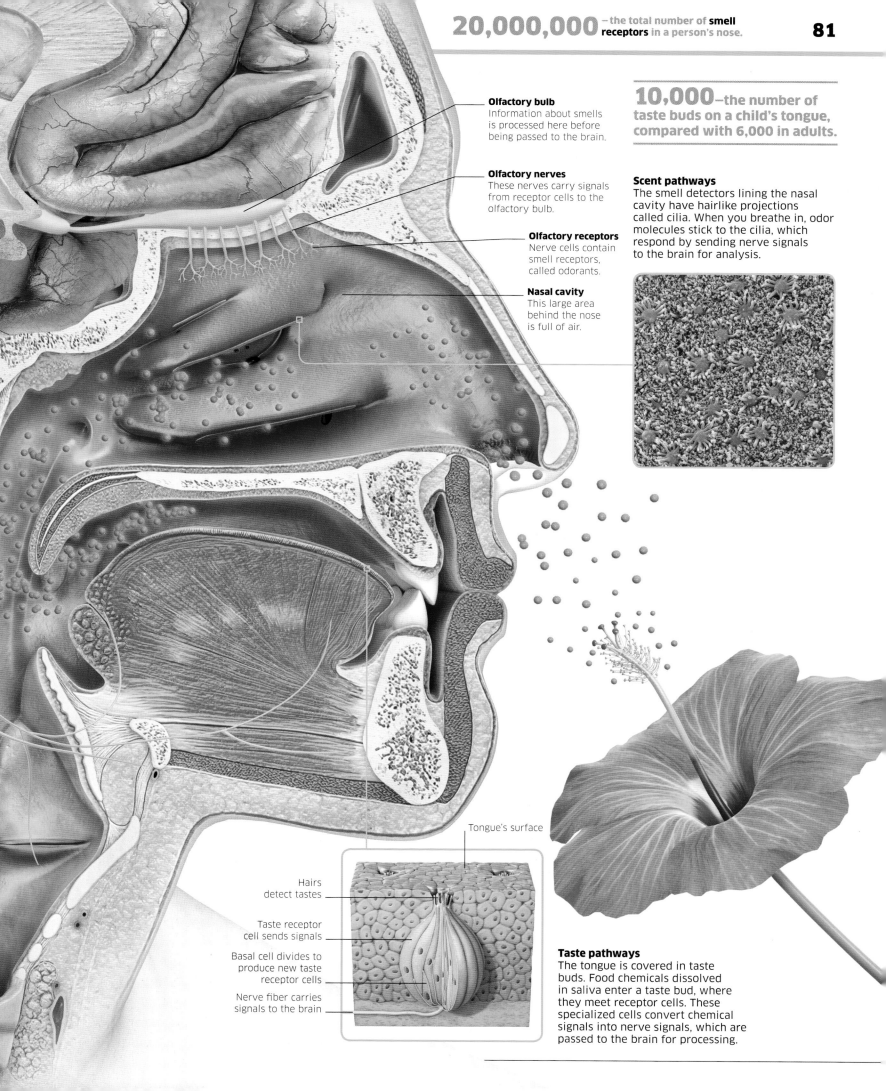

Olfactory bulb
Information about smells is processed here before being passed to the brain.

Olfactory nerves
These nerves carry signals from receptor cells to the olfactory bulb.

Olfactory receptors
Nerve cells contain smell receptors, called odorants.

Nasal cavity
This large area behind the nose is full of air.

10,000 —the number of taste buds on a child's tongue, compared with 6,000 in adults.

Scent pathways
The smell detectors lining the nasal cavity have hairlike projections called cilia. When you breathe in, odor molecules stick to the cilia, which respond by sending nerve signals to the brain for analysis.

Tongue's surface

Hairs detect tastes

Taste receptor cell sends signals

Basal cell divides to produce new taste receptor cells

Nerve fiber carries signals to the brain

Taste pathways
The tongue is covered in taste buds. Food chemicals dissolved in saliva enter a taste bud, where they meet receptor cells. These specialized cells convert chemical signals into nerve signals, which are passed to the brain for processing.

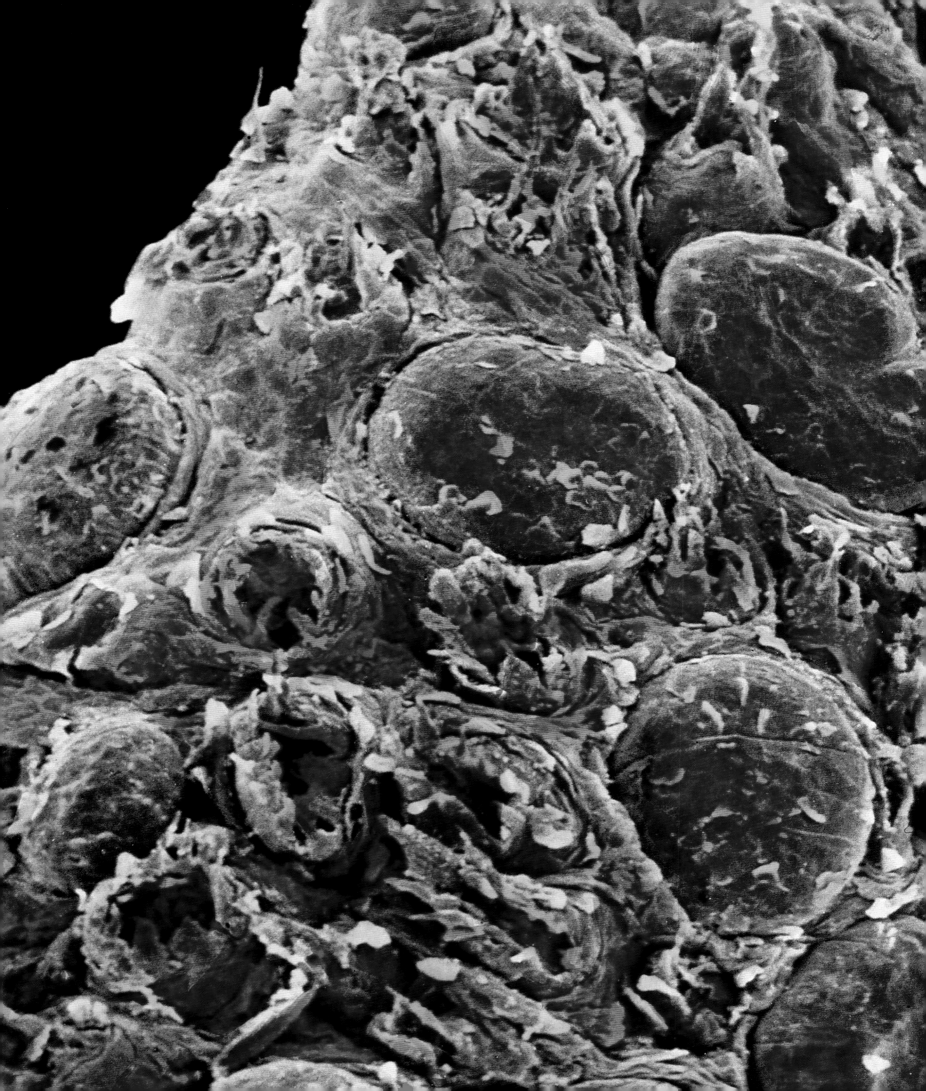

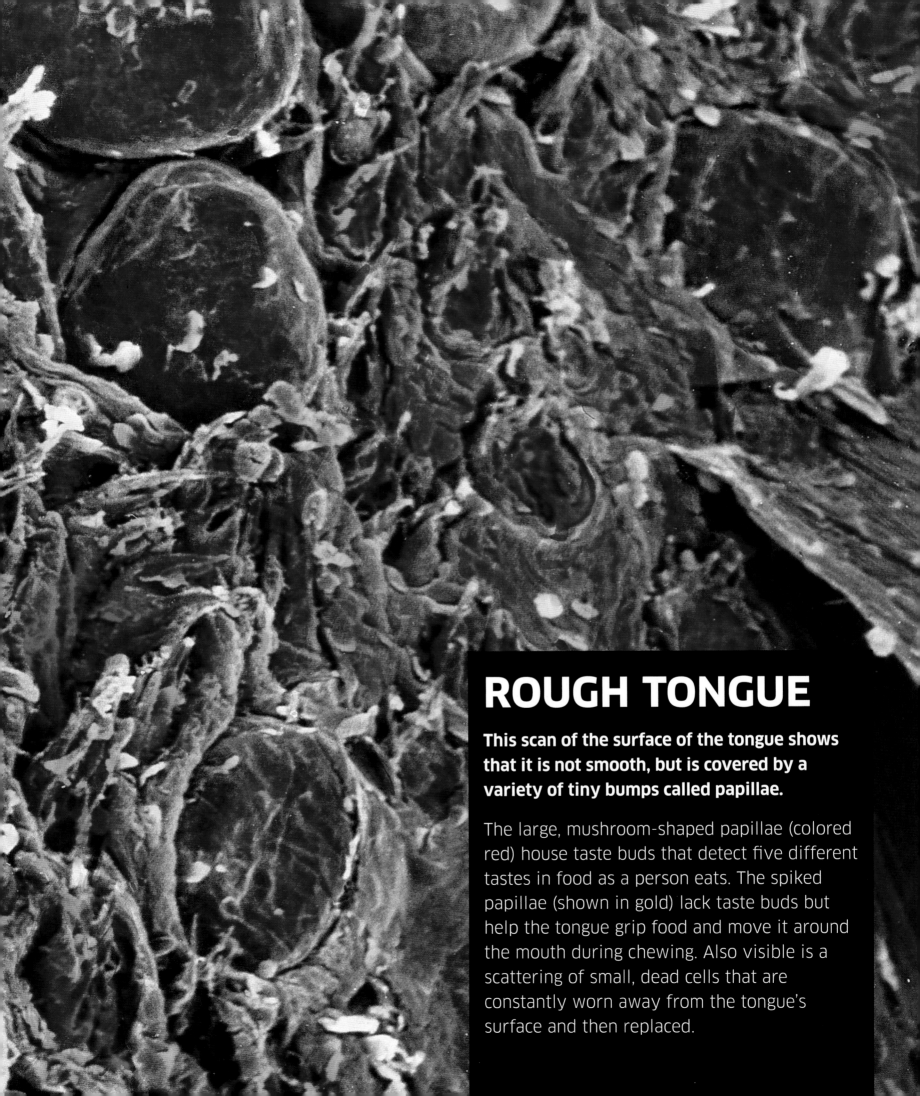

ROUGH TONGUE

This scan of the surface of the tongue shows that it is not smooth, but is covered by a variety of tiny bumps called papillae.

The large, mushroom-shaped papillae (colored red) house taste buds that detect five different tastes in food as a person eats. The spiked papillae (shown in gold) lack taste buds but help the tongue grip food and move it around the mouth during chewing. Also visible is a scattering of small, dead cells that are constantly worn away from the tongue's surface and then replaced.

Eye muscles

Three pairs of muscles control the movements of each eye, allowing it to swivel and roll to look up, down, or from side to side. The muscles are fast-acting, so the eye can easily follow a moving object.

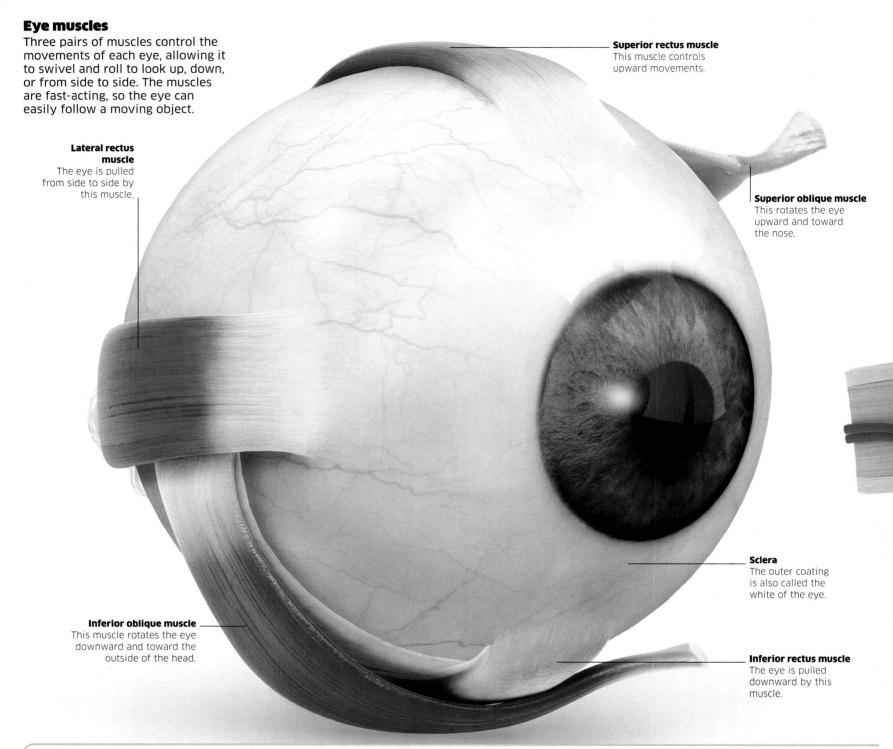

Lateral rectus muscle
The eye is pulled from side to side by this muscle.

Superior rectus muscle
This muscle controls upward movements.

Superior oblique muscle
This rotates the eye upward and toward the nose.

Sclera
The outer coating is also called the white of the eye.

Inferior oblique muscle
This muscle rotates the eye downward and toward the outside of the head.

Inferior rectus muscle
The eye is pulled downward by this muscle.

How vision works

When rays of light from an object hit the cornea (outer shell of the eye) they are bent (refracted). The rays then refract more as they pass through the transparent lens. With distant objects, light is refracted mainly by the cornea—the thin lens only refracts light a little. With nearer objects, the lens becomes wider and it does more of the refraction.

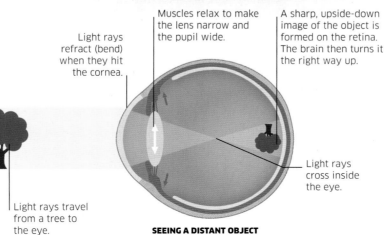

Light rays refract (bend) when they hit the cornea.

Muscles relax to make the lens narrow and the pupil wide.

A sharp, upside-down image of the object is formed on the retina. The brain then turns it the right way up.

Light rays travel from a tree to the eye.

Light rays cross inside the eye.

SEEING A DISTANT OBJECT

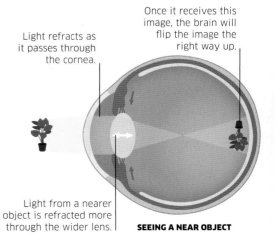

Light refracts as it passes through the cornea.

Once it receives this image, the brain will flip the image the right way up.

Light from a nearer object is refracted more through the wider lens.

SEEING A NEAR OBJECT

415 million—the number of times an **eye blinks** in an average lifetime.

The cornea is the only tissue in the human body that **doesn't contain blood vessels**.

130 million—the number of **light-sensitive** cells in the retina.

85

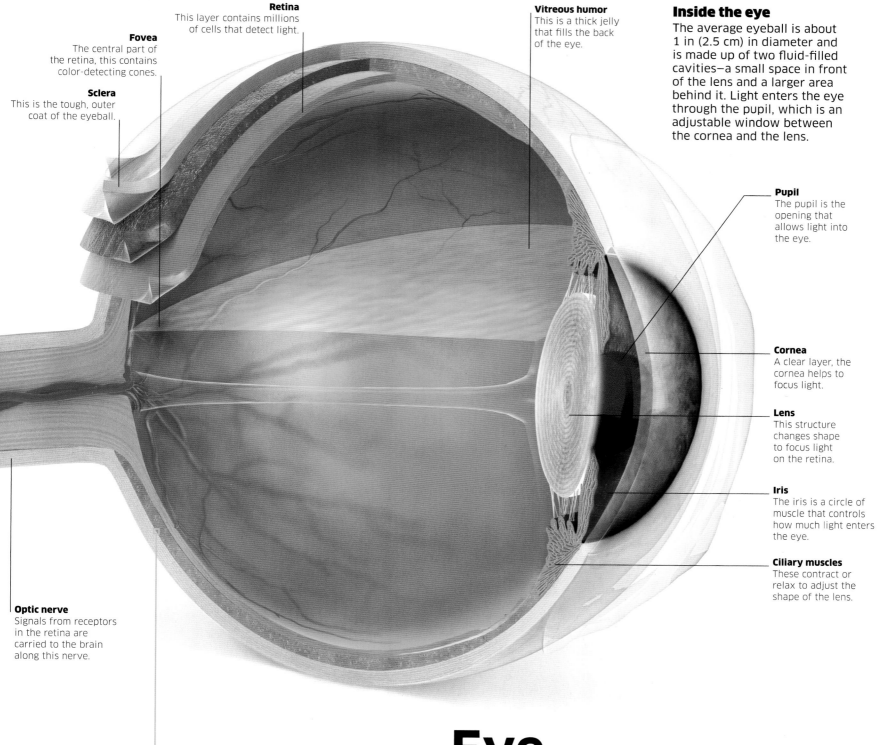

Retina
This layer contains millions of cells that detect light.

Fovea
The central part of the retina, this contains color-detecting cones.

Sclera
This is the tough, outer coat of the eyeball.

Vitreous humor
This is a thick jelly that fills the back of the eye.

Inside the eye
The average eyeball is about 1 in (2.5 cm) in diameter and is made up of two fluid-filled cavities—a small space in front of the lens and a larger area behind it. Light enters the eye through the pupil, which is an adjustable window between the cornea and the lens.

Pupil
The pupil is the opening that allows light into the eye.

Cornea
A clear layer, the cornea helps to focus light.

Lens
This structure changes shape to focus light on the retina.

Iris
The iris is a circle of muscle that controls how much light enters the eye.

Ciliary muscles
These contract or relax to adjust the shape of the lens.

Optic nerve
Signals from receptors in the retina are carried to the brain along this nerve.

Light detectors
This microscope image shows rods (green) and cones (blue)—the two types of light receptor cell on the retina. Rods pick up dim light, while cones detect color and detail. Then they send information about what they record to the brain via the optic nerve.

Eye

The role of the eyes is to collect vast amounts of visual information, which the brain turns into 3-D pictures of the world around us.

Each eye has a built-in lens to give a picture of the world and a bank of sensors to record it. Human eyes can focus on anything from a close-up speck of dust to a galaxy across the universe, and work in both faint moonlight and dazzling sunshine. The lens in each eye focuses light rays together on the back of the eyeball. Receptors record the patterns of light, shade, and colors, then send them to the brain to make an image.

VISION

The human eye is excellent at picking up different colors and fine details. The position of the two eyes also means they can provide a tremendous range of visual information about what is being looked at. The powerful vision-processing areas of the brain then interpret this torrent of data into highly detailed mental images—which your memory then helps you to recognize.

COLOR VISION

Human eyes can see in color thanks to 127 million light-sensitive cells on the back of the retina. These light detectors, called rods and cones, capture light rays from the lenses to create colored images.

Rods and cones

About 120 million rods are sensitive to low light. They see in black and white and provide only minimal detail. About 7 million cones see color and detail, but only in bright light.

Rod cells
The rods work well in dim light. They provide information about the whole image in shades of gray.

Cone cells
The cones detect color and detail at the center of the image, but only work in bright light.

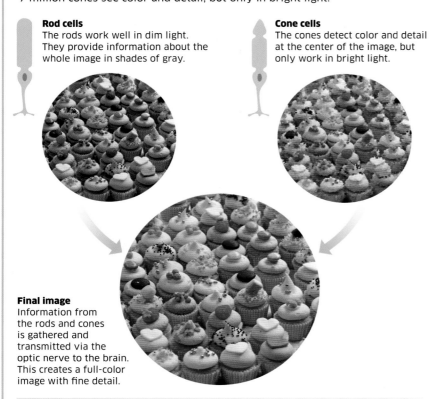

Final image
Information from the rods and cones is gathered and transmitted via the optic nerve to the brain. This creates a full-color image with fine detail.

Three colors

There are three types of color-detecting cones inside the eyes. They are sensitive to red, blue, or green. But combined, they can detect millions of colors, all made of mixtures of these three basic colors.

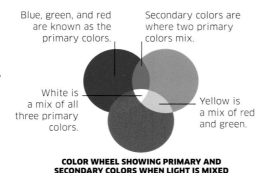

Blue, green, and red are known as the primary colors.

Secondary colors are where two primary colors mix.

White is a mix of all three primary colors.

Yellow is a mix of red and green.

COLOR WHEEL SHOWING PRIMARY AND SECONDARY COLORS WHEN LIGHT IS MIXED

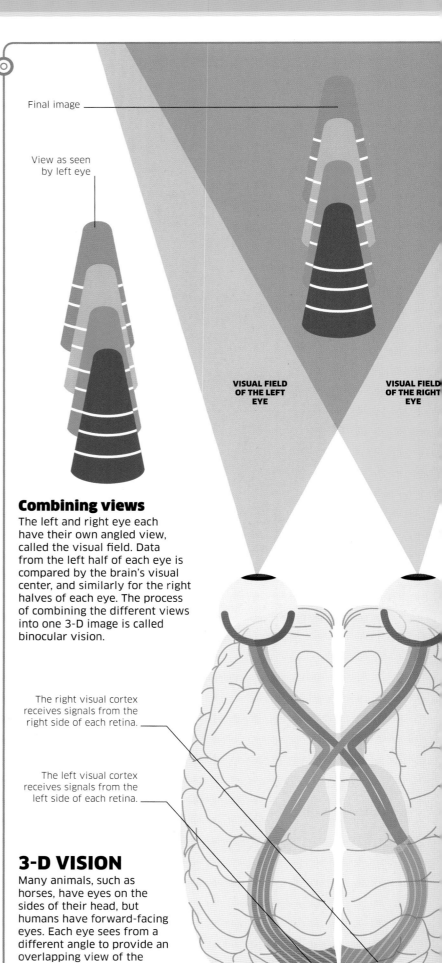

Final image

View as seen by left eye

VISUAL FIELD OF THE LEFT EYE

VISUAL FIELD OF THE RIGHT EYE

Combining views

The left and right eye each have their own angled view, called the visual field. Data from the left half of each eye is compared by the brain's visual center, and similarly for the right halves of each eye. The process of combining the different views into one 3-D image is called binocular vision.

The right visual cortex receives signals from the right side of each retina.

The left visual cortex receives signals from the left side of each retina.

3-D VISION

Many animals, such as horses, have eyes on the sides of their head, but humans have forward-facing eyes. Each eye sees from a different angle to provide an overlapping view of the scene. The brain uses this to create an image with height, width, and depth.

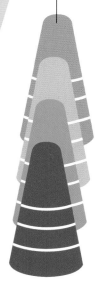

View as seen
by right eye

THE FARTHEST OUR EYES CAN SEE IS THE **ANDROMEDA GALAXY,** ABOUT 2.5 MILLION LIGHT-YEARS AWAY.

Movie magic
The ultimate cinematic experience is a 3-D movie. The film is made by copying what the eyes do. Scenes are shot with two cameras, then special glasses are worn to put the images together. The result makes the audience feel as though they are in the movie.

OPTICAL ILLUSIONS

The brain's task is to make sense of what the eyes see, and it usually gets it right. However, optical illusions can play tricks on the brain because it tries to fill any gaps in the visual information it receives.

Sidewalk painting
Artists can create the illusion of depth by skillful use of techniques such as shading and perspective (making lines meet as if they would in the distance). The brain uses past experience to interpret this scene—wrongly— as a huge chasm in the road.

Moving image
As you look at this image, parts of it seem to move. This is caused by the eyes' light-sensitive cells turning on and off as they react to different parts of the pattern. This fools the eye into thinking it is seeing movement.

EYE PROBLEMS

Sight is a key sense, so maintaining good vision is important to humans. Eyesight often deteriorates as the body ages and the number of light-sensitive rods and cones decreases. Two of the most common eye conditions are problems with focussing and with seeing certain colors.

Out of sight
The most common eye problems are nearsightedness and farsightedness, where distant or near objects can appear blurred. Glasses or contact lenses can help the light to focus in the right place within the eye and make images sharp again.

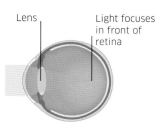

Lens

Light focuses in front of retina

Nearsightedness
Nearsighted people can focus on things that are close, but not on things that are farther away.

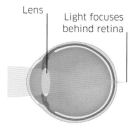

Lens

Light focuses behind retina

Farsightedness
Farsighted people can focus on things at a distance but not on near objects.

Color-blindness
Most eyes can see millions of different colors, but some people cannot distinguish between colors because of injury, illness, or an inherited condition. More boys than girls have color-blindness.

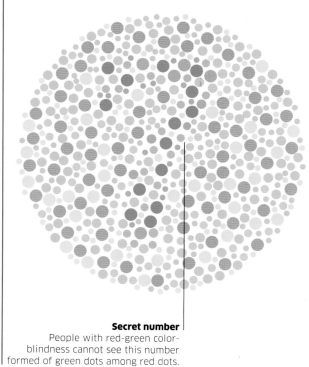

Secret number
People with red-green color-blindness cannot see this number formed of green dots among red dots.

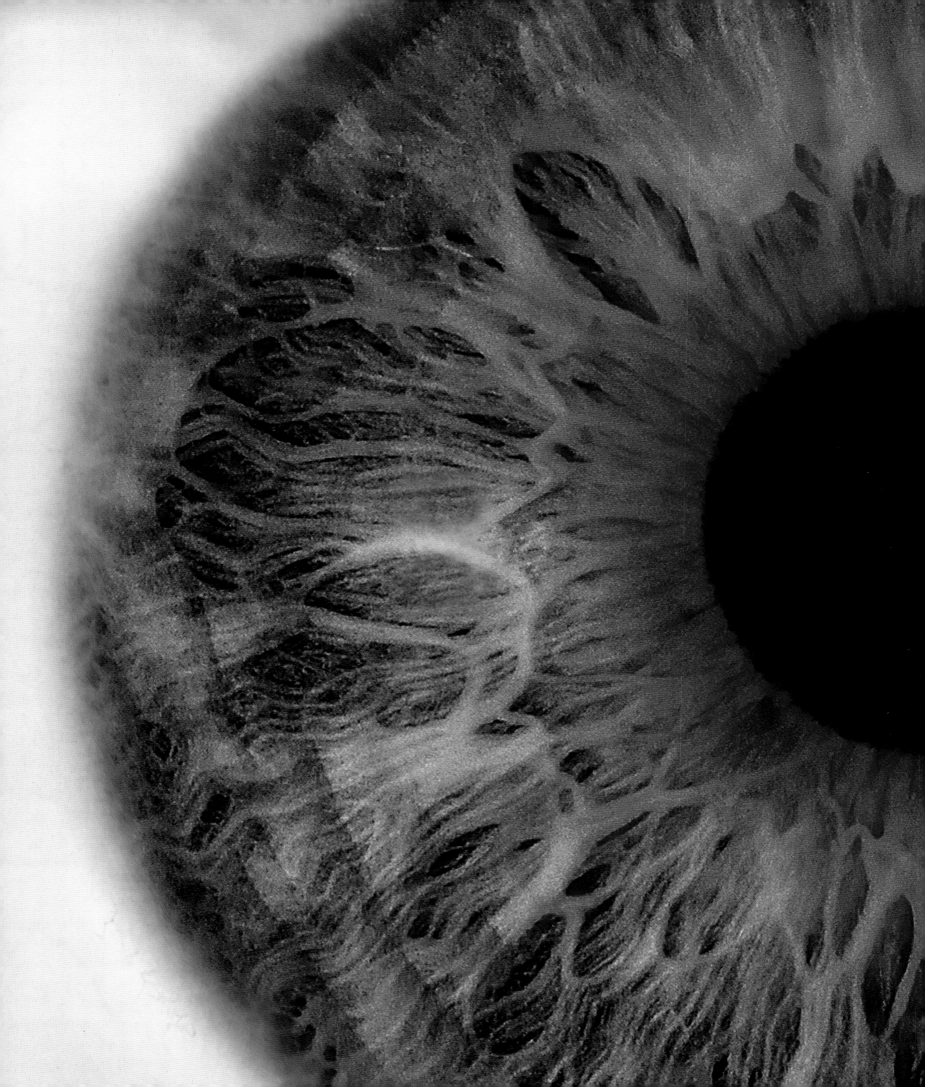

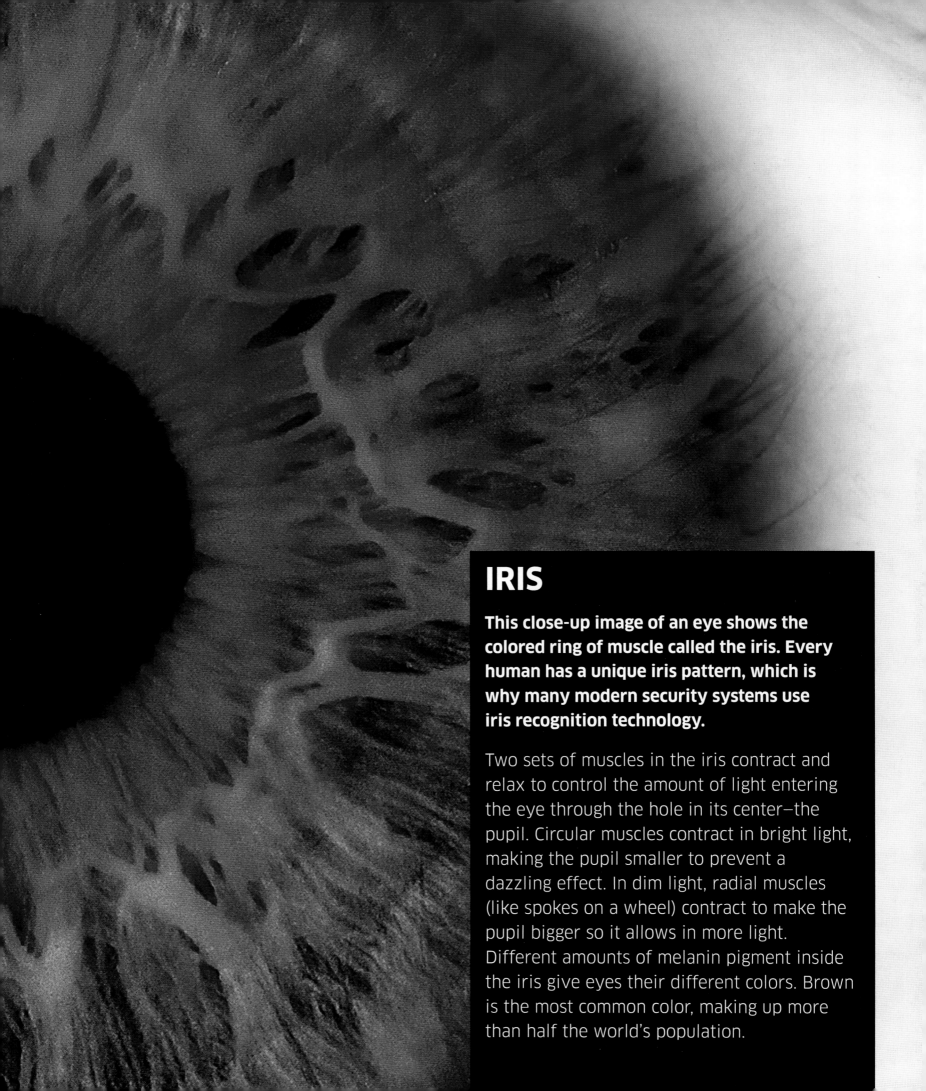

IRIS

This close-up image of an eye shows the colored ring of muscle called the iris. Every human has a unique iris pattern, which is why many modern security systems use iris recognition technology.

Two sets of muscles in the iris contract and relax to control the amount of light entering the eye through the hole in its center—the pupil. Circular muscles contract in bright light, making the pupil smaller to prevent a dazzling effect. In dim light, radial muscles (like spokes on a wheel) contract to make the pupil bigger so it allows in more light. Different amounts of melanin pigment inside the iris give eyes their different colors. Brown is the most common color, making up more than half the world's population.

How hearing works

All sounds make invisible ripples, or waves, in the air. The ear collects sound waves and converts them first into vibrations, then into signals that the brain interprets as sounds.

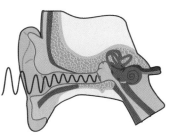

1 Outer ear
Sound waves travel along the ear canal until they hit the eardrum and make it vibrate.

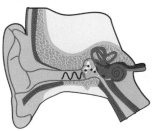

2 Middle ear
The vibrations pass through a series of bones, through the oval window, and into the cochlea.

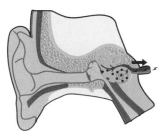

3 Inner ear
Microscopic hairs inside the cochlea convert the vibrations into nerve signals, which are sent to the brain.

Loud and clear

The louder the sound, the bigger the vibrations it makes. Our ears are so sensitive that we can detect even the smallest sound, such as a paper clip dropping on the floor. We measure the loudness of sounds in decibels (dB).

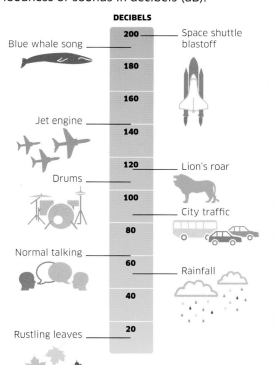

DECIBELS

Blue whale song — 200 — Space shuttle blastoff

180

160

Jet engine — 140

Drums — 120 — Lion's roar

100

City traffic

Normal talking — 80

60 — Rainfall

40

Rustling leaves — 20

Parts of the ear

The ear has three zones, each with different roles. The outer ear collects sounds and funnels them toward the middle ear, where they are converted into vibrations. In the inner ear, the vibrations are transformed again, into signals to send to the brain.

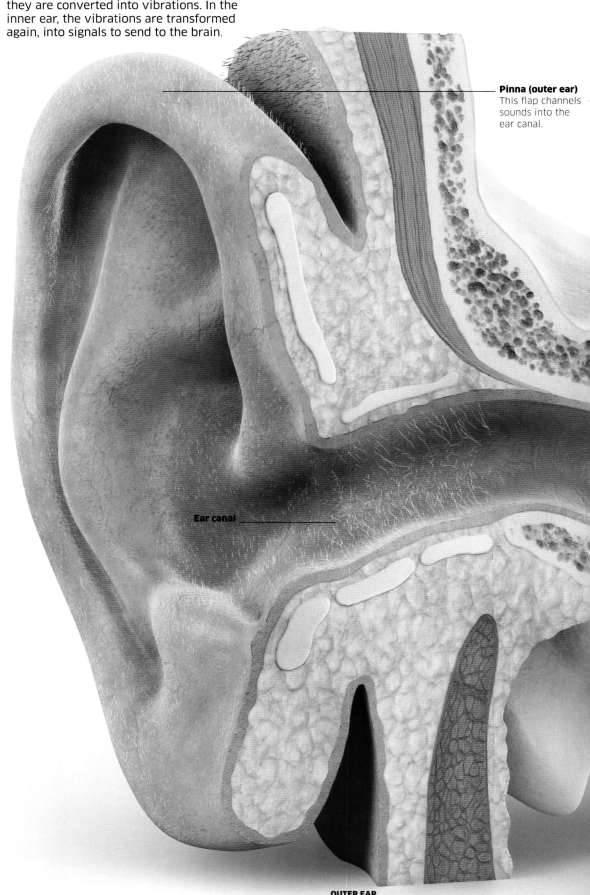

Pinna (outer ear)
This flap channels sounds into the ear canal.

Ear canal

OUTER EAR

The outer ear **continues growing** throughout a person's lifetime.

15,000—the number of **sound-detecting hair cells** in the cochlea.

91

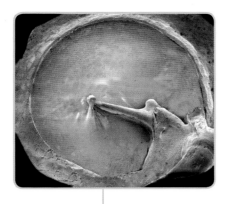

Eardrum
The eardrum is a thin film, about ⅜ in (9 mm) wide, which sits at the entrance to the middle ear and vibrates when sound waves hit it. The eardrum also helps to stop debris from getting inside the ear and damaging it.

Ear

The ear is the body's organ of hearing. It is larger than it looks—only a skin-covered flap is visible on the outside of the head, with the rest of the ear lying hidden from view inside the skull.

The ears collect sound waves and convert them into nerve signals for our brains to decode. Human ears can detect a huge range of different sounds, from high-pitched birdsong to the low rumble of thunder, and from the faintest whisper to the loud roar of a lion.

Stirrup (stapes)
The tiny stirrup bone vibrates and moves the oval window in the cochlea.

Hammer (malleus)
Vibrations from the eardrum are picked up by this bone.

Oval window

Semicircular canals
These three fluid-filled tubes contain sensors that detect movement.

Hair cells
Each hair cell in the cochlea is topped by groups of microscopic hairs. Incoming vibrations bend the hairs by different amounts. These vibration patterns are turned into nerve messages and sent to the brain.

Cochlea
The snail-shaped cochlea is filled with liquid and lined with tiny hair cells that detect vibrations.

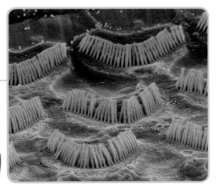

Anvil (incus)
Vibrations from the hammer to the stirrup are transmitted through the anvil.

Smallest bones
The ear contains three of the tiniest bones in the human body. The stirrup bone is the smallest of all, at about the size of a grain of rice.

Anvil

Stirrup | **Hammer**

MIDDLE EAR | INNER EAR

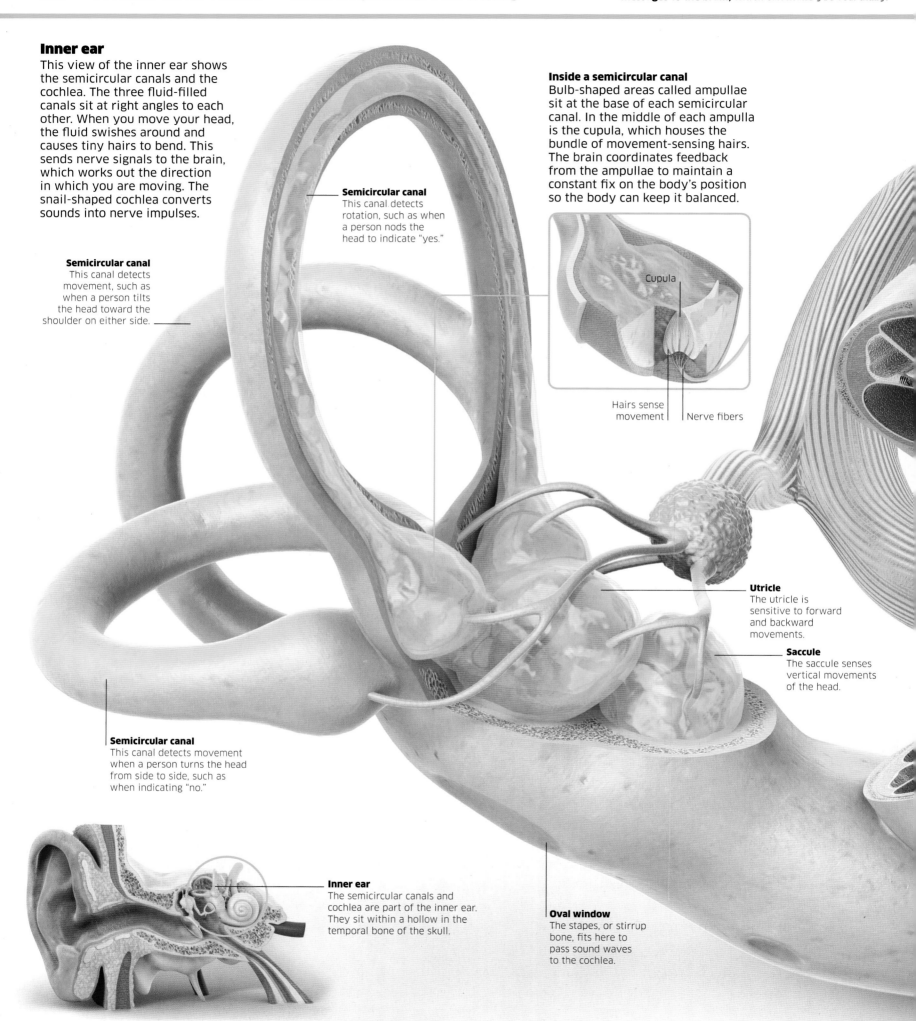

Inner ear
This view of the inner ear shows the semicircular canals and the cochlea. The three fluid-filled canals sit at right angles to each other. When you move your head, the fluid swishes around and causes tiny hairs to bend. This sends nerve signals to the brain, which works out the direction in which you are moving. The snail-shaped cochlea converts sounds into nerve impulses.

Semicircular canal
This canal detects movement, such as when a person tilts the head toward the shoulder on either side.

Semicircular canal
This canal detects rotation, such as when a person nods the head to indicate "yes."

Inside a semicircular canal
Bulb-shaped areas called ampullae sit at the base of each semicircular canal. In the middle of each ampulla is the cupula, which houses the bundle of movement-sensing hairs. The brain coordinates feedback from the ampullae to maintain a constant fix on the body's position so the body can keep it balanced.

Cupula

Hairs sense movement | Nerve fibers

Utricle
The utricle is sensitive to forward and backward movements.

Saccule
The saccule senses vertical movements of the head.

Semicircular canal
This canal detects movement when a person turns the head from side to side, such as when indicating "no."

Inner ear
The semicircular canals and cochlea are part of the inner ear. They sit within a hollow in the temporal bone of the skull.

Oval window
The stapes, or stirrup bone, fits here to pass sound waves to the cochlea.

In an adult, the cochlea is roughly the **same size as a pea**.

1 ¼ in (31.5 mm)—the length of the **tubes of the cochlea** if they were unrolled.

93

Organ of Corti
Running through the middle of the cochlea is the organ of Corti, the main receptor for hearing. Sound waves create vibrations that make wavelike movements in the fluid inside the organ of Corti. These bend the hairs, producing nerve signals, which are sent to the brain to be registered as sounds.

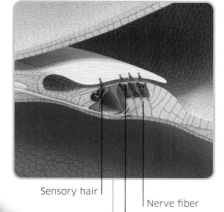

Sensory hair

Nerve fiber

Hair cell

Balance and hearing

In addition to providing our sense of hearing, the ears help us to keep our balance and send vital information to the brain when we move.

The inner ear is the part deepest inside the head. It contains three fluid-filled tubes called semicircular canals. As we move, the fluid inside the canals moves, sending messages to the brain to help us keep our balance. Also in the inner ear is the cochlea, which converts sounds to hearing.

Cochlea
This snail-shaped organ turns vibrations into audible sounds.

Auditory nerve
This nerve carries signals from the ear to the brain.

Balancing act
Different body systems work to keep you balanced. Signals from the inner ear combine with visual signals from the eyes, pressure sensors in the skin, and stretch sensors in the muscles to reveal the body's position. The brain processes this and makes any adjustments to stop the body falling over.

Utricle and saccule
Inside the inner ear are two tiny organs that sense movement of the head in a straight line. The utricle detects forward and backward movement, and the saccule detects up-and-down movement.

The brain takes
0.03 seconds
to send messages to the muscles to correct the body if you start to lose your balance.

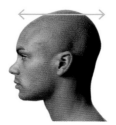

Forward and backward movement, such as traveling in a car, are detected by the utricle.

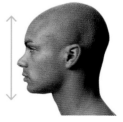

Up-and-down motion, such as riding in an elevator, is sensed by the saccule.

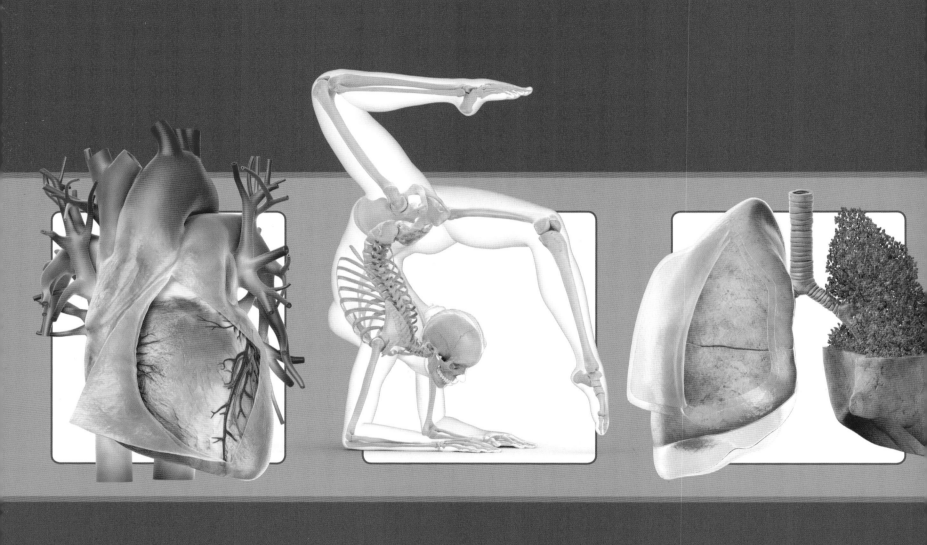

CHEST AND BACK

The chest houses the two powerhouse organs that keep the body running—the heart and lungs. All the body's cells are supplied with essential blood and oxygen thanks to these vital organs. The backbone supports the body and protects the spinal column, which carries messages to and from the brain.

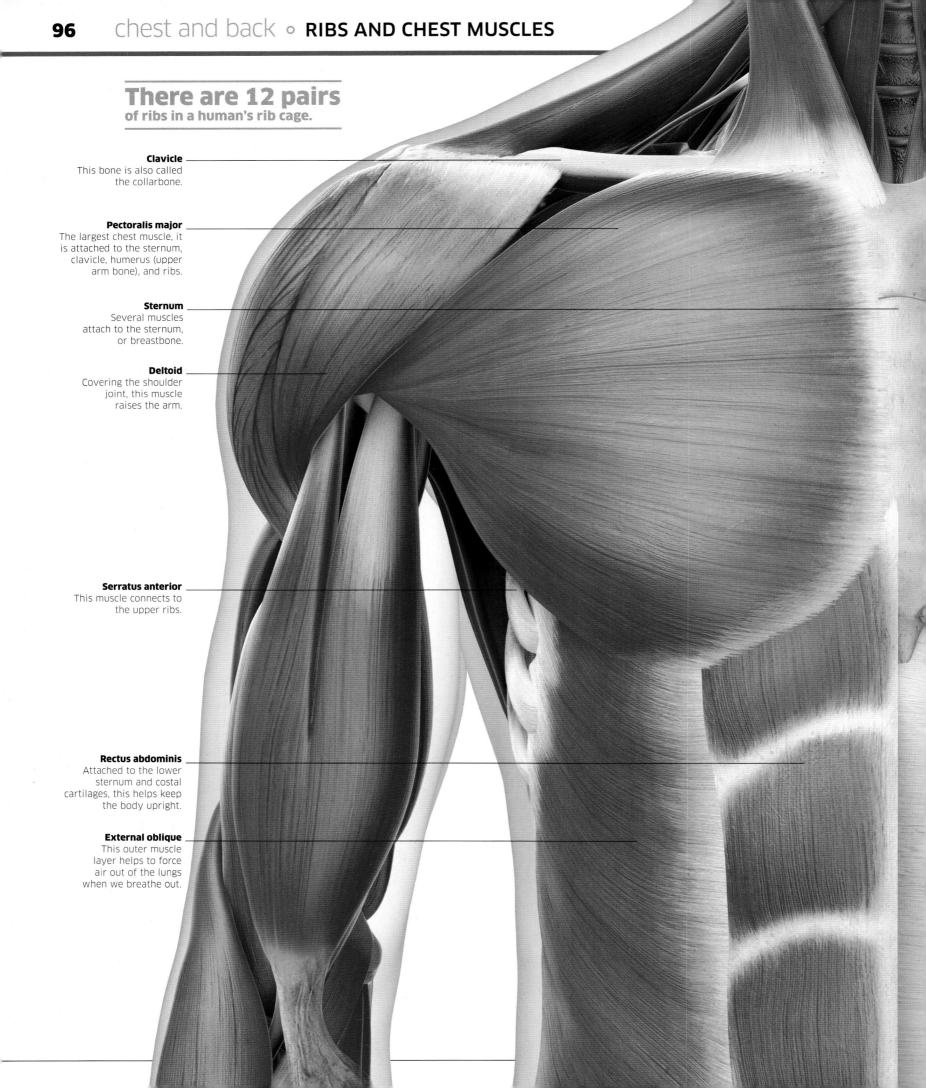

There are 12 pairs
of ribs in a human's rib cage.

Clavicle
This bone is also called the collarbone.

Pectoralis major
The largest chest muscle, it is attached to the sternum, clavicle, humerus (upper arm bone), and ribs.

Sternum
Several muscles attach to the sternum, or breastbone.

Deltoid
Covering the shoulder joint, this muscle raises the arm.

Serratus anterior
This muscle connects to the upper ribs.

Rectus abdominis
Attached to the lower sternum and costal cartilages, this helps keep the body upright.

External oblique
This outer muscle layer helps to force air out of the lungs when we breathe out.

With every inhale, your **rib cage expands by up to 2 in (5 cm)**.

The two lowest pairs of ribs are called **floating ribs** because they attach only to vertebrae and not to the sternum.

97

Ribs and chest muscles

The chest, or thorax, lies between the neck and the abdomen. Inside the thorax lie the heart, lungs, and major blood vessels. The rib cage surrounding them is formed by the backbone, ribs, costal cartilages, and sternum (breastbone).

The rib cage is strong enough to protect the vital organs, but flexible enough to expand and contract for breathing. Attached to the rib cage are the muscles of the chest. Together with the diaphragm, many of these muscles help with breathing.

Costal cartilage
Tough, springy tissue connects the sternum to the ribs.

Internal muscle
When you breathe out, this muscle pulls the rib cage down and out.

Innermost muscle
This muscle lowers the ribs when breathing out.

External muscle
This muscle pulls the rib cage up and out when breathing in.

Intercostal muscles
Between the ribs are three layers of intercostal muscles ("intercostal" simply means "between the ribs"). The muscle fibers run in different directions so the ribs can be pulled in different ways.

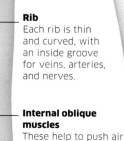

Rib
Each rib is thin and curved, with an inside groove for veins, arteries, and nerves.

Internal oblique muscles
These help to push air out of the lungs when we breathe out.

Muscle movements
The muscles of the chest help with the process of breathing. They pull the ribs up and out, making more space for the lungs to expand as we breathe in. When they relax, the space gets smaller and the air is forced out again.

Back support

The muscles of the neck and back provide a strong support system for the spine—the long line of interlocking bones that helps to keep the upper body stable and upright. Some muscles also help with breathing by lifting and lowering the ribs.

Back muscles pull the spine backward, bend it sideways, or rotate it, allowing the back to perform a wide range of bending and turning movements. Layers of muscle packed around the spine also protect it against injury from pressure or knocks.

Stability and movement

The back has three main muscle layers, which work together to stabilize and move the torso and help with breathing. The deeper layer, shown here, sometimes called the core muscles, holds the body up and keeps you from flopping forward when you bend at the waist.

Developing strength

The layer of stabilizing back muscles plays an important role in a baby's developing ability to sit and move around independently.

Push-ups
Babies begin to build strength in their stabilizing muscles from about three months old. They lie on their tummies and lift their arms in the air to flex these muscles.

Stabilizing muscles get stronger

Sitting up
By nine months old, most babies have developed their stabilizing muscles enough to be able to sit up on their own.

First steps
At around a year old, a baby can stand on her feet and start to walk without help. Stabilizing muscles are still gaining strength, so early attempts can be wobbly.

Larger muscles in the back control movement, while smaller muscles **help with posture**.

Serratus posterior superior
During breathing, this muscle helps lift the ribs.

External intercostal muscle
This is one of a set of muscles that raises the ribs and expands the chest.

Rotatores
These small muscles run all the way up either side of the spine.

Psoas major
This muscle helps to move the hip.

Gluteal muscles
These muscles stabilize the hip, pelvis, and back.

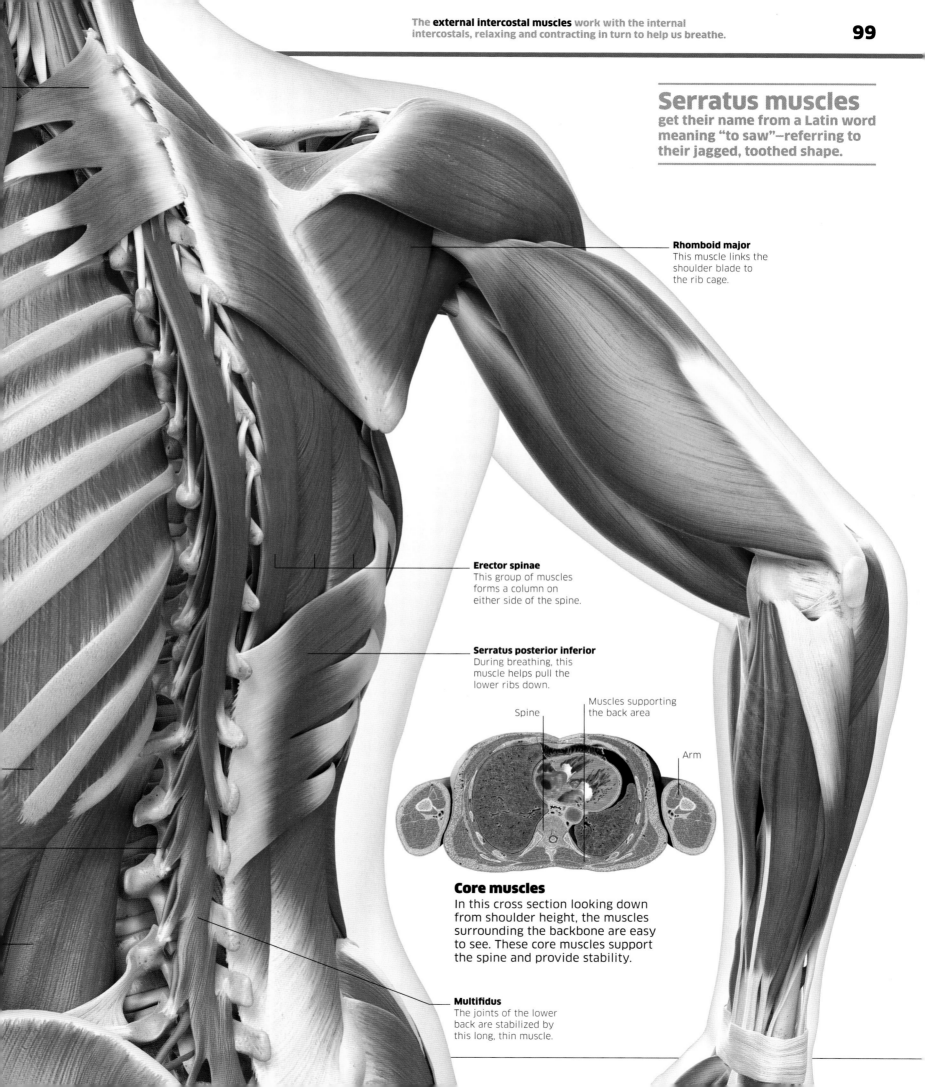

The **external intercostal muscles** work with the internal intercostals, relaxing and contracting in turn to help us breathe.

99

Serratus muscles
get their name from a Latin word meaning "to saw"—referring to their jagged, toothed shape.

Rhomboid major
This muscle links the shoulder blade to the rib cage.

Erector spinae
This group of muscles forms a column on either side of the spine.

Serratus posterior inferior
During breathing, this muscle helps pull the lower ribs down.

Spine

Muscles supporting the back area

Arm

Core muscles
In this cross section looking down from shoulder height, the muscles surrounding the backbone are easy to see. These core muscles support the spine and provide stability.

Multifidus
The joints of the lower back are stabilized by this long, thin muscle.

Backbone

The backbone, also called the spine, runs down the back of the body, from the base of the skull to the coccyx. It provides strong support for the head and body, while allowing the body to twist and bend. It also protects the spinal cord—the thick bundle of nerves that carries messages between the brain and the body.

The human backbone is formed by small, pillar-shaped bones called vertebrae (one is called a vertebra). These stack together to form a strong, flexible, S-shaped column. This shape makes the backbone springy enough to absorb shock during movement, while larger vertebrae in the lower back help to support the upper body's weight. Each vertebra slots into its neighbor to form a flexible but secure tunnel surrounding the spinal cord.

Regions of the backbone

The vertebrae that make up the backbone are often divided into five regions:

■ **Cervical vertebrae**
The seven cervical vertebrae support the head, with the top two vertebrae, the atlas and axis, enabling the head to nod and turn.

■ **Thoracic vertebrae**
The 12 thoracic vertebrae connect with the ribs, forming the back of the rib cage.

■ **Lumbar vertebrae**
There are five lumbar vertebrae, which support most of the body's weight.

■ **Fused bones of the sacrum**
A group of five bones connect the backbone to the pelvic girdle.

■ **Fused bones of the coccyx**
These four bones are an attachment point for muscles, tendons, and ligaments.

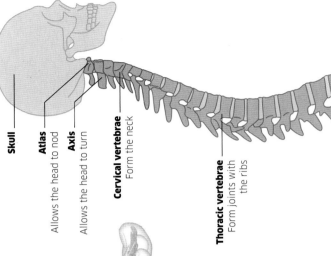

Skull

Atlas
Allows the head to nod

Axis
Allows the head to turn

Cervical vertebrae
Form the neck

Thoracic vertebrae
Form joints with the ribs

Lumbar vertebrae
Form the small of the back

Fused bones of the sacrum

Fused bones of the coccyx

Spine joints

The spurs of bone on the back of each vertebra slot together to form joints that glide back and forth as the spine moves, called facet joints. The shapes of the bones limit how much each joint can move. Disks of cartilage between the bones absorb shock by squishing slightly. They also stop the bones from grinding painfully against each other as they move.

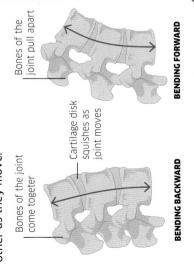

Bones of the joint pull apart

BENDING FORWARD

Bones of the joint come together

Cartilage disk squishes as joint moves

BENDING BACKWARD

33 —the number of bones in the spine, with 9 of them fused together.

Surprisingly flexible

To ensure that the spinal column is well protected, the joints between each vertebra only allow limited movement. But all the small movements add up, allowing the spine to bend backward and forward and side to side, as well as twist and turn.

Hip bone

7 —the number of **vertebrae** in a human's neck, the same number as in a **giraffe's** neck.

25% of the backbone's total length is made up from the **cartilage disks** between the vertebrae.

101

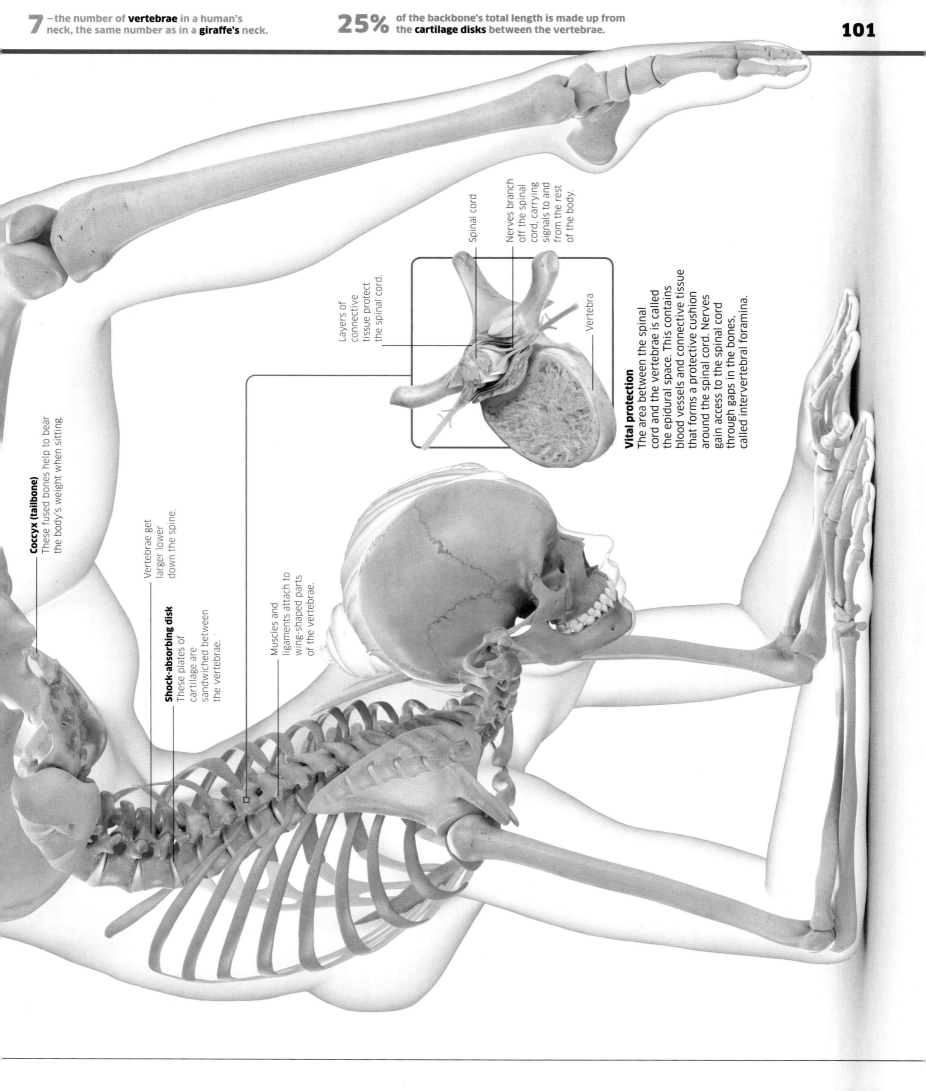

Spinal cord

Nerves branch off the spinal cord, carrying signals to and from the rest of the body.

Layers of connective tissue protect the spinal cord.

Vertebra

Vital protection
The area between the spinal cord and the vertebrae is called the epidural space. This contains blood vessels and connective tissue that forms a protective cushion around the spinal cord. Nerves gain access to the spinal cord through gaps in the bones, called intervertebral foramina.

Coccyx (tailbone)
These fused bones help to bear the body's weight when sitting.

Vertebrae get larger lower down the spine.

Shock-absorbing disk
These plates of cartilage are sandwiched between the vertebrae.

Muscles and ligaments attach to wing-shaped parts of the vertebrae.

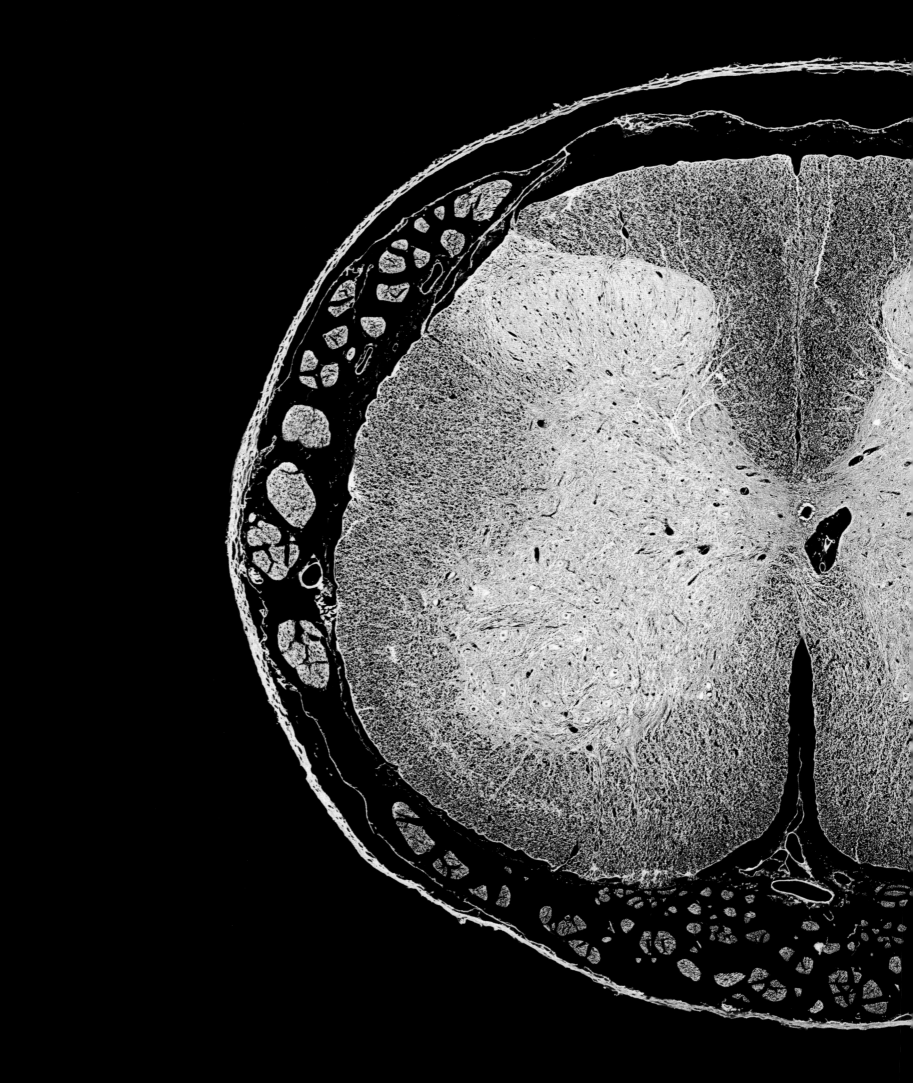

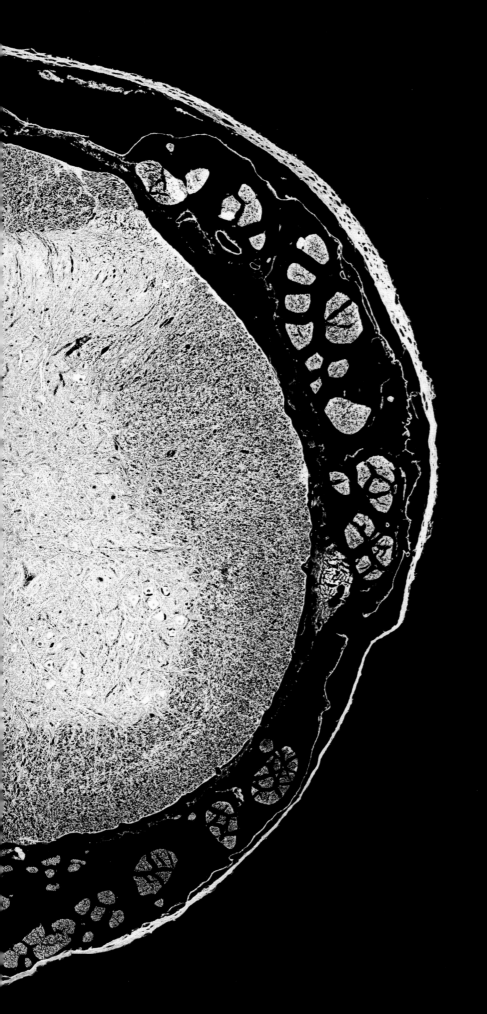

SPINAL CORD

This scan shows a cross-section of the spinal cord in the lower back region. The spinal cord is the body's information superhighway, along which billions of nerve cells carry messages that enable the body to move and function.

It has two main sections: a butterfly-shaped inner mass of gray matter (shown in yellow here) surrounded by outer white matter (shown in pink). White matter is made up of nerve fibers that relay signals to and from the brain. Gray matter contains neurons that receive signals from receptors around the body and send instructions to the muscles.

Heart rate

The heart rate is the number of beats per minute (bpm) that the heart makes. A person's average heart rate varies according to different factors, such as age, gender, and level of fitness.

70 bpm Adult man

78 bpm Adult woman

90 bpm 10-year-old

130 bpm Newborn

A newborn baby's heart is the size of a table tennis ball.

Tight squeeze

The heart sits in the chest, surrounded by the rib cage and between the two lungs, which take up most of the rest of the space in the chest cavity.

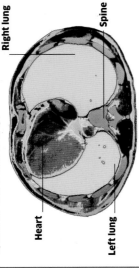

Right lung

Spine

Heart

Left lung

Chest cross-section
This scan shows the chest as if it had been sliced through horizontally. The left lung is smaller than the right lung, as it shares space with the heart.

Vital supplies

To keep the heart beating, the cells need a constant supply of fuel and oxygen. This is delivered by the coronary blood supply—the heart's own network of blood vessels, which penetrate the heart's walls to reach the muscle.

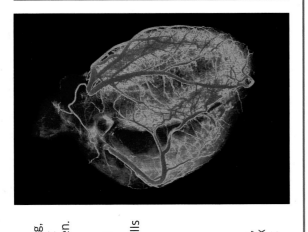

Healthy heart
This colored X-ray of the heart, called an angiogram, shows an intricate network of blood vessels branching off the main arteries.

Heart

The heart is the engine at the center of the body's circulation system. It starts working even before we are born–and from then on, it beats constantly, throughout our lives.

Made from a special kind of muscle not found anywhere else in the body, the hardworking heart contracts and relaxes about 70 times every minute. This rhythmic pumping pushes essential blood out to the body, then fills the heart up again, ready for the next beat.

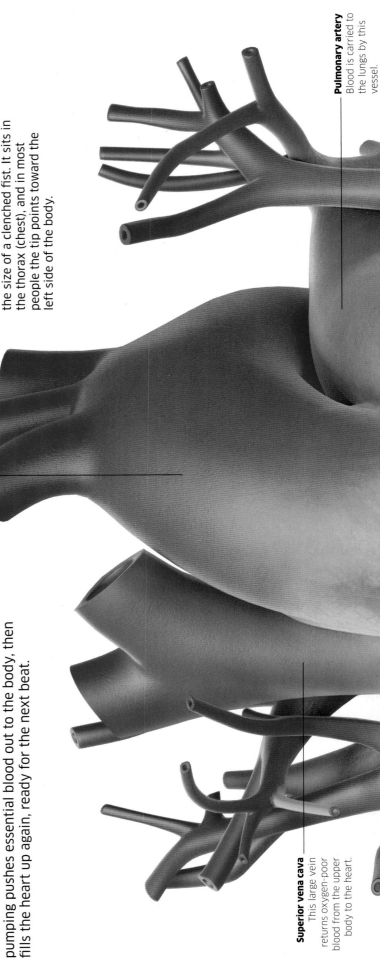

Pulmonary artery
Blood is carried to the lungs by this vessel.

Mighty muscle

A healthy adult's heart is about the size of a clenched fist. It sits in the thorax (chest), and in most people the tip points toward the left side of the body.

Aorta
The body's main artery carries blood from the heart to the rest of the body.

Superior vena cava
This large vein returns oxygen-poor blood from the upper body to the heart.

The **"lub-DUP" sound of a heartbeat** is made by different valves in the heart closing.

2.5 billion—the number of times the **heart will beat** in an average lifetime.

105

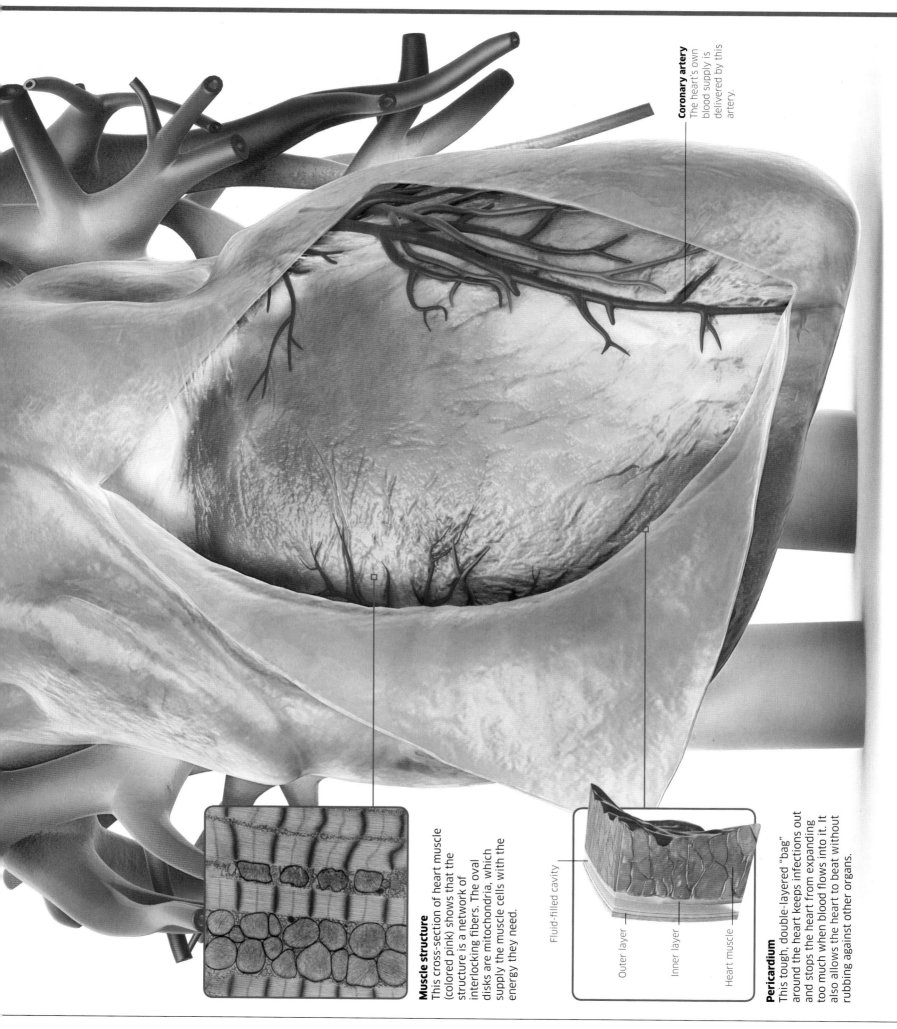

Coronary artery
The heart's own blood supply is delivered by this artery.

Muscle structure
This cross-section of heart muscle (colored pink) shows that the structure is a network of interlocking fibers. The oval disks are mitochondria, which supply the muscle cells with the energy they need.

Fluid-filled cavity

Outer layer

Inner layer

Heart muscle

Pericardium
This tough, double-layered "bag" around the heart keeps infections out and stops the heart from expanding too much when blood flows into it. It also allows the heart to beat without rubbing against other organs.

How the heart works

Although a heartbeat lasts just one second, it has three stages. The rate at which the heart beats is controlled by a pacemaker located in the wall of the right atrium, which sends electrical signals to all parts of the heart.

Key

- Oxygen-rich blood
- Oxygen-poor blood

Blood flows in from the upper body

Blood flows in from the left lung

Left atrium fills with oxygen-rich blood

Right atrium fills with blood

Blood flows in from the lower body

1 Blood flows into the atria
The heart muscle is relaxed and blood enters the upper left and right heart chambers (atria).

Left atrium contracts

Valve opens

Right atrium contracts

Valve opens and right ventricle fills up

Ventricle fills with blood

2 From atria to ventricles
The two atria contract and squeeze blood into the chambers below them (ventricles).

Blood flows to left lung

Ventricles contract, pushing blood out

Blood flows to upper body

Blood flows to right lung

Blood flows to lower body

3 Blood leaves the heart
Last, the ventricles contract and force blood either to the lungs or around the body.

Inside the heart

Each side of the heart has a small upper space, called an atrium, and a larger space below, called a ventricle. During each heartbeat, blood is pumped from atrium to ventricle, then out of the heart. Valves open and close to make sure that the blood only flows in one direction.

Inside the heart

The heart is really two pumps in one, working in a continuous cycle. The right side pumps blood to the lungs, while the left side receives blood back from the lungs, then sends it around the rest of the body.

The heart pumps out about a cup of blood about 70 times a minute, speeding up when necessary to meet body cells' increased demand. Over a lifetime, the heart beats more than 2.5 billion times without resting.

Pulmonary veins
Oxygen-filled blood is carried from the lungs to the heart by these veins.

Pulmonary artery
This major blood vessel delivers oxygen-poor blood to the lungs.

Aorta
The aorta is the body's largest artery.

The average **adult man's heart** weighs around
12 ounces (340 g), about the same as a can of soup.

Water makes up about three-quarters
of the weight of a human heart.

107

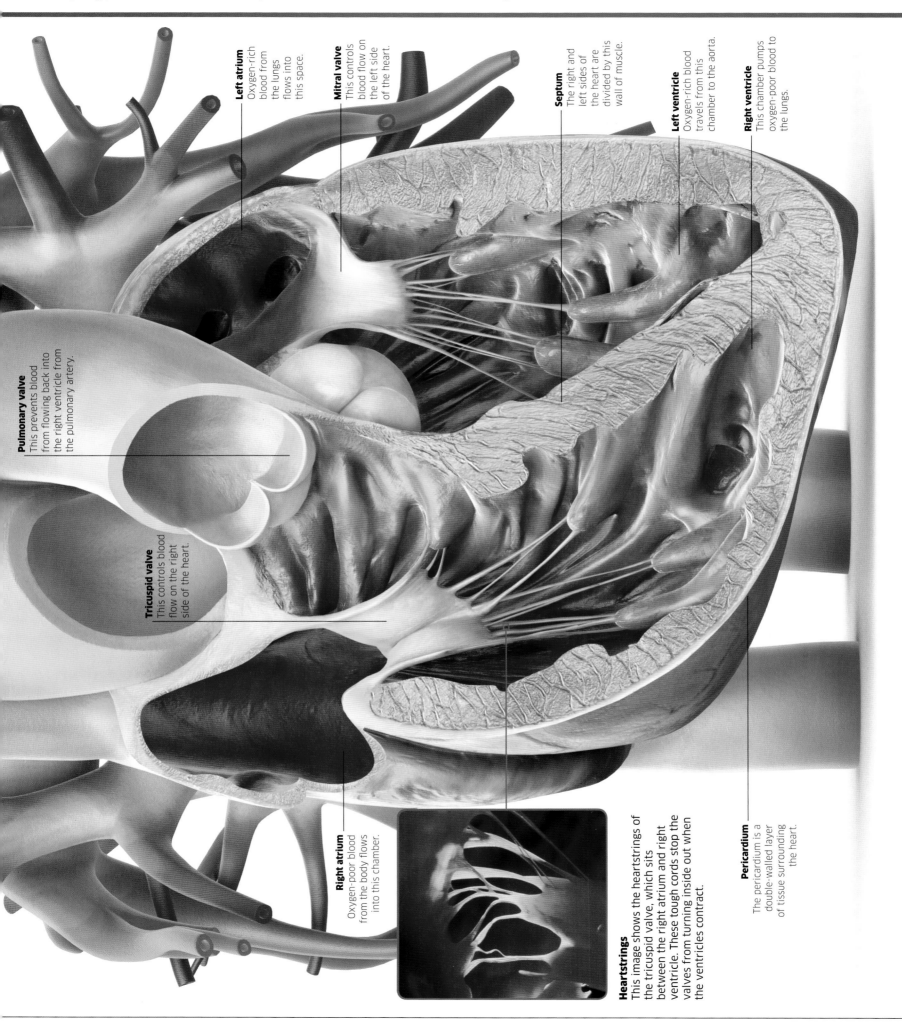

Left atrium
Oxygen-rich blood from the lungs flows into this space.

Mitral valve
This controls blood flow on the left side of the heart.

Septum
The right and left sides of the heart are divided by this wall of muscle.

Left ventricle
Oxygen-rich blood travels from this chamber to the aorta.

Right ventricle
This chamber pumps oxygen-poor blood to the lungs.

Pulmonary valve
This prevents blood from flowing back into the right ventricle from the pulmonary artery.

Tricuspid valve
This controls blood flow on the right side of the heart.

Right atrium
Oxygen-poor blood from the body flows into this chamber.

Heartstrings
This image shows the heartstrings of the tricuspid valve, which sits between the right atrium and right ventricle. These tough cords stop the valves from turning inside out when the ventricles contract.

Pericardium
The pericardium is a double-walled layer of tissue surrounding the heart.

Blood vessels

Pumped by the heart, blood circulates around the human body through millions of blood vessels. These deliver oxygen and other essential substances to the body's cells and tissues.

The three types of blood vessels are arteries, veins, and capillaries. Arteries carry oxygen-rich blood away from the heart. Veins carry oxygen-poor blood back to the heart. These two networks are linked by the smallest blood vessels, capillaries. Oxygen seeps through their thin walls into cells and tissues, while carbon dioxide goes in the other direction, from cells to capillaries.

Elastic layer
These layers allow the artery to stretch and bounce back into shape.

Muscle layer

Elastic layer

Membrane
A thin, protective covering surrounds the inner layer.

Inner layer
The smooth inner lining lets blood flow easily.

Blood
Blood is made up of three types of cells floating in a yellowish liquid called plasma.

Wall of muscle
Arteries' muscular walls stretch to cope with the high-pressure pulses of blood pumped out by the heart. The muscle contracts to make the artery narrower and reduce blood flow, and relaxes to widen it and allow blood to flow more freely.

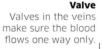

Muscle layer
The layer of muscle is thinner than an artery's.

Valve
Valves in the veins make sure the blood flows one way only.

Membrane

Arteries and veins

The walls of both arteries and veins are made up of three main layers—a tough outer coating, a wall of muscle, and a smooth, inner lining. Arteries have a thicker middle layer of muscle, to control the flow, or pressure, of blood. Pressure needs to be high enough to push blood around the system, but not so strong that it damages delicate capillaries.

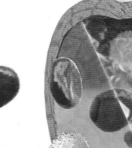

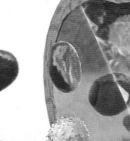

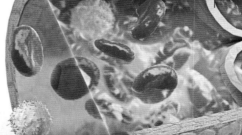

The **biggest arteries and veins** are the width of a thumb, but many capillaries can **only be seen** through a microscope.

98% of the **total length** of the blood vessel network is made up of capillaries.

109

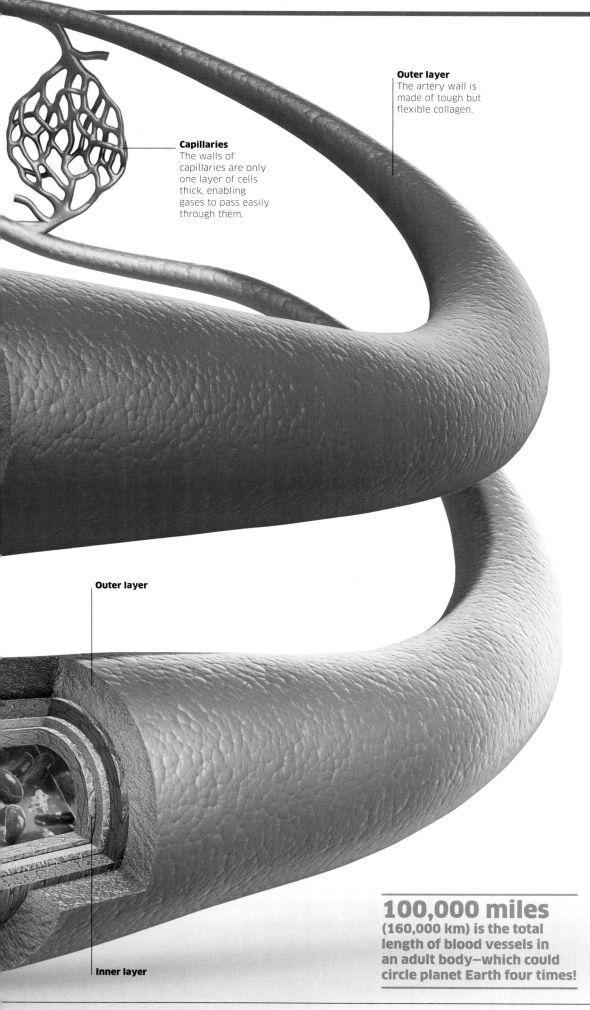

Outer layer
The artery wall is made of tough but flexible collagen.

Capillaries
The walls of capillaries are only one layer of cells thick, enabling gases to pass easily through them.

Outer layer

Inner layer

100,000 miles
(160,000 km) is the total length of blood vessels in an adult body—which could circle planet Earth four times!

Capillary connection

Capillaries connect arteries and veins. The wall of each capillary is formed from an ultra-thin layer of flattened cells. This lets gases and nutrients pass easily through the wall. Some capillaries also have pores, called fenestrations, to make the exchange even quicker.

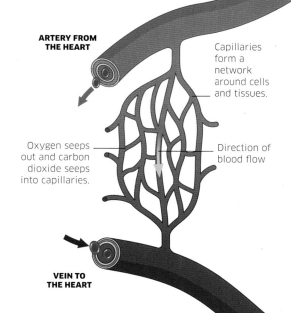

ARTERY FROM THE HEART

Capillaries form a network around cells and tissues.

Oxygen seeps out and carbon dioxide seeps into capillaries.

Direction of blood flow

VEIN TO THE HEART

Vein valves

The long veins in the leg have valves to make sure that blood travels up toward the heart and doesn't fall back down to the feet. When the muscles around the vein contract, they open the valve and push blood upward. When the surrounding muscles relax, the valves close to stop the blood flowing back down.

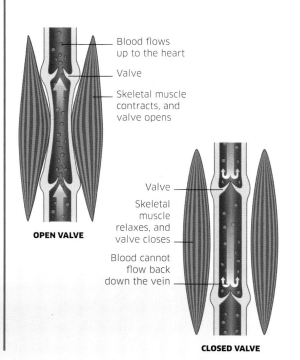

Blood flows up to the heart

Valve

Skeletal muscle contracts, and valve opens

OPEN VALVE

Valve

Skeletal muscle relaxes, and valve closes

Blood cannot flow back down the vein

CLOSED VALVE

BLOOD

Blood circulates endlessly through the human body to keep it alive. This fluid contains trillions of cells and countless chemicals, all floating in watery plasma. Blood is pumped by the heart through a network of blood vessels to deliver nutrients, oxygen, and other essential substances to cells. Blood also transports waste, helps keep the body temperature steady, and fights germs.

TRANSPORTATION SYSTEM

Blood is constantly moving oxygen, nutrients, proteins, and waste products around the body. Some of these help cells grow and function, others are converted into new substances, and the rest are removed from the body.

Oxygen carrier

Red blood cells contain a protein called hemoglobin. Oxygen that enters the blood in the lungs attaches to this hemoglobin and is later released into the body's tissues. It is hemoglobin that gives blood its red color—and the more oxygen hemoglobin carries, the brighter red it becomes.

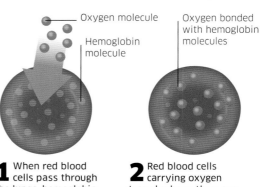

Oxygen released into tissue cell

Oxygen molecule

Hemoglobin molecule

Oxygen bonded with hemoglobin molecules

1 When red blood cells pass through the lungs, hemoglobin binds with oxygen.

2 Red blood cells carrying oxygen travel where they are needed in the body.

3 When the red blood cell arrives at its destination, t[ ] hemoglobin releases oxygen.

WHAT'S IN BLOOD?

Blood consists mostly of a fluid called plasma, together with three types of blood cell—red blood cells, white blood cells, and platelets. They all have different jobs to carry out inside the body.

Blood breakdown

Plasma is made of water with substances dissolved in it, including salts, nutrients, and hormones. Red blood cells take oxygen to cells and remove carbon dioxide. White blood cells hunt and kill bacteria and viruses, while platelets repair damage by plugging a wound and helping blood to clot (thicken).

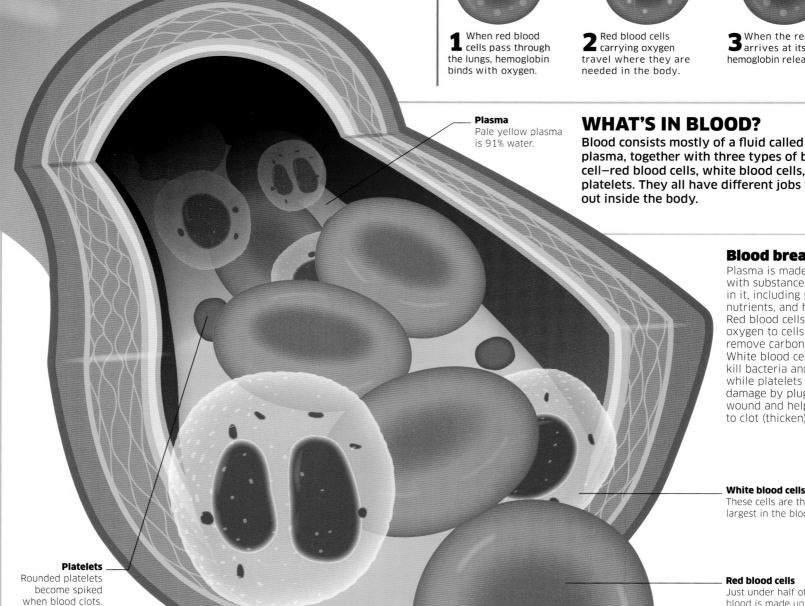

Plasma
Pale yellow plasma is 91% water.

Platelets
Rounded platelets become spiked when blood clots.

White blood cells
These cells are the largest in the blood.

Red blood cells
Just under half of blood is made up of red blood cells.

Transportation superhighway

The bloodstream provides an efficient delivery service, delivering essential fuel and oxygen to cells, and at the same time taking away waste and toxins to keep cells and tissues healthy.

ONE BLOOD CELL GOES THROUGH THE **HEART AND** AROUND THE BODY 1,000 TIMES A DAY.

Oxygen
Red cells pick up oxygen in the lungs and deliver it to all the cells in the body.

Nutrients
Nutrients enter the blood from the digestive system and are delivered around the whole body.

Waste products
Waste is delivered to the liver for recycling, or to the kidneys to be made into urine.

Hormones
The blood delivers chemical messengers, called hormones, to specific destinations.

Body defenses
White cells are carried to fight germs. Platelets are delivered to wound sites.

Carbon dioxide
Carbon dioxide made by cells is delivered to the lungs to be breathed out of the body.

HOW BLOOD CLOTS

After a cut, blood seeps from the wound, triggering an immediate repair process. The blood cells take action immediately. They stop the leak, form a plug, and destroy harmful bacteria. A scab forms, and the clot dissolves when the wound has healed.

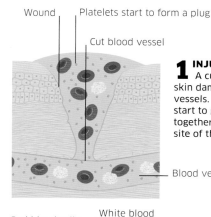

Wound | Platelets start to form a plug
Cut blood vessel
Blood vessel

1 INJURY
A cut in the skin damages blood vessels. Platelets start to group together at the site of the injury.

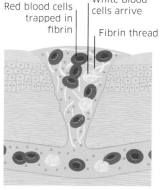

Red blood cells trapped in fibrin | White blood cells arrive
Fibrin thread

2 PLUG
The platelets release chemicals that make fibrin, a sticky threadlike protein. Red cells get stuck in the threads, forming a plug. White blood cells arrive to hunt for germs.

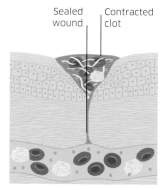

Sealed wound | Contracted clot

3 CLOT
The fibrin threads contract, binding red blood cells and platelets together in a sticky clot, which closes the wound.

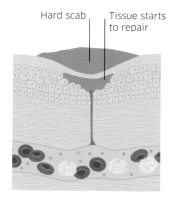

Hard scab | Tissue starts to repair

4 SCAB
The clot near the skin's surface dries out to form a protective scab, which covers the healing wound.

LIFE OF A RED BLOOD CELL

All blood cells are made in red bone marrow. Almost all the bones of young people contain red bone marrow. For adults, it is only found in the skull, ribs, shoulder blades, hips, and the ends of long bones.

Cell cycle

A red blood cell lives for up to 120 days before being swallowed by a type of white blood cell, called a macrophage, in the liver or spleen.

1 New blood cells are made by red bone marrow.

2 A new red blood cell is released into the bloodstream.

5 Useful parts of the old blood cell are recycled.

3 The worn-out red cell is digested by a macrophage.

4 Waste from the blood cell is removed.

BLOOD TYPES

There are four main types of blood—A, B, AB, and O. The type mostly depends on special markers on the surface of red blood cells, called antigens. These help the body to identify blood cells that do not belong to you. Patients who need a blood transfusion must receive the right blood type, or the body will reject the donated blood, making them even more unwell.

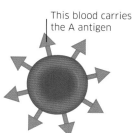

This blood carries the A antigen

Type A
This can be donated to those with A or AB blood types.

B antigen

Type B
This can be donated to those with type B or AB blood.

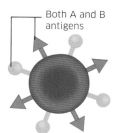

Both A and B antigens

Type AB
This blood can only be donated to other people with the AB blood type.

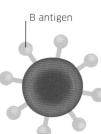

Type O
These blood cells have no antigens and so can be donated to people of any blood type.

Lungs

The two lungs take up most of the space in the chest. Their key function is to get oxygen into, and waste gases out of, the bloodstream. That oxygen is used by the body's cells to release energy, a process that produces waste carbon dioxide.

Breathing draws air rich in oxygen into the lungs through the airways, then pushes air containing carbon dioxide in the opposite direction. Lungs are spongy because they are packed with branching, air-filled tubes that get narrower and narrower before ending in tiny air sacs (alveoli). It is here that oxygen is swapped for carbon dioxide.

Inside the lungs

In the main picture, the left lung has been opened up to show its structure. The lungs' system of airways is called the bronchial tree, because it resembles an upside-down tree. The trachea is the trunk, the bronchi are its branches, and the bronchioles are its twigs.

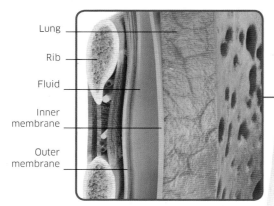

Lung

Rib

Fluid

Inner membrane

Outer membrane

Sliding membranes
Two membranes, called pleurae (one is called a pleura), surround the lungs. A thin layer of fluid between them allows them to slide over one another to ensure the lungs expand and shrink smoothly during breathing.

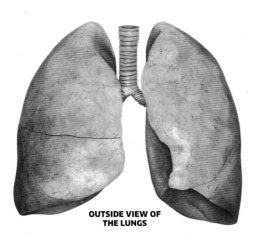

OUTSIDE VIEW OF THE LUNGS

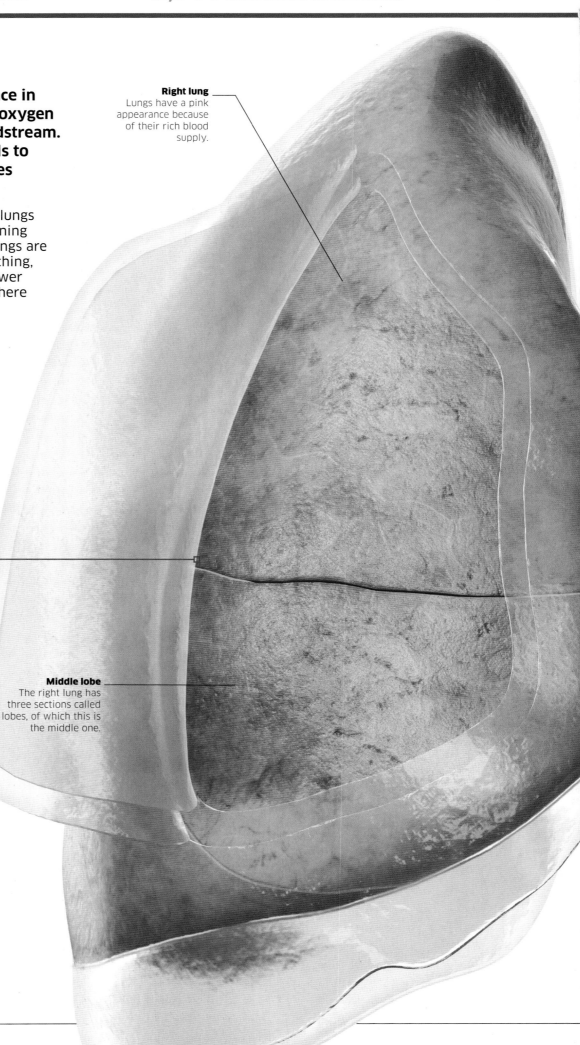

Right lung
Lungs have a pink appearance because of their rich blood supply.

Middle lobe
The right lung has three sections called lobes, of which this is the middle one.

On average, a 10-year-old **breathes in and out** about 20 times every minute.

1,500 miles (2,400 km)—the **total length** of all the lungs' airways (bronchi and bronchioles) put together.

113

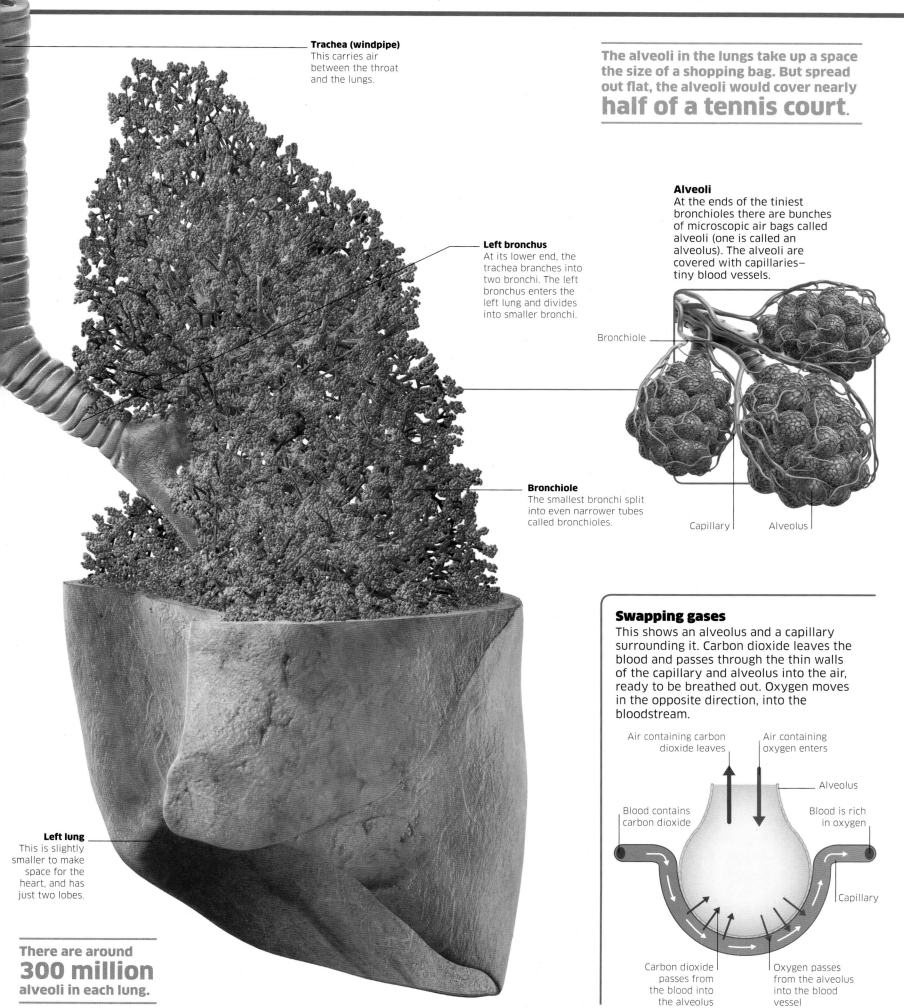

Trachea (windpipe)
This carries air between the throat and the lungs.

The alveoli in the lungs take up a space the size of a shopping bag. But spread out flat, the alveoli would cover nearly **half of a tennis court**.

Left bronchus
At its lower end, the trachea branches into two bronchi. The left bronchus enters the left lung and divides into smaller bronchi.

Alveoli
At the ends of the tiniest bronchioles there are bunches of microscopic air bags called alveoli (one is called an alveolus). The alveoli are covered with capillaries—tiny blood vessels.

Bronchiole

Bronchiole
The smallest bronchi split into even narrower tubes called bronchioles.

Capillary   Alveolus

Left lung
This is slightly smaller to make space for the heart, and has just two lobes.

Swapping gases
This shows an alveolus and a capillary surrounding it. Carbon dioxide leaves the blood and passes through the thin walls of the capillary and alveolus into the air, ready to be breathed out. Oxygen moves in the opposite direction, into the bloodstream.

Air containing carbon dioxide leaves

Air containing oxygen enters

Alveolus

Blood contains carbon dioxide

Blood is rich in oxygen

Capillary

Carbon dioxide passes from the blood into the alveolus

Oxygen passes from the alveolus into the blood vessel

There are around
300 million
alveoli in each lung.

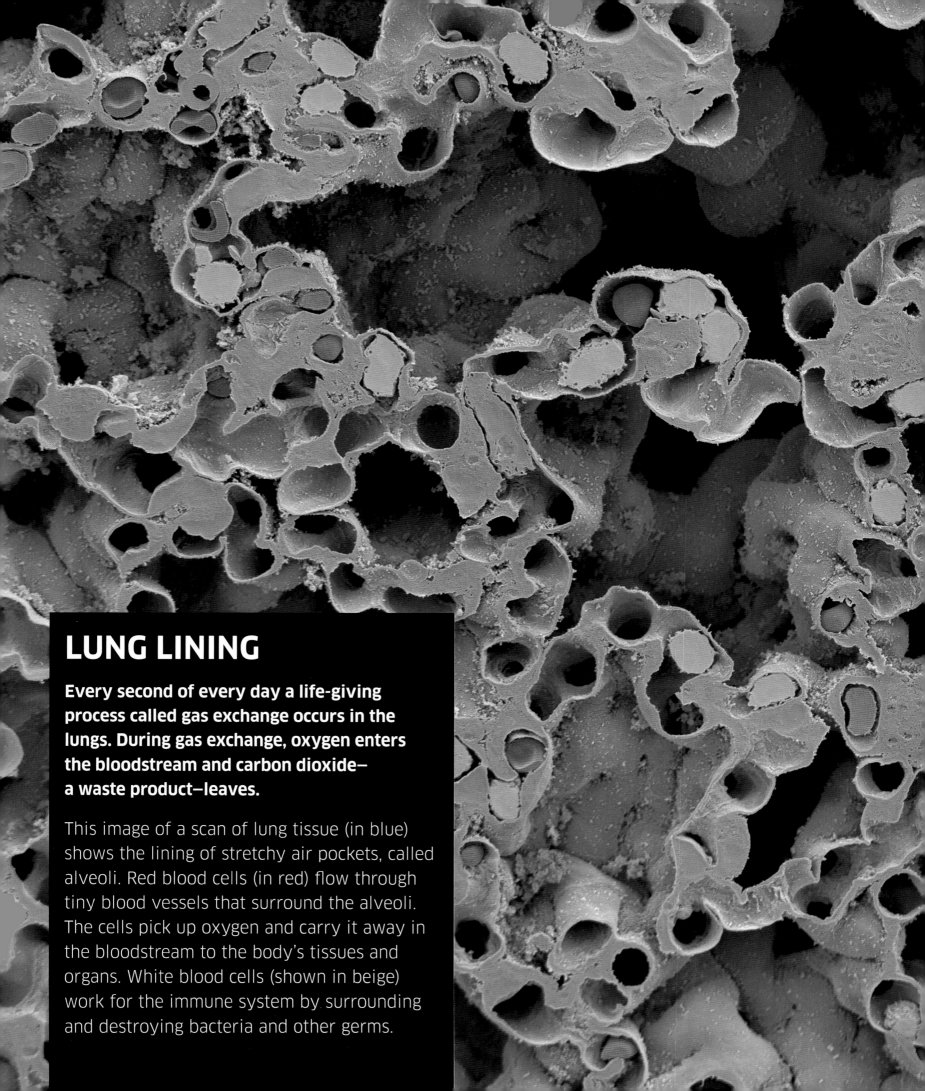

LUNG LINING

Every second of every day a life-giving process called gas exchange occurs in the lungs. During gas exchange, oxygen enters the bloodstream and carbon dioxide— a waste product—leaves.

This image of a scan of lung tissue (in blue) shows the lining of stretchy air pockets, called alveoli. Red blood cells (in red) flow through tiny blood vessels that surround the alveoli. The cells pick up oxygen and carry it away in the bloodstream to the body's tissues and organs. White blood cells (shown in beige) work for the immune system by surrounding and destroying bacteria and other germs.

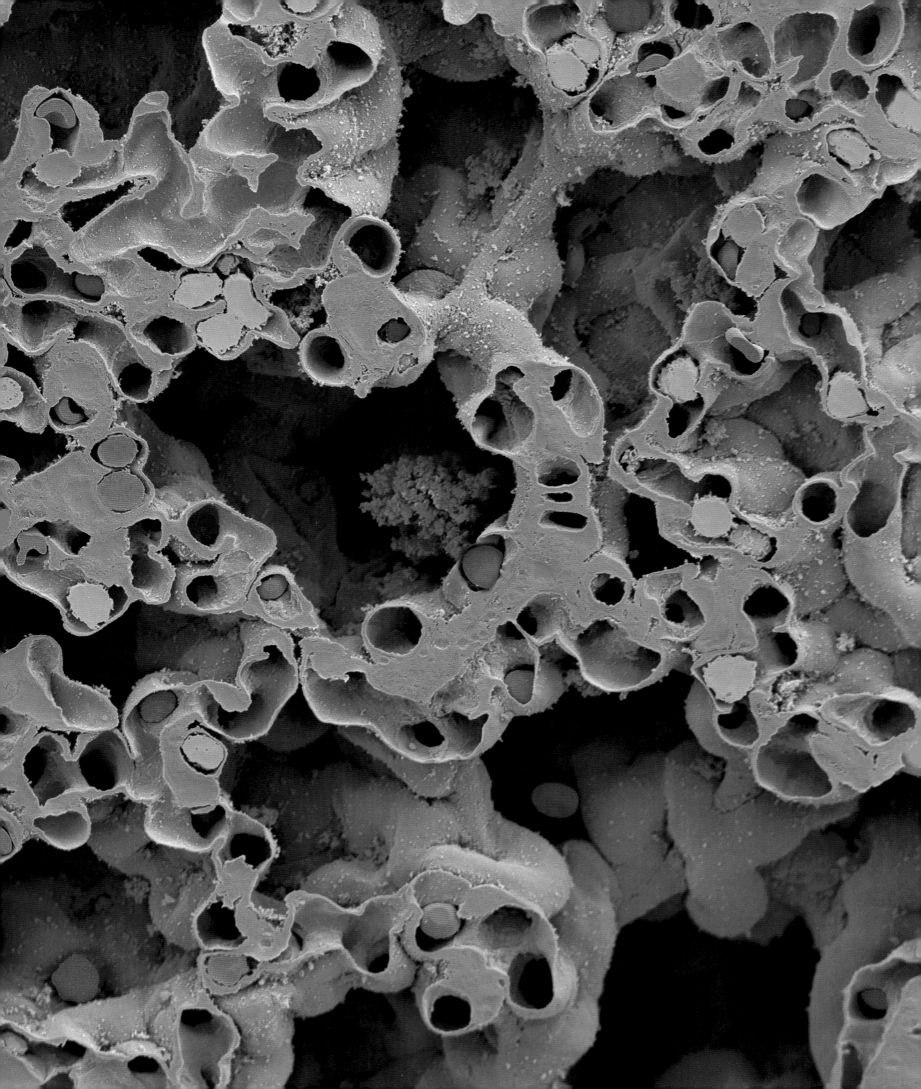

BREATHING AND SPEECH

Humans need to breathe almost constantly in order to provide all the body's cells with the oxygen they need to keep working. We don't need to remember to breathe—the brain makes sure we do it automatically, even when we're asleep. But we can also take control of our breathing, so that we can perform actions such as talking, singing, playing a wind instrument, or just blowing out the candles on a birthday cake. The breath is used for other actions, too, such as sneezing and coughing.

FUELING THE MUSCLES

With each breath we take, oxygen is delivered to the muscle cells to provide the energy that powers movement. The faster the body moves or the harder it works, the more oxygen the cells need. So our breathing speeds up in order to take in, then deliver, more oxygen to where it is needed.

A PERSON WHO LIVES **TO THE AGE OF 80 WILL TAKE ABOUT 700 MILLION** BREATHS IN THEIR LIFETIME.

HOW BREATHING WORKS

When the lungs take a breath in, they expand—but they can't do this on their own. To make them suck in air, the lungs are pulled open by the muscles around them. Then, to breathe out, the muscles relax and the lungs become smaller again, so air is squeezed back out. The muscles used for breathing are the diaphragm, which is below the lungs, and the intercostal muscles, between the ribs.

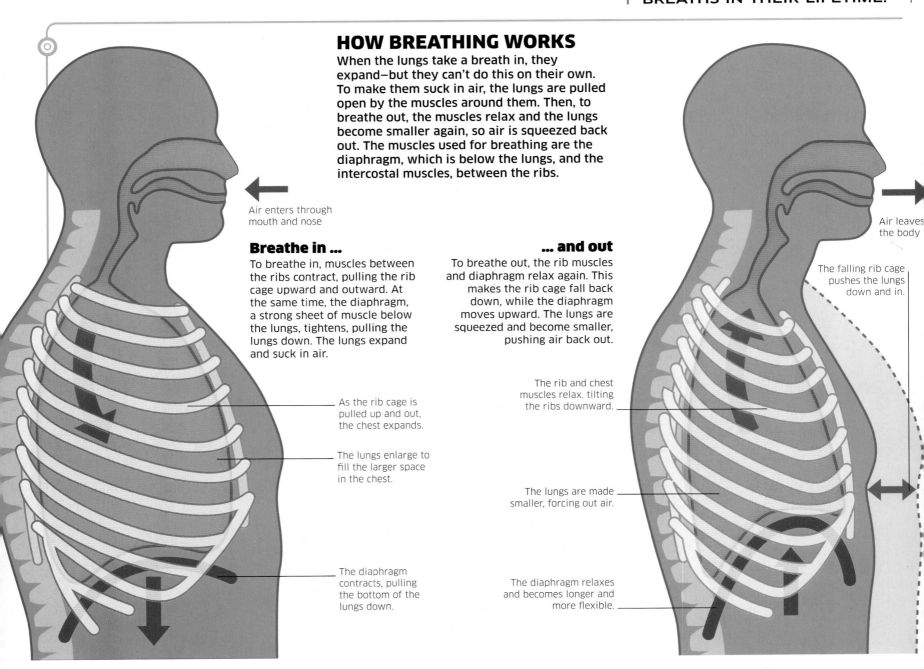

Air enters through mouth and nose

Air leaves the body

Breathe in ...

To breathe in, muscles between the ribs contract, pulling the rib cage upward and outward. At the same time, the diaphragm, a strong sheet of muscle below the lungs, tightens, pulling the lungs down. The lungs expand and suck in air.

... and out

To breathe out, the rib muscles and diaphragm relax again. This makes the rib cage fall back down, while the diaphragm moves upward. The lungs are squeezed and become smaller, pushing air back out.

The falling rib cage pushes the lungs down and in.

As the rib cage is pulled up and out, the chest expands.

The lungs enlarge to fill the larger space in the chest.

The rib and chest muscles relax, tilting the ribs downward.

The lungs are made smaller, forcing out air.

The diaphragm contracts, pulling the bottom of the lungs down.

The diaphragm relaxes and becomes longer and more flexible.

Breathing rates

Breathing rate, or speed, depends on a person's age, size, health, and fitness level as well as on what they are doing. This shows a typical adult's breathing rates when they are taking part in different activities.

Reading
15 breaths per minute

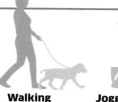
Walking
20 breaths per minute

Jogging
40 breaths per minute

Running fast
Up to 70 breaths per minute

Fitness and breathing

When we exercise, we breathe heavily to take in extra oxygen. With regular exercise, the lungs increase their ability to hold air, and our bodies get more efficient at using the oxygen they take in. This means we don't have to breathe as fast to get the same amount of oxygen to the muscles.

Fighting fit
The more physically fit a person is, the easier they will find it to work out in the gym, dance, or run for a bus, without panting or getting out of breath.

UNUSUAL BREATHS

Normal breathing happens in a regular, repeated pattern. Sometimes, though, there's a different kind of breath, such as a cough, sneeze, or hiccup.

Sneezing
When something irritating gets inside the nose, the brain's response is to trigger a sneeze to clear the air passages. After a sharp breath, muscles in the chest and abdomen contract to force the air back out, carrying the intruding particles with it.

Snoring
Sometimes, the breaths we take while asleep can be heard—in fact, the sound can be loud enough to wake the sleeper. Snoring is caused by relaxed tissues vibrating as air passes over them.

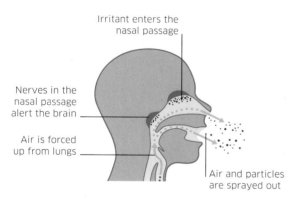

Irritant enters the nasal passage

Nerves in the nasal passage alert the brain

Air is forced up from lungs

Air and particles are sprayed out

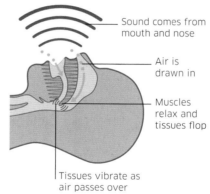

Sound comes from mouth and nose

Air is drawn in

Muscles relax and tissues flop

Tissues vibrate as air passes over

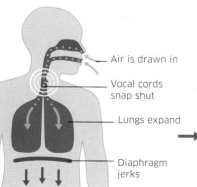

Air is drawn in

Vocal cords snap shut

Lungs expand

Diaphragm jerks

Hiccups
Hiccups happen when nerves around the diaphragm get irritated, for example, by eating quickly. The diaphragm jerks, making the lungs suddenly suck in air. This makes the vocal cords snap shut, making a "hic!" sound.

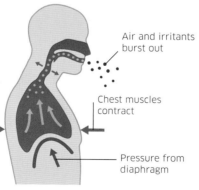

Air and irritants burst out

Chest muscles contract

Pressure from diaphragm

Coughing
Coughing occurs when the body tries to clear something irritating, such as smoke, from the airways. The vocal cords close, so that no air can get through. Then the lungs push air against the cords so they suddenly open, releasing an explosive breath.

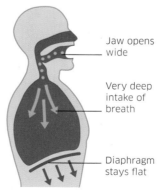

Jaw opens wide

Very deep intake of breath

Diaphragm stays flat

Yawning
A yawn is a deep breath with the mouth wide open, stretching the eardrums and muscles around the throat. Though we often yawn when we're tired, no one knows exactly what yawning is for. It may help to cool the brain, or help to keep you awake and alert.

THE HUMAN VOICE

In addition to supplying the body with oxygen, breathing is also essential for another job: making sounds using the voice. Humans are social beings, so communicating with those around us is very important. We use our voices to deliver information or express our feelings through talking, laughing, or even singing.

How speaking works

As air is breathed out, it passes through the voice box (larynx), below the back of the tongue. Stretched across the larynx are two flexible membranes called the vocal cords. When we want to speak, muscles pull the vocal cords closer together. Air pushes through the small gap, making the cords vibrate to produce a sound. This sound is shaped into a series of words by moving the mouth, lips, and tongue into different positions.

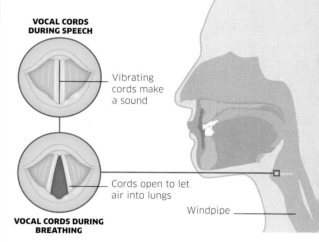

VOCAL CORDS DURING SPEECH

Vibrating cords make a sound

VOCAL CORDS DURING BREATHING

Cords open to let air into lungs

Windpipe

High and low pitch

People's voices have different tones and pitches. Men tend to have deeper voices, as their vocal cords are long and thick, producing a lower sound. Women have higher-pitched voices, and children's are the highest of all, because their vocal cords are much shorter.

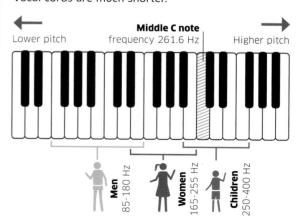

Lower pitch

Middle C note
frequency 261.6 Hz

Higher pitch

Men
85–180 Hz

Women
165–255 Hz

Children
250–400 Hz

Range of the human voice
We measure pitch in hertz (Hz), which describes how fast the vocal cords vibrate per second (frequency).

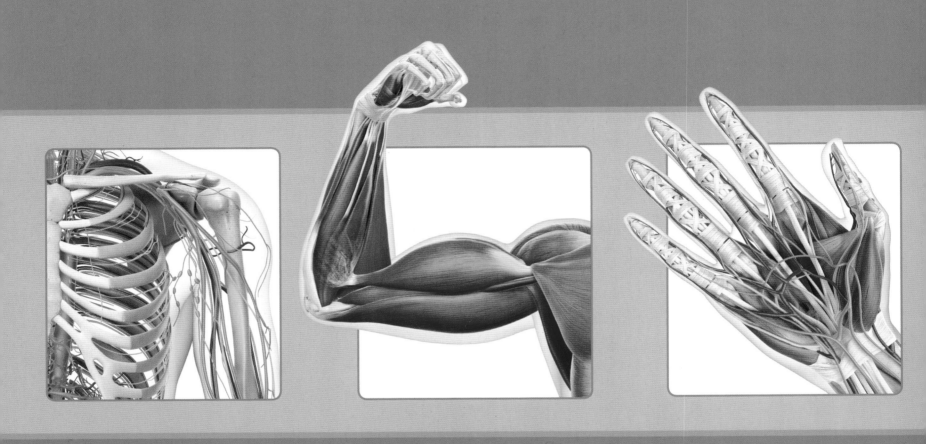

ARMS AND HANDS

The upper limbs are the body's most flexible parts. Shoulder and elbow joints allow the arms to move in all directions. Attached to the arms are our versatile hands. They have countless capabilities, allowing us to touch, lift, throw, and grip. A team of muscles, tendons, and ligaments move and support these limbs.

The shoulder is the **only joint** in the body that can be rotated in a full circle (360°).

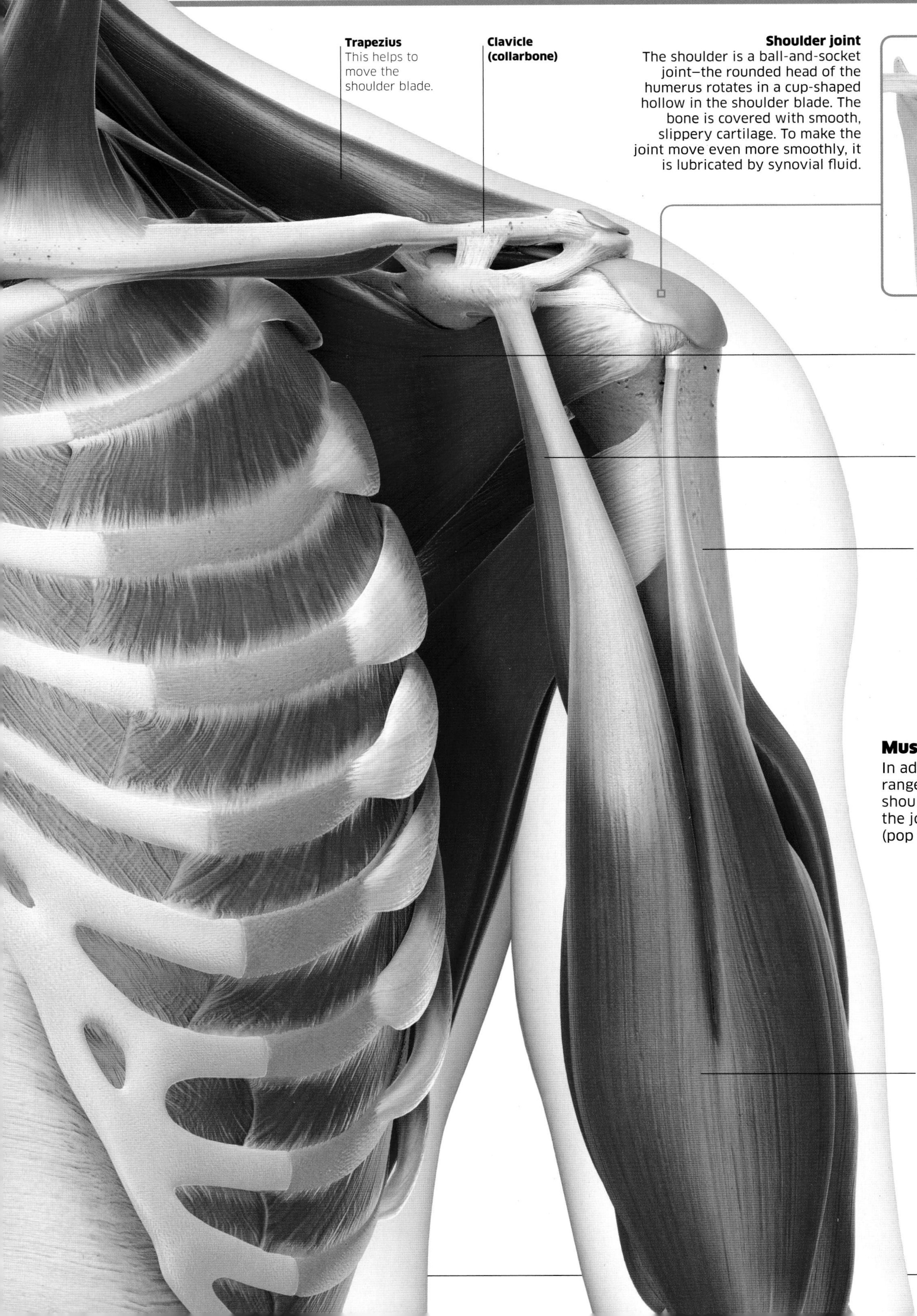

Trapezius
This helps to move the shoulder blade.

Clavicle (collarbone)

Shoulder joint
The shoulder is a ball-and-socket joint—the rounded head of the humerus rotates in a cup-shaped hollow in the shoulder blade. The bone is covered with smooth, slippery cartilage. To make the joint move even more smoothly, it is lubricated by synovial fluid.

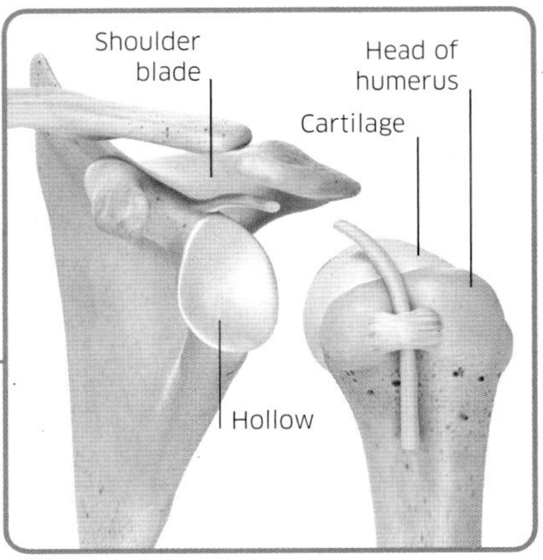

Shoulder blade

Head of humerus

Cartilage

Hollow

Subscapularis
The arm can be twisted inward by this muscle.

Coracobrachialis
This muscle helps to flex the shoulder and pull the upper arm in toward the body.

Humerus
The humerus is the bone of the upper arm.

Muscles and bones
In addition to controlling a wide range of arm movements, the shoulder muscles also stabilize the joint so it doesn't dislocate (pop out of its socket).

Biceps brachii
This is the muscle that bends the elbow.

7 **different muscles** connect the arm bone to the shoulder blade.

105 mph (169 kph) is the **fastest ever recorded throw** of a ball—by a baseball pitcher in 2010.

Shoulder

The shoulder joint—where the upper arm and shoulder blade meet—is the most flexible joint in the body. This mobility, combined with long arms and grasping hands, enables humans to perform a huge range of arm movements.

The bony framework of the shoulder joint is formed by three bones—the shoulder blade (scapula), the collarbone (clavicle), and the top of the upper arm bone (humerus). Deep muscles make the joint stable, while an outer layer of muscles pulls on the bones to move the joint.

Axillary artery
The job of this artery is to supply blood to the shoulder and arm.

Axillary vein
The function of this vein is to carry blood from the arm to the heart.

Lymph node
Lymph nodes trap toxins and germs so they can be eliminated from the body.

Median nerve
The muscles that bend the hands and fingers are controlled by this nerve.

Blood, nerves, and lymph nodes

The shoulder area is rich in lymph nodes, which play a major role in fighting infections. It's also the point at which major blood vessels branch off to supply blood to the arms and hands.

Throwing a ball

This sequence shows the range of muscles, and the amount the shoulder rotates in order to perform a throwing action.

1 Preparing to throw
Muscles in the shoulder, back, and arm contract to raise the arm and pull it backward.

2 Snapping forward
Just before throwing, the chest and upper arm muscles contract to lift the arm up and forward, rotating the shoulder joint.

3 Following through
As the ball is released, chest and side muscles contract to pull the arm down and around the body, rotating the shoulder farther.

Arm and elbow

Walking on two legs has freed our arms up to evolve a huge range of movements. The shoulder joint is the basis for arm flexibility, but the hinged elbow joint provides even more movement.

The three bones that form the elbow joint—the humerus, ulna, and radius—interact with one another so that the forearm forms a hinge with the upper arm, and can also rotate almost 180°. These different kinds of movement are helpful when we eat, for example—the hand can reach out to pick an apple, twist it off its stem, then bring the fruit to the mouth.

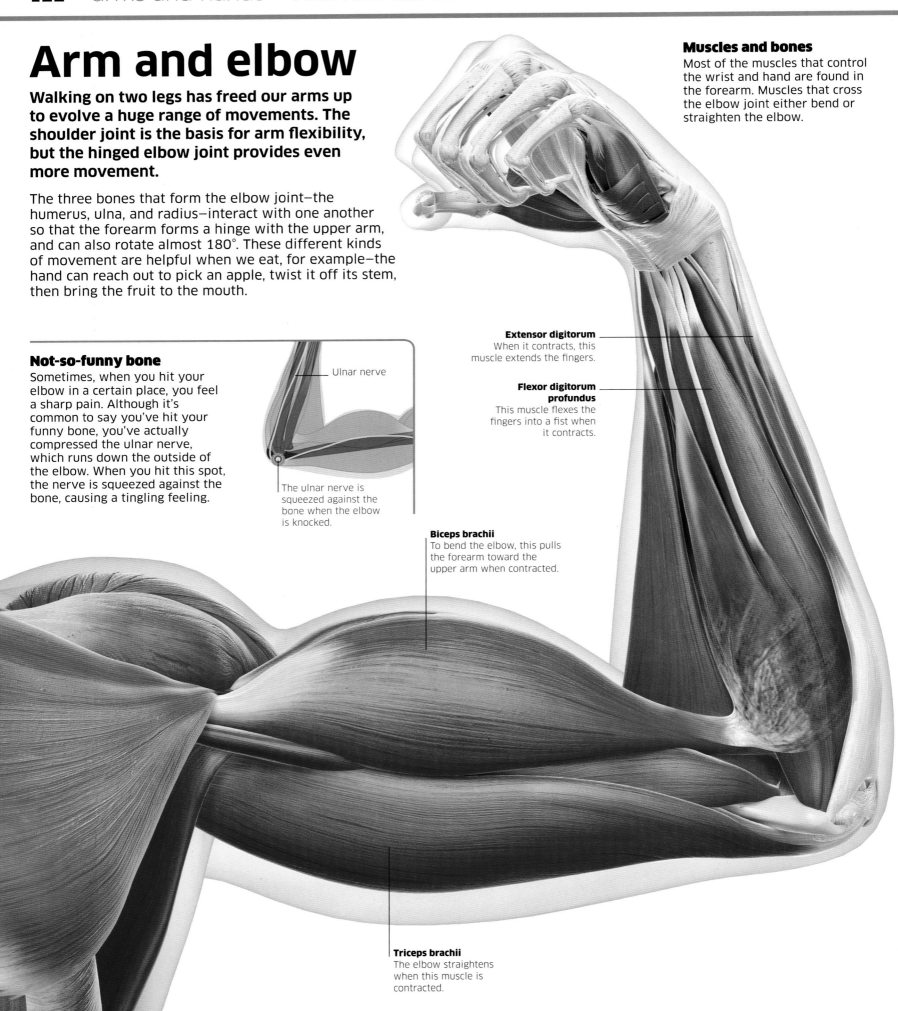

Muscles and bones
Most of the muscles that control the wrist and hand are found in the forearm. Muscles that cross the elbow joint either bend or straighten the elbow.

Not-so-funny bone
Sometimes, when you hit your elbow in a certain place, you feel a sharp pain. Although it's common to say you've hit your funny bone, you've actually compressed the ulnar nerve, which runs down the outside of the elbow. When you hit this spot, the nerve is squeezed against the bone, causing a tingling feeling.

Ulnar nerve

The ulnar nerve is squeezed against the bone when the elbow is knocked.

Extensor digitorum
When it contracts, this muscle extends the fingers.

Flexor digitorum profundus
This muscle flexes the fingers into a fist when it contracts.

Biceps brachii
To bend the elbow, this pulls the forearm toward the upper arm when contracted.

Triceps brachii
The elbow straightens when this muscle is contracted.

50% of all **adult bone breakages** happen to one of the arm bones.

The bony lump at the **very tip of the elbow** is called the olecranon (pronounced oh-LEK-ra-non).

123

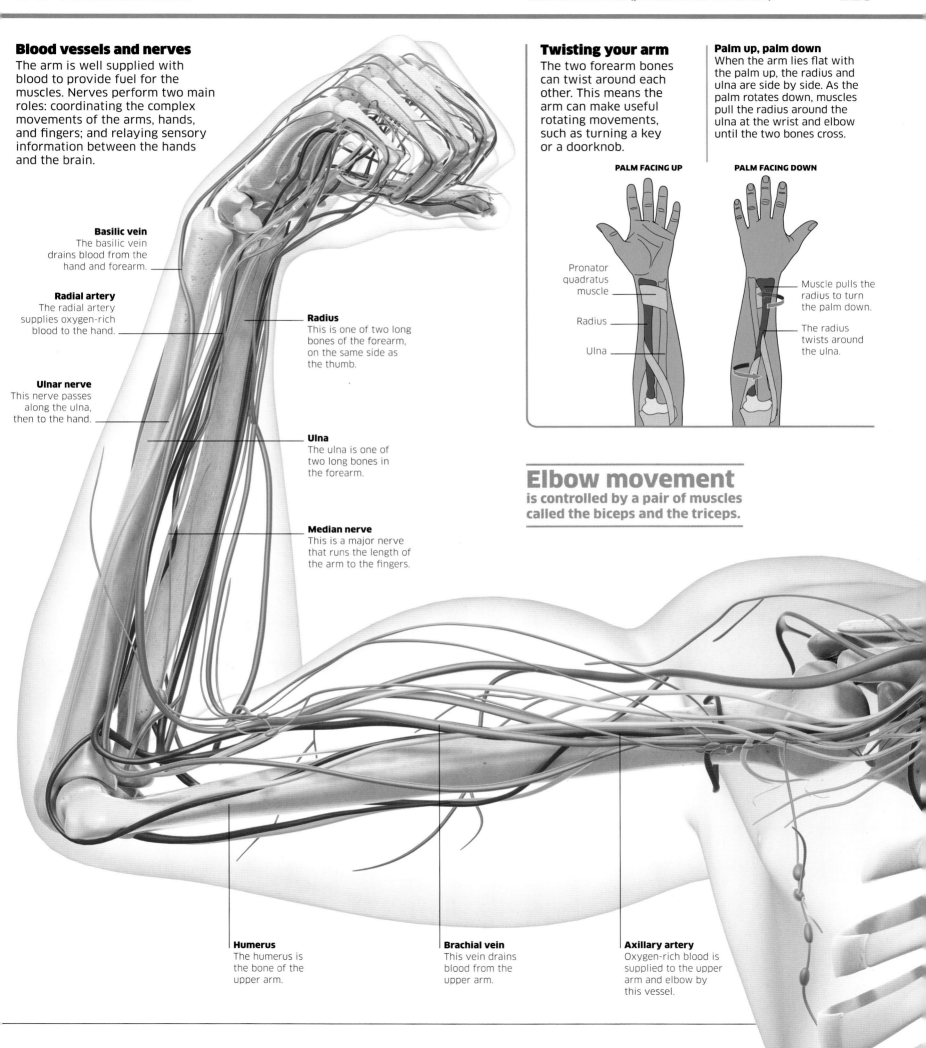

Blood vessels and nerves

The arm is well supplied with blood to provide fuel for the muscles. Nerves perform two main roles: coordinating the complex movements of the arms, hands, and fingers; and relaying sensory information between the hands and the brain.

Basilic vein
The basilic vein drains blood from the hand and forearm.

Radial artery
The radial artery supplies oxygen-rich blood to the hand.

Ulnar nerve
This nerve passes along the ulna, then to the hand.

Radius
This is one of two long bones of the forearm, on the same side as the thumb.

Ulna
The ulna is one of two long bones in the forearm.

Median nerve
This is a major nerve that runs the length of the arm to the fingers.

Humerus
The humerus is the bone of the upper arm.

Brachial vein
This vein drains blood from the upper arm.

Axillary artery
Oxygen-rich blood is supplied to the upper arm and elbow by this vessel.

Twisting your arm

The two forearm bones can twist around each other. This means the arm can make useful rotating movements, such as turning a key or a doorknob.

Palm up, palm down

When the arm lies flat with the palm up, the radius and ulna are side by side. As the palm rotates down, muscles pull the radius around the ulna at the wrist and elbow until the two bones cross.

PALM FACING UP

Pronator quadratus muscle

Radius

Ulna

PALM FACING DOWN

Muscle pulls the radius to turn the palm down.

The radius twists around the ulna.

Elbow movement
is controlled by a pair of muscles called the biceps and the triceps.

Flexible joints

Wherever two or more bones meet, they form a joint. Some of these joints aren't moveable, such as the skull, but most are flexible, allowing some movement between the bones.

Joints give skeletons flexibility for all the different ways we move our bodies—from running and jumping to picking up objects, or sitting down. It is still the muscles that make the movement happen by pulling on the bones, but the kind of movement each joint makes depends on the shape of the ends of the bones that meet.

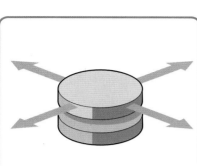

Plane joint
Also called a gliding joint, this is where two flat-ended bones slide against each other. This type of joint is found in the ankles and wrists.

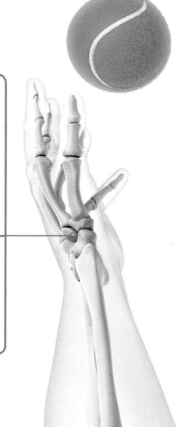

Fixed joint
The different bones of an adult's skull form fixed joints. They are securely fused together and don't allow any movement.

Pivot joint
This allows one bone to swivel around another. In the forearm, the ulna forms a pivot with the radius just below the elbow, allowing the arm to twist palm-up or palm-down.

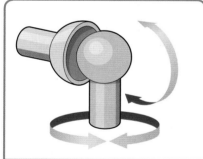

Ball and socket
The ball-shaped head of one bone fits into the cup shape of another bone. This type of joint allows for a wide range of movement and is found in the shoulder and the hip.

Head and neck
A pivot joint at the top of the backbone allows the head to swivel from side to side.

Types of joint

There are six different types of moving joint in the body. Each of them allows a different range of movements. The arms and hands contain examples of all of these types of joint, but they are found in other parts of the body, too.

The only human bone that doesn't have a joint is the **hyoid bone** of the lower jaw.

Cartilage moving against cartilage is **eight times more slippery** than **ice**.

125

Inside a joint

The six types of joint described here are all synovial joints. They allow movement while protecting the bones from damage when they move against each other. Bone ends are covered with smooth, slippery cartilage, which helps reduce friction. The space between the bones is filled with a liquid called synovial fluid. This lubricates the joint and provides a liquid cushion between the bones. Non-synovial joints, such as the sutures of the skull, do not move.

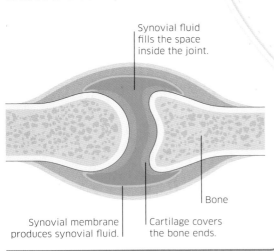

Synovial fluid fills the space inside the joint.

Synovial membrane produces synovial fluid.

Cartilage covers the bone ends.

Bone

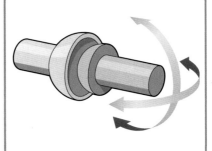

Condyloid joint

This joint is found in the knuckles and toes. An oval, rounded bone fits into an oval, cup-shaped bone. This enables side-to-side and up-and-down movement, so you can spread your fingers apart and move them up and down.

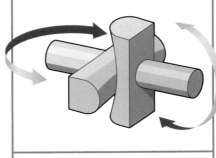

Saddle joint

This is found at the base of the thumb where two U-shaped bones meet, allowing the thumb to rotate in two directions. This enables the thumb to touch each fingertip, as well as sweep across the palm of the hand.

Hinge joint

Just as a door hinge only allows a door to open or close, the hinge joint at the elbow lets the arm bend and straighten. The knee is also a hinge joint.

300 is the approximate number of joints in the body.

MIGHTY MUSCLES

Every movement you make uses muscles. They allow you to smile, walk, lift, and run. Muscles also move blood around the body and food through the digestive system. Some muscles must be ordered by the brain to move, while others work without us even thinking about them.

MUSCLE STRUCTURE

Muscles are packed full of parallel bundles of fibers. These consist of many cells, called myocytes. When they contract, the muscle shortens and creates a pulling action. There are three types of muscle in the body.

Skeletal muscle
This type of muscle pulls on bones to move the skeleton. Skeletal muscle is made of long, cylindrical cells called muscle fibers, each crammed with threads called myofibrils. These contain long protein filaments that slide over each other to make muscles contract.

Blood vessels supply oxygen to muscle fibers.

Bundle of muscle fibers

Myofibril

MUSCLE MOTION

Muscles work by contracting, which means they shorten. As a muscle contracts, it pulls on whatever it is attached to. In general, the larger the muscle, the more pulling power it has. Muscles can pull but not push, which is why they work in pairs, acting in opposite directions. When one muscle pulls, its partner muscle relaxes.

BUILD UP YOUR MUSCLES **BY GETTING A GOOD NIGHT'S REST. DURING DEEP SLEEP, HORMONES ARE RELEASED THAT** STIMULATE THE MUSCLES TO GROW AND REPAIR THEMSELVES.

Pulling together

All the skeletal muscles work in pairs. In the upper arm, the biceps and triceps muscles work as a team to bend and straighten the arm. The triceps pulls the forearm down, and the biceps pulls it up again.

Triceps
When the triceps muscle contracts, it straightens the arm at the elbow. The biceps, opposite the triceps, is relaxed.

Muscle attachment
The triceps is attached to the shoulder blade at this point.

Firmly fixed
The biceps is attached to the shoulder blade at these two points.

Biceps
When the biceps contracts, it pulls the forearm bones up and bends the arm. The triceps muscle is relaxed.

Biceps

Triceps

Tendons
Muscles are firmly attached to bones by tendons.

ELBOW STRAIGHTENED

ELBOW BENT

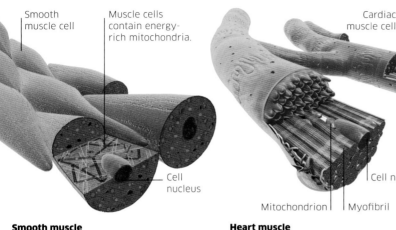

Smooth muscle cell

Muscle cells contain energy-rich mitochondria.

Cell nucleus

Cardiac muscle cell

Cell nucleus

Mitochondrion | Myofibril

Smooth muscle
Arranged in muscular sheets, smooth muscle makes things move along inside the body. For example, it mixes food in the stomach and pushes it through the intestines.

Heart muscle
This type of muscle is found only in the heart, where it is used to pump blood around the body. Heart muscle never gets tired, and it never stops working.

MOVING MESSAGES

Muscles receive their instructions from nerves. Signals from the brain travel down the spinal cord, and then go out to the muscles along nerves. Nerves branch out so they reach each part of the muscle. The signals tell the muscles to contract, and the body moves.

Nerve-muscle junction
Signals from the brain are passed via nerves to muscle fibers. The contact point where they meet is called a nerve-muscle junction.

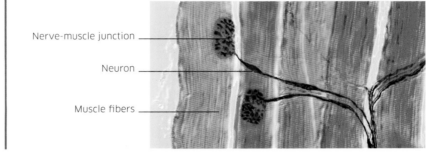

Nerve-muscle junction

Neuron

Muscle fibers

TWITCH TYPES

Muscles are either fast-twitch or slow-twitch. Fast-twitch muscles contract quickly to generate lots of power. Slow-twitch muscles contract slowly and generate less power, but they work for longer without tiring. A healthy body has an equal split of fast- and slow-twitch muscle.

HEAT GENERATORS

Working muscles use oxygen to make energy. A by-product of this chemical process is the production of heat. The harder muscles work, the hotter they become. Shivering in cold weather is caused by your muscles twitching, trying to make more heat.

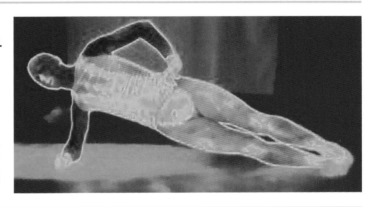

Hot spots
This thermogram image, showing the hottest parts of the body in red, demonstrates how hard this athlete is working his arm and lower leg muscles.

Speedy sprint
Athletes use their fast-twitch muscles for competitive high-speed sprints. These fibers shorten rapidly but tire quickly.

MAINTAINING MUSCLE

Muscles must be kept strong and healthy, so the body can move easily and function properly. Diet and exercise play a major part in building and maintaining muscle.

Muscle food
Protein, such as that found in pulses such as beans and lentils, meat, nuts, and fish, is needed for building and repairing muscle. Carbohydrates such as cereals, bread, and pasta provide energy for muscles to work. A balanced, healthy diet will provide enough protein and carbohydrates for muscles to stay healthy and active.

FISH

PULSES

NUTS

CEREAL

BREAD

PASTA

Resistance training
Some people build bigger muscles by resistance training. Regular exercise of this kind forces muscles to contract repetitively, which builds and strengthens them. It also tears muscle fibers, which then grow back bigger. Weight training, gymnastics, and some kinds of dancing are all forms of resistance training.

Steady walk
Walkers and climbers use their slow-twitch muscles to cover long distances. These fibers contract gradually but keep going.

Lifting weights causes tiny tears in muscle fibers, which the body repairs.

The repaired muscle fibers are bulkier than before, so muscles grow bigger.

SKELETAL MUSCLE

Body movement is controlled by skeletal muscle. About 650 skeletal muscles move the arms, legs, fingers, and toes. This colored scan shows a section of skeletal muscle.

The muscle (shown pink) is attached to the bones via flexible cords, called tendons (shown green). The series of ridges across the muscle show its two interlocking proteins, actin and myosin. When the actin slides over myosin, the muscle contracts. The darker areas show actin and myosin overlapping, while the paler areas show actin alone. When skeletal muscle contracts, its tendon pulls on bone to make the body move.

27—the number of bones in a **human hand**.

A quarter of the part of the brain that controls movement is devoted to **hand movements**.

Hand

Because humans walk upright on two feet, it leaves our hands free to take on other tasks. Human hands are incredibly versatile tools, able to perform a huge range of movements.

The hand's adaptability is made possible by the combination of a framework of small, flexible bones, including long finger bones and a highly moveable thumb. This structure is overlaid with an intricate network of muscles and tendons, which move the bones.

Left hand, palm up

The two main arteries of the arm meet in the palm, before branching into smaller blood vessels. Running through the palm are the long tendons that connect to the forearm muscles. These muscles, along with smaller ones in the palm, control the movements of the fingers.

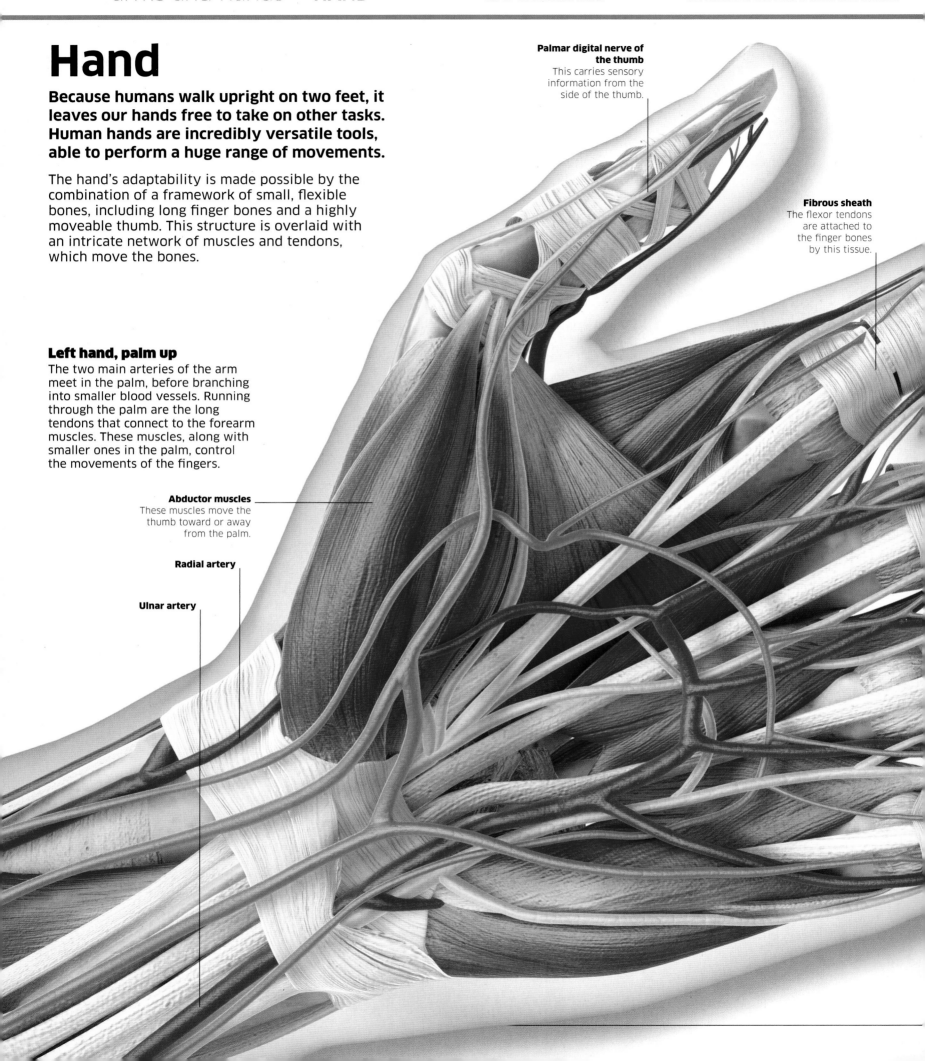

Palmar digital nerve of the thumb
This carries sensory information from the side of the thumb.

Fibrous sheath
The flexor tendons are attached to the finger bones by this tissue.

Abductor muscles
These muscles move the thumb toward or away from the palm.

Radial artery

Ulnar artery

The fingertips contain **more nerve endings** than any other part of our skin.

The fingers contain **no muscles,** just tendons that are moved by muscles in the arm and palm.

131

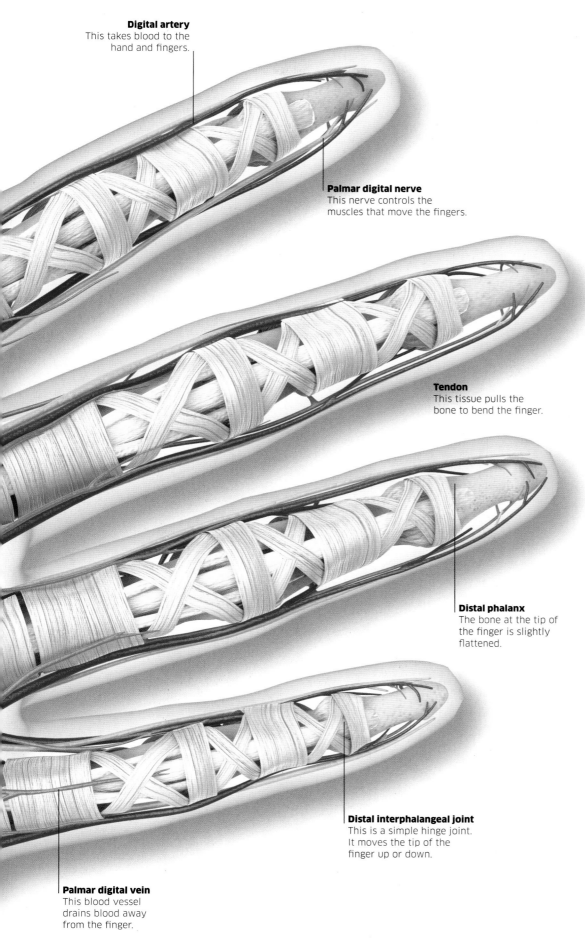

Digital artery
This takes blood to the hand and fingers.

Palmar digital nerve
This nerve controls the muscles that move the fingers.

Tendon
This tissue pulls the bone to bend the finger.

Distal phalanx
The bone at the tip of the finger is slightly flattened.

Distal interphalangeal joint
This is a simple hinge joint. It moves the tip of the finger up or down.

Palmar digital vein
This blood vessel drains blood away from the finger.

Bones
The 27 bones of the hand are made up of 8 small wrist bones (carpals), 5 palm bones (metacarpals), and 14 finger bones (phalanges; one is called a phalanx).

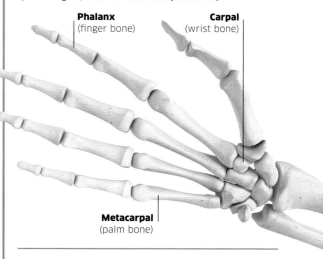

Phalanx
(finger bone)

Carpal
(wrist bone)

Metacarpal
(palm bone)

Muscles and tendons
The fingers are bent and straightened by tendons that extend from the forearm muscles and attach to the finger bones.

Middle finger bends when bone is pulled by tendon

Nerves and blood vessels
Nerves control movement and send signals to the brain from sensors in the skin. Arteries and veins carry blood to and from muscles, tendons, and skin.

Fingertips are rich in nerve endings.

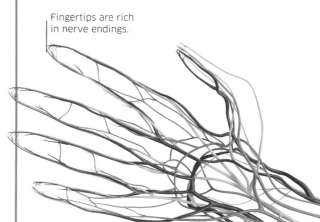

8 **muscles control all the** movements of the thumb.

Hands in action

Humans have the ability to move their thumbs to touch—or oppose—each of the fingers on the same hand. This simple ability means that our hands are able to pick up, handle, and grip objects with incredible precision and dexterity.

Opposable thumbs were crucially valuable to early humans, who used them to make tools, throw spears, and pick berries. This advantage over other mammals helped make humans the dominant species on Earth. Modern humans rely on their hands just as much as our ancestors did—for instance, to write, paint, draw, play musical instruments, use tools, and operate technology.

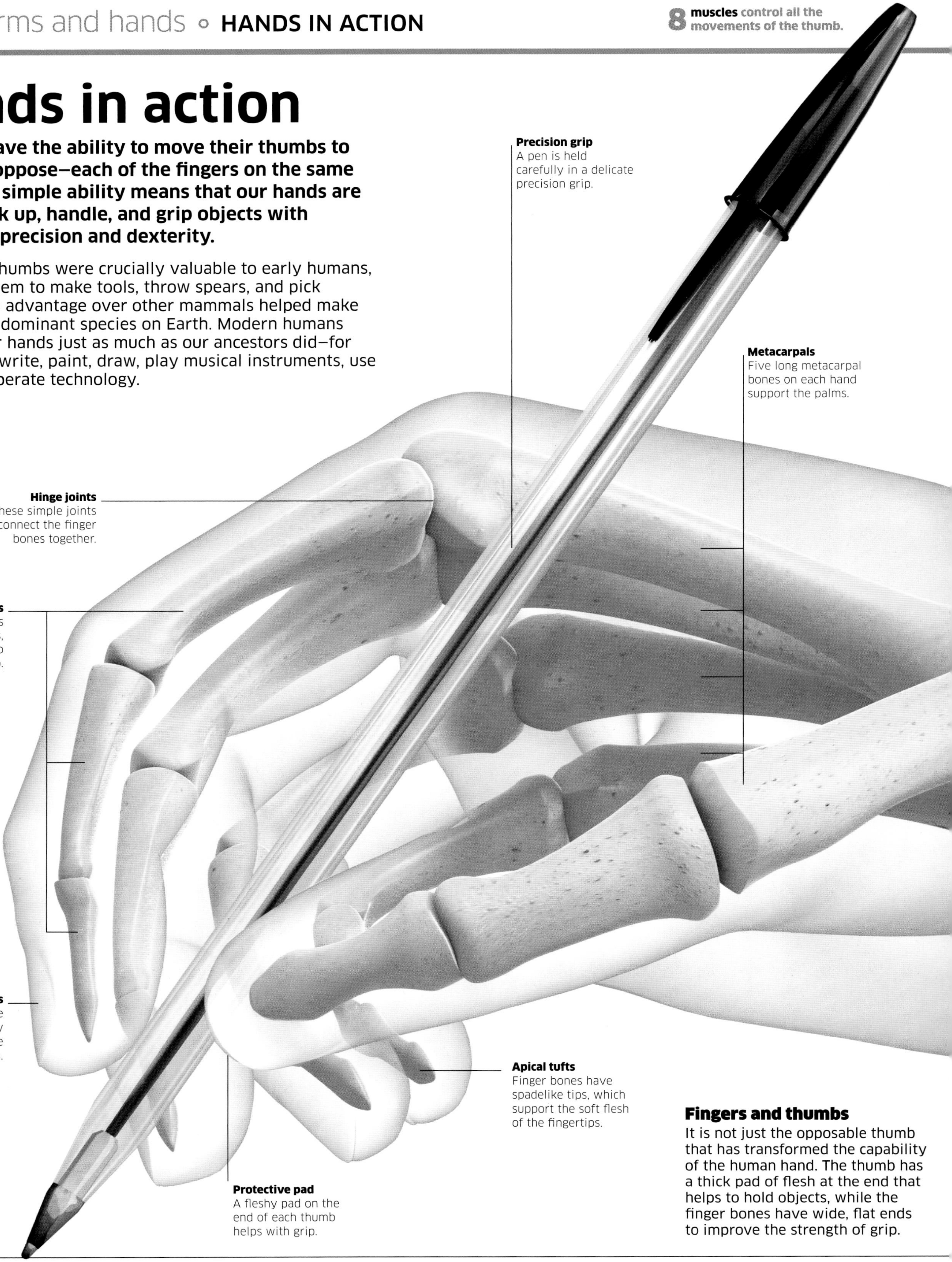

Precision grip
A pen is held carefully in a delicate precision grip.

Metacarpals
Five long metacarpal bones on each hand support the palms.

Hinge joints
These simple joints connect the finger bones together.

Phalanges
Every finger has three phalanges, but the thumb has only two.

Nails
Nails heighten the sense of touch by putting pressure on the fingertips.

Apical tufts
Finger bones have spadelike tips, which support the soft flesh of the fingertips.

Protective pad
A fleshy pad on the end of each thumb helps with grip.

Fingers and thumbs
It is not just the opposable thumb that has transformed the capability of the human hand. The thumb has a thick pad of flesh at the end that helps to hold objects, while the finger bones have wide, flat ends to improve the strength of grip.

Most **apes and monkeys** also have opposable thumbs, but the **human thumb is the most mobile.**

The palm of your hand contains **3,200 sweat glands** per square inch (500 per square centimeter).

133

Researchers have found that the area of the brain that controls the thumbs is much more active in people who use touchscreens every day.

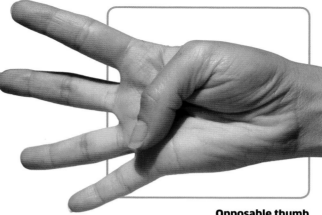

Flexible framework
The multiple joints and bones of the hand provide flexible and versatile movement.

Muscle movements
Many of the hand's intricate movements are produced by muscle tendons that cross the wrist.

Opposable thumb
Thumbs move in the opposite way to fingers, which is why they are called opposable. It is the unique arrangement of bones, joints, and muscles in the thumb and wrist that allows this type of movement.

Carpals
The eight small carpal bones make up the wrist.

Saddle joint
At the base of the thumb, a specialized joint allows the thumb to move in all directions without twisting.

Power and precision
The way we use our hands to grip different things affects the amount of force applied to the object. Hand grips can be described as either power or precision, depending on the position of the hand.

Power grip
A power grip is one in which the fingers curl tightly around an object, forming a cylinder or sphere shape with the hand. This position gives the maximum holding force. Fingers can be close together or spread apart, such as when holding a ball.

CYLINDRICAL GRIP   **SPHERICAL GRIP**

Precision grip
A precision grip is one in which the hand pinches an object between the thumb and fingertips. This gives extremely fine control over movements, but only 25 percent of the strength of a power grip.

PRECISION OR PINCH GRIP

Communicating with hands
People use hand gestures every day to communicate. A greeting could be an informal wave hello or good-bye, or a formal handshake. A thumbs up or down can quickly convey good or bad news. Some hand gestures are used so widely that they are recognized across different cultures.

Sign language
The dexterity of human hands has led to the creation of sign language, which allows people with hearing problems to communicate using a recognized range of hand movements.

THANK YOU   **SORRY**

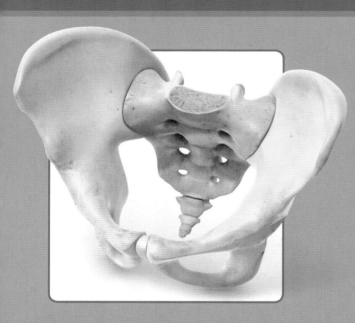
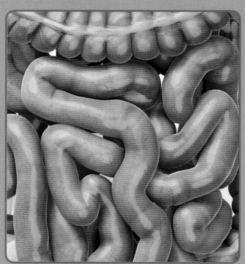
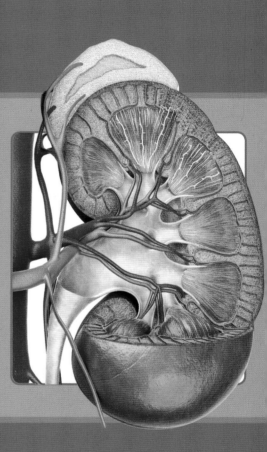

ABDOMEN AND PELVIS

The abdomen contains hardworking organs from many of the body's systems. Most of them help to digest food, clean the blood, or dispose of waste. Supporting them from beneath is a strong framework of bone and muscle called the pelvis.

Inside the abdomen

Many of the body's most important organs lie in the abdomen, the area between the chest and pelvis.

The abdomen contains organs belonging to various body systems, including most of the digestive system, the urinary system, and the reproductive organs. This area is protected by the muscles and other tissues of the abdominal wall. This wall and many of the organs are covered with a slippery membrane called the peritoneum, which allows them to slide over each other.

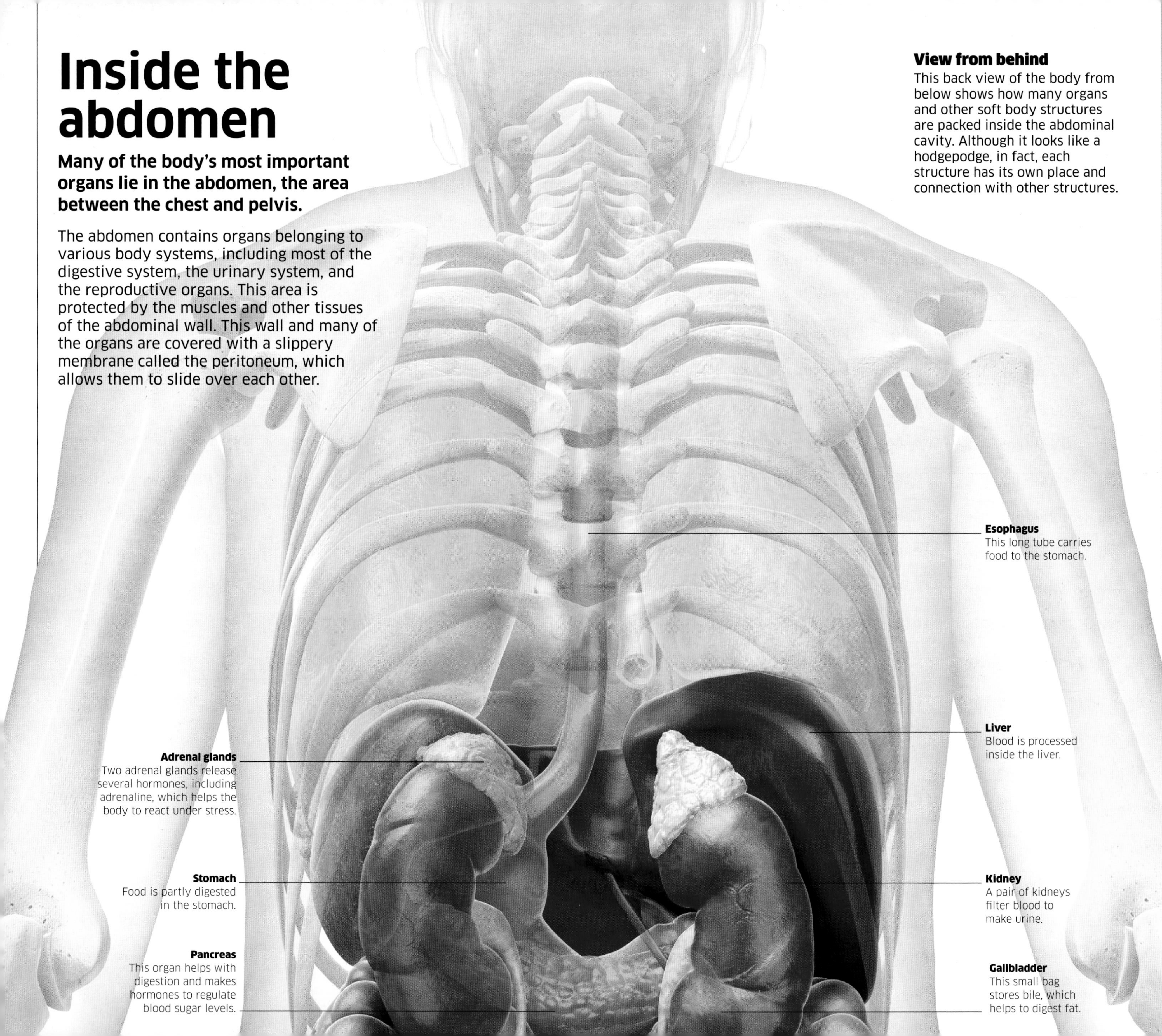

View from behind

This back view of the body from below shows how many organs and other soft body structures are packed inside the abdominal cavity. Although it looks like a hodgepodge, in fact, each structure has its own place and connection with other structures.

Esophagus
This long tube carries food to the stomach.

Liver
Blood is processed inside the liver.

Kidney
A pair of kidneys filter blood to make urine.

Gallbladder
This small bag stores bile, which helps to digest fat.

Adrenal glands
Two adrenal glands release several hormones, including adrenaline, which helps the body to react under stress.

Stomach
Food is partly digested in the stomach.

Pancreas
This organ helps with digestion and makes hormones to regulate blood sugar levels.

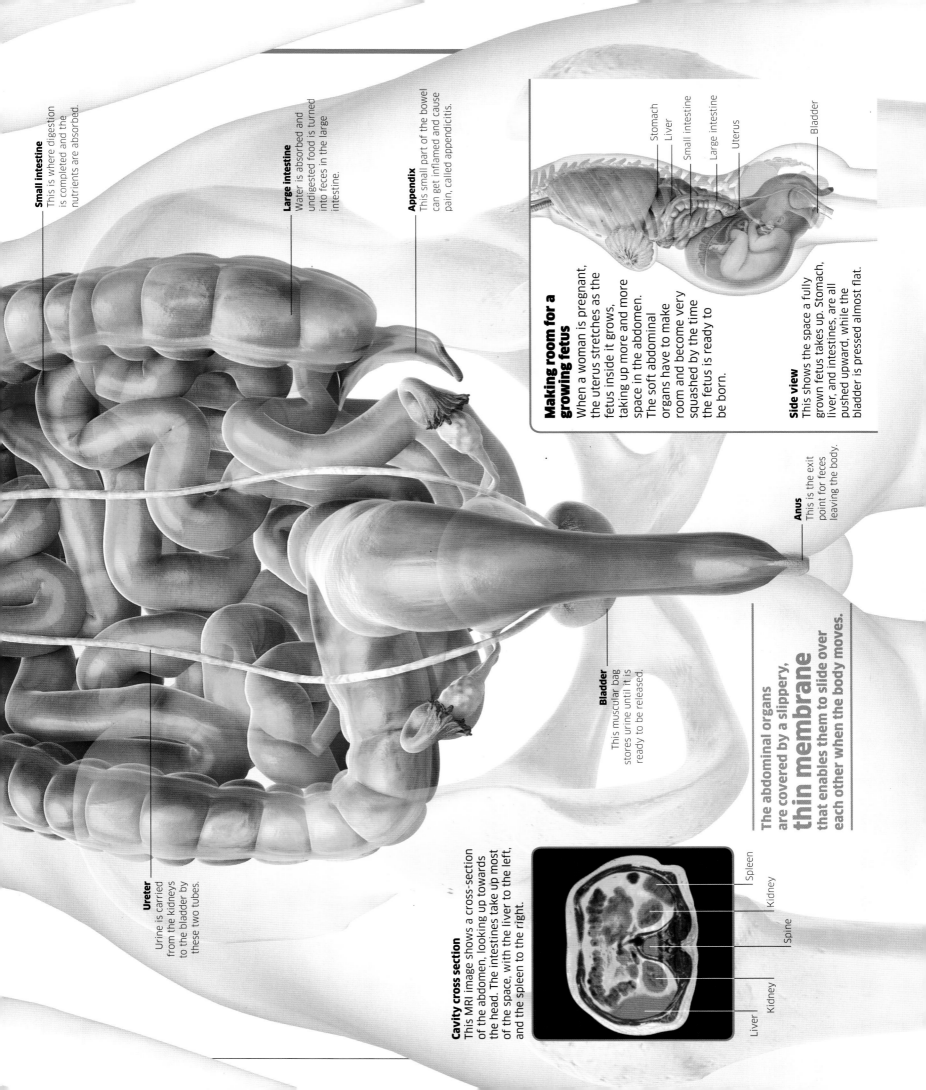

Small intestine
This is where digestion is completed and the nutrients are absorbed.

Large intestine
Water is absorbed and undigested food is turned into feces in the large intestine.

Appendix
This small part of the bowel can get inflamed and cause pain, called appendicitis.

Ureter
Urine is carried from the kidneys to the bladder by these two tubes.

Cavity cross section
This MRI image shows a cross-section of the abdomen, looking up towards the head. The intestines take up most of the space, with the liver to the left, and the spleen to the right.

Spleen

Kidney

Spine

Kidney

Liver

Anus
This is the exit point for feces leaving the body.

Bladder
This muscular bag stores urine until it is ready to be released.

The abdominal organs are covered by a slippery, thin **membrane** that enables them to slide over each other when the body moves.

Making room for a growing fetus

When a woman is pregnant, the uterus stretches as the fetus inside it grows, taking up more and more space in the abdomen. The soft abdominal organs have to make room and become very squashed by the time the fetus is ready to be born.

Stomach

Liver

Small intestine

Large intestine

Uterus

Bladder

Side view
This shows the space a fully grown fetus takes up. Stomach, liver, and intestines, are all pushed upward, while the bladder is pressed almost flat.

In and out

After the stomach fills, it takes up to four hours for food to be turned into chyme, which is then gradually emptied into the duodenum.

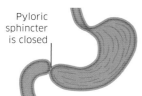

Pyloric sphincter is closed

1 Before a meal The sight and smell of food triggers the release of gastric juice into the empty, fist-sized stomach.

Food is mixed with gastric juice

2 During a meal The stomach fills with food and expands like a balloon. Waves of contraction of the stomach wall mix food with gastric juice.

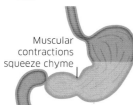

Muscular contractions squeeze chyme

3 After 1–2 hours Partially digested and churned, the food is turned into chyme, which is pushed toward the pyloric sphincter.

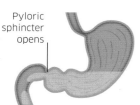

Pyloric sphincter opens

4 After 3–4 hours The pyloric sphincter opens at intervals and the stomach wall contracts to squirt small amounts of chyme into the duodenum.

Being sick

Vomiting, or throwing up, can happen when toxins (poisons) released by bacteria irritate the stomach's lining. In response, the brain tells the diaphragm and abdominal muscles to contract and squeeze the stomach, forcing its contents upward and out of the mouth to remove the irritation.

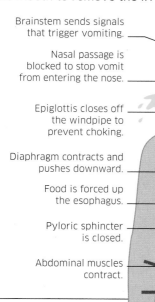

Brainstem sends signals that trigger vomiting.

Nasal passage is blocked to stop vomit from entering the nose.

Epiglottis closes off the windpipe to prevent choking.

Diaphragm contracts and pushes downward.

Food is forced up the esophagus.

Pyloric sphincter is closed.

Abdominal muscles contract.

Stomach

Seconds after swallowing, food enters the stomach, the J-shaped, stretchy bag that links the esophagus to the small intestine. While food is stored in the stomach it is churned into a creamy liquid called chyme. This is released gradually into the small intestine, where digestion is completed.

Two types of digestion happen in the stomach. First, food is doused in acidic gastric juice that contains pepsin, an enzyme that digests proteins. Second, muscles in the stomach's wall create waves of contractions that crush and churn food into mushy chyme.

Inside view

The stomach's wall has three muscle layers that run in different directions. During digestion, these contract in turn to churn food while mixing it with acidic gastric juice. Thick mucus stops gastric juice from damaging the stomach's own delicate lining.

Gastric juice contains hydrochloric acid, which is strong enough to **kill most of the harmful bacteria** that can enter the body in the food we eat.

Pyloric sphincter
Normally closed to keep food in the stomach, this ring of muscle opens slightly once food has been processed (as shown here) to allow a controlled flow of chyme into the duodenum.

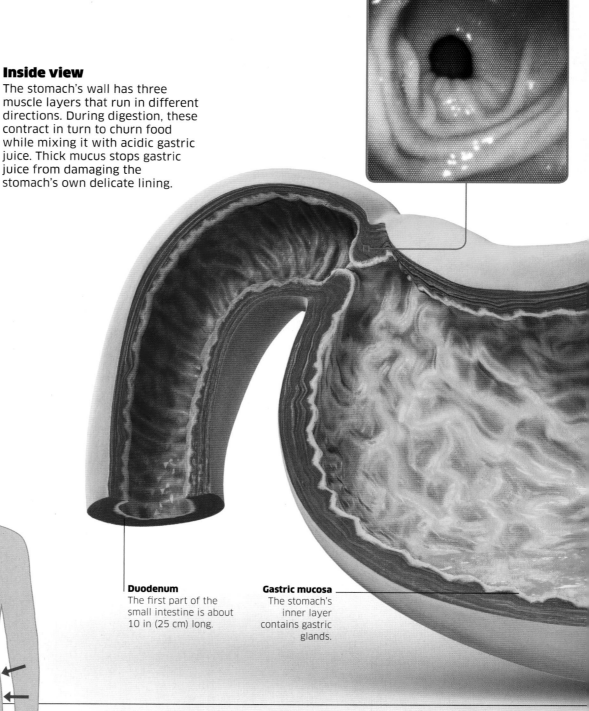

Duodenum
The first part of the small intestine is about 10 in (25 cm) long.

Gastric mucosa
The stomach's inner layer contains gastric glands.

The squelchy noises the stomach makes are caused by mushed-up food **squirting into the intestines**.

3.5 million—the number of **gastric pits** in an average human stomach. **139**

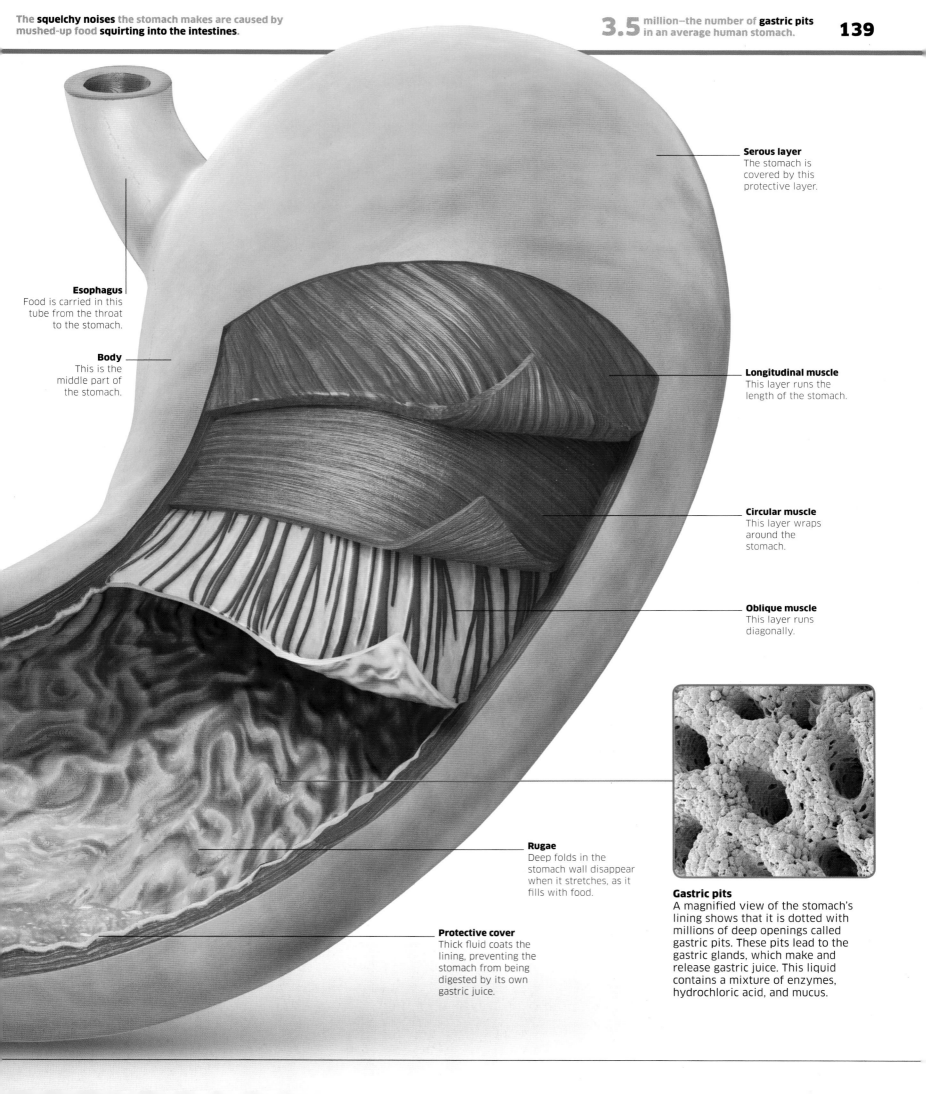

Serous layer
The stomach is covered by this protective layer.

Esophagus
Food is carried in this tube from the throat to the stomach.

Body
This is the middle part of the stomach.

Longitudinal muscle
This layer runs the length of the stomach.

Circular muscle
This layer wraps around the stomach.

Oblique muscle
This layer runs diagonally.

Rugae
Deep folds in the stomach wall disappear when it stretches, as it fills with food.

Protective cover
Thick fluid coats the lining, preventing the stomach from being digested by its own gastric juice.

Gastric pits
A magnified view of the stomach's lining shows that it is dotted with millions of deep openings called gastric pits. These pits lead to the gastric glands, which make and release gastric juice. This liquid contains a mixture of enzymes, hydrochloric acid, and mucus.

FOOD AND NUTRITION

Nutrition is the food your body needs to grow, move, and keep all its parts working. The body can make some of the substances it needs, but the rest have to come from the food we eat. The digestive system breaks food down into simple chemicals called nutrients that the body can use. Nutrients energize the cells ready for work, provide material for new tissues, and help to repair injuries.

ESSENTIALS FOR LIFE

There are six essential types of nutrient that the body needs to work efficiently. Three of them—carbohydrates, proteins, and fats—have to be broken down by the digestive system into simpler substances that can be absorbed into the bloodstream. Vitamins, minerals, and water can be absorbed directly through the lining of the gut.

Fats
These provide energy and help the brain and nervous system to work efficiently.

Proteins
Proteins help to build cells and repair damage.

Carbohydrates
These provide energy for the body.

Vitamins and minerals
Micronutrients from vitamins and minerals help body parts to work.

Water
Water keeps blood and cells working and helps to flush out waste.

FOOD FOR ENERGY

Everything our body does—breathing, sleeping, running, or just thinking—uses energy. Energy also keeps trillions of body cells working. The food you eat supplies energy that keeps the body going.

Energy levels

Different foods contain varying amounts of energy when broken down inside the body. The energy the body gets from a particular food or drink is measured in calories. The amount of energy a body needs depends on many factors. Teenagers need more energy than adults because they are still growing. Men need to take in more calories than women as they are usually bigger and have more energy-consuming muscle.

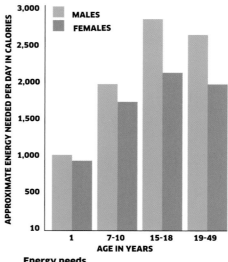

Karate kicks
People who participate in sports use up to three times more calories than inactive people.

Energy needs
People's individual energy needs vary a huge amount. Very active people use a lot of energy, so they need more calories from their food.

Chart: APPROXIMATE ENERGY NEEDED PER DAY IN CALORIES vs AGE IN YEARS (MALES, FEMALES); values ranging 10 to 3,000; ages 1, 7-10, 15-18, 19-49

Using energy

Everything we eat contains a certain amount of energy, and everything we do uses energy. Balancing the calories we take in with the activities we do is key to staying healthy.

Fueling activity
A banana contains about 100 calories. Depending on the activity that you do, that amount of energy will fuel you for different lengths of time.

FAST SWIMMING 10 MINUTES

BALLET 15 MINUTES

WALKING 20 MINUTES

CASUAL CYCLING 25 MINUTES

FRISBEE 30 MINUTES

SLEEPING 2 HOURS

A CYCLIST COMPETING IN THE **TOUR DE FRANCE** BURNS ABOUT **5,000 CALORIES** DURING EACH STAGE **OF THE RACE.**

Vitamins and minerals

Vitamins and minerals are essential substances, called micronutrients, that the body needs in small amounts to work at its best.

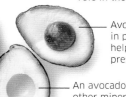

Versatile vitamins
There are 13 different vitamins, each with a specific role in the body's processes.

Avocados are rich in potassium, which helps control blood pressure.

An avocado also contains other minerals, such as zinc, copper, iron, and magnesium.

Full of minerals
Avocados are an excellent source of minerals, and also contain four different vitamins.

VITAMIN	Body benefits	Good sources
A	Eyesight; growth; sense of taste	Liver, carrots, leafy vegetables, dairy products
B1	Brain and nervous system; muscles; heart	Liver, eggs, meat, nuts, whole grains
B2	Eyesight; skin; hair and nails; growth	Liver, fish, dairy products, leafy vegetables
B3	Brain; blood circulation; skin	Fish, meat, eggs
B5	Hormone production; blood	Eggs, chicken, tomatoes
B6	Brain and nervous system; blood; digestion	Fish, chicken, pork, beans, bananas
B7	Helps break down fat; important for growth	Chicken, meat, eggs
B9	Also called folic acid, it is vital for a baby's development	Leafy vegetables, cereals, meat
B12	Brain and nervous system; blood	Eggs, seafood, meat, dairy products
C	Immune system; keeping cells healthy	Citrus fruit, tomatoes, leafy veg, potatoes
D	Bones; teeth; immune system	Sunlight, oily fish, eggs, dairy products
E	Immune system; skin; muscles	Seed and nut oils, green vegetables, butter, eggs
K	Helping blood to clot	Leafy vegetables, cereals, meat

THE RIGHT BALANCE

A healthy diet means not only eating the essential nutrients, but also getting the proportions right. We don't have to achieve an exact balance with every meal, but a balanced diet overall keeps the body working at its best.

Dietary portions
This chart shows the balanced diet that most doctors currently recommend. Fruit and vegetables, and carbohydrates, make up most of the intake, with smaller amounts of protein, dairy products, and oils.

Water
A good daily intake of water is also essential—about 6-8 glasses is ideal.

Fruit and vegetables should make up at least one-third of our diet.

CARBOHYDRATES

Treats
Very sugary or fatty snacks should only be occasional treats.

FRUIT AND VEGETABLES

Starchy foods such as bread, rice, and pasta should make up about one-third of our diet.

Choose oils and spreads that contain unsaturated fats, such as olive oil.

OILS AND SPREADS

Good sources of protein are fish, beans and pulses, chicken, and red meat.

Just under 10% of our diet should be made of dairy food such as milk, cheese, and yogurt.

PROTEINS

DAIRY

FOOD OR SUPERFOOD?

Most experts agree that no single food is good or bad for our health. Some foods that are especially rich in nutrients are called "superfoods"—but even these should form part of a varied and balanced diet.

Quinoa
Pronounced "keen-wa," this South American grain is very high in protein and contains all the amino acids the body needs.

Blueberries
Some studies suggest that eating this fruit improves blood circulation and boosts mental function.

Beets
Research has shown that this vegetable can help lower blood pressure and improve exercise performance.

EXPERTS RECOMMEND
EATING AT LEAST FIVE HELPINGS OF FRUIT **AND VEGETABLES** A DAY TO BE HEALTHY.

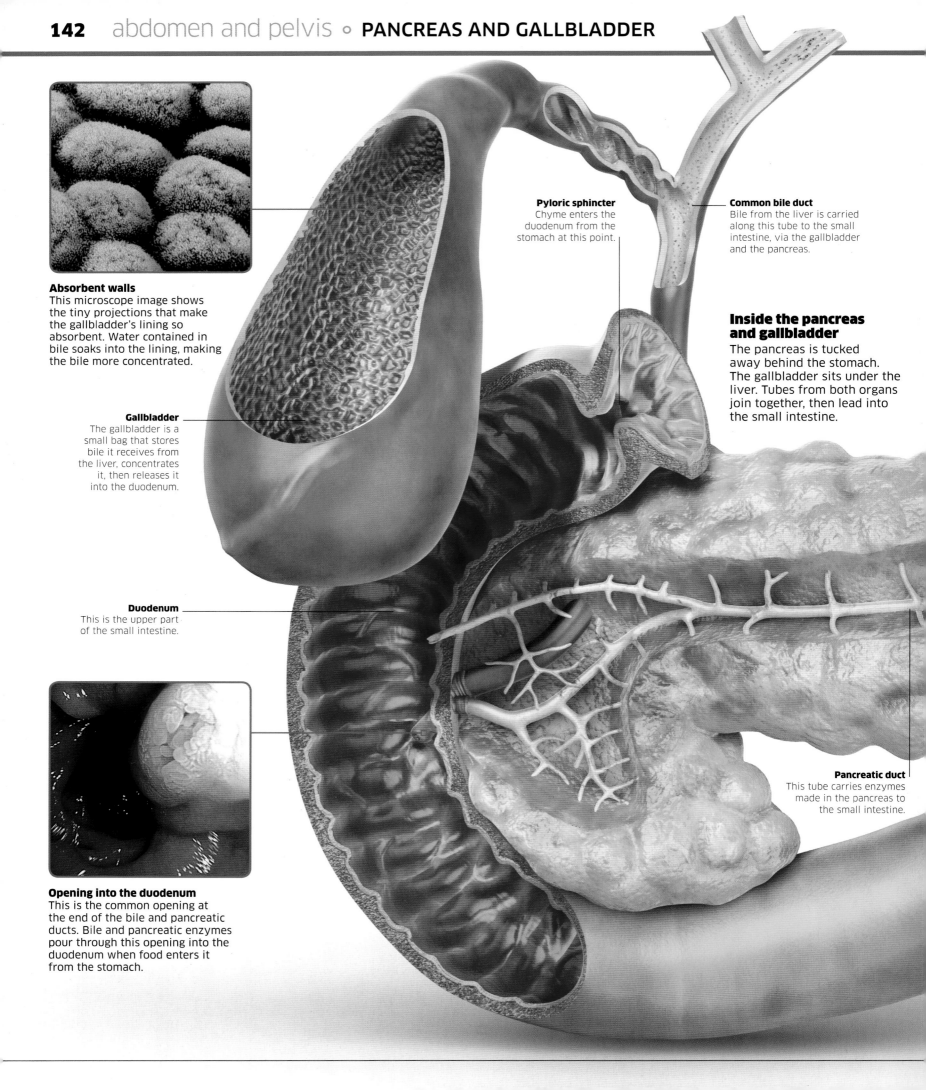

Absorbent walls
This microscope image shows the tiny projections that make the gallbladder's lining so absorbent. Water contained in bile soaks into the lining, making the bile more concentrated.

Pyloric sphincter
Chyme enters the duodenum from the stomach at this point.

Common bile duct
Bile from the liver is carried along this tube to the small intestine, via the gallbladder and the pancreas.

Inside the pancreas and gallbladder
The pancreas is tucked away behind the stomach. The gallbladder sits under the liver. Tubes from both organs join together, then lead into the small intestine.

Gallbladder
The gallbladder is a small bag that stores bile it receives from the liver, concentrates it, then releases it into the duodenum.

Duodenum
This is the upper part of the small intestine.

Pancreatic duct
This tube carries enzymes made in the pancreas to the small intestine.

Opening into the duodenum
This is the common opening at the end of the bile and pancreatic ducts. Bile and pancreatic enzymes pour through this opening into the duodenum when food enters it from the stomach.

An adult's **gallbladder** is about the size of a small pear. The **pancreas** is as big as a banana.

1.7 fluid ounces (50 ml)—the capacity of an adult's **gallbladder** (about three tablespoons).

143

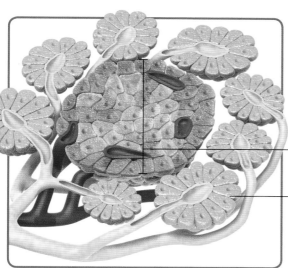

Inside the pancreas
The pancreas contains about one million islets of Langerhans, flowerlike clusters of cells that release the hormones which help the body to store or use glucose. The islets are surrounded by cells that make digestive enzymes.

Islet of Langerhans contains hormone-producing cells

Outer parts of the cluster contain digestive-enzyme-producing cells

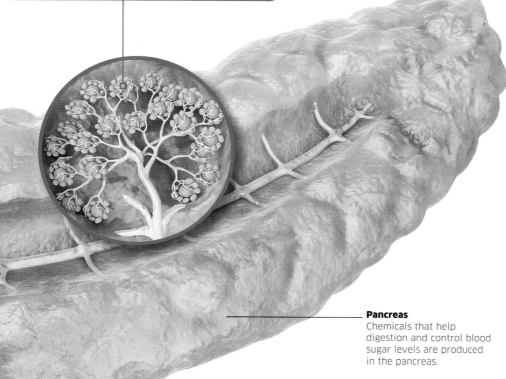

Pancreas
Chemicals that help digestion and control blood sugar levels are produced in the pancreas.

Pancreas and gallbladder

The pancreas and gallbladder play key roles in the next stage of food digestion, which takes place when food arrives in the small intestine from the stomach. Without them, the small intestine could not work properly.

The pancreas and gallbladder release different substances into the small intestine. The pancreas releases pancreatic juice, which is full of enzymes—chemicals that break food into smaller parts, so they can be absorbed into the blood. It also produces hormones that control the amount of sugar in the blood. The gallbladder stores, processes, and releases bile, a liquid that helps the body to digest fat.

Breaking down food
Bile and digestive enzymes work together in the small intestine to digest food. Different enzymes target specific types of foods, dividing them into simpler ingredients so they can easily be absorbed by the body.

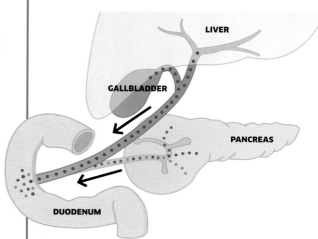

LIVER

GALLBLADDER

PANCREAS

DUODENUM

Key

- **BILE**   breaks down fats
- **LIPASE**   helps to digest fats
- **AMYLASE**   helps to digest sugars
- **PROTEASE**   helps to digest proteins

The route to the duodenum
This shows the route of bile and the digestive enzymes protease, lipase, and amylase as they make their way to the duodenum.

Important insulin
The pancreas produces insulin—the vital hormone that allows glucose in the bloodstream to enter the body's cells and be used as energy. Type-1 diabetes is a condition that causes the pancreas to stop making insulin. Cells are starved of the glucose they need, while blood glucose rises to dangerous levels and causes health problems. To keep healthy, diabetics must inject artificial insulin into their bodies daily.

Daily dose
Many diabetics use a small pump, implanted under the skin, which releases measured doses of insulin at regular intervals.

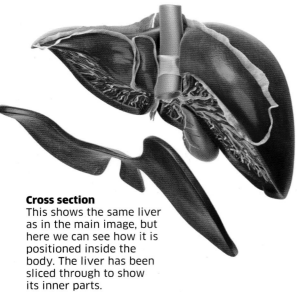

Cross section
This shows the same liver as in the main image, but here we can see how it is positioned inside the body. The liver has been sliced through to show its inner parts.

Liver list

The liver performs hundreds of essential processing, manufacturing, and recycling tasks in the body.

Breaking down
The liver breaks down substances into parts the body can use or get rid of, such as:
• chemicals from food
• medicines
• germs entering in food

Recycling
It also breaks up dead blood cells so their ingredients can be used again.

Building up
Nutrients are used to make new substances that the body needs, such as:
• proteins for building body parts
• chemicals to heal injuries
• bile, which helps to digest fat

Storage
Useful body substances are stored, then released when necessary, such as:
• glucose for energy
• minerals, such as iron and copper
• vitamins A, D, K, and B12

Heating
The liver even gives out heat to help warm the body.

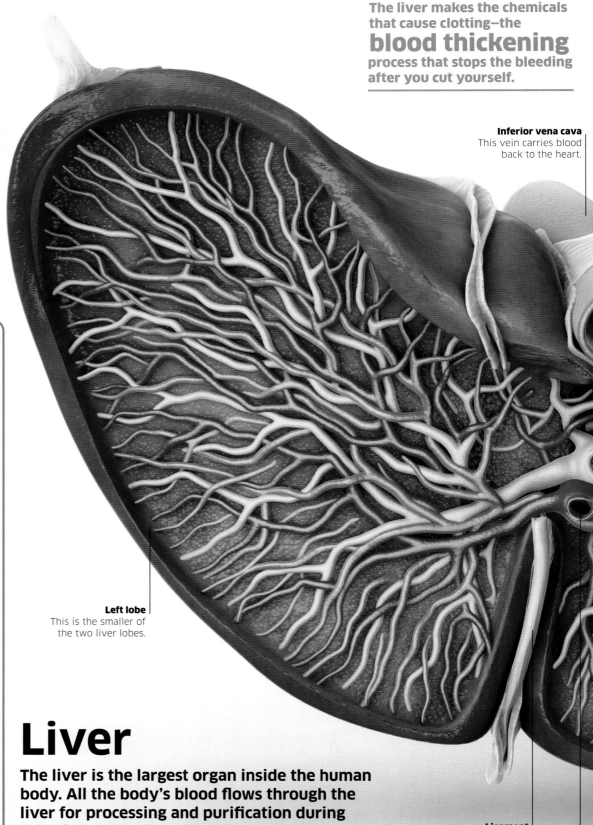

The liver makes the chemicals that cause clotting—the **blood thickening** process that stops the bleeding after you cut yourself.

Inferior vena cava
This vein carries blood back to the heart.

Left lobe
This is the smaller of the two liver lobes.

Ligament
This connective tissue lies between the two main lobes.

Hepatic artery
Oxygen-rich blood is supplied to the liver by this artery.

Liver

The liver is the largest organ inside the human body. All the body's blood flows through the liver for processing and purification during this vital stage of the digestive system.

The liver has many different roles, but one of the most important is controlling the chemical makeup of the blood to keep body conditions stable. Nutrient-rich blood from the small intestine flows directly into the liver, which makes these nutrients more useful for the body and removes harmful chemicals. The liver also makes bile, a fluid used by the small intestine to help digest fats.

15% of the **body's blood** is inside the liver at any time.

The liver **filters blood** at a rate of 3 pints (1.4 liters) every minute.

1 million—the approximate number of blood-filtering **lobules** inside a liver.

145

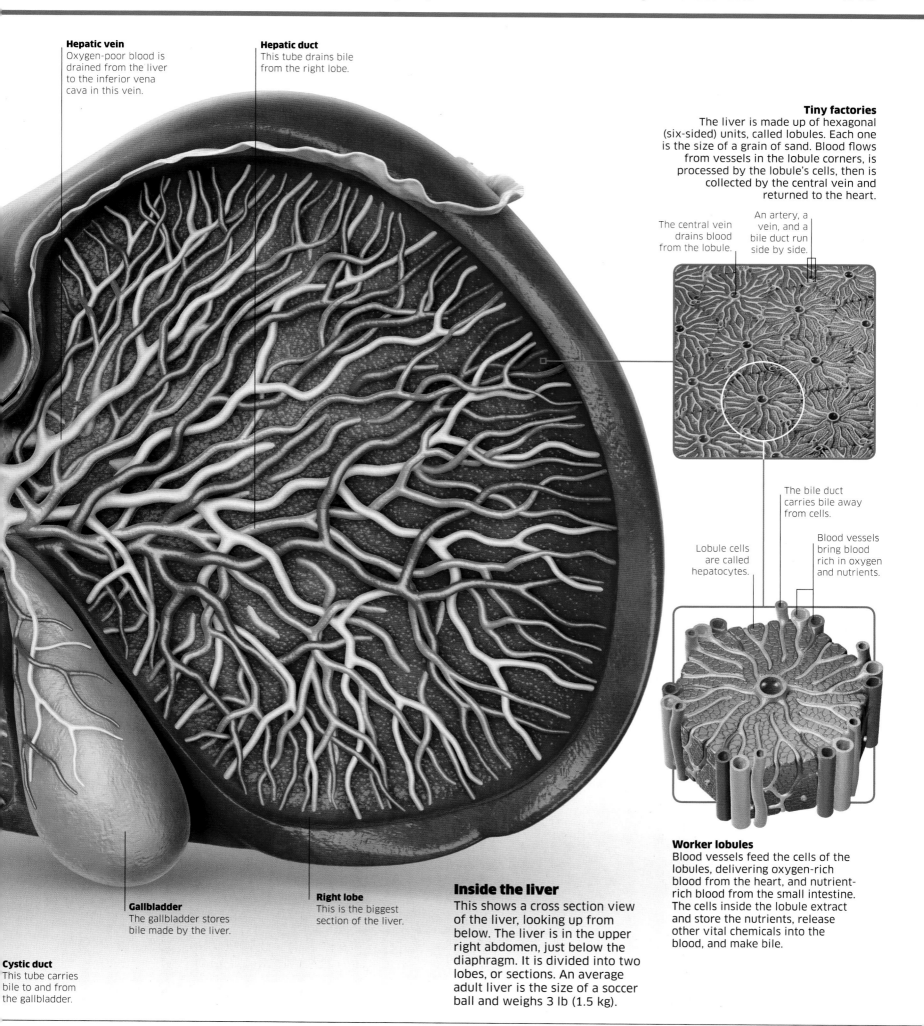

Hepatic vein
Oxygen-poor blood is drained from the liver to the inferior vena cava in this vein.

Hepatic duct
This tube drains bile from the right lobe.

Tiny factories
The liver is made up of hexagonal (six-sided) units, called lobules. Each one is the size of a grain of sand. Blood flows from vessels in the lobule corners, is processed by the lobule's cells, then is collected by the central vein and returned to the heart.

The central vein drains blood from the lobule.

An artery, a vein, and a bile duct run side by side.

The bile duct carries bile away from cells.

Lobule cells are called hepatocytes.

Blood vessels bring blood rich in oxygen and nutrients.

Gallbladder
The gallbladder stores bile made by the liver.

Right lobe
This is the biggest section of the liver.

Cystic duct
This tube carries bile to and from the gallbladder.

Inside the liver
This shows a cross section view of the liver, looking up from below. The liver is in the upper right abdomen, just below the diaphragm. It is divided into two lobes, or sections. An average adult liver is the size of a soccer ball and weighs 3 lb (1.5 kg).

Worker lobules
Blood vessels feed the cells of the lobules, delivering oxygen-rich blood from the heart, and nutrient-rich blood from the small intestine. The cells inside the lobule extract and store the nutrients, release other vital chemicals into the blood, and make bile.

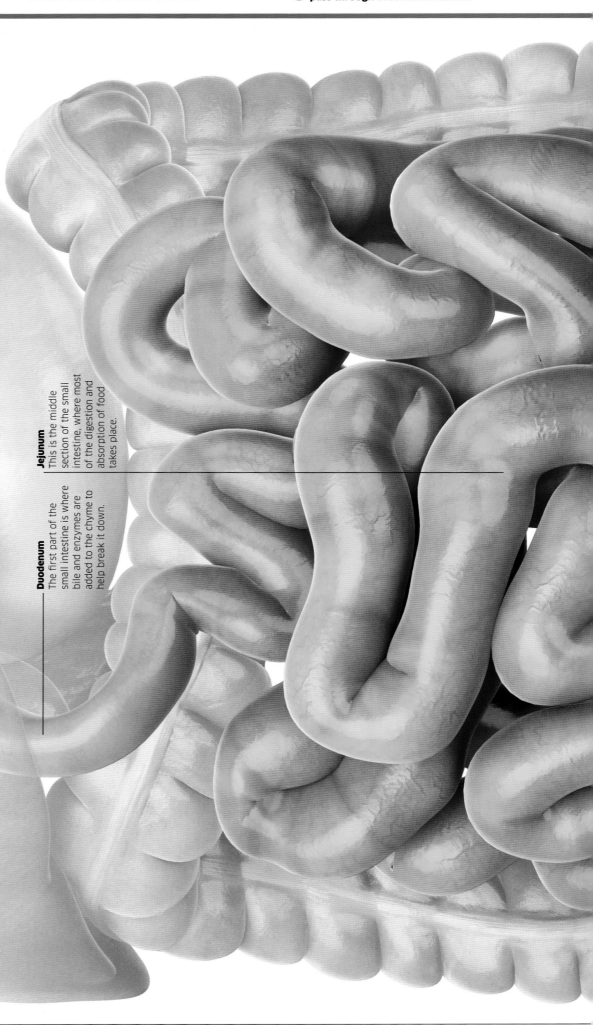

Small intestine

The small intestine is the longest part of the digestive system. It's where most of the digestive process takes place, releasing the nutrients in food so that they can be used to fuel the body's cells.

By the time food reaches the small intestine, the stomach has turned it into a liquid called chyme. This chyme is squirted into the duodenum, the first part of the small intestine, along with bile from the gallbladder and enzymes from the pancreas, which break the chyme down even more. Finally, when most of the food has been broken down into simple nutrients, these pass through the walls of the small intestine and into the bloodstream. The remaining food progresses to the next stage—the large intestine.

If you stretched out the small intestine, it would be longer than four adults lying **head to toe.**

Bundled up

The small intestine is at the front of the lower abdomen, surrounded by the large intestine and other organs. Although it's very long—more than 20 ft (6 m)—the small intestine fits into this space because it is bundled up in a series of loops and coils.

Jejunum
This is the middle section of the small intestine, where most of the digestion and absorption of food takes place.

Duodenum
The first part of the small intestine is where bile and enzymes are added to the chyme to help break it down.

The word villus comes from a **Latin word** meaning "shaggy hair."

If the small intestine were **flattened out**, its area would be about **320 sq ft** (30 sq m)—bigger than 10 double beds put together.

147

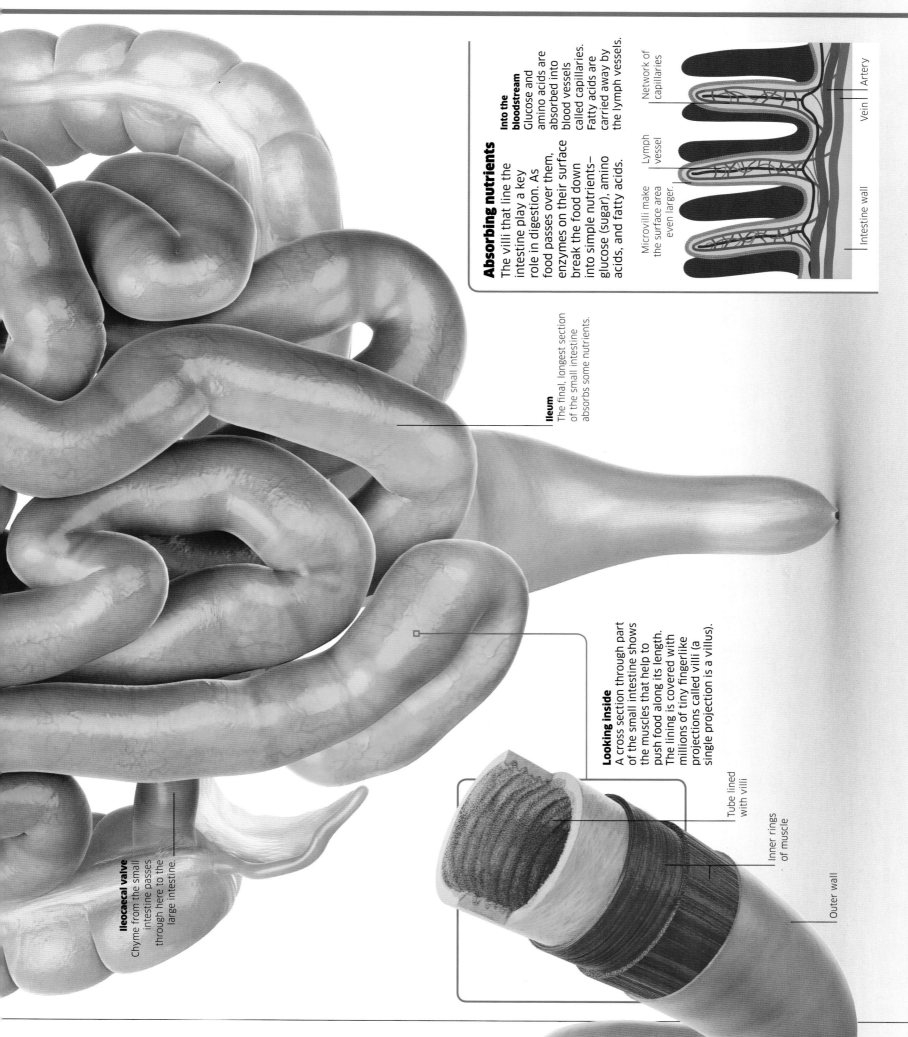

Absorbing nutrients

The villi that line the intestine play a key role in digestion. As food passes over them, enzymes on their surface break the food down into simple nutrients—glucose (sugar), amino acids, and fatty acids.

Into the bloodstream
Glucose and amino acids are absorbed into blood vessels called capillaries. Fatty acids are carried away by the lymph vessels.

Network of capillaries

Microvilli make the surface area even larger.

Lymph vessel

Vein | Artery

Intestine wall

Ileum
The final, longest section of the small intestine absorbs some nutrients.

Looking inside
A cross section through part of the small intestine shows the muscles that help to push food along its length. The lining is covered with millions of tiny fingerlike projections called villi (a single projection is a villus).

Tube lined with villi

Inner rings of muscle

Outer wall

Ileocaecal valve
Chyme from the small intestine passes through here to the large intestine.

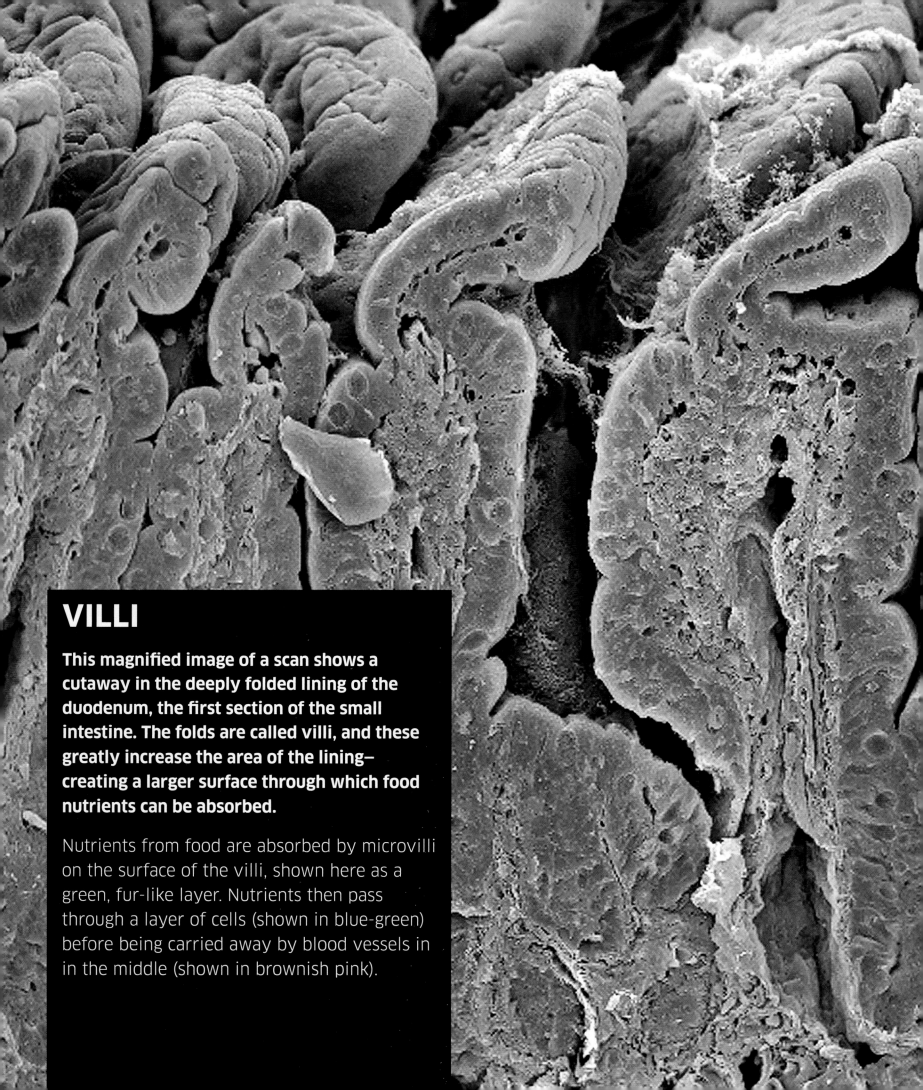

VILLI

This magnified image of a scan shows a cutaway in the deeply folded lining of the duodenum, the first section of the small intestine. The folds are called villi, and these greatly increase the area of the lining– creating a larger surface through which food nutrients can be absorbed.

Nutrients from food are absorbed by microvilli on the surface of the villi, shown here as a green, fur-like layer. Nutrients then pass through a layer of cells (shown in blue-green) before being carried away by blood vessels in in the middle (shown in brownish pink).

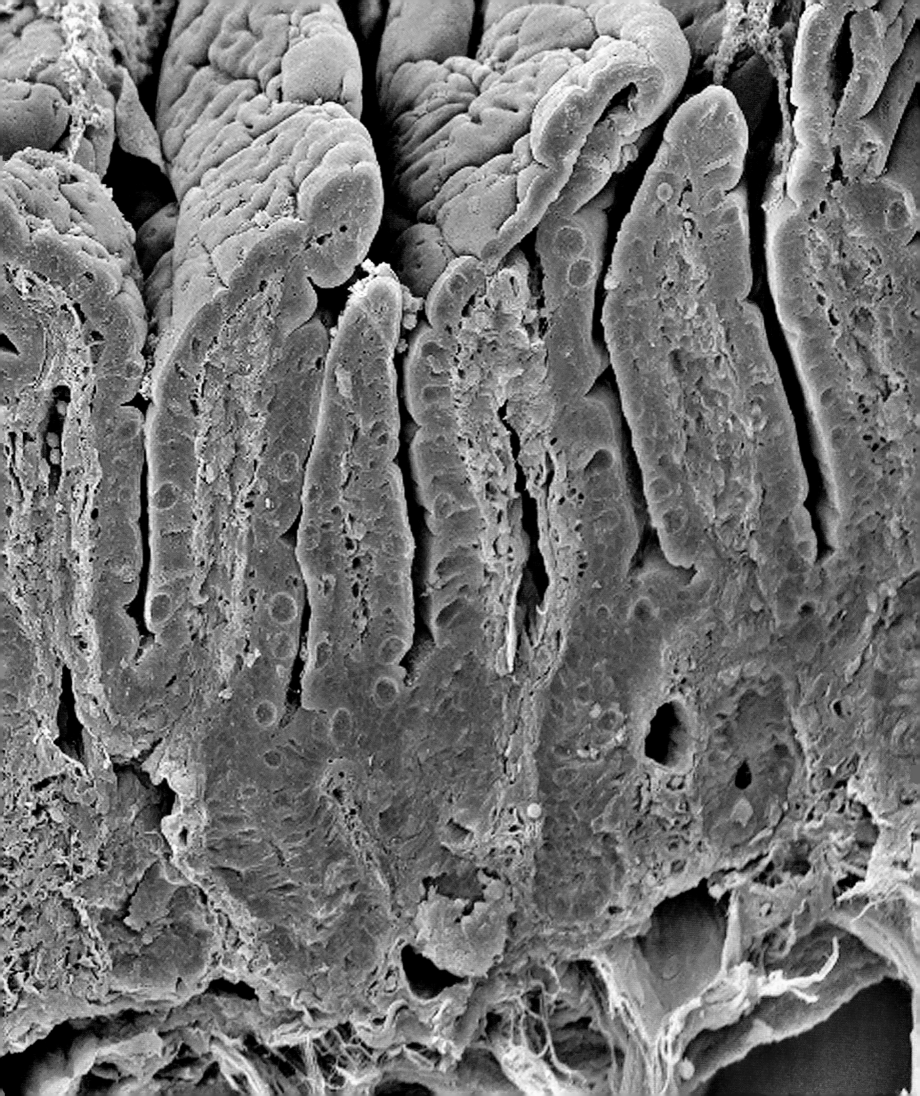

150   abdomen and pelvis ○ **LARGE INTESTINE**

The **ancient Egyptians** called the
appendix "the worm of the intestines."

Large intestine

The large intestine is the final stage of the digestive system. It's where most of the water, and the last few nutrients, are taken from the chyme that enters from the small intestine. It then moves unusable waste out of the body.

Most nutrients have been taken from the food before it gets to the large intestine—but there is still vital work for it to do. Here, trillions of bacteria help to break the remaining food down into valuable nutrients. The large intestine is wider than the small intestine, but it's not nearly as long.

Bacteria in the large intestine produce a number of **different vitamins,** especially vitamin K and biotin, a B vitamin.

Up, across, and down
The large intestine is a wide tube that goes around the small intestine. The tube goes up, across the abdomen, then down again. It has a lumpy appearance because of the way the muscles in its wall contract.

Transverse colon
Passing just below the stomach, this is the middle part of the large intestine.

Gut bacteria
Trillions of bacteria live in the large intestine. Most are either harmless, or actively help to complete digestion by processing the remaining nutrients that could not be digested by enzymes. However, some microorganisms that enter the digestive system can cause illness.

BIFIDOBACTERIA

Ascending colon
On the right side of the abdomen, this section of the intestine rises from the cecum.

Descending colon
This section passes down the left side of the abdomen.

700 —the number of different types of **bacteria** in the large intestine.

4½ lb (2 kg)—the total **weight** of all the bacteria that live in the intestines.

151

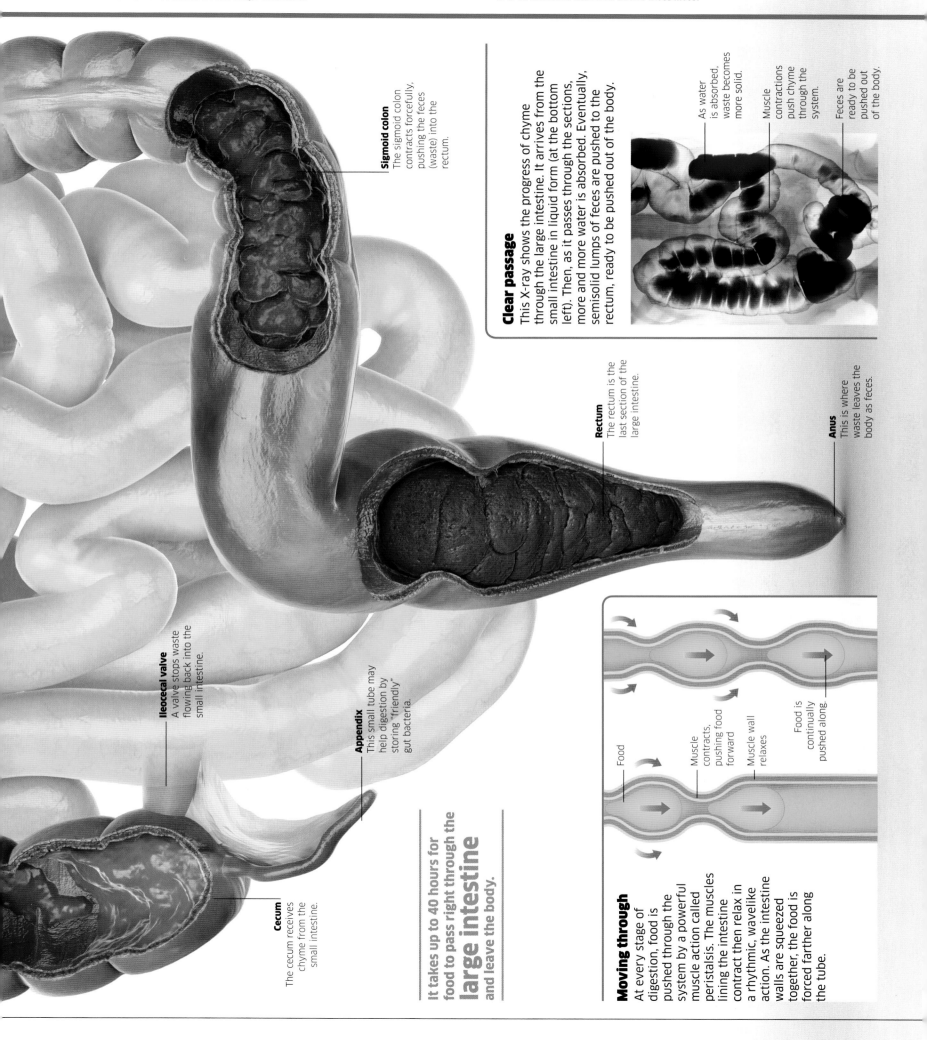

Sigmoid colon
The sigmoid colon contracts forcefully, pushing the feces (waste) into the rectum.

Clear passage

This X-ray shows the progress of chyme through the large intestine. It arrives from the small intestine in liquid form (at the bottom left). Then, as it passes through the sections, more and more water is absorbed. Eventually, semisolid lumps of feces are pushed to the rectum, ready to be pushed out of the body.

As water is absorbed, waste becomes more solid.

Muscle contractions push chyme through the system.

Feces are ready to be pushed out of the body.

Rectum
The rectum is the last section of the large intestine.

Anus
This is where waste leaves the body as feces.

Ileocecal valve
A valve stops waste flowing back into the small intestine.

Appendix
This small tube may help digestion by storing "friendly" gut bacteria.

Cecum
The cecum receives chyme from the small intestine.

It takes up to 40 hours for food to pass right through the

large intestine

and leave the body.

Moving through

At every stage of digestion, food is pushed through the system by a powerful muscle action called peristalsis. The muscles lining the intestine contract then relax in a rhythmic, wavelike action. As the intestine walls are squeezed together, the food is forced farther along the tube.

Food

Muscle contracts, pushing food forward

Muscle wall relaxes

Food is continually pushed along.

152 abdomen and pelvis ○ **PELVIS**

Pelvis shapes help archaeologists determine
whether the skeletons they find are **male** or **female**.

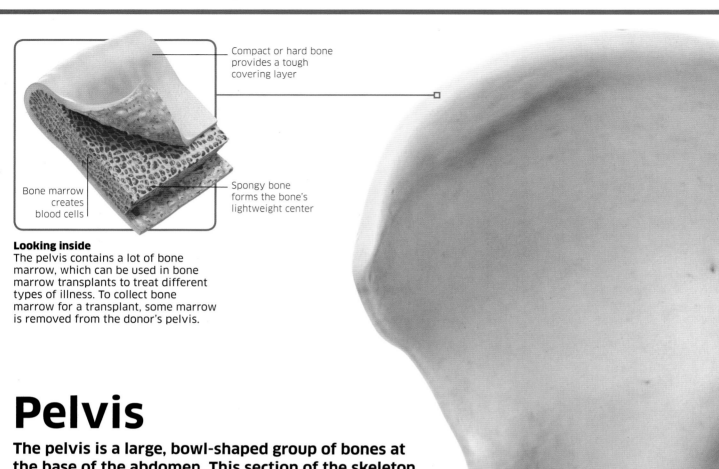

Compact or hard bone
provides a tough
covering layer

Bone marrow
creates
blood cells

Spongy bone
forms the bone's
lightweight center

Looking inside
The pelvis contains a lot of bone
marrow, which can be used in bone
marrow transplants to treat different
types of illness. To collect bone
marrow for a transplant, some marrow
is removed from the donor's pelvis.

Pelvis

**The pelvis is a large, bowl-shaped group of bones at
the base of the abdomen. This section of the skeleton
is made up of several bones fused and linked together.
It surrounds and protects the soft organs inside the
lower abdomen.**

The pelvis has many functions. It supports the intestines and
bladder, and the space in the middle allows waste from the
intestines and bladder to leave the body. In women, the pelvis
supports the uterus as it expands to hold a growing baby and
also provides the baby's route out of the body during
childbirth. Many muscles in the back, abdomen, and legs are
anchored to the pelvis, helping to keep the body upright. The
pelvis allows us to stand, walk, and run without falling over.

Fixed joint
These bones are
held firmly together
by strong ligaments.

Pelvic cavity
The intestines and
bladder are contained
here, surrounded by
the protective pelvis.

Pubis
The pubis is
one of the two
smallest bones
in the pelvis.

Pubic symphysis
This strong cartilage joint
connects the two pubis
bones together.

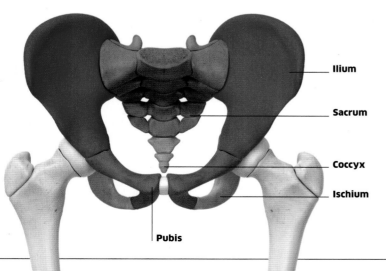

Ilium

Sacrum

Coccyx

Ischium

Pubis

Child's pelvis
At birth, a baby's pelvic bones
are still each in three parts—the
ilium, ischium, and pubis. During
childhood, these slowly fuse
together. This image shows the
pelvis of a four-year-old child,
with the different bones colored
so we can see them more easily.

23 —the age when all the bones in the **pelvis are fully fused**.

An **elephant's** pelvis is the **size of an armchair!**

Organs don't fall through the pelvis because there is a layer of strong muscles, called **the pelvic floor**, beneath.

153

Pelvic girdle
The pelvis is made up of two hip bones, one on each side. Each hip bone has three parts—the ilium, ischium, and pubis. They connect to the sacrum—the lower part of the spine—to form a ringlike shape, called the pelvic girdle.

Sacrum
At the base of the spine, this triangular-shaped bone connects the two hip bones.

Ilium
The largest bone in the pelvis is the ilium, or hip bone. One on each side connects the muscles used to stand and walk.

Spine
The spine, or backbone, is a column of bones that runs from the pelvis to the neck.

Holes
Small holes in the bones are for nerves and blood vessels.

Coccyx
Below the sacrum is the coccyx, or tailbone—all that remains of the tail of our distant ancestors.

Hip joint
The ball-shaped top of the thigh bone sits in this hollow, creating the ball-and-socket hip joint.

Ischium
The lowest bone in the pelvis, the ischium carries all the weight when the body is sitting down.

Male and female
The male pelvis is usually tall and narrow, while the female's is wider, with a larger space in the middle, called the pelvic inlet, to allow babies to pass through in childbirth.

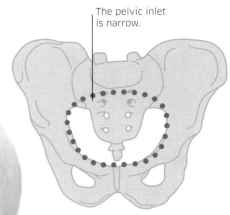

The pelvic inlet is narrow.

MALE PELVIS

The pelvic inlet is much wider, for a baby to go through.

FEMALE PELVIS

Standing up
From four-legged ape-like creatures, we evolved into humans that walk on two legs. As a result, the human pelvis became shorter, rounder, and more upright, so the abdomen could be supported on top of the legs.

Upright pelvis for walking

Pelvis tilted forward for semi-upright movement

GORILLA   **HUMAN**

Kidneys

Your two kidneys filter and clean the blood by removing toxic chemicals. Like the heart, the kidneys are at work every second of every day, producing a continuous flow of clean blood.

As blood circulates, it picks up waste substances produced by the body's cells. These would poison you if they were not removed from the body. The kidneys extract the toxins and excess water from the blood and process them to make urine. In addition to cleaning the blood, the kidneys also release hormones, stimulate red blood cell production, and keep the body's water content balanced. They release more urine if you have drunk a lot and less if you are dehydrated.

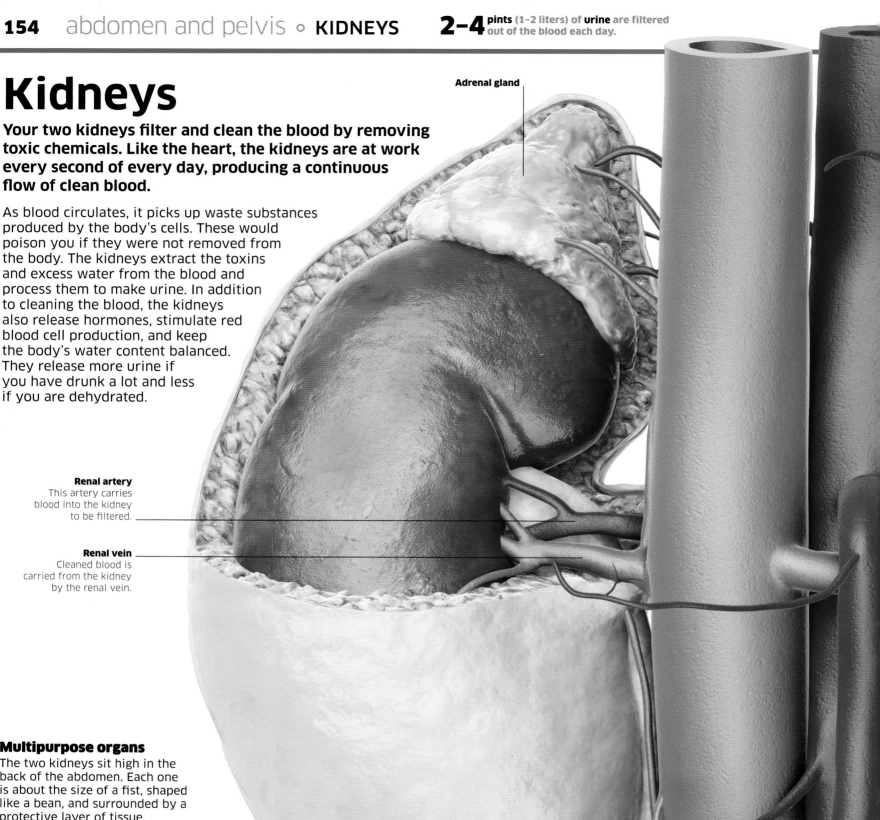

Adrenal gland

Renal artery
This artery carries blood into the kidney to be filtered.

Renal vein
Cleaned blood is carried from the kidney by the renal vein.

Multipurpose organs
The two kidneys sit high in the back of the abdomen. Each one is about the size of a fist, shaped like a bean, and surrounded by a protective layer of tissue.

The average pair of kidneys produces

93,000 pints
(44,000 liters) of urine in a lifetime—that's 550 bathtubs full!

Outer casing
The kidneys and adrenal glands are wrapped in a layer of fat and strong outer tissue.

The amount of **blood that flows** through the kidneys in a lifetime could fill **18 Olympic swimming pools.**

It takes **just under an hour** for the kidneys to clean all the blood in your body.

155

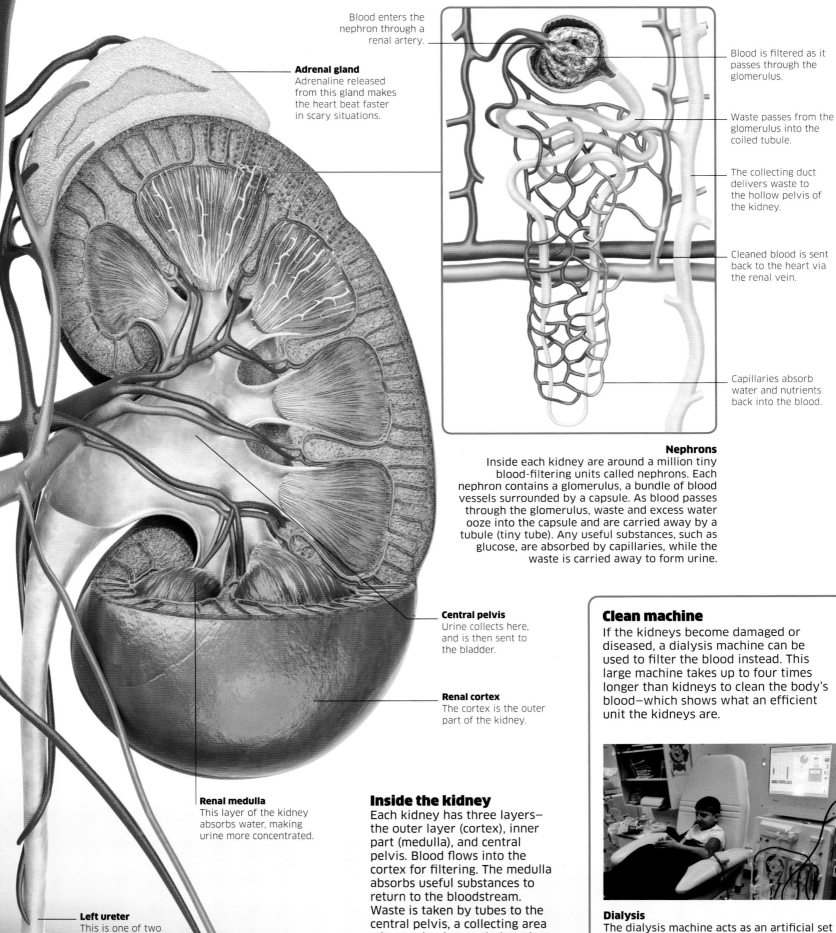

Blood enters the nephron through a renal artery.

Adrenal gland
Adrenaline released from this gland makes the heart beat faster in scary situations.

Blood is filtered as it passes through the glomerulus.

Waste passes from the glomerulus into the coiled tubule.

The collecting duct delivers waste to the hollow pelvis of the kidney.

Cleaned blood is sent back to the heart via the renal vein.

Capillaries absorb water and nutrients back into the blood.

Central pelvis
Urine collects here, and is then sent to the bladder.

Renal cortex
The cortex is the outer part of the kidney.

Renal medulla
This layer of the kidney absorbs water, making urine more concentrated.

Left ureter
This is one of two tubes that carry urine down to the bladder.

Nephrons
Inside each kidney are around a million tiny blood-filtering units called nephrons. Each nephron contains a glomerulus, a bundle of blood vessels surrounded by a capsule. As blood passes through the glomerulus, waste and excess water ooze into the capsule and are carried away by a tubule (tiny tube). Any useful substances, such as glucose, are absorbed by capillaries, while the waste is carried away to form urine.

Inside the kidney
Each kidney has three layers—the outer layer (cortex), inner part (medulla), and central pelvis. Blood flows into the cortex for filtering. The medulla absorbs useful substances to return to the bloodstream. Waste is taken by tubes to the central pelvis, a collecting area where urine is emptied out into two tubes called ureters, and then passes to the bladder.

Clean machine
If the kidneys become damaged or diseased, a dialysis machine can be used to filter the blood instead. This large machine takes up to four times longer than kidneys to clean the body's blood—which shows what an efficient unit the kidneys are.

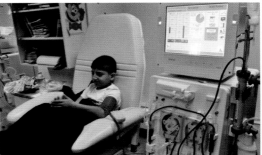

Dialysis
The dialysis machine acts as an artificial set of kidneys. Blood flows from the body to the machine, toxic waste and excess fluid are removed, and the cleaned blood is returned.

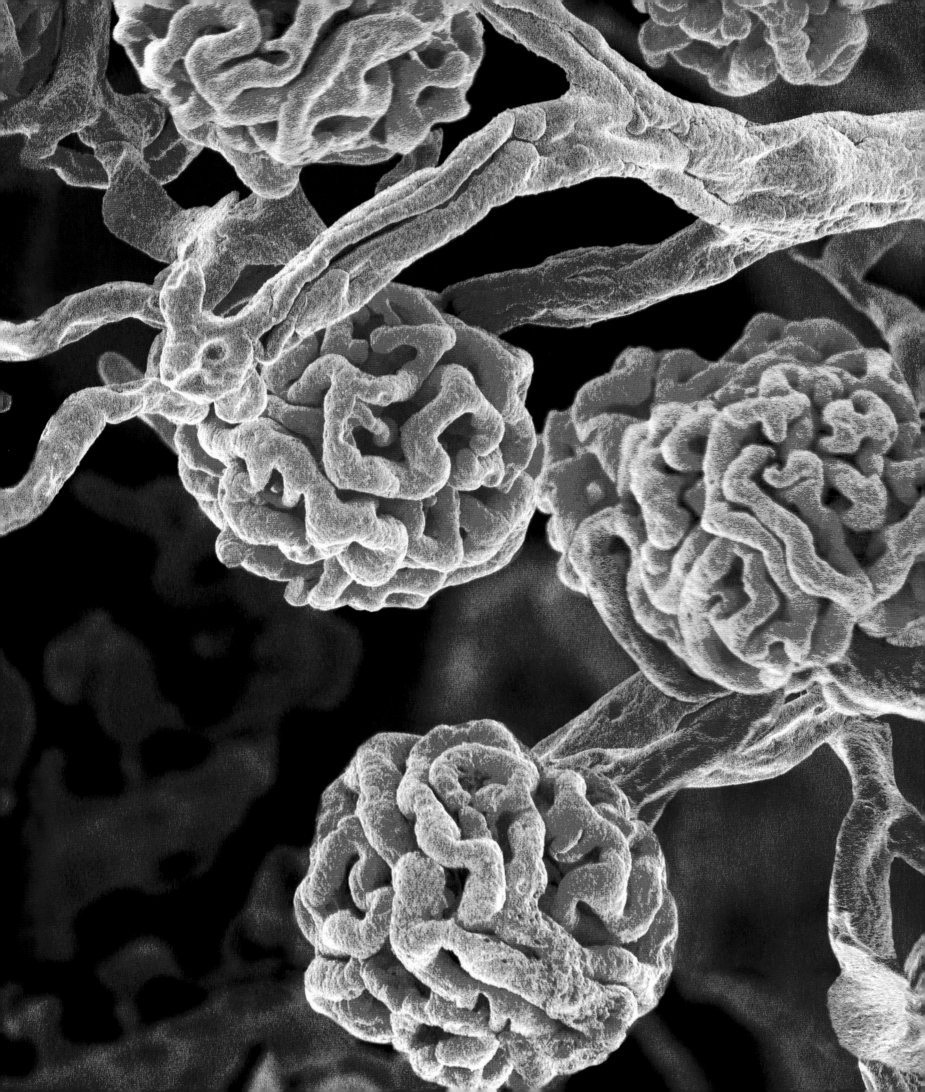

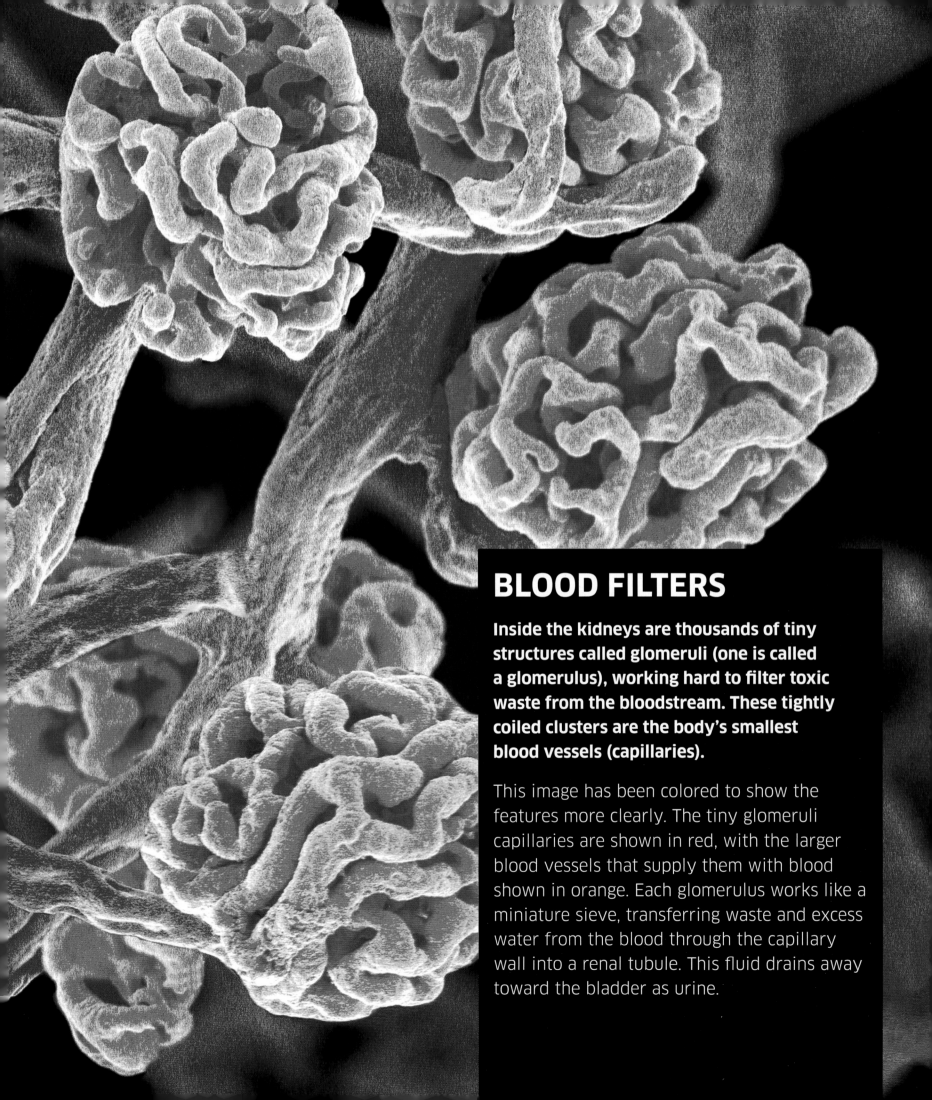

BLOOD FILTERS

Inside the kidneys are thousands of tiny structures called glomeruli (one is called a glomerulus), working hard to filter toxic waste from the bloodstream. These tightly coiled clusters are the body's smallest blood vessels (capillaries).

This image has been colored to show the features more clearly. The tiny glomeruli capillaries are shown in red, with the larger blood vessels that supply them with blood shown in orange. Each glomerulus works like a miniature sieve, transferring waste and excess water from the blood through the capillary wall into a renal tubule. This fluid drains away toward the bladder as urine.

WATER FOR LIFE

The body needs water to stay alive. Every cell, tissue, and organ relies on a regular water supply to function properly. Water makes up more than half of the body. It is found inside cells, as well as in blood and other fluids, such as lymph, tears, saliva, sweat, and urine. The brain constantly monitors water levels inside the body so it can make sure it maintains the correct balance.

WATER LEVELS

The amount of water in a person depends on their age, gender, and weight. The more water-rich muscles they have, the higher their water content. As we grow older, muscles shrink and water levels drop.

Bodies of water

A newborn baby is almost three-quarters water—and the proportion of water in the body drops gradually from then on. Men contain more water than women, as they usually have more water-containing muscle.

74%
NEWBORN BABY

60%
MAN

50%
WOMAN

40%
ELDERLY PERSON

Body chemistry

Water is an essential ingredient of body cells. The millions of chemical reactions that power life take place in the water contained in the body's cells. Different body tissues contain varying amounts of water, depending on their function. Muscle contains three times more water than bone.

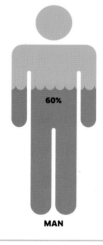
BLOOD 83% WATER

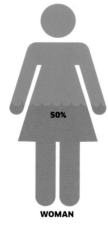
MUSCLE 75% WATER

FAT 25% WATER

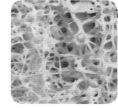
BONE 22% WATER

AN AVERAGE HUMAN **CAN SURVIVE FOR AROUND 100 HOURS** WITHOUT DRINKING WATER.

IN AND OUT

The body needs the right amount of water inside it. We constantly lose water, so we eat and drink to replace it and maintain the correct balance.

Water ways
This image shows how the water we take in compares with the water that exits in different ways, such as breathing, sweating, and urinating.

WATER IN

WATER OUT

Urine, 60%
Most of the water we lose is in the form of urine, produced by the kidneys.

Drinks, 60%
Most of the fluid entering the body comes from regular drinking.

Food, 30%
All the foods we eat contain some water.

Breathing out, 25%
Water inside the lungs exits with exhaled air.

Sweat, 8%
The body keeps cool by sweating, when water evaporates on the skin's surface.

Feces, 4%
Solid waste leaving the body contains some water.

Metabolic water, 10%
This is made by chemical activity inside the cells, as they turn fuel and oxygen into energy.

Other, less than 3%
This includes saliva, tears, mucus, and blood.

WORKING WATER

Water does many different jobs. It helps provide a transportation system around the body. It also regulates body temperature and lubricates parts so they work better.

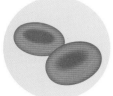

Blood
Blood is mostly water, so it flows easily through blood vessels.

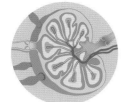

Lymph
Watery lymph flows around the body, recycling chemicals and fighting germs.

Saliva
Saliva moistens foods to help with eating and also kills germs in the mouth.

Sweat
Sweat is released through skin pores to help cool the body down.

Urine
Urine is a mix of excess water and chemicals from the blood.

Joints
Many moving joints have a lubricating layer of liquid, called synovial fluid.

Tissue fluids
Body tissues contain water, with lean tissue holding more than fatty tissue.

Cell cytoplasm
Cells need water for the chemical reactions that take place inside them.

URINE TEST

Urine can provide valuable clues about health. Dark urine is a sign that a person is dehydrated and needs to drink more. Tests can also detect pregnancy, some infections, hormone changes, and diabetes.

Urine sample
To test urine, a testing strip is dipped into a sample. The colored bands react to different chemicals in the urine, revealing any abnormalities.

What is in urine?

Urine is 94 percent water. The rest is made up of dissolved substances the body has no use for. They include sodium, which is excess salt, and urea, the waste produced by the liver.

WATER MAKES UP 94% OF URINE

Urea, 3.5%
Sodium, 1%
Other substances, 1.5%

WATER BALANCE

The hypothalamus in the brain is responsible for monitoring water levels. If it detects too little or too much water, it responds by telling the pituitary gland to release hormones that communicate with the kidneys and other organs.

Too little water

A shortage of water in the body is called dehydration. The body needs to take in more water and also to conserve the water already inside it.

■ **Low water alert**
The pituitary gland releases a hormone into the bloodstream.

■ **Feeling thirsty**
The hormone triggers an urge to drink.

■ **Dry mouth**
The mouth feels dry, as water is sent to areas that need it more.

■ **Kidneys**
The kidneys receive instructions to remove less water from the blood, so the body produces less urine.

A HUMAN DRINKS AN **AVERAGE OF 158,500 PINTS (75,000 LITERS)** OF WATER IN A LIFETIME.

Too much water

Too much water in the body is called overhydration. This condition is rare, but can be caused by illness or by drinking a large amount very quickly. Cells become too waterlogged to work and the blood pressure becomes too high.

■ **High water alert**
The hypothalamus orders blood vessels to widen, which reduces blood pressure.

■ **Kidneys**
The kidneys are ordered to extract more water from the blood, making more urine.

SALTWATER

The water inside our bodies is salty—in fact, it is as salty as seawater. Salt, or sodium, helps maintain the body's water balance—the amount of salt dissolved in the blood tells the hypothalamus how much water the kidneys should release as urine, and how much to keep. Alongside potassium, salt also plays an essential role in helping nerve cells make signals.

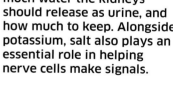

Salt sizes
Salt makes up about 0.4 percent of our body weight. A child's body contains the equivalent of 28 teaspoons of salt, while an adult's body has 40 teaspoons.

Female reproduction

From her teenage years to about her mid-fifties, the role of a woman's reproductive organs is, in combination with a man's sex cells (sperm), to create new human life—a baby.

A woman's main reproductive organs are her ovaries and uterus. The two ovaries are where eggs are stored, then released at regular intervals. If an egg is fertilized by male sperm, the job of the uterus is to nurture and protect the egg as it develops—first into an embryo, then a fetus, which grows into a baby, ready to be born.

Inside the reproductive system

This cross section shows a side view of the female reproductive organs. The uterus is in the middle of the lower abdomen, between the bladder and the rectum. The two ovaries are on either side of the uterus, connected to it by the fallopian tubes.

Ripe egg
This egg is mature and ready for release.

Follicle

Immature egg

Medulla
This contains blood vessels.

Inside an ovary
The ovaries contain many thousands of immature eggs, each enclosed in a baglike follicle. Every month, hormones trigger a process where one of the eggs starts to outgrow the others. When it is mature, the egg is released from the ovary.

Preparing for pregnancy

Every month or so, a woman's body goes through the process of preparing for a possible pregnancy. This sequence is called the menstrual cycle.

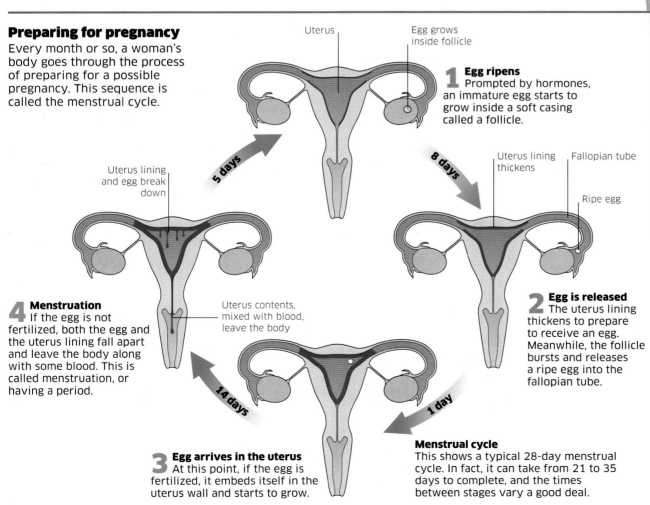

Uterus

Egg grows inside follicle

1 Egg ripens
Prompted by hormones, an immature egg starts to grow inside a soft casing called a follicle.

5 days

8 days

Uterus lining thickens

Fallopian tube

Ripe egg

Uterus lining and egg break down

4 Menstruation
If the egg is not fertilized, both the egg and the uterus lining fall apart and leave the body along with some blood. This is called menstruation, or having a period.

Uterus contents, mixed with blood, leave the body

2 Egg is released
The uterus lining thickens to prepare to receive an egg. Meanwhile, the follicle bursts and releases a ripe egg into the fallopian tube.

14 days

1 day

3 Egg arrives in the uterus
At this point, if the egg is fertilized, it embeds itself in the uterus wall and starts to grow.

Menstrual cycle
This shows a typical 28-day menstrual cycle. In fact, it can take from 21 to 35 days to complete, and the times between stages vary a good deal.

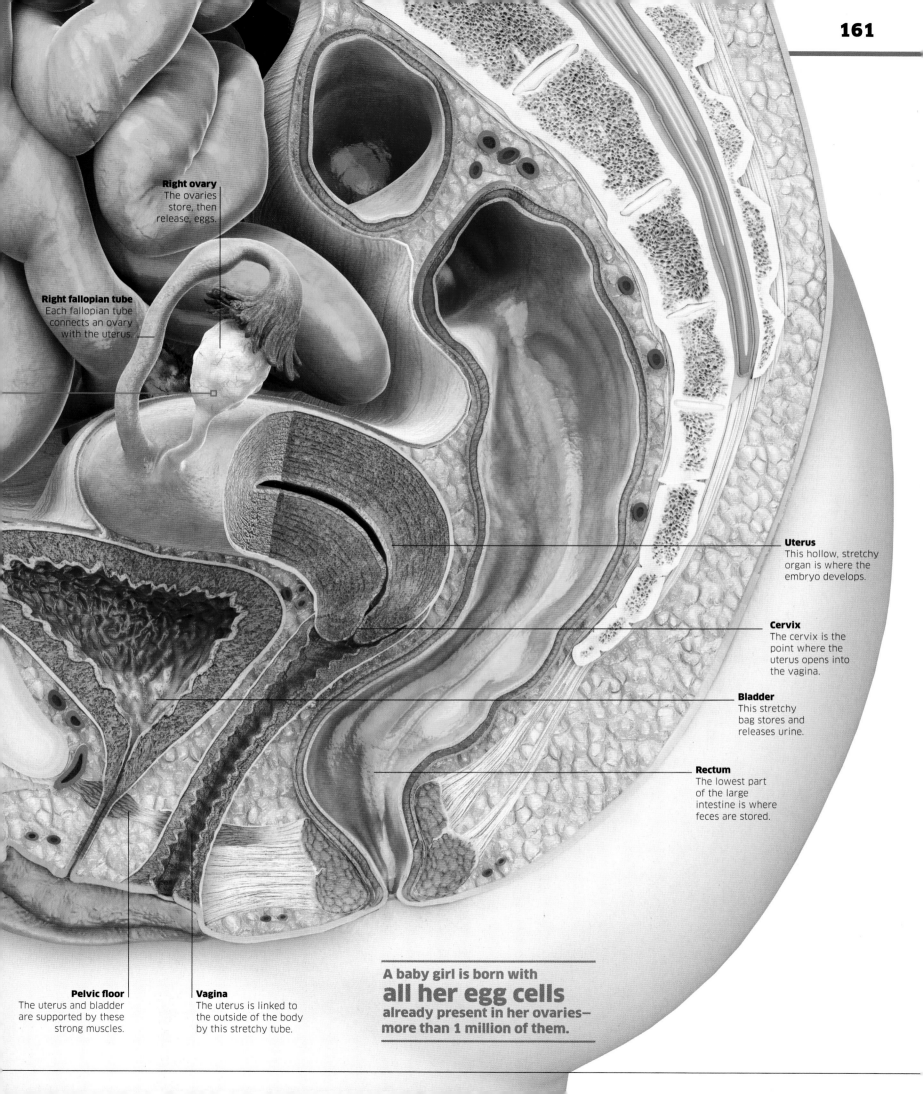

Right ovary
The ovaries
store, then
release, eggs.

Right fallopian tube
Each fallopian tube
connects an ovary
with the uterus.

Uterus
This hollow, stretchy
organ is where the
embryo develops.

Cervix
The cervix is the
point where the
uterus opens into
the vagina.

Bladder
This stretchy
bag stores and
releases urine.

Rectum
The lowest part
of the large
intestine is where
feces are stored.

Pelvic floor
The uterus and bladder
are supported by these
strong muscles.

Vagina
The uterus is linked to
the outside of the body
by this stretchy tube.

A baby girl is born with
all her egg cells
already present in her ovaries—
more than 1 million of them.

Inside the reproductive system

The testes and penis, which are outside the body, are connected by a series of internal tubes and glands. The whole male reproductive system is adapted to produce, mature, and transport sperm to where they can fertilize a female egg.

A man's testes make about
100 million
sperm every day.

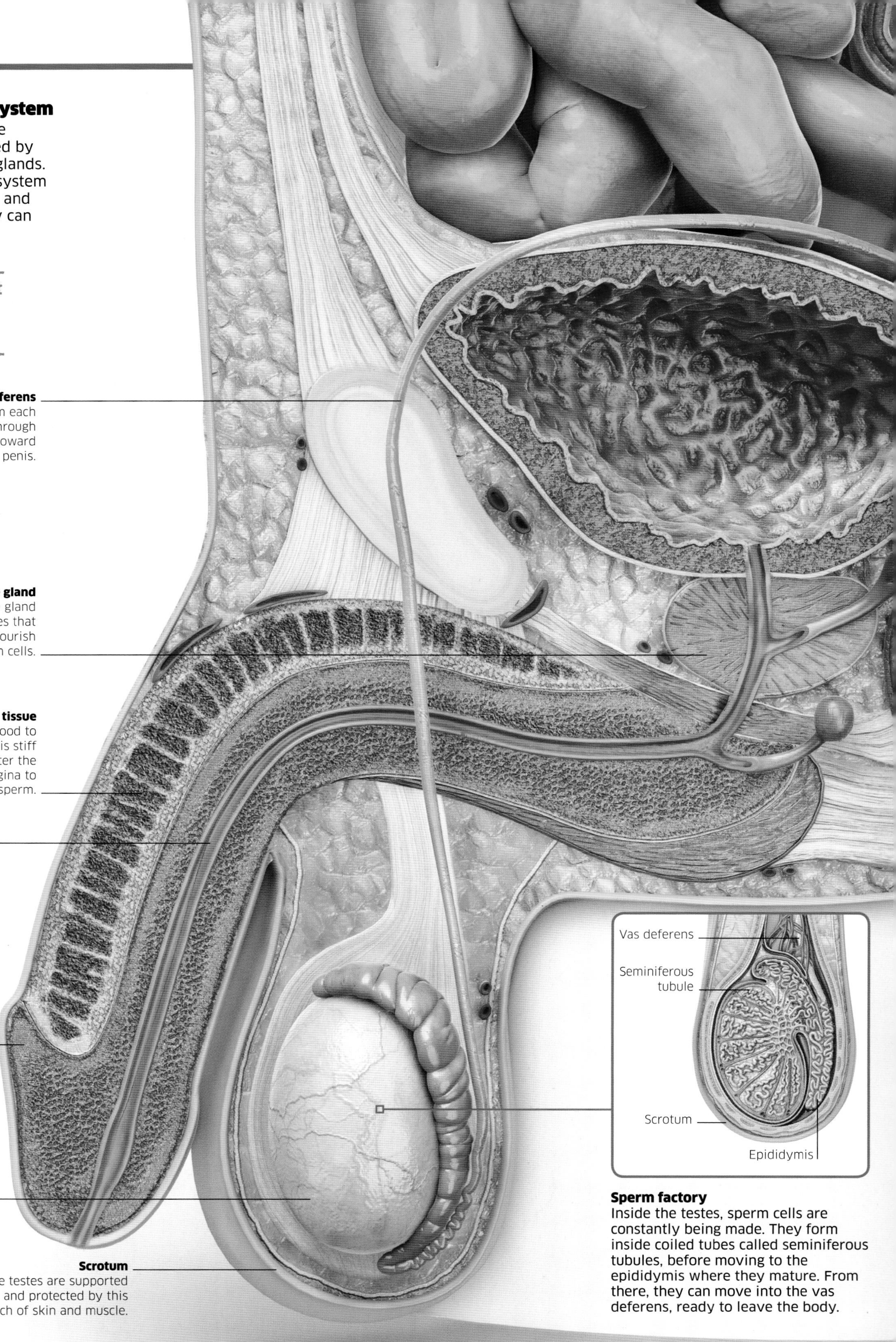

Vas deferens
Sperm from each testis pass through this tube toward the penis.

Prostate gland
The prostate gland adds substances that protect and nourish the sperm cells.

Erectile tissue
This fills with blood to make the penis stiff enough to enter the woman's vagina to deliver sperm.

Urethra
Sperm-carrying semen leaves the body through this tube.

Penis
The penis transfers sperm into a woman's vagina.

Testis
Also called testicles, the two testes make and release sperm cells.

Scrotum
The testes are supported and protected by this pouch of skin and muscle.

Vas deferens

Seminiferous tubule

Scrotum

Epididymis

Sperm factory
Inside the testes, sperm cells are constantly being made. They form inside coiled tubes called seminiferous tubules, before moving to the epididymis where they mature. From there, they can move into the vas deferens, ready to leave the body.

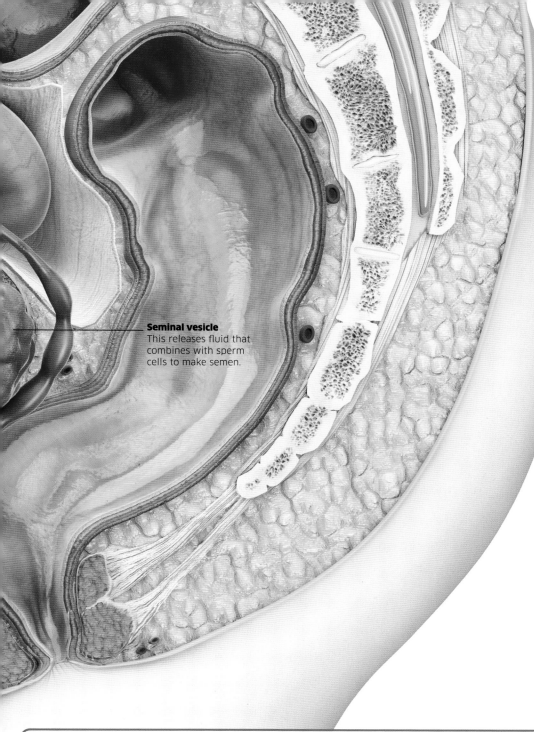

Seminal vesicle
This releases fluid that combines with sperm cells to make semen.

Sperm cells

Sperm cells are among the tiniest human cells, but the nucleus carries half the genetic instructions for creating a new life. Sperm are well adapted to produce enough energy for the long swim to the female egg.

Nucleus

The midpiece is packed with energy-producing mitochondria.

The tail's whiplike action propels the sperm forward.

Male reproduction

The male reproductive organs' role in creating new life is to make sperm (sex cells). The sperm swim to a female egg, where one of them joins with it to create a fertilized egg that will grow into a baby.

A man's main reproductive organs are the testes and penis. The two testes are where sperm are made and stored. Each testis is connected to a tube, which carries the sperm to the penis. On the way, the sperm mix with other substances to make a liquid called semen. During the act of sexual intercourse, the penis becomes stiff and is inserted into a woman's vagina, where it releases the sperm-containing semen.

Fertilization race

To join with an egg, sperm cells must complete the 8–12 in (20–30 cm) journey from the woman's vagina, via the uterus, to the egg in her fallopian tube. This is the equivalent of a 6-mile (10-km) swim for a human. Millions of sperm begin the journey, but just a few survive to reach the egg—and only one will fertilize it.

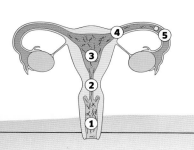

0 HOURS

UP TO 72 HOURS

Sperm ___ Egg

① **Vagina** 250 million sperm	**②** **Cervix** 70 million sperm	**③** **Uterus** 100,000 sperm	**④** **Fallopian tube** A few thousand sperm	**⑤** **Egg** Fewer than 50 sperm
The race begins The vagina is an acidic environment for the sperm. Millions don't make it beyond this stage.	**Through the gap** The surviving sperm swim through the entrance to the uterus, which is slightly open.	**The race gets tough** Many sperm fail to get through the cervix's protective mucus. The successful ones now face attack from immune system cells in the uterus.	**The last effort** Uterus muscles contract to push the sperm toward the fallopian tubes. Half of them swim toward the correct tube, where the egg is.	**Fertilization** A handful of sperm arrive at the egg. Only one succeeds in burrowing through the egg's outer layer to fertilize it.

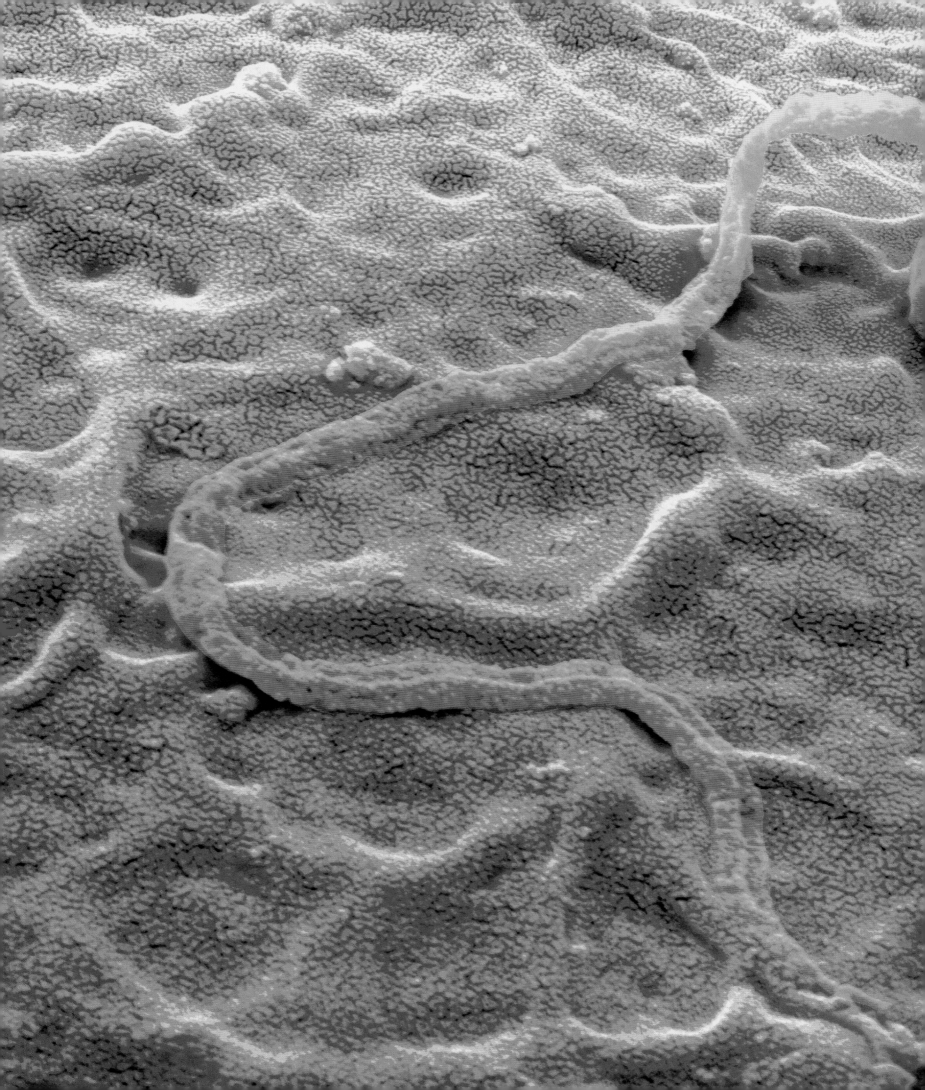

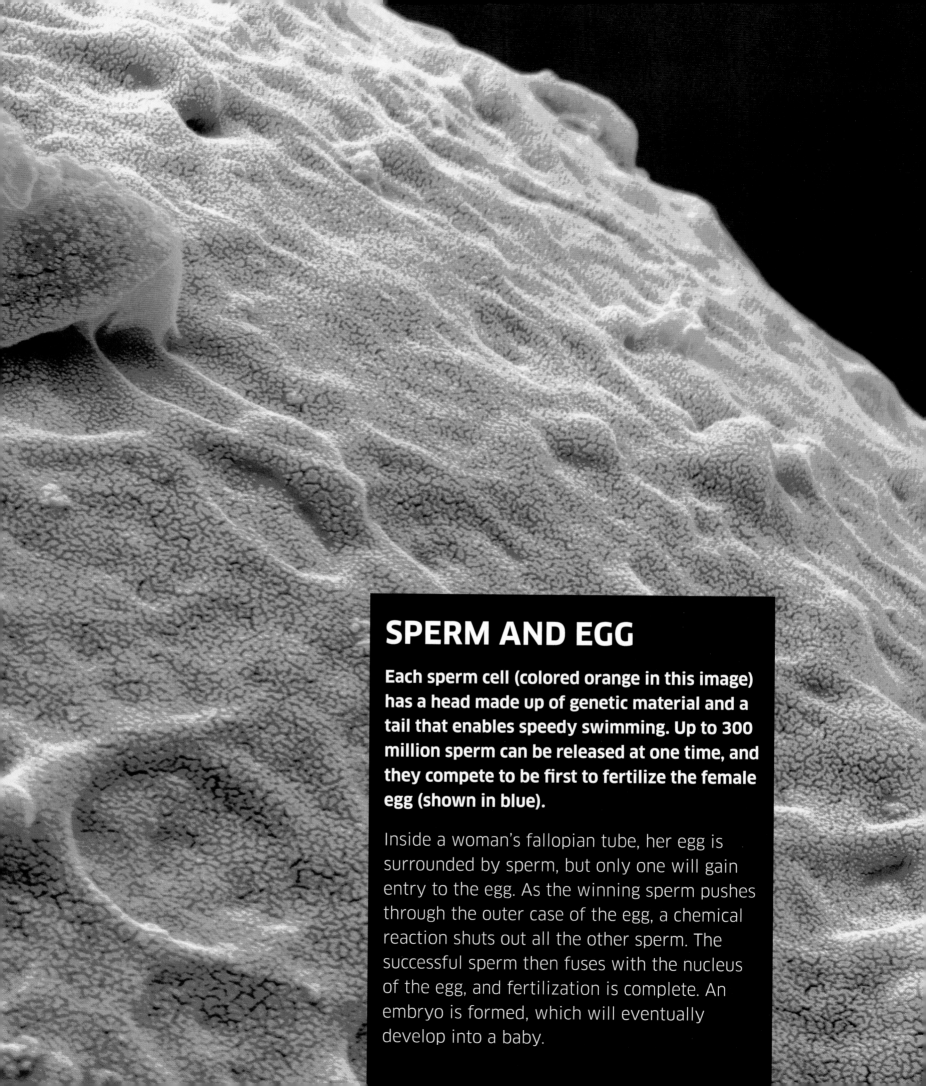

SPERM AND EGG

Each sperm cell (colored orange in this image) has a head made up of genetic material and a tail that enables speedy swimming. Up to 300 million sperm can be released at one time, and they compete to be first to fertilize the female egg (shown in blue).

Inside a woman's fallopian tube, her egg is surrounded by sperm, but only one will gain entry to the egg. As the winning sperm pushes through the outer case of the egg, a chemical reaction shuts out all the other sperm. The successful sperm then fuses with the nucleus of the egg, and fertilization is complete. An embryo is formed, which will eventually develop into a baby.

The growing fetus

Once a sperm cell and an egg cell join, the fertilized egg begins to grow inside the woman's uterus. During pregnancy the female body becomes a complete support system for the unborn baby.

It takes almost nine months for the fertilized egg to become a fully formed baby. Throughout this time, the uterus provides protection and warmth. As the baby develops, the uterus stretches until it is larger than any other organ in the body. The growing fetus shows in the pregnant woman's "bump" at the front of her abdomen.

A fetus begins its development as a single cell—and nine months later, the newborn baby's body consists of about 3 trillion cells.

Villi
The placenta is packed with tiny fingerlike growths. They absorb oxygen and nutrients from the mother's blood, ready to pass to the fetus.

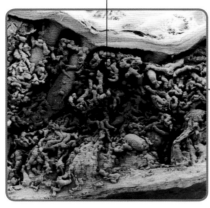

Placenta
The placenta, which is attached to the lining of the uterus, is the fetus's life-support system. It supplies the baby with oxygen and fuel, and also takes waste away, via the umbilical cord.

Amniotic fluid
The amniotic fluid is a mixture of water and nutrients that helps the fetus to grow and cushions it from knocks and jolts.

Uterus
The stretchy uterus expands as the fetus grows inside it.

Skin
A white substance called vernix gives the skin a waterproof coating.

Stages of growth

For the first eight weeks of pregnancy the developing baby is called an embryo. After eight weeks it is known as a fetus. The fetus develops quickly, doubling in weight every five weeks and changing shape as more body parts grow.

Week 5
The embryo is the size of an apple seed. It already has buds from which the arms and legs will grow.

Week 10
The fetus is the size of an olive. All the major organs have grown, new limbs are moving, and its heartbeat is three times faster than that of an adult.

Week 20
The fetus is as long as a banana. It has a big head, a growing brain, and fingers and toes. When the eyes first open, at about week 26, they will be able to detect light and dark.

Full-term fetus
After about 40 weeks, the fetus is fully developed and weighs about 7 lb 12 oz (3.5 kg). It fits tightly inside the uterus, surrounded bya liquid called amniotic fluid. There is little room to move, so it keeps a curled-up position with its limbs bent.

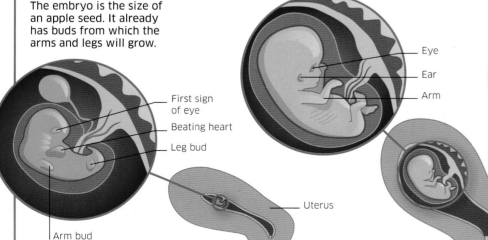

First sign of eye
Beating heart
Leg bud
Arm bud
Uterus
Eye
Ear
Arm
Big head
Eyes shut
Fingers form
Toes form

First breath

When the baby is ready to be born, the mother goes into labor. Giving birth can take anything from less than hour to more than 24 hours. Strong contractions of the uterus push the baby out. The newborn starts to breathe for herself, taking oxygen from the air instead of via the umbilical cord.

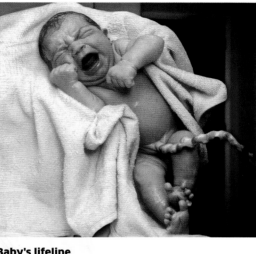

Baby's lifeline
Throughout pregnancy, the umbilical cord connected the fetus to its mother. As soon as the baby is born, the cord is no longer needed and can be cut off.

Umbilical cord
Oxygen is supplied to the fetus through the blood vessels of the umbilical cord.

Head
The head of the fetus is positioned downward, ready for birth.

Mucus plug
A layer of thick mucus seals the entrance to the uterus, keeping out infection.

Birth canal
Also called the vagina, this is the narrow passage the baby will pass along to be born.

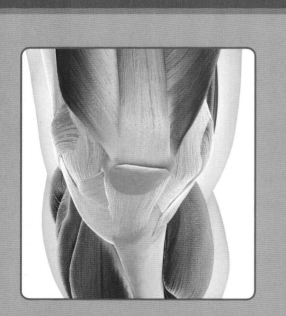

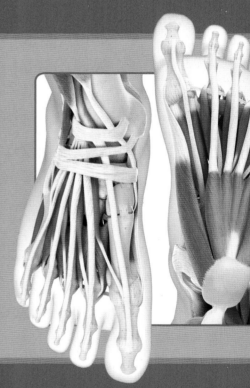

LEGS AND FEET

Our lower limbs are strong, flexible, and powerful. As we move, the bones, joints, and muscles work together to drive our bodies forward. Our feet form a secure base, carry our body weight, and push against the ground to help us walk.

The **gluteus maximus** or buttock muscle is the **biggest muscle** in the human body.

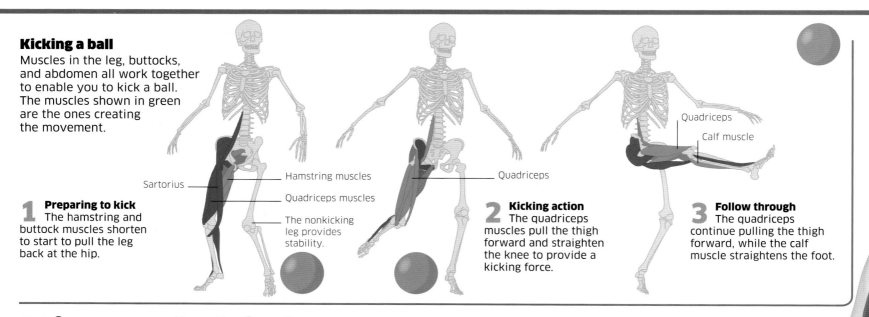

Kicking a ball

Muscles in the leg, buttocks, and abdomen all work together to enable you to kick a ball. The muscles shown in green are the ones creating the movement.

Sartorius

Hamstring muscles

Quadriceps muscles

The nonkicking leg provides stability.

1 Preparing to kick
The hamstring and buttock muscles shorten to start to pull the leg back at the hip.

Quadriceps

2 Kicking action
The quadriceps muscles pull the thigh forward and straighten the knee to provide a kicking force.

Quadriceps

Calf muscle

3 Follow through
The quadriceps continue pulling the thigh forward, while the calf muscle straightens the foot.

Hip and thigh

Unlike most mammals, humans walk upright on two legs. The joints, muscles, and bones of the hip and thigh have to support the downward push of your body as you walk, run, or jump, so they need to be very strong and stable.

The hip and thigh are connected at the hip joint. This joint has to be able to move in a wide range of directions, while staying firm and strong so you don't fall over. When we perform movements such as kicking a ball or dancing, the body is often balanced on just one leg at a time. This means that each side has to be able to hold up the whole body.

Inside the hip and thigh

The femur, or thighbone, connects to the lower part of the pelvis. Surrounding these bones are some of the body's most powerful muscles, which work both to control movement and to pull the body upright.

Gluteus maximus (buttock muscle)
The gluteus maximus is a powerful muscle that helps extend the thigh.

Adductor magnus
The thigh is pulled inward by this muscle.

Semimembranosus
This muscle bends the knee and extends the hip.

Gracilis
The hip is pulled inward by this muscle.

Swinging hips

The mobile hip joint enables the legs to move in three main ways: from side to side, up and down, and rotating, both inward and outward.

Adduction and abduction
This is the sideways movement toward and away from the midline of the body.

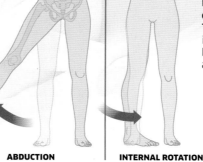

Internal and external rotation
The leg is turned in toward the body, or outward away from it.

ADDUCTION

ABDUCTION

INTERNAL ROTATION

EXTERNAL ROTATION

EXTENSION

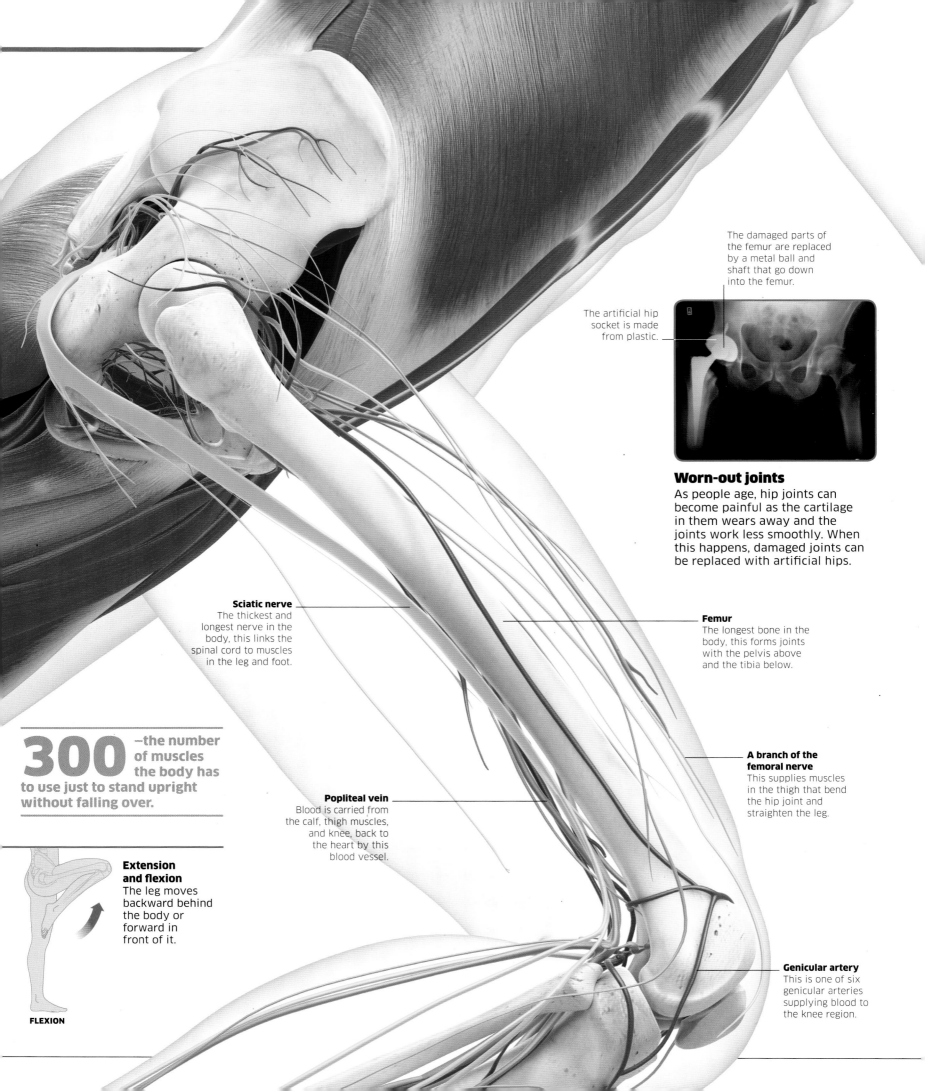

The damaged parts of the femur are replaced by a metal ball and shaft that go down into the femur.

The artificial hip socket is made from plastic.

Worn-out joints

As people age, hip joints can become painful as the cartilage in them wears away and the joints work less smoothly. When this happens, damaged joints can be replaced with artificial hips.

Sciatic nerve
The thickest and longest nerve in the body, this links the spinal cord to muscles in the leg and foot.

Femur
The longest bone in the body, this forms joints with the pelvis above and the tibia below.

A branch of the femoral nerve
This supplies muscles in the thigh that bend the hip joint and straighten the leg.

300 —the number of muscles the body has to use just to stand upright without falling over.

Popliteal vein
Blood is carried from the calf, thigh muscles, and knee, back to the heart by this blood vessel.

Extension and flexion
The leg moves backward behind the body or forward in front of it.

FLEXION

Genicular artery
This is one of six genicular arteries supplying blood to the knee region.

Inside a bone

The bones in a human body are strong to support our mass, but light enough for us to move around easily. They are also slightly flexible, so they are less likely to snap if they are knocked or jarred. Their remarkable structure is what gives bones these different qualities.

A bone's outer layer is made of hard, heavy, compact bone. Within this is a layer of spongy bone—tiny struts of hard bone with spaces in between. This honeycomb structure makes bones light but strong. Like tooth enamel, bone is made of calcium minerals, which make it hard. But unlike enamel, it also contains a stretchy substance called collagen, which gives flexibility.

Longest bone
The femur, or thighbone, is the longest and heaviest bone in the body. The femur is tremendously strong, to withstand the massive forces exerted on it during walking, running, or jumping.

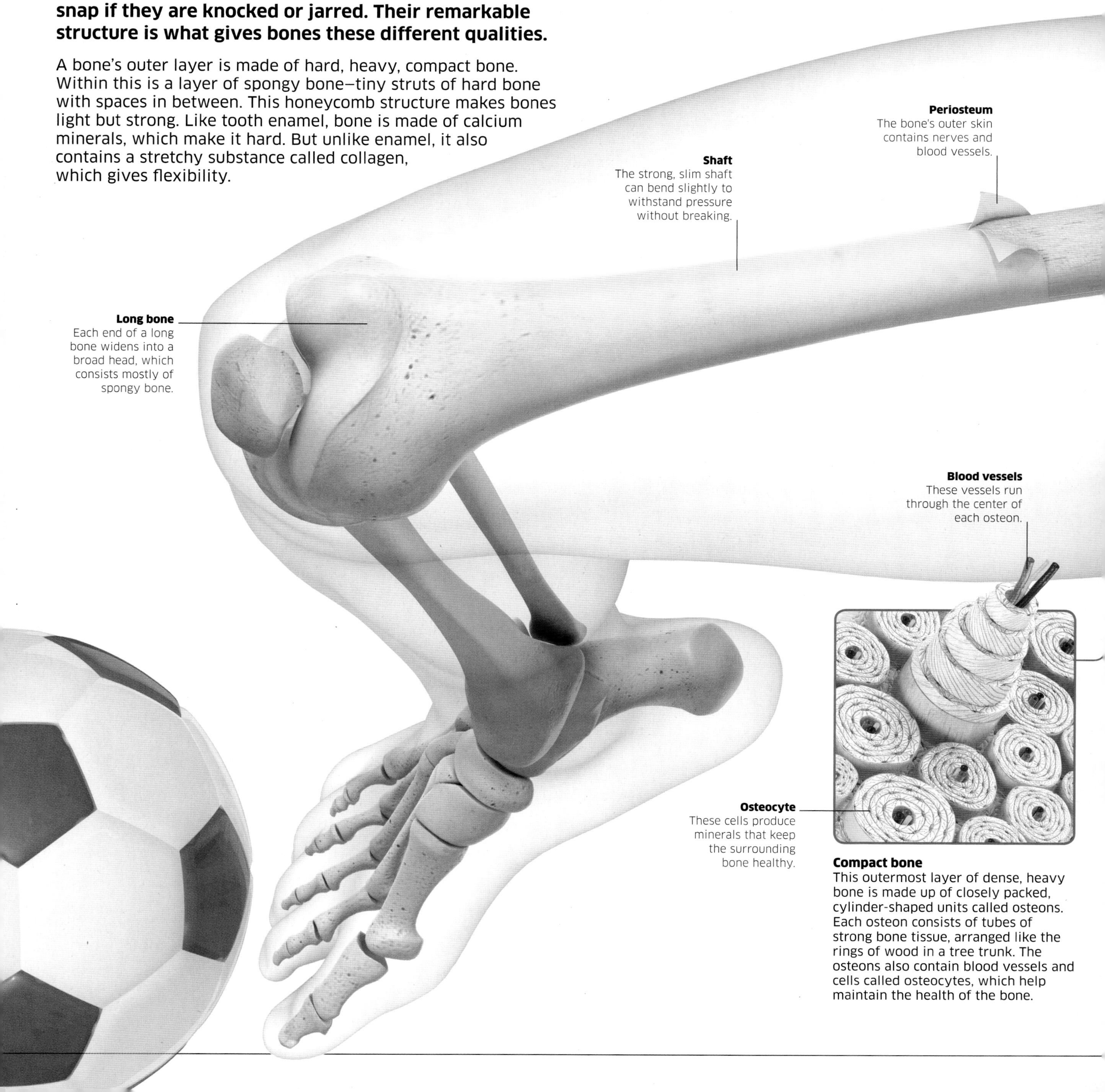

Periosteum
The bone's outer skin contains nerves and blood vessels.

Shaft
The strong, slim shaft can bend slightly to withstand pressure without breaking.

Long bone
Each end of a long bone widens into a broad head, which consists mostly of spongy bone.

Blood vessels
These vessels run through the center of each osteon.

Osteocyte
These cells produce minerals that keep the surrounding bone healthy.

Compact bone
This outermost layer of dense, heavy bone is made up of closely packed, cylinder-shaped units called osteons. Each osteon consists of tubes of strong bone tissue, arranged like the rings of wood in a tree trunk. The osteons also contain blood vessels and cells called osteocytes, which help maintain the health of the bone.

Human bone is **five times stronger** than a **steel bar** of the same weight.

15%
of an adult's mass is taken up by their bones.

Spongy bone
This honeycomblike bone has spaces in it, like a sponge—but it's firm, not squishy.

Blood vessels
These supply energy-giving oxygen and nutrients.

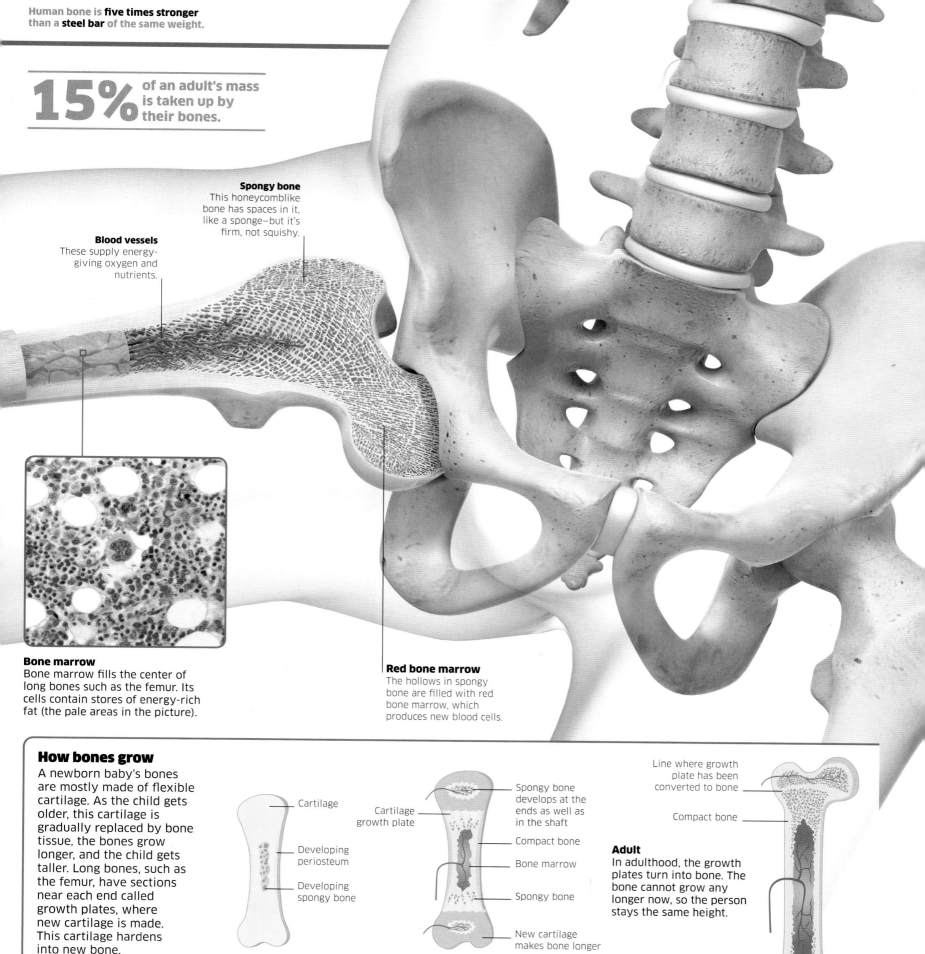

Bone marrow
Bone marrow fills the center of long bones such as the femur. Its cells contain stores of energy-rich fat (the pale areas in the picture).

Red bone marrow
The hollows in spongy bone are filled with red bone marrow, which produces new blood cells.

How bones grow
A newborn baby's bones are mostly made of flexible cartilage. As the child gets older, this cartilage is gradually replaced by bone tissue, the bones grow longer, and the child gets taller. Long bones, such as the femur, have sections near each end called growth plates, where new cartilage is made. This cartilage hardens into new bone.

Cartilage

Developing periosteum

Developing spongy bone

Newborn baby
Spongy bone first starts to form in the shaft, in the middle of the bone.

Cartilage growth plate

Spongy bone develops at the ends as well as in the shaft

Compact bone

Bone marrow

Spongy bone

New cartilage makes bone longer

Nine-year-old child
The bone shaft has hardened into bone. Growth plates at each end produce new cartilage, making the bone longer.

Line where growth plate has been converted to bone

Compact bone

Adult
In adulthood, the growth plates turn into bone. The bone cannot grow any longer now, so the person stays the same height.

Spongy bone

Layer of cartilage still covers bone ends, enabling joints to move easily

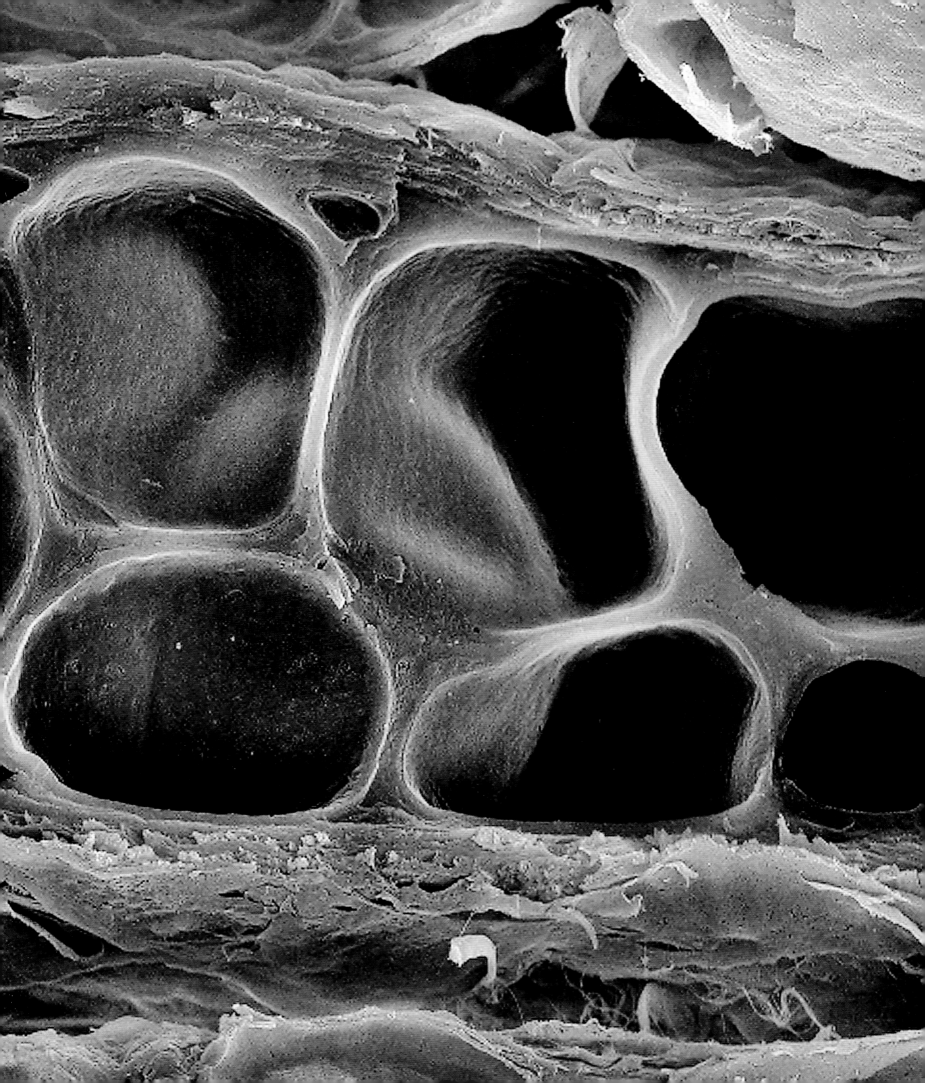

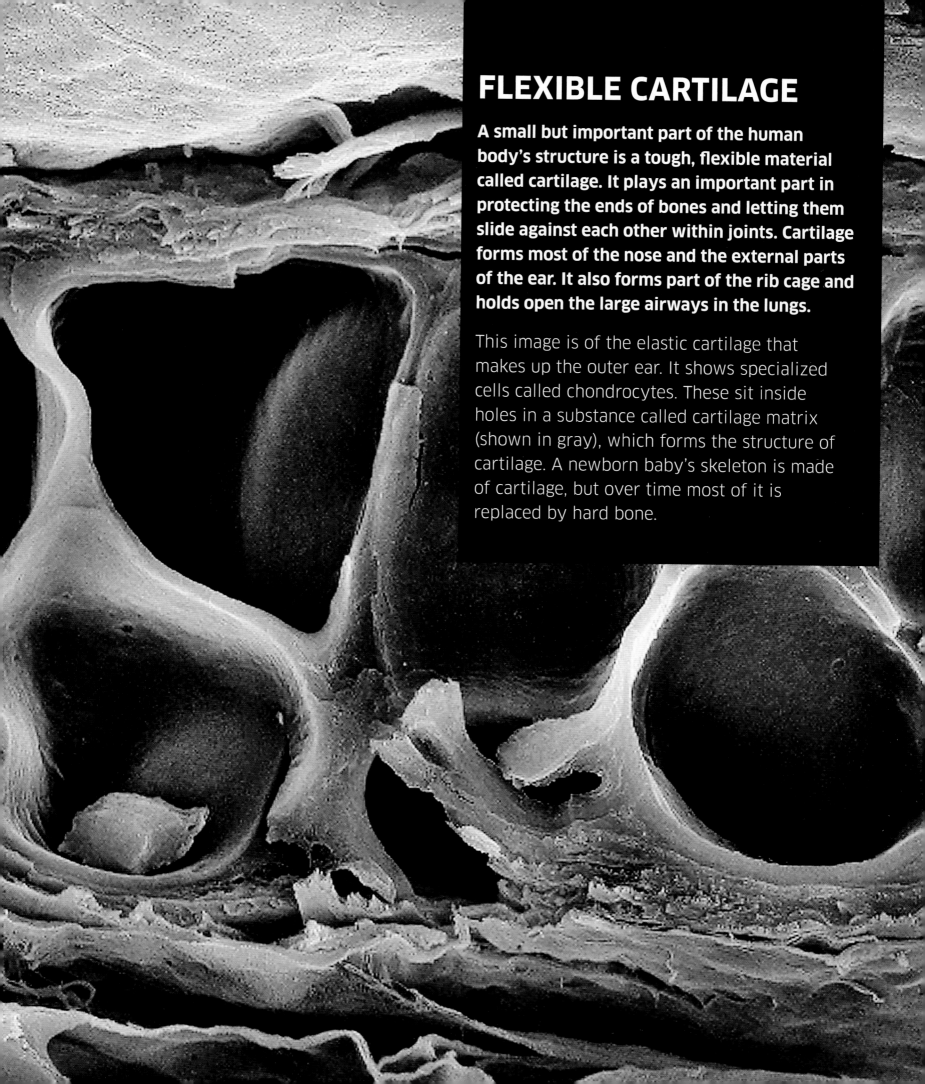

FLEXIBLE CARTILAGE

A small but important part of the human body's structure is a tough, flexible material called cartilage. It plays an important part in protecting the ends of bones and letting them slide against each other within joints. Cartilage forms most of the nose and the external parts of the ear. It also forms part of the rib cage and holds open the large airways in the lungs.

This image is of the elastic cartilage that makes up the outer ear. It shows specialized cells called chondrocytes. These sit inside holes in a substance called cartilage matrix (shown in gray), which forms the structure of cartilage. A newborn baby's skeleton is made of cartilage, but over time most of it is replaced by hard bone.

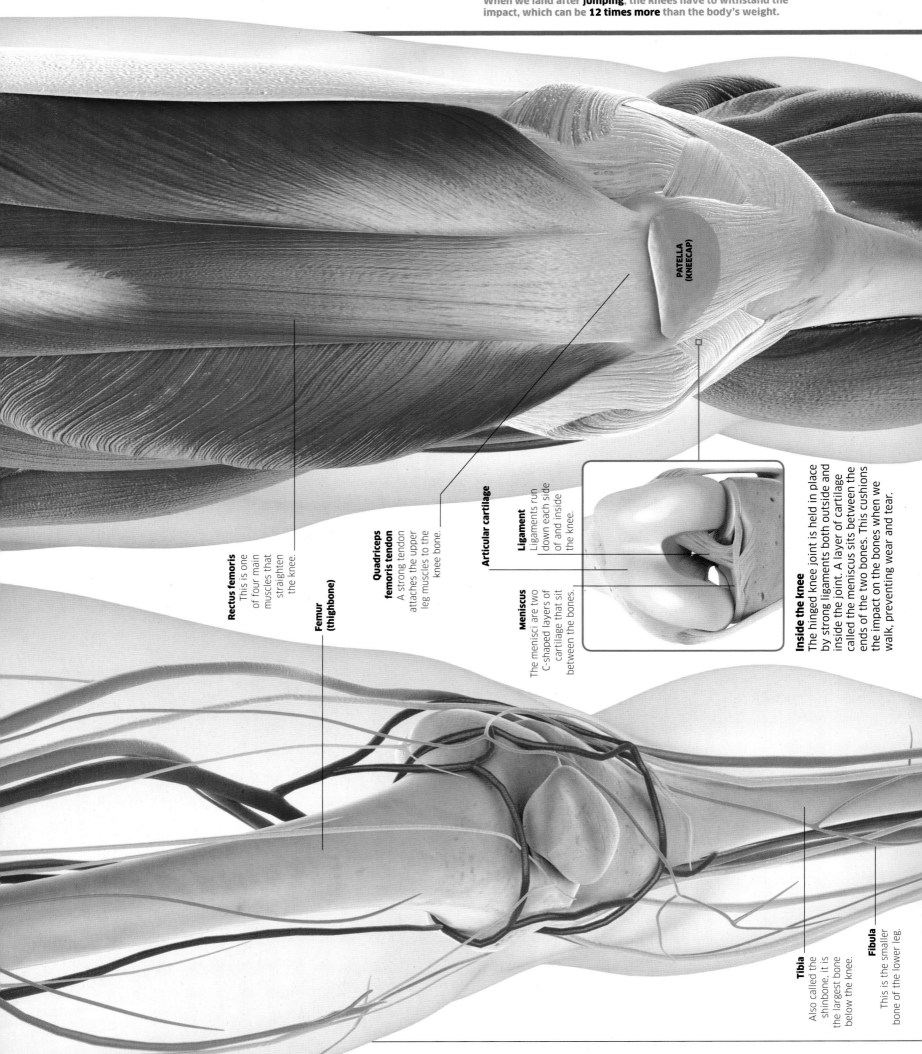

PATELLA (KNEECAP)

Rectus femoris
This is one of four main muscles that straighten the knee.

Femur (thighbone)

Quadriceps femoris tendon
A strong tendon attaches the upper leg muscles to the knee bone.

Articular cartilage

Ligament
Ligaments run down each side of and inside the knee.

Meniscus
The menisci are two C-shaped layers of cartilage that sit between the bones.

Inside the knee
The hinged knee joint is held in place by strong ligaments both outside and inside the joint. A layer of cartilage called the meniscus sits between the ends of the two bones. This cushions the impact on the bones when we walk, preventing wear and tear.

Tibia
Also called the shinbone, it is the largest bone below the knee.

Fibula
This is the smaller bone of the lower leg.

155° is the **angle a typical knee** can flex (bend), enabling us to kneel and squat.

A child's kneecaps do not **harden into bone** until he or she is about three years old.

177

Extensor digitorum longus
This muscle helps move the toes.

Extensor retinaculum
Two bands of connective tissue secure the tendons that cross the front of the ankle.

Tibialis anterior
The foot is bent upward by this muscle.

Great saphenous vein
Blood is carried away from the lower leg and foot by this vein.

Muscles

The lower leg muscles work to bend and straighten the ankle, foot, and toes. They help a person to stand, walk, run, and jump.

Broken bones

Although the lower leg bones are strong, they are among the most often broken bones. Breaks are especially common in people who play sports. The bone heals after a few months, although it may take several years for it to get back to its normal shape.

1 Immediately after injury
Blood fills the area around the break and forms a clot. The surrounding tissue is swollen and painful.

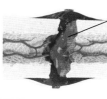

Clot forms

2 After a few days
Cartilage tissue starts to replace the clot. It forms a swelling called a callus, which joins the bone ends and gives some strength back.

Soft callus made of cartilage

New bone tissue

3 One month later
The soft callus is replaced by a hard callus of fast-growing spongy bone, then later by harder, compact bone. After about a year, the healing is complete and all swelling has gone.

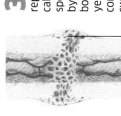

A hard callus of spongy bone is gradually replaced by compact bone.

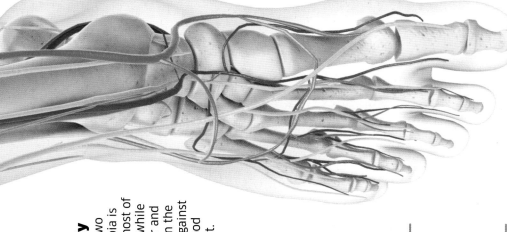

Bones, nerves, and blood supply

The lower leg has two main bones. The tibia is thicker and bears most of the body's weight, while the fibula is smaller and thinner. The veins in the legs have to fight against gravity to carry blood back up to the heart.

The tibia
is the second longest bone in the human body, after the femur.

Knee and lower leg

The leg bones are the strongest in the body. They support our full weight and withstand the impact of walking and running. The knee joint, which connects the thighbones and shinbones, is one of the body's largest joints.

Besides providing a hinge between the lower and upper leg bones, the knee has an extra bone, the kneecap. This protects the joint and helps to anchor the knee's tendons, giving the leg muscles more leverage and pulling power.

Ankle and foot

The ankles and feet must carry the weight of the rest of the body. They work together like a spring, pushing off from the ground during running or jumping, and acting as shock absorbers for landing.

Feet are complex body parts. Including the ankle joint, each foot has more than 100 bones, muscles, and ligaments. Whether standing, walking, climbing, or running, the feet can adopt different positions to help the body stay balanced. Feet also have thick skin and toenails to cushion and protect them.

150 million—the number of steps your feet are likely to take in a lifetime.

Feet first
Each foot consists of 26 bones—14 toe bones, called phalanges, five long bones in the middle, called metatarsals, and seven bones, called tarsals, forming the heel and ankle.

Key

■ Phalanges
■ Metatarsals
■ Tarsals

Bones and nerves
The bones in the foot create a roughly triangular shape, which helps to make it more stable. The arrangement is similar to the hands, but the feet are less flexible because toes are much shorter than fingers. A bundle of nerves provides the ankle and foot with sensation, and the nerves also let the muscles know when to contract.

Superficial fibular nerve
This nerve carries signals from sensors in the feet to the brain.

Anterior tibial artery
This artery carries blood to the front of the lower leg and the top of the foot.

Fibula
Paired with the tibia, this is the thinner leg bone.

Tibia
This is the largest bone in the lower leg.

Ankle bone
These hard bumps on either side of the ankle are the ends of the tibia and fibula bones in the leg.

Talus
The upper tarsal, or talus, forms the ankle joint with the leg bones.

Lateral cuneiform bone
This wedgelike bone is in the center of the foot.

Cuboid
This outer foot bone connects the heel with the fourth and fifth toes.

Great saphenous vein
This vein helps to drain blood from the foot.

Phalange
The toe bones are phalanges—the big toe has two, while the others have three.

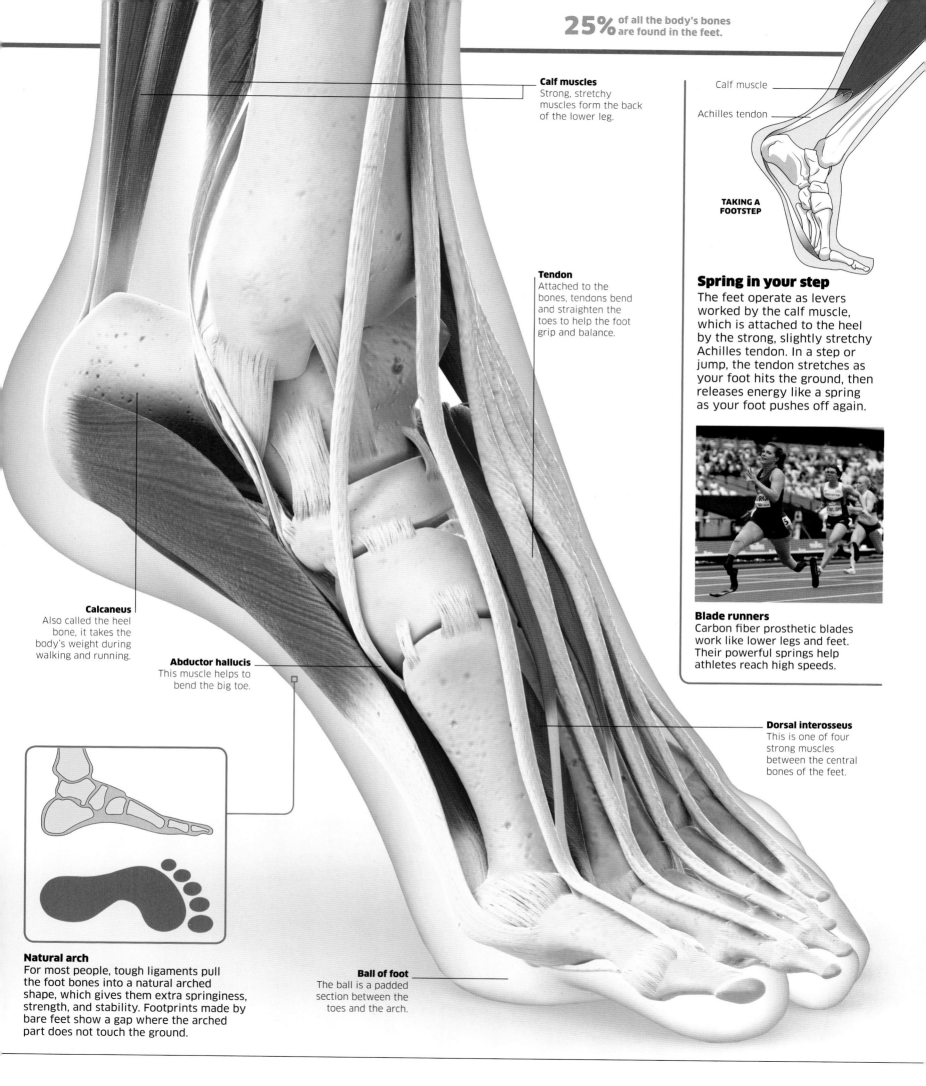

Calf muscles
Strong, stretchy muscles form the back of the lower leg.

Tendon
Attached to the bones, tendons bend and straighten the toes to help the foot grip and balance.

Calf muscle

Achilles tendon

TAKING A FOOTSTEP

Spring in your step
The feet operate as levers worked by the calf muscle, which is attached to the heel by the strong, slightly stretchy Achilles tendon. In a step or jump, the tendon stretches as your foot hits the ground, then releases energy like a spring as your foot pushes off again.

Blade runners
Carbon fiber prosthetic blades work like lower legs and feet. Their powerful springs help athletes reach high speeds.

Calcaneus
Also called the heel bone, it takes the body's weight during walking and running.

Abductor hallucis
This muscle helps to bend the big toe.

Dorsal interosseus
This is one of four strong muscles between the central bones of the feet.

Natural arch
For most people, tough ligaments pull the foot bones into a natural arched shape, which gives them extra springiness, strength, and stability. Footprints made by bare feet show a gap where the arched part does not touch the ground.

Ball of foot
The ball is a padded section between the toes and the arch.

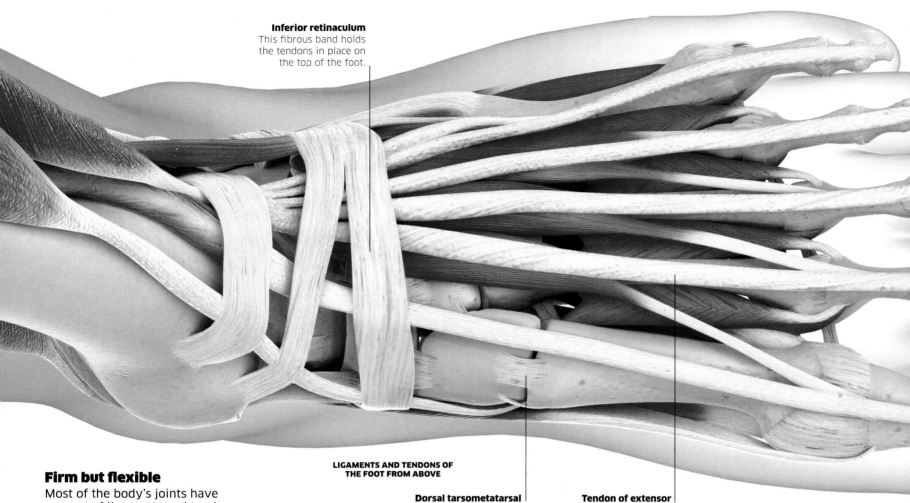

Inferior retinaculum
This fibrous band holds the tendons in place on the top of the foot.

LIGAMENTS AND TENDONS OF THE FOOT FROM ABOVE

Firm but flexible

Most of the body's joints have a group of ligaments and tendons around them. This can be seen with the ankle and foot joints shown in these two images, from above and below. Ligaments allow a joint to move freely, while preventing it from coming loose or falling apart.

Dorsal tarsometatarsal ligament
This is one of the many ligaments that join bones within the foot.

Tendon of extensor digitorum longus muscle
This is one of the tendons connecting this leg muscle to the toes.

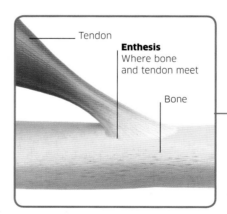

Tendon

Enthesis
Where bone and tendon meet

Bone

Making connections

At the point where tendons and ligaments join to bones, they spread out to cover a larger surface, which gives a stronger grip. Fibers, made of a protein called collagen, grow into the top layer of bone at an attachment site called an enthesis.

Ligaments and tendons

Bones and muscles allow the body to move and change position. However, they could not work without ligaments and tendons—superstrong bands that make firm but flexible connections between bones, joints, and muscles.

Strong, slightly stretchy ligaments hold together the different bones around joints such as the knee, elbow, or shoulder. Tendons do a different job. They are the tough bands that attach a muscle to a bone.

4,000 –the approximate number of tendons in the human body.

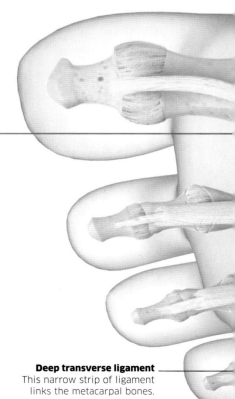

Deep transverse ligament
This narrow strip of ligament links the metacarpal bones.

People are ⅜ in (1 cm) shorter when they go to bed at night, because the joints in the spine compress as they walk around during the day.

900 –the approximate number of **ligaments** in the body.

181

Phalanges
These are the jointed bones of the toes.

Double-jointed
People with flexible bodies are often described as "double-jointed". However, these people don't have unusual joints, but extra-stretchy ligaments. Acrobats and gymnasts often have naturally loose ligaments, but still must train hard to achieve maximum flexibility.

Head held high
One of the most important ligaments in the body is the nuchal ligament, which attaches the skull to the neck bones, helping to keep the head upright and stable.

The nuchal ligament runs down the back of the neck.

Muscles add stability.

Tendons attach the muscles firmly to bones.

Stringy structure
Both ligaments and tendons are made of many bundles of collagen fibers. Collagen is a tough, stringlike protein found in many body tissues, such as bone and skin.

Densely packed collagen fibers

Tough casing

Tendon of flexor hallucis longus
This is the muscle at the back of the leg that bends the toe down.

Achilles tendon
This is the strongest and thickest tendon. It connects the calf muscle to the back of the heel.

Calcaneus (heel bone)

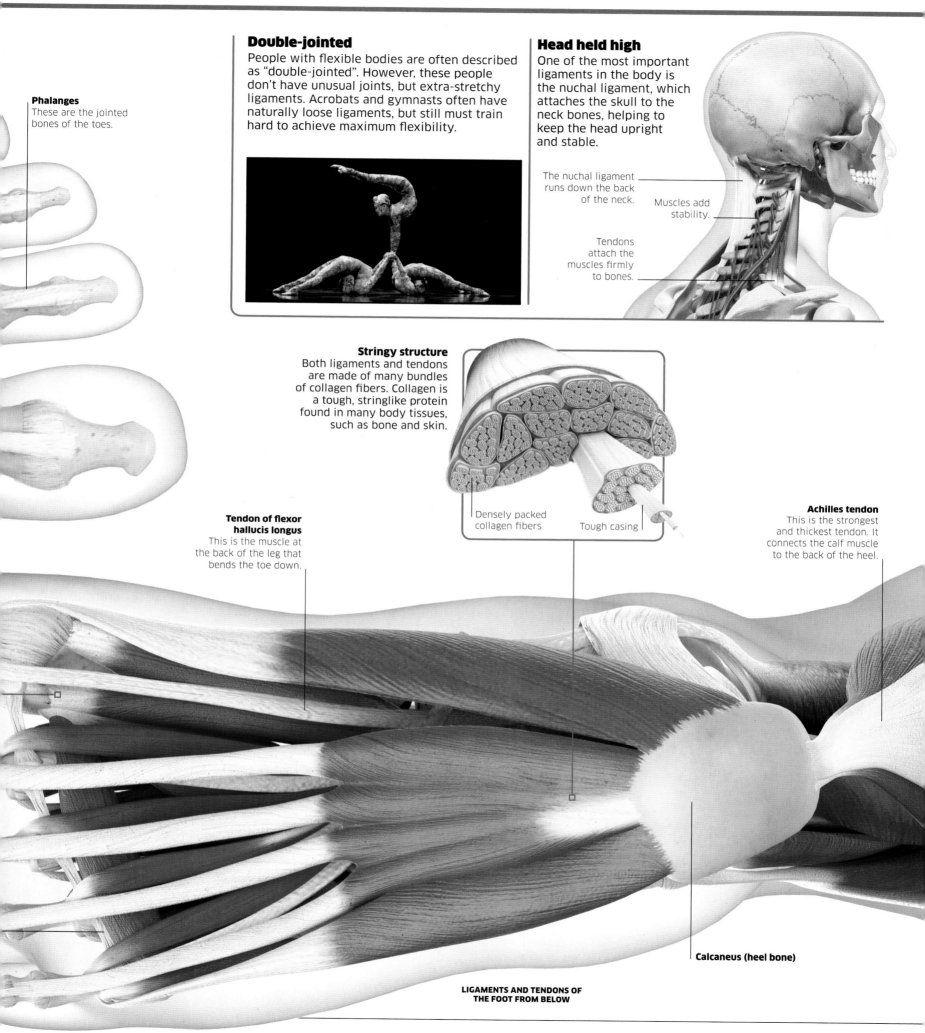

LIGAMENTS AND TENDONS OF THE FOOT FROM BELOW

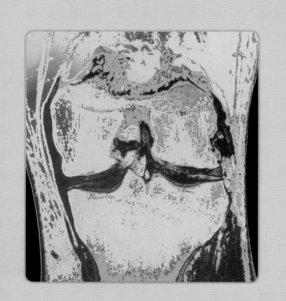

BODY SCIENCE

More is known about the human body today than ever before. Technology allows us to view the body in stunning detail, and we now understand how our lifestyle impacts health. Scientists are evolving revolutionary treatments for disease and injury, and they are even figuring out how humans could adapt to life in space!

1665: Hooke's discoveries
English researcher Robert Hooke publishes *Micrographia*, which contains drawings of things he has seen through his microscope. He coins the term "cell" for the smallest unit of life he finds.

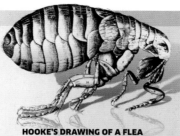

HOOKE'S DRAWING OF A FLEA

1735: Surgical success
French-born English surgeon Claudius Amyand removes the inflamed appendix of Hanvil Anderson, a young patient. To much amazement, Hanvil recovers from surgery.

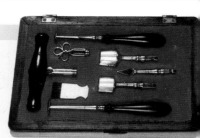

18TH-CENTURY SURGICAL INSTRUMENTS

EARLY DEPICTION OF CIRCULATION

1628: William Harvey
English doctor William Harvey explains the closed circuit of veins and arteries carrying blood around the body in the circulatory system. He understands that the heart works like a pump.

COMPOUND MICROSCOPE

1590: Compound microscope
Dutch eyeglass-maker Zacharias Janssen is said to have invented the compound microscope, a magnifying device with two or more lenses. Medical research is changed forever by this breakthrough.

Medical milestones

Humans have looked for ways to cure illnesses and heal injuries for thousands of years. The earliest people could only pray to their gods, or hope for good fortune. Gradually, as medical science progressed and knowledge of the body grew, more effective treatments were developed.

New generations of doctors and scientists build on the breakthroughs of the past. Today, we know more than ever before about how our bodies work, but there is still a lot to discover. We never stop learning about the incredibly complex machine that keeps us all alive.

c. 390 CE: Public hospital
A Roman noblewoman named Fabiola sets up the first public hospital in western Europe. She works as a nurse in her hospital and is made Saint Fabiola after her death.

SAINT FABIOLA

SURGICAL INSTRUMENTS FROM ANCIENT ROME

c. 129–200 CE: Galen
Galen is a Greek doctor who cares for several Roman emperors. He makes many discoveries by dissecting monkeys and pigs. He acts as physician to the gladiators of his hometown, Pergamon.

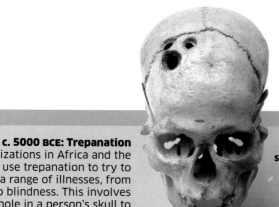

c. 5000 BCE: Trepanation
Early civilizations in Africa and the Americas use trepanation to try to cure a range of illnesses, from epilepsy to blindness. This involves drilling a hole in a person's skull to release evil spirits.

SKULL BEARING MARKS OF TREPANATION

c. 2650 BCE: Imhotep
Ancient Egyptian Imhotep is the most celebrated healer of his time, diagnosing illnesses and devising treatments for more than 200 diseases. He is worshiped as a god in Egypt, Greece, and Rome.

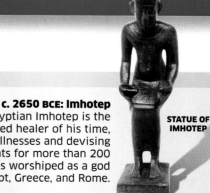

STATUE OF IMHOTEP

Before anaesthetics, surgery had to be speedy. Surgeon **Robert Liston** was said to be able to **amputate a leg** in just 30 seconds.

The **first blood transfusion** took place in 1818 when blood was transferred from a donor to a patient using a syringe.

185

1796: Smallpox vaccination
English doctor Edward Jenner performs the first successful vaccination against disease. He injects a boy with pus from a cowpox blister, and the boy becomes immune to smallpox.

PORTRAIT OF EDWARD JENNER

1816: First stethoscope
French doctor René Laennec invents the stethoscope. This simple wooden tube has evolved to become the twin earpieces now used by modern medics to listen to heartbeats.

LAENNEC'S STETHOSCOPE

EARLIEST SURVIVING EYEGLASSES

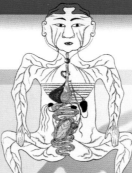

1306: First eyeglasses
A pair of eyeglasses is mentioned for the first time. This occurs in a sermon by Friar Giordano da Pisa.

1242: Blood revelation
Ibn an-Nafis of Damascus is the first to describe blood circulating between the heart and lungs. Galen had thought blood crossed from one heart chamber to the other, but an-Nafis was correct.

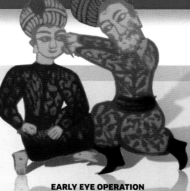

c. 1020: Cataract cure
Ammar bin Ali al-Mawsili of Iraq invents a glass tube that works like a syringe, sucking cataracts from the eyes of patients.

EARLY EYE OPERATION

c. 1025: Canon of Medicine
Persian philosopher Avicenna publishes his *Canon of Medicine*, used by doctors as a textbook for the next 500 years and translated into many languages.

PAGE FROM *CANON OF MEDICINE*

ERASISTRATUS AND HEROPHILOS

c. 250 BCE: School of anatomy
Greek doctors Erasistratus and Herophilos open a school of anatomy in Alexandria, Egypt. They make important discoveries about the heart and brain, but supposedly dissect live criminals in the process!

c. 420 BCE: Hippocrates
Ancient Greek physician Hippocrates is one of the first to realize that diseases have natural, not magical causes. The Hippocratic Oath, a vow of integrity for medical professionals, is named after him.

STATUE OF HIPPOCRATES

STATUE OF SUSHRUTA

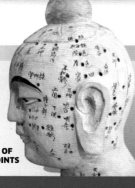

c. 2500 BCE: Acupuncture
The healing practice of acupuncture is developed in China. Fine needles are inserted at specific points under the skin to relieve pain or cure illnesses.

CHINESE MODEL OF ACUPUNCTURE POINTS

c. 500 BCE: Sushruta Samhita
Indian physician Sushruta publishes the *Sushruta Samhita*, a huge work on medicine and surgery. It becomes one of the founding texts of Ayurveda, the traditional Indian system of health, well-being, and healing.

1849: Pioneering doctor
British-born Elizabeth Blackwell becomes the first woman to qualify as a doctor in both the US and the UK. She goes on to practice in London and New York City.

PORTRAIT OF ELIZABETH BLACKWELL

1860: Airborne diseases
French scientist Louis Pasteur proves that infectious diseases can be spread through the air by bacteria and other microorganisms.

LOUIS PASTEUR

1953: Surgical pump
American inventor John Gibbon creates the heart-lung machine, a pump that takes over for the heart and lungs during surgery. This is used in a successful open-heart operation.

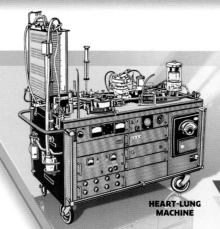

HEART-LUNG MACHINE

1933: Electron microscope
German scientists Ernst Ruska and Max Knoll produce the first electron microscope. The device revolutionizes medical imaging, by producing more powerful pictures than optical microscopes.

RUSKA WITH HIS MICROSCOPE

1953: DNA structure
James Watson, Francis Crick, and Rosalind Franklin show that DNA, the chemical molecule that sets the pattern for growth and development, has a structure like a spiral staircase. This is called a double helix.

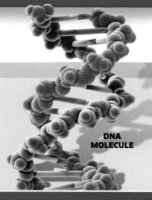

DNA MOLECULE

1954: Kidney transplant
American surgeon Joseph Murray performs the first successful human kidney transplant, in Boston. The recipient, Richard Herrick, lives another eight years.

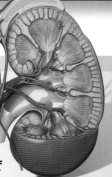

CROSS-SECTION OF A HUMAN KIDNEY

1996: Cloning sheep
Dolly the sheep is the first mammal ever to be cloned—grown in a laboratory from a single stem cell. Cloning has huge potential for treating and preventing human illness.

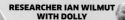

RESEARCHER IAN WILMUT WITH DOLLY

1980–83: Laser scalpels
Researchers Rangaswamy Srinivasan, Samuel Blum, and James J. Wynne use excimer lasers to cut biological tissue. This work becomes vital to the development of laser eye surgery.

LASER EYE SURGERY

2003: Human Genome Project
Scientists announce that the Human Genome Project is complete—we now have an electronic map of human DNA, which may help to treat, cure, or prevent inherited diseases.

SEQUENCE OF HUMAN DNA

2010: Robot operation
DaVinci and McSleepy, a robot surgeon and anesthetist, perform the first all-robotic operation. Human surgeons control robots' movements from a control room.

ROBOT SURGEON

3% of the world's population died from **Spanish flu** in 1918.

A **bionic eye** was successfully tested on 30 people with impaired vision in 2007—the eye is **now available** in Europe and the US.

187

1865: Antiseptic treatments
English surgeon Joseph Lister applies carbolic acid to the wound of a young boy. These antiseptic treatments kill germs and prevent infections. Lister becomes known as the "father of modern surgery."

19TH-CENTURY ANTISEPTIC SPRAYER

1895: X-ray imaging
German physicist Wilhelm Röntgen discovers X-rays, which he uses to make images of the insides of the human body for the first time. The first ever X-ray features the hand of Röntgen's wife.

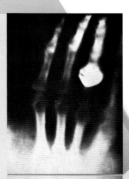

FIRST EVER HUMAN X-RAY

1928: Development of antibiotics
Scottish scientist Alexander Fleming unintentionally grows a mold that kills bacteria. He has discovered penicillin, the world's first antibiotic. By the 1940s, penicillin is mass-produced and has since saved millions of lives as treatment against bacterial infection.

FLEMING'S PENICILLIN DISH

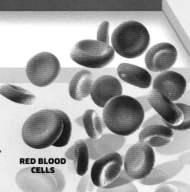

RED BLOOD CELLS

1901: Blood breakthrough
Austrian biologist Karl Landsteiner finds and names the blood types, which are later called A, B, AB, and O. Today, doctors match a patient's blood type when giving a transfusion (injection of new blood).

1955: Polio vaccine
American virologist Jonas Salk introduces a vaccine for polio, a disease that affects children. It is hoped polio will be wiped out by 2018.

JONAS SALK

1967: Heart transplant
South African surgeon Christiaan Barnard performs the first heart transplant operation. A 56-year-old man receives the heart of a young woman, who had been killed in a car accident.

CHRISTIAAN BARNARD

1979: Global vaccinations
The United Nation's World Health Organization declares smallpox the first disease to be officially wiped out, following a worldwide vaccination initiative.

LOGO OF THE WORLD HEALTH ORGANIZATION

DAMADIAN (ON THE LEFT) WITH HIS MRI SCANNER AND A PATIENT

1974: MRI scanner
Armenian-American Raymond Damadian gets a patent for parts of a magnetic resonance imaging (MRI) machine, a device that uses magnetic fields to make medical images.

2013: Stem cell science
In Japan, scientists grow tiny human livers from stem cells. The process could end the shortage of donor organs and save millions of lives.

STEM CELLS

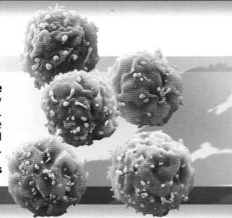

2016: Genetic editing
Scientists make big advances with CRISPR, a biological system of altering DNA. It may soon be possible for doctors to replace faulty sections of our genetic sequence to prevent disease.

ILLUSTRATION OF DNA EDITING

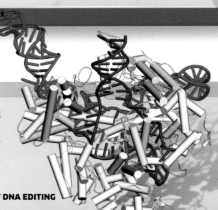

THE INSIDE STORY

For most of history, knowledge of the human body has come from our own eyes—by examining the living and the dead, people have tried to understand the body and how to cure illness. In 1895, the discovery of X-rays first made it possible to see images of a living body's internal structure. Since then, many more methods of looking inside the body have been developed. Doctors now rely on imaging techniques to improve diagnosis, surgery, and treatment.

Single-photon emission computed tomography (SPECT)

This technique works with gamma rays, a type of radiation. Images can either be of 2-D sections or layered into 3-D combinations. SPECT is used for investigating the body's processes, such as blood flow.

Heart imaging
Doctors use one type of SPECT scanning to see the flow of blood in the heart. The SPECT scan can help them decide if all parts of the heart muscle are getting the blood they need. This scan shows a healthy heart.

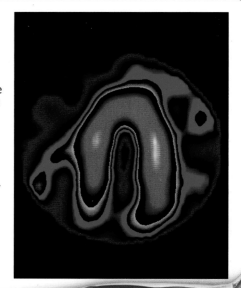

Electroencephalography (EEG)

This imaging technique uses electrodes positioned on the head to monitor electrical activity in the brain. EEGs pick up on changes in levels of brain activity to help diagnose conditions such as epilepsy.

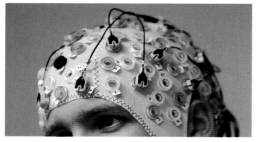

Brain activity
Electrodes attached to this man's head supply information about his brain's activity.

Positron emission tomography (PET)

Radioactive chemicals (radionuclides) are injected into the body. These show high and low levels of cell activity and can detect cancers or unusual action in the brain.

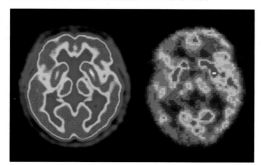

Active and sleeping brains
These two PET scans compare the brain activity of a person when they are awake (left) and asleep (right).

Magnetoencephalography (MEG)

MEG scanners record electric currents in the brain, and the magnetic forces they generate. The readings produce digital images of the brain in action, which are sometimes called "pictures of thinking."

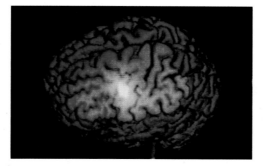

Nerve cells in action
The bright area in this MEG brain scan is where a group of nerve cells are sending commands to muscles to move a finger.

Computerized tomography (CT)

CT scanners rotate around a person and make X-ray images of 2-D "slices" of the body. These images can be layered on top of each other to produce more helpful 3-D images.

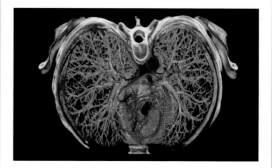

Lungs and heart
This CT scan shows a pair of lungs (green) and a heart (red). By looking at CT scans, doctors can tell whether internal organs are healthy.

Ultrasound

This scanning technique makes images from sound waves. Ultrasound is very safe and is used to check on the health of organs and of babies in the uterus. Many ultrasound scanners are small enough to use by hand.

Kidney
This ultrasound is measuring a healthy kidney inside the abdomen.

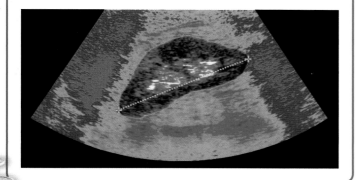

Endoscopy

An endoscope is a thin, flexible tube with a camera at the end. Doctors insert the tube through one of the body's openings, such as the mouth, then watch the images it produces on a monitor.

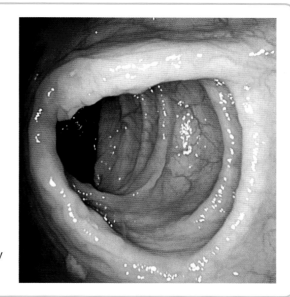

Endoscope image
This endoscope image shows a healthy large intestine. It provides a clear view of the muscular rings and many of the blood vessels in the wall of the intestine. Endoscopy is used to check for ulcers and other problems.

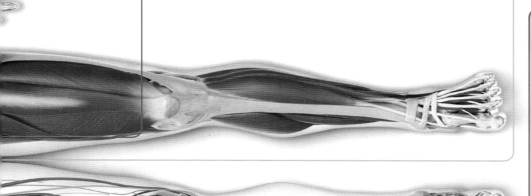

X-rays

X-rays are a type of high-energy radiation. Rays are beamed through the body and onto photographic film. Harder body parts, such as bone, absorb the rays and make a clear image on the film. Soft tissue is not as visible, because the rays pass easily through it.

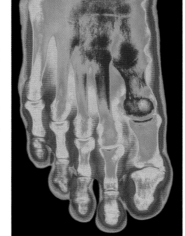

Foot bones
The bones of a right foot show up yellow, green, and blue in this colored X-ray. The red and purple areas are soft tissue.

Magnetic resonance imaging (MRI)

MRI scanners use powerful magnets to stimulate the body's tissues, which causes them to give off radio waves. The radio waves can then be used to create detailed pictures of structures inside the body.

Inside a knee
This MRI scan shows a man's knee. The yellow areas are bone, with cartilage showing in blue. This type of scan is often used to diagnose sports injuries.

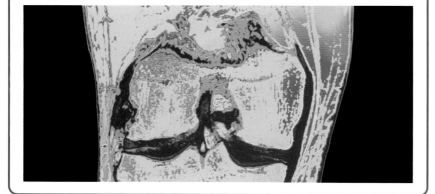

Angiogram

For this type of scan, a patient is first injected with a special dye that shows up on X-rays. The dye highlights blood vessels that are out of shape or blocked.

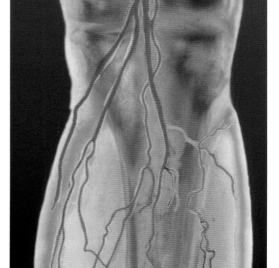

Knee and leg arteries
The arteries in the knee and lower leg are seen clearly as mauve tubes in this angiogram.

HEALTHY HUMANS

In the 21st century, people across the globe are generally healthier than ever, and live longer. Improvements in food, hygiene, and living conditions have transformed many lives. Medical breakthroughs, access to hospitals, and vaccination programs have prevented disease and provided successful treatments. But people can also play their own part in adopting a healthier lifestyle. With more known about the benefits of a good diet, regular exercise, and plenty of sleep, many people are enjoying better health.

MAKING PROGRESS

About 200 years ago, only half of newborn babies in the world would have lived to five years old, but now more than 90 percent of them survive. Worldwide, the average age that people can expect to reach is now 70 years old, which is twice as long as in 1913. Global health programs, such as those run by the United Nations, have played a key role in this progress.

RECIPE FOR HEALTH

Many factors contribute to good health. Most people in developed countries can make choices about their lifestyle that will help them stay well. However, people in the developing world have fewer choices and living healthily can be a challenge for them.

A good diet

It is important to eat a balanced diet, in the right amounts—too little or too much food can harm health. The World Health Organization estimates that 39 percent of adults on Earth are overweight, whereas 14 percent are undernourished. The vast majority of hungry people live in developing countries.

Fish for health
This Japanese market sells all kinds of seafood. The average Japanese person eats 3 oz (85 g) of fish per day, which is almost as much as an American eats in a whole week. This fish-rich diet may be a factor in Japan being one of the world's healthiest nations.

Health care

Today's improved health care means many diseases can be prevented and treated, and people can also be helped in emergencies. Efficient health systems transform communities, with access to clinics, doctors and midwives, and medicines. Health education helps people spot the signs of illness so they can get medical treatment in time.

Raised standards
In Rwanda, a community health care program has helped women to give birth more safely. There has been a huge increase in the number of babies who survive childbirth.

Winding down

The human brain needs sleep to function properly. At the end of the day, the body begins to release chemicals to restrict neuron activity. This reduces brain power for a night of rest and maintenance.

Sleepyheads
In general, the younger the person, the more sleep they need. Babies sleep for up to 16 hours a day, while adults stay healthy on about seven hours' rest.

Bar chart — RECOMMENDED HOURS OF SLEEP PER NIGHT (y-axis: 0 to 16). BABIES: 16, CHILDREN: 12, TEENAGERS: 10, ADULTS: 7.

Drinking water

Unsafe drinking water is one of the biggest threats to human health. Millions of people still die every year from diseases carried in water. In addition to germs, contamination can also come from naturally occurring chemicals such as arsenic. Providing safe water is a swift way to improve the health of entire communities.

Water pump
Public water projects can save lives in rural areas. These people in the Central African Republic are collecting water from a newly repaired pump.

ONE IN EVERY NINE PEOPLE HAS NO ACCESS TO A SAFE WATER SUPPLY.

CHALLENGES TO HEALTH

Some of the factors that affect health are beyond our control as individuals. Natural disasters, wars, and epidemics all put health at risk. The environment in which we live also has an influence on our well-being. Scientists continue to research ways to reduce the impact of the health challenges that people face.

Working the body

The human body is built for activity. Regular exercise strengthens the heart and helps the brain, hair, and skin stay healthy. In the developed world, most people don't get enough exercise—in the UK, recent studies show that 80 percent of adults do not even do the minimum recommended amount of exercise.

Going underground
The human body copes well with the most physically demanding jobs, such as mining. But other factors, such as dust, fumes, or accidents, can make these jobs risky to health.

Climate change

There is overwhelming evidence that Earth's climate is changing. This change is bringing hotter temperatures, extreme weather, rising sea levels, and periods of drought. Some of the risks to humans of climate change include hunger caused by failed crops, an increase in infectious disease, and injuries due to storms and floods.

Drop in disease

Huge advances have been made in controlling infectious diseases. In the USA in 1900, these illnesses caused 53 percent of deaths, but by 2010, this figure had dropped to 3 percent. The main factors in this drop have been: better living conditions so germs cannot spread so easily, antibiotics to kill disease-causing bacteria, and vaccinations, which give immunity to diseases.

Beating polio
This boy is receiving a vaccination against polio, a serious childhood disease. Since a vaccine was developed in the 1950s, polio cases have decreased by 99 percent.

Safer sanitation

The safe disposal of human waste stops it from contaminating land, food, and water, or attracting harmful insects. The United Nations estimates that 2.4 billion people do not have access to safe toilets.

Communal latrine
This simple toilet, or latrine, has improved life for a village in Liberia.

Air pollution

Smoke from factories and fires, exhaust fumes, and chemical pollution all pose risks to people's health. Illnesses caused by air pollution include asthma, heart disease, and some cancers. It is estimated that in 2012, 3.7 million people died worldwide as a direct result of air pollution.

Protective masks
In some parts of the world, people wear masks to filter out particles from heavily polluted air.

Flood damage
This aerial view shows the impact of flooding in Germany in 2016. Flooding can cause homelessness, loss of farmland, and a rise in water-borne diseases such as typhoid or cholera.

Antibiotic resistance

One of the most important advances in medicine is the use of antibiotics to treat infection. However, some microbes are now becoming resistant to all known antibiotics. Without new treatments, lives could be lost to diseases that were once curable.

Resistant bacteria
This sequence shows how a small number of mutated bacteria can quickly become dominant over unmutated bacteria.

Key  Normal bacteria   Resistant bacteria Dead bacteria

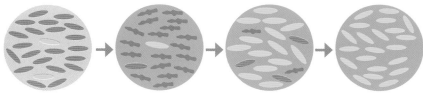

Stage 1 A few bacteria adapt to become resistant to antibiotics.

Stage 2 An antibiotic kills most of the "normal" bacteria.

Stage 3 The resistant bacteria now have room to multiply.

Stage 4 The drug-resistant strain of bacteria takes over.

FUTURE BODIES

Scientists are constantly researching new ways to make us feel better and live longer. Some are working to prevent and cure disease by working on the body's DNA and genetic makeup. Others are developing bionic body parts to replace limbs and internal organs. These advances are transforming the lives of people around the world.

GENETIC MEDICINE

In the 1980s, discoveries about the structure of DNA–the molecule in body cells that directs growth and development–led to a new field of genetic medicine. Scientists are still learning how to use information from our genes to predict and cure health problems. In the future, it might be possible to alter our genetic makeup to avoid diseases.

Genetic testing

For people who have inherited genes for a specific illness or disorder, genetic testing is a lifesaver. Movie star Angelina Jolie was found to carry a mutated version of the gene BRCA1, giving her an 87 percent chance of developing a form of breast cancer. By choosing to have surgery in advance of any diagnosis, her cancer risk reduced to just 5 percent.

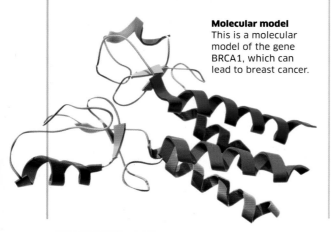

Molecular model
This is a molecular model of the gene BRCA1, which can lead to breast cancer.

Panel testing

It is not always necessary to scan the complete DNA chain. Panel testing can check for genetic mutations more quickly than ever before.

DNA panel
This revolutionary gene panel can test 60 different potentially mutated genes at once, to determine who might be at risk of disease.

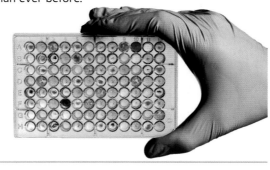

Gene editing

Scientists have found how to use enzymes called nucleases to target, remove, and replace sections of a DNA strand. The latest technologies allow researchers to remove specific areas of the DNA molecule with amazing precision. With this ability, scientists hope to be able to identify faulty genes that cause inherited diseases such as cystic fibrosis, Huntington's disease, and certain cancers.

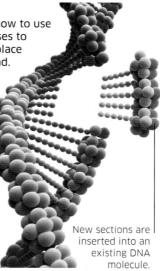

New sections are inserted into an existing DNA molecule.

NANOMEDICINE

In the future, engineers could develop tiny nanobots and inject them into the bloodstream to destroy bacteria, repair damaged cells, and deliver medicines or new strands of DNA. Miniature biotech machines are one-tenth the width of a human hair, and use proteins as motors, sensors, and arms.

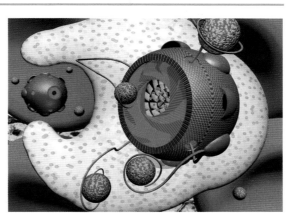

Capturing germs
Called the Pathogen Rustler, this nanobot design would involve using artificial white blood cells as minuscule robot "cowboys," ready to lasso germs and bacteria with their retractable arms.

BIONIC BODIES

Prosthetics are artificial replacements for parts of the body. Scientists are now experimenting with prosthetics that communicate more directly with the human brain. In the future, it could become common for humans to have both natural and artificial body parts, with feedback passing freely between the two.

Exoskeletons

Severe spinal cord injuries and other illnesses can make walking difficult or even impossible. American company Ekso Bionics has designed a powered exoskeletal suit to help with these problems. Originally intended to give workers superstrength when lifting heavy loads, the suit is now used to help wheelchair users regain the motor skills they need to walk independently.

Battery pack powers the exoskeleton

Motor

Computer

Bionic suit
This suit helps to rehabilitate people who have suffered strokes and spinal injuries by correcting posture and assisting them as they walk.

Braces attach the exoskeleton to the user's legs.

Bionic eyes

Many millions of people have severe problems with their eyesight. Developing bionic eyes proves an ongoing challenge for biotechnologists. Visual prosthetic solutions include Argus II, which fits to the eye, and the MVG system, which fits to the brain.

MVG system
Australia's Monash Vision Group (MVG) has designed a device to help people who have damage to the optic nerve. It works in a similar way to the Argus II (shown below), except that the electronic chipset is fitted to the brain, rather than the eye.

MVG SYSTEM

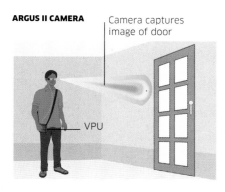

ARGUS II CAMERA

Camera captures image of door

VPU

Electronics case

Image is flipped by the eye to see the door the right way up.

Retina

Implant

Antenna

Electrodes produce visual patterns read by the user.

1 IMAGE CAPTURE
The US device Argus II is designed for people with damaged retinas. A tiny camera mounted on a pair of glasses records the view and converts it into an electrical signal, which is sent to a video processing unit (VPU).

2 ANTENNA
The processed video signal is then sent to a radio transmitter antenna on the side of the glasses. Next, the transmitted signal is picked up by a receiver attached to the eye and finally relayed to a retinal implant inside the eye.

3 ELECTRODES
The signal reaches electrodes placed inside the eye, which stimulate the retina's remaining working cells. They pass the signal along the optic nerve to the brain, and recognizable patterns of light are seen.

Synthetic skin

In the 21st century new advances in synthetic skin are making artificial limbs much more realistic and usable. Innovative technologies mean that the material has as much sensitivity to touch as human skin. Users may in future be able to feel with their prosthetic limbs, just as well as with natural ones.

Helping hand
This revolutionary, touch-sensitive hand has been designed by an American-South Korean team. It is made of silicon and gold, with a flexible plastic covering. Tiny electronic sensors can pick up on heat, cold, and moisture, just like human skin.

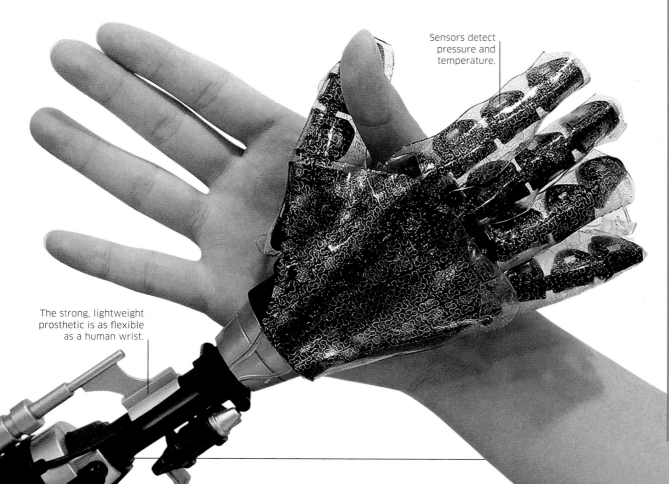

Sensors detect pressure and temperature.

The strong, lightweight prosthetic is as flexible as a human wrist.

The body contains special cells, called stem cells. Every day they divide and produce 300 billion new cells. There are about 200 cell types with different jobs to do. Scientists can now trigger certain genes in the stem cells to make them develop in set ways.

Stem solutions

Stem cells can be steered along many paths. They can be used to create insulin-producing pancreas cells, which could be implanted into diabetic people. This could lead to a cure for diabetes.

Cell cultures
These pots hold stem cells, which may one day be implanted into people to repair damaged cells.

BIOPRINTING

Human organs for transplants are always in short supply. American surgeon Anthony Atala is one of the researchers who believes the solution could lie in bioprinting—making custom-made body parts using a 3-D printer.

Printing a kidney

To make their artificial kidney, the researchers first make a CAT scan (multi-layered X-ray) of an existing kidney. This scan is then used to program the printer to build the new organ.

Organ print
The kidney is made up of layer after layer of bio-ink, a mixture of gel and human cells.

BODIES IN SPACE

Living in space has a dramatic impact on the human body. Scientists research ways for astronauts to stay in space, while minimizing risks to their health. Orbiting 240 miles (390 km) above Earth, the International Space Station (ISS) provides a home and workplace to astronauts for months at a time. Air comes from an onboard supply, radiation levels are high, and even everyday activities can be a huge physical challenge.

DANGER ZONE

Without a space suit, a human in space would quickly die. Aside from the lack of oxygen to breathe, temperatures reach highs and lows that the body cannot cope with. Levels of radiation mean that a human stands no chance of survival. ISS astronauts experience 16 sunrises every 24 hours, which can disrupt their sleep and make them dangerously tired.

Radiation hazards

A huge magnetic field surrounds Earth, which helps to protect people against radiation from the sun and space. A space suit protects against ultraviolet (UV) rays from the sun and provides some protection against the high-energy cosmic rays coming from beyond our solar system.

Galactic cosmic rays
These tiny particles come from outside our solar system. Without protection, they can cause cancers.

Trapped radiation
Fragments of atoms whiz around Earth's magnetic field. This trapped radiation can damage body cells.

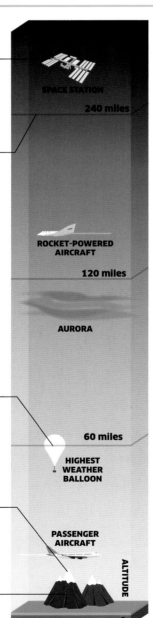

5. Space workplace
The ISS orbits 240 miles (390 km) above Earth, which creates a variety of health challenges for astronauts.

SPACE STATION

240 miles

4. Freezing cold and boiling hot
Temperatures in space can change dramatically very quickly. On the sunny side of the ISS, for example, the temperature reaches 250°F (121°C). On the shady side, it falls to –250°F (–157°C).

ROCKET-POWERED AIRCRAFT

120 miles

AURORA

3. Oxygen omission
At a height of 60 miles (100 km), there is no oxygen in the atmosphere.

60 miles

2. Altitude sickness
At the top of Mount Everest there is 33% of the oxygen there is at sea level, so people suffer from altitude sickness.

HIGHEST WEATHER BALLOON

1. Oxygen assistance
Most mountain climbers have to use extra oxygen from a tank at heights over 21,000 ft (6,500 m).

PASSENGER AIRCRAFT

ALTITUDE

0

SURVIVING SPACE

There is no air to breathe in space, so an astronaut would die very quickly from a shortage of oxygen. Technologies such as the latest space suits and breathing apparatus make it possible to stay in space safely, but the impact still takes its toll on the body. Astronauts must go through intensive testing before the mission, regular health checks while in space, and rehabilitation once they return home.

Essential oxygen

This shows how oxygen, which is essential for human life, gradually disappears from the atmosphere above Earth.

ASTRONAUTS IN SPACE
DO NOT SNORE
SINCE GRAVITY DOESN'T PULL THE TONGUE BACK **WHEN THEY SLEEP.**

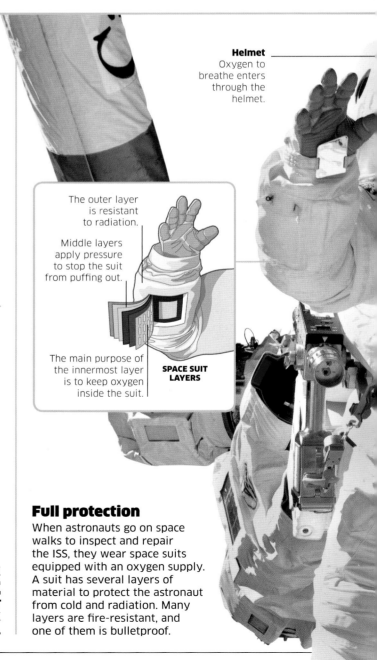

Helmet
Oxygen to breathe enters through the helmet.

The outer layer is resistant to radiation.

Middle layers apply pressure to stop the suit from puffing out.

The main purpose of the innermost layer is to keep oxygen inside the suit.

SPACE SUIT LAYERS

Full protection

When astronauts go on space walks to inspect and repair the ISS, they wear space suits equipped with an oxygen supply. A suit has several layers of material to protect the astronaut from cold and radiation. Many layers are fire-resistant, and one of them is bulletproof.

Solar flare particles
The sun fires fast-moving particles, called solar flare particles. These can damage astronauts' equipment.

Ultraviolet radiation
This strong radiation travels in sunlight. Exposure to it can cause serious harm to the eyes.

Space sleep
On Earth there is a sunrise about every 24 hours, but for astronauts on the ISS the sun rises over Earth every 90 minutes. Astronauts tie their sleeping bags down to stop them from floating. They also use eye masks and ear plugs to block out the light and noise of the station.

Sunrise from space
This is one of the many daily sunrises seen from the ISS looking toward Earth.

Visor
The transparent visor is coated with chemicals that filter the sun's radiation.

Gloves
Tiny heaters inside the gloves keep hands warm.

BODY BATTLES
Conditions in space mean the body is faced with very different challenges from life on Earth. Gravity in a spaceship orbiting Earth is tiny compared with the pull on Earth. This microgravity makes astronauts float in space as though they are weightless. Since their bodies are not working hard, astronauts exercise to keep their muscles and bones strong.

Muscle power
Without a specialized fitness regime, astronauts would lose up to 40 percent of their muscle mass in a few months. This is the equivalent of a 30-year-old's muscles deteriorating to resemble those of an 80-year-old.

Return to Earth
Astronauts back on Earth have weakened muscles and may struggle to walk. This Russian astronaut (cosmonaut) is being carried after a space mission.

Weaker bones
For every month in the microgravity of space, astronauts can lose up to 1 percent of their bone density—which means that the inner network of spongy bone gets more fragile and liable to break.

Outer case of compact bone

Brittle interior of weakened bone

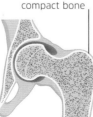

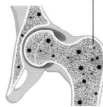

BONE BEFORE A SPACE MISSION

BONE AFTER A SPACE MISSION

Space osteopenia
When astronauts' bones don't have to work against Earth's gravity when they move, they become weaker and less dense. This condition is known as space osteopenia.

Stretchy spine
The human spine expands and relaxes without the continual pressure of gravity. As a result, astronauts grow taller in space by about 3 percent. The extra height is lost within months of returning to Earth.

Tall story
American astronaut Garrett Reisman had grown almost 2 in (5 cm) taller by the end of his five months on the ISS.

Floating fluids
On Earth the body relies on gravity to help blood and other fluids circulate down through the organs and tissues. In the microgravity of space, blood is pushed up into the upper body, where it floats around without being pulled back down. The upper body swells, the face becomes puffy, and the legs shrink. Blood can also put pressure on the eye's optic nerve, blurring the vision.

Long stay
Astronaut Scott Kelly spent more than a year in space, where he experienced many of the symptoms of poor circulation that scientists expected to see.

Liquid balance
As fluid gathers in the upper body, the brain is fooled into thinking the body has too much water. This means astronauts urinate more often and must drink regularly to avoid becoming dehydrated.

SPACE WORKOUT

This picture shows British astronaut Tim Peake working out on an exercise bench on the International Space Station. The device monitors his muscles and heart as he goes through his fitness program.

Without regular exercise, astronauts would experience bone and muscle loss. This is because there is low gravity in space, so the body doesn't have to work as hard as it does on Earth. Astronauts spend two and a half hours every day on treadmills, bikes, and other fitness devices. They have to be strapped on to the equipment so they don't float away. Exercise is also important for astronauts' mental health—to keep them alert and prevent them from getting bored.

RECORD BREAKERS

The human body is the most incredible machine on Earth, but sometimes it is pushed to the limit. The body may have to contend with natural disasters, a harsh environment, or simply the challenge of competition or adventure. As people push the boundaries of human capability, new records are set. Medical advances also make their mark, helping the population grow taller and stronger, and live longer.

UNDER THE SEA

Some people can train themselves to cope with the lack of oxygen that comes when they hold their breath for a long time. This ability is useful for making long underwater dives.

Japanese ama
Pearl divers (called ama) can hold their breath for several minutes underwater.

Deep dive

For thousands of years people in the fishing industry have dived into the sea to catch fish and find shells. The Japanese ama and the Bajau of Malaysia and Indonesia swim to depths of 130 ft (40 m).

HIGH LIFE

The higher the altitude, the harder the body has to work to get enough oxygen. At first, the blood pressure and heart rate rise, and a person takes more breaths. Then the body adapts by increasing the number of red blood cells that carry oxygen, and developing more blood vessels in the muscles.

Mount Everest
(29,029 ft; 8,848 m)
7.7%

Oxygen levels
The air at sea level contains 20.9 percent of usable oxygen, making it easy for the blood to carry oxygen to body cells. Heading to higher ground causes oxygen levels to drop as the air gets thinner.

Aconcagua, Argentina
(22,838 ft; 6,961 m)
9%

La Rinconada
The world's highest town is La Rinconada in the Peruvian Andes. About 50,000 people live at 16,730 ft (5,100 m), with effective oxygen at 11 percent. People acclimatize so well that they mine for gold here.

Denali (Mount McKinley), US
(20,308 ft; 6,190 m)
9.5%

Kilimanjaro, Kenya
(19,341 ft; 5,895 m)
10%

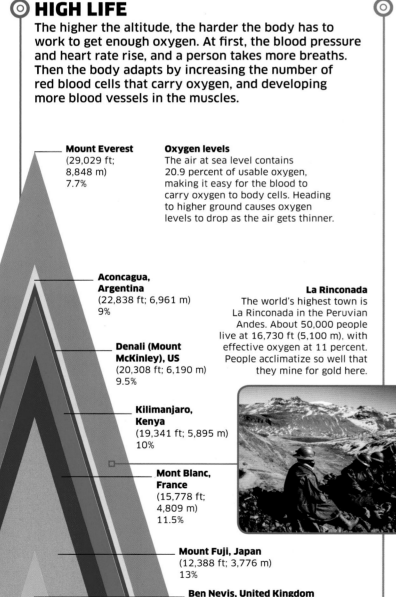

Mont Blanc, France
(15,778 ft; 4,809 m)
11.5%

Mount Fuji, Japan
(12,388 ft; 3,776 m)
13%

Ben Nevis, United Kingdom
(4,413 ft; 1,345 m)
18%

Sea level
OXYGEN LEVEL: 20.9%

SPEED AND ENDURANCE

In the world of sports, athletes continually strive to be faster and stronger. And when people find themselves in the harshest environments, they have to endure huge physical challenges to survive.

Faster and faster

In 1912, the record for the 100 m sprint was 10.6 seconds. At the Mexico Olympics in 1968, American Jim Hines became the first man to officially break the 10-second barrier, aided by low air resistance at high altitude. In 2009, Jamaican Usain Bolt broke all records with 9.572 seconds. It took a whole century for the sprint time to drop by one second.

Power performance
Bolt's muscular arms propel him forward at high speed.

Champion stride
Exceptionally long legs produce powerful strides.

Free diving

Holding your breath underwater without an oxygen tank is now a popular competitive sport, called free diving. Some divers breathe pure oxygen before going underwater and also breathe hard to get rid of toxic carbon dioxide (CO_2). The human body seems to be able to respond to long dives by making changes in blood circulation so that not so much oxygen is used up.

Diving champion
In 2016, free diver Aleix Segura Vendrell held his breath underwater for a record-breaking 24 minutes.

Endurance tests

The human body is built to endure huge physical challenges or even periods without food. Accidents, such as being lost in the wilderness or trapped underground, force people into a fight for survival. Others choose to push their bodies to the limit by taking part in extreme sports and endurance events.

Underground rescue
In 2010, 33 miners were rescued from a collapsed copper pit in Chile. They were stranded 2,300 ft (700 m) below the surface for 69 days, making it the longest underground entrapment in history.

Desert challenge
The hardy participants of Morocco's Marathon des Sables (Desert Marathon) trek through sand dunes and rocky terrain for 156 miles (251 km) in scorching temperatures of 122°F (50°C).

LONG LIFE

The life expectancy of a human has risen steadily over the centuries, with women generally living longer than men. Europe is the longest-lived continent, while African countries take all three places at the bottom of the table. Poverty and lack of health care are the main health risks that many African people face.

Staying alive

Japan is usually agreed to be the longest-living nation—experts believe that its wealth, excellent health care, and healthy diet are the main factors. Japanese people can expect to live more than 30 years longer than those in Sierra Leone, the country with the shortest life expectancy.

	RANK	COUNTRY		LIFE EXPECTANCY (Years)
TOP 3	1	●	Japan	83.7
	2	+	Switzerland	83.4
	3	☾	Singapore	83.1
BOTTOM 3	181		Central African Republic	55.5
	182		Angola	52.4
	183		Sierra Leone	50.1

TALL STORIES

Humans are growing—people in the 21st century are taller than those from previous centuries. Currently the tallest men are from the Netherlands, while the tallest women are from Latvia.

Latvia woman: +6 in
1914
5 ft 1 in
(155.5 cm)
2014
5 ft 7 in
(169.8 cm)

Kenya woman: +1 in
1914
5 ft 1 in
(155.9 cm)
2014
5 ft 2 in
(158.2 cm)

Netherlands man: +5 in
1914
5 ft 7 in
(169.4 cm)
2014
6 ft
(182.5 cm)

India man: +1 in
1914
5 ft 4 in
(162 cm)
2014
5 ft 5 in
(164.9 cm)

Dizzy heights

The world's tallest known person in history was American Robert Pershing Wadlow (1918–1940). He measured 8 ft 11 in (2.72 m), which is taller than an Asian elephant. His height was due to an overactive pituitary gland, which produces a hormone that makes the body grow.

Oldest age

According to official records, the oldest person ever was Jeanne Calment of Arles, France, who reached 122 years, 164 days. She was born in 1875 and died in 1997. She credited a diet plentiful in olive oil and chocolate for her long, healthy life.

TODAY, THERE ARE 450,000 PEOPLE AGED OVER 100 YEARS IN THE WORLD. BY 2050, THERE WILL BE 2.2 MILLION.

Growing population

In 2014, a study found that men and women in every country were taller than 100 years ago, although height gains varied hugely. These increases are likely due to better nutrition, hygiene, and health care.

Giant of Illinois
Record-breaking Robert Pershing Wadlow is seen next to a friend of normal size.

Glossary

ABDOMEN
The lower part of the body, between the chest and the pelvis, which contains most of the digestive organs.

ABDUCTOR MUSCLE
A muscle that pulls a limb away from the midline of the body.

ADDUCTOR MUSCLE
A muscle that pulls a limb toward the midline of the body.

ABSORPTION
The process by which nutrients from digested food pass through the wall of the small intestine and into the blood.

ADRENALINE
A hormone that prepares the body for sudden action at times of danger or excitement.

ALLERGY
An illness caused by overreaction of the body's immune system to a normally harmless substance.

**ALVEOLI
(singular alveolus)**
Tiny air bags in the lungs through which oxygen enters, and carbon dioxide leaves, during breathing.

AMINO ACID
A simple molecule used by the body to build proteins. The digestive system breaks down proteins in food into amino acids.

ANTIBODY
A substance that sticks to germs and marks them for destruction by white blood cells.

ANTIGEN
A foreign substance, such as a bacterium, which triggers the immune system to respond.

AORTA
The largest artery of the body, arising from the left side of the heart. The aorta supplies oxygen-rich blood to all other arteries except for the pulmonary artery.

ARTERY
A blood vessel that carries blood away from the heart to the body's tissues and organs.

ATRIUM
One of two chambers in the upper part of the heart.

AXON
A long fiber that extends from a nerve cell (neuron). It carries electrical signals away from the cell at high speed.

**BACTERIA
(singular bacterium)**
A small type of microorganism. Some types cause disease in humans, while others help to keep the body functioning properly.

BLOOD
Red liquid tissue, which contains several types of cell. Blood carries oxygen, nutrients, salts and other minerals, and hormones around the body. It also collects wastes for disposal and helps defend the body against infection.

BLOOD VESSEL
A tube that carries blood through the body. The main types of blood vessel are arteries, capillaries, and veins.

BONE
The strong, hard body part made mainly of calcium minerals. There are 206 bones in the human body.

BRAIN STEM
The lower part of the brain, which connects to the spinal cord. The brain stem controls functions such as breathing and heart rate.

BRONCHIOLE
A tiny tube through which air passes on its way in or out of the lungs.

**BRONCHUS
(plural bronchi)**
One of the two main branches of the trachea (windpipe), a tube that leads into each lung.

CAPILLARY
A tiny blood vessel that carries blood between arteries and veins.

CARBOHYDRATE
A food group including sugars and starches that provides the body's main energy supply.

CARBON DIOXIDE
The waste gas that is expelled from the body by breathing out.

CARDIAC MUSCLE
A type of muscle found only in the heart.

CARDIOVASCULAR SYSTEM
This body system consists of the heart, blood, and a vast network of blood vessels. It is also called the circulatory system.

CARTILAGE
A tough, flexible type of connective tissue that helps support the body and covers the ends of bones and joints.

CELL
One of the trillions of tiny living units that form the human body.

CELL BODY
Part of a nerve cell (neuron) that contains its nucleus.

CENTRAL NERVOUS SYSTEM
The brain and spinal cord together make up the central nervous system.

CEREBELLUM
The area of the brain behind the brain stem. The cerebellum is concerned with balance and the control of fine movement.

CEREBRAL CORTEX
The folded outer layer of the brain. The cerebral cortex is responsible for high-level brain functions such as thinking, memory, and language.

CEREBRAL HEMISPHERE
One of the two symmetrical halves into which the main part of the brain (the cerebrum) is split.

CEREBRUM
The largest part of the brain, it contains the centers for thought, personality, the senses, and voluntary movement. It is made up of two halves, called hemispheres.

CHROMOSOME
A threadlike package of DNA found in the nucleus of every body cell. A normal cell has a total of 46 chromosomes, arranged in 23 pairs.

CILIA
Microscopic hairlike structures that project from the surface of some body cells.

CLAVICLE
Also called the collarbone, one of two slender bones that make up part of the shoulder girdle.

CONE CELLS
Receptor cells in the back of the eye, which detect different colors and send messages back to the brain for interpretation.

CONTRACTION
The shortening of a muscle to move one part of the body.

CRANIAL NERVE
One of the 12 pairs of nerves that emerge from the brain.

DENDRITE
A short branch that extends from a nerve cell, or neuron, and carries incoming electrical signals from other nerve cells.

DENTINE
The hard, bonelike material that shapes a tooth and forms its root.

DIAPHRAGM
The dome-shaped sheet of muscle that separates the thorax (chest) from the abdomen and plays a key role in breathing.

DIGESTION
The process that breaks down food into simple substances that the body can absorb and use.

DISEASE
Any problem with the body that makes someone unwell. Infectious diseases are those caused by germs.

DNA (deoxyribonucleic acid)
Long molecule found inside the nucleus of body cells. DNA contains coded instructions that control how cells work and how the body grows and develops.

EMBRYO
Term used to describe a developing baby in the first eight weeks following fertilization.

ENAMEL
The hardest material in the body. It covers the exposed part of a tooth with a thin, hard layer.

ENDOCRINE GLAND
A type of gland that makes hormones and releases them into the bloodstream.

ENZYME
A substance that speeds up a chemical reaction in the body.

EPIGLOTTIS
The flap of tissue that closes the windpipe during swallowing to stop the food from entering.

ESOPHAGUS
The muscular tube through which food passes from the throat to the stomach.

EXTENSOR
A muscle that extends or straightens a joint, such as the triceps brachii, which straightens the arm at the elbow.

FAT
A substance found in many foods that provides energy and important ingredients for cells.

FECES
Solid waste made up of undigested food, dead cells, and bacteria, which is expelled from the body via the anus.

FEMUR
The largest bone in the body, located in the leg between the pelvis and the knee.

FERTILIZATION
The joining of a female egg (ovum) and male sperm to make a new individual.

FETUS
The name given to a baby developing in the uterus from the ninth week after fertilization until it is born.

FLEXOR
A muscle that bends a joint, for example, the biceps brachii, which bends the arm at the elbow.

FORAMEN
A hole or opening in a bone through which blood vessels and nerves can pass.

FRONTAL LOBE
The foremost of the four lobes that make up each hemisphere of the cerebrum. The frontal lobes help with mental processes, such as planning and decision-making.

GASTRIC
Describes something relating to the stomach, such as gastric juice.

GENES
Part of DNA, genes contain instructions that control the way the body looks and how it works. Genes are passed on from parents to their children.

GENOME
All the DNA contained in a set of chromosomes. In humans there are 46 chromosomes.

GERM
A tiny living thing (microorganism) that can get into the body and cause illness. Bacteria and viruses are types of germ.

GLAND
A group of specialized cells that make and release a particular substance, such as an enzyme or a hormone.

GLUCOSE
A simple sugar that circulates in the bloodstream and is the main energy source for the body's cells.

HEMOGLOBIN
A substance in red blood cells that carries oxygen around the body.

HEPATIC
Describes something relating to the liver, such as the hepatic artery.

HIPPOCAMPUS
A part of the brain that helps to process long-term memories.

HORMONE
A chemical produced by glands in order to change the way a part of the body works. Hormones are carried by the blood.

HUMERUS
The long bone in the arm that extends from the shoulder to the elbow.

HYPOTHALAMUS
The small structure in the base of the brain that controls many body activities, including temperature and thirst.

IMMUNE SYSTEM
A collection of cells and tissues that protect the body from disease by searching out and destroying germs and mutated cells.

INFECTION
If germs invade your body and begin to multiply, they cause an infection. Some diseases are caused by infections.

IRIS
The colored part of the eye. The iris controls the pupil.

JOINT
A connection between two bones. Most joints allow the body to move. The hip and shoulder joints are two of the most mobile.

KERATIN
A tough, waterproof protein found in hair, nails, and skin.

LARYNX
A structure at the top of the windpipe that generates sound when a person speaks. The sound is created by folds of vibrating tissue called vocal cords.

LIGAMENT
A tough band of tissue that holds bones together where they meet at joints.

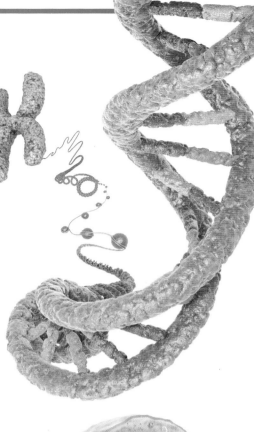

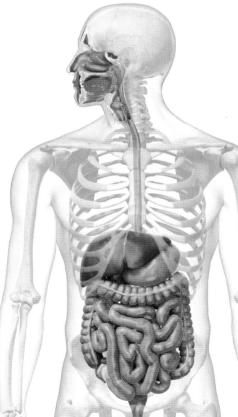

LUNG
One of two organs used for breathing. Lungs take up most of the space in the chest and are part of the body's respiratory system.

LYMPH
Liquid that is picked up from tissues, flows through the lymphatic system, and is returned to the bloodstream.

LYMPHATIC SYSTEM
A network of vessels that collect fluid from body tissues and filter it for germs, before returning the fluid to the bloodstream.

LYMPHOCYTE
A white blood cell specialized to attack a specific kind of germ. Some lymphocytes make antibodies.

MACROPHAGE
A white blood cell that swallows and destroys germs such as bacteria, mutated cells, or debris in damaged tissue.

MAGNETIC RESONANCE IMAGING (MRI)
A technique that uses magnetism and radio waves to produce images of the inside of the body.

METABOLISM
A term used to describe all the chemical reactions going on inside your body, especially within cells.

MINERAL
A naturally occurring chemical, such as salt, calcium, or iron, that you need to eat to stay healthy.

MITOCHONDRIA (singular mitochondrion)
Tiny structures found inside cells that release energy to power the cell's activity.

MITOSIS
The division of a cell into two new and identical cells.

MOTOR NEURON
A type of nerve cell that carries signals from the central nervous system to the muscles, telling them to contract or relax.

MUCUS
A thick, slippery fluid produced in the mouth, nose, throat, and intestines.

MUSCLE
A type of tissue. Most muscles contract to cause movement.

NASAL CAVITY
The hollow space behind the nose through which air flows during breathing.

NERVE
A bundle of fibers through which instructions pass to and from the central nervous system.

NERVE IMPULSE
A tiny electrical signal that is transmitted along a nerve cell at high speed.

NEURON
A term for a nerve cell. Neurons carry information around the body as electrical signals.

NEUTROPHIL
The most common type of white blood cell, which targets and defends the body from harmful bacteria.

NUCLEUS
The control center of a cell. It contains DNA-carrying chromosomes.

NUTRIENTS
The basic chemicals that make up food. The body uses nutrients for fuel, growth, and repair.

OCCIPITAL LOBE
One of the four lobes that make up each hemisphere of the cerebrum. The occipital lobe is the area that controls sight.

ORGAN
A group of tissues that form a body part designed for a specific job. The heart and lungs are organs.

ORGANELLE
A tiny structure within a cell that carries out a particular role.

OVARIES
A pair of glands that store, then release, a woman's eggs (ova).

OVUM (plural, ova)
Also called an egg, the sex cell that is released from a woman's ovaries.

OXYGEN
A gas, found in air, that is vital for life. Oxygen is breathed in, absorbed by the blood and used by cells to release energy.

PARIETAL LOBE
One of the four lobes that make up each hemisphere of the cerebrum. The parietal lobe interprets touch, pain, and temperature.

PATHOGEN
A microorganism that causes disease. Pathogens include bacteria and viruses, and they are sometimes called germs.

PELVIS
A large bony frame that the legs are connected to. It is made up of the hip bones and those at the base of the spine.

PERISTALSIS
A wave of muscle contractions in the wall of a hollow organ that, for example, pushes food down the esophagus during swallowing.

PHAGOCYTE
A general name for white blood cells, such as macrophages, which track down and kill pathogens.

PHALANGES
The bones of the fingers, thumbs, and toes.

PHARYNX
A tube that runs from the nasal cavity to the esophagus. It is also called the throat.

PHOTORECEPTOR
A type of cell found in the eye that sends signals to the brain when it detects light. The two types of photoreceptors in the eye are rods and cones.

PLASMA
A pale yellow liquid that makes up the greater part of blood, and in which the three types of blood cells float.

PLEXUS
A network of nerves or blood vessels.

PROTEIN
Vital nutrients that help the body build new cells.

PULMONARY
Describes something relating to the lungs, such as the pulmonary artery or pulmonary vein.

PULMONARY ARTERY
The artery that carries oxygen-poor blood to the lungs to pick up oxygen. Other arteries carry blood that is rich in oxygen.

PULMONARY VEIN
The vein that carries oxygen-rich blood from the lungs to the heart. All other veins carry blood that has low levels of oxygen.

RECEPTOR
A nerve cell, or the ending of a neuron, which responds to a stimulus such as light or sound.

RED BLOOD CELL
A cell that contains hemoglobin, a protein that carries oxygen and makes the blood red.

REFLEX
A rapid, automatic reaction that is out of a person's control, such as blinking when something moves toward the eyes.

RENAL
Describes something relating to the kidney, such as the renal vein.

RETINA
A layer of light-sensitive neurons lining the back of each eye. The retina captures images and relays them to the brain as electrical signals.

RIB CAGE
A flexible, protective framework of 12 pairs of bones. The rib cage surrounds soft organs in the chest, such as the heart and lungs.

ROD CELL
A light-sensitive cell in the back of the eye. Rod cells work in dim light but do not detect color.

SALIVA
The liquid in the mouth. Saliva helps a person taste, swallow, and digest food.

SCANNING
Any technique that is used to create images of organs and soft tissues inside the body.

SCAPULA
One of the two large, flat bones that form the back of the shoulder. It is also called the shoulder blade.

SEBUM
An oily substance that keeps the skin soft, flexible, and waterproof.

SEMEN
A fluid that contains sperm (male sex cells).

SENSE ORGAN
An organ, such as the eye or ear. It contains receptors that detect changes inside or outside the body, and sends nerve signals to the brain, enabling you to see, hear, balance, taste, and smell.

SENSORY NEURON
A type of nerve cell that carries signals from the sense organs to the central nervous system.

SENSORY RECEPTOR
A specialized nerve cell or the end of a sensory neuron that detects a stimulus, such as light, scent, touch, or sound.

SKELETAL MUSCLE
A type of muscle that is attached to the bones of the skeleton and which moves the body.

SMOOTH MUSCLE
A type of muscle that is found in the walls of hollow organs, such as the small intestine and bladder. Smooth muscle contracts slowly and rhythmically.

SPERM (singular and plural)
A male's sex cells, which are made in, and released from, a man's testes.

SPHINCTER
A ring of muscle around a body opening that opens and closes to allow the flow of material, such as food or urine, through it.

SPINAL CORD
The thick column of nerve cells that runs down the backbone and connects your brain to the rest of the body.

SPINAL NERVE
One of the 31 pairs of nerves that branch out from the spinal cord.

SUTURE
An immovable joint between two bones such as those that make up the pelvis and skull.

SYNAPSE
The junction where two nerve cells (neurons) meet but do not touch.

SYNOVIAL JOINT
A movable joint, such as the knee or elbow, in which the space between bones is filled with lubricating synovial fluid.

TASTE BUD
A receptor on the surface of the tongue that detects different flavors in food and drink.

TENDON
A cord of tough connective tissue that attaches muscle to bone.

THALAMUS
The mass of nerve tissue that lies deep within the brain and receives and coordinates sensory information.

THORACIC CAVITY
The area inside the thorax (chest) containing organs such as the lungs and heart.

THORAX
The upper part of the trunk (the central part of the body) between the abdomen and the neck. Also called the chest.

TISSUE
A group of cells of the same or similar type that work together to perform a particular task. Muscle is a type of tissue. Blood is tissue in liquid form.

TONGUE
The movable, muscular organ attached to the floor of the mouth. It is the main organ for taste and is also essential for speech.

TOXIN
A poisonous substance released into the body, often by disease-causing bacteria.

TRACHEA
Also known as windpipe, the tube that links the larynx to the bronchi, and carries air toward and away from the lungs.

ULTRASOUND
An imaging technique that uses high-frequency sound waves to produce images of body tissues or a developing fetus.

URETHRA
The tube that carries urine from the bladder outside the body. In males, it also transports semen.

UTERUS
The hollow, stretchy organ in which the fetus grows and is nourished until birth. The uterus is sometimes called the womb.

VEIN
A blood vessel that carries blood toward the heart.

VENTRICLE
One of two chambers (left and right) in the lower part of the heart.

VERTEBRA
One of the bones that make up the backbone.

VIRUS
A tiny, infectious, nonliving agent that causes disease by invading, and multiplying inside, body cells.

VITAMIN
One of a number of substances, required in small amounts in the diet to keep the body healthy.

VOCAL CORDS
The small folds of tissue in the larynx (voice box) that vibrate to create the sounds of speech.

WHITE BLOOD CELL
A cell found in the blood that is involved in defending the body against pathogens.

X-RAY
An imaging technique that reveals body structures, especially bones, by passing a type of radiation through the body onto photographic film.

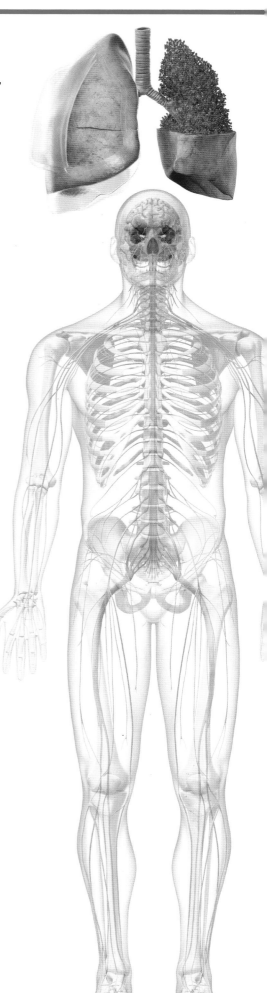

Index

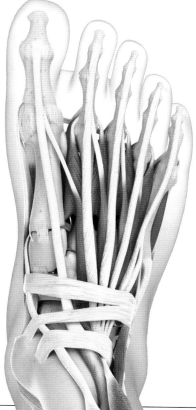

Acknowledgments

The publisher would like to thank the following people for their assistance in the preparation of this book:
Shaila Brown for editorial guidance and Helen Leech for editorial assistance; Neetika Malik Jhingan, Govind Mittal, and George Mihic for design assistance; Steve Crozier for retouching; Katie John for proofreading; Hilary Bird for the index.

Smithsonian Enterprises:
Kealy E. Gordon, Product Development Manager
Ellen Nanney, Licensing Manager
Brigid Ferraro, Vice President, Education and Consumer Products
Carol LeBlanc, Senior Vice President, Education and Consumer Products
Chris Liedel, President

Reviewers for the Smithsonian:
Dr. Don E. Wilson, Curator Emeritus, Department of Vertebrate Zoology, National Museum of Natural History

The publisher would like to thank the following for their kind permission to reproduce photographs:
(Key: a-above; b-below/bottom; c-center; f-far; l-left; r-right; t-top)

6 Science Photo Library: Keith R. Porter (cl). **8 Dorling Kindersley:** Colin Keates / Natural History Museum, London (br). **Science Photo Library:** Keith R. Porter (cr). **8-9 SuperStock:** Science Photo Library (tc). **9 Science Photo Library:** Alvin Telser (fcl, cl, c). **12-13 Science Photo Library**. **15 123RF.com:** luchschen (br). **17 Getty Images:** Indranil Mukherjee / AFP (cra). **23 123RF.com:** Wavebreak Media Ltd (ca). **24 Alamy Stock Photo:** Panther Media GmbH / micut (cl). **iStockphoto.com:** Artem_Furman (bl); Mikolette (tr). **25 Alamy Stock Photo:** Cultura Creative (RF) / Ben Pipe Photography (br); Gallo Images / David Malan (bl). **iStockphoto.com:** antorti (bc). **31 Science Photo Library:** Biosphoto Associates (fbr); R. Bick, B Pointdexer / UT Medical School (bc, br). **40-41 Science Photo Library:** Thomas Deernick / NCMIR. **44 Dreamstime.com:** Syda Productions (r). **Science Photo Library:** Steve Gschmeissner (bl). **45 123RF.com:** stockyimages (cl). **Alamy Stock Photo:** Jim West (bl). **Dreamstime.com:** Saaaaa (tc). **Paul Thompson, UCLA**

School of Medicine: Time-Lapse Map of Brain Development. Paul Thompson (USC) and Judith Rapoport (NIMH) (cb). **50 Science Photo Library:** James Cavallini (cl, cr); Dennis Kunkel Microscopy (tc, cla, ca, bc); Steve Gschmeissner (bl, br). **51 Science Photo Library:** Juergen Berger (ca); Steve Gschmeissner (cra, fcra); Dr. John Brackenbury (bc). **52-53 Science Photo Library**. **64 Science Photo Library:** K H Fung (clb). **66 Science Photo Library:** Science Picture co (cl). **71 Science Photo Library:** Ted Kinsman (clb). **72-73 Science Photo Library:** Tom Barrick, Chris Clark / SGHMS. **74 Alamy Stock Photo:** Sport Picture Library (cra). **75 Alamy Stock Photo:** SIBSA Digital Pvt. Ltd. (cr). **77 Science Photo Library:** Steve Gschmeissner (cra). **79 Science Photo Library:** Eye of Science (cra). **80 Dreamstime.com:** Katarzyna Bialasiewicz (bl). **81 Science Photo Library:** Steve Gschmeissner (cr). **82-83 Science Photo Library:** Prof. P. Motta / Dept. Of Anatomy / University "La Sapienza", Rome. **85 Science Photo Library:** Omikron (bl). **86 123RF.com:** Baloncici (cl). **87 Depositphotos Inc:** Tristan3D (tr). **Dreamstime.com:** Eveleen007 (br). **Getty Images:** Fuse / Corbis (clb); Edgar Mueller (ca). **91 Science Photo Library:** Steve Gschmeissner (tl, cr); Veisland (crb). **93 123RF.com:** Volodymyr Melnyk (cr). **98 123RF.com:** anatols (bl); Patryk Kośmider (clb); sam74100 (fclb). **99 Science Photo Library:** Bo Veisland (cb). **102-103 Getty Images:** Steve Gschmeissner / Science Photo Library. **104 Science Photo Library:** (clb); GCA (cl). **105 Science Photo Library:** Steve Gschmeissner (bl). **107 Science Photo Library:** Philippe Plailly (bc). **108 Science Photo Library:** Overseas (cb). **114-115 Science Photo Library:** Thomas Deernick / NCMIR. **117 123RF.com:** Wavebreak Media Ltd (tl). **127 123RF.com:** Todd Arena (br); Vladislav Zhukov (bl). **Dreamstime.com:** Berc (clb). **Science Photo Library:** Joseph Giacomin / Cultura (cr); Kent Wood (cra). **128-129 Science Photo Library:** Steve Gschmeissner. **133 123RF.com:** Phanuwat Nandee (cr); Sayam Sompanya (cra); wckiw (br). **Dreamstime.com:** Flynt (fcra); Typhoonski (tc); Konstantin Zykov (fcr). **137 Robert Steiner MRI Unit, Imperial College London:** Dr Declan O'Regan, MRC London Institute of Medical Sciences (bc). **138 Science**

Photo Library: Dr. K. F. R. Schiller (cr). **139 Science Photo Library:** Steve Gschmeissner (br). **142 Science Photo Library:** Gastrolab (bl); Steve Gschmeissner (tl). **143 Dreamstime.com:** Clickandphoto (br). **148-149 Science Photo Library:** Steve Gschmeissner. **150 Science Photo Library:** Scimat (cr). **151 Science Photo Library:** (tr). **155 Alamy Stock Photo:** ZUMA Press, Inc. (br). **156-157 Science Photo Library:** Susumu Nishinaga. **158 Science Photo Library:** Dennis Kunkel Microscopy (clb, cb); Steve Gschmeissner (bl); Ted Kinsman (bc). **159 Dreamstime.com:** Alexander Raths (tr); Wxin (bl). **Getty Images:** Digital Art / Corbis (cr). **164-165 Science Photo Library:** Thierry Berrod, Mona Lisa Productions. **171 Alamy Stock Photo:** A Room With Views (cra). **173 Science Photo Library:** Steve Gschmeissner (cl). **174-175 Science Photo Library:** Steve Gschmeissner. **179 Getty Images:** Dan Mullan (cr). **181 Getty Images:** Tristan Fewings (ca). **182 NASA:** (c). **Science Photo Library:** Simon Fraser (cl); Tek Image (cr). **184 Alamy Stock Photo:** ART Collection (cr). **The Trustees of the British Museum:** Peter Hayman (br). **National Museum of Health and Medicine:** Alan Hawk (c). **Science Photo Library:** (tc, tr); Photo Researchers (cla); Science Source (crb). **Science Museum, London:** Adrian Whicher (bc). **185 Alamy Stock Photo:** Art Directors & TRIP / Harish Luther / ArkReligion.com (br). **Getty Images:** De Agostini / A. Dagli Orti (cla); DEA / A. Dagli Orti (cb). **Science Photo Library:** (tr); Paul D. Stewart (tl); Sheila Terry (ca); New York Public Library Picture Collection (cl); National Library of Medicine (cr); John Greim (bl). **Wellcome Images http://creativecommons.org/licenses/by/4.0/:** (clb). **186 Getty Images:** Colin McPherson / Corbis (clb). **Science Photo Library:** (cla); National Library of Medicine (tc); Humanities and Social Sciences Library / New York Public Library (tr); Thomas Hollyman (cra); Evan Otto (c); Alexander Tsiaras (cb); J. C. Revy, ISM (bc); Dr P. Marazzi (br). **187 Getty Images:** Bettmann (cb); PhotoQuest (cl); Mondadori Portfolio (cr). **Science Photo Library:** (tr); St. Mary's Hospital Medical School (cla); Sebastian Kaulitzki (ca); Steve Gschmeissner (bl); Molekuul (br); Dorling Kindersley (tl). **World Health Organisation:** (clb). **188 Alamy Stock Photo:** Roger Bacon / Reuters (cl). **Science Photo Library:**

Centre Jean Perrin / ISM (fbl); Sovereign, ISM (br); Hank Morgan (bl, bc); ISM (tr). **189 Science Photo Library:** (tl); Gastrolab (tr); Simon Fraser (bl); Mehau Kulyk (cr); BSIP VEM (br). **190 123RF.com:** myroom (clb). **Alamy Stock Photo:** Paul Felix Photography (bc). **Getty Images:** William Campbell / Corbis (cra). **191 Alamy Stock Photo:** Olivier Asselin (cr); My Planet (tr); SOPA Images Ltd (crb); dpa picture alliance (bl). **Getty Images:** Jean Chung (tl). **192 123RF.com:** angellodeco (c). **Courtesy of Ekso Bionics:** (br). **Copyright 1999 by Tim Fonseca:** (bc). **Science Photo Library:** Evan Oto (clb); Alfred Pasieka (cb). **193 Getty Images:** New York Daily News Archive (tc). **Science Photo Library:** Tek Image (cr). **Seoul National University:** Dae-Hyeong Kim / Nature Communications 5, 5747, 2014 (b). **Wake Forest Institute for Regenerative Medicine:** (br). **194-195 NASA:** (bc). **195 NASA:** (cra, crb); Reid Wiseman (cla); Bill Ingalls (c); ESA (br). **196-197 NASA:** ESA. **198 123RF.com:** yokokenchan (tr). **Getty Images:** Al Bello (br); Sebastian Castaneda / Anadolu Agency (cb). **199 Alamy Stock Photo:** Sergey Orlov (cla). **Getty Images:** Bettmann (br); Pascal Parrot / Sygma (cra); Government of Chile / Handout / Corbis (cl); Pierre Verdy / AFP (bl)

Cover images: *Front:* **Dorling Kindersley:** Arran Lewis b

All other images © Dorling Kindersley
For further information see: www.dkimages.com

SPACE!

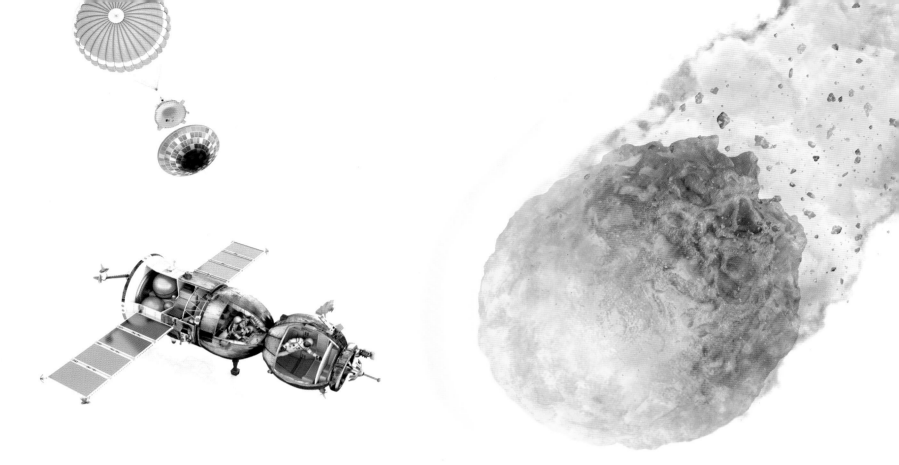

DK SMITHSONIAN☀

SPACE!

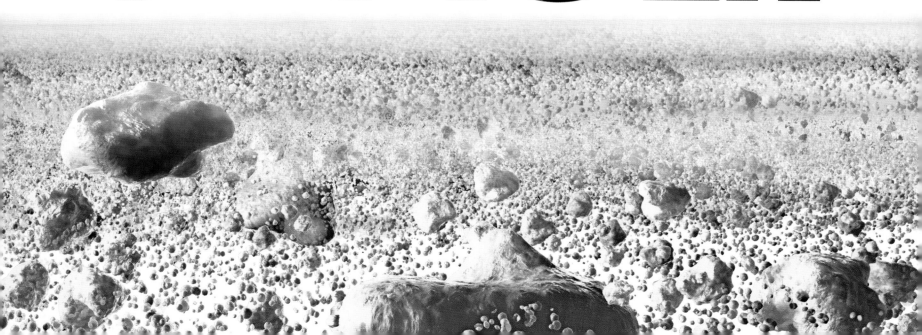

SECOND EDITION

DK LONDON
Managing editor Rachel Fox   **Managing art editor** Owen Peyton Jones
US Editor Kayla Dugger   **US Executive editor** Lori Cates Hand
Production editor Gillian Reid   **Production controller** Laura Andrews
Jacket design development manager Sophia MTT
Publisher Andrew Macintyre   **Associate publishing director** Liz Wheeler
Art director Karen Self   **Publishing director** Jonathan Metcalf

Consultants Jacqueline Mitton, Ian Ridpath, Giles Sparrow

DK DELHI
Project art editor Mansi Agrawal   **Project editor** Vatsal Verma
Senior picture researcher Surya Sankash Sarangi
Managing editor Kingshuk Ghoshal   **Managing art editor** Govind Mittal
Senior DTP designer Shanker Prasad   **DTP designer** Vikram Singh
Senior jacket designer Suhita Dharamjit

FIRST EDITION

DK LONDON
Senior editor Ben Morgan   **Senior art editor** Smiljka Surla
Editor Steve Setford   **Designer** Jacqui Swan
Contributors Robert Dinwiddie, John Farndon, Geraint Jones,
Ian Ridpath, Giles Sparrow, Carole Stott
Scientific consultant Jacqueline Mitton
Illustrators Peter Bull, Jason Harding, Arran Lewis
Jacket design development manager Sophia MTT
Jacket designer Laura Brim   **Jacket editor** Claire Gell
Producer, pre-production Nikoleta Parasaki   **Producer** Mary Slater
Managing editor Paula Regan   **Managing art editor** Owen Peyton Jones
Publisher Andrew Macintyre   **Associate publishing director** Liz Wheeler
Art director Karen Self   **Design director** Stuart Jackman
Publishing director Jonathan Metcalf

DK DELHI
Senior editor Bharti Bedi   **Senior art editor** Nishesh Batnagar
Project editor Priyanka Kharbanda   **Art editors** Heena Sharma, Supriya Mahajan
Assistant editor Sheryl Sadana   **DTP designer** Nityanand Kumar
Senior DTP designers Shanker Prasad, Harish Aggarwal
Picture researcher Deepak Negi   **Jacket designer** Dhirendra Singh
Managing editor Kingshuk Ghoshal   **Managing art editor** Govind Mittal

This American Edition, 2021
First American Edition, 2015
Published in the United States by DK Publishing
1450 Broadway, Suite 801, New York, NY 10018

Copyright © 2015, 2021 Dorling Kindersley Limited
DK, a Division of Penguin Random House LLC
22 23 24 10 9 8 7 6 5 4 3 2 1
001–334974–Jan 23

A catalog record for this book is available from the Library of Congress.
ISBN: 978-0-7440-2892-8

DK books are available at special discounts when purchased in bulk
for sales promotions, premiums, fund-raising, or educational use. For
details, contact: DK Publishing Special Markets,
1450 Broadway, Suite 801, New York, NY 10018
SpecialSales@dk.com

Printed and bound in China

For the curious
www.dk.com

Smithsonian

Established in 1846, the Smithsonian
is the world's largest museum and research
complex, dedicated to public education, national
service, and scholarship in the arts, sciences, and
history. It includes 19 museums and galleries and the
National Zoological Park. The total number of artifacts,
works of art, and specimens in the Smithsonian's
collection is estimated at 155.5 million.

MIX
Paper from
responsible sources
FSC™ C018179

This book was made with
Forest Stewardship Council™
certified paper—one small step
in DK's commitment to a
sustainable future.
For more information go to
www.dk.com/our-green-pledge

CONTENTS

THE SOLAR SYSTEM

THE SOLAR SYSTEM

Our local neighborhood in space is called the solar system. At its heart is the Sun, an ordinary star that is so close it floods our planet with light. Trapped in its orbit by gravity are Earth and seven other planets, their many moons, and millions of comets and asteroids.

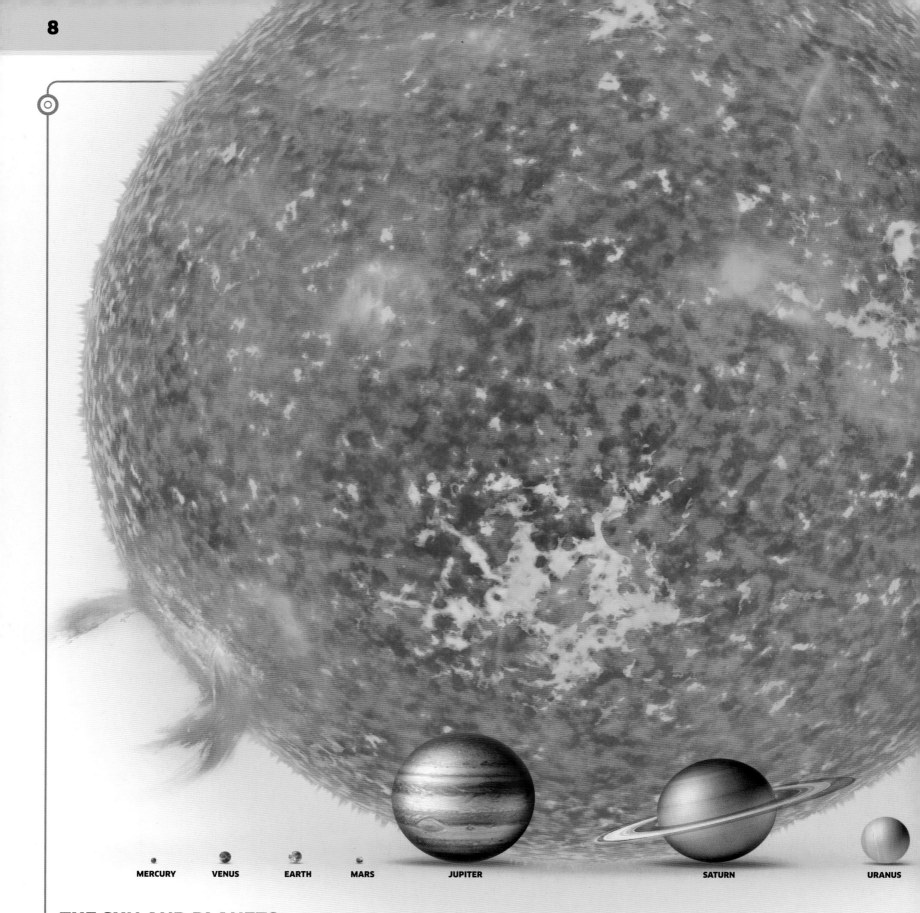

MERCURY   **VENUS**   **EARTH**   **MARS**   **JUPITER**   **SATURN**   **URANUS**

THE SUN AND PLANETS

The Sun is huge compared to even the biggest of the planets, Jupiter, and it contains 99.8 percent of the Solar System's entire mass. At nearly 870,000 miles (1.4 million km) wide, the Sun is 10 times wider than Jupiter and over 1,000 times more massive. Yet even Jupiter is gigantic compared to Earth. The Solar System's eight planets form two distinct groups. The inner planets—Mercury, Venus, Earth, and Mars—are solid balls of rock and metal. In contrast, the outer planets are giants—enormous, swirling globes made mostly of liquid and gas.

1.3 million—the number of times Earth's volume could fit inside the Sun.

SUN

The Sun's family

The Solar System is a vast disk of material at least 1.9 trillion miles (3 trillion km) across, with the Sun at its center. Most of it is empty space, but scattered throughout are countless solid objects bound to the Sun by gravity and orbiting (traveling around) it, mostly in the same direction. The biggest objects are almost perfectly round and are called planets. There are eight of them, ranging from the small rocky planet Mercury to gigantic Jupiter. The Solar System also has hundreds of moons, millions of asteroids, and possibly millions or billions of comets.

NEPTUNE

ORBITAL PLANE

The orbits of the planets and most asteroids around the Sun are aligned, making a flat shape known as a plane. This means they rarely bump into each other. Comets, though, can be in orbits at any angle.

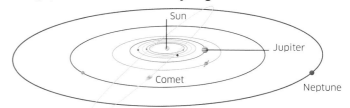

Sun
Jupiter
Comet
Neptune

How orbits work

To understand how orbits work, English scientist Isaac Newton imagined cannonballs being fired into space. If a cannonball flies so fast that the curvature of its fall matches Earth's curvature, it will keep flying forever, orbiting the planet.

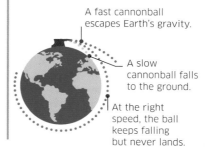

A fast cannonball escapes Earth's gravity.

A slow cannonball falls to the ground.

At the right speed, the ball keeps falling but never lands.

MINOR BODIES

Besides the planets, there are so many other bodies in the Solar System that astronomers have not been able to identify them all. Bodies more than 125 miles (200 km) or so wide, such as dwarf planets and large moons, are round. Smaller objects are lumpy in shape.

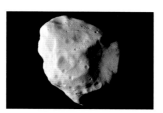

Asteroids
There are millions of these rocky lumps, most of which circle the Sun in an area between Mars and Jupiter: the Asteroid Belt. A few asteroids have orbits that take them perilously close to Earth or other planets.

Comets
Comets are icy bodies that travel in from the outer Solar System, forming bright tails as they come close enough to the Sun for the ice to evaporate. Many comets are thought to come from a vast cloud called the Oort Cloud, far beyond the planets.

Dwarf planets
The force of gravity pulls large objects into a spherical shape over time. Dwarf planets have enough gravity to become spherical but not enough to sweep the area around their orbits clear of other objects. The total number of dwarf planets is unknown.

Moons
Most of the planets and many of the other objects in the Solar System have moons—natural satellites that orbit them, in the same way that the planets orbit the Sun. Nineteen of these moons are large enough to be round, and two of them are larger than the planet Mercury.

STRUCTURE

The Solar System has no clear outer edge and is so big that distances are measured not in miles, but in astronomical units (AU). One astronomical unit is the average distance from Earth to the Sun.

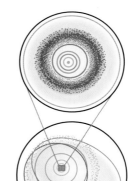

Inner Solar System
Circling nearest to the Sun are the four inner planets: Mercury, Venus, Earth, and Mars. Beyond Mars lies the Asteroid Belt, and beyond the Asteroid Belt is Jupiter (orbit in orange) at 5 AU from the Sun.

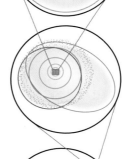

Outer Solar System
Beyond the orbits of Jupiter, Saturn, Uranus, and Neptune is a ring of icy bodies known as the Kuiper Belt, some 30–50 AU from the Sun. Two of the largest objects in the Kuiper Belt are Pluto (orbit in purple) and Eris (orbit in red).

Beyond Pluto
One of the most distant Solar System objects known is Sedna, a minor body whose elongated orbit takes it as far from the Sun as 937 AU. Sedna's journey around the Sun takes 11,400 years to complete. The Sun would look so tiny from Sedna that you could blot it out with a pin.

Oort Cloud
Far beyond Sedna's orbit is the Oort Cloud—a vast ball of icy bodies possibly reaching 100,000 AU from the Sun. Some comets are thought to come from the Oort Cloud. The Sun's gravity is so weak here that objects in the cloud can be dislodged by the gravity of other stars.

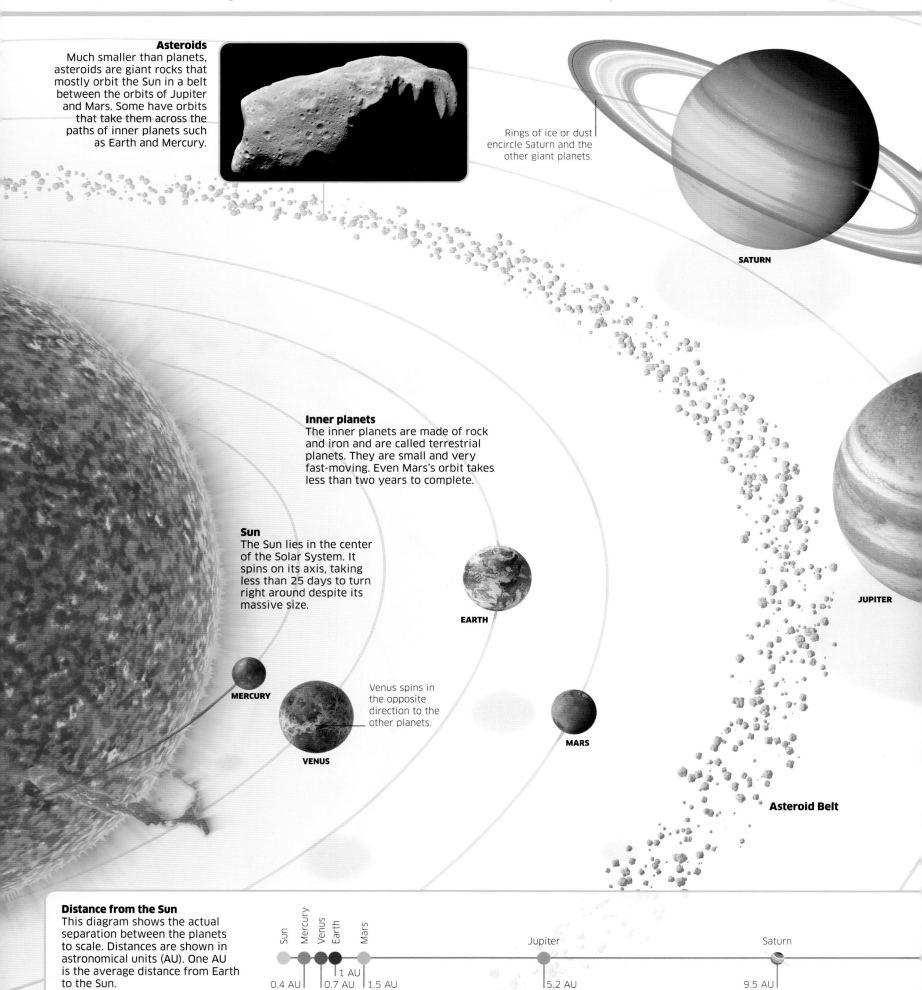

Asteroids
Much smaller than planets, asteroids are giant rocks that mostly orbit the Sun in a belt between the orbits of Jupiter and Mars. Some have orbits that take them across the paths of inner planets such as Earth and Mercury.

Rings of ice or dust encircle Saturn and the other giant planets.

SATURN

Inner planets
The inner planets are made of rock and iron and are called terrestrial planets. They are small and very fast-moving. Even Mars's orbit takes less than two years to complete.

Sun
The Sun lies in the center of the Solar System. It spins on its axis, taking less than 25 days to turn right around despite its massive size.

EARTH

JUPITER

Venus spins in the opposite direction to the other planets.

MERCURY

MARS

VENUS

Asteroid Belt

Distance from the Sun
This diagram shows the actual separation between the planets to scale. Distances are shown in astronomical units (AU). One AU is the average distance from Earth to the Sun.

Sun | Mercury | Venus | Earth | Mars | Jupiter | Saturn

1 AU

0.4 AU | 0.7 AU | 1.5 AU | 5.2 AU | 9.5 AU

250 million years—the time it takes for the Solar System to complete **one orbit of the Milky Way Galaxy**.

11

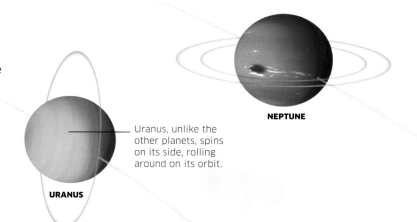

Comets
Comets are giant lumps of ice and dust that have highly elliptical orbits. They can spend centuries in the outer reaches of the Solar System before swooping close to the Sun and developing tails as they warm up.

NEPTUNE

Uranus, unlike the other planets, spins on its side, rolling around on its orbit.

URANUS

Kuiper Belt
Beyond the planets is a belt of icy bodies, some of which are large enough to be classed as dwarf planets. These objects are so far from the Sun that they can take hundreds of years to complete one orbit.

Giants
The outer planets are all much bigger than the inner planets. They are made mostly of liquid over a rocky core. This liquid merges gradually into an atmosphere of gas on the outside.

Jupiter spins around faster than any other planet, completing one rotation in under 10 hours. The speed of the surface layer at its equator is 27,000 mph (43,000 kph).

Every object in space is
spinning around,
from planets and moons to
stars, black holes, and galaxies.

Around the Sun

Trapped by the Sun's gravity, the eight planets of the Solar System travel around the central star on nearly circular paths, spinning like tops as they go.

The farther a planet is from the Sun, the longer its orbit takes and the slower it travels. The farthest planet, Neptune, takes 165 years to get around the Sun and moves at just over 3 miles (5 km) per second. Earth, meanwhile, bowls through space nearly six times as fast, and Mercury, the planet nearest to the Sun, whizzes around it in just 88 days at a speedy 30 miles (50 km) per second. The planets' orbits are not circular. Instead, they follow slightly oval paths, known as ellipses, that take them closer to the Sun at one point. Mercury's orbit is the most elliptical: its farthest point from the Sun is more than 50 percent farther than its nearest point.

Uranus

Neptune

19 AU

30 AU

New Sun
The Sun contains 99.8 percent of the material now in the Solar System.

Rocky planets
Grains of rock and metal collected in the inner part of the young Solar System, which was much hotter than the outer zone. This material would form the inner planets—Mercury, Venus, Earth, and Mars—which have rocky outer layers and cores of iron.

Birth of the Solar System

The planets of the Solar System formed from gas and grains of dust and ice surrounding the newly formed Sun.

The Solar System was born inside a vast, dark cloud of gas and dust. About five billion years ago, something triggered a burst of star formation in the cloud—possibly a nearby star exploded, sending a shock wave rippling through the cloud. Hundreds of pockets of gas were squeezed into clumps. Their gravity pulled in more and more gas, making the clumps larger and denser. This made them heat up inside and start to glow. Eventually, the cores of the clumps got so hot and dense that nuclear reactions began and they became stars. One of those stars was our Sun.

Oldest rocks
Meteorites are space rocks that fall onto Earth. They include the oldest rocks known to science. Many are leftovers from the cloud of debris that formed the planets.

The giant planets contain **99 percent** of the mass of the Solar System outside the Sun.

Collisions between **many smaller objects** finally produced just **four rocky planets** in the Solar System.

13

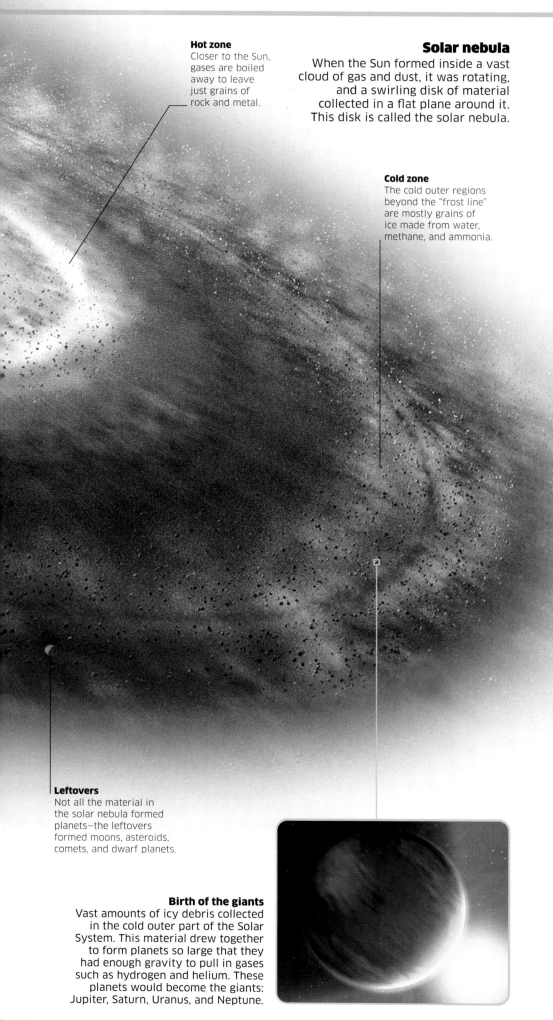

Hot zone
Closer to the Sun, gases are boiled away to leave just grains of rock and metal.

Cold zone
The cold outer regions beyond the "frost line" are mostly grains of ice made from water, methane, and ammonia.

Solar nebula
When the Sun formed inside a vast cloud of gas and dust, it was rotating, and a swirling disk of material collected in a flat plane around it. This disk is called the solar nebula.

Leftovers
Not all the material in the solar nebula formed planets—the leftovers formed moons, asteroids, comets, and dwarf planets.

Birth of the giants
Vast amounts of icy debris collected in the cold outer part of the Solar System. This material drew together to form planets so large that they had enough gravity to pull in gases such as hydrogen and helium. These planets would become the giants: Jupiter, Saturn, Uranus, and Neptune.

The Solar System forms
The Solar System formed 4.6 billion years ago, when a clump of gas and dust was pulled together by its own gravity inside a giant cloud. The collapsing mass gave birth to our Sun, surrounded by a flattened spinning disk (the solar nebula) from which the planets formed.

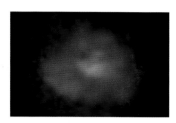

Collapsing clump
Within the giant cloud, a pocket of gas began to shrink, possibly because a shock wave from a supernova (exploding star) disturbed the cloud.

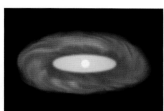

Spinning disk
As the clump shrank, it began spinning, turning faster and faster until it formed a disk. Its center began to heat up.

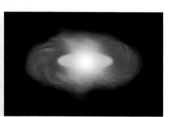

The Sun is born
Nuclear reactions began in the dense center, which began to shine as a star. The leftover matter formed a disk called the solar nebula.

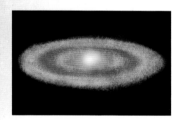

Planetesimals
Gravity caused the particles in the disk to clump together, forming billions of tiny planets, or planetesimals.

Planets form
The planetesimals crashed into each other, sticking together and growing into fewer, larger planets.

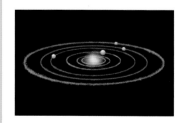

Migration
The orbits of the giant planets changed. Neptune and Uranus moved farther out, pushing smaller icy bodies into even more distant orbits.

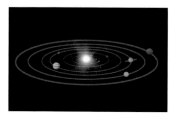

The Solar System today
By about 3.9 billion years ago, the Solar System had settled down into its present pattern of planets.

The Sun

Our Sun is a typical star—a vast, glowing ball made mostly of super-hot hydrogen and helium gas.

The Sun has been shining for nearly 5 billion years and will probably continue to shine for another 5 billion. More than a million times larger in volume than Earth, it contains over 99 percent of the Solar System's mass. The tremendous force of gravity generated by this mass keeps the planets of the Solar System trapped in orbit around it. The Sun's source of power lies buried deep in its core, where temperatures soar to 27 million °F (15 million °C). The intense heat and pressure in the core trigger nuclear fusion reactions, turning 4.4 million tons (4 million tonnes) of matter into pure energy every second. This energy spreads upward to the seething surface of the Sun, where it floods out into space as light and other forms of radiation.

Core
Nuclear energy is generated in the Sun's core. The nuclei (centers) of hydrogen atoms are forced together to form helium nuclei—a process called nuclear fusion.

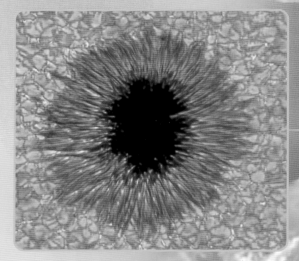

Sunspots
Sometimes dark patches appear on the Sun, often in groups. Called sunspots, they look darker because they are about 3,500°F (2,000°C) cooler than the rest of the surface. They last only a few weeks and are caused by the Sun's magnetic field.

FAST FACTS

Diameter: 865,374 miles (1,392,684 km)

Mass (Earth = 1): 333,000

Surface temperature: 9,930°F (5,500°C)

Core temperature: 27 million °F (15 million °C)

Prominence
Giant eruptions of hot gas sometimes burst out from the Sun. Called prominences, they follow loops in the Sun's invisible magnetic field.

2 billion billion billion tons (tonnes)—the mass of the Sun.

In 1947, the **Great Sunspot** could be **seen** at sunset with the **naked eye**.

15

Convective zone
Below the Sun's surface is the convective zone, an area in which pockets of hot gas rise, cool, and then sink back down again. This movement carries energy from the core toward the surface.

Radiative zone
Deep beneath the convective zone is the dense, hot radiative zone. Energy travels through this part of the Sun as radiation.

Spicules
Jets of gas called spicules cover the entire Sun.

Photosphere
The outer part of the Sun is transparent to light, creating the illusion of a surface. This apparent surface is called the photosphere and has a grainy appearance, caused by pockets of hot gas rising from deep below.

EARTH TO SAME SCALE

Speed of light

Traveling at the speed of light, it takes a mere eight minutes for the Sun's energy to travel across space to reach Earth. However, it can take up to 100,000 years for energy to travel through the star's dense interior to reach its surface.

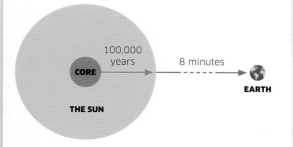

100,000 years

CORE

8 minutes

EARTH

THE SUN

Northern lights

As well as producing heat and light, the Sun flings out streams of deadly high-energy particles, forming the "solar wind." Earth's magnetic field protects us from these particles like an elastic cage, but when a strong blast of them disturbs the magnetic field, trapped particles cascade down into the atmosphere. They set off brilliant light displays near the poles, called auroras or the northern and southern lights.

Solar cycle

The number of sunspots on the Sun varies in a regular cycle, reaching a peak every 11 years or so before dying down again. This happens because of the way the Sun rotates. The star's equator spins 20 percent faster than its poles, causing the Sun's magnetic field to get tangled up. Every 11 years, it gets so tangled that it breaks down before forming afresh.

The Sun spins much faster at its equator than at its poles.

The difference in speeds twists magnetic field lines out of shape.

The twisted field lines burst in loops from the surface, creating sunspots.

16 the solar system · **MERCURY**

176 Earth days—the **length of a day** on Mercury from sunrise to sunrise.

Mercury

The planet Mercury is a giant ball of iron covered in a shallow layer of rock. It is the smallest planet and the one closest to the Sun.

Mercury is the speedster of the planets, completing its journey around the Sun in just 88 Earth days at the brisk pace of 108,000 mph (173,000 kph), which is faster than any other planet. Scorched by the Sun's heat, Mercury's dusty, Moon-like surface is hotter than an oven by day but freezing at night. Deep under the surface, a giant core of iron almost fills the planet's interior. The oversized core suggests that Mercury was once struck with such violence that most of its rocky outer layers were blasted away into space.

Mercury's cliffs
Among Mercury's most distinctive features are long, winding cliffs called rupes, shown in this artist's impression. They probably formed at least three billion years ago when the young planet was cooling and shrinking, which made its surface wrinkle.

Craters on Mercury, such as the Mendelssohn Crater, are named after writers, artists, and composers.

Around the Sun
Mercury takes 88 Earth days to orbit the Sun. As it travels, its shape as seen through a telescope appears to change because we see different parts of the planet lit by sunlight.

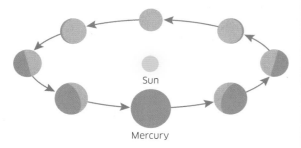

Sun

Mercury

Deep impact
The Caloris Basin, seen here in false color, is one of the biggest impact craters in the solar system. The crater is 960 miles (1,550 km) wide, but the collision that produced it was so violent that debris was flung more than 600 miles (1,000 km) beyond the crater rim.

Caloris Basin

Cracked planet
On the opposite side of Mercury from the Caloris Basin is a strange area of jumbled hills. Scientists think shock waves from the giant impact traveled all the way through Mercury and converged here, cracking the ground.

Impact

Hills

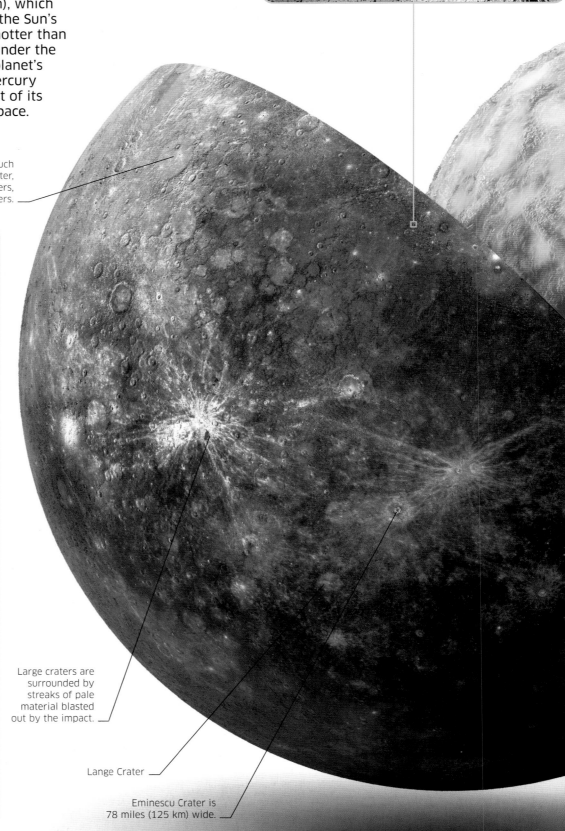

Large craters are surrounded by streaks of pale material blasted out by the impact.

Lange Crater

Eminescu Crater is 78 miles (125 km) wide.

30 miles (50 km) per second—the **speed at which Mercury orbits** the Sun.

806°F (430°C)—the **peak daytime temperature** on Mercury.

−292°F (−180°C)—the temperature during the **coldest part of the night**.

17

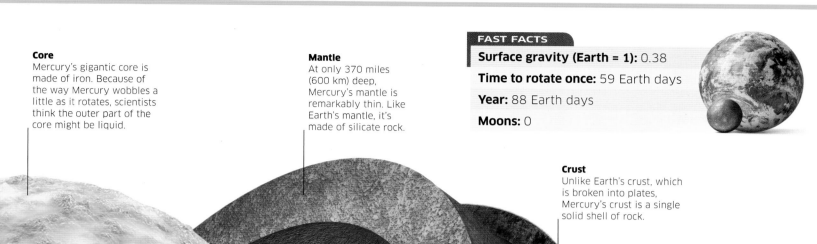

Core
Mercury's gigantic core is made of iron. Because of the way Mercury wobbles a little as it rotates, scientists think the outer part of the core might be liquid.

Mantle
At only 370 miles (600 km) deep, Mercury's mantle is remarkably thin. Like Earth's mantle, it's made of silicate rock.

FAST FACTS

Surface gravity (Earth = 1): 0.38

Time to rotate once: 59 Earth days

Year: 88 Earth days

Moons: 0

Crust
Unlike Earth's crust, which is broken into plates, Mercury's crust is a single solid shell of rock.

Atmosphere
Because Mercury's gravity is weak and its surface is blasted by solar radiation, its atmosphere is thin and contains only a trace of gas.

Scar face
Impacts billions of years ago have left Mercury thoroughly pitted by craters. Because the planet is small, it doesn't have enough gravity to hold on to a thick atmosphere, and there's no air to stop meteorites from crashing into it.

At the base of the mantle is a solid layer of iron sulfide. On Earth this mineral forms shiny rocks known as "fool's gold."

Venus

Our nearest neighbor in space, Venus is very similar to Earth in size. However, the furnacelike surface of this rocky planet bears little resemblance to our world.

Venus is cloaked in swirls of yellowish clouds. Unlike Earth's clouds, which contain life-giving water, these clouds are made of deadly sulfuric acid. The atmosphere is so thick that pressure on the planet's surface is 92 times that on Earth—enough to crush a car flat. At 860°F (460°C), the surface is also hotter than that of any other planet in the Solar System.

Volcanoes

Venus has more volcanoes than any other planet in the Solar System. Half a billion years ago, the entire surface of the planet was remade by volcanic eruptions. We can't see if any of the volcanoes are active, as Venus's thick clouds hide them from view. However, scientists have detected unusual heat from the largest volcano, Maat Mons (below), which suggests it might be active.

Deadly clouds

Venus's dense atmosphere is about 97 percent carbon dioxide. A thick layer of cloud, about 35 miles (60 km) above the surface, hides the planet's surface entirely. These clouds are made of drops of sulfuric acid.

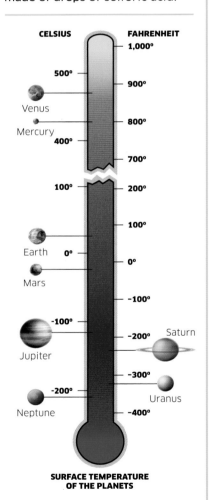

SURFACE TEMPERATURE OF THE PLANETS

Hot planet

Venus is hot not just because it is close to the Sun, but also because its air contains so much carbon dioxide. Like glass in a greenhouse, carbon dioxide traps the Sun's heat. This greenhouse effect warms Earth, too, because of the water vapor and carbon dioxide in the air, but it is much weaker than on Venus.

Many craters on the surface, called coronas, were made not by impacts but by collapsing volcanoes.

Blank areas in the model of Venus are regions that the Magellan spacecraft did not survey.

The Dali Chasma is a 1,243-mile (2,000-km) long network of canyons and valleys.

Venus rotates so slowly that **its day lasts longer than its year**.

1,600 The **number of volcanoes** on the surface of Venus.

5 miles (8 km)—the height of Venus's tallest volcano, **Maat Mons**.

19

FAST FACTS

Surface gravity (Earth = 1): 0.91

Moons: 0

Year: 225 Earth days

Time to rotate once: 243 Earth days

Pancake domes

Unlike volcanoes on Earth, those on Venus rarely erupted explosively. Instead, they oozed lava slowly. In some places, thick lava has piled up on the surface to form squat, rounded volcanoes called pancake domes.

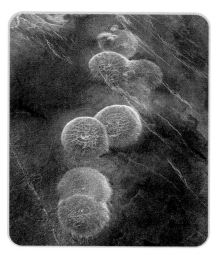

Core

Like the other rocky planets, Venus probably has a red-hot core made mostly of iron. The inner core is likely to be solid, but the outer part may be partly liquid.

The surface consists of bare rock and is so hot that an astronaut would be burned to a cinder in just a few minutes.

Mantle

Venus's mantle of rock is kept slightly soft by heat from the core. Over millions of years, the soft rock slowly churns about.

Crust

Unlike Earth's crust, that of Venus is quite thick and rarely moves, merely bulging up in places every now and then.

Atmosphere

Venus has the thickest, densest atmosphere of all the rocky planets, with a permanent blanket of cloud that covers the entire planet. The cloud-free view on the left side of this 3D model was created from radar data sent to Earth by the Magellan spacecraft.

Earth

Of all the planets known to science, ours is the only one known to harbor life and to have vast oceans of liquid water on the surface.

Earth's distance from the Sun and its moderately thick atmosphere mean it never gets very hot or very cold at the surface. In fact, it is always just the right temperature for water to stay liquid, making life as we know it possible. That is very different from scorching Venus, where all water boils away, and icy Mars, where any water seems to be frozen. Life on Earth began around 3.8 billion years ago, soon after the newly formed planet cooled down, allowing water to form oceans. Since then, living organisms have slowly transformed the planet's surface, coloring the land green and adding oxygen to the atmosphere, which makes our air breathable.

Life in water
Water is essential to all forms of life on Earth because the chemical reactions that keep organisms alive happen in water. Most scientists think life began in water, possibly at the bottom of the sea, where volcanic chimneys might have provided essential warmth and nutrients. Today, oceans contain some of the most diverse natural habitats on the planet, such as the coral reefs of tropical seas.

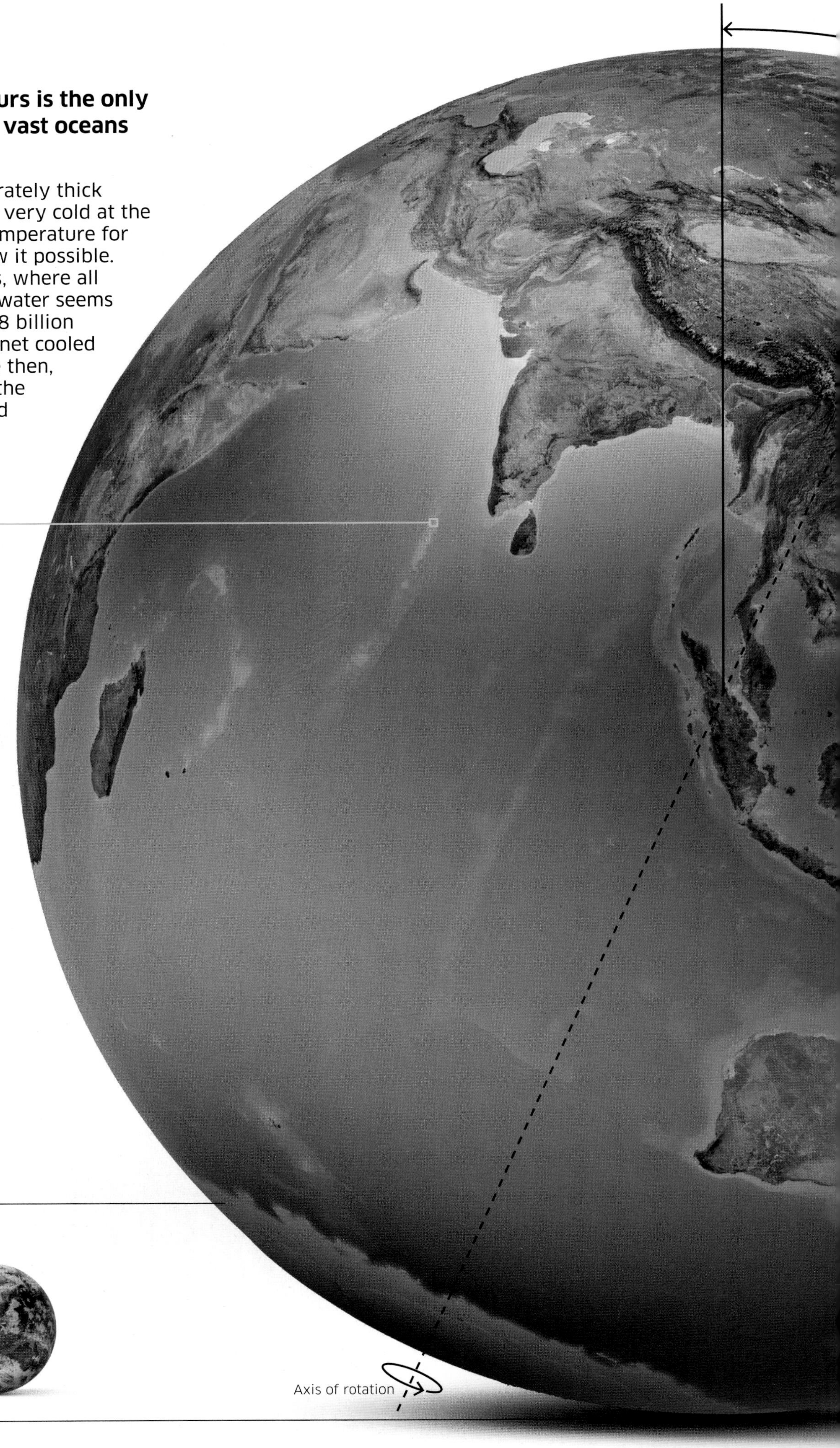

Polar ice
Because Earth's poles receive so little warmth from the Sun, they are permanently cold and are covered in ice. An icy continent sits over Earth's South Pole, but an icy ocean sits at the North Pole.

FAST FACTS

Time to rotate once: 23.9 hours

Year: 365.26 days

Moons: 1

Average temperature: 59°F (15°C)

Axis of rotation

600 The number of volcanoes that have erupted in the last **10,000 years**.

1,036 mph (1,667 kph)—the **speed** at which **Earth rotates** at the equator.

−136°F (−93°C)—the **lowest recorded temperature** on Earth.

21

Tilt

23.4°

Earth does not spin upright, as compared to its path around the Sun. Instead, it is tilted over at an angle of 23.4°. The planet also wobbles very slowly, causing its tilt to swing from 22.1° to 24.5° every 42,000 years.

Living organisms have been found in rock **3 miles (5 km) deep underground** and in the air 10 miles (16 km) high in the atmosphere.

Continents

Most of Earth's land is concentrated in large masses called continents. Over millions of years, the continents very slowly move around the planet, colliding and breaking up to form new patterns.

Life on land

For billions of years, life existed only in water. Then, 475 million years ago, tiny plants inched their way out of swamps and onto land. From this small beginning, life spread over the continents, covering the wettest places with dense forests.

Watery planet

Water covers more than two-thirds of Earth's surface. Scientists think much of it came from comets or asteroids that crashed into the planet early in its history.

Orbit and seasons

Earth's tilt causes different parts of the planet to lean toward the Sun or away from it during the year, creating seasons. When the northern hemisphere leans toward the Sun, the weather is warmer and days are longer, causing summer. When it leans away from the Sun, the weather is colder and nights are longer, causing winter. The seasons are reversed for the southern hemisphere.

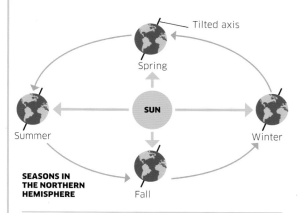

Tilted axis

Spring

SUN

Summer

Winter

SEASONS IN THE NORTHERN HEMISPHERE

Fall

Human influence

In recent centuries, our species has changed Earth's surface so much that our influence is visible from space. As well as lighting up the planet's night side with electricity, we have changed the atmosphere and climate and have replaced large areas of natural ecosystems with farmland and cities.

Deserts

Not all of Earth's surface is covered by life. Deserts don't have enough water to sustain lush forests, and only special kinds of plants and animals can survive in them. Some of Earth's deserts resemble landscapes of other planets. The deserts of central Australia even have the same reddish color as Martian deserts, thanks to iron oxide in the soil—the chemical that gives Mars its color.

Inside Earth

If you could pull Earth apart with your hands, you'd discover it's made of distinct layers that fit together like the layers of an onion.

Earth is made almost entirely of rock and metal. When the young planet was forming and its interior was largely molten, heavy materials like metal sank all the way to the center, while lighter materials such as rock settled on top. Today, Earth's interior is mostly solid, but it is still very hot, with temperatures rising to 10,800°F (6,000°C) in the core, which is hotter than the surface of the Sun. This powerful inner heat keeps the planet's interior slowly moving.

Volcanic action
Most of the rock in Earth's crust and mantle is solid. However, pockets of molten rock form where plates collide or in hotspots where heat wells up from Earth's core. In such places, molten rock may erupt from the surface, forming volcanoes.

Stormy skies
Water from the oceans creates clouds in the lower part of Earth's atmosphere. The layer of clouds gives us rain, snow, and storms such as this hurricane over Florida.

Oceans
Earth is the only planet with a large amount of liquid water on the surface, which makes it possible for life to flourish here. About 97 percent of the water is in the oceans, but there is also water in the air, in rivers and lakes, and in ice.

Atmosphere
Earth is cocooned from space by an atmosphere of gases. The composition has remained unchanged for the last 200 million years, with 78 percent nitrogen, 21 percent oxygen, and small traces of other gases such as carbon dioxide.

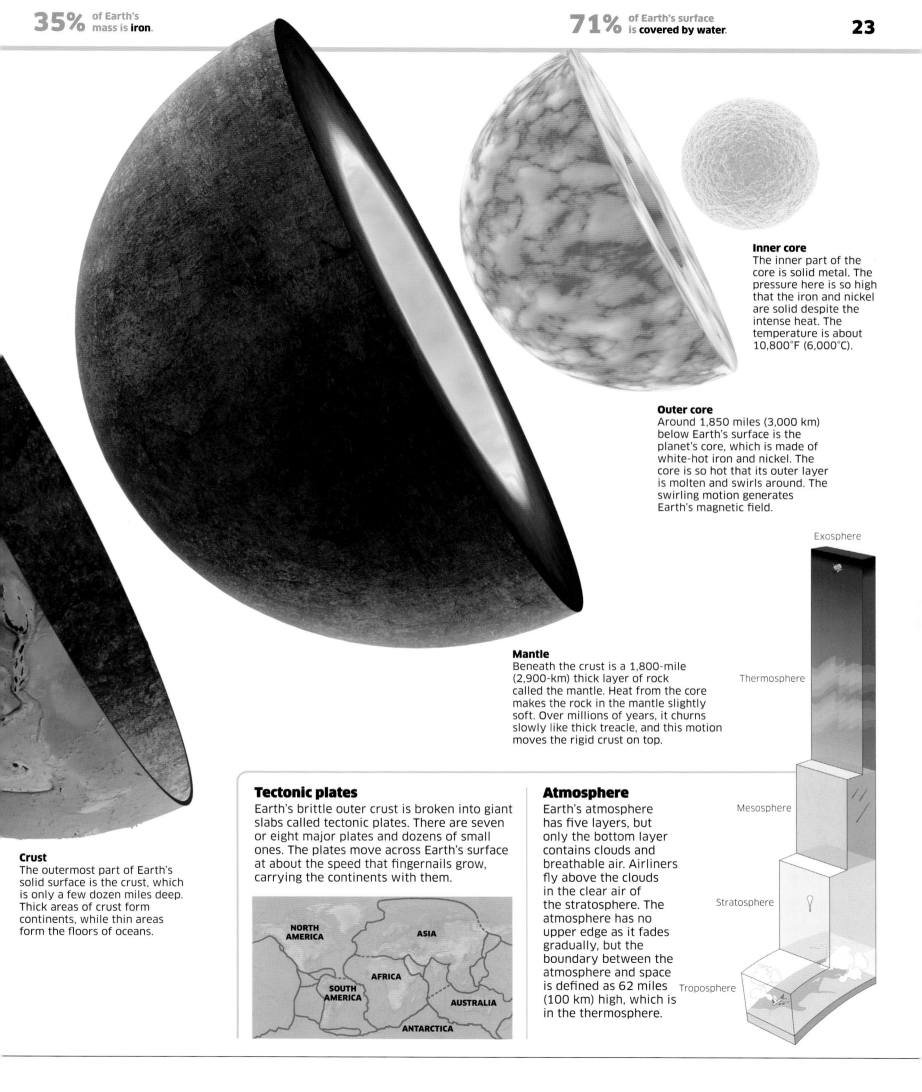

Inner core
The inner part of the core is solid metal. The pressure here is so high that the iron and nickel are solid despite the intense heat. The temperature is about 10,800°F (6,000°C).

Outer core
Around 1,850 miles (3,000 km) below Earth's surface is the planet's core, which is made of white-hot iron and nickel. The core is so hot that its outer layer is molten and swirls around. The swirling motion generates Earth's magnetic field.

Exosphere

Thermosphere

Mantle
Beneath the crust is a 1,800-mile (2,900-km) thick layer of rock called the mantle. Heat from the core makes the rock in the mantle slightly soft. Over millions of years, it churns slowly like thick treacle, and this motion moves the rigid crust on top.

Mesosphere

Crust
The outermost part of Earth's solid surface is the crust, which is only a few dozen miles deep. Thick areas of crust form continents, while thin areas form the floors of oceans.

Tectonic plates
Earth's brittle outer crust is broken into giant slabs called tectonic plates. There are seven or eight major plates and dozens of small ones. The plates move across Earth's surface at about the speed that fingernails grow, carrying the continents with them.

NORTH AMERICA

ASIA

AFRICA

SOUTH AMERICA

AUSTRALIA

ANTARCTICA

Atmosphere
Earth's atmosphere has five layers, but only the bottom layer contains clouds and breathable air. Airliners fly above the clouds in the clear air of the stratosphere. The atmosphere has no upper edge as it fades gradually, but the boundary between the atmosphere and space is defined as 62 miles (100 km) high, which is in the thermosphere.

Stratosphere

Troposphere

24 the Solar System ∘ **THE MOON**

838 lb (380 kg)—the amount of **Moon rock brought to Earth** by Apollo astronauts.

How the Moon formed

Scientists have various theories about how the Moon formed. Most think it formed when a small planet smashed into the young Earth around 4.5 billion years ago. The impact destroyed the small planet and tipped over Earth's axis of rotation. Debris was flung into space to form a cloud. Over time, the debris particles stuck together to become the Moon.

Weak gravity

The force of gravity, which pulls things to the ground, is much weaker on the Moon than on Earth, because the Moon has less mass. Astronauts weigh one-sixth of their Earth weight on the Moon and would be able to jump six times higher if they didn't have heavy spacesuits.

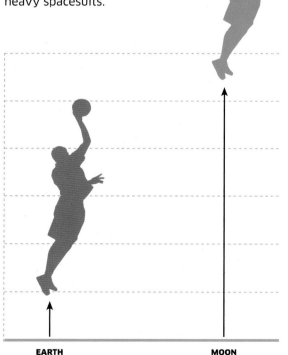

EARTH　　　　**MOON**

Inner core
In the center of the Moon is a ball of incredibly hot but solid iron about 300 miles (500 km) wide. Its temperature is about 2,400°F (1,300°C).

Outer core
Surrounding the inner core is a layer of iron that may have melted, thanks to lower pressure. This outer core is about 430 miles (700 km) wide.

Lower mantle
Heat from the core has probably melted the bottom of the mantle, which is made of rock.

The Moon

So near and bright that we can see it even in daytime, the Moon is the only object in space whose surface features are visible to the naked eye.

The Moon is a quarter as wide as Earth, making it the largest moon relative to its parent planet in the Solar System. It is also the largest and brightest object in the night sky by far, and its fascinating surface—scarred with hundreds of thousands of impact craters—is a spectacular sight through binoculars or telescopes. The Moon formed about 4.5 billion years ago, shortly after Earth, but unlike Earth, its surface has hardly changed in billions of years. The dark "seas," or maria, on its near side are flat plains formed by giant floods of lava that erupted about 3 billion years ago. Surrounding these are the lunar highlands, their ancient hills and valleys littered with the debris of countless meteorite impacts.

FAST FACTS

Time to orbit Earth: 27.32 Earth days

Mass (Earth = 1): 0.167

Distance from Earth: 239,227 miles (385,000 km)

Average diameter: 2,159 miles (3,474 km) wide

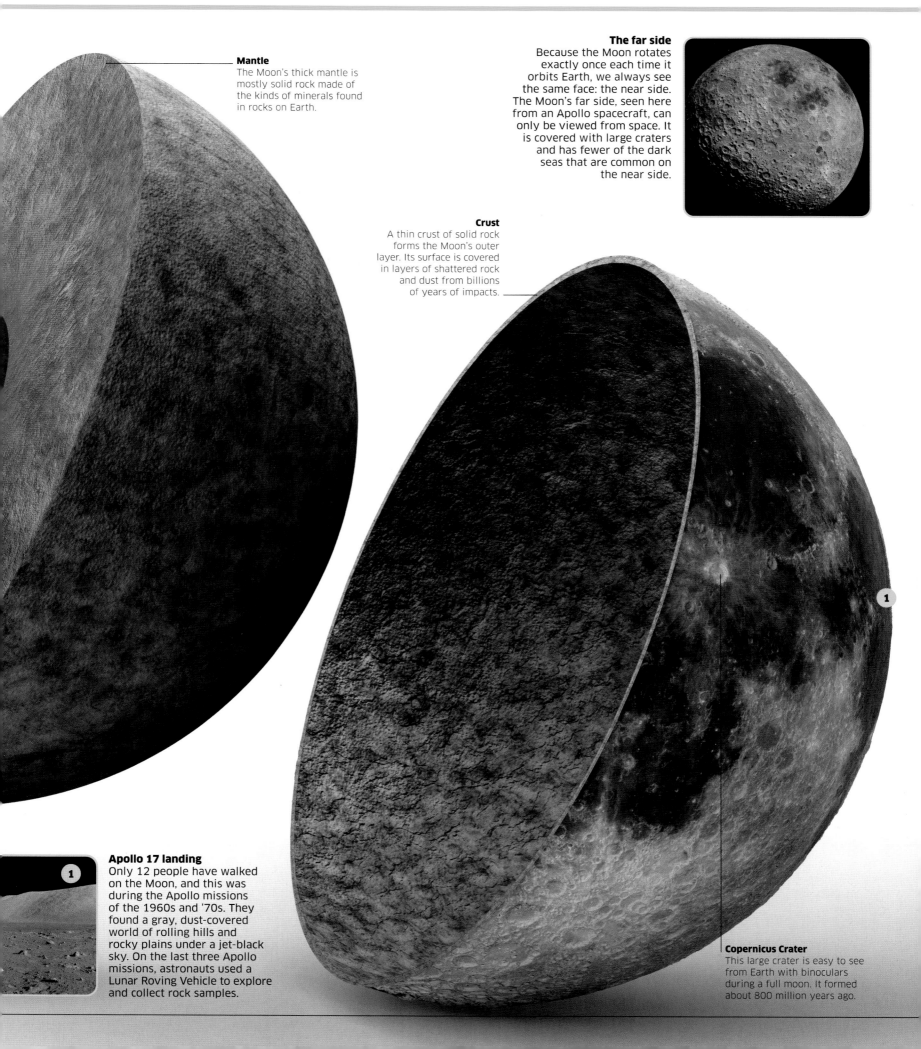

49 The number of times the Moon could **fit inside Earth**.

248°F (120°C)—**midday temperature** at the Moon's equator.

2,288 mph (3,683 kph)—the **speed** at which the **Moon orbits Earth**.

25

Mantle
The Moon's thick mantle is mostly solid rock made of the kinds of minerals found in rocks on Earth.

The far side
Because the Moon rotates exactly once each time it orbits Earth, we always see the same face: the near side. The Moon's far side, seen here from an Apollo spacecraft, can only be viewed from space. It is covered with large craters and has fewer of the dark seas that are common on the near side.

Crust
A thin crust of solid rock forms the Moon's outer layer. Its surface is covered in layers of shattered rock and dust from billions of years of impacts.

Apollo 17 landing
Only 12 people have walked on the Moon, and this was during the Apollo missions of the 1960s and '70s. They found a gray, dust-covered world of rolling hills and rocky plains under a jet-black sky. On the last three Apollo missions, astronauts used a Lunar Roving Vehicle to explore and collect rock samples.

Copernicus Crater
This large crater is easy to see from Earth with binoculars during a full moon. It formed about 800 million years ago.

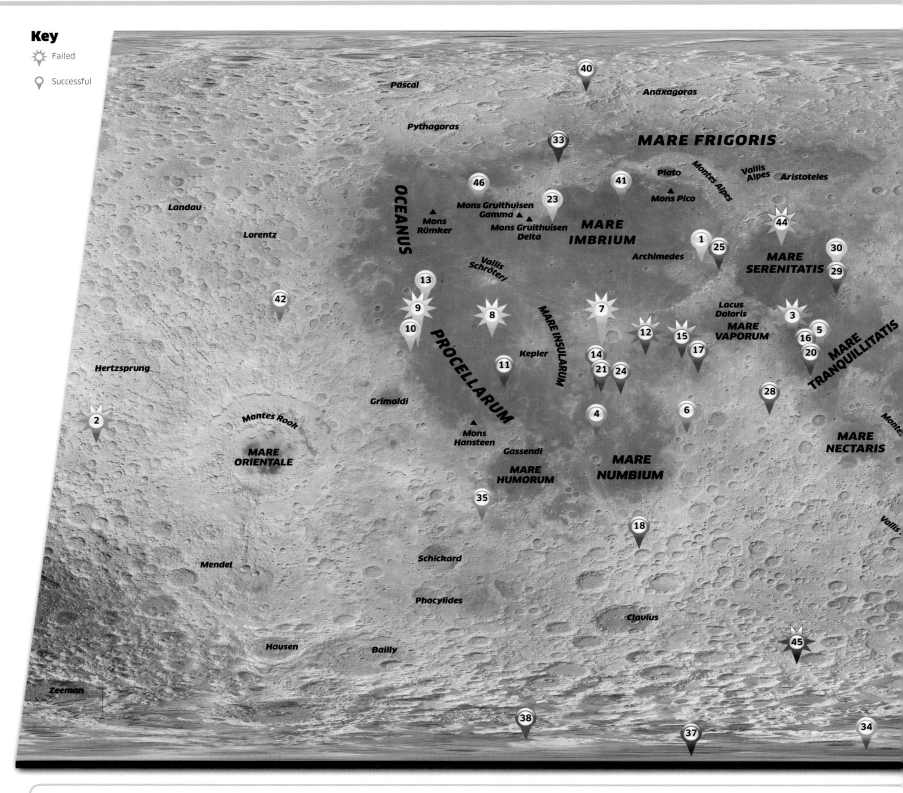

Key

☼ Failed

📍 Successful

Landmark missions

Most lunar spacecraft were launched as part of a series of similar missions. The US's Ranger Program, for example, included nine missions, only three of which were successful. The first 20 or so years of Moon missions were driven by rivalry between the US and USSR, who saw conquering space as a sign of military might or political strength.

Ranger program

The US Ranger spacecraft of the early 1960s were designed not to land on the Moon, but to crash into it. In the moments before impact, they beamed back stunning images of the surface, revealing craters of ever smaller size within larger craters.

Lunokhod

Russia's Lunokhod ("moonwalker") rovers looked like bathtubs on wheels but were a great success. Lunokhod 1 was the first rover to explore another world. It traveled nearly 7 miles (11 km) in 1970–1971 and took thousands of pictures. Powered by solar panels, it hibernated at night.

India's Moon Impact Probe of 2008 **crashed at high speed** into the Moon **to throw up debris** off the surface.

China's Chang'e 4 was the **first spacecraft** to land on the **dark side** of the Moon, which is **not visible from Earth**.

27

Exploring the Moon

Spacecraft have paid more visits to Earth's neighbor than any other body in the Solar System, and the Moon remains the only world beyond Earth that people have set foot on.

It takes only four days for a spacecraft to reach the Moon, which makes it an obvious target for robotic explorers. More than 100 missions to the Moon have been attempted, and more than 40 spacecraft have landed on it; their landing sites are shown on this map. Making a controlled, soft touchdown on the Moon is difficult, so most landers have performed "hard landings," crashing into the lunar surface at speed. The first hard landing was in 1959, and the first soft landing took place in 1966. Remarkably, just three years later, the US Apollo 11 mission placed two humans on the Moon and returned them safely to Earth.

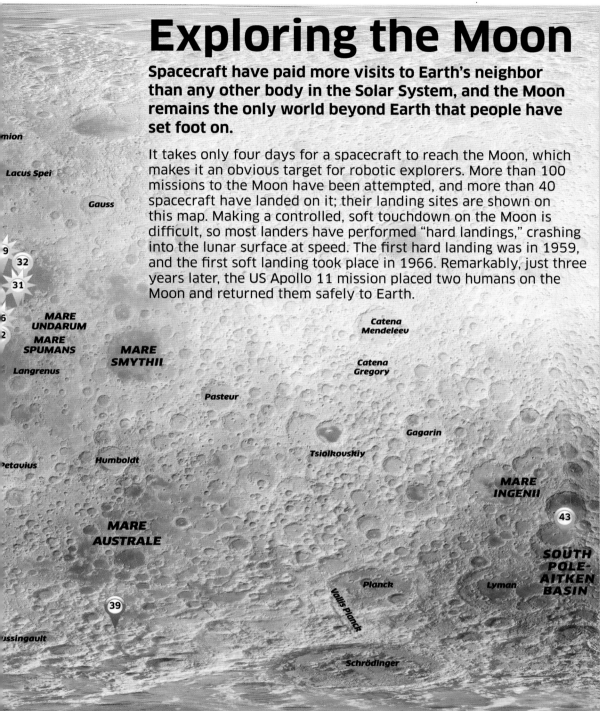

	Name	Year	Country
1	Luna 2	1959	
2	Ranger 4	1962	
3	Ranger 6	1964	
4	Ranger 7	1964	
5	Ranger 8	1965	
6	Ranger 9	1965	
7	Luna 5	1965	
8	Luna 7	1965	
9	Luna 8	1965	
10	Luna 9	1966	
11	Surveyor 1	1966	
12	Surveyor 2	1966	
13	Luna 13	1966	
14	Surveyor 3	1967	
15	Surveyor 4	1967	
16	Surveyor 5	1967	
17	Surveyor 6	1967	
18	Surveyor 7	1968	
19	Luna 15	1969	
20	Apollo 11	1969	
21	Apollo 12	1969	
22	Luna 16	1970	
23	Luna 17/Lunokhod 1	1970	
24	Apollo 14	1971	
25	Apollo 15	1971	
26	Luna 18	1971	
27	Luna 20	1972	
28	Apollo 16	1972	
29	Apollo 17	1972	
30	Luna 21/Lunokhod 2	1973	
31	Luna 23	1974	
32	Luna 24	1976	
33	Hiten*	1993	
34	Lunar prospector*	1999	
35	SMART-1*	2006	esa
36	Chang'e 1*	2007	
37	Chandrayaan 1*	2008	
38	LCROSS	2009	
39	SELENE*	2009	
40	GRAIL*	2012	
41	Chang'e 3/Yutu	2013	
42	LADEE*	2014	
43	Chang'e 4/Yutu-2	2018	
44	Beresheet	2019	
45	Vikram/Pragyaan	2019	
46	Chang'e 5	2020	

*Lunar orbiters that impacted at the end of their missions.

Apollo program
The success of Russia's Luna Program led their American rivals to invest billions of dollars in the Apollo program, which succeeded in landing six crewed craft on the Moon between 1969 and 1972. Later Apollo missions took a kind of car, the Lunar Roving Vehicle (LRV).

Yutu rover
China's Yutu rover arrived on the Moon in 2013, the first lunar rover since Lunokhod 2 in 1973. Although successful at first, it became unable to fold up its solar panels in preparation for the freezing lunar nights and was damaged by the cold. It drove a short distance after landing with the Chang'e 3 spacecraft.

2,050 miles (3,300 km)—the diameter of the **largest impact crater** in the solar system: Utopia Planitia on Mars.

Impact craters

Asteroids, comets, and meteorites fly through space at such terrific speeds that they release devastating energy when they collide with planets and moons, vaporizing solid rock in an instant. The scars they leave behind are called impact craters.

Meteorite impacts have scarred the rocky planets and moons with countless craters. Our Moon is covered with craters, but Earth has far fewer—on Earth, craters are destroyed by erosion and other forces, while those on the Moon remain preserved for billions of years. Many of the Moon's craters formed early in the solar system's history, when the inner planets were bombarded by asteroids. Collisions are much more rare today, but they still pose a deadly risk to Earth.

Lunar impact

The explosive force of a meteorite impact comes not just from the object's size but also from its speed. A typical meteorite is traveling at about 45,000 mph (70,000 kph) when it collides with a body such as the Moon, as shown here. This means it has 1,000 times as much kinetic energy as an equal-sized rock traveling at the speed of a car. When the meteorite collides, much of this kinetic energy turns into heat, causing rock in the ground to melt or even vaporize (turn to gas).

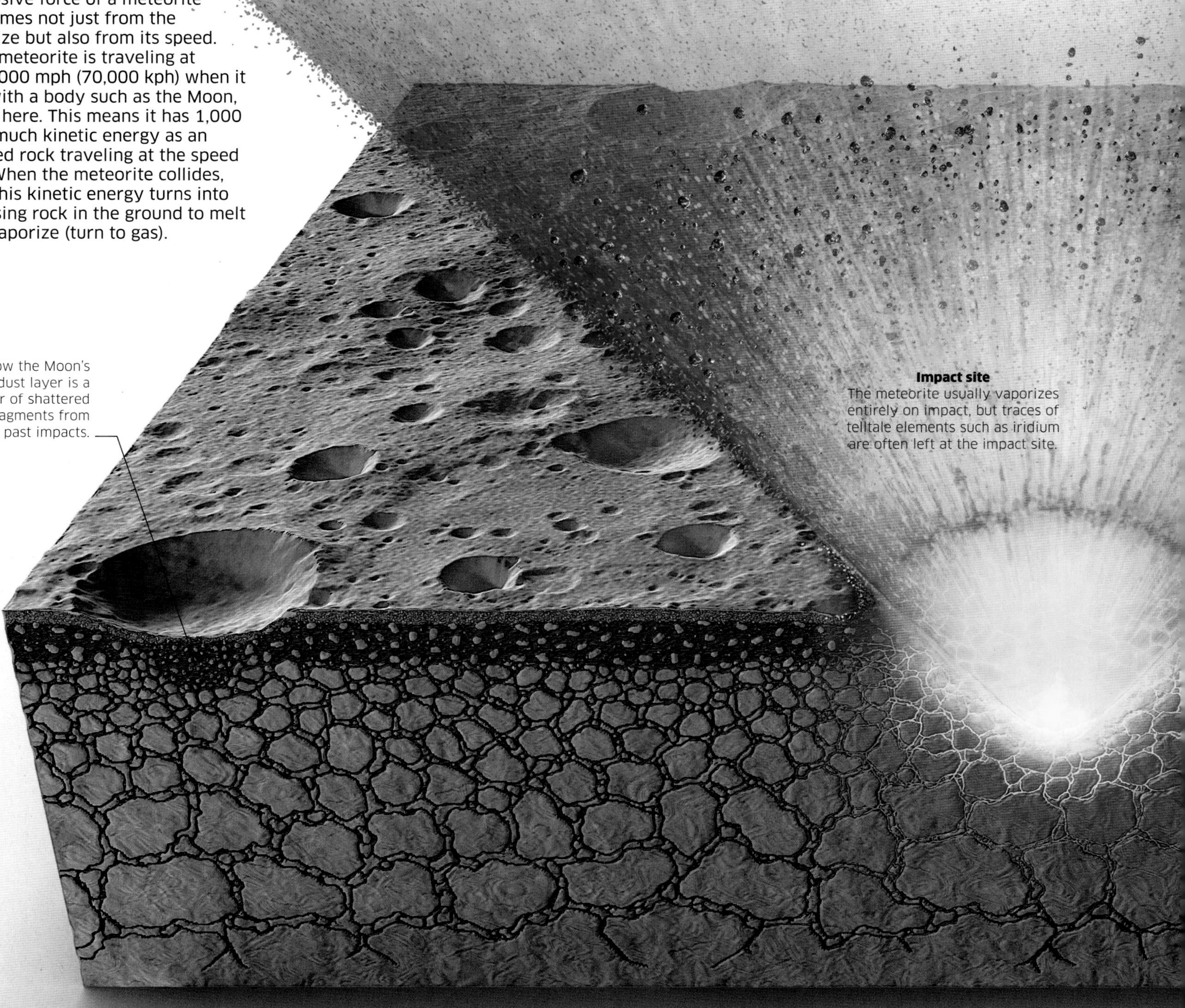

Ejecta curtain
After the meteorite hits, fragments of pulverized rock called ejecta are flung out in a vast cone and fall back to the ground far from the impact site.
Below the Moon's surface dust layer is a deep layer of shattered rock fragments from past impacts.
Impact site
The meteorite usually vaporizes entirely on impact, but traces of telltale elements such as iridium are often left at the impact site.

Vredefort crater in South Africa—the largest
crater on Earth—is around **2 billion years old**.

The Aitken Basin impact crater on the Moon's
south pole is **1,550 miles (2,500 km) wide**.

29

Barringer Crater

Barringer Crater (also known as Meteor
Crater) in Arizona was the first site
on Earth to be identified as an impact
crater. Measuring 0.7 miles (just over 1 km)
wide, it formed some 50,000 years ago
when a nickel-iron meteorite only 160 ft
(50 m) or so wide struck the ground at
around 30,000 mph (50,000 kph). The
collision unleashed a thousand times more
energy than the Hiroshima atomic bomb.

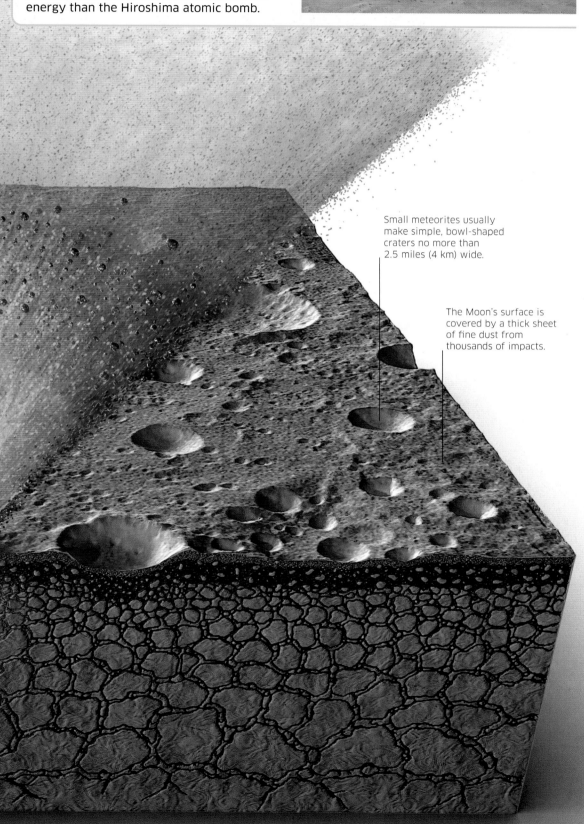

Small meteorites usually
make simple, bowl-shaped
craters no more than
2.5 miles (4 km) wide.

The Moon's surface is
covered by a thick sheet
of fine dust from
thousands of impacts.

How craters form

It takes a mere ten minutes for an impact
crater to fully form, but most of the action
happens in the split second after impact,
when the release of kinetic energy causes
an effect like a nuclear explosion. Small
impacts leave bowl-shaped pits, but
larger impacts create more complex
craters with central hills or terraces.

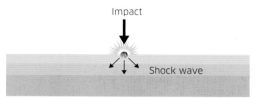

Impact

Shock wave

1 Contact
The meteorite smashes into the Moon,
compressing the surface dramatically and
sending a devastating shock wave through
the ground, pulverizing lunar rock.

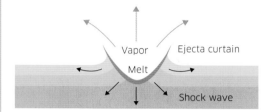

Vapor   Ejecta curtain
Melt

Shock wave

2 Transient crater forms
Energy released by the impact vaporizes
the meteorite and much of the surface rock.
Debris is thrown out in an ejecta curtain,
forming a deep but transient crater.

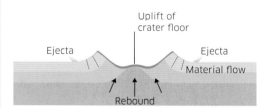

Uplift of
crater floor

Ejecta   Ejecta
Material flow
Rebound

3 Collapse and rebound
The force of a large impact is so great that
the pulverized ground flows like a liquid. The
sides of the transient crater collapse, and
the crater floor rebounds like water splashing,
creating a central hill.

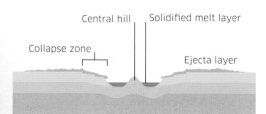

Central hill   Solidified melt layer

Collapse zone   Ejecta layer

4 Final crater
After a crater forms, its shape may
remain unchanged for a long time, unless
altered by volcanic or other geological
activity. On the Moon, old craters frequently
have younger craters within them.

Eclipses

A total solar eclipse is an amazing event. For a few minutes, the Sun disappears behind the Moon and day turns suddenly to night.

Eclipses happen when Earth and the Moon line up with the Sun and cast shadows on each other. When the Moon casts a shadow on Earth, our view of the Sun is blocked and we see a solar eclipse. When the Moon swings behind Earth and passes through Earth's shadow, we see a lunar eclipse—the Moon darkens and turns an unusual reddish color.

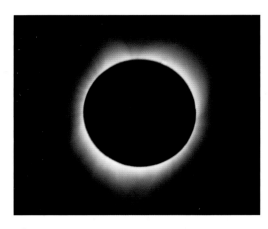

The corona

During a total solar eclipse, the Sun's spectacular outer atmosphere, which is normally impossible to see, becomes visible. Called the corona, it consists of billowing streams of hazy gas surrounding the Sun like a glowing white halo.

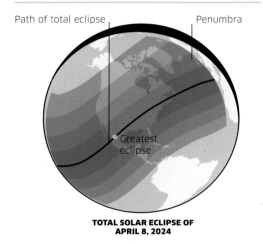

Path of total eclipse

Penumbra

Greatest eclipse

TOTAL SOLAR ECLIPSE OF APRIL 8, 2024

Eclipse path

Astronomers can predict eclipses years in advance. This diagram shows where the total solar eclipse of 2024 will be visible. It will pass across North America from the East coast of central Mexico at 18:07 (universal time) to the east coast of Newfoundland, Canada, at 19:46.

Solar eclipse

On most of its monthly orbits around Earth, the Moon does not line up directly with the Sun. When the Moon's main shadow (umbra) does sweep across Earth, it is only a few miles wide, so a total eclipse is visible only from a narrow strip across the globe. People viewing from the outer part of the shadow (the penumbra) barely notice the eclipse, as the Sun is not completely covered. Because Earth is rotating, the umbra sweeps across the planet's surface quickly, giving viewers in any one spot only a couple of minutes to see it.

MOON'S ORBIT

SUNLIGHT

SUN

108 minutes—the **longest lunar eclipse** in the last century.

In 1504, Christopher Columbus amazed the native people of Jamaica by correctly predicting a **lunar eclipse**.

The eclipsed Moon can appear **red, yellow, orange, or brown**.

31

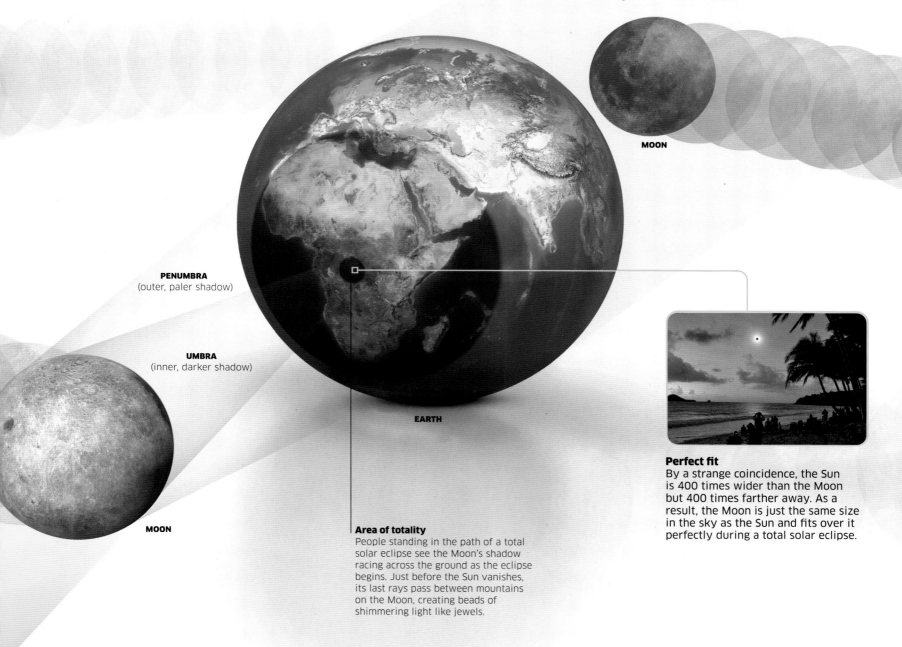

Lunar eclipse

In a total lunar eclipse, Earth's shadow covers the entire Moon. The Moon doesn't disappear from the night sky altogether, though, because some sunlight is deflected by Earth's atmosphere. This weak light is reddish like the light from a sunset, so it changes the Moon's color.

MOON

PENUMBRA
(outer, paler shadow)

UMBRA
(inner, darker shadow)

EARTH

MOON

Perfect fit
By a strange coincidence, the Sun is 400 times wider than the Moon but 400 times farther away. As a result, the Moon is just the same size in the sky as the Sun and fits over it perfectly during a total solar eclipse.

Area of totality
People standing in the path of a total solar eclipse see the Moon's shadow racing across the ground as the eclipse begins. Just before the Sun vanishes, its last rays pass between mountains on the Moon, creating beads of shimmering light like jewels.

Red Moon
Total lunar eclipses happen on average about once a year and are easy to see because anyone on Earth's night side can watch. Over several hours, Earth's shadow slowly creeps across the Moon's face, giving the remaining bright part of the Moon a peculiar shape. The period of totality, when the Moon turns red, can last nearly two hours.

Surface temperatures on Mars can plunge to **-225°F (-143°C)**.

The **most recent volcanic eruption** on Mars happened **2 million years ago**.

Mars

Mars is the second-nearest planet to Earth. It is a freezing desert world that may once have harbored life.

Mars is half Earth's size and much colder, but its arid surface looks oddly familiar, with rocky plains, rolling hills, and sand dunes much like those on Earth. The dusty ground is tinged brownish red by rust (iron oxide) and makes Mars look reddish from Earth, which is why the ancient Greeks and Romans named the planet after their god of war. Mars may have been warmer and wetter in the past, and there are signs that water once flowed across its surface, carving out gullies and laying down sedimentary rock. There may even be fossils of microscopic alien life forms hidden in the ground.

On the surface
The first soft landing on Mars was made by the Soviet probe Mars 3 in 1971. More than 25 spacecraft have successfully flown close to, orbited, or landed on Mars. Ten of these were landers that successfully returned data. Many missions to Mars have ended in failure, but some successful missions have placed robotic rovers on the planet, such as the car-sized rover Curiosity (above), which arrived in 2012.

Core
Mars's small, hot core is mostly iron, but unlike Earth's core, it is largely solid. Only the outer layer is partially molten.

Like Earth, Mars has permanent caps of ice at the poles.

Surface
The desertlike surface is made of rocky plains and valleys, rolling hills, mountains, and canyons. Sandy areas are pale; areas of bare rock look darker.

Valles Marineris
A gigantic canyon system called Valles Marineris is etched deep in the planet's surface near its equator.

Olympus Mons
Mars is home to the largest volcano in the Solar System: Olympus Mons. Its summit is 14 miles (22 km) high, making it three times taller than Mount Everest, though its slopes are so wide and gentle that a visitor would barely see it. Unlike Earth's volcanoes, those on Mars could keep growing for millions of years because the planet's crust doesn't move around.

Mars has the largest dust storms in the Solar System.

Only **24 out of the first 47** attempted missions to Mars were at least partially successful.

33

FAST FACTS

Surface gravity (Earth = 1): 0.38

Time to rotate once: 24.6 hours

Year: 687 Earth days

Moons: 2

Crust

The crust is made mostly of volcanic rock, covered in dust. Unlike Earth's crust, which is broken into moving plates, the Martian crust is a solid shell.

Mantle

Under the crust is Mars's mantle: a deep layer of silicate rock. In the past, the planet's internal heat kept the mantle soft enough to move like treacle, warping the crust and creating volcanoes.

Moons

Mars has two small, potato-shaped moons: Phobos, named after the Greek god of fear; and Deimos, named after the Greek god of terror. The moons may be asteroids that flew close to Mars and were captured by the planet's gravity.

PHOBOS   **DEIMOS**

Orbit and seasons

Mars rotates in just under 25 hours, making its day much the same as Earth's. Its year, though, is much longer, lasting 687 days. As Mars is tilted on its axis, like Earth, it has four seasons—winter, spring, summer, and fall—but they are all freezing cold and bone dry.

Atmosphere

Mars has a thin atmosphere made mostly of carbon dioxide gas. Strong winds sometimes whip up clouds of dust from the arid ground.

Billions of years ago, vast rivers flowed on the Martian surface, carving out giant valleys.

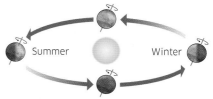

Summer   Winter

SEASONS IN NORTHERN HEMISPHERE

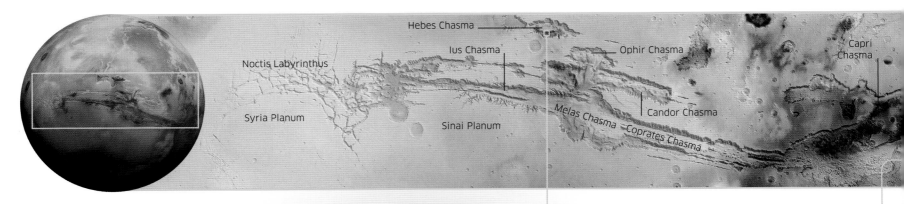

Noctis Labyrinthus

Hebes Chasma

Ius Chasma

Ophir Chasma

Capri Chasma

Syria Planum

Sinai Planum

Melas Chasma

Candor Chasma

Coprates Chasma

Sand dunes
Windblown sand collects on the floor of the Valles Marineris, forming huge dunes. In this false-color photo from the Mars Reconnaissance Orbiter, the reddish Martian sand appears blue. The patterns are continually changing as the dunes slowly migrate, blown by the wind.

Flood channels
In and around Valles Marineris are smaller valleys called outflow channels. These might have formed when ice suddenly melted, triggering floods, or they might have been created by volcanic eruptions.

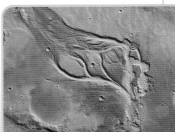

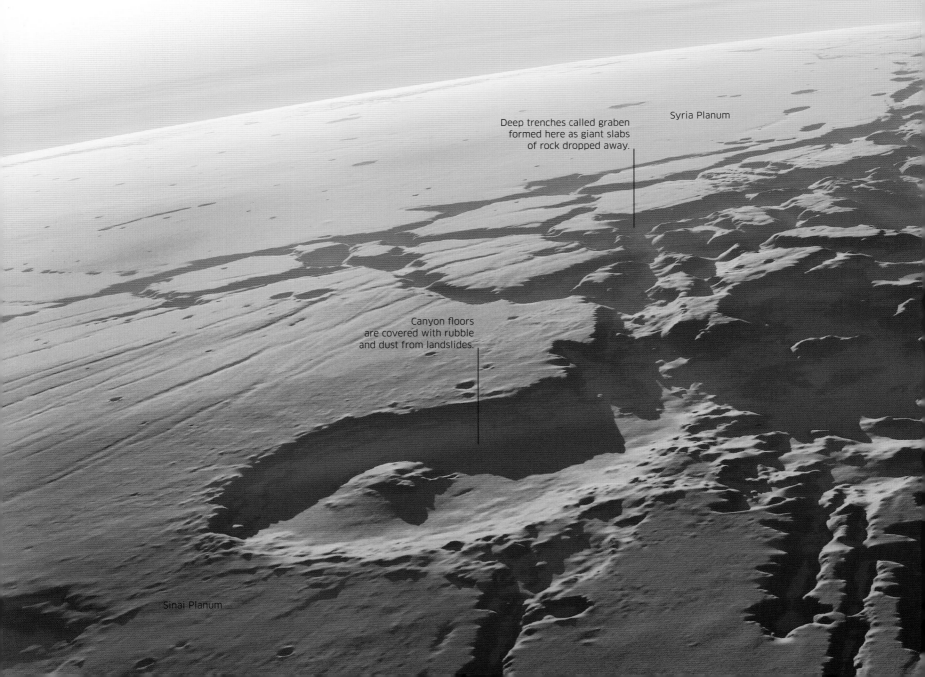

Syria Planum

Deep trenches called graben formed here as giant slabs of rock dropped away.

Canyon floors are covered with rubble and dust from landslides.

Sinai Planum

Valles Marineris is long enough to stretch from **New York to Los Angeles**.

The canyons contain **one-fifth of all the sand dunes** on Mars.

35

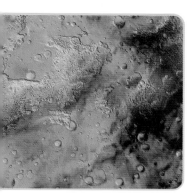

Valles Marineris

Five times as long and almost four times as deep as Earth's Grand Canyon, the massive Valles Marineris canyon system on Mars is one of the wonders of the Solar System.

Named after the Mariner 9 spacecraft that discovered it in 1972, Valles Marineris is a gigantic crack that first ripped open early in Mars's history as nearby volcanoes made the planet's crust bulge. Today, it stretches a fifth of the way around Mars and resembles a vast slash in the planet's face. Over billions of years, floods have gouged out deeper channels and landslides have destroyed valley walls, creating an amazingly varied landscape of canyons, cliffs, and dunes.

Maze of the night

At its western end, the Valles Marineris splits into a maze of steep-walled canyons known as Noctis Labyrinthus, or "maze of the night." The valleys here are rich in water-related minerals. Two billion years ago, when the rest of Mars was dry, they may have been moist enough to harbor life.

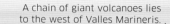

A chain of giant volcanoes lies to the west of Valles Marineris.

Some of the canyons in Noctis Labyrinthus are over 16,400 ft (5,000 m) deep.

Formation

Valles Marineris began to form around 3.5 billion years ago, when volcanic activity made a nearby region of the Martian crust bulge and split. Powerful forces pulled the crust apart, causing a central section to drop and form a deep valley. The valley grew wider over time as its walls eroded.

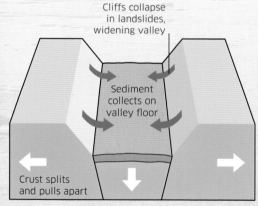

Cliffs collapse in landslides, widening valley

Sediment collects on valley floor

Crust splits and pulls apart

Valley floor sinks

Size

The immense Valles Marineris is more than 2,500 miles (4,000 km) long and up to 4.3 miles (7 km) deep. It dwarfs the Grand Canyon in Arizona, which is about 500 miles (800 km) long and 1 mile (1.6 km) deep.

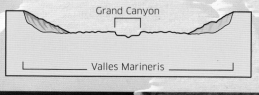

Grand Canyon

Valles Marineris

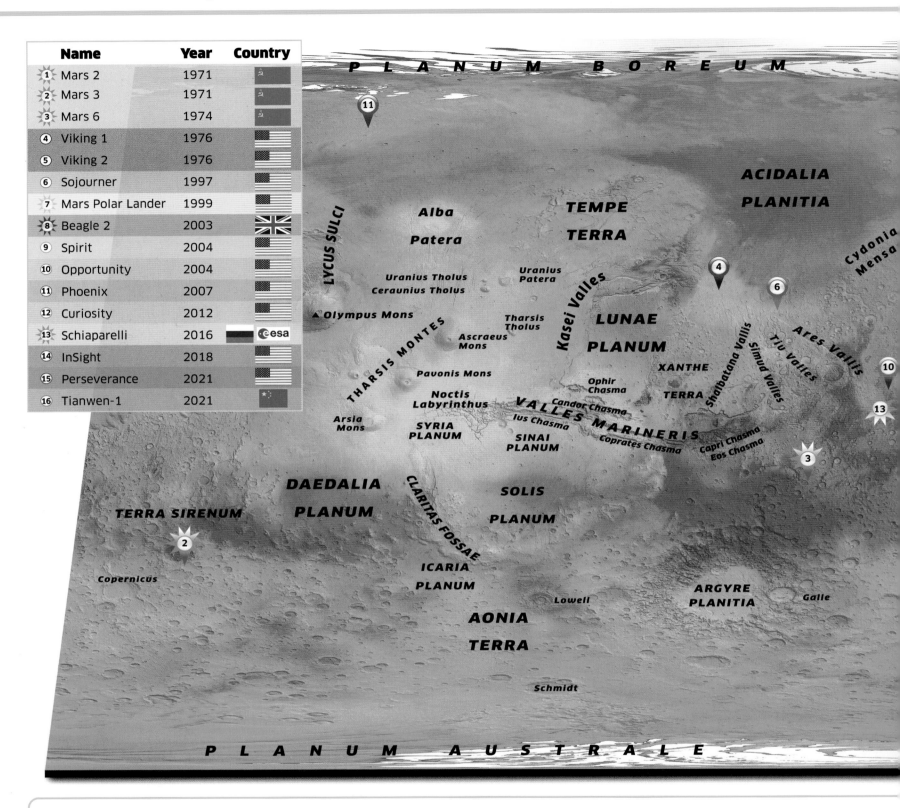

Name	Year	Country
1 Mars 2	1971	☭
2 Mars 3	1971	☭
3 Mars 6	1974	☭
4 Viking 1	1976	🇺🇸
5 Viking 2	1976	🇺🇸
6 Sojourner	1997	🇺🇸
7 Mars Polar Lander	1999	🇺🇸
8 Beagle 2	2003	🇬🇧
9 Spirit	2004	🇺🇸
10 Opportunity	2004	🇺🇸
11 Phoenix	2007	🇺🇸
12 Curiosity	2012	🇺🇸
13 Schiaparelli	2016	esa
14 InSight	2018	🇺🇸
15 Perseverance	2021	🇺🇸
16 Tianwen-1	2021	🇨🇳

Viking invaders

In July 1976, Viking 1 became the first spacecraft to land on Mars, followed in September by Viking 2 (above). The landers tested the Martian soil for biological activity but found no evidence of life.

Bounce-down on Mars

The Pathfinder spacecraft used airbags to land safely on Mars in 1997. It bounced five times before coming to a stop. The airbags then deflated and the spacecraft's side panels folded open like petals to allow a small rover to drive out.

6 years, 3 months, 22 days—the length of time **Viking 1 continued to work** on Mars.

330 ft (100 m)—the distance that the **Sojourner rover traveled** on Mars.

37

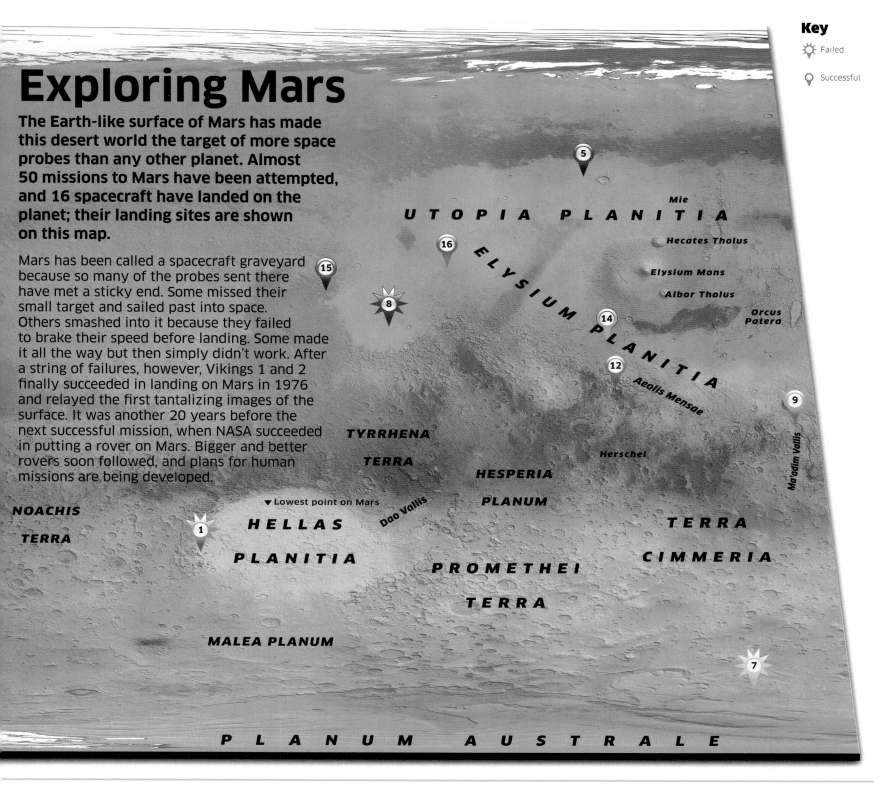

Key

☼ Failed

◗ Successful

Exploring Mars

The Earth-like surface of Mars has made this desert world the target of more space probes than any other planet. Almost 50 missions to Mars have been attempted, and 16 spacecraft have landed on the planet; their landing sites are shown on this map.

Mars has been called a spacecraft graveyard because so many of the probes sent there have met a sticky end. Some missed their small target and sailed past into space. Others smashed into it because they failed to brake their speed before landing. Some made it all the way but then simply didn't work. After a string of failures, however, Vikings 1 and 2 finally succeeded in landing on Mars in 1976 and relayed the first tantalizing images of the surface. It was another 20 years before the next successful mission, when NASA succeeded in putting a rover on Mars. Bigger and better rovers soon followed, and plans for human missions are being developed.

UTOPIA PLANITIA

Mie

Hecates Tholus

Elysium Mons

Albor Tholus

Orcus Patera

ELYSIUM PLANITIA

Aeolis Mensae

Ma'adim Vallis

TYRRHENA TERRA

Herschel

HESPERIA PLANUM

▼ Lowest point on Mars

Dao Vallis

NOACHIS TERRA

HELLAS PLANITIA

PROMETHEI TERRA

TERRA CIMMERIA

TERRA

MALEA PLANUM

PLANUM AUSTRALE

Curiosity rover

The Curiosity rover is the most successful Martian visitor so far and has sent back a huge amount of data. On August 6, 2013, Curiosity marked the anniversary of its landing by playing "Happy Birthday" out loud—the first time music had been played on another planet.

Ingenuity

The Perseverance rover carried a small helicopter, called Ingenuity, to test whether it would fly, and whether similar machines could be useful on future missions. Ingenuity became the first powered, controlled helicopter on another planet when it flew to a height of 33 ft (10 m) on the first of its many flights.

Red planet

The rust-colored landscapes of Mars remind us of sandy deserts on Earth, but the temperature here is as cold as Earth's South Pole in midwinter.

Mars would be deadly to humans without spacesuits, but robotic rovers can operate there. NASA's car-sized Curiosity rover took this photo of its tracks on February 9, 2014– day 538 of its tour of Mars. The distant hills form part of the rim of a 96-mile (155-km) wide crater that Curiosity is searching for signs that Mars may once have been suitable for life.

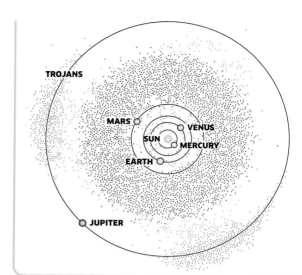

Asteroid Belt

Most asteroids are in a donut-shaped belt between the orbits of Mars and Jupiter, but there are also scattered asteroids among the inner planets and large groups of asteroids in the same orbit as Jupiter, known as "Trojans." The belt often looks crowded in illustrations, but in reality, the asteroids are so far apart that passengers on a spacecraft flying through the belt probably wouldn't see a single one. The total mass of all the asteroids in the belt is only 4 percent of the Moon's mass.

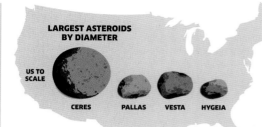

LARGEST ASTEROIDS BY DIAMETER

US TO SCALE

CERES PALLAS VESTA HYGEIA

Size

Large asteroids are very rare—only 26 asteroids are known to be more than 125 miles (200 km) wide. However, there are hundreds of thousands of asteroids wider than 0.6 mile (1 km) and millions of smaller ones.

Asteroids

Millions of rocks known as asteroids hurtle around the inner Solar System, most of them in a belt between the orbits of Mars and Jupiter. They range in size from pebbles to monsters hundreds of miles wide.

Asteroids are leftovers from the cloud of rubble that gave birth to the planets. Most of the rubble in the inner Solar System collected together to become the rocky planets, but the rocks near Jupiter were disturbed by the giant planet's gravity and failed to build up. The Asteroid Belt is what remains today of that debris. Asteroids follow their own orbits around the Sun, spinning as they go, like planets. They are also called minor planets, and the largest asteroid of all—Ceres—is classed as a dwarf planet. Asteroids occasionally collide, forming craters or even smashing into each other. Less often, they crash into moons and planets.

Head and body
The shape of Toutatis suggests it might have formed from two asteroids that stuck together, a small asteroid forming the "head" (left) and a larger one forming the "body." Most asteroids have an irregular shape, but the largest ones pull themselves into a sphere through their own gravity.

2001 The year of the **first soft landing** on an asteroid.

2069 The year that the asteroid Toutatis will next **pass close to Earth**.

0 The chance of Toutatis **hitting Earth** in the next **600 years**.

41

Because of its potato shape, Toutatis spins around two axes. As a result, it tumbles through space like **a badly thrown football.**

Ceres

This image of the cratered surface of Ceres, taken by NASA's Dawn spacecraft, has been enhanced to bring out detail. Dawn orbited asteroid Vesta in 2011–2012, then flew on to study Ceres from 2015 to 2017. Unlike most asteroids, Ceres is rich in water, and salty water coming up to the surface leaves behind bright patches of crystals when it evaporates.

Craters
Asteroids are pockmarked with craters caused by collisions with smaller asteroids.

Toutatis

In 1989, French astronomer Christian Pollas discovered the 3 mile (5 km) wide asteroid 4179 Toutatis, shown in the artist's impression above. Toutatis is a near-Earth asteroid, which means its orbit sometimes brings it close to Earth. When it passed Earth in 2004, it was just four times farther away than the Moon. Asteroids as big as Toutatis hit Earth about once every 20 million years but have the potential to wipe out the entire world population. Today, astronomers keep a close eye on asteroids that wander close to our planet. About 25,000 near-Earth asteroids have been found, of which about 1,000 are more than 0.6 mile (1 km) wide—large enough to make a crater the size of a big city.

Shooting stars and meteorites

The shooting stars we sometimes see streaking across the night sky are not stars at all, but tiny flecks of space rock. Millions of these rock fragments, called meteoroids, hurtle into Earth's atmosphere every year.

Most meteoroids come from the Asteroid Belt or from comets, but a few are chipped off the Moon or Mars by meteorite impacts. They are usually no bigger than a grain of sand, but even tiny grains hit the atmosphere so hard and fast—at up to 44 miles (71 km) per second—that they make the air glow brightly as they ram into it, causing the streak of light we call a meteor or shooting star. Most meteoroids burn up entirely in the atmosphere, but a few really big ones survive to crash into the ground as meteorites.

Incoming meteorite

When a big space rock hits the atmosphere, the effect is dramatic. The air in its path is squeezed violently and heated until it glows brilliantly. As the rock tears through the air, its outer layers are scorched and blasted away, forming trails of vapor and smoke that stream out behind it. A large stony meteoroid can get so hot that it bursts in midair, exploding in a dazzling flash and unleashing a deep roar that carries for miles.

Rocks in the sky

Meteoroids the size of sand grains become meteors (shooting stars), which are only visible at night. Those as big as soccer balls can create brilliant "fireballs" that are visible even by day and may leave a trail of smoke. Some big stony meteoroids hit the atmosphere with such force, they explode in midair. The blast from these "airburst meteors" can flatten trees. Meteoroids that reach the ground and survive are called meteorites.

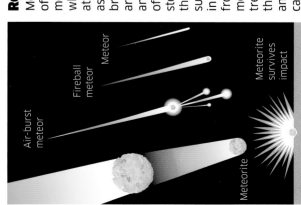

Air-burst meteor

Fireball meteor

Meteor

Meteorite survives impact

Meteorite

Meteor showers

At certain times of year, Earth passes through the trail of dust left in space by a comet, sometimes causing over 100 visible meteors an hour. They all appear to come from the same point, called the radiant. Impressive meteor showers include the Perseids in August and the Geminids in December.

Radiant

Big hitters

The largest meteorite in North America is the Willamette meteorite in the American Museum of Natural History. Discovered in 1902 in Oregon, this massive chunk of iron weighs 16.5 tons (15 tonnes). It is thought to have landed about 13,000 years ago.

WILLAMETTE METEORITE IN THE AMERICAN MUSEUM OF NATURAL HISTORY, NEW YORK

Every day, more than **100 meteorites** weighing at least 0.35 oz (10 g) reach Earth's surface.

In 1908, **a meteor airburst over Siberia** flattened 770 square miles (2,000 square km) of trees.

4.55 billion years—the **age of most meteoroids.**

43

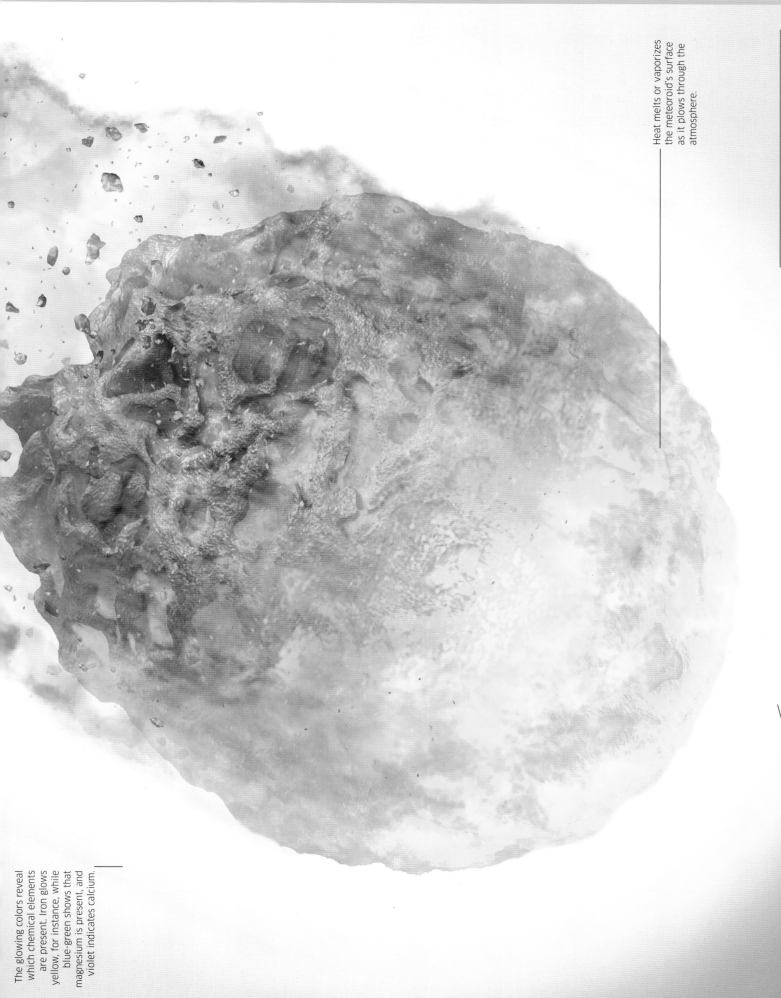

Heat melts or vaporizes the meteoroid's surface as it plows through the atmosphere.

110 tons (100 tonnes) of meteors and meteorites collide with Earth every day—about the same weight as 20 elephants.

The glowing colors reveal which chemical elements are present. Iron glows yellow, for instance, while blue-green shows that magnesium is present, and violet indicates calcium.

Ahead of the meteorite, air is compressed with such force that it becomes white-hot and glows.

Comets and asteroids have been observed **crashing into Jupiter.**

−234°F (−148°C)—the **temperature** of Jupiter's cloud tops.

Jupiter

The largest planet of all, Jupiter is more than twice as massive as all the other planets combined. Unlike rocky worlds, such as Earth or Mars, Jupiter is a gas giant—a vast, spinning globe of gas and liquid with no solid surface.

Jupiter is 1,300 times greater in volume than Earth, and the pull of its gravity is so great that it bends the paths of comets and asteroids flying through the Solar System. Despite the planet's great size, it spins quickly, giving it a day less than 10 hours long. The rapid rotation makes Jupiter bulge visibly at its equator and whips its colorful clouds into horizontal stripes and swirling storms. The largest storm—the Great Red Spot—is bigger than Earth. Lightning can be seen flickering through the dark on Jupiter's night side, and the whole planet is surrounded by belts of lethal radiation that would be extremely dangerous for humans.

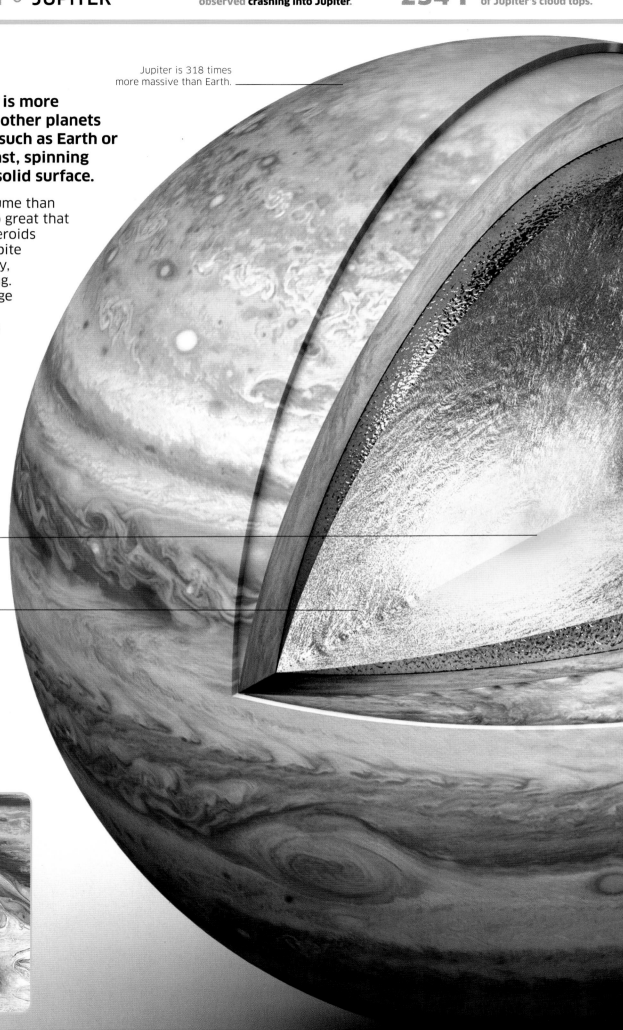

Jupiter is 318 times more massive than Earth.

Core
Jupiter has a large diffuse core where heavier elements blend with hydrogen and helium. At about 27,032–36,032°F (15,000–20,000°C), the center is hotter than the Sun's surface.

Extent of core
The core extends about halfway to the surface, gradually blending with the layer above.

Storm spots
Storms in Jupiter's atmosphere form ovals of different colors. The 7,450 mile (12,000 km) wide Great Red Spot has been raging for several hundred years. Its red color is probably caused by sunlight breaking up chemicals in the tops of the highest clouds.

225 mph (360 kph)—**typical wind speed** on Jupiter.

29 miles (46 km) per second—the **speed at which the Galileo probe** entered Jupiter's atmosphere.

Jupiter gives out **1.6 times more energy** than falls on it due to **internal heating** of the planet.

45

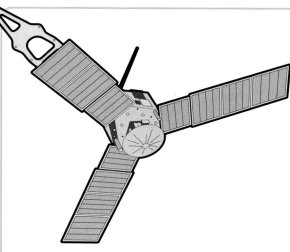

Polar lights
Spectacular light displays called auroras (seen here in ultraviolet light) sometimes occur at Jupiter's poles. Like Earth's northern and southern lights, they are caused by charged particles from space that crash into the atmosphere and make the gas atoms glow. The auroras on Jupiter are up to 100 times brighter than those on Earth.

Liquid metallic layer
Under huge pressure, the hydrogen deep inside Jupiter behaves like a liquid metal. Helium and neon are probably also present in this layer.

Liquid layer
Above the metallic layer is a vast sea of liquid hydrogen. This sea has no surface; instead, it gradually thins out at the top, merging with the gas in Jupiter's atmosphere.

Atmosphere
Hydrogen gas makes up 90 percent of Jupiter's atmosphere. The rest is mostly helium, with small amounts of other elements.

Winds blow in opposite directions in neighboring cloud bands, causing swirling patterns at the boundaries.

Cloud layer
The cloud layer is only 30 miles (50 km) thick. Most of the clouds are thought to consist of frozen ammonia crystals.

FAST FACTS

Surface gravity (Earth = 1): 2.36

Time to rotate once: 9.9 hours

Year: 12 Earth years

Moons: At least 79

Juno spacecraft
NASA's Juno spacecraft went into orbit around Jupiter in July 2016. Its mission was to study Jupiter's gravity, magnetic field, and composition and to take images of the planet. Juno has changed scientists' views about Jupiter's core. They now think it is a mix of hydrogen, helium, and heavier elements extending halfway to the surface.

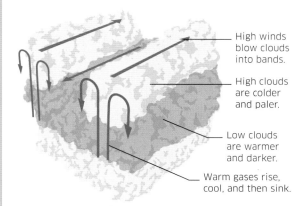

High winds blow clouds into bands.

High clouds are colder and paler.

Low clouds are warmer and darker.

Warm gases rise, cool, and then sink.

Cloud bands
Jupiter's colorful bands are made up of clouds at different heights. In the paler bands, gases are rising and forming high icy clouds. Gaps between these bands of high clouds allow us to see down to the warmer cloud layers below, which are darker in color.

Tenuous rings
Jupiter's faint rings were first seen in 1979 in images taken by Voyager 1. They have since been detected from Earth by viewing the planet in infrared light. The rings consist mainly of dust from Jupiter's smaller moons.

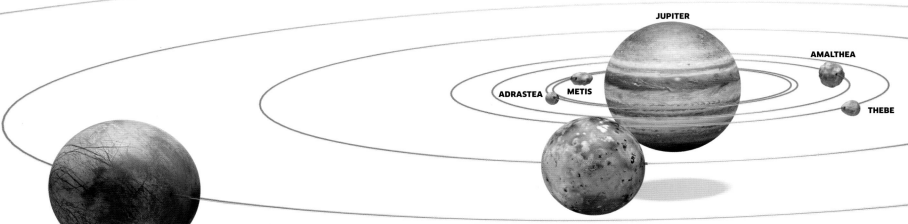

JUPITER

AMALTHEA

ADRASTEA   METIS

THEBE

Io
Caught in a tug-of-war between the gravity of Jupiter and the other Galilean moons, Io is torn by powerful forces that have melted its insides. Molten rock, rich in colorful sulfur chemicals, erupts all over its surface from giant volcanoes.

Europa
Europa's icy surface is covered in strange grooves and cracks. Just as Earth's crust of rock is broken into colliding fragments, so Europa's crust of ice is broken into sheets that push and pull in opposite directions. Water from a salty ocean deep underground erupts from the cracks and freezes, creating new ground.

Ganymede
This large moon is nearly 10 percent wider than Mercury and would be called a planet if it orbited the Sun rather than Jupiter. Its surface is a jigsaw of ancient dark areas with lots of craters and younger paler areas with few craters. Eruptions of slushy ice from underground have resurfaced the younger areas.

Moons of Jupiter

Jupiter's huge mass makes the pull of its gravity very strong. As a result, the giant planet has trapped at least 70 tiny moons to add to its original eight. These small moons were originally asteroids or comets, but they flew close enough to Jupiter to be captured into orbit by its gravity. The original eight moons are large, and four of them are like small planets.

Jupiter's four largest moons are called the Galilean moons, because they were discovered by the great Italian astronomer Galileo Galilei in 1610. These four worlds are very different. The innermost moon, Io, has hundreds of active volcanoes. Next is Europa, which is covered in ice, though a hidden ocean lies below—one of the few places in the Solar System that might harbor life. Ganymede is the Solar System's largest moon and the only one with a magnetic field. Callisto is covered in craters. Its surface is considered the oldest of any moon or planet in the Solar System.

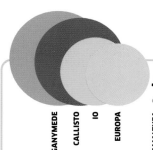

Jupiter's moons to scale

GANYMEDE | CALLISTO | IO | EUROPA | AMALTHEA | HIMALIA | THEBE | ELARA | PASIPHAE | CARME | METIS | LYSITHEA | SINOPE | ANANKE | LEDA | ADRASTEA | CALLIRRHOE | THEMISTO | PRAXIDIKE | IOCASTE | TAYGETE | KALYKE | MEGACLITE | DIA | HELIKE | HARPALYKE | HERMIPPE | THYONE | CHALDENE | AOEDE | EUKELADE | ISONOE | EIRENE | AUTONOE | EUANTHE | AITNE | ERINOME | EURYDOME | HEGEMONE | ARCHE | JUPITER LXX | ERSA | PANDIA | EUPORIE | EUPHEME | JUPITER LV | THELXINOE | ORTHOSIE | S/2003 J16 | MNEME | HERSE | KALE | JUPITER LXI | PHILOPHROSYNE | S/2003 J10 | S/2003 J23 | KALLICHORE | PASITHEE | JUPITER LI | KORE | CYLLENE | S/2003 J2 | SPONDE | S/2003 J4 | JUPITER LXVIII | JUPITER LXIV | JUPITER LXVI | JUPITER LXIII | JUPITER LXVII | JUPITER LIX | S/2003 J12 | JUPITER LXXII | JUPITER LII | JUPITER LVI | S/2003 J9 | VALETUDO | JUPITER LIV | JUPITER LXIX

Jupiter's moon Io is the **most volcanically active world** in the entire Solar System.

Jupiter's moon Ganymede is **larger than the planet Mercury.**

47

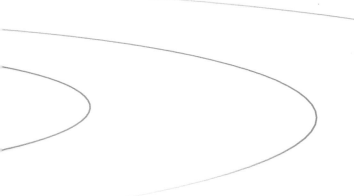

Callisto

The Solar System's most heavily cratered object, Callisto is peppered with meteorite scars. The large number of craters shows that its surface is very old. Oddly, there are very few small craters on Callisto. Scientists think small craters gradually fade away as the ice in their rims evaporates into space, leaving small hills.

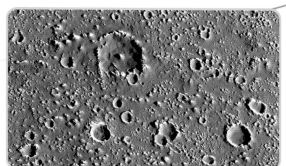

Outer moons

Jupiter's many outer moons are only a few miles wide and orbit the planet in a messy cloud. The inner moons travel in the same direction as Jupiter's rotation, and their circular orbits line up neatly with Jupiter's equator. In contrast, the outer moons orbit in both directions, and their orbits are often wildly tilted or oval. This pattern suggests that most of them are captured objects.

Meteorites have blasted holes in Callisto's dark surface, revealing the pale ice below.

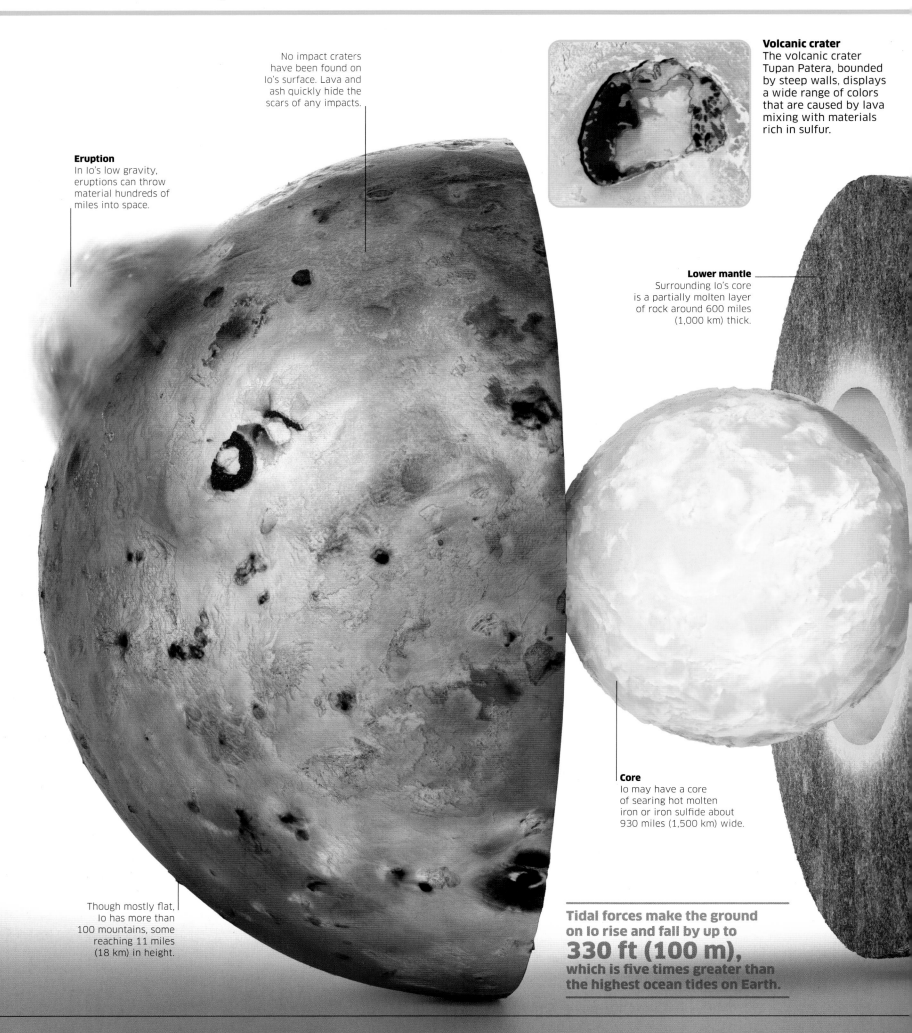

No impact craters have been found on Io's surface. Lava and ash quickly hide the scars of any impacts.

Volcanic crater
The volcanic crater Tupan Patera, bounded by steep walls, displays a wide range of colors that are caused by lava mixing with materials rich in sulfur.

Eruption
In Io's low gravity, eruptions can throw material hundreds of miles into space.

Lower mantle
Surrounding Io's core is a partially molten layer of rock around 600 miles (1,000 km) thick.

Core
Io may have a core of searing hot molten iron or iron sulfide about 930 miles (1,500 km) wide.

Though mostly flat, Io has more than 100 mountains, some reaching 11 miles (18 km) in height.

Tidal forces make the ground on Io rise and fall by up to 330 ft (100 m), which is five times greater than the highest ocean tides on Earth.

2 trillion watts—the **power of the electric current** that flows between Io and Jupiter.

Io is exposed to such **high radiation levels** that an astronaut on the surface would die within hours.

49

Time to orbit Jupiter: 1.77 Earth days

Mass (Earth = 1): 0.015

Surface temperature: –262°F (–163°C)

Diameter: 2,262 miles (3,643 km)

IO   THE MOON

Molten upper mantle
A 30-mile- (50-km-) thick layer of molten rock probably lies under the moon's crust.

Atmosphere
Io has a thin atmosphere of sulfur dioxide that freezes onto the ground at night and evaporates by day. Constant strong winds blow from the sunny side of Io to the dark side.

This active volcano, called Pele, has a lava lake in its central crater.

Crust
Io has a 25-mile- (40-km-) thick crust of rock covered with solidified lava and sulfur chemicals from eruptions. The varying colors come from different forms of sulfur.

Io

The most volcanically active body in the solar system, Jupiter's moon Io is constantly spewing matter into space from its eruptions. Its blotchy, lava-covered face is a world away from the icy terrain of Jupiter's other moons.

This moon's volcanic eruptions don't just affect Io itself. They pump huge amounts of material into space, forming a vast, doughnut-shaped ring of charged particles around Jupiter, called a plasma torus. The plasma torus allows electric currents to flow through space between Jupiter and Io, triggering lightning storms in Jupiter and causing gases around Io to glow. The existence of Io's volcanoes was predicted by scientists before the Voyager 1 spacecraft had a close encounter with the moon in 1979. The incredible images Voyager took confirmed the scientists' predictions: Io erupts so frequently that the moon is literally turning itself inside out.

Tidal heating
The cause of Io's volcanic activity is gravity. As it orbits Jupiter, Io is stretched in different directions by the gravitational pull of Jupiter and the other moons. These tidal forces keep changing Io's shape, causing friction that heats up and melts its interior.

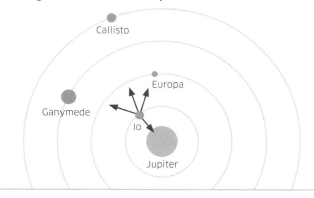

Callisto

Europa

Ganymede

Io

Jupiter

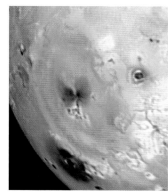

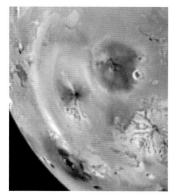

Changing face
Io's appearance can change quickly because of its frequent eruptions. These two images taken five months apart show how fallout from an eruption blanketed a 250-mile- (400-km-) wide area with black material. The red ring is fallout from another volcano, called Pele.

50   the Solar System ○ **SATURN**

764 The number of times Earth's volume could **fit inside Saturn**.

Saturn

The spectacular rings around this giant planet make it one of the wonders of our Solar System. Saturn is the second-biggest planet after Jupiter, and like Jupiter, it has a huge family of moons.

Saturn is a gas giant—a vast, spinning globe made of chemicals that exist as gases on Earth, such as hydrogen. Saturn is 96 percent hydrogen, but only the outer layers are gas. Deep inside the planet, the hydrogen is compressed into a liquid by the weight of the gas above it. Saturn is almost as wide as Jupiter but has less than a third of its mass, making Saturn far less dense. In fact, it is the least dense planet of all. It is also the least spherical: Saturn spins so fast that it bulges at the equator, making it wider than it is tall. Like Jupiter, it has a stormy outer atmosphere driven by powerful winds that sweep its clouds into horizontal bands.

Saturn's poles turn blue in winter, an effect caused by sunlight being scattered by relatively cloud-free air.

Atmosphere
Saturn's atmosphere is mostly hydrogen and helium, with clouds of ammonia ice and water ice on top. Horizontal winds sweep the creamy-colored clouds into bands like those on Jupiter, but with fewer large eddies and storms.

Liquid hydrogen layer
The huge weight of Saturn's atmosphere squeezes the hydrogen underneath into a liquid, forming a vast internal ocean. This sea of liquid hydrogen has no surface—instead, it gradually merges into the gas layer above it.

Rings
Saturn's rings are made of fragments of water ice orbiting the planet in an almost perfectly flat plane. The ice reflects the Sun's light, often making the rings look very bright.

FAST FACTS

Surface gravity (Earth = 1): 1.02

Time to rotate once: 10.7 hours

Year: 29 Earth years

Moons: At least 82

Lightning on Saturn is **10,000 times stronger** than lightning on Earth.

Saturn is the only planet in the Solar System that is **less dense than water**.

1979 The year Saturn was first **visited by a spacecraft**.

51

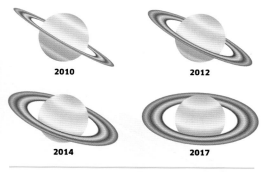

POLAR HEXAGON

POLAR HURRICANE

Polar hexagon
Around the north pole, clouds form a mysterious hexagonal pattern that has persisted for decades. Each side of the hexagon is wider than Earth. It may be a long-lived wave, but no such pattern is seen at the south pole. In its center is a raging hurricane, shown here in false color, in which wind speeds reach 330 mph (530 kph)—five times faster than in a hurricane on Earth.

Core
At the planet's center, there might be a core made of a mixture of rock and the metals iron and nickel.

Liquid metallic layer
At great depths, the pressure is so intense that the hydrogen turns into a liquid metal. An additional layer of liquid helium may surround the core.

Changing view
Saturn is tilted on its axis, so our view of the rings from Earth changes as Saturn orbits the Sun. When the rings are side-on (2010), they are almost invisible. It takes around 15 years for the rings to go from full view to almost invisible and back again.

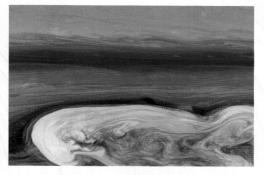

2010

2012

2014

2017

Elongated storm
In 2011, a huge storm broke through Saturn's hazy surface and quickly spread eastward. After a few months, it had spread all the way around the planet, stirring up the clouds into swirls and ripples (shown here in false color).

Mission to Saturn
The Cassini spacecraft, packed with scientific instruments to study Saturn and its rings and moons, arrived in orbit around the planet in 2004 and operated until 2017. The data and images it sent back have transformed our understanding of Saturn. Cassini released a separate probe, Huygens, that parachuted onto the surface of Saturn's biggest moon, Titan.

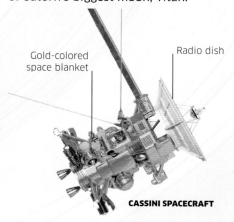

Gold-colored space blanket

Radio dish

CASSINI SPACECRAFT

Saturn's rings

The vast circle of icy debris orbiting Saturn may be the remains of a moon that broke apart in the past. Visible even in small telescopes, Saturn's rings are thousands of miles in diameter but only a few yards thick.

Each particle in Saturn's rings is in orbit around the planet, trapped by the gas giant's gravity. The floating chunks of ice also attract each other through gravity, and they are pulled by the gravity of Saturn's moons. All these forces combine to make the material in the rings bunch up at certain distances from Saturn and thin out at others, forming a series of distinct rings and gaps. All the giants have ring systems, but those of Jupiter, Uranus, and Neptune are much fainter than Saturn's.

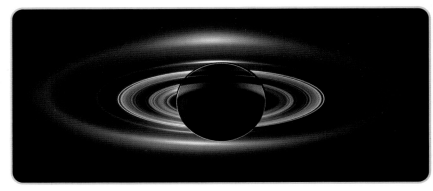

Through Cassini's eyes

The Cassini spacecraft studied the rings in detail while it was in orbit around Saturn. In July 2013, Cassini slipped into Saturn's shadow and captured incredible pictures of its rings lit from behind by the Sun. The images reveal hazy, blue outer rings that are not normally visible. The largest of these—the E ring—is a cloud of microscopic ice grains from geysers erupting on Saturn's moon Enceladus.

Ring system

The main parts of Saturn's rings are given letters, and the gaps within them are named after famous astronomers. The gravitational tug of Saturn's moon Mimas creates the biggest gap, known as the Cassini Division.

Cassini Division

C ring

B ring

Encke Gap

A ring

Main rings

The artist's impression below shows the most densely packed part of Saturn's main rings: the B ring. Fragments of ice here occasionally collide and break. The newly exposed icy surfaces capture the sunlight, making Saturn's rings much brighter than the dark, dusty rings of the other giant planets.

The icy bodies in the rings range in size from tiny icy grains to boulders as big as houses.

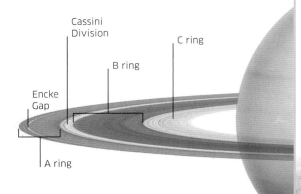

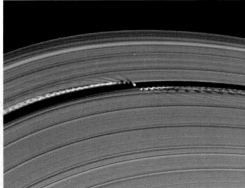

Shepherd moons

Some of Saturn's moons orbit the planet within the rings. The gravity of these "shepherd moons" sweeps their orbits clear, herding the icy debris elsewhere. Saturn's moon Daphnis (above) also kicks up waves in the rings as it hurtles around the planet.

A comet or asteroid hit Saturn's D ring in 1983, causing wobbles in the ring material that lasted for **over 30 years**.

The rings have their own very faint atmosphere, mostly made of oxygen.

Most of the ice lies in a very flat plane, but large blocks of ice rise above it, and there are "bumps" up to 2.5 miles (4 km) high.

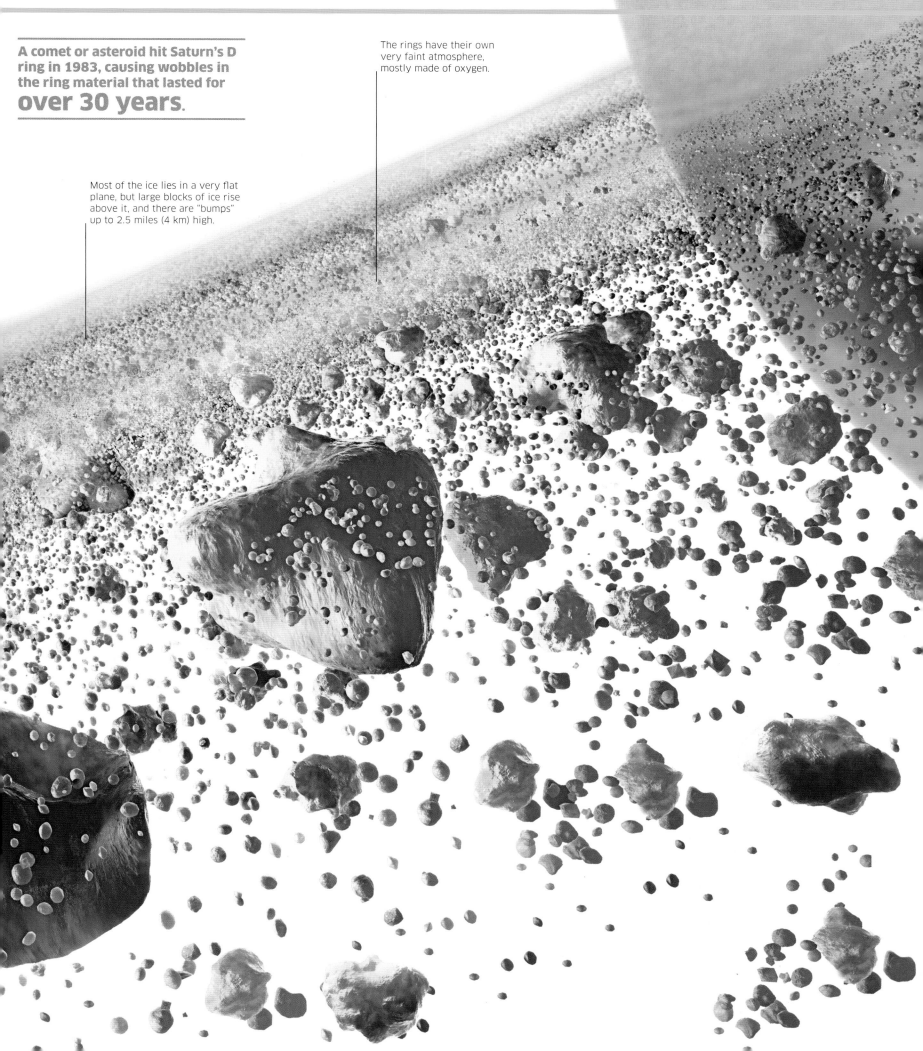

Ring world

Saturn's breathtaking rings are made of billions of sparkling fragments of ice that range from small grains to chunks the size of a bus.

The first person to see the rings was the Italian astronomer Galileo, who called them "ears." Since then, telescopes and spacecraft have revealed even more detail in the rings, which are made up of thousands of individual ringlets. This image is a mosaic of 126 photos captured by the Cassini spacecraft in 2004. Gravity has pulled the material in the rings into a plane so incredibly thin that a scale model of Saturn's main rings, made using standard copy paper, would require a disk of paper about 1.3 miles (2 km) wide.

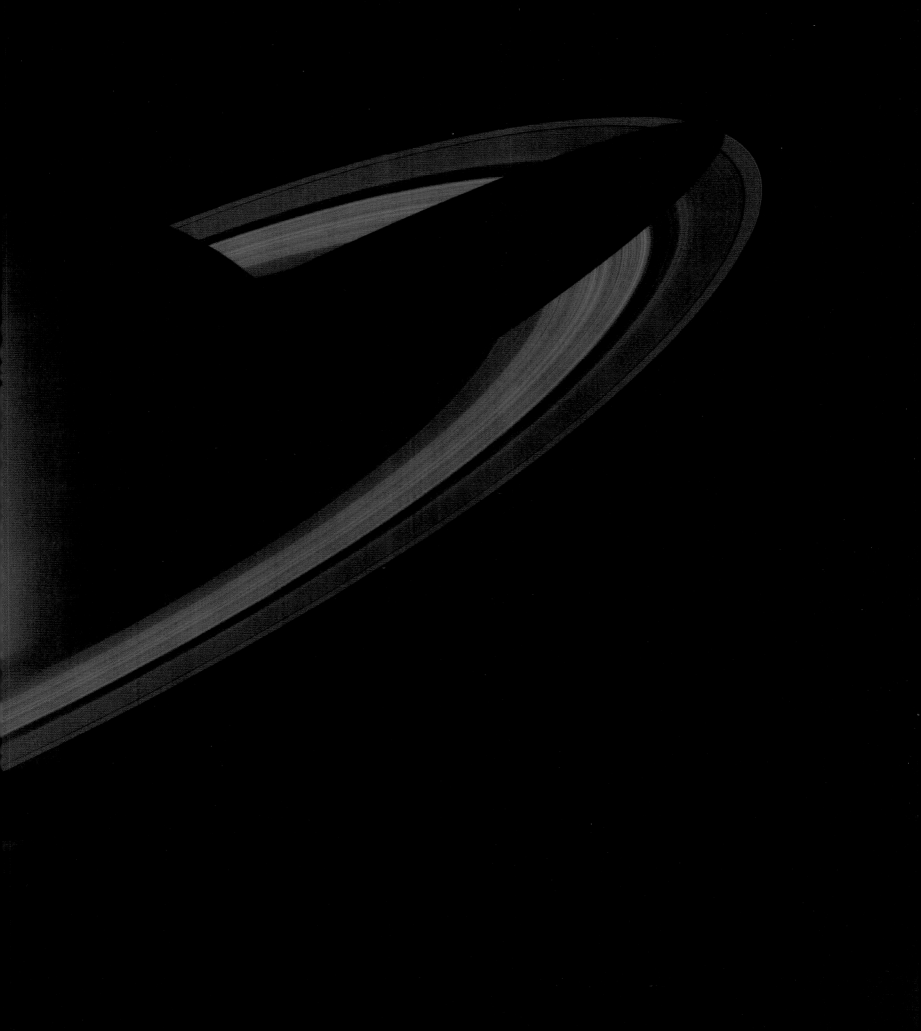

56   the Solar System ○ MOONS OF SATURN

45   The number of Saturn's moons **discovered** with the Subaru Telescope, Hawaii.

Moons of Saturn

There are more known moons orbiting Saturn than any other planet. They form a complex system, and their orbits fall into several distinct groups.

Saturn has at least 82 known moons, but the true number may be far greater. The innermost moons are part of Saturn's ring system, and several have prominent ridges around their equators, where they have accumulated icy material from the rings. Beyond the rings are Saturn's largest moons, which are hundreds of miles wide and mostly have icy crusts. Largest of all is Titan, which is bigger than the planet Mercury. The inner moons and the large moons all move in the same direction as Saturn's rotation, which suggests they formed at the same time as the planet. Farther out, however, is a chaotic cloud of tiny moons that orbit at wild angles.

Most large moons of Saturn are **tidally locked,** which means they always keep the same side facing Saturn.

Orbits of the outer moons

Far from Saturn are dozens of small moons in tilted, noncircular orbits. Many of these orbit in the opposite direction of the main moons. This suggests they formed elsewhere and were captured by Saturn's gravity.

Saturn | Hyperion

Rhea
Saturn's second-largest moon has an icy surface with intriguing discolored patches around the equator, which suggest it may once have had rings.

Titan
This is Saturn's largest moon and the second-largest moon in the Solar System. It has a thick, hazy atmosphere that hides the surface from view.

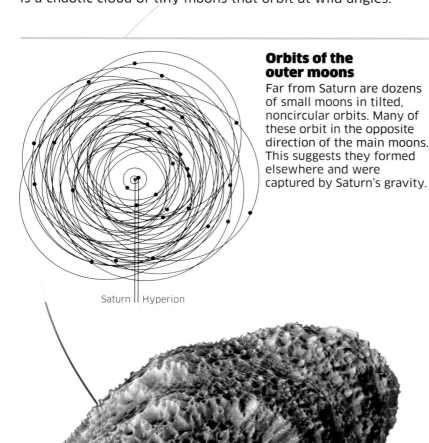

Hyperion
This peculiar moon has so many deep craters that it looks like a bath sponge. It tumbles as it flies through space, its axis of rotation wobbling due largely to the pull of gravity from Titan. Measurements show that Hyperion is partly empty; large hollows must exist under its surface.

53 The number of Saturn's moons that had **been named** by 2020.

Every four years, Saturn's moons Epimetheus and Janus **swap orbits**.

Rhea and Dione both have very thin **oxygen atmospheres**.

57

Dione

Prometheus

Atlas

Polydeuces

Daphnis

Telesto

Mimas

Tethys

Pandora

Pan

Calypso

Epimetheus

Enceladus

Janus

Pallene

Methone

Helene

Ice world

Enceladus's icy exterior is the most reflective surface of any body in the Solar System. Although the snow-white ground is frozen solid, an ocean of liquid water may lie hidden underneath. Near the south pole, jets of gas and ice grains erupt from ice volcanoes. Much of the ice falls back to the surface, coating Enceladus with volcanic snow.

SATURN

Saturn's largest 25 moons to scale

TITAN · RHEA · IAPETUS · DIONE · TETHYS · ENCELADUS · MIMAS · HYPERION · PHOEBE · JANUS · EPIMETHEUS · PROMETHEUS · PANDORA · SIARNAQ · HELENE · ALBIORIX · ATLAS · PAN · TELESTO · PAALIAQ · CALYPSO · YMIR · KIVIUQ · TARVOS · IJIRAQ

58   the Solar System ○ **TITAN**

1655 The year Titan was **discovered** by Dutchman **Christiaan Huygens**.

Titan

Saturn's largest moon, Titan, has some tantalizing similarities with Earth. It has nitrogen-rich air, cloudy skies, mountains, rivers, and lakes. However, this chilly world is far too cold for life as we know it.

In 1980, when the Voyager 1 spacecraft returned the first close-up images of Titan, the scientists back on Earth were disappointed. A thick, orange haze covered the Moon, hiding the surface from view. However, the haze turned out to be a fascinating mix of the kind of carbon chemicals that existed on Earth billions of years ago, before life began. In the distant future, when the Sun brightens and Titan warms up, conditions on the surface may become just right for life.

Crust
As hard as solid rock, water ice probably makes up most of Titan's outer crust.

Seeing through the clouds
A layer of haze surrounds Titan, making it impossible to photograph the surface from space. However, the Cassini spacecraft had a radar system that could "see" through the haze by bouncing radio waves off the ground.

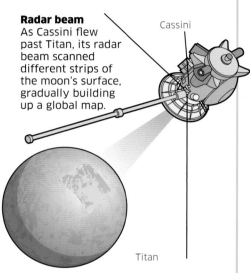

Radar beam
As Cassini flew past Titan, its radar beam scanned different strips of the moon's surface, gradually building up a global map.

Cassini

Titan

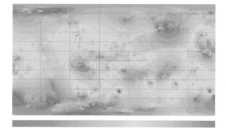

-5,900 FT (-1,800 M)   2,000 FT (600 M)

Mapping Titan
Cassini's map of Titan shows the height of the ground in color. The mountain peaks are red. Some of the mountains may be ice volcanoes, from which a mix of water and ammonia erupts. As the liquid flows down the sides, it freezes, making the volcano grow.

Distant shores
This Cassini radar view has been color-coded to show low-lying, smooth areas as blue and higher, rougher areas as orange. The colors reveal Titan's lakes and rivers. These contain not water but carbon chemicals such as ethane.

Surface view
In January 2005, the European Space Agency's Huygens space probe landed on Titan's surface. Once released from the orbiting Cassini spacecraft, Huygens took three weeks to reach Titan and then parachute down to the surface to return the first images of the hidden world below. This photo shows "rocks" of ice littering the bed of what was once a lake. The smoggy orange sky casts a gloomy light across the whole landscape.

FAST FACTS

Distance from Saturn: 900 million miles (1.4 billion km)

Mass (Earth = 1): 0.002

Time to rotate once: 16 Earth days

Size: 3,200 miles (5,150 km) wide

95% The proportion of **nitrogen** in Titan's **atmosphere**.

The **same side** of Titan always faces its parent planet, Saturn.

Titan is the **second-largest moon in the Solar System**, after Jupiter's moon Ganymede.

59

Polar lakes
On Earth, clouds, rain, and lakes are made of water; on Titan, they are made of chemicals called ethane and methane. Both are invisible gases on Earth, but Titan is so cold that they turn into a liquid there. They form droplets in the air that fall as rain, feeding lakes near the north pole, like the one in this artist's impression.

Atmosphere
Titan's air is mostly nitrogen, like Earth's air. The nitrogen may have been delivered to Titan by comets crashing into it.

Core
Titan's core could be either solid rock or a mixture of ice and rock all the way to the center.

Mantle
The top of Titan's mantle might be made of liquid water, forming a hidden ocean. Deeper down, the mantle consists of ice.

The lower part of the mantle is thought to consist of a special kind of ice that forms under high pressure.

60   the Solar System ◦ **URANUS**

42 years—the **length of one night** at Uranus's north and south poles.

Uranus

In 1781, the astronomer William Herschel peered through the telescope in his garden in England and saw what he thought was a comet. It turned out to be something much more exciting: a new planet.

Uranus is an ice giant much like Neptune, but tipped on its side. For two centuries after Herschel discovered Uranus, very little was learned about it, except that it has moons, rings, and an unusual tilt. Only one spacecraft—Voyager 2–has ever visited the planet, and the pictures it sent back in 1986 revealed a disappointingly boring, pale blue globe with a few faint wisps of cloud. Unlike the other giant planets, Uranus gives off relatively little heat. It does, however, have a strong but lopsided magnetic field.

Uranian moons

Uranus has 27 known moons. The largest, Titania, is 980 miles (1,577 km) wide. The smallest are Trinculo and Cupid, which are only about 11 miles (18 km) wide. All the moons are named after characters from the works of William Shakespeare and the poet Alexander Pope.

TRINCULO
CUPID
FERDINAND
MARGARET
FRANCISCO
MAB
PERDITA
STEPHANO
CORDELIA
OPHELIA
SETEBOS
PROSPERO
BIANCA
DESDEMONA
CALIBAN
ROSALIND
CRESSIDA
BELINDA
JULIET
PORTIA
SYCORAX
PUCK
MIRANDA
ARIEL
UMBRIEL
OBERON
TITANIA

Weird moon

The surface of Uranus's icy moon Miranda is one of the strangest in the Solar System. It looks like a jumble of pieces that do not quite fit together, but no one knows how it became like that. Its features include the highest cliff in the Solar System, Verona Rupes, which may be 12 miles (20 km) high.

ARTIST'S IMPRESSION OF VERONA RUPES

FAST FACTS

Surface gravity (Earth = 1): 0.89

Time to rotate once: 17.2 hours

Year: 84 Earth years

Moons: At least 27

Rings

Uranus is surrounded by a set of narrow rings, most of which were discovered in 1977, when they passed in front of a star. More rings, sharing orbits with small moons, were found later.

Atmosphere

Hydrogen and helium are the main gases in Uranus's atmosphere, but there is also plenty of methane, which gives the planet its pale blue color.

Mantle

Water, methane, and ammonia combine to form a slushy mixture of ice and liquid in Uranus's mantle. At the base of the mantle, there may be a sea of diamonds.

63 **Earths** would be able to **fit inside** Uranus.

13 The **number of known rings** around Uranus.

−371°F (−224°C)—the **minimum temperature** in Uranus's **atmosphere**.

61

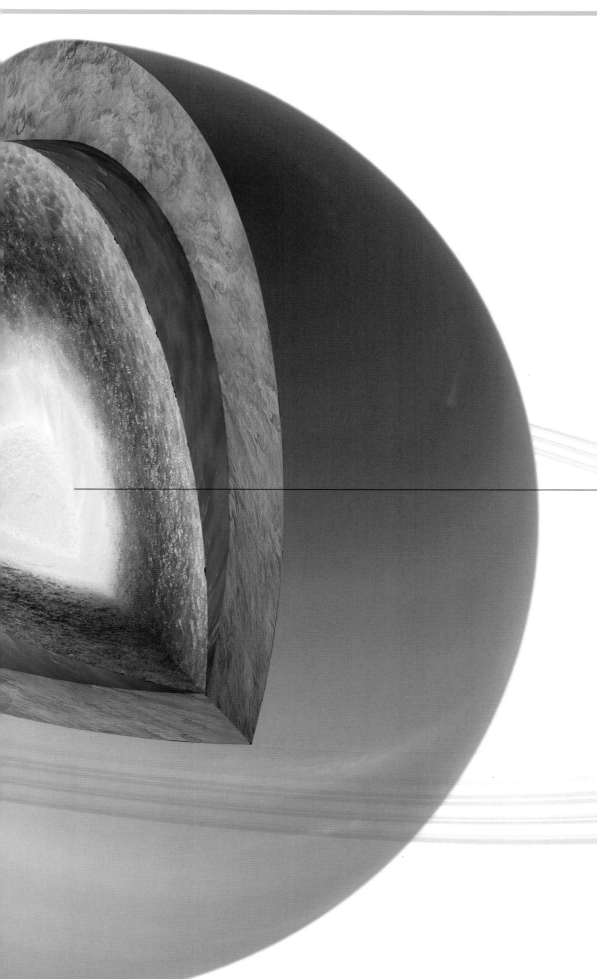

On a roll

Most planets rotate upright like spinning tops, but Uranus's axis of rotation is tipped over on its side. This gives the planet and its moons extreme seasons. In the winter hemisphere, the pole is in constant darkness for 42 years, while the summer pole is in constant sunlight.

Axis

SUN

Summer

Winter

Core

At the planet's center is a core of possibly molten rock, iron, and nickel, with a temperature of more than 9,000°F (5,000°C).

Storm clouds

Uranus looked almost featureless to the cameras on the Voyager 2 spacecraft in 1986. However, this detailed image taken in 2012 by an infrared camera on one of the Keck telescopes in Hawaii reveals turbulent cloud bands and storms similar to those on Jupiter.

Neptune

The Solar System's outermost planet has a striking blue color like Earth. Similar in size and structure to Uranus, Neptune is a giant ball of hot liquid surrounded by a gas atmosphere.

Neptune was the last planet to be discovered and was found thanks to math. Astronomers had noticed that Uranus wandered off its predicted path as though pulled by the gravity of a hidden planet. When they calculated where the mystery world should be and looked through a telescope, they saw Neptune. Just 17 days later, in October 1846, they also saw Neptune's icy moon Triton. Only Voyager 2 has visited Neptune. It flew past the planet in 1989 and sent back pictures of white clouds in Neptune's sky, blown into streaks by furious winds, and faint rings around the gas giant. Triton turned out to be a fascinating world of erupting geysers and frozen nitrogen lakes, surrounded by a thin atmosphere.

Rings
Neptune is surrounded by several thin, faint rings made mostly of dust.

A layer of liquid diamond might surround Neptune's core.

Dust rings

Neptune's rings are made of dark dust that's hard to see, but Voyager 2 took this photo when they were lit from behind by the Sun. The rings have thick and thin sections, making them uneven.

Neptune's moons

For over a century, Triton was Neptune's only known moon, but 14 others have now been discovered. After Triton, the next largest moon is Proteus, at 260 miles (420 km) wide. Nereid has a highly stretched orbit: it swoops close to Neptune before flying seven times farther out.

TRITON

PROTEUS NEREID LARISSA GALATEA DESPINA THALASSA NAIAD HALIMEDE NESO SAO LAOMEDEIA PSAMATHE S/2004 N1

NEPTUNE

The astronomer Galileo Galilei saw Neptune 234 years before its discovery but didn't realize it was a planet.

Geysers on Triton
Voyager 2 discovered huge geysers on Triton. Jets of nitrogen gas blast icy grains up to 5 miles (8 km) above the surface, shown here in an artist's impression. These are caught by the wind and form dark streaks where they settle back on the ground.

Mantle
The mantle is a hot, dense liquid composed mainly of water, methane, and ammonia. This layer is more than 10 times the mass of Earth.

Core
In the center is a white-hot core of rock and iron that is larger than Earth. The temperature here is over 9,000°F (5,000°C).

Triton
Neptune's largest moon is almost as big as Earth's moon. With a surface temperature of -391°F (-235°C), it is one of the coldest places in the Solar System. It orbits in the "wrong" direction, moving the opposite way to Neptune's rotation. This suggests Triton was captured by Neptune's gravity.

Stormy skies
Raging winds tear across Neptune's sky, blowing at up to 1,300 mph (2,100 kph)—nearly 10 times faster than a hurricane on Earth. Storms come and go. Voyager 2 photographed the Great Dark Spot in 1989 (left), a giant storm that had vanished by the time the Hubble Space Telescope looked at Neptune in 1994.

Atmosphere
Neptune's outer layer is made of hydrogen and helium, with increasing amounts of water, ammonia, and methane at greater depths. Its blue color comes from methane.

The clouds are blown around the planet by winds of up to 1,300 mph (2,100 kph).

FAST FACTS
Surface gravity (Earth = 1): 1.12
Time to rotate once: 16.1 hours
Year: 165 Earth years
Moons: At least 14

Beyond Neptune

Billions of rocky and icy objects orbit the Sun. Although some weave paths between the planets, most orbit farther out. Called "trans-Neptunian objects," they are leftovers from the Solar System's formation, and many are fascinating worlds in their own right.

There are small objects scattered throughout the Solar System. Some even have tiny moons or a ring. The rocky ones nearer to the Sun, mostly orbiting in the region between Mars and Jupiter, are known as asteroids. Those farther out consist mainly of ice. A few of the largest that are roundish in shape have been designated "dwarf planets" by astronomers. The most well-known is Pluto, which was once classed as a major planet.

Haumea
The dwarf planet Haumea is egg-shaped rather than round. Its shape is too small to see with a telescope, but astronomers figured it out by studying how it reflects different amounts of light as it rotates. Haumea has two moons, Hi'aka and Namaka, shown in this artist's impression.

Eris
The dwarf planet Eris was discovered in 2005 and has a greater mass than Pluto. It belongs to the scattered disk— a group of icy objects that travel far north and south of the Kuiper Belt disk.

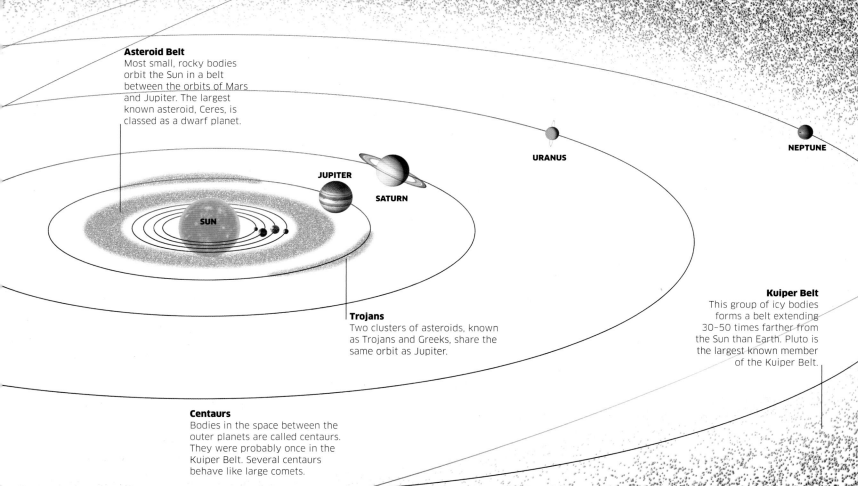

Asteroid Belt
Most small, rocky bodies orbit the Sun in a belt between the orbits of Mars and Jupiter. The largest known asteroid, Ceres, is classed as a dwarf planet.

JUPITER

SATURN

SUN

URANUS

NEPTUNE

Trojans
Two clusters of asteroids, known as Trojans and Greeks, share the same orbit as Jupiter.

Kuiper Belt
This group of icy bodies forms a belt extending 30–50 times farther from the Sun than Earth. Pluto is the largest known member of the Kuiper Belt.

Centaurs
Bodies in the space between the outer planets are called centaurs. They were probably once in the Kuiper Belt. Several centaurs behave like large comets.

1992 The year in which the **first object beyond Pluto** was discovered.

248 years – the time taken for Pluto to **orbit the Sun once.**

–382°F (–230°C)–the **average surface temperature** on Pluto.

65

Pluto's surface
Pluto is about two-thirds the size of Earth's moon. The plains of its icy surface are mainly frozen nitrogen and methane, while its mountains are made of water ice. This image, taken by the New Horizons spacecraft, is close to this dwarf planet's natural color.

Charon
Pluto's largest moon, Charon, is about half as wide as Pluto. It is made of rock and ice, and its gray surface is frozen water. Tidal forces have locked Charon's orbit so that it always hovers above the same place on Pluto's surface and keeps the same face pointing toward Pluto. This image was taken by New Horizons in 2015.

Earth's moon weighs about **six times** more than the dwarf planet Pluto.

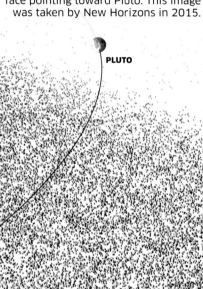

PLUTO

New Horizons mission
NASA's nuclear-powered New Horizons spacecraft visited Pluto and its five moons in 2015. After its encounter, the 880 lb (400 kg) craft set off toward other Kuiper Belt objects, and in 2019, it flew by Arrokoth—the most distant object in the Solar System visited by a spacecraft.

LARGEST KNOWN TRANS-NEPTUNIAN OBJECTS

Earth to scale

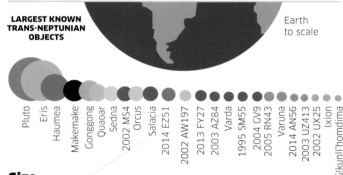

Pluto · Eris · Haumea · Makemake · Gongong · Quaoar · Sedna · 2002 MS4 · Orcus · Salacia · 2014 EZ51 · 2002 AW197 · 2013 FY27 · 2003 AZ84 · Varda · 1995 SM55 · 2004 GV9 · 2005 RN43 · Varuna · 2014 AN56 · 2003 UZ413 · 2002 UX25 · Ixion · G!kúnǁʼhòmdímà

Size
Though small relative to Earth, some trans-Neptunian objects rival larger moons in the Solar System. Four have been recognized as dwarf planets: Eris, Pluto, Haumea, and Makemake. However, many other objects beyond Neptune could possibly qualify as dwarf planets.

Solar System

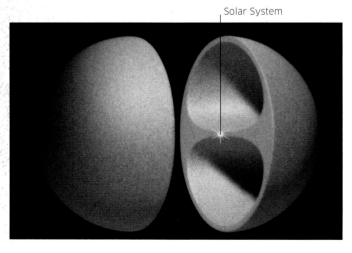

Oort Cloud
Beyond the Kuiper Belt lies a roughly spherical cloud of icy bodies that probably stretches a quarter of the way to the nearest star. Many comets are likely to originate from this planetary deep freeze.

Structure of a comet

The cloud of gas and dust that surrounds the nucleus is called the coma. The coma's largest part, visible in ultraviolet light, is made of hydrogen. Both tails follow the comet's motion around the Sun.

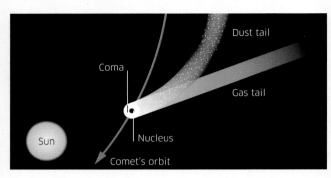

Around the Sun

The orbits of comets are typically elliptical (oval). Only when comets come close to the Sun do their tails develop. The time taken to make one orbit varies enormously—Comet Encke, a short-period comet, takes only three years to orbit the Sun, but long-period comets can take millions of years.

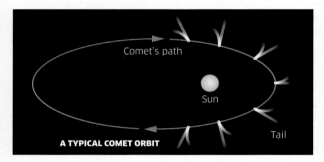

A TYPICAL COMET ORBIT

SIZE OF COMET 67P RELATIVE TO A CITY

Comet 67P

The best-studied comet in history is the 3-mile (5-km) wide Comet 67P, which was explored by the European spacecraft Rosetta that arrived at it in 2014. Rosetta released a separate probe called Philae to make the first soft landing (as opposed to a violent impact) on a comet nucleus. The harpoon meant to anchor Philae to the comet failed to fire on landing, causing Philae to bounce hundreds of yards into space. It bounced twice before settling.

Comets

Comets are strange but beautiful sights, like stars with glowing tails. Dozens of comets are discovered each year as they swoop through the inner Solar System and around the Sun, though most are not visible to the naked eye.

For thousands of years, people were puzzled by comets or even frightened by them, seeing their unexpected appearance as bad omens. We now know these visitors from the outer Solar System are simply ancient lumps of ice and dust—leftovers from the cloud of rubble from which the planets formed billions of years ago. When comets venture close to the Sun, the ice warms up and releases gas and dust into a gigantic cloud and tails. Comets have changed little since they first formed, which makes them a prime target for space scientists who want to learn more about the early Solar System.

Crust
A crust of jet-black dust makes the surface of the nucleus darker than coal. Comet nuclei are among the darkest objects in the Solar System.

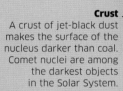

Tall tails
Comets look as though they are streaking through space with their tails stretched out behind them, but that's just an illusion. In reality, the tails always point away from the Sun, whichever way a comet is traveling. There are two main tails: a gas tail (blue in the photo of Comet Hale–Bopp on left) and a dust tail (white). The gas tail points almost directly away from the Sun, but the dust tail bends back toward the comet's path.

355 **million miles** (570 million km)—the longest measured comet gas tail.

Comet dust trails that cross Earth's orbit cause **meteor showers**.

The first comet to have its orbital path calculated was **Comet Halley**.

67

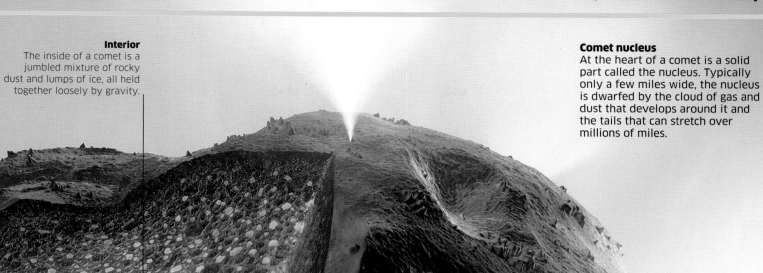

Interior
The inside of a comet is a jumbled mixture of rocky dust and lumps of ice, all held together loosely by gravity.

Comet nucleus
At the heart of a comet is a solid part called the nucleus. Typically only a few miles wide, the nucleus is dwarfed by the cloud of gas and dust that develops around it and the tails that can stretch over millions of miles.

Jets of gas and dust
The Sun's warmth makes ice in the comet evaporate to form gas. Jets of gas erupt from the sunward side of the nucleus, carrying dust grains with them.

Coma
A vast cloud of dust, gas, and ice particles called a coma builds up around the nucleus as a comet approaches the Sun. Rarely, a coma can grow larger than the Sun.

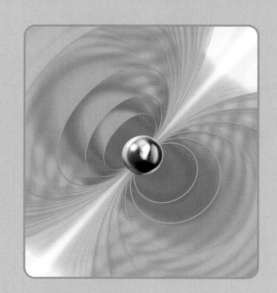

STARS

On a dark night you can see thousands of stars twinkling in the sky, but there are countless trillions more scattered across the fathomless depths of space. Like our Sun, all stars are dazzling balls of hot gas that can shine for billions of years, powered by nuclear fusion.

How stars work

A star is a brilliant, shining ball of extremely hot gas, mainly hydrogen, that generates fantastic amounts of energy in its core. This energy travels out through the star until it reaches the surface, where it escapes into space as light, heat, and other types of radiation invisible to our eyes. Stars are bright and hot because of the vast quantity of energy they generate.

PARTS OF A STAR

Stars vary tremendously in their size, but all of them have the same parts. Every star has an extremely hot central region, or core, that produces energy; one or more layers of gas through which this energy travels outward; a very hot surface; and an atmosphere.

SUN

An average star

Our Sun is an ordinary star that looks huge to us because it's so close. Sun-sized stars have two layers through which energy moves outward from the core: an inner layer where it travels by radiation, and an outer layer that carries it by convection (rising and falling currents). In larger stars, these two layers are the other way around, while some smaller stars have only a convection layer. Like all stars, the Sun has a brilliant surface that emits light and heat.

How stars shine

The energy produced by a star is released by nuclear fusion in its core. This process involves the nuclei (central parts) of atoms joining together to make more massive nuclei. Fusion can only occur at the extremely high temperatures present in star cores.

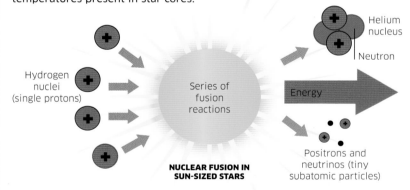

Hydrogen nuclei (single protons)

Series of fusion reactions

Energy

Helium nucleus

Neutron

Positrons and neutrinos (tiny subatomic particles)

NUCLEAR FUSION IN SUN-SIZED STARS

Forces in stars

Most stars exist in a stable state through a delicate balance between two forces: gravity, which pushes matter inward; and pressure, generated by energy released from the core, which pushes matter outward.

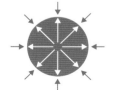

Forces in balance
In a normal star, the inward push of gravity balances the outward pressure.

Star turns into red giant
The cores of old stars heat up. The extra heat boosts the outward pressure, so the star swells.

Collapse to black hole
When a particularly large star dies, gravity may cause its core to collapse to form a black hole.

STARLIGHT

As well as visible light, stars emit invisible types of radiation, such as ultraviolet rays and microwaves, all of which travel as waves. The whole range of these different radiations, including light, is called the electromagnetic (EM) spectrum. Stars are too distant for us to visit them to study, but we can tell a lot about them from the light and other radiation they emit.

These two stars look equally bright in the night sky, but in reality, star A is brighter but farther away.

Star brightness

A star's brightness, or magnitude, can be stated either as how bright it looks or how bright it really is. These differ, as stars vary in their distance from Earth, which affects how bright they appear. Oddly, a star's brightness is measured on a scale in which a small number denotes a bright star and a large number indicates a dim star.

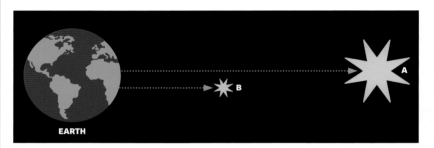

EARTH

The electromagnetic spectrum

Light travels as a wave, and we see light waves of different lengths as colors: red light, for example, has longer waves than blue. Stars produce energy in a huge range of wavelengths, most of which are invisible to our eyes. Many astronomers study stars by using wavelengths we cannot see.

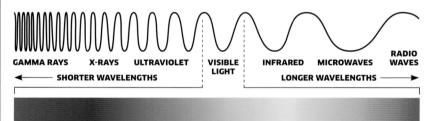

| GAMMA RAYS | X-RAYS | ULTRAVIOLET | VISIBLE LIGHT | INFRARED | MICROWAVES | RADIO WAVES |

← SHORTER WAVELENGTHS   LONGER WAVELENGTHS →

Studying stars

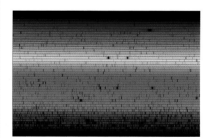

By studying the spectrum of a star, astronomers can figure out many of the chemical elements it contains. Each chemical element in the star's atmosphere absorbs particular wavelengths in the spectrum of radiation from the hotter gas beneath, producing a unique pattern, like a fingerprint. The dark gaps in the spectrum of light from our Sun (above) are caused by 67 different elements.

Variable stars

Some stars regularly vary in both size and brightness. These stars are constantly trying to reach an equilibrium between the inward-pulling gravitational force and the outward-pushing pressure. They swell and shrink in regular cycles, varying from a few hours to a few years—being brightest (and hottest) when smallest, and dimmest (and coolest) when biggest.

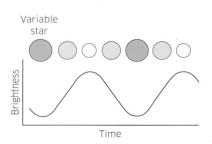

Variable star

Brightness

Time

HOW FAR ARE THE STARS?

All stars other than the Sun are situated at incredible distances from Earth, which is why they appear as just pinpricks of light in the night sky. They are so far away that a special unit is needed to express their distance. This unit is the light-year, which is the distance light travels in a year. A light-year is about 6 trillion miles (10 trillion km).

Nearby stars

There are 33 stars lying within 12.5 light-years of the Sun, some of which belong to multiple star systems containing two or three stars (binary or trinary systems). Many of these nearby stars are small, dim ones called red dwarfs, but a few are larger, dazzling yellow, orange, and white stars. The diagram below shows their positions in space, relative to the Sun at the center.

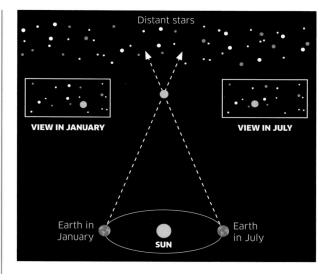

Distant stars

VIEW IN JANUARY

VIEW IN JULY

Earth in January

SUN

Earth in July

Measuring distance

There are various ways of measuring how far away stars are. One clever technique is to view the same star at two distinct times of year, when Earth is at opposite sides of its orbit around the Sun. If a star is nearby, its position relative to more distant stars appears to shift between these two points of view (an effect known as parallax). The amount of shift can be used to calculate exactly how far away it is. Using this method, astronomers have worked out that Proxima Centauri—the star closest to the Sun—is about 4.2 light-years away.

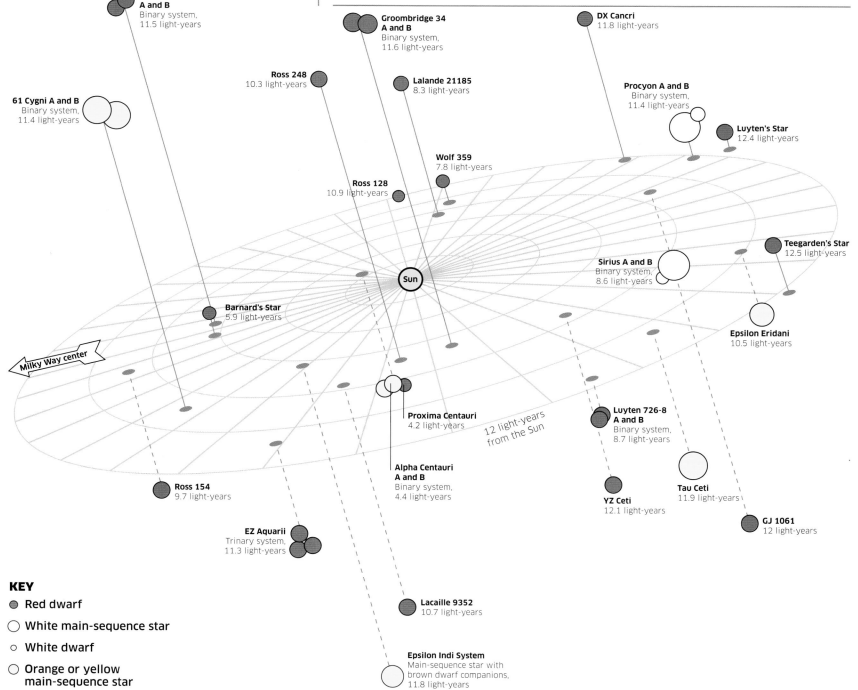

Struve 2398 A and B
Binary system, 11.5 light-years

Groombridge 34 A and B
Binary system, 11.6 light-years

DX Cancri
11.8 light-years

Ross 248
10.3 light-years

Lalande 21185
8.3 light-years

Procyon A and B
Binary system, 11.4 light-years

61 Cygni A and B
Binary system, 11.4 light-years

Luyten's Star
12.4 light-years

Wolf 359
7.8 light-years

Ross 128
10.9 light-years

Teegarden's Star
12.5 light-years

Sirius A and B
Binary system, 8.6 light-years

Sun

Barnard's Star
5.9 light-years

Epsilon Eridani
10.5 light-years

Milky Way center

Proxima Centauri
4.2 light-years

12 light-years from the Sun

Luyten 726-8 A and B
Binary system, 8.7 light-years

Ross 154
9.7 light-years

Alpha Centauri A and B
Binary system, 4.4 light-years

Tau Ceti
11.9 light-years

YZ Ceti
12.1 light-years

GJ 1061
12 light-years

EZ Aquarii
Trinary system, 11.3 light-years

KEY

- Red dwarf
- White main-sequence star
- White dwarf
- Orange or yellow main-sequence star

Lacaille 9352
10.7 light-years

Epsilon Indi System
Main-sequence star with brown dwarf companions, 11.8 light-years

Types of stars

In the night sky, all stars look like tiny pinpricks of light. However, stars differ greatly in size, color, brightness, and life span.

The smallest are tiny dwarf stars less than a thousandth of the Sun's volume. The largest are 8 billion times greater in volume than the Sun. The largest stars are also billions of times brighter than the smallest stars. The characteristics of a star depend mainly on how much matter it contains—its mass. The more massive a star is, the hotter and brighter it will be, but the shorter its life span. This is because big stars burn through their nuclear fuel much faster. Astronomers use the color, size, and brightness of stars to classify them into a number of groups.

Giant stars

The largest stars are aging stars that have swelled and brightened enormously toward the end of their lives. Giant stars are up to 200 times wider than the Sun and can be thousands of times more luminous. Supergiants and hypergiants are up to 2,000 times wider than the Sun and up to a billion times brighter.

Dwarf stars

Dwarf stars make up the majority of stars and are relatively small and dim. They include stars about the size of the Sun or somewhat larger and many smaller stars called red dwarfs. They also include white dwarfs—the tiny, dense remnants of giant stars that have lost their outer layers.

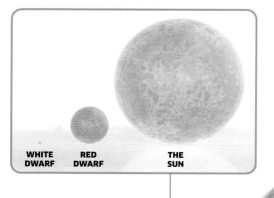

WHITE
DWARF

RED
DWARF

THE
SUN

ORANGE
GIANT

RED
GIANT

BLUE
SUPERGIANT

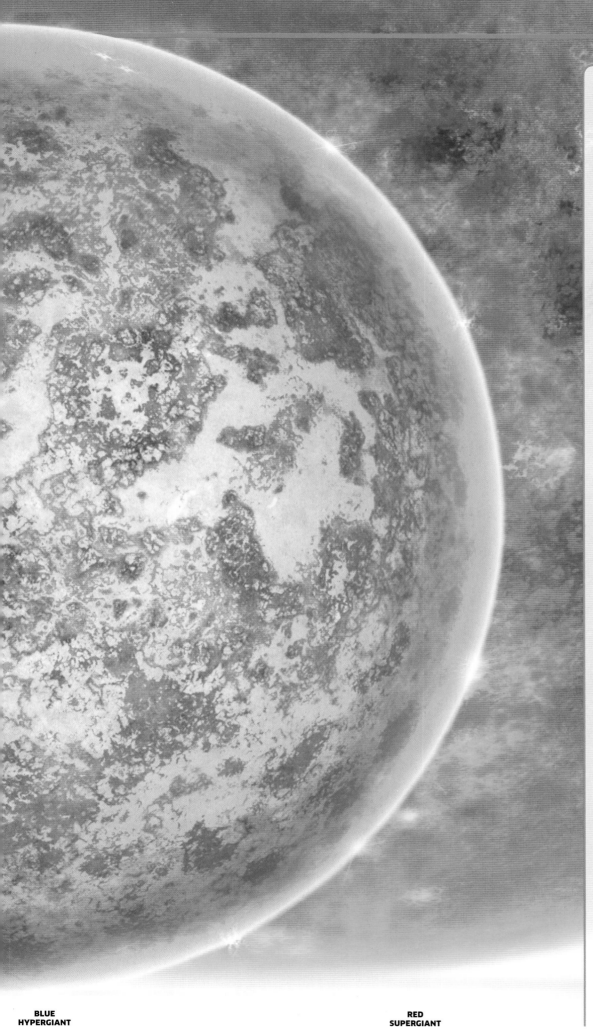

Colors

A star's color depends on how hot its surface is. The hottest stars produce a bluish light, while cooler stars are an orangish red. You can see these colors on a clear night by using binoculars to look closely at different stars.

Color	Temperature
Blue	80,000°F (45,000°C)
Bluish white	55,000°F (30,000°C)
White	22,000°F (12,000°C)
Yellowish white	14,000°F (8,000°C)
Yellow	12,000°F (6,500°C)
Orange	9,000°F (5,000°C)
Red	6,500°F (3,500°C)

Star chart

About 100 years ago, two astronomers discovered an ingenious way of classifying stars that also shows the stage each star has reached in its life. The astronomers—Ejnar Hertzsprung and Henry Russell—did this by making a graph of stars with temperature along the bottom and brightness up the side. Most stars, including our Sun, fall into a band on the diagram called the main sequence; these are small to medium stars in a range of colors. The other stars, including giants and dwarfs, form separate groups. These are older stars that would have been in the main sequence millions of years ago.

Blue supergiant

Red supergiant

Blue and bluish white giants

Orange giants

White giants

Yellow giants

Red giants

BRIGHTER

DIMMER

Main-sequence stars

Red dwarfs

White dwarfs

◄— HOTTER

COOLER —►

Seeing stars

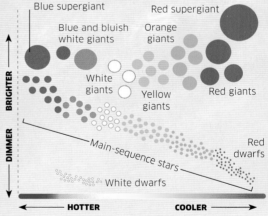

Supergiant stars are easy to see if you look for the famous constellation of Orion, the Hunter. Orion's shoulder is a red supergiant called Betelgeuse, which is one of the largest stars in the northern sky. Orion's foot is a blue supergiant, Rigel.

Betelgeuse

Rigel

ORION

BLUE HYPERGIANT

RED SUPERGIANT

Orion Nebula
At a distance of 1,500 light-years from Earth, this colorful gas cloud is the closest star-forming region to Earth. The Orion Nebula contains massive young stars giving off enormous amounts of energy, which makes the surrounding gases glow brightly. You can see the Orion Nebula easily by using binoculars to look at the constellation of Orion, but the colors will be much fainter than shown here.

Trapezium stars
In the heart of the Orion Nebula is a cluster of very bright, newly formed stars called the Trapezium. These stars are up to 30 times more massive than our Sun, and their intense energy illuminates much of the surrounding cloud.

This gas cloud is separated from the main part of the nebula by dark dust lanes and is lit up by a young star at its center.

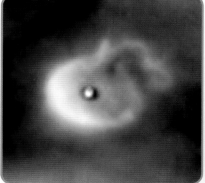

Star babies
The youngest stars in the Orion Nebula are still surrounded by dense disks of gas and dust. The Hubble Space Telescope has photographed more than 200 of these disks, which are also known as proplyds. Planets may eventually form from the gas and dust in them.

Star birth

New stars and planets are born in vast clouds of interstellar gas and dust in a process that can take millions of years.

The gas clouds that give birth to stars are known as molecular clouds and are made of hydrogen gas. While most of the hydrogen is spread out incredibly thinly across space, denser clumps can form if something disturbs the cloud. Once that happens, the clumps of gas may begin to shrink due to gravity and pull in more gas, concentrating it at their centers. Eventually, the core regions become so dense and hot that stars ignite. These brilliant newborn stars may illuminate the clouds in which they formed, creating a dazzling display of light and color.

Nair al Saif is the brightest star in Orion's sword.

50 million years—how long it can take for a
solar system to form inside a gas cloud.

700 The approximate **number of stars**
within the Orion Nebula.

75

Intense ultraviolet radiation from young stars makes atoms in the gas clouds emit light. Each element emits a characteristic color. Hydrogen, for instance, glows red. The colors in this photograph are enhanced.

Bubble-shaped region containing hot gas

Fierce stellar winds from massive newborn stars create arcs of gas and dust.

Wisps of hydrogen gas and dust

The dark areas are dust clouds that block light.

How a star forms

Star formation begins when a gas and dust cloud in deep space is subjected to a trigger event, such as a nearby supernova or an encounter with a nearby star. Once the cloud starts to collapse, gravity does the rest of the work to form a star.

Clumps form
Pockets of dense gas form in a molecular cloud (a huge cloud of cold, dark gas and dust).

Clump contracts
The force of gravity makes a gas clump shrink and pull in more gas from around it.

Spinning disk
The clump shrinks to form a hot, dense core surrounded by a spinning disk of matter. Jets of gas shoot out from its poles.

Star ignites
When the center is hot enough, nuclear fusion begins and a star is born. A disk of matter still orbits the young star.

Disk disperses
The leftover material is either dispersed into space or clumps together to form planets, moons, and other objects.

Stellar nurseries

Our galaxy contains many star-birth regions. The Horsehead Nebula looks like a silhouette of a horse's head in ordinary light but is pink in the infrared image below. The Carina Nebula, four times larger than the Orion Nebula, is famous for a gargantuan dust-gas pillar known as Mystic Mountain.

HORSEHEAD NEBULA

MYSTIC MOUNTAIN IN THE CARINA NEBULA

Exoplanets

The first exoplanet—a planet outside our Solar System orbiting an ordinary star—was discovered in 1995. Since then, astronomers have found more than 4,000 of these alien worlds, some of which are similar to Earth and may even harbor life.

Until the 1990s, the only planets known to science were the eight planets that orbit our Sun. People suspected that planets might orbit other stars, but such worlds were impossible to detect because of the vast distances separating them from us. However, as telescopes became more advanced, astronomers began to notice faint changes in the color or intensity of light from distant stars, which suggested planets were passing in front of them. Careful studies followed, and the first exoplanet was confirmed in 1995. Thousands of extrasolar systems have now been discovered, some with up to eight planets. These range from small, probably rocky worlds like Earth to giants with rings 200 times wider than Saturn's. There may be hundreds of billions of exoplanets in our galaxy.

Astronomers reckon there could be
11 billion Earth-like
habitable exoplanets in our galaxy.

The Kepler-62 system

In 2013, the Kepler space telescope discovered five exoplanets orbiting the star Kepler-62, which lies 1,200 light-years from Earth. The picture below is an artist's impression of the planets, which are too far away to photograph. Two of them orbit in the star's "habitable zone," where the temperature is right for life. Like all newly discovered exoplanets, the planets in Kepler-62 have catalog names but may receive proper names in the future.

Dense clouds may cover Kepler-62d, which is likely to have a thick atmosphere.

Sun-scorched
The planet Kepler-62b orbits very close to the star, zipping around it every six days. Its surface temperature is 887°F (475°C)—probably too hot for life.

Mars-sized
Kepler-62c is about the size of Mars. It is fiercely hot, with a surface temperature of 572°F (300°C).

Largest planet
Kepler-62d's size suggests it has enough gravity to hold onto a thick atmosphere. Its surface is hotter than boiling water.

The **most massive** known exoplanet
has about **30 times** the mass of Jupiter.

Aldebaran, in the constellation Taurus,
is the **brightest known star with an exoplanet**.

77

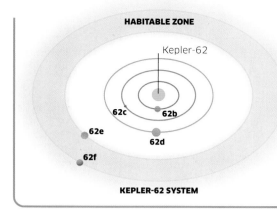

KEPLER-62 SYSTEM

Habitable zone

Two of the planets in the Kepler-62 system orbit in an area known as the habitable zone (or "Goldilocks zone"), where temperatures are just right for water to exist as a liquid on a planet's surface. Many scientists think liquid water is essential for life to flourish.

First photo of an exoplanet

This infrared image in false color, taken in 2004, was the first direct photo of an exoplanet. The planet, which appears as a red blob, is a type known as a "hot Jupiter"—a boiling-hot gas giant. It orbits around a brown dwarf called 2M1207 about 172 light-years from Earth.

Worlds beyond

This artist's impression shows how the Kepler-62 system might look from the planet 62f. Planet 62e looms in the sky nearby, while the other three planets and the Kepler-62 star are visible in the background.

Kepler-62e is likely to be a rocky planet with a thick atmosphere and possibly oceans or ice on its surface.

Earth-like

Kepler-62e is one of the most Earth-like planets known. Its surface temperature is 32°F (0°C), which means it may have liquid water, a cloudy atmosphere, and even life.

Cold Earth

Kepler-62f is similar to 62e but colder. It may have surface water and ice. Its year is 267 days long, and its surface gravity is probably stronger than Earth's.

The atmosphere contains
significant amounts
of water vapor.

Orange star

The orange dwarf star HD 189733 A has only
one known exoplanet—the hot Jupiter HD
189733 b, which orbits its parent star every
2.2 days. The planet was detected from a
slight dimming it causes in the star's light each
time it passes between the star and Earth.

The temperature of the planet's atmosphere is over 1,800°F (1,000°C), making the planet inhospitable to life as we know it.

Blue planet

This artist's impression shows one of the nearest hot Jupiters: HD 189733 b, which is 63 light-years from Earth. Its deep blue color is due to vast numbers of silicate particles—glass rain—in its atmosphere.

Every second, several million pounds of hydrogen boil away from the surface of HD 189733 b.

Hot Jupiters

Many of the planets that have been detected outside our own solar system are of a type called "hot Jupiters"—weird, exotic gas giants that are about the size of Jupiter or larger, but much hotter because they orbit close to their stars.

Hot Jupiters orbit at a distance of 1–46 million miles (2–75 million km) from their stars—much closer than Jupiter, which orbits hundreds of millions of miles from the Sun. These star-snuggling worlds are scorched by their stars, producing extreme weather conditions in their atmospheres, including howling winds, temperatures high enough to melt steel, and molten-glass rain. Scientists think that hot Jupiters must have originated farther away from their stars and then migrated toward them, since there would not have been enough material so close to a star for such huge planets to form there.

Death of hot Jupiters

Hot Jupiters often have violent deaths. Some spiral in toward their parent star and are consumed. Others boil away into space, leaving behind just a rocky or metallic core.

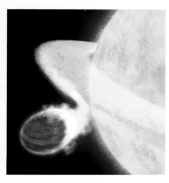

Pulled in by gravity
The hot Jupiter WASP-12 orbits so close to its star that gravity is distorting it and ripping off its atmosphere.

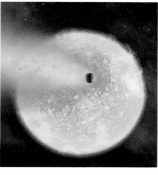

Loss of atmosphere
The atmosphere of HD 209458 b is boiling away into space at a rate of thousands of tons per second, forming a long tail of hydrogen.

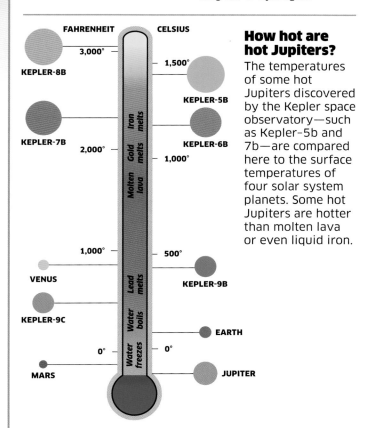

How hot are hot Jupiters?

The temperatures of some hot Jupiters discovered by the Kepler space observatory—such as Kepler-5b and 7b—are compared here to the surface temperatures of four solar system planets. Some hot Jupiters are hotter than molten lava or even liquid iron.

Wild orbits

Upsilon Andromedae b was one of the first hot Jupiters to be detected. It is one of four planets orbiting a star 44 light-years away. Shown here are three of the planets' orbits, which are tilted at wildly different angles.

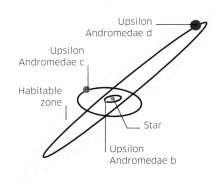

Upsilon Andromedae d
Upsilon Andromedae c
Habitable zone
Star
Upsilon Andromedae b

GAS CLOUD

PROTOSTAR

PROTOSTAR

PROTOSTAR

RED DWARF

Star birth
All stars are born from clumps of gas and dust that contract under the influence of gravity to form hot, spinning structures called protostars. Starbirth clouds are found scattered throughout the spiral arms of the Milky Way, as well as in other galaxies.

Small stars
The smallest stars (with masses up to a quarter of our Sun's) are relatively cool and dim and are known as red dwarfs. These can shine for hundreds of billions of years. As they age, their surface temperature increases and they eventually become blue dwarfs. Then they cool to white dwarfs, and finally to cold, dead black dwarfs.

Medium stars
Stars about the same mass as the Sun last for billions to tens of billions of years. They swell into red giant stars at the end of their lives. A red giant undergoes a peaceful death, shedding its outer layers to form a ghostly cloud of wreckage called a planetary nebula.

The red supergiant
Betelgeuse
is expected to explode as a supernova any day in the next 100,000 years.

Massive stars
Stars with the highest mass—more than eight times the mass of the Sun—have the shortest lives, measured in millions to hundreds of millions of years. Usually white to blue in color for most of their lives, they redden as they age and die in the most spectacular and violent way possible.

Lives and deaths of stars

Stars shine as long as they can maintain the delicate balance between the inward pull of their own gravity and the outward pressure of energy from the core. How long this lasts depends on how much matter a star starts off with.

Massive stars have relatively short lives because they quickly use up their hydrogen fuel in nuclear reactions. The most massive stars die in stupendous explosions called supernovas. Small stars have less fuel but they use it slowly and can last for hundreds of billions of years before they gradually fade away. Medium-mass stars, like the Sun, evolve along an intermediate path and end up as beautiful objects called planetary nebulae when they die.

Red supergiant
When a massive star has fused all the hydrogen fuel in its core, it starts producing energy by fusing together helium atoms. Eventually the core runs out of helium, but it continues to force together atoms to form heavier and heavier elements until iron atoms are formed. At the same time, the star swells into a red supergiant. When the core turns into iron, it can no longer produce enough energy to withstand the inward pull of the star's gravity and the star collapses violently and then explodes in a supernova.

The very largest stars may have life
spans as short as **3 million years**.

Our Sun will **become a red giant** in 5 billion years
and may grow large enough to **swallow Earth**.

81

Star's light
begins to dim

BLUE DWARF

BLACK DWARF

Life stories

Contrasted here are the life stories of
the three main types of stars: low-mass
stars (top row); medium-mass stars
like the Sun (middle row); and massive
stars (bottom row). Small stars have
the longest lives. In fact, they live
for so long that no red dwarf in the
universe has yet evolved to the blue
dwarf or black dwarf stage.

White dwarf
Left at the heart of a planetary
nebula is all that remains of the
red giant's core: a small, brilliant
star called a white dwarf. This
causes the surrounding cloud
to shine. Over a long period of
time it cools to a black dwarf.

BLACK DWARF

Red giant
A red giant forms when a
medium-mass star runs out of
hydrogen in its core. The core
begins to use helium as a fuel,
while hydrogen is "burned" as
a fuel in a shell surrounding
the core. At the same time, the
star expands to a giant size.

When all its fuel is
used up, the outer
layers of a red
giant are shed.

Planetary nebula
A planetary nebula is a glowing cloud
of material shed by a red giant, often
with a beautiful and complex shape.
Planetary nebulae last for only a few
tens of thousands of years.

Supernova
When it can produce no more energy by
nuclear fusion reactions, a red supergiant
disintegrates in a supernova explosion.
The star's outer layers dissipate into
space while its core continues to collapse
on itself. Depending on its mass, the core
of the star implodes to form either
a neutron star or a black hole.

Neutron star
If the remaining core has between 1.4 and 3
times as much mass as our Sun, it collapses
to about the size of a city and becomes a
neutron star—an incredibly compact object
made of neutrons that spins at a furious rate.
Neutron stars are so dense that a single
teaspoonful of their matter has a mass of
about 10 million tons.

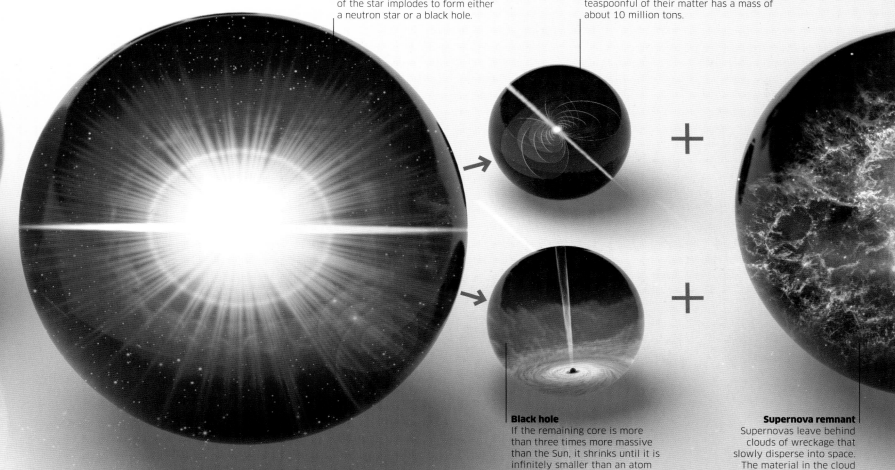

Black hole
If the remaining core is more
than three times more massive
than the Sun, it shrinks until it is
infinitely smaller than an atom
and forms a black hole—a region
of space from which nothing (not
even light) can escape.

Supernova remnant
Supernovas leave behind
clouds of wreckage that
slowly disperse into space.
The material in the cloud
may eventually form new
stars, repeating the cycle
of star birth and death.

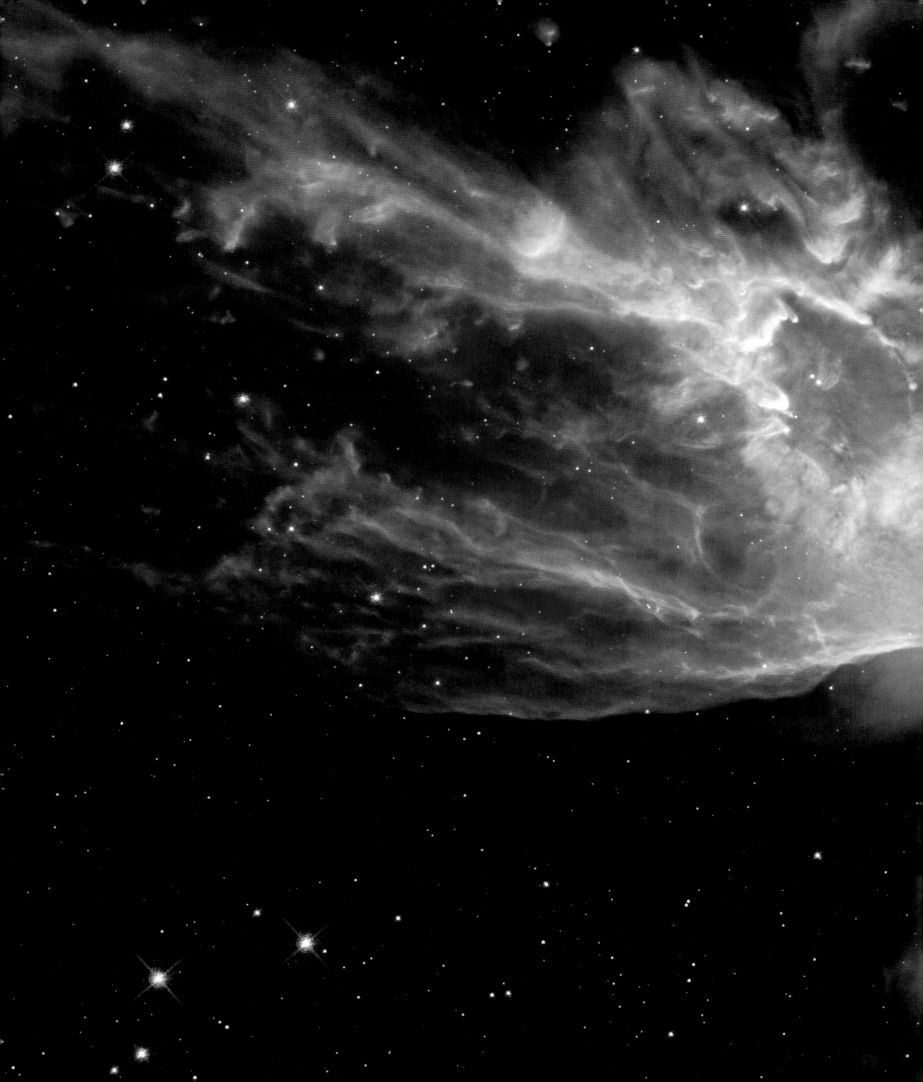

Butterfly Nebula

When stars like our Sun die, they cast off their outer layers as glowing clouds of wreckage. These ghostly remains are known as planetary nebulae.

Planetary nebulae were so named because the first to be noticed were round in shape, like planets. Others, however, fling their gas in two directions to form wings or a figure-eight shape. The Butterfly Nebula, captured here by the Hubble Space Telescope, is about 500 times wider than our solar system, and the gas in its wings is hurtling through space at 590,000 mph (950,000 kph). Hidden in its heart is all that remains of the original star's core—a tiny, feeble star called a white dwarf.

Red supergiants

The largest stars in the universe are red supergiants. These are massive stars that have swollen to a vast size as they grow old.

All stars produce energy by the process of nuclear fusion. Inside the star's core, the temperature and pressure are so high that hydrogen atoms are forced together, fusing them into helium atoms—a process that releases colossal amounts of energy. Massive stars use up the fuel in the core quickly and then begin to balloon in size as nuclear fusion spreads out from the core. The outer layers of the most massive stars expand into an immense sphere of glowing gas, forming a red supergiant. Eventually, the star disintegrates in a sudden and violent explosion called a supernova, leaving behind either a tiny neutron star or a black hole.

Hydrogen-fusing shell

Convective layer
Pockets of hot gas rise within the convective layer, before cooling and sinking back down. This process of rising and falling is called convection.

Structure
This model reveals the inner structure of a red supergiant in the last moment of its life, before a supernova explosion destroys it. The size of the core, which is minuscule relative to the supergiant's full extent, is exaggerated in our model. After hydrogen runs out, the core fuses a succession of heavier elements, forming a series of shells in the star's center. The heaviest element a star can fuse is silicon, which powers the star for about a day, causing iron to build up. When the star attempts to fuse iron, it explodes.

Helium-fusing shell

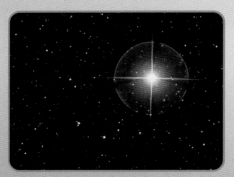

Our local red supergiant
The red supergiant closest to Earth is a star called Antares, which is 880 times wider than our Sun. Although 550 light-years away, Antares is easily visible in the night sky. It could explode in a supernova at any point in the next million years or so, but it poses no threat to Earth.

Outer layers
The outer part of the star consists of thinly spread hydrogen gas. There is no distinct surface. Instead, the gas fades gradually into the emptiness of space.

SIZE OF THE SUN FOR COMPARISON

A supernova explosion can **outshine an entire galaxy**.

The red supergiant **Antares** is over **57,000 times brighter** than the Sun.

85

Core
Nuclear fusion takes place only in the core, where elements such as hydrogen are fused to make heavier elements.

Iron core

Silicon-fusing shell

Oxygen-fusing shell

Neon-fusing shell

Carbon-fusing shell

Warm color
The outer layer of a red supergiant has a temperature of about 6,900°F (3,800°C), which is much lower than the surface temperature of a Sun-like star. The cooler surface gives the star its reddish color.

Life and death of a supergiant

Two powerful forces govern the life of a star: gravity, which pulls matter in the star inward, and pressure, which pushes matter outward. Normally balanced, these forces can become unbalanced at the end of a star's life.

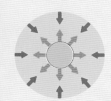

1 HYDROGEN BURNING
For most of a star's life, its core turns hydrogen into helium by nuclear fusion. The energy this releases maintains pressure that pushes the star's matter outward, balancing the inward pull of gravity.

2 HELIUM BURNING
When hydrogen in the core runs out, massive stars begin to fuse helium. Hydrogen burning spreads to a shell outside the inner core, causing the star's outer layers to expand.

3 MULTILAYER CORE
When helium in the core runs out, the star starts to fuse carbon to form neon. Next it fuses neon into oxygen. A series of shells forms in the core region, fusing different elements.

4 COLLAPSE
When the core finally tries to fuse iron, disaster ensues. Iron fusion cannot maintain outward pressure, so gravity overwhelms the core. It collapses to the size of a city in a split second, rushing inward at a quarter of the speed of light.

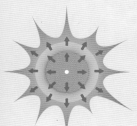

5 EXPLOSION
As temperatures in the core soar, a flood of particles called neutrinos is released. The star's collapsing outer layers rebound off this flood, causing a catastrophic explosion brighter than a billion Suns: a supernova.

Supersize stars

If a typical red supergiant were placed in the center of our solar system, it would extend out to between the orbits of Mars and Jupiter. In contrast, a large red giant would reach out only to about Earth's orbit.

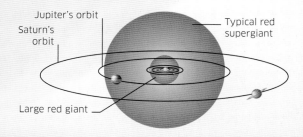

Jupiter's orbit

Saturn's orbit

Typical red supergiant

Large red giant

Neutron stars

When a huge star self-destructs in a supernova explosion, one of two things may happen. The core of a particularly massive star, crushed by its own stupendous gravity, shrinks until it is tinier than an atom and becomes a black hole. The core of a smaller star, however, shrinks to the size of a city to become a neutron star.

Neutron stars are the tiniest, densest stars known and can pack the mass of the whole Sun into an area smaller than London. They are so compact that a mere pinhead of matter has more than twice the mass of the largest supertanker on Earth. All neutron stars spin around at a furious rate, some rotating as fast as 700 times a second. We know this because neutron stars send out beams of radiation that sweep around the sky as they spin, making them appear to flash on and off if they sweep across Earth. Neutron stars that flash like this are called pulsars.

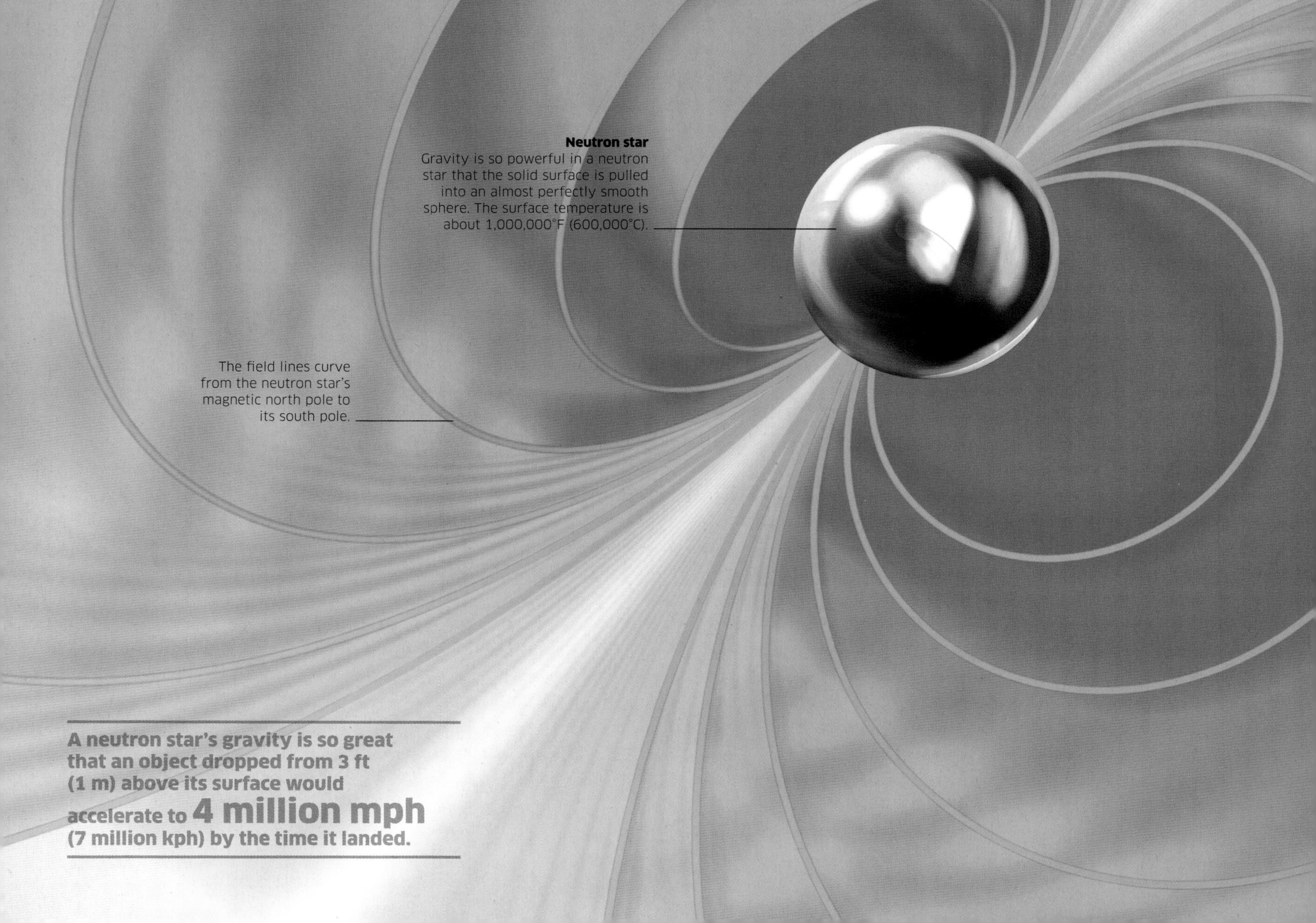

Neutron star
Gravity is so powerful in a neutron star that the solid surface is pulled into an almost perfectly smooth sphere. The surface temperature is about 1,000,000°F (600,000°C).

The field lines curve from the neutron star's magnetic north pole to its south pole.

A neutron star's gravity is so great that an object dropped from 3 ft (1 m) above its surface would accelerate to 4 million mph (7 million kph) by the time it landed.

100 million—the estimated **number** of neutron stars in our galaxy.

A neutron star's solid surface is **10 billion times stronger** than steel.

The **highest "mountains"** on a neutron star are **less than 0.19 in (5 mm) tall.**

87

Pulsars

Astronomers have discovered around 2,000 pulsars (flashing neutron stars) since the first one was spotted in 1967. These neutron stars have powerful magnetic fields and produce beams of radio waves from their magnetic poles. As the star spins around its axis of rotation, the two radio beams sweep out cone shapes across the sky, causing them to pulse where they sweep across Earth. The slowest pulsars send out about five pulses of radio waves a second. The fastest send out 716 pulses a second.

Radiation beam
A neutron star emits beams of radiation from its magnetic poles. The radiation may take the form of radio waves, X-rays, gamma rays, or even visible light.

Magnetic field
The magnetic field of a neutron star can be a quadrillion times more powerful than Earth's magnetic field. It rotates at the same speed as the star.

Inside a neutron star

Most stars are made of gas, but a neutron star has a crust of solid iron about 0.6 miles (1 km) thick. Beneath this is a sea of subatomic particles called neutrons, crammed together by powerful gravity, forming a kind of liquid that doesn't exist on Earth.

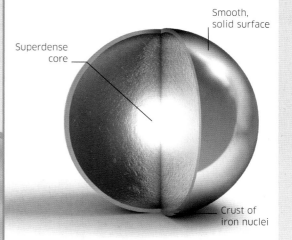

Smooth, solid surface

Superdense core

Crust of iron nuclei

Size

At 9–15 miles (15–25 km) wide, neutron stars are about as big as a city. Compared to other stars, however, they are tiny. Their density produces very powerful gravity at the surface. An average man on one would weigh 7.7 billion tons (7 billion tonnes).

NEUTRON STAR COMPARED TO VANCOUVER, CANADA

Density

The material that makes up a neutron star is so dense that a single teaspoonful brought to Earth would weigh more than the entire world population. A soccer ball made from neutron star matter would weigh 5.5 trillion tons (5 trillion tonnes)—about the same as Mount Everest.

 = **5.5 TRILLION** TONS

Black holes

Black holes are among the strangest objects in the universe. The pull of their gravity is so great that nothing can escape from them—not even light.

Most black holes form when massive stars run out of fuel and die in an explosion. The dead star's core—unable to resist the crushing force of its own gravity—collapses, shrinking in milliseconds until it is infinitely smaller than an atom. The core becomes what scientists call a singularity: an object so impossibly small that it has zero size but infinite density. Anything straying within a certain distance of the singularity is doomed to be pulled in by gravity and disappear forever. The point of no return forms a spherical boundary around the singularity called an event horizon, which marks how close you can safely get.

Event horizon
Anything that crosses this boundary from the outside can never escape.

Types of black hole
Two main types of black holes exist: stellar and supermassive. Stellar black holes form when enormous stars explode as supernovas at the ends of their lives. Supermassive black holes are bigger and are found at the centers of galaxies, often surrounded by a whirlpool of intensely hot, glowing matter.

Some scientists think black holes may **evaporate and disappear** over time by leaking heat energy.

The swirling clouds of matter around supermassive black holes are the **brightest objects in the universe.**

Some black holes rotate **thousands of times** per second.

89

Lensing
Black holes bend light. In this artist's impression, light from the accretion disk is bent to form a glowing halo around the black hole.

Singularity
Hidden in the black hole's center is a singularity, where matter has been squeezed into a point of infinite density.

Accretion disk
Gas, dust, and disintegrated stars spiral around some black holes in a disk. The material in the disk is not doomed—it may stay in orbit, just as planets orbit stars.

The first black hole image
In April, 2019, scientists released the first ever image of a black hole. The breakthrough image was created using an international network of telescopes collectively called the Event Horizon Telescope (EHT) and shows galaxy M87's supermassive black hole surrounded by its gold-colored accretion disc.

Spaghettification
The gravitational pull of a black hole rises so steeply nearby that an astronaut falling into one would be stretched like spaghetti and torn apart.

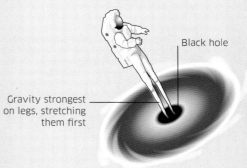

Black hole

Gravity strongest on legs, stretching them first

Bending light and stretching time
Black holes have such powerful gravity that they bend light like giant lenses. If Earth orbited a black hole, an observer would see a highly distorted image of the planet, like the one above. According to Albert Einstein's theory of relativity, black holes also slow down time. If an astronaut spent only an hour or so near a black hole, he might return to Earth to find that many years had passed.

Wormholes
Einstein's theory of relativity says that massive objects bend the four combined dimensions of space and time (space-time). Some experts have speculated that black holes might warp space-time so much that they could create shortcuts, called wormholes, between different parts of the universe or different times. There is no direct evidence that wormholes exist.

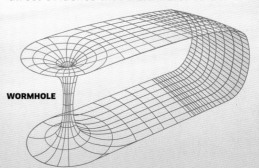

WORMHOLE

The pole star, **Polaris**, is actually a **triple star system**.

Some star pairs take **millions of years** to orbit each other.

Star clusters

Large groups of stars are called clusters. These can contain anything from a few dozen to several million stars. There are two main types of star clusters: globular and open. The Milky Way galaxy contains many examples of both.

Globular cluster

These are roughly spherical collections of up to several million ancient stars that formed at the same time. The example above is the Great Globular Cluster in Hercules.

Open cluster

Open clusters are loosely bound collections of young stars that formed around the same time from the same cloud of gas. The example here is the Butterfly Cluster in the constellation Scorpius.

Multiple stars

Unlike many other stars, our Sun is a loner with no companions. Most of the stars we can see in the night sky belong to multiple star systems—that is, two or more stars orbiting each other, held together by gravity.

Pairs of stars that simply orbit each other are called binary systems, but there are also systems of three, four, or more stars, with complicated orbital patterns. Some pairs of stars are so close together that material flows between them. These stars are called interacting binaries. As the stars age, the system can develop in a variety of dramatic ways. For example, in an X-ray binary, material flows from a normal or giant star to an extremely dense companion—a neutron star or a black hole—and gives off powerful X-rays as it spirals inward. Alternatively, material spilling from a normal or giant star onto a white dwarf may cause the dwarf to produce occasional brilliant blasts of light called novas.

One side of the donor star becomes distorted as gas is pulled toward the white dwarf by gravity.

The gas forms a funnel shape as it is pulled off the giant star.

Accretion disk
Gravity causes the material in this disk to spiral in toward the star at the center. As it does so, vast amounts of energy are released as heat and radiation.

White dwarf
A white dwarf star is the remains of a previous giant star that lost its outer layers. It is extremely dense: one teaspoon of white dwarf material weighs about 15 tons.

Interacting binary

Here, gas flows from a red giant to a nearby white dwarf, forming a swirling disk as it spirals in toward the dwarf star. The white dwarf becomes unstable as its mass increases, causing nuclear explosions at its surface. From Earth, these outbursts of light look like new stars appearing, which is why they are called novae, from the Latin word *nova*, meaning new.

Donor star
In an interacting binary, the star that is losing material to its companion is called the donor. It is usually the larger star in a pair—in this case, a red giant.

Relatively cool, low-density hydrogen gas

Type 1a supernova

The transfer of gas onto a white dwarf star can lead not just to nova outbursts but eventually, scientists think, to a cataclysmic explosion called a Type 1a supernova. This happens because the mass lost by the white dwarf during each nova blast is less than the mass it gains between outbursts, so it slowly grows. Finally, it becomes so massive that it is totally destabilized, triggering a supernova.

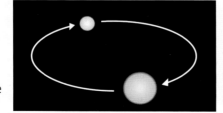

1 PAIR OF ORBITING STARS
Two interacting binary stars are orbiting relatively close to each other. One is a yellow star like our own Sun. Its smaller, denser companion is a white dwarf star.

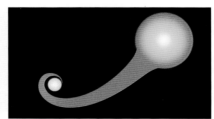

2 MATTER TRANSFER
As the Sun-like star ages, it swells to become a red giant. Some of its gas spills onto the smaller white dwarf star. This can lead to a series of surface outbursts, or novas.

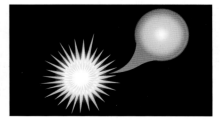

3 WHITE DWARF EXPLODES
The white dwarf's mass increases until it becomes unstable and explodes as a Type 1a supernova. The explosion may cause the red giant star to be blown away.

Star cloud

Every single tiny dot in this image of our galaxy's center is a star, possibly with a family of planets.

Our eyes can make out about 6,000 stars in the whole night sky, but that's only a ten-millionth of the total number of stars in our galaxy. Most are hidden behind clouds of dust, but the telescope that created this image used infrared light to see them. The image shows an area of sky about the size of your fist held at arm's length. The bright patch is the center of the Milky Way, where a supermassive black hole lies hidden.

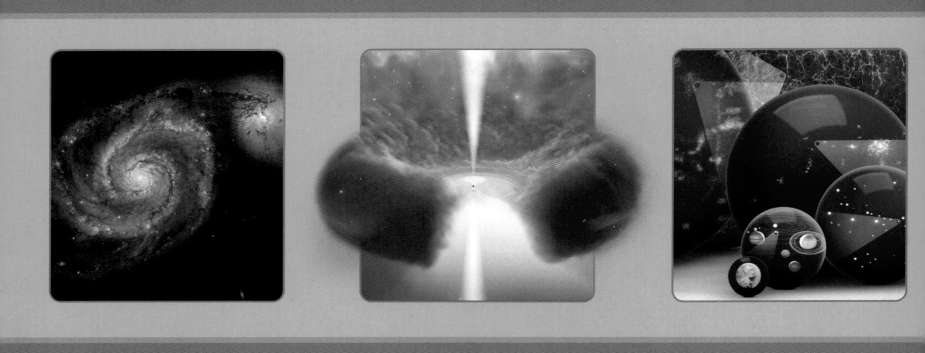

GALAXIES

Our Sun is just one of perhaps 200 billion stars that are held together in space by gravity to form a galaxy—a vast, swirling collection of stars, dust, gas, and invisible matter. There are billions of galaxies in the universe, stretching as far as we can see in every direction.

The cosmos

The cosmos, or Universe, is everything that exists—not just on Earth or in the Solar System, but also across the mind-bogglingly vast expanses of space. The cosmos includes the galaxy of stars to which our Sun belongs, countless billions of other galaxies, and unfathomable stretches of emptiness between the galaxies. Scientists who study the cosmos are called cosmologists. While astronomers study the stars and galaxies, cosmologists try to find out how and when the Universe began, why it has changed over time, and what its eventual fate will be.

WHAT'S THE UNIVERSE MADE OF?

The Universe is made of matter and energy. Matter includes visible objects such as stars, but also a mysterious invisible substance called dark matter, which we can only detect through its gravity. Energy includes radiation, such as light, and dark energy. Almost nothing is known of dark energy except that it is causing the Universe to expand faster and faster.

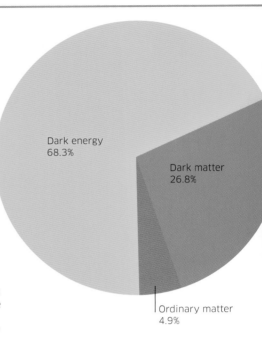

Dark energy
68.3%

Dark matter
26.8%

Ordinary matter
4.9%

Mass-energy

Scientists have found that matter and energy are interchangeable forms of the same thing, called mass-energy. This pie chart shows how the total mass-energy of the Universe divides up into ordinary matter, dark matter, and dark energy.

EARTH

THE SUN
8 light-minutes

NEAREST STAR TO SUN (PROXIMA CENTAURI)
4.2 light-years

NEAREST RED SUPERGIANT STAR (ANTARES)
550 light-years

CENTER OF THE MILKY WAY
27,000 light-years

NEAREST SPIRAL GALAXY (ANDROMEDA)
2.5 million light-years

FARTHEST VISIBLE GALAXIES
Tens of billions of light-years

COSMIC DISTANCES

Outside the Solar System, distances in space are so huge that we need special units to measure them. One light-year is the distance that light, moving at around 670 million mph (1 billion kph), travels in a whole year—about 6 million million miles (9.5 million million km). The most distant objects we can see mark the limit of the observable Universe, but the whole Universe extends much farther.

THE EXPANDING UNIVERSE

About 100 years ago, astronomers discovered that distant galaxies are rushing away from us at great speed. This isn't just because they are flying through space—it's because space itself is expanding, making the farthest galaxies rush away the fastest. The discovery meant the Universe must once have been much smaller and possibly began with a sudden, dramatic expansion from a single point. This idea, known as the Big Bang theory, is the best explanation for how the Universe began. More recently, scientists have discovered that the expansion is getting faster.

Expanding space

Although the Universe is expanding, it isn't expanding *into* anything. Instead, space itself is expanding. One way to visualize this tricky idea is to imagine a two-dimensional universe on the surface of a balloon. As the balloon inflates, the galaxies get farther apart.

The space between the galaxies expands, though the galaxies remain the same size.

Galaxies were much closer together in the distant past.

BILLIONS OF YEARS AGO

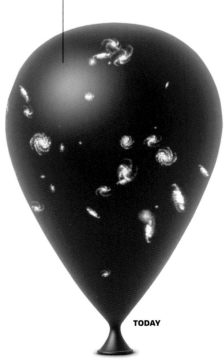

TODAY

Ordinary matter

Everything we can see or touch—from our own bodies to Earth, the planets, and stars—is made up of what astronomers call ordinary matter. Atoms are made of ordinary matter, and most of the ordinary matter in the Universe is concentrated in galaxies, such as those dotted throughout the Hubble Space Telescope image above.

Dark matter

Most of the matter in the Universe is not ordinary matter, but dark matter, which is impossible to see. Dark matter can only be detected by the gravity it exerts. In the picture above, which shows a cluster of many galaxies, the area colored blue shows where astronomers think dark matter lies, based on their calculations.

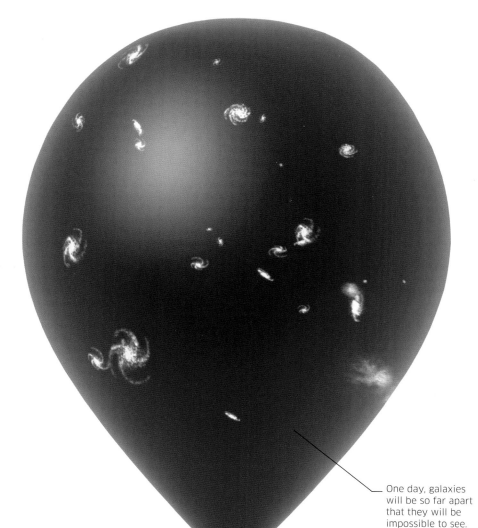

One day, galaxies will be so far apart that they will be impossible to see.

BILLIONS OF YEARS IN THE FUTURE

GRAVITY

The force of gravity is the most important force at large scales in the Universe. It is gravity that holds planets together in the Solar System, keeps stars together in galaxies, and groups galaxies together into galaxy clusters.

Law of gravity

The English scientist Isaac Newton discovered how gravity works more than 300 years ago. He was the first person to realize that the force of gravity keeps the Moon in orbit around Earth and keeps the planets in orbit around the Sun.

CLOCKWORK MODEL OF THE SOLAR SYSTEM

Space-time

Newton's law of gravity allowed scientists to predict the motion of planets with great accuracy, but it wasn't perfect. In 1915, German-born scientist Albert Einstein published an even more accurate theory. Einstein said that gravity happens because massive objects bend the fabric of space and time, a bit like a heavy ball on a rubber sheet. A star, for instance, distorts space-time, causing planets to circle around it.

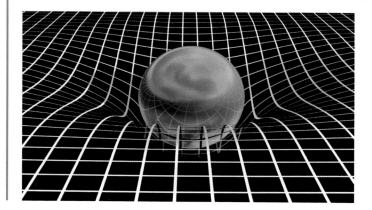

Milky Way

Seen from the southern hemisphere in winter, the Milky Way's central area forms a spectacular band of light stretching across the night sky.

Although the Milky Way is a spiral galaxy, we see its disk as a plane because we are inside it. The bright cloud on the right marks the star-packed heart of the galaxy. The dark lanes are vast interstellar dust clouds that block the light of the stars behind them. Here, photographers on Castlepoint Beach in New Zealand try to capture the galaxy in all its midwinter glory.

1923 The year in which **Edwin Hub-ble** proved that there are galaxies beyond our own.

12–13 billion years—the **age of** the Milky Way Galaxy.

Galaxies

Like nearly all stars, the Sun belongs to a huge collection of stars held together by gravity: a galaxy. Our galaxy is just one of hundreds of billions of galaxies floating in the vastness of the Universe.

On very clear, dark nights, you can sometimes see a band of milky light across the sky. The light comes from stars in the main part of our own galaxy, the Milky Way. The Milky Way is disk-shaped, but because we are inside it, we see its light as a band. It is so huge that its size defies imagination. It would take 150 billion years to cross the Milky Way at the speed of an airliner, and even the nearest star would take 6 million years to reach. Almost everything the naked eye can see in the sky belongs to the Milky Way. Beyond it, countless other galaxies stretch in all directions as far as telescopes can see.

Milky Way

The Milky Way is shaped like two fried eggs back-to-back. In the center is a bulge containing most of the galaxy's stars, and around this is a flat disk. The disk is made up of spiral arms that curve out from the center. There are two major spiral arms and several minor ones. In the heart of the central bulge is a black hole 4 million times more massive than the Sun.

The Milky Way contains about 200 billion stars.

Scutum–Centaurus Arm
This is one of the two main spiral arms of the galaxy. The area where it joins the central bar is rich in star-forming clouds.

Dark lane formed by dust

Barred spiral
The Milky Way is classed as a barred spiral galaxy because the central bulge is bar-shaped.

Norma Arm

Eagle Nebula
Glowing clouds of gas and dust occur throughout our galaxy. The dark pillars in this image of the Eagle Nebula are clouds of dust and hydrogen thousands of times larger than the Solar System. Inside these clouds, new stars are forming.

Galactic center
The bright white region seen here marks the center of our galaxy. This is an extremely active place. At its heart, matter spirals into a gigantic black hole. The reddish areas next to the center are large arcs of glowing gas.

Solar System
Our Solar System orbits the galactic center once every 225 million years, traveling at about 120 miles (200 km) per second. So far, it has completed only 23 orbits.

120,000 light-years—the width of the **Milky Way** Galaxy.

95% of the mass in our galaxy is **dark matter**.

200 billion—the **estimated number of galaxies in the observable Universe**.

101

Orion Arm
Our Solar System is located close to the inner edge of this small arm, which is about 10,000 light-years long. Many of the brightest stars in the night sky can be found in this arm.

Carina–Sagittarius Arm
Situated inside the Orion Arm, this minor spiral arm is rich in bright nebulae and star clusters.

Nebula

Outer Arm

Perseus Arm
A major arm of the Milky Way, this is around 100,000 light-years long and curves around the outside of the Orion Arm, which includes our Solar System. Numerous star clusters and nebulae dot the Perseus Arm.

Galaxy shapes

Galaxies come in various shapes and sizes, from fuzzy clouds with no clear shape to beautiful spirals with graceful, curving arms. The main types of galaxy shape are shown below. Whatever the shape, all galaxies spin—though their individual stars do not all orbit the center at the same speed. As the stars in a galaxy orbit, they may pass in and out of crowded areas, like cars passing through traffic jams. These crowded areas appear to us as spiral arms.

Spiral
These galaxies consist of a central hub of stars surrounded by a flat rotating disk containing stars, gas, and dust. The material in the disk is concentrated into two or more spiral arms, which curve outward. The spiral galaxy here, known as Bode's Galaxy, is relatively close to our own, at 12 million light-years away.

Barred spiral
This type is similar to a spiral except that a straight bar of stars, dust, and gas runs across the center, connecting curved or spiral arms. Our own galaxy, the Milky Way, is a barred spiral, as is NGC 1365 (left). At 200,000 light-years across, NGC 1365 is one of the largest galaxies known.

Elliptical
These galaxies can be spherical, rugby ball–shaped, or even cigar-shaped, with no clear internal structure. They contain mostly very old red stars, which give the galaxy an orange or reddish hue, but little gas and dust. Their stars follow a variety of orbits. M60, shown here, is quite a large elliptical galaxy.

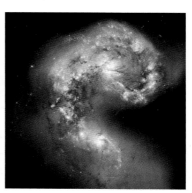

Irregular
Galaxies of this type have no particular shape or symmetry. Some are made by collisions between two galaxies. For example, the Antennae Galaxies (left) were separate spirals until 1.2 billion years ago, when they started merging.

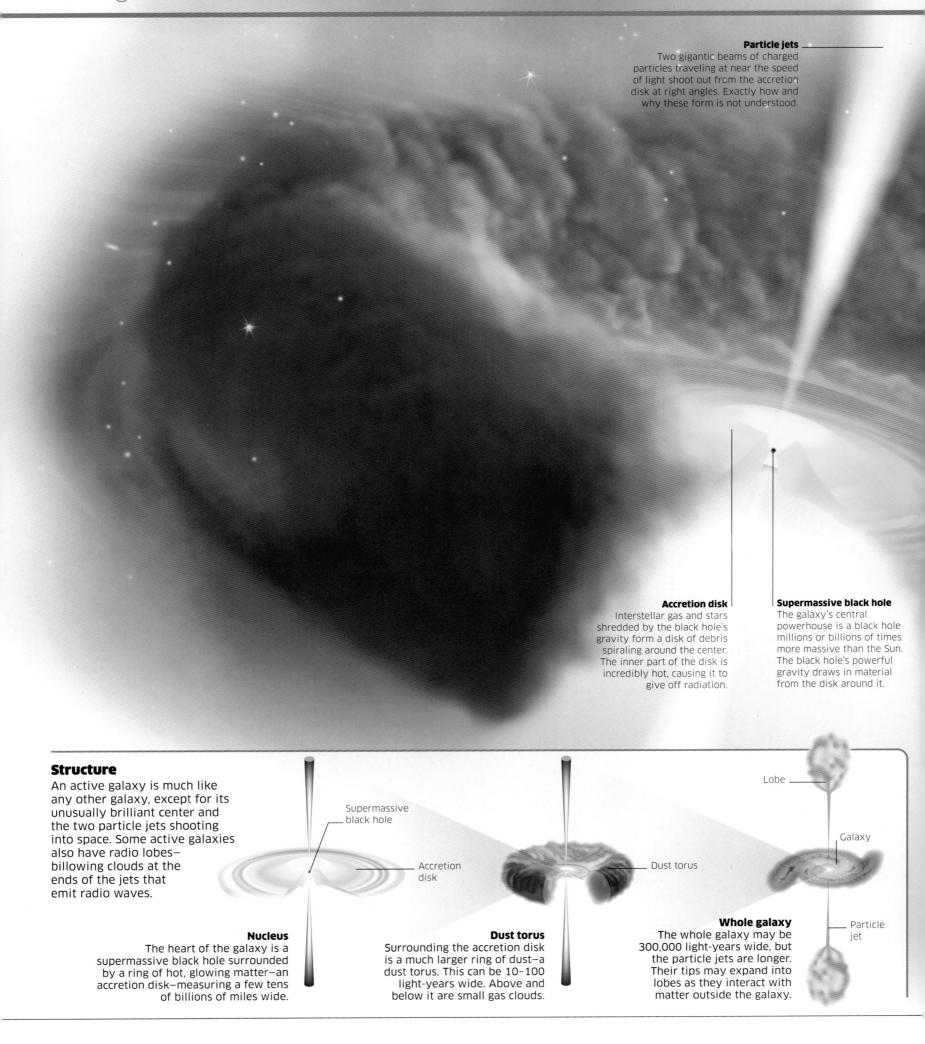

Particle jets
Two gigantic beams of charged particles traveling at near the speed of light shoot out from the accretion disk at right angles. Exactly how and why these form is not understood.

Accretion disk
Interstellar gas and stars shredded by the black hole's gravity form a disk of debris spiraling around the center. The inner part of the disk is incredibly hot, causing it to give off radiation.

Supermassive black hole
The galaxy's central powerhouse is a black hole millions or billions of times more massive than the Sun. The black hole's powerful gravity draws in material from the disk around it.

Structure

An active galaxy is much like any other galaxy, except for its unusually brilliant center and the two particle jets shooting into space. Some active galaxies also have radio lobes— billowing clouds at the ends of the jets that emit radio waves.

Supermassive black hole

Accretion disk

Dust torus

Lobe

Galaxy

Particle jet

Nucleus
The heart of the galaxy is a supermassive black hole surrounded by a ring of hot, glowing matter—an accretion disk—measuring a few tens of billions of miles wide.

Dust torus
Surrounding the accretion disk is a much larger ring of dust—a dust torus. This can be 10–100 light-years wide. Above and below it are small gas clouds.

Whole galaxy
The whole galaxy may be 300,000 light-years wide, but the particle jets are longer. Their tips may expand into lobes as they interact with matter outside the galaxy.

Light from the farthest **quasars** has taken over **12 billion years** to reach us.

A **quasar** can emit **100,000 times more light** than our own galaxy.

103

Active galaxies

Galaxies glow in the darkness of space thanks to the light from their stars. A few galaxies, however, also blast out vast amounts of light and other types of radiation from their cores. These are active galaxies.

The center, or nucleus, of an active galaxy emits a staggeringly large amount of electromagnetic radiation. This energy floods out into space not only as visible light, but also as radio waves, X-rays, ultraviolet radiation, and gamma rays. The radiation comes from an intensely hot and dense disk of matter spiraling around and into a black hole possibly a billion times the mass of the Sun—a supermassive black hole. Active galaxies also fling out jets of particles that penetrate deep into intergalactic space. These strange galaxies include some of the most distant objects we can see, such as quasars—objects so astonishingly far away that their light has taken billions of years to reach us, meaning they probably no longer exist.

Dust torus
In some active galaxies, a ring (torus) of gas and dust blocks our view of the central black hole and accretion disk.

Beyond the dust torus are the stars and clouds of gas and dust that make up the bulk of the galaxy.

Types of active galaxies

Active galaxies seen from different angles or distances can look very different. As a result, astronomers have distinct names for what look like different objects but are actually part of the same family.

Radio galaxies
When seen with a radio telescope, radio galaxies are flanked by gigantic, billowing clouds called lobes. Those on Hercules A (above) are nearly 10 times longer than our Milky Way Galaxy.

Seyfert galaxies
These galaxies have much brighter centers than normal galaxies. Most, such as NGC 1566 above, are spiral in shape.

Quasars
Quasars, such as 3C 273 above, are the brightest objects in the Universe. They are active galactic nuclei billions of light-years from Earth.

Blazars
When a jet from an active galaxy's nucleus points toward Earth, we see a blazar. Some astronomers think M87 (above) is a nearby blazar.

104 galaxies ○ **COLLIDING GALAXIES**

When galaxies merge, the **black holes at their centers** may also merge.

Colliding galaxies

Neighboring galaxies sometimes drift close enough for the force of gravity to make them collide. Flying into each other at millions of miles an hour, they crash in a blaze of fireworks as colliding gas clouds give birth to thousands of new stars.

Because the stars in a galaxy are so far apart, galaxies can collide without any of their stars crashing into one another. In fact, during a collision, two galaxies can pass right through each other. Nevertheless, the gravitational tug of war wreaks havoc on the galaxies' shapes, tearing spiral arms apart and flinging billions of stars into space. Often the collision slows down the movement of the galaxies so much that a second or third pass-through happens. In time, the two galaxies may merge to form one larger galaxy.

The Whirlpool Galaxy has two very clear spiral arms. It was the first galaxy to be described as a spiral.

The dark stripes are "lanes" of dust that block the light from the stars behind them.

The Whirlpool Galaxy has a very bright center because it is what astronomers call an active galaxy—one in which huge amounts of light are being released by gas and dust spiraling into a central black hole.

Clusters of hundreds of thousands of hot, newborn stars blaze with a bluish light.

Whirlpool Galaxy

About 300 million years ago, the Whirlpool Galaxy was struck by a dwarf galaxy that now appears to dangle from one of the larger galaxy's spiral arms. The dwarf galaxy, called NGC 5195, may already have passed through the Whirlpool Galaxy twice. The gravity of the dwarf galaxy has stirred up gas clouds inside the Whirlpool, triggering a burst of star formation. On a dark night, you can see this galactic collision through a small telescope in the constellation of Canes Venatici.

4 billion years—time left until the **Milky Way and Andromeda Galaxies collide**.

The galaxy that will form when the **Milky Way and Andromeda merge** has already been given a name: **Milkdromeda**.

105

One arm of the Whirlpool Galaxy seems to have been tugged out by gravity toward the dwarf galaxy, which lies behind it.

This dark lane is a bridge of dust joining the two galaxies. It blocks the light from the stars behind, which tells us that the dwarf galaxy must be farther away than the Whirlpool Galaxy.

The shape of the dwarf galaxy has been distorted by the collision. Any spiral arms it may once have had are no longer visible.

The bright pink areas are clouds of gas and dust that have been stirred up by the collision, causing millions of new stars to form.

Oddball galaxies

The Universe contains many strange-looking galaxies that do not seem to fit into the usual galaxy classification system. Astronomers reckon many of these oddities are the result of collisions, mergers, or other interactions between two or more galaxies.

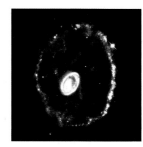

Cartwheel Galaxy
This bizarre object formed when a spiral galaxy bumped into a smaller companion 200 million years ago. The shock wave it produced rearranged the galaxies into a bluish ring and central bright portion.

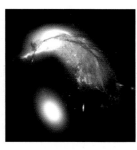

The Porpoise
Here, what was once a spiral galaxy is being reshaped by the gravity of a galaxy below it. The end result looks like a porpoise leaping over a fuzzy oval ball. A burst of newly formed blue stars forms the porpoise's nose.

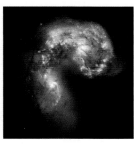

Antennae Galaxies
These intertwined spiral galaxies are going through a "starburst" phase. Clouds of dust and gas are compressing each other, causing stars to form rapidly. The areas of star formation glow with brilliant pink and blue colors.

Future galactic merger

Our own galaxy—the Milky Way—is hurtling toward the neighboring Andromeda Galaxy at 250,000 mph (400,000 kph). Billions of years from now, they will collide and eventually merge. Above is an artist's idea of how the collision might look from Earth around the time it starts, with the Andromeda Galaxy (left) grown to an enormous size in the night sky.

106 galaxies ∘ **GALAXY CLUSTERS**

10,000 The **number of galaxies** in the richest galaxy clusters.

Nearby clusters

Spread out in many directions from the Local Group are other galaxy clusters, a few of which are shown below. Clusters are grouped into even bigger structures called superclusters.

Abell 1689
This buzzing hive of galaxies is one of the biggest clusters known.

Virgo cluster
Two elliptical galaxies resembling eyes lie near the center of this cluster.

Leo cluster
The Leo cluster is part of a huge sheet of galaxies known as the Great Wall.

Abell 1185
This cluster contains an odd-looking galaxy called the Guitar (left).

Gravitational lensing

Galaxy clusters contain so much matter that their gravity can bend light rays passing close by. As a result, they act like giant lenses in space and can distort the shapes of more distant galaxies as viewed from Earth. This effect is known as gravitational lensing.

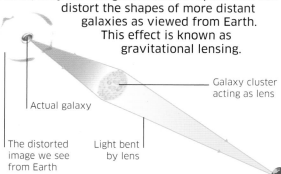

Galaxy cluster acting as lens

Actual galaxy

The distorted image we see from Earth

Light bent by lens

Sunburst Arc
The curved streaks in this image are multiple images of a galaxy almost 11 billion light-years from Earth. This galaxy's appearance is warped and magnified by the gravity of a massive galaxy cluster 4.6 billion light-years from Earth.

Local Group

Our home galaxy belongs to a cluster called the Local Group. The Local Group has three large spiral or barred spiral galaxies (the Milky Way, Andromeda, and Triangulum) and more than 50 smaller dwarf and irregular galaxies. They are spread out over a region roughly 10 million light-years across. Many of the smaller galaxies are clustered around the two largest spirals.

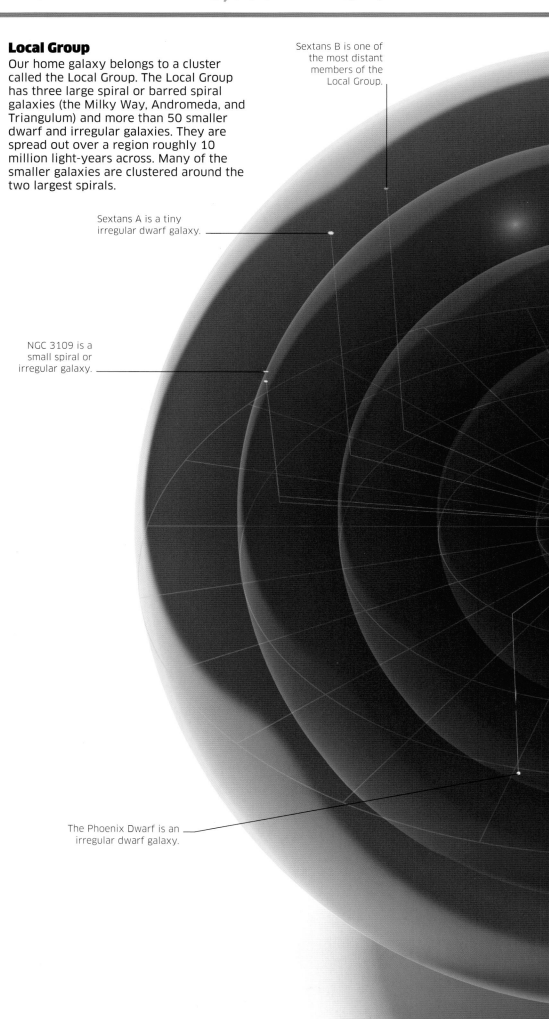

Sextans B is one of the most distant members of the Local Group.

Sextans A is a tiny irregular dwarf galaxy.

NGC 3109 is a small spiral or irregular galaxy.

The Phoenix Dwarf is an irregular dwarf galaxy.

90% of the mass in galaxy clusters is **dark matter**.

The **Triangulum Galaxy** is the **most distant object** visible to the naked eye.

There are **billions** of galaxy clusters in the Universe.

107

Milky Way
Our home galaxy is a barred spiral and is the second-largest galaxy in the Local Group (after Andromeda). A swarm of small galaxies surrounds it.

Galaxy clusters

Galaxies are held together in clusters by gravity, sometimes orbiting each other and often colliding. These clusters typically measure a few million light-years across.

Some galaxy clusters are quite sparse and contain only a few galaxies. The cluster that our own Milky Way Galaxy belongs to is one of these. Other clusters are much denser and contain hundreds or even thousands of galaxies, often arranged chaotically but sometimes forming a neat, spherical pattern. A giant elliptical galaxy usually lies at the center of these dense clusters. Galaxy clusters don't just contain galaxies. They also contain large amounts of thin, hot gas and mysterious dark matter, which we can't see.

IC10 is flying toward the Milky Way at 217 miles (350 km) per second.

Andromeda Galaxy
The largest galaxy in our cluster is Andromeda—a beautiful barred spiral some 140,000 light-years wide that has about a trillion stars. On a dark night with no light pollution, it can be seen quite easily through binoculars or even with the naked eye as a gray smudge. We see the galaxy nearly edge-on.

M110 is a dwarf elliptical galaxy.

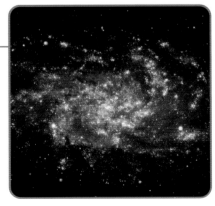

Triangulum Galaxy
Sometimes called the Pinwheel Galaxy or M33, Triangulum is a spiral galaxy. It is the third-largest galaxy in the Local Group. About 50,000 light-years wide, from Earth, it appears almost face-on. It is visible through binoculars or, less easily, with the naked eye on a very dark night.

The Wolf-Lundmark-Melotte Galaxy lies on the edge of the Local Group.

The shape of space

The three dimensions of space are "bent" by the gravitational pull of all the matter in the universe into a fourth dimension, which we cannot see. Since this is hard to visualize, scientists use the metaphor of a two-dimensional rubber sheet to explain the idea. Scientists used to think that the rubber sheet might be bent in any of three ways, depending on how densely packed with matter the universe is. We now know that the observable universe has a "flat" shape.

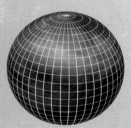

Closed
A dense universe would bend itself into a closed shape. In such a universe, traveling in a straight line would eventually bring you back to your starting point.

Open
If the universe is of low density, it might extend into an "open" shape. In this case, it would be infinite in size and have no outer edge.

Flat
Our universe appears to have just the right concentration of matter to have a "flat" shape. This suggests it will keep expanding forever, and like an open universe it might be infinite in size.

1 Earth
Our home world is a small, rocky planet floating in the enormous emptiness of space. Our nearest neighboring planet, Venus, is about a 15-minute journey away at the speed of light.

2 Solar system
Earth belongs to a family of planets and other objects that orbit the Sun. The farthest planet, Neptune, is 4.5 hours away at the speed of light, but the whole solar system is over 3 light-years wide.

3 Local stars
The closest star to the Sun is about 4 light-years away. Within 16 light-years of the Sun, there are 43 star systems containing 60 stars. Some of these star systems may have families of planets too.

4 Milky Way
The Sun and its neighboring stars occupy a tiny fraction of the Milky Way galaxy—a vast, swirling disk containing 400 billion stars and enormous clouds of gas and dust. It is over 100,000 light-years wide.

100 billion trillion—the estimated **number of stars** in the observable universe.

109

The universe

Everything in the universe is a part of something bigger. Earth is part of the solar system, which lies in the Milky Way galaxy, which is just a tiny bit of the whole universe.

The scale of the universe defies imagination. Astronomers use light as a yardstick to measure distance because nothing can cross the vast expanses of interstellar space faster. Yet even one light-year—the distance light travels in a whole year, or 6 trillion miles (10 trillion km)—is dwarfed by the largest structures observed in the known universe. Only a fraction of the universe is visible to us: the part of the universe from which light has had time to reach Earth since the Big Bang. The true extent of the universe is unknown—it may even be infinite in size.

Edge of observable universe

Orion arm of the Milky Way

5. Virgo supercluster
Our galaxy is just one of tens of thousands of galaxies that are clustered together in a group called the Virgo supercluster. This vast array of galaxies is more than 100,000 light-years across.

6. Supercluster filaments
Superclusters form a web of massive, threadlike structures called filaments, which occupy about 5 percent of the visible universe. Between these are immense, bubblelike voids.

7. Observable universe
The part of the universe we can see is about 93 billion light-years across, with Earth at the center. It contains millions of superclusters, forming a vast, foamlike structure. What lies beyond is unknown.

The Milky Way and nearby galaxies are being drawn toward a mysterious concentration of mass in intergalactic space called the **Great Attractor**.

110 galaxies ○ **THE BIG BANG**

1 billionth of a trillionth of a trillionth of a second—the time the universe took to expand from nothing to the size of a soccer field.

Afterglow of the Big Bang

A faint afterglow of the Big Bang exists throughout space. This radiation was released when the universe was about 380,000 years old and still extremely hot. The image on the right is a map of the radiation across the whole sky. The variations in intensity, shown in color, are due to minute variations in density in the early universe. Gravity, working on these tiny variations, created the uneven distribution of matter we can see in the universe today, with clusters of galaxies separated by immense voids.

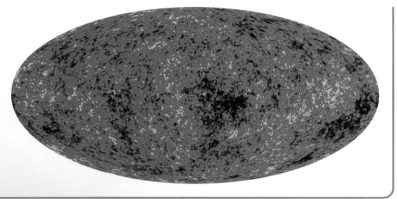

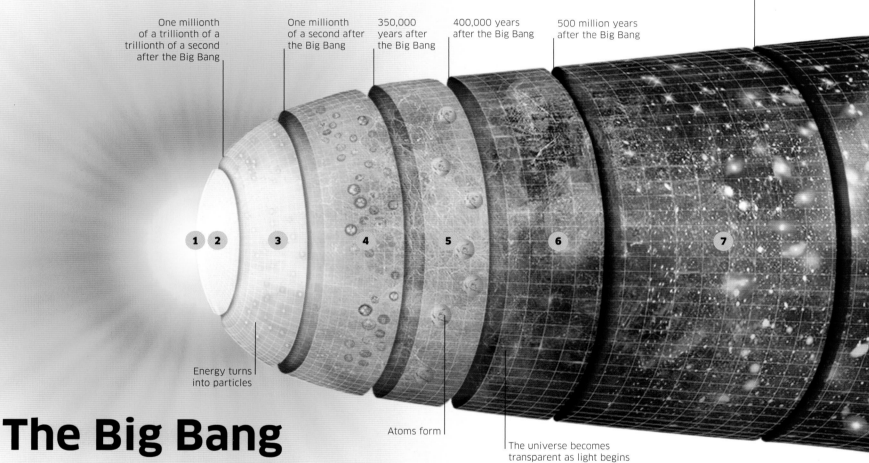

One millionth of a trillionth of a trillionth of a second after the Big Bang

One millionth of a second after the Big Bang

350,000 years after the Big Bang

400,000 years after the Big Bang

500 million years after the Big Bang

3 billion years after the Big Bang

Energy turns into particles

Atoms form

The universe becomes transparent as light begins to pass freely through space.

The Big Bang

About 14 billion years ago, the universe suddenly appeared from nowhere as a tiny concentration of pure energy. It then expanded trillions of trillions of times in an instant—an event known as the Big Bang.

In the first millisecond of existence, the intense energy of the newborn universe produced a vast number of subatomic particles (particles smaller than atoms). Some of these joined together to form the nuclei (centers) of atoms—the building blocks of all the matter we see in the universe today. But it wasn't until the universe was about 380,000 years old that actual atoms formed, and it wasn't until hundreds of millions of years later that galaxies and stars appeared. As well as producing energy and matter, the Big Bang also gave rise to four basic forces that govern the way everything in the universe works, from the force of gravity to the forces that hold atoms together. Ever since the Big Bang, the universe has continued to expand and cool down, and it will probably continue doing so forever.

1 The universe starts as an unimaginably hot point of energy, infinitely smaller than a single atom.

2 In a tiny fraction of a second, it expands to the size of a city, and the rate of inflation then slows. This is not an explosion of matter into space, but an expansion of space itself.

3 So far, the universe is just energy. But soon, a seething mass of tiny particles and antiparticles (the same as their corresponding particles, but with the opposite electric charge) form from this energy. Most of these cancel out, turning back into energy, but some are left over.

4 The leftover matter begins to form protons and neutrons.

By now, the universe is about a millionth of a second old. Within a few minutes, the neutrons and many of the protons join to form atomic nuclei.

5 About 380,000 years later, the universe has cooled enough for atomic nuclei to combine with electrons to make hydrogen and helium atoms.

6 The universe is now a vast cloud of hydrogen and helium atoms. Light can pass more easily through space, so the universe becomes transparent. Gravity acts on tiny variations in the gas cloud, pulling the gas into clumps that will eventually become galaxies.

7 Around 550 million years after the Big Bang, the first stars ignite in the densest parts of these gas clumps. By 600 million years after the Big Bang,

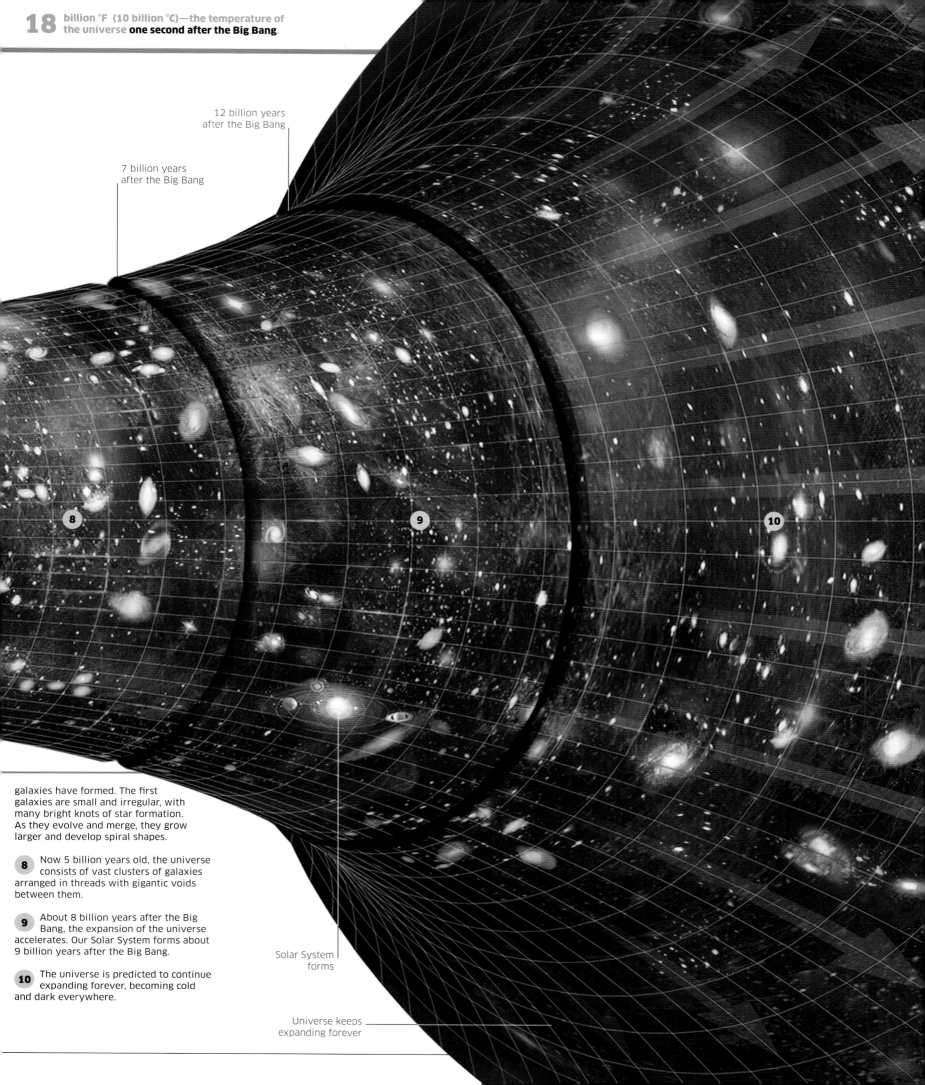

12 billion years
after the Big Bang

7 billion years
after the Big Bang

8

9

10

galaxies have formed. The first
galaxies are small and irregular, with
many bright knots of star formation.
As they evolve and merge, they grow
larger and develop spiral shapes.

8 Now 5 billion years old, the universe
consists of vast clusters of galaxies
arranged in threads with gigantic voids
between them.

9 About 8 billion years after the Big
Bang, the expansion of the universe
accelerates. Our Solar System forms about
9 billion years after the Big Bang.

10 The universe is predicted to continue
expanding forever, becoming cold
and dark everywhere.

Solar System
forms

Universe keeps
expanding forever

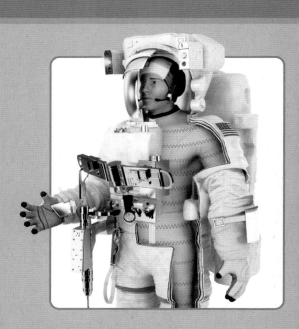

EXPLORING SPACE

People have studied the stars and planets for centuries, but it wasn't until 1957 that the first human-made object went into orbit, marking the beginning of the Space Age. Since then, thousands of rockets have been launched, hundreds of people have become astronauts, and 12 men have walked on the Moon.

SPACE TAXIS

NASA's space shuttle was a unique spacecraft with a partially reusable design. After taking off vertically like a rocket, it landed back on Earth like a plane. Five different shuttles operated between 1981 and the shuttle's retirement in 2011. Many of the missions were for building the International Space Station (ISS).

The main part of the shuttle system was called the orbiter.

Booster rockets fell back to Earth after launch to be collected and reused.

ATLANTIS LIFTING OFF FROM KENNEDY SPACE CENTER

Soyuz
Russia's Soyuz craft have been operating since the 1960s and are now used to ferry astronauts to the ISS.

Orion
For future trips to the Moon, asteroids, and Mars, Orion will be launched by the US's Space Launch System (SLS) rocket.

Crew Dragon
SpaceX's Crew Dragon craft carried its first crew to the International Space Station (ISS) in 2020 and its second one in 2021.

Boeing Starliner
This future craft, designed to be reused 10 times, will ferry crews of up to seven to the International Space Station.

Space exploration

Space starts a mere 60 miles (100 km) above our heads. It is a short journey away—less than 10 minutes by rocket—but it is a dangerous and difficult one. We've been sending spacecraft to explore the Solar System for only 60 years or so, but we've been using telescopes to explore the skies for more than 400 years, and our curiosity about the cosmos goes back millennia. The more we discover, the more we want to explore.

LAUNCH SITES

There are about 30 launch sites on Earth, nine of which are shown below. The best place to launch from is near the equator, where a rocket gets an extra push from Earth's spin. The largest launch site is Baikonur, which sends spacecraft to the International Space Station.

PLESETSK, RUSSIA
YASNY, RUSSIA
JIUQUAN, CHINA
VANDENBERG, US
BAIKONUR, KAZAKHSTAN
TANEGASHIMA, JAPAN
MOJAVE DESERT, US
CAPE CANAVERAL/ KENNEDY SPACE CENTER, US
XICHANG, CHINA
SRIHARIKOTA, INDIA
KOUROU, FRENCH GUIANA

LAUNCH VEHICLES

Rockets are built not to explore space themselves, but to launch other smaller vehicles into orbit, such as satellites or planetary spacecraft. The smaller vehicle usually travels in the rocket's nose. Built to make the journey only once, rockets are destroyed as they fall back to Earth and burn up. The larger the rocket, the heavier and more complicated the cargo it can carry. Most rockets carrying spacecraft are launched by the US, Russia, and Europe.

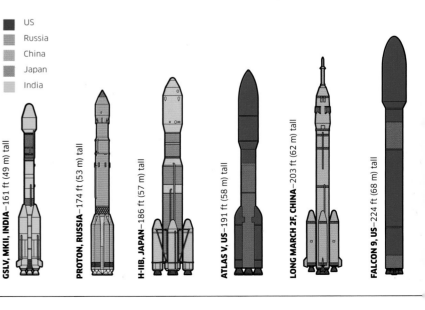

- US
- Russia
- China
- Japan
- India

GSLV, MKII, INDIA—161 ft (49 m) tall
PROTON, RUSSIA—174 ft (53 m) tall
H-IIB, JAPAN—186 ft (57 m) tall
ATLAS V, US—191 ft (58 m) tall
LONG MARCH 2F, CHINA—203 ft (62 m) tall
FALCON 9, US—224 ft (68 m) tall

SPACE EXPLORERS

Over 130 spacecraft have successfully left Earth to explore the Solar System. All have been robotic, except for the crewed Apollo craft that went to the Moon. Powered by the Sun or by radioactive chemicals, robotic craft can work for years, peering down onto planets from orbit or landing to explore the surface. They send data and often spectacular images back to Earth.

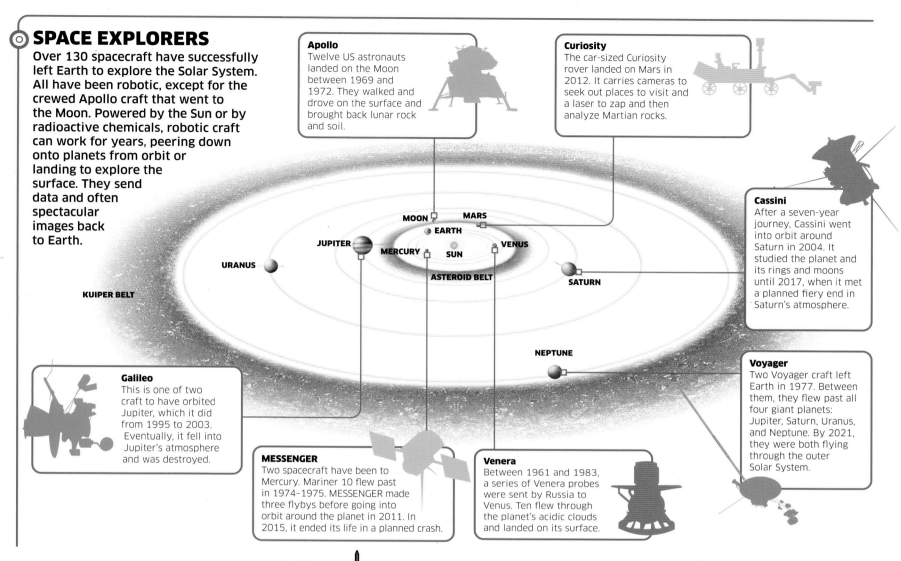

Apollo
Twelve US astronauts landed on the Moon between 1969 and 1972. They walked and drove on the surface and brought back lunar rock and soil.

Curiosity
The car-sized Curiosity rover landed on Mars in 2012. It carries cameras to seek out places to visit and a laser to zap and then analyze Martian rocks.

Cassini
After a seven-year journey, Cassini went into orbit around Saturn in 2004. It studied the planet and its rings and moons until 2017, when it met a planned fiery end in Saturn's atmosphere.

Galileo
This is one of two craft to have orbited Jupiter, which it did from 1995 to 2003. Eventually, it fell into Jupiter's atmosphere and was destroyed.

MESSENGER
Two spacecraft have been to Mercury. Mariner 10 flew past in 1974–1975. MESSENGER made three flybys before going into orbit around the planet in 2011. In 2015, it ended its life in a planned crash.

Venera
Between 1961 and 1983, a series of Venera probes were sent by Russia to Venus. Ten flew through the planet's acidic clouds and landed on its surface.

Voyager
Two Voyager craft left Earth in 1977. Between them, they flew past all four giant planets: Jupiter, Saturn, Uranus, and Neptune. By 2021, they were both flying through the outer Solar System.

MOON, MARS, EARTH, JUPITER, MERCURY, SUN, VENUS, URANUS, ASTEROID BELT, SATURN, NEPTUNE, KUIPER BELT

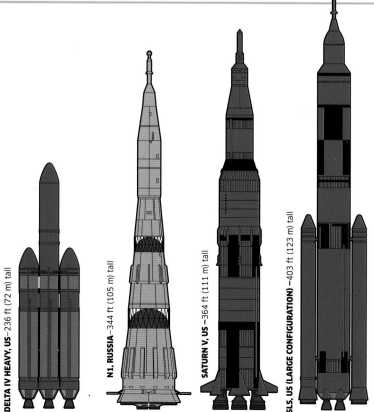

DELTA IV HEAVY, US—236 ft (72 m) tall
N1, RUSSIA—344 ft (105 m) tall
SATURN V, US—364 ft (111 m) tall
SLS, US (LARGE CONFIGURATION) —403 ft (123 m) tall

SEEING THE INVISIBLE

As well as producing light that our eyes can see, objects in space produce other kinds of radiation that are invisible to us. All types of radiation travel as waves. Astronomers use special telescopes to capture waves of different lengths, from radio waves, which have long wavelengths, to gamma rays, which are very short.

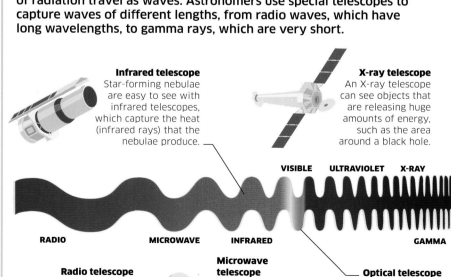

Infrared telescope
Star-forming nebulae are easy to see with infrared telescopes, which capture the heat (infrared rays) that the nebulae produce.

X-ray telescope
An X-ray telescope can see objects that are releasing huge amounts of energy, such as the area around a black hole.

RADIO, MICROWAVE, INFRARED, VISIBLE, ULTRAVIOLET, X-RAY, GAMMA

Radio telescope
Radio waves are the longest. They have revealed galaxies that would otherwise remain unseen.

Microwave telescope
Telescopes that capture microwaves allow us to see the afterglow of the Big Bang.

Optical telescope
Optical telescopes use visible light but magnify the image, letting us see farther than the naked eye.

20,000 years ago
In Africa, people mark pieces of bone with what may be the first record of Moon phases. Farmers follow the cycles of the Sun and Moon to plan their crops.

5,000–1,000 years ago
For ancient peoples, astronomy is part of religion. Many sacred monuments, such as Stonehenge in England, are built to align with the Sun or constellations.

Discovering space

The history of astronomy and the study of the heavens spans thousands of years, linking ancient religious sites with high-tech 21st-century observatories and spacecraft.

Since the dawn of history, people have looked into the night sky and wondered what the countless points of light were. It wasn't until fairly recently that we realized the stars are suns like ours, but incredibly far away. Just as early seafarers explored the world in search of new lands, modern explorers have sailed into space on voyages of discovery. Only a few people have visited another world, but scores of robotic probes have ventured to the planets on our behalf.

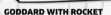

1926: Rocket science
American engineer Robert Goddard successfully fires the first liquid-fueled rocket. It rises 41 ft (12 m) into the air before fizzling out. Over the next 15 years, he launches another 34 rockets, some of which soar to heights of more than 1.2 miles (2 km).

GODDARD WITH ROCKET

FRUIT FLY

1947: First animals in space
The US adapts captured German V2 rockets, used as deadly weapons in World War II, to send the first living creatures into space. The earliest astro-animals are fruit flies, followed by monkeys. The missions aim to see how animals' bodies respond to being in space.

SPACE SHUTTLE COLUMBIA

1976–1977: Mars and beyond
Two American space robots, Viking 1 and 2, land on Mars, carry out soil tests, and send back color images. In 1977, the space probe Voyager 2 blasts off, eventually flying by Jupiter, Saturn, Uranus, and Neptune.

1971–1973: Living in space
Space stations allow astronauts to spend weeks in orbit. The first, in 1971, is the Russian Salyut 1. The US follows with its own, Skylab, in 1973.

SKYLAB SPACE STATION

1981: Shuttle launch
The 1980s see missions begin for the space shuttle, the first reusable crewed orbiter. Shuttles will remain in service until 2011. In 1986, the Russians start to build the Mir space station.

1990: Hubble
The Hubble Space Telescope is placed in orbit. It reveals many distant wonders of space never seen before.

PILLAR AND JETS IN THE CARINA NEBULA

2009–2012: Kepler Observatory
NASA launches the Kepler Observatory, which uses a special light-measuring device to search for planets orbiting distant stars.

ARTIST'S IMPRESSION OF KEPLER SPACECRAFT

If undisturbed, **footprints** left by astronauts on the Moon will stay visible for at least **100 million years**.

18 The number of **astronauts who have died** during spaceflight missions.

117

STONEHENGE, ENGLAND

COPERNICUS'S DRAWING OF THE SOLAR SYSTEM

1540s: A shocking idea

Polish astronomer Nicolaus Copernicus writes a book about a shocking new idea. He suggests that the Sun, not Earth, is at the center of the Solar System.

ISAAC NEWTON'S TELESCOPE

1890s: Science fiction

The first science fiction novels hit the market. Books like *The War of the Worlds* and *The Time Machine*, both written by H. G. Wells, arouse public interest in space exploration and also inspire serious science projects.

1600s: Telescopes

Italian astronomer Galileo Galilei greatly improves telescope design, and the Solar System can now be seen clearly. English scientist Isaac Newton explains how gravity holds the planets in orbit around the Sun.

1957: Sputnik

In Russia, rocket scientists achieve two firsts this year. They send up the first artificial satellite, Sputnik 1, and a month later, they launch Sputnik 2, which carries Laika, the first dog to go into orbit. As planned, Laika perishes at the end of the mission.

1961: First person in space

Russian cosmonaut Yuri Gagarin becomes the first person in space, orbiting Earth in a flight lasting just over 100 minutes. Later in the decade, the Russians achieve the first human spacewalk (1965) and the first soft landing on the Moon by a spacecraft (1966).

STATUE OF YURI GAGARIN IN MOSCOW, RUSSIA

LUNOKHOD 1

1970: First rover

Russians launch the first Lunar Roving Vehicle: Lunokhod 1, a remote-control, eight-wheeled buggy. It soft lands on the Moon and operates for 11 days, sending back pictures and taking soil samples.

1969: Humans on the Moon

The United States' Apollo 11 craft lands the first people on the Moon: Neil Armstrong and Buzz Aldrin. The astronauts stay for nearly 24 hours, collecting Moon rocks and taking photographs of the lunar surface.

RYUGU

2018: Asteroid explorer

Japan's Hayabusa-2 mission enters orbit around a small asteroid called Ryugu, surveying it for 17 months, deploying rovers to its surface, and capturing samples of its material for return to Earth in 2020.

Into the future

Over the coming decades, a focus of space research will be the continuing hunt for distant planets that might harbor life. A crewed mission to Mars by 2050 may be feasible.

118 exploring space ○ **TELESCOPES**

798 The **number of segments** in the main mirror of the Extremely Large Telescope (ELT).

Telescopes

The first telescopes were little more than hand-held wooden tubes, but they allowed astronomers to discover mountains on the Moon and moons around Jupiter. Today's giant telescopes let us see billions of light-years into the far reaches of space.

Like eyes, telescopes collect light and focus it to create an image. Unlike our eyes, however, telescopes can train their sights on tiny targets and can add together the light they receive over a long period. The bigger a telescope is, the more light it can collect and the sharper the image. With a large telescope, we can zoom in on distant galaxies or volcanoes on Mars. The first telescopes used glass lenses, but big lenses bend under their own weight, so astronomers switched to mirrors to make telescopes bigger. In the largest telescopes, dozens of segments are arranged together to form one giant, curved mirror. Earth's atmosphere blurs our view of space, so large professional telescopes are built on mountains, where the air is dry and still, or launched into space.

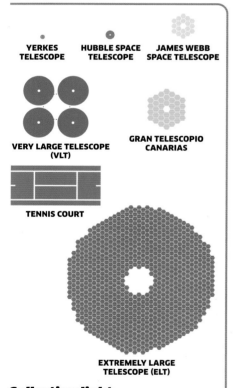

YERKES TELESCOPE

HUBBLE SPACE TELESCOPE

JAMES WEBB SPACE TELESCOPE

VERY LARGE TELESCOPE (VLT)

GRAN TELESCOPIO CANARIAS

TENNIS COURT

EXTREMELY LARGE TELESCOPE (ELT)

Collecting light

A key part of a telescope is the mirror or lens that collects light. The world's largest telescope lens (in the Yerkes telescope in the US) is only 40 in (1 m) wide. Mirrors made of hexagonal segments in a honeycomb pattern can be far bigger. The ELT mirror will be nearly four times larger in area than a tennis court.

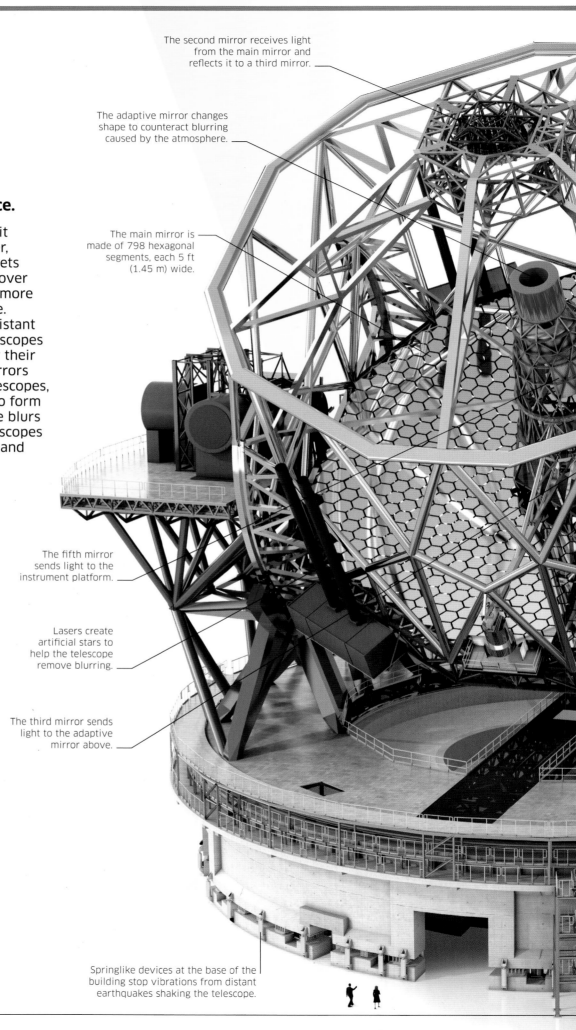

The second mirror receives light from the main mirror and reflects it to a third mirror.

The adaptive mirror changes shape to counteract blurring caused by the atmosphere.

The main mirror is made of 798 hexagonal segments, each 5 ft (1.45 m) wide.

The fifth mirror sends light to the instrument platform.

Lasers create artificial stars to help the telescope remove blurring.

The third mirror sends light to the adaptive mirror above.

Springlike devices at the base of the building stop vibrations from distant earthquakes shaking the telescope.

12,000 The approximate **number of professional astronomers** in the world.

The largest telescopes can collect **100 million times more light** than the human eye.

119

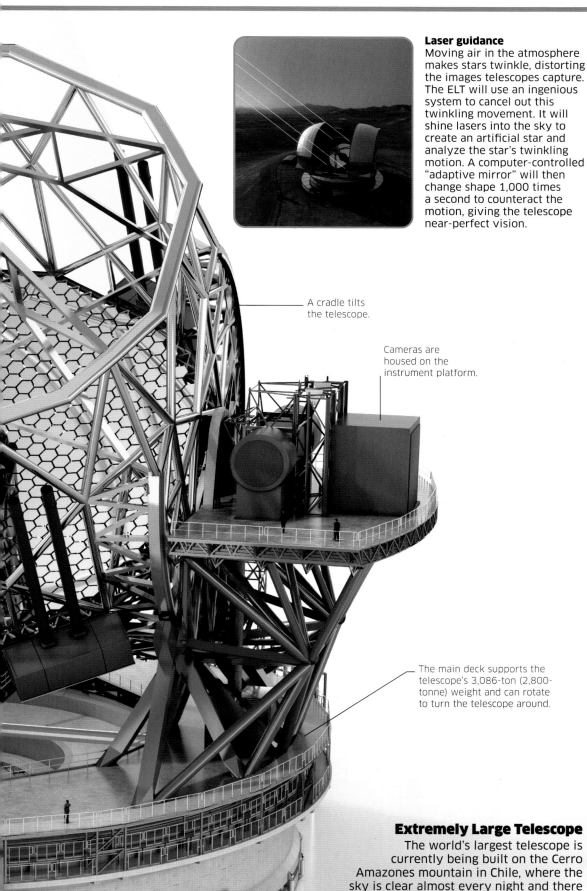

A cradle tilts the telescope.

Cameras are housed on the instrument platform.

The main deck supports the telescope's 3,086-ton (2,800-tonne) weight and can rotate to turn the telescope around.

Extremely Large Telescope

The world's largest telescope is currently being built on the Cerro Amazones mountain in Chile, where the sky is clear almost every night and there are excellent views of the southern stars. Called the Extremely Large Telescope (ELT), it will be as tall as a 15-story building, and its enormous mirror will gather more light than all 13 of the world's current largest telescopes combined. A computer-controlled "adaptive mirror" will make the images as sharp as those of a space telescope.

Laser guidance

Moving air in the atmosphere makes stars twinkle, distorting the images telescopes capture. The ELT will use an ingenious system to cancel out this twinkling movement. It will shine lasers into the sky to create an artificial star and analyze the star's twinkling motion. A computer-controlled "adaptive mirror" will then change shape 1,000 times a second to counteract the motion, giving the telescope near-perfect vision.

How simple telescopes work

A telescope uses a lens or a mirror to collect light from distant objects and focus it to create an image. In simple telescopes, the image is viewed through an eyepiece lens that magnifies the image. Telescopes that use lenses to capture light are called refractors. Those that use mirrors are called reflectors.

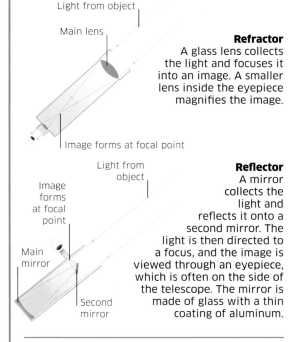

Light from object

Main lens

Refractor
A glass lens collects the light and focuses it into an image. A smaller lens inside the eyepiece magnifies the image.

Image forms at focal point

Light from object

Image forms at focal point

Reflector
A mirror collects the light and reflects it onto a second mirror. The light is then directed to a focus, and the image is viewed through an eyepiece, which is often on the side of the telescope. The mirror is made of glass with a thin coating of aluminum.

Main mirror

Second mirror

In a different light

Telescopes collect wavelengths of energy other than light. Each wavelength reveals different details in an object. A typical galaxy, such as the Andromeda Galaxy below, gives off energy in many wavelengths. X-rays, for instance, come from very hot areas, and radio waves come from colder areas.

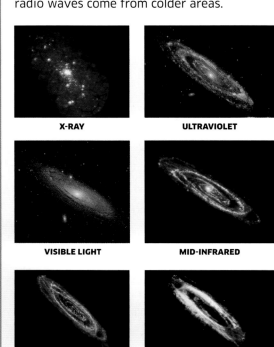

X-RAY　　　　**ULTRAVIOLET**

VISIBLE LIGHT　　　　**MID-INFRARED**

FAR-INFRARED　　　　**RADIO**

120

43.5 ft (13.2 m)—the length of Hubble, about the size of a **tour bus**.

40 million—the approximate **number of stars** Gaia looks at every day.

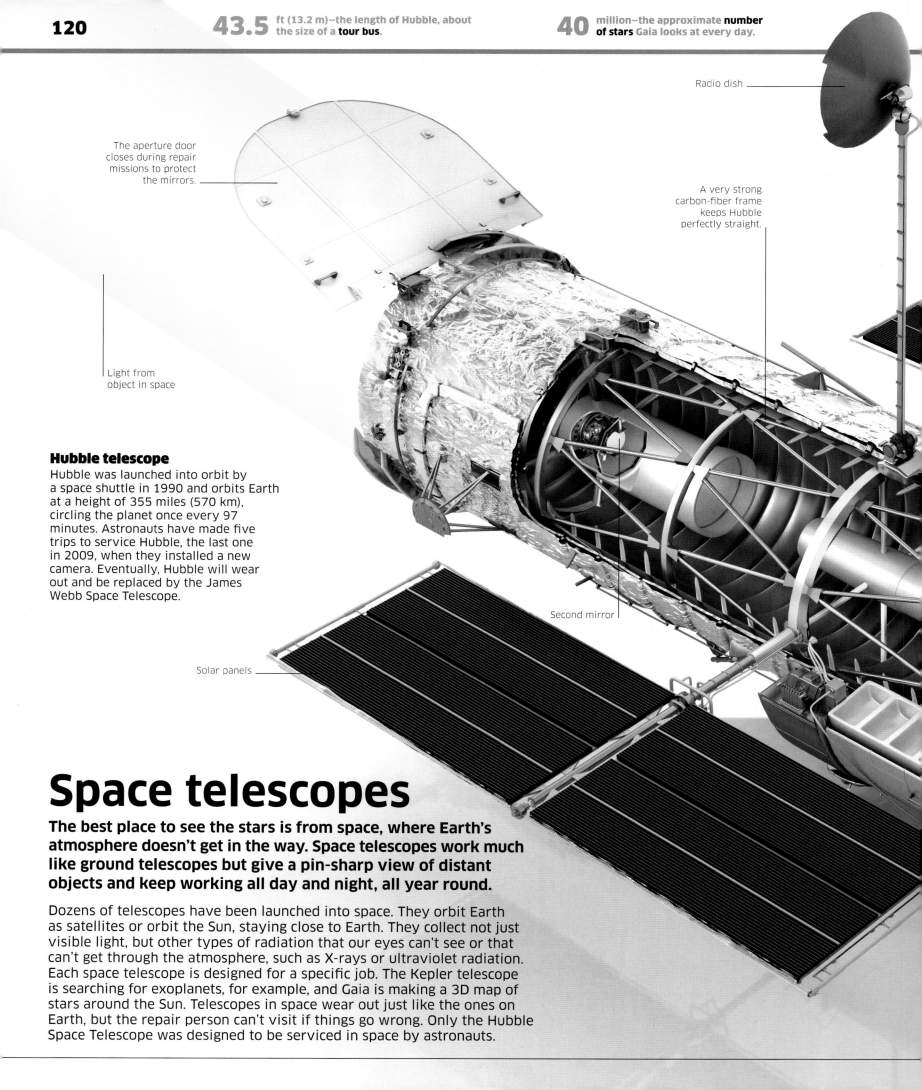

Radio dish

The aperture door closes during repair missions to protect the mirrors.

A very strong carbon-fiber frame keeps Hubble perfectly straight.

Light from object in space

Hubble telescope

Hubble was launched into orbit by a space shuttle in 1990 and orbits Earth at a height of 355 miles (570 km), circling the planet once every 97 minutes. Astronauts have made five trips to service Hubble, the last one in 2009, when they installed a new camera. Eventually, Hubble will wear out and be replaced by the James Webb Space Telescope.

Second mirror

Solar panels

Space telescopes

The best place to see the stars is from space, where Earth's atmosphere doesn't get in the way. Space telescopes work much like ground telescopes but give a pin-sharp view of distant objects and keep working all day and night, all year round.

Dozens of telescopes have been launched into space. They orbit Earth as satellites or orbit the Sun, staying close to Earth. They collect not just visible light, but other types of radiation that our eyes can't see or that can't get through the atmosphere, such as X-rays or ultraviolet radiation. Each space telescope is designed for a specific job. The Kepler telescope is searching for exoplanets, for example, and Gaia is making a 3D map of stars around the Sun. Telescopes in space wear out just like the ones on Earth, but the repair person can't visit if things go wrong. Only the Hubble Space Telescope was designed to be serviced in space by astronauts.

1 billion–the approximate number of pixels in Gaia's camera–the **largest camera in space**.

120 gigabytes–the **amount of data** Hubble sends to Earth each week.

The James Webb's mirror will collect **seven times** more light than Hubble's mirror.

121

Main mirror
The 7.87-ft (2.4-m) wide main mirror in the Hubble Space Telescope collects light and reflects it onto a second mirror. The second mirror reflects the beam back through a hole in the middle of the main mirror to a suite of cameras and scientific instruments. Hubble's main mirror is almost perfectly smooth. If it were scaled up to the size of Earth, the biggest bump on its surface would be just 6 in (15 cm) high.

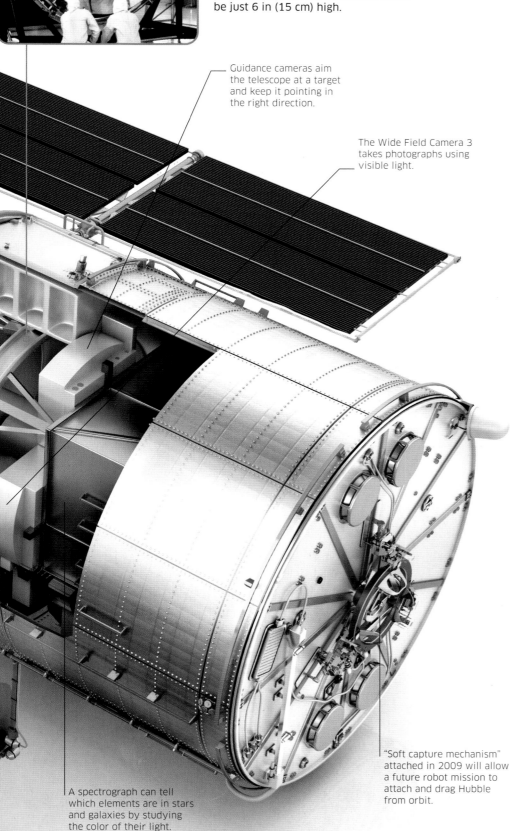

Guidance cameras aim the telescope at a target and keep it pointing in the right direction.

The Wide Field Camera 3 takes photographs using visible light.

"Soft capture mechanism" attached in 2009 will allow a future robot mission to attach and drag Hubble from orbit.

A spectrograph can tell which elements are in stars and galaxies by studying the color of their light.

Looking deep
When we look into space, we are looking back in time. Since its launch, Hubble has let us see deeper and deeper into space, revealing young galaxies in the early Universe. The James Webb Space Telescope will look even deeper to see newborn galaxies.

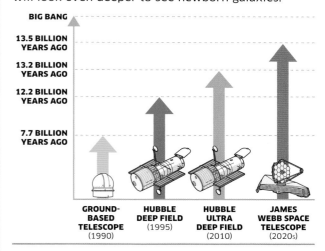

BIG BANG

13.5 BILLION YEARS AGO

13.2 BILLION YEARS AGO

12.2 BILLION YEARS AGO

7.7 BILLION YEARS AGO

GROUND-BASED TELESCOPE (1990)

HUBBLE DEEP FIELD (1995)

HUBBLE ULTRA DEEP FIELD (2010)

JAMES WEBB SPACE TELESCOPE (2020s)

Hubble hits
Astronomers have processed the data from Hubble to create many beautiful images, including galaxies, star-birth regions such as the Eagle Nebula, and dying stars such as the Cat's Eye Nebula.

SOMBRERO GALAXY

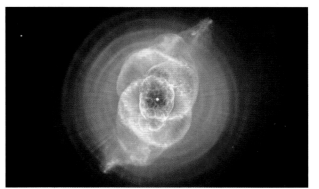

CAT'S EYE NEBULA

EAGLE NEBULA

Rockets

It takes a staggering amount of energy to break free from Earth's gravitational pull and fly into space. The only vehicles capable of doing this are rockets, which harness the explosive power of burning fuel to lift cargo such as satellites and spacecraft into orbit. Most of a rocket's weight is fuel, and nearly all of it is consumed in the first few minutes, burning at a rate of up to 16½ tons (15 tonnes) every second.

People used rockets as weapons for hundreds of years before they became safe and powerful enough to reach space. Since an early German V-2 rocket reached outer space in 1944, rockets have gotten larger and more complicated. A modern rocket is really several rockets in one, with separate "stages" stacked cleverly together. When the lowest stage runs out of fuel, it drops off, making the remaining vehicle lighter. The stage above then ignites. The cargo is usually in the uppermost stage, under the rocket's nose. Most rockets are built to fly to space only once and are destroyed as their parts fall back to Earth.

Launch pad
The SLS's space journey will start at the Kennedy Space Center in Florida. Launch pad 39B was once used by the Apollo Moon missions and the Space Shuttle.

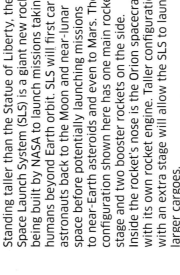

Space Launch System
Standing taller than the Statue of Liberty, the Space Launch System (SLS) is a giant new rocket being built by NASA to launch missions taking humans beyond Earth orbit. SLS will first carry astronauts back to the Moon and near-lunar space before potentially launching missions to near-Earth asteroids and even to Mars. The configuration shown here has one main rocket stage and two booster rockets on the side. Inside the rocket's nose is the Orion spacecraft, with its own rocket engine. Taller configurations with an extra stage will allow the SLS to launch larger cargoes.

How rockets work
Most of the body of a rocket is taken up by huge tanks containing fuel and an oxidizer (a chemical needed to make fuel burn). Once ignited, these two chemicals react explosively to make hot gases, which rush out of the rear nozzle. The rush of hot gases creates the force of thrust that pushes the rocket forward.

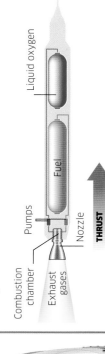

Liquid oxygen

Fuel

Pumps

Combustion chamber

Exhaust gases

Nozzle

THRUST

Escape rocket
The nose cone is a small rocket designed to carry the crew module away safely during an emergency.

Steering engines for escape rocket

Crew module
This is the only part of the Orion spacecraft that will return to Earth, using a parachute to splash down in the ocean.

To the Moon and beyond
NASA's Artemis program will use SLS launches to assemble a space station in orbit around the Moon, as seen in this artist's impression. This Lunar Gateway station will act as a base for landings on the lunar surface, and eventually as a staging point for assembly of larger Orion-based spacecraft needed to reach Mars.

2,755 tons (2,500 tonnes)—the weight of the SLS rocket, analogous to **7.5 jet airliners**.

44 million horsepower—the combined power of the SLS's two **booster rockets**.

2 The average number of **rocket launches** from Earth every week.

123

Cargo weight

The heavier a rocket's cargo, the more fuel is needed to lift it, which adds further to the weight. The Saturn V rocket used for the Apollo Moon missions carried a cargo as heavy as 24 elephants, but the whole rocket weighed as much as 400 elephants.

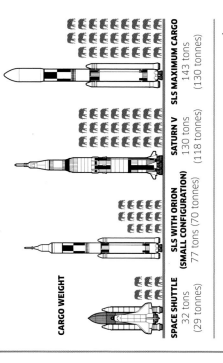

CARGO WEIGHT

SLS MAXIMUM CARGO
143 tons
(130 tonnes)

SATURN V
130 tons
(118 tonnes)

SLS WITH ORION
(SMALL CONFIGURATION)
77 tons (70 tonnes)

SPACE SHUTTLE
32 tons
(29 tonnes)

Thrust

The force that pushes a rocket is called thrust. To reach low Earth orbit, a rocket must generate enough thrust to reach a speed of 18,000 mph (29,000 kph)—nine times faster than a bullet.

MAXIMUM TOTAL THRUST

SLS
8.4 million pounds
(37 million Newtons)

SPACE SHUTTLE
7.8 million pounds
(35 million Newtons)

SATURN V
7.6 million pounds
(34 million Newtons)

Main engines

At the base of the rocket are four RS-25 engines—the same kind of engine that was used to power space shuttles. Working together, the SLS's main engines and boosters produce as much power as 13,400 train engines.

Service module
The central section of the Orion spacecraft carries fuel and other supplies.

Spacecraft engine
Orion's engine will be able to propel the craft to Mars in three to four months.

Boosters
Two booster rockets provide most of the thrust needed for liftoff. They produce enough power in two minutes to supply 92,000 homes for a whole day.

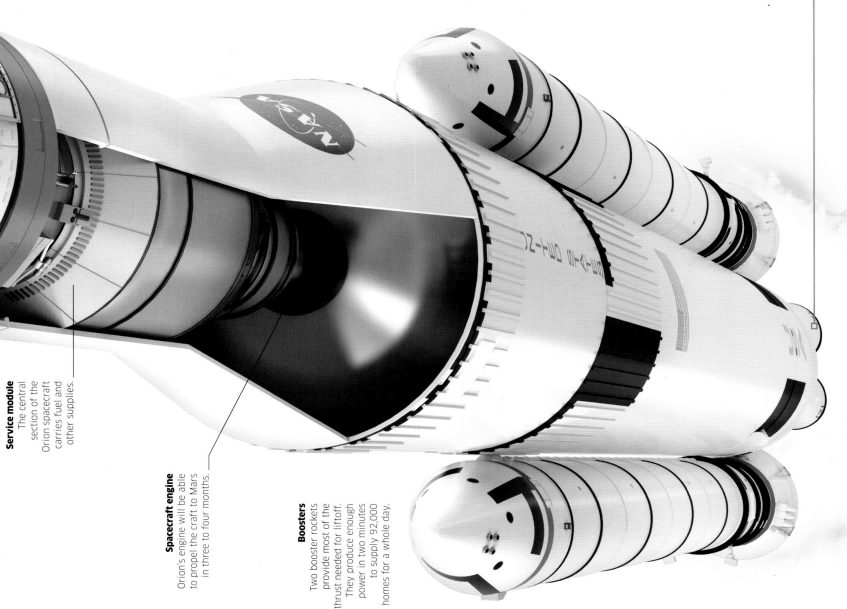

124 exploring space · **FIRST PERSON IN SPACE**

6 The **number of crewed spaceflights** made in the Vostok spacecraft.

First person in space

In 1961, Russian pilot Yuri Gagarin became the first person in space when he made a daredevil 108-minute trip around Earth in a tiny spacecraft called Vostok 1. Since then, more than 500 people have been to space.

The race to put the first person in space began in October 1957, when Russia's uncrewed Sputnik 1 became the first spacecraft to orbit the planet. Sputnik 2 followed later that year, carrying a dog named Laika—a stray from the streets of Moscow. The craft was not designed to return to Earth, so Laika died during the mission. About three years later, Yuri Gagarin made his historic trip, and within six weeks of his return, the US pledged to put humans on the Moon. The first space travelers were jet pilots who were used to dangerous, physically grueling flights and had been trained to use ejector seats and parachutes. But even for these pilots, space travel posed a deadly risk. Of the 100 or so uncrewed missions before Gagarin's flight, half ended in failure, and prior to Vostok 1, no one was certain that a human could travel to space and return alive to Earth.

The descent module was covered by a heat shield material to protect it from temperatures of about 5,400°F (3,000°C) as it reentered the atmosphere.

The walls were insulated to reduce noise and vibration.

Air tanks for cabin

SERVICE MODULE

Radio antenna

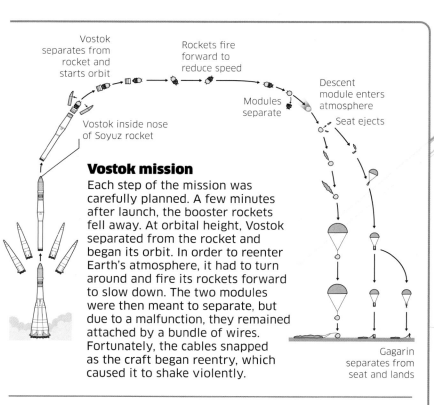

Vostok separates from rocket and starts orbit

Rockets fire forward to reduce speed

Vostok inside nose of Soyuz rocket

Modules separate

Descent module enters atmosphere

Seat ejects

Gagarin separates from seat and lands

Vostok mission

Each step of the mission was carefully planned. A few minutes after launch, the booster rockets fell away. At orbital height, Vostok separated from the rocket and began its orbit. In order to reenter Earth's atmosphere, it had to turn around and fire its rockets forward to slow down. The two modules were then meant to separate, but due to a malfunction, they remained attached by a bundle of wires. Fortunately, the cables snapped as the craft began reentry, which caused it to shake violently.

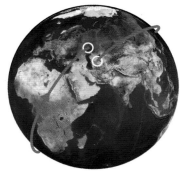

Around the world
Gagarin took off from the Baikonur Cosmodrome (space center) in Kazakhstan and traveled east around the planet, taking 108 minutes to complete a single orbit. Vostok's modules separated when he was over Africa, and Gagarin landed shortly afterward in a grassy field near the Russian town of Engels.

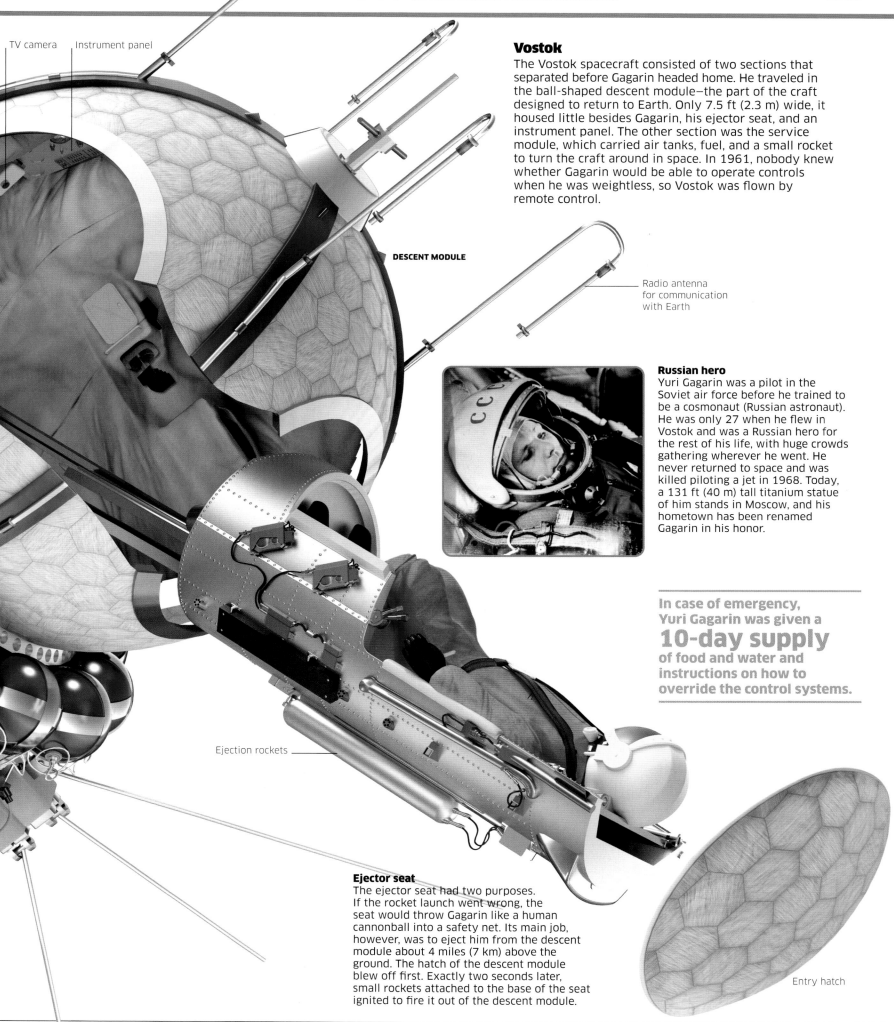

1963 The year of the **first spaceflight by a woman** (Russian engineer Valentina Tereshkova).

125

TV camera   Instrument panel

Vostok

The Vostok spacecraft consisted of two sections that separated before Gagarin headed home. He traveled in the ball-shaped descent module—the part of the craft designed to return to Earth. Only 7.5 ft (2.3 m) wide, it housed little besides Gagarin, his ejector seat, and an instrument panel. The other section was the service module, which carried air tanks, fuel, and a small rocket to turn the craft around in space. In 1961, nobody knew whether Gagarin would be able to operate controls when he was weightless, so Vostok was flown by remote control.

DESCENT MODULE

Radio antenna for communication with Earth

Russian hero

Yuri Gagarin was a pilot in the Soviet air force before he trained to be a cosmonaut (Russian astronaut). He was only 27 when he flew in Vostok and was a Russian hero for the rest of his life, with huge crowds gathering wherever he went. He never returned to space and was killed piloting a jet in 1968. Today, a 131 ft (40 m) tall titanium statue of him stands in Moscow, and his hometown has been renamed Gagarin in his honor.

In case of emergency, Yuri Gagarin was given a

10-day supply

of food and water and instructions on how to override the control systems.

Ejection rockets

Ejector seat

The ejector seat had two purposes. If the rocket launch went wrong, the seat would throw Gagarin like a human cannonball into a safety net. Its main job, however, was to eject him from the descent module about 4 miles (7 km) above the ground. The hatch of the descent module blew off first. Exactly two seconds later, small rockets attached to the base of the seat ignited to fire it out of the descent module.

Entry hatch

126 exploring space ○ **SPACE PROBES**

6 The number of Saturn's
moons discovered by Cassini.

Types of space probe

Most space probes simply fly past or orbit their target, but some attempt to land. Landers may stay put on the surface or rove around. Probes such as Huygens are released by an orbiter to enter a planet's or moon's atmosphere. All types have power, communication systems, and scientific instruments onboard.

DEEP IMPACT

Flyby and impactor

As Deep Impact flew by the comet Tempel 1 in July 2005, it released an impactor that "bombed" the comet's surface, releasing gas and dust.

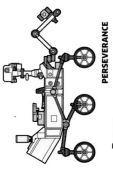

PERSEVERANCE

Rover

Five wheeled rovers have explored the surface of Mars. In February 2021, Perseverance landed on Mars on a mission to hunt for signs of past Martian life.

GALILEO

Orbiter and probe

From 1995 to 2003, Galileo orbited Jupiter and flew close to its larger moons. It released a probe to study the top 100 miles (160 km) of Jupiter's atmosphere.

PHILAE

Lander

Released by the Rosetta spacecraft, this fridge-sized lander touched down on the nucleus of a comet in late 2014. Philae took the first images from a comet.

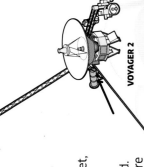

VOYAGER 2

Flyby

Voyager 2, launched in 1977, flew past Jupiter, Saturn, Uranus, and Neptune. The only craft to have visited the outer two planets, it is now heading out into deep space.

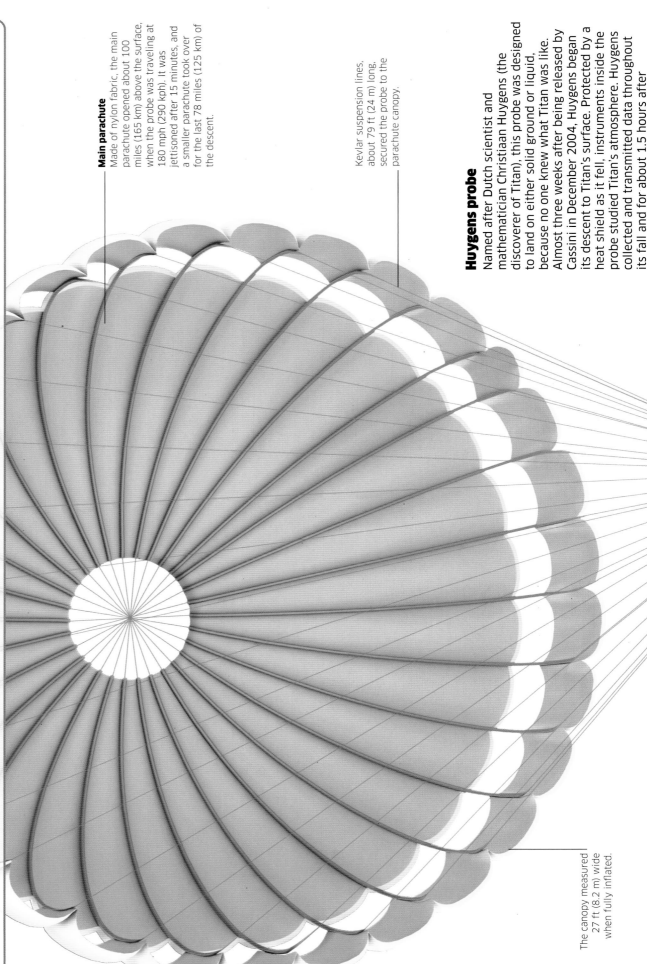

Main parachute

Made of nylon fabric, the main parachute opened about 100 miles (165 km) above the surface, when the probe was traveling at 180 mph (290 kph). It was jettisoned after 15 minutes, and a smaller parachute took over for the last 78 miles (125 km) of the descent.

Kevlar suspension lines, about 79 ft (24 m) long, secured the probe to the parachute canopy.

Huygens probe

Named after Dutch scientist and mathematician Christiaan Huygens (the discoverer of Titan), this probe was designed to land on either solid ground or liquid, because no one knew what Titan was like. Almost three weeks after being released by Cassini in December 2004, Huygens began its descent to Titan's surface. Protected by a heat shield as it fell, instruments inside the probe studied Titan's atmosphere. Huygens collected and transmitted data throughout its fall and for about 1.5 hours after landing—on a soft but solid surface.

The canopy measured 27 ft (8.2 m) wide when fully inflated.

Voyager 1 is the **most distant spacecraft** from Earth and has left the Solar System forever.

14 The **number of asteroids** visited by spacecraft.

3 billion miles (5 billion km) and 9.5 years—**New Horizons' journey to Pluto.**

127

Space probes

Robotic spacecraft can work for years at a time in remote locations and in harsh conditions that humans could never endure.

Each craft is designed for a specific mission. It could be orbiting Mars, which is what Mars Express does, or traveling with a comet as it flies around the Sun, like Rosetta. Once these craft have reached their destinations, their onboard instruments test and record conditions on these faraway worlds. Some craft, such as Cassini-Huygens, are two in one. Cassini, the bigger of the two, left Earth for Saturn in 1997 with Huygens attached to its side. After a seven-year journey, the pair arrived at the planet. Then Huygens started its own mission, parachuting down onto Titan, the largest of Saturn's many moons.

Inside Huygens

Under Huygens's covers was a platform of instruments. Fixed to the lower side of this platform were instruments that analyzed the gases in Titan's air and the materials on the ground. Another instrument measured the probe's landing speed and determined what the landing site was like.

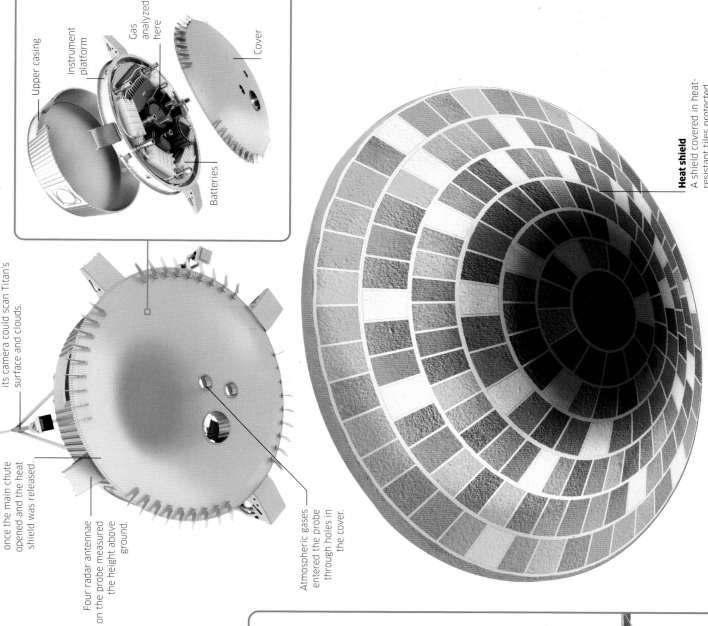

Upper casing

Instrument platform

Gas analyzed here

Cover

Batteries

Bridle

The three-legged bridle allowed Huygens to fall steadily, even in gusty winds. It also helped the probe rotate slowly so that its camera could scan Titan's surface and clouds.

Probe

Instruments inside the probe started to work once the main chute opened and the heat shield was released.

Four radar antennae on the probe measured the height above ground.

Atmospheric gases entered the probe through holes in the cover.

Heat shield

A shield covered in heat-resistant tiles protected Huygens when it slammed into Titan's atmosphere and began to slow down. After doing its job, the shield dropped off.

Getting there

On its way to Saturn, Cassini-Huygens got help from Venus twice, and Earth and Jupiter once each. Too heavy to fly direct, it flew by these planets and was boosted by their gravity, giving the craft the speed needed to reach Saturn.

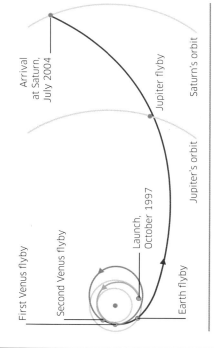

First Venus flyby

Second Venus flyby

Launch, October 1997

Earth flyby

Jupiter's orbit

Saturn's orbit

Jupiter flyby

Arrival at Saturn, July 2004

Cassini spacecraft

Cassini is the fourth craft to visit Saturn and the first to orbit it. About the size of a small bus, it has 12 instruments to study the planet, its rings, and its moons. It is so far away that messages between Cassini and Earth take over an hour.

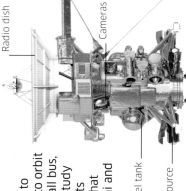

Radio dish

Cameras

Fuel tank

Radioactive power source

Main rocket engines

128 exploring space ○ **ROVERS**

100,000 The approximate **number of TV pictures** captured by Russia's Lunokhod rovers on the Moon.

Rovers

Most spacecraft that touch down on other worlds have to stay put where they land. Rovers, however, are built to explore. These sophisticated robots are sent commands by radio signal from Earth but are programmed to find their own way around.

The smallest rovers are the size of a microwave oven; the largest are as big as a car. Solar panels provide power, and an internal computer serves as a rover's "brain." Rovers are packed with scientific instruments, from special cameras to onboard chemical laboratories. They use radio antennae to send their data and discoveries back to a control center on Earth.

A radio antenna communicates with Earth.

Spirit rover

The rover Spirit, shown here, was one of a pair of identical rovers that landed on opposite sides of Mars in 2004. Spirit lost power in 2010, but its twin, Opportunity, operated until 2018. The rovers received commands from Earth in the morning and sent back data in the afternoon, once they had finished traveling, taking pictures, and testing rock.

An extendable "arm" with an elbow, a wrist, and a handful of tools can reach out to touch objects.

Rock drill

Opportunity used its drill to grind the surface off rocks so it could obtain deeper samples for chemical analysis. The rock shown here, nicknamed "Marquette Island," is about the size of a basketball and is unlike any of the rocks around it. It may have been thrown out of an impact crater some distance away.

Wheels

The four corner-wheels have motors that make them swivel, allowing the rover to turn. It can turn right around on the spot.

20 minutes–the time taken for a **message from a Mars rover** to reach Earth.

7.5 months–the approximate length of the **journey from Earth to Mars**.

100 watts–**Opportunity's power consumption**, which is about the same as a **house light bulb**.

129

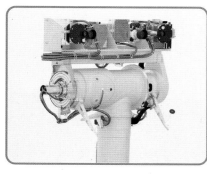

Panoramic camera

Four cameras held on a mast at head height served as Opportunity's eyes. Two "pancams" took color photos of the Martian landscape, helping scientists choose places to visit. Two "navcams" took 3D images of the ground, helping the rover plan its route.

Finding the way

Rovers are given destinations, but they find their own way there using their cameras and onboard computers to calculate the safest path. They travel only a few centimeters a second and stop every few seconds to reassess the route. Opportunity's top speed was 0.11 mph (0.18 kph), but its average speed was a fifth of this.

TRACKS LEFT BY OPPORTUNITY

Rover records

Earth's Moon was the first world to be explored by rovers, but today it is Mars that is most famous for its small population of rovers, including Opportunity, which holds the record for the greatest distance traveled by a rover.

OPPORTUNITY 2004–2018
28.1 MILES (45.1 KM)

LUNOKHOD 2 1973
24.2 MILES (39 KM)

APOLLO 17 LUNAR ROVING VEHICLE (LRV) 1972
22.2 MILES (35.7 KM)

APOLLO 15 LRV 1971
17.3 MILES (27.8 KM)

APOLLO 16 LRV 1972
16.8 MILES (27.1 KM)

CURIOSITY 2012–
16 MILES (25.8 KM)

LUNOKHOD 1 1970–1971
6.5 MILES (10.5 KM)

SPIRIT 2004–2010
4.8 MILES (7.7 KM)

YUTU-2 2019–
0.4 MILES (0.7 KM)

SOJOURNER 1997
0.06 MILES (0.1 KM)

— **ON MARS**

YUTU 2013–2014
0.06 MILES (0.1 KM)

— **ON THE MOON**

- - - **STILL ACTIVE**

PERSEVERANCE 2021–
0.9 MILES (1.48 KM)

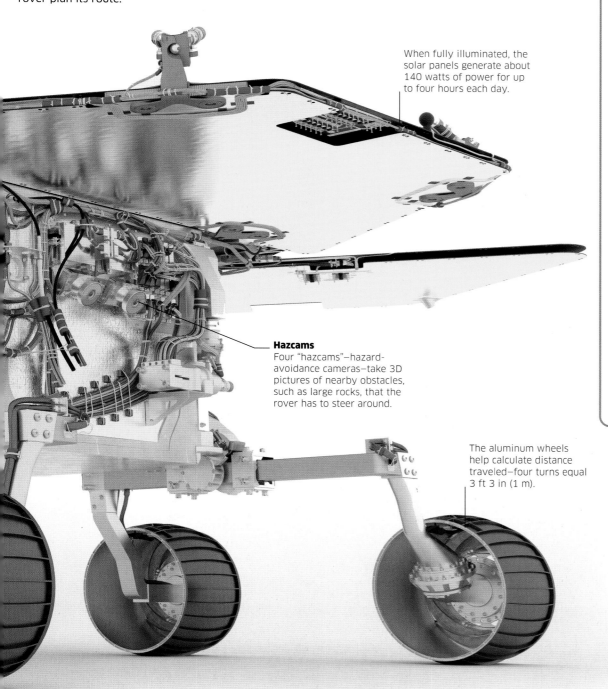

When fully illuminated, the solar panels generate about 140 watts of power for up to four hours each day.

Hazcams

Four "hazcams"–hazard-avoidance cameras–take 3D pictures of nearby obstacles, such as large rocks, that the rover has to steer around.

The aluminum wheels help calculate distance traveled–four turns equal 3 ft 3 in (1 m).

Balancing act

Like their predecessors Spirit and Opportunity, Curiosity and Perseverance use a "rocker-bogie" suspension arrangement to link their wheels to the rover body. This clever system allows the wheels to ride over bumpy ground while the rover's body stays level.

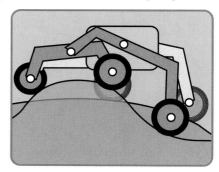

1 month—the length of time life-support systems on Soyuz can **keep the crew alive.**

Back to Earth
Only the Descent Module returns to Earth—the other two modules are jettisoned and burn up in Earth's atmosphere. The Descent Module's thrusters control its return before it is slowed by a series of parachutes. Three and a half hours after leaving the International Space Station, it lands in open country in Kazakhstan. The crew are helped out and flown away by helicopter.

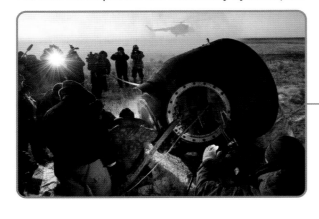

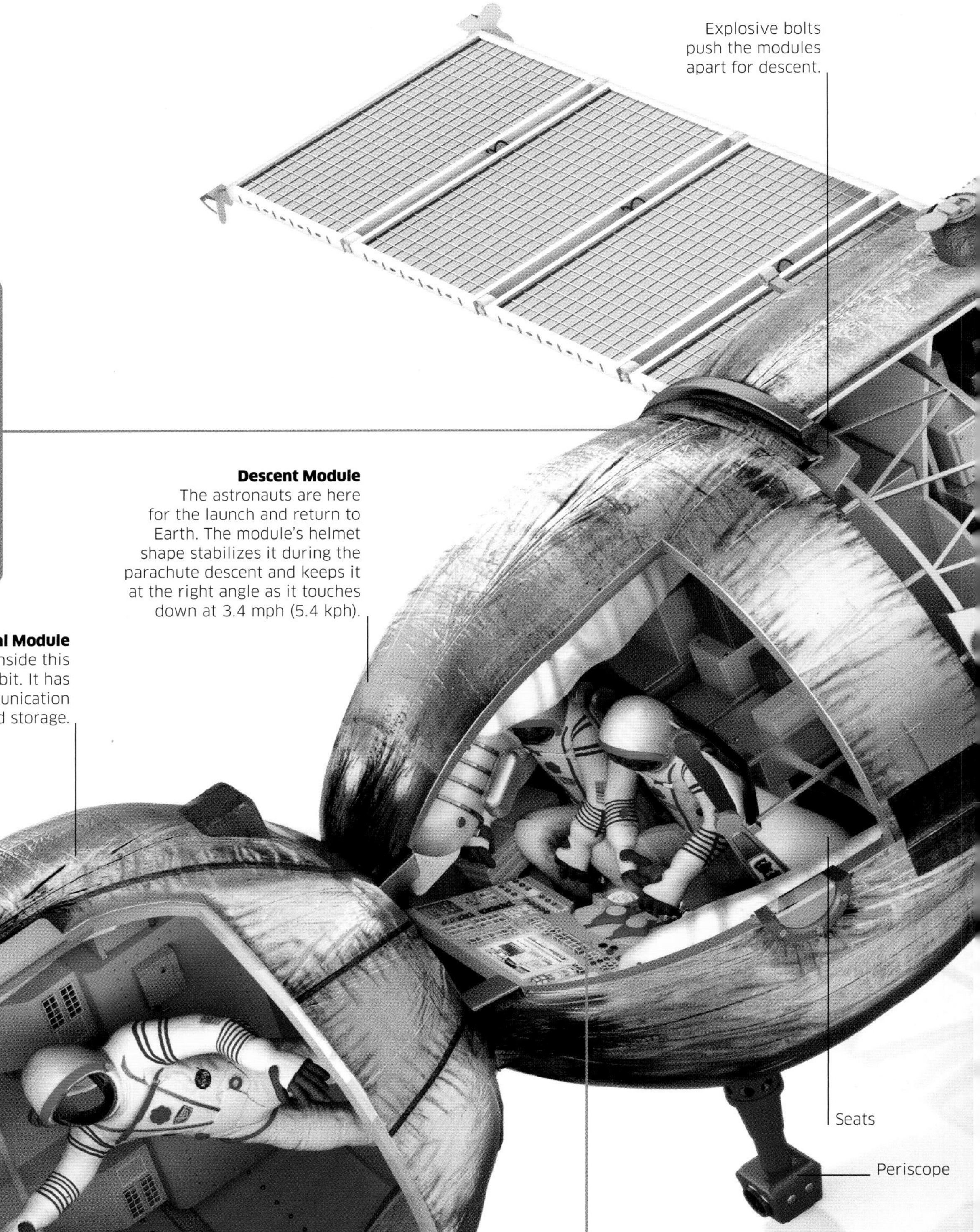

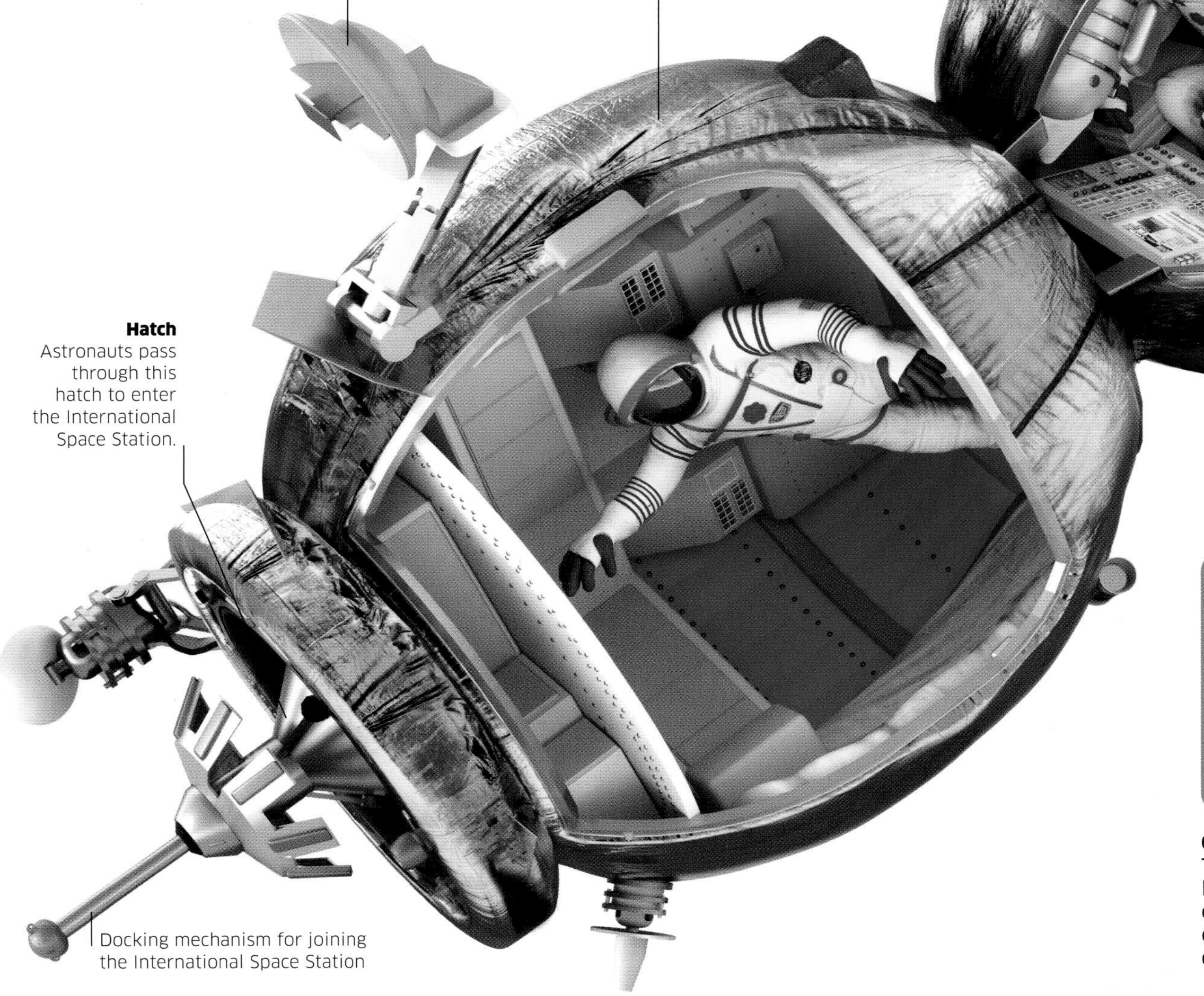

Explosive bolts push the modules apart for descent.
Descent Module
The astronauts are here for the launch and return to Earth. The module's helmet shape stabilizes it during the parachute descent and keeps it at the right angle as it touches down at 3.4 mph (5.4 kph).
This antenna transmits pulses to calculate the craft's position when docking with the International Space Station.
Orbital Module
The crew live inside this module during orbit. It has a bathroom, communication equipment, and storage.
Hatch
Astronauts pass through this hatch to enter the International Space Station.
Seats
Periscope
Docking mechanism for joining the International Space Station

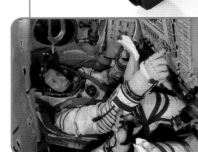

Cockpit
The crew of three sit elbow to elbow for launch and return. In front of them is the control desk with guidance and navigation controls to maneuver the craft. Above the desk is the hatch into the Orbital Module.

355 The number of people who have **flown in a space shuttle**.

131

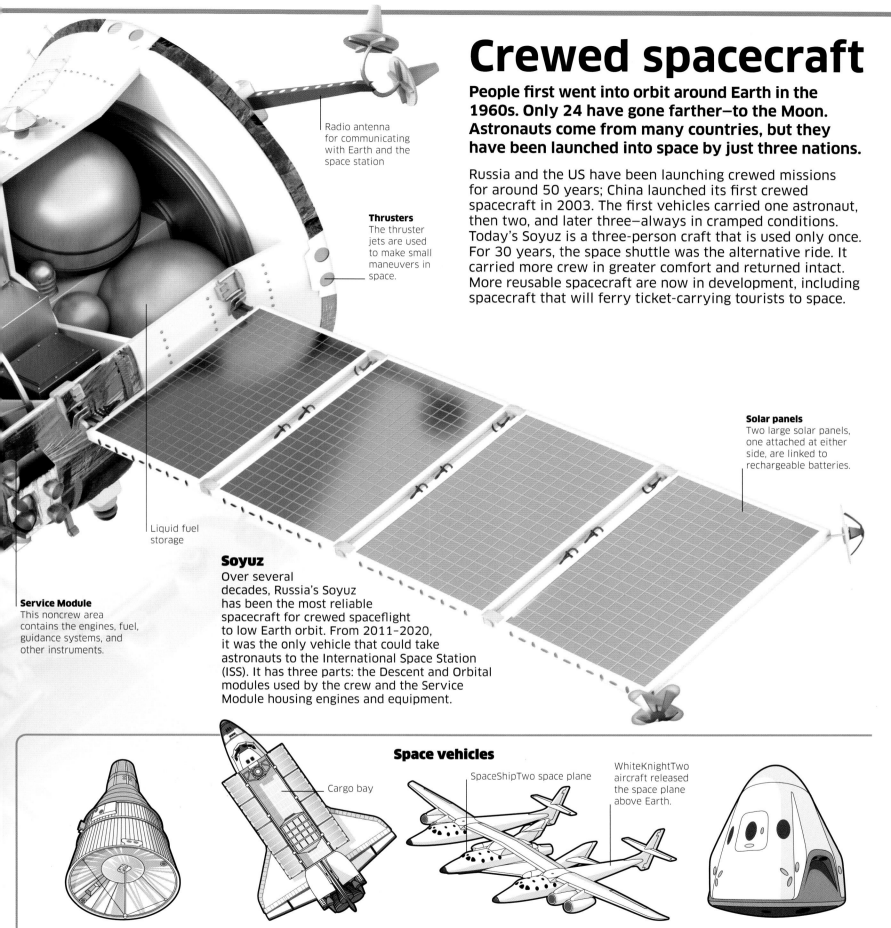

Radio antenna
for communicating
with Earth and the
space station

Thrusters
The thruster
jets are used
to make small
maneuvers in
space.

Solar panels
Two large solar panels,
one attached at either
side, are linked to
rechargeable batteries.

Service Module
This noncrew area
contains the engines, fuel,
guidance systems, and
other instruments.

Liquid fuel
storage

Soyuz
Over several
decades, Russia's Soyuz
has been the most reliable
spacecraft for crewed spaceflight
to low Earth orbit. From 2011–2020,
it was the only vehicle that could take
astronauts to the International Space Station
(ISS). It has three parts: the Descent and Orbital
modules used by the crew and the Service
Module housing engines and equipment.

Crewed spacecraft

**People first went into orbit around Earth in the
1960s. Only 24 have gone farther—to the Moon.
Astronauts come from many countries, but they
have been launched into space by just three nations.**

Russia and the US have been launching crewed missions
for around 50 years; China launched its first crewed
spacecraft in 2003. The first vehicles carried one astronaut,
then two, and later three—always in cramped conditions.
Today's Soyuz is a three-person craft that is used only once.
For 30 years, the space shuttle was the alternative ride. It
carried more crew in greater comfort and returned intact.
More reusable spacecraft are now in development, including
spacecraft that will ferry ticket-carrying tourists to space.

Space vehicles

Cargo bay

SpaceShipTwo space plane

WhiteKnightTwo
aircraft released
the space plane
above Earth.

Gemini
One of the first US crewed
spacecraft was Gemini, which
took 10 two-man crews into
orbit in 1965–1966. There, they
made America's first spacewalk.

Space shuttle
The five space shuttles flew
crews of up to eight into space
between 1981 and 2011. In
total, the reusable shuttle fleet
completed 21,030 orbits of Earth.

SpaceShipTwo
Developed from the reusable SpaceShipOne,
Virgin Galactic's SpaceShipTwo, designed
for space tourism, made its first crewed flight to
space in July 2021. It used a rocket to climb to
the edge of space after being released mid-air.

Crew Dragon
Capable of being reused up to five
times, SpaceX's Crew Dragon first
carried astronauts to the ISS in 2020.
It is launched from a Falcon 9 rocket
and can carry up to seven passengers.

Space Shuttle

The Space Shuttle was the world's first reusable spacecraft, designed to carry a crew of 2–8 astronauts to space and back.

NASA's fleet of five Shuttles operated for 30 years, launching 135 times and spending a total of 3.6 years in flight. Launched with the aid of two disposable solid-fuel rockets, they reached orbit in only 8 minutes, accelerating from 0 to 16,000 mph (25,000 kph). The shuttle program ended in 2011, having lasted twice the 15-year life span it was originally designed for.

134 exploring space ○ **APOLLO PROGRAM**

195 hours, 18 minutes—the **total length** of the **first Apollo mission** to the Moon.

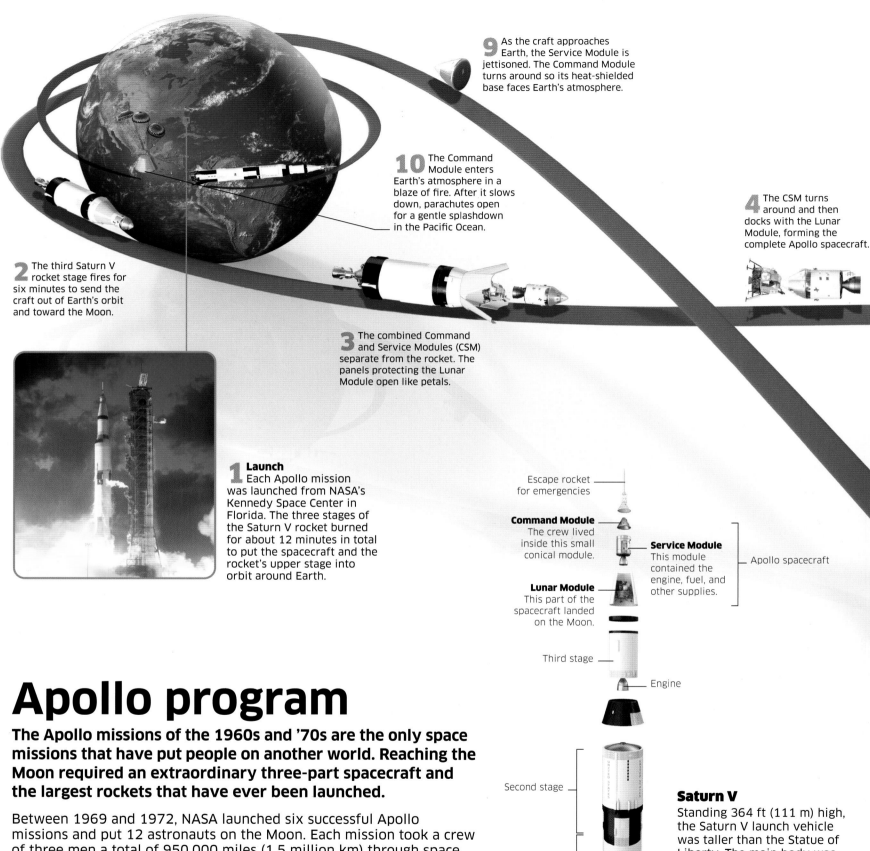

9 As the craft approaches Earth, the Service Module is jettisoned. The Command Module turns around so its heat-shielded base faces Earth's atmosphere.

10 The Command Module enters Earth's atmosphere in a blaze of fire. After it slows down, parachutes open for a gentle splashdown in the Pacific Ocean.

4 The CSM turns around and then docks with the Lunar Module, forming the complete Apollo spacecraft.

2 The third Saturn V rocket stage fires for six minutes to send the craft out of Earth's orbit and toward the Moon.

3 The combined Command and Service Modules (CSM) separate from the rocket. The panels protecting the Lunar Module open like petals.

1 Launch
Each Apollo mission was launched from NASA's Kennedy Space Center in Florida. The three stages of the Saturn V rocket burned for about 12 minutes in total to put the spacecraft and the rocket's upper stage into orbit around Earth.

Escape rocket for emergencies

Command Module
The crew lived inside this small conical module.

Service Module
This module contained the engine, fuel, and other supplies.

Apollo spacecraft

Lunar Module
This part of the spacecraft landed on the Moon.

Third stage

Engine

Apollo program

The Apollo missions of the 1960s and '70s are the only space missions that have put people on another world. Reaching the Moon required an extraordinary three-part spacecraft and the largest rockets that have ever been launched.

Between 1969 and 1972, NASA launched six successful Apollo missions and put 12 astronauts on the Moon. Each mission took a crew of three men a total of 950,000 miles (1.5 million km) through space on a looping, figure-eight journey to the Moon and back. Launched by the gigantic Saturn V rocket—which had to be built anew for each trip—the astronauts traveled in an Apollo spacecraft made of three parts that could separate. The spiderlike Lunar Module carried two men down to the lunar surface. The remaining crew member stayed in the cone-shaped, silvery Command Module, which also carried the crew home. Attached to this was the cylindrical Service Module, housing the spacecraft's rocket engine, fuel, and supplies.

Second stage

First stage

Engines

Saturn V
Standing 364 ft (111 m) high, the Saturn V launch vehicle was taller than the Statue of Liberty. The main body was made of three different rockets, or stages, stacked together. The Apollo spacecraft, tiny by comparison, was on top. The main rockets fired in sequence, each stage propelling the sections above to greater speeds and heights before running out of fuel and falling back to Earth.

15 tons (13.6 tonnes)—the quantity of fuel **burned every second** during launch.

300 The **total number of hours** Apollo astronauts spent on the Moon.

In 1970, Apollo 13 was **damaged by an explosion** on the way to the Moon and had to return to Earth.

135

Command and Service Modules

The Command and Service Modules flew as a single unit (the CSM) for most of each mission. Astronauts lived in the Command Module—the conical front part—which had five triple-glazed windows for viewing the Moon, Earth, and docking maneuvers. The living quarters were cramped and had very basic facilities, with no bathroom. Instead, astronauts used plastic bags or a special hose connected to the vacuum of space.

Mission control

The nerve center of each Apollo mission was the control room at Johnson Space Center in Houston, Texas. Here, scientists and engineers kept a round-the-clock watch over the spacecraft and talked to the crew via radio. The crew remained in continual radio contact with mission control except when the spacecraft traveled behind the Moon.

5 The Apollo spacecraft sails to the Moon, a journey of about three days. It slows down to enter lunar orbit.

The Apollo program cost **$24 billion** and employed 400,000 people at its peak.

7 The Lunar Module separates from the CSM and lands on the Moon. The CSM stays in orbit with one astronaut on board.

8 The top half of the Lunar Module returns to orbit and docks with the CSM, allowing the crew to get back on board. The Lunar Module is then abandoned in space, and the CSM sets off for Earth.

6 Once the craft is safely in lunar orbit, two astronauts go through a hatch into the Lunar Module, ready for their descent to the Moon.

Lunar lander

In the greatest adventure that humans have ever been part of, six Apollo spacecraft touched down on the Moon between 1969 and 1972. The 12 people who landed explored the lunar surface and returned with bags of precious rock samples.

When Apollo astronaut Neil Armstrong set foot on the Moon on July 20, 1969 (US time), it marked the end of a race between the US and Soviet Union that had dominated the early years of space exploration. Armstrong flew to the lunar surface with colleague Buzz Aldrin in the Apollo 11 Lunar Module, nicknamed Eagle, while their colleague Michael Collins remained in orbit in the Apollo Command Module. Armstrong had to take manual control of the Eagle in the last minutes of a hair-raising descent after realizing the planned landing site was unsafe. He touched down with only 30 seconds of fuel left, then made his famous announcement to the whole world: "Tranquility Base here. The Eagle has landed."

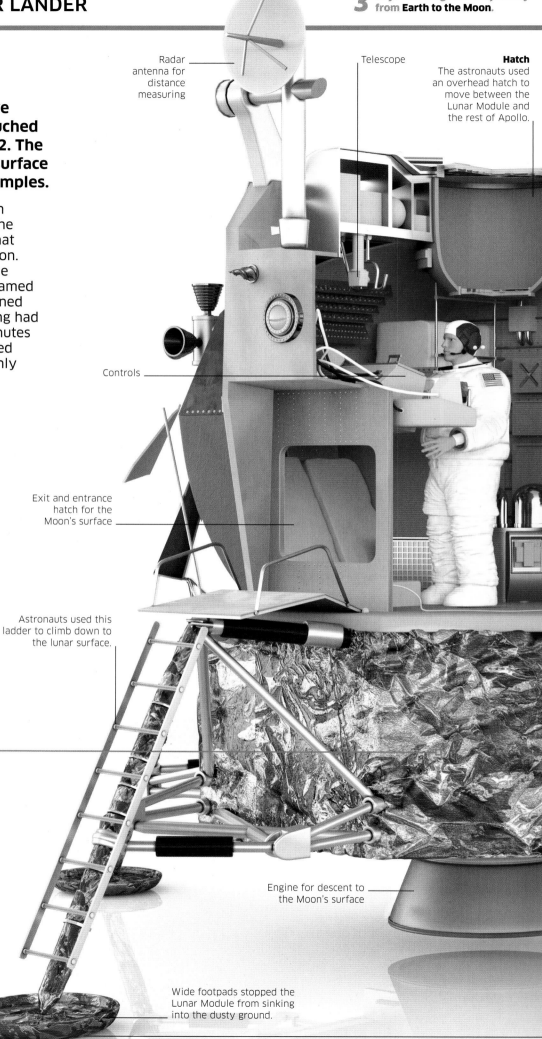

Radar antenna for distance measuring

Telescope

Hatch
The astronauts used an overhead hatch to move between the Lunar Module and the rest of Apollo.

Controls

Exit and entrance hatch for the Moon's surface

Astronauts used this ladder to climb down to the lunar surface.

Ascent stage lifts off

Descent stage stays put

Engine for descent to the Moon's surface

Wide footpads stopped the Lunar Module from sinking into the dusty ground.

Lift off
When it was time to leave, the ascent engine fired. It lifted the ascent stage back into lunar orbit, where the craft docked with the Command and Service Modules. The two lunar astronauts moved back into the Command Module, stowing their rock samples and cameras. The ascent stage was then jettisoned to crash back into the lunar surface.

The **last person to stand on the Moon** was
Eugene Cernan, on December 14, 1972.

80 hours—the total time spent **outside the Lunar Module**
by the 12 astronauts who visited the Moon.

137

SERVICE MODULE   COMMAND MODULE   LUNAR MODULE

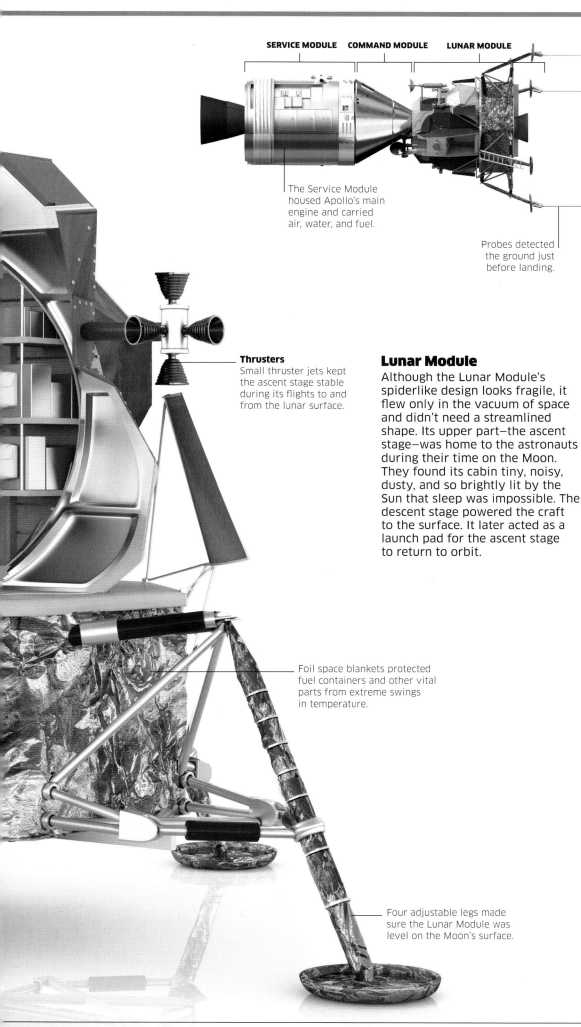

The Service Module
housed Apollo's main
engine and carried
air, water, and fuel.

Probes detected
the ground just
before landing.

Apollo spacecraft

There were three parts to the Apollo craft. The
crew traveled in the Command Module. Once
at the Moon, two astronauts transferred to the
Lunar Module for the descent to the surface.
The third stayed in the combined Command
and Service Modules, orbiting the Moon while
awaiting their return. The Command Module
was the only part of Apollo to return to Earth.

More than 500 million

people watched Neil Armstrong on live
TV when he left the Lunar Module and
stepped onto the Moon.

Thrusters
Small thruster jets kept
the ascent stage stable
during its flights to and
from the lunar surface.

Lunar Module

Although the Lunar Module's
spiderlike design looks fragile, it
flew only in the vacuum of space
and didn't need a streamlined
shape. Its upper part—the ascent
stage—was home to the astronauts
during their time on the Moon.
They found its cabin tiny, noisy,
dusty, and so brightly lit by the
Sun that sleep was impossible. The
descent stage powered the craft
to the surface. It later acted as a
launch pad for the ascent stage
to return to orbit.

Lunar gravity

Gravity on the Moon is only one-sixth as
strong as gravity on Earth. Not only do all
things on the Moon weigh one-sixth of their
Earth weight, but lunar hills are also six
times easier to climb. And, as Apollo 16's
commander John Young found out, you can
jump six times higher on the Moon's surface.

Foil space blankets protected
fuel containers and other vital
parts from extreme swings
in temperature.

Memento

Apollo craft and equipment, including six
descent stages and three Moon buggies, are
still on the Moon. David Scott and James
Irwin of Apollo 15 left other mementos in
the dusty soil: a list of 14 American and
Russian astronauts who lost their lives and a
small figure representing a fallen astronaut.

Four adjustable legs made
sure the Lunar Module was
level on the Moon's surface.

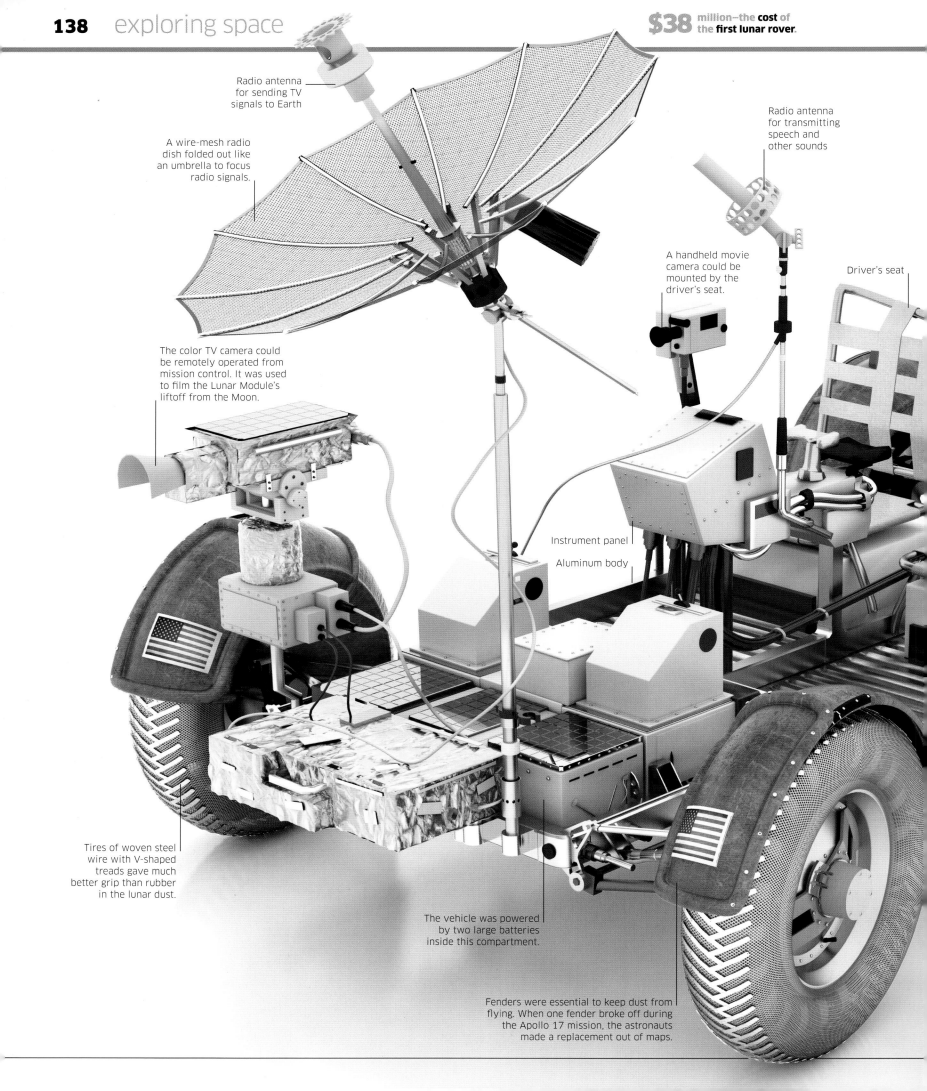

Radio antenna for sending TV signals to Earth

A wire-mesh radio dish folded out like an umbrella to focus radio signals.

Radio antenna for transmitting speech and other sounds

The color TV camera could be remotely operated from mission control. It was used to film the Lunar Module's liftoff from the Moon.

A handheld movie camera could be mounted by the driver's seat.

Driver's seat

Instrument panel

Aluminum body

Tires of woven steel wire with V-shaped treads gave much better grip than rubber in the lunar dust.

The vehicle was powered by two large batteries inside this compartment.

Fenders were essential to keep dust from flying. When one fender broke off during the Apollo 17 mission, the astronauts made a replacement out of maps.

56 miles (90 km)—the **total distance traveled** by all three lunar rovers.

11.2 mph (18 kph)—the **top speed** achieved by the LRV on the Moon.

4.6 miles (7.6 km)—the **greatest distance** a rover traveled from the landing site.

139

The tool caddy at the back carried equipment for collecting samples, including brushes, a hammer, a scoop, and a rake.

The seats were made of aluminum tubing with nylon webbing and had Velcro seatbelts.

Handhold

Under-seat storage allowed astronauts to collect up to 60 lb (27 kg) of rock samples.

Moon buggy

The first Apollo astronauts had to explore the Moon on foot. On the last three missions, astronauts took a Lunar Roving Vehicle (LRV)—a battery-powered buggy that allowed them to travel for miles.

Built from the lightest materials possible, the LRV weighed a mere 77 lb (35 kg) in the Moon's low gravity—about twice the weight of a mountain bike on Earth. Four sturdy metal wheels, each equipped with its own motor, steering, and brake, enabled the LRV to ride safely over craters and rocks while maintaining grip in the loose lunar dust. Apollo 11 astronauts could walk only 330 ft (100 m) or so from the landing site in their bulky suits, but with the LRV to carry them, the crew of Apollo 17 traveled a total of 22 miles (36 km) as they explored and collected samples. Three LRVs were sent to the Moon, and all remain there today. Their last job was to use an onboard camera to film their drivers lifting off for the return to Earth.

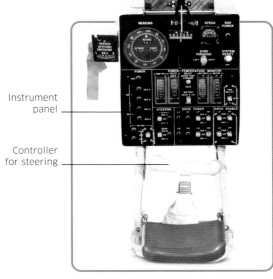

Instrument panel

Controller for steering

Controls
The instrument panel showed speed, direction, tilt, battery power, and temperature. The LRV had no steering wheel. Instead, the driver used a T-shaped controller to steer, accelerate, and brake. The LRV also had a map holder and storage space for tools and rock samples.

Unpacking the LRV

The LRV was designed to fold flat so it could travel to the Moon attached to the side of the Lunar Module. One astronaut had to climb the ladder and undo the clips that held the LRV securely in place so it could be pulled down.

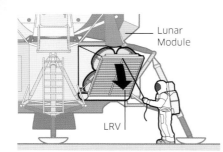

Lunar Module

LRV

1 LOWERING THE LRV
Getting the LRV down to the ground required both astronauts to pull on a series of straps in careful sequence. Pulleys took care of the rest.

Rear wheels

2 CHASSIS UNFOLDS
Lowering the LRV caused the rear wheels to fold out and lock into place automatically. The rover's seats were now facing upward.

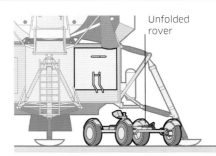

Unfolded rover

3 LRV DISCONNECTED
The front wheels also unfolded and locked in place automatically. Finally, the astronauts raised the seats and other parts by hand.

140 exploring space ∘ **SPACESUIT**

25 The **number of times a suit is used** on the International Space Station.

Spacesuit

A modern spacesuit is far more than just protective clothing. It serves as a wearable spacecraft, creating a safe, Earth-like environment for the human body.

In the early days of space travel, a spacesuit was made in one piece, tailored to fit the astronaut who would wear it. Today, astronauts working outside the International Space Station wear a one-size-fits-all suit made of many parts. A semirigid top fits onto pants, and a helmet, gloves, boots, and life-support backpack all go on top. Beneath the suit is a comfortable, one-piece garment containing tubes of flowing water to keep the body cool. On the outside of the suit are controls, tethers that attach the astronaut to the space station, and tools for the jobs to be done.

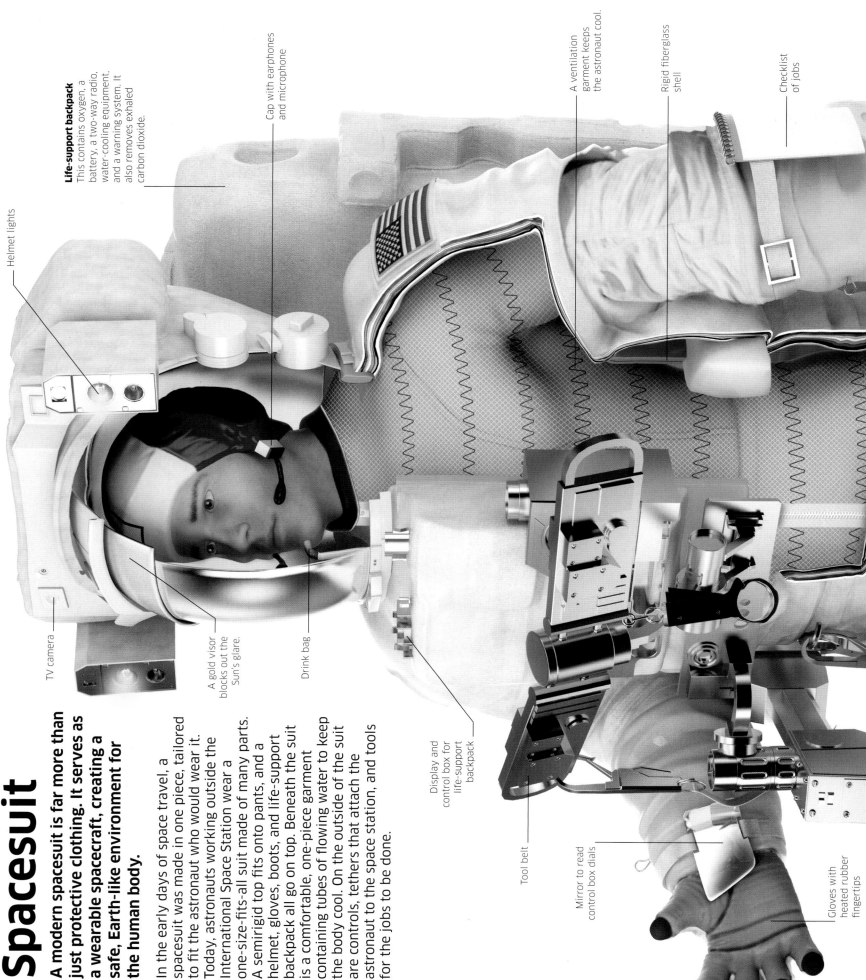

Life-support backpack
This contains oxygen, a battery, a two-way radio, water-cooling equipment, and a warning system. It also removes exhaled carbon dioxide.

Cap with earphones and microphone

A ventilation garment keeps the astronaut cool.

Rigid fiberglass shell

Checklist of jobs

Helmet lights

TV camera

A gold visor blocks out the Sun's glare.

Drink bag

Display and control box for life-support backpack

Tool belt

Mirror to read control box dials

Gloves with heated rubber fingertips

$12 million—the cost of a **single spacesuit**.

A **modern spacesuit** is 280 lb (127 kg) on Earth but is **weightless in space**.

300 ft (92 m)— the total **length of water tubes** in the ventilation garment worn under a spacesuit.

141

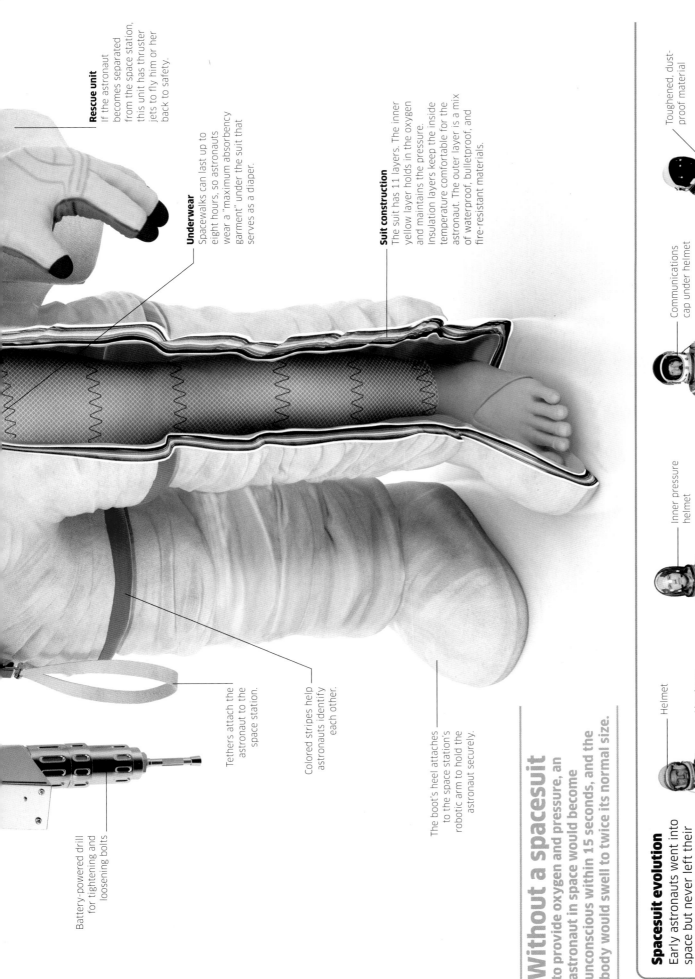

Rescue unit
If the astronaut becomes separated from the space station, this unit has thruster jets to fly him or her back to safety.

Underwear
Spacewalks can last up to eight hours, so astronauts wear a "maximum absorbency garment" under the suit that serves as a diaper.

Suit construction
The suit has 11 layers. The inner yellow layer holds in the oxygen and maintains the pressure. Insulation layers keep the inside temperature comfortable for the astronaut. The outer layer is a mix of waterproof, bulletproof, and fire-resistant materials.

Battery-powered drill for tightening and loosening bolts

Tethers attach the astronaut to the space station.

Colored stripes help astronauts identify each other.

The boot's heel attaches to the space station's robotic arm to hold the astronaut securely.

Without a spacesuit
to provide oxygen and pressure, an astronaut in space would become unconscious within 15 seconds, and the body would swell to twice its normal size.

Spacesuit evolution
Early astronauts went into space but never left their craft. They wore pressure suits like those used by fighter pilots. As the role of astronauts changed to include "spacewalks" outside the craft, their clothing evolved. Today, astronauts wear a flight suit for journeys, casual clothes while in the space station, and a spacesuit for spacewalks.

Mercury
America's Mercury astronauts, who flew between 1961 and 1963, wore silver pressure suits with straps and zippers for a snug fit.

Helmet

Aluminum-coated nylon gave the suit a silver color.

Apollo
The astronauts who went to the Moon in the late 1960s used the same flexible suit for both flying and walking on the lunar surface.

Inner pressure helmet

Inner layers of Apollo suit (outer "white" layers are not shown)

First shuttle suit
In 1981, the first shuttle astronauts wore an escape suit based on a US Air Force pressure suit. A bright orange version was later introduced.

Communications cap under helmet

xEMU suit
NASA's latest Extravehicular mobility unit (EMU) spacesuit is designed for flexible working on the Moon and Mars, as well as in the weightlessness of space.

Toughened, dust-proof material

Flexible sleeves with sensitive gloves

Spacewalk

The airless vacuum of space is deadly to the human body. Without a suit, an astronaut would die in under a minute.

A spacesuit shields the body from the ferocious heat of the Sun and the extreme cold of shadows in airless space. It also exerts pressure on an astronaut's body in a way that compensates for the absence of air pressure and prevents body fluids from simply boiling out of the skin. Here, NASA astronaut Jessica Meir works on an upgrade to the International Space Station's power systems while circling Earth at a speed of 17,100 mph (27,600 kph). This was the third of Meir's three record-breaking all-female spacewalks with Christina Koch during ISS Expedition 61 in 2019–2020.

144 exploring space ∘ **SPACE STATIONS**

437.7 days—the **longest single stay in space**, by Valerie Poliakov on the Mir space station.

Space stations

Only three people have spent more than a year continuously in space, all of them on board a space station. These giant, orbiting spacecraft allow astronauts to spend long periods living and working off the planet.

More than 10 crewed space stations have orbited Earth since 1971. The first one, Salyut 1, was small enough to be launched in one piece but had room for three people. Larger space stations are built in orbit by joining roomlike parts called modules, which are constructed on Earth and launched separately. Astronauts used this method to build the International Space Station (ISS), fixing the first parts together in 1998. It is the largest man-made object ever to orbit Earth and is easily visible to the naked eye, looking like a bright star that sweeps across the sky in just a few minutes. The ISS is used for scientific research, but space stations may one day be used as staging posts for crewed missions to the planets.

International Space Station
Inside, the ISS is as spacious as a six-bedroom house. Most of the space is taken up by work areas such as laboratories. The crew of six work nine hours a day, five days a week, performing experiments and exercising to keep fit.

Kibo
The largest module is this Japanese science laboratory, used for a wide range of science experiments.

Canadarm2
This robotic arm with seven motorized joints moves equipment and astronauts.

Harmony
This American module has four small wall closets that serve as bedrooms.

Columbus
Astronauts use this European laboratory module to study the effect of weightlessness on animals, plants, and the human body.

How big is it?
The ISS is about the size of a soccer field and is more than 50 percent longer than a Boeing 747 (the world's longest passenger aircraft). It weighs about 496 tons (450 tonnes), which is about as much as 375 average-sized cars.

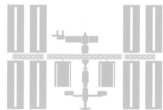

BOEING 747
233 ft (71 m) long

INTERNATIONAL SPACE STATION
357 ft (109 m) long

Orbit
Traveling at 17,100 mph (27,600 kph), the ISS circles Earth once every 90 minutes or so, crossing from the southern to northern hemisphere and back again on each orbit. Because Earth rotates, the ISS passes over a different part of the planet on each pass, tracing out the blue line below.

In the lab
Inside the US Destiny laboratory, an astronaut upgrades Robonaut, the first humanoid robot in space. Considered one of the crew, Robonaut does simple and routine tasks inside the station. Eventually, Robonaut will work outside alongside spacewalking astronauts.

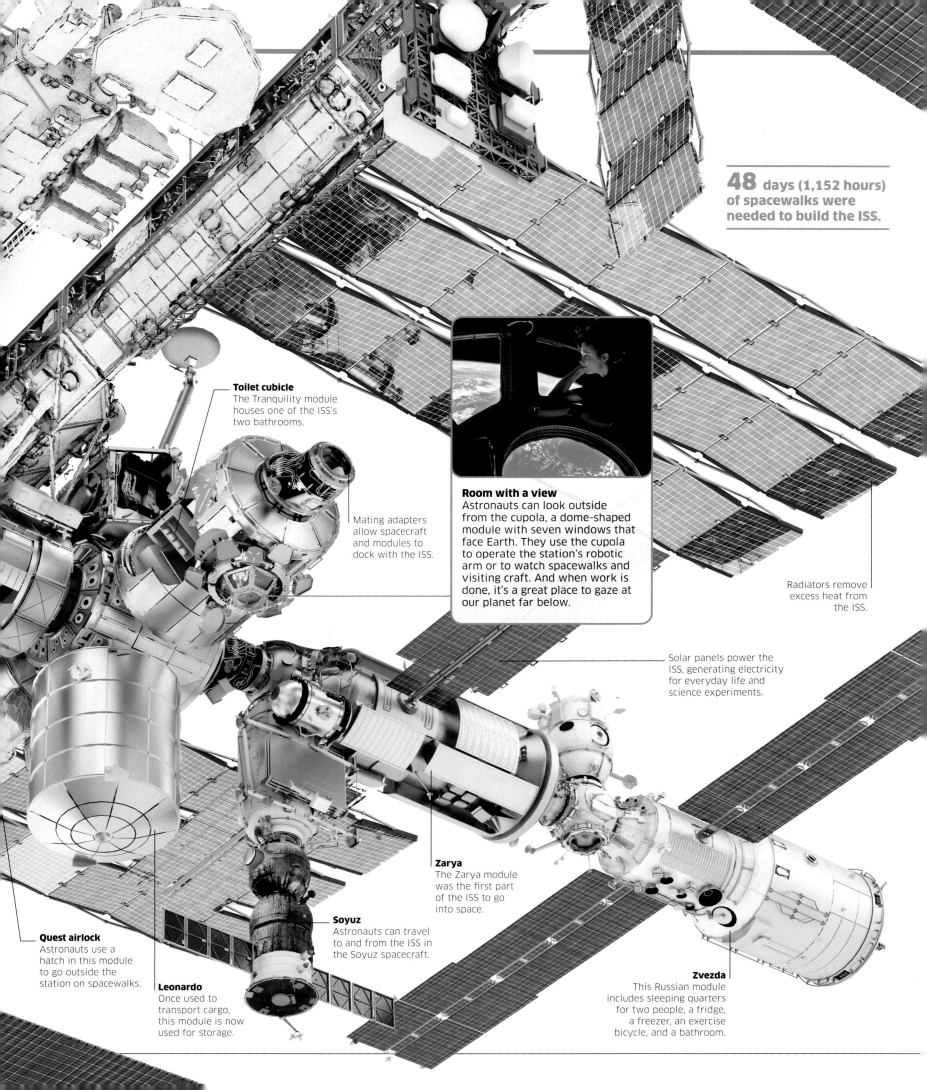

48 days (1,152 hours) of spacewalks were needed to build the ISS.

Toilet cubicle
The Tranquility module houses one of the ISS's two bathrooms.

Mating adapters allow spacecraft and modules to dock with the ISS.

Room with a view
Astronauts can look outside from the cupola, a dome-shaped module with seven windows that face Earth. They use the cupola to operate the station's robotic arm or to watch spacewalks and visiting craft. And when work is done, it's a great place to gaze at our planet far below.

Radiators remove excess heat from the ISS.

Solar panels power the ISS, generating electricity for everyday life and science experiments.

Zarya
The Zarya module was the first part of the ISS to go into space.

Quest airlock
Astronauts use a hatch in this module to go outside the station on spacewalks.

Soyuz
Astronauts can travel to and from the ISS in the Soyuz spacecraft.

Leonardo
Once used to transport cargo, this module is now used for storage.

Zvezda
This Russian module includes sleeping quarters for two people, a fridge, a freezer, an exercise bicycle, and a bathroom.

Future exploration

Although no humans have left Earth orbit since the last Apollo Moon mission in 1972, current proposals aim to send a new generation of astronauts to the Moon, and also farther afield to Mars.

The US space agency NASA, China, and Russia all hope to launch crewed lunar missions in coming decades. NASA and China also have their sights on Mars, which is a much more ambitious target. The costs, technical challenges, and risks involved in a human mission to Mars are enormous. In the meantime, robotic spacecraft and rovers are likely to continue exploring the Solar System, advancing our knowledge of the planets without the dangers or costs of crewed expeditions.

Martian base
This artist's impression shows one proposed idea for a Mars base. The main building is constructed from a series of landers that arrive separately and are joined together by robotic rovers already on the ground. The technology needed to build a base of this sophistication may not exist for decades.

Because Mars has a thin atmosphere and a weak magnetic field, dangerous levels of radiation reach the surface. Living quarters would need to be heavily shielded or underground.

Modular landers bring vital supplies from Earth.

Ice mixed with the Martian soil can be melted and processed using solar electricity, producing water, oxygen, and even rocket fuel for the return journey to Earth.

–85°F (–65°C)–the **average temperature** on the surface of Mars.

147

Greenhouse

Long-term settlers on Mars would have to produce their own food in greenhouses. The plants would need a large supply of water, which would be difficult to provide, as well as warmth, air, and artificial light. Growing plants outdoors on Mars would be impossible, as the temperature is too low and there is no liquid water.

Living quarters

Because buried dwellings would have no windows, settlers would use screens to see outside and to keep in touch with Earth. However, live conversations with Earth would not be possible, as radio signals from Mars take about 40 minutes to get there and back.

Inflatable homes

Constructing large buildings on Mars would be impossible, so settlers would either have to live inside landers or bring cleverly packaged dwellings that could be erected simply. One solution might be to use inflatable dwellings. Because the air pressure on Mars is very low, any dwellings would need to withstand being filled with pressurized air.

Solar panels provide power. Although Mars is farther from the Sun than Earth, its thinner air lets more solar energy reach the ground.

Steps into the future

The future of space exploration is likely to be a partnership between commercial companies and government agencies. Companies such as Virgin Galactic and SpaceX will offer suborbital and orbital trips to civilian space tourists, as well as launches to the International Space Station. Meanwhile, NASA will concentrate its efforts on the Moon and beyond.

Suborbital tourism

Virgin Galactic's SpaceShipTwo (named VSS Unity) made its first flight with paying passengers in July 2021. It carried four space tourists (left) to the edge of space on a trip that included four minutes of weightlessness. In the same month, Blue Origin's New Shepard craft made its first crewed suborbital flight.

Return to the Moon

As part of its Artemis program, NASA is developing the Human Landing System (HLS)–a spacecraft that can be docked to Orion and which will carry astronauts to and from the lunar surface.

The search for life

The Universe is a huge place. In our home galaxy, there may be as many as 100 billion stars with planets, yet our galaxy is just one of possibly 200 billion galaxies. It seems unlikely, therefore, that Earth is the only place with life. Large telescopes all over the world are searching space for evidence that life could exist elsewhere. We probably won't come across any little green men—in fact, it may be hard to recognize life if we do find it. An unexplained radio signal, a hint of hidden water, a rock that might contain tiny fossils: these are the sorts of clues scientists are looking for.

IS ANYBODY OUT THERE?

In 1961, astronomer Frank Drake devised a method for estimating how many civilizations might be sending out radio signals in our galaxy. Known as the Drake Equation, this formula involves seven factors, written as symbols, which have to be multiplied together. The values of some of the factors can only be guessed at, so the equation gives only a very rough idea of our chances of finding extraterrestrials.

RADIO SIGNALS

If alien civilizations do exist somewhere, it's possible they have discovered how to use radio waves to send signals to each other, just as we do with phones, TV, and radio broadcasts. So one way of finding aliens is simply to search for their radio signals traveling through space. SETI (search for extraterrestrial intelligence) projects do this, using huge radio dishes to scan the skies for distinctive signals. We can also use radio telescopes to send out our own messages, aiming them at likely destinations in our galaxy. So far, neither approach has brought success.

The Wow! signal

In 1977, a scientist at an American radio observatory noticed that a signal from space was unusually strong. Thrilled that it might be a message from aliens, he wrote "Wow!" on a printout. Sadly, the Wow! signal was never detected again.

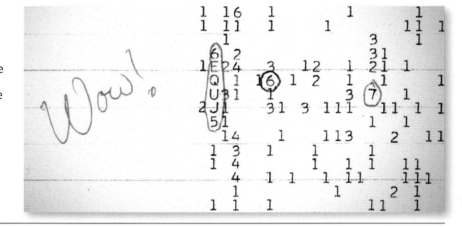

Searching the skies

The Allen Telescope Array in California is a group of 42 radio telescopes—each 20 ft (6.1 m) in diameter—designed to scan the skies for SETI signals, as well as mapping natural radio emissions from distant galaxies.

$$N = R^* \times f_p \times n_e \times f_l \times f_i \times f_c \times L$$

N — Number of alien civilizations that are sending out radio signals

R* — The rate at which new stars form in our galaxy each year

f_p — The fraction of such stars that have a family of orbiting planets

n_e — For each star, the number of planets that have the right conditions for life

f_l — The fraction of such planets on which life appears

f_i — The fraction of life-supporting planets on which intelligent life develops

f_c — The fraction of civilizations that develop radio technology

L — The lifespan of each civilization, judged by how long it continues to send messages

The Arecibo message

In 1974, astronomers used the giant Arecibo radio telescope in Puerto Rico to send a coded message toward a star cluster 25,000 light-years away. The signal lasted three minutes and consisted of a stream of binary numbers that, when decoded, forms a simple picture telling aliens about life on Earth. Because the signal will take 25,000 years to reach its target—and any reply will take another 25,000 years to come back—the message was symbolic rather than a serious attempt to communicate.

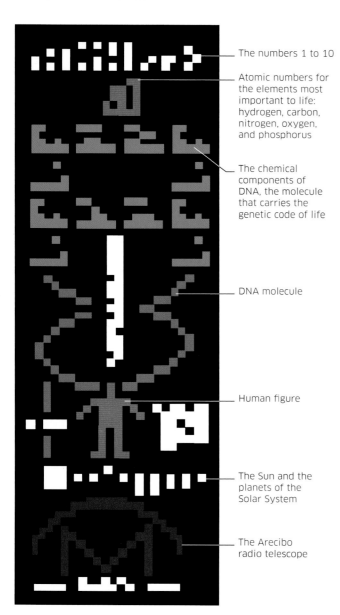

- The numbers 1 to 10
- Atomic numbers for the elements most important to life: hydrogen, carbon, nitrogen, oxygen, and phosphorus
- The chemical components of DNA, the molecule that carries the genetic code of life
- DNA molecule
- Human figure
- The Sun and the planets of the Solar System
- The Arecibo radio telescope

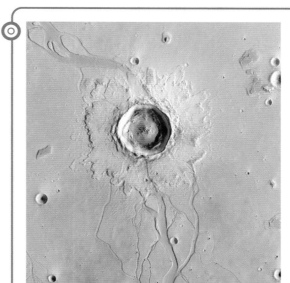

SEARCHING THE SOLAR SYSTEM

Although we have yet to find evidence of life in other parts of our Solar System, spacecraft have found evidence of liquid water, which is vital to life on Earth. Hidden oceans exist under the surface of some moons, and water almost certainly once flowed on Mars.

Mars

Photographs of Mars strongly suggest that water has flowed across its surface in the past, if only for brief periods. Long ago, Mars may have been warmer and wetter, allowing rivers and lakes to exist on the surface. Future Martian landers may try to find out whether there are any buried fossils from Mars's remote past.

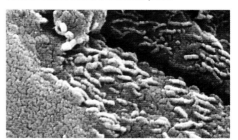

Martian meteorite
In 1996, scientists amazed the world when they announced the discovery of what looked like fossilized bacteria inside a Martian meteorite found in Antarctica. This evidence of extraterrestrial life seemed so strong that US president Bill Clinton made a televized statement about the discovery. Since then, scientists have argued about the structures inside meteorite ALH84001, which some claim are merely mineral deposits.

Under the ice

Hidden below the icy surface of Jupiter's moon Europa (left), there likely exists a huge saltwater ocean, warmed by strong tides. Because water and warmth are key to the development of life, Europa is high on scientists' list of Solar System locations to search for life. Saturn's moon Enceladus probably also has a liquid-water ocean beneath an ice covering, and this, too, might be a place that could harbor life.

THE NIGHT SKY

You don't need to board a rocket to see space—just walk outside on a clear night and look up. The constellations are easy to see with the naked eye, but with binoculars you can see more—from the moons of Jupiter to starbirth nebulae and even whole galaxies.

The celestial sphere

The celestial sphere is an imaginary sphere around Earth on which any object in the sky can be precisely mapped, just as locations on Earth can be mapped on a globe. Different parts of the sphere are visible from different areas of Earth, and because our planet is continually rotating, different areas of the sphere come into view over the course of a night. Stars and other distant objects stay fixed in more or less the same place on the celestial sphere for long periods of time, but objects in the Solar System, such as the Sun, Moon, and planets, are always moving.

WHAT IS THE CELESTIAL SPHERE?

Think of the celestial sphere as a giant glass ball around Earth with stars pinned to its surface. Because Earth rotates, the celestial sphere also appears to rotate. Like Earth, it has north and south poles and is divided into northern and southern hemispheres by an equator. We can pinpoint any location on Earth with measurements called latitude and longitude. The celestial sphere uses a similar system, but the numbers are called declination and right ascension.

Earth's axis

North celestial pole

Lines of declination measure positions north or south of the celestial equator.

MARS

The Sun and planets appear to move around the sky close to a line called the ecliptic.

Sun's motion

SUN

The celestial equator lies directly above Earth's equator.

THE SPINNING SKY

It's impossible to see the whole celestial sphere at once because Earth gets in the way. However, because Earth rotates and travels around the Sun, different parts of the celestial sphere come into view at different times. How much you can see, and how the stars move, depends on whereabouts on Earth you live.

Key to spheres
- ● Observer
- ···· Observer's horizon
- ■ Stars always visible
- ■ Stars visible at some time
- ■ Stars never visible

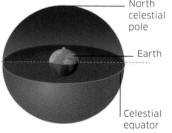

North celestial pole

Earth

Celestial equator

View from the North Pole
From here, you can only see the northern half of the celestial sphere–the other half is never visible. As Earth rotates, the stars move in circles around the celestial pole, which is directly overhead.

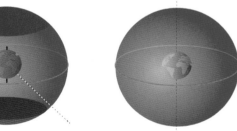

View from midlatitudes
From midlatitude regions such as the US and Europe, you can always see the constellations around the celestial pole, but the other constellations change during the night and during the year.

View from the equator
From the equator, you can see the entire celestial sphere over the course of a year. The north and south celestial poles lie on the horizon, making polar constellations hard to see.

Through the year

Earth's night side faces different parts of the celestial sphere over the course of the year as we orbit the Sun. Because of this, different constellations come in and out of view as the months pass. Stars are easiest to see in winter, because the nights are longer and the darkness is much deeper. In summer, nights are shorter and the sky doesn't get so dark, so stars look fainter.

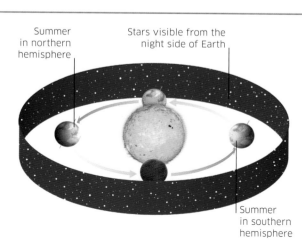

Summer in northern hemisphere

Stars visible from the night side of Earth

Summer in southern hemisphere

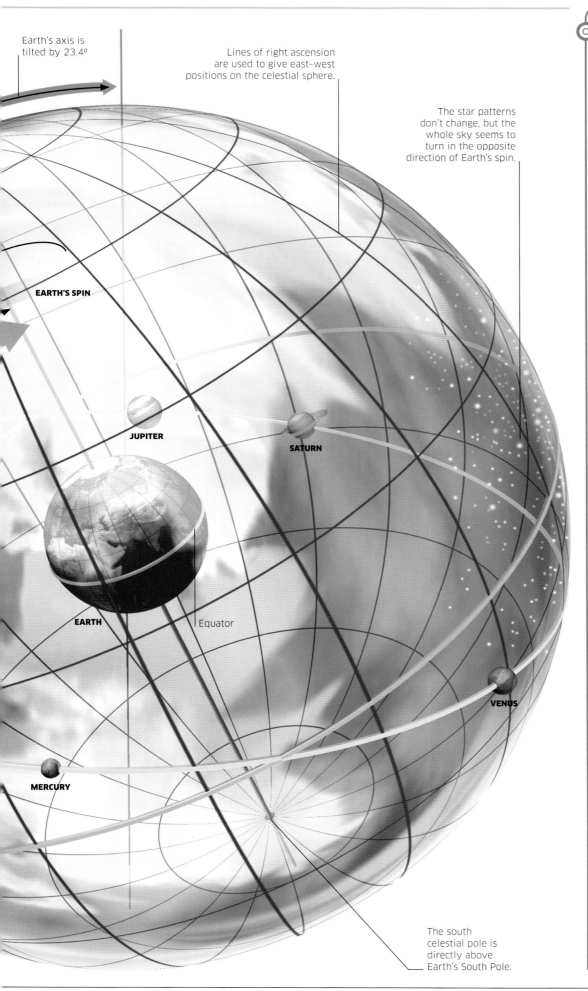

Earth's axis is tilted by 23.4°

Lines of right ascension are used to give east-west positions on the celestial sphere.

The star patterns don't change, but the whole sky seems to turn in the opposite direction of Earth's spin.

EARTH'S SPIN

JUPITER

SATURN

EARTH

Equator

VENUS

MERCURY

The south celestial pole is directly above Earth's South Pole.

ORIGINS

In ancient times, people didn't know that Earth rotates, so they naturally thought that the Sun and stars were moving around us. Ancient stargazers thought Earth was the center of the Universe, surrounded by a set of glass spheres—one for the stars and separate spheres for the Moon, each planet, and the Sun.

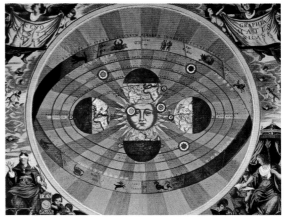

ILLUSTRATION OF THE COPERNICAN SYSTEM, 1661

Sun in the middle

About 500 years ago, Polish astronomer Nicolaus Copernicus realized he could predict the movements of the planets better by assuming the Sun was in the middle rather than Earth. His revolutionary theory showed that Earth was not the center of creation.

The zodiac

The Sun's path along the ecliptic takes it through 13 constellations: 12, called the signs of the zodiac, have long been seen as having special significance. The 13th, Ophiuchus, is often overlooked.

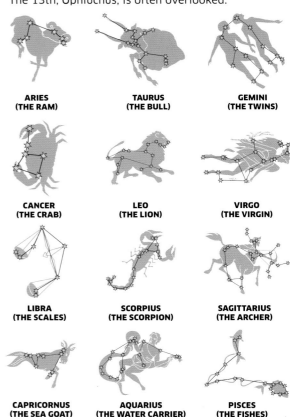

ARIES (THE RAM)

TAURUS (THE BULL)

GEMINI (THE TWINS)

CANCER (THE CRAB)

LEO (THE LION)

VIRGO (THE VIRGIN)

LIBRA (THE SCALES)

SCORPIUS (THE SCORPION)

SAGITTARIUS (THE ARCHER)

CAPRICORNUS (THE SEA GOAT)

AQUARIUS (THE WATER CARRIER)

PISCES (THE FISHES)

Practical stargazing

One of the things that makes astronomy such a great hobby is that everybody can join in. On a typical dark night, a person with good vision can see up to 3,000 stars, so there are plenty of interesting features to find with the naked eye and learn about. Before getting started, it's best to understand a few basics, such as the way the stars and other objects move across the sky and how astronomers keep track of them. Armed with this essential knowledge, anyone can go out and begin to identify the constellations or learn to spot red giants, star-birth nebulae, or even whole galaxies millions of light-years from Earth.

⊙ BASIC EQUIPMENT

The essentials for a night of stargazing are warm clothes, a star chart of some sort, and a flashlight to see by. If you have a smartphone or tablet, you can download various apps that will show the night sky visible from your location at any time and date. However, many people prefer to use a circular chart called a planisphere.

Night vision
It takes about 20 minutes for your eyes to fully adjust to darkness so that you can see the faintest stars. Avoid bright light or you'll ruin your night vision. If you need to use a flashlight, a red one is best, as it won't affect your ability to see in the dark.

⊙ SIZING UP THE SKY

Astronomers treat the sky as if it were a huge sphere surrounding Earth. Distances between objects are measured in degrees. There are 360 degrees in a circle, so the distance around the whole sky is 360 degrees. The Moon is about half a degree wide.

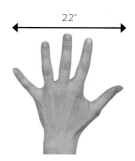

Handspan
A hand held at arm's length with fingers spread widely covers an angle of about 22 degrees between the outstretched little finger and thumb.

Finger joints
The top part of an index finger is about 3 degrees wide. The middle part is 4 degrees wide, and the bottom part is 6 degrees wide.

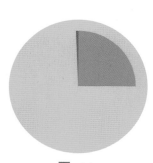

Finger width
The tip of a finger pointing upward at arm's length is about 1 degree wide and can completely cover a full moon.

- ■ 1 degree
- ■ 90 degrees
- ■ 360 degrees

Mapping the stars

You can measure the exact position of a star at any moment with two numbers. One is altitude: the star's height above the horizon, measured in degrees. The other is azimuth: the angle from due north, measured in degrees clockwise. The star below, for example, has an altitude of 45 degrees and an azimuth of 25 degrees.

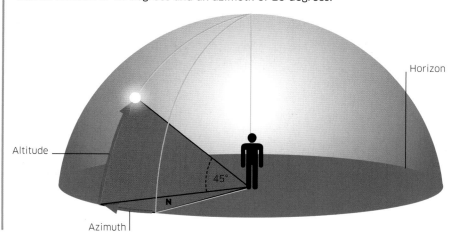

Horizon

Altitude

45°

N

Azimuth

⊙ UNDER DARK SKIES

The key to good stargazing is to find the darkest, clearest skies available. Professional observatories are often located on high mountaintops in remote areas, but the most important thing is simply to get away from city lights and the glow of "light pollution." Under a truly dark sky, the Milky Way is an unforgettable sight.

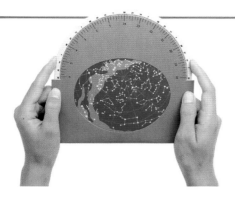

Planisphere
This astronomer's tool consists of a circular star chart and an overlay with an oval window. When the time and date marked around the edges of the two layers are correctly aligned, the stars shown in the window will mirror those in the sky above.

Optical Instruments

Binoculars and telescopes will boost your stargazing. Their big lenses or mirrors collect much more light than a human eye can, revealing very faint objects such as nebulae and galaxies. Their eyepieces, meanwhile, create a magnified image of a small part of the sky, allowing stargazers to separate closely spaced objects, such as double stars, and see more detail on the Moon and planets.

Binoculars
Binoculars have two large, light-collecting lenses and use prisms to direct light into magnifying eyepieces. Good binoculars will allow you to see Jupiter's moons, but you need steady hands to stop the image shaking.

Telescopes
A telescope has either an objective lens or a large primary mirror. It collects much more light than binoculars. The eyepiece gives a highly magnified image of a smaller area of sky. A tripod or other mount is used to steady the telescope and stop it from wobbling.

Milky Way
Our home galaxy is visible on clear, moonless nights as a wash of milky light across the sky. The best time to see it is late summer in the northern hemisphere and late winter in the southern hemisphere.

THE CHANGING SKY

Watch the sky for more than a few minutes and you'll notice that the stars move slowly around the sky, rising in the east and setting in the west. This is an illusion caused by Earth's rotation, and the pattern of movement varies between different parts of the world.

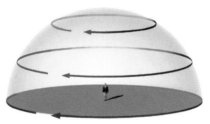

Motion at the North Pole
If you watched the sky from Earth's North Pole, no stars would ever rise or set. Instead, they would simply move in circles around the Pole Star, which never moves.

Motion at midlatitudes
From most parts of the world, some stars stay visible throughout the night, traveling in a circle, while other stars rise and set.

Motion at the equator
At the equator, all stars rise in the east, cross the sky, and set in the west. The constellations visible at night change gradually over the course of a year.

Moving constellations

Earth's orbit around the Sun means that the positions of the constellations in the sky appear to change. You'll notice this if you view the same constellation at the same time over several weeks.

APRIL 1, 8 P.M.

APRIL 8, 8 P.M.

APRIL 15, 8 P.M.

Northern star hopping

To the untrained eye, the night sky can look like a bewildering mass of stars. A good way to make sense of it is to look for well-known landmarks and then trace imaginary lines from these to other constellations. This technique is called star hopping and is easy to do with the naked eye, though you can see more if you have binoculars or a telescope. The chart on this page shows how to star hop around the north celestial pole, which is visible to people who live in Earth's northern hemisphere.

FINDING THE WAY

This tour of the northern sky starts with a famous pattern of stars called the Big Dipper or Plough. You can use the Big Dipper as a signpost to find the Pole Star and other sights nearby. Some are quite faint, so you will need a clear, dark night to see them all.

1 THE FIRST STEP is to find the Big Dipper and locate the two stars farthest from its "handle," which are known as the Pointers. Draw an imaginary line through the Pointers and extend it to a bright star. This is the Pole Star, and it is always due north.

2 EXTEND THE LINE from the Pointers past the Pole Star to reach the faint constellation Cepheus, which looks a bit like a lopsided house. Binoculars will reveal the bright red Garnet Star at the base of the house—the reddest star visible to the naked eye and one of the largest stars known.

3 NOW DRAW A LINE from the third star in the Big Dipper's handle through the Pole Star to find the constellation Cassiopeia, which looks like a flattened "W." If you have binoculars, look for a star cluster just below the central peak of the "W." This star cluster is called NGC 457.

4 THE LARGE BUT FAINT and shapeless constellation Draco (the Dragon) is best seen under very dark skies. A line from the fourth star in the Big Dipper's handle cuts across the dragon's body and carries on to its head, a pattern of stars called the Lozenge.

5 TRACK DOWN one of the brightest galaxies in the sky with binoculars: follow a diagonal line across the Big Dipper's rectangle of stars and continue in the same direction, looking for a pair of tiny fuzzy patches. These are the galaxies M81 and its fainter companion M82.

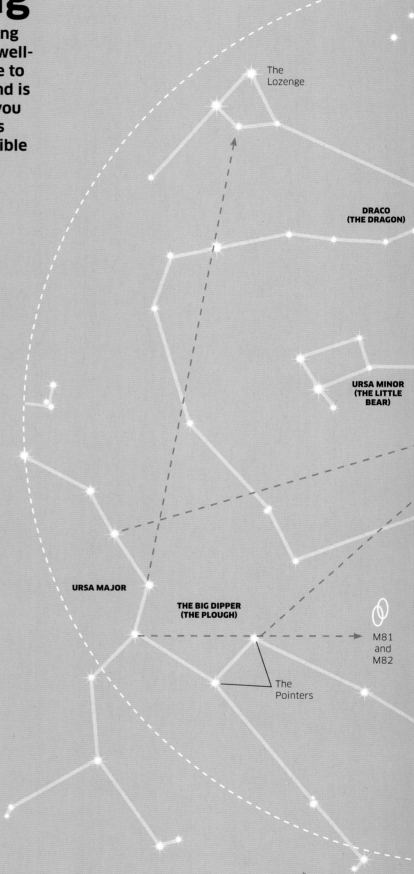

The Lozenge

DRACO
(THE DRAGON)

URSA MINOR
(THE LITTLE BEAR)

URSA MAJOR

THE BIG DIPPER
(THE PLOUGH)

M81
and
M82

The Pointers

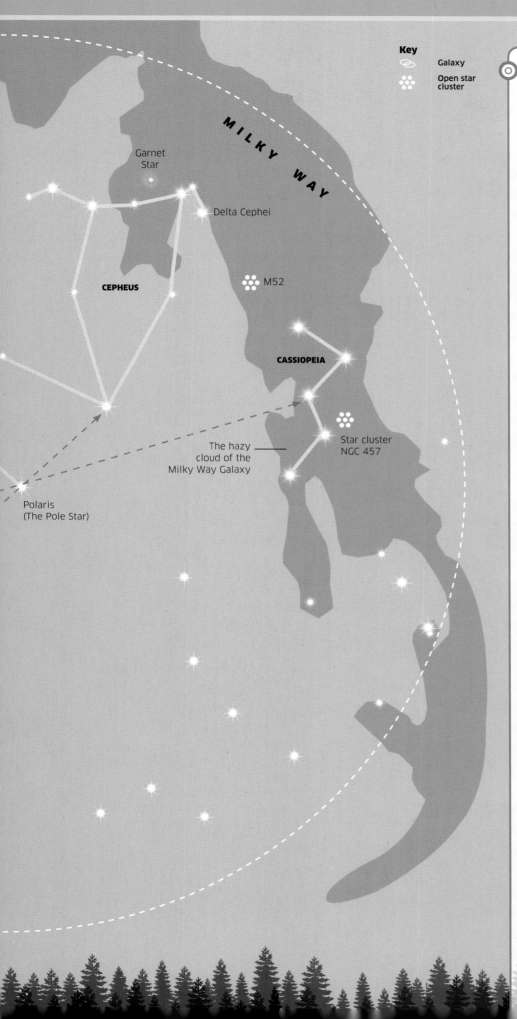

M I L K Y   W A Y

Garnet Star

Delta Cephei

CEPHEUS

M52

CASSIOPEIA

Star cluster NGC 457

The hazy cloud of the Milky Way Galaxy

Polaris (The Pole Star)

Key

⊘ Galaxy

⬡ Open star cluster

◎ WHAT TO SEE

Close to the band of the Milky Way, we can see densely packed stars, clusters, and nebulae. Away from it, we can only see a few relatively nearby stars and some distant galaxies across the gulf of intergalactic space.

Big and Little bears
The brightest seven stars of the constellation Ursa Major, the Great Bear, form the familiar pattern known as the Big Dipper or Plough. Following the Pointers to the Pole Star reveals a similar pattern of seven stars called Ursa Minor, the Little Bear.

Pole Star
Because Earth rotates, stars move across the sky during the night, circling the north celestial pole. However, one star barely moves: the Pole Star, which lies in the tail of the Little Bear (Ursa Minor). Sailors used to use this guiding star to find north on clear nights.

Cassiopeia and the Milky Way
The constellation of Cassiopeia lies embedded in the northern reaches of the Milky Way, the pale band of countless distant stars that wraps its way around the sky. This makes Cassiopeia a rich hunting ground for star clusters and other deep-sky objects.

M81 and M82
The bright spiral galaxy M81 (top), also called Bode's Galaxy, lies about 12 million light-years from Earth. Nearby in the night sky is M82 (bottom), an irregular cloud of distant stars that is also known as the Cigar Galaxy.

Southern star hopping

This chart shows you how to star hop your way around some of the top sights in the southern night sky, visible to people who live in Earth's southern hemisphere. The southern sky gives stargazers a fantastic view of our Milky Way Galaxy and the bright constellations Carina, Centaurus, and the Southern Cross. There are many celestial wonders to spot, from colorful nebulae and star clusters to whole galaxies.

◎ FINDING THE WAY

Southern stargazers don't have a pole star to guide them, and the constellations closest to the pole are faint and unremarkable. Fortunately, the Milky Way runs close by and is packed with bright stars and other landmarks. The Southern Cross (Crux) and the so-called Southern Pointers make good starting points for finding your way around the sky.

1 FIRST, IDENTIFY the Southern Cross (not to be confused with the False Cross) and the Southern Pointer stars Alpha and Beta Centauri. Draw a line from Beta Centauri to the bottom of the Southern Cross and carry on for the same distance again to reach the famous Carina Nebula. This complex mix of a star-forming nebula and a massive star on the brink of explosion is well worth exploring with binoculars.

2 TWO BEAUTIFUL STAR CLUSTERS lie close to the Carina Nebula: NGC 3532 and the Southern Pleiades (IC 2602). This second cluster contains five or six naked-eye stars—see how many you can count. (You'll see more by looking slightly to one side of it.) Then use binoculars to view many more.

3 NEXT, FOLLOW A LINE from the top of the Southern Cross, past the Carina Nebula, and onward by the same distance again. Here, you'll find the deceptive pattern of the False Cross, and just beyond it the star cluster IC 2391. This impressive jewelry box of stars is best appreciated through binoculars.

4 NOW FOLLOW THE downward (longer) bar of the Southern Cross and cross an empty area of the sky to reach the Small Magellanic Cloud. This small galaxy orbits our own Milky Way Galaxy and contains hundreds of millions of stars. Nearby is an impressive globular cluster of stars known as 47 Tucanae.

5 FINALLY, RETURN to the Southern Pointers and follow a line from Alpha Centauri to discover three bright stars that form a triangle shape—the unimaginatively named constellation Triangulum Australe.

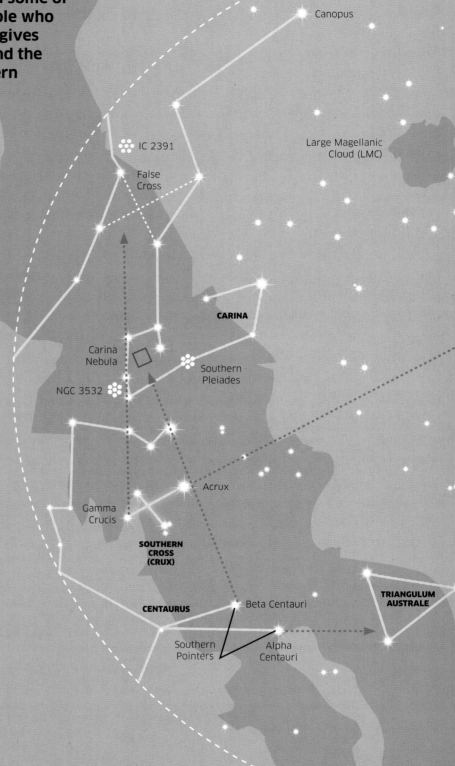

Canopus

IC 2391

Large Magellanic Cloud (LMC)

False Cross

CARINA

Carina Nebula

Southern Pleiades

NGC 3532

Acrux

Gamma Crucis

SOUTHERN CROSS (CRUX)

CENTAURUS

Beta Centauri

TRIANGULUM AUSTRALE

Southern Pointers

Alpha Centauri

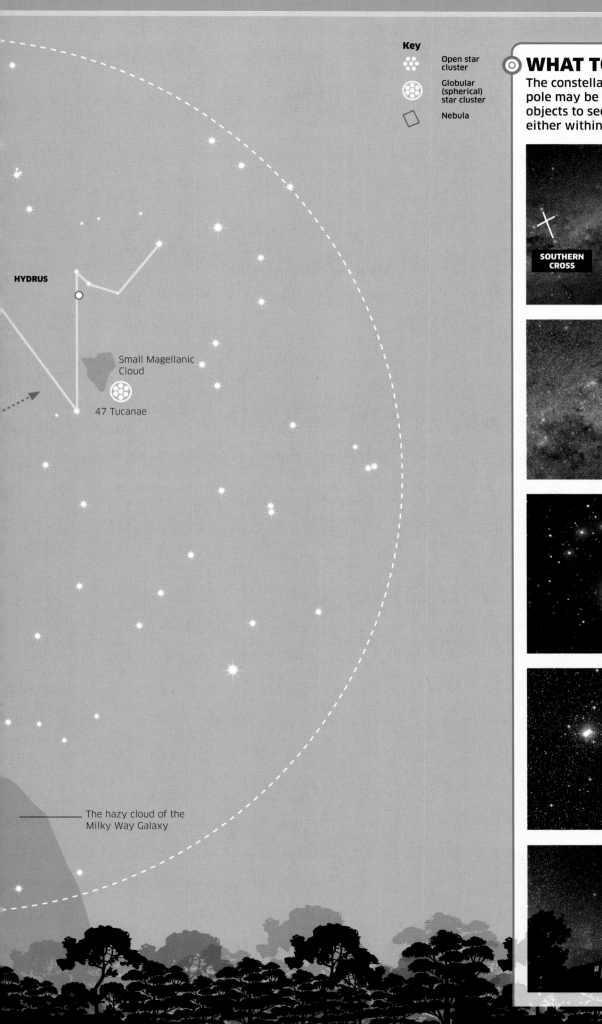

HYDRUS

Small Magellanic Cloud

47 Tucanae

The hazy cloud of the Milky Way Galaxy

Key

Open star cluster

Globular (spherical) star cluster

Nebula

WHAT TO SEE

The constellations directly around the south celestial pole may be faint, but there are many other interesting objects to see a little farther afield. Most of these lie either within the band of the Milky Way or close to it.

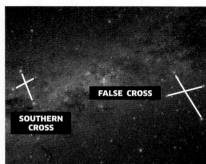

False Cross
The False Cross is made of bright stars from the constellations Carina and Vela. It mimics the shape of the true Southern Cross, which is why the two are often confused. However, the False Cross is slightly larger.

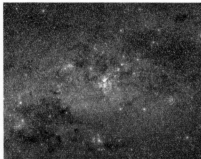

Carina Nebula
The Carina Nebula is a vast, star-forming gas cloud about 7,500 light-years from Earth. Deep inside, it is a massive star nearing the end of its life that will eventually explode in a supernova. Photographs capture the red color of the Carina Nebula, but to the naked eye, it appears white.

Southern Pleiades
The Southern Pleiades cluster (IC 2602) is an open cluster—a group of young stars that formed in the same gas cloud. It is visible to the naked eye, but binoculars will reveal more of the stars within it. There are around 60 stars in total.

Open cluster IC 2391
This bright open cluster likely originated from the same star-forming cloud as the Southern Pleiades, since it has a similar age (about 50 million years) and is a similar distance from Earth (500 light-years).

Large and Small Magellanic clouds
These irregular galaxies are satellites of our own galaxy, the Milky Way. In southern skies, they look like small, detached clumps of the Milky Way. The large cloud is about 160,000 light-years from Earth, while the small cloud is around 210,000 light-years away.

Star maps

From Earth, about 6,000 stars are visible to the naked eye, though you can only see about half of these from any location at any one time.

Over a year, you can see all the stars in either the north or south celestial hemisphere—depending on whether you are north or south of the equator—and some of the stars in the other celestial hemisphere, too.

Northern sky

Most of the constellation names in the northern hemisphere come from the ancient Greeks. They are often linked to myths, such as the story of Perseus and Andromeda, but some of the fainter stars lie in more modern constellations.

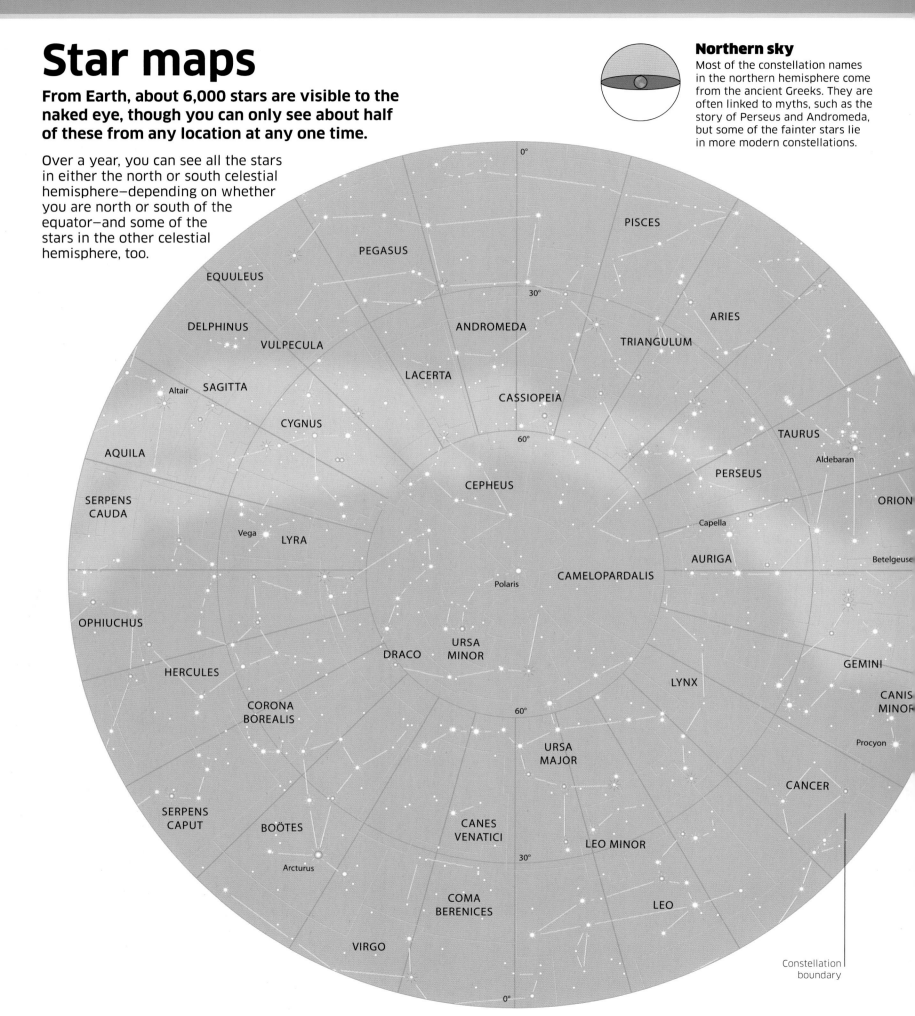

Constellation boundary

Key

These maps show fairly bright stars, down to magnitude 5.0. There are many more faint stars visible to the naked eye.

○ Yellow star
✳ Red star
○ Orange star
○ White star
○ Blue star

◎ Magnitude brighter than 0.0
◎ Magnitude brighter than 1.0
○ Magnitude brighter than 2.0

○ Magnitude brighter than 3.0
· Magnitude brighter than 4.0
· Magnitude brighter than 5.0

Southern sky

Southern hemisphere stars close to the celestial equator (around the edges of the map) were visible to ancient Greek astronomers, who grouped them into mythological constellations. Names for constellations around the south celestial pole were proposed by astronomers working from the late 16th century onward.

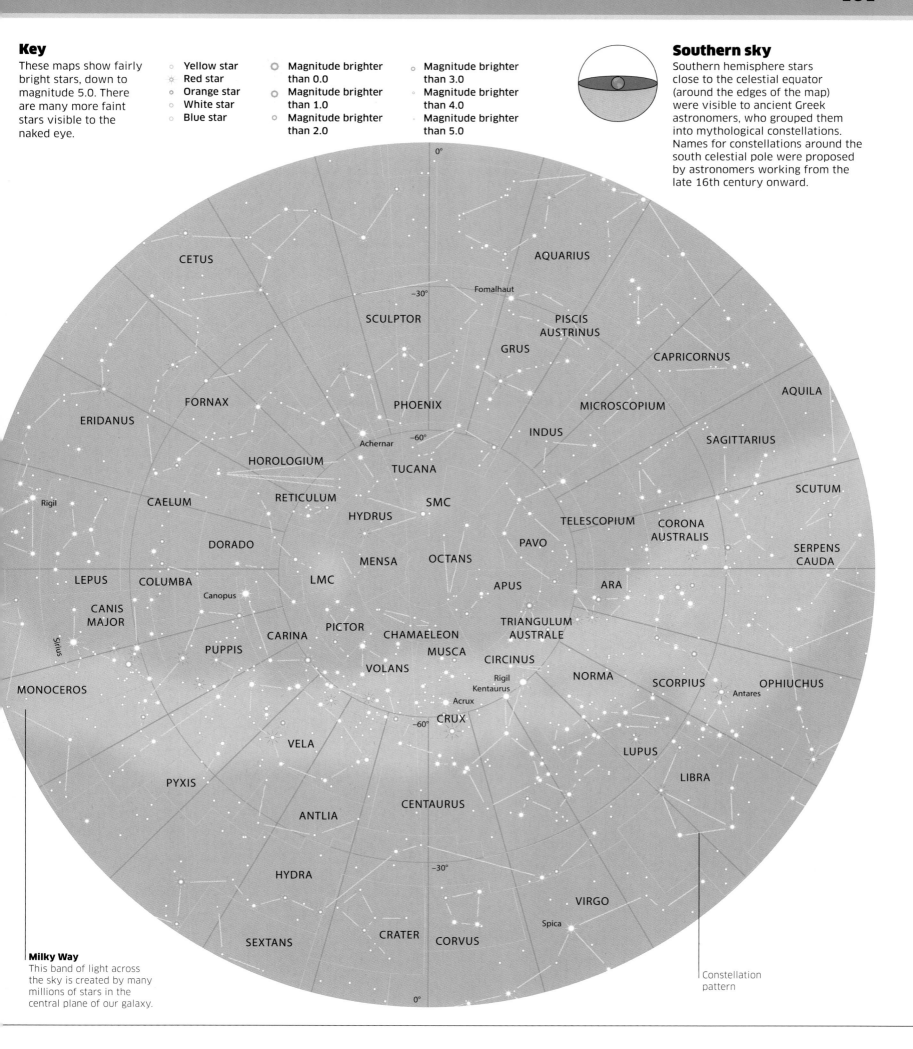

Milky Way
This band of light across the sky is created by many millions of stars in the central plane of our galaxy.

Constellation pattern

CETUS
AQUARIUS
−30°
Fomalhaut
SCULPTOR
PISCIS AUSTRINUS
GRUS
CAPRICORNUS
FORNAX
PHOENIX
MICROSCOPIUM
AQUILA
ERIDANUS
INDUS
Achernar
−60°
SAGITTARIUS
HOROLOGIUM
TUCANA
SCUTUM
RETICULUM
SMC
Rigil
CAELUM
HYDRUS
TELESCOPIUM
CORONA AUSTRALIS
SERPENS CAUDA
DORADO
PAVO
LEPUS
COLUMBA
MENSA
OCTANS
APUS
ARA
LMC
Canopus
CANIS MAJOR
PICTOR
TRIANGULUM AUSTRALE
CARINA
CHAMAELEON
PUPPIS
MUSCA
CIRCINUS
NORMA
SCORPIUS
OPHIUCHUS
VOLANS
Rigil Kentaurus
Antares
Sirius
Acrux
MONOCEROS
CRUX
−60°
LUPUS
VELA
LIBRA
PYXIS
CENTAURUS
ANTLIA
−30°
HYDRA
VIRGO
Spica
SEXTANS
CRATER
CORVUS
0°
0°

Constellations

Since the earliest times, people have looked for patterns in the stars. The people of ancient Greece knew 48 constellations, named after mythical beings, though the patterns bear little resemblance to the beings they are named after. Today scientists recognize 88 constellations. These modern constellations are not just patterns of stars—they are whole segments of the sky that fit together like a jigsaw puzzle to form a complete sphere.

KEY

Deep-sky objects

Galaxy	Globular cluster	Open cluster	Planetary nebula or supernova remnant	Black hole or X-ray binary	Other deep-sky object

Star magnitudes

-1.5-0	0-0.9	1.0-1.9	2.0-2.9	3.0-3.9	4.0-4.9	5.0-5.9	6.0-6.9

Constellation widths

Hand symbols are used to indicate a constellation's apparent size in the sky. A spread hand at arm's length spans about 22° of sky, while a closed hand covers about 10°. Combinations of these symbols are used to convey the full width and depth of the constellation.

CEPHEUS

The constellation Cepheus is named after a mythical king, the husband of Queen Cassiopeia. In Greek mythology, King Cepheus and Queen Cassiopeia were told by an oracle that they must sacrifice their daughter, Princess Andromeda, to a sea monster to stop it from destroying their coastline. In a dramatic rescue, Andromeda was saved from the monster's jaws by the warrior Perseus. All the characters from this myth have constellations named after them. The stars of Cepheus form a shape like a house with a pointed roof. The most famous of its stars is Delta Cephei.

NORTHERN HEMISPHERE

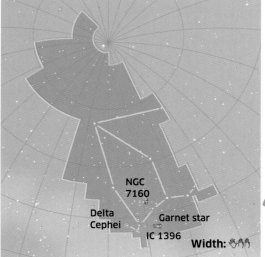

NGC 7160

Delta Cephei

Garnet star

IC 1396

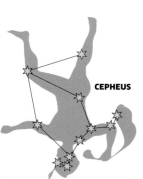

CEPHEUS

Width: 🖐🤚🤚

URSA MINOR

This constellation represents a small bear with a long tail. At the tip of its tail lies the Pole Star, called Polaris, which is the brightest star in the constellation. Ursa Minor is sometimes called the Little Dipper, because its main stars form a shape that looks like a smaller version of the Big Dipper in the constellation Ursa Major. It was one of the original constellations known to the ancient Greeks.

NORTHERN HEMISPHERE

🔭 Things to look for

Polaris
Most stars move around the sky, but Polaris stays still and is always due north. Sailors have long used this star to find their way.

URSA MINOR (THE LITTLE BEAR)

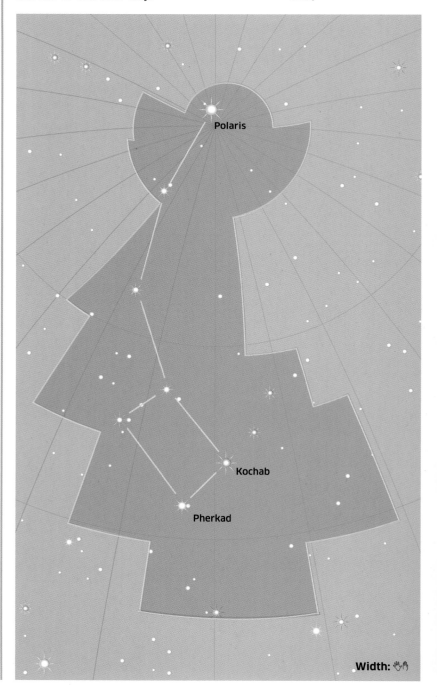

Polaris

Kochab

Pherkad

Width: 🖐🤚

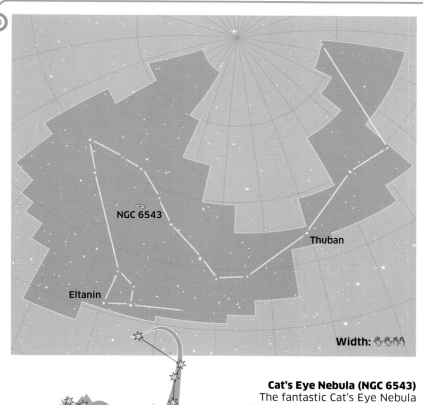

NGC 6543

Thuban

Eltanin

Width: 🖐🖐🖐

DRACO
(THE DRAGON)

DRACO

Draco is a constellation representing a dragon. In Greek mythology, this was the dragon slain by the warrior Heracles, who is represented by a neighboring constellation. The dragon's head is formed by four stars near the border with Hercules. The ancient Greeks visualized Heracles with one foot on the dragon's head. From the head, its body curls like a snake across the sky between Ursa Minor and Ursa Major. Draco's brightest star, Eltanin, lies in the dragon's head.

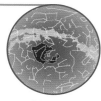

NORTHERN HEMISPHERE

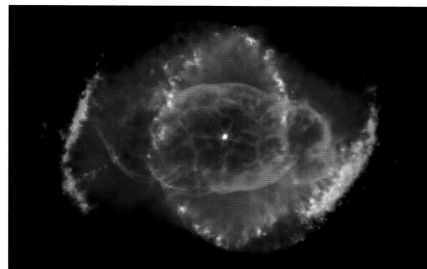

Cat's Eye Nebula (NGC 6543)
The fantastic Cat's Eye Nebula in Draco is seen here as pictured by the Hubble Space Telescope. The Cat's Eye is a type of object known as a planetary nebula, consisting of gas thrown off from a dying star. This nebula is also known by its catalog number NGC 6543.

CASSIOPEIA

A mythical queen from ancient Greece—the wife of King Cepheus and the mother of Princess Andromeda—inspired the name of this constellation. On star maps, she is depicted sitting in a chair and combing her hair. In the sky, the main stars of Cassiopeia form a W-shape, which is easy to recognize but does not really look much like a person sitting in a chair. Cassiopeia contains several interesting clusters of stars. The brightest of them can be seen with binoculars and small telescopes.

CASSIOPEIA

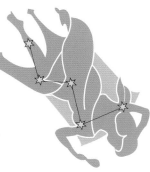

Star cluster M103
This star cluster in Cassiopeia is visible through small telescopes. Its three brightest stars form a line across the center. The star at the top right actually lies closer to us than the others, so it is not really a member of the cluster at all.

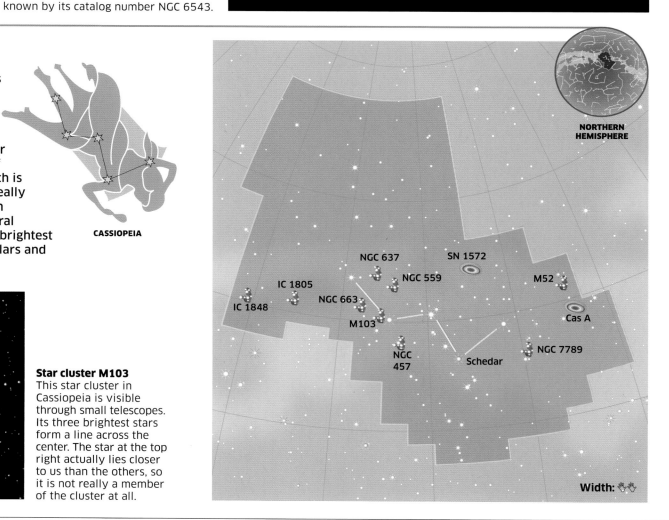

NORTHERN HEMISPHERE

NGC 637
SN 1572
IC 1805
NGC 559
M52
IC 1848
NGC 663
NGC 457
M103
Cas A
Schedar
NGC 7789

Width: 🖐🖐

CAMELOPARDALIS

Dutch astronomer Petrus Plancius devised this strangely named constellation in 1612. It represents a giraffe. The Greeks called giraffes "camel leopards" because of their long necks and spotted bodies, which is where Camelopardalis gets its name. It is difficult to spot because it contains only faint stars.

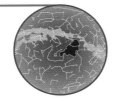

NORTHERN HEMISPHERE

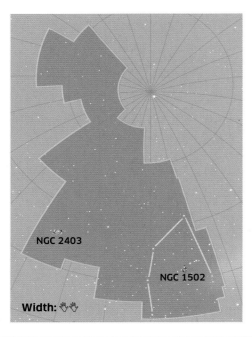

NGC 2403

NGC 1502

Width: 🖐🖐

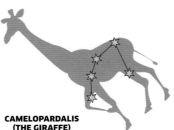

CAMELOPARDALIS (THE GIRAFFE)

LYNX

This is a faint constellation squeezed in between the constellations Ursa Major and Auriga. Polish astronomer Johannes Hevelius created it in 1687. Hevelius had very sharp eyesight, and he named the constellation Lynx because, he said, you would have to be lynx-eyed to see it. It has a number of interesting double and triple stars that can be studied with a small telescope.

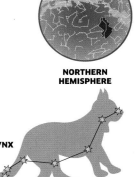

NORTHERN HEMISPHERE

LYNX

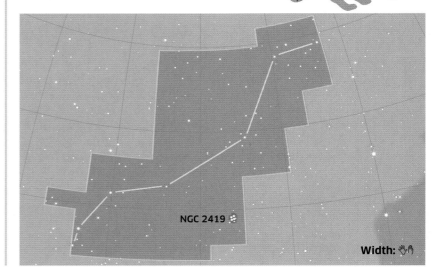

NGC 2419

Width: 🖐

AURIGA

The constellation Auriga is easy to find because it contains the star Capella, one of the brightest stars in the entire sky. To the ancient Greeks, the constellation represented a charioteer carrying a goat and two baby goats on his arm. Capella was the goat and the two fainter stars were the babies. Among the objects of interest in Auriga is a row of three star clusters, M36, M37, and M38, all visible through binoculars. The star that once marked the charioteer's right foot has now been transferred to Taurus the bull, which lies to the south.

AURIGA (THE CHARIOTEER)

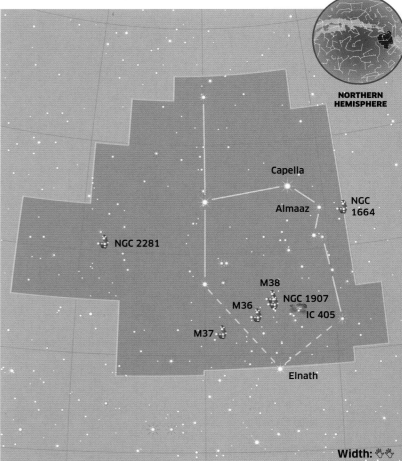

NORTHERN HEMISPHERE

Capella

NGC 1664

Almaaz

NGC 2281

M38

NGC 1907

M36

IC 405

M37

Elnath

Width: 🖐🖐

Flaming Star Nebula
The Flaming Star Nebula (IC 405) is a giant cloud of gas lit up by a hot star called AE Aurigae. The nebula can only be seen through a large telescope.

URSA MAJOR

This large constellation's name is Latin for the Great Bear, which it represents. Seven of its brightest stars form a saucepan shape, popularly known as the Big Dipper (or Plough), which is one of the best-known features in the entire sky. The two stars in the bowl of the saucepan farthest from the handle, called Merak and Dubhe, are known as the Pointers because they point toward the Pole Star, Polaris. The curving handle of the saucepan points toward the bright star Arcturus in the nearby constellation Boötes.

**URSA MAJOR
(THE GREAT BEAR)**

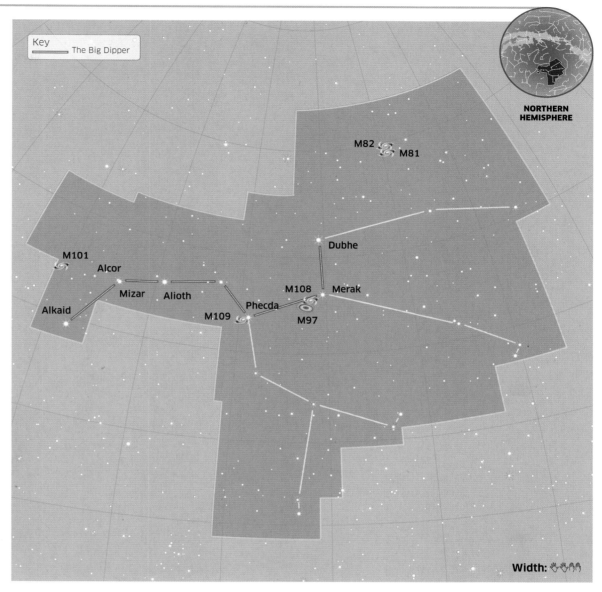

Key
—— The Big Dipper

**NORTHERN
HEMISPHERE**

M82 M81

Dubhe

M101

Alcor

Mizar Alioth

M108 Merak

Alkaid

M109 Phecda

M97

Width:

Spiral galaxy M81

In the northern part of Ursa Major lie two contrasting galaxies, known by their catalog numbers M81 and M82. M81 is a beautiful spiral, shown in this Hubble Space Telescope image (above). M82 is irregular in shape. It is thought to be undergoing a burst of star formation resulting from an encounter with M81 millions of years ago. M81 and M82 both lie about 12 million light-years away.

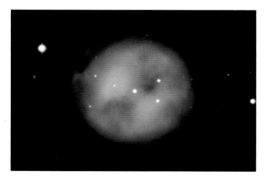

Owl Nebula

Just under the bowl of the Big Dipper, a glowing cloud of gas called M97 can be seen through a telescope. It is also called the Owl Nebula because of the two darker spots that look like the eyes of an owl. It is a planetary nebula made of gas thrown off from a dying star.

Spiral galaxy M101

Near the end of the handle of the Big Dipper lies the spiral galaxy M101. Although it is too faint to see without binoculars or a telescope, its spiral arms show up clearly on photographs. It is sometimes called the Pinwheel Galaxy.

👓 Things to look for

Mizar This is the second star in the handle of the Big Dipper. Next to it is a fainter star called Alcor, which can also be seen with the naked eye.

CANES VENATICI

This constellation was named after a pair of hunting dogs by Polish astronomer Johannes Hevelius in 1687. There are only two stars of any note in the constellation, but it also contains many interesting galaxies. Most famous of these is the Whirlpool Galaxy. This can be seen through binoculars as a faint patch of light, but a large telescope is needed to make out its spiral shape. Another object of note is the globular star cluster M3 near the constellation's southern border.

Sunflower Galaxy
Another beautiful spiral galaxy in Canes Venatici is the Sunflower Galaxy (M63), seen here through a large telescope. The star on the right is not connected with the galaxy but is much closer to us.

Whirlpool Galaxy
Seen here is a Hubble Space Telescope view of the Whirlpool Galaxy (M51), a vast spiral of stars some 30 million light-years away. Behind it, near the end of one of its arms, is a smaller galaxy, which astronomers think will one day merge with it.

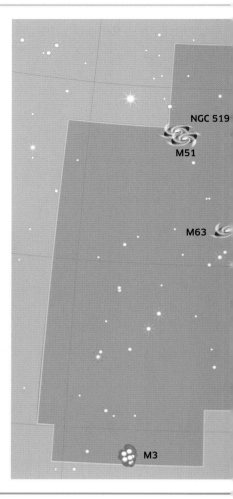

NGC 519

M51

M63

M3

BOÖTES

Boötes represents a man herding the Great Bear around the pole. He is sometimes referred to as the herdsman or bear driver. This constellation contains Arcturus, the brightest star in the northern half of the sky. It is a giant star and looks pale orange to the eye.

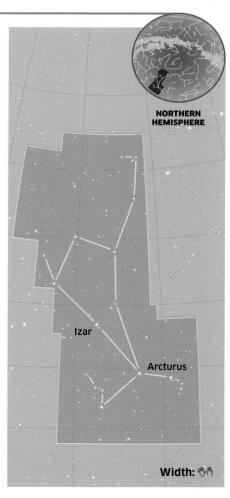

NORTHERN HEMISPHERE

Izar

Arcturus

Width: 🖐🖐

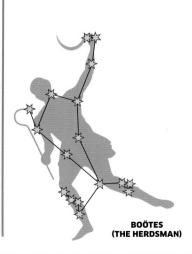

BOÖTES (THE HERDSMAN)

HERCULES

This constellation is named after Heracles, the strong man of Greek mythology (known as Hercules by Romans). In star charts he is often depicted brandishing a club and with one foot on the head of Draco, the dragon, which he killed in a fight. The stars of Hercules are not particularly bright, so the constellation can be difficult to find. Its most noticeable feature is a squashed square of four stars known as the Keystone, which marks the body of Hercules. On one side of the Keystone lies the globular cluster M13.

HERCULES

Star cluster M13
The globular cluster M13 is a ball of about 300,000 stars some 25,000 light-years away. It can be seen as a hazy patch through binoculars. Telescopes are needed to see the individual stars.

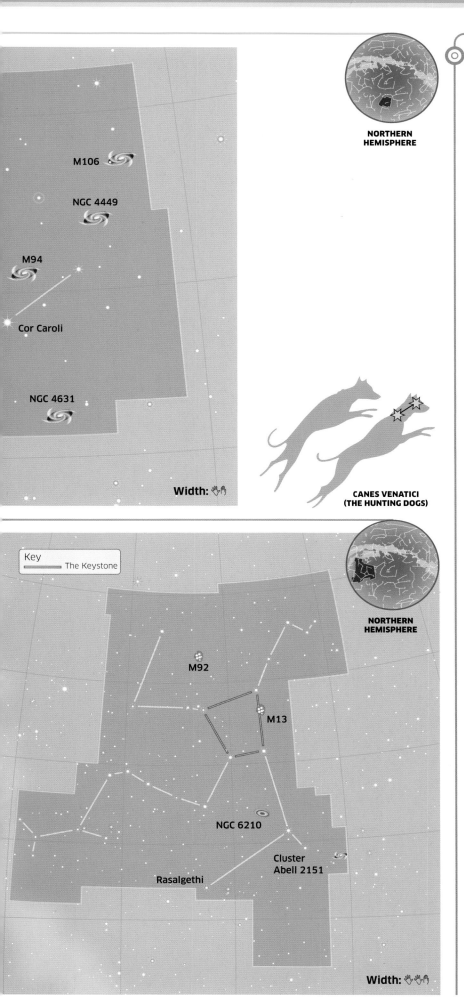

M106

NGC 4449

M94

Cor Caroli

NGC 4631

Width: 🖐🤏

NORTHERN
HEMISPHERE

**CANES VENATICI
(THE HUNTING DOGS)**

Key
— The Keystone

NORTHERN
HEMISPHERE

M92

M13

NGC 6210

Cluster
Abell 2151

Rasalgethi

Width: 🖐🖐🤏

LYRA

NORTHERN
HEMISPHERE

The constellation Lyra represents a small harp,
known to the Greeks as a lyre. In mythology,
it was the instrument played by the musician
Orpheus. Lyra is easy to spot because it contains
Vega, the fifth-brightest star in the entire sky,
25 light-years away. Vega forms one corner
of the Summer Triangle—a triangle formed by
bright stars in three different constellations.

LYRA (THE LYRE)

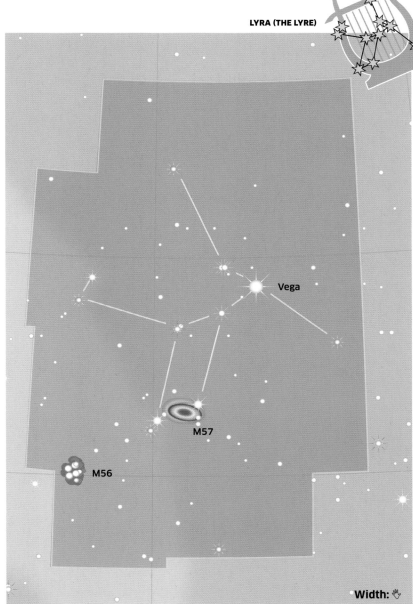

Vega

M57

M56

Width: 🖐

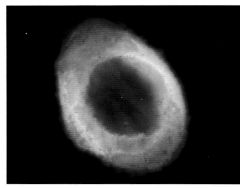

Ring Nebula
The Ring Nebula (M57), seen
here through the Hubble
Space Telescope, is a shell of
glowing gas. At its center is
a white dwarf, the remains
of the star that lost its outer
layers to form the nebula.

CYGNUS

The ancient Greeks visualized Cygnus as a swan flying along the Milky Way. Its brightest star, Deneb, marks its tail, while the star Albireo is its beak. In mythology, the swan was the disguise used by the god Zeus when he visited Queen Leda of Sparta. The overall shape of the constellation resembles a large cross, so it is sometimes known as the Northern Cross. One of the most exciting objects in Cygnus lies in the swan's neck—a black hole called Cygnus X-1. The black hole itself cannot be seen from Earth, but satellites in space have detected X-rays from hot gas falling into it from a nearby star.

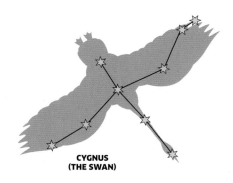

CYGNUS
(THE SWAN)

👀 Things to look for

Albireo In the head of the swan lies a beautiful colored double star known as Albireo. To the naked eye it appears as a single star, but small telescopes show it as a pair. The brighter star is orange, and the fainter one is blue-green.

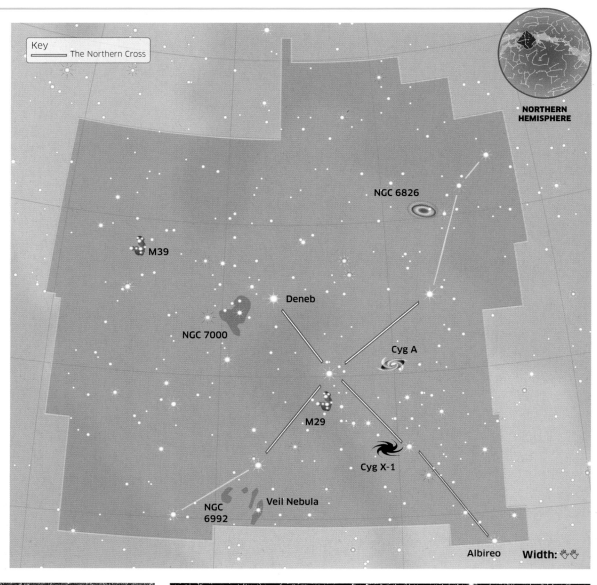

Key
— The Northern Cross

NORTHERN HEMISPHERE

NGC 6826

M39

Deneb

NGC 7000

Cyg A

M29

Cyg X-1

Veil Nebula

NGC 6992

Albireo   Width: 👋👋

North America Nebula
Near Deneb lies a cloud of gas popularly known as the North America Nebula (NGC 7000) because of its shape, which resembles the continent of North America. The nebula cannot be seen without a telescope and shows up best in color photographs like the one here.

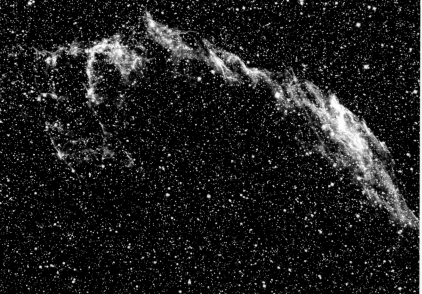

Veil Nebula
In one wing of the swan lie streamers of gas from a star that exploded as a supernova thousands of years ago. The shattered remains of that star are splashed across an area wider than six full moons, forming the Veil Nebula.

ANDROMEDA

This constellation is named after a princess of Greek mythology who was chained to a rock by her parents, King Cepheus and Queen Cassiopeia, as a sacrifice to a sea monster. Fortunately, she was rescued in the nick of time by the hero Perseus, who lies next to her in the sky. Andromeda's head is marked by the star known as Alpheratz. In ancient times, this star was shared with the constellation Pegasus.

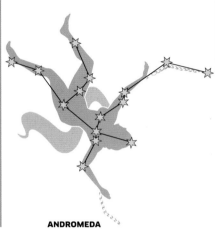

ANDROMEDA

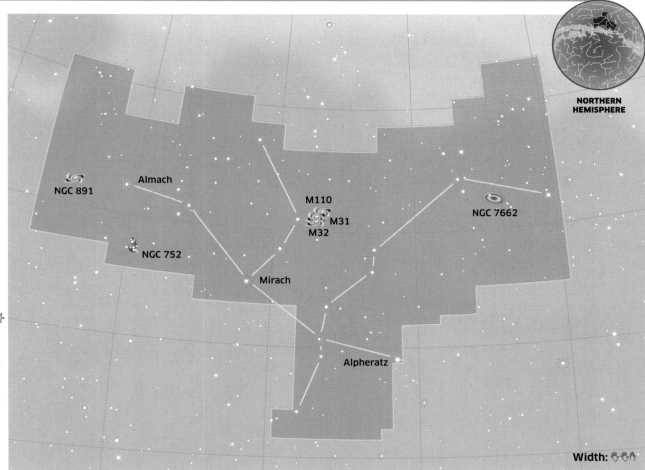

NORTHERN HEMISPHERE

NGC 891

Almach

M110

M31

M32

NGC 7662

NGC 752

Mirach

Alpheratz

Width: 🖐🖐🖐

LACERTA

This small figure represents a lizard scuttling between Andromeda and Cygnus. It was devised in 1687 by the Polish astronomer Johannes Hevelius from some faint stars that had not previously been part of any constellation. Of particular note is an object called BL Lacertae. Once thought to be an unusual variable star, it is now known to be the core of an active galaxy.

LACERTA (THE LIZARD)

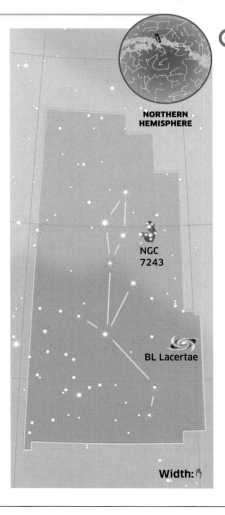

NORTHERN HEMISPHERE

NGC 7243

BL Lacertae

Width: 🖐

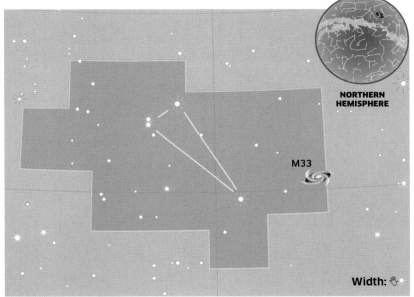

NORTHERN HEMISPHERE

M33

Width: 🖐

TRIANGULUM

To the ancient Greeks, this small, triangular constellation just south of Andromeda represented either the delta of the Nile River or the island of Sicily. Its main feature is M33, a spiral galaxy faintly visible through binoculars. M33 lies nearly 3 million light-years away and is the third-largest member of our Local Group of galaxies.

TRIANGULUM (THE TRIANGLE)

PERSEUS

The constellation Perseus is named after a hero of Greek mythology who was sent to cut off the head of Medusa, an evil character known as a Gorgon. In the sky, Perseus is seen holding his sword aloft in his right hand, with the head of Medusa in his left. The head is marked by the variable star Algol.

NORTHERN HEMISPHERE

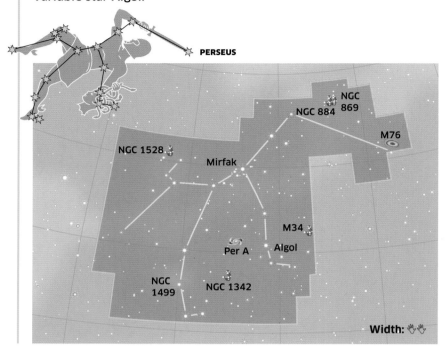

PERSEUS

NGC 869
NGC 884
M76
NGC 1528
Mirfak
M34
Per A
Algol
NGC 1499
NGC 1342

Width: 🖐️🖐️

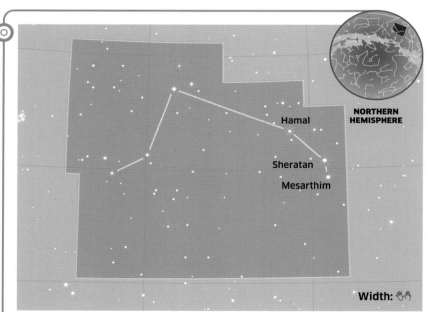

NORTHERN HEMISPHERE

Hamal

Sheratan
Mesarthim

Width: 🖐️🖐️

ARIES

Aries represents a ram with a golden fleece in Greek mythology. According to legend, Jason and the Argonauts made an epic voyage from Greece to the Black Sea to collect and bring back the fleece. The constellation's most obvious feature is a crooked line of three stars south of Triangulum. The most southerly (and faintest) of these stars, Mesarthim, is a double star that is easily divided by small telescopes.

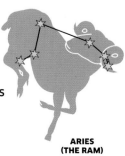

ARIES
(THE RAM)

CANCER

This constellation represents a crab that had a minor role in Greek mythology. According to the story, when Heracles was fighting the multiheaded Hydra, the crab bit him but was then crushed underfoot. Cancer is the faintest of the 12 constellations of the zodiac. Near its center is a large, hazy star cluster with several alternative names: the Beehive, Praesepe, the Manger, or simply M44.

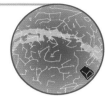

NORTHERN HEMISPHERE

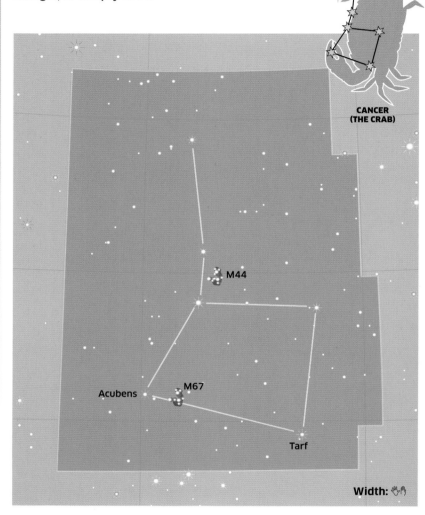

CANCER
(THE CRAB)

M44

Acubens
M67

Tarf

Width: 🖐️🖐️

Beehive Cluster
M44 is an open cluster made of stars that lie about 577 light-years from Earth. While the cluster can be seen by the naked eye, most of its stars are visible only with binoculars or a telescope.

TAURUS

Taurus the bull is one of the most magnificent and interesting constellations in the sky. In Greek mythology, the god Zeus turned himself into a bull to carry off Princess Europa to the island of Crete. The brightest star in the constellation is Aldebaran, a red giant that marks the glinting eye of the bull. The star at the tip of the bull's right horn, Elnath, was once shared with Auriga to the north.

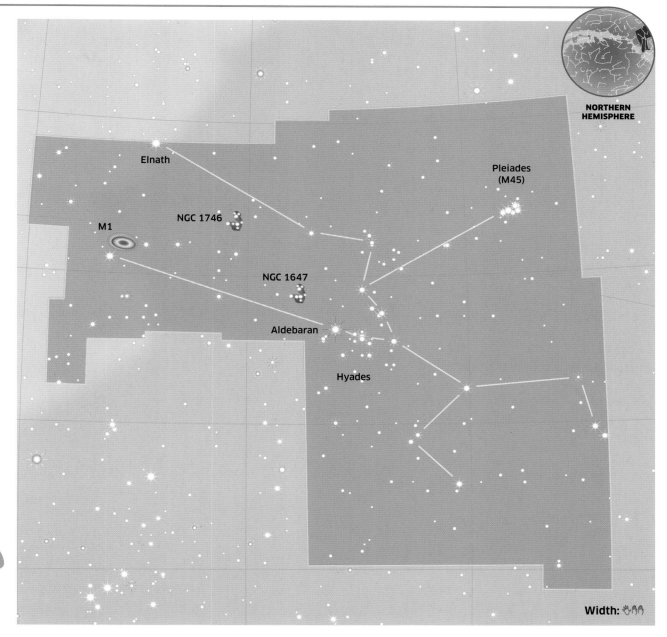

NORTHERN
HEMISPHERE

Elnath

Pleiades
(M45)

NGC 1746

M1

NGC 1647

Aldebaran

Hyades

Width: ✋👌👌

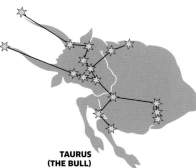

**TAURUS
(THE BULL)**

Pleiades

The Pleiades Cluster, popularly known as the Seven Sisters, is a beautiful star group. Six or more stars can be seen with the naked eye, and binoculars show dozens. Photographs reveal even more, along with a haze of dust that surrounds them.

Crab Nebula

In the year 1054, a new star appeared temporarily in Taurus. This was a supernova, the most violent form of stellar explosion. Now only visible through telescopes, the star's shattered remains can be seen as the Crab Nebula (M1). This image was taken with the Hubble Space Telescope.

Hyades

The face of the bull is marked by a V-shaped group of stars called the Hyades, easily visible to the naked eye. The bright star Aldebaran (in yellow) appears to be one of the Hyades but is, in fact, closer to us and lies in front of the cluster by chance.

GEMINI

Gemini represents the mythical twins Castor and Pollux. The two brightest stars in the constellation are named after the twins and mark their heads. A small telescope shows that Castor is a double star. These two stars orbit each other every 500 years or so. Larger telescopes show a fainter red dwarf near them. Special instruments have revealed that each of these three stars is itself a close double, making Castor a family of six stars, all linked by gravity.

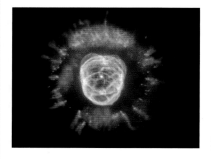

Eskimo Nebula
The Eskimo Nebula (NGC 2392) is a remarkable planetary nebula. It gets its popular name from its resemblance to a face surrounded by a fur-lined hood. Another name for it is the Clown-face Nebula.

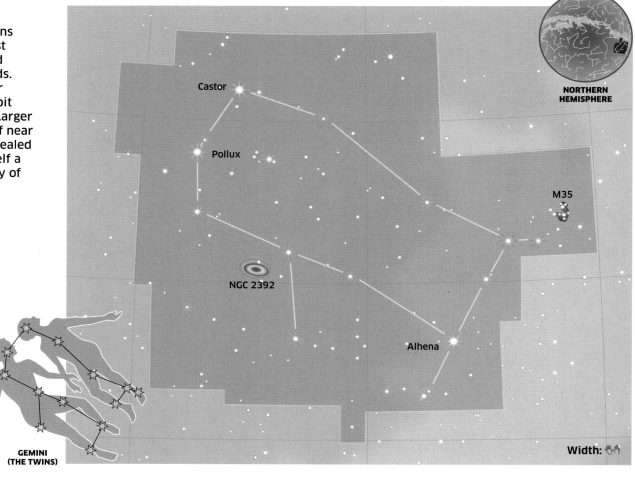

NORTHERN HEMISPHERE

Castor

Pollux

M35

NGC 2392

Alhena

Width:

GEMINI (THE TWINS)

LEO MINOR

This small constellation represents a lion cub. Polish astronomer Johannes Hevelius introduced it in 1687. Leo Minor contains very few objects of interest. The star R Leonis Minoris is a red giant. Its brightness varies at regular intervals—it can be seen with binoculars at its brightest but is not visible even through small telescopes at its dimmest.

NORTHERN HEMISPHERE

LEO MINOR (THE LITTLE LION)

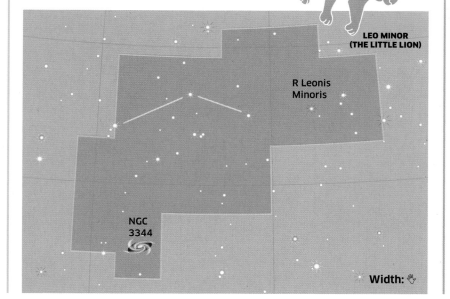

R Leonis Minoris

NGC 3344

Width:

COMA BERENICES

This is a faint but interesting constellation near the tail of Leo, the lion. The ancient Greeks imagined it as the hair of Queen Berenice of Egypt. She cut off her hair to thank the gods after her husband returned safely from fighting a war in Asia. Dozens of faint stars form a wedge-shaped group called the Coma Star Cluster, easily seen in binoculars.

NORTHERN HEMISPHERE

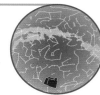

COMA BERENICES (BERENICE'S HAIR)

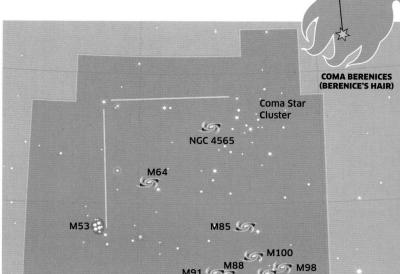

Coma Star Cluster

NGC 4565

M64

M53

M85

M100

M91   M88   M98

M99

Width:

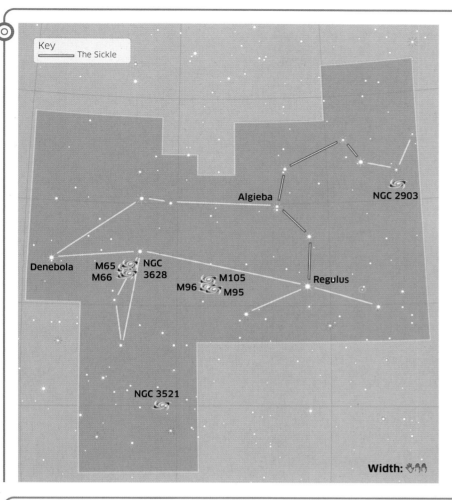

Key
The Sickle

Algieba

NGC 2903

Denebola

M65
M66

NGC
3628

M105

M96
M95

Regulus

NGC 3521

Width: 🖐👊👊

LEO

This is one of the few constellations that really looks like what it is supposed to represent—in this case, a crouching lion. In Greek mythology, it was said to be the lion slain by the warrior Heracles as one of his 12 labors. An arc of stars called the Sickle (marked here in purple) forms the lion's head and chest. Leo's brightest star, Regulus, lies at the base of the Sickle. One of the stars in the Sickle, Algieba, can be seen as a double star through small telescopes.

NORTHERN HEMISPHERE

LEO (THE LION)

Spiral galaxy M66
M66 is a beautiful spiral galaxy that lies underneath the hind quarters of Leo, the lion. It forms a pair with another galaxy, M65. They can be glimpsed with small telescopes under good conditions, but large instruments help to see them clearly.

VIRGO

Virgo is the second-largest constellation. In Greek mythology, it represented both the goddess of justice and the goddess of agriculture. The main stars of Virgo form a lazy "Y" shape. The constellation's brightest star, Spica, is at the base of the Y. The star Porrima, in the middle of the Y, is a double star divisible with a small telescope. In the bowl of the Y is the Virgo Cluster—a cluster of more than 1,000 galaxies about 55 million light-years away.

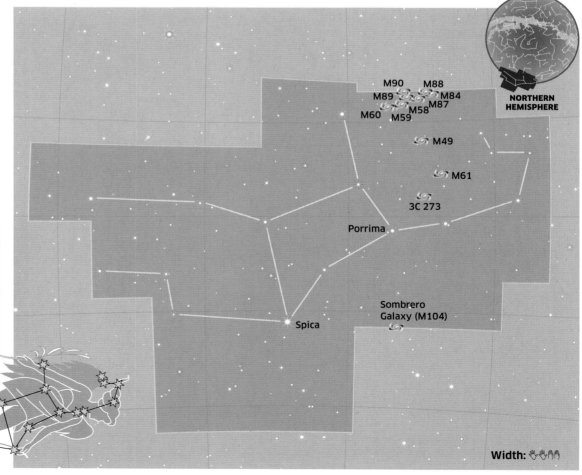

M90 M88
M89 M84
M87
M60 M59
M58

NORTHERN HEMISPHERE

M49

M61

3C 273

Porrima

Spica

Sombrero Galaxy (M104)

VIRGO (THE VIRGIN)

Width: 🖐🖐👊👊

Sombrero Galaxy
The Sombrero Galaxy (M104) is a spiral galaxy seen edge-on that resembles a Mexican sombrero hat. This view of it was taken by the Hubble Space Telescope. The Sombrero is 30 million light-years away, closer to us than the Virgo Cluster of galaxies.

LIBRA

The scales of justice are represented by Libra and are held by the goddess of justice, Virgo, who lies next to Libra in the sky. Libra's stars represented the claws of the scorpion, Scorpius, until Roman times.

SOUTHERN HEMISPHERE

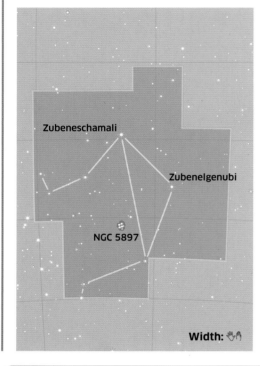

Zubeneschamali

Zubenelgenubi

NGC 5897

Width: 🖐🖐

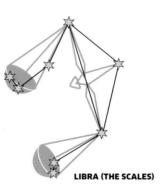

LIBRA (THE SCALES)

🔭 Things to look for

Zubenelgenubi This is a wide, double star easily spotted with binoculars or even sharp eyesight. Its strange name comes from the Arabic for "the southern claw."

SERPENS

The constellation Serpens represents a large snake being held by the man in the constellation Ophiuchus. The head of the snake lies on one side of Ophiuchus, the tail on the other. This is the only example of a constellation being split into two. However, the two halves count as only one constellation. Near the neck of the snake lies M5, one of the best globular clusters in the northern skies, just visible through binoculars. Binoculars will also show an open cluster called IC 4756 near the snake's tail.

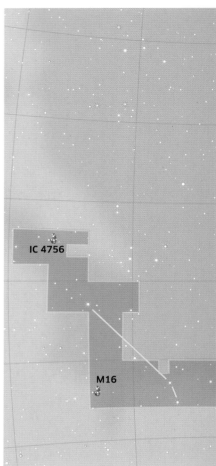

IC 4756

M16

SERPENS (THE SERPENT)

CORONA BOREALIS

Shaped like a horseshoe, this constellation represents the jeweled crown worn by Princess Ariadne of Crete when she married the god Dionysus. Within the arc of the crown lies a very unusual variable star, R Coronae Borealis. This is a yellow supergiant that suddenly drops in brightness every few years.

CORONA BOREALIS (THE NORTHERN CROWN)

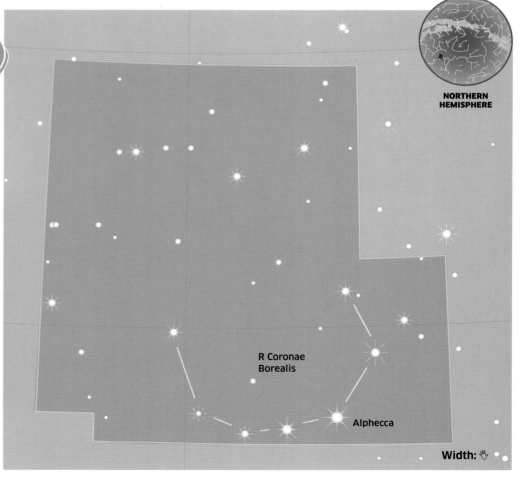

NORTHERN HEMISPHERE

R Coronae Borealis

Alphecca

Width: 🖐

Jewel in the crown
Alphecca is the brightest member of the arc of seven stars that makes up the northern crown, Corona Borealis.

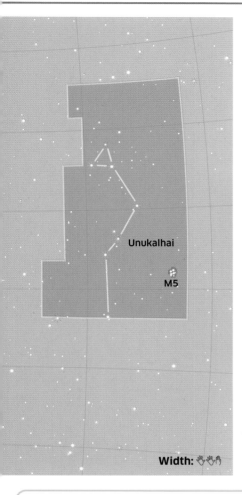

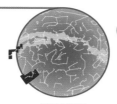

Unukalhai

M5

Width:

Eagle Nebula
In the tail section of Serpens lies
a star cluster called M16, visible
through binoculars. Surrounding it
is a glowing cloud of gas called the
Eagle Nebula, seen here through a
large telescope in Chile.

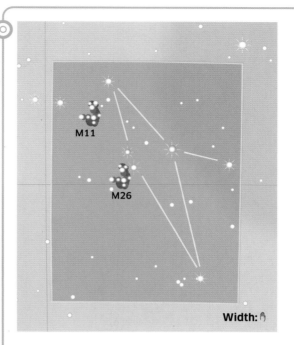

M11

M26

Width:

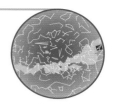

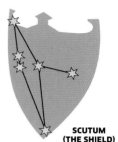

SCUTUM
(THE SHIELD)

SCUTUM

This small constellation represents a shield. It was created
in the late 17th century by the Polish astronomer Johannes
Hevelius. One of the brightest parts of the Milky Way lies in
the northern half of this constellation and is known as the
Scutum Star Cloud. Near the border with the constellation
Aquila is M11, a star cluster often called the Wild Duck
Cluster because its shape resembles a flock of birds in flight.

OPHIUCHUS

This constellation represents the god of medicine.
In the sky, he is depicted holding a large snake:
the constellation Serpens. Ophiuchus contains
several globular clusters that can be seen with
binoculars and small telescopes. The brightest
of them are M10 and M12.

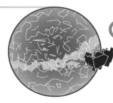

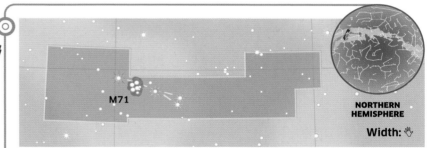

M71

Width:

SAGITTA

The third-smallest constellation in the
sky, Sagitta represents an arrow. It was
one of the original constellations known to
the ancient Greeks, who said that the arrow was
shot either by Heracles, which lies next to it, or by
one of the gods. Although its stars are faint, it is
quite easy to recognize.

SAGITTA
(THE ARROW)

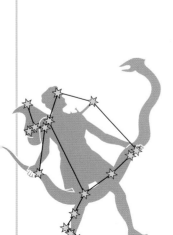

OPHIUCHUS
(THE SERPENT HOLDER)

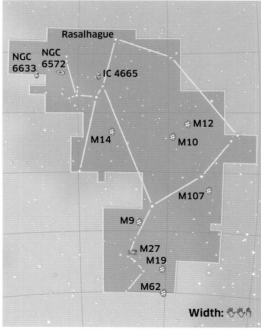

Rasalhague

NGC
6633

NGC
6572

IC 4665

M14

M12

M10

M107

M9

M27

M19

M62

Width:

Globular cluster M71
Sagitta contains a faint globular
cluster, M71, visible through
small telescopes. It measures
about 27 light-years wide and
is thought to be about 10 billion
years old.

AQUILA

Aquila represents a flying eagle, one of the disguises that was said in mythology to have been adopted by the Greek god Zeus. Its main star is Altair, which marks one corner of the Summer Triangle—a famous triangle made of bright stars from different constellations. The other two stars of the triangle are Vega in Lyra and Deneb in Cygnus. The most interesting feature in Aquila is Eta Aquilae, one of the brightest examples of the type of variable star known as a Cepheid.

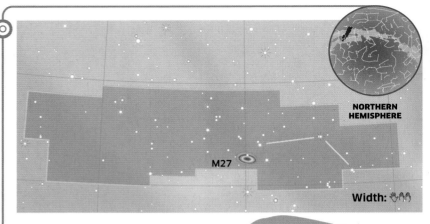

NORTHERN HEMISPHERE

AQUILA (THE EAGLE)

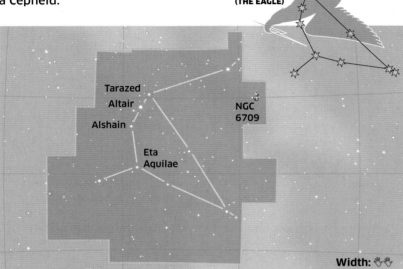

Tarazed
Altair
Alshain
NGC 6709
Eta Aquilae

Width: 🖐️🤚

VULPECULA

Polish astronomer Johannes Hevelius named this faint constellation in the late 17th century. It represents a fox. An attractive object for binoculars is a group of stars called the Coathanger, shaped like a bar with a hook on top.

M27

NORTHERN HEMISPHERE

Width: 🖐️🤚🤚

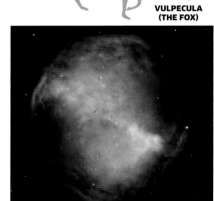

VULPECULA (THE FOX)

Dumbbell Nebula
A famous object in the constellation Vulpecula is the Dumbbell Nebula (M27). This planetary nebula (a shell of gas thrown off from a dying star) can be seen with binoculars on clear nights.

DELPHINUS

This attractive constellation represents a dolphin. In mythology, this was the dolphin that rescued the Greek musician Arion when he jumped overboard from a ship to escape a band of robbers. The constellation's two brightest stars bear the odd names Sualocin and Rotanev. Read backward, they spell Nicolaus Venator, the name of an Italian astronomer who is thought to have cunningly named them after himself.

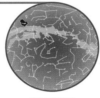

NORTHERN HEMISPHERE

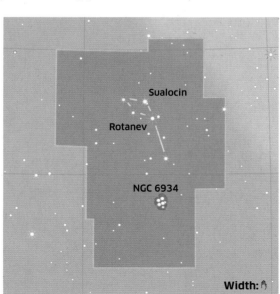

Sualocin
Rotanev
NGC 6934

Width: ☝️

DELPHINUS (THE DOLPHIN)

EQUULEUS

Equuleus is the second-smallest constellation in the sky, representing the head of a foal. It lies next to the large flying horse Pegasus and was one of the constellations known to the ancient Greeks. There is little of interest in it apart from a double star, Gamma Equulei, that can easily be divided with binoculars.

NORTHERN HEMISPHERE

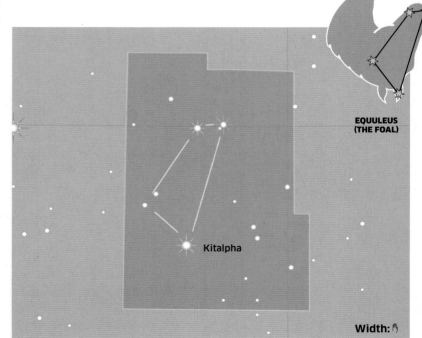

EQUULEUS (THE FOAL)

Kitalpha

Width: ☝️

PEGASUS

This large constellation of the northern sky represents a flying horse in Greek mythology. Its most noticeable feature is a pattern called the Great Square, formed by four stars that outline the horse's body. However, only three stars of the Square actually belong to Pegasus, as the fourth is over the border in Andromeda (although, in the past, it was shared by the two constellations). The Square is so large that 30 full moons placed side by side could fit inside it. The horse's nose is marked by the star Enif.

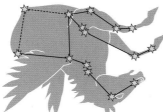

**PEGASUS
(THE WINGED HORSE)**

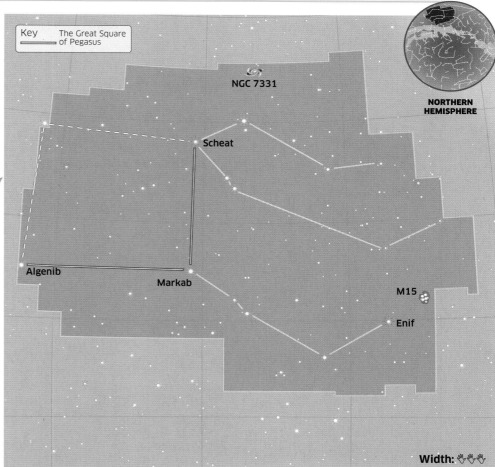

NGC 7331

NORTHERN HEMISPHERE

Scheat

Algenib

Markab

M15

Enif

Width: 🖐🖐

Globular cluster M15
Near the star Enif lies M15, one of the finest globular clusters in northern skies. This is easily visible through binoculars as a fuzzy patch. Telescopes reveal it as a vast ball of stars.

AQUARIUS

The constellation Aquarius represents a young man pouring water from a jar. The jar is represented by a little group of stars around Zeta Aquarii. A string of fainter stars cascading southward represents the flow of water. In the north of the constellation lies the globular cluster M2, visible as a faint patch through binoculars. Two famous planetary nebulae (remains of dying stars) can be found in Aquarius with telescopes.

**AQUARIUS
(THE WATER CARRIER)**

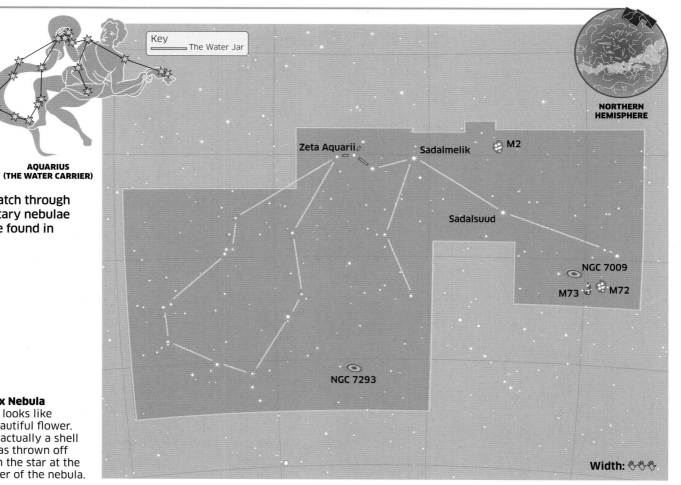

Key   The Water Jar

NORTHERN HEMISPHERE

Zeta Aquarii

Sadalmelik

M2

Sadalsuud

NGC 7009

M73   M72

NGC 7293

Width: 🖐🖐🖐

Helix Nebula
This looks like a beautiful flower. It is actually a shell of gas thrown off from the star at the center of the nebula.

PISCES

Pisces represents two fish with their tails tied together by ribbons. The star Alrescha marks the knot joining the two ribbons. The constellation depicts the Greek myth in which Aphrodite and her son Eros turned themselves into fish to escape from a monster, Typhon. A loop of seven stars called the Circlet marks the body of one of the fish. Pisces includes M74, a beautiful face-on spiral galaxy just visible through small telescopes.

NORTHERN HEMISPHERE

PISCES (THE FISHES)

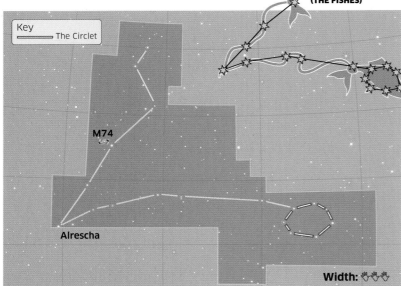

Key
— The Circlet

M74

Alrescha

Width: 🖐🖐🖐

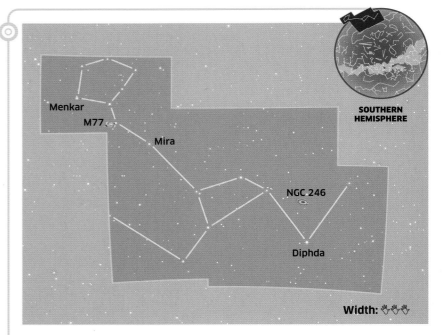

SOUTHERN HEMISPHERE

Menkar

M77

Mira

NGC 246

Diphda

Width: 🖐🖐🖐

CETUS

Cetus, the sea monster, is the fourth-largest constellation. In Greek mythology, Andromeda was chained to a rock as a sacrifice to the monster, but Perseus saved her. In the neck of Cetus lies Mira, a famous variable star. When at its brightest, Mira is easily visible to the naked eye, but it fades from view for months at a time.

CETUS (THE SEA MONSTER)

CANIS MAJOR

The constellation Canis Major and nearby Canis Minor represent the dogs of Orion. Canis Major contains the brightest star in the night sky, Sirius, which lies 8.6 light-years away. South of Sirius is the star cluster M41, which is just visible to the naked eye under clear dark skies and is a beautiful sight through binoculars.

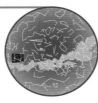

SOUTHERN HEMISPHERE

CANIS MAJOR (THE LARGE DOG)

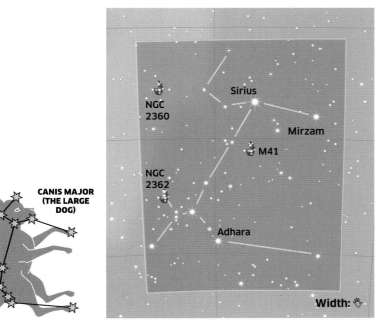

NGC 2360

Sirius

Mirzam

M41

NGC 2362

Adhara

Width: 🖐

CANIS MINOR

Canis Minor is the smaller of the two dogs of Orion. Its main star, Procyon, is the eighth brightest in the sky. Procyon forms a large triangle with the other Dog Star (Sirius in Canis Major) and Betelgeuse in Orion. Both Procyon and Sirius are orbited by white dwarf stars, but these companions can be seen only with large telescopes. There is little else of interest in this constellation.

SOUTHERN HEMISPHERE

CANIS MINOR (THE LITTLE DOG)

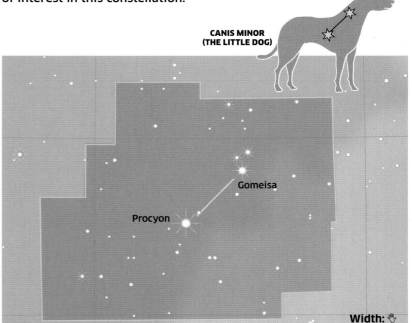

Gomeisa

Procyon

Width: 🖐

ORION

This constellation represents a giant hunter of Greek mythology. In the sky, he is depicted raising his club and shield against Taurus the bull, the constellation next to him. The bright star Betelgeuse marks Orion's right shoulder and Rigel is his left foot. Betelgeuse is a red supergiant, which varies slightly in brightness, while Rigel, another supergiant star, is hotter and bluer. One feature that makes Orion easy to identify is the line of three stars that mark his belt. From the belt hangs his sword, which contains one of the treasures of the sky, the Orion Nebula.

**ORION
(THE HUNTER)**

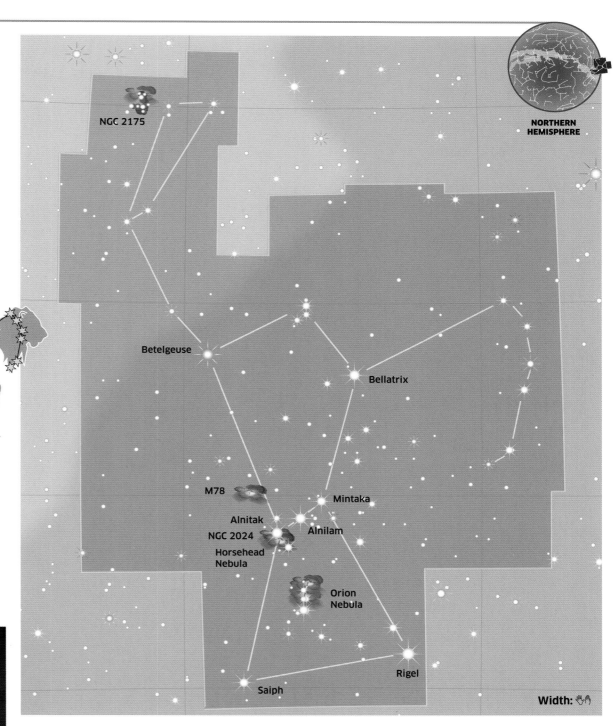

NORTHERN
HEMISPHERE

NGC 2175

Betelgeuse

Bellatrix

M78

Alnitak

NGC 2024

Horsehead
Nebula

Mintaka

Alnilam

Orion
Nebula

Rigel

Saiph

Width: ✋✋

Trapezium
At the center of the Orion Nebula lies a group of four stars called the Trapezium, which can be seen through small telescopes. Light from these newborn stars helps make the surrounding gas glow.

Horsehead Nebula
Looking like a knight in a celestial chess game, the Horsehead Nebula is a dark cloud of dust, seen here through a large telescope in Chile. The nebula is located just below the star Alnitak in Orion's belt. The background nebula is faint and the Horsehead shows up well only on photographs.

Orion Nebula
The Orion Nebula, a large star-forming cloud of gas, looks like a patch of mist in binoculars and small telescopes, but when pictured by the Hubble Space Telescope, its full complexity and color can be seen.

MONOCEROS

This constellation represents a unicorn, the mythical beast with a single horn. Dutch astronomer and map-maker Petrus Plancius introduced it in the early 17th century in a gap between Greek constellations. One feature of interest is Beta Monocerotis, which is an excellent triple star for small telescopes. Three attractive star clusters for binoculars or small telescopes are M50, NGC 2244, and NGC 2264.

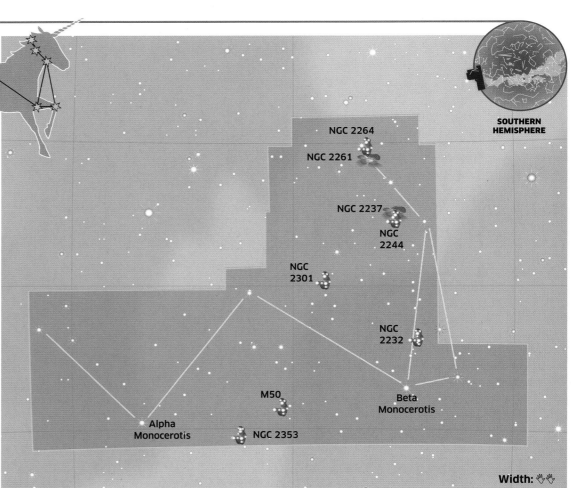

SOUTHERN HEMISPHERE

NGC 2264
NGC 2261
NGC 2237
NGC 2244
NGC 2301
NGC 2232
M50
Beta Monocerotis
Alpha Monocerotis
NGC 2353

Width: 🖐🖐

Rosette Nebula
The star cluster NGC 2244 lies within a flowerlike cloud of gas known as the Rosette Nebula. The star cluster can easily be seen with binoculars, but the nebula, glowing like a pink carnation, shows up only on photographs.

HYDRA

This is the largest constellation of all, stretching more than a quarter of the way around the sky. In Greek mythology, Hydra was a monster with many heads, although in the sky it has only one head, represented by a loop of five stars. Its brightest star is called Alphard, meaning "the solitary one," because it lies in a fairly blank area of sky. M48, near the border with Monoceros, is a star cluster visible through binoculars and small telescopes.

SOUTHERN HEMISPHERE

HYDRA (THE WATER SNAKE)

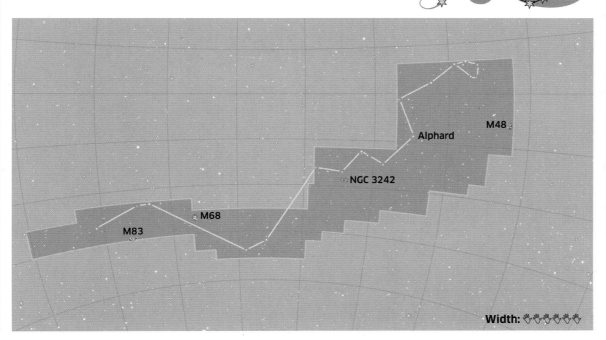

M48
Alphard
NGC 3242
M68
M83

Width: 🖐🖐🖐🖐🖐

Spiral galaxy M83
Sometimes known as the Southern Pinwheel, M83 is a beautiful spiral galaxy 15 million light-years away. It can be seen as a faint patch through small telescopes, but larger instruments are needed to bring out the beauty of its spiral arms.

ANTLIA

This is a small, faint southern constellation invented in the 1750s by the French astronomer Nicolas-Louis de Lacaille. Its name, which means "pump," commemorates the invention of a kind of air pump. The constellation's most impressive feature is a spiral galaxy called NGC 2997. This is too faint to see with small telescopes but shows up beautifully on photographs, which reveal clouds of pink gas dotted along its arms.

SOUTHERN HEMISPHERE

ANTLIA (THE AIR PUMP)

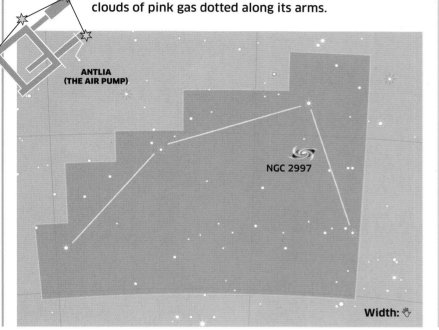

NGC 2997

Width: 🖐

SEXTANS

A faint constellation that was invented in the late 17th century by the Polish astronomer Johannes Hevelius, Sextans represents an instrument called a sextant, which was used for measuring star positions. Sextans contains the Spindle Galaxy (NGC 3115), a galaxy several times larger than our Milky Way.

SOUTHERN HEMISPHERE

SEXTANS (THE SEXTANT)

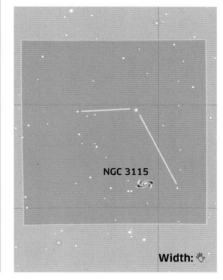

NGC 3115

Width: ✋

Spindle Galaxy
This galaxy appears rod-shaped because we see it edge-on. It is also known by its catalog number NGC 3115.

CRATER

The word "crater" is Latin for cup, and this constellation represents the cup of the Greek god Apollo. In Greek mythology, Apollo sent a crow to fetch water in the cup. The greedy bird was late because it stopped to eat figs. It blamed the delay on a snake, but Apollo realized what had happened and punished the crow for lying by placing it in the sky, along with the cup and the snake. Crater contains no major objects of interest for users of small telescopes.

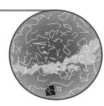

SOUTHERN HEMISPHERE

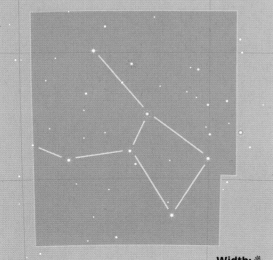

Width: 🖐

CRATER (THE CUP)

CORVUS

Corvus represents a crow that was sent to fetch water in a cup by the god Apollo. It lies next to Crater, which represents the cup. Both lie on the back of Hydra, the water snake. The constellation's most amazing feature is a pair of colliding galaxies called the Antennae—NGC 4038 and 4039. Large telescopes reveal long streamers of gas and stars stretching away from the galaxies like the antennae (feelers) of an insect.

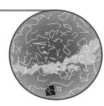

SOUTHERN HEMISPHERE

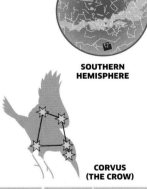

CORVUS (THE CROW)

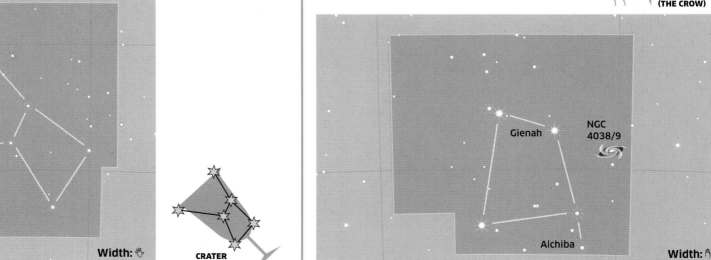

Gienah

NGC 4038/9

Alchiba

Width: ✊

CENTAURUS

Centaurs were mythical creatures of ancient Greece, half-man, half-horse. This constellation represents a centaur called Chiron, who taught the children of the Greek gods. Small telescopes show that its brightest star, Alpha Centauri, is a double star. There is also a third star: a red dwarf called Proxima Centauri, which is the closest star to the Sun at 4.2 light-years away.

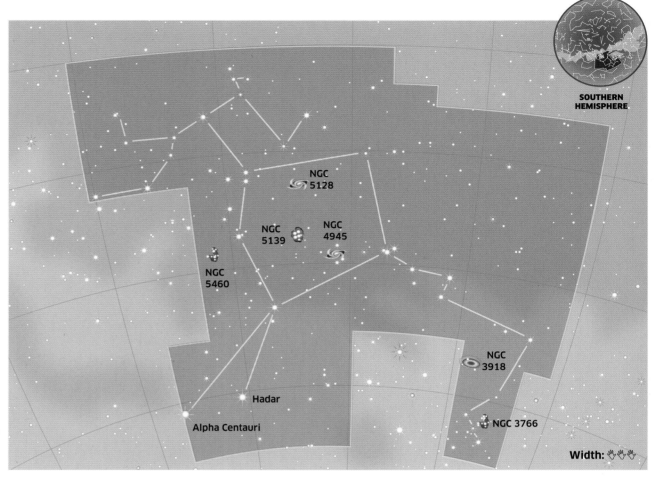

SOUTHERN HEMISPHERE

NGC 5128

NGC 5139

NGC 4945

NGC 5460

NGC 3918

Hadar

Alpha Centauri

NGC 3766

Width:

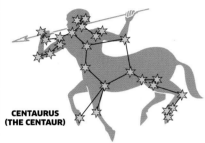

CENTAURUS
(THE CENTAUR)

CRUX

Popularly known as the Southern Cross, this is the smallest of all the 88 constellations. Its brightest star, Acrux, is a double star that is easily separated by small telescopes. Near Mimosa lies NGC 4755, popularly known as the Jewel Box, a beautiful cluster of stars easily visible through binoculars and small telescopes. A dark cloud of dust called the Coalsack Nebula can be seen against the bright Milky Way background.

SOUTHERN HEMISPHERE

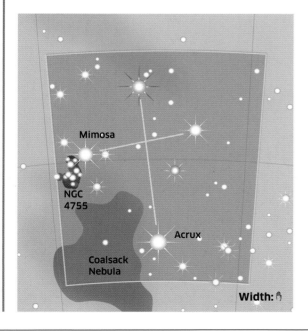

Mimosa

NGC 4755

Acrux

Coalsack Nebula

Width:

CRUX
(THE SOUTHERN CROSS)

LUPUS

This constellation represents a wolf. Ancient Greek astronomers imagined it as being held on a spear by Centaurus, the centaur. Lupus contains several interesting double stars. In the southern part of the constellation lies a star cluster with the catalog number NGC 5822.

SOUTHERN HEMISPHERE

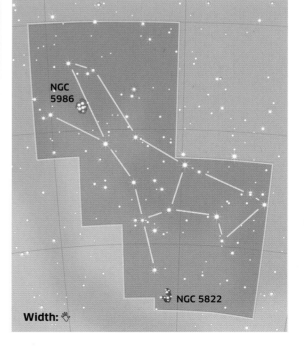

NGC 5986

NGC 5822

Width:

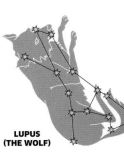

LUPUS
(THE WOLF)

SAGITTARIUS

This constellation represents an archer drawing his bow and is depicted as a centaur. The eight main stars of Sagittarius form a shape known as the Teapot. Near the lid of the Teapot lies M22, a large globular cluster easily visible through binoculars. There are several fine nebulae in Sagittarius, including the Trifid Nebula (M20).

SAGITTARIUS (THE ARCHER)

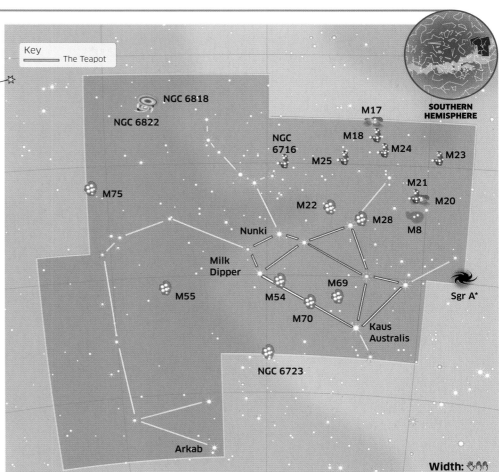

Key
—— The Teapot

NGC 6818
NGC 6822
M17
M18
NGC 6716
M24
M23
M25
M21
M75
M20
M22
M28
M8
Nunki
Milk Dipper
M69
M55
M54
Sgr A*
M70
Kaus Australis
NGC 6723
Arkab

SOUTHERN HEMISPHERE

Width: 🤚🤚🤚

Trifid Nebula
The Trifid Nebula (M20) is a colorful combination of pink gas and blue dust. Its full beauty is revealed on photographs taken with large telescopes, as seen here.

SCORPIUS

This constellation represents the scorpion that stung Orion to death in a story from Greek mythology. At the scorpion's heart lies Antares, a red supergiant hundreds of times larger than the Sun. Next to Antares is M4, a large globular cluster visible through binoculars. At the end of the scorpion's curling tail is a large star cluster, M7, just visible to the naked eye as a brighter spot in the Milky Way. Near to it is M6, smaller and best seen through small telescopes. Another beautiful star cluster for binoculars is NGC 6231.

SOUTHERN HEMISPHERE

SCORPIUS (THE SCORPION)

Sco X-1
M80
Antares
M4
M6
NGC 6383
M7
Shaula
NGC 6322
NGC 6231
NGC 6124
NGC 6388
NGC 6178

Width: 🤚🤚

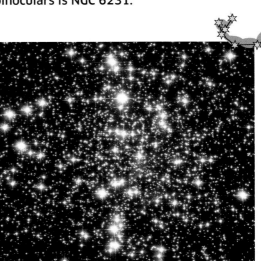

Star cluster M4
This sparkling photo from the Hubble Space Telescope shows the heart of the M4 globular cluster, 7,200 light-years from Earth.

CAPRICORNUS

This constellation is shown as a goat with the tail of a fish. It is said to represent the Greek god Pan, who had the horns and legs of a goat. He grew the fish tail when he jumped into a river to escape from a monster called Typhon. A feature of interest is Algedi, a wide double star, which is easily divided with binoculars or even good eyesight. Dabih is another double, but needs binoculars or a small telescope to divide.

SOUTHERN HEMISPHERE

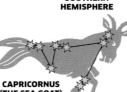

CAPRICORNUS (THE SEA GOAT)

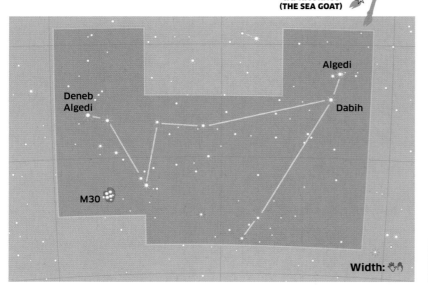

Algedi
Deneb Algedi
Dabih
M30
Width: 🖐✋

MICROSCOPIUM

This faint constellation of the southern sky was invented in the 1750s by the French astronomer Nicolas-Louis de Lacaille, who studied the southern stars from the Cape of Good Hope in southern Africa. Lacaille invented many new constellations representing scientific instruments—in this case, a microscope.

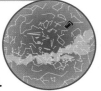

SOUTHERN HEMISPHERE

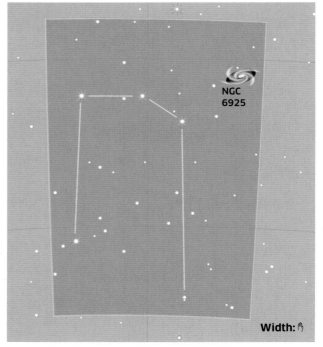

NGC 6925
Width: ✋

MICROSCOPIUM (THE MICROSCOPE)

PISCIS AUSTRINUS

To the ancient Greeks, this constellation represented a large fish drinking water flowing from a jar held by Aquarius to its north. Its brightest star is Fomalhaut, which lies 25 light-years away. The name Fomalhaut comes from Arabic and means "fish's mouth."

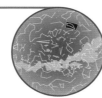

SOUTHERN HEMISPHERE

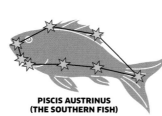

PISCIS AUSTRINUS (THE SOUTHERN FISH)

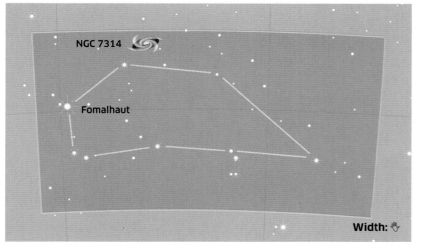

NGC 7314
Fomalhaut
Width: 🖐

SCULPTOR

Invented in the 1750s by the French astronomer Nicolas-Louis de Lacaille, this constellation represents a sculptor's studio. Its stars are faint, but it contains a number of interesting galaxies. Most impressive of these is NGC 253, a spiral galaxy 13 million light-years away, seen nearly edge-on and just visible in small telescopes. NGC 55 is another edge-on spiral. Dust clouds and areas of star formation make it look patchy, and it can be seen clearly only with larger telescopes.

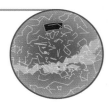

SOUTHERN HEMISPHERE

THE SCULPTOR

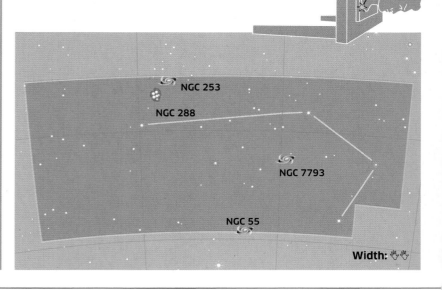

NGC 253
NGC 288
NGC 7793
NGC 55
Width: 🖐🖐

FORNAX

French astronomer Nicolas-Louis de Lacaille came up with this constellation in the 1750s. It represents a furnace used for chemical experiments. On its border lies the Fornax Cluster of galaxies, which is located about 65 million light-years away.

SOUTHERN HEMISPHERE

NGC 1097

NGC 1365

NGC 1316

Width: 🖐🖐

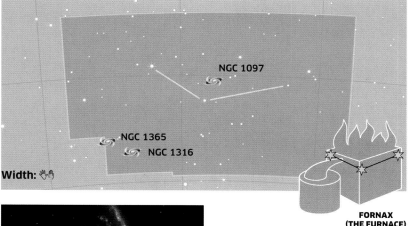

FORNAX (THE FURNACE)

Barred spiral galaxy NGC 1365
A prominent member of the Fornax cluster, NGC 1365 is a barred spiral galaxy. Large telescopes are needed to see its full size and shape.

CAELUM

Caelum is another of the small, faint constellations of the southern sky that were invented in the 1750s by the French astronomer Nicolas-Louis de Lacaille. It represents a chisel used by engravers. Caelum is squeezed into the gap between Eridanus and Columba. There is little in the constellation of interest to users of binoculars and small telescopes.

SOUTHERN HEMISPHERE

CAELUM (THE CHISEL)

Width: 🖐

ERIDANUS

To the ancient Greeks, this large constellation represented a river, either the Nile in Egypt or the Po in Italy. In the sky it meanders from the left foot of Orion deep into the southern sky. Its brightest star is Achernar, at the southern end of the river.

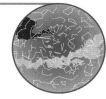

SOUTHERN HEMISPHERE

Barred spiral galaxy NGC 1300
Seen here in a Hubble view is a classic example of a barred spiral galaxy. NGC 1300 lies about 70 million light-years from us. Large telescopes are needed to see it.

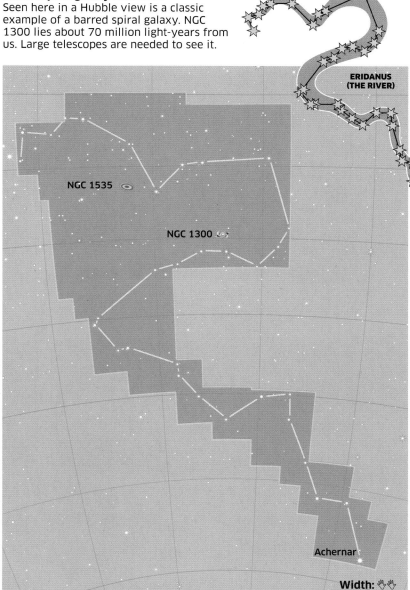

ERIDANUS (THE RIVER)

NGC 1535

NGC 1300

Achernar

Width: 🖐🖐

LEPUS

Lepus represents a hare scampering under the feet of the hunter Orion. It was one of the constellations known to the ancient Greeks. The name of its brightest star, Arneb, means "hare" in Arabic. An interesting feature in this constellation is Gamma Leporis, an attractive double star that can be divided with binoculars. Another object of interest is NGC 2017, a small group of stars, the brightest of which can be seen through small telescopes.

SOUTHERN HEMISPHERE

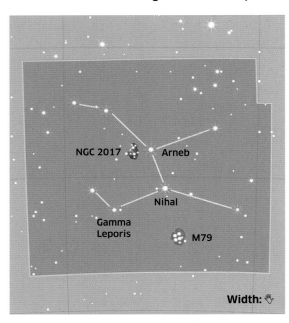

NGC 2017
Arneb
Nihal
Gamma Leporis
M79

Width: ✋

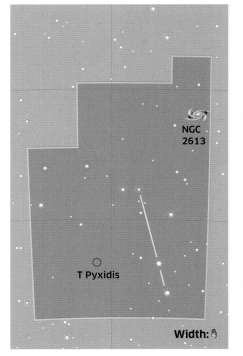

LEPUS (THE HARE)

COLUMBA

This constellation was devised in 1592 by the Dutch astronomer Petrus Plancius, using stars between Lepus and Canis Major that were not part of any Greek constellation. It is said to represent the dove that Noah sent from the biblical Ark to find dry land. Columba's brightest star is called Phact, from the Arabic meaning "ring dove."

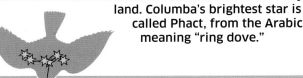

SOUTHERN HEMISPHERE

COLUMBA (THE DOVE)

Phact
Wazn
NGC 1792
NGC 1851

Width: ✋

PYXIS

French astronomer Nicolas-Louis de Lacaille devised this faint southern constellation in the 1750s, during his survey of the southern sky. Pyxis depicts a magnetic compass as used on ships. The constellation's most remarkable star is T Pyxidis, a recurrent nova–a kind of star that brightens from time to time. It has been seen to flare up six times since 1890. Further outbursts could occur at any time.

SOUTHERN HEMISPHERE

NGC 2613

T Pyxidis

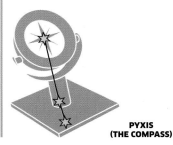

PYXIS (THE COMPASS)

Width: ✋

PUPPIS

Puppis was once part of a much larger Greek constellation called Argo Navis, the ship of Jason and the Argonauts. It depicted the ship's stern. Puppis lies in a rich part of the Milky Way and contains many bright star clusters. M46 and M47 lie side by side and create a brighter patch in the Milky Way. NGC 2451 and NGC 2477 are two more clusters that lie close together. Binoculars give a good view of them both.

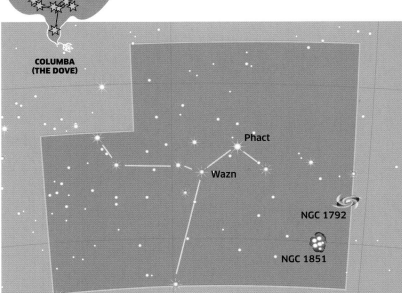

M47
M46
M93
NGC 2571
NGC 2439
NGC 2546
NGC 2451
Naos
NGC 2477

SOUTHERN HEMISPHERE

PUPPIS (THE STERN)

Width: ✋

Star cluster M47
M47 is a large and scattered cluster of a few dozen stars in the north of Puppis, visible with binoculars. The rich view in this image was captured through a large professional telescope.

VELA

Vela represents the sails of Argo Navis, the ship of Jason and the Argonauts. Argo Navis was a large Greek constellation that was split into three smaller parts. The other two parts are Puppis and Carina. Two stars in Vela combine with a pair of stars in Carina to form the False Cross, sometimes mistaken for the real Southern Cross. Around another star is a large cluster called IC 2391, bright enough to be visible to the naked eye.

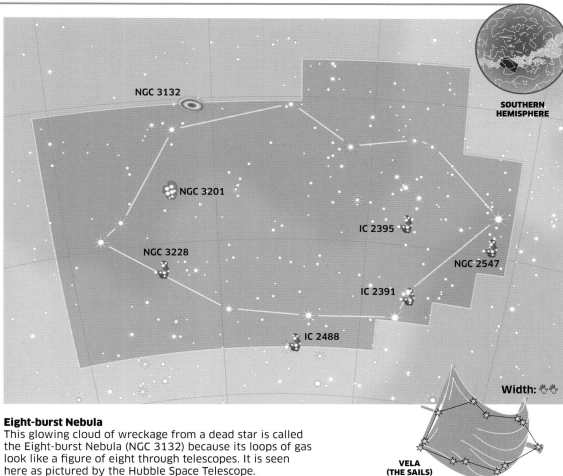

SOUTHERN
HEMISPHERE

NGC 3132

NGC 3201

IC 2395

NGC 3228

NGC 2547

IC 2391

IC 2488

Width: 🖐🖐

VELA
(THE SAILS)

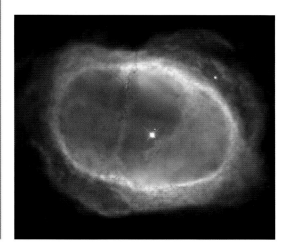

Eight-burst Nebula
This glowing cloud of wreckage from a dead star is called the Eight-burst Nebula (NGC 3132) because its loops of gas look like a figure of eight through telescopes. It is seen here as pictured by the Hubble Space Telescope.

CARINA

Carina is one of the three parts into which the large Greek constellation of Argo Navis, the ship of Jason and the Argonauts, was split. It depicts the ship's keel, or hull. This constellation contains the second-brightest star in the night sky, Canopus. A pair of stars in Carina form half of the False Cross, completed by two stars in Vela.

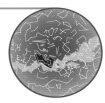

SOUTHERN
HEMISPHERE

NGC
3293

IC
2581

NGC
3114

Canopus

NGC 2516

NGC
3532

NGC
3372

NGC 2808

IC 2602

Width: 🖐🖐🖐

Southern Pleiades
The large star cluster IC 2602, called the Southern Pleiades, is a glorious sight through binoculars.

CARINA
(THE KEEL)

Carina Nebula
The Carina Nebula (NGC 3372) is a large, V-shaped cloud of gas visible to the naked eye. Its brightest part surrounds the star Eta Carinae, a peculiar variable star that has thrown off shells of gas in the past.

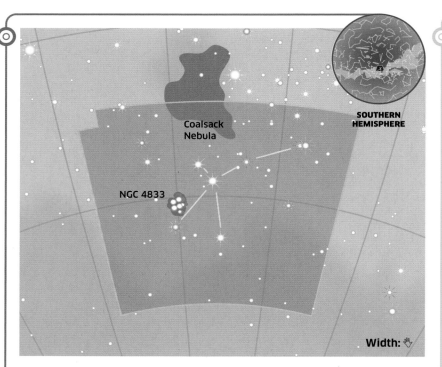

SOUTHERN HEMISPHERE

Coalsack Nebula

NGC 4833

Width: 🖐

MUSCA

This constellation of the southern sky was invented at the end of the 16th century by Dutch seafarers. It represents a fly. Part of the dark Coalsack Nebula spills into Musca from Crux, which lies to the north. Of note is NGC 4833, a globular cluster that can be seen through binoculars and small telescopes.

MUSCA (THE FLY)

CIRCINUS

This small southern constellation was created in the 1750s by the French astronomer Nicolas-Louis de Lacaille. Most of his constellations represented instruments from science and the arts. He visualized Circinus as a pair of dividing compasses used by surveyors and navigators. Its brightest star is a double.

SOUTHERN HEMISPHERE

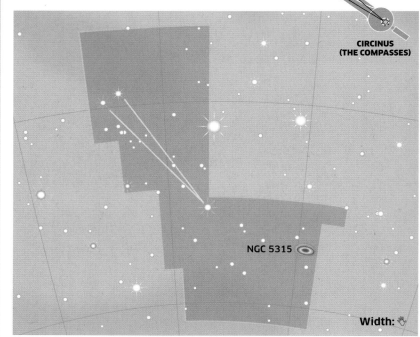

CIRCINUS (THE COMPASSES)

NGC 5315

Width: 🖐

NORMA

Norma was introduced in the 1750s by the French astronomer Nicolas-Louis de Lacaille. It represents a level as used by draftsmen and builders. Objects of note include the star Gamma Normae, which consists of a wide pair of unrelated stars, both separately visible to the naked eye, and NGC 6087, a large, rich star cluster visible through binoculars.

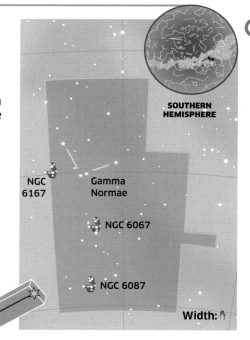

SOUTHERN HEMISPHERE

NGC 6167

Gamma Normae

NGC 6067

NGC 6087

NORMA (THE LEVEL)

Width: 🖐

Star cluster NGC 6067
NGC 6067 is a rich cluster of stars in central Norma, visible through binoculars and small telescopes. It covers an area of sky about half the apparent diameter of the full moon.

TRIANGULUM AUSTRALE

At the end of the 16th century, Dutch explorers who sailed to the East Indies created a dozen new constellations among the southern stars. The smallest of them was Triangulum Australe, the southern triangle. It is smaller than the northern triangle, Triangulum, but its stars are brighter. The main object of interest in Triangulum Australe is the star cluster NGC 6025 on its northern border, visible through binoculars.

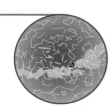

SOUTHERN HEMISPHERE

TRIANGULUM AUSTRALE (THE SOUTHERN TRIANGLE)

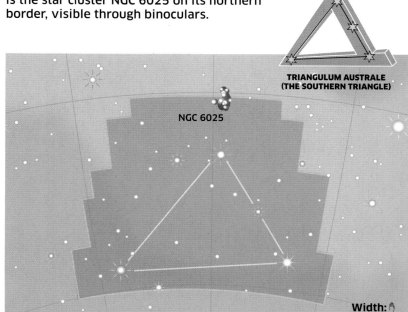

NGC 6025

Width: 🖐

ARA

The constellation Ara was known to the ancient Greeks. To them it depicted the altar on which the gods of Mount Olympus swore an oath of loyalty before fighting the Titans, their sworn enemies. An attractive star cluster in Ara is NGC 6193. None of the stars of Ara is of particular interest.

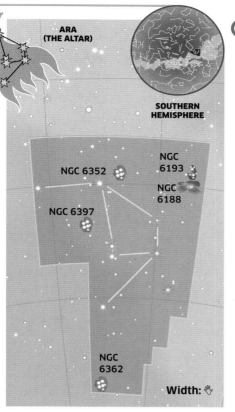

ARA
(THE ALTAR)

SOUTHERN HEMISPHERE

NGC 6352

NGC 6193

NGC 6188

NGC 6397

NGC 6362

Width: ✋

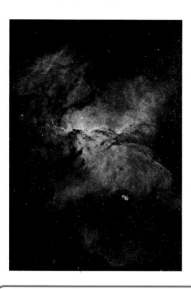

Star birth nebula NGC 6188
Ultraviolet radiation from the stars in NGC 6193 lights up the sulfur, hydrogen, and oxygen atoms in the star birth nebula NGC 6188, as seen in this Hubble photo.

TELESCOPIUM

French astronomer Nicolas-Louis de Lacaille came up with this faint constellation in the 1750s to commemorate the telescope, the astronomer's basic tool. The constellation has since been reduced in size. Besides a globular cluster and a wide pair of unrelated stars, which can be seen separately with binoculars or even good eyesight, there is little of note.

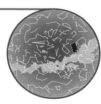

SOUTHERN HEMISPHERE

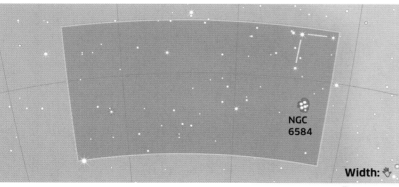

NGC 6584

Width: ✋

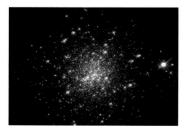

Globular cluster NGC 6584
NGC 6584 is a faint and distant globular cluster and can be seen well through a large telescope. It is seen here as photographed by the Hubble Space Telescope.

TELESCOPIUM
(THE TELESCOPE)

CORONA AUSTRALIS

This small constellation lies under the feet of Sagittarius. It represents a crown or wreath and was one of the constellations known to the ancient Greeks. Although faint, Corona Australis is fairly easy to spot, as its main stars form a noticeable arc. An interesting object for small telescopes is the globular cluster NGC 6541.

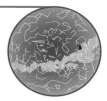

SOUTHERN HEMISPHERE

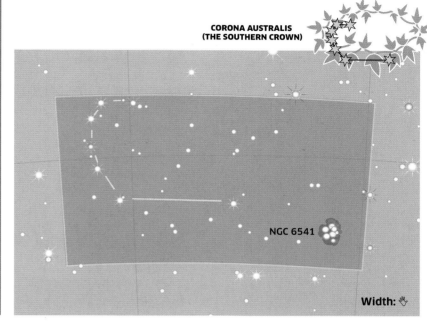

CORONA AUSTRALIS
(THE SOUTHERN CROWN)

NGC 6541

Width: ✋

INDUS

Indus is one of the 12 southern constellations introduced at the end of the 16th century by Dutch seafarers. This constellation was visualized as a native hunter brandishing a spear. Indus has an interesting double star that can be divided by a small telescope.

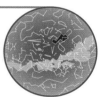

SOUTHERN HEMISPHERE

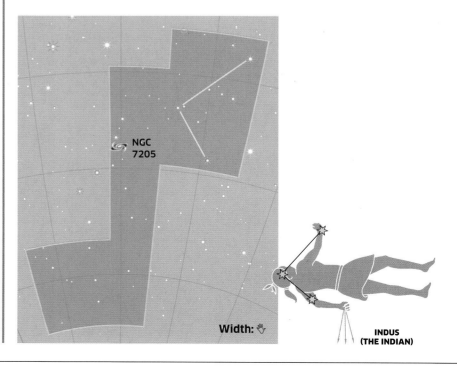

NGC 7205

Width: ✋

INDUS
(THE INDIAN)

GRUS

Grus represents a crane, a long-necked wading bird. It is one of the constellations invented in the late 16th century by Dutch seafarers. In the bird's neck lie two wide double stars. Both pairs can be divided with the naked eye. The stars in each pair are actually at different distances from us and so are not related– they are just optical doubles and not true binaries.

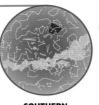

SOUTHERN HEMISPHERE

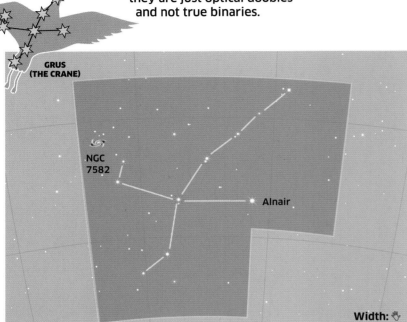

GRUS (THE CRANE)

NGC 7582

Alnair

Width: 🤚

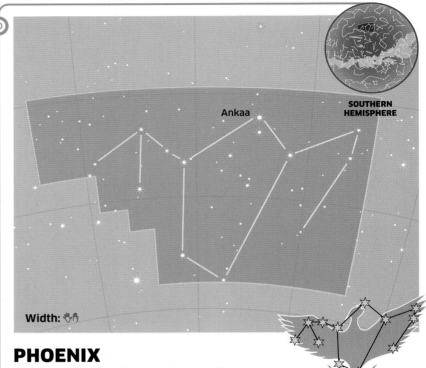

Ankaa

SOUTHERN HEMISPHERE

Width: 🤚🤏

PHOENIX

This constellation lies near the southern end of the river Eridanus. Phoenix is the largest of the 12 new constellations that were created at the end of the 16th century by Dutch explorers sailing to the East Indies. It represents the mythical bird that was said to be reborn from its own ashes every 500 years.

THE PHOENIX

TUCANA

Dutch navigators came up with this southern constellation in the late 16th century. It represents a toucan, a tropical bird with a large beak. Tucana contains the Small Magellanic Cloud (SMC), a mini-galaxy about 200,000 light-years away from us. To the naked eye, the SMC looks like a separate part of the Milky Way. The globular clusters 47 Tucanae and NGC 362 lie on either side of the SMC but are actually much closer to us.

SOUTHERN HEMISPHERE

TUCANA (THE TOUCAN)

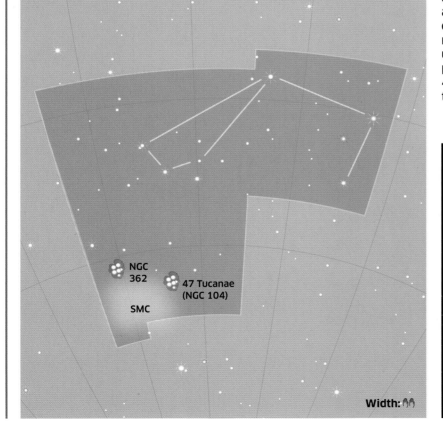

NGC 362

47 Tucanae (NGC 104)

SMC

Width: 👐

Globular cluster 47 Tucanae
To the naked eye, the globular cluster 47 Tucanae (NGC 104) looks like a single fuzzy star, but through large telescopes it breaks up into a swarm of individual points of light, as seen here. It lies about 16,000 light-years away from us.

HYDRUS

Representing a sea snake, this constellation slithers between the Large and Small Magellanic Clouds (LMC and SMC). Hydrus was created by Dutch explorers in the 16th century. It should not be confused with Hydra, the large water snake, which has been known since ancient Greek times. Hydrus has a pair of red giants, Pi Hydri, that look like a double star but are unrelated and lie at different distances from us. Pi Hydri can be seen separately through binoculars.

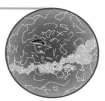

SOUTHERN HEMISPHERE

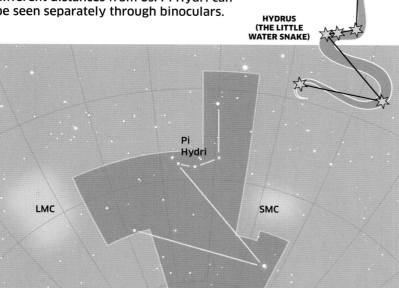

HYDRUS (THE LITTLE WATER SNAKE)

Pi Hydri

LMC

SMC

Width: 🖑

HOROLOGIUM

Horologium represents a clock with a long pendulum, as used in observatories for accurate timekeeping in the days before electronic clocks. It is one of the southern constellations honoring scientific and technical instruments that were introduced by the French astronomer Nicolas-Louis de Lacaille in the 1750s. Horologium is faint and contains few objects of interest for small telescopes.

SOUTHERN HEMISPHERE

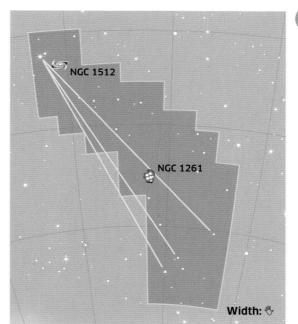

NGC 1512

NGC 1261

HOROLOGIUM (THE PENDULUM CLOCK)

Width: 🖑

Zeta Reticuli

NGC 1313

SOUTHERN HEMISPHERE

Width: ✊

RETICULUM

This small southern constellation is one of 14 invented in the 1750s by the French astronomer Nicolas-Louis de Lacaille when he mapped the southern stars from the Cape of Good Hope in southern Africa. Reticulum represents the cross-hairs in the eyepiece of Nicolas's telescope, which helped him measure the positions of stars accurately. Of note is Zeta Reticuli, a pair of yellow stars that can be separated through binoculars.

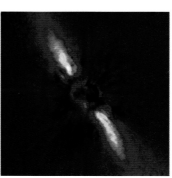
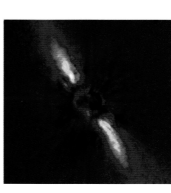

RETICULUM (THE NET)

PICTOR

This is yet another constellation invented in the 1750s by the French astronomer Nicolas-Louis de Lacaille. It represents an artist's easel. Pictor contains an interesting double star, Iota Pictoris, which can be easily separated through small telescopes.

SOUTHERN HEMISPHERE

PICTOR (THE PAINTER'S EASEL)

Beta Pictoris
The second brightest star in Pictor, Beta Pictoris is surrounded by a disk of dust and gas. Planets are thought to be forming from the disk. This disk can be seen only through large telescopes with special equipment.

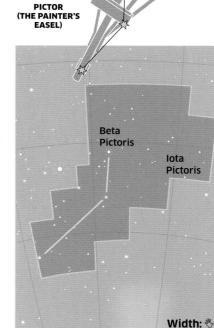

Beta Pictoris

Iota Pictoris

Width: 🖑

DORADO

Dutch seafarers created this southern constellation in the late 16th century. It represents a type of tropical fish called a dorado but is also known as the Goldfish. The main feature of Dorado is the Large Magellanic Cloud (LMC), the bigger of the two companion galaxies of the Milky Way. Another point of interest is the Tarantula Nebula (NGC 2070), which appears as a hazy star.

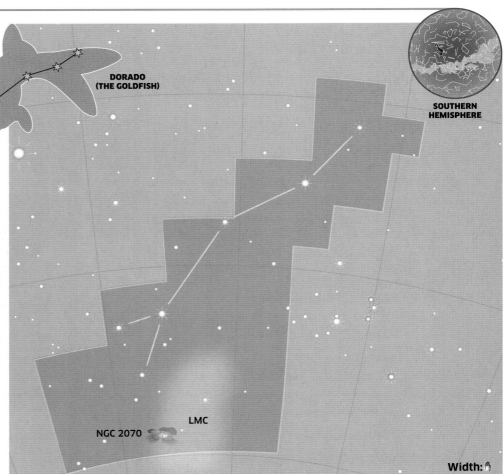

DORADO
(THE GOLDFISH)

SOUTHERN
HEMISPHERE

LMC

NGC 2070

Width: ✋

Large Magellanic Cloud
The Large Magellanic Cloud (LMC) can easily be seen with the naked eye, and looks like a detached part of our galaxy. Binoculars reveal many star clusters and nebulae within it.

VOLANS

This constellation was invented in the late 16th century by Dutch explorers who sailed to the East Indies, surveying the stars of the southern sky on the way. It represents a flying fish—one of the exotic creatures they saw on their voyages. Gamma and Epsilon Volantis are double stars that can easily be distinguished by small telescopes.

SOUTHERN
HEMISPHERE

VOLANS
(THE FLYING FISH)

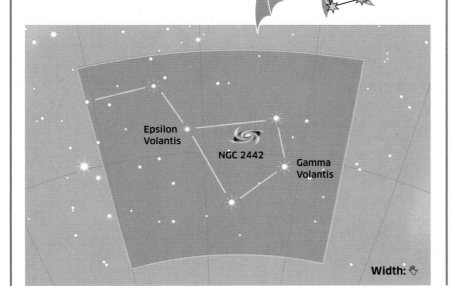

Epsilon
Volantis

NGC 2442

Gamma
Volantis

Width: ✋

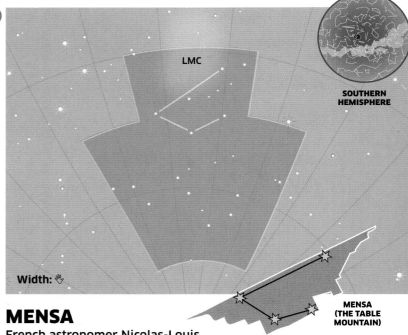

LMC

SOUTHERN
HEMISPHERE

Width: ✋

MENSA
(THE TABLE
MOUNTAIN)

MENSA

French astronomer Nicolas-Louis de Lacaille devised this constellation in the 1750s. He measured the positions of thousands of southern stars from an observatory near the foot of Table Mountain at the Cape of Good Hope, South Africa. This constellation was named Mensa—which means "table" in Latin—to celebrate the mountain. Mensa contains part of the Large Magellanic Cloud (LMC). All of Mensa's stars are faint, and none of them is of interest for users of small telescopes.

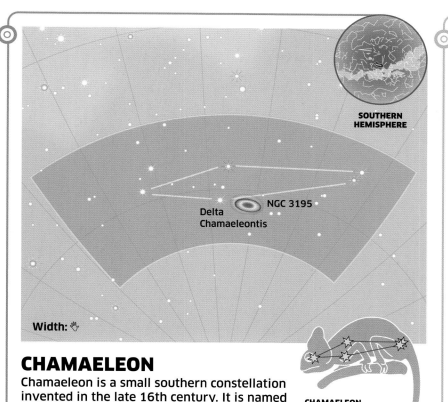

SOUTHERN HEMISPHERE

NGC 3195

Delta Chamaeleontis

Width: 🖐

CHAMAELEON

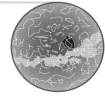

CHAMAELEON (THE CHAMELEON)

Chamaeleon is a small southern constellation invented in the late 16th century. It is named after the lizard that can change its skin color to match its surroundings. Next to it lies Musca, the Fly, which is appropriate because chameleons eat flies. Of interest is Delta Chamaeleontis, a wide double star that is easily seen with binoculars.

APUS

SOUTHERN HEMISPHERE

Dutch explorers sailing to the East Indies in the late 16th century devised Apus. This constellation represents a bird of paradise, a kind of bird known for its beautiful plumage, which in the past was used to decorate hats and other items of clothing. Delta Apodis is a wide pair of unrelated red giant stars, which can be seen separately with the naked eye or in binoculars.

APUS (THE BIRD OF PARADISE)

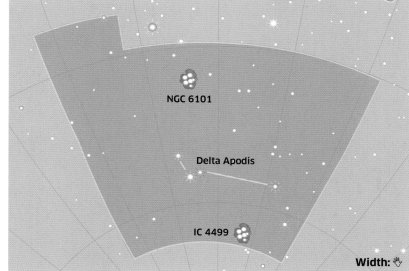

NGC 6101

Delta Apodis

IC 4499

Width: 🖐

PAVO

Pavo represents a peacock, a bird with a glorious, fanlike tail. It is one of the 12 southern constellations introduced by Dutch seafarers at the end of the 16th century. Items of note include NGC 6752, a large and bright globular cluster, easily visible in binoculars; and NGC 6744, a beautiful spiral galaxy with a short central bar, best seen in photographs.

SOUTHERN HEMISPHERE

PAVO (THE PEACOCK)

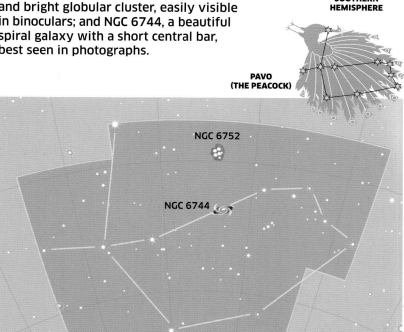

NGC 6752

NGC 6744

Width: 🖐🖐

SOUTHERN HEMISPHERE

Sigma Octantis

Width: 🖐

OCTANS (THE OCTANT)

OCTANS

Octans contains the south pole of the sky. Unlike the northern hemisphere, there is no bright pole star in the southern sky. The closest visible star to the south celestial pole is Sigma Octantis, but it is very faint. Octans was introduced in the 1750s by the French astronomer Nicolas-Louis de Lacaille. It represents a navigation instrument known as an octant, the forerunner of the sextant.

REFERENCE

The reference section is packed with facts and figures about planets, spacecraft missions, stars, and galaxies, and tells you the best time to see shooting stars, comets, and eclipses. A glossary explains many of the terms used in this book.

Solar System data

Our Solar System consists of the Sun and all the objects under its gravitational influence, including the eight planets and their moons, and an unknown number of dwarf planets, asteroids, comets, and smaller objects. The most distant objects—comets orbiting in the Oort Cloud—can be as far as a light-year from the Sun.

The Sun weighs about **670 times** as much as all the planets and other objects in the Solar System combined.

THE PLANETS

A planet is officially defined as an object in direct orbit around the Sun, with enough mass to pull itself into a ball and strong-enough gravity to force other objects out of broadly similar orbits. Today, astronomers recognize eight planets—four relatively small, rocky (or "terrestrial") worlds close to the Sun and four much larger giant planets farther out.

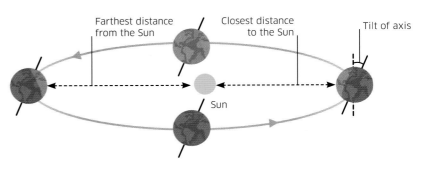

Farthest distance from the Sun — Closest distance to the Sun — Tilt of axis — Sun

A PLANET'S ORBIT AROUND THE SUN

PLANET DATA

	Mercury	Venus	Earth	Mars	Jupiter	Saturn	Uranus	Neptune
Diameter	3,032 miles (4,880 km)	7,522 miles (12,104 km)	7,926 miles (12,756 km)	4,220 miles (6,792 km)	88,846 miles (142,984 km)	74,896 miles (120,536 km)	31,762 miles (51,118 km)	30,774 miles (49,528 km)
Mass (Earth = 1)	0.06	0.82	1	0.11	318	95	14	17
Time of one rotation	1,408 hours	5,833 hours	23.9 hours	24.6 hours	9.9 hours	10.7 hours	17.2 hours	16.1 hours
Surface gravity (Earth = 1)	0.38	0.91	1	0.38	2.36	1.02	0.89	1.12
Tilt of axis	0.01°	2.6°	23.4°	25.2°	3.1°	26.7°	82.2°	28.3°
Number of moons	0	0	1	2	79+	82+	27+	14+
Closest distance to the Sun	29 million miles (46 million km)	67 million miles (107 million km)	91 million miles (147 million km)	128 million miles (207 million km)	460 million miles (741 million km)	841 million miles (1,353 million km)	1,703 million miles (2,741 million km)	2,761 million miles (4,445 million km)
Farthest distance from the Sun	43 million miles (70 million km)	68 million miles (109 million km)	95 million miles (152 million km)	157 million miles (249 million km)	507 million miles (817 million km)	940 million miles (1,515 million km)	1,866 million miles (3,004 million km)	2,825 million miles (4,546 million km)
Time to orbit the Sun	88 Earth days	225 Earth days	365.26 days	687 Earth days	12 Earth years	29 Earth years	84 Earth years	165 Earth years
Average orbital speed	30 miles (48 km) per second	22 miles (35 km) per second	19 miles (30 km) per second	15 miles (24 km) per second	8 miles (13 km) per second	6 miles (10 km) per second	4 miles (7 km) per second	3 miles (5 km) per second

METEOR SHOWERS

After being ejected from a comet or asteroid, many grains of rock get concentrated into narrow streams. When Earth's orbit crosses these streams, the grains burn up in our atmosphere as meteors (shooting stars), causing predictable meteor showers.

MAJOR METEOR SHOWERS

Name	Peak date	Most meteors	Parent comet/asteroid
Quadrantids	January 4	120 per hour	2003 EH1
Lyrids	April 22	10 per hour	C/1861 G1 (Thatcher)
Eta Aquarids	May 5	30 per hour	1P/Halley
Perseids	August 12	100 per hour	109P/Swift-Tuttle
Geminids	December 14	120 per hour	3200 Phaethon

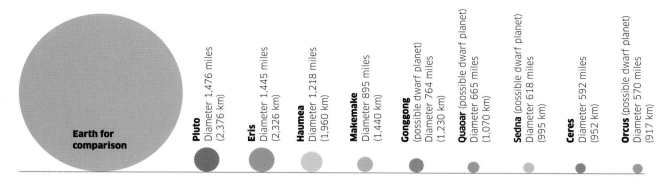

Earth for comparison

Pluto Diameter 1,476 miles (2,376 km)

Eris Diameter 1,445 miles (2,326 km)

Haumea Diameter 1,218 miles (1,960 km)

Makemake Diameter 895 miles (1,440 km)

Gonggong (possible dwarf planet) Diameter 764 miles (1,230 km)

Quaoar (possible dwarf planet) Diameter 665 miles (1,070 km)

Sedna (possible dwarf planet) Diameter 618 miles (995 km)

Ceres Diameter 592 miles (952 km)

Orcus (possible dwarf planet) Diameter 570 miles (917 km)

DWARF PLANETS

A dwarf planet is a spherical object in an independent orbit around the Sun that lacks the strong gravity required to clear its orbit of other objects. Dwarf planets are mostly found in the Kuiper Belt and scattered disk zones beyond the orbit of Neptune, but they include Ceres—the largest asteroid in the Main Asteroid Belt.

COMETS

Most comets are deep-frozen, icy objects lurking at the outer edges of the Solar System, but a small number have fallen into orbits that periodically bring them closer to the Sun and cause them to burst into life.

COMET HALE-BOPP

SOME PERIODIC COMETS

Name	Orbital period	Sightings	Next due
1P/Halley	75 years	30	July 2061
2P/Encke	3 years, 3 months	64	October 2023
6P/d'Arrest	6 years, 6 months	20	March 2028
9P/Tempel	5 years, 5 months	14	January 2022
17P/Holmes	6 years, 10 months	10	January 2028
21P/Giacobini–Zinner	6 years, 6 months	16	March 2025
29P/Schwassmann–Wachmann	15 years	8	March 2034
39P/Oterma	19 years	4	July 2023
46P/Wirtanen	5 years, 5 months	11	April 2024
50P/Arend	8 years, 3 months	9	May 2024
55P/Tempel-Tuttle	33 years	5	May 2031
67P/Churyumov Gerasimenko	6 years, 5 months	7	April 2028
81P/Wild	6 years, 5 months	5	November 2022
109P/Swift-Tuttle	133 years	5	July 2126

ECLIPSES

By sheer coincidence, the Sun and Moon appear almost exactly the same size in Earth's skies. As a result, the Moon can sometimes pass in front of the Sun, blocking out its disk to create a solar eclipse. Total solar eclipses, which block the disk completely to reveal the tenuous outer solar atmosphere, are rare and very localized, but partial eclipses are more frequently seen.

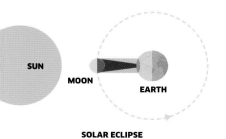

SUN
MOON
EARTH

SOLAR ECLIPSE

TOTAL SOLAR ECLIPSES

Date	Location
April 8 2024	Mexico, central US, east Canada
August 12 2026	Arctic, Greenland, Iceland, Spain
August 2 2027	Morocco, Spain, Algeria, Libya, Egypt, Saudi Arabia, Yemen, Somalia
July 22 2028	Australia, New Zealand
November 25 2030	Botswana, South Africa, Australia
March 30 2033	East Russia, Alaska
March 20 2034	Africa, the Middle East, Asia
September 2 2035	China, Korea, Japan, Pacific
July 13 2037	Australia, New Zealand
December 26 2038	Australia, New Zealand, South Pacific
December 15 2039	Antarctica
April 30 2041	Angola, Congo, Uganda, Kenya, Somalia
April 20 2042	Malaysia, Indonesia, the Philippines, Northern Pacific
April 9 2043	North America, Northeast Asia
August 23 2044	North America
August 12 2045	North America, Central America, South America

Exploring the planets

Since the late 1950s, we have sent dozens of robotic spacecraft beyond Earth's orbit, mostly aimed at other planets. Some perform brief flyby missions en route to another destination, but others stay longer. Orbiters become long-term satellites of planets, while landers and rovers touch down to examine or even explore the surface.

Rocky worlds

Earth's immediate neighbors, Venus and Mars, have been subject to intense study by a variety of spacecraft, not all of which can be listed here—those mentioned below include all major successes, as well as notable firsts and some interesting failures. The innermost planet, Mercury, moves so quickly in its orbit that it is hard to reach and rarely visited.

MESSENGER

Mercury

Mission	Country of origin	Arrival date	Type	Status
Mariner 10	US	1974	Multiple flybys	Success
MESSENGER	US	2011	Orbiter	Success
BepiColombo	Europe/Japan	2025	Orbiter	En route

Venera

Magellan

Venus

Mission	Country of origin	Arrival date	Type	Status
Mariner 2	US	1962	Flyby	Success
Venera 4	USSR/Russia	1967	Flyby	Success
Mariner 5	US	1967	Flyby	Success
Venera 7	USSR/Russia	1970	Lander	Success
Venera 9	USSR/Russia	1975	Orbiter/lander	Success
Pioneer Venus Orbiter	US	1978	Orbiter	Success
Pioneer Venus Multiprobe	US	1978	Atmospheric probe	Success
Venera 11	USSR/Russia	1978	Flyby/lander	Success
Venera 15	USSR/Russia	1983	Orbiter	Success
Vega 1	USSR/Russia	1985	Flyby/lander/balloon	Partial success (lander failure)
Vega 2	USSR/Russia	1985	Flyby/lander/balloon	Success
Magellan	US	1990	Orbiter	Success
Venus Express	Europe	2006	Orbiter	Success
Akatsuki	Japan	2015	Orbiter	Success

Mariner

Mars Express

Mars

Mission	Country of origin	Arrival date	Type	Status
Mariner 4	US	1965	Flyby	Success
Mariner 6	US	1969	Flyby	Success
Mariner 7	US	1969	Flyby	Success
Mariner 9	US	1971	Orbiter	Success
Mars 2	USSR/Russia	1971	Orbiter/lander	Partial success (lander failure)

Viking 1	US	1976	Orbiter/lander	Success
Viking 2	US	1976	Orbiter/lander	Success
Phobos 2	USSR/Russia	1989	Phobos orbiter/lander	Partial success (lander failure)
Mars Pathfinder	US	1997	Lander/rover	Success
Mars Global Surveyor	US	1997	Orbiter	Success
Mars Odyssey	US	2001	Orbiter	Success
Mars Express/Beagle 2	Europe	2003	Orbiter/lander	Partial success (lander failure)
MER-A Spirit	US	2004	Rover	Success
MER-B Opportunity	US	2004	Rover	Success
Mars Reconnaissance Orbiter	US	2006	Orbiter	Success
Phoenix	US	2008	Lander	Success
Curiosity	US	2012	Rover	Success
Mars Orbiter Mission (Mangalyaan)	India	2014	Orbiter	Success
MAVEN	US	2014	Orbiter	Success
EXOMARS	Europe/Russia	2016	Orbiter/lander	Partial success (lander failure)
Insight	US	2018	Orbiter/lander	Success
Hope	UAE	2021	Orbiter	Success
Tianwen-1	China	2021	Orbiter/rover	Success
Perseverance	US	2021	Rover	Success

Giants

The giant planets have no surfaces to investigate, but their atmospheres, rings, and moons are all intriguing. After an initial wave of flyby missions that surveyed the giants in the 1970s and '80s, Jupiter and Saturn have both been surveyed by long-term orbiters. A probe has entered Jupiter's atmosphere, and a lander has touched down on Saturn's largest moon, Titan.

Juno

Galileo

Jupiter

Mission	Country of origin	Arrival date	Type	Status
Pioneer 10	US	1973	Flyby	Success
Pioneer 11	US	1974	Flyby	Success
Voyager 1	US	1979	Flyby	Success
Voyager 2	US	1979	Flyby	Success
Galileo	US	1995	Orbiter/atmospheric probe	Success
Cassini	US and Europe	2000	Flyby	Success
New Horizons	US	2007	Flyby	Success
Juno	US	2016	Orbiter	Success

Saturn

Mission	Country of origin	Arrival date	Type	Status
Pioneer 11	US	1979	Flyby	Success
Voyager 1	US	1980	Flyby	Success
Voyager 2	US	1981	Flyby	Success
Cassini/Huygens	US and Europe	2004	Orbiter/Titan lander	Success

Uranus and Neptune

Mission	Country of origin	Arrival date	Type	Status
Voyager 2	US	Uranus 1986, Neptune 1989	Flyby	Success

Stars and galaxies

The vast majority of objects in the night sky lie far beyond our solar system. All the individual stars we can see are members of our own Milky Way galaxy, as are most of the star clusters and nebulae visible through amateur instruments. There are also countless other galaxies far beyond our own, most of them too distant to see.

There are about **200 billion** galaxies in the observable universe and about as many stars in the Milky Way.

Closest stars

Many of the closest stars to Earth are red dwarfs, often in binary or multiple systems and so faint that they are hard to see despite their proximity. There are also a few Sun-like stars, and a couple of brilliant white stars, each paired with a burned-out white dwarf companion. Also close to Earth are many starlike objects called brown dwarfs—failed stars that are not massive enough to trigger nuclear fusion in their core.

KEY

- ● Red dwarf
- ○ White main-sequence star
- ○ Yellow main-sequence star
- ○ White dwarf
- ● Orange main-sequence star
- ● Brown dwarf

Star type	Designation	Distance	Constellation	Apparent magnitude	Visibility
○	Sun	8 light minutes	–	–26.7	Naked eye
●	Proxima Centauri	4.2 light-years	Centaurus	11.1	Telescope
● ●	Alpha Centauri A/B	4.4 light-years	Centaurus	0.01/1.34	Naked eye
●	Barnard's Star	6.0 light-years	Ophiuchus	9.5	Telescope
● ●	Luhman 16 A/B	6.6 light-years	Vela	10.7	Telescope
●	WISE 0655-0714	7.2 light-years	Hydra	13.9	Telescope
●	Wolf 359	7.8 light-years	Leo	13.4	Telescope
●	Lalande 21185	8.3 light-years	Ursa Major	7.5	Binoculars
○ ○	Sirius A/B	8.6 light-years	Canis Major	–1.46/8.44	Naked eye/telescope
● ●	Luyten 726-8	8.7 light-years	Cetus	12.5/13.0	Telescope
●	Ross 154	9.7 light-years	Sagittarius	10.4	Telescope
●	Ross 248	10.3 light-years	Andromeda	12.3	Telescope
○	Epsilon Eridani	10.5 light-years	Eridanus	3.73	Naked eye
●	Lacaille 9352	10.7 light-years	Piscis Austrinus	7.3	Binoculars
●	Ross 128	10.9 light-years	Virgo	11.1	Telescope
●	WISE 1506+7027	11.1 light-years	Ursa Minor	14.3	Telescope
● ● ●	EZ Aquarii A/B/C	11.3 light-years	Aquarius	13.3/13.3/14.0	Telescope
○ ○	Procyon A/B	11.4 light-years	Canis Minor	0.4/10.7	Naked eye/telescope
● ●	61 Cygni A/B	11.4 light-years	Cygnus	5.2/6.0	Naked eye/binoculars
● ●	Struve 2398 A/B	11.5 light-years	Draco	8.9/9.7	Telescope
● ●	Groombridge 34 A/B	11.6 light-years	Andromeda	8.1/11.1	Telescope

Brightest star

Star brightness is measured by apparent magnitude. The brightest stars have the lowest number; 6 is roughly the limit of naked-eye visibility in a clear, dark sky. The Sun, with a magnitude of –26.7, is the brightest object in our skies, but at night thousands of stars are visible to the naked eye, and millions more can be seen through binoculars or a telescope.

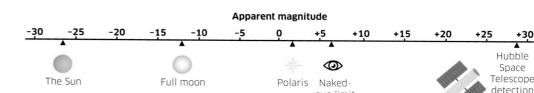

Apparent magnitude

| -30 | -25 | -20 | -15 | -10 | -5 | 0 | +5 | +10 | +15 | +20 | +25 | +30 |

The Sun | Full moon | Polaris | Naked-eye limit | Hubble Space Telescope detection limit

Nebulae

Nebulae are clouds of interstellar gas and dust of various shapes and sizes, ranging from huge star-forming complexes to the smoke rings puffed out by dying stars. Below are a few of the brightest nebulae.

Name: Carina Nebula

Designation: NGC 3372

Constellation: Carina

Magnitude: 1

Distance: 6,500 light-years

Type: Emission nebula

Visibility: Naked eye

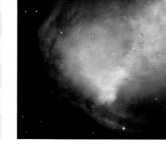

Name: Dumbbell Nebula

Designation: M27

Constellation: Vulpecula

Magnitude: 7.5

Distance: 1,360 light-years

Type: Planetary nebula

Visibility: Binoculars

Name: Orion Nebula

Designation: M42

Constellation: Orion

Magnitude: 4

Distance: 1,340 light-years

Type: Emission nebula

Visibility: Naked eye

Name: Helix Nebula

Designation: NGC 7293

Constellation: Aquarius

Magnitude: 7.6

Distance: 700 light-years

Type: Planetary nebula

Visibility: Binoculars

Name: Lagoon Nebula

Designation: M8

Constellation: Sagittarius

Magnitude: 6

Distance: 4,100 light-years

Type: Emission nebula

Visibility: Naked eye

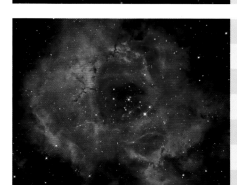

Name: Rosette Nebula

Designation: NGC 2237

Constellation: Monoceros

Magnitude: 9

Distance: 5,200 light-years

Type: Emission nebula

Visibility: Binoculars

Galaxies

The brightest galaxies in the sky tend to be those closest to the Milky Way. This table lists some of the most interesting galaxies that can be observed with binoculars or the naked eye.

KEY

 Irregular   Barred spiral

Spiral   Elliptical

Type	Name	Designation	Constellation	Apparent magnitude	Distance	Visibility
Barred spiral	Large Magellanic Cloud	LMC	Dorado/Mensa	0.9	160,000 light-years	Naked eye
Irregular	Small Magellanic Cloud	SMC	Tucana	2.7	200,000 light-years	Naked eye
Spiral	Andromeda Galaxy	M32	Andromeda	3.4	2.5 million light-years	Naked eye
Spiral	Triangulum Galaxy	M33	Triangulum	5.7	2.9 million light-years	Binoculars
Elliptical	Centaurus A	NGC 5128	Centaurus	6.8	13.7 million light-years	Binoculars
Spiral	Bode's Galaxy	M81	Ursa Major	6.9	11.8 million light-years	Binoculars
Spiral	Southern Pinwheel	M83	Hydra	7.5	15.2 million light-years	Binoculars
Barred spiral	Sculptor Galaxy	NGC 253	Sculptor	8.0	11.4 million light-years	Binoculars

Glossary

ANTENNA
A rod- or dishlike structure on spacecraft and telescopes used to transmit and receive radio signals.

APHELION
The point in the orbit of a planet, comet, or asteroid at which it is farthest from the Sun.

ASTEROID
A small, irregular Solar System object made of rock and/or metal that orbits the Sun.

ASTEROID BELT
A donut-shaped region of the Solar System, between the orbits of Mars and Jupiter, that contains a large number of orbiting asteroids.

ASTRONAUT
A person trained to travel and live in space.

ATMOSPHERE
The layer of gas that surrounds a planet. Also the outermost layer of gas around the Sun or a star.

ATOM
The smallest particle of a chemical element that can exist on its own.

AURORA
Patterns of light that appear near the poles of some planets. Solar wind particles are trapped by a planet's magnetic field and drawn into its atmosphere, where they collide with atoms and cause them to give off light.

AXIS
The imaginary line that passes through the center of a planet or star and around which the planet or star rotates.

BIG BANG
The explosion that created the Universe billions of years ago. According to the Big Bang theory, the Universe began in an extremely dense and hot state and has been expanding ever since. The Big Bang was the origin of space, time, and matter.

BLACK HOLE
An object in space with such a strong gravitational pull that nothing, not even light, can escape from it.

BLAZAR
An active galaxy with a supermassive black hole at its center.

CHARGED PARTICLE
A particle that has a positive or negative electrical charge.

CHROMOSPHERE
A gaseous layer above the surface of a star, such as the Sun. Along with the corona, it forms the star's outer atmosphere.

COMET
An object made of dust and ice that travels around the Sun in an elliptical orbit. As it gets near the Sun, the ice starts to vaporize, creating a tail of dust and gas.

CONSTELLATION
A named area of the sky (defined by the International Astronomical Union). The whole sky is divided into 88 constellations. Many are based around distinctive patterns of stars.

CORONA
The outermost part of the Sun or a star's atmosphere, seen as a white halo during a solar eclipse.

COSMONAUT
A Russian astronaut.

CRATER
A bowl-shaped depression on the surface of a planet, moon, asteroid, or other body.

CRUST
The thin, solid outer layer of a planet or moon.

DARK ENERGY
The energy that scientists believe is responsible for the acceleration in the expansion of the Universe.

DARK MATTER
Invisible matter that can be detected only by the effect of its gravity.

DENSITY
The amount of matter that occupies a certain volume.

DWARF PLANET
A planet that is big enough to have become spherical but hasn't managed to clear all the debris from its orbital path.

ECLIPSE
An astronomical event in which an object either passes into the shadow of another object or temporarily blocks an observer's view. During a solar eclipse, the shadow of the Moon falls on Earth. In a lunar eclipse, the shadow of Earth falls on the Moon.

ELECTROMAGNETIC RADIATION
Energy waves that can travel through space and matter. Visible light, X-rays, and microwaves are all forms of electromagnetic radiation.

EQUATOR
The imaginary line around the center of a planet, halfway between its north and south poles.

ESCAPE VELOCITY
The minimum speed at which an object has to travel to escape the gravity of a planet or moon. Earth's escape velocity is 7 miles (11.2 km) per second.

EXOPLANET
A planet that orbits a star other than the Sun.

GALAXY
A collection of millions or trillions of stars, gas, and dust held together by gravity.

GAMMA RAY
An electromagnetic energy wave that has a very short wavelength.

GLOBULAR CLUSTER
A large, ball-shaped cluster of old stars tightly packed together.

GRANULATION
Mottling on the surface of the Sun or another star.

GRAVITY
The force that pulls all objects that have mass and energy toward one another. It is the force that keeps moons in orbit around planets and planets in orbit around the Sun.

HABITABLE
Suitable for living in or on.

HEMISPHERE
One half of a sphere. Earth is divided into northern and southern hemispheres by the equator.

HERTZSPRUNG–RUSSELL DIAGRAM
A diagram showing a star's temperature and brightness in relation to other stars.

INFRARED
Electromagnetic radiation with wavelengths shorter than radio waves but longer than visible light. It is the primary form of radiation emitted by many objects in space.

LAUNCH VEHICLE
A rocket-powered vehicle that is used to send spacecraft or satellites into space.

LIGHT-YEAR
The distance traveled by light in a vacuum in one year.

LITHOSPHERE
The solid, hard outer layer of a planet or moon.

MAGNETIC FIELD
A field of force that may, for example, be created by a planet, star, or galaxy and surround it.

MAGNITUDE
The brightness of an object in space given as a number. Bright objects have low or negative numbers and dim objects have high numbers.

MAIN-SEQUENCE STAR
An ordinary star, such as our Sun, that shines by converting hydrogen to helium. Main-sequence stars lie on the main band of the Hertzsprung–Russell diagram.

MANTLE
A thick layer between the core and the crust of a planet or moon.

MARE
A large, flat area on the Moon's surface that looks dark when viewed from Earth. These areas were originally thought to be lakes or seas but are now known to be floods of solidified lava.

MATTER
Something that exists as a solid, liquid, or gas.

MESOSPHERE
The layer of atmosphere 30–50 miles (50–80 km) above Earth.

METEOR
A streak of light, also called a shooting star, seen when a meteoroid burns up due to friction on entering Earth's atmosphere.

METEORITE
A meteoroid that reaches the ground and survives impact. Meteorites are usually classified according to their composition as stony, iron, or stony-iron.

METEOROID
A particle of rock, metal, or ice traveling through space.

MICROWAVE
Electromagnetic radiation with wavelengths longer than infrared and visible light but shorter than radio waves.

MILKY WAY
The barred spiral galaxy that contains the Solar System and is visible to the naked eye as a band of faint light across the night sky.

MODULE
A portion of a spacecraft.

NEBULA
A cloud of gas and/or dust in space.

NEUTRINO
A subatomic particle produced by nuclear fusion in stars, as well as in the Big Bang.

NEUTRON
A subatomic particle that does not have an electrical charge. It is found in all atomic nuclei except those of hydrogen.

NEUTRON STAR
A dense collapsed star that is mainly made of neutrons.

NUCLEAR FUSION
A process in which two atomic nuclei join to form a heavier nucleus and release large amounts of energy.

NUCLEUS
The compact central core of an atom or galaxy. The solid body of a comet.

ORBIT
The path taken by an object around another when affected by its gravity. The orbits of planets are mostly elliptical in shape.

ORBITER
A spacecraft that is designed to orbit an object but not land on it.

PARTICLE
An extremely small part of a solid, liquid, or gas.

PAYLOAD
Cargo or equipment carried into space by a rocket or a spacecraft.

PENUMBRA
The lighter outer shadow cast by an object. A person inside this region can see part of the source of light causing the shadow. Also the lighter, less cool region of a sunspot.

PERIHELION
The point in the orbit of a planet, comet, or asteroid at which it is closest to the Sun.

PHASE
The portion of a moon or planet that is seen to be lit by the Sun. The Moon passes through a cycle of different phases every 30 days.

PHOTOSPHERE
The thin gaseous layer at the base of the Sun's atmosphere from which visible light is emitted.

PLANET
A spherical object that orbits a star and is sufficiently massive to have cleared its orbital path of debris.

PLANETARY NEBULA
A glowing cloud of gas around a star at the end of its life.

PLANETESIMALS
Small rocky or icy objects formed in the early Solar System that were pulled together by gravity to form planets.

PLANISPHERE
A disk-shaped star map with an overlay that shows which part of the sky is visible at particular times and dates.

PLASMA
A highly energized form of gas. The Sun is made of plasma.

PROBE
An uncrewed spacecraft that is designed to explore objects in space and transmit information back to Earth (especially one that explores the atmosphere or surface of an object).

PROMINENCE
A large, flamelike plume of plasma emerging from the Sun's photosphere.

PULSAR
A neutron star that sends out beams of radiation as it spins.

QUASAR
Short for "quasi-stellar radio source," a quasar is the immensely luminous nucleus of a distant active galaxy with a supermassive black hole at its center.

RED GIANT
A large, luminous star with a low surface temperature and a reddish color. It "burns" helium in its core rather than hydrogen and is nearing the final stages of its life.

ROVER
A vehicle that is driven remotely on the surface of a planet or moon.

SATELLITE
An object that orbits another object larger than itself.

SEYFERT GALAXY
An active galaxy, often spiral in shape, with a supermassive black hole at the center.

SOLAR FLARE
The brightening of a part of the Sun's surface, accompanied by a release of huge amounts of electromagnetic energy.

SOLAR WIND
A continuous flow of fast-moving charged particles from the Sun.

SPACE-TIME
A combination of three dimensions of space—length, breadth, height—with the dimension of time.

SPACEWALK
Activity by an astronaut in space outside a spacecraft, usually to conduct repairs or test equipment.

STAR
A huge sphere of glowing plasma that generates energy by nuclear fusion in its core.

STRATOSPHERE
The layer of the atmosphere 5–30 miles (8–50 km) above Earth's surface.

SUBATOMIC PARTICLE
Any particle smaller than an atom.

SUNSPOT
A region of intense magnetic activity in the Sun's photosphere that appears darker than its surroundings.

THERMOSPHERE
The layer of the atmosphere 50–375 miles (80–600 km) above Earth's surface.

THRUST
The force from an engine that propels a rocket or spacecraft forward.

TRANSIT
The passage of a planet or star in front of another, larger object.

TROPOSPHERE
The layer of the atmosphere 4–12 miles (6–20 km) above Earth's surface.

ULTRAVIOLET RADIATION
Electromagnetic radiation with wavelengths shorter than visible light but longer than X-rays.

UMBRA
The darker central shadow cast by an object. A person inside this region cannot see the source of light causing the shadow. Also the darker, cooler region of a sunspot.

X-RAY
Electromagnetic radiation with wavelengths shorter than ultraviolet radiation but longer than gamma rays.

Index

Acknowledgments

The publisher would like to thank the following people for their assistance in the preparation of this book:
Ann Baggaley, Virien Chopra, Rohini Deb, Upamanyu Das, and Ashwin Khurana for editorial assistance; Nick Sotiriadis, Bryan Versteeg, and the Maltings Partnership for additional illustrations; Steve Crozier for image retouching; Harish Aggarwal, Priyanka Sharma, and Saloni Singh for the jacket; Caroline Stamps for proofreading; and Helen Peters for the index.

Curator for the Smithsonian (for the first edition):
Andrew Johnston, Geographer, Center for Earth and Planetary Studies, National Air and Space Museum, Smithsonian

Smithsonian Enterprises:
Kealy Gordon, Product Development Manager
Jill Corcoran, Director of Licensed Publishing
Janet Archer, DMM Ecom and D-to-C
Carol LeBlanc, President, SE

The publisher would like to thank the following for their kind permission to reproduce their photographs:

(Key: a-above; b-below/bottom; c-center; f-far; l-left; r-right; t-top)

2 NASA: Tony Gray and Tom Farrar (cl). **3 Dreamstime.com:** Peter Jurik (cb). **ESO:** The design for the E-ELT shown here is preliminary. http://creativecommons.org/licenses/by/3.0 (cr). **9 ESA:** OSIRIS Team MPS / UPD / LAM / IAA / RSSD / INTA / UPM / DASP / IDA (clb). **ESO:** E. Slawik http://creativecommons.org/licenses/by/3.0 (clb/Hale-bopp). **NASA:** (bl). **Science Photo Library:** Detlev Van Ravenswaay (clb/Pluto). **10 NASA:** JPL (tc). **12 Science Photo Library:** Jean-Claude Revy, A. Carion, ISM (br); Mark Garlick (clb). **13 NASA:** JPL-Caltech / T. Pyle (SSC) (bc). **14 BBSO / Big Bear Solar Observatory:** (clb). **15 Corbis:** Daniel J. Cox (crb). **16 NASA:** (clb). **17 NASA:** Johns Hopkins University Applied Physics Laboratory / Carnegie Institution of Washington (br). **18 NASA:** (tl); JPL (cra). **19 NASA:** JPL (tr). **20 FLPA:** Chris Newbert / Minden Pictures (cl). **21 Corbis:** Frans Lanting (cb, bc). **NASA:** Robert Simmon, using Suomi NPP VIIRS data provided courtesy of Chris Elvidge (NOAA National Geophysical Data Center). Suomi NPP is the result of a partnership between NASA, NOAA, and the Department of Defense. (crb). **22 Corbis:** Stocktrek Images (cra). **NASA:** Hal Pierce, NASA / GSFC (cl). **24 Getty Images:** Dana Berry (cla). **NASA:** (br). **25 NASA:** (tr). **29 Corbis:** Jim Wark / Visuals Unlimited (tc). **30 NASA:** Carla Thomas (tl). **31 Alamy Images:** Alexey Stiop (bc). **Corbis:** Brian Cassey / epa (tl). **32 Corbis:** Walter Myers / Stocktrek Images (bl). **NASA:** JPL / MSSS / Ed Truthan (tc). **33 NASA:** JPL-Caltech / University of Arizona (crb, fcrb). **34 ESA:** DLR / FU Berlin (cra). **NASA:** JPL / University of Arizona (ca). **34-35 NASA:** (tl). **Kees Veenenbos:** (b). **36 NASA:** (bc); Edward A. Guinness (bl). **37 NASA:** JPL-Caltech (bc); JPL-Caltech / ASU / MSSS (br). **38-39 NASA:** JPL-Caltech / MSSS. **41 NASA:** JPL-Caltech / UCLA / MPS / DLR / IDA (tr). **42 Alamy Stock Photo:** Citizen of the Planet / Scott Murphy (br). **44 NASA:** (bl). **45 NASA:** Hubble Heritage Team (STScI / AURA) Acknowledgment: NASA / ESA, John Clarke (University of Michigan) (tc); JPL, Galileo Project, (NOAO), J. Burns (Cornell) et al. (crb). **47 NASA:** JPL (c). **48 NASA:** JPL / University of Arizona (tr). **49 NASA:** JPL / University of Arizona (br). **51 NASA:** (br); JPL-Caltech / SSI (tl, tc, cr). **52 NASA:** JPL-Caltech / SSI (tr, clb). **54-55 NASA:** JPL-Caltech / SSI. **58 NASA:** ESA / NASA / JPL / University of Arizona (c); JPL-Caltech / ASI / JHUAPL / Cornell / Weizman (cl); JPL-Caltech / ASI / USGS (bl). **61 W.M. Keck Observatory:** Lawrence Sromovsky, University of Wisconsin-Madison (br). **62 Corbis:** NASA / Roger Ressmeyer (clb). **63 NASA:** JPL (cb). **Dr. Dominic Fortes, UCL:** (tc). **64 NASA:** (tr). **65 NASA:** (tr); Johns Hopkins University Applied Physics Laboratory / Southwest Research Institute / Alex Parker (ca, tl). **66 Corbis:** Andrew Bertuleit Photography (clb). **ESA:** Rosetta / MPS for OSIRIS Team MPS / UPD / LAM / IAA / SSO / INTA / UPM / DASP / IDA (clb/comet). **ESO:** E. Slawik (bc) http://creativecommons.org/licenses/by/3.0. **74 NASA:** ESA and L. Ricci (ESO) (cb); K.L. Luhman (Harvard-Smithsonian Center for Astrophysics, Cambridge, Mass.); and G. Schneider, E. Young, G. Rieke, A. Cotera, H. Chen, M. Rieke, R. Thompson (Steward Observatory, University of Arizona, Tucson, Ariz.) http://creativecommons.org/licenses/by/3.0 (cl). **75 NASA:** ESA, and the Hubble Heritage Team (AURA / STScI) (crb); ESA, M. Livio and the Hubble 20th Anniversary Team (STScI) (br). **77 ESO:** http://creativecommons.org/licenses/by/3.0 (tr). **Danielle Futselaar / SETI Institute (Collaborative work):** (cra). **79 NASA:** ESA / G. Bacon (cra); ESA, Alfred Vidal-Madjar (Institut d'Astrophysique de Paris, CNRS) (fcra). **82-83 NASA:** ESA and the Hubble SM4 ERO Team. **84 Science Photo Library:** Royal Observatory, Edinburgh (bl). **87 Corbis:** Chris Cheadle / All Canada Photos (crb). **88 NASA:** JPL-Caltech (bl). **89 A. Riazuelo, IAP/UPMC/CNRS:** (cr). **90 Adam Block/Mount Lemmon SkyCenter/University of Arizona (Board of Regents):** T. Bash, J. Fox (clb). **Sergio Eguivar:** (cla). **92-93 Two Micron All Sky Survey, which is a joint project of the University of Massachusetts and the Infrared Processing and Analysis Center/California Institute of Technology, funded by the National Aeronautics and Space Administration and the National Science Foundation**. **94 NASA:** ESA, S. Beckwith (STScI), and The Hubble Heritage Team (STScI / AURA) (cl). **96-97 Science Photo Library:** Take 27 Ltd. (bc). **97 Alamy Images:** Paul Fleet (br). **Chandra X-Ray Observatory:** X-ray: NASA / CXC / CfA / M.Markevitch et al.; Optical: NASA / STScI; Magellan / U.Arizona / D.Clowe et al.; Lensing Map: NASA / STScI; ESO WFI; Magellan / U.Arizona / D.Clowe et al. http://creativecommons.org/licenses/by/3.0 (tr). **Dorling Kindersley:** Whipple Museum of History of Science, Cambridge (cr). **NASA:** R. Williams (STScI), the Hubble Deep Field Team (tl). **98-99 Mark Gee**. **100 CFHT/Coelum:** J.-C. Cuillandre & G. Anselmi (clb/M16). **NASA:** ESA, SSC, CXC, and STScI (clb). **101 NASA:** CXC / SAO, JPL-Caltech, Detlef Hartmann (cra); CXC / MSU / J.Strader et al, Optical: NASA / STScI (crb); ESA / Hubble (br). **SSRO:** R.Gilbert, D.Goldman, J.Harvey, D.Verschatse, D.Reichart (cr). **103 NASA:** ESA, S. Baum, and C. O'Dea (RIT), R. Perley and W. Cotton (NRAO / AUI / NSF), and the Hubble Heritage Team (STScI / AURA) (cra); ESA / Hubble & Flickr user Det58 (cr); ESA and the Hubble Heritage Team (STScI / AURA); Acknowledgment: P. Cote (Herzberg Institute of Astrophysics) and E. Baltz (Stanford University) (br). **ESA / Hubble:** Hubble & NASA (crb). **105 NASA:** ESA, Curt Struck and Philip Appleton (Iowa State University), Kirk Borne (Hughes STX Corporation), and Ray Lucas (STSI) (cra); ESA and the Hubble Heritage Team (STScI / AURA) (cr); ESA and the Hubble Heritage Team (STScI / AURA)-ESA / Hubble Collaboration (crb); ESA; Z. Levay and R. van der Marel, STScI; T. Hallas; and A. Mellinger (br). **106 Adam Block / Mount Lemmon SkyCenter / University of Arizona (Board of Regents):** (cl). **CFHT / Coelum:** J.-C. Cuillandre & G. Anselmi (c). **ESO:** Digitized Sky Survey 2 http://creativecommons.org/licenses/by/3.0 (ca). **NASA:** ESA, the Hubble Heritage Team (STScI / AURA), J. Blakeslee (NRC Herzberg Astrophysics Program, Dominion Astrophysical Observatory), and H. Ford (JHU) (cla). **ESA / Hubble:** (bl). **107 NASA:** ESA / Hubble & Digitized Sky Survey 2. Acknowledgment: Davide De Martin (ESA / Hubble) (crb); Swift Science Team / Stefan Immler (br). **110 NASA:** WMAP Science Team (tc). **114 Alamy Stock Photo:** Military News (bc). **NASA:** (clb, bl); Tony Gray and Tom Farrar (ca); JPL-Caltech (cb). **116-117 Dreamstime.com:** Justin Black (tc). **116 Dreamstime.com:** Jahoo (cr). **NASA:** (ca, bl, crb); JPL (cb); Ames / JPL-Caltech (br); ESA and M. Livio and the Hubble 20th Anniversary Team (STScI) (bc). **117 Alamy Images:** DBI Studio (c); Danil Roudenko (br). **Dorling Kindersley:** The Science Museum, London (tr). **Shutterstock.com:** Uncredited / AP (bl). **Getty Images:** Universal History Archive (ca). **NASA:** (tc, cb); Hubble Heritage Team, D. Gouliermis (MPI Heidelberg) et al., (STScI / AURA), ESA (bc). **118-119 European Southern Observatory:** The design for the E-ELT shown here is preliminary http://creativecommons.org/licenses/by/3.0. **119 ESA:** Herschel / PACS / SPIRE / J. Fritz, U. Gent (br). **ESO:** L. Calçada http://creativecommons.org/licenses/by/3.0 (tc). **Adam Evans:** (crb/Visible). **NASA:** GALEX, JPL-Caltech (fcrb); ROSAT, MPE (crb); JPL-Caltech / Univ. of Ariz. (fcrb/mid-infrared). **Science Photo Library:** Dr. Eli Brinks (fbr). **121 NASA:** (tl); Hubble Heritage team, JPL-Caltech / R. Kennicutt (Univ. of Arizona), and the SINGS Team (cr); ESA, HEIC, and The Hubble Heritage Team (STScI / AURA), R. Corradi (Isaac Newton Group of Telescopes, Spain) and Z. Tsvetanov (NASA) (crb); ESA and the Hubble Heritage Team (STScI / AURA) (br). **122 NASA:** (br); Artist concept (tl). **123 NASA:** (cra). **124 NASA:** F. Espenak, GSFC (bl). **125 Rex Features:** Sovfoto / Universal Images Group (c). **128 NASA:** JPL-Caltech / Cornell (bl). **129 NASA:** JPL-Caltech / Cornell University (ca). **130 ESA:** T. Peake (br). **NASA:** Bill Ingalls (cla). **132-133 NASA**. **134 NASA:** (cl). **135 Corbis:** Bettmann (cra). **NASA:** (tc). **137 NASA:** (crb, br). **139 NASA:** J.L. Pickering (cr). **141 NASA:** (br, cra); JSC (crb); Joel Kowsky (cra). **142-143 Alamy Stock Photo:** Geopix. **144 NASA:** (crb). **145 NASA:** Tracy Caldwell Dyson (ca). **146-147 Bryan Versteeg:** (Mars Habitat artworks). **147 Getty Images:** Virgin Galactic / Handout / Anadolu Agency (bl). **Alamy Stock Photo:** Stocktrek Images, Inc. (br). **148 Ohio State University Radio Observatory:** North American Astrophysical Observatory (cr). **Science Photo Library:** Dr. Seth Shostak (b). **149 ESA:** DLR / FU Berlin (G. Neukum) (c). **NASA:** (crb); Galileo Project, JPL, Ted Stryk (bc). **NRAO :** SETi (bl). **150 Corbis:** Rick Fischer / Masterfile (cl). **NASA:** NASA, ESA, K. Kuntz (JHU), F. Bresolin (University of Hawaii), J. Trauger (Jet Propulsion Lab), J. Mould (NOAO), Y.-H. Chu (University of Illinois, Urbana), and STScI, Canada-France-Hawaii Telescope / J.-C. Cuillandre / Coelum, G. Jacoby, B. Bohannan, M. Hanna / NOAO / AURA / NSF (c). **Peter Michaud (Gemini Observatory):** AURA, NSF (cr). **153 Corbis:** (cra). **154 Dreamstime.com:** Andrew Buckin (tr). **154-155 Corbis:** Bryan Allen (bc). **156 Corbis:** Rick Fischer / Masterfile (cra). **157 Corbis:** Alan Dyer, Inc. / Visuals Unlimited (br). **Peter Michaud (Gemini Observatory):** AURA, NSF (cr). **Science Photo Library:** Eckhard Slawik (crb). **159 Corbis:** Alan Dyer, Inc. / Visuals Unlimited (tr, br, cra). **Chris Picking:** (cr). **Science Photo Library:** Celestial Image co. (crb). **163 NASA:** J. P. Harrington (U. Maryland) and K. J. Borkowski (NCSU) (cr). **NOAO / AURA / NSF:** Hillary Mathis, N. A. Sharp (bl). **164 NOAO / AURA / NSF:** Adam Block (bl). **165 NASA:** NASA, ESA and the Hubble Heritage Team STScI / AURA). Acknowledgment: A. Zezas and J. Huchra (Harvard-Smithsonian Center for Astrophysics) (cl); NASA, ESA, K. Kuntz (JHU), F. Bresolin (University of Hawaii), J. Trauger (Jet Propulsion Lab), J. Mould (NOAO), Y.-H. Chu (University of Illinois, Urbana), and STScI, Canada-France-Hawaii Telescope / J.-C. Cuillandre / Coelum, G. Jacoby, B. Bohannan, M. Hanna / NOAO / AURA / NSF (bc). **NOAO / AURA / NSF:** (bl). **166 Adam Block / Mount Lemmon SkyCenter / University of Arizona (Board of Regents):** (c, br). **NASA:** ESA, S. Beckwith (STScI), and The Hubble Heritage Team (STScI / AURA) (tc). **167 NASA:** The Hubble Heritage Team (AURA / STScI / NASA) (br). **168 Adam Block / Mount Lemmon SkyCenter / University of Arizona (Board of Regents):** (bl). **NOAO / AURA / NSF:** N. A. Sharp, REU program (br). **170 NASA:** Stuart Heggie (br). **171 Corbis:** Tony Hallas / Science Faction (bl). **NASA:** ESA / ASU / J. Hester (bc). **Jose Mtanous:** (crb). **172 NASA:** Andrew Fruchter (STScI) (cla). **173 NASA:** The Hubble Heritage Team (STScI / AURA) (clb). **Science Photo Library:** NASA / JPL-CALTECH / CXC / Ohio State University / C. Grier et al. / STScI / ESO / WFI (cr). **174 Corbis:** Roger Ressmeyer (bl). **175 ESO:** http://creativecommons.org/licenses/by/3.0 (ca). **NASA:** ESA / Hubble (br). **176 ESO:** http://creativecommons.org/licenses/by/3.0 (cr). **177 ESO:** VISTA / J. Emerson. Acknowledgment: Cambridge Astronomical Survey Unit http://creativecommons.org/licenses/by/3.0 (bl). **NOAO / AURA / NSF:** (cl). **179 ESO:** http://creativecommons.org/licenses/by/3.0 (bc). **NASA:** ESA, K. L. Luhman (Harvard-Smithsonian Center for Astrophysics, Cambridge, Mass.); and G. Schneider, E. Young, G. Rieke, A. Cotera, H. Chen, M. Rieke, R. Thompson (Steward Observatory, University of Arizona, Tucson, Ariz.) (bl); ESA, M. Robberto (Space Telescope Science Institute / ESA) and the Hubble Space Telescope Orion Treasury Project Team (br). **180 Corbis:** Visuals Unlimited (cla). **ESO:** http://creativecommons.org/licenses/by/3.0 (br). **181 Chandra X-Ray Observatory:** ESO / VLT (cra). **183 ESO:** http://creativecommons.org/licenses/by/3.0 (cla). **NASA:** STScI, Wikisky (br). **185 ESO:** http://creativecommons.org/licenses/by/3.0 (cl). **NASA:** ESA and The Hubble Heritage Team (STScI / AURA). Acknowledgment: P. Knezek (WIYN) (cra). **186 ESO:** http://creativecommons.org/licenses/by/3.0 (bc). **187 Roberto Mura:** (bl). **NASA:** ESA, N. Smith (University of California, Berkeley), and The Hubble Heritage Team (STScI / AURA) (br); The Hubble Heritage Team (STScI / AURA / NASA) (cl). **188 Meire Ruiz:** (bl). **189 John Ebersole:** (cl). **Science Photo Library:** NASA / ESA / STScI (bl). **190 ESO:** M.-R. Cioni / VISTA Magellanic Cloud survey. Acknowledgment: Cambridge Astronomical Survey Unit http://creativecommons.org/licenses/by/3.0 (br). **191 ESO:** (crb). **192 ESO:** Y. Beletsky (LCO) http://creativecommons.org/licenses/by/3.0 (cla). **194 Corbis:** Dennis di Cicco (cr). **NASA:** JPL-Caltech (cl). **NOAO / AURA / NSF:** SSRO / PROMPT / CTIO (c). **197 Corbis:** Dennis di Cicco (cl). **201 Brian Davis:** (crb). **ESO:** (cra). **NASA:** ESA, The Hubble Heritage Team (AURA / STScI) (cla); ESA, M. Robberto (Space Telescope Science Institute / ESA), and the Hubble Space Telescope Orion Treasury Project Team (cl); JPL-Caltech (cr). **NOAO / AURA / NSF:** SSRO / PROMPT / CTIO (clb)

For further information see:
www.dkimages.com

SCIENCE!

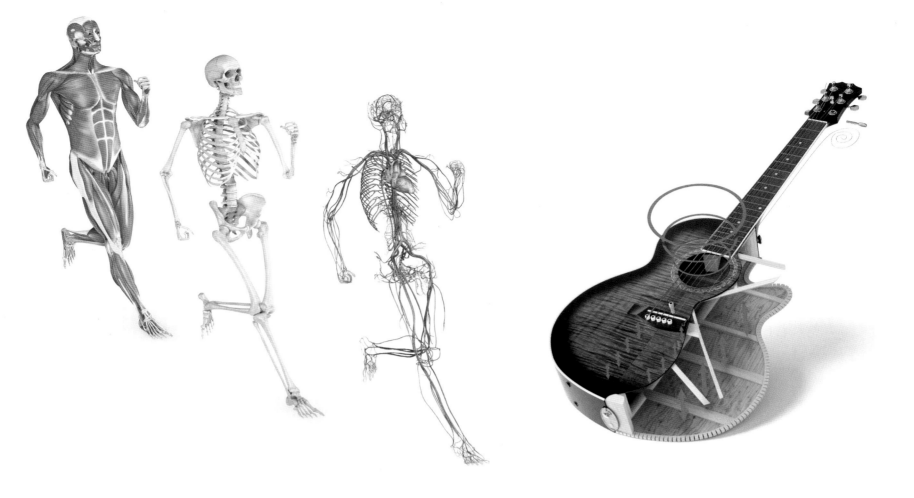

DK SMITHSONIAN ✳

SCIENCE!

Written by: Abigail Beall, Jack Challoner, Adrian Dingle, Derek Harvey, Bea Perks
Consultant: Jack Challoner

Illustrators: Peter Bull, Jason Harding, Stuart Jackson-Carter — SJC Illustration,
Jon @ KJA, Arran Lewis, Sofian Moumene, Alex Pang, Jack Williams

Penguin Random House

DK UK:
Senior Editor Georgina Palffy
Senior Art Editor Stefan Podhorodecki
Editors Vicky Richards, Anna Streiffert Limerick, Alison Sturgeon
US Editor Megan Douglass
Designers David Ball, Gregory McCarthy, Sadie Thomas
Managing Editor Francesca Baines
Managing Art Editor Philip Letsu
Jacket Design Development Manager Sophia MTT
Jacket Editor Amelia Collins
Jacket Designer Surabhi Wadhwa Gandhi
Producer (Pre-Production) Jacqueline Street
Producer Jude Crozier
Publisher Andrew Macintyre
Art Director Karen Self
Associate Publishing Director Liz Wheeler
Design Director Philip Ormerod
Publishing Director Jonathan Metcalf

DK India:
Managing Jackets Editor Saloni Singh
Jacket Designer Tanya Mehrotra
Senior DTP Designer Harish Aggarwal
Jackets Editorial Coordinator Priyanka Sharma
Picture Research Manager Taiyaba Khatoon
Picture Researcher Deepak Negi

First American Edition, 2018
Published in the United States by DK Publishing
1450 Broadway, Suite 801, New York, NY 10018

Copyright © 2018 Dorling Kindersley Limited
DK, a Division of Penguin Random House LLC
22 23 24 10 9 8 7 6 5 4 3 2 1
001–334974–Jan 23

A catalog record for this book is available from the Library of Congress.
ISBN 978-1-4654-7363-9

DK books are available at special discounts when purchased in bulk for sales promotions, premiums, fund-raising, or educational use. For details, contact: DK Publishing Special Markets, 1450 Broadway, Suite 801, New York, NY 10018
SpecialSales@dk.com

Printed and bound in China

For the curious
www.dk.com

THE SMITHSONIAN
Established in 1846, the Smithsonian is the world's largest museum and research complex, dedicated to public education, national service, and scholarship in the arts, sciences, and history. It includes 19 museums and galleries and the National Zoological Park. The total number of artifacts, works of art, and specimens in the Smithsonian's collection is estimated at 154 million.

CONTENTS

MATTER

ENERGY & FORCES

LIFE

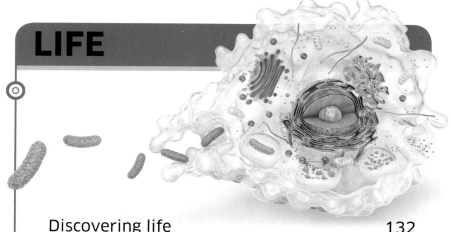

REFERENCE

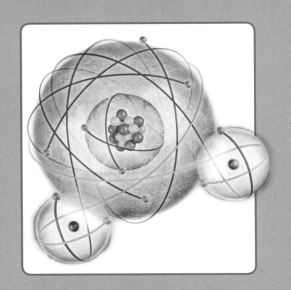

MATTER

The ground beneath your feet, the air around you, and the stars in the sky are made of matter. You are made of matter, too. All matter is made of minute particles called atoms, which join together in countless ways to form an astonishing variety of substances.

1855 The **bunsen burner** is invented by German scientist **Robert Bunsen.**

1909

1913

pH scale invented
Danish chemist Søren Peder Lauritz Sørensen invents the pH scale, which is used to judge whether a substance is an acid, neutral, or base.

Electron shells
The Danish scientist Niels Bohr proposes a model of the atom that shows how electrons occupy shells and orbit around the nucleus.

MODERN TIMES

Modern chemistry
Advances in technology allowed chemists and other scientists to invent new materials by reproducing natural materials synthetically or rearranging atoms through nanotechnology.

New elements
Polish-French scientist Marie Curie and her husband, Pierre, discover two new radioactive elements, radium and polonium. Radium is later used in radiotherapy to treat cancer.

1898

CATHODE RAY TUBE

1897

The Atomic Age
The discovery of radioactivity led to a better understanding of what lies inside an atom, and more research into subatomic particles. This knowledge was put to use in medicine and health care.

Discovery of electrons
English scientist J. J. Thomson discovers electrons using a cathode ray tube. This is the first step toward understanding the structure of atoms.

1890 – 1945

Discovering matter

Thousands of years of questioning, experimentation, and research have led to our understanding of matter as we know it today.

Following the earliest explorations of matter by our prehistoric ancestors, Greek philosophers were among the first people to attempt to classify matter and explain its behavior. Over time, scientists found more sophisticated ways of analyzing different types of matter and discovered many of the elements. The Industrial Revolution saw the invention of new synthetic materials using these elements, while greater understanding of the structure of atoms led to significant advances in medicine. New substances and materials with particularly useful properties are still being discovered and invented to this day.

1772 / 1774

Discovery of oxygen
Swedish chemist Carl Scheele builds a contraption to capture oxygen by heating various compounds together. English scientist Joseph Priestley also discovers oxygen by showing that a candle can't burn without it.

1789

Antoine Lavoisier
French chemist Antoine Lavoisier publishes *Elements of Chemistry*, which lists the 33 known elements divided into four types: gases, metals, non-metals, and earths.

SCHEELE'S OXYGEN APPARATUS

Timeline of discoveries
From prehistory to the present day, people have sought to understand how matter behaves and to classify different types. Over the years, this has led to the discovery of new matter and materials.

Prehistory to antiquity
The earliest discoveries of how matter behaves were made not by scientists, but by prehistoric ancestors trying to survive. During antiquity, philosophers spent a lot of time trying to work out what matter is.

Making fire
Our ancestors learn to make fire using combustion (although they don't know that at the time).

Copper and bronze
Smelting of copper (extracting it from its ore through heat) is discovered. Bronze (copper smelted with tin) is first produced in 3200 BCE.

Greek philosophers
Empedocles suggests that everything is made of four elements: air, earth, fire, and water. Democritus suggests that all matter consists of atoms.

BEFORE 500 CE

790,000 BCE

3200 BCE

420 BCE

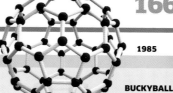

1661 Robert Boyle's *The Sceptical Chymist* develops a **theory of atoms**.

1958

1985

2004

BUCKYBALL

GRAPHENE

Carbon dioxide monitoring
American scientist Charles David Keeling starts to monitor the rise of carbon dioxide in the atmosphere. His Keeling Curve graph is still used to study climate change.

Buckyball discovery
Scientists at Rice University in Houston discover a new form of carbon called buckminsterfullerene, or buckyball.

World's thinnest material
Graphene (a layer of carbon atoms just one atom thick) is produced at the University of Manchester, UK. It is the world's thinnest material, but 200 times stronger than steel.

1945 – PRESENT

1870

1869

1890–1945

Synthetic materials
The first synthetic materials made from cellulose are invented: celluloid (moldable plastic) in 1870 and viscose rayon in 1890.

Mendeleev's periodic table
Russian chemist Dmitri Mendeleev arranges the 59 known elements into groups based on their atomic mass and properties. This periodic table enables him to predict the discovery of three more elements.

VISCOSE, SYNTHETIC SILK

GAY-LUSSAC EXPERIMENTING WITH AIR PRESSURE IN HOT-AIR BALLOON

1803

19TH CENTURY

Industrial Revolution
Driven by the thirst for modernization, chemists identified more elements and invented ways to use them in medicine, in creating new materials, and in advanced industrial technologies.

Dalton's atomic theory
English chemist John Dalton argues that all matter is composed of atoms and atoms of the same element are identical. He compiles a list of elements based on their atomic mass, then known as atomic weight.

Structure of water
French chemist Joseph Louis Gay-Lussac experiments with gases and pressure and finds that water is made up of two parts hydrogen and one part oxygen.

1805

DALTON'S ATOMIC MODELS

1800 – 1890

1527

Age of Discovery
The Renaissance brought both rediscovery of antique knowledge and a quest for fresh ideas. Scientists began to test, experiment, and document their ideas, publishing their findings and working hard to classify matter.

17TH CENTURY

Salts, sulfurs, and mercuries
Swiss chemist Theophrastus von Hohenheim works out a new classification for chemicals, based on salts, sulfurs, and mercuries.

1600 – 1800

Classifying elements
Persian physician Al-Razi divides elements into spirits, metals, and minerals depending on how they react with heat.

Middle Ages
In Asia and the Islamic world, alchemists experimented to find the elixir of life and to make gold. By the late Middle Ages, European alchemists were working toward the same goal.

Gunpowder
While they are looking for the elixir of life, Chinese alchemists accidentally invent gunpowder by mixing saltpeter with sulfur and charcoal.

500 CE – 1600

855 CE

900

MIDDLE AGES

WHAT IS MATTER?

The air around you, the water you drink, the food you eat, your own body, the stars, and the planets—all of these things are matter. There is clearly a huge variety of different types of matter, but it is all made of tiny particles called atoms, far too small to see. About ninety different kinds of atom join together in many combinations to make all the matter in the universe.

PARTICLES OF MATTER

Matter is made of atoms—but in many substances, those atoms are combined in groups called molecules, and in some they exist as ions: atoms that carry an electric charge. Both atoms and ions can bond together to form compounds.

Atoms and molecules

An atom is incredibly small: you would need a line of 100,000 of them to cover the width of a human hair. Tiny though they are, atoms are made of even smaller particles: protons, neutrons, and electrons. Different kinds of atom have different numbers of these particles. Atoms often join, or bond, in groups called molecules. A molecule can contain atoms of the same kind or of different kinds.

It's a matter of water

Water is one of the most abundant substances on Earth. More than two thirds of the surface of Earth is covered by water. Animals contain lots of water, too—nearly two thirds of a cat's mass is water, for example. Water is made up of H_2O molecules, each made up of atoms of hydrogen and oxygen.

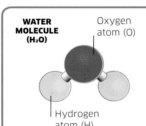

WATER MOLECULE (H_2O)
Oxygen atom (O)
Hydrogen atom (H)

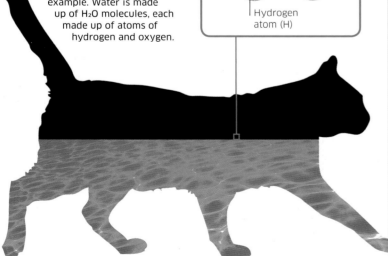

ELEMENTS, COMPOUNDS, AND MIXTURES

Everything around us is matter, but it is a bit more complex than that. Elements can exist on their own, but usually bond together chemically with other elements to form compounds or appear in mixtures (substances in which the "ingredients" are not chemically bonded, but simply mixed together). A mixture can consist of two or more elements, an element and a compound, or two or more separate compounds.

What's what?

Everything can be sorted into different categories of matter, depending on whether it is a pure substance or a mixture of different substances. This diagram shows the main types.

Cut diamond

Pure substances
Matter is pure if it is made of just one kind of substance. That substance can be an element or a compound. Diamond, a form of the element carbon, is a pure substance. So is salt (sodium chloride), a compound of the elements sodium and chlorine.

Elements
An element, such as gold, is a pure substance, made of only one kind of atom. Iron, aluminum, oxygen, carbon, and chlorine are other examples of elements. All elements have different properties, and are sorted into a chart called the periodic table (see pp.28–29).

Compounds
A compound is a pure substance that consists of atoms of different elements bonded together. In any particular compound, the ratio of the different kinds of atoms is always the same. In salt there are equal numbers of sodium and chlorine atoms (1:1), while water contains twice as many hydrogen as oxygen atoms (2:1).

Stainless steel—an alloy of iron, carbon, and chromium—is a homogeneous mixture.

Homogeneous mixtures
In a homogeneous mixture, particles of different substances are mixed evenly, so the mixture has the same composition throughout. They can be solid (steel), liquid (honey), or gas (air).

Solutions
All homogeneous mixtures are solutions, but the most familiar are those where a solid has been dissolved in a liquid. An example is salt water—in which the salt breaks down into ions that mix evenly among the water molecules. In sugary drinks, the sugar is also dissolved—no grains of sugar float around in the solution.

The air in a balloon is a homogeneous mixture of several gases, mostly the elements nitrogen and oxygen.

Matter
Matter can be solid, liquid, or gas. Most of the matter around you, from planets to animals, is composed of mixtures of different substances. Only a few substances exist naturally in completely pure form.

A frog is made of compounds and mixtures.

An ice cream is an impure substance—a mixture of many different ingredients.

A sandwich is a mixture of several substances.

Impure substances
If a substance is impure, it means that something has been mixed into it. For example, pure water consists of only hydrogen and oxygen. But tap water contains minerals, too, which makes it an impure substance. All mixtures are impure substances.

Mixtures
There are many different kinds of mixtures, depending on what substances are in the mix and how evenly they mix. The substances in a mixture are not bound together chemically, and can be separated. Rocks are solid mixtures of different minerals that have been pressed or heated together.

A leaf is a very complex uneven mixture.

Muddy water is a suspension: it may look evenly mixed at first, but the larger mud particles soon separate out.

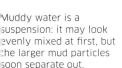

Heterogeneous mixtures
In a heterogeneous mixture, particles of different substances are mixed unevenly. Examples are concrete (a mixture of sand, cement, and stone) and sand on a beach, which consists of tiny odd-sized particles of eroded rock, sea shells, and glass fragments.

Suspensions
Suspensions are liquids that contain small particles that do not dissolve. If they are shaken, they can appear evenly mixed for a short time, but then the particles separate out and you can see them with your naked eye.

Colloids
A colloid looks like an even mixture, but no particles have been completely dissolved. Milk, for example, consists of water and fat. The fat does not dissolve in water, but floats around in minute blobs that you cannot see without a microscope. A cloud is a colloid of tiny water droplets mixed in air.

STATES OF MATTER
Most substances exist as solids, liquids, or gases—or as mixtures of these three states of matter. The particles of which they are made (the atoms, molecules, or ions) are in constant motion. The particles of a solid vibrate but are held in place—that's why a solid is rigid and keeps its shape. In a liquid, the particles are still attracted to each other, but can move over each other, making it fluid. In a gas, the particles have broken free from each other, and move around at high speed.

Changing states of matter
With changes in temperature, and sometimes in pressure, one state can change into another. If it is warm, a solid ice cube melts into liquid water. If you boil the water, it turns into gaseous steam. When steam cools down, it turns back into a liquid, such as the tiny droplets of mist forming on a bathroom window. Only some substances, including candle wax, exist in all three states.

Gases
Near the wick, the temperature is high enough to vaporize the liquid wax, forming a gas of molecules that can react with the air. This keeps the flame burning.

Liquid
In the heat of the flame, the wax melts, and the molecules can move over each other and flow.

Solid
Solid wax is made of molecules held together. Each wax molecule is made of carbon and hydrogen atoms.

Plasma, the fourth state of matter
When gas heats up to a very high temperature, electrons break free from their atoms. The gas is now a mixture of positively charged ions and negatively charged electrons: a plasma. A lightning bolt is a tube of plasma because of the extremely high temperature inside it. In space, most of the gas that makes up the sun, and other stars in our universe, is so hot it is plasma.

Atomic proportions

You would have to enlarge an atom to a trillion times its size to make it as big as a football stadium. Even at that scale, the atom's electrons would be specks of dust flying around the stadium, and its nucleus would be the size of a marble.

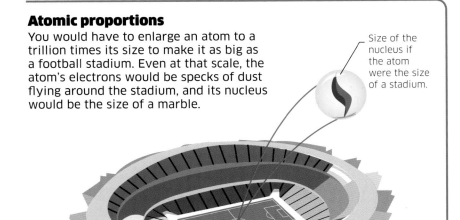

Size of the nucleus if the atom were the size of a stadium.

Atoms

You, and all the things around you, are made of tiny particles called atoms—particles so minuscule that even a small grain of sand is made up of trillions of them.

Atoms were once thought to be the smallest possible parts of matter, impossible to split into anything smaller. But they are actually made of even smaller particles called protons, neutrons, and electrons. Atoms join, or bond, in many different ways to make every different kind of material. A pure substance, consisting of only one type of atom, is called an element. Some familiar elements include gold, iron, carbon, neon, and oxygen. To find out more about the elements, see pp.28–41.

Atomic structure

The nucleus at the center of an atom is made of protons and neutrons. The protons carry a positive electric charge. The neutrons carry no charge—they are neutral. Around the nucleus are the electrons, which carry a negative electric charge. It is the force between the positively charged protons and the negatively charged electrons that holds an atom together.

Particles of an atom

Every atom of an element has the same number of electrons as it has protons, but the number of neutrons can be different. Below are the particles of one atom of the element carbon.

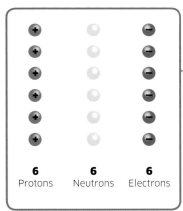

6	**6**	**6**
Protons	Neutrons	Electrons

Carbon atom

The number of protons in an atom's nucleus is called the atomic number. This defines what an element is like: each element has a different atomic number, as shown in the periodic table (see pp.28–29). For the element carbon, shown here, the atomic number is 6. An atom's number of electrons is also equal to its atomic number.

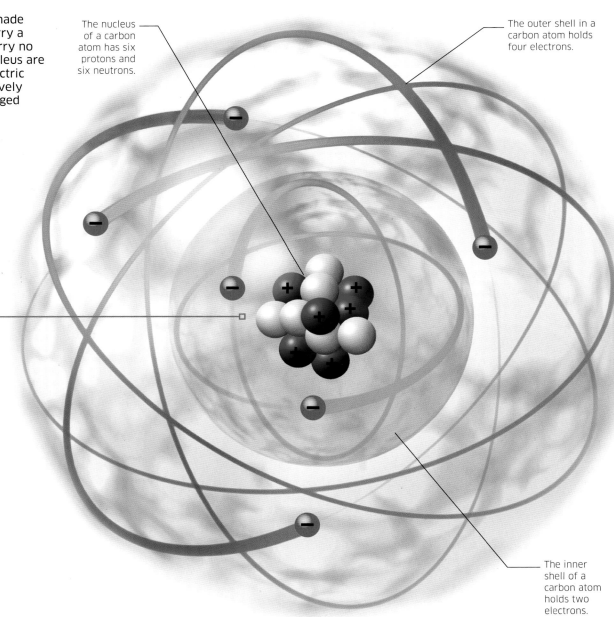

The nucleus of a carbon atom has six protons and six neutrons.

The outer shell in a carbon atom holds four electrons.

The inner shell of a carbon atom holds two electrons.

Atoms of the **element helium** are **the smallest** of all **atoms**.

1803 The year **schoolteacher John Dalton** presented his **theory** about **what atoms are** and what they do.

13

Electrons and electron shells

An atom's electrons are arranged around the nucleus in shells. Each shell can hold a certain number of electrons before it is full: the inner shell can hold 2, the next shell 8, the third one 18, and so on. The heaviest atoms, with large numbers of electrons, have seven shells. Atoms that don't have full outer shells are unstable. They seek to share, or exchange, electrons with other atoms to form chemical compounds. This process is known as a chemical reaction. Atoms with a filled outer shell are stable, and therefore very unreactive.

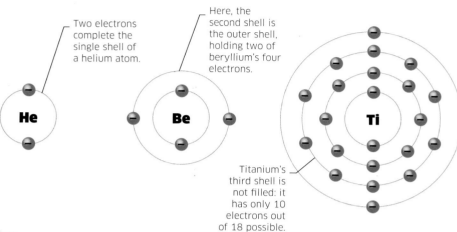

Two electrons complete the single shell of a helium atom.

He

Here, the second shell is the outer shell, holding two of beryllium's four electrons.

Be

Ti

Titanium's third shell is not filled: it has only 10 electrons out of 18 possible.

Helium
The gas helium has the atomic number 2. All its atoms have two electrons, which is the maximum number the first shell can hold. With a full outer shell, helium atoms are very unreactive.

Beryllium
The second shell of an atom can hold up to eight electrons. The metal beryllium (atomic number 4) has a filled inner shell, but only two electrons in its outer shell, making it quite reactive.

Titanium
The metal titanium (atomic number 22) has four shells. It has two electrons in its outer shell, even though the third shell is not full. It is quite common for metals to have unfilled inner shells.

Atomic mass and isotopes

The mass of an atom is worked out by counting the particles of which it is made. Protons and neutrons are more than 1,800 times heavier than electrons, so scientists only take into account those heavier particles, and not the electrons. All atoms of a particular element have the same number of protons, but there are different versions of the atoms, called isotopes, that have different numbers of neutrons. The relative atomic mass of an element is the average of the different masses of all its atoms.

Isotopes of sodium
All atoms of the element sodium (atomic number 11) have 11 protons, and nearly all have 12 neutrons. So the relative atomic mass is very close to 23, but not exactly.

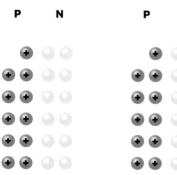

Sodium-22
The sodium isotope with 11 neutrons in its atoms has a mass of 22.

Sodium-23
Sodium-23, the most common sodium isotope, has 11 protons and 12 neutrons.

Sodium-24
This sodium isotope has a mass of 24: 11 protons and 13 neutrons.

Atoms and matter

It is difficult to imagine how atoms make the world around you. Everyday objects don't look as if they consist of tiny round bits joined together: they look continuous. It can help to zoom in closer and closer to an everyday material, such as paper, to get the idea.

Paper
Paper is made almost entirely of a material called cellulose, which is produced inside plant cells, usually from trees. Cellulose is hard-wearing and can absorb inks and paints.

Cellulose fiber
Cellulose forms tiny fibers, each about one thousandth of a millimeter in diameter. The fibers join together, making paper strong and flexible.

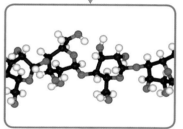

Cellulose molecule
Each cellulose fiber is made of thousands of molecules. A cellulose molecule is a few millionths of a millimeter wide. It is made of atoms of different elements: carbon (black), oxygen (red), and hydrogen (white).

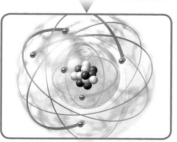

Carbon atom
A typical cellulose molecule contains a few thousand carbon atoms. Each carbon atom has six electrons that form bonds with atoms of the other two elements.

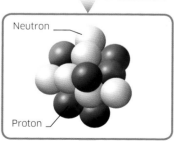

Neutron

Proton

Nucleus
Most of the carbon atom is empty space. Right at the center, about one trillionth of a millimeter across, is the nucleus, made of six protons and six neutrons.

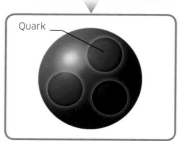

Quark

Quarks
Each particle in the nucleus is made of even smaller particles, called quarks. Each proton—and each neutron—is made of three quarks, held together by particles called gluons.

Molecules

A molecule consists of two or more atoms joined, or bonded, together. Many familiar substances, such as sugar or water, are made up of molecules. Molecules are so small that even a small drop of water contains trillions of them.

All the molecules of a particular compound (chemically bonded substance) are identical. Each one has the same number of atoms, from at least two elements (see pp.28–29), combined in the same way. The bonds that hold molecules together form during chemical reactions but they can be broken as atoms react with other atoms and rearrange to form new molecules. It is not only compounds that can exist as molecules. Many elements exist as molecules, too, but all the atoms that make up these molecules are identical, such as the pair of oxygen atoms that make up pure oxygen (O_2).

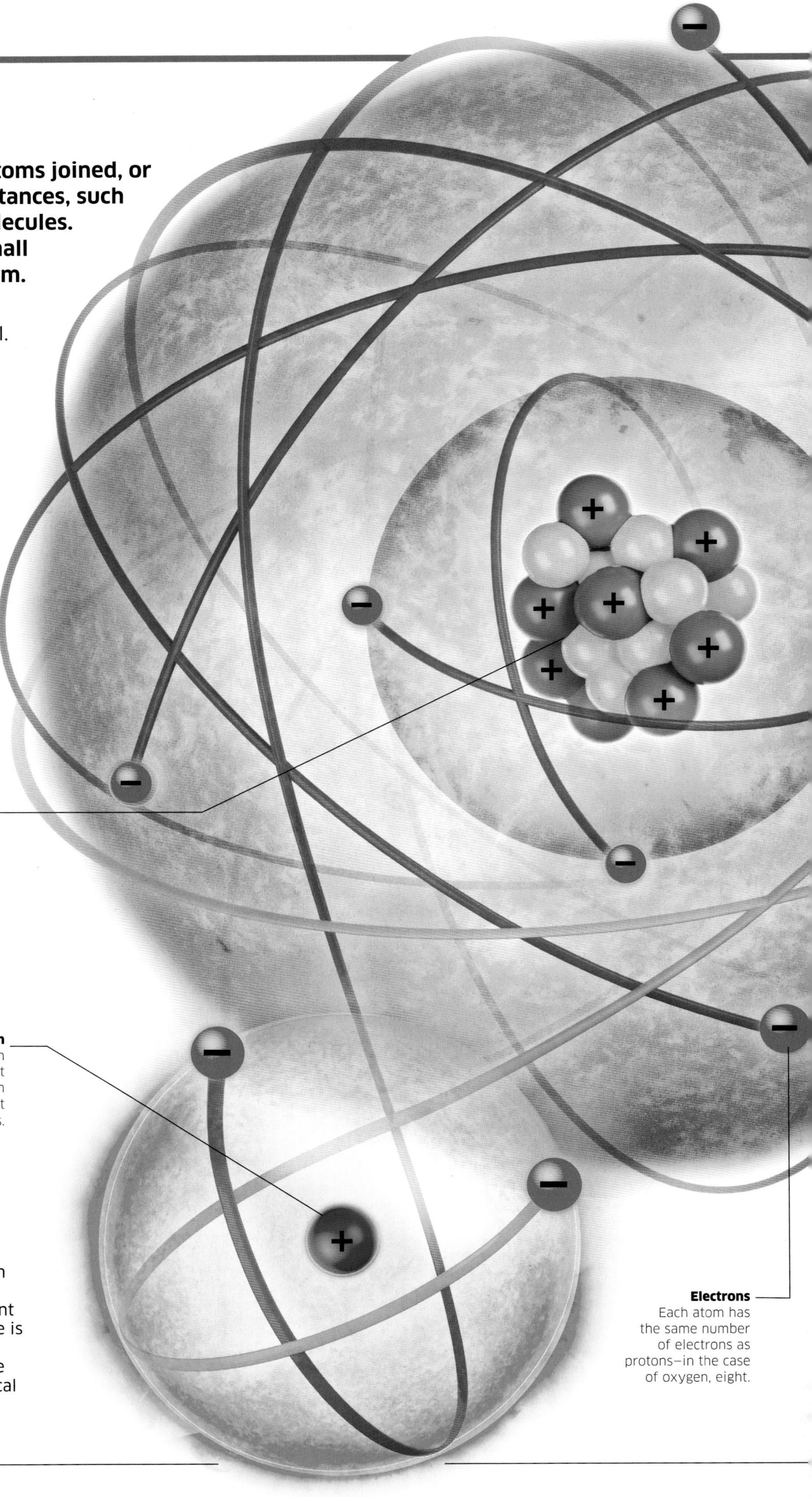

Nucleus of oxygen atom
The oxygen atom has eight protons and eight neutrons in its nucleus. Protons (shown in green) have a positive charge while neutrons (white) are neutral.

Nucleus of hydrogen atom
The hydrogen atom is the only atom that consists of just one proton in its nucleus, and does not contain any neutrons.

Water molecule

Imagine dividing a drop of water in half, and then in half again. If you could keep doing this, you would eventually end up with the smallest amount of water: a water molecule. Every water molecule is made up of one oxygen atom and two hydrogen atoms. The atoms are held together as a molecule because they share electrons, in a type of chemical bond called a covalent bond (see also p.16).

Electrons
Each atom has the same number of electrons as protons—in the case of oxygen, eight.

Around **90 types of atom** combine to make **millions of types of molecule**.

DNA is a supersized molecule that contains around **10 billion atoms**.

15

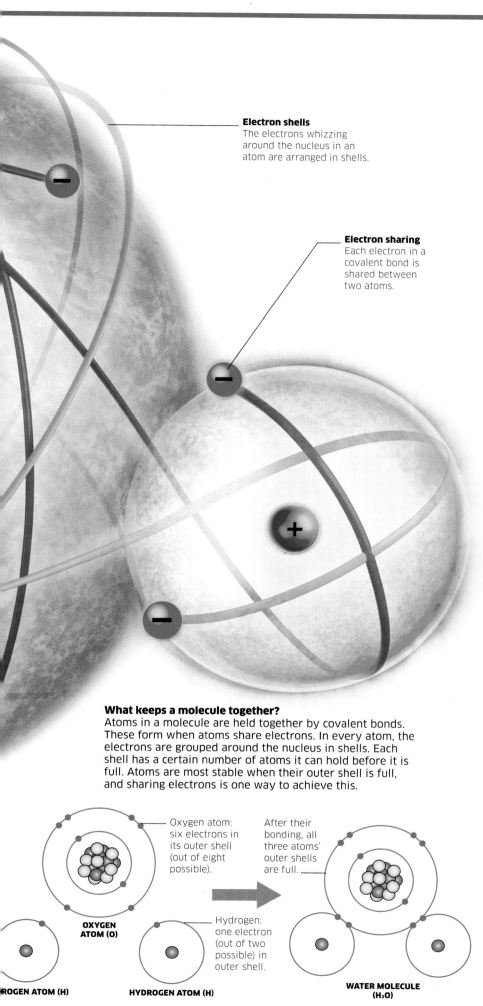

Electron shells
The electrons whizzing around the nucleus in an atom are arranged in shells.

Electron sharing
Each electron in a covalent bond is shared between two atoms.

What keeps a molecule together?

Atoms in a molecule are held together by covalent bonds. These form when atoms share electrons. In every atom, the electrons are grouped around the nucleus in shells. Each shell has a certain number of atoms it can hold before it is full. Atoms are most stable when their outer shell is full, and sharing electrons is one way to achieve this.

Oxygen atom: six electrons in its outer shell (out of eight possible).

After their bonding, all three atoms' outer shells are full.

OXYGEN ATOM (O)

Hydrogen: one electron (out of two possible) in outer shell.

ROGEN ATOM (H)   HYDROGEN ATOM (H)

WATER MOLECULE (H₂O)

Elements and compounds

Most elements are made up of single atoms, but some are made of molecules of two or more identical atoms. When two elements react, their molecules form a new compound.

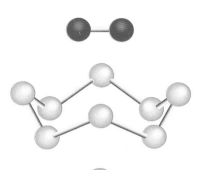

Oxygen
The gas oxygen (O_2) is made of molecules, each containing two oxygen atoms.

Sulfur
Pure sulfur (S), a solid, normally exists as molecules of eight sulfur atoms bonded together.

Sulfur dioxide (SO₂)
When sulfur and oxygen molecules react, their bonds break to make new bonds and a new substance forms.

Representing molecules

Scientists have different ways of representing molecules to understand how chemical reactions happen. Here, a molecule of the gas compound methane (CH_4), made of one carbon atom and four hydrogen atoms, is shown in three ways.

Lewis structure
The simplest way to represent a molecule is to use the chemical symbols (letters) and lines for covalent bonds.

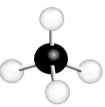

Ball and stick
Showing the atoms as balls and the bonds as sticks gives a three-dimensional representation of a molecule.

Space filling
This method is used when the space and shape of merged atoms in a molecule are more important to show than bonds.

Macromolecules

While some compounds are made of small molecules consisting of just a few atoms, there are many compounds whose molecules are made of thousands of atoms. This molecular model shows a single molecule of a protein found in blood, called albumin. It contains atoms of many different elements, including oxygen, carbon, hydrogen, nitrogen, and sulfur.

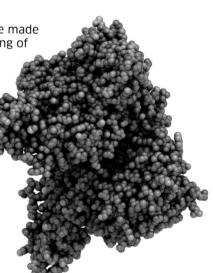

Bonding

Matter is made of atoms. Most of them are joined, or bonded, together. The bonds that hold atoms together are formed by the outermost parts of each atom: the electrons in the atom's outer shell.

There are three main types of bonding: ionic, covalent, and metallic. An ionic bond forms when electrons from one atom transfer to another, so that the atoms become electrically charged and stick together. A covalent bond forms when electrons are shared between two or more atoms. In a metal, the electrons are shared freely between many metal atoms. All chemical reactions involve bonds breaking and forming.

To bond or not to bond

The number of electrons an atom has depends upon how many protons are in its nucleus. This number is different for each element (see p.28). The electrons are arranged in "shells," and it is the electrons in the outermost shell that take part in bonding. An atom is stable when the outermost shell is full (see p.13). The atoms of some elements have outermost shells that are already full—they do not form bonds easily. But most atoms can easily lose or gain electrons, or share them with other atoms, to attain a full outer shell. These atoms do form bonds and take part in chemical reactions.

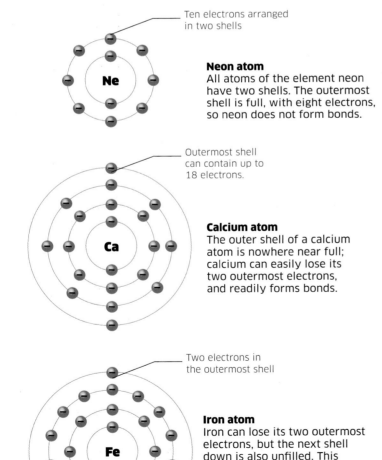

Ten electrons arranged in two shells

Neon atom
All atoms of the element neon have two shells. The outermost shell is full, with eight electrons, so neon does not form bonds.

Outermost shell can contain up to 18 electrons.

Calcium atom
The outer shell of a calcium atom is nowhere near full; calcium can easily lose its two outermost electrons, and readily forms bonds.

Two electrons in the outermost shell

Iron atom
Iron can lose its two outermost electrons, but the next shell down is also unfilled. This means that iron (and most other transition metals) can form all three types of bond—ionic, covalent, and metallic.

Ionic bonding

Many solids are made of ions: atoms, or groups of atoms, that carry an electric charge because they have either more or fewer negative electrons than positive protons. Ions form when atoms (or groups of atoms) lose or gain electrons in order to attain full outer electron shells. Electrical attraction between positive ions (+) and negative ions (-) causes the ions to stick together, forming a crystal.

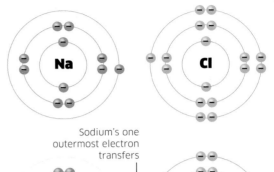

Two atoms
Neither sodium (Na) nor chlorine (Cl) atoms have filled outer shells. Sodium will easily give up its outermost electron.

Sodium's one outermost electron transfers

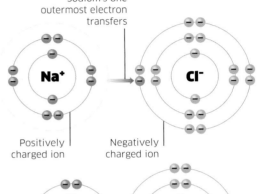

Electron transfer
Chlorine readily accepts the electron, so now both atoms have filled outer shells. They have become electrically charged and are now ions.

Positively charged ion

Negatively charged ion

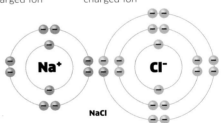

NaCl

Electrical attraction
The positive sodium ion and the negative chlorine ion are attracted to each other. They have become a compound called sodium chloride (NaCl).

Sodium ions and chlorine ions are held together by electrical attraction.

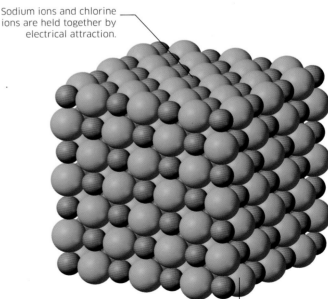

Ionic crystal
Ions of opposite electric charge are attracted to each other, and they form a regular pattern called a crystal. Many solids are ionic crystals, such as salt.

Salt crystal
The ions arrange in a regular pattern, forming a crystal of the compound sodium chloride (NaCl), or table salt.

The **atoms in your DNA** are held together by **covalent bonds**.

4 The **number of bonds** each **carbon atom can form**, making it one of the best atoms at **making up many different compounds**.

17

Covalent bonding

Another way atoms can attain full outer electron shells is by sharing electrons in a covalent bond. A molecule is a group of atoms held together by covalent bonds (see pp.14–15). Some elements exist as molecules formed by pairs of atoms, for example chlorine, oxygen, and nitrogen. Covalent bonds can be single, double, or triple bonds.

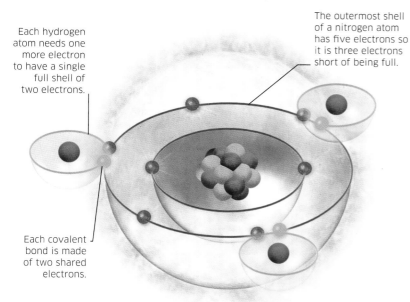

Each hydrogen atom needs one more electron to have a single full shell of two electrons.

The outermost shell of a nitrogen atom has five electrons so it is three electrons short of being full.

Each covalent bond is made of two shared electrons.

AMMONIA MOLECULE (NH₃)

Ammonia molecule
A molecule of the compound ammonia (NH_3) is made of atoms of nitrogen (N) and hydrogen (H). The shell closest to the nucleus of an atom can hold only two electrons. Hydrogen and helium are the only elements with just one shell.

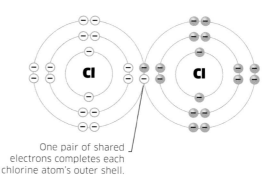

Single bond
Some pairs of atoms share only one electron each, forming a single bond.

One pair of shared electrons completes each chlorine atom's outer shell.

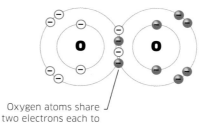

Double bond
Sometimes, pairs of atoms share two electrons each, forming a double bond.

Oxygen atoms share two electrons each to fill their outer shell.

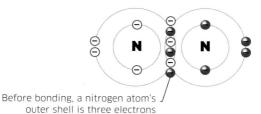

Triple bond
In some pairs of atoms, three electrons are shared, forming a triple bond.

Before bonding, a nitrogen atom's outer shell is three electrons short, so it forms a triple bond.

Metallic bonding

In a metal, the atoms are held in place within a "sea" of electrons. The atoms form a regular pattern—a crystal. Although the electrons hold the atoms in place, they are free of their atoms, and can move freely throughout the crystalline metal. This is why metals are good conductors of electricity and heat.

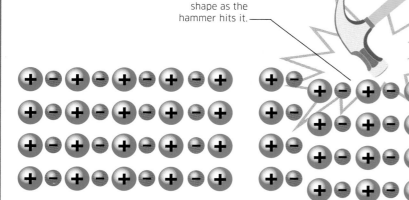

The metal changes shape as the hammer hits it.

Conducting heat and electricity
An electric current is a flow of electric charge. In a metal, negatively charged electrons can move freely, so electric current can flow through them. The mobile electrons are also good at transferring heat within a metal.

Malleable metals
Metal atoms are held in place by metallic bonding, but are able to move a little within the "sea" of electrons. This is why metals are malleable (change shape when beaten with a hammer) and ductile (can be drawn into a wire).

Getting into shape
With some heat and a hammer, metals can be shaped into anything from delicate jewelry to sturdier objects, such as this horseshoe. Horseshoes used to be made of iron, but these days metal alloys such as steel (see p.63) are more common.

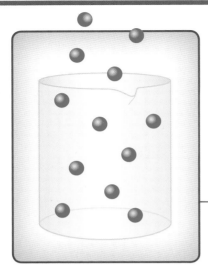

Gas state
The particles of a gas, such as oxygen, or the water vapor in the polar bear's breath, are not tightly held together by bonds. Without these forces keeping them together, they move freely in any direction.

Air
Air is a mixture of gases: mostly nitrogen (78 percent), oxygen (21 percent), and small proportions of argon and carbon dioxide.

Solids, liquids, and gases

There are four different states of matter: solid, liquid, gas, and plasma. Everything in the universe is in one of those states. States can change depending on temperature and pressure.

All pure substances can exist in all of the three states common on Earth—solid, liquid, and gas. What state a substance is in is determined by how tightly its particles (atoms or molecules) are bound together. When energy (heat) is added, the tightly packed particles in a solid increase their vibration. With enough heat, they start moving around and the solid becomes a liquid. At boiling point, molecules start moving all over the place and the liquid becomes gas. Plasma is a type of gas so hot that its atoms split apart.

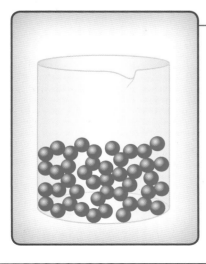

Liquid state
The particles of a liquid, such as water, are less tightly packed than in a solid and not neatly arranged, and they have weaker bonds. That is why liquids flow and spread, taking the shape of any container.

Salt water
Salty seawater has a lower freezing point than freshwater, which freezes at 32°F (0°C). Because salt disrupts the bonds between water molecules, seawater stays liquid until about 28°F (-2°C).

Water is one of the few substances that **expand** when **freezing**.

67 percent of freshwater on Earth is in its solid state in the form of **ice caps and glaciers**.

19

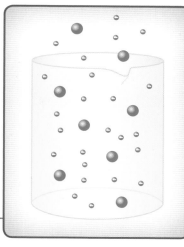

Plasma
Plasma, which makes up the sun and stars, is the most common matter in the universe. Intense heat makes its atoms separate into positively charged nuclei and negatively charged electrons that whiz about at very high speed.

Aurora borealis
Collisions between plasma from space and gases in the atmosphere energize atmospheric atoms, which release light when they return to normal energy levels.

States of matter
Water exists in three states. Here we see it as solid ice, liquid seawater, and gaseous water vapor exhaled by the polar bear. Water vapor is invisible until it cools and condenses to form steam, a mist of liquid droplets—the same happens when a pan of water boils. In the Arctic Circle, the spectacular northern lights (aurora borealis) reveal the presence of plasma, the fourth state of matter.

Changing states of matter
Adding or removing energy (as heat) causes a state change. Solids melt into liquids, and liquids vaporize into gas. Some solids can turn straight to gas; some gases into solids.

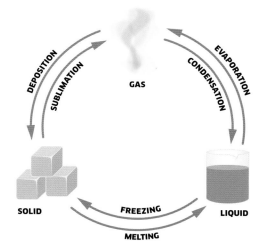

DEPOSITION SUBLIMATION GAS CONDENSATION EVAPORATION

SOLID FREEZING LIQUID

MELTING

Sublimation
Solid carbon dioxide is known as dry ice. With lowered pressure and increased heat it becomes CO_2 gas—this is called sublimation. When a gas goes straight to solid, the term is deposition.

Melting and freezing
All pure substances have a specific melting and freezing point. How high or low depends on how their molecules are arranged.

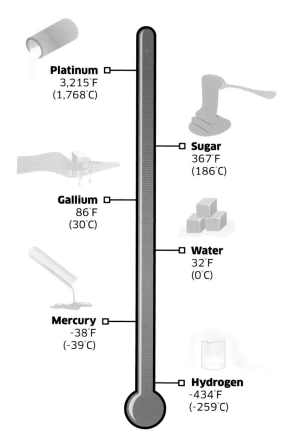

Platinum
3,215˚F
(1,768˚C)

Sugar
367˚F
(186˚C)

Gallium
86˚F
(30˚C)

Water
32˚F
(0˚C)

Mercury
-38˚F
(-39˚C)

Hydrogen
-434˚F
(-259˚C)

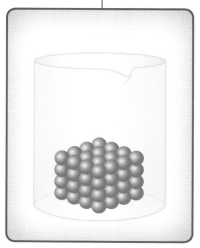

Solid state
In a solid, such as ice, particles are held together by bonds and sit tightly packed. The particles vibrate slightly but they don't move around, so solids keep their shape.

Mixtures

When two or more substances are mixed together, but do not bond chemically to make a compound, they form a mixture. In a mixture, substances can be separated by physical means.

Mixtures are all around us, both natural and man-made. Air is a mixture of gases. Soil is a mixture of minerals, biological material, and water. The pages of this book are a mixture of wood pulp and additives, and the ink on the pages is a mixture of pigments. There are different types of mixtures. Salt dissolved in water is a solution. Grainy sand mixed with water forms a suspension. A colloid is a mix of tiny particles evenly dispersed, but not dissolved, in another substance; mist is a colloid of minute droplets of water in air. Evenly distributed mixtures are homogeneous, uneven mixtures are heterogeneous (see also pp.10–11).

Spray
Sea spray is a heterogeneous mixture of air and seawater.

Salty solution
The salt water in the sea is a solution: a homogeneous mixture of water and dissolved salts. When seawater evaporates, salt crystals are formed.

Sand
Sand is a heterogeneous mixture: a close look reveals tiny pieces of eroded rock, crushed shells, glass, and even bits of plastic.

Organic matter
Fish and other sea creatures release organic matter, such as waste and old scales, into the sea.

Mixtures in nature

Most substances in nature are mixtures, including seawater, rocks, soil, and air. Understanding how to separate these mixtures provides us with an important supply of natural resources, for example by removing salt from seawater and separating gases, such as argon, from air.

Seaweed
Dead and decaying algae also contribute organic matter to the seawater mix.

More than **5½ million tons** of **gold** are dispersed as tiny particles in the world's oceans.

Seawater is an important source of the useful element **magnesium**, an alkaline earth metal. **21**

Sea foam
Sea foam forms at the water's edge when wind and waves whip up air and water to frothy bubbles which mix with biological material excreted from algae and other sea life.

Rock
Lots of different minerals can make up the solid mixture that forms rocks. Most of the minerals that are present in seawater come from eroded rock.

Seawater
The oceans are full of materials dissolved as well as dispersed (scattered) in water: salts, gases, metals, organic compounds, and microscopic organisms. This type of uneven mixture is called a suspension.

Separating mixtures

There are many ways to separate mixtures, whether it is to extract a substance or analyze a mixture's contents. Different techniques work for different substances depending on their physical properties.

Filtration
Filtration separates insoluble solids from liquids, which pass through the filter.

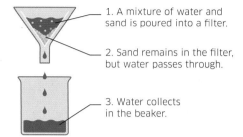

1. A mixture of water and sand is poured into a filter.

2. Sand remains in the filter, but water passes through.

3. Water collects in the beaker.

Chromatography
How fast substances in a liquid mixture, such as ink, separate depends on how well they dissolve—the better they dissolve, the further up the soaked paper they travel with the solvent.

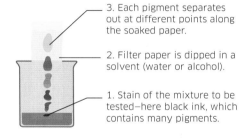

3. Each pigment separates out at different points along the soaked paper.

2. Filter paper is dipped in a solvent (water or alcohol).

1. Stain of the mixture to be tested—here black ink, which contains many pigments.

Distillation
This method separates liquids according to their boiling point. The mixture is heated, and the substance that boils first evaporates and can be collected as it condenses.

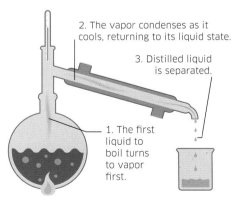

2. The vapor condenses as it cools, returning to its liquid state.

3. Distilled liquid is separated.

1. The first liquid to boil turns to vapor first.

Magnetism
Passing a magnet over a mixture of magnetic and nonmagnetic particles removes the magnetic ones.

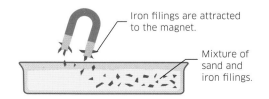

Iron filings are attracted to the magnet.

Mixture of sand and iron filings.

Rocks and minerals

The chemistry of Earth is dominated by the huge variety of rocks and minerals that shape the landscape around us.

There are thousands of different kinds of rocks and minerals. What they are like depends on the chemical elements they contain, and the way these elements are grouped together. A rock is a mixture of different minerals, arranged as billions of tiny grains. Each mineral is usually a compound of two or more elements chemically bonded together. Many of these form beautiful crystals. Sometimes, a mineral is an element in its raw form—such as copper or gold.

The rock cycle

Solid rocks look like they must stay the same forever, but in fact they change over thousands or millions of years. Some melt under the influence of Earth's internal heat and pressure. Others get eroded by wind and rain. The three main forms of rock are linked in a cycle that changes one form into another. The cycle is driven slowly, but inevitably, by a set of dramatic movements deep within the Earth.

Most of the ocean floor is made of **igneous basalt rock**, much younger than most rocks on land.

Sedimentary rock
Fragments of rock broken away by weathering and erosion join together to form sedimentary rocks, such as sandstone (below) and limestone. The fragments gather in layers at the bottom of lakes and oceans, and get compacted and cemented together under their own weight. Eventually, uplift pushes this rock up to the surface.

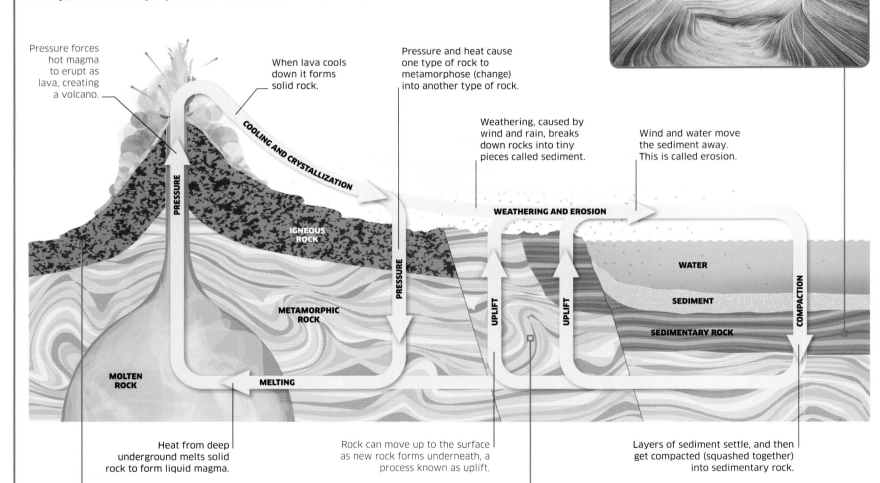

Pressure forces hot magma to erupt as lava, creating a volcano.

When lava cools down it forms solid rock.

COOLING AND CRYSTALLIZATION

Pressure and heat cause one type of rock to metamorphose (change) into another type of rock.

Weathering, caused by wind and rain, breaks down rocks into tiny pieces called sediment.

Wind and water move the sediment away. This is called erosion.

WEATHERING AND EROSION

PRESSURE

IGNEOUS ROCK

PRESSURE

WATER

UPLIFT

UPLIFT

SEDIMENT

COMPACTION

METAMORPHIC ROCK

SEDIMENTARY ROCK

MOLTEN ROCK

MELTING

Heat from deep underground melts solid rock to form liquid magma.

Rock can move up to the surface as new rock forms underneath, a process known as uplift.

Layers of sediment settle, and then get compacted (squashed together) into sedimentary rock.

Igneous rock
The interior of the Earth is so hot it melts solid rock, forming a liquid called magma. When magma cools down it solidifies and crystallizes to form igneous rock, such as granite (formed underground) and basalt (seen left) from lava erupted from volcanoes.

Metamorphic rock
Rocks that get buried deep underground are squeezed and heated under pressure. But instead of melting the rock, this rearranges its crystals to form metamorphic rock. For example, buried limestone changes into marble, as in this cave.

Earth's upper mantle, just beneath the crust, consists mainly of **very hot peridotite**, a green igneous rock.

Dark green imperial jade is one of the **rarest and most precious** minerals in the world.

23

Elements of Earth's crust

Planet Earth is mostly made up of the elements iron, oxygen, silicon, and magnesium, with most of the iron concentrated in Earth's core. But Earth's outer layer, the crust, is made from minerals of many different elements, such as silicates (containing silicon and oxygen). This diagram shows which elements are most common in the crust.

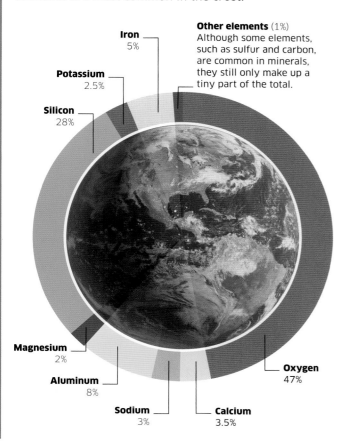

Iron 5%

Potassium 2.5%

Silicon 28%

Other elements (1%) Although some elements, such as sulfur and carbon, are common in minerals, they still only make up a tiny part of the total.

Magnesium 2%

Aluminum 8%

Sodium 3%

Calcium 3.5%

Oxygen 47%

Native elements

In Earth's crust, most elements exist combined with others in mineral compounds. But some, called native elements, appear in pure form. About 20 elements can be found in pure form, including metals, such as copper and gold, and non-metals, such as sulfur and carbon.

Sulfur
Powder and crystals of pure sulfur from volcanic gases accumulate around volcanic vents. In the rock cycle, it gets mixed into rocks. It also forms part of many mineral compounds.

Mineral compounds

There are more than 4,000 different kinds of minerals. Scientists classify them according to which elements they contain, and sort them into a few main groups. The group name tells which is the main element in all minerals in that group. All sulfide minerals, for example, contain sulfur. Many minerals exist in ores—rocks from which metals can be extracted—or as pretty gem crystals (see p.24).

Hematite
This oxide contains lots of iron, making it an important iron ore.

Rose quartz
This is a pink form of quartz, one of the silicates made up of only silicon and oxygen.

Oxides
Different metals combine with oxygen to form these hard minerals. They are in many ores, making these valuable sources of metal. Many make fine gems.

Silicates
All silicates, the most common group, contain silicon and oxygen. Some include other elements, too. The rock granite is made of three silicates, including quartz.

Baryte
The element barium combined with sulphur and oxygen makes baryte, which comes in many different forms.

Chalcopyrite
Both copper and iron can be sourced from ores containing this sulfide.

Sulfates
A sulfur and oxygen compound combines with other elements to form sulfates. Most common are gypsum, which forms cave crystals (see pp.26–27), and baryte.

Sulfides
Metals combined with sulfur, but no oxygen, form sulfides. Sulfides make up many metal ores. Many are colorful, but are usually too soft to use as gemstones.

Malachite
Copper combines with carbon and oxygen to give this useful and decorative mineral its green color.

Fluorite
Calcium and fluorine make up this mineral, which comes in many different colors.

Carbonates
Compounds of carbon and oxygen combine with other elements to form carbonates. Many are quite soft. Some exist in rocks such as chalk and limestone.

Halides
These minerals contain one or more metals combined with a halogen element (fluorine, chlorine, bromine, or iodine; see p.40). Rock salt is an edible halide.

Crystals

A crystal is a solid material, made of atoms set in a repeating 3-D pattern. Crystals form from minerals when molten magma cools to become solid rock. Crystals of some substances, such as salt, sugar, and ice, are formed through evaporation or freezing.

The shapes and colors of mineral crystals depend on the elements from which they are made and the conditions (the temperature and pressure) under which they formed. The speed at which the magma cools decides the size of the crystals. Crystals can change under extreme pressure in the rock cycle (see p.22), when one rock type changes into another.

Crystal structures

Crystals have highly ordered structures. This is because the atoms or molecules in a crystal are arranged in a 3-D pattern that repeats itself exactly over and over again. Most metals have a crystalline structure, too.

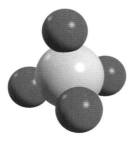

Quartz tetrahedron
The molecule that makes up quartz is in the shape of a tetrahedron, made of four oxygen atoms and one silicon atom.

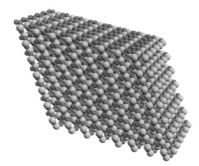

Quartz crystal
A quartz crystal consists of a lattice of tetrahedrons, repeated in all directions.

One mineral, two gem crystals

Crystals of the mineral corundum come in many colors, thanks to different impurities in the crystal structure. Often cut and polished to be used as gems, the best known are sapphire (usually blue) and ruby (red).

BLUE CORUNDUM: SAPPHIRE

RED CORUNDUM: RUBY

CUT RUBY CRYSTAL SET IN A RING

Quartz crystals

The crystal quartz is one of the most common minerals in Earth's crust. It comes in many different forms and colors—but they all share the same formula: silicon dioxide, or SiO_2. Some of the best known include rock crystal (transparent), rose quartz (pink), tiger-eye (yellow-brown), citrine (yellow), and amethyst (purple). Their beauty makes them popular for jewelry, whether in natural form, tumbled, or cut and polished.

Amethyst geode
A geode is formed when gas bubbles are trapped in cooling lava. The crystals lining the walls of the geode grow when hot substances containing silicon and oxygen, as well as traces of iron, seep into the cavities left by the bubbles.

The purple color of amethyst comes from iron impurities in the crystal structure.

The outer shell of the geode is normally a volcanic, igneous rock such as basalt.

Crystal systems

The shape of a crystal is determined by how its atoms are arranged. This decides the number of flat sides, sharp edges, and corners of a crystal. Crystals are sorted into six main groups, known as systems, according to which 3-D pattern they fit.

Cubic
Gold, silver, diamond, the mineral pyrite (above), and sea salt all form cubic crystals.

Tetragonal
Zircon, a silicate mineral, is a typical tetragonal crystal, looking like a square prism.

Hexagonal and trigonal
Apatite is a hexagonal crystal, with six long sides. Trigonal crystals have three sides.

Monoclinic
Orthoclase (above) and gypsum crystals are monoclinic, one of the most common systems.

The **largest quartz crystal cluster** in the world is 9.8 ft (3 m) tall and weighs more than **30,000 lb (14,000 kg)**.

25

Prisms of rock crystal, a colorless type of quartz

The trigonal crystal system of quartz is visible here.

Ice crystals

In an ice crystal, water molecules are aligned hexagonally. These crystals form when water vapor in the air freezes straight to a solid. If liquid water freezes slowly, it will form simple hexagonal crystals, but without the delicate branches and shapes of a snowflake crystal.

The unique pattern of a snowflake is based on a six-sided shape (hexagon).

Snowflake
A snowflake is a six-sided ice crystal. Each snowflake grows into a different variation on this shape, depending on how it drifts down from the sky. No two snowflakes are the same.

Sugar and salt crystals

Crystals of sea salt and crystals of sugar are more different than they look. Salt crystals are highly ordered six-sided cubes, while sugar crystals are less well ordered hexagonal prisms.

Sea salt belongs to the cubic crystal system, but when the crystals form quickly they take a pyramid shape.

Sea salt crystals
Crystals of sea salt (sodium chloride) are held together by ionic bonds (see p.16). When salt water evaporates, the dissolved minerals left behind form salt crystals.

Liquid crystals

In nature, cell membranes and the solution produced by silkworms to spin their cocoons are liquid crystals. The molecules in liquid crystals are highly ordered, but they flow like a liquid.

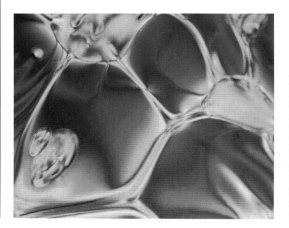

Liquid crystals at work
Man-made liquid crystals, such as the ones seen here, are used in liquid crystal displays (LCDs) in TV screens, digital watches, and mobile phones. They do not produce light, but create clear images by altering the way light passes through them.

Axinite, a silicate mineral (see p.23)

Orthorhombic
The mineral topaz forms beautiful orthorhombic crystals, often with a pyramid-like top.

Triclinic
The least symmetrical of all, triclinic crystals include axinite (above) and turquoise.

Crystal cave

In extremely hot and humid conditions, these scientists are investigating the largest crystals ever found, in the Giant Crystal Cave, Naica, Mexico.

The crystals are made of selenite, a form of the mineral gypsum (calcium sulfate), which is the main ingredient of plaster and blackboard chalk. The crystals form very slowly from calcium, sulfur, and oxygen dissolved in hot water. This water was heated by magma in a geological fault beneath the cave. The largest crystals weigh 55 tons and are 39 ft (12 m) long.

THE ELEMENTS

Shiny gold, tough iron, smelly chlorine, and invisible oxygen—what do they have in common? They are all elements: substances made of only one type of atom that cannot be broken down into a simpler substance. But they can combine with other elements to form new substances, known as compounds. Everything around us is made up of elements, either in pure form or combined. Water, for example, is made of the elements hydrogen and oxygen. There are 118 known elements, of which around 90 exist naturally. The rest have been created in laboratory experiments.

Atomic number
This is the number of protons in the atom's nucleus. The element iron has an atomic number of 26, which means it has 26 protons (and 26 electrons).

Atomic mass number
An atom's mass is how many protons and neutrons it has. This number shows the relative atomic mass (the average mass of all an element's atoms, see p.13).

26	55.845
Fe	
IRON	

Name
In English, some element names look very different to their symbol. We say "iron" rather than "ferrum," its original Latin name.

Chemical symbol
An element has the same symbol all over the world, while the name can be different in different languages.

The periodic table
In 1869, the Russian scientist Dmitri Mendeleev came up with a system for how to sort and classify all the elements. In his chart, the atomic number increases left to right, starting at the top left with hydrogen, with an atomic number of 1. Arranging elements in rows and columns reveals patterns. For example, elements from the same column, or group, react in similar ways and form a part of similar compounds.

Elemental information
An element's place in the table is decided by its atomic number. Each element has a "tile" showing its atomic number, its chemical symbol, and its atomic weight (weights in brackets are estimates for unstable elements). The symbol is an abbreviation of the element's original name. This name was often invented by the person who discovered the element.

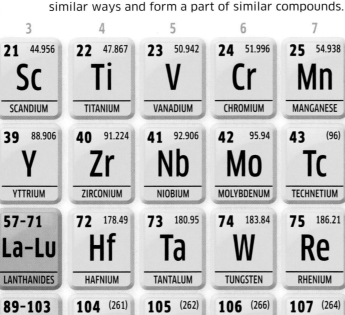

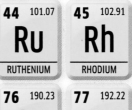

The periodic table:

Group 1 — 1 | 1.0079 **H** HYDROGEN

1	2		3	4	5	6	7	8	9	10	11	12
3, 6.941 **Li** LITHIUM	4, 9.0122 **Be** BERYLLIUM											
11, 22.990 **Na** SODIUM	12, 24.305 **Mg** MAGNESIUM											
19, 39.098 **K** POTASSIUM	20, 40.078 **Ca** CALCIUM		21, 44.956 **Sc** SCANDIUM	22, 47.867 **Ti** TITANIUM	23, 50.942 **V** VANADIUM	24, 51.996 **Cr** CHROMIUM	25, 54.938 **Mn** MANGANESE	26, 55.845 **Fe** IRON	27, 58.933 **Co** COBALT	28, 58.693 **Ni** NICKEL	29, 63.546 **Cu** COPPER	30, 65.39 **Zn** ZINC
37, 85.468 **Rb** RUBIDIUM	38, 87.62 **Sr** STRONTIUM		39, 88.906 **Y** YTTRIUM	40, 91.224 **Zr** ZIRCONIUM	41, 92.906 **Nb** NIOBIUM	42, 95.94 **Mo** MOLYBDENUM	43, (96) **Tc** TECHNETIUM	44, 101.07 **Ru** RUTHENIUM	45, 102.91 **Rh** RHODIUM	46, 106.42 **Pd** PALLADIUM	47, 107.87 **Ag** SILVER	48, 112.41 **Cd** CADMIUM
55, 132.91 **Cs** CAESIUM	56, 137.33 **Ba** BARIUM		57-71 **La-Lu** LANTHANIDES	72, 178.49 **Hf** HAFNIUM	73, 180.95 **Ta** TANTALUM	74, 183.84 **W** TUNGSTEN	75, 186.21 **Re** RHENIUM	76, 190.23 **Os** OSMIUM	77, 192.22 **Ir** IRIDIUM	78, 195.08 **Pt** PLATINUM	79, 196.97 **Au** GOLD	80, 200.59 **Hg** MERCURY
87, (223) **Fr** FRANCIUM	88, (226) **Ra** RADIUM		89-103 **Ac-Lr** ACTINIDES	104, (261) **Rf** RUTHERFORDIUM	105, (262) **Db** DUBNIUM	106, (266) **Sg** SEABORGIUM	107, (264) **Bh** BOHRIUM	108, (277) **Hs** HASSIUM	109, (268) **Mt** MEITNERIUM	110, (281) **Ds** DARMSTADTIUM	111, (282) **Rg** ROENTGENIUM	112, (285) **Cn** COPERNICIUM

Lanthanides and actinides
Periods 6 and 7 each contain 14 more elements than periods 4 and 5. This makes the table too wide to fit easily in books, so these elements are shown separately. All elements in the actinides group are radioactive.

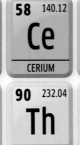

57, 138.91 **La** LANTHANUM	58, 140.12 **Ce** CERIUM	59, 140.91 **Pr** PRASEODYMIUM	60, 144.24 **Nd** NEODYMIUM	61, (145) **Pm** PROMETHIUM	62, 150.36 **Sm** SAMARIUM	63, 151.96 **Eu** EUROPIUM	64, 157.25 **Gd** GADOLINIUM	65, 158.93 **Tb** TERBIUM
89, (227) **Ac** ACTINIUM	90, 232.04 **Th** THORIUM	91, 231.04 **Pa** PROTACTINIUM	92, 238.03 **U** URANIUM	93, (237) **Np** NEPTUNIUM	94, (244) **Pu** PLUTONIUM	95, (243) **Am** AMERICIUM	96, (247) **Cm** CURIUM	97, (247) **Bk** BERKELIUM

Periodic table key

- ■ Alkali metals
- ▨ Alkaline earth metals
- ▫ Transition metals
- ▨ Lanthanide metals
- ▫ Actinide metals
- ■ Other metals
- ▨ Metalloids
- ▨ Other non-metals
- ▨ Halogens
- ■ Noble gases

Key to atomic models on pp.30–41.

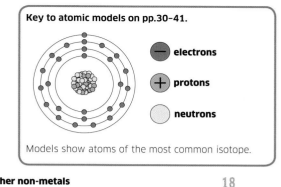

- − electrons
- + protons
- ○ neutrons

Models show atoms of the most common isotope.

Other non-metals
These include three elements essential for life on Earth—carbon, nitrogen, and oxygen.

13	14	15	16	17	18
					2 4.0026 **He** HELIUM
5 10.811 **B** BORON	**6** 12.011 **C** CARBON	**7** 14.007 **N** NITROGEN	**8** 15.999 **O** OXYGEN	**9** 18.998 **F** FLUORINE	**10** 20.180 **Ne** NEON
13 26.982 **Al** ALUMINUM	**14** 28.086 **Si** SILICON	**15** 30.974 **P** PHOSPHORUS	**16** 32.065 **S** SULFUR	**17** 35.453 **Cl** CHLORINE	**18** 39.948 **Ar** ARGON
31 69.723 **Ga** GALLIUM	**32** 72.64 **Ge** GERMANIUM	**33** 74.922 **As** ARSENIC	**34** 78.96 **Se** SELENIUM	**35** 79.904 **Br** BROMINE	**36** 83.80 **Kr** KRYPTON
49 114.82 **In** INDIUM	**50** 118.71 **Sn** TIN	**51** 121.76 **Sb** ANTIMONY	**52** 127.60 **Te** TELLURIUM	**53** 126.90 **I** IODINE	**54** 131.29 **Xe** XENON
81 204.38 **Tl** THALLIUM	**82** 207.2 **Pb** LEAD	**83** 208.96 **Bi** BISMUTH	**84** (209) **Po** POLONIUM	**85** (210) **At** ASTATINE	**86** (222) **Rn** RADON
113 (284) **Nh** NIHONIUM	**114** (289) **Fl** FLEROVIUM	**115** (288) **Mc** MOSCOVIUM	**116** (293) **Lv** LIVERMORIUM	**117** (294) **Ts** TENNESSINE	**118** (294) **Og** OGANESSON

66 162.50 **Dy** DYSPROSIUM	**67** 164.93 **Ho** HOLMIUM	**68** 167.26 **Er** ERBIUM	**69** 168.93 **Tm** THULIUM	**70** 173.04 **Yb** YTTERBIUM	**71** 174.97 **Lu** LUTETIUM
98 (251) **Cf** CALIFORNIUM	**99** (252) **Es** EINSTEINIUM	**100** (257) **Fm** FERMIUM	**101** (258) **Md** MENDELEVIUM	**102** (259) **No** NOBELIUM	**103** (262) **Lr** LAWRENCIUM

UNDERSTANDING THE PERIODIC TABLE

Within the table are blocks of elements that behave in similar ways. On the left are the most reactive metals. Most everyday metals occur in the middle of the table in a set called the transition metals. Non-metals are mostly on the right of the table and include both solids and gases.

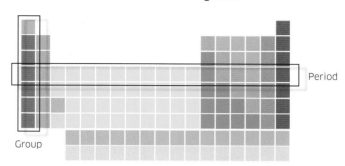

Period

Group

Building blocks

The periodic table is made up of rows called periods and columns called groups. As we move across each period, the elements change from solid metals (on the left) to gases (on the right).

Periods

All elements in a period have the same number of electron shells in their atoms. For example, all elements in the third period have three shells (but a different number of electrons).

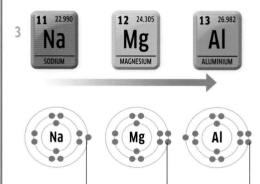

One electron in outer shell. Two electrons in outer shell. Three electrons in outer shell.

Shrinking atoms
As you move along each row (period) of the table, the atoms of each element contain more protons and electrons. Each atom has the same number of electron shells, but for each step to the right, there are more positively charged protons pulling the shells inward. This "shrinks" the atom, and makes it more tightly packed.

Groups

The elements in a group react in similar ways because they have the same number of electrons in their outer shell (see p.13). For example, while the elements in group 1 all have different numbers of electrons, and shells, they all have just one electron in their outer shell.

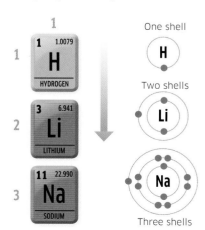

One shell

Two shells

Three shells

Growing atoms
Atoms get bigger and heavier as we move down each column (group). This is because the atoms of each element below have more protons and more electrons than the element above. As shells fill up with electrons (see p.13), a new shell is added each time we move another step down a group, down to the next period.

Transition metals

What we usually think of as "metals" mostly belong to the group of elements known as transition metals. Most are hard and shiny. They have many other properties in common, including high boiling points and being good at conducting heat and electricity.

The transition metals make up the biggest element block in the periodic table, spreading out from group 3 through to group 12, and across four periods (see pp.28–29). This wide spread indicates that, although they are similar in many ways, they vary in others, such as how easily they react and what kinds of compounds they form.

Some of these metals have been known for more than 5,000 years. Some were only discovered in the 20th century. This is a selection of some of the 38 transition metals.

GOLD
Aurum
Discovered: c. 3000 BCE

Since ancient times, gold has been treasured because of its great beauty, and also because it doesn't get damaged by corrosion—it keeps its yellow sheen and does not rust. Easy to shape, it can be seen in jewelry, Egyptian masks, building decorations, and also in electronics. It doesn't easily react or form compounds with other elements.

Atomic structure
- − 79
- + 79
- ○ 118

79 196.97
Au
GOLD

Gold nugget
In nature, pure gold can be found in nuggets such as this or, more commonly, as grains inside rocks.

SILVER
Argentum
Discovered: c. 3000 BCE

Like gold and copper, silver was one of the elements known and used by the earliest civilizations. It is valuable and easy to mold and used to be made into coins. Today, coins are made of alloys (see pp.62–63). Silver is still one of the most popular metals and is used for jewelry and decorative objects.

Atomic structure
- − 47
- + 47
- ○ 60

47 107.87
Ag
SILVER

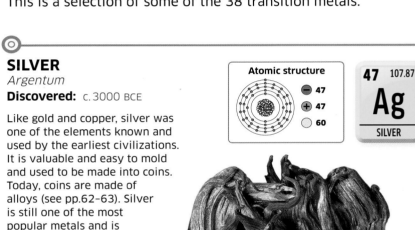

Chunk of silver
Silver metal reacts with the sulfur in air, which produces a black coating. That is why silver needs polishing to stay shiny.

OSMIUM
Osmium
Discovered: 1803

This rare, blue-shimmering metal is incredibly dense—a tennis ball-sized lump of osmium would have a mass of 7.7 lb (3.5 kg). If exposed to air, it reacts with oxygen to form a poisonous oxide compound, so for safe use it needs to be combined with other metals or elements. The powder used to detect fingerprints contains osmium.

Atomic structure
- − 76
- + 76
- ○ 116

76 190.23
Os
OSMIUM

Hard but brittle
This sample of refined osmium looks solid enough, but the tiny cracks all over it show that it is fragile in its pure form.

Manganese is a transition metal which exists in tiny traces in **nuts and pineapples**.

The heavy transition metal **tungsten** has the **highest melting point** of any metal: **6,177.2°F (3,414°C).**

31

COBALT
Cobaltum
Discovered: 1739

Cobalt is somewhat similar to iron, its neighbor on the periodic table. The metal is often added to alloys, including those used to make permanent magnets. A cobalt compound has long been used to produce "cobalt blue," a deep, vibrant blue for paints and dyes.

Atomic structure
- 27
+ 27
○ 32

27 58.933
Co
COBALT

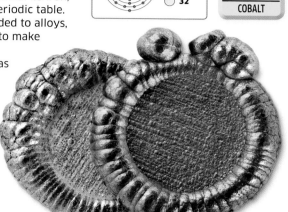

Cobalt color
Extracted from its ore, pure cobalt metal is silvery gray in appearance.

NICKEL
Niccolum
Discovered: 1751

This useful metal, which does not rust, is one of the ingredients in stainless steel (see p.63). It is also used to protect ships' propellers from rusting in water. Its best-known role is perhaps in the various alloys used to make coins, including the US 5-cent coin that is called a nickel.

Atomic structure
- 28
+ 28
○ 30

28 58.693
Ni
NICKEL

Pure nickel
These samples of pure nickel have been shaped into tiny balls.

TITANIUM
Titanium
Discovered: 1791

Known for its strength, this metal was named after the Titans, the divine and tremendously forceful giants of Greek mythology. Titanium is hard but also lightweight, and resistant to corrosion. This super combination of properties makes it perfect for use in artificial joints and surgical pins, but also in watches and in alloys for the aerospace industry. It is, however, a very expensive material.

Laboratory sample
Although titanium is a common element in Earth's crust, it usually only exists in mineral compounds, not as a native element. Pure titanium has to be extracted and refined.

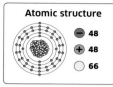

CADMIUM
Cadmium
Discovered: 1817

Although it has some uses in industry and laser technology, this metal is now known to be highly toxic and dangerous to humans. If ingested, it can react like calcium, an essential and useful element, but will replace the calcium in our bones. This causes bones to become soft and easy to break.

Atomic structure
- 48
+ 48
○ 66

48 112.41
Cd
CADMIUM

Poisonous pellet
This sample of pure cadmium has been refined in a laboratory.

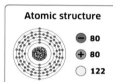

MERCURY
Hydrargentum
Discovered: 1500 BCE

Famous for being the only metal that is liquid at room temperature, mercury has fascinated people for thousands of years. Only freezing to a solid at near -38°F (-39°C), it has long been used to measure temperature. But it is also poisonous, so thermometers now use other methods.

Atomic structure
- 80
+ 80
○ 122

80 200.59
Hg
MERCURY

Quick liquid
Mercury is also known as quicksilver, and it is easy to see why.

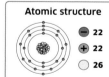

When titanium reacts with oxygen in the air it gets a duller gray coating. This actually works as a protection against corrosion.

Atomic structure
- 22
+ 22
○ 26

22 47.867
Ti
TITANIUM

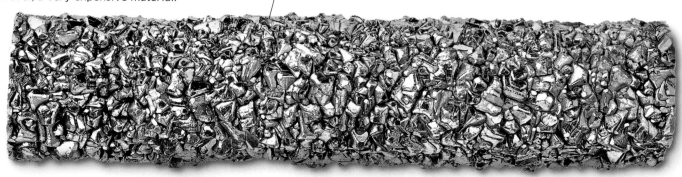

LITHIUM
Lithium
Discovered: 1817

Lithium is the lightest of all metals. It has been used in alloys in the construction of spacecraft. In more familiar uses, we find lithium in batteries, and also in compounds used to make medicines.

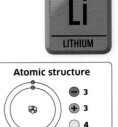

3	6.941
Li	
LITHIUM	

Atomic structure

- − 3
- + 3
- ○ 4

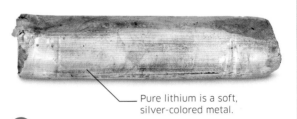

Pure lithium is a soft, silver-colored metal.

More metals

Most of the elements known to us are metals. In addition to the transition metals, there are five other metal groups in the periodic table, featuring a wide range of properties.

The alkali metals and alkaline earth metals are soft, shiny, and very reactive. The elements known as "other metals" are less reactive and have lower melting points. Underneath the transition metals are the lanthanides, which used to be called "rare earth metals," but turned out not to be rare at all, and the radioactive actinides. Whatever the group, these metals are all malleable, and good conductors of electricity and heat.

SODIUM
Natrium
Discovered: 1807

So soft it can easily be cut with a knife and very reactive, sodium is more familiar to us when in compounds such as common salt (sodium chloride). It is essential for life, and plays a vital role in our bodies.

11	22.990
Na	
SODIUM	

Atomic structure

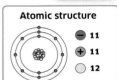

- − 11
- + 11
- ○ 12

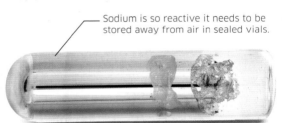

Sodium is so reactive it needs to be stored away from air in sealed vials.

MAGNESIUM
Magnesium
Discovered: 1755

Magnesium is an important metal because it is both strong and light in weight. The oceans are a main source of magnesium, but it's quite expensive to produce, so recycling it is crucial. As a powder, or thin strip, it is flammable and burns with a bright white light. It is often used in fireworks and flares.

12	24.305
Mg	
MAGNESIUM	

Atomic structure

- − 12
- + 12
- ○ 12

Magnesium is refined to produce a pure, shiny gray metal.

POTASSIUM
Kalium
Discovered: 1807

Along with sodium, the alkali metal potassium helps to control the nervous system in our bodies. We get it from foods such as bananas, avocados, and coconut water. It is added to fertilizers and is also part of a compound used in gunpowder.

19	39.098
K	
POTASSIUM	

Atomic structure

- − 19
- + 19
- ○ 20

Highly reactive, potassium is often stored in oil to stop it reacting.

CALCIUM
Calcium
Discovered: 1808

Our bodies are full of calcium, the fifth most common element on Earth. It makes teeth and bones strong, which is why it is important to eat calcium-rich foods, such as broccoli and oranges. It is also a vital part of compounds used to make cement and plaster.

20	40.078
Ca	
CALCIUM	

Atomic structure

- − 20
- + 20
- ○ 20

Pure metal samples such as this one are prepared using chemical processes. In nature, calcium is part of many minerals, but it doesn't exist on its own.

Aluminum is the most common metal in **Earth's rocky crust.**

Uranium, an actinide metal, was the first known **radioactive element.**

Atoms of the **artificial element Moscovium break apart** as soon as they have been made.

33

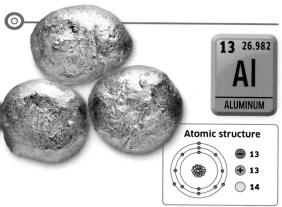

13	26.982
Al	
ALUMINUM	

TIN
Stannum
Discovered: c. 3000 BCE

Tin was once smelted with copper to produce the alloy bronze—which led to the Bronze Age. Today it is used in alloys to plate other metal objects, such as pots and "tin cans."

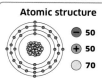

50	118.71
Sn	
TIN	

Atomic structure
- 50
+ 50
○ 70

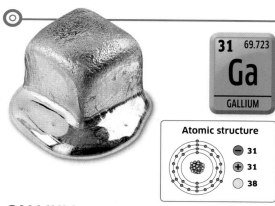

31	69.723
Ga	
GALLIUM	

Atomic structure
- 31
+ 31
○ 38

ALUMINUM
Aluminium
Discovered: 1825

Light and easy to shape, this metal is the main part of alloys used for anything from kitchen foil to aircraft parts. Much of it is recycled, as extracting it from mineral ores to produce pure metal is expensive and very energy-consuming.

Atomic structure
- 13
+ 13
○ 14

GALLIUM
Gallium
Discovered: 1875

Famous as an element with a melting point at just above room temperature, gallium metal melts in your hand. In commercial applications, gallium is a vital element in the production of semi-conductors for use in electronics.

THALLIUM
Thallium
Discovered: 1861

This soft, silvery metal is toxic in its pure state. It was commonly put to use as rat poison, but sometimes ended up killing humans, too. Combined with other elements it can be useful, for example to improve the performance of lenses.

81	204.38
Tl	
THALLIUM	

Atomic structure
- 81
+ 81
○ 124

BISMUTH
Bismuthum
Discovered: 1753

Bismuth is a curious element. It is what is known as a heavy metal, similar to lead, but not very toxic. It is a tiny bit radioactive. It was not defined as an individual element until the 18th century, but has been known and used as a material since ancient times. For example in Egypt, at the time of the pharaohs, it added shimmer to makeup. It is still used in cosmetics today.

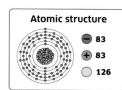

Atomic structure
- 83
+ 83
○ 126

83	208.96
Bi	
BISMUTH	

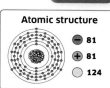
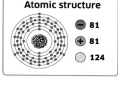

Toxic thallium in its pure form, safely kept in a vial.

Bismuth crystals
Brittle and gray in its pure metal form, bismuth can produce spectacular multicolored crystals as an oxide compound.

INDIUM
Indium
Discovered: 1863

A very soft metal in its pure state, indium is part of the alloy indium tin oxide, or ITO. This material is used in touch screens, LCD TV screens, and as a reflective coating for windows.

49	114.82
In	
INDIUM	

Atomic structure
- 49
+ 49
○ 66

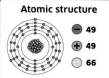

34 matter ○ **METALLOIDS**

Human **hair, skin, and nails** need **silicon** to stay healthy.

Metalloids

Also known as semi-metals, the metalloids are an odd collection of elements that show a wide range of chemical and physical properties. Sometimes they act like typical metals, sometimes like non-metals. One example of their behavior as both is their use as semi-conductors in modern electronics.

In the periodic table, the metalloids form a jagged diagonal border between the metals on the left, and the non-metals to the right. Some scientists disagree regarding the exact classification of some elements in this part of the periodic table, precisely because of this in-between status. Some of the elements shown here are toxic, some are more useful than others, some are very common, and some very rare. But they are all solid at room temperature.

Silicon sample
Pure silicon, such as this sample refined in a laboratory, shatters easily.

SILICON
Silicium
Discovered: 1823

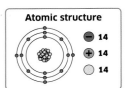

Atomic structure
- 14
+ 14
○ 14

14 28.086
Si
SILICON

Most of us are familiar with silicon, even if we don't know it. It is the second most abundant element in the Earth's crust, only after oxygen, and appears in many different silicate minerals. Mixed with other elements, silicon, a typical semi-conductor, is at the heart of the electronics industry—used in microchips and solar panels. Silicone baking molds contain silicon, too.

Silicate minerals
Silicon is more or less everywhere, found in the silicate compounds that are better known to us as sand, quartz, talc, and feldspar, and in rocks made up of these minerals. Silicates also include minerals whose crystals make luxurious gems, such as amethyst, opal, lazurite, jade, and emerald. All these contain silica (silicon and oxygen), and sometimes other elements, too (see p.23).

Genesis rock
Collected on the moon by Apollo 15 in 1971, this rock contains feldspar, a type of silicate mineral.

Moon mineral
It is not just on Earth that silicates abound. The surface of the moon is made of 45 percent silica.

Orthoclase
This feldspar is what gives pink granite its color.

Feldspar minerals
A widespread group of silicate minerals, feldspars contain aluminum as well as silica, and often other elements, too, including calcium, sodium, and potassium. They form common rocks, such as granite. The pretty crystal called moonstone is also a type of feldspar.

Silicate sands
Desert sand is chiefly composed of silica, a silicon and oxygen compound with the chemical name silicon dioxide. Sand started out as rock that was gradually broken up and eroded into finer and finer grains. In the Sahara (left), this process started some 7 million years ago.

Tellurium is **named after Tellus**, the **Latin name** for **planet Earth**.

2 The **number of Nobel Prizes** won by **Marie Curie**, whose **daughter Irene** also won the Nobel Prize in **chemistry**.

35

BORON
Boron
Discovered: 1808

A hard element, boron gets even harder when combined with carbon as boron carbide. This is one of the toughest materials known, used in tank armor and bulletproof vests. Boron compounds are used to make heat-resistant glass.

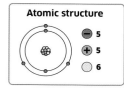

Atomic structure
- −5
- +5
- 6

5 10.811
B
BORON

Dark and twisted
Pure boron is extracted from minerals in the deserts of Death Valley.

GERMANIUM
Germanium
Discovered: 1886

In the history of the periodic table, germanium is an important element. In 1869, in his first table, Mendeleev predicted that there would be an element to fill a gap below silicon. It was discovered 17 years later, and did indeed fit there. Today germanium is used together with silicon in computer chips.

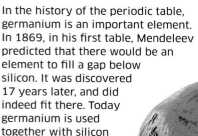

Atomic structure
- −32
- +32
- 42

32 72.64
Ge
GERMANIUM

Pure germanium
Refined germanium is shiny but brittle.

ARSENIC
Arsenicum
Discovered: 1250

Arsenic is an element with a deadly reputation. Throughout history, it has been used to poison people and animals, in fiction as well as in real life. Oddly, in the past it has been used as a medicine, too. It is sometimes used in alloys to strengthen lead, a soft, poisonous metal.

Atomic structure
- −33
- +33
- 42

33 74.922
As
ARSENIC

Dark matter
Pure arsenic can be refined from mineral compounds.

ANTIMONY
Stibium
Discovered: 1600 BCE

Antimony comes from stibnite, a naturally occurring mineral that also contains sulfur. Stibnite used to be ground up and made into eye makeup by ancient civilizations, as seen on Egyptian scrolls and death masks. Known as kohl, its Arabic name, it is still used in cosmetics in some parts of the world.

Atomic structure
- −51
- +51
- 70

51 121.76
Sb
ANTIMONY

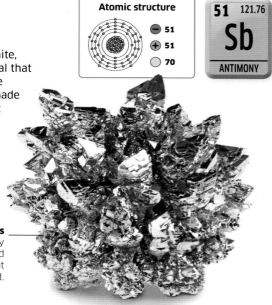

Brittle crystals
This laboratory sample of refined antimony is hard but easily shattered.

TELLURIUM
Tellurium
Discovered: 1783

A rare element, in nature tellurium exists in compounds with other elements. It has a few specialist uses. It is used in alloys to make metal combinations easier to work with. It is mixed with lead to increase its hardness, and help to prevent it being damaged by acids. In rubber manufacture, it is added to make rubber objects more durable.

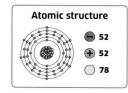

Atomic structure
- −52
- +52
- 78

52 127.60
Te
TELLURIUM

Refined tellurium
Silvery crystals of tellurium are often refined from by-products of copper mining.

POLONIUM
Polonium
Discovered: 1898

This highly radioactive and toxic element will forever be associated with the great scientist Marie Curie. Along with her husband Pierre, she discovered the element while researching radioactivity. She named it after her native Poland.

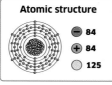

Atomic structure
- −84
- +84
- 125

84 (209)
Po
POLONIUM

Uraninite
Tiny amounts of polonium exist in this uranium ore.

36   matter ∘ SOLID NON-METALS

The **human body** contains lots of **phosphorus**, **85 percent** of which is in **our teeth and bones**.

Solid non-metals

Unlike metals, most non-metals do not conduct heat or electricity, and are known as insulators. They have other properties that are the opposite of those of metals, too, such as lower melting and boiling points.

On the right side of the periodic table are the elements that are described as non-metals. These include the halogens and the noble gases (see pp.40–41). There is also a set known as "other non-metals," which contains the elements carbon, sulfur, phosphorus, and selenium, all solids at room temperature. All of these exist in different forms, or allotropes. The "other non-metals" set of elements also includes a few gases (see pp.38–39).

Raw graphite
The surface of pure graphite looks metallic but is soft and slippery.

Raw diamond
Formed deep underground, raw diamonds are found in igneous (volcanic) rocks.

A clear diamond crystal like this can be cut into a precious gem.

PHOSPHORUS
Phosphorus
Discovered: 1669

Atomic structure

⊖ 15
⊕ 15
○ 16

15 30.974
P
PHOSPHORUS

As a German alchemist boiled urine to produce the mythical philosopher's stone, he discovered a glowing, and very reactive, material instead. He named it phosphorus. It has a number of forms. The two most common are known as red phosphorus and white phosphorus.

Red phosphorus
More stable than white phosphorus, this form is used in safety matches and fireworks.

White phosphorus
White phosphorus needs to be stored in water because it bursts into flames when in contact with air. It can cause terrible burns.

CARBON
Carbonium
Discovered: Prehistoric times

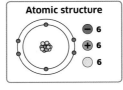

Atomic structure

⊖ 6
⊕ 6
○ 6

6 12.011
C
CARBON

Carbon is at the center of all life. This element forms the backbone of almost all the most important biological molecules. DNA, amino acids, proteins, fats, and sugars all contain multiple joined carbon atoms, bonded with other atoms, to form the molecules that make living organisms work. Carbon is in our bodies, in our food, in plants, and in most fuels we use for heating and transportation. It appears as crystal-clear diamond as well as soft graphite.

Carbon allotropes
Allotropes are different forms of the same element. Carbon has three main allotropes: diamond, graphite, and buckminsterfullerene. It is the way the carbon atoms are arranged and bonded that determines which allotropes exist, and what their chemical and physical properties are.

Diamond
Diamond, an extremely hard allotrope of carbon, has its atoms arranged in a three-dimensional, rigid structure, with very strong bonds holding all of the atoms together.

Graphite
The "lead" in pencils is actually clay mixed with graphite, an allotrope in which the atoms bond in layers of hexagons. These can slide over each other, making it soft and greasy.

The **largest rough diamond** ever found, mined in South Africa, was just over **4 in (10 cm)** long.

The **Brazil nut** is the richest source of the form of **selenium** that the **human body needs**.

37

SULFUR
Sulfur
Discovered: 1777

This element has a distinctive yellow color. Many compounds containing sulfur have a strong smell—for example, in rotten eggs and when onions are cut, it is sulfur that is at work. In ancient times it was known as brimstone, but it was only in 1777 that the French scientist Antoine Lavoisier discovered that it was in fact an element.

Atomic structure
– 16
+ 16
○ 16

16 32.065
S
SULFUR

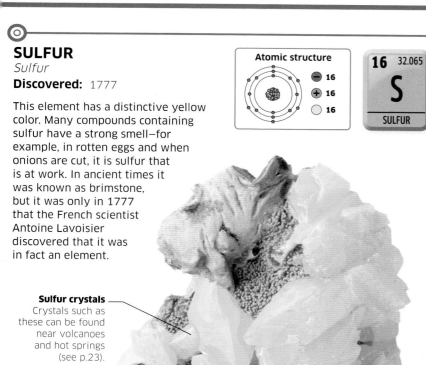

Sulfur crystals
Crystals such as these can be found near volcanoes and hot springs (see p.23).

SELENIUM
Selenium
Discovered: 1817

Named after the Greek word *selene*, meaning "moon," selenium exists in three forms: red, gray, and black selenium. This is an element we need in just the right amount for our bodies to stay healthy, and it is a useful ingredient in anti-dandruff shampoo, but in some compounds it can be very toxic.

Atomic structure
– 34
+ 34
○ 46

34 78.96
Se
SELENIUM

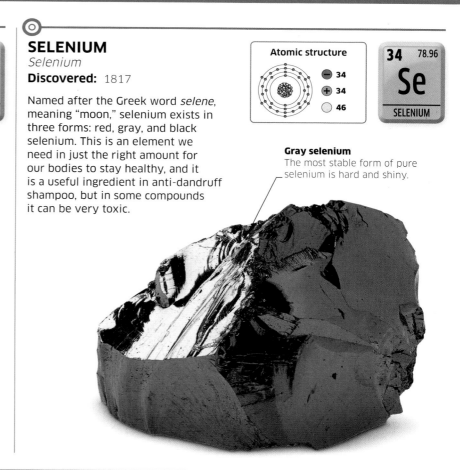

Gray selenium
The most stable form of pure selenium is hard and shiny.

Carbon fiber
In modern materials technology, carbon fibers that are one-tenth of a hair in thickness, but very tough, can be used to reinforce materials such as metals, or plastic (as seen above, enlarged many times).

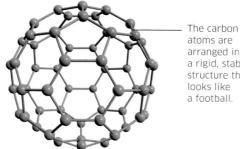

The carbon atoms are arranged in a rigid, stable structure that looks like a football.

Buckminsterfullerene
Nicknamed a buckyball, buckminsterfullerene is any spherical molecule of carbon atoms, bonded in hexagons and pentagons. There are typically 60 atoms in a "ball." They exist in soot, but also in distant stars, and were only discovered in 1985.

Carbon fossil fuels
The substances we call hydrocarbon or fossil fuels include coal, natural gas, and oil. These fuels were formed over millions of years from decaying dead organisms. They are made up mainly of carbon and hydrogen, and when they burn they produce carbon dioxide gas (see p.50–51).

Coal
A long, slow process turned trees that grew on Earth some 300 million years ago into coal that we can mine today. As dead trees fell, they started to sink deep down in boggy soil. They slowly turned into peat, a form of dense soil, which can be burned when dried. Increasing heat and pressure compacted the peat further, turning it into lignite, a soft, brown rock. Even deeper down, the intense heat turned the lignite into solid coal.

Oil and natural gas
The crude oil that is used to make diesel and gasoline is known as petroleum, meaning "oil from the rock." Millions of years ago, a layer of dead microorganisms covered the seabeds. It was slowly buried under mud and sand, gradually breaking down into hydrocarbons. Heat and pressure changed mud into rock and organic matter into liquid, or gas. This bubbled upward until it reached a "lid" of solid rock, and an oil (or gas) field was formed.

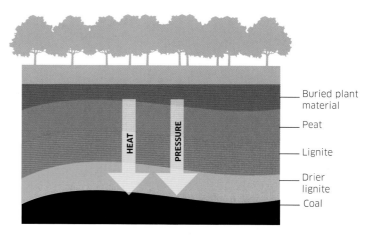

HEAT
PRESSURE

Buried plant material
Peat
Lignite
Drier lignite
Coal

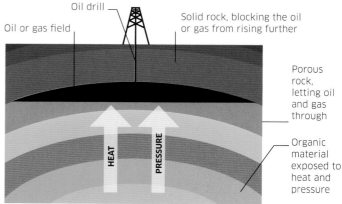

Oil drill
Oil or gas field
Solid rock, blocking the oil or gas from rising further

HEAT
PRESSURE

Porous rock, letting oil and gas through

Organic material exposed to heat and pressure

Hydrogen, oxygen, and nitrogen

Among the non-metal elements, these three gases are vital to us in different ways. A mixture of nitrogen and oxygen makes up most of the air we breathe, while hydrogen is the most abundant element in the universe.

Each of these gases has atoms that go in pairs: they exist as molecules of two atoms. That is why hydrogen is written as H_2, oxygen as O_2, and nitrogen as N_2. All three elements are found in compounds, such as DNA and proteins, that are vital for all forms of life on Earth.

HYDROGEN
Hydrogenium
Discovered: 1766

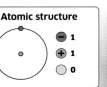

Atomic structure
- 1
+ 1
0

1 1.0079
H
HYDROGEN

Hydrogen is the simplest of all the elements. Its lightest, and most common, isotope has atoms made of a single proton and a single electron, but no neutrons. Hydrogen gets its name from the Greek *hydro* and *genes* meaning "water forming;" when it reacts with oxygen it makes water, or H_2O.

Hydrogen in the universe
Although rare in Earth's atmosphere, hydrogen makes up more than 88 percent of all matter in the universe. Our sun is not much more than a ball of very hot hydrogen. The hydrogen fuses together to produce helium (see p.41), the second element in the periodic table. In the process, a vast amount of energy is produced.

Hydrogen as fuel
A very reactive element that will burn easily, hydrogen can be used as a fuel. When mixed with oxygen, it forms an explosive mixture. The rocket of a spacecraft uses liquid hydrogen, mixed with liquid oxygen, as fuel. In fuel cells, used in electric cars, the chemical reaction between hydrogen and oxygen is converted to electricity. This combustion reaction produces only water, not water and carbon dioxide as in gasoline-fueled engines, making it an environmentally friendly fuel.

NITROGEN
Nitrogenium
Discovered: 1772

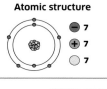

Atomic structure
- 7
+ 7
7

7 14.007
N
NITROGEN

In a nitrogen molecule (N_2), the two atoms are held together with a strong triple bond. The molecule is hard to break apart, which means nitrogen does not react readily with other substances. It is a very common element, making up 78 percent of the air on Earth. It is extremely useful, too. We need it in our bodies and, as part of the nitrogen cycle (see p.186), it helps plants to grow. Where plants and crops need extra help, it is added to fertilizers.

Explosive stuff
Molecules of nitrogen are not reactive, but many compounds containing nitrogen react very easily. These are found in many explosives, such as TNT, dynamite, and gunpowder, and in fireworks, too. On its own, compressed nitrogen gas is used to safely but powerfully blast out paintballs in paintball guns.

Liquid nitrogen
Nitrogen only condenses to liquid if it is cooled to -321°F (-196°C). This means that it is extremely cold in liquid form, instantly freezing anything it comes into contact with. This is useful for storing sensitive blood samples, cells, and tissue for medical use.

Jupiter is covered in **seas of liquid hydrogen**, formed as the **hydrogen in its atmosphere** condenses.

As a gas, oxygen is transparent, but in **its liquid form** it is pale blue.

39

OXYGEN
Oxygenium

Discovered: 1774

The element that we depend on to stay alive, oxygen was only recognized as an element in the late 18th century. Many chemists from different countries had for years been trying to work out precisely what made wood burn, and what air was made of, and several came to similar conclusions at roughly the same time. Oxygen is useful to us in many different forms and roles, some of which are described here.

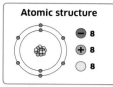

Atomic structure

− 8
+ 8
8

8   15.999

O

OXYGEN

STRATOSPHERE

OZONE LAYER

TROPOSPHERE

Most of the harmful UV radiation from the sun is absorbed by the ozone layer.

The ozone layer encircles Earth at a height of around 65,000 ft (20 km).

Fire
Three things are required for a fire to burn: there must be fuel, a source of heat such as a match, and oxygen gas. Without oxygen, no combustion (burning) can take place. Some fire extinguishers spray a layer of foam on the fire to prevent oxygen feeding it.

If a burning candle is placed in a jar, once the oxygen in the jar has been used up the flame soon flickers and goes out.

Air
Approximately 21 percent, or one fifth, of the air in Earth's atmosphere is oxygen gas. In the lower atmosphere, the oxygen we breathe is the most common form of oxygen—molecules made up of two oxygen atoms (O_2). Higher above us, however, is the ozone layer that protects us from harmful ultraviolet rays from the sun. Ozone (O_3) is another form, or allotrope, of oxygen, with three oxygen atoms in its molecules.

Life on Earth
Our planet is the only one that has oxygen in its atmosphere. This is necessary for us to breathe. Oxygen is produced by photosynthesis, the process by which plants produce the food they need to live and grow. Water—which enabled life in the first place, millions of years ago, and is crucial to the survival of life in all forms—also contains oxygen. Even the ground is full of oxygen, in the form of different mineral compounds (see pp.22–23).

Life
All animals need oxygen to break down food and produce energy in a vital process called respiration.

Land
Most of Earth's crust is made of rocks that contain oxygen compounds, such as these granite boulders.

Water
Perhaps the most important compound on Earth, water covers two thirds of our planet.

Halogens and noble gases

On the right-hand side of the periodic table are the non-metals known as halogens (group 17) and noble gases (group 18).

The word "halogen" means "salt-forming," and refers to the fact that these elements easily form salt compounds with metals. These include sodium chloride–common table salt–and those metal salts that give fireworks their colors, such as barium chloride which makes green stars. The noble gases don't form bonds with other "common" elements and are always gases at room temperature.

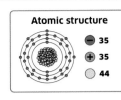

Atomic structure
- 35
+ 35
○ 44

35 79.904 Br BROMINE

BROMINE
Bromum
Discovered: 1826

One of only two elements that are liquids at room temperature (the other is mercury), bromine is toxic and corrosive. It forms less harmful salt compounds, such as those found in the Dead Sea in the Middle East.

A liquid halogen
A drop of pure, dark orange-brown bromine fills the rest of the glass sphere with paler vapor.

FLUORINE
Fluor
Discovered: 1886

A pale yellow gas, fluorine is an incredibly reactive element. On its own, it is very toxic, and ready to combine with even some of the least reactive elements. It will burn through materials such as glass and steel. When added to drinking water and toothpaste in small doses, it helps prevent tooth decay.

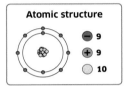

Atomic structure
- 9
+ 9
○ 10

9 18.998 F FLUORINE

Calming mixture
In this glass vial, fluorine has been mixed with the noble gas helium to keep it from reacting violently.

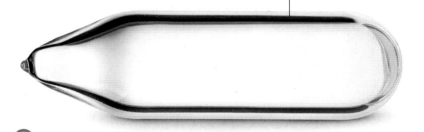

CHLORINE
Chlorum
Discovered: 1774

Like its periodic neighbor fluorine, chlorine is a very reactive gas. It is so poisonous that it has been used in chemical warfare, in World War I for example. It affects the lungs, producing a horrible, choking effect. Its deadly properties have been put to better use in the fight against typhoid and cholera: when added to water supplies, it kills the bacteria that cause these diseases. It is also used to keep swimming pools clean, and in household bleach.

Atomic structure
- 17
+ 17
○ 18

17 35.453 Cl CHLORINE

Chlorine is a pale green gas.

IODINE
Iodium
Discovered: 1811

The only halogen that is solid at room temperature, iodine will sublime, which means it turns straight from a solid into a gas. It can be used as a disinfectant in medicine, and it is an essential element for human health, in small amounts.

Atomic structure
- 53
+ 53
○ 74

53 126.90 I IODINE

Iodine sublimation
The dark purple, almost black solid turns into a paler gas.

TENNESSINE
Tennessine
Discovered: 2010

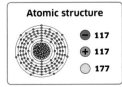

Atomic structure
- 117
+ 117
○ 177

117 294 Ts TENNESSINE

A latecomer among the halogens, this artificial element only got its name in 2016, six years after being created. It doesn't exist naturally, but is produced, a few atoms at a time, by crashing smaller atoms into one another until they stick together. The element is so new that so far, almost nothing is known about its chemistry. It is named after the US state of Tennessee, home to the laboratory where much of the research into making it took place.

Fluorine is part of a compound **used to create** the layer in **nonstick pans** that stops food getting stuck.

Helium is named after **Helios, the Greek god of the sun**, as it was **discovered in the cloud of gas** surrounding the sun.

41

NEON
Neon
Discovered: 1898

Neon might be the most well-known of the noble gases because of its use in bright advertising signs and lighting. Like the other members of the noble gases group, it is inert (doesn't react with other elements), and quite rare. Neon is present in air in small quantities; in fact, air is the only source of this element. To extract the neon, air is cooled until it becomes liquid. Then it is heated up again and, through distillation, the different elements present in air can be harvested as they vaporize. Neon can be used as a refrigerant and, when combined with helium, it can be used in lasers.

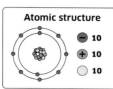
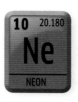

Neon red?
When electricity is passed through neon gas, it glows a stunning red. In fact, only red neon signs are actually made of neon. Other "neon" colors come from other noble gases—argon, for example, gives blue colors.

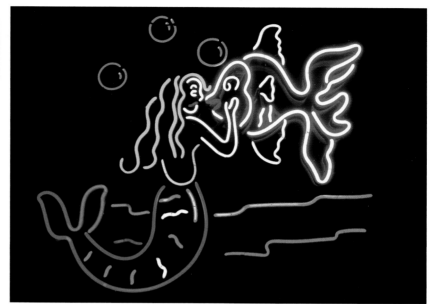

HELIUM
Helium
Discovered: 1895

Helium is a very light gas; only hydrogen is lighter. That is why it is put in all kinds of balloons. Airships, weather balloons, and party balloons can all be filled with the gas to make them rise and remain in the air. Helium is very unreactive. Because of this, it forms few compounds. Like neon, it can also be used as a cooling agent.

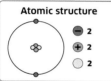

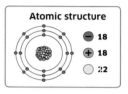

ARGON
Argon
Discovered: 1894

After nitrogen and oxygen, argon is the third most abundant gas in Earth's atmosphere. It is unreactive in nature, and doesn't conduct heat very well. Its name, from the Greek word *argos*, even means "idle." It can be put to good use, however—for example in welding and to protect fragile museum artifacts from decaying in oxygen-rich air.

Welding flame
Argon gas is used in welding to prevent water vapor and oxygen gas reacting with the metal.

Dying star
The Crescent Nebula is made of gases thrown off by a dying star. Most of what remains of the star is helium, produced by millions of years of nuclear fusion.

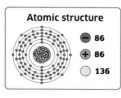

RADON
Radon
Discovered: 1900

Radon is a colorless gas which is released from minerals in the ground that contain the element uranium. Dangerously radioactive, radon can be a serious health risk. Breathing it in can cause lung cancer. It is present everywhere, but usually at very low levels. In areas where higher levels of radon are likely, home radon testing kits are sometimes provided.

Volcanic mud
Radon is present in volcanic springs and the mud surrounding them. Scientists often monitor the levels to make sure the groundwater in the area is safe to drink.

CHEMICAL REACTIONS

A chemical reaction is what happens when one substance meets and reacts with another and a new substance is formed. The substances that react together are called reactants, and those formed are called products. In a chemical reaction, atoms are only rearranged, never created or destroyed.

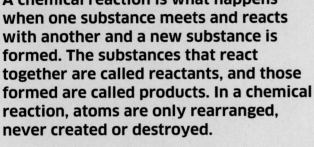

A change in color of a substance often indicates that a reaction has happened.

DIFFERENT REACTIONS

There are many types of reaction. They vary depending on the reactants involved and the conditions in which they take place. Some reactions happen in an instant, and some take years. Exothermic reactions give off heat while endothermic reactions cool things down. The products in a reversible reaction can turn back into the reactants, but in an irreversible reaction they cannot. Redox reactions involve two simultaneous reactions: reduction and oxidation.

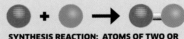

SYNTHESIS REACTION: ATOMS OF TWO OR MORE REACTANTS JOIN TOGETHER

DECOMPOSITION REACTION: ATOMS OF ONE REACTANT BREAK APART INTO TWO PRODUCTS

DISPLACEMENT REACTION: ATOMS OF ONE TYPE SWAP PLACES WITH THOSE OF ANOTHER, FORMING NEW COMPOUNDS

Three kinds of reaction

Reactions can be classified in three main groups according to the fate of the reactants. As shown above, in some reactions the reactants join together, in others they break apart, and in some their atoms swap places.

REACTION BASICS

Chemical reactions are going on around us all the time. They help us digest food, they cause metal to rust, wood to burn, and food to rot. Chemical reactions can be fun to watch in a laboratory–they can send sparks flying, create puffs of smoke, or trigger dramatic color changes. Some happen quietly, however, without us even noticing. The important fact behind all these reactions is that all the atoms involved remain unchanged. The atoms that were there at the beginning of the reactions are the same as the atoms at the end of the reaction. The only thing that has changed is how those atoms have been rearranged.

Reactants and products

The result of a chemical reaction is a chemical change, and the generation of a product or products that are different from the reactants. Often, the product looks nothing like the reactants. A solid might be formed by two liquids, a yellow liquid might turn blue, or a gas might be formed when a solid is mixed with a liquid. It doesn't always seem as if the atoms in the reactants are the same as those in the products, but they are.

Chemical equations

The "law of conservation of mass" states that mass is neither created nor destroyed. This applies to the mass of the atoms involved in a reaction, and can be shown in a chemical equation. Reactants are written on the left, and products on the right. The number of atoms on the left of the arrow always equal those on the right. Everything is abbreviated: "2 H_2" means two molecules of hydrogen, with two atoms in each molecule.

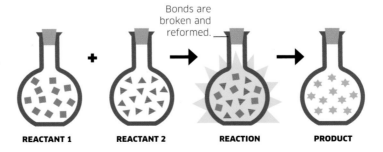

Bonds are broken and reformed.

REACTANT 1   REACTANT 2   REACTION   PRODUCT

2 HYDROGEN MOLECULES (2 H_2)   1 OXYGEN MOLECULE (O_2)   2 WATER MOLECULES (2 H_2O)

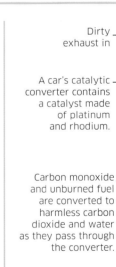

Dirty exhaust in

A car's catalytic converter contains a catalyst made of platinum and rhodium.

Carbon monoxide and unburned fuel are converted to harmless carbon dioxide and water as they pass through the converter.

Cleaner exhaust out

Catalysts

Catalysts are substances that make chemical reactions go faster. Some reactions can't start without a catalyst. Catalysts help reactants interact, but they are not part of the reaction and remain unchanged. Different catalysts do different jobs. Cars use catalysts that help reduce harmful engine fumes by speeding up their conversion to cleaner exhausts.

Quick or slow?
Bread dough made with yeast rises slowly through fermentation. In this process, chemical compounds in the yeast react with sugar to produce bubbles of carbon dioxide gas, which make the dough rise. With baking soda, the reaction is between an acid and an alkali, which generates carbon dioxide in an instant.

Hot or cold?
It takes energy to break the bonds between atoms, while energy is released when new bonds form. Often, more energy is released than it takes to break the bonds. That energy is released as heat, such as when a candle burns. This is an exothermic reaction. If the energy released is less than the energy required to break the bonds, the reaction takes energy from its surroundings and both become colder. That reaction is endothermic.

Redox reactions
Redox reactions involve reduction (the removal of oxygen, or addition of electrons) and oxidation (the addition of oxygen or removal of electrons). When an apple turns brown in the air, a chemical inside the apple is oxidized, and oxygen from the air is reduced.

Reversible or irreversible?
Rusting is a redox reaction that, like an apple going brown, is irreversible. In a reversible reaction, certain products can turn back into their original reactants.

WHY DO REACTIONS HAPPEN?

Different chemical reactions happen for different reasons, including temperature, pressure, and the type and concentration of reactants. Chemical reactions involve the breaking and making of bonds between atoms. These bonds involve the electrons in the outer shell of each atom. It is how the electrons are arranged in atoms of different elements that decides which atoms can lose electrons and which ones gain them.

Why do atoms react?
Atoms that can easily lose electrons are likely to react with atoms that need to fill their outer shell. There are different types of bonds depending on how the atoms do this: covalent, ionic, and metallic (see pp.16–17). A water molecule (below) has covalent bonds.

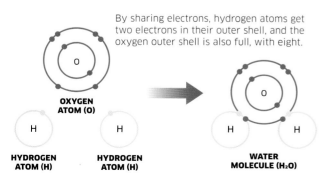

By sharing electrons, hydrogen atoms get two electrons in their outer shell, and the oxygen outer shell is also full, with eight.

OXYGEN ATOM (O)

HYDROGEN ATOM (H)   **HYDROGEN ATOM (H)**

WATER MOLECULE (H₂O)

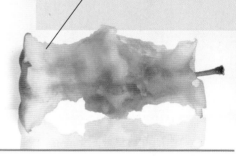

Increasing reactivity →

POTASSIUM	— Reacts with water
SODIUM	
CALCIUM	
MAGNESIUM	
ALUMINUM	— Reacts with diluted acids
ZINC	
IRON	
COPPER	
SILVER	
GOLD	— Hardly reacts at all

Metal reactivity series
A reactivity series sorts elements according to how readily they react with other elements. The most reactive is at the top; the least reactive at the bottom. It helps predict how elements will behave in some chemical reactions.

Potassium
Potassium is the most reactive metal in the series. Adding a lump of potassium to water causes the potassium to react instantly: it whizzes around on the surface of the water and bursts into spectacular flames.

Compounds

When two or more elements join together by forming chemical bonds, they make up a new, different substance. This substance is known as a compound.

Compounds are not just mixtures of elements. A mixture can be separated into the individual substances it contains, but it is not easy to turn a compound back into the elements that formed it. For example, water is a compound of hydrogen and oxygen. Only through a chemical reaction can it be changed back into these separate elements. A compound is made of atoms of two or more elements in a particular ratio. In water, for example, the ratio is two hydrogen atoms and one oxygen atom for every water molecule.

Fascinating formula

The chemical formula of a compound tells you which elements are present, and in what ratio. The compound sulfuric acid (H_2SO_4) is made of molecules that each contain two hydrogen atoms, one sulfur atom, and four oxygen atoms.

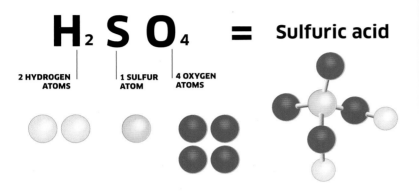

H_2 **S** O_4 = **Sulfuric acid**

2 HYDROGEN ATOMS **1 SULFUR ATOM** **4 OXYGEN ATOMS**

Great ways to bond

There are two types of bond that can hold the atoms in a compound together: covalent and ionic (see pp.16–17). Covalent bonds form between non-metal atoms. Ionic bonds form between metal and non-metal atoms.

Covalent compounds
Covalent compounds, such as sugar, form molecules in which the atoms form covalent bonds. They melt and boil at lower temperatures than ionic compounds. When they dissolve in water, they do not conduct electricity.

Salt lowers the freezing point of water, so it is used for melting ice and snow on roads.

Ionic compounds
Ionic compounds consist of ions. An ion is an electrically charged particle, formed when an atom has lost or gained electrons. Ions bond together, forming crystals with high melting points. Salt is an ionic compound.

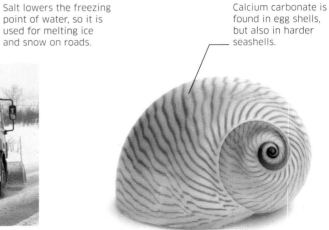

Calcium carbonate is found in egg shells, but also in harder seashells.

Best of both
Most compounds combine ionic and covalent bonding. In calcium carbonate, for example, calcium ions form ionic bonds with carbonate ions. Each carbonate ion contains carbon and oxygen atoms held together by covalent bonds.

Nothing like their elements

When atoms of different elements join to make new compounds, it is hard to tell what these elements are from looking at the compound. For example, no carbon is visible in carbon dioxide (CO_2), and no sodium in table salt, or sodium chloride (NaCl).

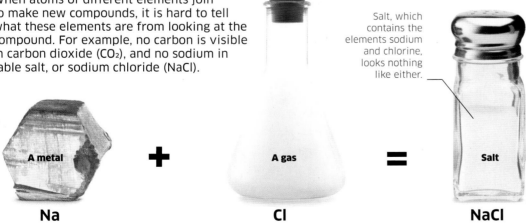

Salt, which contains the elements sodium and chlorine, looks nothing like either.

A metal + **A gas** = **Salt**

Na
Sodium

Cl
Chlorine

NaCl
Sodium chloride

Look what they have become
In chemical reactions, atoms from different elements regroup into new, different atom combinations. The resulting substances often look, and feel, completely different, too. For instance, sodium is a shiny metal, and chlorine is a pale green gas, but together they make sodium chloride (salt), a white crystal.

Pyrite, a form of iron sulfide

Iron sulfide
Iron sulfide, a compound of iron and sulfur, exists in several forms. Iron filings and yellow sulfur powder can be fused together to form a black solid called iron (II) sulfide (FeS). The mineral pyrite (FeS_2, above), known as "fool's gold," is another form of iron sulfide. Unlike iron, neither of these compounds is magnetic.

1862 The year **the first plastic**, Parkesine, was **presented to the public**. It was used to **make buttons**.

Cellulose, a **natural polymer**, is used to make **cellophane**, often used in **candy wrappers**.

45

Polymers

Some molecules join together in a chain to form long polymers (meaning "many parts"). The smaller molecules that make up the polymer are called monomers. There are many important polymers in living things. Cellulose, which makes up wood, is the most abundant natural polymer on Earth. The DNA in our bodies, and starch in foods such as pasta, rice, and potatoes are also polymers. Polymers can be man-made, too. Synthetic polymers include a vast array of different plastics.

Plastic polymers and recycling

The first man-made polymers were attempts to reproduce the natural polymers silk, cellulose, and latex (see pp.58–59). Today, plastics play a massive role in the way we live, but they also pose a serious risk to the environment. In 1988, an identification code was developed to make plastic recycling easier. The code's symbols let the recyclers know what plastic an object is made of, which matters when it is time to process and recycle it.

What makes a polymer

A polymer is like a long string of beads, with each bead, or monomer, in the string made up of exactly the same combination of atoms. Shorter ones, with just two monomers, are called dimers, while those with three are known as trimers.

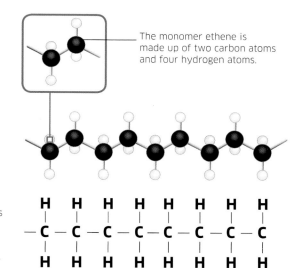

The monomer ethene is made up of two carbon atoms and four hydrogen atoms.

Polyethylene polymer
A string of ethene monomers is known as polyethylene (or polyethene/polythene). There are several thousand ethene monomers in a polyethylene polymer.

Type of plastic	Symbol	Properties	Use
Polyethylene terephthalate	1 PET or PETE	Clear, lightweight but strong and heat-resistant. Good barrier to gas, moisture, alcohol, and solvents.	• Water bottles • Food jars • Ovenproof film
High-density polyethylene	2 HDPE	Tough; can be stretched without breaking, and easy to process. Resistant to moisture and solvents.	• Milk containers • Trash cans with wheels • Juice bottles
Polyvinyl chloride	3 PVC	Strong; resistant to chemicals and oil. Rigid PVC is used in construction; flexible PVC in inflatables.	• Pipes • Toys and inflatables • Flooring
Low-density polyethylene	4 LDPE	Flexible and tough, can withstand high temperatures. Good resistance to chemicals. Easy to process.	• Plastic bags • Snap-on lids • Six-pack rings
Polypropylene	5 PP	Tough, flexible, and long lasting. High melting point. Resistant to fats and solvents.	• Hinges on flip-top lids • Plastic medicine bottles • Concrete additives
Polystyrene	6 PS	Can be solid or foamed. Good for insulation and easy to shape, but slow to biodegrade.	• Disposable foam cups • Plastic cutlery • Packaging
Miscellaneous	7 Miscellaneous	Other plastics such as acrylic, nylon, polylactic acid, and plastic multi-layer combinations.	• Baby bottles • Safety glasses • "Ink" in 3-D printers

Acids and bases

Chemical opposites, acids and bases react when they are mixed together, neutralizing one another. Bases that are soluble in water are called alkalis. All alkalis are bases, but not all bases are alkalis.

Bases and acids can be weak or strong. Many ingredients in food contain weak acids (vinegar, for instance) or alkalis (eggs), while strong acids and alkalis are used in cleaning products and industrial processes. Strong acids and alkalis break apart entirely when dissolved in water, whereas weak acids and alkalis do not.

Corrosive power

Strong acids and alkalis can cause serious burns to skin. Very strong acids and alkalis can burn through metal, and some can even dissolve glass. While dangerous, their corrosive power can be useful, for instance, for etching glass or cleaning metals.

Is it an acid or a base?

The acidity of a substance is measured by its number of hydrogen ions—its "power of hydrogen" or pH. Water, with a pH of 7, is a neutral substance. A substance with a pH lower than 7 is acidic; one with a pH above 7 is alkaline. Each interval on the scale represents a tenfold increase in either alkalinity or acidity. For instance, milk, with a pH of 6, is ten times more acidic than water, which has a pH of 7. Meanwhile, seawater, with a pH of 8, is ten times more alkaline than pure water.

Hydrogen ions (H⁺)

determine whether a solution is an acid or an alkali. Acids are H⁺ donors while alkalis are H⁺ acceptors.

The pH scale

Running from 0 to 14, the pH scale is related to the concentration of hydrogen ions (H^+). A pH of 7 is neutral. A pH of 1 indicates a high concentration of hydrogen ions (acidic). A pH of 14 shows a low concentration (alkaline).

The litmus test

A version of the litmus test has been used for hundreds of years to tell whether a solution is acidic or alkaline. Red litmus paper turns blue when dipped into an alkali. Blue litmus paper turns red when dipped into an acid.

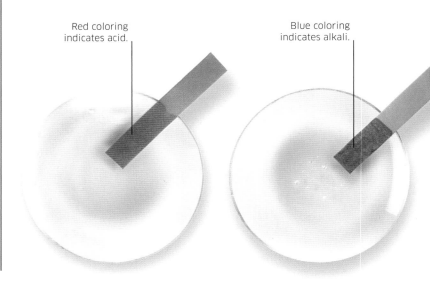

Red coloring indicates acid.

Blue coloring indicates alkali.

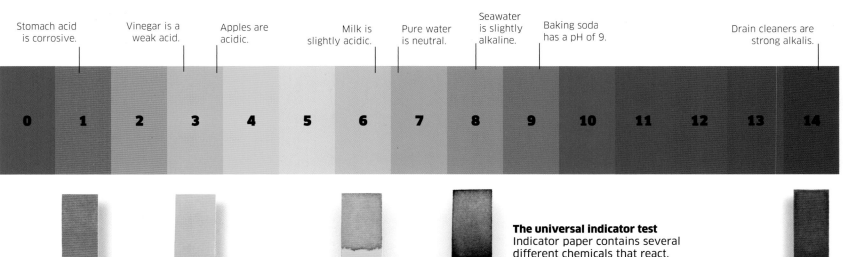

Stomach acid is corrosive.

Vinegar is a weak acid.

Apples are acidic.

Milk is slightly acidic.

Pure water is neutral.

Seawater is slightly alkaline.

Baking soda has a pH of 9.

Drain cleaners are strong alkalis.

0 1 2 3 4 5 6 7 8 9 10 11 12 13 14

The universal indicator test

Indicator paper contains several different chemicals that react, turning a range of colors in response to different pH values. Dipping indicator paper into an unknown solution reveals its pH.

Gardeners use **coffee grounds** to lower the pH of soil around **acid-loving plants such as roses**.

Soapy water is strongly **alkaline**.

Stomach acid is almost as **corrosive as battery acid,** but our stomachs produce a **mucus that protects us** from damage.

47

It's all about the ions

The difference between an acid and an alkali comes down to their proportion of positively charged particles called hydrogen ions (H⁺). When an acidic compound is dissolved in water, it breaks up, releasing H⁺ ions: it has an increased proportion of positively charged ions. When an alkaline compound dissolves in water it releases negatively charged particles called hydroxide ions (OH⁻). Acids are called H⁺ donors; alkalis are called H⁺ acceptors.

Acid
There are more positively charged H⁺ ions than negatively charged OH⁻ ions in an acid.

Neutral
A neutral solution contains equal numbers of positive H⁺ and negative OH⁻ ions.

Base
There are more negatively charged OH⁻ ions than positively charged H⁺ ions in an alkali.

Mixing acids and bases

The reaction between an acid and an alkali produces water and a salt. It is called a neutralization reaction. The H⁺ ions in the acid react with the OH⁻ ions in the alkali, resulting in a substance that is neither acid nor alkali. Different acids and alkalis produce different salts when they react.

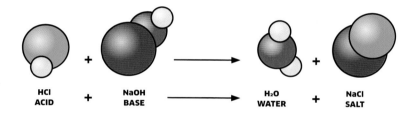

| HCl
ACID | + | NaOH
BASE | → | H₂O
WATER | + | NaCl
SALT |

Neutralization formula
When hydrochloric acid (HCl) reacts with the alkali sodium hydroxide (NaOH), they produce a neutral solution that consists of water (H₂O) and a well-known salt—sodium chloride (NaCl), or table salt.

Acids and bases in agriculture
Farmers monitor soil pH levels carefully. Soils are naturally acidic or alkaline, and different crops prefer a higher or lower pH. Farmers can reduce the soil pH by adding certain fertilizers, or raise the soil pH with alkalis, such as lime (calcium hydroxide).

Kitchen chemistry

The kitchen is a great place to see acids and alkalis in action. Weak acids—found in lemon juice and vinegar—can preserve or improve the flavor of food. When baking, we use weak alkalis present in baking soda to help cakes to rise. Strong acids and alkalis are key ingredients in a range of cleaning products. They are so powerful that protective gloves must be worn when using them.

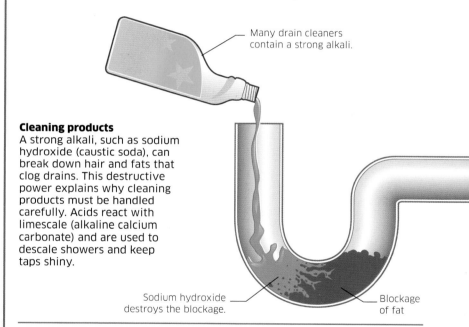

Many drain cleaners contain a strong alkali.

Cleaning products
A strong alkali, such as sodium hydroxide (caustic soda), can break down hair and fats that clog drains. This destructive power explains why cleaning products must be handled carefully. Acids react with limescale (alkaline calcium carbonate) and are used to descale showers and keep taps shiny.

Sodium hydroxide destroys the blockage.

Blockage of fat

Bubbles made by carbon dioxide

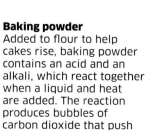

Baking powder
Added to flour to help cakes rise, baking powder contains an acid and an alkali, which react together when a liquid and heat are added. The reaction produces bubbles of carbon dioxide that push the cake mixture upward.

Crystal forest

If you dip a piece of pure metal into a solution in which another metal is dissolved, something quite magical may happen.

These delicate crystals have formed on a piece of zinc placed in a solution of lead nitrate. The magic is in fact a chemical reaction known as metal displacement, seen here in a photograph taken through a microscope. The more reactive metal (zinc) displaces the less reactive metal (lead) from its nitrate compound, so instead of lead nitrate and zinc, we end up with pure lead and a solution of zinc and nitrate ions. The lead atoms join together in regular patterns, forming crystals of pure lead.

50   matter ○ **COMBUSTION**

Space rockets use combustion to take off, fueled by **liquid hydrogen**.

Combustion

Combustion is the reaction between a fuel—such as wood, natural gas, or oil—and oxygen. The combustion reaction releases energy in the form of heat and light. Fuel needs a trigger (a match or a spark) before combustion can start.

Combustion is at work in bonfires, fireworks, and when we light a candle. But more than just a spectacle, it is essential to the way we live. Most of the world's power stations generate electricity using the combustion of fossil fuels such as coal, oil, and gas. Most cars, semi trucks, boats, and planes are driven by engines powered by combustion. Scientists are working hard to create alternatives to what is now understood to be a potentially wasteful and harmful source of energy. But for now we all rely on it to keep warm and to get where we need.

Campfire chemistry

Dry wood contains cellulose (made of the elements carbon, hydrogen, and oxygen). It burns well in oxygen, which makes up about one fifth of air.

Carbon dioxide
Carbon dioxide (CO_2) is produced when wood burns. Known as a greenhouse gas, it contributes to global warming if there is too much of it in the atmosphere.

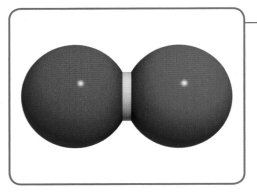

Oxygen
For combustion to work, there needs to be a good supply of the element oxygen. Oxygen in the air exists as molecules made up of two oxygen atoms, with the chemical formula O_2.

Water vapor
The combustion of cellulose, which makes up about half the dry mass of wood, produces water (H_2O) as well as carbon dioxide (CO_2). In the heat of a fire, the water evaporates as steam.

A balanced reaction

During combustion, substances known as reactants are transformed into new substances called products. The reaction rearranges the atoms of the reactants. They swap places, but the number of each is the same. Energy (heat and light) is released when the bonds that hold the initial molecules together are broken and new ones are formed.

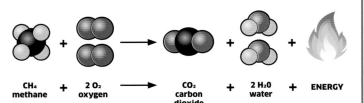

| CH_4 methane | + | $2\ O_2$ oxygen | → | CO_2 carbon dioxide | + | $2\ H_2O$ water | + | ENERGY |

Methane combustion
Above is the reaction formula for the combustion of methane (natural gas). The number of carbon (C), hydrogen (H), and oxygen (O) atoms is the same on each side of the arrow, but the substances they make up have changed.

Early man first learned to **make fire** around 1 million years ago.

1777 The year French chemist **Antoine Lavoisier** proved that **oxygen** is involved in combustion.

51

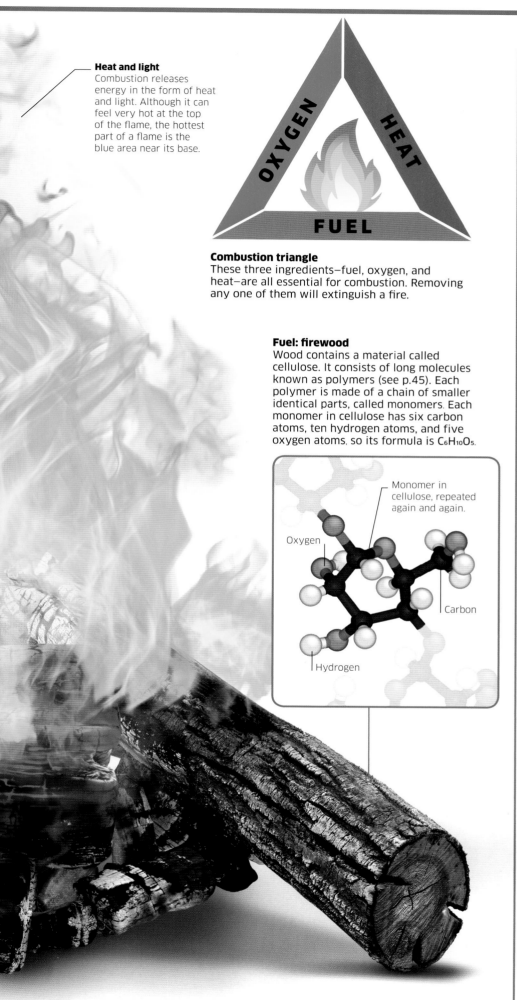

Heat and light
Combustion releases energy in the form of heat and light. Although it can feel very hot at the top of the flame, the hottest part of a flame is the blue area near its base.

Combustion triangle
These three ingredients—fuel, oxygen, and heat—are all essential for combustion. Removing any one of them will extinguish a fire.

Fuel: firewood
Wood contains a material called cellulose. It consists of long molecules known as polymers (see p.45). Each polymer is made of a chain of smaller identical parts, called monomers. Each monomer in cellulose has six carbon atoms, ten hydrogen atoms, and five oxygen atoms, so its formula is $C_6H_{10}O_5$.

Monomer in cellulose, repeated again and again.

Oxygen

Carbon

Hydrogen

Fuel efficiency and the environment
Different fuels release different amounts of energy. They also produce different amounts of carbon dioxide when they burn. Wood is least efficient and produces the most carbon dioxide, which makes it the least environmentally friendly fuel.

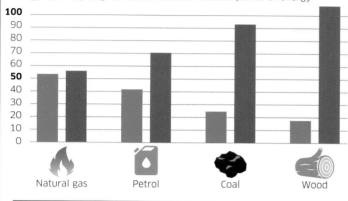

Energy values of different fuels
- Energy content (kJ per gram of fuel)
- Quantity (mg) of carbon dioxide released per kJ of energy

| | Natural gas | Petrol | Coal | Wood |

Fireworks
Fireworks shoot up in the air and explode into colorful displays thanks to combustion. The fuel used is charcoal, mixed with oxidizers (compounds providing oxygen) and other agents. The colors come from different metal salts.

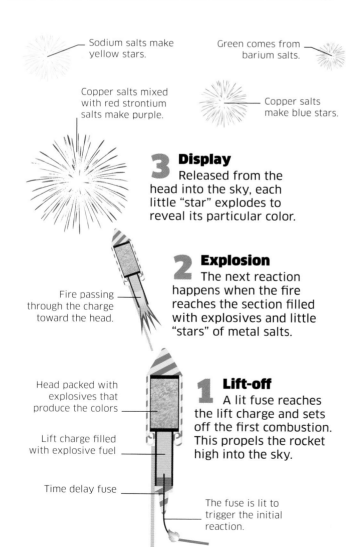

Sodium salts make yellow stars.

Green comes from barium salts.

Copper salts mixed with red strontium salts make purple.

Copper salts make blue stars.

3 Display
Released from the head into the sky, each little "star" explodes to reveal its particular color.

2 Explosion
The next reaction happens when the fire reaches the section filled with explosives and little "stars" of metal salts.

Fire passing through the charge toward the head.

1 Lift-off
A lit fuse reaches the lift charge and sets off the first combustion. This propels the rocket high into the sky.

Head packed with explosives that produce the colors

Lift charge filled with explosive fuel

Time delay fuse

The fuse is lit to trigger the initial reaction.

52 matter ∘ **ELECTROCHEMISTRY**

1799 The year Italian scientist **Alessandro Volta** invented **the first** electrical battery.

Electrochemistry

Electricity and chemical reactions are closely linked, and together fall under the heading electrochemistry. Electrochemistry is the study of chemical processes that cause electrons to move.

An electric current is a steady flow of electrons, the tiny negative particles that whizz around in the shells of atoms. Electrons can flow in response either to a chemical reaction taking place inside a battery, or to a current delivered by the main electrical grid.

Electricity is key to electrolysis. This process is used in industries to extract pure elements from ionic compounds (see p.44) that have been dissolved in a liquid known as an electrolyte. Electrolysis can also be used to purify metals, and a similar process can be used to plate (cover) objects with a metal. The result depends on the choice of material of the electrodes and, in particular, the exact contents of the electrolyte.

Ions and redox reactions

Chemical reactions where electrons are transferred between atoms are called oxidation-reduction (redox) reactions. Atoms that have lost or gained electrons become ions, and are electrically charged. Atoms that gain electrons become negative ions (anions). Atoms that lose electrons become positive ions (cations). These play an important role in electrolysis.

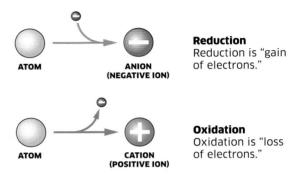

ATOM → **ANION (NEGATIVE ION)**

Reduction
Reduction is "gain of electrons."

ATOM → **CATION (POSITIVE ION)**

Oxidation
Oxidation is "loss of electrons."

Electrolysis

Ionic compounds contain positive and negative ions. They can be separated using electricity, by a process called electrolysis. If electricity passes through an electrolyte (an ionic compound that has been dissolved in water), the negative ions in the electrolyte will flow toward the positive electrode and the positive ions will flow toward the negative electrode. The products created in the process will depend on what is in the electrolyte. This diagram shows how water (H_2O) can be split back into its original pure elements, oxygen and hydrogen. The two gases can be trapped and collected as they bubble up along the electrodes.

Water as electrolyte
The electric current makes each neutral water molecule (H_2O) split up into electrically charged ions: a positive hydrogen ion (H^+) and a negative hydroxide ion (OH^-).

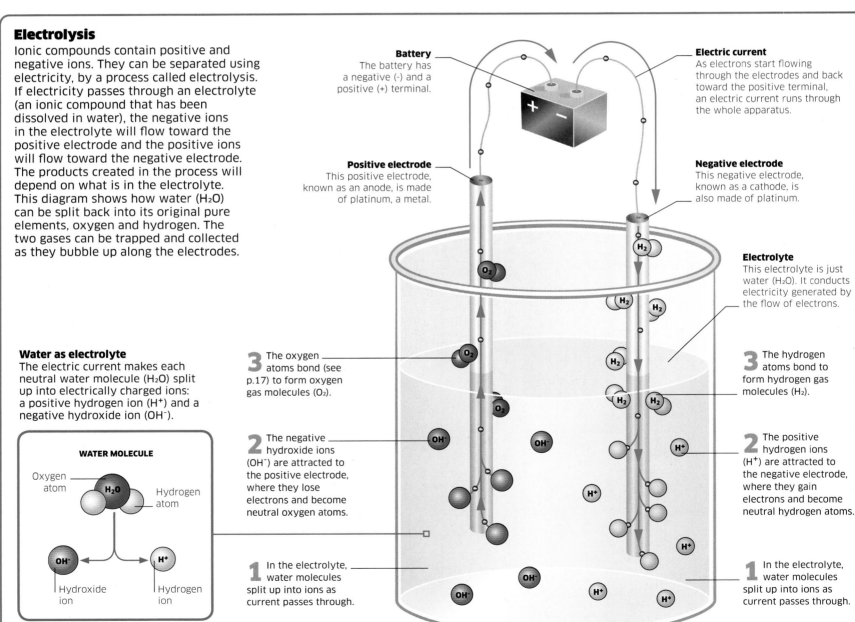

Battery
The battery has a negative (-) and a positive (+) terminal.

Electric current
As electrons start flowing through the electrodes and back toward the positive terminal, an electric current runs through the whole apparatus.

Positive electrode
This positive electrode, known as an anode, is made of platinum, a metal.

Negative electrode
This negative electrode, known as a cathode, is also made of platinum.

Electrolyte
This electrolyte is just water (H_2O). It conducts electricity generated by the flow of electrons.

WATER MOLECULE

Oxygen atom — H_2O — Hydrogen atom

OH^- Hydroxide ion ← → H^+ Hydrogen ion

3 The oxygen atoms bond (see p.17) to form oxygen gas molecules (O_2).

2 The negative hydroxide ions (OH^-) are attracted to the positive electrode, where they lose electrons and become neutral oxygen atoms.

1 In the electrolyte, water molecules split up into ions as current passes through.

3 The hydrogen atoms bond to form hydrogen gas molecules (H_2).

2 The positive hydrogen ions (H^+) are attracted to the negative electrode, where they gain electrons and become neutral hydrogen atoms.

1 In the electrolyte, water molecules split up into ions as current passes through.

1807 The year British chemist **Sir Humphry Davy** discovered the **elements** potassium and sodium **through electrolysis**.

The **human body contain electrolytes** that regulate nerve and muscle functions, which rely on a **weak electric current**.

53

Electroplating

Similar to electrolysis, electroplating is a process that coats a cheaper metal with a more expensive metal, such as silver. To turn a cheap metal spoon into a silver-plated spoon, the cheap metal spoon is used as a cathode (negative electrode) and a silver bar is used as the anode (positive electrode). These two electrodes are bathed in an electrolyte that contains a solution of the expensive metal, in this case silver nitrate solution.

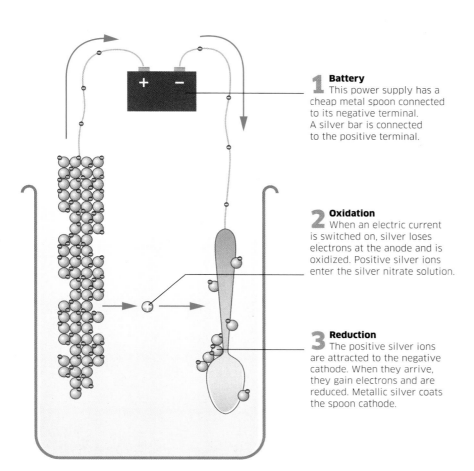

1 Battery
This power supply has a cheap metal spoon connected to its negative terminal. A silver bar is connected to the positive terminal.

2 Oxidation
When an electric current is switched on, silver loses electrons at the anode and is oxidized. Positive silver ions enter the silver nitrate solution.

3 Reduction
The positive silver ions are attracted to the negative cathode. When they arrive, they gain electrons and are reduced. Metallic silver coats the spoon cathode.

Gray tarnish showing that oxidation has taken place.

Oxidation in air
Silver oxidizes when exposed to air, so silver plated items eventually lose their shine as a gray tarnish forms on the surface. Polishing removes the tarnish but the plating might be damaged.

Galvanizing
Steel or iron can be prevented from rusting (a form of oxidation) by coating them in the metal zinc, a process called galvanizing. These nails have been galvanized.

Purifying metals

The copper that is extracted from copper ore is not pure enough to become electrical wiring. It has to be purified by electrolysis. Impure copper acts as the anode, and pure copper as the cathode. These electrodes lie in a solution of copper sulfate.

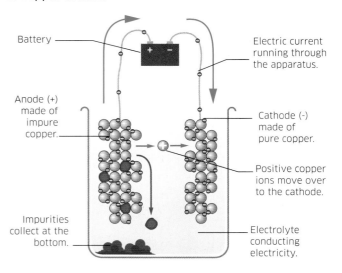

Battery

Electric current running through the apparatus.

Anode (+) made of impure copper.

Cathode (-) made of pure copper.

Positive copper ions move over to the cathode.

Impurities collect at the bottom.

Electrolyte conducting electricity.

Electrorefining

Pure copper is used to make electrical wiring and components. Here you can see copper purification, called electrorefining, being carried out on a massive scale in a factory, in the process described above.

Electrochemistry in batteries

Batteries turn chemical energy into electrical energy (see p.92). This is the opposite of electrolysis, which turns electrical energy into chemical energy. In a battery, it is the anode that is negative and the cathode that is positive. The reaction at the anode is still oxidation and at the cathode it is still reduction.

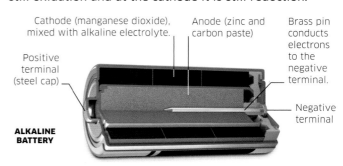

Cathode (manganese dioxide), mixed with alkaline electrolyte.

Anode (zinc and carbon paste)

Brass pin conducts electrons to the negative terminal.

Positive terminal (steel cap)

Negative terminal

ALKALINE BATTERY

Hot metal

Ignite a mixture of chemicals called thermite and you'll need to stand back! These chemicals react together very quickly, producing enormous amounts of heat.

A thermite reaction is a spectacular display, but also serves a practical purpose: it is used to extract molten iron from iron oxide for welding. It takes a lot of heat to start the reaction, which then releases enough heat to melt the iron. The process most commonly uses a mixture of iron oxide and aluminum. A slim ribbon of magnesium is inserted into the mixture as a fuse. When ignited, it starts the reaction, breaking the bonds between the iron and oxygen atoms. Aluminum then bonds with the released oxygen, producing more heat. This in turn breaks more bonds and melts the leftover iron.

MATERIALS

The word "materials" describes the kind of matter we use for making and building things. Every object is made of a material—a hard material or a soft material, a rough or a smooth, a multicolored or a plain gray one. Nature has come up with millions of different materials, and people have developed millions more. You might think that is more than enough materials, but researchers are continually discovering amazing new natural materials, and inventing incredible new synthetic materials.

NATURAL OR SYNTHETIC?

People have used natural materials—such as wool, leather, and rubber—for thousands of years. Today we also make materials using chemicals. These synthetic materials have unique properties and make us less reliant on precious natural materials, but they can be difficult to dispose of in an environmentally friendly way.

Natural leather
Leather is made from animal skin. People have worn leather since the Stone Age, and still do. Leather can be molded into shape, retains heat, is fairly waterproof, and resists tears.

Synthetic trainer
The synthetic materials in this sports shoe offer several advantages over leather. They are easier and cheaper to produce, and have more flexibility, but they probably won't last as long.

CHOOSING MATERIALS

Different materials suit different purposes—there is no single "best material." It all depends on what you want a material to do. Among their many properties, materials vary according to how hard they are, what they feel like, how strong or elastic they are, and whether or not they are waterproof.

Composite materials
Sometimes the properties of one material are not enough, so two or more materials are combined into a composite. There are different composites. Concrete is made from strong stones, sand to fill the gaps, and cement to bind it all together. It stays together thanks to a chemical reaction that sets it. It can be made even stronger by adding steel bars in wet concrete. Fiberglass is a type of plastic reinforced with glass fibers. It is lightweight and easy to mold, and is used to make anything from bathtubs to boats and surfboards.

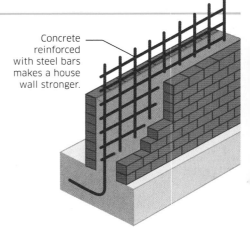

Concrete reinforced with steel bars makes a house wall stronger.

Properties of materials
This chart lists some of the properties we need to think about when choosing a material for a certain product, and some common materials. Some of these properties are relative: marble, for example, is hard, but for a rock it is quite soft, which is why sculptors have chosen it to carve into statues since ancient times.

Material	Hardness	Texture	Strength	Elasticity	Water resistance
Wood	From soft (balsa) to hard (mahogany)	Rough unless polished	Strength varies	Can be elastic or rigid	Some woods are more waterproof
Glass	Very hard (does not flex under pressure)	Smooth	Not very strong; shatters on impact	Not elastic	Waterproof
Diamond	One of the hardest materials known	Smooth when cut	Strong	Not elastic	Waterproof
Marble	Hard (but soft for a rock)	Smooth	Strong	Not elastic	Waterproof
Wool	Soft natural fibers	Rough or smooth	Strong fibers	Elastic in wool yarn and clothing	Not waterproof
Kevlar®	Hard synthetic fibers	Smooth	Strong	Elastic	Waterproof
Nylon	Hard synthetic	Smooth	Strong	Elastic in tights; less so in rope	Waterproof
Steel	Hard metal alloy	Smooth	Strong	Elastic, particularly in springs	Waterproof
Copper	Soft metal	Smooth	A weak metal	Not elastic	Waterproof

LASTING MATERIALS

Materials last for different lengths of time. Some materials decay in a matter of weeks, while some last for tens of thousands of years. The materials that survive for millennia provide a fascinating window into the way our ancestors used to live.

Viking long ship
Several Viking longships dating back more than a thousand years have been discovered intact in burial mounds. These ships were built of wood such as oak. Wood normally decays after a few hundred years, but the organisms that break it down need oxygen. There was no oxygen supply around the ships that lay buried, so the wood survived. Hulls of sunken wooden sailing ships survive underwater for the same reason.

The Oseberg ship, dating from 800 CE, was found in a burial mound in Norway.

Roman amphitheater
Rome's Colosseum is made of several materials—a rock called travertine; another rock made of volcanic ash, called tuff; and concrete. It was built in 80 CE as an amphitheater. Since then it has been through wars and used as housing, factories, shops, and a fortress, but the basic materials have remained in place.

NEW MATERIALS

Material scientists—chemists, physicists, and engineers—research and deliver a steady stream of exciting new materials. Some materials resist damage, some heal themselves. There are plastics that conduct electricity, and wall coverings that reduce pollution. Environmental concerns are leading to materials designed to use fewer natural resources and to decompose without harmful waste.

Nanotechnology
Nanotechnology deals with materials that are between 1 and 100 nanometers wide or long. A nanometer is a millionth of a millimeter (making a housefly about 5 million nanometers long). This means new materials can be designed by moving and manipulating atoms.

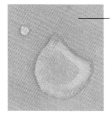

This fabric is coated with water-repellent nanoparticles made of aluminium oxide.

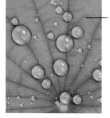

The surface of a lotus leaf is naturally "nanostructured" to repel water.

Aerogel
Aerogels are incredibly lightweight. Normal gels have a liquid and a solid component. In aerogels, the liquid is replaced by air—more than 99.8 percent of an aerogel is air. It protects from both heat and cold. Possible uses include insulation for buildings, space suits, and sponges for mopping up chemical spills.

REUSING AND RECYCLING

Reusing and recycling materials reduces the need to produce ever more of the materials we use a lot. This helps conserve raw materials, and cuts harmful carbon emissions. Materials production today considers the full life-cycle of a product—from reducing the raw materials and energy needed to produce it in the first place, to preventing materials from ending up in landfills and oceans.

The recycling sorting process
Different materials must be recycled in separate ways, and some things that get put in recycling bins cannot be recycled at all. The vast amount of materials we throw away gets processed in huge recycling centers.

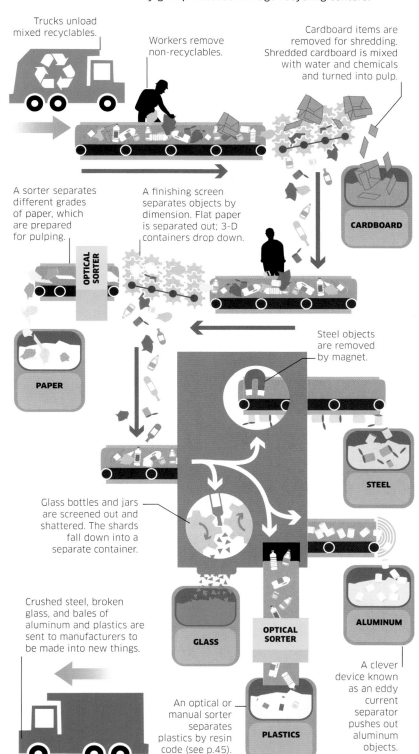

58 matter ○ NATURAL MATERIALS

600 The **number of trees** needed to build a medieval **warship**.

Natural materials

Early humans learned to use the materials they found around them to make tools, clothes, and homes. Many natural materials are still used in the same way, while others are combined to make new ones.

Some natural materials come from plants (for example wood, cotton, and rubber), others from animals (silk and wool), or from Earth's crust (clay and metals). Their natural properties—bendy or rigid, strong or weak, absorbent or waterproof—have been put to good use by humans for millions of years. People have also learned to adjust these properties to suit their needs. Soft plant fibers and animal wool are spun into longer, stronger fibers. Animal skins are treated to make leather to wear. Skins were also used to make parchment to write on; now we use paper made from wood. Metals are mixed to make stronger materials called alloys (see pp.62-63).

Materials from animals

Animals, from insects to mammals, are a rich source of materials. The skin of pigs, goats, and cows can be treated and turned into leather. Caterpillars called silkworms spin themselves cocoons that can be unraveled into fine silk threads. Sheep grow thick, waterproof hair that can be cut off, or shorn, and spun into wool thread used for knitting or woven into fabrics.

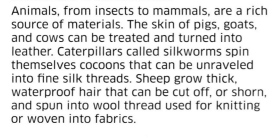

The silk used for these bright scarves has been dyed. Natural silk is pale in color, and its tone depends on what the silkworms are eating.

Silk
Silkworms and their moth parents have been farmed for more than 5,000 years. A cocoon can produce up to 2,950 ft (900 m) of silk thread that can be made into beautiful fabrics.

Wool
Sheep have been bred for their wool for more than 6,000 years. An average sheep produces wool for about eight sweaters a year—or 60 pairs of socks. Today, wool is often mixed with acrylic fibers.

Different breeds of sheep produce different types of wool.

Wool yarn
Wool is washed, then spun into long fibers, and dyed.

Materials from plants

Plant materials have played a key role in humanity's success as a species. Wood has provided shelters, tools, and transportation, while cotton and flax (a plant used to make linen) have clothed people for thousands of years. Plant materials can be flexible or rigid, heavy or light, depending on the particular combination of three substances in their cell walls: lignin, cellulose, and hemicellulose.

Latex and rubber
Today, a lot of rubber is synthetic, but natural rubber comes from latex, a fluid that can be tapped from certain types of trees. It contains a polymer that makes it elastic.

Cotton
Fluffy cotton, consisting mainly of cellulose, protects the cotton plant's seeds. It is picked and spun into yarn or thread. The texture of cotton fabrics vary depending on how they are woven.

Wood
Different types of wood have different properties, including color, texture, weight, and hardness, making them suitable for different things. Wood pulp is used to make paper. A lot of wood is harvested from wood plantations.

Bamboo, a fast-growing, treelike grass, can be turned into a fabric that is soft, breathable, and absorbs sweat, making it good for sportswear.

Glass was first made in Ancient Egypt and Mesopotamia in **around 2,000 BCE.**

59

Keeping it natural
Natural materials, such as rubber, cotton, and different types of wood, are used in a wide range of everyday items, such as the ones seen here.

Vulcanized tires
Adding sulfur to natural rubber, a process called vulcanization, increases its durability.

Elastic, not plastic
Rubber gloves are often made of flexible latex.

Thin but strong
Cellulose polymer chains line up together to give cotton thread its strength.

Absorbent cotton
Cotton is great for towels and cotton swabs as it is soft and can absorb up to 27 times its weight in water.

Cotton swabs

Steady support
Lignin is the substance that holds cellulose and hemicellulose fibers together and makes wood stiff and strong—useful properties for ladders.

Curved wood
Some woods, such as maple and spruce, can be bent into shape using steam. They are good for making violins and other string instruments.

Materials from Earth's crust
Earth materials range from sand, clay, and rocks to minerals and metals. Materials from the earth have always been important for building. If you look at buildings, you can usually see what materials lie underground in the area—flint or slate, sandstone, limestone, marble, or clay. These materials are also essential for practical and decorative cookware, earthenware, and utensils.

Clay and clay products
Clay, a mixture of the minerals silicon dioxide and aluminum oxide, has many uses. To make bricks, natural clay is mixed with water and pressed into shape before being dried. It is then baked at very hot temperatures to make it waterproof. Pottery is made in a similar way, but with clay of finer particles.

Earthenware pottery is fired at temperatures of around 1,830°F (1,000°C).

Sand and glass
Glass is made from sand. It is usually the sand common in deserts, which consists of the mineral silica. Beach sand often has traces of other substances, making less clear glass. Carefully chosen additives color the glass. The ingredients are melted together at 2,732°F (1,500°C) before being shaped into window panes, drinking glasses, or bottles.

Eyeglass lenses used to be made of pure glass. Today they are often plastic.

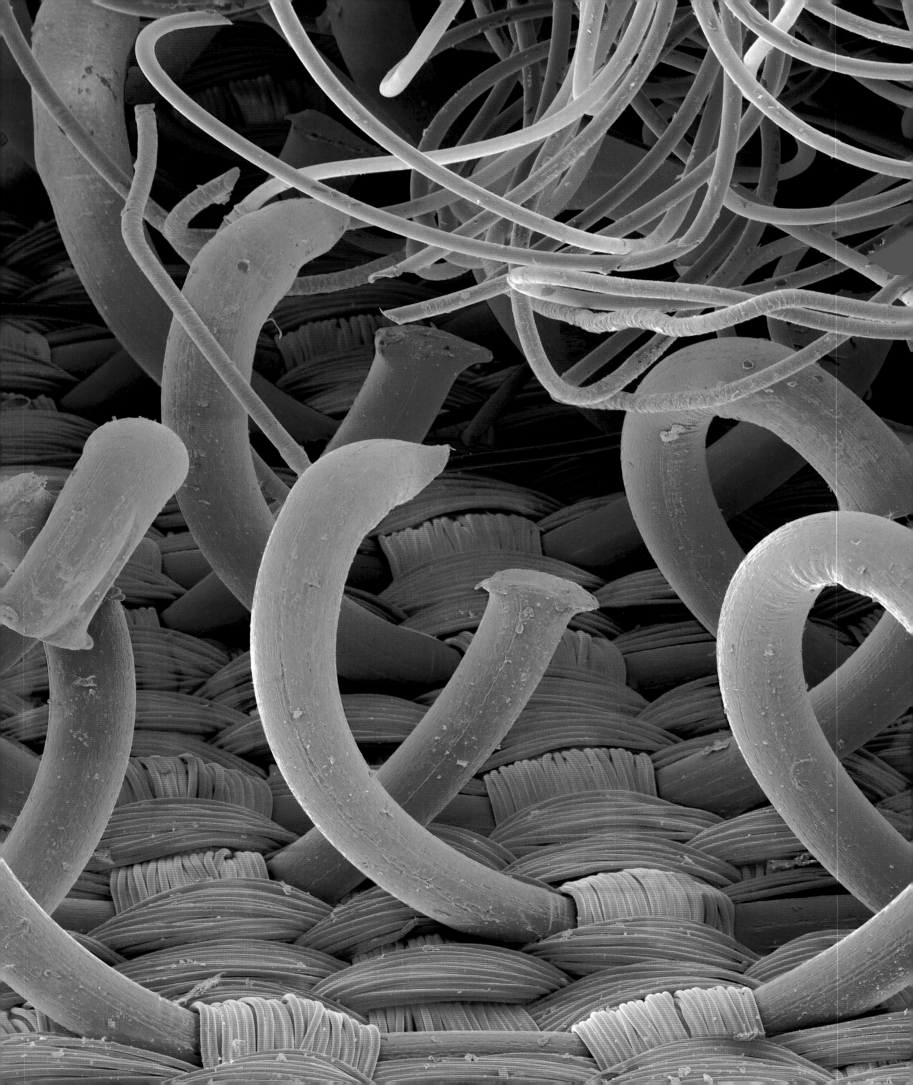

Hook and loop

Most people are familiar with Velcro®, a quick and easy fastener on clothing, shoes, and bags. This is what it looks like close-up.

This false-colored image, captured by an electron microscope, shows the small, soft loops (blue) that catch in the sturdy hooks (green) when the two strips are pressed together. Velcro® is made from nylon or polyester. It was invented by the Swiss engineer George de Mestral in 1941, after he noticed that hooked burdock seeds stuck to his dog's fur and to his own clothing.

Alloys

An alloy is a mixture of at least two different elements, at least one of which is a metal. Alloys are used to make many things, including car and airplane parts, musical instruments, jewelry, and medical implants.

In many alloys, all the elements are metal. However, some alloys contain non-metals, such as carbon. The ingredients of an alloy are carefully chosen for the properties they bring to the alloy, whether to make it stronger, more flexible, or rust-resistant. All alloys have metallic properties, are good electrical conductors, and have advantages over pure metals.

Early alloys

The first man-made alloy was bronze. It was developed around 5,000 years ago by smelting (heating) copper and tin together. This was the start of the Bronze Age, a period in which this new, strong alloy revolutionized the making of tools and weapons. Some thousand years later, people learned to make brass from copper and zinc.

Bronze weapons
Bronze can be hammered thin, stretched, and molded. These objects, made in Mesopotamia around 2000 BCE, were designed to fit on a mace (a clublike weapon).

Atomic arrangements

It is how the atoms are arranged in a material that decides how it behaves in different conditions. Atoms of pure metals are regularly arranged, but in alloys this arrangement is disrupted. The atoms of the main component of an alloy may be of a similar size, or much bigger, than those of the added one. They can be arranged in several ways.

Identical atoms of pure metals

Pure metals
The atoms in a pure metal such as gold (left) are neatly arranged. Under pressure, they will slide over one another, causing cracking.

Zinc atoms replace copper atoms in a brass alloy used for trumpets.

Substitutional alloys
Atoms of the added component take up almost the same space as atoms of the main one. This distorts the structure and makes it stronger.

Tiny carbon atoms sit between large iron atoms, making steel very strong.

Interstitial alloys
These alloys, such as steel used for bridges, are strong: smaller atoms fill the gaps between larger ones, preventing cracking or movement.

Interstitial carbon atoms and substitutional nickel or chromium atoms make stainless steel strong as well as non-rusting.

Combination alloys
Some alloys have a combination of atom arrangements to improve their properties. An example is stainless steel, used in cutlery.

Alloys in coins

Coins used to be made of gold and silver, but these metals are too expensive and not hard-wearing enough for modern use. Several different alloys are used for coins today. They are selected for their cost, hardness, color, density, resistance to corrosion, and for being recyclable.

EU €2-coin
Outer ring: copper (75%), nickel (25%). Center: copper (75%), zinc (20%), nickel (5%).

British £1-coin
Outer ring: copper (76%), zinc (20%), nickel (4%). Inner ring: copper (75%), nickel (25%).

Egyptian £1-coin
Outer ring: steel (94%), copper (2%), nickel plating (4%). Inner ring: steel (94%), nickel (2%), copper plating (4%).

Australian $1-coin
Copper (92%), nickel (2%), aluminum (6%).

Sterling silver, used in most silver **jewelry**, is in fact an **alloy**, containing **7.5 percent copper**.

Mercury makes up about half of **amalgam**, an **alloy** sometimes used as **dental filling**; the rest is **silver, copper, and tin**.

63

Clever alloys

All alloys are developed to be an improvement on the individual metals from which they were made. Some alloys are an extreme improvement. Superalloys, for example, have incredible mechanical strength, resistance to corrosion, and can withstand extreme heat and pressure. These properties makes them very useful in aerospace engineering, as well as in the chemical industries. Memory alloys, or smart alloys, often containing nickel and titanium, "remember" their original shape.

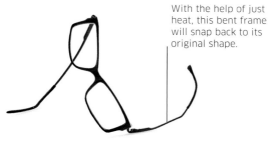

With the help of just heat, this bent frame will snap back to its original shape.

Memory alloys
An object made from a memory alloy can return to its original shape if it has been bent. Simply applying heat restores the alloy to the shape it was in.

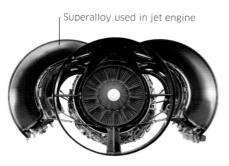

Superalloy used in jet engine

Superalloys
These high-performance alloys hold their shape in temperatures close to their high boiling points of around 1,832°F (1,000°C).

Spanish piece-of-eight
These legendary Spanish coins were made of silver. From the 15th to the 19th centuries, they were used throughout the vast Spanish Empire, and in other countries, too.

Japanese 50-yen coin
Copper (75%) and nickel (25%).

US dime (10-cent) coin
Copper (91.67%) and nickel (8.33%).

Swedish 10-krona coin
An alloy known as "Nordic gold," also used in euro cents: copper (89%), aluminum (5%), zinc (5%), tin (1%).

Aluminum alloys

The metal aluminum is lightweight, resistant to corrosion, and has a high electrical conductivity. It is useful on a small scale (as foil, for example) but, because it is soft, it needs to be alloyed with other elements to be strong enough to build things. Aluminum alloys are often used in car bodies and bicycle frames.

Light, rust-proof frame made of an aluminum alloy

Steel

Iron, a pure metal, has been used since the Iron Age, some 3,000 years ago. But although it is very strong, iron is also brittle. There were some early iron alloys, but the strongest one, steel, came into common use during the Industrial Revolution in the 19th century. There are two ways of making steel: it can be produced from molten "pig iron" (from iron ore) and scrap metal in a process called basic oxygen steelmaking (BOS), or from cold scrap metal in the electric arc furnace (EAF) process. Impurities, such as too much carbon, are removed, and elements such as manganese and nickel are added to produce different grades of steel. The molten steel is then shaped into bars or sheets ready to make into various products.

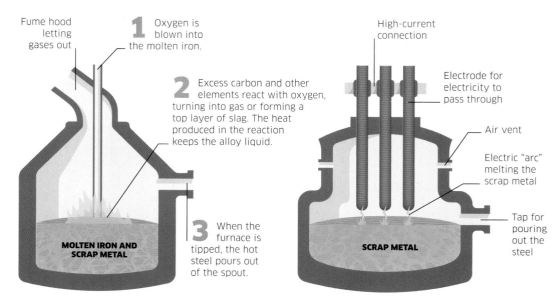

Fume hood letting gases out

1 Oxygen is blown into the molten iron.

2 Excess carbon and other elements react with oxygen, turning into gas or forming a top layer of slag. The heat produced in the reaction keeps the alloy liquid.

3 When the furnace is tipped, the hot steel pours out of the spout.

MOLTEN IRON AND SCRAP METAL

High-current connection

Electrode for electricity to pass through

Air vent

Electric "arc" melting the scrap metal

Tap for pouring out the steel

SCRAP METAL

Basic oxygen steelmaking (BOS)
Oxygen is blown through molten "pig iron" and scrap metal to reduce its carbon content and other impurities. Then alloying elements are added, turning the molten metal into steel.

Electric arc furnace (EAF)
Cold scrap metal is loaded into the furnace. An electric current forms an "arc" (a continuous spark), which melts the metal. The final grade of steel is determined by adding alloying elements.

10 billion tons of **plastics** have been **made** since the 1950s.

Materials technology

Synthetic materials are born in laboratories. Using their knowledge of elements and compounds, chemists can develop new materials with unique properties, created for specific tasks.

Materials created artificially perform different functions depending on their chemistry—the arrangements of their atoms or molecules, and how they react. Research constantly brings new materials to meet new challenges, ranging from synthetic textiles and biodegradeable plastics to the vast range of high-performance materials that make up a racing car.

Fuel tank
Combining bullet-proof Kevlar® and flexible rubber keeps the tank light, strong, and less likely to crack on impact.

Brakes
Adding carbon fiber to brake discs keeps them light and able to resist temperatures of up to 2,192°F (1,200°C).

Exhaust
This is formed from a 0.04 inch (1 mm) thick heat-resistant steel alloy first made for the aerospace industry.

Engine
Precise regulations decide which materials can be used for the many parts of a Formula One engine—no composites are allowed.

Racing car

Formula One cars rely on materials that can withstand extreme heat and pressure. The structure must be rigid in some parts and flexible in others; some parts are heavy while some have to be light. The drivers are also exposed to heat and pressure—and speeds over 200 mph (320 km/h)—and rely on synthetic materials to keep safe. Their clothing is made with layers of Nomex®, a fire-resistant polyamide (a type of plastic) used for fire and space suits. Kevlar®, similar to Nomex® but so strong it is bullet proof, is used to reinforce various car parts as well as the driver's helmet.

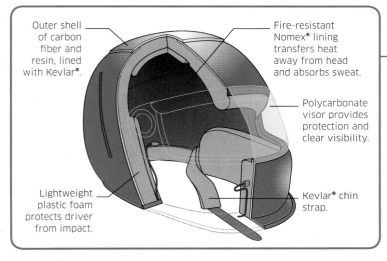

Outer shell of carbon fiber and resin, lined with Kevlar®.

Fire-resistant Nomex® lining transfers heat away from head and absorbs sweat.

Polycarbonate visor provides protection and clear visibility.

Lightweight plastic foam protects driver from impact.

Kevlar® chin strap.

Helmet anatomy

Drivers are subjected to extreme G-forces when braking and cornering. This puts great strain on their necks. To help keep their heads up, their helmets must be as light as possible. Highly specialized materials are used for the helmets, which need to be light and comfortable, yet strong and able to absorb impacts and resist penetration in case of an accident.

The **lightest man-made** solid is **aerogel**, which is both **fireproof** and insulating.

A **waterproof superglue** that could one day be **used to heal wounds** is based on the **sticky slime** that keeps **mussels** stuck to rocks.

65

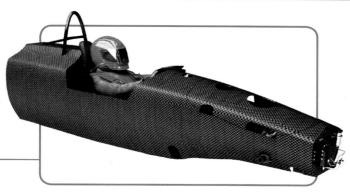

Survival cell

The monocoque, or survival cell, surrounds the cockpit where the driver sits. It is made of a strong, stiff carbon-fiber composite that can absorb the full energy of an impact without being damaged. Carbon fiber is much lighter than steel or aluminium, helping the car go faster and use less fuel.

Mimicking nature

Many synthetic materials were invented to replace natural materials that were too hard, or too expensive, to extract or harvest. For example, nylon was invented to replace silk in fabrics, and polyester fleece can be used instead of wool. Ever advancing technology makes it possible to imitate some amazing materials, such as spider silk, which is tougher than Kevlar®, stronger than steel, yet super flexible.

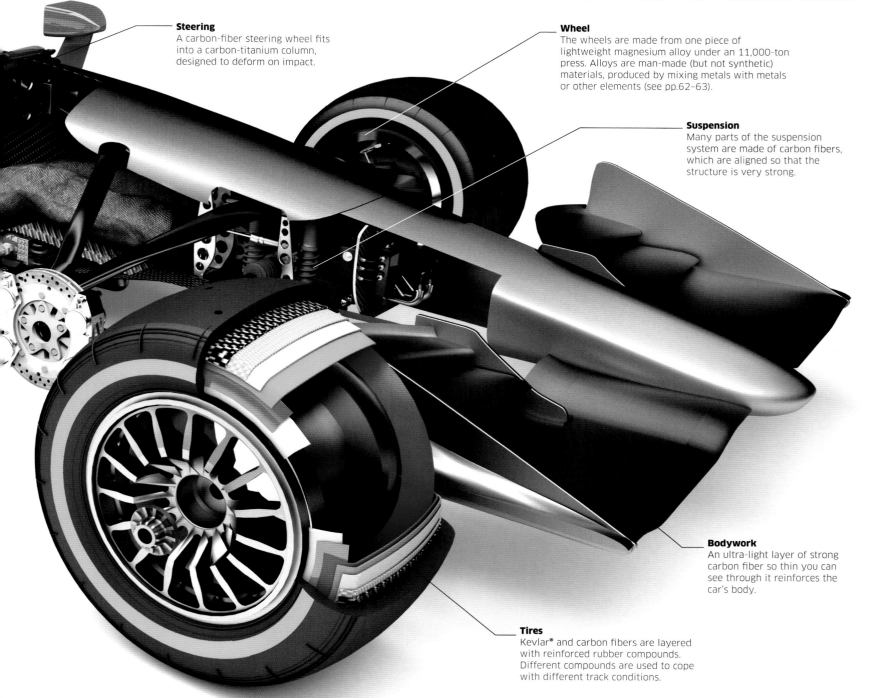

Steering
A carbon-fiber steering wheel fits into a carbon-titanium column, designed to deform on impact.

Wheel
The wheels are made from one piece of lightweight magnesium alloy under an 11,000-ton press. Alloys are man-made (but not synthetic) materials, produced by mixing metals with metals or other elements (see pp.62–63).

Suspension
Many parts of the suspension system are made of carbon fibers, which are aligned so that the structure is very strong.

Bodywork
An ultra-light layer of strong carbon fiber so thin you can see through it reinforces the car's body.

Tires
Kevlar® and carbon fibers are layered with reinforced rubber compounds. Different compounds are used to cope with different track conditions.

ENERGY AND FORCES

Energy and forces are essential concepts in science; nothing can happen without them. Forces change the motion of an object, and energy is behind everything that changes—from a flower opening to an exploding bomb. The amount of energy in the universe is fixed; it cannot be created or destroyed.

The modern age
Scientific discovery and technology go hand in hand as astronomers and physicists use computer science and particle accelerators to expand our knowledge of the universe.

Relativity
Einstein's General Theory of Relativity explains that what we perceive as gravity is an effect of the curvature of space and time.

MODEL OF THE EXPANDING UNIVERSE

Big Bang theory
Belgian priest and physicist Georges Lemaître comes up with the theory of an ever-expanding universe that began with the Big Bang–the source of all energy and forces.

20TH CENTURY

1916

1927

Radio waves
German physicist Heinrich Hertz proves that electromagnetic waves exist.

1876

1848

Combustion engine
German engineer Nikolaus Otto develops the internal combustion engine. It uses understanding gained over two hundred years of how the temperature, volume, and pressure of gases relate.

THERMOMETER

Absolute zero
Scottish scientist Lord Kelvin calculates the lowest possible temperature–at which particles almost cease to vibrate–as –460°F (–273°C), calling it absolute zero.

OTTO'S ENGINE

RADIO MAST

1886

Discovering energy and forces

People have been asking questions about how the world around them works, and using science to find answers for them, for thousands of years.

From the forces that keep a ship afloat and the magnetism that helps sailors to navigate the oceans with a compass, to the atoms and subatomic particles that make up our world and the vast expanses of space, people through history have learned about the universe by observation and experiment. In ancient and medieval times, as the tools available to study the world were limited, so was knowledge of science. The modern scientific method is based on experiments, which are used to test hypotheses (unproven ideas). Observed results modify hypotheses, improving our understanding of science.

Gravity
English scientist Isaac Newton (left) explains how gravity works after an apple falls on his head.

18TH CENT

ISAAC NEWTON

1687

1678

Wave theory of light
Dutch scientist Christiaan Huygens announces his theory that light travels in waves. This is contested by Newton's idea that light is made of particles.

LIGHT AS A WAVE

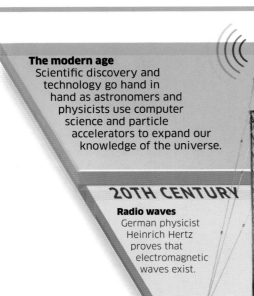

Ancient and medieval ideas
The ancient Greeks and Romans used debate to help them understand the universe, while Arab and Chinese scholars studied mathematics and natural phenomena such as rainbows and eclipses.

Buoyancy
The Greek thinker Archimedes realizes the force pushing upward on an object in water is equal to the weight of water displaced.

Magnetic compass
The Chinese create primitive compasses with lodestone, a naturally occurring magnet.

Light vision
Arab scholar Alhazen suggests that light is emitted from objects into the eye, not the reverse.

BEFORE 1500

240 BCE

200 BCE

1011 CE

Computer science
British code-breaker Alan Turing develops the first programmable computer, laying the foundations of modern computer science.

BOMBE CODE-BREAKING MACHINE

NUCLEAR EXPLOSION

Nuclear energy
Italian–American physicist Enrico Fermi leads a US team that builds the world's first nuclear fission reactor. In 1945, the first atomic bomb is dropped on Hiroshima.

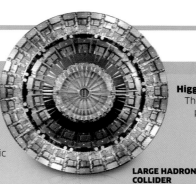

LARGE HADRON COLLIDER

Higgs boson
The Higgs boson particle is identified, confirming the Standard Model of particle physics developed in the 1970s.

1890-PRESENT

1936

1942

2012

1831

1799

Energy conservation
German physicist Hermann von Helmhotz states that energy cannot be created or destroyed, it can only change its form.

PERPETUAL MOTION MACHINE

Electromagnetic induction
After electricity and magnetism are linked, English scientist Michael Faraday uses electromagnetic induction to generate electricity.

FARADAY'S COIL

Current electricity
Italian inventor Alessandro Volta creates an electric current by stacking disks of zinc, copper, and cardboard soaked in salt water in alternate layers—the first battery.

VOLTAIC PILE

Timeline of discoveries
Since ancient times, debate and experiment have led to discoveries that further human understanding of how the world works—but there are still many questions left to answer.

1700-1890

1847

NEWCOMEN ENGINE

The Industrial Revolution
Scientific principles understood by the 18th century were applied to large-scale practical machines during the Industrial Revolution. The power of electricity was unlocked, which led the way for a surge in new technology.

1712

Steam engine
Thomas Newcomen, an English engineer, builds the world's first practical steam engine. It is followed by James Watt's more efficient engine and Richard Trevithick's steam locomotive.

Static electricity
German scientist Ewald Georg von Kleist invents the Leyden jar, a device that can store a static electric charge and release it later.

LEYDEN JAR

1700-1890

1712

1643

1604

1600

Atmospheric pressure
Italian physicist Evangelista Torricelli creates a simple barometer that demonstrates atmospheric pressure.

BAROMETER

Falling bodies
In a letter to theologian Paolo Sarpi, Italian scientist Galileo outlines his theory that all objects fall at the same rate, regardless of mass or shape.

GALILEO'S EXPERIMENT WITH FALLING BODIES

Earth's magnetism
English scientist William Gilbert theorizes that the Earth must have a huge magnet inside.

1500-1700

Bending light
German monk Theodoric of Freiburg uses bottles of water and water droplets in rainbows to understand refraction.

16TH CENTURY

A new age of science
The scientific revolution, from the mid-16th to the late 18th centuries, transformed understanding of astronomy and physics. This period saw the development of the scientific method of experiment and observation.

Solar system
Polish astronomer Nicolaus Copernicus states that the Earth and planets orbit around the sun.

NICOLAUS COPERNICUS

GILBERT'S MAGNET

1300

1543

ENERGY

Energy is all around us—the secret power behind everything in our world, from a bouncing ball to an exploding star. Energy is what makes things happen. It is what gives objects the ability to move, to glow with heat and light, or to make sounds. The ultimate source of all energy on Earth is the sun. Without energy, there would be no life.

TYPES OF ENERGY

Energy exists in many different forms. They are all closely related and each one can change into other types.

Potential energy
This is stored energy. Climb something, and you store potential energy to jump, roll, or dive back down.

Mechanical energy
Also known as elastic energy, this is the potential stored in stretched objects, such as a taut bow.

Nuclear energy
Atoms are bound together by energy, which they release when they split apart in nuclear reactions.

Chemical energy
Food, fuel, and batteries store energy within the chemical compounds they are made of, which is released by reactions.

Sound energy
When objects vibrate, they make particles in the air vibrate, sending energy waves traveling to our ears, which we hear as sounds.

Heat energy
Hot things have more energy than cold ones, because the particles inside them jiggle around more quickly.

Electrical energy
Electricity is energy carried by charged particles called electrons moving through wires.

Light energy
Light travels at high speed and in straight lines. Like radio waves and X-rays, it is a type of electromagnetic energy.

Kinetic energy
Moving things have kinetic energy. The heavier and faster they are, the more kinetic energy they have.

Measuring energy

Scientists measure energy in joules (J). One joule is the energy transferred to an object by a force of 1 newton (N) over a distance of 1 meter (m), also known as 1 newton meter (Nm).

• Energy of the sun
The sun produces four hundred octillion joules of energy each second!

• Energy in candles
A candle emits 80 J—or 80 W—of energy (mainly heat) each second.

• Energy of a light bulb
An LED uses 15 watts (W), or 15 J, of electrical energy each second.

• Energy in water
To raise water temperature 1.8°F (1°C) takes 1 calorie (1/1,000 kilocalories).

• Energy in food
The energy released by food is measured in kilo-calories: 1 kcal = 4,184 J.

• Tiny amounts of energy
Ergs measure tiny units of energy. There are 10 million ergs in 1 J.

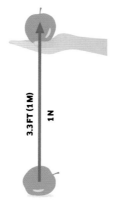

Lifting an apple
One joule is roughly equivalent to lifting an apple 3.3 ft (1 m).

CONSERVATION OF ENERGY

There's a fixed amount of energy in the universe that cannot be created or destroyed, but it can be transferred from one object to another and converted into different forms.

Energy conversion

The total amount of energy at the start of a process is always the same at the end, even though it has been converted into different forms. When you switch on a lamp, for example, most of the electrical energy is converted into light energy—but some will be lost as heat energy. However, the total amount of energy that exists always stays the same.

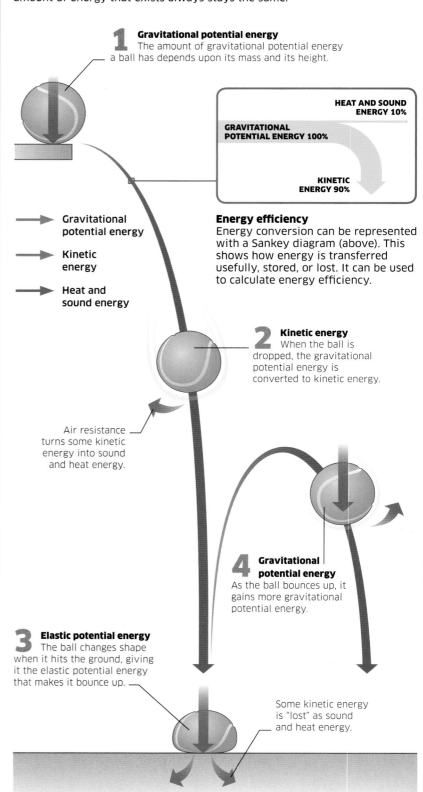

1 **Gravitational potential energy**
The amount of gravitational potential energy a ball has depends upon its mass and its height.

HEAT AND SOUND ENERGY 10%
GRAVITATIONAL POTENTIAL ENERGY 100%
KINETIC ENERGY 90%

→ Gravitational potential energy

→ Kinetic energy

→ Heat and sound energy

Energy efficiency
Energy conversion can be represented with a Sankey diagram (above). This shows how energy is transferred usefully, stored, or lost. It can be used to calculate energy efficiency.

2 **Kinetic energy**
When the ball is dropped, the gravitational potential energy is converted to kinetic energy.

Air resistance turns some kinetic energy into sound and heat energy.

4 **Gravitational potential energy**
As the ball bounces up, it gains more gravitational potential energy.

3 **Elastic potential energy**
The ball changes shape when it hits the ground, giving it the elastic potential energy that makes it bounce up.

Some kinetic energy is "lost" as sound and heat energy.

ENERGY SOURCES

People in the industrialized world use a lot of energy in homes, business, and industry, for travel and transportation. The energy used comes from primary sources such as fossil fuels, nuclear energy, and hydropower. Crude oil, natural gas, and coal are called fossil fuels because they were formed over millions of years by heat from Earth's core and pressure from rock on the remains (fossils) of plants and animals (see p.37).

Energy consumption

Most energy consumed in the US is from nonrenewable sources, with more than 80 percent derived from fossil fuels. Despite advances, just 10 percent comes from renewable sources, of which nearly half is from biomass.

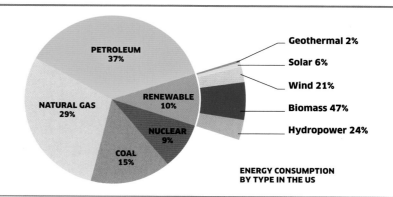

PETROLEUM 37%

NATURAL GAS 29%

RENEWABLE 10%

NUCLEAR 9%

COAL 15%

Geothermal 2%
Solar 6%
Wind 21%
Biomass 47%
Hydropower 24%

ENERGY CONSUMPTION BY TYPE IN THE US

Nonrenewable sources

Fossil fuels are limited resources on our planet, which create greenhouse gases (see pp.128–129) and toxic pollutants. Nuclear energy produces fewer greenhouse gases, but leaves harmful waste.

Crude oil
Liquid hydrocarbons found deep underground.

Natural gas
Hydrocarbon gas formed millions of years ago.

Coal
Solid hydrocarbons made by heat and pressure.

Nuclear energy
Energy released by splitting uranium atoms.

Renewable sources

Energy produced by resources that cannot run out, such as sunlight, wind, and water, is more sustainable. Their use does not produce greenhouse gases and other harmful waste products. Biomass releases carbon dioxide, however, and must be offset by planting new trees.

Biomass
Fuel from wood, plant matter, and waste.

Geothermal energy
Heat deep inside the Earth, in water and rock.

Wind power
Moving air caused by uneven heating of Earth.

Solar energy
The sun's radiation, converted into heat.

Hydropower
The energy of falling or flowing water.

Tidal and wave power
The motion of tides and wind-driven waves.

Energy use

In the developed world, industry and transportation are the most energy-hungry sectors, while efficiency has reduced energy consumption in the home.

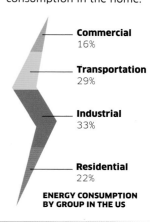

Commercial 16%

Transportation 29%

Industrial 33%

Residential 22%

ENERGY CONSUMPTION BY GROUP IN THE US

ELECTRICAL GRID

Regardless of the primary energy source, most energy is delivered to users as electrical energy. The network of cables used to distribute electricity to homes, offices, and factories is called the electrical grid. Many sources, including wind and solar, feed into the grid, but the majority of electricity is generated in power stations, which use the energy released by burning fossil fuels to power huge electrical generators.

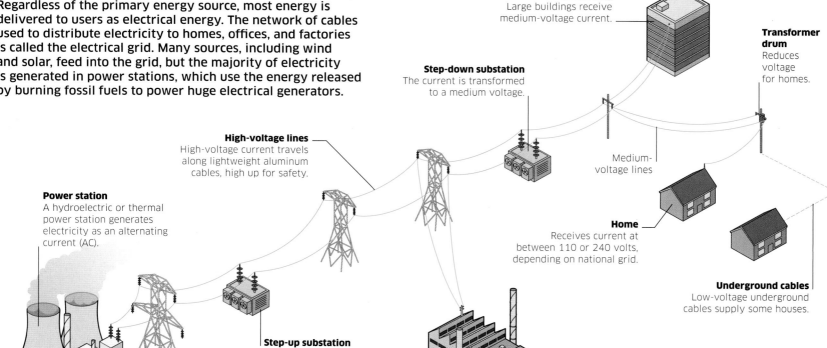

Office building
Large buildings receive medium-voltage current.

Transformer drum
Reduces voltage for homes.

Step-down substation
The current is transformed to a medium voltage.

High-voltage lines
High-voltage current travels along lightweight aluminum cables, high up for safety.

Medium-voltage lines

Power station
A hydroelectric or thermal power station generates electricity as an alternating current (AC).

Home
Receives current at between 110 or 240 volts, depending on national grid.

Underground cables
Low-voltage underground cables supply some houses.

Step-up substation
A transformer boosts the current to a high voltage before it enters the grid.

Factory
Industry receives high-voltage current.

Metals are good heat conductors because their electrons are free to move and pass energy on.

Copper, gold, silver, and aluminum are all good conductors of heat.

Heat transfer

Heat in this pan of boiling water can be seen to move in three ways—radiation, conduction, and convection—between the heat source, the metal pan, and the water.

Heat distribution
A thermogram (infrared image) reveals how heat is distributed from the hottest point, the flame, to the coldest, the wooden spoon and stove.

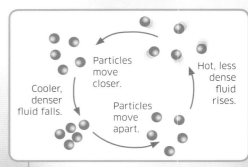

Convection
As a fluid (liquid or gas) heats up, the particles of which it is made move apart, so the fluid becomes less dense and rises. As it moves away from the heat source, the fluid cools down, its density increases, and it falls.

Particles move closer. Cooler, denser fluid falls. Hot, less dense fluid rises. Particles move apart.

Thermal insulation
Materials such as plastic and wood are thermal insulators, which do not conduct heat.

Heat

Heat is energy that increases the temperature of a substance or makes it change state—from a liquid to a gas, for example. Heat can move into or within a substance in three ways: conduction, convection, or radiation.

Atoms and molecules are always moving around. The energy of their movement is called kinetic energy. Some move faster than others, and the temperature of a substance is the average kinetic energy of its atoms and molecules.

Hot particles emit yellow light.

Particles move less away from heat source.

Heat source

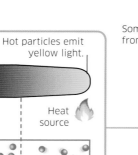

Conduction

When the particles (atoms or molecules) of a solid are heated, they move faster, bumping into other particles and making them move faster, too. The movement of the particles conducts heat away from the heat source. As the temperature increases in a metal, the particles lose heat as thermal radiation, making the metal glow red, yellow, and then white hot.

Radiation from pan
Some radiant heat is lost from the side of the pan.

Radiation from flame
Heat moves as radiant energy waves through a gas or vacuum. This is how the sun heats Earth.

Radiation absorbed by stove
The matte black surface of the stove absorbs some heat radiation.

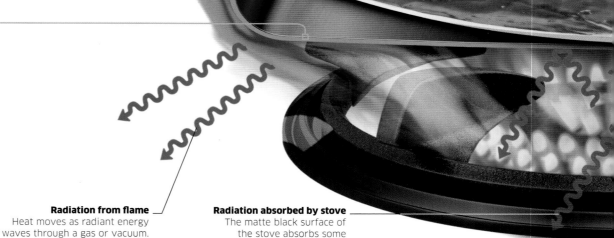

Heat energy always passes from hot objects or materials to cooler ones.

The sun is the main source of heat on Earth.

The temperature range on Earth is less than 250°F (150°C).

73

Convection currents in air

In the daytime, warm air rises from the land and cool air flows in from the sea, creating a sea breeze. At night, warm air rises from the sea and cool air flows out to sea.

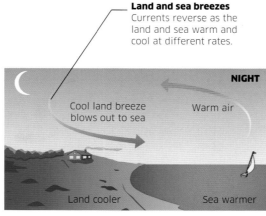

Land and sea breezes
Currents reverse as the land and sea warm and cool at different rates.

DAY

Warm air rises

Cool sea breeze blows in from sea

Land warmer

Sea cooler

NIGHT

Cool land breeze blows out to sea

Warm air

Land cooler

Sea warmer

Steel
The steel lining the pan is a less good heat conductor than copper, but also less reactive, so it is slower to corrode.

Copper
The copper exterior of the pan is a good conductor of heat, but corrodes easily.

Radiation reflected off pan
The shiny metal exterior absorbs heat radiation from the flame, but also reflects some back.

Measuring temperature

Temperature measures how hot or cold an object is by taking the average value of its heat energy. It is measured in degrees Celsius (°C), Fahrenheit (°F), or Kelvin (K). A degree is the same size on the °C scale and K scale. All atoms stop moving at absolute zero (0K).

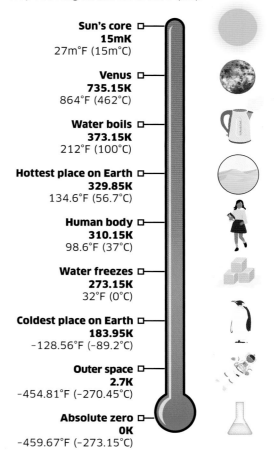

Sun's core
15mK
27m°F (15m°C)

Venus
735.15K
864°F (462°C)

Water boils
373.15K
212°F (100°C)

Hottest place on Earth
329.85K
134.6°F (56.7°C)

Human body
310.15K
98.6°F (37°C)

Water freezes
273.15K
32°F (0°C)

Coldest place on Earth
183.95K
-128.56°F (-89.2°C)

Outer space
2.7K
-454.81°F (-270.45°C)

Absolute zero
0K
-459.67°F (-273.15°C)

Heat loss and insulation

Heat is easily lost from our homes through floors, walls, roofs, windows, and doors. To increase energy efficiency by reducing heat loss, materials that are poor conductors—such as plastics, wood, cork, fiberglass, and air—can be used to provide insulation.

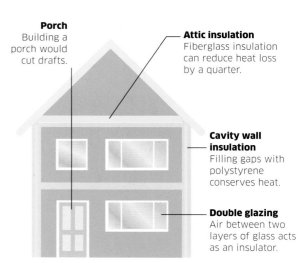

Porch
Building a porch would cut drafts.

Attic insulation
Fiberglass insulation can reduce heat loss by a quarter.

Cavity wall insulation
Filling gaps with polystyrene conserves heat.

Double glazing
Air between two layers of glass acts as an insulator.

74 energy and forces ○ **NUCLEAR ENERGY**

449 The number of **operational nuclear reactors in the world**, with many more being built.

Nuclear energy

Nuclear reactions are a highly efficient way of releasing energy. Smashing atomic particles together sets off a chain reaction—producing enough heat to generate large amounts of electricity.

Most elements have several slightly different forms, called isotopes. Each isotope of an element has a different number of neutrons. Radioactive isotopes have too many or too few neutrons, making them unstable. Isotopes of heavy elements, such as uranium and plutonium, may break apart, or decay, producing radiation. Atomic nuclei can also be broken apart (fission) or joined together (fusion) artificially to release energy, which can be harnessed in nuclear power stations and weapons.

Nuclear reactor

Nuclear fission power stations are found all over the world. They all use the same basic principles to generate electricity. Firstly, atoms are smashed apart in the reactor to release heat energy. This energy passes into a nearby chamber to heat up water and produce large quantities of steam. The steam powers spinning turbines attached to a generator, which converts this kinetic energy into the electricity that is pumped out to the world.

Protective dome
A concrete dome around the reactor absorbs radiation.

Control rods
Control rods lowered into the core slow the reaction by absorbing excess neutrons.

Fuel rods
Rods of nuclear fuel are lowered to start a fission reaction.

Reactor core
Atomic nuclei split inside the reactor, releasing heat energy.

Steam
The water heated in the tank evaporates into steam, which passes along pipes to the turbines.

Turbines
A series of turbines are spun around by the steam.

Heated water
Water inside the reactor is heated as the reaction takes place.

Inner loop
Water from the reactor heats up a tank of water, before flowing back into the reactor.

Outer loop
Water from the turbine unit returns to the steam generator, ready to be heated again.

Cherenkov radiation
The atomic particles in the reactor travel incredibly fast. In doing so, they generate a type of radiation called Cherenkov radiation, which makes the water surrounding the reactor glow an eerie blue color.

Types of radiation

When unstable nuclei break apart, or decay, they may release three types of radiation: alpha, beta, and gamma. Alpha and beta radiation are streams of particles released by atomic nuclei. Gamma rays, released during alpha and beta decay or even by lightning, are a form of electromagnetic radiation—similar to light, but more powerful and dangerous.

British physicists **John Cockcroft and Ernest Walton** carried out the **first artificial nuclear fission** in 1932.

11 percent of the world's electricity is provided by nuclear power plants.

75

Electricity pylons
These carry power lines that transmit electricity from the power station to electricity users.

Generator
The generator converts energy from the turbines into electricity.

Condenser loop
Cooled water is pumped back to the turbine, ready to be heated again.

Cooling towers
Large towers receive the steam and condense it back into water.

Nuclear fission

The nuclei of atoms can split apart or join together, forming new elements and releasing energy. A large atomic nucleus splitting in two is called nuclear fission. A neutron hits the nucleus of a uranium atom, causing it to split, or fission, in two. More neutrons are released as a result, and these hit more nuclei, creating a chain reaction. The extra energy that is released ends up as heat that can be used to generate electricity.

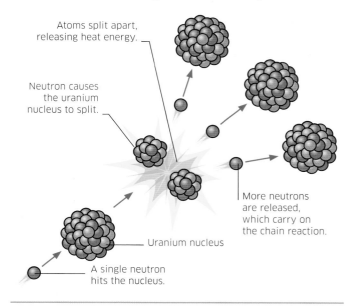

Atoms split apart, releasing heat energy.

Neutron causes the uranium nucleus to split.

More neutrons are released, which carry on the chain reaction.

Uranium nucleus

A single neutron hits the nucleus.

Nuclear fusion

The process in which two smaller atomic nuclei join together is called fusion. Two isotopes of hydrogen are smashed into each other to make helium, releasing heat energy and a spare neutron. Fusion takes place in stars, but has not yet been mastered as a viable form of producing energy on Earth, due to the immense heat and pressure needed to start the process.

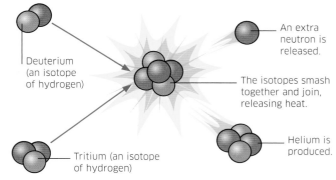

Deuterium (an isotope of hydrogen)

An extra neutron is released.

The isotopes smash together and join, releasing heat.

Tritium (an isotope of hydrogen)

Helium is produced.

Alpha radiation
Some large nuclei release a positively charged particle made of two protons and two neutrons, called an alpha particle.

Beta radiation
In some nuclei, a neutron changes to a proton, creating an electron called a beta particle, which shoots out of the nucleus.

Gamma radiation
Gamma rays are electromagnetic waves released during alpha and beta decay.

Containing radiation

Radiation can be extremely harmful to human health and containing it can be tricky. Alpha, beta, and gamma radiation can pass through different amounts of matter because they have different speeds and energy. Alpha particles can be stopped by just a sheet of paper, or skin. Beta rays can pass through skin but not metal. Gamma rays can only be stopped by a sheet of lead or thick concrete.

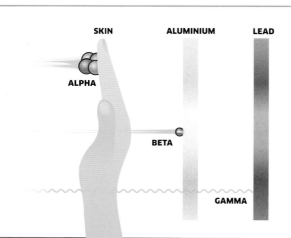

SKIN   ALUMINIUM   LEAD

ALPHA

BETA

GAMMA

76 energy and forces ∘ **SOUND**

Ultrasonic waves have a **frequency higher than audible sound waves**.

The **frequency** of sound **doubles every time the pitch rises an octave**.

Acoustic guitar sounds

When a player plucks the strings of a guitar, each string vibrates at a different frequency to produce a note of a different pitch—higher- or lower-sounding. The pitch of the note produced depends on the length, tension, thickness, and density of the string. The strings' vibration passes into the body of the instrument, which causes air inside and outside it to vibrate, making a much louder sound.

String thickness and density
The thickness of strings affects their frequency and pitch: the thickest string creates the lowest frequency and lowest-pitch notes. Strings made of more dense materials will have a lower pitch.

Sound waves
Vibrating air comes out of the sound hole in waves that spread out evenly in all directions like the ripples in a pool of water.

Sound hole
Air at the sound hole oscillates, adding resonance.

Soundboard
The large surface area of the soundboard (also known as the top plate) vibrates, creating sound energy.

Saddle and bridge
The string vibrations are transmitted to the saddle and bridge of the guitar.

Vibrating soundboard

Vibrating air

Braces
On the inside of the top and back plates, braces add structural support to the guitar. The geometric pattern they are arranged in affects the sound made.

Hollow body
The hollow body amplifies sound energy traveling through the guitar.

Sounds louder than **85 decibels** can **damage human hearing**.

Sound can't travel through a **vacuum**, so **space is silent**.

77

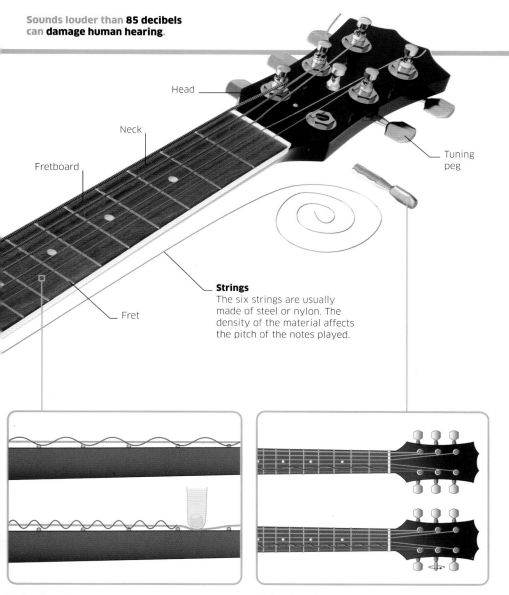

Head

Neck

Fretboard

Fret

Tuning peg

Strings
The six strings are usually made of steel or nylon. The density of the material affects the pitch of the notes played.

String length
Frets (raised bars) are spaced along the fretboard on the front of the neck. The player presses a string down on the fretboard to shorten its length, increasing the frequency and raising the pitch of the sound.

String tension
Turning the tuning pegs enables the player to tighten or loosen the strings, adjusting the pitch so that the guitar is in tune. As the strings are tightened, the frequency increases, raising the pitch.

Sound

Sound carries music, words, and other noises at high speed. It travels in waves, created by the vibration of particles within a solid, liquid, or gas.

If you pluck a guitar string, it vibrates. This disturbs the air around it, creating a wave of high and low pressure that spreads out. When the wave hits our ears, the vibrations are passed on to tiny hairs in the inner ear, which send information to the brain, where it is interpreted. What distinguishes sounds such as human voices from one another is complex wave shapes that create distinctive quality and tone.

20 Hz to 20 kHz—the normal range of human hearing. This range decreases as people get older. Children can usually hear higher frequencies than adults.

How sound travels
Sounds waves squeeze and stretch the air as they travel. They are called longitudinal waves because the particles of the medium they are traveling through vibrate in the direction of the wave.

Vibrating particles
As vibrations travel through air, particles jostle each other to create high-pressure areas of compression and low-pressure areas of rarefaction.

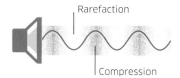

Rarefaction

Compression

Amplitude and loudness
The energy of a sound wave is described by its amplitude (height from center to crest or trough), corresponding to loudness.

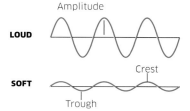

Amplitude

LOUD

SOFT

Crest

Trough

Frequency and pitch
A sound wave's pitch is defined by its frequency—the number of waves that pass a point in a given time. It is measured in hertz (Hz).

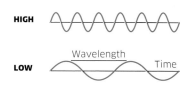

HIGH

LOW

Wavelength

Time

Speed of sound in different materials
Sound moves fastest in solids, because the particles are closer together, and slowest in gases, such as air, because the particles are further apart. The speed of sound is measured in miles per hour.

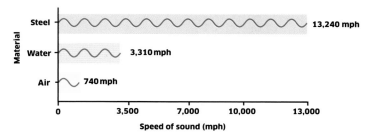

Material	
Steel	13,240 mph
Water	3,310 mph
Air	740 mph

0   3,500   7,000   10,000   13,000

Speed of sound (mph)

The decibel range
Loudness describes the intensity of sound energy, and is measured in decibels (dB) on a logarithmic scale, so 20 dB is 10 times more intense than 10 dB, or twice as loud. Human hearing ranges from 0 to 150 dB.

LEAF FALLING NEARBY (10 dB)
Barely audible

WHISPERING IN EAR (30 dB)
Quiet

SPEAKING NEAR YOU (60 dB)
Moderate

VIOLIN AT ARM'S LENGTH (90 dB)
Loud

FRONT OF ROCK GIG (120 dB)
Very loud

FIREWORK AT CLOSE RANGE (150 dB)
Painfully loud

Artificial light

Sprawling cities across the East Coast at night are clearly visible in this photograph taken by astronauts aboard the International Space Station (ISS).

Long Island and New York can be seen on the right, Philadelphia, Pittsburgh, and other major cities in the center. Streetlights and lights in homes and gardens contribute to the glow. For people on the ground, some of the light is reflected back by a haze of dust and water vapor, creating light pollution that makes it hard to see the stars in the night sky.

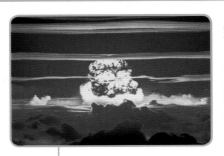

Gamma rays
The highest-energy waves, with wavelengths the size of an atomic nucleus, gamma rays are emitted by nuclear fission in weapons and reactors and by radioactive substances. Gamma radiation is very harmful to human health.

Visible light
This is the range of wavelengths that is visible to the human eye. Each drop in a raindrop is like a tiny prism that splits white light into the colors of the spectrum.

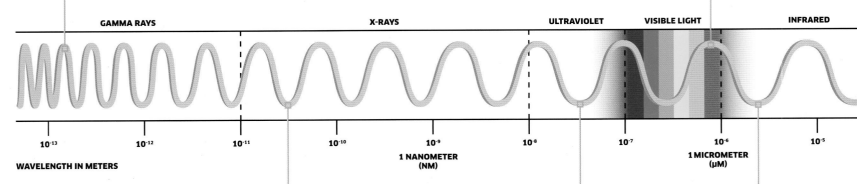

| GAMMA RAYS | X-RAYS | ULTRAVIOLET | VISIBLE LIGHT | INFRARED |

10^{-13} 10^{-12} 10^{-11} 10^{-10} 10^{-9} 10^{-8} 10^{-7} 10^{-6} 10^{-5}

WAVELENGTH IN METERS

1 NANOMETER (NM)

1 MICROMETER (µM)

X-rays
With the ability to travel through soft materials but not hard, dense ones, X-rays are used to look inside the body and for security bag checks.

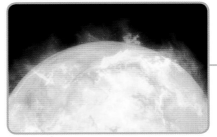

Ultraviolet (UV)
Found in sunlight, UV radiation can cause sunburn and eye damage. The shortest, most harmful wavelengths are blocked by the ozone layer.

Infrared
Known as heat radiation, infrared is invisible, but special cameras are able to detect it and "see" the temperature of objects such as these penguins.

Electromagnetic radiation

Light is one of several types of wave energy called electromagnetic radiation, which also includes radio waves, X-rays, and gamma radiation.

Electromagnetic radiation reaches us from the sun, stars, and distant galaxies. The Earth's atmosphere blocks most types of radiation, but allows radio waves and light, which includes some wavelengths of infrared and ultraviolet, to pass through.

The electromagnetic spectrum beyond visible light was discovered between 1800, when British astronomer William Herschel first observed infrared, and 1900, when French physicist Paul Villard discovered gamma radiation.

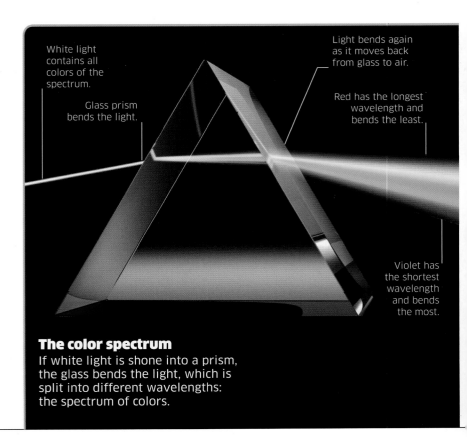

White light contains all colors of the spectrum.

Glass prism bends the light.

Light bends again as it moves back from glass to air.

Red has the longest wavelength and bends the least.

Violet has the shortest wavelength and bends the most.

The color spectrum
If white light is shone into a prism, the glass bends the light, which is split into different wavelengths: the spectrum of colors.

All electromagnetic waves travel through space at the **speed of light**, which is **299,792,458 m/s** (commonly rounded to 300,000 km/s).

Extremely low frequency (ELF) radio waves are used to **communicate with submarines.**

81

Microwaves
On Earth, microwaves are used for radar, cell phone, and satellite communications. Scientists have captured images (left) of microwaves left over from the Big Bang at the birth of the universe.

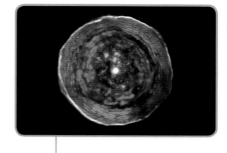

Radio waves
The longest waves on the spectrum, radio waves carry TV as well as radio signals. Radio telescopes are able to capture radio waves emitted by sources in space and convert them into images, such as this star (left).

Waves at this end of the spectrum have the least energy and lowest frequencies.

MICROWAVE

RADIO WAVES

| 10⁻³ | 10⁻² | 10⁻¹ | 1 | 10¹ | 10² | 10³ | 10⁴ | 10⁵ |

10^{-3} 10^{-2} 10^{-1} 1 10^{1} 10^{2} 10^{3} 10^{4} 10^{5}

1 MILLIMETER (MM)   1 METER (M)   1 KILOMETER (KM)

The electromagnetic spectrum
There are electromagnetic waves over a wide range of wavelengths, from gamma waves, which have the shortest wavelength and highest energy, to radio waves, which have the longest wavelength and lowest energy. All electromagnetic waves are invisible, except for those that make up light. As you move along the spectrum, different wavelengths are used for a variety of tasks, from sterilizing food and medical equipment to communications.

The dividing line between some types of electromagnetic radiation is distinct, whereas other types overlap. Microwaves, for example, are the shortest wavelength radio waves, ranging from 1 mm to 1 m.

Electromagnetic waves
All types of electromagnetic radiation are transverse waves that transfer energy from place to place and can be emitted and absorbed by matter. Electromagnetic radiation travels as waves of electric and magnetic fields that oscillate (vibrate) at right angles to each other and to the direction of travel.

Direction of travel

Electric field

Magnetic field

Seeing color
We see color based on information sent to the brain from light-sensitive cells in the eye called cones. There are three types of cone, which respond to red, green, or blue light. We see all colors as a mix of these three colors. Objects reflect or absorb the different colors in white light. We see the reflected colors.

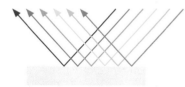

White object
White objects reflect all the colors that make up the visible light spectrum, which is why they appear white.

Light scattering
When sunlight hits Earth's atmosphere, air molecules, water droplets, and dust particles scatter the light, but they don't scatter the colors equally. This is why the sky is blue, clouds are white, and sunsets red.

Blue sky
The blue of the sky is caused by air molecules in the atmosphere, which scatter short-wavelength light at the blue end of the spectrum. Larger water and dust particles scatter the full spectrum as white light. The bluer the sky, the purer the air.

Black object
Black objects absorb all the colors of the visible light spectrum and reflect none. They also absorb more heat.

Green object
We see green objects because they reflect only the green wavelengths of visible light.

Red sunset
When the sun is low in the sky, light takes a longer path through the atmosphere, more light is scattered, and shorter wavelengths are absorbed. At sunrise and sunset, clouds may appear red, reflecting the color of light shining on them.

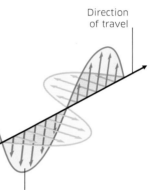

1 million threads of **fiber-optic cable** can fit in a ½ in- (12.7 mm-) diameter tube.

Telephone network

Cell phones connect to base stations, each providing coverage of a hexagonal area called a cell. Each cell has a number of frequencies or channels available to callers. As cell phones each connect to a particular base station, the same frequencies can be used for callers using base stations elsewhere. Landline calls go through local and main exchanges.

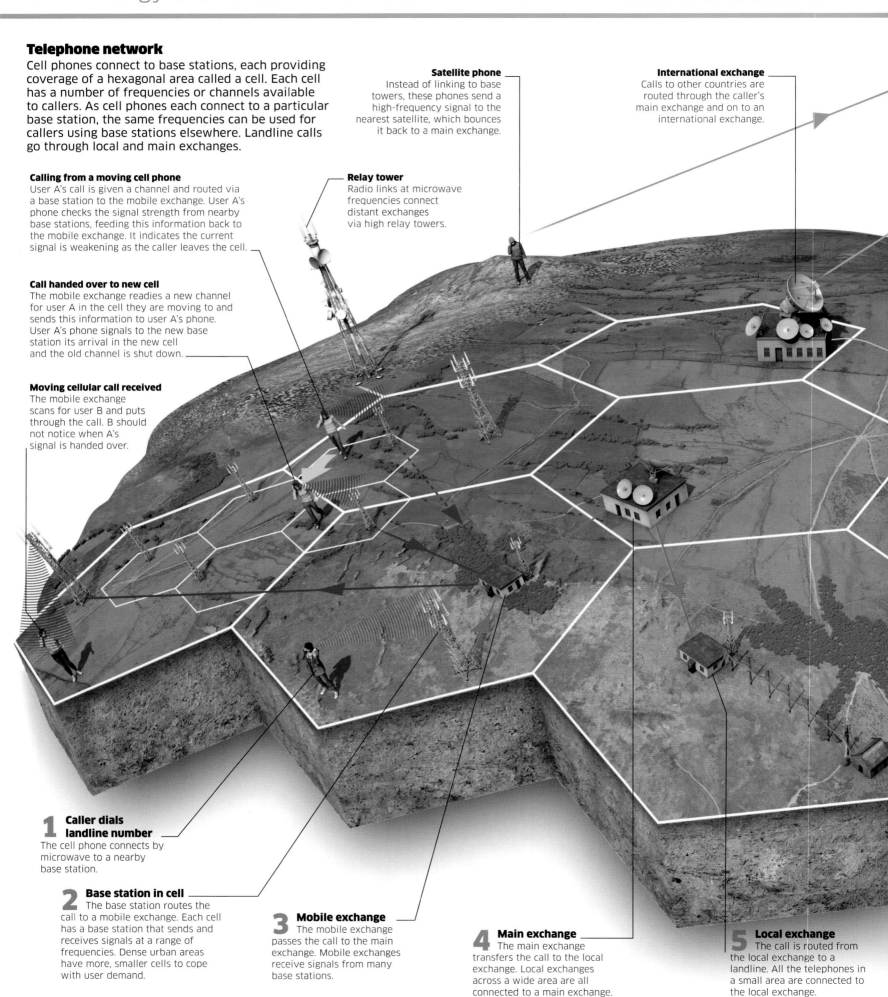

Satellite phone
Instead of linking to base towers, these phones send a high-frequency signal to the nearest satellite, which bounces it back to a main exchange.

International exchange
Calls to other countries are routed through the caller's main exchange and on to an international exchange.

Calling from a moving cell phone
User A's call is given a channel and routed via a base station to the mobile exchange. User A's phone checks the signal strength from nearby base stations, feeding this information back to the mobile exchange. It indicates the current signal is weakening as the caller leaves the cell.

Relay tower
Radio links at microwave frequencies connect distant exchanges via high relay towers.

Call handed over to new cell
The mobile exchange readies a new channel for user A in the cell they are moving to and sends this information to user A's phone. User A's phone signals to the new base station its arrival in the new cell and the old channel is shut down.

Moving cellular call received
The mobile exchange scans for user B and puts through the call. B should not notice when A's signal is handed over.

1 Caller dials landline number
The cell phone connects by microwave to a nearby base station.

2 Base station in cell
The base station routes the call to a mobile exchange. Each cell has a base station that sends and receives signals at a range of frequencies. Dense urban areas have more, smaller cells to cope with user demand.

3 Mobile exchange
The mobile exchange passes the call to the main exchange. Mobile exchanges receive signals from many base stations.

4 Main exchange
The main exchange transfers the call to the local exchange. Local exchanges across a wide area are all connected to a main exchange.

5 Local exchange
The call is routed from the local exchange to a landline. All the telephones in a small area are connected to the local exchange.

24,000 miles (39,000 km) is the length of the **world's longest fiber-optic submarine telecommunications cable**.

60 The approximate **percentage** of the **world's population** that **owns a cell phone**.

83

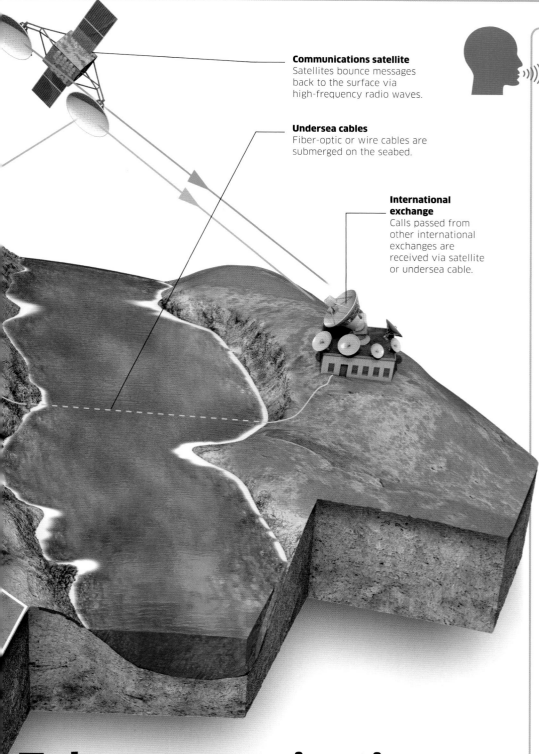

Communications satellite
Satellites bounce messages back to the surface via high-frequency radio waves.

Undersea cables
Fiber-optic or wire cables are submerged on the seabed.

International exchange
Calls passed from other international exchanges are received via satellite or undersea cable.

Telecommunications

Modern telecommunications use electricity, light, and radio as signal carriers. The global telephone network enables us to communicate worldwide, using radio links, fiber-optic cables, and metal cables.

Signals representing sounds, images, and other data are sent as either analog signals, which are unbroken waves, or as digital signals that send binary code as abrupt changes in the waves. Radio waves transmit radio and TV signals through the air around Earth, while microwave wavelengths are used in cell phones, Wi-Fi, and Bluetooth. Cables carry signals both above and below ground—as electric currents along metal wires, or as pulses of light that reflect off the glass interiors of fiber-optic cables.

Speech conversion
Our voices are converted from analog signals to digital ones to make calls.

1 A cell phone captures sound as a continuously varying or analog signal. The signal is measured at various points and each point is given a value. Here a point on the signal is measured as 3, which is shown as its binary equivalent of 0011. The phone's analog to digital converter produces strings of these binary numbers (see p.95).

2 The 1s and 0s of the binary number 0011 become off/off/on/on. The phone transmits the on/off values, encoding them as sudden changes to the signal's waves. The signal passes from base station to mobile exchange to base station.

3 The phone receives the digital signal and interprets the on/off transmission as strings of binary numbers. The phone's digital to analog converter turns the binary numbers back into analog information.

4 The phone's speaker sends an analog signal we hear as a sound wave.

The ionosphere and radio waves
The ionosphere is a region of the atmosphere that contains ions and free electrons. This causes it to reflect some lower-frequency, longer-wavelength radio waves over large distances.

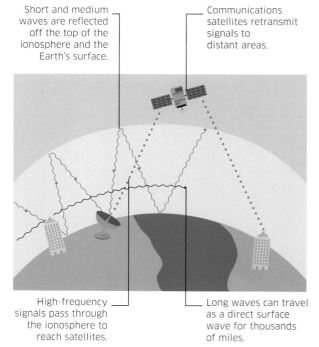

Short and medium waves are reflected off the top of the ionosphere and the Earth's surface.

Communications satellites retransmit signals to distant areas.

High-frequency signals pass through the ionosphere to reach satellites.

Long waves can travel as a direct surface wave for thousands of miles.

84 energy and forces ○ **LIGHT**

The **sun's surface**, at 10,000°F (5,500°C), **glows white hot** with a continuous spectrum of wavelengths.

Light

Light is a type of electromagnetic radiation. It is carried by a stream of particles, called photons, that can also behave like a wave.

The most important source of light on Earth is the sun. Sunlight is produced by energy generated in the sun's core. Like the sun, some objects such as candles emit (send out) light—they are luminous. In contrast, most objects reflect and/or absorb light. Light travels as transverse waves, like ripples in water; the direction of wave vibration is at right angles to the direction that the light travels.

Light and matter

A material appears shiny, dull, or clear depending on whether it transmits, reflects, or absorbs light rays. Most materials absorb some light.

Transparent
Light passes through transparent (clear) materials. The light is transmitted, bending as it changes speed.

Opaque (matte)
Dull, opaque materials have a rough surface that absorbs some light, and reflects and scatters the rest.

Translucent
Materials that are translucent (milky) let light through, but scatter it in different directions.

Opaque (shiny)
Shiny, opaque materials have a smooth surface that reflects light in a single beam.

Sources of light

Light is a form of energy. It is produced by two distinct processes: incandescence and luminescence. Incandescence is the emission of light by hot objects. Luminescence is the emission of light without heat.

Photons

If an atom gains energy, electrons orbiting the nucleus jump to higher orbits, or "energy levels." When the electrons return to their original orbits, they release photons of light, or other electromagnetic radiation.

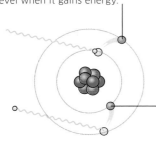

Excited atom
Electron jumps to higher level when it gains energy.

Atom calms down
Electron gives out photon as it returns to its original orbit.

Incandescence

Incandescent light sources produce light because they are hot. The hotter an object, the more of the visible color spectrum it produces. Incandescent light produces all the colors in its range in a continuous spectrum.

Color spectrum
A spectroscope image shows the spectrum of colors a light source emits.

Toaster grill
A grill or the element of a toaster, at about 1,110°F (600°C), will glow with only red light. It also emits light in the infrared range.

Candle flame
A candle flame, at about 1,550°F (850°C), produces some green and yellow light, as well as red, so it glows with a bright yellow light.

Incandescent light bulb
The filament of an old-style light bulb, at about 4,500°F (2,500°C), produces nearly all the spectrum. Missing some blue light, it has a yellow tinge.

Luminescence

A luminescent light source produces light by electrons losing energy in atoms. Energy is lost in exact amounts, which determine the color of the light produced, depending on the chemistry of the luminescent material.

Bioluminescence
Bioluminescent animals such as fireflies produce a single wavelength of yellowish-green light by oxidizing a molecule called luciferin.

Light-emitting diode (LED)
An LED may produce two or more colors. Energy-saving LEDs produce red, green, and blue light, chosen to give an impression of white light.

Compact fluorescent lamp
Luminescent paints on the inside of glass produce red, green, and blue light, giving an impression of white light (not a continuous spectrum).

Lasers

A laser produces an intense beam of light of a single wavelength. The light is concentrated in a "lasing medium" such as crystal. In a crystal laser, light from a coiled tube "excites" atoms in a tube made of crystals, such as ruby. The photons of light that these excited atoms produce reflect between the tube's mirrored ends and escape as a powerful beam. We say the light is coherent, because the waves are in step.

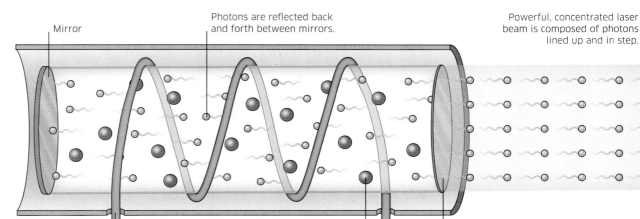

Mirror

Photons are reflected back and forth between mirrors.

Powerful, concentrated laser beam is composed of photons lined up and in step.

A flash tube is a powerful lamp whose light excites electrons in the crystal.

Excited atoms give off photons, which excite other atoms, too.

Light emerges from partial (semi-silvered) mirror.

Laser is an acronym for **light amplification by stimulated emission of radiation**.

Today, the **double-slit experiment** is used to demonstrate wave-particle duality—that **light behaves as both waves and particles**.

85

Diffraction and interference

Light waves spread out when they pass through tiny gaps or holes. The smaller the gap, the more spreading (diffraction) that occurs. When two or more waves meet, they add together or cancel each other out, forming bigger or smaller waves. This is known as interference.

Double-slit experiment

To prove that light behaves as a wave, not a particle, in 1801 English scientist Thomas Young shone light through slits to demonstrate that light waves diffract and interfere like waves in water.

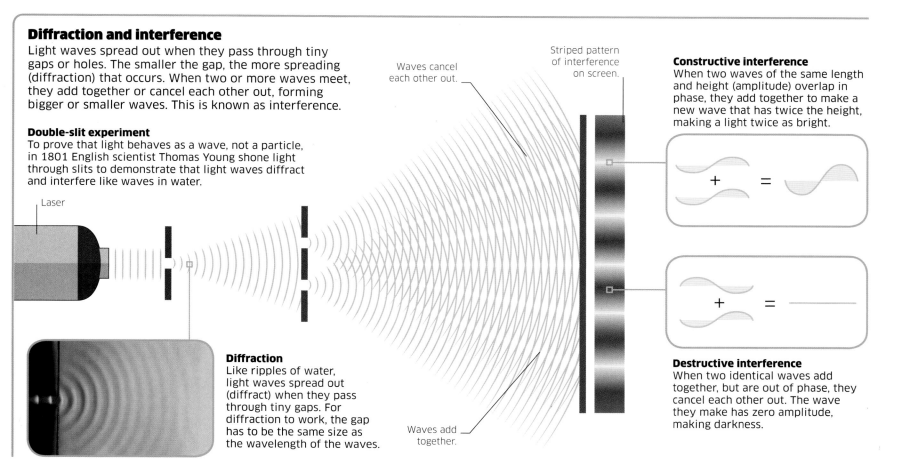

Laser

Waves cancel each other out.

Striped pattern of interference on screen.

Waves add together.

Diffraction

Like ripples of water, light waves spread out (diffract) when they pass through tiny gaps. For diffraction to work, the gap has to be the same size as the wavelength of the waves.

Constructive interference

When two waves of the same length and height (amplitude) overlap in phase, they add together to make a new wave that has twice the height, making a light twice as bright.

+ =

Destructive interference

When two identical waves add together, but are out of phase, they cancel each other out. The wave they make has zero amplitude, making darkness.

+ =

Reflection

Light rays bounce off a smooth surface, such as a mirror, in a single beam. This is called specular reflection. If the surface is rough, the rays bounce off randomly in different directions. This is called diffuse reflection.

The law of reflection

A light ray beamed at a mirror bounces off again at exactly the same angle, or, in more scientific terms, the angle of incidence is equal to the angle of reflection.

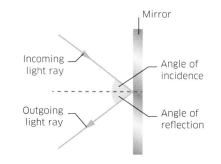

Mirror

Incoming light ray

Angle of incidence

Outgoing light ray

Angle of reflection

Reverse images

Mirrors don't reverse things left to right—writing looks reversed because you've turned it around. What mirrors do is to reverse things back to front along an axis at right angles to the mirror.

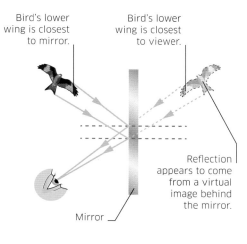

Bird's lower wing is closest to mirror.

Bird's lower wing is closest to viewer.

Reflection appears to come from a virtual image behind the mirror.

Mirror

Refraction

Light rays travel more slowly in more dense substances such as water and glass than in air. The change in speed causes light to bend (refract) as it passes from air to glass or water and back. How much a material refracts light is known as its refractive index.

Bending light

Light rays slow down and bend as they pass from air to glass, and speed up and bend outward as they pass from glass to air. The refractive index of air is 1. For glass, it is around 1.60, depending on the quality of the glass, whereas for diamond—which is harder and denser—it is 2.40.

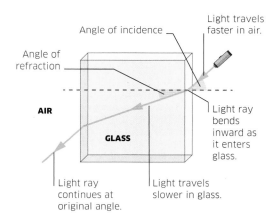

Light travels faster in air.

Angle of incidence

Angle of refraction

AIR

GLASS

Light ray bends inward as it enters glass.

Light ray continues at original angle.

Light travels slower in glass.

Real and apparent depth

Refraction makes an object in water appear nearer the surface. Because our brains assume that light rays travel in a straight line, rather than bending, we see the object in the water higher up than it really is. For a person under water, the reverse applies: an object on land appears higher up than it is.

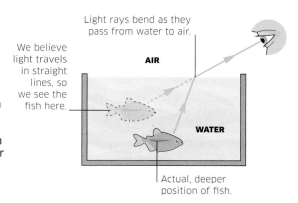

Light rays bend as they pass from water to air.

We believe light travels in straight lines, so we see the fish here.

AIR

WATER

Actual, deeper position of fish.

Types of telescope

Refracting telescopes use lenses to gather and focus light. Reflecting telescopes do the same with mirrors—huge space telescopes use very large mirrors. Compound telescopes combine the best of lenses and mirrors.

Refracting telescope

A large convex lens focuses light rays to a mirror that reflects the light into the eyepiece, where a lens magnifies the image. Lenses refract the light, causing color distortion.

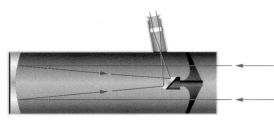

Reflecting telescope

A concave mirror reflects and focuses light to a secondary mirror, which reflects it into an eyepiece, where a lens magnifies the image. There is no color distortion.

Compound telescope

The most common type of telescope, this combines lenses and mirrors to maximize magnification and eliminate distortion.

Telescopes

Powerful telescopes make faint objects, such as distant stars and galaxies, easier to see. They work by first gathering as much light as they can, using either a lens or a mirror, and then focusing that light into a clear image.

There are two main types of telescope: refracting, which focus light using lenses, and reflecting, which focus light using mirrors. Optical telescopes see visible light, but telescopes can also look for different kinds of electromagnetic radiation: radio telescopes receive radio waves and X-ray telescopes image X-ray sources. Telescopes use large lenses compared to microscopes, which are used to look at things incredibly close up, while binoculars work like two mini telescopes side by side.

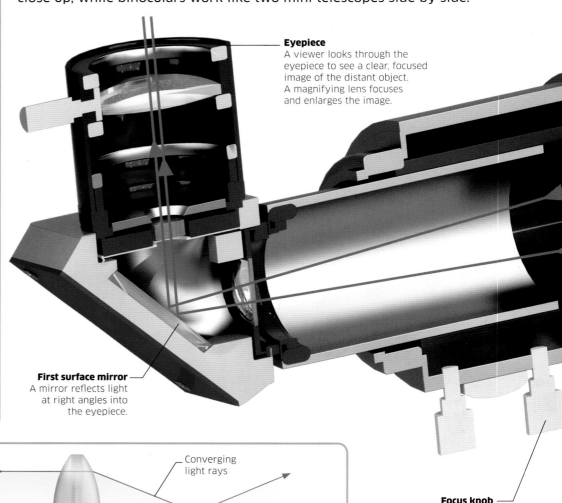

Eyepiece
A viewer looks through the eyepiece to see a clear, focused image of the distant object. A magnifying lens focuses and enlarges the image.

First surface mirror
A mirror reflects light at right angles into the eyepiece.

Focus knob
Twisting the knob adjusts the focal length to focus the image.

Convex and concave lenses

Convex, or converging, lenses take light and focus it into a point behind the lens, called the principal focus. This is the type of lens used in the glasses of a short-sighted person. By contrast, concave, or diverging, lenses spread light out. When parallel rays pass through a concave lens, they diverge as if they came from a focal point—the principal focus— in front of the lens.

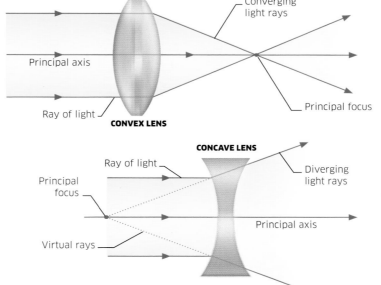

Converging light rays

Principal axis

Ray of light

Principal focus

CONVEX LENS

CONCAVE LENS

Ray of light

Diverging light rays

Principal focus

Principal axis

Virtual rays

A GERMAN-DUTCH LENS MAKER **CALLED HANS LIPPERSHEY DEVELOPED THE EARLIEST** REFRACTING TELESCOPE **IN THE YEAR 1608.** GALILEO IMPROVED THE DESIGN.

Isaac Newton created the first reflecting telescopes to get around the problem of color distortion.

The **Hubble Space Telescope** can see as far as **13 billion light-years away**, to a distant galaxy called **MACS0647-JD**.

When you look at a star **5,000 light-years away**, you are looking back in time; the light you are seeing left the star **5,000 years ago**.

87

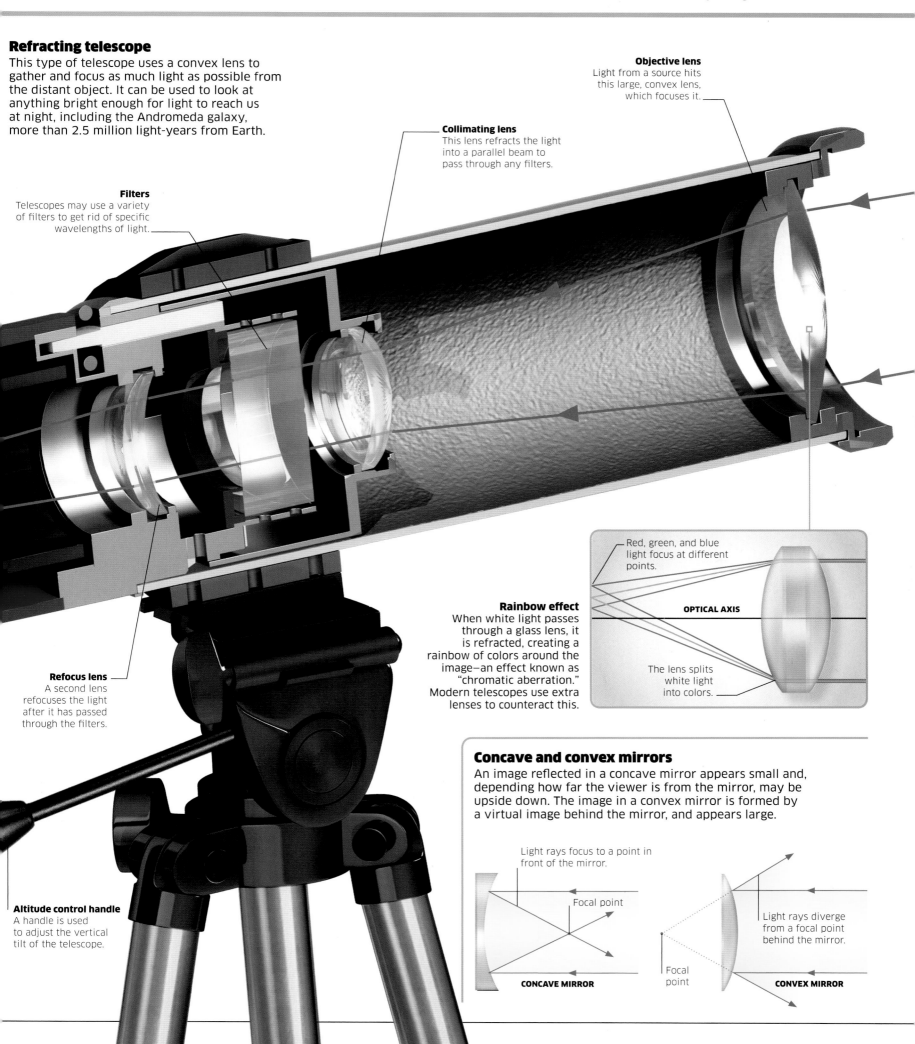

Refracting telescope

This type of telescope uses a convex lens to gather and focus as much light as possible from the distant object. It can be used to look at anything bright enough for light to reach us at night, including the Andromeda galaxy, more than 2.5 million light-years from Earth.

Objective lens
Light from a source hits this large, convex lens, which focuses it.

Collimating lens
This lens refracts the light into a parallel beam to pass through any filters.

Filters
Telescopes may use a variety of filters to get rid of specific wavelengths of light.

Red, green, and blue light focus at different points.

OPTICAL AXIS

The lens splits white light into colors.

Rainbow effect
When white light passes through a glass lens, it is refracted, creating a rainbow of colors around the image—an effect known as "chromatic aberration." Modern telescopes use extra lenses to counteract this.

Refocus lens
A second lens refocuses the light after it has passed through the filters.

Altitude control handle
A handle is used to adjust the vertical tilt of the telescope.

Concave and convex mirrors

An image reflected in a concave mirror appears small and, depending how far the viewer is from the mirror, may be upside down. The image in a convex mirror is formed by a virtual image behind the mirror, and appears large.

Light rays focus to a point in front of the mirror.

Focal point

CONCAVE MIRROR

Focal point

Light rays diverge from a focal point behind the mirror.

CONVEX MIRROR

Magnetism

Magnetism is an invisible force exerted by magnets and electric currents. Magnets attract iron and a few other metals, and attract or repel other magnets. Every magnet has two ends, called its north and south poles, where the forces it exerts are strongest.

A magnetic material can be magnetized or will be attracted to a magnet. Iron, cobalt, nickel—and their alloys—and rare earth metals are all magnetic, which means they can be magnetized by stroking with another magnet or by an electric current. Once magnetized, these materials stay magnetic unless demagnetized by a shock, heat, or an electromagnetic field (see p.93). Most other materials, including aluminum, copper, and plastic, are not magnetic.

Unlike poles attract, like poles repel

The invisible field of force around a magnet is called a magnetic field. Iron filings show how the magnetic field loops around the magnet from pole to pole.

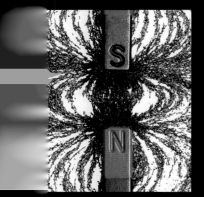

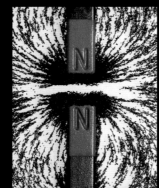

Attraction
Unlike or opposite poles (a north pole and a south pole) attract each other. Iron filings reveal the lines of force running between unlike poles.

Repulsion
Like poles (two north or two south poles) repel each other. Iron filings show the lines of force being repelled between like poles.

Magnetic induction

An object made of a magnetic material, such as a steel paper clip, is made of regions called domains, each with its own magnetic field. A nearby magnet will align the domain's fields, turning the object into a magnet. The two magnets now attract each other—that is why paper clips stick to magnets. Stroking a paper clip with a magnet can align the domains permanently.

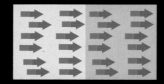

Domains scattered
In an unmagnetized object, the domains point in all directions.

Domains aligned
When a magnet is nearby, the domain's fields align in the object.

Magnetic compass

Made of magnetized metal and mounted so that it can spin freely, the needle of a magnetic compass lines up in a north-south direction in Earth's magnetic field. Because the Earth's magnetic North Pole attracts the north, or north-seeking, pole of other magnets, it is in reality the south pole of our planet's magnetic field.

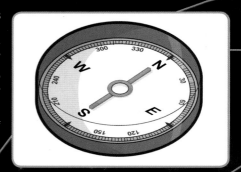

A teardrop-shaped magnetic field

Earth's magnetic field protects us from the harmful effects of solar radiation. In turn, a stream of electrically charged particles from the sun, known as the solar wind, distorts the magnetic field into a teardrop shape and causes the auroras—displays of light around the poles (see pp.90-91).

Distortion of the magnetosphere
The stream of charged particles from the sun compresses Earth's magnetic field on the side nearest the sun and draws the field away from Earth into a long "magnetotail" on the far side.

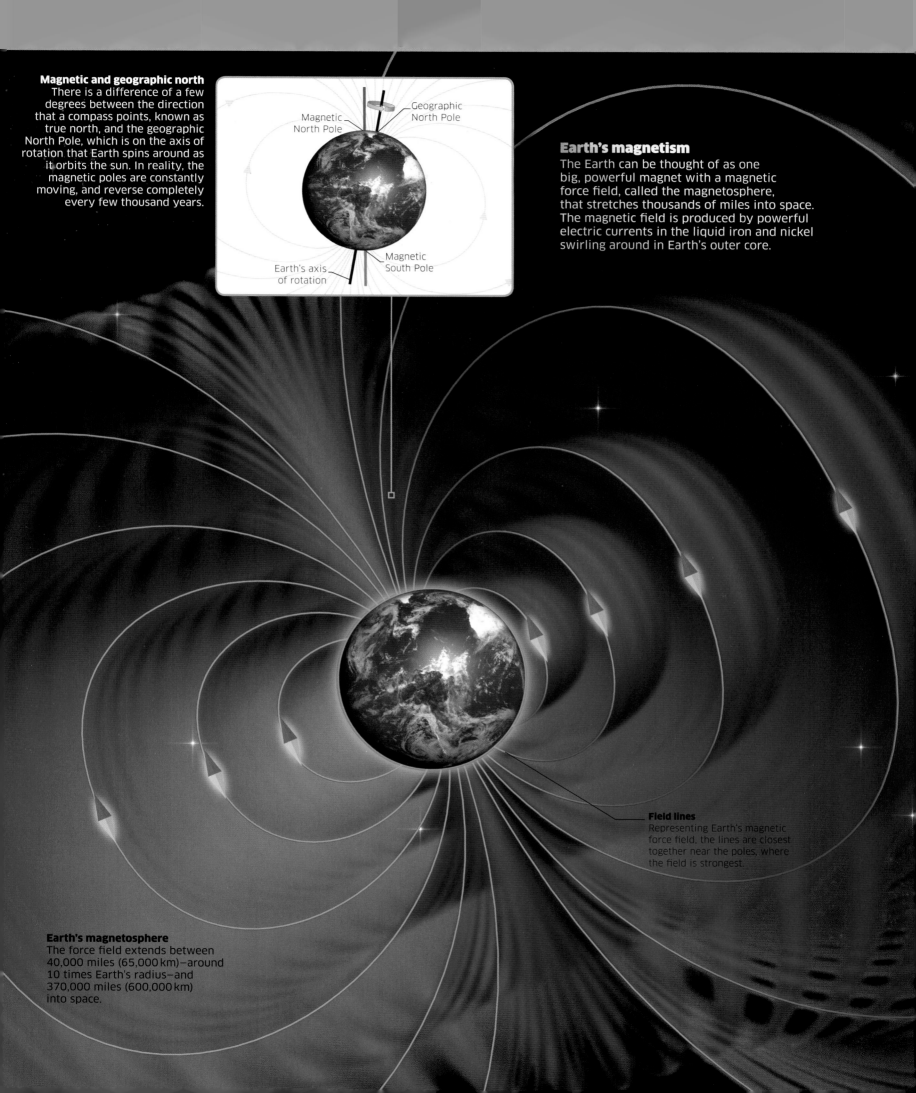

Magnetic and geographic north
There is a difference of a few degrees between the direction that a compass points, known as true north, and the geographic North Pole, which is on the axis of rotation that Earth spins around as it orbits the sun. In reality, the magnetic poles are constantly moving, and reverse completely every few thousand years.

Magnetic North Pole

Geographic North Pole

Earth's axis of rotation

Magnetic South Pole

Earth's magnetism
The Earth can be thought of as one big, powerful magnet with a magnetic force field, called the magnetosphere, that stretches thousands of miles into space. The magnetic field is produced by powerful electric currents in the liquid iron and nickel swirling around in Earth's outer core.

Field lines
Representing Earth's magnetic force field, the lines are closest together near the poles, where the field is strongest.

Earth's magnetosphere
The force field extends between 40,000 miles (65,000 km)–around 10 times Earth's radius–and 370,000 miles (600,000 km) into space.

Aurora borealis

The spectacular natural light show known as the aurora borealis, or northern lights, is a dazzling spectacle of ribbons and sheets of green, yellow, and pink light.

The cause of the aurora is a stream of charged particles ejected from the surface of the sun, known as the solar wind. These particles are guided toward the poles by Earth's magnetic field. When they hit oxygen and nitrogen molecules in the atmosphere, electrons in the molecules emit colored light. The northern lights—and aurora australis, or southern lights, around the South Pole—occur whenever the solar wind blows, typically about two hundred nights a year.

Electricity

A useful form of energy that can be converted to heat, light, and sound, electricity powers the modern world.

Atoms contain tiny particles called electrons that carry negative electrical charge. These orbit the positively charged atomic nucleus, but can become detached. Static electricity is the build-up of charge in an object. Current electricity is when charge flows.

Current electricity

When an electric charge flows through a metal, it is called an electric current. The current is caused by the drift of negatively charged electrons through a conductor in an electrical circuit. Individual electrons actually travel very slowly, but pass electrical energy along a wire very fast.

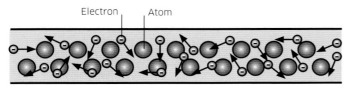

Electron   Atom

No current
If a conductor wire is not connected to a power supply, the free electrons within it move randomly in all directions.

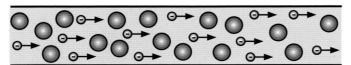

Direct current (DC)
If the wire is given energy by a battery, electrons drift toward the positive pole of the power supply. If the charge flows in one direction, it is known as direct current (DC).

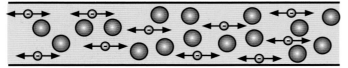

Alternating current (AC)
Electrical grid electricity runs on an alternating current (AC) supply. The charge changes direction periodically, sending the electrons first one way and then the other.

Copper wire is a good conductor.

Plastic is an insulator.

Conductors and insulators

Charged particles can flow through some substances but not others. In metals, electrons move between atoms. In solutions of salts, ions (positively charged atoms) can also flow. These substances are known as conductors. Current cannot pass through insulators, such as plastic, which have no free electrons. Semi-conductors such as silicon have atomic structures that can be altered to control the flow of electricity. They are widely used in electronics.

Static electricity

Electricity that does not flow is called static electricity. A static charge can be produced by rubbing two materials together, transferring electrons from one to the other. Objects that gain electrons become negatively charged, while objects that lose electrons become positively charged.

Attraction and repulsion
Rubbing balloons against your hair will charge the balloons with electrons, leaving your hair positively charged. The negative charge of the balloons will attract the positive charge of your hair.

Static discharge
When ice particles within a cloud collide, they gain positive and negative charge. Lightning is an electrical discharge between positive and negative parts of a thunderstorm cloud and the ground.

Making electricity

In order to make electrons move, a source of energy is needed. This energy can be in the form of light, heat, or pressure, or it can be the energy produced by a chemical reaction. Chemical energy is the source of power in a battery-powered circuit.

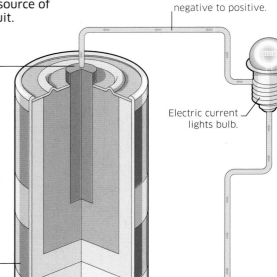

Current flows from negative to positive.

Carbon anode (+)

Electric current lights bulb.

Zinc casing is cathode (–).

Battery
A standard battery produces an electric current using carbon and zinc conductors and a chemical paste called an electrolyte (see pp.52–53). In a circuit, the current flows from the negative electrode (cathode) to the positive electrode (anode). Lithium batteries, which have manganese cathodes and lithium anodes, produce a stronger voltage (flow of electrons).

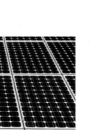

Solar cell
Light falling onto a "photovoltaic" cell, such as a solar cell, can produce an electric current. Light knocks electrons out of their orbits around atoms. The electrons move through the cell as an electric current.

In 1600, English scientist William Gilbert observed
a link between "the amber effect" and magnetism.

In 1752, American statesman and scientist Benjamin Franklin **flew a kite
with a key on its string into a thunderstorm** to prove lightning is electrical.

93

Electric circuits

An electric circuit is the path around which a current of electricity flows. A simple circuit includes a source of electrical energy (such as a battery) and conducting wires linking components (such as switches, bulbs, and resistors) that control the flow of the current. Resistance is the degree to which materials resist the flow of current.

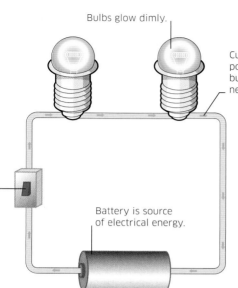

Bulbs glow dimly.

Current flows from positive to negative, but electrons flow from negative to positive.

Switch makes or breaks circuit.

Battery is source of electrical energy.

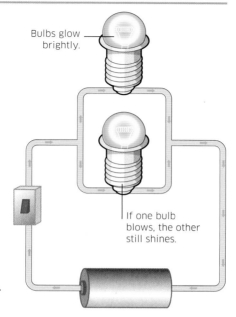

Bulbs glow brightly.

Parallel circuit
A parallel circuit has two or more branches, so that each branch gets the full voltage from the source. If the circuit is broken on one of the branches, it continues to flow through the others.

If one bulb blows, the other still shines.

Series circuit

In a series circuit, all the components are connected one after another, so that they share the voltage of the source. If the circuit is broken, electricity ceases to flow.

Electromagnetism

Moving a wire in a magnetic field causes a current to flow through the wire, while an electric current flowing through a wire generates a magnetic field around the wire. This creates an electromagnet—a useful device because its magnetism can be switched on and off.

Electromagnetic field

When an electric current flows through a wire, it generates rings of magnetic field lines all around it. You can see this by placing a compass near a wire carrying a current. The stronger the current, the stronger the magnetism.

Magnetic field

Direction of current

Electric motors

In an electric motor, a current flows through a coil of wire between the poles of a magnet. The magnetic field that the coil produces interacts with the field of the magnet, forcing the coil to turn. The rotating coil can be attached to a drive shaft to power a machine.

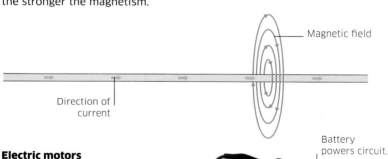

Battery powers circuit.

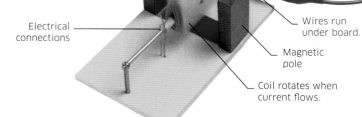

Electrical connections

Wires run under board.

Magnetic pole

Coil rotates when current flows.

Solenoid

A coil of wire carrying a current produces a stronger magnetic field than a straight wire. This coil creates a common type of electromagnet called a solenoid. Winding a solenoid around an iron core creates an even more powerful magnetic field.

North pole

Loops make rings of magnetic field.

Direction of current

Electric generators

In a generator, a current is produced by rotating a wire coil between a magnet's poles, or by rotating a magnet while the coil is static. Generators can be big enough to power a city, or small, portable devices for supplying electricity to individuals.

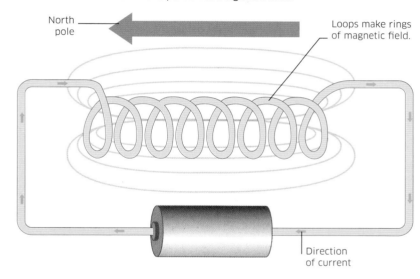

Galvanometer registers voltage.

Coil spins between magnets.

Wires run under board.

Electronics

Electric current is caused by a drift of electrons through a circuit. An electronic device uses electricity in a more precise way than simple electric appliances, to capture digital photos or play your favorite songs.

While it takes a large electric current to boil water, electronics use carefully controlled electric currents thousands or millions of times smaller, and sometimes just single electrons, to operate a range of complex devices. Computers, smartphones, amplifiers, and TV remote controls all use electronics to process information, communicate, boost sound, or switch things on and off.

Printed circuit board (PCB)
The "brain" of a smartphone is on its printed circuit board—a premanufactured electronic circuit unique to a particular device. The PCB is made from interconnected microchips, each of which is constructed from a tiny wafer of silicon and has an integrated circuit inside it containing millions of microscopic components.

Motherboard
The main printed circuit board, which is the phone's main processor, is also referred to as a mainboard or logic board.

Digital camera

Front-facing camera

Battery

The metal casing acts as an antenna.

Fingerprint sensor components

Lightning USB connector port

Micro SIM card

Micro SIM card tray

Wi-Fi antenna

Electronic components
Electronic circuits are made of building blocks called components. A transistor radio may have a few dozen, while a processor and memory chip in a computer could have billions. Four components are particularly important and appear in nearly every circuit.

Diode
Diodes make electric current flow in just one direction, often converting alternating to direct current.

Resistor
Resistors reduce electric current so it is less powerful. Some are fixed and others are variable.

Transistor
Transistors switch current on and off or convert small currents into bigger ones.

Capacitor
Capacitors store electricity. They are used to detect key presses on touch screens.

Smartphone
Cell phones are now so advanced that they are really hand-sized computers. As well as linking to other digital devices, they contain powerful processor chips and plenty of memory to store applications.

Smartphones today are more powerful than the NASA computers that sent Apollo 11 to the moon.

95

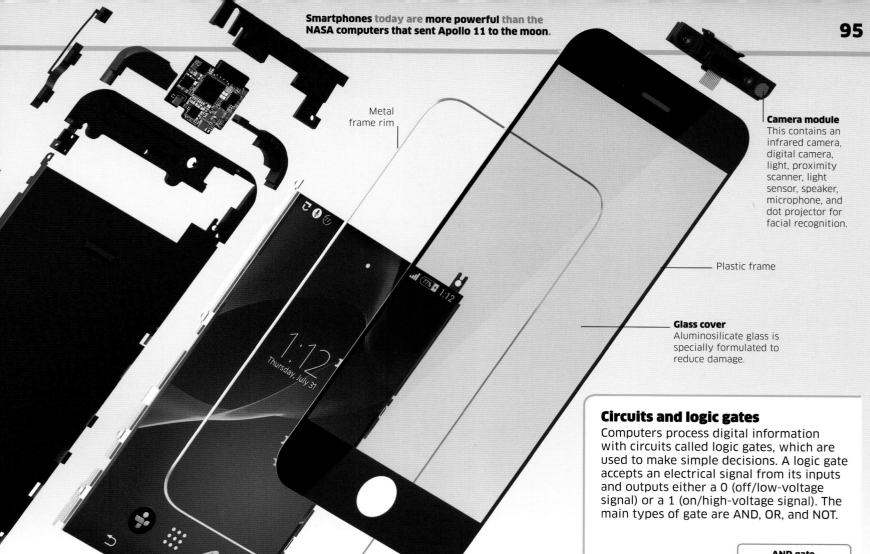

Metal frame rim

Camera module
This contains an infrared camera, digital camera, light, proximity scanner, light sensor, speaker, microphone, and dot projector for facial recognition.

Plastic frame

Glass cover
Aluminosilicate glass is specially formulated to reduce damage.

Touch screen
A grid of sensors registers touch as electrical signals, which are sent to the processor. This interprets the gesture and relates it to the app being run.

Circuits and logic gates

Computers process digital information with circuits called logic gates, which are used to make simple decisions. A logic gate accepts an electrical signal from its inputs and outputs either a 0 (off/low-voltage signal) or a 1 (on/high-voltage signal). The main types of gate are AND, OR, and NOT.

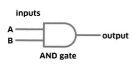

inputs

A
B

output

AND gate

AND gate		
Input A	Input B	Output
1	0	0
0	1	0
0	0	0
1	1	1

AND gate
This compares the two numbers and switches on only if both the numbers are 1. There will only be an output if both inputs are on.

Digital electronics

Most technology we use today is digital. Our devices convert information into numbers or digits and process these numbers in place of the original information. Digital cameras turn images into patterns of numbers, while cell phones send and receive calls with signals representing strings of numbers. These are sent in a code called binary, using only the numerals 1 and 0 (rather than decimal, 0–9).

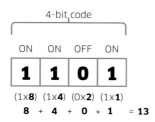

4-bit code

ON	ON	OFF	ON
1	**1**	**0**	**1**

(1x**8**) (1x**4**) (0x**2**) (1x**1**)

8 + 4 + 0 + 1 = 13

Binary numbers
In binary, the position of 1s and 0s corresponds to a decimal value. Each binary position doubles in decimal value from right to left (1, 2, 4, 8) and these values are either turned on (x1) or off (x0). In the 4-bit code shown, the values of 8, 4, and 1 are all "on," and when added together equal 13.

Analog to digital

A sound wave made by a musical instrument is known as analog information. The wave rises and falls as the sound rises and falls. A wave can be measured at different points to produce a digital version with a pattern more like a series of steps than a wave form.

Sampling
The size of a wave is "sampled" or measured at different times and its value recorded as a string of numbers.

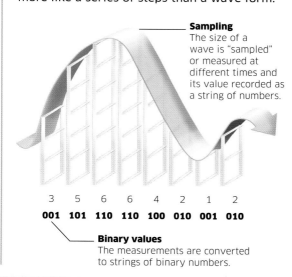

3	5	6	6	4	2	1	2
001	**101**	**110**	**110**	**100**	**010**	**001**	**010**

Binary values
The measurements are converted to strings of binary numbers.

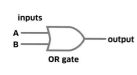

inputs

A
B

output

OR gate

OR gate		
Input A	Input B	Output
0	0	0
0	1	1
1	0	1
1	1	1

OR gate
This switches on if either of the two numbers is 1. If both numbers are 0, it switches off. There will be an output if one or both inputs are on.

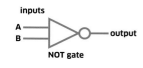

inputs

A
B

output

NOT gate

NOT gate	
Input	Output
0	1
1	0

NOT gate
This reverses (inverts) whatever goes into it. A 0 becomes a 1, and vice versa. The output is only on if the input is off. If the input is on, the output is off.

FORCES

Invisible forces are constantly at play in our day-to-day life, from the wind rustling the leaves of trees to the tension in the cables of a suspension bridge. A force is any push or pull. Forces can change an object's speed or direction of motion, or can change its shape. English scientist Isaac Newton figured out how forces affect motion over three hundred years ago (see pp.98–99). His principles are still applied in many fields of science, engineering, and in daily life today.

WHAT IS A FORCE?

A force can be a push or a pull. Although you can't see a force, you can often see what it does. A force can change the speed, direction, or shape of an object. Motion is caused by forces, but forces don't always make things move—balanced forces are essential for building stability.

Contact forces

When one object comes into contact with another and exerts a force, this is called a contact force. Either a push or a pull, this force changes the direction, speed, or shape of the object.

Changing direction
If a player bounces a ball against a wall during practice, the wall exerts a force on the ball that changes its direction.

Changing speed
When a player kicks, back-heels, or volleys a soccer ball, the force that is applied changes the ball's speed.

Changing shape
Kicking or stepping on the soccer ball applies a force that momentarily squashes it, changing the ball's shape.

Non-contact forces

All forces are invisible, but some are exerted without physical contact between objects. The closer two objects are to each other, the stronger is the force.

Gravity
Gravity is a force of attraction between objects with mass. Every object in the universe pulls on every other object.

Magnetism
A magnet creates a magnetic field around it. If a magnetic material is brought into the field, a force is exerted on it.

Static electricity
A charged object creates an electric field. If another charged object is moved into the field, a force acts on it.

Weight, gravity, and mass

Weight is not the same as mass, which is a measure of how much matter is in an object. Weight is the force acting on that matter and is the result of gravity. The mass of an object is the same everywhere, but its weight can change.

Measuring forces
Forces can be measured using a force meter, which contains a spring connected to a metal hook. The spring stretches when a force is applied to the hook. The bigger the force, the longer the spring stretches and the bigger the reading. The unit of force is the newton (N).

Calculating weight
Mass is measured in kilograms (kg). Weight can be calculated as mass x gravity (N/kg). The pull of gravity at Earth's surface is roughly 10 N/kg, so an object with a mass of 1 kg weighs 10 N.

BALANCED AND UNBALANCED FORCES

Not all forces acting on an object make it move faster or in a different direction: forces on a bridge must be balanced for the structure to remain stable. In a tug of war, there's no winner while the forces are balanced; it takes a greater force from one team to win.

Balanced forces
If two forces acting on an object are equal in size but opposite in direction, they are balanced. An object that is not moving will stay still, and an object in motion will keep moving at the same speed in the same direction.

The tension in the rope is 500 N.

250 N   250 N

Unbalanced forces
If two forces acting on an object are not equal, they are unbalanced. An object that is not moving will start moving, and an object in motion will change speed or direction.

150 N   350 N

DEFORMING FORCES

When a force acts on an object that cannot move, or when a number of different forces act in different directions, the whole object changes shape. The type of distortion an object undergoes depends on the number, directions, and strengths of the forces acting upon it, and on its structure and composition—if it is elastic (returns to its original shape) or plastic (deforms easily but does not return to its original shape). Brittle materials fracture, creep, or show fatigue if forces are applied to them.

Compression
When two or more forces act in opposite directions and meet in an object, it compresses and bulges.

Tension
When two or more forces act in opposite directions and pull away from an elastic object, it stretches.

Torsion
Turning forces, or torques, that act in opposite directions twist the object.

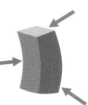

Bending
When several forces act on an object in different places, the object bends (if malleable) or snaps.

Resultant forces

A force is balanced when another force of the same strength is acting in the opposite direction. Overall, this has the same effect as no force at all.

RESULTANT FORCE: 0 N

When opposing teams pull with equal force, the resultant force is 0 N.

RESULTANT FORCE: 200 N

One team pulls with more force than the other. The resultant force is 200 N.

TURNING FORCES

Instead of just moving or accelerating an object in a line, or sending an object off in a straight line in a different direction, forces can also be used to turn an object around a point known as an axis or a pivot. This kind of force works on wheels, seesaws, and fairground rides such as carousels. The principles behind these turning forces are also used in simple machines (see pp.106–107).

Moment

When a force acts to turn an object around a pivot, the effect of the force is called its moment. The turning effect of a force depends on the size of the force and how far away from the pivot the force is acting. Calculated as force (N) x distance (m), moment is measured in newton meters (Nm).

Sitting closer to the pivot of a seesaw increases the moment.

A greater weight increases the moment.

The center of a seesaw is its pivot.

Centripetal forces

A constant force has to be applied to keep an object turning in a circle, obeying Newton's first law of motion (see pp.98–99). Known as centripetal force, it pulls the turning object toward the center of rotation—imagine a yo-yo revolving in a circle on its string—continually changing its direction, while the motion changes its speed. Without this force, the object would move in a straight line away from the center.

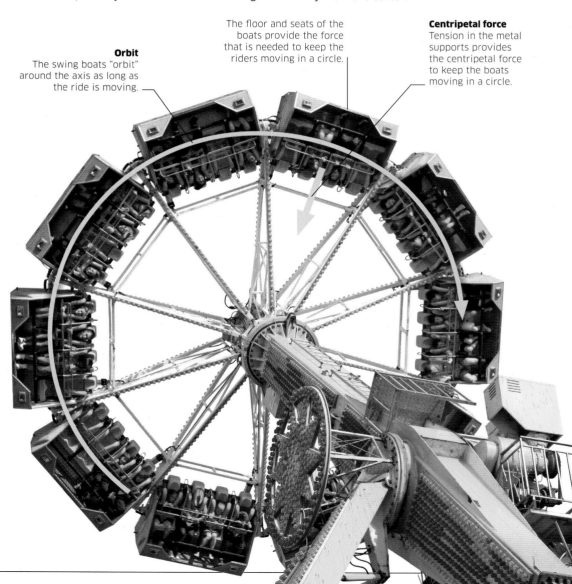

The floor and seats of the boats provide the force that is needed to keep the riders moving in a circle.

Orbit
The swing boats "orbit" around the axis as long as the ride is moving.

Centripetal force
Tension in the metal supports provides the centripetal force to keep the boats moving in a circle.

In frictionless space, **spacecraft travel at a constant velocity**—obeying Newton's first law of motion.

Laws of motion

When a force acts on an object that is free to move, the object will move in accordance with Newton's three laws of motion.

English physicist and mathematician Isaac Newton published his laws of motion in 1687. They explain how objects move—or don't move—and how they react with other objects and forces. These three scientific laws form the basis of what is known as classical mechanics. Modern physics shows that Newton's laws are not perfectly accurate, but they are still useful in everyday situations.

First law of motion

Any object will remain at rest, or move in a straight line at a steady speed, unless an external force acts upon it. So, a soccer ball is stationary until it is kicked and then moves until other forces stop it. This is known as inertia. If all external forces are balanced, the object will maintain a constant velocity. For an object that is not moving, this is zero.

At rest
Gravity acts on the ball, but the ground stops it from moving so it remains at rest.

Force causes motion
The impact of a cleat kicking the ball applies a force that accelerates the ball.

Force stops motion
The ball slows down due to friction and stops when it meets a cleat.

Second law of motion

When a force acts on an object, the object will generally move in the direction of the force. This causes a change in velocity, known as acceleration. The larger the force, the greater an object's acceleration will be. The more massive an object is, the greater the force needed to accelerate it. This is written as force = mass x acceleration.

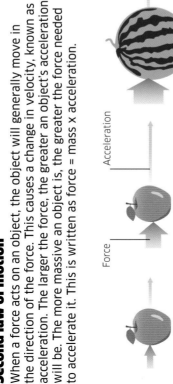

Force

Acceleration

Small mass, small force
A force causes an object to accelerate, changing its velocity per second, at a certain rate.

Small mass, double force
If the mass stays the same but the force doubles, the object will accelerate at twice the rate.

Double mass, double force
If the mass doubles and the force doubles again, the rate of acceleration stays the same.

Ariane 5

The Ariane 5 rocket is a launch vehicle used to deliver massive payloads, such as communication satellites, into orbit. Causing a rocket to accelerate upward requires enormous forces to overcome the gravity pulling it downward. Hot gases expand, exerting forces on the walls of the combustion chamber to lift the rocket. The walls of the chamber produce a reaction force that pushes back on the gases, which escape at high speed through the nozzles at the bottom of the engine. These forces create acceleration.

A global navigation system is carried into orbit.

A communication satellite is mounted in the upper stage.

Vehicle equipment bay
The rocket's "brain," this contains equipment that guides and tracks the rocket.

Upper cryogenic stage
The upper stage is powered by a separate engine to position satellites in orbit.

Liquid oxygen tank contains 165 tons of oxidizer.

Main cryogenic stage
The main stage holds liquid hydrogen that mixes with liquid oxygen in the combustion chamber to combust.

Liquid hydrogen tank contains 28 tons of fuel.

Fairing protects satellites during lift-off.

THRUST

NET FORCE

852 tons—the weight of Ariane 5 at liftoff. Its **liftoff thrust is 1,477 tons**.

To reach a low Earth orbit, **a rocket must generate enough thrust to reach a speed of 18,000 mph (29,000 km/h)**. **99**

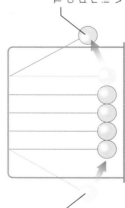

Solid rocket booster
Two solid-propellant boosters deliver more than 90 percent of thrust in a short blast at liftoff.

Vulcain 2 engine
The main engine burns for 10 minutes to provide thrust.

Fuel combusts in the combustion chamber, generating hot gases at high pressure.

Rocket nozzle expels hot exhaust gases, which push backward.

WEIGHT

Newton's three laws at work

A rocket taking off shows Newton's laws in action. Before liftoff, the rocket's enormous weight—the result of gravity pulling it down toward Earth—is balanced by the upward force of the launch pad so it remains stationary (first law). Fuel combustion in the engines creates thrust, propelling the rocket forward (second law). The thrust that pushes the rocket forward is a reaction to the hot exhaust gases pushing backward (third law).

Velocity, speed, and acceleration

Speed is a measure of the rate at which a distance is covered. Velocity is not the same as speed; it measures direction as well as speed of movement. Acceleration measures the rate of change of velocity. Speeding up, turning, and slowing down are all acceleration.

Increasing speed
When a force is applied to an object, its speed increases—it accelerates.

Changing direction
When an object changes direction, its velocity changes. This is also a type of acceleration.

Decreasing speed
When a force slows a moving object down, its speed decreases—it decelerates, or accelerates negatively.

Third law of motion

Forces come in pairs, and any object will react to a force applied to it. The force of reaction is equal and acts in an opposite direction to the force that produces it. If one object is immobile, then the other will move. If both objects can move, then the object with less mass will accelerate more than the other. Every action has an equal and opposite reaction.

Skateboarder moves but wall stays put.

Skateboarders move in opposite directions at same velocity.

Action
If a skateboarder pushes a wall, the wall pushes back with a reaction force that causes the skater to roll away from it.

Reaction
If one skateboarder pushes another, action and reaction cause both skaters to roll away from each other.

Momentum

A moving object keeps moving because it has momentum. It will keep moving until a force stops it. However, when it collides with another object, momentum will be transferred to the second object.

Newton's cradle
Energy is conserved when the balls collide.

As the left ball hits the line of other balls, its velocity decreases and its momentum falls to zero.

The momentum of the first ball passes to the right ball, increasing its velocity.

Relative velocity

The velocity of an object is its speed in a particular direction. Two objects traveling at the same speed but in opposite directions, or at different speeds in the same direction, have different velocities.

Same direction, same speed
The relative velocity of the two cars is 0mph (0km/h).

CAR TRAVELING AT 30MPH (50KM/H)

CAR TRAVELING AT 30MPH (50KM/H)

Same direction, different speeds
The relative velocity of the two cars is 10mph (15km/h).

CAR TRAVELING AT 40MPH (65KM/H)

CAR TRAVELING AT 30MPH (50KM/H)

Opposite direction, same speed
The relative velocity of cars on a collision course is 60mph (100km/h).

CAR TRAVELING AT 30MPH (50KM/H)

CAR TRAVELING AT 30MPH (50KM/H)

Friction

Friction is a force that occurs when a solid object rubs against or slides past another, or when it moves through a liquid or a gas. It always acts against the direction of movement.

The rougher surfaces are and the harder they press together, the stronger the friction—but friction occurs even between very smooth surfaces. Friction can be useful—it helps us to stand, walk, and run—but it can also be a hindrance, slowing movement and making machines inefficient. A by-product of friction is heat.

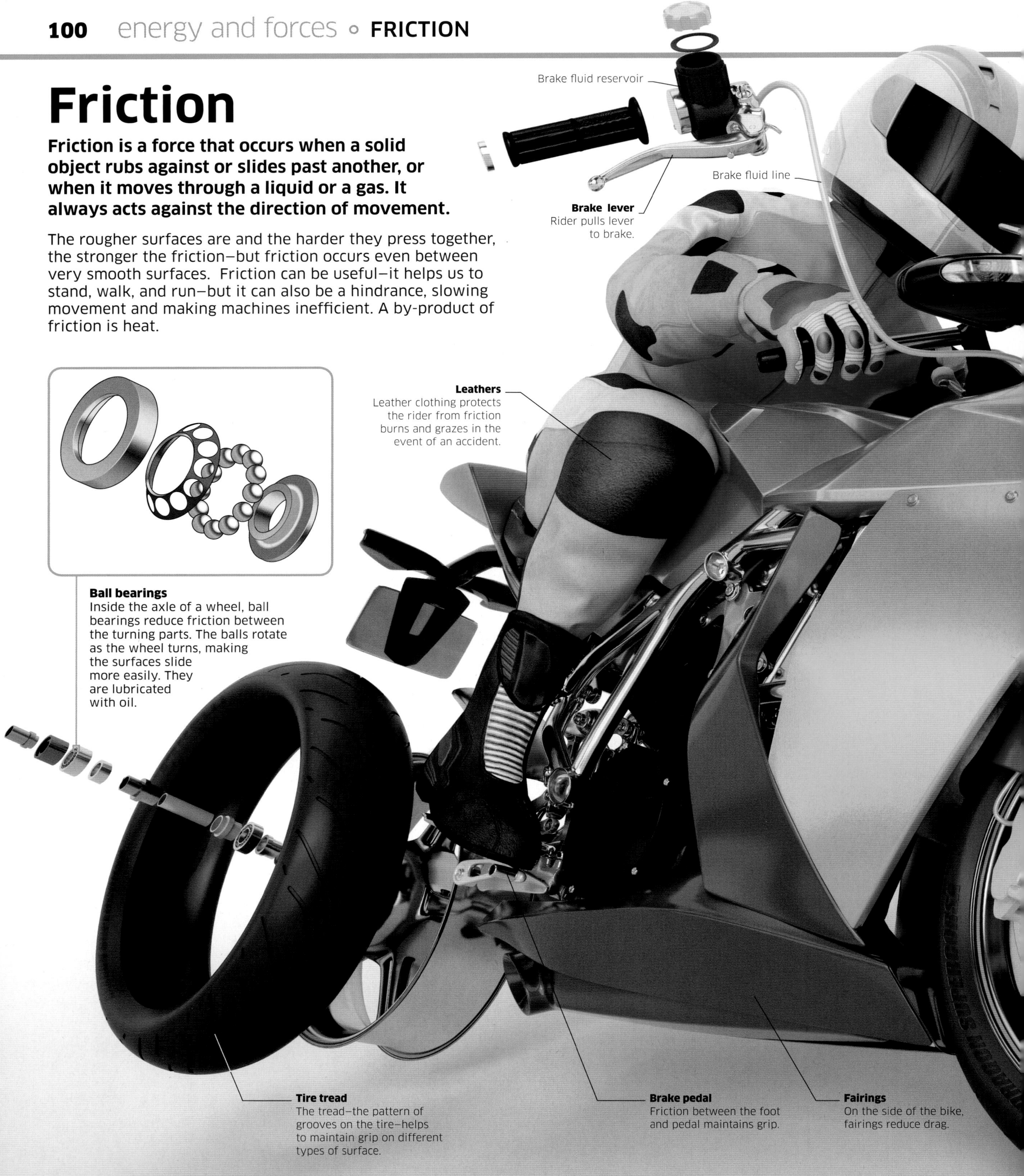

Brake fluid reservoir

Brake fluid line

Brake lever
Rider pulls lever to brake.

Leathers
Leather clothing protects the rider from friction burns and grazes in the event of an accident.

Ball bearings
Inside the axle of a wheel, ball bearings reduce friction between the turning parts. The balls rotate as the wheel turns, making the surfaces slide more easily. They are lubricated with oil.

Tire tread
The tread—the pattern of grooves on the tire—helps to maintain grip on different types of surface.

Brake pedal
Friction between the foot and pedal maintains grip.

Fairings
On the side of the bike, fairings reduce drag.

Fish and aquatic mammals such as **whales and dolphins** have **streamlined body shapes** to reduce water resistance.

If the re-entry angle of a spacecraft is too steep, the braking effect due to **atmospheric friction will cause the spacecraft to break up**.

101

Friction in a motorcycle

The force of friction both helps and hinders a motorcycle rider. Friction between the tires and ground is essential for movement and grip, and is the force behind braking. Drag, the friction that occurs between air and the bike, slows the rider down, and friction between moving parts makes the bike less efficient.

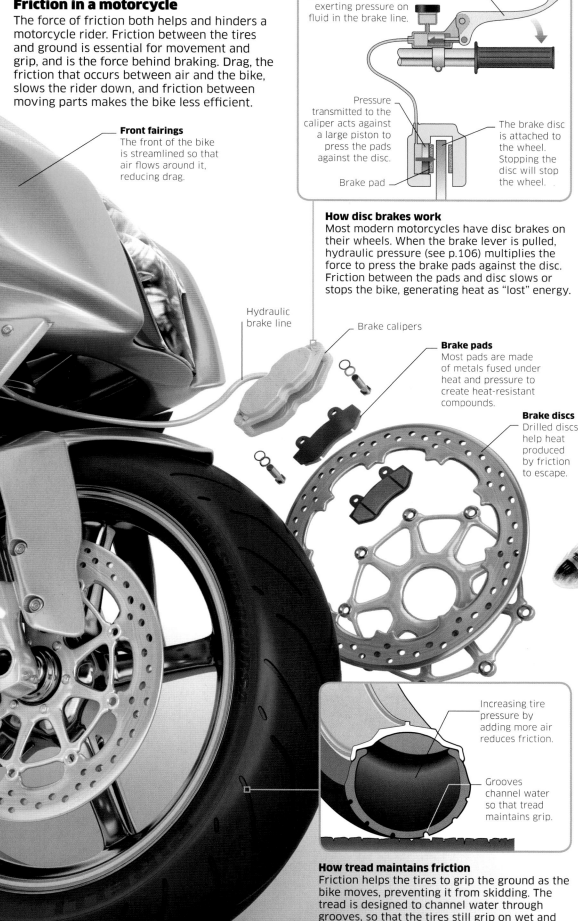

Front fairings
The front of the bike is streamlined so that air flows around it, reducing drag.

Pulling a lever pushes a small piston, exerting pressure on fluid in the brake line.

Pressure transmitted to the caliper acts against a large piston to press the pads against the disc.

Brake pad

The brake disc is attached to the wheel. Stopping the disc will stop the wheel.

How disc brakes work
Most modern motorcycles have disc brakes on their wheels. When the brake lever is pulled, hydraulic pressure (see p.106) multiplies the force to press the brake pads against the disc. Friction between the pads and disc slows or stops the bike, generating heat as "lost" energy.

Hydraulic brake line

Brake calipers

Brake pads
Most pads are made of metals fused under heat and pressure to create heat-resistant compounds.

Brake discs
Drilled discs help heat produced by friction to escape.

Increasing tire pressure by adding more air reduces friction.

Grooves channel water so that tread maintains grip.

How tread maintains friction
Friction helps the tires to grip the ground as the bike moves, preventing it from skidding. The tread is designed to channel water through grooves, so that the tires still grip on wet and muddy roads.

Fluid resistance (drag)

When an object moves through a fluid, it pushes the fluid aside. That requires energy, so the object slows down—or has to be pushed harder; this is known as form drag. Fluid also creates friction as it flows past the object's surface; this is called skin friction.

Water resistance
When a boat moves through water, it pushes water out of the way. The water resists, rising up as bow and stern waves and creating transverse waves in the boat's wake.

Air resistance

When an object moves through air, the drag is called air resistance. The bigger and less streamlined the object and the faster the object is moving, the greater the drag. When spacecraft re-enter the atmosphere, moving very fast, the drag heats their surfaces to as much as 2,750°F (1,500°C).

Helpful and unhelpful friction

It is tempting to think of friction as an unhelpful force that slows movement, but friction can be helpful, too. Without friction between surfaces, there would be no grip and it would be impossible to walk, run, or cycle. However, the boot is on the other foot for skiers, snowboarders, and skaters, who minimize friction to slide.

Reducing friction
The steel blades of ice skates reduce friction, enabling skaters to glide across ice.

Increasing friction
The treads of rubber-soled mountain boots increase friction and grip for climbers.

102 energy and forces ○ **GRAVITY**

51 lb (23 kg)—the **weight on Mars**, due to lower gravity, of a person weighing **137 lb (62 kg) on Earth**.

Law of Falling Bodies

Gravity pulls more strongly on heavier objects—but heavier objects need more force to make them speed up than lighter ones. Galileo was the first person to realize, in 1590, that any two objects dropped together should speed up at the same rate and hit the ground together. We are used to lighter objects falling more slowly—because air resistance slows them more.

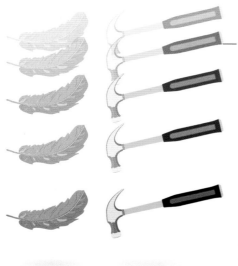

In the near-frictionless environment of the moon, a heavy hammer and a light feather fall at the same rate.

Falling in a vacuum
In 1971, astronaut Dave Scott proved Galileo right when he dropped a feather and a hammer on the moon.

Law of Universal Gravitation

In 1687, English scientist Isaac Newton came up with his Law of Universal Gravitation. It states that any two objects attract each other with a force that depends on the masses of the objects and the distance between them.

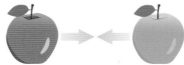

Equal and opposite
The gravitational force between two objects pulls equally on both of them—whatever their relative mass—but in opposite directions.

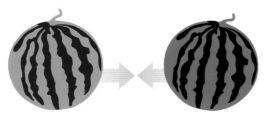

Double the mass
If one object's mass is doubled, the gravitational force doubles. If the mass of both objects is doubled (as here), the force is four times as strong.

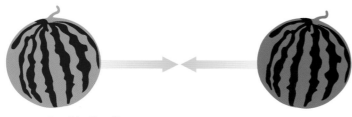

Double the distance
If the distance between two objects is doubled, the gravitational force is quartered.

Gravity and orbits

Newton used his understanding of gravity (see left) and motion to work out how planets, including Earth, remain in their orbits around the sun. He realized that without gravity Earth would travel in a straight line through space. The force of gravity pulls Earth toward the sun, keeping it in its orbit. Earth is constantly falling toward the sun, but never gets any closer. If Earth slowed down or stopped moving, it would fall into the sun!

Elliptical orbit
Earth's orbit around the sun is in fact elliptical (an oval), not circular.

Speed of travel
If Earth was not speeding through space, gravity would pull it into the sun.

Earth
Based on the strength of its gravitational force, the mass of Earth is estimated to be 6.5 sextillion tons!

The force of gravity 62 miles (100 km) above Earth is

3 percent less
than at sea level on Earth.

32.2 ft/s²—the **rate** at which a **falling** object accelerates toward Earth.

Gravity is the weakest of the four fundamental forces: strong nuclear, electromagnetic, weak nuclear, and gravitational.

103

Gravity

Gravity is a force of attraction between two objects. The more mass the objects have and the closer they are to each other, the greater the force of attraction.

Earth's gravity is the gravitational force felt most strongly on the planet: it is what keeps us on the ground and keeps us from floating off into space. In fact, we pull on Earth as much as Earth pulls on us. Gravity also keeps the planets in orbit around the sun, and the moon around Earth. Without it, each planet would travel in a straight line off into space.

The best way scientists can explain gravity is with the General Theory of Relativity, formulated by Albert Einstein in 1915. According to this theory, gravity is actually caused by space being distorted around objects with mass. As objects travel through the distorted space, they change direction. So, according to Einstein, gravity is not a force at all!

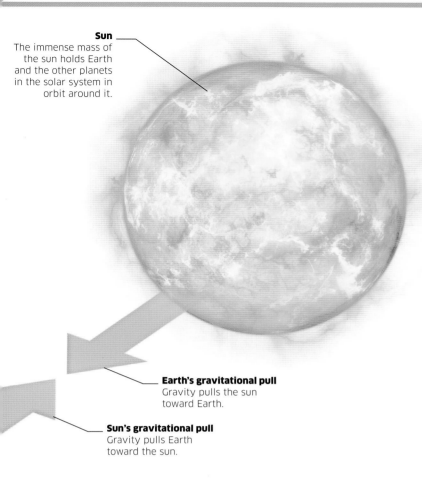

Sun
The immense mass of the sun holds Earth and the other planets in the solar system in orbit around it.

Earth's gravitational pull
Gravity pulls the sun toward Earth.

Sun's gravitational pull
Gravity pulls Earth toward the sun.

Earth's orbit
Earth orbits around the sun because the sun's mass is much great than its own.

Earth's direction of travel
In the absence of gravity, Earth would move in a straight line.

Mass and weight

Mass is the amount of matter an object contains, which stays the same wherever it is. It is measured in kilograms (kg). Weight is a force caused by gravity. The more mass an object has and the stronger the gravity, the greater its weight. Weight is measured in newtons (N).

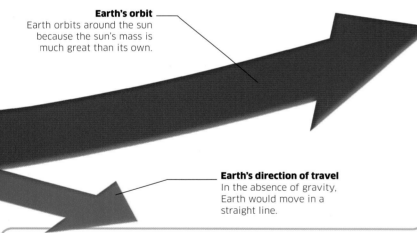

EARTH

Child with mass of 66 lb (30 kg) weighs 300 N.

MOON

Child has mass of 66 lb (30 kg), but weighs 50 N.

Weight on Earth and moon
The moon's gravity is a sixth of Earth's, which means your weight on the moon would be one sixth of your weight on Earth.

Tides

The gravitational pull of the moon and the sun cause the oceans to bulge outward. The moon's pull on the oceans is strongest because it is closest to Earth, and it is the main cause of the tides. However, at certain times of each lunar month, the sun's gravity also plays a role, increasing or decreasing the height of the tides.

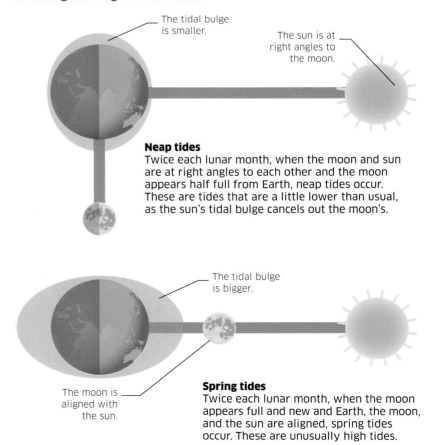

The tidal bulge is smaller.

The sun is at right angles to the moon.

Neap tides
Twice each lunar month, when the moon and sun are at right angles to each other and the moon appears half full from Earth, neap tides occur. These are tides that are a little lower than usual, as the sun's tidal bulge cancels out the moon's.

The tidal bulge is bigger.

The moon is aligned with the sun.

Spring tides
Twice each lunar month, when the moon appears full and new and Earth, the moon, and the sun are aligned, spring tides occur. These are unusually high tides.

104   energy and forces ○ **PRESSURE**

Whales can withstand dramatic pressure changes
because their **bodies are more flexible** than human bodies.

Pressure

Pressure is the push on a surface created by one or more forces. How much pressure is exerted depends upon the strength of the forces and the area of the surface. Walk over snow in snowshoes and you won't sink in—but walk on grass in stiletto heels and you will.

Solids, liquids, and gases can apply pressure onto a surface because of their weight, pressing down on it. The pressure applied by liquids and gases can be increased by squashing them. Pressure is measured in pounds per square inch (psi) or in newtons per square meter (N/m²)—also called Pascals (Pa).

Atmospheric and water pressure

Near sea level, the weight of the air around us presses with a force of about 15 psi (100,000 Pa). Pressure decreases with altitude, because there is less air above pressing down. In the ocean, pressure increases quickly with depth, since water is denser than air.

250 miles (400 km)
As a Soyuz spacecraft travels to the International Space Station (ISS), which orbits at 250 miles (400 km), gas molecules are so few and far between that air pressure is almost nonexistent. The space station's atmosphere is maintained at the same pressure as sea level.

115,000 ft (35,000 m)
As weather balloons ascend into the stratosphere, they expand from 6 ft 6 in (2 m) to 26 ft (8 m) across as air pressure decreases to just 0.1 psi (1,000 Pa). The gas molecules within the balloon spread out as pressure from outside diminishes.

60,000 ft (18,000 m)
Above this altitude—the Armstrong limit—humans cannot survive in an unpressurized environment. Air pressure is 1 psi (7,000 Pa) and exposed body fluids such as saliva and moisture in the lungs will boil away—but not blood in the circulatory system.

36,000 ft (11,000 m)
This is the cruising altitude of passenger jets. As a plane lifts off, your ears may pop due to the change in pressure: air trapped in the inner ear stays at the same pressure, but air pressure outside changes, exerting a force on your eardrum. Pressure falls to 3 psi (23,000 Pa) on the plane's exterior.

28,871 ft (8,848 m)
At Everest's summit, atmospheric pressure is one third of that at sea level: 4.5 psi (33,000 Pa). It is hard to make tea as water boils at 162°F (72°C)—not hot enough for a good brew. Liquids boil when the particles of which they are made move fast enough to have the same pressure as air—so when pressure falls, the boiling point is lower.

Felix Baumgartner makes a record-breaking skydive from 127,852 ft (38,964 m).

Pilots of fighter jets cruising at 50,000 ft (15,000 m) wear pressure suits.

130,000 ft
(40,000 m)

**ABOVE
SEA LEVEL**

115,000 ft
(35,000 m)

98,000 ft
(30,000 m)

82,000 ft
(25,000 m)

65,500 ft
(20,000 m)

130,000 ft
(40,000 m)

The **record altitude for a jet plane** with a pressurized cockpit **is 123,520 ft (37,649 m)**, set by a Russian MiG-25M.

The **record depth for a scuba dive**, set by Egyptian diver Ahmed Gabr is **1,090 ft (332.5 m)** below sea level.

105

18,000 ft (5,500 m)
One half of the atmosphere is contained between Earth's surface and 18,000 ft (5,500 m), where air pressure is 7.3 psi (50,000 Pa). The other half is between this altitude and 100,000 ft (30,000 m).

17,400 ft (5,300 m)
At Everest base camp, atmospheric pressure is about half that at sea level. Altitude sickness is common as air pressure falls to 7.4 psi (51,000 Pa) and there is a low concentration of gas molecules. Climbers pause here to acclimatize and few go higher without extra oxygen.

5,000 ft (1,500 m)
Air pressure decreases to 12 psi (84,000 Pa) at this altitude and breathing is difficult. Lower air density means there are fewer molecules in the same volume of air so people have to breathe faster and deeper to take in the same amount of oxygen.

0 ft (0 m)
At sea level, the pressure pushing down on the surface, known as "one atmosphere," is 15 psi (101,000 Pa). It is the result of the weight of all the air above that surface.

-32 ft (-9.75 m)
Atmospheric pressure is double that at sea level: 30 psi (200,000 Pa). This means that a 32-ft (9.75-m) column of water weighs as much as the entire column of air above it from outer space to 0 ft (0 m).

-130 ft (-40 m)
The normal depth limit for a qualified scuba diver. Pressure here is 73 psi (500,000 Pa)—nearly five times sea level. The spongy tissue of the lungs begins to contract, making it hard to breathe. Diving tanks contain compressed, oxygen-enriched air to overcome this.

-13,000 ft (-4,000 m)
The average depth of the oceans is six times that of the maximum crush depth of most modern submarines, which can survive pressure of 5,800 psi (40 million Pa)—four hundred times What it is at sea level.

-36,070 ft (-10,994 m)
The *Deepsea Challenger* submersible dove close to the deepest known point in Earth's ocean, Challenger Deep in the Marianas Trench, where pressure is 16,040 psi (110 million Pa)—more than a thousand times atmospheric pressure at sea level.

Skydivers typically jump from 11,500 ft (3,500 m).

Herbert Nitsch makes a record-breaking free dive to -702 ft (-214 m).

Russian submarine *Komsomolets K-278* dives to -3,346 ft (-1,020 m).

-13,000 ft (-4,000 m)

BELOW SEA LEVEL

33,000 ft (10,000 m)

16,500 ft (5,000 m)

0 ft (0 m)

-16,500 ft (-5,000 m)

-36,000 ft (-11,000 m)

Simple machines

A machine is anything that changes the size or direction of a force, making work easier. Simple machines include ramps, wedges, screws, levers, wheels, and pulleys.

Complex machines such as cranes and diggers combine a number of simple machines, but whatever the scale, the physical principles remain the same. Many of the most effective machines are the simplest—a sloping path (ramp); a knife (wedge); a jar lid (screw); scissors, nutcrackers, and tweezers (levers); a faucet (wheel and axle); or hoist (pulley), for example. Hydraulics and pneumatics use the pressure in fluids (liquids and gases) to transmit force.

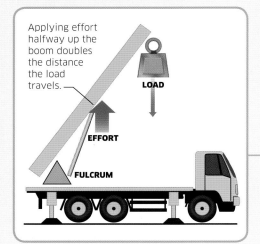

Applying effort halfway up the boom doubles the distance the load travels.

LOAD

EFFORT

FULCRUM

Lever
The crane's boom is a long, third-class lever. When a hydraulic ram applies a force greater than the load between the load and the fulcrum, the crane lifts the load.

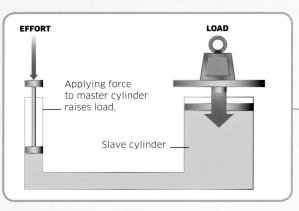

EFFORT

LOAD

Applying force to master cylinder raises load.

Slave cylinder

Hydraulics
A hydraulic system makes use of pressure in a liquid by applying force (effort) to a "master" cylinder, which increases fluid pressure in a "slave" cylinder. The hydraulic ram lifts the crane's boom by using pressure from fluid in the cylinder to push a piston.

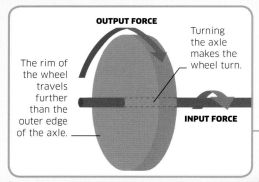

OUTPUT FORCE

Turning the axle makes the wheel turn.

The rim of the wheel travels further than the outer edge of the axle.

INPUT FORCE

Wheel and axle
A wheel with an axle can be used in two ways: either by applying a force to the axle to turn the wheel, which multiplies the distance traveled; or by applying a force to the wheel to turn the axle, like a spanner.

Ramp and wedge
Also known as an inclined plane, a ramp reduces the force needed to move an object from a lower to a higher place. A wedge acts like a moving inclined plane, applying a greater force to raise an object.

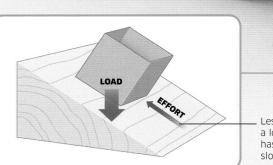

LOAD

EFFORT

Less effort is needed to push a load up a ramp, but the load has to move further along the slope than it moves vertically.

The tool known as **Archimedes' screw pump** has been used to **transport water for irrigation** since the 7th century BCE.

107

Single fixed pulley

Compound pulley

EFFORT

LOAD

EFFORT

LOAD

Pulley
Using a rope around a wheel, pulleys make it easier to raise or lower a load. A single fixed pulley changes the direction of movement. A compound (block and tackle) pulley reduces the effort, too.

Bevel gear controls direction of rotation.

INPUT FORCE

OUTPUT FORCE

Gears
Gears are toothed wheels that transmit force and come in four main types. In all of them, one gear wheel turns faster or slower than the other or moves in a different direction. In "bevel" gears, two wheels interlock to change the direction of rotation.

Types of lever
A lever is a bar that tilts on a fulcrum or pivot. If you apply force (effort) to one part of a lever, the lever swings on the fulcrum to raise a load. Levers work in three ways, depending on the relative position of the fulcrum, load, and effort on the bar.

Load and effort are equal because the distance between them and the fulcrum is equal.

LOAD

EFFORT

FULCRUM

First-class levers
The fulcrum is in between the effort and the load—as in a beam scale or a pair of scissors (two levers hinged at a fulcrum).

The effort is twice as far from the fulcrum as the load, so the force needed to lift it is halved.

INPUT FORCE

OUTPUT FORCE

Screw turns to raise load.

Screw
An auger—the screwlike drill bit of this boring tool—is a ramp that winds around itself, with a wedge at the tip. It is used to lift earth as it excavates. Other screws, such as light bulbs or wood and masonry screws, hold things together.

LOAD

FULCRUM

EFFORT

Second-class levers
The fulcrum is at one end and effort is applied to the other, with a load between—as in a wheelbarrow or nutcracker.

The load moves twice as far as the effort, because it is twice as far from the fulcrum.

LOAD

FULCRUM

EFFORT

Third-class levers
The fulcrum is at the end, with load at the other end and effort applied in between—as in a hammer or a pair of tweezers.

Compound machines
A big mechanical crane and digger combines a number of simple machines with a powerful engine to make light work of heavy lifting and excavation.

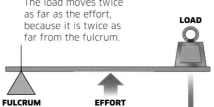

Most solids are denser than their liquid forms, but water is an exception: ice is less dense than water, which is why ice cubes and icebergs float.

Floating

Why does an apple float but a gold apple of the same size sink? How do ships carrying a cargo across the sea stay afloat? And what makes a balloon float in air?

Fluids (liquids and gases) exert pressure on the surface of any object immersed in them. Pressure in a fluid increases with depth, so the pressure pushing upward on the bottom of an object is greater than the pressure pushing downward on the top. This results in an upward force, called "upthrust." If the upthrust on an object is greater than, or equal to, its weight, the object floats. If the upthrust is less than its weight, the object sinks. Same-sized objects of different densities weigh more or less, so one object may float while another of the same size sinks.

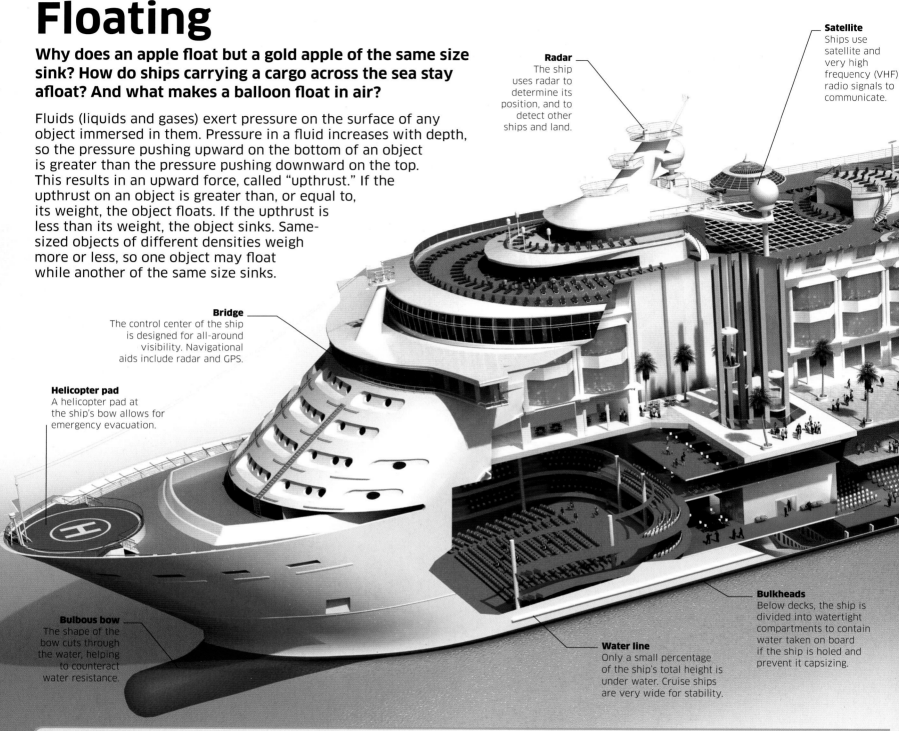

Radar
The ship uses radar to determine its position, and to detect other ships and land.

Satellite
Ships use satellite and very high frequency (VHF) radio signals to communicate.

Bridge
The control center of the ship is designed for all-around visibility. Navigational aids include radar and GPS.

Helicopter pad
A helicopter pad at the ship's bow allows for emergency evacuation.

Bulbous bow
The shape of the bow cuts through the water, helping to counteract water resistance.

Water line
Only a small percentage of the ship's total height is under water. Cruise ships are very wide for stability.

Bulkheads
Below decks, the ship is divided into watertight compartments to contain water taken on board if the ship is holed and prevent it capsizing.

Water density

When ocean trade routes opened up around the globe, sailors were surprised to find their carefully loaded ships sank when they got near the equator. This was because the density of warm tropical waters was less than that of cool northern waters, and so provided less upthrust. When the ships entered freshwater ports, the water density was lower still, and ships were even more likely to sink.

TROPICAL FRESH WATER

Warm water that is not salt has a low density, so a ship floats low in it.

TROPICAL SEAWATER

Salt water has a higher density than fresh water, so a ship floats higher.

SUMMER TEMPERATE SEAWATER

As salt water cools, its density increases and a ship becomes more buoyant.

WINTER NORTH ATLANTIC SEAWATER

In the freezing cold waters of the North Atlantic, ships float high in the water.

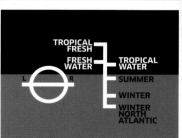

The Plimsoll line
On a ship's hull, this mark shows the depth to which the ship may be immersed when loaded. This varies with a ship's size, type of cargo, time of year, and the water densities in port and at sea.

Greek philosopher **Archimedes first established the principle of buoyancy**, or how things float, in the **2nd century BCE**.

109

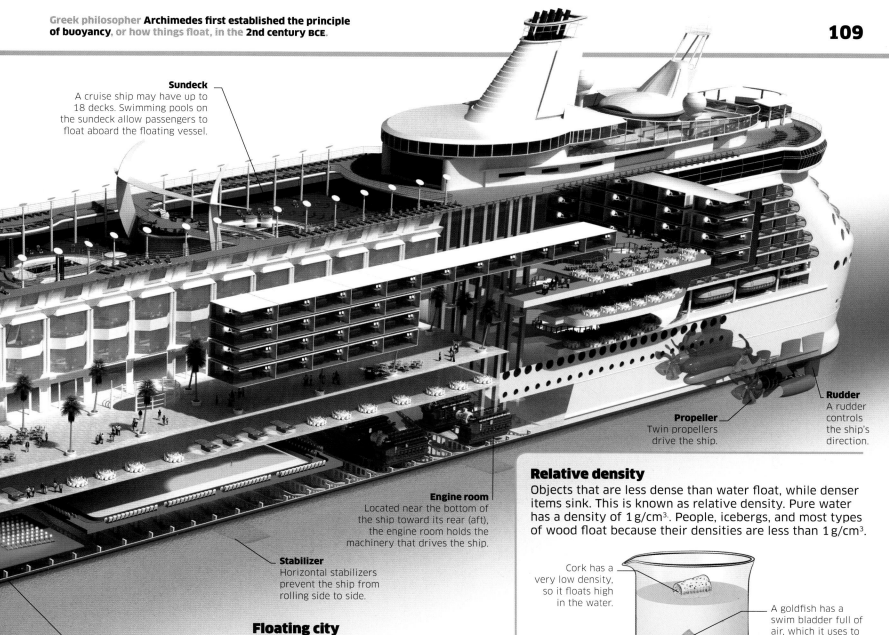

Sundeck
A cruise ship may have up to 18 decks. Swimming pools on the sundeck allow passengers to float aboard the floating vessel.

Rudder
A rudder controls the ship's direction.

Propeller
Twin propellers drive the ship.

Engine room
Located near the bottom of the ship toward its rear (aft), the engine room holds the machinery that drives the ship.

Stabilizer
Horizontal stabilizers prevent the ship from rolling side to side.

Hull
Welded construction maximizes the strength of the hull. Some ships are designed with a stronger double hull.

Floating city
Vast cruise ships can carry nearly 10,000 people, along with fuel, food, water, and cargo (known as dead weight), and the ship's machinery (lightweight), displacing 110,230 tons of water. How can these juggernauts of the sea float?

Relative density
Objects that are less dense than water float, while denser items sink. This is known as relative density. Pure water has a density of $1\,g/cm^3$. People, icebergs, and most types of wood float because their densities are less than $1\,g/cm^3$.

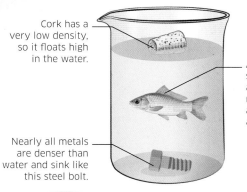

Cork has a very low density, so it floats high in the water.

A goldfish has a swim bladder full of air, which it uses to regulate its density, allowing it to float at different depths.

Nearly all metals are denser than water and sink like this steel bolt.

How boats float
Water exerts pressure on any object immersed in it. Pressure increases with depth, so the pressure on the underneath of an object is greater than the pressure on the top. The difference results in a force known as upthrust, or buoyancy. If the upthrust on a submerged object is equal to the object's weight, the object will float.

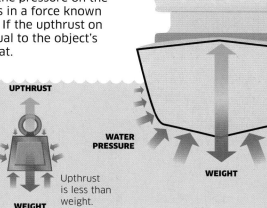

UPTHRUST — Upthrust balances weight.

UPTHRUST

WATER PRESSURE

WEIGHT

Sink or swim
A solid block of steel sinks because its weight is greater than upthrust, but a steel ship of the same weight floats because its hull is filled with air so its density overall is less than the density of water.

UPTHRUST

WEIGHT

Upthrust is less than weight.

Floating in air
Like water, air exerts pressure on objects with a force called upthrust that equals the weight of air pushed aside by the object. Few objects float in air because it is light, but the air in hot-air balloons is less dense than cool air.

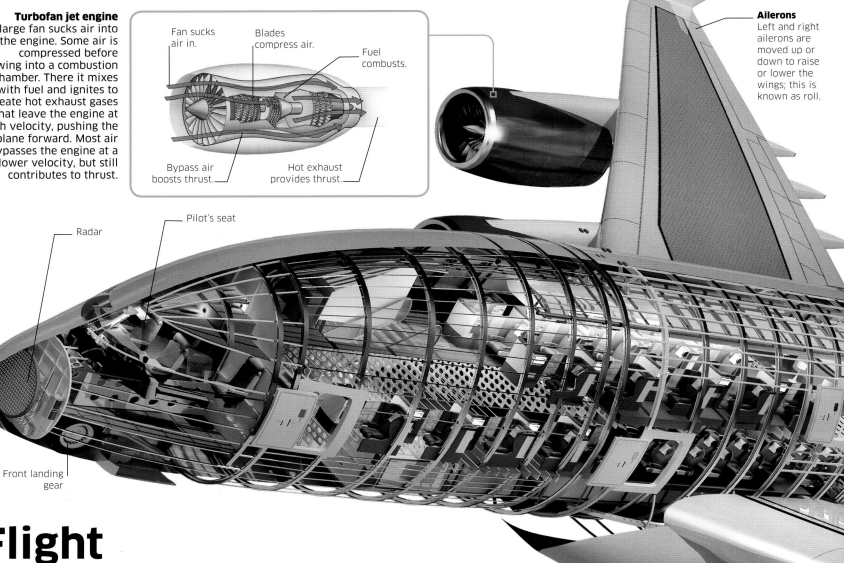

Turbofan jet engine
A large fan sucks air into the engine. Some air is compressed before flowing into a combustion chamber. There it mixes with fuel and ignites to create hot exhaust gases that leave the engine at high velocity, pushing the plane forward. Most air bypasses the engine at a lower velocity, but still contributes to thrust.

Fan sucks air in.

Blades compress air.

Fuel combusts.

Bypass air boosts thrust.

Hot exhaust provides thrust.

Ailerons
Left and right ailerons are moved up or down to raise or lower the wings; this is known as roll.

Radar

Pilot's seat

Front landing gear

Flight

Dynamics is the science of movement, and aerodynamics is movement through air. In order to fly, planes use thrust and lift to counteract the forces of drag and gravity.

Just over a hundred years since the first powered flight, today more than 100,000 planes fly every day and it seems normal to us that an airliner weighing as much as 619 tons when laden can take to the skies. To take off, a plane must generate enough lift to overcome gravity, using the power of its engines to create drag-defying thrust.

Airbus A380
The Airbus 380 is the world's biggest passenger aircraft: 234 ft (73 m) long with a wing span of 262 ft (79.8 m), it can seat 555 people on two decks and carry 165 tons of cargo.

The forces of flight

Four forces act upon an airplane traveling through the air: thrust, lift, gravity, and drag. Thrust from the engines pushes the plane forward, forcing air over the wings, which creates lift to get it off the ground, while gravity pulls the plane downward, and drag – or air resistance – pulls it backward. In level flight at a constant speed, all four of these forces are perfectly balanced.

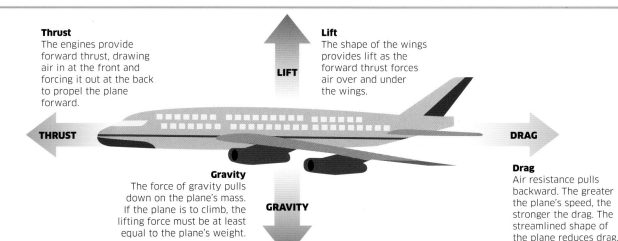

Thrust
The engines provide forward thrust, drawing air in at the front and forcing it out at the back to propel the plane forward.

Lift
The shape of the wings provides lift as the forward thrust forces air over and under the wings.

LIFT

THRUST

DRAG

Drag
Air resistance pulls backward. The greater the plane's speed, the stronger the drag. The streamlined shape of the plane reduces drag.

Gravity
The force of gravity pulls down on the plane's mass. If the plane is to climb, the lifting force must be at least equal to the plane's weight.

GRAVITY

289 tons—the **maximum fuel capacity** of an Airbus A380.

180 mph (280 km/h)—the **average take-off speed** of a jet airliner.

111

Airfoil

The cross-section of a plane's wing has a shape called an airfoil, which forces air to speed up over the top surface and slow down beneath. The aerofoil is angled so that air passing under the wing is forced downward. Air passing over the wing is forced downward too. The angle also creates an area of very low pressure above the wing. As a result of the wing pushing the air downward and the pressure difference above and below the wing, the air pushes the wing (and plane) upward.

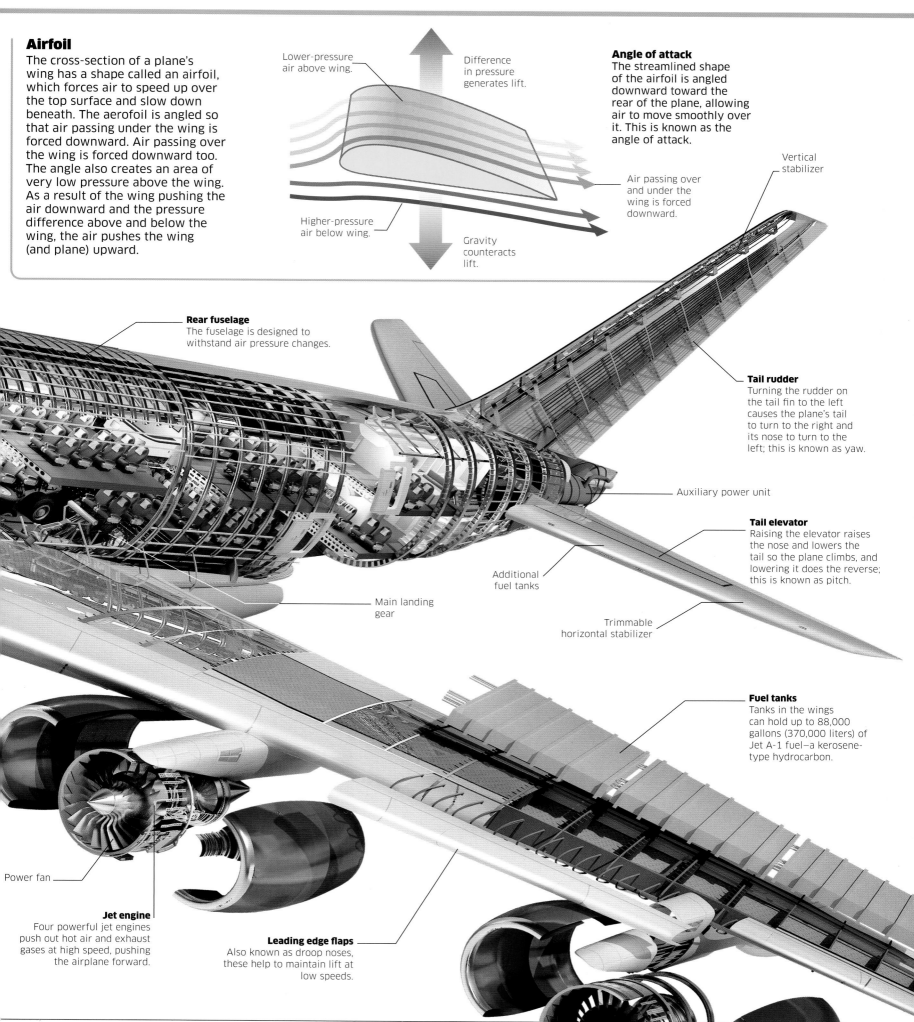

Lower-pressure air above wing.

Difference in pressure generates lift.

Higher-pressure air below wing.

Gravity counteracts lift.

Angle of attack
The streamlined shape of the airfoil is angled downward toward the rear of the plane, allowing air to move smoothly over it. This is known as the angle of attack.

Air passing over and under the wing is forced downward.

Vertical stabilizer

Rear fuselage
The fuselage is designed to withstand air pressure changes.

Tail rudder
Turning the rudder on the tail fin to the left causes the plane's tail to turn to the right and its nose to turn to the left; this is known as yaw.

Auxiliary power unit

Tail elevator
Raising the elevator raises the nose and lowers the tail so the plane climbs, and lowering it does the reverse; this is known as pitch.

Additional fuel tanks

Main landing gear

Trimmable horizontal stabilizer

Fuel tanks
Tanks in the wings can hold up to 88,000 gallons (370,000 liters) of Jet A-1 fuel—a kerosene-type hydrocarbon.

Power fan

Jet engine
Four powerful jet engines push out hot air and exhaust gases at high speed, pushing the airplane forward.

Leading edge flaps
Also known as droop noses, these help to maintain lift at low speeds.

SPACE AND EARTH

All of space, matter, energy, and time make up the universe—a vast, ever-expanding creation that is so big it would take billions of years to cross it, even when traveling at the speed of light. Within the universe are clumps of matter called galaxies, and within those are planets like our own—Earth.

THE EXPANSION OF SPACE

Astronomers on Earth can observe galaxies moving away from us, but in reality they are moving away from every other point in the universe as well. These galaxies are not moving into new space—all of space is expanding and pulling them away from each other. This effect can be imagined by thinking of the universe as a balloon. As the balloon inflates, the rubber stretches and individual points on it all move further away from each other.

Huge expanses of space will come between galaxies in the future.

Although the galaxies remain the same size, the distance between them has grown.

Galaxies used to be more tightly clumped together.

BILLIONS OF YEARS AGO

TODAY

BILLIONS OF YEARS IN THE FUTURE

THE BIG BANG

The universe came into existence around 13.8 billion years ago in a cataclysmic explosion known as the Big Bang. Starting out as tinier than an atom, it rapidly expanded—forming stars, and clusters of stars called galaxies. A large part of this expansion happened incredibly quickly—it grew by a trillion kilometers in under a second.

The universe is dark until stars form.

Stars form.

379,000 years after the Big Bang, this afterglow light was emitted. It can still be seen in the universe today.

Expansion quickly happens.

The universe begins from nothing.

① ② ③ ④ ⑤ ⑥ ⑦

First galaxies form.

1 The universe suddenly appears. At this stage, it is made up of pure energy and reaches extreme temperatures.

2 Rapid expansion (inflation) takes place, transforming the universe from a tiny mass smaller than a fraction of an atom into a gigantic space the size of a city.

3 Matter is created from the universe's energy. This starts out as minuscule particles and antiparticles (the same mass as particles but with an opposite electric charge). Many of these converge and cancel each other out, but some matter remains.

4 The universe is still less than a second old when the first recognizable subatomic particles start to form. These are protons and neutrons—the particles that make up the nucleus of an atom.

5 Over the next 379,000 years, the universe slowly cools, until eventually atoms are able to form. This development changes the universe from a dense fog into an empty space punctuated by clouds of hydrogen and helium gas. Light can now pass through it.

THE OBSERVABLE UNIVERSE

When we look at distant objects in the night sky, we are actually seeing what they looked like millions, or even billions, of years ago, because that is how long the light from them has taken to reach us. All of the space we can see from Earth is known as the observable universe. Other parts lie beyond that, but are too far away for the light from them to have reached us yet. However, using a space-based observatory such as the Hubble Space Telescope, we can capture images of deep space and use them to decipher the universe's past.

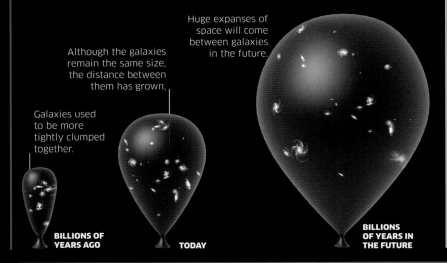

HUBBLE DEEP FIELD

HUBBLE ULTRA DEEP FIELD

FIRST GALAXIES

FIRST STARS

DARK AGES

RADIATION ERA

Hubble imaging
The Hubble Space Telescope has been operating since 1990 and has captured thousands of images of the universe. Many of these have been compiled to create amazing views of the furthest (and therefore oldest) parts of the universe we can see. These are known as Deep Field images.

The first Hubble Deep Field observed one part of the night sky over 10 days. It revealed galaxies formed less than a billion years after the Big Bang.

The later Hubble Ultra Deep Field image (above) shows even further into the past, picturing galaxies formed 13 billion years ago, when the Universe was around 800 million years old.

There are regions of space further back in time that Hubble and other powerful space telescopes cannot see.

6 Just over half a million years after the Big Bang, the distribution of matter in the universe begins to change. Tiny denser patches of matter begin to be pulled closer together by gravity.

8 Stars form in groups within the universe's vast clouds of gas. The first groups become the first galaxies. Most of these are relatively small, but later merge to form larger galaxies that stretch for hundreds of millions of light-years.

10 Our solar system comes into being after 9 billion years, formed from the collapse of a large nebula (a cloud of gas and dust). Material first forms into the sun, and then other clumps become the variety of planets surrounding it, including Earth.

This NASA probe was launched in 2001 to measure the size and properties of the universe.

11 →

12 →

11 In the future, the universe will continue to expand and change, and our solar system will not last for ever. The sun is very slowly getting hotter, and when the universe is 20 billion years old, it will also expand in size–an event likely to destroy Earth.

7 The effects of gravity begin to create more and more clumps of matter, until large spheres of gas, called stars, are formed. The universe is now 300 million years old. These stars produce the energy to sustain themselves by nuclear fusion.

9 Around 8 billion years after the Big Bang, the expansion of the universe begins to accelerate.

Solar system forms.

12 Scientists do not know exactly how the universe will end, but it is predicted to keep expanding and become incredibly cold and dark– a process known as the "Big Chill."

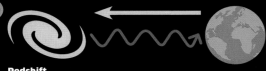

Redshift
When an object (a distant galaxy) is moving away from the observer (us), its wavelengths get longer. The light it produces therefore shifts into the red end of the light spectrum. More distant galaxies have greater redshift– supporting the theory that the universe is expanding.

Blueshift
A few nearby galaxies are actually moving toward us. Their wavelengths will be shorter, shifting the light they produce to the blue end of the spectrum.

DISCOVERING THE BIG BANG

Scientists did not always believe in the theory of an expanding universe and the Big Bang. However, during the 20th century, several discoveries were made which supported this idea. In 1929, American astronomer Edwin Hubble observed that the light coming from distant galaxies appeared redder than it should be. He attributed this to a phenomenon called redshift, suggesting that galaxies must be moving away from us. Another piece of evidence was the discovery of cosmic background radiation–microwaves coming from all directions in space that could only be explained as an after effect of the Big Bang.

Cosmic background radiation
This image, captured by NASA's Wilkinson Microwave Anisotropy Probe, shows a false color depiction of the background radiation that fills the entire universe. This is the remains of the intense burst of energy that was released by the Big Bang.

Most of a **galaxy's mass** is made up of **dark matter**.

It is estimated that there are **2 trillion galaxies** in the parts of **the universe** we can see.

Galaxies

Unimaginably huge collections of gas, dust, stars, and even planets, galaxies come in many shapes and sizes. Some are spirals, such as our own galaxy, others are like squashed balls, and some have no shape at all.

When you look up at the sky at night, every star you see is part of our galaxy, the Milky Way. This is part of what we call the Local Group, which contains about 50 galaxies. Beyond it are countless more galaxies that stretch out as far as telescopes can see. The smallest galaxies in the universe have a few million stars in them, while the largest have trillions. The Milky Way lies somewhere in the middle, with between 100 billion and 1 trillion stars in it. The force of gravity holds the stars in a galaxy together, and they travel slowly around the center. A supermassive black hole hides at the heart of most galaxies.

Astronomers have identified four types of galaxies: spiral, barred spiral, elliptical, and irregular. Spiral galaxies are flat spinning disks with a bulge in the center, while barred spiral galaxies have a longer, thinner line of stars at their center, which looks like a bar. Elliptical galaxies are an ellipsoid, or the shape of a squashed sphere—these are the largest galaxies. Then there are irregular galaxies, which have no regular shape.

MILKY WAY

Type: *Barred spiral*
Diameter: *100,000 light years*

Our own galaxy, the Milky Way, is thought to be a barred spiral shape, but we cannot see its shape clearly from Earth because we are part of it. From our solar system, it appears as a pale streak in the sky with a central bulge of stars. From above, it would look like a giant whirlpool that takes 200 million years to rotate.

Galactic core

Infrared and X-ray images reveal intense activity near the galactic core. The galaxy's center is located within the bright white region. Hundreds of thousands of stars that cannot be seen in visible light swirl around it, heating dramatic clouds of gas and dust.

Solar system
Our solar system is in a minor spiral arm called the Orion arm.

Side view of the Milky Way
Viewed from the side, the Milky Way would look like two fried eggs back to back. The stars in the galaxy are held together by gravity and travel slowly around the galactic heart in a flat orbit.

Our **sun** lies between **25,000 and 28,000 light years** from the **center of the Milky Way**.

The **largest galaxies** in the universe stretch up to **2 million light years long**.

The word **galaxy** comes from the **Greek** term *galaxias kyklos*, which means **milky circle**.

115

ANDROMEDA

Type: *Spiral*
Distance: *2,450,000 light years*

Our closest large galaxy, Andromeda—a central hub surrounded by a flat, rotating disc of stars, gas, and dust—can sometimes be seen from Earth with the naked eye. In 4.5 billion years, Andromeda is expected to collide with the Milky Way, forming one huge elliptical galaxy.

MESSIER 87

Type: *Elliptical*
Distance: *53 million light years*

M87, also known as Virgo A, is one of the largest galaxies in our part of the universe. The galaxy is giving out a powerful jet of material from the supermassive black hole at its center, energetic enough to accelerate particles to nearly the speed of light.

SMALL MAGELLANIC CLOUD

Type: *Dwarf (irregular)*
Distance: *197,000 light years*

The dwarf galaxy SMC stretches 7,000 light years across. Like its neighbor the Large Magellanic Cloud (LMC), its shape has been distorted by the gravity of our own galaxy. Third closest to the Milky Way, it is known as a satellite galaxy because it orbits our own.

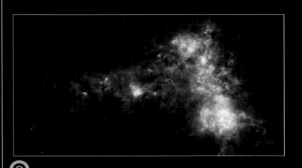

CARTWHEEL GALAXY

Type: *Ring (irregular)*
Distance: *500 million light years*

The Cartwheel Galaxy started out as a spiral. However, 200 million years ago it collided with a smaller galaxy, causing a powerful shock throughout the galaxy, which tossed lots of the gas and dust to the outside, creating its unusual shape.

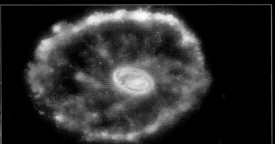

ANTENNAE GALAXIES

Type: *Merging spirals*
Distance: *45 million–65 million light years*

Around 1.2 billion years ago, the Antennae Galaxies were two separate galaxies: one barred spiral and one spiral. They started to merge a few hundred million years ago, when the antennae formed and are expected to become one galaxy in about 400 million years.

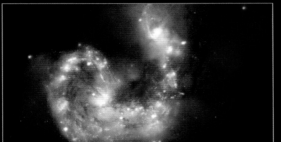

WHIRLPOOL GALAXY

Type: *Colliding spiral and dwarf*
Distance: *23 million light years*

About 300 million years ago, the spiral Whirlpool Galaxy was struck by a dwarf galaxy, which now appears to dangle from one of its spiral arms. The collision stirred up gas clouds, triggering a burst of star formation, which can be seen from Earth with a small telescope.

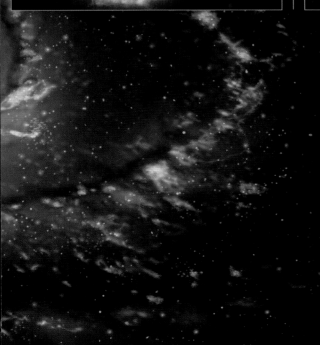

Active galaxies

Some galaxies send out bright jets of light and particles from their centers. These "active" galaxies can be grouped into four types: radio galaxies, Seyfert galaxies, quasars, and blazars. All are thought to have supermassive black holes at their core, known as the active galactic nuclei, which churn out the jets of material.

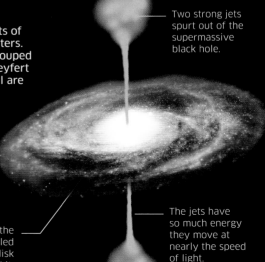

Two strong jets spurt out of the supermassive black hole.

The jets have so much energy they move at nearly the speed of light.

The material near the center of the supermassive black hole is called the accretion disk. An opaque disk of dust and gas gathers around it.

Star life cycle

Stars are born in vast clouds of cold, dense interstellar gas and dust that evolve until, billions of years later, they run out of fuel and die.

The clouds that give birth to stars consist mainly of hydrogen gas. New stars are huge, spinning globes of hot, glowing gas—mainly hydrogen with some helium. Most of this material is packed into the stars' cores, setting off nuclear reactions—fueled by hydrogen—that form helium and release energy in the form of heat and light. When most of the hydrogen is used up, stars may fade away, expand, or collapse in on themselves.

1 Interstellar cloud
Stars are born in huge clouds of dense, cold gas and dust. A supernova explosion or star collision can trigger star birth.

2 Fragments form
The cloud breaks up into fragments. Gravity pulls the most massive and dense of these into clumps.

3 Protostar forms
Gravity pulls more material into the protostar's core. Density, pressure, and temperature build up.

4 Spinning disk
The material being pulled in starts to spin round, blowing out jets of gas.

5 Main sequence star
The core becomes so hot and dense that nuclear reactions occur and the star shines.

6 Planets form
Debris spinning around the star may clump together to form planets, moons, comets, and asteroids.

7 Stable star
The glowing core produces an outward pressure that balances the inward pull of gravity.

Birth, life, and death of a star

Stars start out their life as clouds of gas and dust, called nebulae. After millions of years, these clouds begin to pull inward because of the gravity of the gas and dust. As it is squeezed, the cloud heats up to form a young star, known as a protostar. If this reaches 27 million degrees Fahrenheit, it is hot enough to start nuclear fusion—the reaction needed for a star to form. The energy produced prevents a star from collapsing under its own weight and makes it shine. What happens when the fuel runs out and the star dies depends on how much dust gathered in the first place.

The sun has existed for about

4.5 billion years,

and has burned about half of

its hydrogen fuel.

Death of a small star
Stars with less than half the mass of the sun, called red dwarfs, fade away slowly. Once the hydrogen in the core is used up, the star begins to feed off hydrogen in its atmosphere, shrinking—over up to a trillion years—to become a black dwarf.

Black dwarf
When all fuel is used up and its light is extinguished, the star becomes a cinder the size of Earth.

Star continues to shrink and fade.

Light intensity fades out.

Star begins to shrink.

Death of a medium-sized star
When a star with the same mass as our sun has used up its hydrogen (after about 10 billion years) nuclear fusion spreads out from the core, making the star expand into a red giant. The core collapses until it is hot and dense enough to fuse helium. When this, too, runs out, the star becomes a white dwarf, its outer layers spreading into space as a cloud of debris.

Neutron stars are the smallest, most dense stars in the universe–6 miles (10 km) in diameter but with up to 30 times as much mass as our sun.

Energy released in the center of the sun takes millions of years to reach its surface.

117

If you sorted all the stars into piles, the biggest pile, by far, would be

red dwarfs–stars

with less than half of the sun's mass.

Death of a massive star
Stars more than eight times the mass of our sun will be hot enough to become supergiants. The heat and pressure in the core become so intense that nuclear fusion can fuse helium and larger atoms to create elements such as carbon or oxygen. As this happens, the stars swell into supergiants, which end their lives in dramatic explosions called supernovae. Smaller supergiants become neutron stars, but larger ones become black holes.

Red supergiant
Nuclear fusion carries on inside the core of the supergiant, forming heavy elements until the core turns into iron and the star collapses.

Star types
The Hertzsprung-Russell diagram is a graph that astronomers use to classify stars. It plots the brightness of stars against their temperature to reveal distinct groups of stars, such as red giants (dying stars) and main sequence stars (ordinary stars). Astronomers also classify stars by color, which relates to temperature. Red is the coolest color, seen in stars cooler than 6,000°F (3,500°C). Stars such as our sun are yellowish white and average around 10,000°F (6,000°C). The hottest stars are blue, with surface temperatures above 21,000°F (12,000°C).

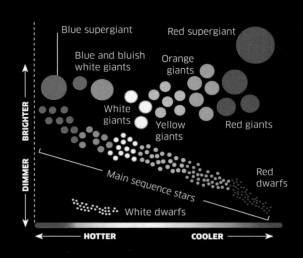

Blue supergiant · Red supergiant · Blue and bluish white giants · Orange giants · White giants · Yellow giants · Red giants · BRIGHTER · DIMMER · Main sequence stars · Red dwarfs · White dwarfs · HOTTER · COOLER

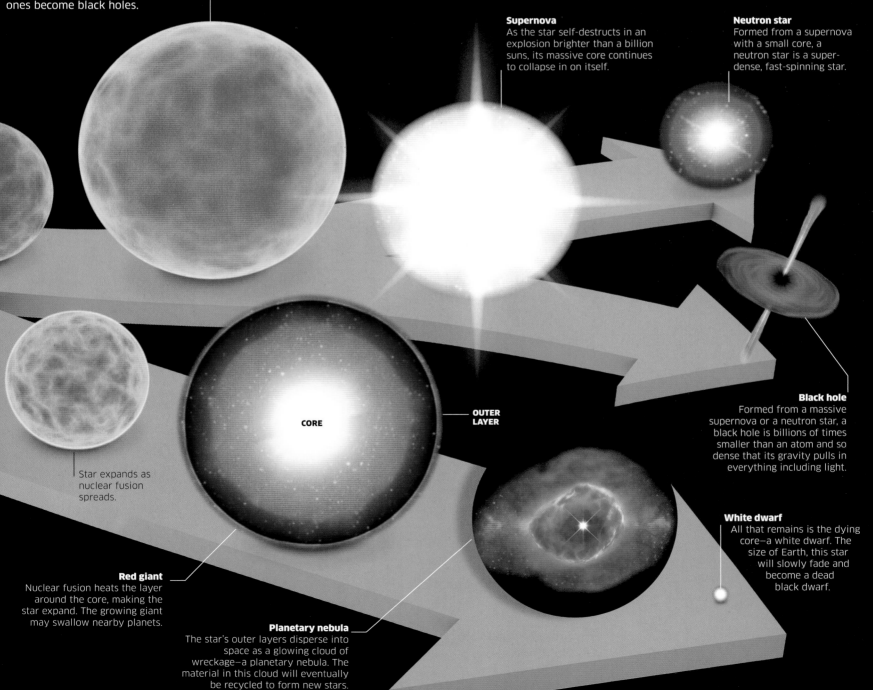

Supernova
As the star self-destructs in an explosion brighter than a billion suns, its massive core continues to collapse in on itself.

Neutron star
Formed from a supernova with a small core, a neutron star is a super-dense, fast-spinning star.

CORE

OUTER LAYER

Black hole
Formed from a massive supernova or a neutron star, a black hole is billions of times smaller than an atom and so dense that its gravity pulls in everything including light.

Star expands as nuclear fusion spreads.

White dwarf
All that remains is the dying core–a white dwarf. The size of Earth, this star will slowly fade and become a dead black dwarf.

Red giant
Nuclear fusion heats the layer around the core, making the star expand. The growing giant may swallow nearby planets.

Planetary nebula
The star's outer layers disperse into space as a glowing cloud of wreckage–a planetary nebula. The material in this cloud will eventually be recycled to form new stars.

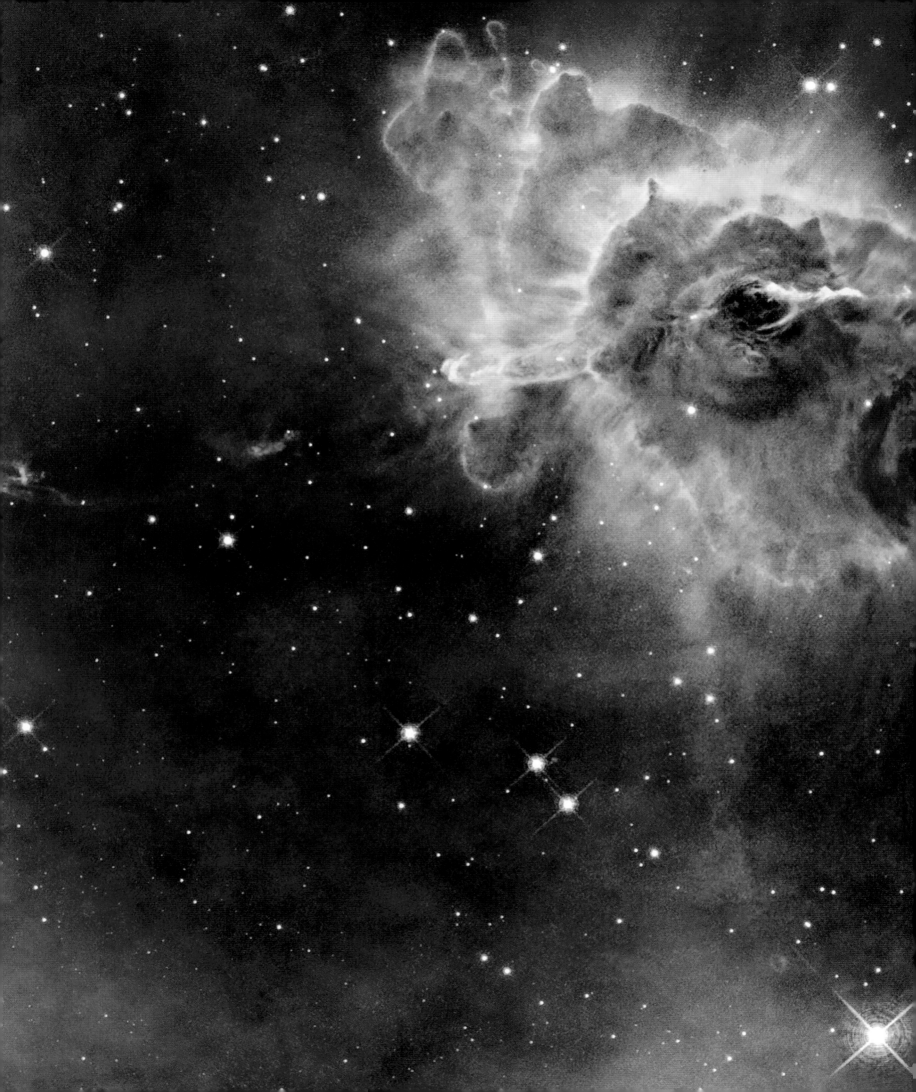

Carina Nebula

This remarkable image of part of the Carina Nebula was captured by the Hubble Space Telescope. Inside this enormous pillar of dust and gas, stars are being born.

The nebula comprises mostly hydrogen and helium, but also contains the debris from old stars that exploded long ago. Gravity pulls all of this matter into clumps that heat up and begin to shine, their light and other radiation sculpting the cloud with jets and swirls. The Carina Nebula lies 7,500 light-years away, in our own galaxy, the Milky Way.

Size comparison

With a diameter of nearly 870,000 miles (1.4 million km), the sun is 10 times wider than Jupiter, the biggest of the planets, and over 1,000 times more massive.

Inner planets

The inner four planets are smaller than the outer four. They are called terrestrial planets.

MERCURY VENUS EARTH MARS

Outer planets

The outermost four planets are larger and made up of gas, so they are called the gas giants.

JUPITER   SATURN

URANUS   NEPTUNE

Oort Cloud

The Oort Cloud is a ring of tiny, icy bodies that is thought to extend between 50,000 and 100,000 times farther from the sun than the distance from the sun to Earth—but it's so far away that no one really knows.

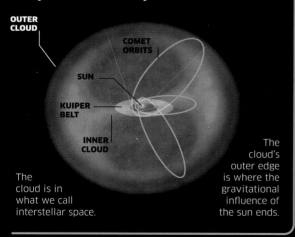

OUTER CLOUD

COMET ORBITS

SUN

KUIPER BELT

INNER CLOUD

The cloud is in what we call interstellar space.

The cloud's outer edge is where the gravitational influence of the sun ends.

Distance from the sun

It is hard to imagine how far Earth is from the sun, and how much bigger the sun is than Earth. If Earth were a peppercorn, the sun would be the size of a bowling ball—100 times bigger.

Kuiper Belt

The Solar System does not end beyond Neptune: the Kuiper Belt (30–55 AU from the sun) is home to smaller bodies that include dwarf planets.

Neptune
Astronomers predicted the existence of the blue planet by its effect on the orbit of Uranus.

Uranus
The icy blue giant rotates on its side as it orbits the sun. Winter on the planet lasts 42 years.

Saturn
The second largest planet, Saturn has 62 moons and is circled by sparkling fragments of ice that form its rings.

Jupiter
More massive than the other planets combined, Jupiter rotates once every 10 hours, whipping its red clouds into stripes and swirling storms.

Comets

These icy bodies develop spectacular tails of gas and dust as they near the sun.

Orbits

The orbits of the planets and most asteroids around the sun are aligned. Comets, though, can orbit at any angle.

Orbiting planets

There are eight planets in the solar system. They form two distinct groups. The inner planets—Mercury, Venus, Earth, and Mars—are solid balls of rock and metal. The outer planets—Jupiter, Saturn, Uranus, and Neptune— are gas giants: enormous, swirling globes made mostly of hydrogen and helium.

The Solar System

The solar system is a huge disk of material, with the sun at its center, that stretches out over 19 billion miles (30 billion km) to where interstellar space begins.

Most of the solar system is empty space, but scattered throughout are countless solid objects bound to the sun by gravity and orbiting around it. These include the eight planets, hundreds of moons and dwarf planets, millions of asteroids, and possibly billions of comets. The sun itself makes up 99.8 percent of the mass of the solar system.

SUN MERCURY VENUS EARTH MARS

JUPITER

SATURN

Earth is 92.9 million miles (149.6 million km) from the sun—or one astronomical unit (AU).

Jupiter is 484 million miles (780 million km) from the sun, which is equal to 5.2 AU.

Saturn orbits on average 890 million miles (1.43 billion km) from the sun, or 9.58 AU.

There are five known dwarf planets:
Ceres, Pluto, Makemake, Eris, and Haumea.

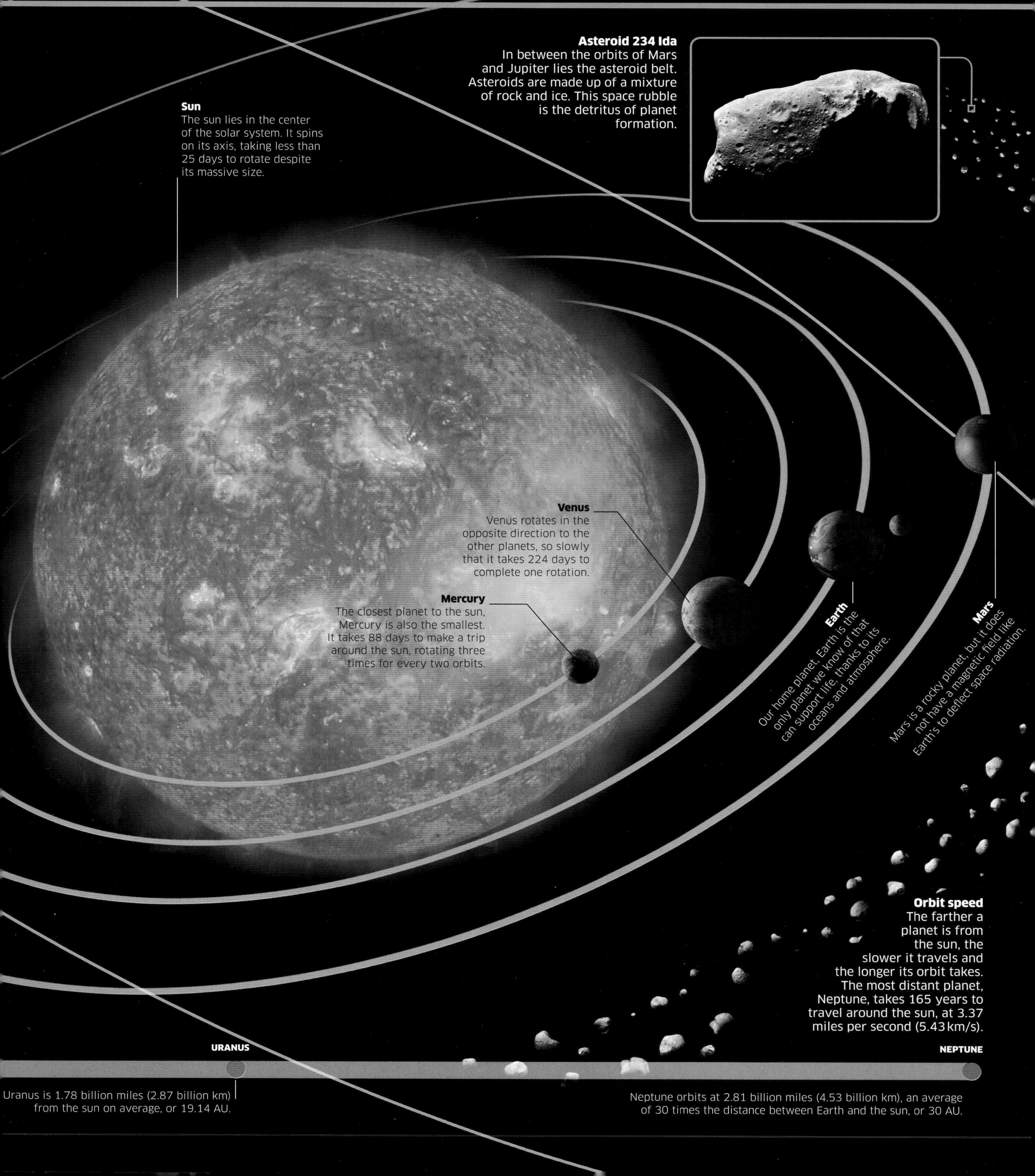

Asteroid 234 Ida
In between the orbits of Mars and Jupiter lies the asteroid belt. Asteroids are made up of a mixture of rock and ice. This space rubble is the detritus of planet formation.

Sun
The sun lies in the center of the solar system. It spins on its axis, taking less than 25 days to rotate despite its massive size.

Venus
Venus rotates in the opposite direction to the other planets, so slowly that it takes 224 days to complete one rotation.

Mercury
The closest planet to the sun, Mercury is also the smallest. It takes 88 days to make a trip around the sun, rotating three times for every two orbits.

Earth
Our home planet, Earth is the only planet we know of that can support life, thanks to its oceans and atmosphere.

Mars
Mars is a rocky planet, but it does not have a magnetic field like Earth's to deflect space radiation.

Orbit speed
The farther a planet is from the sun, the slower it travels and the longer its orbit takes. The most distant planet, Neptune, takes 165 years to travel around the sun, at 3.37 miles per second (5.43 km/s).

URANUS

NEPTUNE

Uranus is 1.78 billion miles (2.87 billion km) from the sun on average, or 19.14 AU.

Neptune orbits at 2.81 billion miles (4.53 billion km), an average of 30 times the distance between Earth and the sun, or 30 AU.

122 energy and forces ○ **EARTH AND MOON**

Earth's **rotation** is getting **slower** by **17 milliseconds every 100 years**.

The seasons

As Earth orbits around the sun, it also rotates around its axis—an imaginary north-south line. This axis is tilted by 23.4° compared to Earth's orbit, so that one part of the planet is always closer to or farther away from the sun, resulting in the seasons.

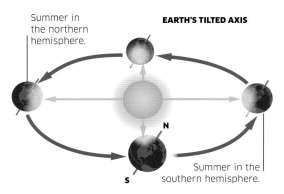

Summer in the northern hemisphere.

EARTH'S TILTED AXIS

N

S

Summer in the southern hemisphere.

Atmosphere

Earth's atmosphere is made up of a mix of gases—78 percent nitrogen, 21 percent oxygen, and a small amount of others, such as carbon dioxide and argon. These gases trap heat on the planet and let us breathe. The atmosphere has five distinct layers.

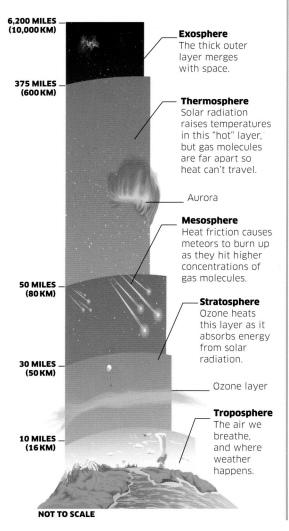

6,200 MILES (10,000 KM)

375 MILES (600 KM)

Exosphere
The thick outer layer merges with space.

Thermosphere
Solar radiation raises temperatures in this "hot" layer, but gas molecules are far apart so heat can't travel.

Aurora

Mesosphere
Heat friction causes meteors to burn up as they hit higher concentrations of gas molecules.

50 MILES (80 KM)

Stratosphere
Ozone heats this layer as it absorbs energy from solar radiation.

30 MILES (50 KM)

Ozone layer

Troposphere
The air we breathe, and where weather happens.

10 MILES (16 KM)

NOT TO SCALE

Earth and Moon

Our home, Earth, is about 4.5 billion years old. With a diameter of just over 7,500 miles (12,000 km), it orbits the sun every 365.3 days and spins on its axis once every 23.9 hours.

Of all the planets in the universe, ours is the only place life is known to exist. Earth is one of the solar system's four rocky planets, and the third from the sun. Its atmosphere, surface water, and magnetic field—which protects us from solar radiation—make Earth the perfect place to live.

Inside Earth

Earth is made up of rocky layers. The outer crust floats on a rocky shell called the mantle. Beneath this is the hot, liquid outer core and solid, inner core.

Outer core
The liquid outer layer of the Earth's core is hot. Made of liquid iron and nickel, it is 1,400 miles (2,300 km) thick.

Oceanic crust
The solid outer layer of rocks is the crust. Under the oceans, it is only about 6 miles (10 km) thick, but it is denser than the continental crust.

Continental crust
The continental crust is the land on which we stand. It is much thicker than the oceanic crust—up to 45 miles (70 km) thick—but is less dense.

Sun
The sun's diameter is 109 times Earth's.

Every year, the **moon drifts** 1.48 in (3.78 cm) **further away from Earth**.

Earth's **inner core spins at a different speed** to the rest of the planet.

More than **300,000 impact craters** wider than **0.6 miles (1 km)** cover the **moon's surface**.

123

The moon
Orbiting Earth every 27 days, the moon is a familiar sight in the night sky. The same side of the moon always faces Earth. The dark side of the moon can only be seen from spacecraft.

Inner core
The iron inner core is just over two-thirds of the size of the moon and as hot as the surface of the sun. It is solid because of the immense pressure on it.

Lower mantle
The lower layer of the mantle contains more than half the planet's volume and extends 1,800 miles (2,900 km) below the surface. It is hot and dense.

Upper mantle
The layer extending 255 miles (410 km) below the crust is mostly solid rock, but it moves as hot, molten rock rises to the surface, cools, and then sinks.

Moon
Our only natural satellite, the moon is almost as old as Earth. It is thought it was made when a flying object the size of Mars crashed into our planet, knocking lots of rock into Earth's orbit. This rock eventually clumped together to form our moon. It is the moon's gravitational pull that is responsible for tides.

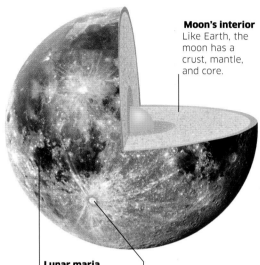

Moon's interior
Like Earth, the moon has a crust, mantle, and core.

Lunar maria
Dark, flat areas known as maria, or seas, are in fact huge plains of solidified lava.

Lunar craters
Craters, formed by asteroid impacts 3.5 billion years ago, pockmark the moon.

Lunar cycle
The moon doesn't produce its own light. The sun illuminates exactly half of the moon, and the amount of the illuminated side we see depends upon where the moon is in its orbit around Earth. This gives rise to the phenomenon known as the phases of the moon.

NEW MOON (0 DAYS)

WAXING CRESCENT

FIRST QUARTER (DAY 7)

WAXING GIBBOUS

FULL MOON (DAY 14)

WANING GIBBOUS

LAST QUARTER (DAY 21)

WANING CRESCENT

NEW MOON (DAY 28)

Earth
Earth's diameter is four times that of the moon, and our planet weighs 80 times more than its satellite.

Earth to sun
The sun is 93 million miles (150 million km) from Earth. It takes light 8 minutes to travel this distance, known as one astronomical unit (AU).

Moon
The moon is 239,000 miles (384,000 km) from Earth.

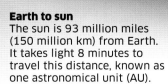

124 energy and forces ○ **TECTONIC EARTH**

34 miles (55 km)—the average width of the 1,850-mile (3,000-km) long East African Rift System of active faults.

Tectonic Earth

Earth's surface is a layer of solid rock split into huge slabs called tectonic plates, which slowly shift, altering landscapes and causing earthquakes and volcanoes.

The tectonic plates are made up of Earth's brittle crust fused to the top layer of the underlying mantle, forming a shell-like elastic structure called the lithosphere. Plate movement is driven by convection currents in the lower, viscous layers of the mantle—known as the asthenosphere—when hot, molten rock rises to the surface and cooler, more solid rock sinks. Most tectonic activity happens near the edges of plates, as they move apart from, toward, or past each other.

Plates move at between ¼ in (7 mm) per year, one-fifth **the rate human fingernails grow,** and 6 in (150 mm) per year—the rate human hair grows.

Continental drift

Over millions of years, continents carried by different plates have collided to make mountains, combined to form supercontinents, or split up in a process called rifting. South America's east coast and Africa's west coast fit like pieces of a jigsaw puzzle. Similar rock and life forms suggest that the two continents were once a supercontinent.

PANGAEA

270 MILLION YEARS AGO

LAURASIA

GONDWANA

180 MILLION YEARS AGO

NORTH AMERICA

AFRICA

SOUTH AMERICA

66 MILLION YEARS AGO

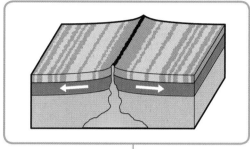

Divergent boundary
As two plates move apart, magma welling up from the mantle fills the gap and creates new plate. Linked with volcanic activity, divergent boundaries form mid-ocean spreading ridges under the sea.

Plate tectonics
Where plates meet, landscape-changing events, such as island formation, rifting (separation), mountain-building, volcanic activity, and earthquakes take place. Plate boundaries fall into three main classes: divergent, convergent, and transform.

Island arc
A series of underwater volcanoes forms a chain of islands, or an archipelago.

Ocean trench
Two ocean plates subduct to form a deep-sea trench.

Mid-ocean ridge
Magma wells up as plates move apart, forming a ridge on the ocean floor.

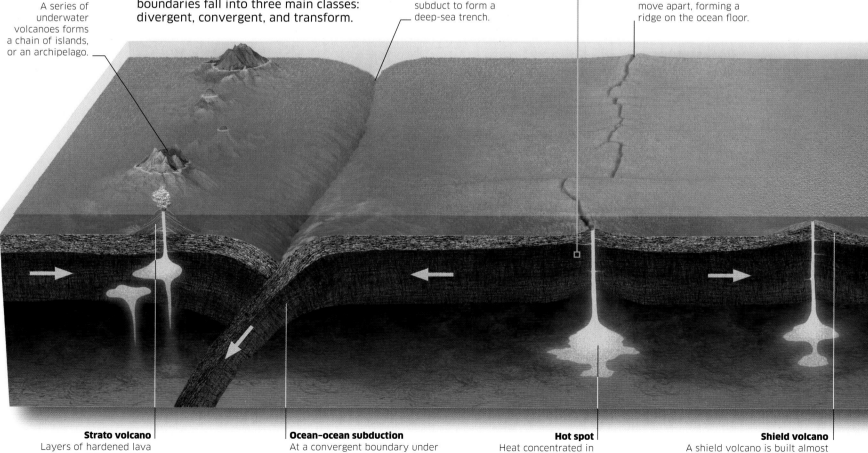

Strato volcano
Layers of hardened lava and ash build up, making these volcanoes steeper than shield volcanoes.

Ocean–ocean subduction
At a convergent boundary under the sea, one oceanic plate slides under the other, creating a mid-ocean trench.

Hot spot
Heat concentrated in some areas of the mantle can erupt as molten magma.

Shield volcano
A shield volcano is built almost entirely of very fluid lava flows, making it quite shallow in shape.

4 billion years old–the age of the oldest parts of Earth's crust.

9.5 The magnitude of the **largest recorded earthquake** in the world, **in Chile on May 22, 1960.**

452 The number of **volcanoes** around the **Pacific Ring of Fire.**

125

Tectonic plates

There are seven large plates and numerous medium-sized and smaller plates, which roughly coincide with the continents and oceans. The Ring of Fire is a zone of earthquakes and volcanoes around the Pacific plate from California in the northeast to Japan and New Zealand in the southwest.

——— CONVERGENT
——— DIVERGENT
——— TRANSFORM
- - - - - UNCERTAIN

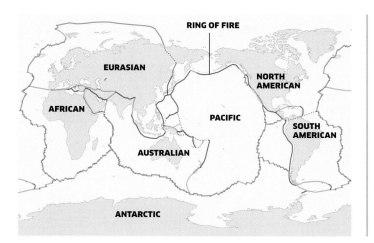

Colliding continents

When continents collide, layers of rock are pushed up into mountain ranges. Continental convergence between the Indian subcontinent and Eurasian landmass formed the Himalayas.

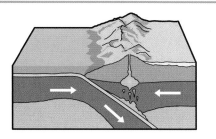

Convergent boundary
As two plates move toward each other, one plate moves down, or subducts, under the other and is destroyed. A deep-sea trench or chain of volcanoes may form, and earthquakes often occur.

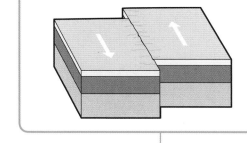

Transform boundary
When plate edges scrape past each other, earthquakes are frequent. The San Andreas fault in California is a famous example.

Sliding plates
Plates sliding past each other may make earthquakes happen.

Volcanic ranges
A chain of volcanoes develops on the side of the plate that is not subducting.

Rift valley
A valley appears where two plates move apart, or rift.

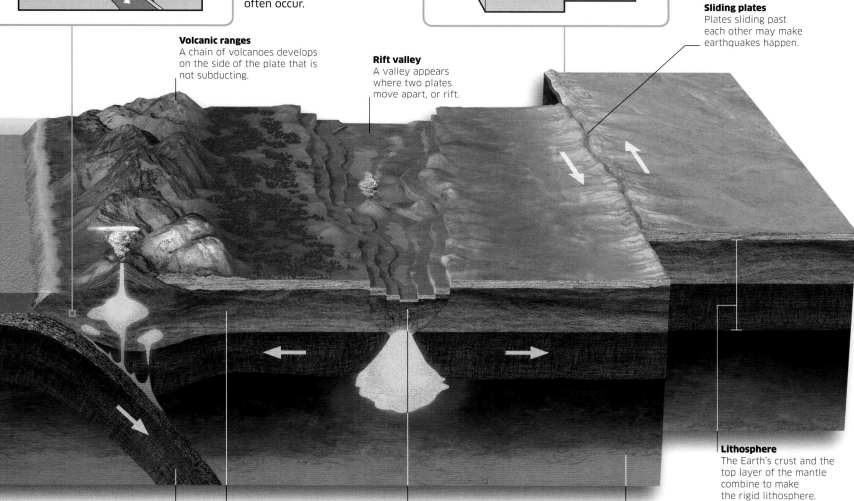

Lithosphere
The Earth's crust and the top layer of the mantle combine to make the rigid lithosphere.

Oceanic-continental subduction
A thinner oceanic plate slides under the thicker continental plate at this boundary.

Continental crust
The Earth's crust is thicker and less dense on land than under the oceans.

Continental rift
When two continental plates move apart, they create a rift—as in East Africa's Rift Valley. Magma rises up through the gap, leading to volcanic activity.

Asthenosphere
Temperature and pressure combine to make the rock in this layer semi-molten.

Storm clouds

Dense, dark clouds gathering overhead mean stormy weather is on the way. Thunderstorms have terrifying power but also an awesome beauty.

Our weather is created by changes in the atmosphere. When air turns cold, it sinks, becoming compressed under its own weight and causing high pressure at Earth's surface. As the air molecules squeeze together, they heat up. The warm air rises, surface pressure drops, and fair weather may follow. But when rapidly rising warm air meets descending cold air, the atmosphere becomes unsettled. Water vapor in the air turns into clouds, the clouds collide, and electric energy builds up. The electricity is released in lightning bolts that strike Earth's surface with cracks of thunder, often accompanied by heavy rainfall.

Supercell storms

One of the most dangerous weather conditions is the supercell storm, when a huge mass of cloud develops a rotating updraft of air, called a mesocyclone, at its center. The cloud cover may stretch from horizon to horizon. Above this, unseen from the ground, a cloud formation known as cumulonimbus towers like a monstrous, flat-topped mushroom into the upper atmosphere. A supercell storm system can rage for many hours, producing destructive winds, torrential rain, and giant hailstones.

MESOCYCLONE

Cumulonimbus
All thunderstorms arise from a type of dense cloud known as a cumulonimbus. In a supercell, this can reach more than 6 miles (10 km) high.

Cold air falls.

REAR FLANK DOWNDRAFT

FORWARD FLANK DOWNDRAFT

WIND

Mesocyclone
Warm air rotates as it rises upward.

Flanking line
A trail of cumulonimbus cloud may develop behind the main supercell.

Cloud base
The base of the supercell forms a dense ceiling that obscures the higher cloud masses from observers on the ground.

Wall cloud
A swirling wall cloud may drop down from the main cloud base—an impressive feature when seen from the ground.

Tornado
The twisting dark funnel of a tornado may descend from the storm cloud.

Lightning discharge from negative cloud to positive ground.

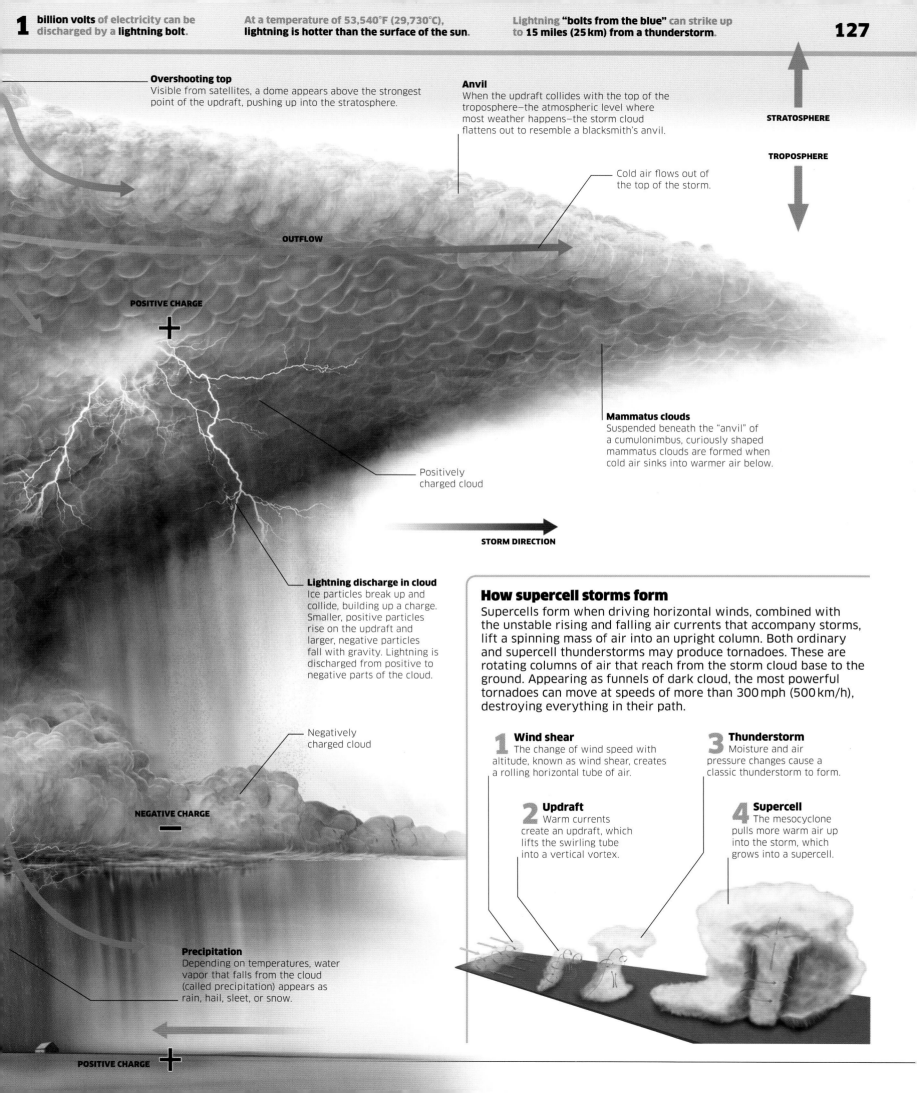

1 billion volts of electricity can be discharged by a lightning bolt.

At a temperature of 53,540°F (29,730°C), lightning is hotter than the surface of the sun.

Lightning "bolts from the blue" can strike up to 15 miles (25 km) from a thunderstorm.

127

Overshooting top
Visible from satellites, a dome appears above the strongest point of the updraft, pushing up into the stratosphere.

Anvil
When the updraft collides with the top of the troposphere—the atmospheric level where most weather happens—the storm cloud flattens out to resemble a blacksmith's anvil.

STRATOSPHERE

TROPOSPHERE

Cold air flows out of the top of the storm.

OUTFLOW

POSITIVE CHARGE

+

Positively charged cloud

Mammatus clouds
Suspended beneath the "anvil" of a cumulonimbus, curiously shaped mammatus clouds are formed when cold air sinks into warmer air below.

STORM DIRECTION

Lightning discharge in cloud
Ice particles break up and collide, building up a charge. Smaller, positive particles rise on the updraft and larger, negative particles fall with gravity. Lightning is discharged from positive to negative parts of the cloud.

How supercell storms form
Supercells form when driving horizontal winds, combined with the unstable rising and falling air currents that accompany storms, lift a spinning mass of air into an upright column. Both ordinary and supercell thunderstorms may produce tornadoes. These are rotating columns of air that reach from the storm cloud base to the ground. Appearing as funnels of dark cloud, the most powerful tornadoes can move at speeds of more than 300 mph (500 km/h), destroying everything in their path.

Negatively charged cloud

1 Wind shear
The change of wind speed with altitude, known as wind shear, creates a rolling horizontal tube of air.

3 Thunderstorm
Moisture and air pressure changes cause a classic thunderstorm to form.

2 Updraft
Warm currents create an updraft, which lifts the swirling tube into a vertical vortex.

4 Supercell
The mesocyclone pulls more warm air up into the storm, which grows into a supercell.

NEGATIVE CHARGE
—

Precipitation
Depending on temperatures, water vapor that falls from the cloud (called precipitation) appears as rain, hail, sleet, or snow.

POSITIVE CHARGE
+

Climate change

For the last half century, Earth's climate has been getting steadily warmer. The world's climate has always varied naturally, but the evidence suggests that this warming is caused by human activity— and it could have a huge impact on our lives.

Humans make the world warmer mainly by burning fossil fuels such as coal and oil, which fill the air with carbon dioxide that traps the sun's heat. This is often referred to as global warming, but scientists prefer to talk about climate change because the unpredictable effects include fueling extreme weather. In future, we can expect more powerful storms and flooding as well as hotter summers and droughts.

Greenhouse effect

The cause of global warning is the greenhouse effect. In the atmosphere, certain gases—known as greenhouse gases—absorb heat radiation that would otherwise escape into space. This causes our planet to be warmer than it would be if it had no atmosphere. The main greenhouses gases are carbon dioxide, methane, nitrous oxide, and water vapor.

2 Reflection
Almost a third of the energy in sunlight is reflected back into space as UV and visible light.

Transportation
Gasoline- and diesel- guzzling trucks and cars, as well as fuel-burning airplanes, produce around 15 percent of greenhouse gases.

Farming and deforestation
Intensively farmed cows, sheep, and goats release huge amounts of methane, a greenhouse gas. Forests absorb carbon dioxide, so deforestation leaves more carbon dioxide in the atmosphere.

1 Light from the sun
The sunlight that passes through the atmosphere is a mixture of types of radiation: ultraviolet (UV—short wave), visible light (medium wave), and infrared (long wave).

Industry
Heavy industry burning fossil fuels for energy adds about 13 percent of global greenhouse gas emissions.

Power stations
Burning coal, natural gas, and oil to generate electricity accounts for more than 30 percent of all polluting carbon dioxide.

3 Absorption
The remaining energy in sunlight is absorbed by the Earth's surface, converted into heat, and emitted into the atmosphere as long-wave, infrared radiation.

26 ft (8 m)—the amount **sea levels** would **rise** if the **polar ice sheets melted**.

50 percent—the **increase** in the amount of **carbon dioxide** in the air **since 1980**.

129

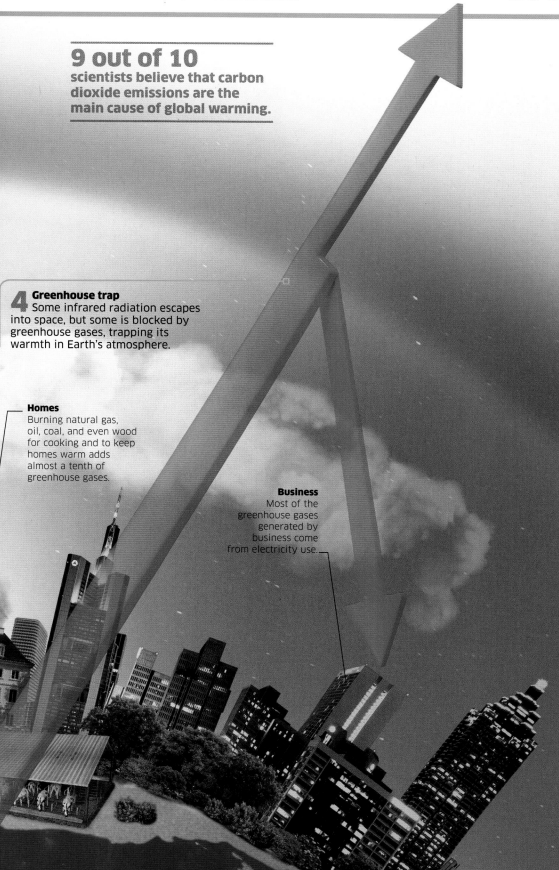

9 out of 10
scientists believe that carbon dioxide emissions are the main cause of global warming.

4 Greenhouse trap
Some infrared radiation escapes into space, but some is blocked by greenhouse gases, trapping its warmth in Earth's atmosphere.

Homes
Burning natural gas, oil, coal, and even wood for cooking and to keep homes warm adds almost a tenth of greenhouse gases.

Business
Most of the greenhouse gases generated by business come from electricity use.

Melting ice caps
Arctic sea ice is melting and the Antarctic ice sheet and mountain glaciers are shrinking fast as the world warms. Melting land ice combined with the expansion of seawater as it warms are raising sea levels. Sea warmth is also adding extra energy into the air, driving storms.

Disappearing ice
The extent of Arctic and Antarctic sea ice shrank to record lows in 2017.

CLIMATE-RELATED DISASTERS
SUCH AS FLOODS, STORMS, AND OTHER **EXTREME WEATHER EVENTS HAVE INCREASED** THREE TIMES SINCE 1980.

Ocean acidification
Carbon dioxide emissions not only contribute to the greenhouse effect. The gas dissolves in the oceans, making them more acidic. Increasing the acidity of seawater can have a devastating effect on fragile creatures that live in it. It has already caused widespread coral "bleaching," and reefs are dwindling.

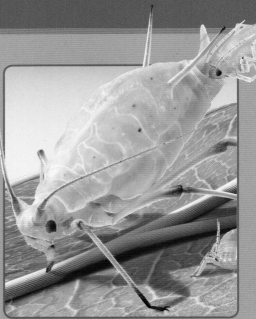

LIFE

There is nothing more complex in the entire universe than living things. Life comes in an extraordinarily diverse range of forms–from microscopic bacteria to giant plants and animals. Each organism has specialized ways of keeping its body working, and of interacting with its environment.

1977

Modern times
In the most recent biological developments, things that were thought to be impossible just a hundred years ago became routine. Faulty body parts could be replaced with artificial replicas and even genes could be changed to switch characteristics.

New worlds
American scientists discover deep-sea animals supported by the chemical energy of volcanic vents— the only life not dependent on the sun and photosynthesis.

1978-1996

New life
The first human "test tube" baby—made with cells fertilized outside the human body—is born in 1978. Then, in 1996, Dolly the sheep becomes the first mammal to be artificially cloned from body cells.

DOLLY THE SHEEP

MODERN TIMES

1960s

Animal behavior
More biologists begin studying the behavior of wild animals. In the 1960s, British biologist Jane Goodall discovers that chimpanzees use tools.

1953

The structure of DNA
American and British scientists James Watson and Francis Crick identify that DNA (the genetic code of life packed into cells) has a double helix shape.

1 9 0 0 - 1 9 7 0

Discovering life

Ever since people first began to observe the natural world around them, they have been making discoveries about life and living things.

Biology—the scientific study of life—emerged in the ancient world when philosophers studied the diversity of life's creatures, and medical experts of the day dissected bodies to see how they worked. Hundreds of years later, the invention of the microscope opened up the world of cells and microbes, and allowed scientists to understand the workings of life at the most basic level. At the same time, new insights helped biologists answer some of the biggest questions of all: the cause of disease, and how life reproduces.

1800s

1856-1865

Inheritance
An Austrian-born monk called Gregor Mendel, carries out breeding experiments with pea plants that help to explain the inheritance of characteristics.

Anesthetics and antiseptics
The biggest steps in surgery happen in the 1800s: anesthetics are used to numb pain, while British surgeon Joseph Lister uses antiseptics to reduce infection.

19th century
The next hundred years saw some of the most important discoveries in biology. Some helped medicine become safer and more effective. Others explained the inheritance of characteristics and the evolution of life.

19TH CENTURY

Timeline of discoveries
More than 2,000 years of study and experiment has brought biology into the modern age. While ancient thinkers began by observing the plants and animals around them, scientists today can alter the very structure of life itself.

Antiquity to 16th century
Ancient civilizations in Europe and Asia were the birthplace of science. Here the biologists of the day described the anatomy (structure) of animals and plants and used their knowledge to invent ways to treat illness.

Describing fossils
Many ancient peoples discover fossils. In 500 BCE, Xenophanes, a Greek philosopher, proposes that they are the remains of animals from ancient seas that once covered the land.

LEECHES

Healing theories
Early medical doctors believe that illness is caused by an imbalance of bodily fluids, called humors, that can be treated with blood-sucking leeches.

Early anatomy
Human anatomy is scrutinized in detail by cutting open dead bodies. Dissections are even public spectacles—the first public one is carried out in 1315.

B E F O R E 1 6 0 0

The **Greek philosopher Aristotle** produced the **first classification** of animals and **separated vertebrates from invertebrates**.

In 2001, scientists published the results of the **Human Genome Project: a catalog of all human genes**.

133

2015

2010s

2017

Artificial parts
False limbs had been used since antiquity, but the 20th century brings more sophisticated artificial body parts. The first bionic eye is implanted in 2015.

Fossil evidence
More discoveries of ancient creatures, often preserved in amber, lead scientists to new conclusions, such as the realization that many dinosaurs had feathers.

Changing genes
In the late 20th century scientists become able to edit the genes of living things. In 2017, some mosquitoes are genetically altered to try and stop the spread of the disease malaria.

1970–PRESENT

1930s

1928

1900s

The rise of ecology
The study of ecology (how organisms interact with their surroundings) emerges in the 1930s, as British botanist Arthur Tansley introduces the idea of ecosystems.

Antibiotics discovered
British biologist Alexander Fleming discovers that a substance–penicillin, the first known antibiotic–stops the growth of microbes. Antibiotics are now used to treat many bacterial infections.

Chromosomes and genes
American scientist Thomas Hunt Morgan carries out experiments on fruit flies, which prove that the units of inheritance are carried as genes on chromosomes.

Early 20th century
Better microscopes and advances in studying the chemical makeup of cells helped to show how all life carries a set of building instructions–in the form of chromosomes and DNA–while ecology and behavior became new topics of focus.

1859

1860s

Evolution
British biologist Charles Darwin publishes a book–*On the Origin of Species*–explaining how life on Earth has evolved by natural selection.

CHARLES DARWIN

Microbes
An experiment by the French biologist Louis Pasteur proves microbes are sources of infection. It also disproves a popular theory which had argued that living organisms could be spontaneously generated from nonliving matter.

MICROBE

20TH CENTURY ▶

1800–1900

1796

1770s

1735

Classifying life VAN LEEUWENHOEK'S MICROSCOPE
Swedish botanist Carl Linnaeus devises a way of classifying and naming plants and animals that is still used today.

1665

Vaccines invented
A breakthrough in medicine, the first vaccine is used by British doctor Edward Jenner to protect against a deadly disease–smallpox.

Photosynthesis discovered
In the 1770s, the experiments of a Dutch biologist, Jan Ingenhousz, show that plants need light, water, and carbon dioxide to make sugar.

Microscopic life
British scientist Robert Hooke views cells down a microscope and inspires a Dutchman, Antony van Leeuwenhoek, to invent his own unique version of a microscope.

1600–1800

1628

Cataloging life
The ancient Greeks are the first to try classifying life, but it is not until the 16th century that species are first cataloged in large volumes.

17th–18th centuries
New scientific experiments added to the wealth of knowledge laid down by the first philosophers. This research helped to answer important questions about life's vital processes, such as blood circulation in animals and photosynthesis in plants.

Blood circulation
A British doctor called William Harvey combines observation with experiment to show how the heart pumps blood around the body.

17TH CENTURY ▶

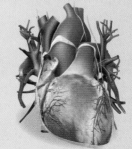

WHAT IS LIFE?

Life can be defined as a combination of seven main actions—known as the characteristics of life—that set living things apart from nonliving things. However big or small, every organism must process food, release energy, and excrete its waste. All will also, to some degree, gather information from their surroundings, move, grow, and reproduce.

Life on a leaf
The characteristics of life can all be seen in action on a thumbnail-sized patch of leaf. Tiny insects, called aphids, suck on the leaf's sap and give birth to the next generation, while leaf cells beneath the aphids' feet generate the sap's sugar.

Sensitivity
Sense organs detect changes in an organism's surroundings, such as differences in light or temperature. Each kind of change—called a stimulus—is picked up by them. With this information, the body can coordinate a suitable response.

Segments near the end of the aphid's antenna contain sense organs.

Antenna
Aphid antennae carry different kinds of sensors, including some that detect odors indicating a leaf is edible.

Nutrition
Food is either consumed or made. Animals, fungi, and many single-celled organisms take food into their body from their surroundings. Plants and algae make food inside their cells, by using light energy from the sun to convert carbon dioxide and water into sugars and other nutrients.

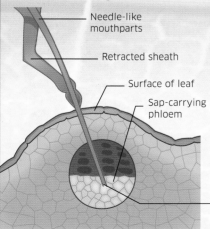

Needle-like mouthparts

Retracted sheath

Surface of leaf

Sap-carrying phloem

Pressure in the leaf's vein forces sap up through the proboscis of the aphid.

Proboscis
Like most other animals, aphids pass food through a digestive system, from which nutrients move into the body's cells. Aphids can only drink liquid sap. They use a sharp proboscis that works like a needle to puncture a leaf vein to get sap.

Movement
Plants are rooted in the ground, but can still move their parts in response to their surroundings—for instance, to move toward a light source. Animals can move their body parts much faster by using muscles, which can even carry their entire body from place to place.

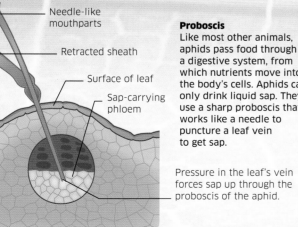

Muscles contract.

Sap is drawn up into the digestive system.

Head muscles
Muscles are found all over an aphid's body. As the aphid eats, muscles in its head contract (shorten) to pull and widen its feeding tube. This allows it to consume the sap more effectively.

Birth
A female aphid gives birth to live young.

Reproduction
By producing offspring, organisms ensure that their populations survive, as new babies replace the individuals that die. Breeding for most kinds of organisms involves two parents reproducing sexually by producing sex cells. But some organisms can breed asexually from just one parent.

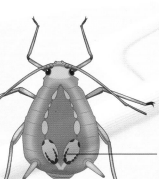

Babies in babies
Some female aphids carry out a form of asexual reproduction where babies develop from unfertilized eggs inside the mother's body. A further generation of babies can develop inside the unborn aphids.

The daughters that are old enough to be born already contain the aphid's granddaughters.

Respiration
Organisms need energy to power their vital functions, such as growth and movement. A chemical process happens inside their cells to release energy, called respiration. It breaks down certain kinds of foods, such as sugar. Most organisms take in oxygen from the environment to use in their respiration.

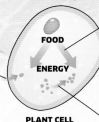

Some energy is used to move materials around, including into and out of cells.

Energy is released from food.

FOOD
ENERGY
PLANT CELL

Some energy is used to build materials inside the cell to help the body grow.

Excretion
Hundreds of chemical reactions happen inside living cells, and many of these reactions produce waste substances that would cause harm if they built up. Excretion is the way an organism gets rid of this waste. Animals have excretory organs, such as kidneys, to remove waste, but plants use their leaves for excretion.

Excretion by leaf
Plant leaves have pores, called stomata, for releasing waste gases, such as oxygen and carbon dioxide.

Growth
All organisms get bigger as they get older and grow. Single cells grow very slightly and stay microscopic, but many organisms, such as animals and plants, have bodies made up of many interacting cells. As they grow, these cells divide to produce more cells, making the body bigger.

Molting
The body of an aphid is covered in a tough outer skin called an exoskeleton. In order to grow, an aphid must periodically shed this skin so its body can get bigger. Its new skin is initially soft and flexible, but soon toughens.

SEVEN KINGDOMS OF LIFE
Living things are classified into seven main groups called kingdoms. Each kingdom contains a set of organisms that have evolved to perform the characteristics of life in their own way.

Archaea
Looking similar to bacteria, many of these single-celled organisms survive in very extreme environments, such as hot, acidic pools.

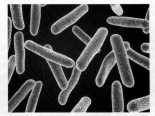

Bacteria
The most abundant organisms on Earth, bacteria are usually single-celled. They either consume food, like animals do, or make it, like plants do.

Algae
Simple relatives of plants, algae make food by photosynthesis. Some are single-celled, but others, such as seaweeds and this *Pandorina*, are multicelled.

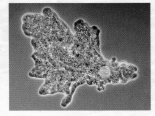

Protozoa
These single-celled organisms are bigger than bacteria. Many of them behave like miniature animals, by eating other microscopic organisms.

Plants
Most plants are anchored to the ground by roots and have leafy shoots to make food by photosynthesis.

Fungi
This kingdom includes toadstools, mushrooms, and yeasts. They absorb food from their surroundings, often by breaking down dead matter.

Animals
From microscopic worms to giant whales, all animals have bodies made up of large numbers of cells and feed by eating or absorbing food.

The fossil record

Fossils from prehistoric times show just how much life has changed across the ages, and how ancient creatures are related to the organisms on Earth today.

Life has been evolving on our planet for more than four billion years—ever since it was just a world of simple microbes. Across this vast expanse of time, more complex animals and plants developed. Traces of their remains—found as fossils in prehistoric rocks—have helped us to work out their ancestry.

EARLIER DINOSAUR ANCESTORS

Like most birds, theropods had feet with three forward-pointing toes, and hollow bones.

170 MILLION YEARS AGO

150 MILLION YEARS AGO

1 Megalosaurus
Theropods, such as *Megalosaurus*, were meat-eating dinosaurs that walked on two legs. Some smaller, feathered theropods were the ancestors of birds.

The origins of birds

Fossilized skeletons show us that the first prehistoric birds were remarkably similar to a group of upright-walking dinosaurs. From these fossils, it is possible to see how their forelimbs evolved into wings for flight, and how they developed the other characteristics of modern birds.

Archaeopteryx fossil
This fossil of *Archaeopteryx* has been preserved in soft limestone. Around the animal's wing bones, the imprints left by the feathers are clearly visible.

How fossils form

Fossils are the remains or impressions of organisms that died more than 10,000 years ago. Some fossils have recorded what is left of entire bodies, but usually only fragments, such as parts of a bony skeleton, have survived.

Skeletons and other hard parts are more likely to leave an impression than soft tissues.

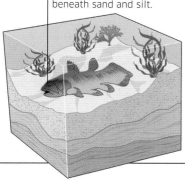

1 Death
Bodies that settled under water or in floodplains could be quickly buried beneath sand and silt.

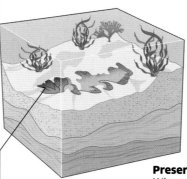

2 Burial
Layers of sediment cover the body and build up into rock on top of it.

3 Reveal
Millions of years later, movements of Earth's crust cause rocks to move upward, exposing the fossil on dry land.

Preserved in time
When organisms in the prehistoric world died, their bodies were more likely to be preserved if they were quickly buried. Rotting under layers of sediment, the body slowly turned into mineral, until the resulting fossil was exposed by erosion.

Over millions of years, groups of organisms split up as they evolve and become adapted to new environments or situations.

4.2 billion years old—the age of the **oldest fossils discovered**. These were tiny microbes in rocks.

On average, **each species survives for about a million years**, before it **becomes extinct or evolves** into something else.

137

Confuciusornis fossil
Lots of preserved *Confuciusornis* specimens have long tail streamers. These are now thought to be exclusive to males and to have been used in displays to attract a mate during breeding season.

Mass extinction

Life in the prehistoric past was occasionally rocked by catastrophic events that wiped out entire groups of organisms. Five mass extinction events have occurred in the last 500 million years. Many may have been caused by climate change and volcanic eruptions, but there is also strong evidence that the event that eliminated the dinosaurs was caused by an asteroid striking the Earth.

Claws on the bird's thumb and third finger may have helped it climb through trees.

2 Archaeopteryx
Thought to be the first true bird, *Archaeopteryx* had feathered wings, but retained dinosaur characteristics, such as clawed forelimbs, a toothed beak, and a bony tail. Its small wing muscles suggest it may not have been able to fly well.

3 Confuciusornis
Thirty million years after *Archaeopteryx*, *Confuciusornis* emerged. It had a tail of feathers that lacked a bony support, and a toothless beak. Its flight feathers were longer than *Archaeopteryx*, but it still could not flap as well as modern birds.

4 Ichthyornis
Living just before the extinction of the dinosaurs, *Ichthyornis* resembled a modern seabird, and was about the size of a gull. Although it had strong flight muscles, its bill still contained sharp teeth that helped it catch fish.

120 MILLION YEARS AGO

90 MILLION YEARS AGO

Ichthyornis had a well-developed breastbone for supporting strong flight muscles.

A mass extinction 66 million years ago drove dinosaurs to extinction, but their bird descendants survived.

PRESENT DAY

5 Ruby-throated hummingbird
A lightweight skeleton and strong muscles help most modern, toothless birds fly with far greater skill than any of their ancestors.

Evolution

All living things are related and united by a process called evolution. Over millions of years, evolution has produced all the species that have ever lived.

Change is a fact of life. Every organism goes through a transformation as it develops and gets older. But over much longer periods of time—millions or billions of years—entire populations of plants, animals, and microbes also change by evolving. All the kinds of organisms alive today have descended from different ones that lived in the past, as tiny variations throughout history have combined to produce entirely new species.

Song thrushes are an important predator of snails, often foraging in bushes and trees to find prey.

The bird smashes a snail on a hard stone to get to the soft body inside.

Natural selection

The characteristics of living things are determined by genes (see pp.180–181), which sometimes change as they are passed down through generations—producing mutations. All the variety in the natural world—such as the colors of snail shells—comes from chance mutations, but not all of the resulting organisms do well in their environments. Only some survive to pass their attributes on to future generations—winning the struggle of natural selection.

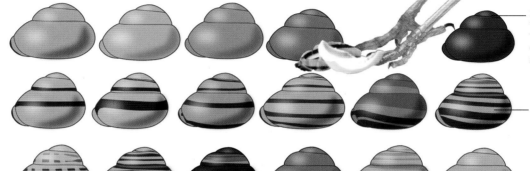

Shells of grove snails vary in color from yellow to dark brown, depending upon the genes they carry.

Some snail genes cause their shells to develop banding patterns.

Dry grassy habitat

Against a background of dry grass, snails with darker shells are most easily spotted, causing the paler ones to survive in greater numbers.

The song thrush hunts by sight, and picks out the most visible snails.

Dark woodland habitat

In woodland, grove snails with shells that match the dark brown leaf litter of the woodland floor are camouflaged and survive, but yellow-shelled snails are spotted by birds.

Brown snails are more likely to survive in woodland, so more will build up in this area over time.

Hedge habitat

In some sun-dappled habitats with a mixture of grass, twigs, and leaves, stripy-shelled grove snails are better disguised, and plain brown or yellow ones become prey.

Stripy shells break up the outline of the snails, so they are not easily seen.

Africa's **Lake Malawi** contains more than **500 species of cichlid fishes** that have **evolved from a single ancestral fish** within the last million years.

50 years is all the time it takes for **some infectious bacteria to evolve resistance** to antibiotic drugs.

139

How new species emerge

Over a long period of evolution, varieties of animals can end up becoming so different that they turn into entirely new species—a process called speciation. This usually happens when groups evolve differences that stop them from breeding outside their group, especially when their surroundings change so dramatically that they become physically separated from others.

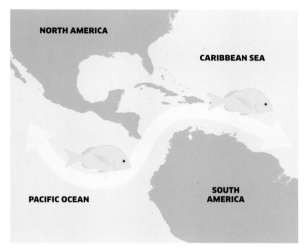

1 Ancestral species
Five million years ago, before North and South America were joined, a broad sea channel swept between the Pacific Ocean in the west and the Caribbean in the east. Marine animals, such as the reef-dwelling porkfish, could easily mix with one another in the open waters. Porkfish from western and eastern populations had similar characteristics and all of them could breed together, so they all belonged to the same species.

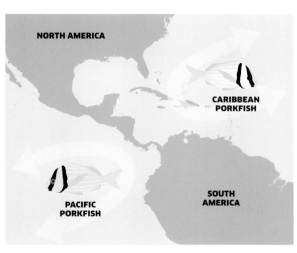

2 Modern species
The shifting of Earth's crust caused North and South America to collide nearly 3 million years ago. This cut off the sea channel, isolating populations of porkfish on either side of Central America. Since then, the two populations have evolved so differently that they can no longer breed with each other. Although they still share a common ancestor, today the whiter Caribbean porkfish and the yellower Pacific porkfish are different species.

Evolution on islands

Isolated islands often play host to the most dramatic evolution of all. Animals and plants can only reach them by crossing vast expanses of water, and—once there—evolve quickly in the new and separate environment. This can lead to some unusual creatures developing—such as flightless birds and giant tortoises.

Out of all the reptiles and land mammals of the Galápagos Islands,
97 percent
are found nowhere else in the world.

Tortoise travels
The famous giant tortoises unique to the Galápagos Islands are descended from smaller tortoises that floated there from nearby South America.

Adaptation

Living things that survive the grueling process of natural selection are left with characteristics that make them best suited to their surroundings. This can be seen in groups of closely related species that live in very different habitats—such as these seven species of bears.

Polar bear
The biggest, most carnivorous species of bear is adapted to the icy Arctic habitat. It lives on fat-rich seal meat and is protected from the bitter cold by a thick fur coat.

Brown bear
The closest relative of the polar bear lives further south in cool forests and grassland. As well as preying on animals, it supplements its diet with berries and shoots.

Black bear
The North American black bear is the most omnivorous species of bear, eating equal amounts of animal and plant matter. This smaller, nimbler bear can climb trees to get food.

Sun bear
The smallest bear lives in tropical Asia and has a thin coat of fur to prevent it from overheating. It has a very sweet tooth and extracts honey from bee hives with its long tongue.

Sloth bear
This shaggy-coated bear from India is adapted to eat insects. It has poorly developed teeth and, instead, relies on long claws and a long lower lip to obtain and eat its prey.

Spectacled bear
The only bear in South America has a short muzzle and teeth adapted for grinding tough plants. It feeds mainly on leaves, tree bark, and fruit, only occasionally eating meat.

Giant panda
The strangest bear of all comes from the cool mountain forests of China. It is almost entirely vegetarian, with paws designed for grasping tough bamboo shoots.

Miniature life

Some organisms are so tiny that thousands of them can live out their lives in a single drop of water.

The minuscule home of the microbe, or microorganism, is a place where sand grains are like giant boulders and the slightest breeze feels like a hurricane. These living things can only be seen through a microscope, but manage to find everything they need to thrive in soil, oceans, or even deep inside the bodies of bigger animals.

GIARDIA
Kingdom: Protozoa

Animal-like microbes that are single-celled are called protozoans. Some, such as amoebas, use extensions of cytoplasm (cell material) to creep along. Others, such as giardia, swim, and absorb their food by living in the intestines of animals.

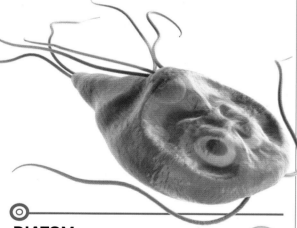

DIATOM
Kingdom: Algae

¹⁄₁₀₀ mm

The biggest algae grow as giant seaweeds, but many, such as diatoms, are microscopic single cells. All make food by photosynthesis, forming the bottom of many underwater food chains that support countless lives.

Diatoms are surrounded by a large cell wall.

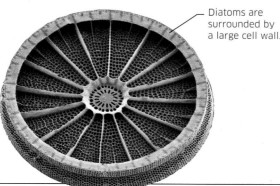

SPIROCHAETE
Kingdom: Bacteria

¹⁄₁₀₀ mm

Any place good for life can be home to bacteria–the most abundant kinds of microorganisms on the planet. They are vital for recycling nutrients, although some–such as the corkscrew-shaped spirochaetes–are parasites that cause disease in humans and other animals.

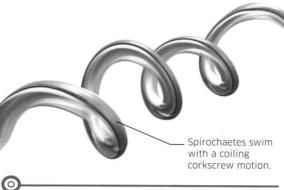

Spirochaetes swim with a coiling corkscrew motion.

PENICILLIUM
Kingdom: Fungi

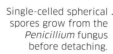

¹⁄₁₀ mm

The microscopic filaments of fungi smother dead material, such as leaf litter, so their digestive juices can break it down. When their food runs out, they scatter dustlike spores, which grow into new fungi.

Single-celled spherical spores grow from the *Penicillium* fungus before detaching.

WATERMEAL
Kingdom: Plants

1 mm

The smallest plant, called watermeal, floats on ponds, blanketing the surface in its millions. A hundred could sit comfortably on a fingertip, each one carrying a tiny flower that allows it to reproduce.

THERMOPLASMA
Kingdom: Archaea

¹⁄₁₀₀₀ mm

These microbes look like bacteria, but are a distinct life form. Many, like the *Thermoplasma volcanium*, live in the most hostile habitats imaginable, such as hot pools of concentrated acid.

Like bacteria, archaea have no cell nucleus and are protected by a tough cell wall.

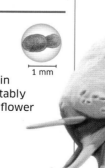
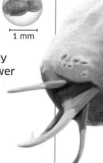

The number of **bacteria in your mouth** is greater than **the number of people on Earth**.

Single-celled microbes were the first life on Earth—4 billion years ago.

141

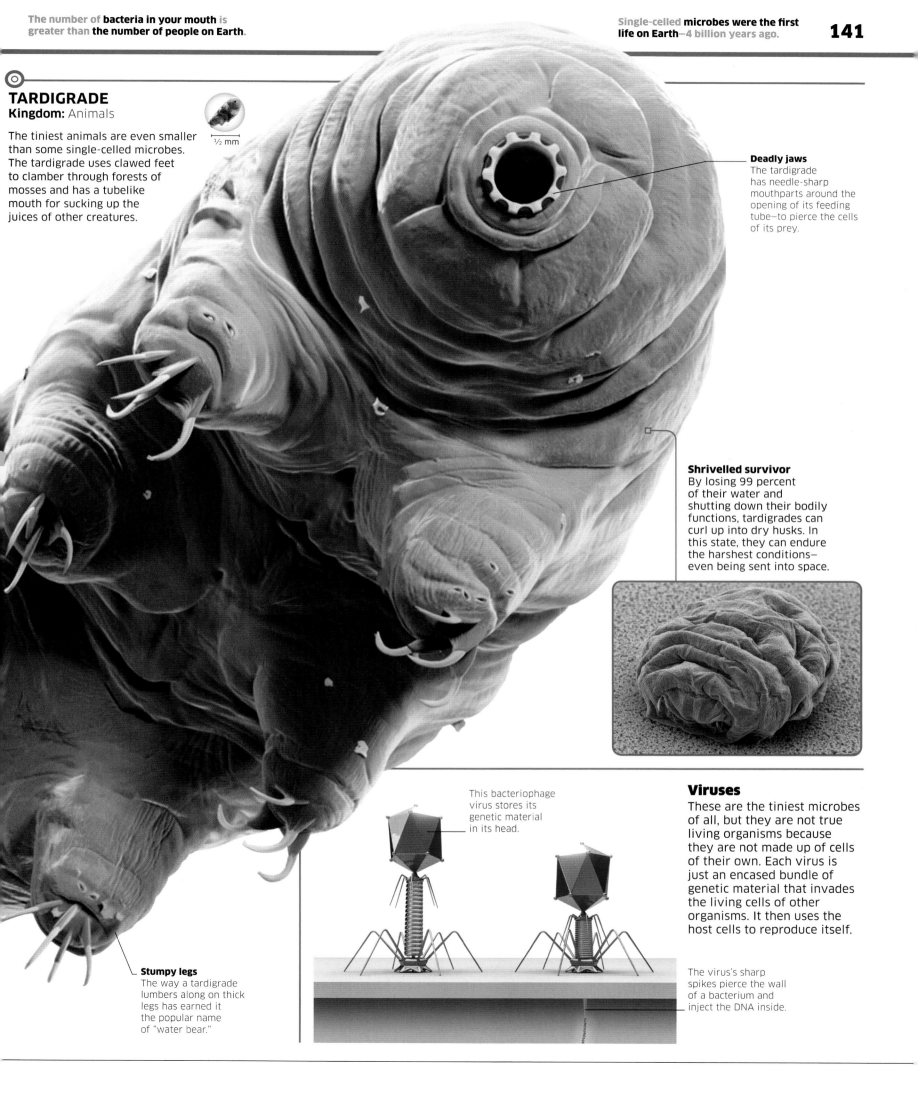

TARDIGRADE
Kingdom: Animals

The tiniest animals are even smaller than some single-celled microbes. The tardigrade uses clawed feet to clamber through forests of mosses and has a tubelike mouth for sucking up the juices of other creatures.

½ mm

Deadly jaws
The tardigrade has needle-sharp mouthparts around the opening of its feeding tube—to pierce the cells of its prey.

Shrivelled survivor
By losing 99 percent of their water and shutting down their bodily functions, tardigrades can curl up into dry husks. In this state, they can endure the harshest conditions—even being sent into space.

This bacteriophage virus stores its genetic material in its head.

Viruses
These are the tiniest microbes of all, but they are not true living organisms because they are not made up of cells of their own. Each virus is just an encased bundle of genetic material that invades the living cells of other organisms. It then uses the host cells to reproduce itself.

The virus's sharp spikes pierce the wall of a bacterium and inject the DNA inside.

Stumpy legs
The way a tardigrade lumbers along on thick legs has earned it the popular name of "water bear."

Cells

The living building blocks of animals and plants, cells are the smallest units of life. Even at this microscopic level, each one contains many complex and specialized parts.

Cells need to be complex to perform all the jobs needed for life. They process food, release energy, respond to their surroundings, and—within their minuscule limits—build materials to grow. In different parts of the body, many cells are highly specialized. Cells in the muscles of animals can twitch to move limbs and those in blood are ready to fight infection.

Centriole
Structural proteins called microtubules are assembled around a cylindrical arrangement known as a centriole.

Golgi apparatus
The Golgi apparatus packages proteins and sends them to where they are needed.

Cytoplasm
The jellylike cytoplasm holds all the cell's parts—known as organelles.

Cell membrane
A thin, oily layer controls the movement of substances into and out of the cell.

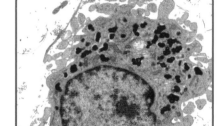

Nucleus
The nucleus (dark purple) controls the activity of the cell. It is packed with DNA (deoxyribonucleic acid)—the cell's genetic material.

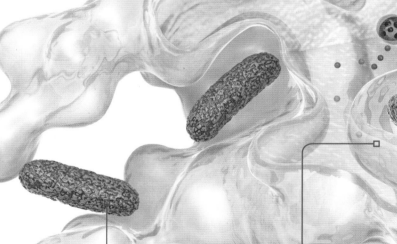

Pseudopodium
One of many fingerlike extensions of cytoplasm helps this kind of cell to engulf bacteria.

1 Bacterium approaches
Bacterial cells are 100 times smaller than blood cells, but potentially cause disease. It is a white blood cell's job to prevent them from invading the body.

2 Food vacuole forms
The blood cell envelops bacteria within its cytoplasm, trapping them in fluid-filled sacs called food vacuoles.

3 Digestion begins
Tiny bags of digestive fluid—called lysosomes—fuse with the food vacuole and empty their contents onto the entrapped bacteria.

Cells eating cells

A white blood cell is one of the busiest cells in a human body, part of a miniature army that destroys potentially harmful bacteria. Many white blood cells do this by changing shape to swallow invading cells: they extend fingers of cytoplasm that sweep bacteria into sacs for digestion.

Bacteria cells look different from those of plants and animals:
they **do not contain a nucleus**, mitochondria, or chloroplasts.

143

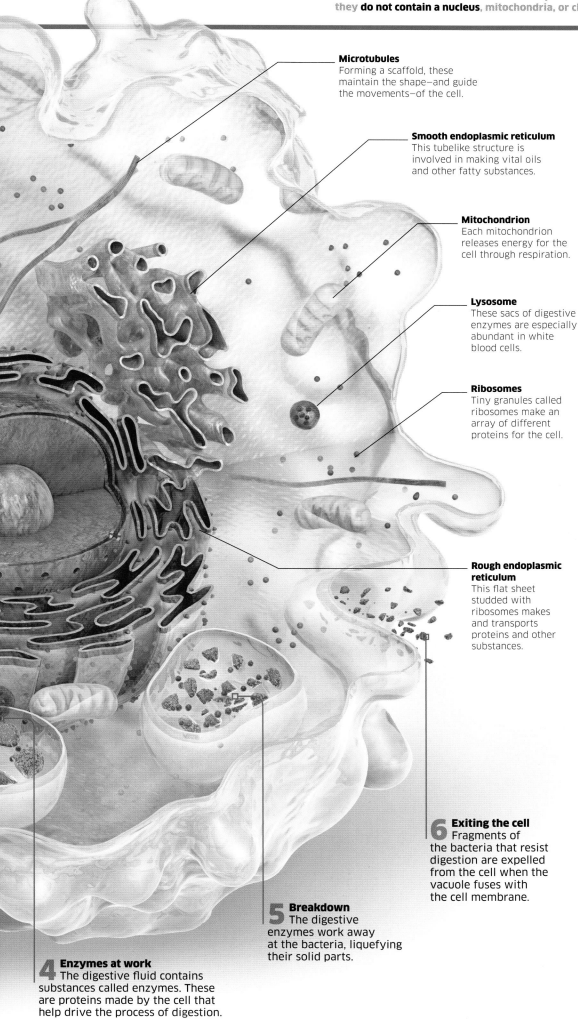

Microtubules
Forming a scaffold, these maintain the shape—and guide the movements—of the cell.

Smooth endoplasmic reticulum
This tubelike structure is involved in making vital oils and other fatty substances.

Mitochondrion
Each mitochondrion releases energy for the cell through respiration.

Lysosome
These sacs of digestive enzymes are especially abundant in white blood cells.

Ribosomes
Tiny granules called ribosomes make an array of different proteins for the cell.

Rough endoplasmic reticulum
This flat sheet studded with ribosomes makes and transports proteins and other substances.

6 Exiting the cell
Fragments of the bacteria that resist digestion are expelled from the cell when the vacuole fuses with the cell membrane.

5 Breakdown
The digestive enzymes work away at the bacteria, liquefying their solid parts.

4 Enzymes at work
The digestive fluid contains substances called enzymes. These are proteins made by the cell that help drive the process of digestion.

Enzymes

Cells make complex molecules called proteins, many of which work as enzymes. Enzymes are catalysts—substances that increase the rate of chemical reactions and can be used again and again. Each type of reaction needs a specific kind of enzyme.

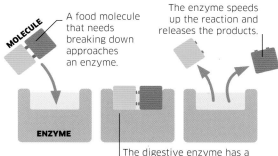

MOLECULE

A food molecule that needs breaking down approaches an enzyme.

The enzyme speeds up the reaction and releases the products.

ENZYME

The digestive enzyme has a specific shape that "locks" onto the food molecule.

Cell variety

Unlike animal cells, plant cells are ringed by a tough cell wall and many have food-making chloroplasts. Both animals and plants have many specialised cells for different tasks.

ANIMAL CELLS

Fat cell
Its large droplet of stored fat provides energy when needed.

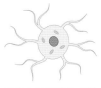

Bone-making cell
Long strands of cytoplasm help this cell connect to others.

Ciliated cell
Hairlike cilia waft particles away from airways.

Secretory cell
These cells release useful substances, such as hormones.

PLANT CELLS

Starch-storing cell
Some root cells store many granules of energy-rich starch.

Leaf cell
Inside this cell, green chloroplasts make food for the plant.

Supporting cell
Thick-walled cells in the stem help support plants.

Fruit cell
Its large sap-filled vacuole helps to make a fruit juicy.

3.3 lb (1.5 kg)—the **weight of the liver**, which is the **largest internal organ** in the human body.

Skeletal system
Some of the hardest parts of the body make up the skeleton. Bone contains living cells but is also packed with hard minerals. This helps it support the stresses and strains of the moving body, and to protect soft organs, too.

Circulatory system
No living cell is very far from a blood vessel. The circulatory system serves as a lifeline to every cell. It circulates food, oxygen, and chemical triggers—such as hormones—as well as transporting waste to the excretory organs.

Digestive system
By processing incoming food, the digestive system is the source of fuel and nourishment for the entire body. It breaks down food to release nutrients, which then seep into the bloodstream to be circulated to all living cells.

Muscular system
The moving parts of the body rely on muscles that contract when triggered to do so by a nerve impulse or chemical trigger. Contraction shortens the muscle, which pulls on a part of the body to cause motion.

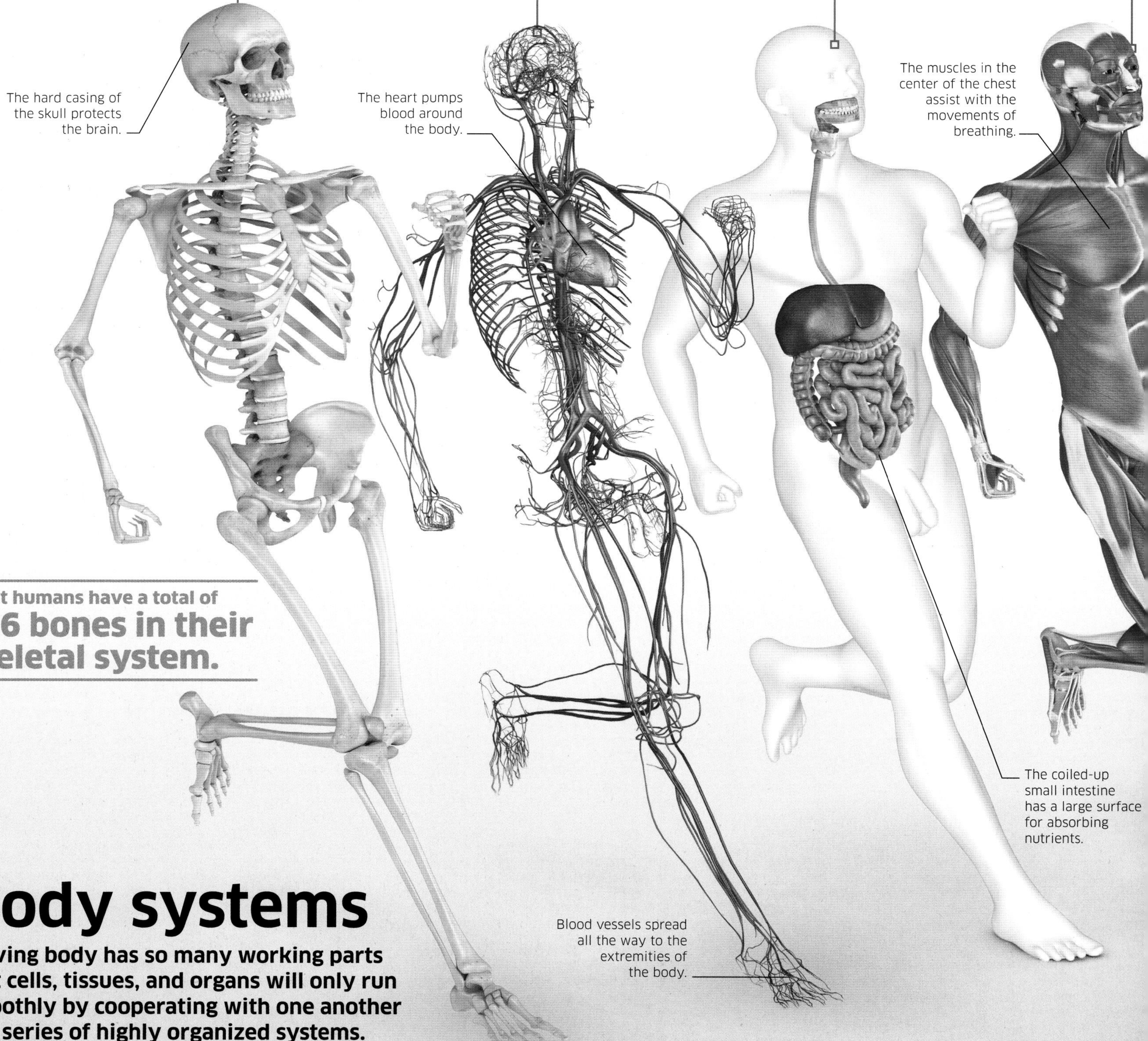

The hard casing of the skull protects the brain.
The heart pumps blood around the body.
The muscles in the center of the chest assist with the movements of breathing.
The coiled-up small intestine has a large surface for absorbing nutrients.
Blood vessels spread all the way to the extremities of the body.

Adult humans have a total of
206 bones in their skeletal system.

Body systems

A living body has so many working parts that cells, tissues, and organs will only run smoothly by cooperating with one another in a series of highly organized systems.

Each system is designed to carry out a particular function essential to life—whether breathing, eating, or reproducing. Just as organs are interconnected in organ systems, the systems interact, and some organs, such as the pancreas, even belong to more than one system.

Human body systems
There are 12 systems of the human body, of which 8 of the most vital are shown here. The others are the urinary system (see pp.162–163), the integumentary system (skin, hair, and nails), the lymphatic system (which drains excess fluid), and the endocrine system (which produces hormones).

Blood is a liquid tissue and contains more than **4 million red blood cells** per cubic millimeter—**the most abundant kind of cell in the human body.**

The skin is the largest organ of all—accounting for more than **10 percent of total human body weight.**

145

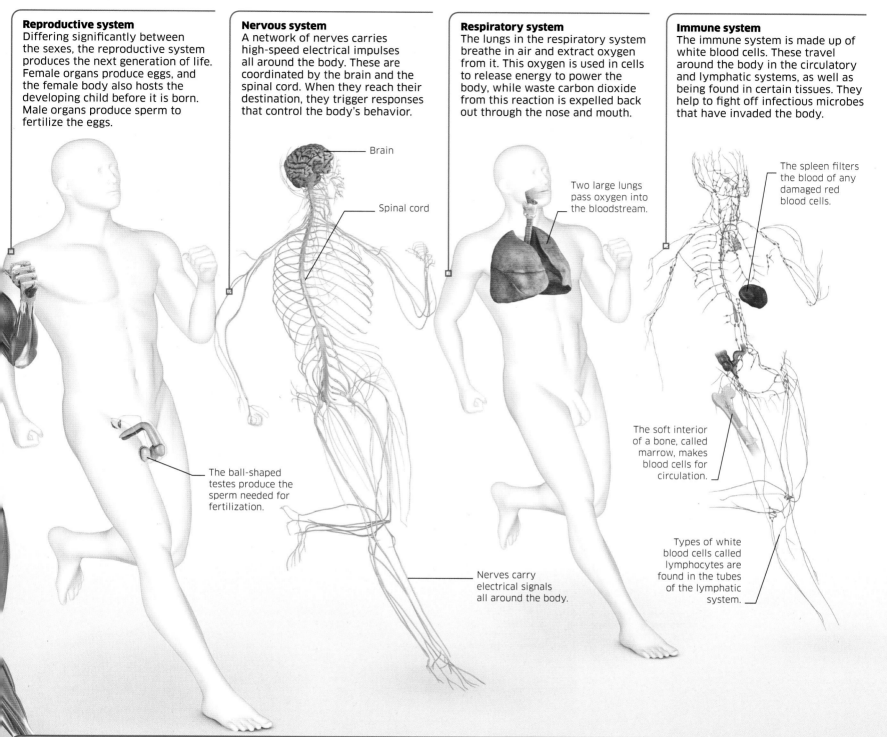

Reproductive system
Differing significantly between the sexes, the reproductive system produces the next generation of life. Female organs produce eggs, and the female body also hosts the developing child before it is born. Male organs produce sperm to fertilize the eggs.

The ball-shaped testes produce the sperm needed for fertilization.

Nervous system
A network of nerves carries high-speed electrical impulses all around the body. These are coordinated by the brain and the spinal cord. When they reach their destination, they trigger responses that control the body's behavior.

Brain

Spinal cord

Nerves carry electrical signals all around the body.

Respiratory system
The lungs in the respiratory system breathe in air and extract oxygen from it. This oxygen is used in cells to release energy to power the body, while waste carbon dioxide from this reaction is expelled back out through the nose and mouth.

Two large lungs pass oxygen into the bloodstream.

Immune system
The immune system is made up of white blood cells. These travel around the body in the circulatory and lymphatic systems, as well as being found in certain tissues. They help to fight off infectious microbes that have invaded the body.

The spleen filters the blood of any damaged red blood cells.

The soft interior of a bone, called marrow, makes blood cells for circulation.

Types of white blood cells called lymphocytes are found in the tubes of the lymphatic system.

Building a body
Each of the trillions of cells that make up a human body are busy with life's vital processes, such as processing food. But cells are also organized for extra tasks in arrangements called tissues, such as muscles and blood. Multiple tissues, in turn, make up organs, each of which has a specific vital function. A collection of organs working together to carry out one process is called a system.

Cell
The basic building blocks of life, cells can be specialized for a variety of different tasks.

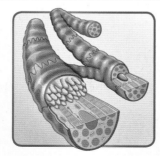

Tissue
Groups of complementary cells work together in tissues that perform particular functions.

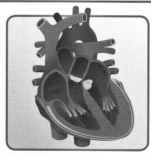

Organ
Combinations of tissues are assembled together to make up organs, such as the human heart.

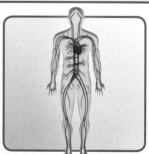

System
Complementary organs are connected into organ systems, which carry out key body processes.

Photosynthesizers
Leaves contain a green pigment called chlorophyll. This traps the energy of sunlight, which is used to build sugars. The process, called photosynthesis, is the origin of virtually all the food chains on Earth.

Flies are drawn to the giant Rafflesia flower because it has the odor of their favorite food: rotting meat.

An indigo flycatcher snatches flies attracted to the foul stench of the Rafflesia flower.

Nutrition

All life needs food—whether it's the sugary sap made in the green leaves of plants, or the solid meals eaten by hungry animals.

Food gives organisms the fuel to power all the living processes that demand energy, such as growth. Animals, fungi, and many microbes consume it from their surroundings—by eating or absorbing the materials of other organisms, living or dead. In contrast, plants and other microbes start with very simple chemical ingredients, such as carbon dioxide and water, and use these to make food inside their cells.

What is food?

The nutrients in food come from a complex mixture of molecules—each one containing carbon, hydrogen, and oxygen as its main elements. Three main groups—carbohydrates, fats, and proteins—make up the bulk of food molecules, although all organisms require different amounts of each type.

A Kinabalu pit viper hunts small mammals and birds.

Oxygen
Carbon
Hydrogen
AMINO ACID
Nitrogen

FATTY ACID

Proteins
Groups of atoms called amino acids link into chains of proteins, which help with growth and repair.

SUGAR

Carbohydrates
Rings of atoms called sugars provide energy and link to form chains of starch.

Fats and oils
Used for storing energy or building cells, these are made of long molecules called fatty acids.

Mycorrhizae
A network of fungus filaments—called mycorrhizae—grows among plant roots. Together, roots and filaments have a feeding partnership: the plants pass sugars to the fungi in exchange for minerals gathered by the fungi.

Predators
Animals that prey on others are called predators. Leeches are famous for sucking blood, but the giant red leech has a taste for meat-grabbing giant earthworms as they emerge from burrows after rainfall.

Tropical rainforests produce nearly **45 billion tons of food** each year.

147

Parasites

Surprisingly, the world's biggest flower is produced by a plant with no leaves. Rafflesia's massive bloom stinks of rotting meat to attract pollinating blowflies, but the rest of the plant grows as spreading tissue inside a tropical vine. A parasite, it steals food from the vine because it cannot photosynthesize for itself.

Hotbed of nutrition

A rainforest floor in Borneo is a busy community of living things, all striving for nourishment. While green-leaved plants make the food upon which, ultimately, everything else depends, a multitude of predators, parasites, and decomposers are fed by living prey and an abundance of dead matter.

Mountain tree shrews nourish the pitchers with their droppings—and are rewarded with a lick of sweet nectar.

Insectivorous plants

Where the soil is low in certain minerals, some plants seek other sources of food. The leaves of pitcher plants develop into vessels that contain pools of fluid for digesting drowning insects and even the droppings of occasional mammals.

Saprophytes

Toadstools and other fungi are saprophytes—meaning that they absorb the liquified remains of dead matter. They are made up of microscopic filaments, called hyphae, that penetrate the soil and cling to dead matter, simultaneously releasing digestive juices and soaking up the digested products.

Soil contains dead matter, which releases minerals into the ground as it decomposes.

Bacteria

Most kinds of bacteria digest dead matter, driving the process of decomposition. Others process the chemical energy in minerals to make their own food and, in doing so, release nitrates—an important source of nitrogen sucked up by plant roots.

Many detritus-eating animals burrow in soil, where they are surrounded by their food.

Detritivores

A forest floor is littered with organic detritus (waste), such as dead leaves. This provides abundant food for detritivores, such as giant blue earthworms, that have the digestive systems to cope with this tough material.

Photosynthesis

Virtually all food chains on Earth begin with photosynthesis—the chemical process in green leaves and algae that is critical for making food.

All around the planet when the sun shines, trillions of microscopic chemical factories called chloroplasts generate enough food to support all the world's vegetation. These vital granules are packed inside the cells of plant leaves and ocean algae. They contain a pigment, called chlorophyll, that makes our planet green and absorbs the sun's energy to change carbon dioxide and water into life-giving sugar.

Waxy layer
The surface of the leaf is coated in a waxy layer to stop it from drying out under the sun's rays.

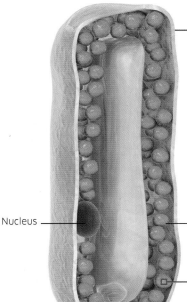

Palisade cell
Oblong-shaped palisade cells form a layer near the surface of the leaf. They contain the most chloroplasts, so they perform the most photosynthesis.

Nucleus

Tightly-packed chloroplasts

Spongy cells
The lower layer of the leaf contains round cells surrounded by air-filled spaces. These spaces help carbon dioxide in the air reach photosynthesizing cells.

Xylem
Tubes called xylem carry water into the leaf.

Phloem
Phloem tubes transport the food made during photosynthesis to other parts of the plant.

Chlorophyll
Chlorophyll is attached to membranes around the disks. Having lots of disks means there is more room for chlorophyll.

Chloroplast
A chloroplast is a bean-shaped granule. Together, all the chloroplasts contain so much of the pigment chlorophyll that the entire leaf appears green.

Fluid around the disks contains chemicals called enzymes that drive the production of sugar.

Inside a leaf
Cells that are near the sunlit surface of a leaf contain the most chloroplasts. Each chloroplast is sealed by transparent oily membranes and encloses stacks of interconnected discs that are at the heart of the photosynthesis process. The discs are covered in green chlorophyll, which traps light energy from the sun. This energy then drives chemical reactions that form sugar in the fluid surrounding the disks.

Epidermis
A single layer of cells, called the epidermis, forms a skin that protects the photosynthesizing layers underneath.

Photosynthesis in winter

During the winter season, some kinds of plants retain their leaves—even though their photosynthesis slows down. Other species drop their leaves and become dormant, having stored up enough food to last them until spring.

Evergreen tree
Pine trees have tough needlelike leaves that can keep working even in freezing temperatures.

Deciduous tree
Many broad-leaved trees drop all their leaves at once in winter and grow a new set in spring.

Bundle sheath
A layer of cells strengthens the bundle of xylem and phloem.

Stoma
The lower epidermis is punctured by pores called stomata that let carbon dioxide into the leaf and oxygen back out.

Guard cells
Two guard cells make up each stoma and control when it opens and closes.

Chemical reactions

Inside a chloroplast, a complex chain of chemical reactions takes place, which uses up water and carbon dioxide and generates sugar and oxygen. The light energy trapped by chlorophyll is first used to extract hydrogen from water, and expel the excess oxygen into the atmosphere. The hydrogen is then combined with carbon dioxide to make a kind of sugar called glucose. This provides the energy the plant needs for all the functions of life.

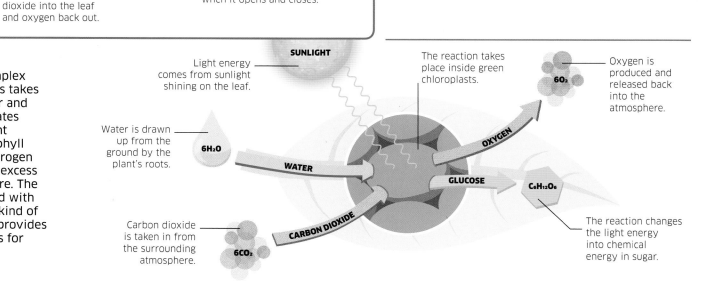

SUNLIGHT

Light energy comes from sunlight shining on the leaf.

The reaction takes place inside green chloroplasts.

Oxygen is produced and released back into the atmosphere.

Water is drawn up from the ground by the plant's roots.

$6H_2O$

WATER

OXYGEN

$6O_2$

GLUCOSE

$C_6H_{12}O_6$

Carbon dioxide is taken in from the surrounding atmosphere.

CARBON DIOXIDE

$6CO_2$

The reaction changes the light energy into chemical energy in sugar.

COLORADO BEETLE
Strategy: Leaf eater

Leaves can be a bountiful source of food, but leaf eaters must first get past a plant's defenses. Many are specialized to deal with particular plants, such as the Colorado beetle, which eats potato plant leaves that are poisonous to other animals.

VAMPIRE BAT
Strategy: Parasite

Some animals obtain food directly from living hosts—without killing them. Blood suckers, such as the vampire bat, get a meal rich in protein. The bat attacks at night, and is so stealthy that the sleeping victim scarcely feels its bites.

HAGFISH
Strategy: Scavenger

Deep-sea hagfishes are scavengers: they feed on dead matter. By tying themselves into knots, they are able to brace themselves against the carcasses of dead whales so that their spiny jawless mouths can rasp away at the flesh.

COCONUT CRAB
Strategy: Fruit and seed eater

Although many fruits and seeds are packed with nutrients, not all are easily accessible. The world's biggest land crab feasts on coconuts—tough "stone fruits" that its powerful claws must force open to reach the flesh inside.

Feeding strategies

All animals need food to keep them alive—in the form of other organisms, such as plants and animals. Many will go to extreme lengths to obtain their nutrients.

Whether they are plant-eating herbivores, meat-eating carnivores, or omnivores that eat many different foods, all animals are adapted to their diets. Every kind of animal has evolved a way for its body to get the nourishment it needs. Some animals only ever drink liquids, such as blood, or filter tiny particles from water, while others use muscles and jaws to tear solid food to pieces.

NILE CROCODILE
Strategy: Predator

Carnivores that must kill to obtain food not only need the skill to catch their prey, but also the strength to overpower it. Some predators rely on speed to chase prey down, but the Nile crocodile waits in ambush instead. It lurks submerged at a river's edge until a target comes to drink, then grabs the prey with its powerful jaws and pulls the struggling animal underwater to drown it.

Mighty bite
The crocodile's jaws can deliver a bite that has three times more force than a lion's.

Easy prey
Zebras are often attacked while crossing large rivers.

Many **predators**, such as spiders, **use disabling venom** to overpower their prey.

The **biggest living animal**–the blue whale–and the **biggest fish**–the whale shark–are both **filter feeders**.

151

LESSER FLAMINGO
Strategy: Filter feeder

The lesser flamingo is nourished almost entirely by the microscopic algae in African salt lakes. Each cupful of water from the lakes is a rich soup containing billions of algae, which the bird filters out with its unusual bill. By lowering its head upside down into the lake and pumping its tongue backward and forward like a piston, water gets drawn into and out of the long bill. A coating of minute brushes on the inner lining of the bill trap the algae, which are then rapidly swallowed by the hungry bird.

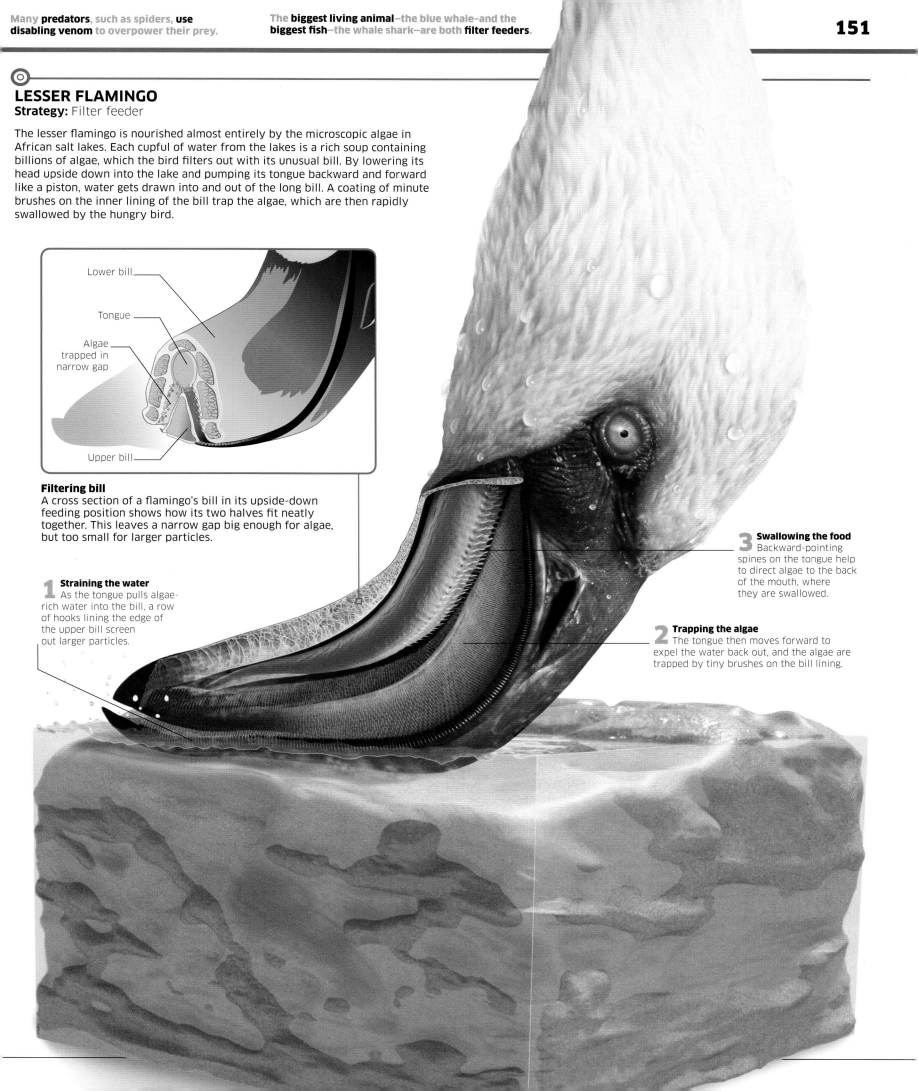

Lower bill

Tongue

Algae trapped in narrow gap

Upper bill

Filtering bill
A cross section of a flamingo's bill in its upside-down feeding position shows how its two halves fit neatly together. This leaves a narrow gap big enough for algae, but too small for larger particles.

1 Straining the water
As the tongue pulls algae-rich water into the bill, a row of hooks lining the edge of the upper bill screen out larger particles.

3 Swallowing the food
Backward-pointing spines on the tongue help to direct algae to the back of the mouth, where they are swallowed.

2 Trapping the algae
The tongue then moves forward to expel the water back out, and the algae are trapped by tiny brushes on the bill lining.

152 life ○ **PROCESSING FOOD**

23 ft (7 m) long—the **length of an adult human intestine**.
It can take **half a day for food to pass along** its length.

Processing food

Eating is only part of the story of how the body gets nourishment. An animal's digestive system must then break down the food so that nutrients can reach cells.

Food contains vital ingredients called nutrients, such as sugars and vitamins. Most animals eat solid food, and the digestive system has to liquefy this food inside the body so these nutrients can seep into the bloodstream. Once dissolved in the blood, they are circulated around the body to get to where they are needed—inside cells.

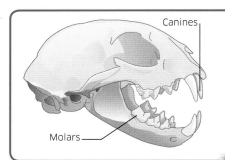

Carnivore teeth
Stabbing canines and sharp-edged, bone-crunching molars help the bobcat kill prey and bite through its skin and bones.

Canines

Molars

Esophagus
The esophagus (food) pipe carries lumps of swallowed food down to the stomach.

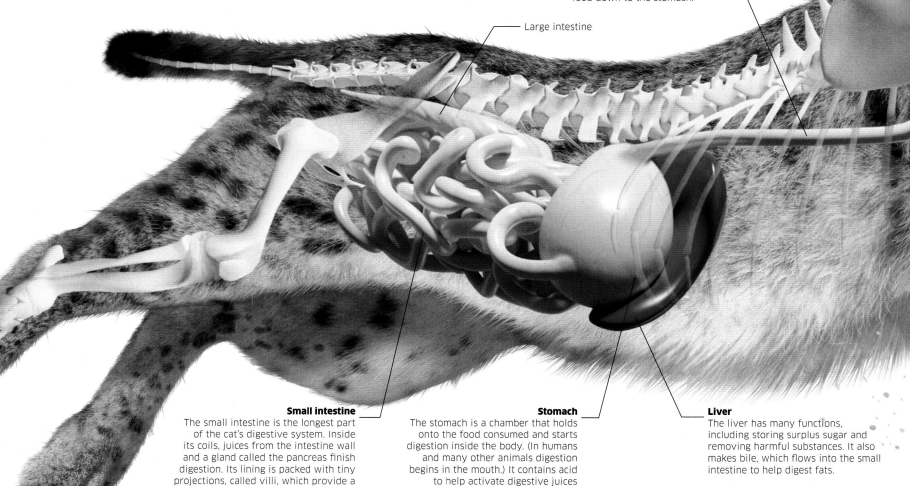

Large intestine

Small intestine
The small intestine is the longest part of the cat's digestive system. Inside its coils, juices from the intestine wall and a gland called the pancreas finish digestion. Its lining is packed with tiny projections, called villi, which provide a large surface area for absorbing nutrients.

Stomach
The stomach is a chamber that holds onto the food consumed and starts digestion inside the body. (In humans and many other animals digestion begins in the mouth.) It contains acid to help activate digestive juices and to kill harmful microbes.

Liver
The liver has many functions, including storing surplus sugar and removing harmful substances. It also makes bile, which flows into the small intestine to help digest fats.

Releasing the nutrients

Biting and chewing by the mouth reduces food into manageable lumps for swallowing, but further processing is needed to extract the nutrients. Muscles in the wall of the digestive system churn food into a lumpy paste and mix it with digestive juices containing chemicals called enzymes. The enzymes help to drive chemical reactions that break big molecules into smaller ones, which are then absorbed into the blood.

Carbohydrates
Starch is digested into sugars, such as glucose.

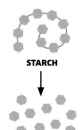

STARCH

↓

GLUCOSE

Proteins
Proteins are digested into amino acids.

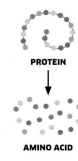

PROTEIN

↓

AMINO ACID

Fats
Fats and oils are broken down to release fatty acids and glycerol.

FATS AND OILS

↓

FATTY ACIDS   GLYCEROL

Digestive systems

A carnivorous bobcat and a herbivorous rabbit both have digestive systems filled with muscles and digestive juices to help break up their food. But they have important differences—each is adapted to the challenges of eating either chewy meat or tough vegetation.

There are more than
100 trillion bacteria
in the digestive tract.

Some plant-eating mammals eat clay, because the minerals in this dense soil **soak up the defensive poisons** found in some plant leaves.

153

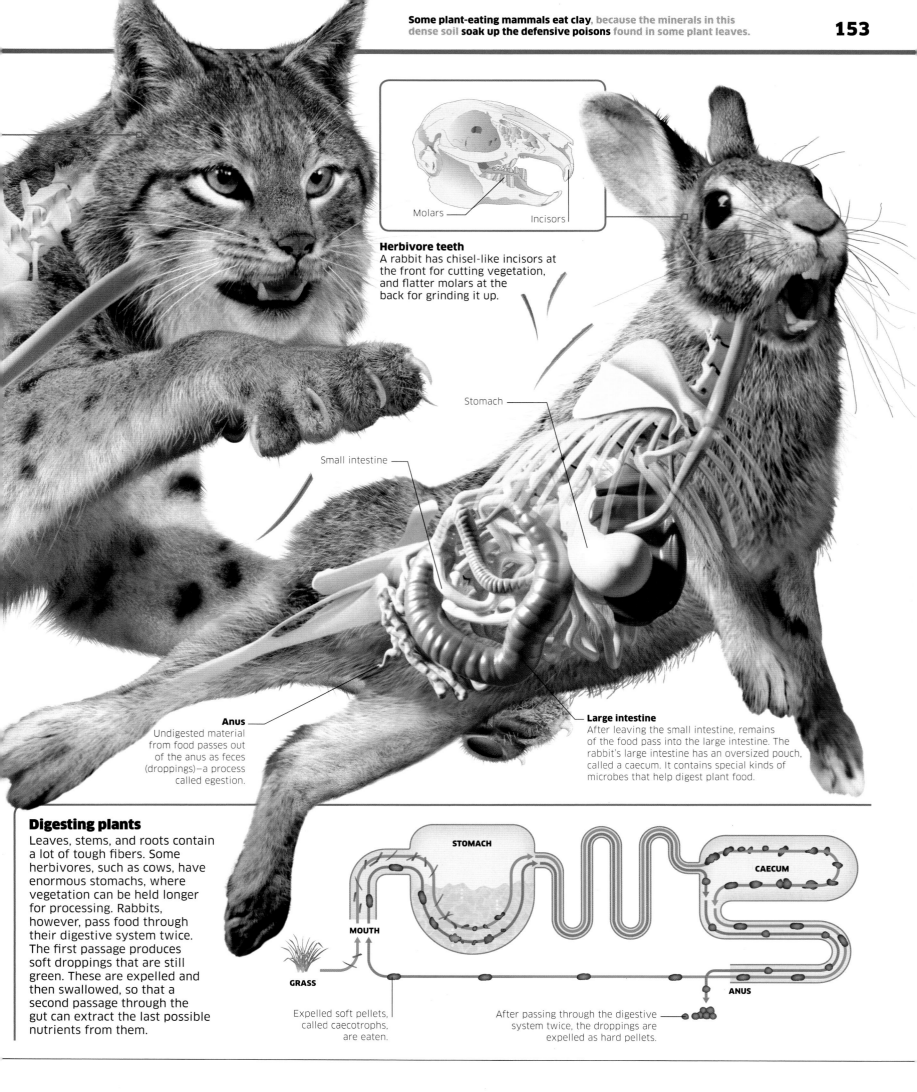

Herbivore teeth
A rabbit has chisel-like incisors at the front for cutting vegetation, and flatter molars at the back for grinding it up.

Molars

Incisors

Stomach

Small intestine

Anus
Undigested material from food passes out of the anus as feces (droppings)—a process called egestion.

Large intestine
After leaving the small intestine, remains of the food pass into the large intestine. The rabbit's large intestine has an oversized pouch, called a caecum. It contains special kinds of microbes that help digest plant food.

Digesting plants
Leaves, stems, and roots contain a lot of tough fibers. Some herbivores, such as cows, have enormous stomachs, where vegetation can be held longer for processing. Rabbits, however, pass food through their digestive system twice. The first passage produces soft droppings that are still green. These are expelled and then swallowed, so that a second passage through the gut can extract the last possible nutrients from them.

STOMACH

CAECUM

MOUTH

GRASS

ANUS

Expelled soft pellets, called caecotrophs, are eaten.

After passing through the digestive system twice, the droppings are expelled as hard pellets.

Plant transpiration

To lift water to their topmost branches, trees need incredible water carrying systems. The tallest ones can pull water with the force of a high-pressure hose.

Plants owe this remarkable ability to impressive engineering. Their trunks and stems are packed with bundles of microscopic pipes. Water and minerals are moved from the soil to the leaves, while food made in the leaves is sent around the entire plant.

3 Pull from above

Water evaporates from the moist tissues inside living leaves. The vapor it generates spills out into the surrounding atmosphere through pores called stomata. This water loss, known as transpiration, is replaced with water arriving from the ground in pipelike xylem vessels.

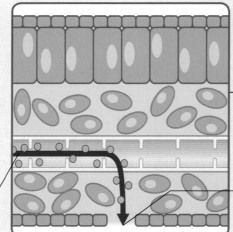

Water moves into the leaf in xylem vessels of the leaf's veins.

Water vapor escapes through pores called stomata.

2 Rising water

The microscopic xylem vessels carry unbroken columns of water through the stem all the way up to the leaves. Water molecules stick together, so as transpiration pulls water into the leaves, all the columns of water rise up through the stem—like water climbing through drinking straws. This is called the transpiration stream.

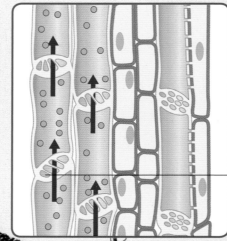

Xylem vessels are made up of stacks of empty dead cells with holes in their ends.

Transpiration

A tree's water carrying system is incredibly efficient and, unlike similar systems in animals, does not require any energy from the organism. The sun's heat causes water to evaporate from the leaves, a process called transpiration, which triggers the tree to pull more water up from the ground.

Bark
Tough outer layers of bark serve to protect the tree's trunk from injury.

1 Absorption from below

Water seeps into the roots from the soil by a process called osmosis. It then passes into tubes called xylem vessels to join the transpiration stream upward. Microscopic extensions to the root, called root hairs, help maximize the absorption area so the tree can pick up large amounts of water and minerals.

Water passes into the root through the root hair.

Xylem vessels

A mature oak tree can **transpire** more than **a bath full of water** every day.

155

Phloem
The innermost layer of the tree's bark, called the phloem, transports food made by photosynthesis in the leaves.

Cambium
A thin layer of actively dividing cells, the cambium generates more xylem and phloem as the tree grows thicker.

Sapwood
This contains the xylem vessels that stream water up the tree.

Heartwood
This is made of old xylem vessels that no longer carry water, but help support the weight of the tree.

Food distribution

Sugars and other food are made in the leaves through photosynthesis (see pp.148–149). They are then carried through pipes called phloem— traveling to roots, flowers, and others parts that cannot make food for themselves.

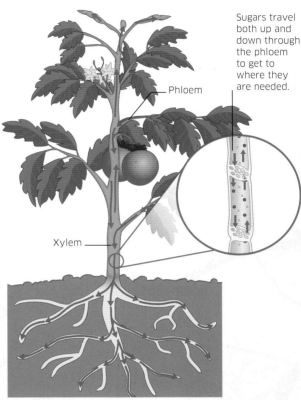

Sugars travel both up and down through the phloem to get to where they are needed.

Phloem

Xylem

Osmosis

When cell membranes stretch between two solutions with different concentrations, water automatically passes across to the higher concentration by a process called osmosis. This happens in plant roots—where root cell membranes are situated between the weak mineral solutions found in soil and the higher concentrations inside the root cells.

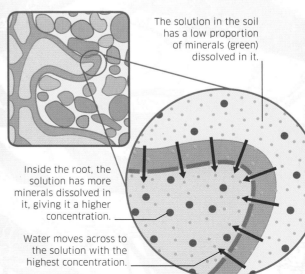

The solution in the soil has a low proportion of minerals (green) dissolved in it.

Inside the root, the solution has more minerals dissolved in it, giving it a higher concentration.

Water moves across to the solution with the highest concentration.

156 life ○ **CIRCULATION**

Some invertebrates have blue blood—colored by copper pigments.

70 times a minute is how fast the **human heart** beats on average.

The heart

The blue whale has the biggest heart of any animal: weighing in at 400 lb (180 kg) and standing as tall as a 12-year-old child. Containing four chambers, it is made of solid muscle, and contracts with a regular rhythm to pump blood out through the body's arteries. When its muscles relax, the pressure inside the chambers dips very low to pull in blood from the veins.

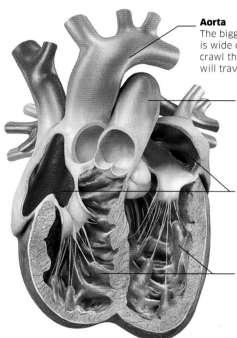

Aorta
The biggest artery in the blue whale is wide enough for a toddler to crawl through. Blood from here will travel around the body.

Pulmonary artery
Unlike in other arteries, the blood flowing through this artery does not carry oxygen, but travels to the lungs to pick it up.

Atria
The two small upper chambers of the heart are called atria. Atria pump blood into the ventricles.

Ventricles
The two larger chambers of the heart are called ventricles. The right ventricle pumps blood to the lungs, and the left pumps it around the rest of the body.

Network of vessels

Thousands of miles of blood vessels run through the body of a blue whale. Thick-walled arteries (shown in red) carry blood away from the heart and thin-walled veins (shown in blue) ferry it back. These both branch off countless times to form a network of microscopic capillaries (smaller blood vessels) that run between the cells.

Circulation

Blood is an animal's essential life support system, transporting food and oxygen around its body and removing waste from cells.

Animals have trillions of cells that need support, and a vast network of tiny tubes called blood vessels stretches throughout their bodies in order to reach them all. A pumping heart keeps blood continually flowing through the blood vessels, and this bloodstream gathers food from the digestive system and oxygen from lungs or gills. When the blood reaches cells, these essentials pass inside, while waste moves back out of the cells and is then carried away by the blood to excretory organs, such as the kidneys.

11 tons of blood are contained within the body of a blue whale. Its heart pumps the equivalent of two baths with every beat.

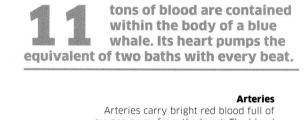

Arteries
Arteries carry bright red blood full of oxygen away from the heart. The blood moves at high pressure, because it is propelled by the heart's strong beat.

Veins
Veins carry purplish-red blood back to the heart. It is harder for the blood to travel in this direction, so muscles push on the veins to help the blood move along.

Arteries leading to the head provide oxygenated blood for the brain.

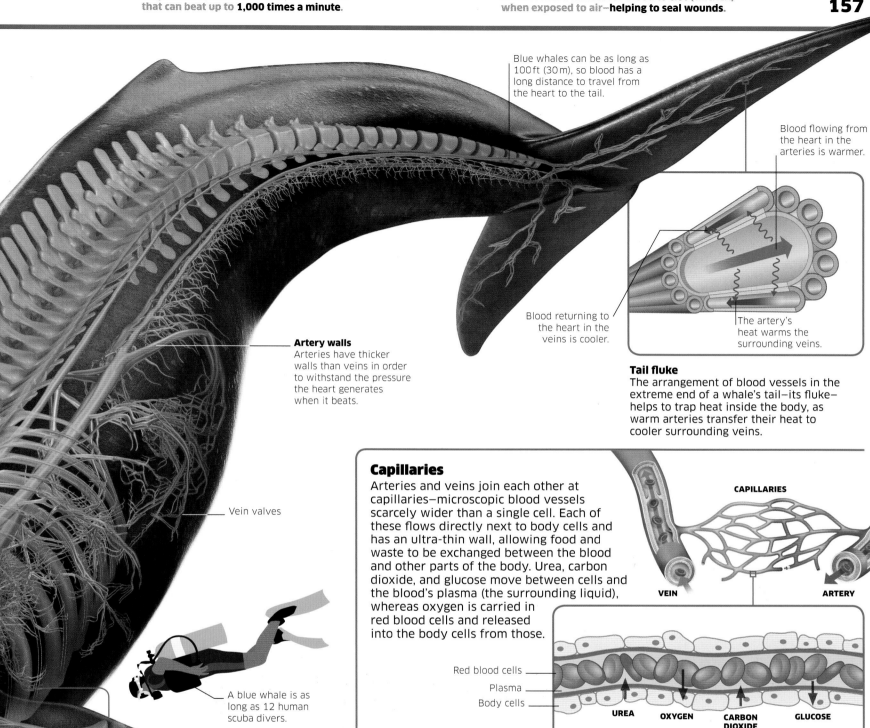

Blue whales can be as long as 100 ft (30 m), so blood has a long distance to travel from the heart to the tail.

Blood flowing from the heart in the arteries is warmer.

Blood returning to the heart in the veins is cooler.

The artery's heat warms the surrounding veins.

Artery walls
Arteries have thicker walls than veins in order to withstand the pressure the heart generates when it beats.

Tail fluke
The arrangement of blood vessels in the extreme end of a whale's tail—its fluke—helps to trap heat inside the body, as warm arteries transfer their heat to cooler surrounding veins.

Vein valves

Capillaries
Arteries and veins join each other at capillaries—microscopic blood vessels scarcely wider than a single cell. Each of these flows directly next to body cells and has an ultra-thin wall, allowing food and waste to be exchanged between the blood and other parts of the body. Urea, carbon dioxide, and glucose move between cells and the blood's plasma (the surrounding liquid), whereas oxygen is carried in red blood cells and released into the body cells from those.

CAPILLARIES

VEIN

ARTERY

Red blood cells
Plasma
Body cells

UREA OXYGEN CARBON DIOXIDE GLUCOSE

A blue whale is as long as 12 human scuba divers.

Blood flows through the vein.

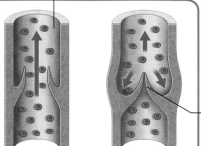

Vein valves
One-way valves in the veins close off behind the blood as it passes through, to stop it flowing back the other way.

Valves close behind the blood so it cannot flow backward.

Double circulation
Mammals have a more efficient circulation than fishes. Blood pumped by a fish's heart moves through the gills to pick up oxygen, travels around the rest of the body, and only then returns back to the heart. However, in mammals, blood returns to the heart directly after the lungs. It then has more pressure when it flows to the cells, making exchanges easier. This is why mammals have four chambers in their hearts—both an upper and lower chamber for each circuit.

GILL CAPILLARIES

OTHER CAPILLARIES

SINGLE CIRCULATION

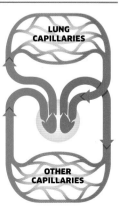

LUNG CAPILLARIES

OTHER CAPILLARIES

DOUBLE CIRCULATION

Breathing with lungs

Land-living vertebrates, such as mammals, birds, and reptiles, breathe with lungs. These air-filled cavities sit inside the chest and have thin walls lined with blood vessels. When the animal breathes in and out, chest muscles expand and deflate the lungs, pulling in oxygen-rich air and removing waste carbon dioxide.

Oxygen and carbon dioxide enter and leave the body through the nose and mouth.

The trachea (windpipe) is a stiff-walled tube that carries air down to the lungs.

A sturdy rib cage protects the lungs, while chest muscles power them.

Breathing

An animal breathes to supply its cells with oxygen— a vital resource that helps to burn up food and release much-needed energy around the body.

All organisms—including animals, plants, and microbes— get energy from respiration, a chemical reaction that happens inside cells. Most do this by reacting food with oxygen, producing carbon dioxide as a waste product. To drive the oxygen into the body, different animals have highly adapted respiratory systems, such as lungs or gills. These can exchange large quantities of gas, carrying oxygen to respiring cells in the bloodstream, and excreting waste carbon dioxide.

Oxygen traveling in the blood is attached to a pigment called hemoglobin—
the substance that gives blood its red color.

Alveoli

The lungs of mammals are made up of millions of microscopic sacs called alveoli. Each sac has an ultra-thin wall covered in a network of blood capillaries. This fine surface allows lots of oxygen and carbon dioxide to move between the air and the blood.

Waste carbon dioxide is transferred back from the blood to the lungs.

Oxygen moves through the very thin walls of the alveoli into the blood capillaries.

Breathing with gills

Gills are feathery extensions of the body that splay out in water so that aquatic animals can breathe. The delicate, blood-filled gills of fish are protected inside chambers on either side of their mouth cavity. A fish breathes by opening its mouth to draw oxygen-rich water over its gills. Some fishes rely on the stream created as they swim forward, but most use throat muscles to gulp water. Oxygen moves from the gills into the blood, while stale water emerges from the gill openings on either side of the head.

Diffusion

Oxygen and carbon dioxide are able to cross the microscopic membrane between the lungs and the blood by diffusion: a process by which molecules naturally move from an area where they are highly concentrated to one in which their numbers are fewer. This happens all around the body, as gases move between blood and respiring cells.

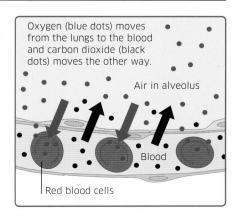

Oxygen (blue dots) moves from the lungs to the blood and carbon dioxide (black dots) moves the other way.

Air in alveolus

Blood

Red blood cells

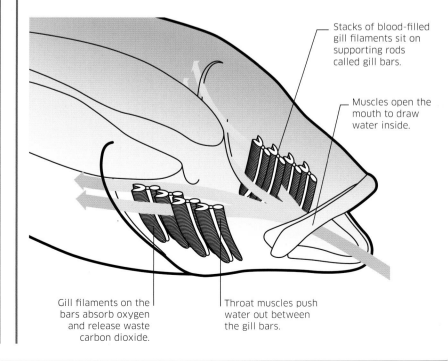

Stacks of blood-filled gill filaments sit on supporting rods called gill bars.

Muscles open the mouth to draw water inside.

Gill filaments on the bars absorb oxygen and release waste carbon dioxide.

Throat muscles push water out between the gill bars.

500 million alveoli are in the human lungs, providing an enormous area for gas exchange.

Some underwater insects breathe with gills, or even carry bubbles of air underwater with them.

159

Breathing with tracheae

Insects and related invertebrates have a breathing system that gets oxygen directly to their muscles. Instead of oxygen being carried in the blood, an intricate network of pipes reaches into the body from breathing holes called spiracles. Each pipe—known as a trachea—splits into tinier branches called tracheoles. The tracheoles are precisely arranged so that their tips penetrate the body's cells. This delivers oxygen-rich air from the surroundings deep into the insect, where respiration takes place.

Tracheole

Trachea

Spiracle

Tracheoles

Microscopic air-filled tracheoles in the body of an insect perform a similar role to blood-filled capillaries in other animals: they pass oxygen into the cells, while carbon dioxide moves out. This direct and efficient system means cells get oxygen delivered straight to them.

COCKROACH

Spiracles
Spiracles can be opened and closed by muscles (green) depending on external conditions.

Tracheoles
Tracheoles have very thin walls to encourage the movement of oxygen directly into cells without passing through blood.

Tracheae
Tracheae do not collapse because their walls are thickened with the same material that makes up the insect's outer skeleton.

Glucose reacts with oxygen inside cells to release energy.

RESPIRING CELL

Carbon dioxide and water are formed as waste products.

GLUCOSE

CARBON DIOXIDE

OXYGEN

WATER

HARD WORKING CELL

MORE GLUCOSE

MORE CARBON DIOXIDE

MORE OXYGEN

MORE WATER

More energy is released to power muscles when the horse is running.

Cellular respiration

The oxygen an animal brings into its body is used in a chemical process called respiration. This mainly takes place in capsules within cells, called mitochondria. Here, energy-rich foods, such as sugars (glucose), are broken down into smaller molecules to release usable energy. The more active an animal is, the more oxygen it needs to keep this reaction running. While oxygen is crucial for most respiration, animals under physical pressure can release a tiny bit of extra energy without oxygen—a process known as anaerobic respiration.

CARBON DIOXIDE

OXYGEN

Glucose from digested food is stored inside cells until it is needed.

CARBON DIOXIDE

OXYGEN

An active animal breathes faster and deeper to supply its cells with more oxygen to get more energy.

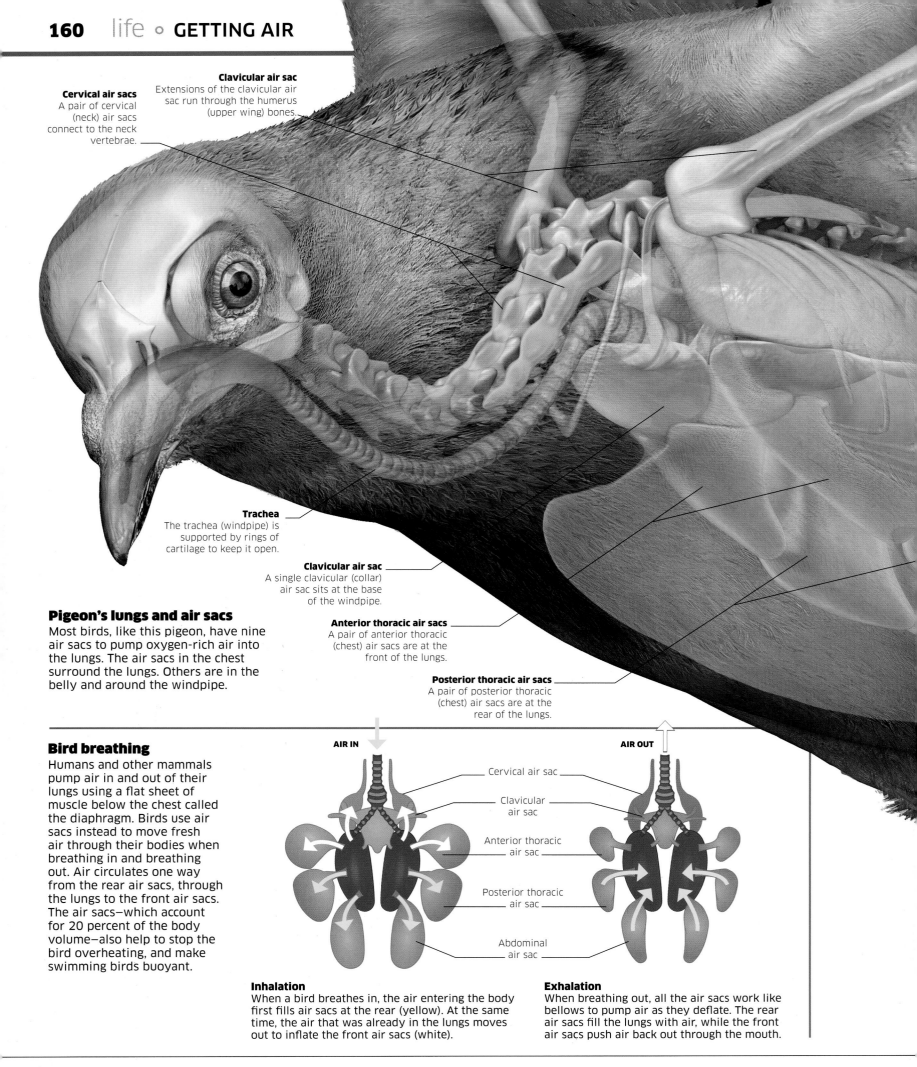

Cervical air sacs
A pair of cervical (neck) air sacs connect to the neck vertebrae.

Clavicular air sac
Extensions of the clavicular air sac run through the humerus (upper wing) bones.

Trachea
The trachea (windpipe) is supported by rings of cartilage to keep it open.

Clavicular air sac
A single clavicular (collar) air sac sits at the base of the windpipe.

Anterior thoracic air sacs
A pair of anterior thoracic (chest) air sacs are at the front of the lungs.

Posterior thoracic air sacs
A pair of posterior thoracic (chest) air sacs are at the rear of the lungs.

Pigeon's lungs and air sacs

Most birds, like this pigeon, have nine air sacs to pump oxygen-rich air into the lungs. The air sacs in the chest surround the lungs. Others are in the belly and around the windpipe.

Bird breathing

Humans and other mammals pump air in and out of their lungs using a flat sheet of muscle below the chest called the diaphragm. Birds use air sacs instead to move fresh air through their bodies when breathing in and breathing out. Air circulates one way from the rear air sacs, through the lungs to the front air sacs. The air sacs—which account for 20 percent of the body volume—also help to stop the bird overheating, and make swimming birds buoyant.

AIR IN

AIR OUT

Cervical air sac

Clavicular air sac

Anterior thoracic air sac

Posterior thoracic air sac

Abdominal air sac

Inhalation
When a bird breathes in, the air entering the body first fills air sacs at the rear (yellow). At the same time, the air that was already in the lungs moves out to inflate the front air sacs (white).

Exhalation
When breathing out, all the air sacs work like bellows to pump air as they deflate. The rear air sacs fill the lungs with air, while the front air sacs push air back out through the mouth.

Getting air

Birds need plenty of energy to fuel active lives. Their beautifully efficient system for getting oxygen to cells is unique—no other animal has one quite like it.

The key to a bird's breathing system lies in big, air-filled sacs that pack the body. They help supply air to the lungs, which—unlike human lungs—are small and rigid. Breathing makes the sacs inflate and deflate like balloons, sweeping fresh air through the lungs. Oxygen continually seeps into the blood and circulates to the cells, so they can release energy in respiration.

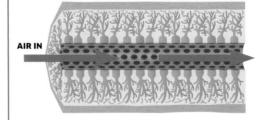

Parabronchi (air-filled tubes) bring air to the air vessels.

AIR IN

Microscopic tubes called capillaries carry blood.

Gaseous exchange
Each lung is filled with tiny air-filled vessels intermingled with microscopic blood vessels, helping to bring oxygen as close to the blood as possible.

Abdominal air sacs
The biggest pair of air sacs are in the abdomen (belly) of the body.

Breathing at high altitudes
Traveling at high altitudes poses a special problem for some high-flying birds, as the air gets so thin that there is little oxygen. The migration route of bar-headed geese takes them over the Himalayas—the highest any known bird has flown. To cope with this, they have bigger lungs than other waterfowl and can breathe more deeply, while the pigment in their blood (hemoglobin) traps oxygen in the thin air especially well.

162 life ○ **BALANCING THE BODY**

60 times a day—how often
human kidneys filter the blood.

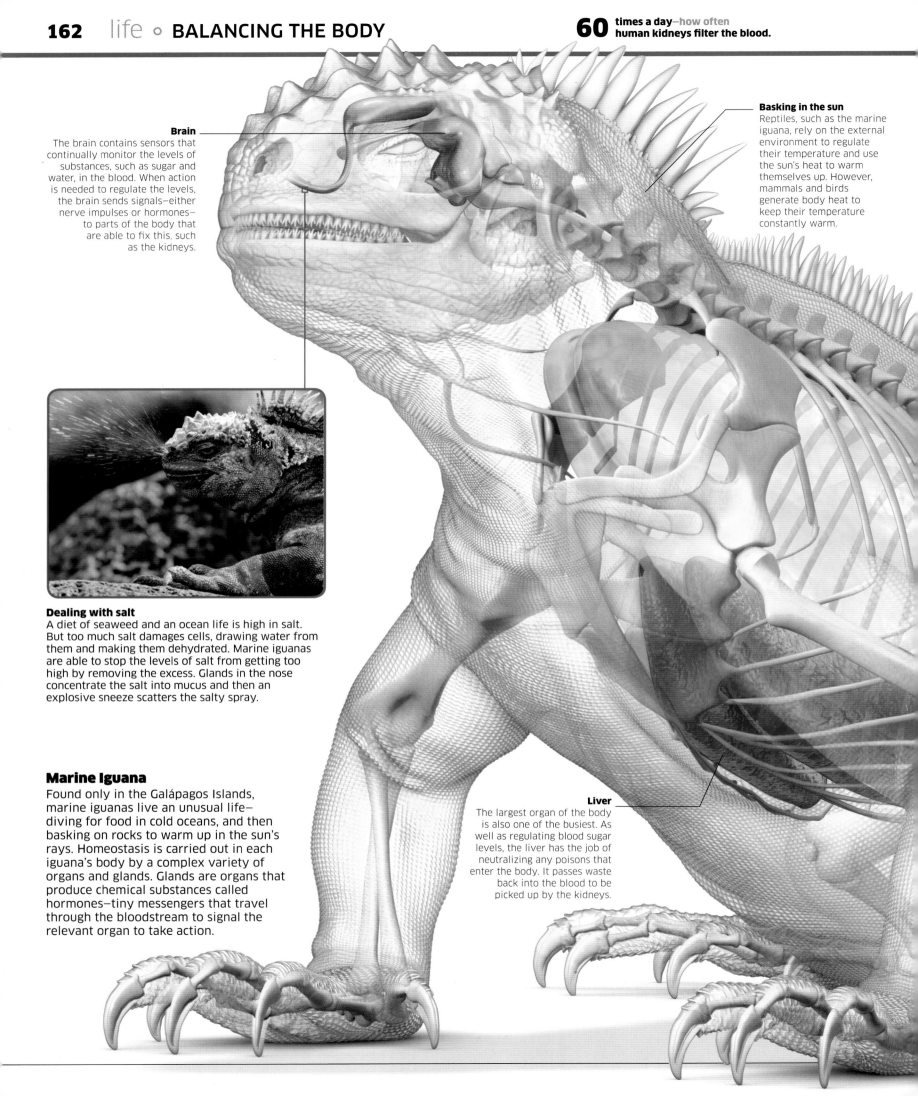

Brain
The brain contains sensors that continually monitor the levels of substances, such as sugar and water, in the blood. When action is needed to regulate the levels, the brain sends signals—either nerve impulses or hormones—to parts of the body that are able to fix this, such as the kidneys.

Basking in the sun
Reptiles, such as the marine iguana, rely on the external environment to regulate their temperature and use the sun's heat to warm themselves up. However, mammals and birds generate body heat to keep their temperature constantly warm.

Dealing with salt
A diet of seaweed and an ocean life is high in salt. But too much salt damages cells, drawing water from them and making them dehydrated. Marine iguanas are able to stop the levels of salt from getting too high by removing the excess. Glands in the nose concentrate the salt into mucus and then an explosive sneeze scatters the salty spray.

Marine Iguana

Found only in the Galápagos Islands, marine iguanas live an unusual life—diving for food in cold oceans, and then basking on rocks to warm up in the sun's rays. Homeostasis is carried out in each iguana's body by a complex variety of organs and glands. Glands are organs that produce chemical substances called hormones—tiny messengers that travel through the bloodstream to signal the relevant organ to take action.

Liver
The largest organ of the body is also one of the busiest. As well as regulating blood sugar levels, the liver has the job of neutralizing any poisons that enter the body. It passes waste back into the blood to be picked up by the kidneys.

99 °F (37°C)—the ideal temperature for enzymes in the human body to function.

500 chemical reactions are performed by human liver cells in order to carry out its everyday functions.

163

Balancing the body

While external conditions may change from rain to shine, the internal environment of an animal's body is carefully controlled to ensure the vital processes of life can take place.

This balancing act is called homeostasis. Complex vertebrate (backboned) animals have especially good systems of homeostasis that regulate factors such as body temperature, blood sugar levels, and water levels. Alongside this, other areas of the body carry out a process called excretion to remove waste, which can be harmful if left to accumulate. This continual regulation gives the body the right set of conditions to carry out all the functions of life, such as processing food and releasing energy.

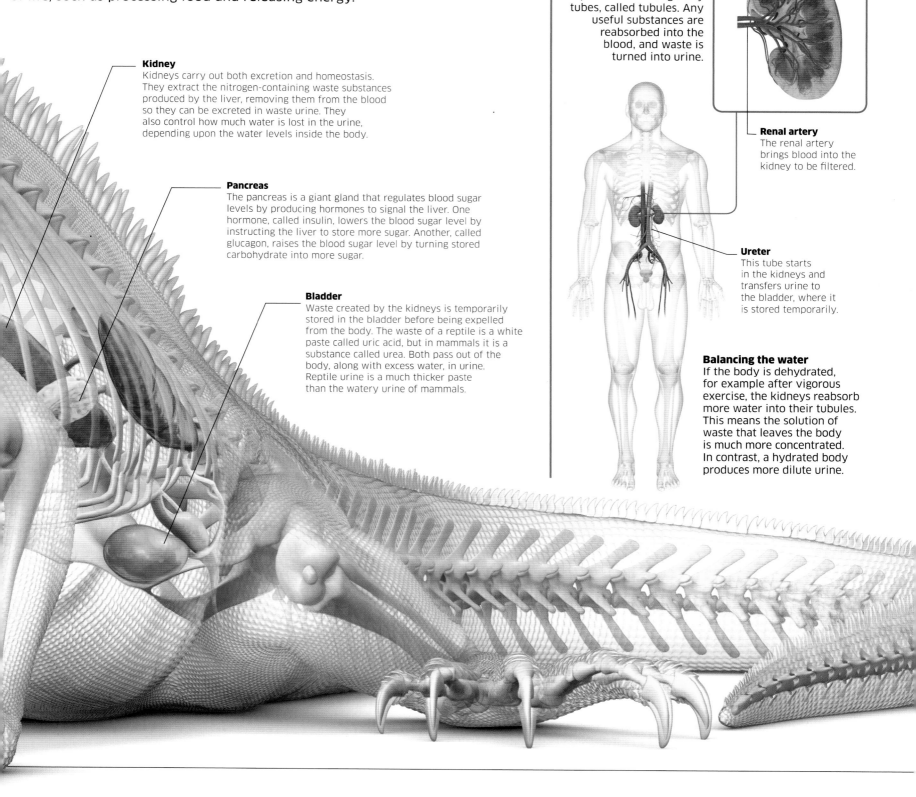

Kidney
Kidneys carry out both excretion and homeostasis. They extract the nitrogen-containing waste substances produced by the liver, removing them from the blood so they can be excreted in waste urine. They also control how much water is lost in the urine, depending upon the water levels inside the body.

Pancreas
The pancreas is a giant gland that regulates blood sugar levels by producing hormones to signal the liver. One hormone, called insulin, lowers the blood sugar level by instructing the liver to store more sugar. Another, called glucagon, raises the blood sugar level by turning stored carbohydrate into more sugar.

Bladder
Waste created by the kidneys is temporarily stored in the bladder before being expelled from the body. The waste of a reptile is a white paste called uric acid, but in mammals it is a substance called urea. Both pass out of the body, along with excess water, in urine. Reptile urine is a much thicker paste than the watery urine of mammals.

Urinary system

Although mammal and reptile kidneys differ in their shape, both contain a complex system of blood vessels and tubes to filter the blood of waste products. These, along with the bladder, make up the urinary system. As well as removing excess water, most kidneys can also excrete in urine any unwanted salt, unlike those of the marine iguana.

Filtering the blood
Kidneys filter liquid, containing waste, directly from the blood. This liquid drains through tiny tubes, called tubules. Any useful substances are reabsorbed into the blood, and waste is turned into urine.

Renal artery
The renal artery brings blood into the kidney to be filtered.

Ureter
This tube starts in the kidneys and transfers urine to the bladder, where it is stored temporarily.

Balancing the water
If the body is dehydrated, for example after vigorous exercise, the kidneys reabsorb more water into their tubules. This means the solution of waste that leaves the body is much more concentrated. In contrast, a hydrated body produces more dilute urine.

Nerve cells and synapses

Cells of the nervous system have lengthy fibers that can carry electrical signals, called nerve impulses, across long distances. When these signals reach small gaps between cells, called synapses, they trigger the release of a chemical across the gap. This chemical then stimulates a new impulse in the next nerve cell.

Nerve impulses travel along the fiber of a neuron.

Most nerve fibers are coated in a fatty sheath that makes the impulses move faster.

The fiber of the first neuron meets another one at a synapse.

Synapses

Tiny chemicals called neurotransmitters cross the gap between nerve cells. They are picked up by receptors on the other side.

Responding to surroundings

A gorilla uses its eyes to help sense tasty food, such as wild celery. As they view the food, the eyes send off nerve impulses (electrical signals) to the brain, which then sends instructions to the gorilla's muscles to rip up the plant and eat it.

1 Seeing the plant
Receptors are cells that sense a change in surroundings—called a stimulus. When the receptors in the eye detect light, or "see" the celery, they set off electrical impulses in the nerve cells that are connected to them.

Nerve fibers

Each nerve contains a bundle of microscopic nerve cell fibers. Some nerves carry both sensory and motor fibers; others carry just one or the other.

Impulses

A nerve impulse is a fast-moving spark of electrical activity that runs along the cell membranes of nerve cells (neurons).

6 Hands respond
Parts of the body that move in response to a nerve impulse are called effectors. Muscles are among the most important effectors of an animal's body. When a nerve impulse arrives at a muscle along a motor neuron, it makes the muscle contract (shorten)—in this case to grip and tear the celery.

Nervous system

The speediest body system has cables that carry messages faster than a racing car, and a central control that is smarter than the best computer.

The cables of the nervous system are its nerves, and its control center is the brain. Every moment that the body senses its surroundings, the entire system sends countless electrical impulses through billions of fibers. The nerves trigger muscles to respond, and the brain coordinates all this complex activity.

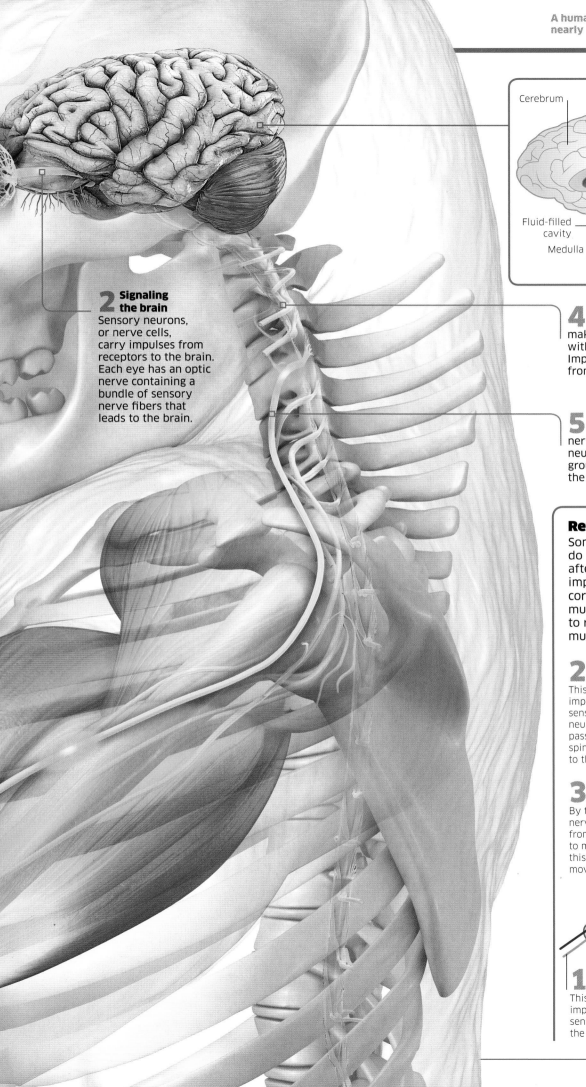

CROSS SECTION

Cerebrum

Fluid-filled
cavity

Medulla

Cerebellum

3 Coordinating a response

The brain coordinates where impulses go in order to control the body's behavior. The cerebrum manages complex actions that demand intelligence, like peeling and breaking up food. More routine actions, such as walking, are controlled by the cerebellum, while the medulla effects internal functions, like breathing.

2 Signaling the brain

Sensory neurons, or nerve cells, carry impulses from receptors to the brain. Each eye has an optic nerve containing a bundle of sensory nerve fibers that leads to the brain.

4 Traveling onward

Together with the brain, the spinal cord makes up the central nervous system. It works with the brain to pass signals around the body. Impulses traveling from the brain branch off from the spinal cord to motor neurons.

5 Signaling the muscles

Cells that carry impulses from the central nervous system to muscles are called motor neurons. Bundles of motor neuron fibers are grouped into nerves that run all the way from the spinal cord to the limb muscles.

Reflex actions

Some automatic responses, called reflex actions, do not involve the brain, such as when you recoil after touching something hot. In these instances, impulses travel from the sense organs to the spinal cord, where relay neurons pass the signal to the muscles. Bypassing the brain allows the impulses to reach the effectors and generate a response much more quickly.

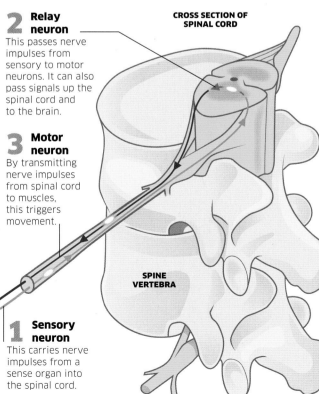

CROSS SECTION OF SPINAL CORD

2 Relay neuron

This passes nerve impulses from sensory to motor neurons. It can also pass signals up the spinal cord and to the brain.

3 Motor neuron

By transmitting nerve impulses from spinal cord to muscles, this triggers movement.

SPINE VERTEBRA

1 Sensory neuron

This carries nerve impulses from a sense organ into the spinal cord.

Vision

Eyes packed with light-sensitive cells enable animals to see. Vertebrates, such as humans, have two camera-like eyes that focus light onto the back of the eye. But some invertebrates rely on many more eyes—the giant clam has hundreds of tiny eyes scattered over its body. Each animal's eyes are specialized in different ways. Some are so sensitive that they can pick up the faintest light in the dark of night or in the deep sea.

Four-eyed fish
When it swims at the surface, this fish's split-level eyes help it to focus on objects above and below the water.

Long-legged fly
Flies and many other insects have compound eyes—made up of thousands of tiny lenses.

Tarsier
This primate's eyes are the biggest of any mammal when compared to the size of its head. They help it see well at night.

Touch

Animals have receptors in their skin that sense when other things come into contact with their body. Some receptors only pick up firm pressures, while others are sensitive to the lightest of touches. Receptor cells are especially concentrated in parts of the body that rely a lot on feeling textures or movement. Human fingertips are crammed with touch receptors, as are the whiskers of many cats, and the unusual nose of the star-nosed mole.

Star-nosed mole
The fleshy nose tentacles of this animal have six times more touch receptors than a human hand.

Senses

Animals sense their surroundings using organs that are triggered by light, sound, chemicals, or a whole range of other cues.

Sense organs are part of an animal's nervous system. They contain special cells called receptors that are stimulated by changes in the environment and pass on signals to the brain and the rest of the body. Through these organs animals can gain a wealth of information about their surroundings, equipping them to react to threats or opportunities. Each kind of animal has sense organs that are best suited to the way it lives.

Taste and smell

Smelling and tasting are two very similar senses, as they both detect chemicals. The tongue has receptors that taste the chemicals dissolved in food and drinks, and receptors inside the nose cavities pick up the chemicals in odors. Some animals that are especially reliant on chemical senses, or that do not have receptors elsewhere, have a concentrated patch of receptors in the roof of their mouth, called a Jacobson's organ.

Mouse senses

Like most mammals, a mouse has a keen nose. It uses smell to communicate with others of its kind: signaling a territorial claim or a willingness to mate. A mouse's tongue detects tastes in food, and both tongue and nose send signals to the brain.

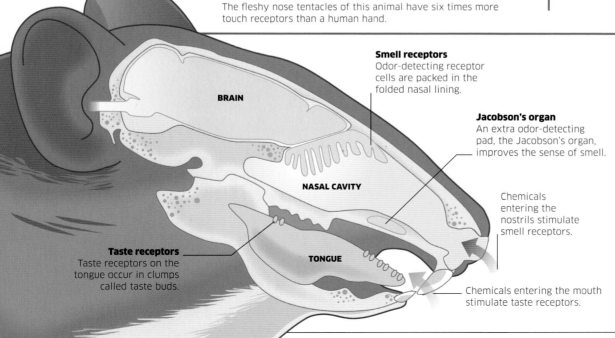

Smell receptors
Odor-detecting receptor cells are packed in the folded nasal lining.

Jacobson's organ
An extra odor-detecting pad, the Jacobson's organ, improves the sense of smell.

Chemicals entering the nostrils stimulate smell receptors.

BRAIN

NASAL CAVITY

Taste receptors
Taste receptors on the tongue occur in clumps called taste buds.

TONGUE

Chemicals entering the mouth stimulate taste receptors.

Sharks have **sensory pits on their snouts for detecting the electrical fields** of prey.

Blood-sucking **mosquitoes are attracted to the body odor and carbon dioxide** produced by their victims.

167

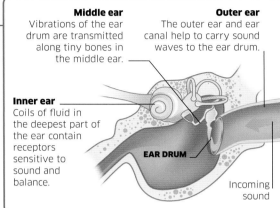

Pinna

Hearing

Animals hear because their ears contain receptors that are sensitive to sound waves. As the waves enter the ear, they vibrate a membrane called an ear drum. The vibrations pass along a chain of tiny bones until they reach the receptors within the inner ear.

Middle ear
Vibrations of the ear drum are transmitted along tiny bones in the middle ear.

Outer ear
The outer ear and ear canal help to carry sound waves to the ear drum.

Inner ear
Coils of fluid in the deepest part of the ear contain receptors sensitive to sound and balance.

EAR DRUM

Incoming sound

Bat-eared fox
In mammals, each ear opening is surrounded by a fleshy funnel for collecting sound, called a pinna. The desert-living bat-eared fox has such large pinnae that it also uses them to radiate warmth to stop it from overheating.

Hearing ranges
The pitch, or frequency, of a sound is measured in hertz (Hz): the number of vibrations per second. Different kinds of animals detect different ranges of pitch, and many are sensitive to ultrasound and infrasound that are beyond the hearing of humans.

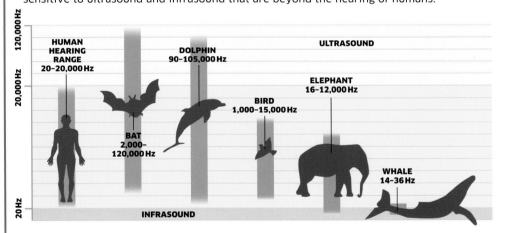

120,000 Hz

20,000 Hz

20 Hz

HUMAN HEARING RANGE
20–20,000 Hz

ULTRASOUND

DOLPHIN
90–105,000 Hz

BAT
2,000–120,000 Hz

BIRD
1,000–15,000 Hz

ELEPHANT
16–12,000 Hz

WHALE
14–36 Hz

INFRASOUND

Snake senses
A snake's tongue has no receptors and instead is used for transferring odors and tastes from prey and enemies to its sense organ in the roof of the mouth. A small nostril picks up additional smells.

Jacobson's organ
Chemicals on the tongue tip are transferred here to be detected.

Smell receptors pass signals along nerves to the brain.

NOSTRIL

Chemicals from the air, surfaces, or food are picked up by the tongue.

BRAIN

The forked tip helps to collect chemicals coming from both the left and the right.

Other ways of sensing the world
The lives of many kinds of animals rely on quite extraordinary sensory systems. Some have peculiar types of receptors that are not found in other animals. These give them the power to sense their surroundings in ways that seem quite unfamiliar to us—such as by picking up electrical or magnetic fields.

Electroreception
The rubbery bill of the platypus—an aquatic egg-laying mammal—contains receptors that detect electrical signals coming from the muscles of moving prey. They help the platypus find worms and crayfish in murky river waters.

Echolocation
Bats and dolphins use echolocation to navigate and find food. By calling out and listening for the echoes bouncing back from nearby objects, they can work out the positions of obstacles and prey.

Fire detection
Most animals flee from fire, but the fire beetle thrives near flames. Its receptors pick up the infrared radiation coming from a blaze, drawing it to burned-out trees where it can breed undisturbed by predators.

Magnetoreception
Birds can sense the earth's magnetic field. By combining this with information about the time of day and position of the sun or stars, they can navigate their way on long-distance migrations.

Balance
All vertebrate animals have balance receptors in their ears to sense the position of their head and tell up from down. These help humans walk upright and stop climbing animals, such as capuchin monkeys, from falling out of trees.

Time
Tiny animals, such as insects, experience time more slowly because their senses can process more information every second. Compared with humans, houseflies see everything in slow motion—helping them to dodge predators.

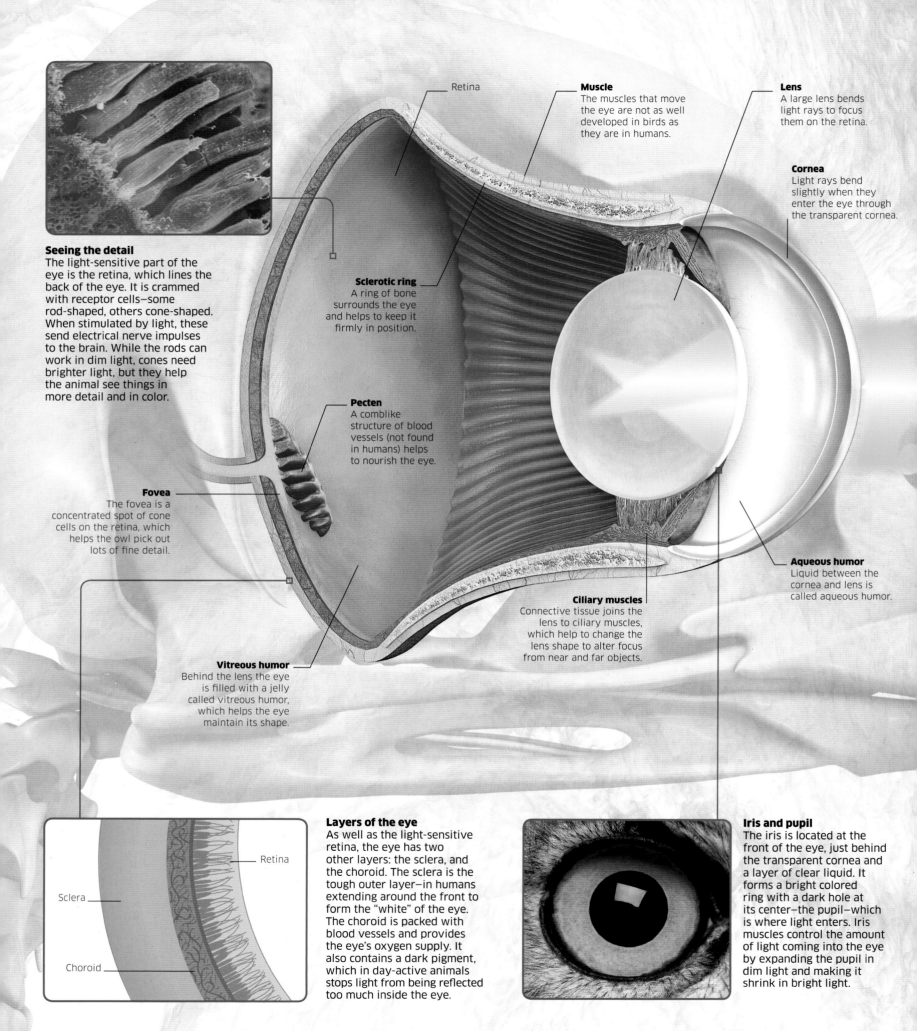

Seeing the detail
The light-sensitive part of the eye is the retina, which lines the back of the eye. It is crammed with receptor cells—some rod-shaped, others cone-shaped. When stimulated by light, these send electrical nerve impulses to the brain. While the rods can work in dim light, cones need brighter light, but they help the animal see things in more detail and in color.

Retina

Muscle
The muscles that move the eye are not as well developed in birds as they are in humans.

Lens
A large lens bends light rays to focus them on the retina.

Cornea
Light rays bend slightly when they enter the eye through the transparent cornea.

Sclerotic ring
A ring of bone surrounds the eye and helps to keep it firmly in position.

Pecten
A comblike structure of blood vessels (not found in humans) helps to nourish the eye.

Fovea
The fovea is a concentrated spot of cone cells on the retina, which helps the owl pick out lots of fine detail.

Vitreous humor
Behind the lens the eye is filled with a jelly called vitreous humor, which helps the eye maintain its shape.

Ciliary muscles
Connective tissue joins the lens to ciliary muscles, which help to change the lens shape to alter focus from near and far objects.

Aqueous humor
Liquid between the cornea and lens is called aqueous humor.

Retina

Sclera

Choroid

Layers of the eye
As well as the light-sensitive retina, the eye has two other layers: the sclera, and the choroid. The sclera is the tough outer layer—in humans extending around the front to form the "white" of the eye. The choroid is packed with blood vessels and provides the eye's oxygen supply. It also contains a dark pigment, which in day-active animals stops light from being reflected too much inside the eye.

Iris and pupil
The iris is located at the front of the eye, just behind the transparent cornea and a layer of clear liquid. It forms a bright colored ring with a dark hole at its center—the pupil—which is where light enters. Iris muscles control the amount of light coming into the eye by expanding the pupil in dim light and making it shrink in bright light.

Nocturnal mammals, such as cats, have **a light-reflective layer** behind their retinas, which **makes their eyes shine** when illuminated.

No animal can see in pitch darkness. All animals must detect at least **a small amount of light** to have vision.

169

Vision

The ability to see allows all animals to build up a detailed picture of their surroundings—vital for finding food and avoiding danger.

When an animal sees the world, its eyes pick up light and use lenses to focus this onto light-sensitive receptor cells. These cells then send signals to the brain, which composes a visual image of everything in the field of view. For animals with the best vision, the image can be finely detailed—even when the light is poor.

Night eyes

The eyes of birds are so big in proportion to their head that they are largely fixed inside their sockets. This means a bird must rotate its flexible neck to look around. Owl eyes, like those of many nocturnal birds, are especially large and are designed for good night vision. Their unusual shape creates room for a larger space at the back of the eye, packed with extra light-sensitive cells.

Seeing color

Receptor cells called cones are what allow animals to see color. These detect different light wavelengths—from short blue wavelengths to long red ones. Animals with more types of cones can see more colors, but those with just one are only able to see the world in black and white.

Humans have three kinds of cones, but dolphins have only one.

Three cones help humans see three primary colors: red, green, and blue, plus all their combinations.

Many day-flying birds have one more type of cone than humans, meaning they
can see ultraviolet.

Near and far

The eye's lens focuses light onto the retina, and can change shape to better focus on either closer objects or those farther away. A ring of muscle controls this shape. It contracts to make the lens rounder for near focus, and relaxes to pull the lens flatter for distant focus.

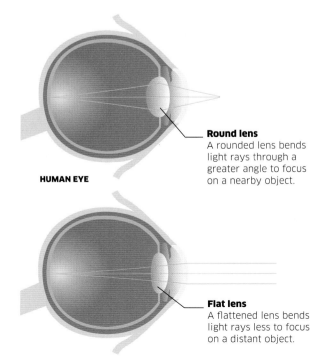

HUMAN EYE

Round lens
A rounded lens bends light rays through a greater angle to focus on a nearby object.

Flat lens
A flattened lens bends light rays less to focus on a distant object.

Binocular vision

When two forward-facing eyes have overlapping fields of view, this is called binocular vision. This gives an animal a three-dimensional view of the world, helping it to judge distance—a skill especially important for predators that hunt prey. Other animals with eyes on the sides of their head have a narrower range of binocular vision, but better all-around vision.

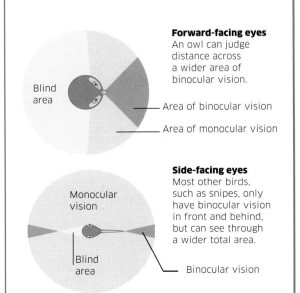

Forward-facing eyes
An owl can judge distance across a wider area of binocular vision.

Blind area

Area of binocular vision

Area of monocular vision

Side-facing eyes
Most other birds, such as snipes, only have binocular vision in front and behind, but can see through a wider total area.

Monocular vision

Blind area

Binocular vision

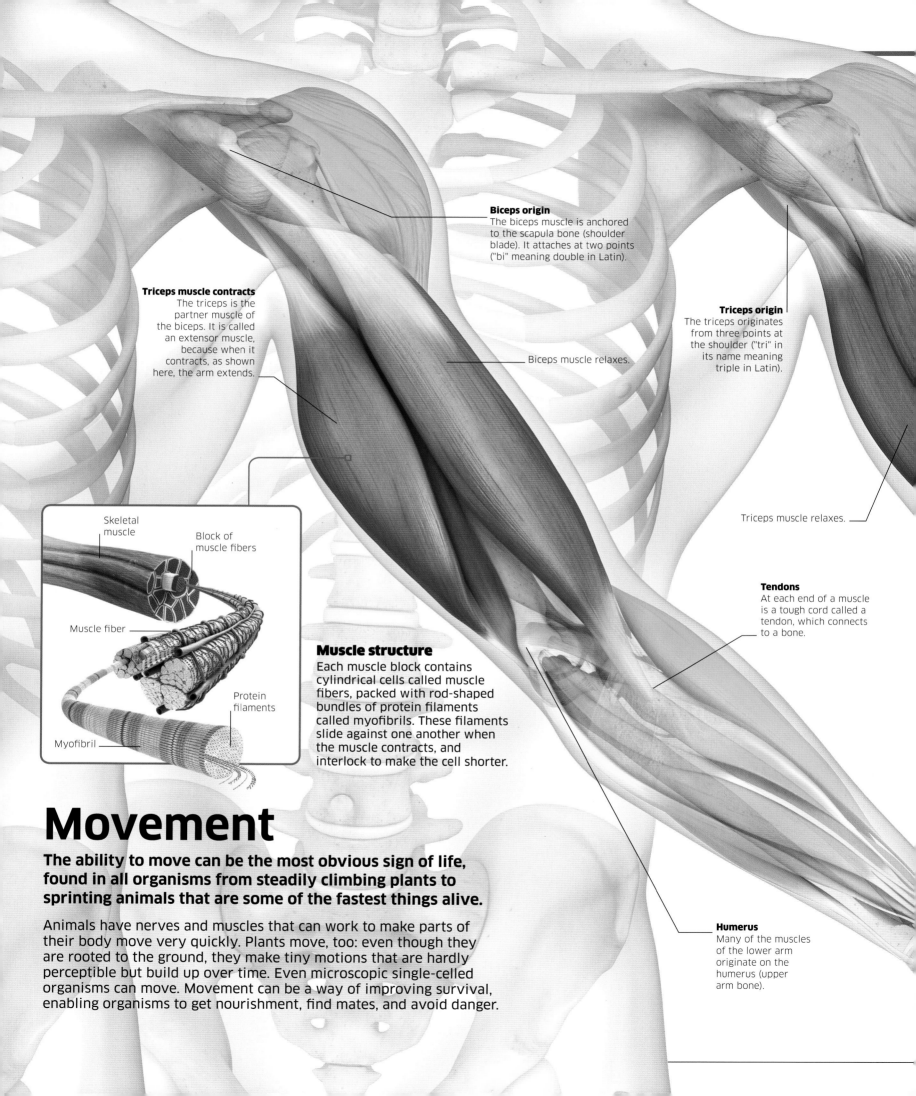

Biceps origin
The biceps muscle is anchored to the scapula bone (shoulder blade). It attaches at two points ("bi" meaning double in Latin).

Triceps muscle contracts
The triceps is the partner muscle of the biceps. It is called an extensor muscle, because when it contracts, as shown here, the arm extends.

Biceps muscle relaxes.

Triceps origin
The triceps originates from three points at the shoulder ("tri" in its name meaning triple in Latin).

Triceps muscle relaxes.

Skeletal muscle

Block of muscle fibers

Muscle fiber

Protein filaments

Myofibril

Muscle structure
Each muscle block contains cylindrical cells called muscle fibers, packed with rod-shaped bundles of protein filaments called myofibrils. These filaments slide against one another when the muscle contracts, and interlock to make the cell shorter.

Tendons
At each end of a muscle is a tough cord called a tendon, which connects to a bone.

Movement

The ability to move can be the most obvious sign of life, found in all organisms from steadily climbing plants to sprinting animals that are some of the fastest things alive.

Animals have nerves and muscles that can work to make parts of their body move very quickly. Plants move, too: even though they are rooted to the ground, they make tiny motions that are hardly perceptible but build up over time. Even microscopic single-celled organisms can move. Movement can be a way of improving survival, enabling organisms to get nourishment, find mates, and avoid danger.

Humerus
Many of the muscles of the lower arm originate on the humerus (upper arm bone).

The snapping movement of a **Venus fly trap** is controlled by an **electrical impulse**.

Heart muscle is **the only muscle that can spontaneously contract** without being triggered by a nerve impulse.

171

It takes a muscle around
twice as long
to relax than to contract.

Biceps muscle contracts
The biceps of the upper arm is called a flexor muscle, because when it contracts, as shown here, it pulls on the lower arm to flex (bend) the elbow joint.

Finger movement
There are no muscles in the fingers—only tendons. These connect to the muscles in the rest of the hand.

Forearm muscles
The muscles in the lower arm control the complex movements of the wrist, hand, and fingers.

Working in pairs
Muscles are made up of bundles of long cells that either contract (shorten) or relax (lengthen) when triggered by the nervous system. The most common type of muscles are those connected to the bones of the skeleton. They pull on the bones when they contract, causing actions like the movement of this arm. Because muscles cannot push, they have to work in pairs—one muscle to pull the arm upward and another to pull it back down.

Rotating the arm
As well as pulling the lower arm toward it, the biceps can also rotate the forearm so the palm of the hand faces upward.

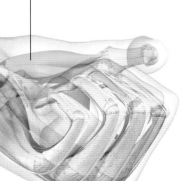

Plant movement
Like animals, plants move to make the most of their environment. The shoot tips of plants are especially sensitive to light and can slowly bend toward a light source. A chemical called auxin (which regulates growth) encourages the shadier side of the shoot to grow more, bending the plant toward the sun.

Auxin (pink) produced in the shoot tip spreads down through the shoot, making it grow upward.

When light shines from one direction, auxin moves to the shadier side.

On the shadier side, the auxin stimulates the plant cells to grow bigger, so that the shoot bends toward the light.

Support structures
Animals have a skeleton to support their bodies and protect their soft organs. This is especially important for large land-living animals that are not supported by water. Skeletons also provide a firm support for contracting muscles, helping animals to have the strength to move around.

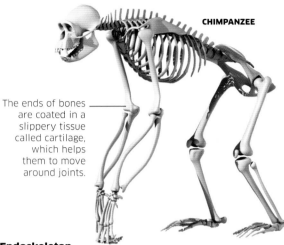

CHIMPANZEE

The ends of bones are coated in a slippery tissue called cartilage, which helps them to move around joints.

Endoskeleton
Vertebrate animals—including fish, amphibians, reptiles, birds, and mammals—have a hard internal skeleton within their bodies. The muscles surround the skeleton and pull on its bones.

The skeleton is thinner and more flexible around the joints.

HORNED GHOST CRAB

Exoskeleton
Many types of invertebrates, such as insects and crustaceans, are supported by an external skeleton that covers their body like a suit of armor with muscles inside. Exoskeletons cannot grow with the rest of the body, so must be periodically shed and replaced.

MOON JELLYFISH

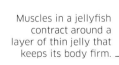

Muscles in a jellyfish contract around a layer of thin jelly that keeps its body firm.

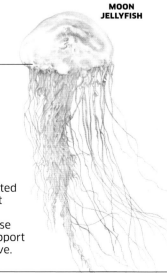

Hydroskeleton
Some kinds of soft-bodied animals, such as sea anemones and earthworms, are supported by internal pouches that stay firm because they are filled with fluid. These water-filled pouches support the muscles as they move.

Pulsating

A jellyfish moves neither forward nor backward, but instead rises and falls in the water. It has a ring of muscles around the rim of its bell. When these contract, the bell closes slightly like a drawstring bag, forcing water out and shooting the animal upward.

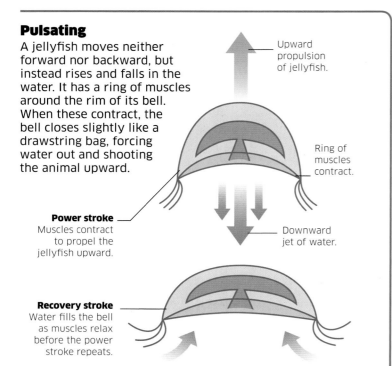

Upward propulsion of jellyfish.

Ring of muscles contract.

Downward jet of water.

Power stroke
Muscles contract to propel the jellyfish upward.

Recovery stroke
Water fills the bell as muscles relax before the power stroke repeats.

Getting around

Whether over land, underwater, or in the air, animals can move themselves around in extraordinary ways when all their muscles work together.

Although all living things move parts of their body to an extent, only animals can truly "locomote". This is when the entire body moves to a different location. Some animals do it without any muscle power at all—riding on ocean currents or getting blown by the wind. But most animals locomote under their own steam. They do so for many different reasons: to find food or a mate, or to escape from predators. Some animals migrate over enormous distances from season to season, or even from day to day.

Tiny, deep ocean pygmy sharks grow no bigger than 8 in (20 cm), but each night **swim 1 mile (1.5 km) up to the surface and back** in order to feed.

Tiger beetles have long legs to give them speed.

Tiger beetle

Predatory tiger beetles are fast sprinters. Like all insects, they have six legs, and when running they lift three simultaneously, leaving three in contact with the ground. However, their big eyes cannot keep up with their speed, meaning their vision is blurred every time they run.

Running

An animal that moves over land needs its muscles to pull against a strong supporting framework. It also needs good balance to stay upright, meaning that its muscles and skeleton must work together with the nervous system. Some animals move slowly, even when in a hurry, but others are born to run. The fastest runners not only have powerful muscles to move their limbs more quickly, but also take much longer strides.

A cheetah can accelerate to **62 mph (100 km/h)** in just three seconds.

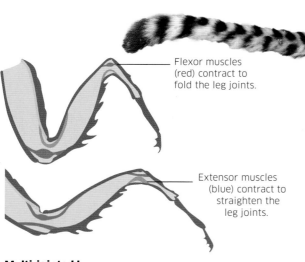

Flexor muscles (red) contract to fold the leg joints.

Extensor muscles (blue) contract to straighten the leg joints.

Multi-jointed leg

Arthropods, including insects, spiders, and crabs, have multi-jointed legs that carry an armorlike outer skeleton, with their muscles attached on the inside. Their muscles work in pairs around each joint—one to flex (bend) and the other to extend.

A flexible spine helps the cheetah's body bend up and down when sprinting.

Long legs deliver long strides.

All four feet are airborne at least twice for each stride.

Cheetah

The cheetah accelerates faster than any other land animal, but it is not just its long legs that help it pick up speed. Humans run on the flats of their feet, but in cats the toes bear the weight—effectively lengthening the limb. The cheetah's flexible backbone helps make its legs swing wider, adding 10 percent to its stride.

The **strongest jumper** is the **froghopper bug**, which leaps **a distance 70 times its body size**.

75 mph (120 km/h)—**the speed of a peregrine falcon** as it dives for prey in the sky. It is **the fastest animal of all**.

173

Burrowing

Life underground comes with special challenges. Burrowers need the strength to dig through soil to create a passage, and the ability to crawl through small openings. Moles use their feet like shovels to claw back the soil, but earthworms bulldoze their way through with their bodies.

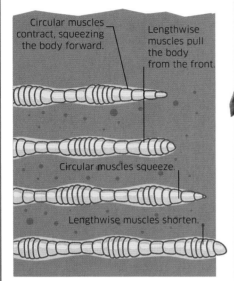

Circular muscles contract, squeezing the body forward.

Lengthwise muscles pull the body from the front.

Circular muscles squeeze.

Lengthwise muscles shorten.

Earthworm
An earthworm has two sets of muscles. One set encircles the body and squeezes to push it forward, like toothpaste from a tube. The other pulls the body forward.

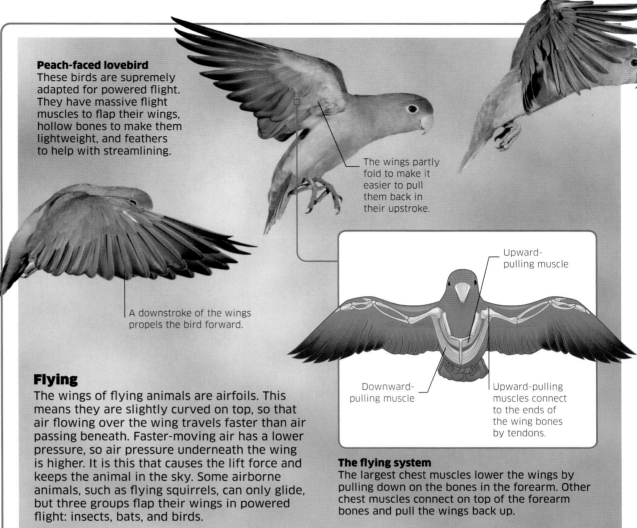

Peach-faced lovebird
These birds are supremely adapted for powered flight. They have massive flight muscles to flap their wings, hollow bones to make them lightweight, and feathers to help with streamlining.

The wings partly fold to make it easier to pull them back in their upstroke.

A downstroke of the wings propels the bird forward.

Upward-pulling muscle

Downward-pulling muscle

Upward-pulling muscles connect to the ends of the wing bones by tendons.

Flying
The wings of flying animals are airfoils. This means they are slightly curved on top, so that air flowing over the wing travels faster than air passing beneath. Faster-moving air has a lower pressure, so air pressure underneath the wing is higher. It is this that causes the lift force and keeps the animal in the sky. Some airborne animals, such as flying squirrels, can only glide, but three groups flap their wings in powered flight: insects, bats, and birds.

The flying system
The largest chest muscles lower the wings by pulling down on the bones in the forearm. Other chest muscles connect on top of the forearm bones and pull the wings back up.

Swimming

Water is thicker than air, so it exerts a bigger force called drag against any animal that moves through it. Swimming animals reduce drag by being streamlined. Even though marine animals, such as fish and dolphins are only distantly related, they both have similar body shapes, to better propel themselves through the water.

Swimming fish
Fish have blocks of muscle in the sides of their body. These contract to bend the body in an "S" shape, sweeping the tail from side to side and propelling the fish forward.

Sailfish
The enormous fin of a sailfish helps to steady its body—letting it get close to prey undetected. However, when the sail is lowered, it gives chase faster than any other fish in the ocean.

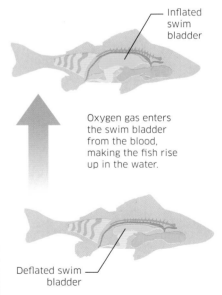

Inflated swim bladder

Oxygen gas enters the swim bladder from the blood, making the fish rise up in the water.

Deflated swim bladder

Controlling buoyancy
Fish are heavier than water, but most bony fish have a gas-filled chamber—the swim bladder—for staying buoyant when swimming. By controlling the volume of gas inside the swim bladder, fish can rise or sink through different water levels.

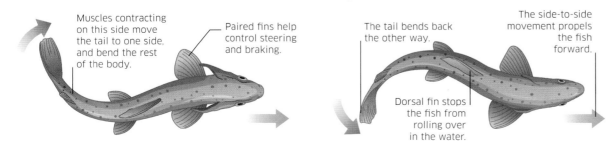

Muscles contracting on this side move the tail to one side, and bend the rest of the body.

Paired fins help control steering and braking.

The tail bends back the other way.

The side-to-side movement propels the fish forward.

Dorsal fin stops the fish from rolling over in the water.

Plant reproduction

Despite being rooted in the ground, plants work hard to ensure the survival of their species. With the help of wind, water, and animals, they fertilize one another and disperse their seeds far and wide.

Flowers are the reproductive organs of most kinds of plants and contain both male and female cells. The male cells—encased in dusty pollen grains—fertilize eggs in the flower's female parts. Each tiny young plant produced is then enclosed inside a seed: a survival capsule that protects its contents until they are ready to germinate.

Stamen
Yellow stamens, which produce dustlike pollen grains, are the male parts of the plant.

Carpenter bees visit the flowers to collect sugary nectar—an energy-rich food.

1 Flowering
The flower's vibrant purple stripes guide a carpenter bee to the nectar glands at its center. Other plants with less attractive flowers may instead scatter their pollen on the wind.

2 Pollination
Yellow stamens brush the insect's hairy body with pollen, which the bees carry with them to the purple clublike stigmas of another plant in the species.

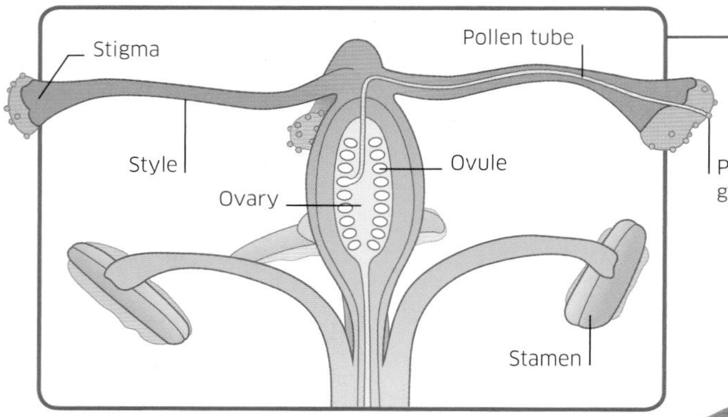

Stigma

Style

Ovary

Ovule

Pollen tube

Pollen grain

Stamen

3 Fertilization
After landing on the stigma, the pollen grains sprout microscopic tubes to carry their male cells down the style to reach the female eggs. Each fertilized egg then grows into an embryo, nestled inside a white capsule called an ovule.

After fertilization, the petals of a flower shrivel and fall off.

Reproduction partnerships
Like many kinds of plants, the passion vine from South America relies on animals to help it reproduce. Large, hairy carpenter bees in search of sweet nectar carry pollen from flower to flower, while birds with a taste for fruit—here the great kiskadee—spread the seeds.

4 Fruiting
When fertilized, the base of the flower begins to develop into a fleshy fruit. The ovules embedded inside harden to form seeds.

Many kinds of flowers are **pollinated by insects**, but others use **birds or even bats**.

The **seeds of fir trees** and related plants develop from **cones instead of flowers**.

175

6 Germination
If seeds land on moist ground, the embryos inside them start to grow and the seeds germinate. Roots grow down to absorb water and minerals, while shoots sprout upward to make leaves.

A new shoot emerges from the split seed capsule.

Leaves spring up as the plant develops.

Stigma
The purple stigmas are female parts of the flower, which collect the pollen grains.

Style
A style connects each stigma to the ovary at its base.

5 Seed dispersal
The fruit turns orange and gets sweeter as it ripens. This attracts fruit-eaters, such as the great kiskadee, which consume the fruit and scatter the plant's seeds in their droppings.

Birds can spread seeds far away from the original plant, but they are not the only way these tiny capsules travel. Other seed species may be carried by wind or water.

Asexual reproduction

Many plants can reproduce asexually–meaning without producing male and female sex cells. Some develop side shoots, or runners, that split away into new plants. A few grow baby plants on their leaves.

Tiny new plants growing on the leaf of a hen-and-chicken fern fall off to produce entirely new ferns.

Reproducing by spores

Mosses and ferns do not produce flowers and seeds, but scatter spores instead. Spores are different from seeds, as they contain just a single cell rather than a fertilized embryo. These cells grow into plants with reproductive organs, which must fertilize each other to develop into mature plants that can produce a new generation of spores.

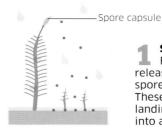

Spore capsule

1 Scattering spores
Fully-grown moss shoots release countless single-celled spores from spore capsules. These are carried by the wind, landing where each can grow into a new plant.

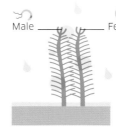

Male — — Female

2 Sex organs develop
Landing on moist ground, the spores grow into tiny, leafy shoots with microscopic sex organs. Male organs produce sperm, and female organs produce eggs.

3 Fertilization
Falling raindrops allow swimming sperm cells to reach the eggs held inside the female sex organs, where they fertilize them.

Spore-producing shoot

4 Spore capsule grows
Each fertilized egg grows into a new spore-producing shoot with a spore capsule, ready to make more spores and repeat the life cycle.

Producing young

The drive to reproduce is one of the most basic instincts in all animals. Many species devote their entire lives to finding a mate and making new young.

The most common way for animals to reproduce is through sexual reproduction—where sperm cells produced by a male fertilize egg cells produced by a female. The fertilized egg then becomes an embryo that will slowly grow and develop into a new animal. Many underwater animals release their sperm and eggs together into open water, but land animals must mate so that sperm are passed into the female's body and can swim inside it to reach her eggs.

Laying eggs on land

In some land animals, such as birds and reptiles, eggs are fertilized inside the mother's body and then laid—usually into a nest. These eggs have a hard, protective shell that encases the embryo inside and stops it from drying out. They also contain a big store of food— the yolk—which nourishes the embryo as it develops. It can take weeks or even months before the baby is big enough to hatch and survive in the world outside.

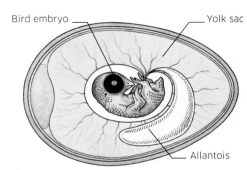

Bird embryo — Yolk sac

Allantois

Inside a bird's egg

The shell of a bird's egg lets in air to help the embryo breathe. The yolk sac provides nutrients as it grows into a chick, while another sac, the allantois, helps collect oxygen and waste.

Giving birth to live young

Except for a few egg-laying species (called monotremes), mammals give birth to live young. The mother must support the growing embryos inside her body—a demanding task that may involve her taking in extra nutrients. The babies grow in a part of the mother's body called the uterus, or womb, where a special organ called a placenta passes them food and oxygen.

A new generation of mice

Some mammals, such as humans, usually give birth to one baby at a time. Others have large litters—like mice, which can produce up to 14 babies at one time. Each one starts as a fertilized egg, grows into an embryo, and then is born just three weeks later.

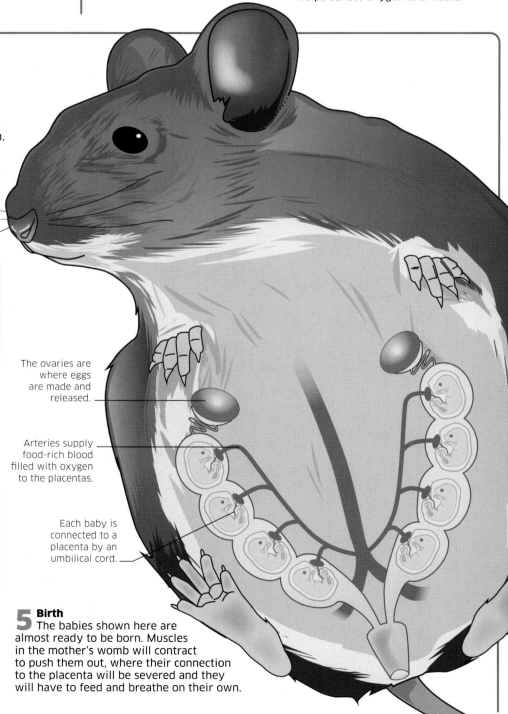

The ovaries are where eggs are made and released.

Arteries supply food-rich blood filled with oxygen to the placentas.

Each baby is connected to a placenta by an umbilical cord.

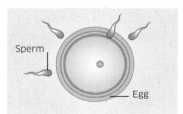

Sperm

Egg

1 Fertilization
When a male mouse mates with a female, thousands of sperm enter her body and swim to her eggs. The first to arrive penetrates an egg—fertilizing it.

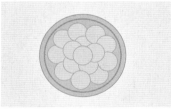

2 Embryo forms
The fertilized egg cell now contains a mixture of genes from the sperm and the egg. It divides multiple times to form a microscopic ball of cells called an embryo.

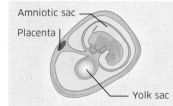

Cell mass

Early stage yolk sac

3 Implantation
The embryo becomes a hollow ball. A cell mass on one side will become the mouse's body. The ball travels into the womb to embed into its wall— an event called implantation.

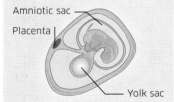

Amniotic sac

Placenta

Yolk sac

4 Placenta grows
The baby mouse begins to form and gets nutrients from first a temporary yolk sac and then a placenta. A fluid-filled bag, the amniotic sac, cushions the embryo.

5 Birth
The babies shown here are almost ready to be born. Muscles in the mother's womb will contract to push them out, where their connection to the placenta will be severed and they will have to feed and breathe on their own.

300 million eggs can be produced by the ocean sunfish at one time—more than any other back-boned animal.

Female seahorses lay their eggs inside a pouch on the male's body, so it is the father that gives birth to them.

177

Laying eggs in water

Fish fertilize their eggs externally, so the females lay unfertilized eggs directly into the water. Instead of having hard shells, fish eggs are usually coated in a soft jelly that will cushion and protect the developing embryos. Most fish do not wait around to see the embryos develop, but simply scatter lots of floating eggs and swimming sperm and leave the outcome to chance. However, some species, such as clown fish, carefully tend to their developing babies.

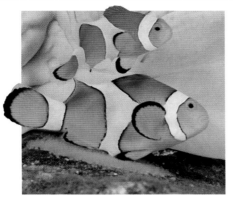

1 Laying and fertilization
A female clown fish lays her eggs onto a hard surface. The male then releases his sperm to fertilize them.

2 Caring for the eggs
During the week it takes for them to hatch, the father guards the eggs, using his mouth to clean them.

3 Hatching
Tiny babies, called fry, break out of the eggs. They grow quickly, feeding on nutrients in their yolk sac.

Investing in babies

All animals spend a lot of time and effort in breeding, but they invest this energy in different ways. Some—such as many insects and most fish—produce thousands of eggs at once, and a few even die after breeding. Others produce just one baby at a time, but spend a lot of time caring for each one.

Breeding lifetimes

Animals must have fully grown reproductive systems before they can breed, and some can take years to develop these. While some animals breed often throughout their long lives, shorter-lived species make up for their limited life spans by producing many babies each time.

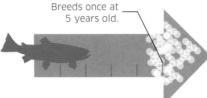

Breeds once at 5 years old.

Sockeye salmon
Salmon swim from the ocean into rivers to scatter millions of eggs. They die after this huge effort, so can only breed once.

The pregnancy of an elephant **lasts for 22 months,** the longest time of any mammal.

Starts breeding at 3 years old.

Can breed until 10 years old.

Common toad
Toads can keep breeding for seven years of their adult life, and each year produce thousands of eggs.

African elephant
It takes so long to rear an elephant calf that elephants only manage it every few years. However, they continue to reproduce for many decades.

Starts breeding at 20 years old.

Continues breeding until 60 years old.

Parental care

The best way to ensure that babies survive is to give them good care when they are at their most vulnerable, but animal parents vary a lot in their degree of devotion. Many invertebrates give limited parental care or none at all. But mammal babies may be nurtured by their parents for many years.

Newborn kangaroos live in a pouch in their mother's bodies, where they continue to grow and develop.

Coral
Adult coral provide no parental care. Young microscopic stages of coral—called larvae—must fend for themselves in the open ocean, where most will get eaten by predators.

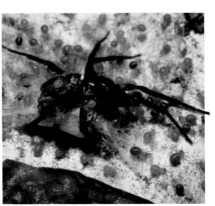

Black lace weaver spider
This spider mother makes the ultimate sacrifice for her babies. After laying more eggs for her young to eat, she encourages them to bite her. This stirs their predatory instincts, and they eat her.

Orangutan
Childhood for this tree-living ape lasts well into the teenage years—just like in humans. During this time, the young will stick close to their mother for protection and learn vital survival skills from her.

A male dragonfly **guards over his pond** and the females in his territory.

1 Mating
A male dragonfly holds onto his mate by hooking the end of his abdomen in the groove of her neck. In this position, he passes sperm into her body to fertilize her eggs.

6 Male dragonfly
As flying adults with 4 in (10 cm) wingspans, dragonflies grow no more. They skim close to the surface of the pond, catching prey in midair.

Delicate wings only emerge in the last stage of its life cycle.

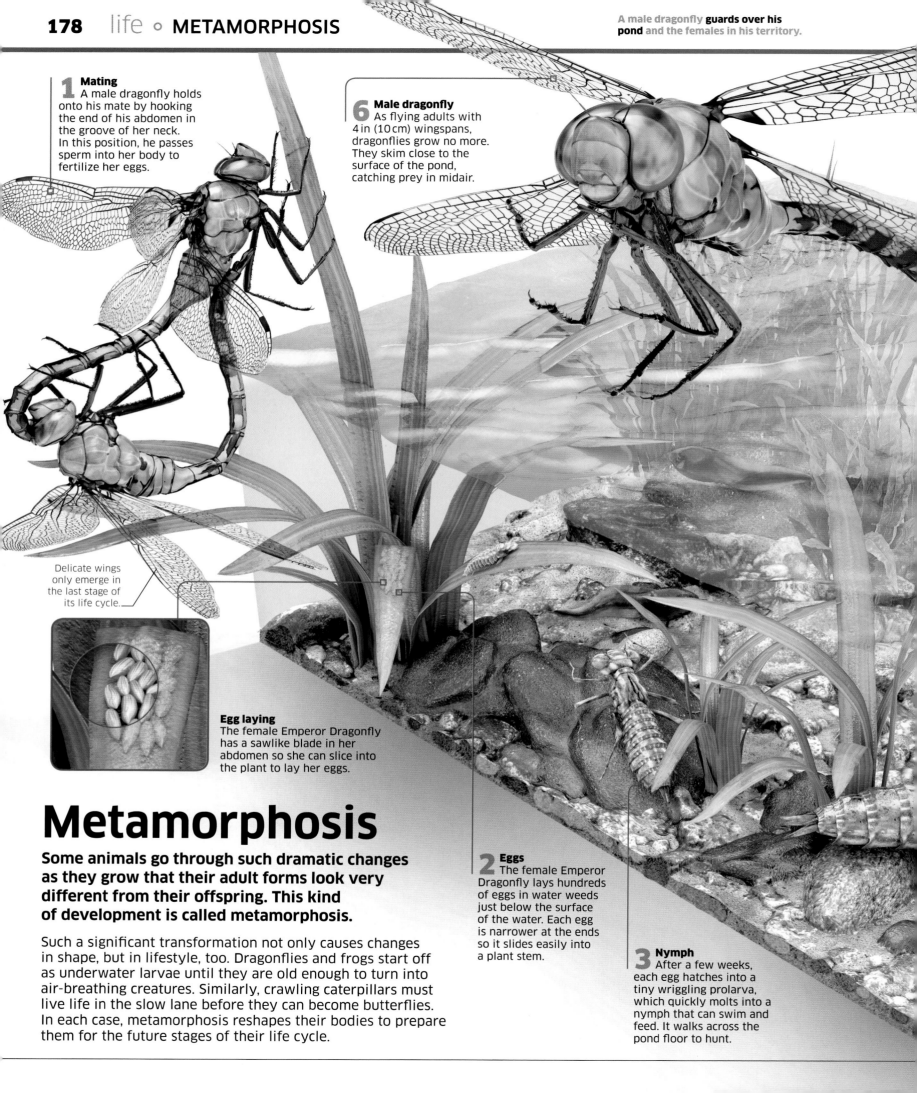

Egg laying
The female Emperor Dragonfly has a sawlike blade in her abdomen so she can slice into the plant to lay her eggs.

Metamorphosis

Some animals go through such dramatic changes as they grow that their adult forms look very different from their offspring. This kind of development is called metamorphosis.

Such a significant transformation not only causes changes in shape, but in lifestyle, too. Dragonflies and frogs start off as underwater larvae until they are old enough to turn into air-breathing creatures. Similarly, crawling caterpillars must live life in the slow lane before they can become butterflies. In each case, metamorphosis reshapes their bodies to prepare them for the future stages of their life cycle.

2 Eggs
The female Emperor Dragonfly lays hundreds of eggs in water weeds just below the surface of the water. Each egg is narrower at the ends so it slides easily into a plant stem.

3 Nymph
After a few weeks, each egg hatches into a tiny wriggling prolarva, which quickly molts into a nymph that can swim and feed. It walks across the pond floor to hunt.

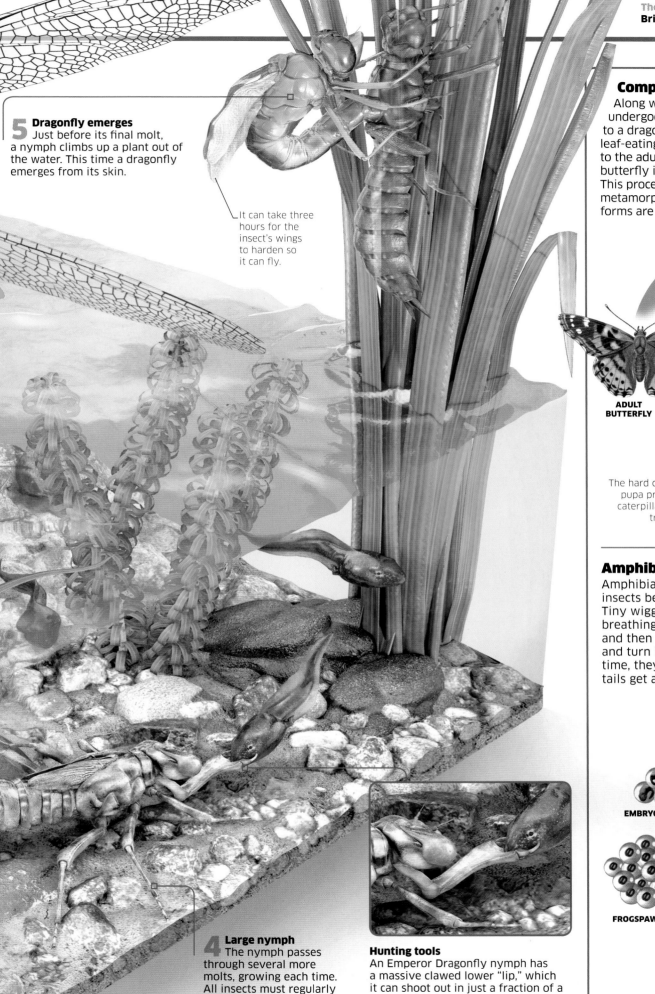

5 Dragonfly emerges
Just before its final molt,
a nymph climbs up a plant out of
the water. This time a dragonfly
emerges from its skin.

It can take three
hours for the
insect's wings
to harden so
it can fly.

Complete metamorphosis

Along with many other insects, a butterfly
undergoes a different kind of metamorphosis
to a dragonfly. Its larva is a caterpillar, a
leaf-eating creature that has no resemblance
to the adult form at all. It changes into a flying
butterfly in a single transformation event.
This process is different to incomplete
metamorphosis, where the multiple larval
forms are smaller versions of the adult.

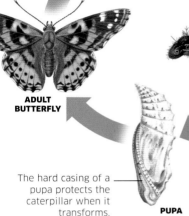

EGG

CATERPILLAR

ADULT
BUTTERFLY

The hard casing of a
pupa protects the
caterpillar when it
transforms.

PUPA

Amphibian life cycle

Amphibians grow more gradually than
insects because they do not need to molt.
Tiny wiggling tadpoles—with gills for
breathing underwater—hatch from frogspawn
and then take weeks or months to get bigger
and turn into air-breathing frogs. During this
time, they steadily grow their legs and their
tails get absorbed back into their bodies.

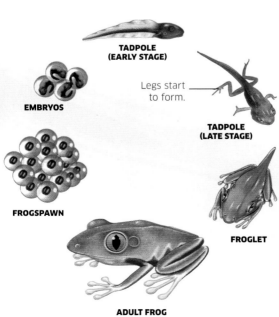

TADPOLE
(EARLY STAGE)

Legs start
to form.

EMBRYOS

TADPOLE
(LATE STAGE)

FROGSPAWN

FROGLET

ADULT FROG

4 Large nymph
The nymph passes
through several more
molts, growing each time.
All insects must regularly
molt their outer skin
because this strong casing
cannot expand as they grow.

Hunting tools
An Emperor Dragonfly nymph has
a massive clawed lower "lip," which
it can shoot out in just a fraction of a
second to grab its prey. The nymphs
can grow over 2 in (5 cm) long—large
enough to grab large prey such as fish.

Packaging the information

Inside the nucleus of every cell in the human body are 46 molecules of DNA, carrying all the information needed to build and maintain a human being. Each molecule is shaped like a twisted ladder—named a double helix—and packaged up into a bundle called a chromosome. Genetic information is carried by the sequence of different chemical units, known as bases, that make up the "rungs" of the ladder.

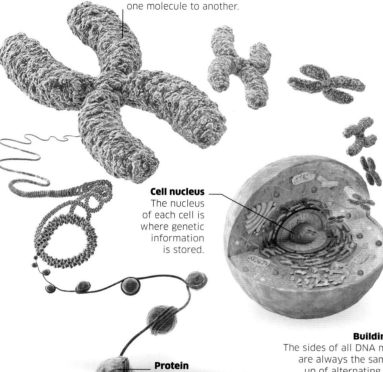

Chromosome
A tightly packed mixture of protein and DNA forms a chromosome. Each chromosome contains one long molecule of DNA. The DNA in this chromosome has replicated to make an X-shape. It is ready to split in two, sending one molecule to one cell and one molecule to another.

Cell nucleus
The nucleus of each cell is where genetic information is stored.

Protein
The DNA double helix is wrapped around balls of protein to help it fit inside the cell.

Genetics and DNA

The characteristics of a living thing—who we are and what we look like—are determined by a set of instructions carried inside each of the body's cells.

Instructions for building the body and keeping it working properly are held in a substance called DNA (deoxyribonucleic acid). The arrangement of chemical building blocks in DNA determines whether a living thing grows into an oak tree, a human being, or any other kind of organism. DNA is also copied whenever cells divide, so that all the cells of the body carry a set of these vital genetic instructions. Half of each organism's DNA is also passed on to the next generation in either male or female sex cells.

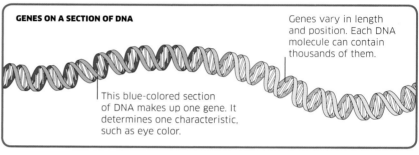

GENES ON A SECTION OF DNA

Genes vary in length and position. Each DNA molecule can contain thousands of them.

This blue-colored section of DNA makes up one gene. It determines one characteristic, such as eye color.

What is a gene?

The information along DNA is arranged in sections called genes. Each gene has a unique sequence of bases. This sequence acts as a code to tell the cell to make a specific protein, which, in turn, affects a characteristic of the body.

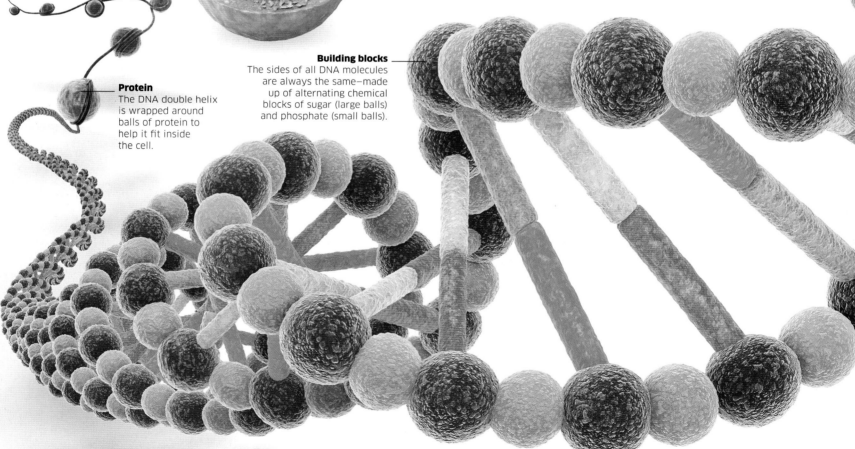

Building blocks
The sides of all DNA molecules are always the same—made up of alternating chemical blocks of sugar (large balls) and phosphate (small balls).

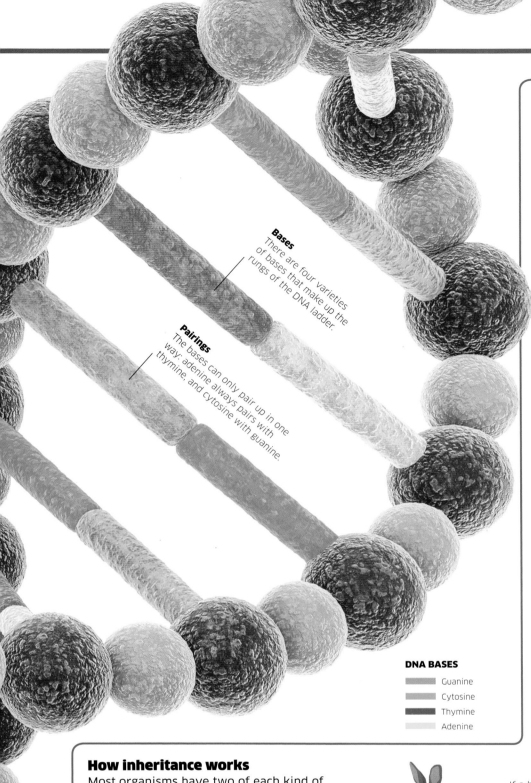

Bases
There are four varieties of bases that make up the rungs of the DNA ladder.

Pairings
The bases can only pair up in one way: adenine always pairs with thymine, and cytosine with guanine.

DNA BASES
- Guanine
- Cytosine
- Thymine
- Adenine

DNA replication

Cells replicate themselves by splitting in two. Therefore, all the instructions held in DNA must be copied before a cell divides, so each new cell will have a full set. The DNA does this by splitting into two strands. Each of these then provides a template for building a new double helix.

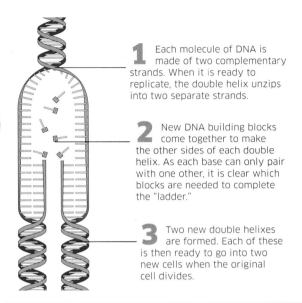

1 Each molecule of DNA is made of two complementary strands. When it is ready to replicate, the double helix unzips into two separate strands.

2 New DNA building blocks come together to make the other sides of each double helix. As each base can only pair with one other, it is clear which blocks are needed to complete the "ladder."

3 Two new double helixes are formed. Each of these is then ready to go into two new cells when the original cell divides.

What gets inherited?

Many human features, such as eye color, hair color, and blood type, are due to particular genes. Different varieties of genes, called alleles, determine variation in these characteristics. Other characteristics, such as height, are affected by many genes working together, but also by other factors, such as diet.

Genes
Some characteristics are only inherited from parents.

EYE COLOR

EARLOBE SHAPE

Genes and environment
Other characteristics are influenced by genes and the environment.

AGE WHEN HAIR TURNS GRAY

EYESIGHT

How inheritance works

Most organisms have two of each kind of gene—one from each parent. Many genes have two or more variations, called alleles, so the genes an animal inherits from its mother and father may be identical or different. When two animals, such as rabbits, reproduce, there are many different combinations of alleles their offspring can receive. Some alleles are dominant (like those for brown fur), and when a baby rabbit has two different alleles it will have the characteristic of the dominant allele. Other alleles are recessive, and babies will only have the characteristic they determine if they have two of them. This explains why some children inherit physical characteristics not seen in their parents.

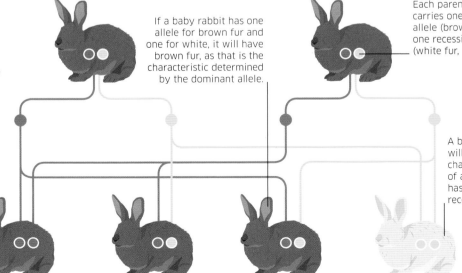

If a baby rabbit has one allele for brown fur and one for white, it will have brown fur, as that is the characteristic determined by the dominant allele.

Each parent rabbit carries one dominant allele (brown fur) and one recessive allele (white fur, or albinism).

A baby rabbit will only have the characteristics of albinism if it has two of the recessive alleles.

A place to live

Every form of life—each species of plant, animal, or microbe—has a specific set of needs that means it can only thrive in suitable places.

Habitats are places where organisms live. A habitat can be as small as a rotting log or as big as the open ocean, but each one offers a different mixture of conditions that suits a particular community of species. There, the inhabitants that are adapted to these conditions—to the habitat's climate, food, and all other factors—can grow and survive long enough to produce the next generation.

Life between the tides

Nowhere can the diversity between habitats be seen better than where the land meets the sea. Conditions vary wildly on a rocky shore—from the submerged pools of the lower levels to the exposed land higher up. As the tide moves in and out daily, many species must be adapted to a life spent partly in the open air and partly underwater.

High shore
Only the toughest ocean species survive on the highest, driest part of the shore. The seaweed here, called channelled wrack, can survive losing more than 60 percent of its water content.

Middle shore
On the middle zone of the shore, a seaweed called bladder wrack spends about 50 percent of its time in the water and 50 percent out of the water as the tide rises and falls.

Lower shore
Life on the lowest part of the shore usually stays covered by seawater—a good habitat for organisms that cannot survive being exposed to the air.

Serrated wrack
Serrated wrack seaweed survives on the lower shore alone—where it is only uncovered when the tides are at their lowest.

Snails
Many animals, such as snails that graze on algae, can only feed when they are underwater.

Many organisms have **urban habitats**—from secretive **house mice** to **large leopards** that roam free in the city of Mumbai, India.

Microscopic **bacteria are found in every community**. There could be **thousands of species** of bacteria in just **a single teaspoon of soil**.

183

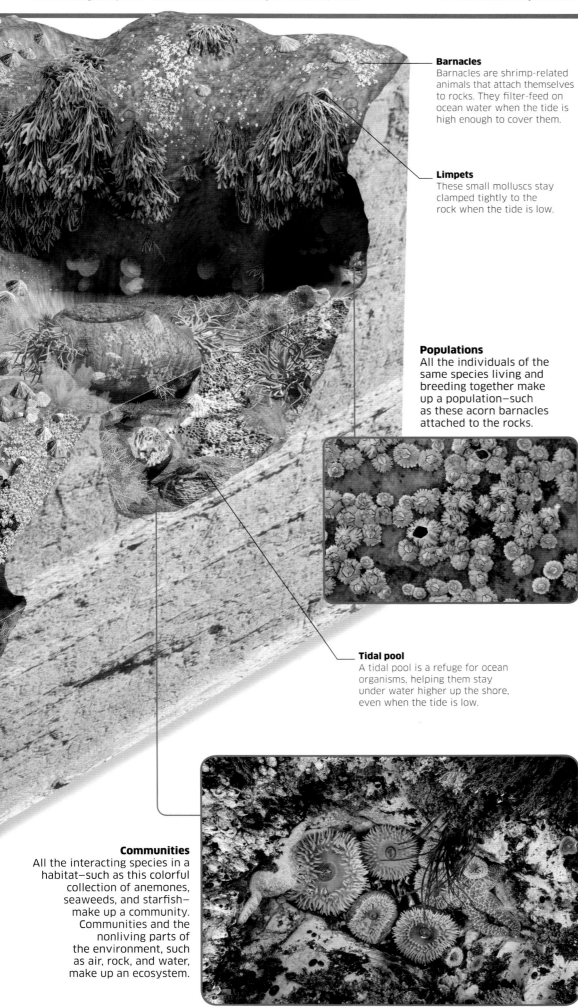

Barnacles
Barnacles are shrimp-related animals that attach themselves to rocks. They filter-feed on ocean water when the tide is high enough to cover them.

Limpets
These small molluscs stay clamped tightly to the rock when the tide is low.

Populations
All the individuals of the same species living and breeding together make up a population—such as these acorn barnacles attached to the rocks.

Tidal pool
A tidal pool is a refuge for ocean organisms, helping them stay under water higher up the shore, even when the tide is low.

Communities
All the interacting species in a habitat—such as this colorful collection of anemones, seaweeds, and starfish—make up a community. Communities and the nonliving parts of the environment, such as air, rock, and water, make up an ecosystem.

Interactions between species

Within a habitat's community, species interact with one another in many ways. Each kind of interaction is called a symbiosis, and there are several different kinds of partnerships: some helpful, and some harmful.

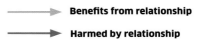

→ Benefits from relationship

→ Harmed by relationship

Mutualism
A flower is pollinated by a bee, while, in return, it provides the insect with nectar.

FLOWER   BEE

Parasitism
A blood-sucking tick gets food from its animal host, but the hedgehog is harmed.

TICK   HEDGEHOG

Predation
Predators take their partnerships to the extreme by killing their prey for food.

TIGER   GOAT

Competition
Scavengers competing for the same carcass each get a smaller share of food.

VULTURE   HYENA

Niches

The conditions required by a species (such as water) and the role the species plays in its habitat is called its niche. No two species have exactly the same niche. The sea goldie and the cardinal tetra share some conditions (both need warm temperatures), but not others (one lives in freshwater, the other in saltwater).

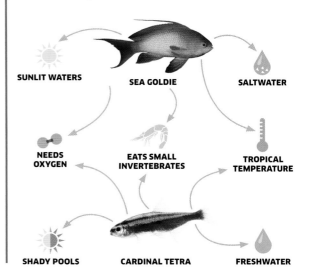

SUNLIT WATERS   SEA GOLDIE   SALTWATER

NEEDS OXYGEN   EATS SMALL INVERTEBRATES   TROPICAL TEMPERATURE

SHADY POOLS   CARDINAL TETRA   FRESHWATER

Oceanic zones

Covering nearly three-quarters of Earth's surface, and reaching down to 9 miles (11 km) at their deepest point, the oceans make up the biggest biome by volume. All life here lives submerged in salty marine waters, but conditions vary enormously from the coastlines down to the ocean's bottom.

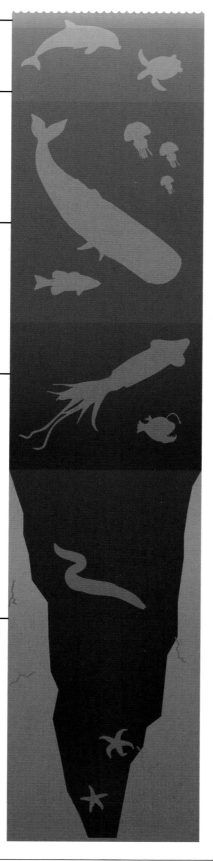

Sunlit zone
(0–650 ft/0–200 m)
Bright sunlight provides energy for ocean food chains that start with algae.

Twilight zone
(650–3,280 ft/200–1,000 m)
Sunlight cannot penetrate far into the ocean. As depth increases, conditions are too dark for algae, but animals thrive.

Midnight zone
(3,280–13,000 ft/ 1,000–4,000 m)
Animals find different ways of surviving in the dark ocean depths. Many use bioluminescence: they have light-producing organs to help them hunt for food or avoid danger.

Abyssal zone
(13,000–19,650 ft/ 4,000–6,000 m)
Near the ocean floor, water pressure is strong enough to crush a car and temperatures are near freezing. Most food chains here are supported by particles of dead matter raining down from above.

Hadal zone
(19,650–36,000 ft/ 6,000–11,000 m)
The ocean floor plunges down into trenches that form the deepest parts of the ocean. But even here there is life—with a few kinds of fishes diving down to 26,000 ft (8,000 m) and invertebrates voyaging deeper still.

Biomes

Places exposed to similar sets of conditions—such as temperature or rainfall—have similar-looking habitats, even when they are as far apart as North America and Asia. These habitat groups are called biomes. Over continents and islands, they include tundra, deserts, grasslands, forests—and freshwater lakes and rivers.

Tundra
Where land is close to the poles, conditions are so cold that the ground is permafrost—meaning it is frozen throughout the year. Here, trees are sparse or cannot grow at all, and the thin vegetation is made up of grasses, lichens, and small shrubs.

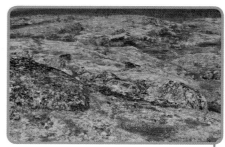

Taiga
The largest land biome is a broad belt of coniferous forest that encircles the world below the Arctic tundra. Conifers, pines, and related trees have needlelike leaves that help them survive low temperatures. They are evergreen—so they retain their tough foliage even in the coldest winters.

Temperate forest
The Earth's temperate zones are between the cold polar regions and the tropics around the equator. Many of the forests that grow in these seasonal regions are deciduous: they produce their leaves during the warm summers, but lose them in the cold winters.

Temperate grassland
Where the climate is too dry to support forests but too wet for desert, the land is covered with grassland—a habitat that supports a wide range of grazing animals. Temperate grasslands experience seasonal changes in temperature, but stay green throughout the year.

Tropical dry and coniferous forest
Some tropical regions have pronounced dry seasons that can last for months. Here, many kinds of trees drop their leaves in times of drought. Others have adaptations that help them to stay evergreen. In places, the forests are dominated by conifers with drought-resistant leaves.

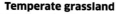

Extremophiles are organisms that **live in extreme habitats**—such as **bacteria that thrive** at **248°F (120°C) around volcanic vents.**

Habitats change: Antarctica is covered in snow and ice today, but **52 million years ago rainforests grew there.**

185

Habitats and biomes

Around Earth, plants, animals, and other organisms live in habitats that are as different as the driest, most windswept deserts and the deepest, darkest oceans.

Conditions vary from one part of the world to another, and they have a big effect on the kinds of living things that can survive together in any place. The freezing cold poles experience a winter of unbroken darkness for half the year, while the equator basks in tropical temperatures year-round. And the world of the oceans reaches from the sunlit surfaces down into the dark abyss.

Freshwater
Rainfall collecting in rivers and lakes creates freshwater habitats. Aquatic plants grow in their shallows and animals swim in the open water or crawl along their muddy or stony bottoms. Where rivers meet the sea, water is affected by the oceans' saltiness.

Mediterranean woodland
A Mediterranean-type climate has hot, dry summers and wet, mild winters. It is most common where lands in the temperate zone are influenced by mild ocean air. Its forests are dominated by trees—such as eucalyptus—that are sclerophyll, meaning they have leathery, heat-resistant leaves.

Montane grassland and shrubland
Temperatures drop with increasing altitude, so the habitat changes in mountain regions. Forests give way to grassland on exposed slopes, which are then replaced with sparser vegetation—called montane tundra—higher up.

Tropical rainforest
Where temperature, rainfall, and humidity remain high all year round, Earth is covered with tropical rainforest. These are the best conditions for many plants and animals to grow, and they have evolved into more different species than in any other land biome.

Desert
In some parts of the world—in temperate or tropical regions—the land receives so little rainfall that conditions are too dry for most grasses and trees. In arid places with hot days and cold nights, succulent plants survive by storing water in roots, stems, or leaves.

Tropical grassland
Grasslands in the tropics support some of the largest, most diverse gatherings of big grazing animals anywhere on Earth. Unlike most plants, grasses grow from the base of their leaves and thrive even when vast numbers of grazers eat the top of their foliage.

Cycles of matter

Many of Earth's crucial materials for life are constantly recycled through the environment.

All the atoms that make up the world around us are recycled in one way or another. Chemical reactions in living things, such as photosynthesis and respiration, drive much of this recycling. These processes help pass important elements like carbon and nitrogen between living things, the soil, and the atmosphere.

Nitrogen gas makes up about two-thirds of Earth's atmosphere.

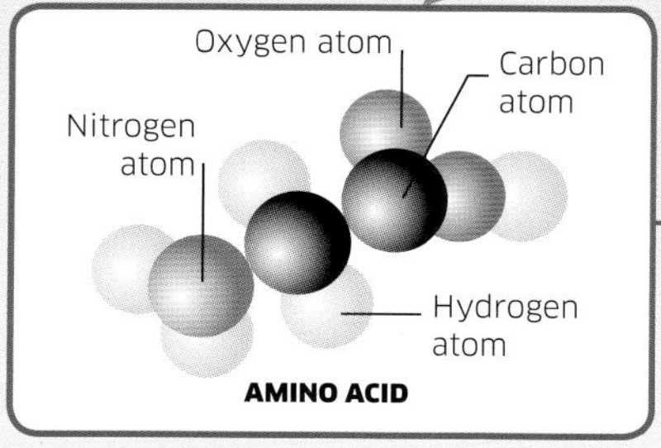

Oxygen atom
Carbon atom
Nitrogen atom
Hydrogen atom
AMINO ACID

Nitrogen in molecules
Molecules containing nitrogen—such as this amino acid—are used by plants, animals, and bacteria. It helps with growth and other vital functions.

Plants use nitrate from the roots to make food. When a leaf falls, it still contains this nitrogen.

NITROGEN MOLECULES

The nitrogen cycle
Nitrogen exists in many forms inside living things, including in DNA, proteins, and amino acids. Animals and many bacteria obtain their nitrogen by feeding on other organisms—dead or alive. Plants absorb it as a mineral called nitrate—a chemical that gets released into the soil through the action of the bacteria.

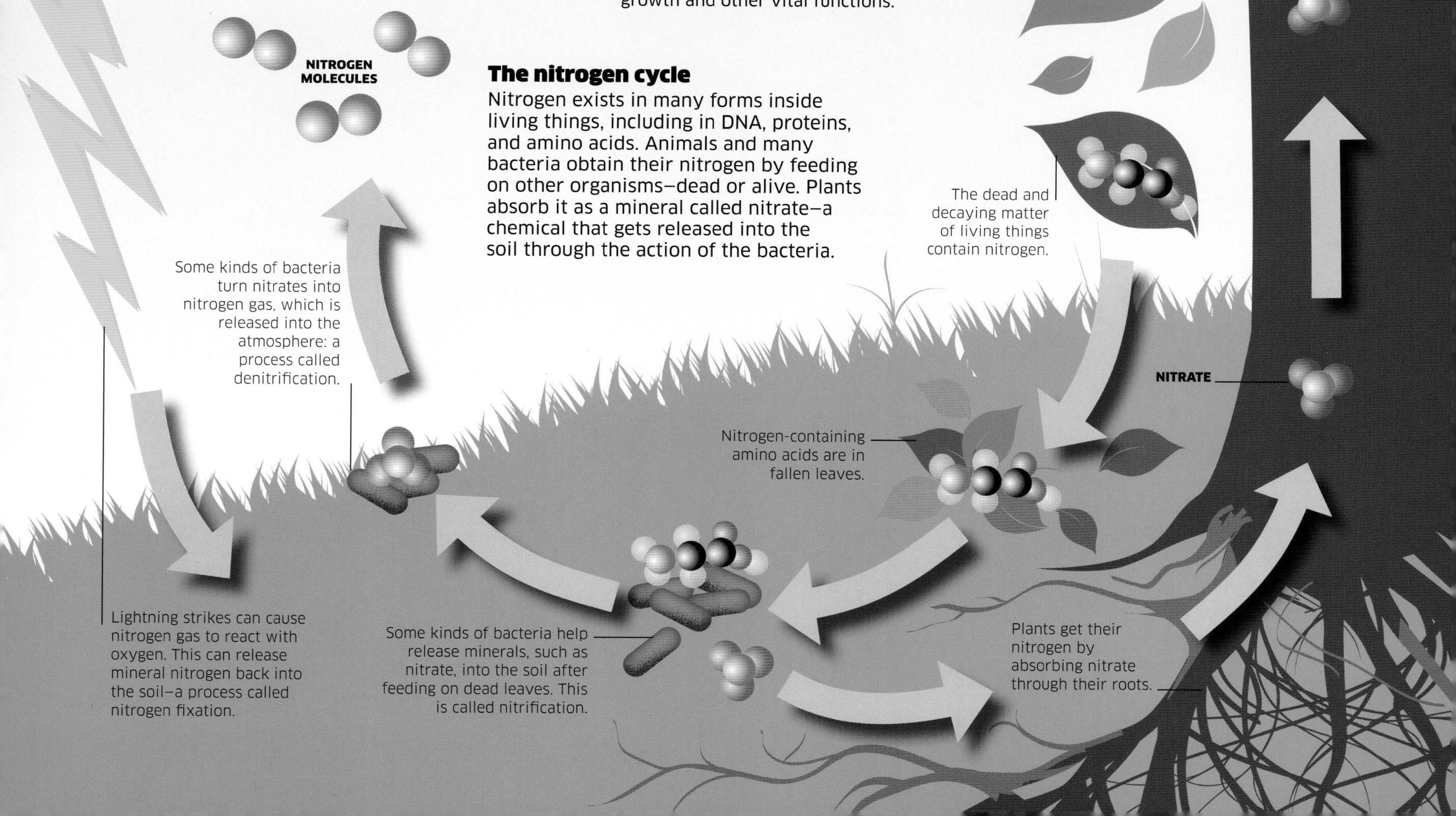

The dead and decaying matter of living things contain nitrogen.

Some kinds of bacteria turn nitrates into nitrogen gas, which is released into the atmosphere: a process called denitrification.

NITRATE

Nitrogen-containing amino acids are in fallen leaves.

Lightning strikes can cause nitrogen gas to react with oxygen. This can release mineral nitrogen back into the soil—a process called nitrogen fixation.

Some kinds of bacteria help release minerals, such as nitrate, into the soil after feeding on dead leaves. This is called nitrification.

Plants get their nitrogen by absorbing nitrate through their roots.

Oceans contain huge amounts of carbon—about
50 times more than the amount in the atmosphere.

187

When a plant is dry,
carbon makes up about
**50 percent
of its weight.**

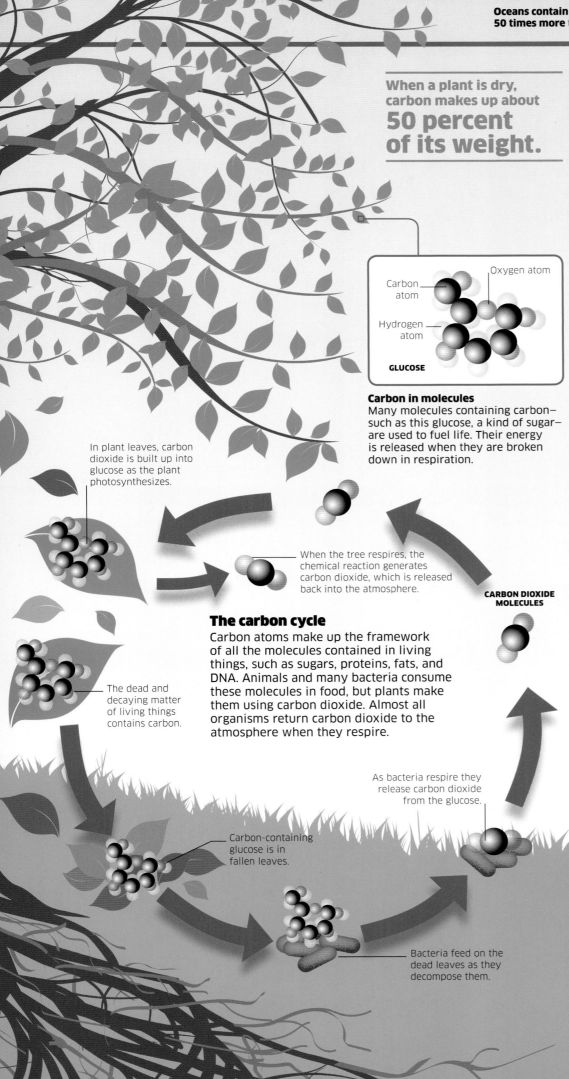

Carbon
atom

Oxygen atom

Hydrogen
atom

GLUCOSE

Carbon in molecules
Many molecules containing carbon—
such as this glucose, a kind of sugar—
are used to fuel life. Their energy
is released when they are broken
down in respiration.

In plant leaves, carbon
dioxide is built up into
glucose as the plant
photosynthesizes.

When the tree respires, the
chemical reaction generates
carbon dioxide, which is released
back into the atmosphere.

**CARBON DIOXIDE
MOLECULES**

The carbon cycle
Carbon atoms make up the framework
of all the molecules contained in living
things, such as sugars, proteins, fats, and
DNA. Animals and many bacteria consume
these molecules in food, but plants make
them using carbon dioxide. Almost all
organisms return carbon dioxide to the
atmosphere when they respire.

The dead and
decaying matter
of living things
contains carbon.

As bacteria respire they
release carbon dioxide
from the glucose.

Carbon-containing
glucose is in
fallen leaves.

Bacteria feed on the
dead leaves as they
decompose them.

Recycling water
Water is made of two elements—hydrogen
and oxygen—and travels through earth, sea,
and sky in the global water cycle. This cycle
is dominated by two processes: evaporation
and precipitation. Liquid water in oceans,
lakes, and even on plant leaves evaporates to
form gaseous water vapor. The water vapor
then condenses to form the tiny droplets
inside clouds, before falling back down to
Earth as precipitation: rain, hail, or snow.

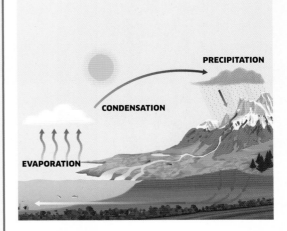

PRECIPITATION

CONDENSATION

EVAPORATION

The water cycle
Recycling of water is driven by the heating
effects of the sun. At it is warmed, surface water
evaporates into the atmosphere, but cools and
condenses to form rain or snow. Rainfall drains or
runs off to oceans and lakes to complete the cycle.

The long-term carbon cycle
Carbon atoms can be recycled between living
organisms and the air within days, but other
changes deeper in the earth take place over
millions of years. Lots of carbon gets trapped
within the bodies of dead organisms either
in the ocean or underground—forming fossil
fuels. It is then only released back into the
atmosphere through natural events such as
volcanic eruptions, or when it is burned by
humans in forms such as coal (see pp.36–37).

Coal mining
At this mining terminal in Australia, carbon-
containing coal is extracted from the ground.

1 Sunlight
When the sun is shining brightly, a single square meter of ocean surface collects more than a thousand joules of energy every second—enough to power a microwave oven.

When seabirds eat fish and return to shore, they transfer some of the energy of the ocean food chain to the land.

2 Phytoplankton
Plankton are tiny organisms that float in the water in billions. They contain algae called phytoplankton that make food by photosynthesis. Because they harness their energy directly from the sun, they are called the producers in a food chain.

3 Zooplankton
Tiny animals, called zooplankton, feed on the phytoplankton. Including a variety of shrimps and fish larvae, these are the primary consumers—animals that eat only algae or plants. They make up the second stage of a food chain.

4 Herring
The Pacific herring is a key link in the ocean food chain—an omnivore that eats both phytoplankton and zooplankton. It is the secondary consumer of the chain, and swims in large shoals that are easily snapped up by bigger predators.

Food waste
In deeper, darker parts of the ocean there is not enough light for photosynthesis, so food chains here often rely on dead organisms falling down through the water.

Photosynthesis by ocean-dwelling phytoplankton generates around
70 percent of the oxygen in the air.

The bodies of dead animals sink into the depths, where they are eaten by scavengers and decomposers.

Some deep-ocean **food chains start with minerals produced from volcanic vents**, rather than sunlight.

Although most primary consumers must eat large numbers of plants, just **one large tree can support thousands of plant-eaters.**

189

An ocean food chain

Near the surface of the ocean, where bright sunlight strikes the water, billions of microscopic algae photosynthesize to make food. In doing so, they kick-start a food chain that ends with some of the biggest meat-eaters on the planet.

Food chains

Living things rely on one another for nourishment. Energy in a food chain travels from the sun to plants, then animals, and finally to predators at the very top of the chain.

The sun provides the ultimate source of energy for life on Earth. Plants and algae change its light energy into chemical energy when they photosynthesize. Vegetarian (herbivorous) animals consume this food and they, in turn, are eaten by meat-eating carnivores. Energy is passed up the chain, and also transfers to scavengers and decomposers (see pp.146–147) when they feed on the dead remains of organisms.

Heat production
The chemical reactions that take place in living organisms generate heat, which escapes into the surrounding water.

Ecological pyramids

The levels of a food chain can be shown stacked up together to make an ecological pyramid. Plants or algae—the producers of food—form the base of the pyramid, with consumers on the higher levels. Each stage of the pyramid can also be shown as the total weight of the organisms on that level—their biomass. Both biomass and, usually, the number of animals decreases toward the top, as energy is lost at each level. Organisms use energy to stay alive and it is given off as waste and heat, leaving less to be passed on.

Only about 10 percent of the energy, and biomass, in any level passes to the one above.

2.2 lb (1 kg)

The amount of biomass decreases at each level.

The number of organisms usually decreases at each higher level of the pyramid.

Primary consumers, such as rabbits, must eat large numbers of plants to get enough energy.

TOP PREDATOR

22 lb (10 kg)

SECONDARY CONSUMERS

220 lb (100 kg)

PRIMARY CONSUMERS

2,200 lb (1,000 kg)

PRODUCERS

6 Great white shark
Being the food chain's top predator means that little else will prey on an adult great white shark. But, like all other organisms, after death the energy in its body will support decomposers that feed on its corpse.

5 Sea lion
Sea lions swim hundreds of yards from the shoreline to reach the best fishing grounds. As they hunt herring, the energy in the fish meat passes into the sea lion's body. Because their herring prey are also meat-eaters, this makes sea lions tertiary consumers.

Threatened species

Human activities, such as habitat destruction and hunting, threaten many species of plants and animals with extinction.

In 1964, the International Union for the Conservation of Nature (IUCN)—the world authority on conservation—started to list endangered species on the Red List. Since then, it has grown to cover thousands of species.

THE RED LIST CRITERIA

Scientists choose a level of threat for each species from among seven categories, depending on the results of surveys and other research. An eighth category includes species that need more study before a decision is made. The numbers of species on the Red List at the end of 2017 are listed below.

- ◎ **Least concern:** 30,385
- ◎ **Near threatened:** 5,445
- ◎ **Vulnerable:** 10,010
- ◎ **Endangered:** 7,507
- ◎ **Critically endangered:** 5,101
- ◎ **Extinct in wild:** 68
- ◉ **Extinct:** 844

Threatened numbers
The Red List has prioritized groups such as amphibians, reptiles, and birds that are thought to be at greatest risk. Most species—especially invertebrates, which make up 97 percent of all animal species—have not yet been assessed.

Back from the brink
The Mauritius pink pigeon population had fallen to just 10 individuals by 1990. Conservation efforts helped to bring the numbers back up to a possible 380 by 2011.

LEAST CONCERN

Widespread and abundant species facing no current extinction threat: some do well in habitats close to humans and have even been introduced into countries where they are not native.

HUMAN
Homo sapiens
Location: Worldwide
Population: 7.5 billion; increasing

MALLARD
Anas platyrhynchos
Location: Worldwide
Population: 19 million; increasing

CANE TOAD
Rhinella marina
Location: Tropical America, introduced elsewhere
Population: Unknown; increasing

NEAR THREATENED

Species facing challenges that may make them threatened in the near future: a decreasing population size increases risk.

JAGUAR
Panthera onca
Location: Central and South America
Population: 64,000; decreasing

Shaggy, reddish feathers

REDDISH EGRET
Egretta rufescens
Location: Central and South America
Population: Unknown; decreasing

Moist skin

JAPANESE GIANT SALAMANDER
Andrias japonicus
Location: Japan
Population: Unknown; decreasing

PISTACHIO
Pistacia vera
Location: Southwestern Asia
Population: Unknown, decreasing

VULNERABLE

Species that may be spread over a wide range or abundant, but face habitat destruction and hunting.

HUMBOLDT PENGUIN
Spheniscus humboldti
Location: Western South America
Population: 30,000–40,000

Enormous colorful wings

ROTHSCHILD'S BIRDWING
Ornithoptera rothschildi
Location: Western New Guinea
Population: Unknown

GOLDEN HAMSTER
Mesocricetus auratus
Location: Syria, Turkey
Population: Unknown; decreasing

Long, paddle-like snout

AMERICAN PADDLEFISH
Polyodon spathula
Location: Mississippi River Basin
Population: More than 10,000

The **passenger pigeon** was once the **most common bird in North America**, but **hunting drove it to extinction**—the last one died in Cincinnati Zoo in 1914.

Conservation projects, such as protecting forest habitats, have increased the number of **giant pandas** in the world—they are **no longer endangered**.

191

◎ ENDANGERED

Species restricted to small areas, with small populations, or both: conservation projects, such as protecting habitats, can help save them from extinction.

WHALE SHARK
Rhincodon typus
Location: Warm oceans worldwide
Population: 27,000–238,000; decreasing

Flat face with forward-facing eyes

CHIMPANZEE
Pan troglodytes
Location: Central Africa
Population: 173,000–300,000; decreasing

FIJIAN BANDED IGUANA
Brachylophus bulabula
Location: Fiji
Population: More than 6,000; decreasing

GURNEY'S PITTA
Hydrornis gurneyi
Location: Myanmar, Thailand
Population: 10,000–17,200; decreasing

Yellow and black under parts on males

◎ CRITICALLY ENDANGERED

Species in greatest danger: some have not been seen in the wild for so long that they may already be extinct; others have plummeted in numbers.

YANGTZE RIVER DOLPHIN
Lipotes vexillifer
Location: Yangtze River
Population: Last seen 2002; possibly extinct

COMMON SKATE
Dipturus batis
Location: Northeastern Atlantic
Population: Unknown; decreasing

SPIX'S MACAW
Cyanopsitta spixii
Location: Brazil
Population: Last seen 2016; possibly extinct in wild

Blue plumage

CHINESE ALLIGATOR
Alligator sinensis
Location: China
Population: Possibly fewer than 150 in wild

Thick armored skin

◎ EXTINCT IN WILD

Species that survive in captivity or in cultivation: a few, such as Père David's deer, have been reintroduced to wild habitats from captive populations.

GUAM KINGFISHER
Todiramphus cinnamominus
Last wild record: Guam, 1986
Population: 124 in captivity

BLACK SOFTSHELL TURTLE
Nilssonia nigricans
Last wild record: Bangladesh, 2002
Population: 700 in artificial pond

PÈRE DAVID'S DEER
Elaphurus davidianus
Last wild record: China, 1,800 years ago
Population: Large captive herds; reintroduced to wild

Long, backward-pointing antlers in males

WOOD'S CYCAD
Encephalartos woodii
Last wild record: South Africa, 1916
Population: A handful of clones of one plant in botanic gardens

◎ EXTINCT

Species no longer found alive in the wild, even after extensive surveys, nor known to exist in captivity or cultivation: under these circumstances, it is assumed that the last individual has died.

GOLDEN TOAD
Incilius periglenes
Last wild record: Costa Rica, 1989
Population: Declared extinct 2004

CAROLINA PARAKEET
Conuropsis carolinensis
Last wild record: US, 1904
Population: Last parakeet died in zoo, 1918

THYLACINE
Thylacinus cynocephalus
Last wild record: Tasmania, 1930
Population: Last thylacine died in zoo, 1936

ST. HELENA GIANT EARWIG
Labidura herculeana
Last wild record: St. Helena, 1967
Population: Declared extinct 2001

REFERENCE

The scope of science stretches far and wide. Scientists study the vast expanse of the universe and everything within it—including the diversity of life and how it evolved. Careful observation, measurements, and experiments help scientists understand the world.

Scale of the universe

The difference in size between the smallest and biggest things in the universe is unimaginably vast—from subatomic particles to galaxies.

No one knows how big the universe is, but it has been expanding since it formed in the Big Bang 13.7 billion years ago. The distances are so great that cosmologists measure them in terms of light-years—the distance light moves in space in a year, which is equal to 6 trillion miles (9.5 trillion kilometers)—and parts of the universe are billions of light-years apart.

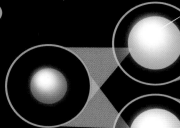

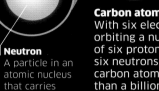

Proton
A particle in an atomic nucleus that carries a positive charge.

Quark
Too small to measure, different kinds of quarks are the subatomic particles that make up protons and neutrons.

Neutron
A particle in an atomic nucleus that carries no charge.

Carbon atom
With six electrons orbiting a nucleus of six protons and six neutrons, a carbon atom is less than a billionth of a meter across.

Limestone rock
Solid mixtures of billions of tiny fossilized shells and mineral fragments make up limestone rock, containing calcium carbonate—a compound that has atoms of calcium, carbon, and oxygen.

Nearest neighbor
Andromeda—the closest major galaxy to our Milky Way—is 2.5 million light-years from Earth.

ANDROMEDA

TRIANGULUM

LOCAL GROUP

MILKY WAY

Group cluster
Our Local Group is within a supercluster that is about 110 million light-years in diameter.

Supercluster
Clusters of galaxies span a region of space ten times bigger than the Local Group. Such a supercluster can contain tens of thousands of galaxies. Our Milky Way is within the Virgo Supercluster. Scientists think there are about 10 million superclusters in the observable universe.

Local Group
The Milky Way is part of a so-called Local Group of about 50 galaxies that stretch across 10 million light-years of space—that's 100 times the diameter of our Milky Way. Galaxies are millions of times farther apart than the stars that are in each one. Andromeda is the biggest galaxy in our Local Group—most others are much smaller.

Traveling at the **speed of light**, it would take **100,000 years** to cross the Milky Way.

The **sun** accounts for **99.8 percent of the mass** of our solar system.

Thousands of exoplanets have been discovered **outside our solar system** since the first one was identified in 1995.

195

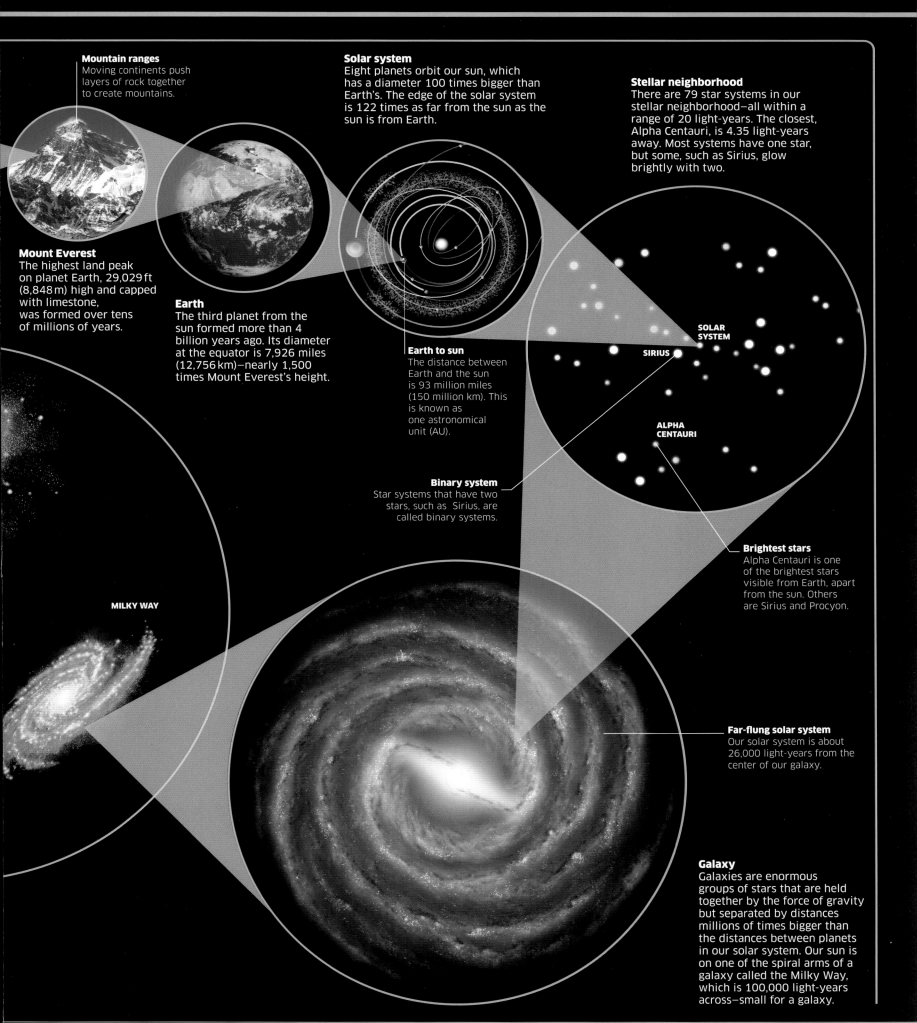

Mountain ranges
Moving continents push layers of rock together to create mountains.

Solar system
Eight planets orbit our sun, which has a diameter 100 times bigger than Earth's. The edge of the solar system is 122 times as far from the sun as the sun is from Earth.

Stellar neighborhood
There are 79 star systems in our stellar neighborhood—all within a range of 20 light-years. The closest, Alpha Centauri, is 4.35 light-years away. Most systems have one star, but some, such as Sirius, glow brightly with two.

Mount Everest
The highest land peak on planet Earth, 29,029 ft (8,848 m) high and capped with limestone, was formed over tens of millions of years.

Earth
The third planet from the sun formed more than 4 billion years ago. Its diameter at the equator is 7,926 miles (12,756 km)—nearly 1,500 times Mount Everest's height.

Earth to sun
The distance between Earth and the sun is 93 million miles (150 million km). This is known as one astronomical unit (AU).

SOLAR
SYSTEM

SIRIUS

ALPHA
CENTAURI

Binary system
Star systems that have two stars, such as Sirius, are called binary systems.

Brightest stars
Alpha Centauri is one of the brightest stars visible from Earth, apart from the sun. Others are Sirius and Procyon.

MILKY WAY

Far-flung solar system
Our solar system is about 26,000 light-years from the center of our galaxy.

Galaxy
Galaxies are enormous groups of stars that are held together by the force of gravity but separated by distances millions of times bigger than the distances between planets in our solar system. Our sun is on one of the spiral arms of a galaxy called the Milky Way, which is 100,000 light-years across—small for a galaxy.

Units of measurement

Scientists measure quantities—such as length, mass, or time—using numbers, so that their sizes can be compared. For each kind of quantity, these measurements must be in units that mean the same thing wherever in the world the measurements are made.

SI units
The abbreviation "SI" stands for *Système International*. It is a standard system of metric units that has been adopted by scientists all over the world so that all their measurements are done in the same way.

Base quantities

Just seven quantities give the most basic information about everything around us. Each is measured in SI units and uses a symbol as an abbreviation. The SI system is metric, meaning that smaller and larger units are obtained by dividing or multiplying by 10, 100, 1,000, etc. Centimeters, for instance, are 100 times smaller than a meter, but kilometers are 1,000 times bigger.

LENGTH
SI unit: meter (m)

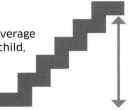

One meter is about the average height of a 3½-year-old child, or five steps up a typical staircase.

- A millionth of a meter (1 micrometer) = the length of a bacterium.
- A thousandth of a meter (1 millimeter) = the diameter of a pinhead.
- 1,000 meters (1 kilometer) = the average distance an adult walks in 12 minutes.

MASS
SI unit: kilogram (kg)

One kilogram is the mass of one liter of water, or about the mass of an average-sized pineapple.

- A thousand trillionth of a kilogram (1 picogram) = the mass of a bacterium.
- A thousandth of a kilogram (1 gram) = the mass of a paper clip.
- 1,000 kilograms (1 metric ton) = the average mass of an adult walrus.

TIME
SI unit: second (s)

One second is the time it takes to swallow a mouthful of food, or to write a single-digit number.

- A thousandth of a second (1 millisecond) = the time taken by the brain to fire a nerve impulse.
- A tenth of a second (1 decisecond) = a blink of an eye.
- 1 billion seconds (1 gigasecond) = 32 years.

TEMPERATURE
SI unit: kelvin (K)

Just one degree rise in temperature can make you feel hot and feverish.

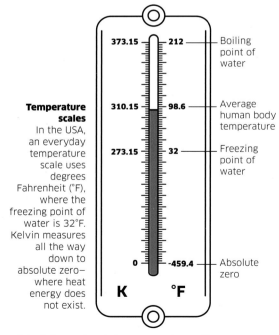

Temperature scales
In the USA, an everyday temperature scale uses degrees Fahrenheit (°F), where the freezing point of water is 32°F. Kelvin measures all the way down to absolute zero—where heat energy does not exist.

K	°F	
373.15	212	Boiling point of water
310.15	98.6	Average human body temperature
273.15	32	Freezing point of water
0	-459.4	Absolute zero

- 0 kelvin = absolute zero, when all objects and their particles are still.
- 1 kelvin = the coldest known object in the universe, the Boomerang Nebula.
- 1,000 kelvin = the temperature inside a charcoal fire.

ELECTRICAL CURRENT
SI unit: ampere (A)

One ampere is about the current running through a 100 W light bulb.

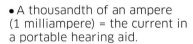

- A thousandth of an ampere (1 milliampere) = the current in a portable hearing aid.
- 100,000 amperes = the current in the biggest lightning strikes.
- 10 thousand billion amperes = the current in the spiral arms of the Milky Way.

LIGHT INTENSITY
SI unit: candela (cd)

One candela is the light intensity given off by a candle flame.

- A millionth of a candela = the lowest light intensity perceived by human vision.
- A thousandth of a candela = a typical night sky away from city lights.
- 1 billion candelas = the intensity of the sun when viewed from Earth.

AMOUNT OF A SUBSTANCE
SI unit: mole (mol)

One mole is a set number of atoms, molecules, or other particles. Because substances all have different atomic structures, one mole of one substance may be very different to that of another.

A mole of gold atoms is in about six gold coins.

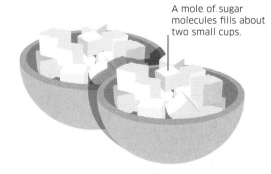

A mole of sugar molecules fills about two small cups.

- A tenth of a mole of iron atoms = the amount of iron in the human body.
- 1,000 moles of carbon atoms = the amount of carbon in the human body.
- 10 million trillion moles of oxygen molecules = the amount of oxygen in Earth's atmosphere.

Derived quantities

Other kinds of quantities are also useful in science, but these are calculated from base quantities using scientific equations. For instance, we combine SI measurements of mass, distance, and time to work out an SI measurement for force. This means that force is said to be a derived quantity.

FORCE
SI unit: newton (N)

One newton is about the force of gravity on a single apple.

$$\text{Force in newtons} = \frac{\text{Mass in kilograms} \times \text{distance in meters}}{\text{Time in seconds}^2}$$

- A 10 billionth of a newton = the force needed to break six chemical bonds in a molecule.
- 10 newtons = the weight of an object with mass of 1 kilogram.

PRESSURE
SI unit: pascal (Pa)

One pascal is about the pressure of one bill of paper money resting on a flat surface.

$$\text{Pressure in pascals} = \frac{\text{Force in newtons}}{\text{Area in meters}^2}$$

- A 10 thousand trillionth of a pascal = the lowest pressure recorded in outer space.
- 1 million pascals (1 megapascal) = the pressure of a human bite.

ENERGY
SI unit: joule (J)

One joule is about the energy needed to lift a medium-sized tomato a height of one meter.

$$\text{Energy in joules} = \text{Force in newtons} \times \text{distance in meters}$$

- A millionth of a joule (1 microjoule) = the energy of motion in six flying mosquitoes.
- 1,000 joules (1 kilojoule) = the maximum energy from the sun reaching 1 square meter of Earth's surface each second.

FREQUENCY
SI unit: hertz (Hz)

One hertz is about the frequency of a human heartbeat: one beat per second.

$$\text{Frequency in hertz} = \frac{\text{Number of cycles}}{\text{Time in seconds}}$$

- 100 hertz = the frequency of an engine cycle in a car running at maximum speed.
- 10,000 hertz = the frequency of radio waves.

POWER
SI unit: watt (W)

One watt is about the power used by a single Christmas tree light.

$$\text{Power in watts} = \frac{\text{Energy in joules}}{\text{Time in seconds}}$$

- A millionth of a watt (1 microwatt) = the power used by a wristwatch.
- 1 billion watts (1 gigawatt) = the power used by a hydroelectric generating station.

POTENTIAL DIFFERENCE
SI unit: volt (V)

Voltage is a measure of the difference in electrical energy between two points—the force needed to make electricity move. One volt is about the voltage in a lemon battery cell.

$$\text{Potential difference in volts} = \frac{\text{Power in watts}}{\text{Current in amperes}}$$

- 100 volts = the electrical grid voltage in the US.

ELECTRICAL CHARGE AND RESISTANCE
SI unit: Charge—coulomb (C)
Resistance—ohm (Ω)

The measurements relating to electricity are all interlinked. Charge is a measure of how positive or negative particles are, and can be calculated from the current and the time. Resistance is a measure of the difficulty a current has in flowing, and can be calculated from the voltage and the current.

Flowing particles carry a charge.

Resistance is a measure of the difficulty current has in flowing through an object. In a narrower section of wire, the current faces more resistance.

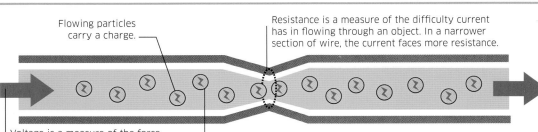

Voltage is a measure of the force that keeps the charges flowing.

Current is the amount of charge flowing through each second.

$$\text{Resistance in ohms} = \frac{\text{Potential difference in volts}}{\text{Current in amperes}}$$

$$\text{Charge in coulombs} = \text{Current in amperes} \times \text{time in seconds}$$

198   reference ○ **CLASSIFYING LIFE**

More than **half of all known animal species belong to the class of insects**, and most of these belong to one order: the beetles.

Classifying life

Scientists have described more than a million and a half different species of living things. They classify them into groups based on how they are related.

There are lots of ways of classifying organisms. Insects, birds, and bats could be grouped as flying animals, and plants could be grouped by how we use them. But neither of these systems shows natural relationships. Biological classification works by grouping related species. Bats, for instance, have closer links to monkeys than they do to birds, because they are both furry mammals that have evolved from the same mammal ancestors.

Single-celled organisms are the most common form of life in some kingdoms—including archaea, bacteria, and protozoans.

Seven kingdoms of organisms

Archaea	Bacteria	Protozoans

More than 30 phyla of animals, including ...

Flatworms	Annelids	Molluscs

12 classes of chordates, including ...

Sea squirts	Jawless fishes	Cartilaginous fishes	Lobe-finned fishes	Ray-finned fishes

29 orders of mammals, including ...

Monotremes	Marsupials	Elephants	Sloths and anteaters	Primates	Rodents	Rabbits, hares, and pikas

15 families of primates, including ...

Dwarf and mouse lemurs	True lemurs	Sifakas and relatives	Bushbabies	Aye-aye	Lorises and relatives	Tarsiers

Scientific names

Every species has a two-part scientific name using Latin words that are internationally recognized in science. The first part identifies its genus group, the second its species. Lions and tigers belong to the *Panthera* genus of big cats, but have different species names.

Panthera leo
Lion

Panthera tigris
Tiger

MAMMALS   TURTLES   LIZARDS AND SNAKES   CROCODILES   BIRDS

Fossils and DNA show that birds are most closely related to crocodiles.

Classifying birds

Modern classification aims to show how organisms are linked by evolution. Birds and reptiles are traditionally in two separate classes. But birds evolved from reptile ancestors (see pp.136–137), so many scientists think they should be a sub-group of the reptiles.

90 percent of plant species are flowering plants. The remainder are spore-producing plants, such as mosses.

Most species on Earth still await discovery. It's possible that **less than 20 percent** have been classified so far.

199

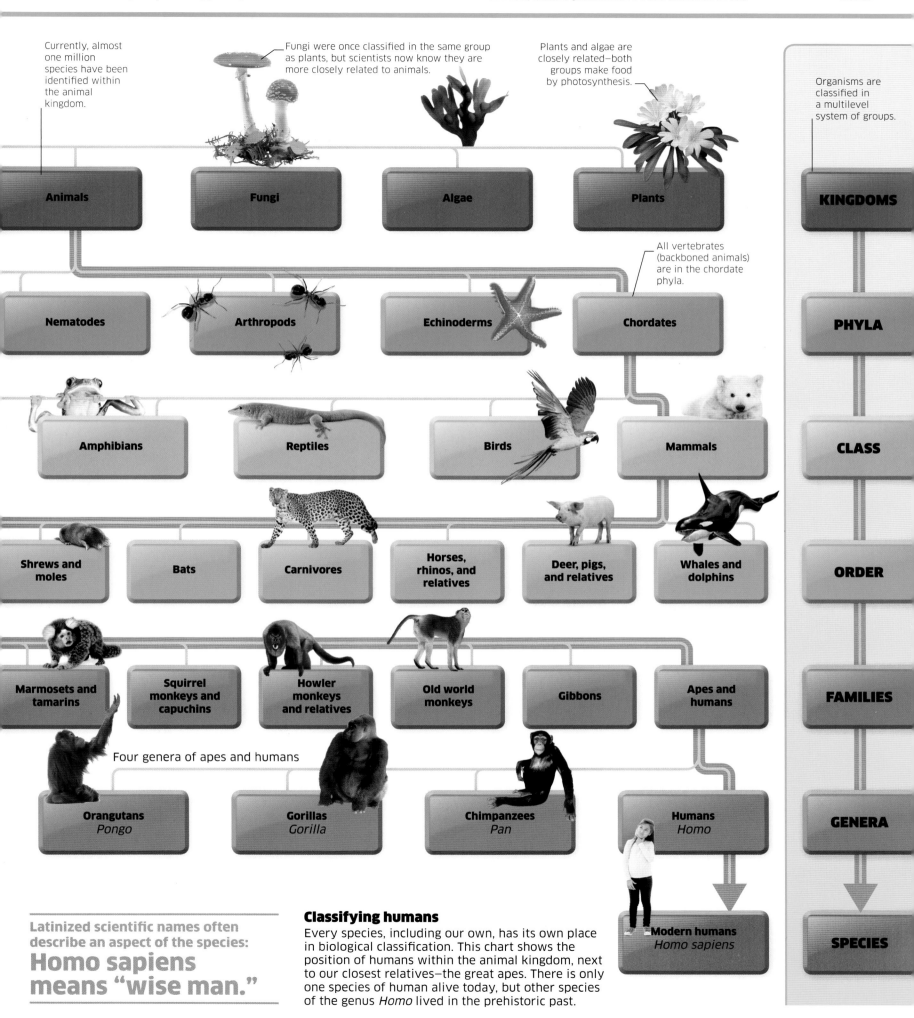

Currently, almost one million species have been identified within the animal kingdom.

Fungi were once classified in the same group as plants, but scientists now know they are more closely related to animals.

Plants and algae are closely related—both groups make food by photosynthesis.

Organisms are classified in a multilevel system of groups.

Animals

Fungi

Algae

Plants

KINGDOMS

All vertebrates (backboned animals) are in the chordate phyla.

Nematodes

Arthropods

Echinoderms

Chordates

PHYLA

Amphibians

Reptiles

Birds

Mammals

CLASS

Shrews and moles

Bats

Carnivores

Horses, rhinos, and relatives

Deer, pigs, and relatives

Whales and dolphins

ORDER

Marmosets and tamarins

Squirrel monkeys and capuchins

Howler monkeys and relatives

Old world monkeys

Gibbons

Apes and humans

FAMILIES

Four genera of apes and humans

Orangutans
Pongo

Gorillas
Gorilla

Chimpanzees
Pan

Humans
Homo

GENERA

Modern humans
Homo sapiens

SPECIES

Latinized scientific names often describe an aspect of the species:

Homo sapiens means "wise man."

Classifying humans

Every species, including our own, has its own place in biological classification. This chart shows the position of humans within the animal kingdom, next to our closest relatives—the great apes. There is only one species of human alive today, but other species of the genus *Homo* lived in the prehistoric past.

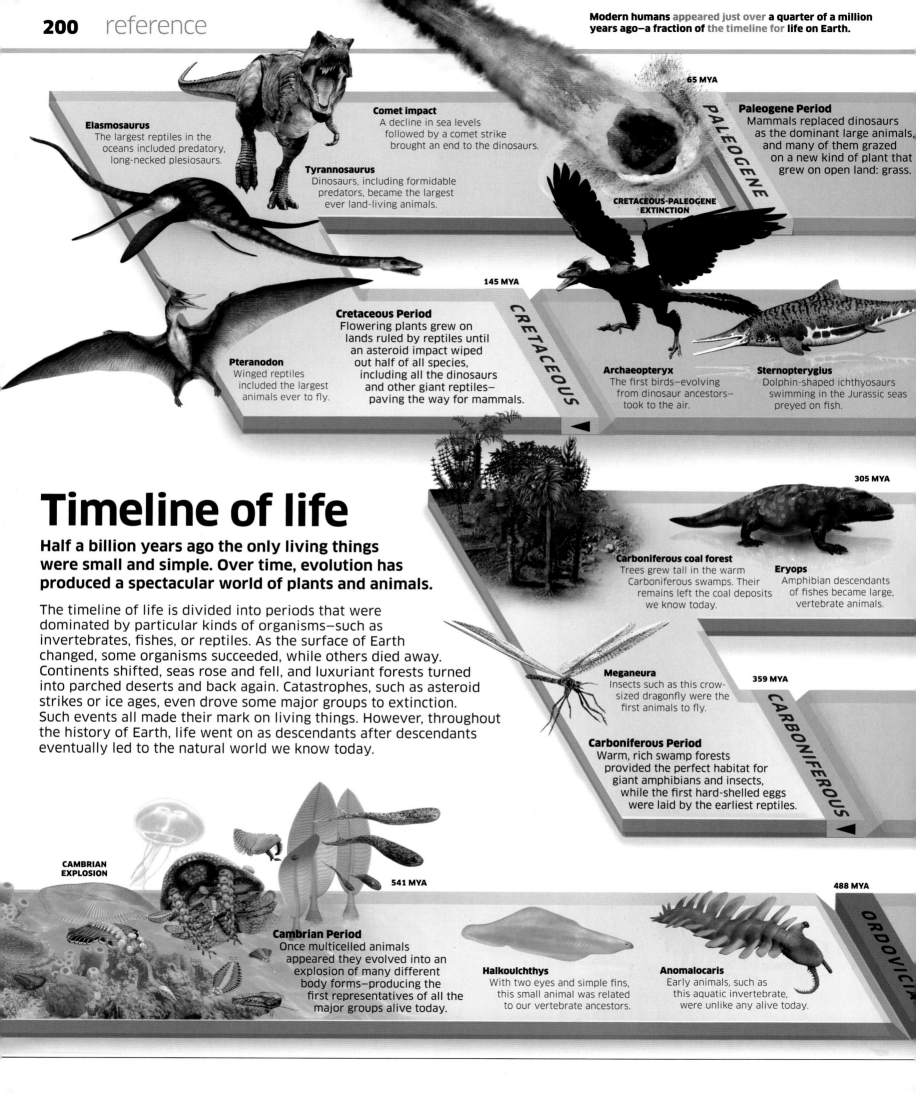

Modern humans appeared just over **a quarter of a million years ago—a fraction of** the timeline for **life on Earth.**

65 MYA

Paleogene Period
Mammals replaced dinosaurs as the dominant large animals, and many of them grazed on a new kind of plant that grew on open land: grass.

PALEOGENE

CRETACEOUS-PALEOGENE EXTINCTION

Elasmosaurus
The largest reptiles in the oceans included predatory, long-necked plesiosaurs.

Comet impact
A decline in sea levels followed by a comet strike brought an end to the dinosaurs.

Tyrannosaurus
Dinosaurs, including formidable predators, became the largest ever land-living animals.

145 MYA

Cretaceous Period
Flowering plants grew on lands ruled by reptiles until an asteroid impact wiped out half of all species, including all the dinosaurs and other giant reptiles—paving the way for mammals.

CRETACEOUS

Pteranodon
Winged reptiles included the largest animals ever to fly.

Archaeopteryx
The first birds—evolving from dinosaur ancestors—took to the air.

Sternopterygius
Dolphin-shaped ichthyosaurs swimming in the Jurassic seas preyed on fish.

305 MYA

Timeline of life

Half a billion years ago the only living things were small and simple. Over time, evolution has produced a spectacular world of plants and animals.

The timeline of life is divided into periods that were dominated by particular kinds of organisms—such as invertebrates, fishes, or reptiles. As the surface of Earth changed, some organisms succeeded, while others died away. Continents shifted, seas rose and fell, and luxuriant forests turned into parched deserts and back again. Catastrophes, such as asteroid strikes or ice ages, even drove some major groups to extinction. Such events all made their mark on living things. However, throughout the history of Earth, life went on as descendants after descendants eventually led to the natural world we know today.

Carboniferous coal forest
Trees grew tall in the warm Carboniferous swamps. Their remains left the coal deposits we know today.

Eryops
Amphibian descendants of fishes became large, vertebrate animals.

Meganeura
Insects such as this crow-sized dragonfly were the first animals to fly.

359 MYA

Carboniferous Period
Warm, rich swamp forests provided the perfect habitat for giant amphibians and insects, while the first hard-shelled eggs were laid by the earliest reptiles.

CARBONIFEROUS

CAMBRIAN EXPLOSION

541 MYA

Cambrian Period
Once multicelled animals appeared they evolved into an explosion of many different body forms—producing the first representatives of all the major groups alive today.

488 MYA

Halkoulchthys
With two eyes and simple fins, this small animal was related to our vertebrate ancestors.

Anomalocaris
Early animals, such as this aquatic invertebrate, were unlike any alive today.

ORDOVICIAN

The earliest evidence of **single-celled fossil life** exists in rocks that are **3.5 billion years old.**

Billions of years ago, algae produced much of the **oxygen** in the air today.

201

Megacerops
Tiny ancestors evolved into large mammals that replaced the dinosaurs.

23 MYA

NEOGENE

Neogene Period
Many familiar groups of mammals, such as rodents, primates, antelopes, and cats, evolved in the Neogene, while flying birds diversified in the skies.

Thylacosmilus
Predatory mammals, including saber-toothed cats, hunted grazers on the open grassland.

2.6 MYA

QUATERNARY

Quaternary Period
Mammals and birds survived Quaternary ice ages, but one species— humans— drove many others to extinction by hunting and habitat destruction, causing the biggest mass extinction of modern times.

Red lines indicate mass extinctions.

201 MYA

TRIASSIC-JURASSIC EXTINCTION

JURASSIC

Jurassic Period
The peak of the Age of Dinosaurs saw the evolution of giant reptiles on land and in the seas, which included the largest land animals of all time.

Asteroid impact
A space rock colliding with Earth wiped out a quarter of all species.

Eoraptor
The first dinosaurs, some two-legged, evolved from small reptiles that survived the Permian-Triassic extinction.

Periods of time
Earth's prehistory is marked by a timescale divided up into geological periods. Each period represents a length of time that has left its mark in rocks with fossils and other evidence.

299 MYA

PERMIAN-TRIASSIC EXTINCTION

PERMIAN

Permian Period
Continents dried up to favor scaly reptiles over amphibians. The period ended with violent eruptions causing the biggest of all mass extinctions.

Dimetrodon
As moist-skinned amphibians declined in a drier world, reptiles such as this carnivore took over.

Triassic Period
New kinds of forests containing conifers and cycads were inhabited by the first dinosaurs until a possible asteroid impact brought about mass extinction.

TRIASSIC

251 MYA

Elginerpeton
Fishes with strong, fleshy fins—such as Elginerpeton—paved the way for the evolution of walking limbs.

Devonian Period
More kinds of fishes evolved in the oceans, while vertebrate animals and trees appeared on land. Climate change near the end of the Devonian Period caused mass extinction.

ATE DEVONIAN XTINCTION

DEVONIAN

375-360 MYA

416 MYA

Climatius
This fish had a sharklike skeleton of rubbery cartilage, but bony, spiny fins.

433 MYA

Ordovician Period
The oceans of the Ordovician teemed with invertebrates and primitive fishes, but ended with an ice age that drained shallow seas and caused a mass extinction.

Orthoceras
This relative of squid had grasping arms and a body inside a long, cone-shaped shell.

ORDOVICIAN EXTINCTION

SILURIAN

Silurian Period
Jawed fishes and coral reefs appeared for the first time, while distant relatives of spiders and centipedes started to crawl onto land.

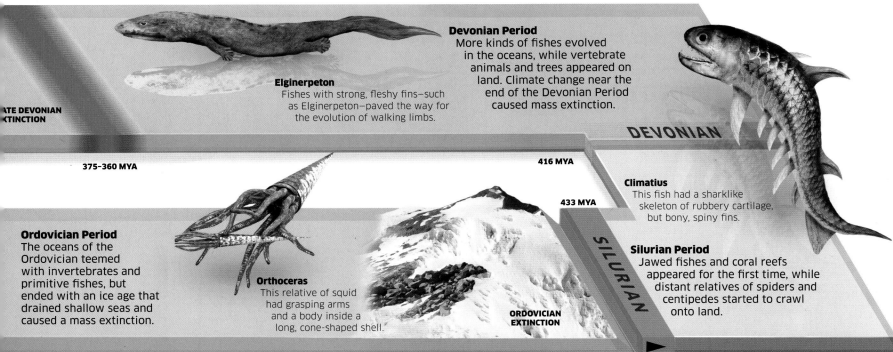

Glossary

ACID
A substance with a pH lower than 7.

ALGAE
Plantlike organisms that can make food using energy from sunlight.

ALKALI
See Base

ALLOY
A mixture of two or more metals, or of a metal and a non-metal.

ANALOG
Relating to signals or information represented by a continuously varying value, such as a wave.

ATMOSPHERE
The layer of breathable gases, such as oxygen and nitrogen, that surrounds Earth.

ATOM
The smallest unit of an element.

BACTERIA
Microscopic organisms with a simple, single-celled form.

BASE
A substance with pH higher than 7. Bases that are soluble in water are called alkalis. Also: one of the four chemicals that make up the "rungs" of a DNA double helix.

BIOLOGY
The science of living things.

BUOYANCY
The tendency of a solid to float or sink in liquids.

CARBOHYDRATE
An energy-rich substance, such as sugar or starch.

CATALYST
A substance that makes a chemical reaction occur much more rapidly, but is not changed by the reaction.

CELL
The smallest unit of life.

CHEMICAL BOND
An attraction between particles, such as atoms or ions.

CHEMICAL REACTION
A process that changes substances into new substances by breaking and making chemical bonds.

CHEMISTRY
The science of matter and elements.

CHROMOSOME
A threadlike structure, found in the nucleus of cells, that is made up of coiled strands of DNA. Humans have 46 chromosomes per body cell.

CLIMATE
The most common weather conditions in an area over a long period of time.

COMBUSTION
A chemical reaction in which a substance reacts with oxygen, releasing heat and flames.

COMPOUND
A chemical substance in which two or more elements have bonded together.

CONCENTRATION
The amount of one substance mixed in a known volume of the other.

CONDENSATION
A process whereby a gas changes into a liquid.

CONDUCTOR
A substance through which heat or electric current flows easily.

COVALENT BOND
A type of chemical bond in a molecule where atoms share one or more electrons.

DNA
A material found in the cells of all organisms that carries instructions for how a living thing will look and function.

DRAG
The resistance force formed when an object pushes through a fluid, such as air or water.

ECOSYSTEM
A community of organisms and the nonliving environment around them.

ELECTRIC CHARGE
How positive or negative a particle is.

ELECTRON
One of the tiny particles inside an atom. It has a negative electric charge.

ELEMENT
A simple substance made of atoms that are all the same kind.

ENERGY
What enables work to be done. Energy exists in many different forms and cannot be created or destroyed, only transferred.

ENZYME
A substance produced in living organisms that acts as a catalyst and speeds up chemical reactions.

EROSION
A process by which Earth's surface rocks and soil are worn away by wind, water, or ice.

EVAPORATION
A process by which a liquid changes into a gas.

EVOLUTION
The process by which Earth's species gradually change over long periods of time, such as millions of years, to produce new species.

EXCRETION
The process by which living organisms expel or get rid of waste produced by cells of the body.

FERTILIZATION
The joining of male and female sex cells so they develop into new life.

FISSION
A splitting apart; nuclear fission is the splitting of the nucleus of an atom.

FOSSIL
The preserved remains or impressions of life from an earlier time.

FOSSIL FUEL
A substance formed from the remains of ancient organisms that burns easily to release energy.

FRICTION
The dragging force that occurs when one object moves over another.

FUSION
A joining together; nuclear fusion is the joining of two atomic nuclei.

GAS
A state of matter that flows to fill a container, and can be compressed.

GENE
One of the tiny units carried on DNA that determine what a living thing looks like and how it functions.

GLUCOSE
A simple carbohydrate, or sugar, made by photosynthesis and then used by cells as a source of energy.

GRAVITY
The force that attracts one object to another and prevents things on Earth from floating off into space.

HABITAT
The area where an animal naturally makes its home.

INHERITANCE
The range of natural characteristics passed on to offspring by parents.

INSULATOR
A material that stops heat moving from a warm object to a colder one.

ION
An atom that has lost or gained one or more electrons and as a result has either a positive or negative electric charge.

IONIC BOND
A type of chemical bond where one or more electrons are passed from one atom to another, creating two ions of opposite charge that attract each other.

ISOTOPE
One of two or more atoms of a chemical element that have different numbers of neutrons compared to other atoms of the element.

LIFT
The upward force produced by an aircraft's wings that keeps it airborne.

LIQUID
A state of matter that flows and takes the shape of a container, and cannot be compressed.

MAGMA
Hot, liquid rock that is found beneath Earth's surface.

MAGNET
An object that has a magnetic field and attracts or repels other magnetic objects.

MASS
A measure of the amount of matter in an object.

MATERIAL
A chemical substance out of which things can be made.

METAL
Any of many elements that are usually shiny solids and good conductors of electricity.

MICROORGANISM
A tiny organism which can only be seen with the aid of a microscope. Also known as a microbe.

MINERAL
A solid, nonliving material occurring naturally and made up of a particular kind of chemical compound.

MOLECULE
A particle formed by two or more atoms joined by covalent bonds.

MONOMER
A molecule that can be bonded to other similar molecules to form a polymer.

NERVE
A fiber that carries electrical messages (nerve impulses) from one part of the body to another.

NEUTRON
One of the tiny particles in an atom. It has no electric charge.

NUCLEUS
The control center inside the cells of most living organisms. It contains genetic material, in the form of DNA. Also: the central part of an atom, made of protons and neutrons.

NUTRIENT
A substance essential for life to exist and grow.

ORBIT
The path taken by an object, for example, a planet, that is circling around another.

ORGAN
A group of tissues that makes up a part of the body with a special function. Important organs include the heart, lungs, liver, and kidneys.

ORGANISM
A living thing.

PARTICLE
A tiny speck of matter.

PHOTOSYNTHESIS
The process by which green plants use the sun's energy to make carbohydrates from carbon dioxide and water.

PHYSICS
The science of matter, energy, forces, and motion.

PIGMENT
A chemical substance that colors an object.

POLLEN
Tiny grains produced by flowers, which contain the male cells needed to fertilize eggs.

POLYMER
A long, chainlike molecule made up of smaller molecules connected together.

PRESSURE
The amount of force that is applied to a surface per unit of area.

PRODUCT
A substance produced by a chemical reaction.

PROTEIN
A type of complex chemical found in all living things, used as enzymes and in muscles.

PROTON
One of the tiny particles inside an atom. It has a positive electric charge.

RADIATION
Waves of energy that travel through space. Radiation includes visible light, heat, X-rays, and radio waves. Nuclear radiation includes subatomic particles and fragments of atoms.

RADIOACTIVE
Describing a material that is unstable because the nuclei of its atoms split to release nuclear radiation.

REACTANT
A substance that is changed in a chemical reaction.

REACTIVE
A substance that is likely to become involved in a chemical reaction.

RESPIRATION
The process occurring in all living cells that releases energy from glucose to power life.

ROOM TEMPERATURE
A standard scientific term for comfortable conditions (for humans), usually a temperature of around 68°F (20°C).

SEX ORGANS
The organs of an organism that allow it to reproduce. They usually produce sex cells: sperm in males, and eggs in females.

SOLID
A state of matter in which an element's atoms are joined together in a rigid structure.

SOLUTE
A substance that becomes dissolved in another.

SOLVENT
A substance that can have other substances dissolved in it.

SYNTHETIC
Man-made chemical.

TISSUE
A group of similar cells that carry out the same function, such as muscle tissue, which can contract.

TOXIC
Causing harm, such as a poison.

ULTRASOUND
Sound with a frequency above that which the human ear can detect.

ULTRAVIOLET
A type of electromagnetic radiation with a wavelength shorter than visible light.

UNIVERSE
The whole of space and everything it contains.

VOLCANO
An opening in Earth's crust that provides an outlet for magma when it rises to the surface.

WAVE
Vibration that transfers energy from place to place, without transferring the matter that it is flowing through.

WAVELENGTH
The distance between wave crests, usually when referring to sound waves or electromagnetic waves.

WEIGHT
The force applied to a mass by gravity.

Index

Acknowledgments

The publisher would like to thank the following people for their assistance in the preparation of this book:

Ben Morgan for editorial and scientific advice; Ann Baggaley, Jessica Cawthra, Sarah Edwards, and Laura Sandford for editorial assistance; Caroline Stamps for proofreading; Helen Peters for the index; Simon Mumford for maps; Phil Gamble, KJA-Artists.com, and Simon Tegg for illustrations; avogadro.cc/cite and www.povray.org for 3D molecular modelling and rendering software.

DK Delhi:
Manjari Rathi Hooda: Head, Digital Operations
Nain Singh Rawat: Audio Video Production Manager
Mahipal Singh, Alok Singh: 3D Artists

Smithsonian Enterprises:
Kealy E. Gordon: Product Development Manager
Ellen Nanney: Licensing Manager
Brigid Ferraro: Vice President, Education and Consumer Products
Carol LeBlanc: Senior Vice President, Education and Consumer Products

Curator for the Smithsonian:
Dr. F. Robert van der Linden, Curator of Air Transportation and Special Purpose Aircraft, National Air and Space Museum, Smithsonian

The Smithsonian name and logo are registered trademarks of the Smithsonian Institution.

The publisher would like to thank the following for their kind permission to reproduce photographs:

(Key: a-above; b-below/bottom; c-centre; f-far; l-left; r-right; t-top)

2 123RF.com: Konstantin Shaklein (tl). **3 Dorling Kindersley:** Clive Streeter / The Science Museum, London (cb). **TurboSquid:** Witalk73 (cra). **6 TurboSquid:** 3d_molier International (c). **10 123RF.com:** scanrail (ca). **Dorling Kindersley:** Ruth Jenkinson / Holts Gems (cra). **11 Dorling Kindersley:** Stephen Oliver (cb). **Dreamstime.com:** Dirk Ercken / Kikkerdirk (cla); Grafner (ca); Ron Sumners / Sumnersgraphicsinc (cl); Kellyrichardsonfl (cb/leaves); Heike Falkenberg / Dslrpix (br). **13 Dreamstime.com:** Wisconsinart (cra). **Science Photo Library:** Dennis Kunkel Microscopy (cra/Cellulose). **15 123RF.com:** molekuul (crb). **19 Dreamstime.com:** Fireflyphoto (cr). **20 Gary Greenberg, PhD / www.sandgrains.com:** (clb). **21 Alamy Stock Photo:** Jim Snyders (tl). **National Geographic Creative:** David Liittschwager (cb). **22 Alamy Stock Photo:** Evan Sharboneau (bl). **Dreamstime.com:** Photographerlondon (cra). **Getty Images:** Wu Swee Ong (bc). **23 Dorling Kindersley:** Ruth Jenkinson / Holts Gems (ca). **Dreamstime.com:** Ali Ender Birer / Enderbirer (cl). **Getty Images:** Alain Bachellier (bl). **24 Alamy Stock Photo:** Björn Wylezich (fclb). **Dorling Kindersley:** Natural History Museum, London (bc). **Getty Images:** De Agostini / A. Rizzi (clb). **National Museum of Natural History, Smithsonian Institution:** (cb). **24-25 Alamy Stock Photo:** Björn Wylezich. **25 Dreamstime.com:** Jefunne Gimpel (cra); Elena Moiseeva (crb). **Science Photo Library:** James Bell (br). **26-27 National Geographic Creative:** Carsten Peter / Speleoresearch & Films (c). **30 Dorling Kindersley:** Ruth Jenkinson / RGB Research Limited (bc). **31 Dorling Kindersley:** Ruth Jenkinson / RGB Research Limited (All images). **32-33 Dorling Kindersley:** Ruth Jenkinson / RGB Research Limited (All images). **34 Alamy Stock Photo:** PjrStudio (clb); Björn Wylezich (tr); Science History Images (crb). **35 Dorling Kindersley:** Ruth Jenkinson / RGB Research Limited. **36 Dorling Kindersley:** Natural History Museum, London (bl); Ruth Jenkinson / RGB Research Limited (c, cl). **37 Dorling Kindersley:** Ruth Jenkinson / RGB Research Limited (cra). **Science Photo Library:** Eye of Science (clb). **38 123RF.com:** Konstantin Shaklein (ca); Romolo Tavani (clb). **Dreamstime.com:** Markus Gann / Magann (tr); Vit Kovalcik / Vkovalcik (crb). **Fotolia:** VERSUSstudio (bl). **39 Alamy Stock Photo:** robertharding (b). **Dreamstime.com:** Hotshotsworldwide (cr). **40 Dorling Kindersley:** Ruth Jenkinson / RGB Research Limited (All images). **41 123RF.com:** Dmytro Sukharevskyy / nevodka (c). **Alamy Stock Photo:** Neon Collection by Karin Hildebrand Lau (tr). **Dreamstime.com:** Reinhold Wittich (bl). **iStockphoto.com:** DieterMeyrl (br). **42 iStockphoto.com:** Claudio Ventrella (cl). **42-43 iStockphoto.com:** MKucova (ca). **43 123RF.com:** Kittiphat Inthonprasit (cl). **iStockphoto.com:** ispain (cra); Claudio Ventrella (ca). **Science Photo Library:** Charles D. Winters (br). **44 123RF.com:** Petra Schüller / pixelelfe (cr). **Alamy Stock Photo:** Alvey & Towers Picture Library (c). **Dorling Kindersley:** Ruth Jenkinson / RGB Research Limited (bl). **Science Photo Library:** (bc). **46 Science Photo Library:** Gustoimages (b). **47 Alamy Stock Photo:** Dusan Kostic (bl). **iStockphoto.com:** clubfoto (br). **48-49 Science Photo Library:** Beauty Of Science. **50 123RF.com:** molekuul (cl). **50-51 TurboSquid:** 3d_molier International (b/charred logs). **51 TurboSquid:** 3d_molier International (bc). **53 123RF.com:** mipan (br). **Alamy Stock Photo:** Blaize Pascall (crb). **Getty Images:** Matin Bahadori (clb); Mint Images - Paul Edmondson (bl). **54-55 Benjamin Lappalainen:** blapphoto (c). **56 123RF.com:** Olegsam (bl). **Dorling Kindersley:** © The Board of Trustees of the Armouries (clb/helmet); Natural History Museum, London (clb/Marble). **Dreamstime.com:** Jianghongyan (clb). **Fotolia:** apttone (clb/diamond). **iStockphoto.com:** Believe_In_Me (cra); Belyaevskiy (ca). **57 123RF.com:** Sangsak Aeiddam (bl). **Dreamstime.com:** Nataliya Hora (cl). **Getty Images:** Anadolu Agency (cla); Pallava Bagla (clb); Science & Society Picture Library (clb/Fabric). **58 123RF.com:** bbtreesubmission (bc); yurok (c). **Alamy Stock Photo:** Tim Gainey (clb); Kidsada Manchinda (cra); Monkey Biscuit (crb); Hemis (br). **Dreamstime.com:** Hugoht (bl). **59 123RF.com:** belchonock (cla); Thuansak Srilao (cra); serezniy (cb); sauletas (cr); gresei (bl); Milic Djurovic (bc); Anton Starikov (crb/Jar); Vladimir Nenov / nenovbrothers (br). **Dreamstime.com:** Valentin Armianu / Asterixvs (crb); Dmitry Rukhlenko / F9photos (ca). **60-61 Science Photo Library:** Clouds Hill Imaging Ltd. **62 123RF.com:** Robyn Mackenzie (crb, br); Matt Trommer / Eintracht (cb). **Alamy Stock Photo:** Interfoto (tr); Kristoffer Tripplaar (cl); seen0001 (clb); Anastasiya Zolotnitskaya (bl). **Dorling Kindersley:** Frits Solvang / Norges Bank (cb/Krone). **Getty Images:** © Santiago Urquijo (clb/Bridge). **63 123RF.com:** Manav Lohia / jackmicro (clb/Dime). **Alamy Stock Photo:** money & coins @ ian sanders (clb/Yen); Zoonar GmbH (tc). **Dorling Kindersley:** Gerard Brown / Bicycle Museum Of America (cr). **Getty Images:** David Taylor-Bramley (tr). **iStockphoto.com:** knape (bl). **Photo courtesy Gabriel Vandervort | AncientResource.com:** (clb). **65 naturepl.com:** Alex Hyde (tr). **66 TurboSquid:** Witalk73 (cl). **68 Dreamstime.com:** Jochenschneider (bc). **69 Dorling Kindersley:** The Science Museum, London (ca, cra, cr, c). **Getty Images:** Oxford Science Archive / Print Collector (crb). **72 Science Photo Library:** Tony Mcconnell (tc). **73 Alamy Stock Photo:** Universal Images Group North America LLC (cla). **74 Science Photo Library:** Patrick Landmann (bc). **76-77 TurboSquid:** Witalk73. **78-79 Science Photo Library:** NASA (c). **80 Dreamstime.com:** Markus Gann / Magann (c). **Getty Images:** Digital Vision (tl); Pete Rowbottom (tc); Matthias Kulka / Corbis (crb). **Science Photo Library:** Gustoimages (cl); Edward Kinsman (cr). **81 ESA:** The Planck Collaboration (tl). **ESO:** ALMA (ESO/NAOJ/NRAO), F. Kerschbaum https://creativecommons.org/licenses/by/4.0 (tc). **Getty Images:** William Douglas / EyeEm (bc). **iStockphoto.com:** Turnervisual (cb). **84 Getty Images:** Don Farrall (fcrb); Wulf Voss / EyeEm (c); Melanie Hobson / EyeEm (cr); Francesco Perre / EyeEm (fcr); James Jordan Photography (cb); Steven Puetzer (crb). **85 Science Photo Library:** Andrew Lambert Photography (cl). **88 Alamy Stock Photo:** Alchemy (fcla, cla); Naeblys (bl). **90-91 Juan Carlos Casado:** STARRYEARTH (c). **92 123RF.com:** iarada (bl); Derrick Neill / neilld (cra). **Dreamstime.com:** Aprescindere (bc). **94 123RF.com:** Norasit Kaewsai / norgal (br). **Science Photo Library:** (fcrb, fbr); Tek Image (tr); Martyn F. Chillmaid (crb). **97 Alamy Stock Photo:** geogphotos (br). **102 Dreamstime.com:** Antartis (crb). **103 Dreamstime.com:** Markus Gann / Magann (tl). **106-107 TurboSquid:** Zerg_Lurker. **107 iStockphoto.com:** Mikita_Kavalenkau (cb). **112-113 NASA:** WMAP Science Team (tr). **112 NASA:** NASA / ESA / S. Beckwith(STScI) and The HUDF Team (cb). **Science Photo Library:** Take 27 Ltd (clb). **113 NASA:** WMAP Science Team (crb). **114-115 Science Photo Library:** Mark Garlick. **114 NASA:** JPL-Caltech / ESA / CXC / STScI (cr). **Science Photo Library:** David A. Hardy, Futures: 50 Years In Space (bl). **115 Dreamstime.com:** Tose (br). **Getty Images:** Robert Gendler / Visuals Unlimited, Inc. (ca). **iStockphoto.com:** plefevre (cla). **NASA:** ESA / JPL-Caltech / STScI (cra); JPL-Caltech (clb); X-ray: NASA / CXC / SAO / J.DePasquale; IR: NASA / JPL-Caltech; Optical: NASA / STScI (cb); ESA, S. Beckwith (STScI) and the Hubble Heritage Team (STScI / AURA) (crb). **118-119 National Geographic Creative:** NASA / ESA (c). **120-121 Science Photo Library:** NASA. **120 Alamy Stock Photo:** Science Photo Library (clb). **Dreamstime.com:** Torian Dixon / Mrincredible (cla). **121 Getty Images:** Photodisc / StockTrek (tr). **123 Dreamstime.com:** Gregsi (tc, cra). **125 Alamy Stock Photo:** TAO Images Limited (tr). **127 Alamy Stock Photo:** Science History Images (br). **129 123RF.com:** mihtiander (crb). **Getty Images:** Sirachai Arunrugstichai (fcrb). **133 Alamy Stock Photo:** World History Archive (bl); Z4 Collection (cb). **Dorling Kindersley:** The Science Museum, London (crb). **Dreamstime.com:** Anetlanda (tc); Koolander (cla); Bolygomaki (clb). **134 Science Photo Library:** Eye of Science (cl). **135 123RF.com:** Eduardo Rivero / edurivero (br). **Dreamstime.com:** Andrey Sukhachev / Nchuprin (cra/Bacteria); Peter Wollinga (crb). **Getty Images:** Roland Birke (cr/Protozoa). **Science Photo Library:** Dennis Kunkel Microscopy (cra); Power And Syred (bc); Gerd Guenther (cr). **136 Science Photo Library:** Chris Hellier (cb). **137 Alamy Stock Photo:** Mopic (cra). **Dreamstime.com:** Steve Byland / Stevebyland (br). **Gyik Toma / Paleobear:** (tl). **138 Alamy Stock Photo:** Dave Watts (tr). **139 123RF.com:** Iakov Filimonov / jackf (tr); Sergey Krasnoshchokov / most66 (cra); Christian Musat (crb/Spectacled bear); Pablo Hidalgo (bc). **Dreamstime.com:** Mikhail Blajenov / Starper (crb); Guoqiang Xue (cr); Ivanka Blazkova / Ivanka80 (cr/Sun bear); Minyun Zhou / Minyun9260 (br). **140 Science Photo Library:** Steve Gschmeissner (bl). **141 Science Photo Library:** Eye of Science (crb). **142 Science Photo Library:** Steve Gschmeissner (cl). **146 Science Photo Library:** Dr Jeremy Burgess (cb). **147 Science Photo Library:** Dennis Kunkel Microscopy (br). **149 Getty Images:** wallacefsk (cr). **iStockphoto.com:** BeholdingEye (fcr). **150 Dorling Kindersley:** Jerry Young (ca). **159 123RF.com:** Anastasija Popova / virgonira (br). **161 Alamy Stock Photo:** FLPA (cb). **Getty Images:** Kiatanan Sugsompian (bc). **162 June Jacobsen:** (cl). **166 Dreamstime.com:** Haveseen (tr); Worldfoto (tl). **Getty Images:** Visuals Unlimited, Inc. / Ken Catania (c). **iStockphoto.com:** lauriek (tc). **167 Alamy Stock Photo:** blickwinkel (cr). **Dorling Kindersley:** Jerry Young (crb/Monkey). **Getty Images:** De Agostini Picture Library (cra/Bat); Yva Momatiuk & John Eastcott / Minden Pictures (tl); Nicole Duplaix / National Geographic (cra). **iStockphoto.com:** arlindo71 (br); sharply_done (crb). **168 iStockphoto.com:** GlobalP (br). **Science Photo Library:** Omikron (tl). **169 Dreamstime.com:** John Anderson / Johnandersonphoto (cra). **172 Dreamstime.com:** Stu Porter / Stuporter (br). **iStockphoto.com:** TommyIX (cl). **173 Getty Images:** Gail Shumway (t); Alexander Safonov (cb). **174 Alamy Stock Photo:** garfotos (tr); Shoot Froot (cra); Richard Garvey-Williams (cl); John Richmond (crb); Brian Haslam (br). **Depositphotos Inc:** danakow (cr). **175 Alamy Stock Photo:** Brian Haslam (cla). **Harald Simon Dahl:** www.flickr.com/photos/haraldhobbit/14007088580/in/photostream (tc). **Getty Images:** Alan Murphy / BIA / Minden Pictures (bl). **SuperStock:** Konrad Wothe / Minden Pictures (cra). **177 Alamy Stock Photo:** Premaphotos (cb); Poelzer Wolfgang (tl). **Getty Images:** David Doubilet (clb); Brook Peterson / Stocktrek Images (tc, tr); Stephan Naumann / EyeEm (crb). **183 Getty Images:** Tim Laman / National Geographic (c); John E Marriott (bc). **184 Alamy Stock Photo:** age fotostock (br). **Dreamstime.com:** Chase Dekker (cra/Taiga); Max5128 (cra); Snehitdesign (c); Jeffrey Holcombe (crb). **185 Dreamstime.com:** Eddydegroot (bl); Denis Polyakov (cla); Ivan Kmit (cra); Szefei (crb); Zlikovec (br). **iStockphoto.com:** ianwool (tl). **186-187 Depositphotos Inc:** Olivier26. **187 iStockphoto.com:** pamspix (br). **188 Getty Images:** Bill Curtsinger / National Geographic (cla). **190 123RF.com:** Anan Kaewkhammul / anankkml (ca). **Alamy Stock Photo:** Mark Daffey (fbl). **Dorling Kindersley:** Cotswold Wildlife Park (tr). **Dreamstime.com:** Natalya Aksenova (clb); Johan Larson / Jaykayl (bl); Wrangel (cl, br); David Spates (c); Anton Ignatenco / Dionisvera (bc); Sailorr (cr). **191 Alamy Stock Photo:** dpa picture alliance (cb). **Dorling Kindersley:** Twan Leenders (cra/Turtle). **Dreamstime.com:** Frozentime (cra/Kingfisher); Isselee (cl); Meunierd (crb/Deer). **194 Science Photo Library:** Sinclair Stammers (tr). **195 Dreamstime.com:** Koolander (cla); Daniel Prudek (tl). **NASA:** JPL-Caltech (bc). **196 Dorling Kindersley:** Rotring UK Ltd (tr). **Dreamstime.com:** Dave Bredeson / Cammeraydave (crb); Tanyashir (bc). **iStockphoto.com:** artisteer (cb). **197 Alamy Stock Photo:** Tetra Images (cr). **Dreamstime.com:** Yu Lan / Yula (c). **iStockphoto.com:** Icsatlos (crb); seb_ra (cb). **198 123RF.com:** Koji Hirano / kojihirano (fcrb); Eric Isselee / isselee (cr/Gibbon). **Dorling Kindersley:** Andrew Beckett (Illustration Ltd) (cb, crb); David J Patterson (ftr); Jerry Young (cl, bl). **Dreamstime.com:** Isselee (clb); Andrey Sukhachev / Nchuprin (tr). **199 123RF.com:** Andrejs Pidjass / NejroN (cra). **Dorling Kindersley:** Natural History Museum, London (tc); Jerry Young (clb, crb). **Dreamstime.com:** Isselee (fcra); Janpietruszka (cla); Piotr Marcinski / B-d-s (br); Volodymyrkrasyuk (cl)

All other images © Dorling Kindersley
For further information see: **www.dkimages.com**